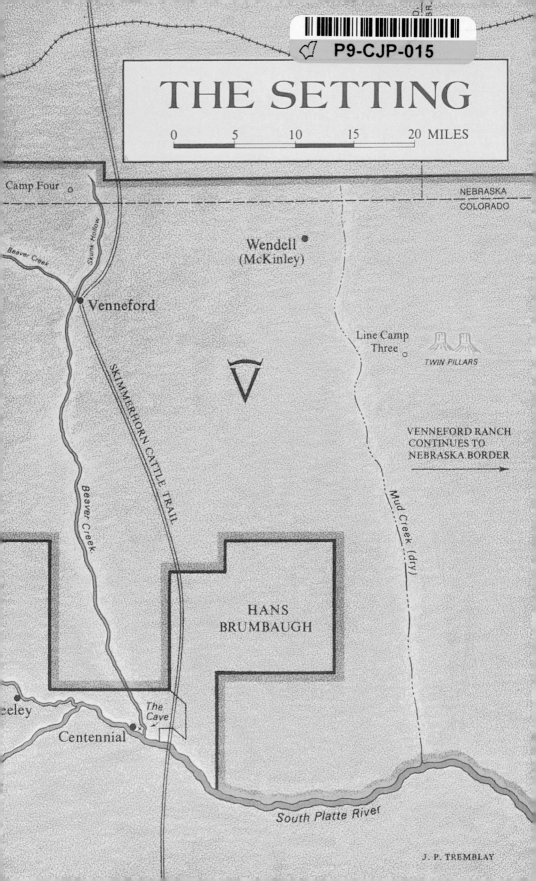

THE SETTING

0   5   10   15   20 MILES

Camp Four

NEBRASKA
COLORADO

Beaver Creek

Skunk Hollow

Wendell
(McKinley)

Venneford

Line Camp
Three

TWIN PILLARS

SKIMMERHORN CATTLE TRAIL

Beaver Creek

VENNEFORD RANCH
CONTINUES TO
NEBRASKA BORDER

Mud Creek (dry)

HANS
BRUMBAUGH

eeley

The
Cave

Centennial

South Platte River

J. P. TREMBLAY

Tales of the South Pacific
The Fires of Spring
Return to Paradise
The Voice of Asia
The Bridges at Toko-Ri
Sayonara
The Floating World
The Bridge at Andau
Hawaii
Report of the County Chairman
Caravans
The Source
Iberia
Presidential Lottery
The Quality of Life
Kent State:
   What Happened and Why
The Drifters
A Michener Miscellany: 1950–1970
Centennial

with A. Grove Day
Rascals in Paradise

CENTENNIAL

CENTENNIAL

JAMES A. MICHENER

Random House 🏠 *New York*

Library of Congress Cataloging in Publication Data

Designed by Antonina Krass

Manufactured in the United States of America

468B975

Acknowledgments

This novel deals with a subject that has concerned me since 1936, when I first came to know the South Platte River. Writing it has been one of the happiest experiences of my life, for it put me in contact with many learned and perceptive people. Among the many to whom I am indebted are these specialists:

Geology: Roger Cuffey and Lauren Wright, Pennsylvania State University; the latter took me on an extended field trip of the Rockies; Gerald Richmond, William Mallory, U. S. Geological Survey; Jack Murphy, Denver Museum of Natural History, who took me on a field trip to dinosaur deposits; Robert Egbert, Phillips Petroleum, who provided preliminary data for the core diagram of Centennial; and especially Ogden Tweto, U.S.G.S., foremost authority on the Rockies, who provided line-by-line checking of the text and the core diagram.

Paleontology: G. Edward Lewis, U.S.G.S.; Don Lindsay, D.M.N.H.; Bertrand Schultz, Mylan Stout, University of Nebraska; G. E. Untermann, Vernal, Utah; Tobe Wilkins, Dinosaur National Monument; Kay McElroy, Greeley, who took me on a field trip to Pawnee Buttes.

Early Man: Frank Frazier, Denver; George Frison, University of Wyoming, who took me on an extended field trip to prehistoric Clovis sites; H. M. Wormington, Denver, who allowed me to read the manuscript of her forthcoming book.

Flint Knapping: Don Crabtree, Kimberley, Idaho; H. M. Wormington, Denver; Bruce Bradley, Cambridge, England, who made a Clovis point for me.

Indian Life: Virginia Trenholm, Cheyenne; Evelyn Nickeson, Kinnear; Nellie Scott, Fort Washakie; Father Lewis O'Neill, S.J., Stephens; Reverend David Duncombe, Ethete, all of Wyoming.

Early St. Louis: John Francis McDermott, University of Southern Illinois; Mrs. Odile Trufanow, Denver; George Brooks, Frances Stader, Missouri Historical Society; and Ernest Kirschten, all of St. Louis.

Old Lancaster: Laura Lundgren, S. E. Dyke, John Ward Willson Loose, Lancaster County Historical Society.

Oregon Trail: Merrill J. Mattes, National Park Service; Gregory M. Franzwa, St. Louis.

Fort Laramie: Charles Sharp, Lewis Eaton, Bill Henry, all of Fort Laramie, who showed the most devoted patience in helping on research and field trips; Roger Kent Heape, Belleville, Illinois, who allowed me to read his unpublished thesis on the Treaty of 1851.

Cattle Trails: C. Boone McClure, Panhandle-Plains Historical Museum, Canyon, Texas; Dean Krakel, Cowboy Hall of Fame, Oklahoma City; Mrs. Laura Peacock, Jacksboro, Texas; Jessie Newton Yarborough, Robert Lee, Texas.

Ranch Life: Farrington Carpenter, Hayden, Colorado; Allen Fordyce, Big Horn; Burrell Nickeson, Kinnear, both of Wyoming. The following graciously allowed me to visit their ranches and ask many questions: J. J. Gibson, 6666 Ranch, Guthrie, Texas; Herman Werner, Van Irvine, Casper; Robert and Martha Gibbs, TY Ranch, Arvada, all of Wyoming; and especially Ronald and Virginia Wolff, Two Bar Ranch, Wheatland, Wyoming, who flew me to various historic sites in their ranch plane.

Sugar Beets: Lyman Andrews, William M. White, Denver, Colorado.

Birds: Gustav Swanson, C.S.U., who took me on a beautiful exploration of the Buttes area.

Denver Stock Show: Willard Simms, Denver; C. W. Ferguson, Miami.

Mexican-Chicano Problems: Corky Gonzales, Bernard Valdez, Jim Kent, Minoru Yasui, Denver; Diputado Abelardo Perez Campos, Francisco Almada, Chihuahua, Mexico, the former having shown me extraordinary courtesy; Susan Sellers, Mexico City, who provided much help on Chicano songs.

Dryland Farming: Isabel Blair, James Reed, Dora Good, all of Sterling, Colorado, the last of whom took me on an extensive field trip to an old line camp.

Cattle Industry: Larry Yarrington, Sterling, Colorado, who gave me a graduate seminar on artificial insemination; Tom Risinger, Jack Winninger, Cody, Wyoming, who introduced me to Simmentals; Russell Staats, Chugwater, Wyoming, custodian of the great Swan Land Cattle Company operation; Joe Gloyd, Frank Robertson, Wheatland, Wyoming; Gene Gressley, University of Wyoming; Bill Wadlow, Wyoming Hereford Ranch, Cheyenne.

Guns: Dabney Otis Collins, Ross Miller, Frank M. Sellers, Denver, the last-named being the world's authority on the Sharps rifle; Vernon Gunnion, Lancaster, expert on Melchior Fordney rifles.

Railroads: Ed Haley, Denver; Bob Richardson, Colorado Railroad Museum, Golden, Colorado.

Irrigation: Felix Sparks, Denver; John W. Nelson, Loveland, Colorado; John E. Moore, U.S.G.S.; Glen G. Saunders, Denver, Colorado; E. V. Richardson and Harvey Johnson, Fort Collins, Colorado, who took me on a thrilling field trip to the irrigation canals in the highest Rockies.

Appaloosas: Ed Roberts, Denver; George B. Hatley, Moscow, Idaho.

My thanks also go to Katherine Halverson, Bill Williams and John Cornelius of the Wyoming State Museum and Archives; Randolph Wagner, Wyoming Travel Commission, who showed me his excellent movie on the Oregon Trail; Tony Bevinetto and Charles McCurdy, Grand Teton National Park; Harold McCracken, Whitney Gallery of Western Art at Cody; the Western Pennsylvania Historical Society; Nebraska State Historical Society; Union Pacific Railroad Museum; and to Tom Ten Eyck of Denver, who took me on field trips to study ecology.

No city could have been more pleasant to work in than Denver, except for repeated traffic tickets, the worst winter in 170 years, the hottest summer in 87, and the nation's most galling gas shortage. Alys Freeze, Western Collection, Denver Public Library, provided invaluable help, and so did the entire staff of that estimable institution.

A group of wise and dedicated scholars read segments to help me avoid gross error: *Geology:* Wright, Cuffey, Tweto, Schumm; *Inhabitants:* Lewis, Schultz, Stout; *Early Man:* Wormington, Crabtree, Bradley; *Indians:* Trenholm; *Oregon Trail:* Mattes, Franzwa; *Trappers:* McDermott; *Fort Laramie:* Heape; *Cattle Trail:* McClure; *Hunters:* Sellers; *Sugar Beets:* Andrews; *Irrigation:* Moore. They must not be charged with such error as has persisted, because in certain instances I decided to stay with my own interpretations.

During my research I was aided at different and crucial times by two gifted members of the *Reader's Digest* staff: Leslie Laird, who had earlier helped me on my book on Kent State, and John Kings, who had for some years been a rancher in Wyoming. Tessa Dalton provided much expert guidance on wildlife. These three accompanied me on extensive field trips to Mexico, Texas, New Mexico, Arizona, Nevada, California, Utah, Idaho, Montana, Wyoming, Nebraska, Oklahoma, Kansas and Missouri. All three were good drivers, amiable storytellers and opposed to smoking.

This is a novel. Its characters and scenes are imaginary. There was no Venneford Ranch, no prairie town of Line Camp, no Skimmerhorn cattle drive in 1868, no Centennial. None of the families depicted here were real, nor founded upon real precedents. There was no Lame Beaver, nor Skimmerhorn nor Zendt nor Grebe. On the other hand, certain background incidents and characters are real. There was a great convocation in 1851 at Fort Laramie. There was a drought in 1931–1935. Jennie Jerome, the mother of Winston Churchill, did frequent the English ranches near Cheyenne. Charles Goodnight, one of the great men of the west, did haul the corpse of his partner home in a lead box. Melchior Fordney, the master gunsmith, was murdered. The South Platte River did behave as described.

Contents

THE
COMMISSION

ONLY ANOTHER WRITER, SOMEONE WHO had worked his heart out on a good book which sold three thousand copies, could appreciate the thrill that overcame me one April morning in 1973 when Dean Rivers of our small college in Georgia appeared at my classroom door.

'New York's trying to get you,' he said with some excitement. 'If I got the name right, it's one of the editors of *US*.'

'The magazine?'

'I could be wrong. They're holding in my office.'

As we hurried along the corridor he said, with obvious good will, 'This could prove quite rewarding, Lewis.'

'More likely they want to verify some fact in American history.'

'You mean, they'd telephone from New York?'

'They pride themselves on being accurate.' I took perverse pleasure in posing as one familiar with publishing. After all, the editors of *Time* had called me once. Checking on the early settlements in Virginia.

Any sophistication I might have felt deserted me when I reached the telephone. Indeed, my hands were starting to sweat. The years had been long and fruitless, and a telephone call from editors in New York was agitating.

'This Dr. Lewis Vernor?' a no-nonsense voice asked.

'Yes.'

'Author of *Virginia Genesis*?'

'Yes.'

'Had to be sure. Didn't want to embarrass either of us.' The voice dropped slightly, as if that part of the discussion were ended. Then with crisp authority it said, 'Dr. Vernor, I'm James Ringold, managing editor here at *US*. Problem is simple. Can you catch a plane from Atlanta this afternoon and report at my office tomorrow morning at nine?' Before I could even gasp, he added, 'We cover expenses, of course.' Then, when

I hesitated because of my surprise, he said, 'I think we may have something that would interest you . . . considerably.' I grew more confused, which gave him time to add, 'And before you leave for the airport, will you discuss schedules with your wife and your college? We shall very probably want to preempt your time from the end of semester right through Christmas.'

I placed my hand over the mouthpiece and made some meaningless gesture toward Dean Rivers. 'Can I fly to New York on the late plane?'

'Of course! Of course!' he whispered with an enthusiasm as great as mine. 'Something big?'

'I don't know,' I whispered back. Then into the phone I said, 'What was your name again?' When he replied, I told him, 'I'll be there.'

In the next hour I called my wife, arranged for Professor Hisken to take my classes and then reported to the president's office, where Dean Rivers had prepared the way with President Rexford by telling him that it sounded like the chance of a century for me and that he, Rivers, recommended that I be given the necessary leave.

Rexford, a tall southern gentleman who had accomplished wonders collecting funds for a college that badly needed them, was always pleased when one of his faculty received outside attention, because in subsequent meetings with businessmen he could allude to the fact that 'we're becoming better known all the time, something of a national force.' He greeted me warmly and asked, 'What's this I hear about *US* wanting to borrow our finest history man for the autumn term?'

'I really know nothing about it, sir,' I replied honestly. 'They want to interview me tomorrow morning, and if I pass muster, they want to offer me a job from term-end to Christmas.'

'When's your next sabbatical?'

'I was planning to spend next spring quarter in the Oregon libraries.'

'I remember. Settlement of the northwest. Mmmmm?'

'I thought that having started in Virginia and then done my study on the Great Lakes, it might be natural for me to—'

'Complete the cycle? Yes. Yes. You do that and you'll be a very valuable man to us, Vernor. A lot of foundations are going to be looking for projects dealing with the American past, and if we could offer you as a man who has done his homework, Virginia to Oregon . . . well, I don't have to tell you that I could generate a lot of interest in a man like that.'

'So you think I should stay here and work on my Oregon project?'

'I haven't said what I think, Vernor. But I know for a fact . . .' Here he rose and moved restlessly about his office, thrusting his arms out in bursts of energy. 'I know that a lot of these foundations would just love to place a project in Georgia. Get them off the hook of appearing too provincial.'

'Then I'll tell the editors—'

'You won't tell them anything. Go. Listen. See what they have to sell.

And if by chance it should fit into your grand design . . . How much do we pay you a quarter?'

'Four thousand dollars.'

'Let's do it this way. If what they have to offer is completely wide of the mark—bears no relation to American settlement—turn 'em down. Stay here the fall and winter quarters, then go out to Oregon in the spring.'

'Yes, sir.'

'But if it does fit in with your intellectual plans, say, something on the Dakotas. And'—he accented the word heavily—'if they'll pay you four thousand or more, I'll grant you fall quarter without pay, and you can take your sabbatical with pay spring quarter and head for Oregon.'

'That's generous,' I said.

'I'm thinking only of myself. Point is, it wouldn't hurt with the foundations if I could say that our man Vernor had done that big writing job for *US*. Gives you a touch of professionalism. That and your two books. And believe me, it's that professionalism that makes you eligible for the big grants.' He stalked about the room, hungrily, then turned and said, 'So you go ahead. Listen. And if it sounds good, call me from New York.'

At eight-thirty next morning I was walking down Avenue of the Americas, among those towering buildings of glass, marveling at how New York had changed since I knew it in 1957 when Alfred Knopf was publishing my first book on Virginia. I felt as if I had been away from America for a generation.

US had offices north of the new CBS building; its glass tower was the most impressive on the avenue. I rode up to the forty-seventh floor and entered a walnut-paneled waiting room. 'I'm early,' I told the girl.

'So am I,' she said. 'Coffee?' She was as bright as the magazine for which she worked, and she put me at my ease. 'If Ringold-san told you nine, nine it will be.'

At one minute after nine she ushered me into his office, where she introduced me to four attractive young editors. James Ringold was under forty and wore his hair combed straight forward, like Julius Caesar. Harry Leeds, his executive assistant, was something past thirty and wore an expensive double-knit in clashing colors. Bill Wright was obviously just a beginner. And Carol Endermann . . . well, I couldn't begin to guess how old she was. She could have been one of my good-looking, leggy graduate students from a tobacco farm in the Carolinas, or just as easily, a self-directed thirty-three-year-old assistant professor at the University of Georgia. I felt I was in the hands of four dedicated people who knew what they were doing, and was sure I would enjoy watching them operate.

'Let me get one thing straight, Vernor,' Ringold said. 'You published *Virginia Genesis* in 1957 with Knopf. How did it sell?'

'Miserably.'

'But they brought it out in paperback two years ago.'

'Yes. It's widely used in universities.'

'Good. I hope you got back your investment on it.'

'With paperbacks, yes.'

'That book I know. Very favorably. Now tell me about your next one.'

'*Great Lakes Ordeal*. Mostly iron and steel development. A lot on immigration, of course.'

'Knopf do it, too?'

'Yes.'

'Miserably?'

'Yes, but it's paying its way . . . in paperback.'

'Delighted to hear it,' Ringold said. 'Harry, tell him how we got onto his name.'

'With pleasure,' young Leeds said. 'Sometime ago we needed expertise of the highest caliber. On a project of some moment. We sent out calls to about thirty certified intellectuals for recommendations—and guess what?' He pointed at me. 'Abou Ben Adhem's name led all the rest!'

'In the profession,' Bill Wright said, 'you have one hell of a reputation.'

'Hence the phone call,' Leeds said.

'Your books may not sell, Vernor,' Wright continued, 'but the brains of this nation know a good man when they read his research.'

Ringold was slightly irritated by young Wright's interruption and now resumed charge. 'What we have in mind, Professor Vernor, is for you to make a research report for us in great depth, but also at great speed. If you devote your entire time from the end of May till Christmas, we feel sure that with your background you can do it. But our schedule is so tight, if you submit it one day late, it won't be worth a damn to us—not one damn.'

'Does that kind of schedule frighten you?' Leeds asked.

'I work on the quarter system,' I said. Either they understood what this meant in way of planning and precise execution, or they didn't. They did.

'Good,' Ringold said. He rose, walked about his desk and said, standing, 'So now we're down to the nitty-gritty. Carol?'

'What we have in mind, Professor Vernor'—I noticed that she used the exact phraseology of her boss—'is to publish in late 1974 a double issue of *US* devoted entirely to an in-depth analysis of one American community. We want you to go to that community, study it from the inside, give us intimate research on whatever aspects of it interest you deeply.'

'The ones that awaken a gut response,' young Wright volunteered.

'We're already prepared to do a quick once-over job,' Miss Endermann said, 'but what we're after is much deeper . . . nothing less than the soul of America . . . as seen in microcosm.'

I gripped the arms of my chair and breathed slowly. This seemed the kind of commission a man like me dreams of. It was what I had tried to do in Virginia after graduating from the university at Charlottesville and what I had followed up with at the Great Lakes when teaching at the University of Minnesota. I at least knew what the problem was.

'Have you identified the community?' I asked. Much would depend upon whether I had competence in the selected area.

'We have,' Ringold said. 'Tell him, Harry.'

'Because the arteries of America have always been so crucial,' Leeds said, 'we determined from the start to focus on a river . . . the ebb and flow of traffic . . . the journeymen up and down . . . the influence of time sweeping past . . .' As he spoke he closed his eyes, and it was apparent that he had chosen the river, and no doubt the specific settlement on it. He opened his eyes and said, 'So, Professor Vernor, I'm afraid we've stuck you with a river.'

'I worked with rivers in Virginia,' I said.

'I know. That's what attracted me to you.'

I was eager to land this job, because it was the kind of work I ought to do before going to Oregon, but I did not want to appear too eager. I sat staring at the floor, trying to collect my thoughts. DeVoto had already done a masterful job on the Missouri River, but he had left some topics undeveloped. I might be able to write a strong report on St. Joseph, or one of the Mandan villages, or even something farther west, say Great Falls. 'I'd not want to compete with DeVoto,' I said tentatively, 'but there's a chance I could do something original on the Missouri.'

'It wasn't the Missouri we had in mind,' Leeds said.

Well, I thought, that's that. Of course, there was still the Arkansas. I could select some settlement like La Junta . . . include Bent's Fort and the massacre at Sand Island. But I insisted upon being honest with these editors, so I told them, 'If your river is the Arkansas, you'd do better choosing someone more fluent in Spanish. To deal with the Mexican land grants, and subjects like that.'

'We weren't interested in the Arkansas,' Leeds said.

'What did you have in mind?'

'The Platte.'

'The Platte!' I gasped.

'None other,' Leeds said.

'That's the sorriest river in America. You've heard all the jokes about the Platte. "Too thick to drink, too thin to plow." That's a nothing river.'

'That's why we chose it,' Leeds said.

Miss Endermann broke in. 'We specifically wanted to avoid notorious places like St. Joseph, one of my favorite cities on earth, because it would be too easy to do. A great deal of American history was drab, just as you said now—a nothing river, "a mile wide and an inch deep." '

'We reasoned, and properly so I'm convinced,' Ringold said, 'that if we can make the Platte comprehensible to Americans, we can inspire them with the meaning of this continent. And goddamnit, that's what we're going to do. We'll leave the drums and bugles and flying eagles to others. We are going to dive into the heart of that lousy river . . .' He stopped in embarrassment. Obviously, the editors of *US* had made a major commitment to the Platte, and I respected their enthusiasm.

'I understand your approach,' I said. 'Now you have to understand that I can't be expected to be a world authority on the Platte. I know about its settlement, its Indians, its irrigation—the general things. But I must not pose as an expert.'

'We know that,' Miss Endermann said eagerly. 'We want you for what you have been, not for what you are. You can immerse yourself in this subject within a week.'

'That's true,' I said. 'I've already reconnoitered the North Platte twice in connection with the Oregon Trail. I know most of the sites along the North Platte, know them well.'

Harry Leeds broke in: 'What we had in mind was the South Platte.'

'Good God!' I couldn't help myself. The South Platte was the most miserable river in the west, a trickle in summer when its water was needed, a raging torrent in spring. It was muddy, often more island than river, and prior to the introduction of irrigation, it had never served a single useful purpose in its halting career. I couldn't think of even one town situated on the South Platte. Yes, there was Julesburg—most evil town along the railroad—burnt by Indians in 1866 or thereabouts.

Then I remembered. 'There is Denver,' I said lamely, 'but if you didn't want a major river, I'm sure you don't want a major city. It isn't Denver, is it?'

Miss Endermann answered my rhetorical question: 'Have you ever heard of Centennial, Colorado?'

For some moments I racked my brain, and from somewhere a tag-end piece of information such as scholars earmark for possible future use surfaced. 'Centennial. Am I wrong in thinking that it had another name? Didn't they change it in 1876 . . . to honor Colorado's entrance into the Union? What was the old name? Rather well known in early chronicles, seems to me. Was it Zendt's Farm?'

'It was,' Miss Endermann said.

'You know, I can't recall a single fact about Zendt's Farm. Gentlemen, I am not well versed in your chosen subject. Sorry.'

I assumed that this was the end of the interview, but I assumed wrong. 'It's for that reason we want you,' Ringold said. 'Listening to your non-faked reactions to a town you never heard of and a river you despise convinces me that you're precisely the man we want. The job's yours if you want it, and we're damned lucky to find you.'

With that he ushered us from his office, instructing Harry Leeds to go over details with me and bring the crowd to Toots Shor's for lunch at twelve sharp. 'We'll discuss money then,' he said, 'but so far as I'm concerned, you're hired, unless your fee is unspeakable.'

Four of us went to Harry Leeds' office, where gigantic photographic blowups of George Catlin's paintings of Indians adorned the walls. 'My tipi,' he said.

We discussed how I would work. I would drive to Centennial as soon as my classes ended, establish contacts with the Denver Public Library, which was some fifty miles away, introduce myself to the faculties at Greeley, Fort Collins and Boulder, and prepare research reports on what had actually happened at Centennial during its history, which had started only in 1844 with the arrival of Zendt and one of the mountain men.

'I might want to go further back,' I suggested.

'The Spanish never settled that far north,' Wright said, 'and the French never settled that far south. Lewis and Clark ignored the Platte altogether. We can start safely with Zendt in 1844.'

I was not to bother about literary style. I was writing neither a doctoral thesis nor a novel. I was simply submitting arbitrarily selected insights as to the character and background of Centennial and its settlers, and I could depend upon the home office to polish whatever segments they might want to publish.

'And regardless of what fee you and Ringold agree upon,' Wright assured me, 'we want you to purchase whatever maps, agricultural studies, reports you need—you name it.'

'We would want you to send them back at the end of the study,' Leeds said.

'How much do you expect me to write?' I asked, still not clear as to the creative relationships.

'By Christmas, a fairly complete reaction to the site.'

'Usually I spend that much time on a chapter,' I said. 'There's a hell of a lot of first-class work been done on the west by some very good men, and I'm not going to presume . . .'

'Vernor,' young Wright explained patiently, 'we are not hiring you to do a research study on the sugar-beet industry of the South Platte. We are hiring you as a sensitive, intelligent man, and all we want from you are some letters which share with us your understanding of what transpired at Centennial, Colorado, between the years 1844 and 1974. Just write us some letters, as if we were your friends . . . your interested friends.'

The other two agreed that that was exactly what they wanted, and we went off to lunch fairly satisfied that the project would work, but at Toots Shor's, a restaurant I had not visited before, I was to receive a series of shocks which altered the whole prospect.

As we entered the restaurant the proprietor, a large man, ambled over to Harry Leeds and shouted, 'Hello, you miserable son-of-a-bitch, haven't they fired you yet?'

Leeds took this in stride, and Shor turned to me, grabbing me by the collar. 'Don't let this crumbum talk you into doing his dirty work. He's known as the literary pimp of Sixth Avenue.' With that he showed us to our table, where James Ringold was waiting.

'He's dead drunk already,' Shor warned me. 'How this stumblebum keeps that magazine goin', I'll never know.'

With that he departed, and Ringold asked Leeds, 'All settled?'

'All settled,' Leeds said. 'We couldn't be happier, right?' He addressed this question to Wright and Endermann, and they nodded.

'Then it's simply a matter of money. Use your car and we'll pay twelve cents a mile. We'll pay your hotel bills, but we do not expect you to take a suite at the Brown Palace. Don't be alarmed if board and keep run a hundred and seventy dollars a week. You can travel as required but you cannot rent airplanes, road graders or dog sleds. Under no circumstances are you ever to be out a penny of your own money, except for whorehouses. We do, however, expect itemized expense sheets, and we pay out money only when they are verified.' I was accustomed to asking Dean Rivers if I might have thirty dollars for a new atlas. This hit me so fast that I simply could not digest the details, but I noticed that young Wright was taking note of everything. 'He'll send you a copy,' Ringold assured me.

'Now as to fee,' he said, 'you're a top professor in Georgia. You're worth a lot of money, and I'm sure they don't pay you according to your worth. I'm not going to haggle. We're asking two quarters of your time, half a year's salary. We'll give you eighteen thousand dollars.'

I could have fainted. After I had sipped a little consommé I said something which led to my next shock. I said, 'Mr. Ringold, that's generous pay and you know it. But if you're gambling so much on this special issue, what if I get sick? Can't provide the manuscript?'

He looked at me in amazement. 'Haven't you told him?' he asked Leeds.

'Never occurred to me,' Leeds said, and the other two shrugged their shoulders as if it had slipped their minds too.

'Vernor,' Ringold said expansively, 'we have the article already written—every word of it. Illustrations and maps are well started. We could go to press next week. All we want from you is assurance that we're on the right track.'

This information staggered me. I was being hired to write not a polished article which would appear under my name, but merely a house report to back up something already completed, a report which might never be published and might not even be used. When the article appeared, a sleazy job at best, there would be this byline: 'Prepared with the assistance of Professor Lewis Vernor, Department of History, Georgia Baptist.' I was being bought, for a good price . . . but I was being bought.

The food went sour and my disappointment must have shown, for Ringold said, reassuringly, 'We always work this way, Vernor. We work like demons month after month on a project . . . best writers in America . . . but at the end we always want someone with real brains to vet the damned thing. That's why we stay in business—facts are important to us, but understandings are vital. We inject a very high percentage of understandings in our rag and we're asking you to help us on our next big project.'

My vanity was destroyed and my intellectual integrity humiliated. 'I think this lunch is over, gentlemen,' I said. I tried to rephrase the sentence so as to include Miss Endermann, and loused things up.

It was young Wright who faced up to the debacle. 'I'm going to make a suggestion. Professor Vernor, as you must know, Mr. Ringold's offer was most generous. I handle these things all the time and I can assure you we would not hesitate to offer Arthur Schlesinger such a deal. We made such a generous offer because we respect you. You thought you were writing an article for us. I understand your confusion. Let me suggest this. Go out to Centennial. Carol's already cased the joint. She'll go with you to see if you respond the way she did. We'll pay someone to take your classes. You can leave tomorrow. Better still, leave tonight. And if you decide to join us, when your report is finished, you'll be free to publish it under your own name—maybe as a book. Six months after our publication the property becomes yours.'

'That's a damned good idea, Wright,' Ringold said. 'That's exactly what we'll do. Vernor, can you fly out to Centennial this afternoon? There's a United plane at three.'

'I'd have to ask President Rexford.'

'Get him on the phone. Toots! You got a phone there?'

For the first time in my life a waiter brought a phone to my table, curling the long black wire across my chair. In a moment I was speaking with President Rexford, but I had barely introduced myself when Ringold took the phone. 'Rexford? Sure I remember you. The Baptist Committee, that's right. We want to borrow your bright boy for one week. We'll pay three hundred dollars for some graduate student to cover for him. Is that a deal?' There was some conversation, after which Ringold handed me the phone. 'He wants to talk with you.'

'Hello, Vernor? Is the project germane to Oregon?'

'Totally. But it's not what we thought at all. I'd just be doing legwork for background stuff.'

'Could it lead to anything substantial?'

'Yes. It's work I would have to do later.'

'Do they pay well?'

'Very.'

'Take it. Fly out to Colorado tonight. Professor Hisken could use the three hundred dollars and we'll forget the graduate student.'

So that afternoon at three Miss Endermann and I boarded the jet for Denver, and because of the time difference we arrived there at four. She hired a car, and while it was still light we drove north. To the west rose the noble Rockies, to the east stretched the prairies, mile upon mile of treeless land. At the end of an hour I saw the sight which had been familiar to all travelers westward, a line of scrawny, limb-broken cotton-woods.

'There's the Platte,' I said, and we entered upon a small north-south road which took us down to the river, one of the strangest in the world. It was quite wide, several hundred yards perhaps, but most of the width was taken up with islands, sand bars, rocks and stumps of trees. Where was the water? There was a little here, some over there, but the spring floods had not yet broken loose, and it was all a stagnant muddy brown. Its principal product seemed to be gravel, endless supplies of gravel waiting to be hauled away by trucks which lined the bank.

Across the Platte lay the little town of Centennial. The sign told the whole story:

CENTENNIAL

COLORADO

Elev. 4618

Pop. 2618

When we turned right into the one-way circle that took us across the Union Pacific tracks and into town, I heard someone shouting, 'Hey! It's Carol!' and I looked over to see a black man standing before a barber-shop.

'Nate!' Carol called. 'How about Mexican food tonight?'

'Like always,' he called back. 'Eight?'

We pulled in behind the barbershop and parked where a sign said that if we did not intend to register at the Railway House, our car would be towed away at a cost of twenty-five dollars. The bellman who came out to greet us recognized Carol, and they too had a reunion.

'I wanted you to stay here, right by the railroad, in order to catch the old flavor,' she explained as we registered, and this was prudent judgment, because everything about the place was old: the smell, the carpets, the uniform of the bellman and my room. But it was likable. Men traveling from one Colorado town to another in times past had climbed down from the Union Pacific and lodged here, and for a historian they had left memories.

At quarter to eight I met Miss Endermann in the lobby and she took me out onto Prairie—not Prairie Street or Avenue or Boulevard. Just Prairie.

'If you're like me,' she said, 'you orient yourself properly at the start. Well, Prairie runs due north and south. The center of town is where Prairie and Mountain cross, because Mountain runs due east and west. We'll walk there.'

We went to the intersection, and she said, 'It all starts from here. West to the Rockies. East to Omaha. South to Denver. North to Cheyenne. Streets begin at the east and run by number up to Tenth Street. Avenues begin at the railroad and run north to Ninth Avenue. It's well laid out.'

We turned east on Mountain and walked four blocks to a noisy restaurant called Flor de Méjico, and there again we were warmly greeted, this time by a robust Mexican introduced to me as Manolo Marquez. 'We knew you'd be back,' he told Miss Endermann. 'Tonight the best in the house, on me.'

He showed us to a table covered by a red-checkered cloth and a well-greased menu which Miss Endermann told me had been invariable for the past five years. 'I hope you like Mexican food,' she said.

"It's not common in Georgia.'

'We'll introduce him to it, Manolo,' she cried. 'Three plates, with a sample of everything. And some Coors beer.' She asked if I knew this Colorado beer, and I said no. 'With Mexican food it's sort of heaven,' she assured me.

The door opened and the black man I had seen on the street entered and came to our table. Miss Endermann kissed him, then said, 'This is my friend and counselor, Nate Person. Not only a good barber but a sagacious one. He knows where the bodies are buried.'

Person, a gray-templed man in his fifties, asked where I was from, and when I said Georgia he laughed. 'That's a state not high on my list.'

'It's getting better,' I assured him.

'High time,' he said evenly.

'You must tell him everything you told me,' Miss Endermann said, and Nate nodded.

I suppose it was a good dinner, but the items that faced me were so unlike what I was accustomed to in Georgia that it all tasted like a hot jumble. 'The toasted thing is a taco,' Miss Endermann explained. To me it was more like French-fried cardboard, and the enchilada and tamale seemed so nearly identical that I never did discover which was which. The stuffed pepper, called a chili relleno, was mostly fried cheese, but the salad was great. So was the small glass of pomegranate juice. And the Coors beer was, as she had predicted, 'as light as a cupful of mountain water.'

After we had finished the dinner, which Miss Endermann and Person gulped as if they hadn't eaten in weeks, I began to experience the most pleasing sensation. It was as if my stomach were in harmony with the world. 'That must have been pretty good food,' I said. 'Tastes better now than it did going down.'

'Join the club,' Miss Endermann said. 'Nate, remember that first time you made me try it? Thought I'd die.'

There was a commotion at the door and Marquez hurried over to greet a tall, gangling westerner who had slouched in. He wore a cowboy hat, a bandanna and crooked-heel boots with fancy spurs. He was what western writers call a 'lean, mean hombre,' but he moved with an easy grace and made himself at home wherever he was.

He came directly to our table, where he grabbed Miss Endermann, pulled her to her feet and kissed her.

'Cisco!' she cried. 'This is too much. I thought you were in Chicago.'

'I was. Got back Monday. Heard you were in town. Knew I'd find you here.'

She introduced him to me as Cisco Calendar, and he let me know at once that he didn't think much of me. He turned a chair around and straddled it, resting his chin on the back. 'Good to see you,' he said to Carol. He spoke elliptically and kept his half-savage face close to hers.

It was obvious that he intended getting Miss Endermann off by himself, and it was just as obvious that she wished it that way, so after a few uneasy moments he said, 'Got the car out here. Wanta take a spin?' She did, and that was the last I saw of this angular, aggressive cowboy.

In the morning Miss Endermann said, 'If you're up to it after the Mexican food, let's reconnoiter.' She drove me up and down the two main streets until my bearings were set. She then took me to the plush northwest segment: 'The Skimmerhorns, the Wendells, the Garretts. Those are the names that count.' In the northeast sector, where the homes were noticeably poorer, she said, 'Zendt's Farm, which started it all, and down here, the original Wendell place. There was a great scandal about it, and you'll want to look into that.'

As we passed the Flor de Méjico in the southeast, she said, 'That's where we ate last night. Down here by the tracks is where Manolo Marquez lives, and along here is Nate Person's barbershop, where we came into town yesterday.' In the remaining sector, the southwest, there was not much: along the tracks the ramshackle home of Cisco Calendar. 'He could afford much better, of course, but that's where his family has always lived.'

That was Centennial, at least the part I would be concerned with. 'Not quite,' Miss Endermann said. 'Two more localities, and they loom large.' And she drove me north on Prairie and well up toward the Wyoming line, where I saw something which astonished me: a massive castle complete with spires and donjon.

'It's Venneford,' she said. 'All the land we'll be on today, and millions of acres more, once belonged to Earl Venneford of Wye. Greatest cattle ranch in the west.'

'Does the noble earl figure in my story?'

'Not unless you want him to,' she said. 'But what we see next is the heart of your story.'

And she drove me east onto dry land such as I had never before seen, bleak and desolate, and at the top of a rise she stopped the car and said,

'This is how they found it. A vast emptiness. Nothing has changed in a million years.'

In no direction could I see any sign that man had ever tried to occupy this enormous land—no house, no trail, not even a fence post. It was empty and majestic, the great prairie of the west.

Miss Endermann interrupted my reflections with a promise: 'When we reach the top of that next hill you'll see something memorable.'

She was right. As we climbed upward through the desolate waste, we reached an elevation from which I looked down upon a compelling sight, one that would preoccupy me for the next half year. It was a village, Line Camp, she said, and once it had flourished, for a tall grain silo remained, but now it was deserted, its shutters banging, its windows knocked in.

We drove slowly, as if in a funeral procession, through the once busy streets marked only by gaping foundation holes where stores and a church had stood. We found only devastation, gray boards falling loose, school desks ripped from their moorings. Somehow I must make the boards divulge their story, but now only hawks visited Line Camp and the stories were forgotten.

Two buildings survived, a substantial stone barn and across from it a low stone edifice to whose door came a very old man to stare at us.

'The only survivor,' Miss Endermann said, and as we watched, even he disappeared.

'What happened?' I asked.

'We want you to tell us,' she said.

It must have been obvious that I was captivated by Centennial and its environs, because at lunch we began to pinpoint my commission, and I said, 'By the way, nobody has told me who wrote the story I'm supposed to fortify.'

'Don't you know?'

'Obviously not.'

'I did.'

'You did?'

'Yes. I researched this story on the scene for five months.'

'I knew . . .' I was confused. 'Of course, I realized that the people here knew you. But I thought you'd been . . .'

'Helping someone else? Helping someone important?'

She asked these questions with such a cutting edge that I thought we'd better get down to cases. 'Miss Endermann,' I said, 'you'll forgive me, but your magazine is asking me to spend a lot of time on this project. May I ask what your credentials are? Do you mind a few questions?'

'Not at all,' she said frankly. 'I'd expect them. I know this is important to you.'

'What do you think of Frank Gilbert Roe?'

Without batting an eye, she said, 'On horses, terrific. On bison, I prefer McHugh.'

This was a sophisticated response, so I proceeded: 'What's your reaction to the Lamanite theory?'

'A despicable aberration of Mormonism.' She stopped and asked apologetically, 'You're not Mormon, are you?' And before I could answer, she said, 'Even if you are, I'm sure you agree with me.'

'I respect the Mormons,' I said, 'but I think their Lamanite theory asinine.'

'I'm so glad,' she said. 'I don't think I could work with someone who took that sort of bull seriously.'

'What was your reaction to the Treaty of 1851?'

'Ah,' she said reflectively. 'Its heart was in the right place. But the government in Washington had such a perverted misunderstanding of the land west of Missouri that there was no chance—none ever—that the Arapaho would be allowed to keep the land they were given. If it hadn't been gold, it would have been something else. Stupidity. Stupidity.'

This young woman knew something. I asked her, 'What is your judgment on the Skimmerhorn massacre?'

'Oh, no!' she protested. 'It's your job to tell us what you think about that. But I will confess this. I've studied the Skimmerhorn papers at Boulder and the court-martial records in Washington, and I've interviewed the Skimmerhorns in Minnesota and Illinois. I know what I think. Six months from now I want to know what you think.'

I had one final question, and this would prove the depth of her investigation. 'Have you done any work on the reports of Maxwell Mercy?'

She burst into laughter and astonished me by rising and kissing me on the cheek. 'You're a real dear,' she said. 'I did my master's thesis under Allan Nevins at Columbia on some unpublished letters I'd found of Captain Mercy. On my bedroom wall at home I have an old photograph of him taken by Jackson at Fort Laramie, and for your personal information I got damned near straight A's at Illinois and honors at the University of Chicago, where I took my doctorate.'

'Then what in hell are you doing knocking around with Cisco Calendar till four o'clock this morning?'

'Because he sends me, you old prude. He sends me.'

Next morning I drove her to Denver, where she caught the plane back to New York. At the ramp she told me, 'Stay the rest of the week. You'll fall in love with this place. I did.' When I wished her luck at the office, she said, 'I'll be working on maps.' Then, impulsively, she grabbed my hands. 'We really need you . . . to make the thing hum. Call us Friday night, saying you're signing on.'

I drove back by way of the university at Boulder because I wanted to consult my old friend, Gerald Lambrook of their history department, and he said, 'I can't see any pitfalls in the arrangement, Lewis. Granted, you're not writing the article and you lose some control, but they're a good outfit and if they say they're going to give it first-class presentation, they will. What it amounts to, they're paying you to do your own basic research.'

Lambrook was an old-style professor, with a book-lined study, sheaves of term papers, which he still insisted on, and even a tweed jacket and a pipe. I worked in a turtleneck and it was sort of nice to know that the old Columbia-Minnesota-Stanford types were around. I had known him at Minnesota and it was easy to renew our old friendship.

'But I'm interested, historically speaking,' he said, 'in the fact that you haven't mentioned the thing for which Centennial is most famous. The area, I mean.'

I asked him what that was, and he said, 'The old Zendt place.'

'I know about it. Saw it yesterday. The fellow from Pennsylvania who wouldn't build a fort but did build a farm.'

'I don't mean the farm. I mean Chalk Cliff, on his first place.'

'Never heard of it.'

'That's where the first American dinosaur was found.'

'The hell it was!'

'That great big one. Went to Berlin, and how we wish we had it back. And then, not far from there, but still on the original farm, the Clovis-point dig. Say, if you're free, I think I could get one of the young fellows from geology to run us up there.' He started making phone calls, between which he told me, 'The university's doing some work up there, I think.' Finally he located an instructor who was taking his students on a field trip to the Zendt dig during the coming week, and he said he'd enjoy refreshing his memory, so off we went, Lambrook and I in my car and young Dr. Elmo Kennedy in his.

We drove north along the foothills of the Rockies, past Estes Park on the west and Fort Collins on the east, till we came to what might have been called badlands. Dr. Kennedy pulled up to inform me, 'We're now entering the historic Venneford spread, and Chalk Cliff lies just ahead. I'll open the gates, you close them.'

We proceeded through three barbed-wire fences behind which white-faced Herefords grazed, and came at last to an imposing cliff, running north and south, forty feet high and chalky white. 'Part of an old fault,' Kennedy explained. 'Pennsylvanian period, if you're interested. At the foot of the cliff, in 1875, down here in the Morrisonian Formation, Professor Wright of Harvard dug out the great dinosaur that can be seen in Berlin.'

'I never knew that,' I confessed. 'I knew the dinosaur. but not its provenance.'

'And two miles up, at the other end of the cliff, is where they found—1935, I think it was—that excellent site with the Clovis points.'

'I have heard about that,' I said, 'but not that it was located near Chalk Cliff.'

We spent the rest of the morning there, inspecting this historic site, after which Lambrook and Kennedy drove back to Boulder. 'Be sure to close the gates,' they warned. That left me some time to inspect the brooding cliff, and as I kicked at the chalky limestone I came upon a fossilized sea shell, a frail, delicate thing now transformed into stone, indubitable proof that this cliff and the land around it had once lain at the bottom of some sea and now stood over five thousand feet above sea level. I tried to visualize the titanic force that must have been involved in such a rearrangement of the earth's surface, and I think it was then I began to see my little object-town Centennial in a rather larger dimension than the editors back in New York saw it.

By back roads I drove east to Line Camp, seeing that desolate spot from a new angle, and was even more fascinated by the compression of history one observed there: Indian campground, cattle station, sheep ranch, dry-land farming, dust bowl, and then abandonment as a site no longer fit for human concern. The place attracted me like a magnet and I wished that I were writing of it and not Centennial, which at this point seemed pretty ordinary to me, but as I drove south, it occurred to me that I must be following the old Skimmerhorn Trail, and when I came to the low bluffs that marked the delineation between the river bottom and the prairie and I was able to look down into Centennial and its paltry railroad, with cottonwoods outlining the south side of the Platte, I had a suspicion that perhaps it too had had its moments of historic significance. What they were, I could not anticipate, but if I took the job I would soon find out.

I was eating lunch at Flor de Méjico—sandwiches, not enchiladas— when I heard a man's voice inquiring, 'Manolo, you have a man from Georgia eating here?' Marquez replied, 'Right over here, Paul,' and he brought a tall, well-dressed rancher-type to my table.

'I'm Paul Garrett,' he said, extending his hand. 'Mind if I sit down?'

I asked him to do so, and he said, 'Heard you were in town. When Miss Endermann was here before we did a lot of work together. And I wondered if you'd like to take a little orientation spin in my plane.'

'Very much!' I said. 'I understand things better when I see the geographical layout. But I'm leaving Friday.'

'I meant right now.'

'I'm free.'

He drove me out to an airstrip east of Beaver Creek, where his pilot waited with a six-seater Beechcraft, and we piled in. Within minutes we were high over the Platte, and for the first time I saw the meanders of this incredible river from aloft. 'The braided river,' one expert had called it with justification, for the strands of the river were so numerous and the islands so interspersed, it did seem as if giant hands had braided the river so that it now hung like a lovely pigtail from the head of the mountains.

Several times we flew up and down the Platte, and I appreciated better how it dominated the area, where it overflowed its banks, where it deposited huge thicknesses of gravel, and how men had siphoned off much of its water into irrigation ditches. It became an intricate system rather than an isolated stretch.

Garrett then directed the pilot to fly north to the Wyoming line, and as we left the river and crossed the arid plains, coming at last to the bluffs which marked the end of Colorado in that direction, he told me, 'This is the old Venneford spread. I want you to see it, because you won't believe it.' He asked the pilot to fly west toward the mountains, and below I saw the shining white expanse of Chalk Cliff.

'I was down there this morning,' I said.

'Good spot. The boundary's a little farther west.' He pointed to an old wire fence, and we dropped low to inspect it. 'That's where the Venneford lands began,' he said. 'Now until I tell you different, everything you see down there once belonged to Earl Venneford of Wye. Everything.'

We sped east for half an hour, over an immense tract of land, and I became fascinated by a phenomenon I had not seen before: at periodic intervals great circles were indented into the surface of the plains, as if gigantic fairies had built magic rings or Indians their tipis of enormous size. I could not imagine what these circles were, and was about to ask Garrett when he said, 'It's still Venneford land.'

We flew for an hour and fifteen minutes, deviating north and south for short excursions to explore arroyos, and at the end of that time he pointed ahead: 'The Nebraska line. That's where the earl's land ended.'

'How much?'

'One hundred and eighty miles east-west, fifty miles north-south.'

'That's nine thousand square miles!' I hesitated. 'Are my figures right?'

'Well over five million acres,' he said.

I stared at the magnitude of the land, the empty, lonely expanse, and guessed that it hadn't been good for much in those days and wasn't good for much now.

'A hundred and eighty miles in one direction,' he said as we turned homeward. 'The foreman would inspect about ten miles a day in his buggy. Eighteen days merely to cover the middle and forget the north and south borders. It's that kind of land, Professor Vernor. It requires more than sixty acres to support one cow-and-calf unit.'

'Miss Endermann told me you'd bought some of it,' I said.

'I've only a hundred and thirty-three thousand acres. Maybe the best part, though.' He asked the pilot to fly north of the Venneford castle, where he outlined a rugged terrain of barren plains, foothills and some attractive low mountains. 'A real challenge,' Garrett said. 'If you come back, come up and look it over.'

'I'd like that,' I said.

'Back east, how many acres to the unit?' he asked as we headed toward Centennial.

'My uncle in Virginia needs only one acre for what you call a unit— bottom land, along the river.'

'There you have the difference between Virginia and Colorado. One to an acre your way. One to sixty our way. That makes your land sixty times better than ours. But we work seventy times harder, so we come out a little bit ahead.'

He drove me back to the hotel and I asked if he'd join me in a drink. 'Never during the day,' he said, and before I could ask further questions, he was gone.

I now had Centennial keyed in, as far as prairie, mountain and river were concerned, so I directed my remaining stay to the town itself. The Garrett plot, at Ninth and Ninth, was a brooding place with a nineteenth-century wooden house dominating scrubby trees. The Morgan Wendell place, one block south, was a handsome ranch-style home covering a large and beautifully landscaped area. But it was the land east of town that preoccupied me, for to a Georgian, what went on there was new. Beaver Creek protected the town from the encroaching prairie. West of the creek lay bottom lands, largely swampy and a place for birds; east of the creek stood Centennial's two commercial enterprises.

North of the highway stood the dominating sugar factory of Central Beet. Its pungent aroma, even in the spring of the year, permeated Centennial with a clean, earthlike smell. To a man like me, reared in the cane country, it seemed profane that men would try to extract sugar from beets, but they did.

South of the highway was something I had never seen before: vast corrals delimited by wooden fences, containing not a shred of grass nor any growing things except hundreds upon hundreds of white-faced cattle, all the same size, all being fattened for the slaughterhouses in Omaha and Kansas City. Never before had I seen so many cattle at one time, and I tried to estimate how many there were. When I reached two hundred in one corral and realized that there were two dozen corrals all equally crammed, I concluded that my original estimate of hundreds had to be multiplied by ten.

The place was like a factory—*Brumbaugh Feed Lots*, the sign said— with overhead conveyors bringing the grain to each corral, and traps for hauling away the manure, and waterpipes everywhere—and all convenient both to the sugarbeet factory, from which came beet pulp for feeding the animals, and to the railroad, which brought in calves and hauled away fattened cattle. What really astonished me was to discover that every animal I saw was either a heifer or a steer—no bulls, no cows, just yearlings bred specially for butchering.

On Thursday afternoon I drove out to Line Camp, and again I was affected by the strange allure of sweeping prairie and lonely vista. I was east of the deserted village when I saw before me a sight of compelling interest: twin pillars rising a sheer five hundred feet from the surrounding land. For miles in every direction there was nothing but empty land, then these twin pillars of red and gray rock shooting skyward.

They were so conspicuous that I was sure they must be named, and I looked about for someone to question, but there was no one. For mile upon mile there was no one, only the silent pillars and a hawk inspecting them from aloft.

The late sun made the red rocks flame and I watched for a long time, trying to guess how such spires could have been left standing, but finding no answer. In Georgia such a phenomenon would have been a natural wonder. 'The Devil's Darning Needles,' or something like that. In the west they were not even marked on the map, so prodigal had nature been with her displays.

Every night I ate dinner at the hotel, and my waiter was a man whose ancestors had come to Centennial with the building of the railroad in the 1880s and had lingered. When Nate Person gave me a haircut he told me that an ancestor of his had come north from Texas with the cattle drives and had lingered. Manolo Marquez had a father who had come north from Chihuahua to work sugar beets and he too had lingered, and it occurred to me that unlike Garvey, Georgia, where my ancestors had lived for three hundred years, everyone in Centennial had arrived within the last hundred and twenty years—just drifting through—and all had lingered.

I was much taken with the town. I had a good time with Marquez and Nate Person. I liked Paul Garrett immensely and wanted to know more about him. And the setting, with that incredible Platte River dominating everything, was much to my taste. What deterred me, then, from telephoning James Ringold and saying, 'I'll take the job'?

Vanity. As simple as that. I hated to play second fiddle, anonymously, to someone else, especially a beginning scholar much younger than myself. I suppose the fact that she was a girl added to my resentment, but in an age of Women's Lib, I was not about to admit that. I feared the whole project was undignified and a potential threat to my professional reputation. I was therefore prepared to inform New York that I could not accept, when I took one last walk Friday afternoon. I was reflecting on the fact that during my visit to Centennial, I had met a black, a Mexican and many Caucasians, but not one Indian. I considered that symbolic of today's west.

I walked idly through North Bottoms in order to catch a better understanding of how Central Beet and Brumbaugh Feed Lots interrelated, when I saw ahead of me a lone workman operating a back-hoe in the extreme elbow of Beaver Creek, and I went over to ask him what he was doing.

'Gonna build a bridge over the creek. So's the beet trucks from the west can enter the plant easier.'

As I watched him gouging the back-hoe into the soft earth, I became aware of a third man who had joined us. He introduced himself as Morgan Wendell, director of Wendell Real Estate, 'Slap Your Brand on a Hunk of Land.' He had left his offices, walked across Mountain and come through the North Bottoms to stand not far from me. I could not imagine why the digging of foundations for a bridge abutment should have concerned him, but he was obviously perturbed, and for good reason, apparently, for just as he took his place by me, the swinging arm of the back-hoe slammed down into the soft earth with extra force, hit rock and fell into a hole. It required considerable dexterity for the operator to manipulate his machine out of this difficulty, but he succeeded. I watched the maneuvering with interest; Morgan Wendell watched with horror.

When the back-hoe was again free, the driver climbed down to inspect what had trapped him. I too moved forward to peer into the hole. But Morgan Wendell elbowed us both aside and took command.

'You'd better quit work at this spot,' he told the operator. 'Sink hole or something. Work on the other side.'

'They told me to work here,' the man said.

'I'm telling you to work over there.'

'Who are you?'

'Morgan Wendell. I own the land on this side.'

'Oh!' He shrugged his shoulders, cranked up his machine and drove it ponderously along the creek to Mountain, crossing over to the eastern side.

As soon as he was gone, Morgan Wendell looked at me and said, 'Well, that's that,' and he began edging me away from the hole. I showed no inclination to go, whereupon a very firm hand gripped my arm and led me back toward town. I decided that prudence required my acquiescence, for Morgan Wendell was a tall, heavy-set man who weighed a good deal more than I and had a much longer reach.

When we got to First Street, just opposite Wendell Place, the old headquarters of the family, I said, as casually as I could, 'Well, I'll have some chili at Flor de Méjico.'

'It's good there,' he said.

When I left him, keeping my glance carefully ahead but watching as much as I could out of the corner of my eye, I saw him rush back to the exposed hole and climb in. He was there for some time, perhaps fifteen minutes, after which he climbed out carrying something wrapped in his coat. He walked south along the bank of Beaver Creek, crossed the highway and went into his office building.

As soon as he was out of sight I ran to the opening, climbed down and found myself inside a cave, not large but very secure . . . until the back-hoe punctured the roof. It had been formed, I judged, by the action of water on soft limestone and must have been very old. Along the western side there was a small bench, not formed by man yet appearing almost to have been made as a piece of built-in furniture. At the far end of this bench lay an item which Morgan Wendell had apparently overlooked: a small bone, which I suspected was human.

I placed it in my pocket and climbed out of the little cave. I was none too soon, for the back-hoe operator, who was then on the other side of the creek, was now directed by Morgan Wendell to bring his lumbering machine back to the western side, come up the creek bank and begin filling in the cave and tamping it down with his machine. When he had finished, Wendell inspected the job and satisfied himself that no one would be likely to detect that a long-lost cave had been accidentally laid bare that afternoon.

I returned to my room at the Railway Arms and put in a person-to-person call to James Ringold at *US*: 'This is Vernor. I'll take the job.' I heard him call out to Leeds and Wright: 'Get Carol. Good news.'

I said, 'But I'll have to do the work my way.'

'Wouldn't want you to do it any other way.'

'My first reports may go a little deeper than you intended,' I warned.

'It's your ideas we want.'

'But I'll get it done by Christmas.'

'Jingle bells, jingle bells' sounded over the telephone—three male voices, joined later by a soprano. It would be an interesting time till Christmas.

THE
LAND

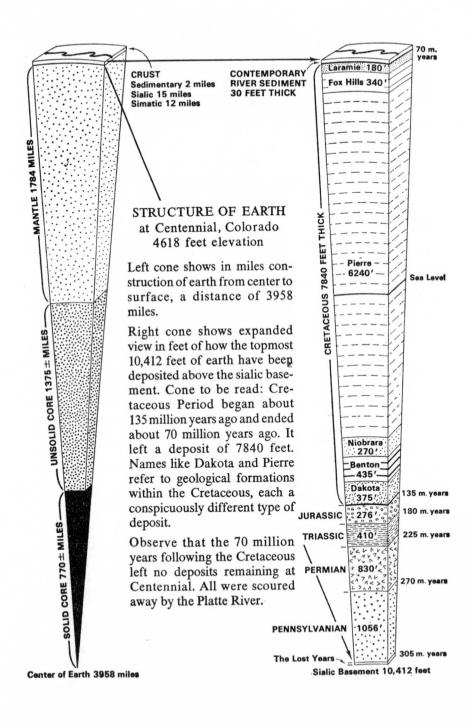

CRUST
Sedimentary 2 miles
Sialic 15 miles
Simatic 12 miles

CONTEMPORARY
RIVER SEDIMENT
30 FEET THICK

MANTLE 1784 MILES

UNSOLID CORE 1375 ± MILES

SOLID CORE 770 ± MILES

Center of Earth 3958 miles

STRUCTURE OF EARTH
at Centennial, Colorado
4618 feet elevation

Left cone shows in miles construction of earth from center to surface, a distance of 3958 miles.

Right cone shows expanded view in feet of how the topmost 10,412 feet of earth have been deposited above the sialic basement. Cone to be read: Cretaceous Period began about 135 million years ago and ended about 70 million years ago. It left a deposit of 7840 feet. Names like Dakota and Pierre refer to geological formations within the Cretaceous, each a conspicuously different type of deposit.

Observe that the 70 million years following the Cretaceous left no deposits remaining at Centennial. All were scoured away by the Platte River.

70 m. years

Laramie 180'
Fox Hills 340'

CRETACEOUS 7840 FEET THICK

Pierre
6240'

Sea Level

Niobrara 270'

Benton 435'

Dakota 375'

JURASSIC 276'

TRIASSIC 410'

PERMIAN 830'

PENNSYLVANIAN 1056'

The Lost Years

Sialic Basement 10,412 feet

135 m. years
180 m. years
225 m. years

270 m. years

305 m. years

WHEN THE EARTH WAS ALREADY ANCIENT, of an age incomprehensible to man, an event of basic importance occurred in the area which would later be known as Colorado.

To appreciate its significance, one must understand the structure of the earth, and to do this, one must start at the vital center.

Since the earth is not a perfect sphere, the radius from center to surface varies. At the poles it is 3950 miles and at the equator 3963. At the time we are talking about, Colorado lay about the same distance from the equator as it does now, and its radius was 3956. Those miles were composed in this manner.

At the center then, as today, was a ball of solid material, very heavy and incredibly hot, made up mostly of iron; this extended for about 770 miles. Around it was a cover about 1375 miles thick, which was not solid, but which could not be called liquid either, for at that pressure and that temperature, nothing could be liquid, as we know that word. It permitted movement, but it did not easily flow. It transmitted heat, but it did not bubble. It is best described as having characteristics with which we are not familiar, perhaps like a warm plastic.

Around this core was fitted a mantle of dense rock 1784 miles thick whose properties are difficult to describe, though much is known of them. Strictly speaking, this rock was in liquid form, but the pressures exerted upon it were such as to keep it more rigid than a bar of iron. The mantle was a belt which absorbed both pressure and heat from many directions and was, consequently, under considerable stress. From time to time throughout this story, the pressures will become so great that some of the mantle material will force its way toward the surface of the earth, undergoing marked change in the process. The resultant body of molten liquid, called magma, will solidify to produce the igneous rock, granite, but if it is still in liquid form as it approaches the surface, lava results. It was in the mantle that many of the movements originated which would determine what was to happen next to the visible structure of the earth, and although we shall not often refer again to the mantle, we must remember it deep beneath our feet, accumulating stress and generating enormous heat as it prepares for its next dramatic excursion toward the surface, producing the magma which will appear as either granite or lava.

At the top of the mantle, only twenty-seven miles from the surface, rested the earth's crust, where life would develop. What was it like? It can be described as the hard scum that forms at the top of a pot of boiling porridge. From the fire at the center of the pot, heat radiates not only upward but in all directions. The porridge bubbles freely at first when it is thin, and its motion seems to be always upward, but as it thickens, one can see that for every slow bubble that rises at the center of the pan, part of the porridge is drawn downward at the edges; it is this slow reciprocal rise and fall which constitutes cooking. In time, when enough of this convection has taken place, the porridge exposed to air begins to thicken perceptibly, and the moment the internal heat stops or diminishes, it hardens into a crust.

This analogy has two weaknesses. The flame that keeps the geologic pot bubbling does not come primarily from the hot center of the earth, but rather from the radioactive structure of the rocks themselves. And as the liquid magma cools, different types of rock solidify: heavy dark ones rich in iron settle toward the bottom; lighter ones like quartz move to the top.

The crust was divided into two distinct layers. The lower and heavier, twelve miles thick, was composed of a dark, dense rock known by the made-up name of sima, indicating the predominance of silicon and magnesium. The upper and lighter layer, fifteen miles thick, was composed of lighter rock known by the invented word sial, indicating silicon and aluminum. The subsequent two miles of Colorado's rock and sediment would eventually come to rest on this sialic layer.

Three billion, six hundred million years ago the crust had formed, and the cooling earth lay exposed to the developing atmosphere. The surface as it then existed was not hospitable. Temperatures were too high to sustain life, and oxygen was only beginning to accumulate. What land had tentatively coagulated was insecure, and over it winds of unceasing fury were starting to blow. Vast floods began to sweep emerging areas and kept them swamplike, rising and falling in the agonies of a birth that had not yet materialized. There were no fish, no birds, no animals, and had there been, there would have been nothing for them to eat, for grass and trees and worms were unknown.

There were in existence, even under these inhospitable conditions, elements like algae from which recognizable life would later develop, but the course of their future development had not yet been determined.

The earth, therefore, stood at a moment of decision: would it continue as a mass with a fragile covering incapable of sustaining either structures or life, or would some tremendous transformation take place which would alter its basic surface appearance and enlarge its capacity?

Sometime around three billion, six hundred million years ago, the answer came. Deep within the crust, or perhaps in the upper part of the mantle, a body of magma began to accumulate. Its concentration of heat was so great that previously solid rock melted partially. The lighter materials were melted first and moved upward through the heavier material that was left behind, coming to rest at higher elevations and in enormous quantities.

Slowly but with irresistible power it broke through the earth's crust and burst into daylight. In some cases, the sticky, almost congealed magma may have exploded upward as a volcano whose ash would cover thousands of square miles, or, if the magma was of a slightly different composition, it would pour through fissures as lava, spreading evenly over all existent features to a depth of a thousand feet.

As the magma spread, the central purer parts solidified into pure granite. Most of it, however, was trapped within the crust, and slowly cooled and solidified into rock deep below the surface.

What degree of time was required for this gigantic event to complete itself? It almost certainly did not occur as a vast one-time cataclysm although it might have, engulfing all previous surface features in one titanic wrenching which shook the world. More likely, convective movements in the mantle continued over millions of years. The rising internal heat accumulated eon after eon, and the resultant upward thrust still continues imperceptibly.

The earth was at work, as it is always at work, and it moved slowly. A thousand times in the future this irresistible combination of heat and movement would change the aspect of the earth's surface.

This great event of three billion, six hundred million years ago was different from many similar events for one salient reason: it intruded massive granite bodies which, when the mountains covering it were eroded away, would stand as the permanent basement rock. In later times it would be penetrated, wrenched, compressed, eroded and savagely distorted by cataclysmic forces of various kinds. But through three billion, six hundred million years, down to this very day, it would endure. Upon it would be built the subsequent mountains; across it would wander the rivers; high above its rugged surface animals would later roam; and upon its solid foundations homesteads and cities would rest.

A relatively short distance below the surface of the earth it rides, this infinitely aged platform, this permanent base for action. How do we know of its existence? From time to time, in subsequent events which we shall observe, blocks of this basement rock will be pushed upward, where they can be inspected, and tested, and analyzed, and even dated. At other memorable spots throughout Colorado this incredibly ancient rock will be broken by faults in the earth's crust, and large blocks of it will be uplifted to form the cores of present-day mountain ranges.

It is beautiful to see, as it sticks its head into daylight, a hard, granitic pink or gray-blue substance as clean and shining as if it had been created yesterday. You find it unexpectedly along canyon walls, or at the peaks of mountains or occasionally at the edge of some upland meadow, standing inconspicuously beside alpine flowers. It is a part of life, an almost living thing, with its own stubborn character formed deep in the bowels of the earth, once compressed by titanic forces and heated to hundreds of degrees. It is a poem of existence, this rock, not a lyric but a slow-moving epic whose beat has been set by eons of the world's experience.

Often the basement rock appears not as granite but as unmelted gneiss, and then it is even more dramatic, for in its contorted structure you can see proof of the crushing forces it has undergone. It has been fractured, twisted, folded over to the breaking point and reassembled into new arrangements. It tells the story of the internal tumult that has always accompanied the genesis of new land forms, and it reminds us of the wrenching and tearing that will be required when new forms rise into being, as they will.

It must be understood that basement rock is not a specific kind of rock, for its components change from place to place. It has been well defined as the 'layer of rock below which lies ignorance.' In some places it hides far below sea level; at others it marks the tops of mountains fourteen thousand feet high. Throughout most of the United States it lies hidden, but in Canada it is exposed over large areas, forming a shield. Nor was it all laid down at the same time, for variations in its dating are immense. In Minnesota it was deposited more than three and a half billion years ago; in Wyoming, only two and a half billion years ago; and in Colorado, only a few miles to the south, at the relatively recent date of one billion seven hundred million years ago.

After the basement rock had been accumulated at Centennial, later than almost anywhere else in the United States, one of the most extraordinary events occurred. About two billion years of history vanished, leaving no recoverable record. By studying other parts of the west, and by making shrewd extrapolations, we can construct guesses as to what must have happened, but we have no proof. The rocks which should have been at hand to tell the story have either been destroyed beyond recognition or were never deposited in the first place. We are left in ignorance.

This situation is not confined to the small area around Centennial, although there the gap is spectacular. At no spot in North America have we been able to find an unbroken sequence of rocks from earliest basement to recent sediment. Always there is a tantalizing gap. Over short distances it can have amazing variations in time and extent; for example, during the missing years at Centennial, massive accumulations of granite which would later form Pikes Peak were being assembled only a few miles to the south.

For hundreds of millions of years at a time Centennial must have lain at the bottom of the sea which at intervals covered much of America. Then grains of sediment, eroded from earth masses remaining above sea level, would drift in silently and fall upon the basement, building with infinite slowness a sedimentary rock which might ultimately stand five thousand feet thick.

At other intervals the new-forming land would rise from the sea to be weathered by storm and wind and creeping rivers long vanished. This cycle of beneath-sea, above-sea was repeated at least a dozen times; repeatedly magma sent upward by the mantle broke through the crust and crept over the land; repeatedly erosion cut it away and left new forms much different from their predecessors.

The time required! The slow passage of years! The constant alterations! Now part of an uplifted mountain, now sunk at the bottom of some sea, Centennial experienced wild fluctuations. Because of the erratic wanderings of the earth, it stood sometimes fairly close to the equator, with a baking sun overhead; at subsequent times it might be closer to the north pole, with ice in winter. It was swamp during one eon, a desert the next. Whenever it came to temporary rest, it should have been exhausted, a worn-out land, but always new energies surged up from below, generating new experiences.

Those lost two billion years lie upon the consciousness of man the way vague memories of ghosts survive in the recollections of childhood. When man did finally arrive on the scene, he would be the inheritor of those vanished years, and everything he did would be limited to some degree by what had happened to his earth in those forgotten years, for it was then that its quality was determined, its mineral content, the value of its soil and the salinity of its waters.

About three hundred and five million years ago occurred what can be called the first event which left an identifiable record at Centennial, and with it our story begins. Within the mantle, forces developed which produced a penetration of the earth's crust. The basement broke into discrete blocks, some of which were pushed upward higher than their surroundings, to relieve the pressure from below.

The resulting mountains covered much of central Colorado, following fairly closely the outlines that the historical Rocky Mountains would later occupy, and at the conclusion of five or ten million years they constituted a major range.

It was not born in cataclysm. There was no dramatic opening of earth from which fully formed mountains emerged. Nor was there any excess of volcanism. Instead there was the slow, unceasing uplift of rock until the new mountains stood forth in considerable majesty. They were the Ancestral Rockies, and since they left behind them rocks which can be analyzed, we can construct for them a logical history.

They were not soaring peaks, like their successors, but they did rise from sea level and would have seemed higher above their pediment than today's Rockies, which although they lift far into the sky, take their start from plains already high.

From the moment of their birth they participated in a startling series of events. No sooner had they pushed their crests above the flat surface of the land than small streams began to nibble at their flanks, eating away small fragments of rock and sand. High winds tore at their low summits, and freezing winters broke away protuberances. At intervals earthquakes toppled insecure rocks; at other times inland seas lashed at their feet, eroding them further.

As the mountains increased in age, the small streams grew into rivers, and as they increased in volume, they also increased in carrying power, and soon they were conveying broken bits of mountain downward, cutting as they went and forming great alluvial fans along the margins of the range.

In a beautiful interrelationship, the mountains continued to push upward at about the rate at which the eroding forces were tearing them down. Had the mountains been permitted to grow unimpeded, they might have reached heights of twenty thousand feet; as it was, the system of balances kept them at some undetermined elevation, perhaps no more than three or four thousand feet.

And then, for some reason, the upward pressures ceased, and over a period of forty million years this once formidable range was razed absolutely flat by erosion, with not a single peak remaining as a memento of what had been one of the earth's outstanding features. The fabled Ancestral Rockies, a masterpiece of landscape, vanished, its component rocks reduced to rubble and scattered across the growing plains of eastern Colorado, Kansas and Nebraska. Mountains that had commanded the landscape had become pebbles.

Later, as if to seal off even the record of their existence, the land upon which they had stood was submerged spasmodically over a period of eighty to ninety million years in the Jurassic and Cretaceous periods, the era of the dinosaurs. Clay, silt and sand were moved in by rivers emptying into the inland sea, filtering down slowly, silently in the darkness, accumulating in soft layers. But with the passage of time and the weight of water and sediment pressing down, it gradually solidified into layers of rock thousands of feet thick. Thus the roots of the once great mountains were sealed off, as if the forces which had erected them in the first place had reconsidered, erased them and then buried the evidence.

It is essential to comprehend the meaning of time. When a mountain ten thousand feet high vanishes over a period of forty million years, what has happened? Each million years it loses two hundred and fifty feet, which means each thousand years it loses three inches. The loss per year would be minuscule and could not have been detected while it was happening.

This extremely slow average rate does not preclude occasional catastrophes like earthquakes or floods which might compress into one convulsion the losses for an average millennium. Nor does it mean that the debris could be easily removed. These mountains covered an extensive land area, and even a trivial average loss, if applied over that total area, would require much riverine action to carry the eroded materials away.

The fact remains that an enormous mountain range had vanished.

Since this seems a prodigal action, extremely wasteful of motion and material, a caution must be voiced. The rocks that were lifted from the depths of the earth to form the Ancestral Rockies had been used earlier in the construction of other mountain ranges whose records have now vanished. When those predecessor ranges were eroded away, the material that composed them was deposited in great basins, mainly to the west.

The earth was much like a prudent man who has an allotted span of life and a given amount of energy. Using both wisely, conserving where possible, he can enjoy a long and useful life; but no matter how prudent, he will not escape ultimate death. The earth uses its materials with uncanny thrift; it wastes nothing; it patches and remodels. But always it expends a little of its heat, and in the end—at some unpredictable day billions of years from now—that fire will diminish and earth, like man, will die. In the meantime, its resources are conserved.

While the Ancestral Rockies were disappearing, an event which was to leave still-visible consequences was reaching its climax along the eastern shore of what would later be known as the United States. The time was about two hundred and fifty million years ago; during preceding periods, reaching very far into the past, a building process of beautiful complexity had been operating. Into the deep ocean depressions east of the wandering shoreline, prehistoric and very ancient mountains had deposited sediments that had accumulated to a remarkable depth; at some places they were forty thousand feet thick. With the passage of time and in the presence of great pressure, they had of course formed into rock. Thrust and compression, uplift and subsidence had crumpled these rocks into contorted shapes.

The stage was now set for an event which would elevate the rocks into a mountain range. It occurred when the subterranean plate on which rested the crust that was later to become part of the continent of Africa began to move slowly westward. In time the migration of this plate became so determined—and perhaps it was matched by a comparable movement of the American plate eastward—that collision became inevitable. The predecessor of the Atlantic Ocean was squeezed so severely that it was entirely eliminated. The continents came into actual contact, so that such living things as then existed could move from America to Africa and back again over land.

As the inexorable collision continued, there had to be some kind of dislocation along the edges that were bearing the brunt. It seems probable that the edge of the African plate turned under, its rocky components returning to the crust and perhaps even back into the mantle. We know that the edge of the American plate was thrust upward to produce the Appalachian Mountains, not some ancestral Appalachians, but the roots of the very mountains we see today.

After some twenty million years of steady growth the Appalachians stood forth as a more considerable range than the Ancestral Rockies had been. They were, of a certainty, some of the world's most impressive mountains, soaring thousands of feet into the air.

Inevitably, as soon as they began to emerge, the tearing-down process commenced. First the continental plates drifted apart, with Africa and the Americas winding up in roughly the positions they occupy today. The Atlantic Ocean as it exists today started to develop, its deep inclines providing a basin for the catchment of rock and silt eroded from the heights. Volcanoes operated and at intervals enormous fractures occurred, allowing vast segments of the range to rise while others fell.

As early as a hundred million years ago the Appalachians—only a truncated memory of their original grandeur—began to assume their present shape; they are thus one of the oldest landscape features of the United States. At this time the Appalachians had no competition from the Rocky Mountains, for that range had not yet emerged; indeed, most of America from the Appalachians to Utah was nothing but a vast sea from which substantial land would rise only much later.

The Appalachians play no further part in this story—except that a stubborn Dutchman who grew up along their flank will travel westward to Centennial in his Conestoga—and in their present condition they seem a poor comparison to the Rockies. They are no longer high; they contain no memorable landscape; they do not command great plains; and they are impoverished where minerals like gold and silver are concerned. But they are the majestic harbingers of our land; they served their major purpose long before man existed, then lingered on as noble relics to provide man with an agreeable home when he did arrive. They are mountains of ancient destiny, and to move among them is to establish contact with a notable period of our history.

They have been mentioned here to provide a counterbalance to the great things that were about to happen in the west. About seventy million years ago much of the western part of America lay beneath a considerable sea, and if this configuration had persisted, the eastern United States would have been an island much like Great Britain, but dominated by the low-lying Appalachians.

But beneath the surface of the inland sea great events portended. The combined weight of sediment and water, pressing down upon a relatively weak basin area, coincided with an upsurge of magma from the mantle. As before, these magmatic pressures from below pushed upward huge blocks of the basement, and bent the more flexible layered rocks above the basement until a massive mountain range had been erected. The range, running from northern Canada almost to Mexico, was both longer and wider than the Ancestral Rockies had ever been and placed somewhat farther east. Its major elevations stood very high, and as these areas were uplifted, the inland sea was drained off.

The mountain range was composed in part of rock that had formerly been utilized in the Ancestral Rockies—which is why we know so much about those ancient mountains we have never seen—and formed one of the world's major structural forms, which it still does.

The Rockies are therefore very young and should never be thought of as ancient. They are still in the process of building and eroding, and no one today can calculate what they will look like ten million years from now. They have the extravagant beauty of youth, the allure of adolescence, and they are mountains to be loved.

Their history is reasonably clear. Not all were born as a result of basement block uplift, for certain mountains were squeezed upward by vast forces acting laterally. Others may have arisen as a result of some movement of the American plate. And we have visible proof that some of the southern mountains were built by spectacular action.

About sixty-seven million years ago volcanic activity of considerable range and intensity erupted throughout Colorado. As the mountains rose, the crust cracked and allowed lava to rise to the surface in great quantity. Lava flows were extensive, but so were explosions of gaseous ash, which sometimes accumulated to a depth of several hundred feet, compressing itself finally into rock which still exists.

Especially awesome were the vast clouds of gaseous matter which drifted eastward, with internal temperatures rising to thousands of degrees. Whatever they passed over they killed instantly through the exhaustion of oxygen, and when their temperatures fell, the clouds fell too. Their contents then solidified to form crystalline rock, one cloud producing enough to blanket large areas to a depth of seven or eight feet. In other areas, lakes were formed, dammed by lava flows from volcanic fields.

Now for the first time we come to the river which will command our attention for the remainder of this story. It was born coincident with the rise of the New Rockies, called into being to carry rainfall and melting snow down from the heights. For millions of years it was not the dominant river of the region; in fact, five competing rivers led eastward from the Rockies, their long-abandoned courses still discernible in the drylands. They lost their identity because of a peculiarity; an arm of our river began to cut southward along the edge of the mountain range, and in doing so, it captured one after another of the competing rivers, until they no longer ran eastward as independent rivers but coalesced to form the Platte.

When the Rockies were younger, and therefore higher than now, the river had to be of a goodly size. We can deduce this from the amount of material it was required to carry. The area covered by its deposits was about three hundred and twenty miles long and one hundred and forty wide. Depending upon how thick the overlay was, the river had to transport more than seven thousand cubic miles of rubble.

In those early days it was wide and turbulent. It was capable of carrying huge rocks, which it disintegrated into fragments of great cutting power, but its main burden was sand and silt. Its flow was irregular; at times it would wander fifty miles wide across plains; for long periods it would hold to one channel. During these years it labored continuously at its job of building the plains of middle America.

About forty million years ago the building process was aided by a cataclysmic event. To the southwest a group of volcanoes burst into action, and so violent were their eruptions, volcanic ash drifted across the sky for half a thousand miles, held aloft by great windstorms. The ash, blackening the sky as it passed, blanketed the area when it fell. Perhaps at some point an entire volcano may have exploded in one super burst, commanding the heavens with its burden of fire and lava; eruptions continued over a period of fifteen million years, and the wealth of ash that fell upon Colorado accumulated to a depth of thousands of feet. Combining with clay, it formed one of the principal rocks of the region.

It is difficult to comprehend the violence of this period. Twenty-three known volcanoes operated in Colorado, some of them much larger than Vesuvius or Popocatepetl. Obviously, they could not have been in constant eruption; there had to be periods of long quiescence, but it does seem likely that some acted in concert, energized by a common agitation within the mantle. They deposited an incredible amount of new rock, more than fourteen thousand cubic miles of it in all.

They glowed through the nights, illuminating in ghostly flashes the mountains and plains they were creating. At times they sponsored earthquakes, and then for some mysterious reason, possibly because the molten magma was exhausted, they died, one after another, until there were no active volcanoes in the region, only the clearly defined calderas which still stand to mark this age of violence.

About fifteen million years ago the area underwent a massive dislocation in a process that extended for ten million years. The entire central portion of America experienced a massive uplifting. Perhaps the continental plate was undergoing some major adjustment, or there may have been a sizable disruption within the mantle. At any rate, the surfaces—both mountains and valleys to the west, and the low-lying flat plains to the east—rose. Colorado was uplifted to its present altitude. Rivers like the Missouri, which then ran north to the Arctic Ocean, began to take form, and the outlines of our continent assumed more or less their present shape. Many subsequent adjustments of a minor nature would still occur—for example, at this time North and South America were not yet joined—but the shapes we know were discernible.

About one million years ago the Ice Age began to send its rapacious fingers down from the north polar ice cap. Because of intricate changes in climate, triggered perhaps by variations in the carbon dioxide content of the earth's atmosphere or by accumulations of volcanic dust which intercepted the sun's heat that otherwise would have reached the earth, large sheets of ice began to accumulate where none had been before.

The glaciers invading North America reached so far south and were so thick, they imprisoned water that normally belonged to the oceans, which meant that shorelines which had lain submerged for the preceding millions of years now lay exposed. The great western glacier did not quite reach Centennial; it halted some distance to the north. But at high elevations in the New Rockies, small glaciers did form and filled the valleys, and when they moved slowly to lower levels they gouged out the valley bottoms and carved the standing rocks, so that much of the beauty of the New Rockies stems from the work of the glaciers.

They arrived in the mountains at spaced intervals, the first major one appearing about three million years ago; the last, only fifteen thousand years ago. But of course, at high, cold altitudes like the topmost New Rockies small glaciers persisted and still exist.

As the mountain glaciers melted they produced unprecedented amounts of water, which created floods of gigantic proportion. They cascaded down with fierce velocity and submerged traditional rivers, causing them to expand many times their customary width. Much detritus was borne down from the mountains, most of it with sharp cutting edges, and it was this mixture of copious water and cutting rock which planed down the lands to the east.

Sometimes, high in the Rockies, the glacier would impound a temporary rock-and-ice barrier, and behind it an enormous lake would be formed. It would exist for decades or centuries. Then, one day, there would be a violent cracking sound, and with one vast rush the contents of the lake would surge forth, miles wide until it roared into some confining canyon, when it would compress into a devastating liquid missile, shooting along with terrifying force, uprooting every living thing and ripping away huge boulders from the walls of the canyon before rushing at last onto the plains.

There it would reach the river. A wall of water would fan out across the plains, engulfing both the river and its tributaries. Churning, roaring, twisting, it would scour everything before it as it scratched and clawed its way eastward. In the space of an afternoon, such a flood might carve away deposits which had required ten million years to accumulate.

It was the river which had laid down the new land; it was the river which took it away. The endless cycle of building up, tearing down and rebuilding, using the same material over and over, was contributed to by the river. It was the brawling, undisciplined, violent artery of life and would always be.

The major characteristics of land around Centennial were now fairly well determined and there is little more to report. There were, however, four special places of no great consequence in the grand scheme of things but around which much of this story will revolve.

The first was a chalk cliff running north-south some miles northwest of Centennial. Its basic components had been laid down some two hundred and seventy million years ago during that period when the Ancestral Rockies were disintegrating and washing out to sea. At the bottom of this sea huge beds of limestone accumulated in flat layers, one above the other like sheaves of paper in a pile. This limestone was infinitely older than the New Rockies and constituted yet another example of how the earth's material was used, broken down, accumulated, conserved and reissued in new form.

For about one hundred million years this limestone bed lay flat, sometimes exposed but usually at the bottom of some sea. Then internal turbulence within the mantle uplifted the area so that it stood as high as some mountains. No sooner had it moved into its elevated position than it was visited by a racking accident: a large fault wrenched the surface of the earth, depressed the area and cracked the limestone along its north-south axis. The eastern portion dropped some eighty feet below its previous level, while the western half rose twenty, forming a white chalk cliff about one hundred feet high.

There it stood, one hundred and thirty-six million years ago, a chalky white cliff with a rain forest on its upper plateau and a great swamp bathing its feet, ready for the dramatic incidents which would occur along its margin.

The second place was a moderately high mountain valley to the west of Centennial and slightly to the south. A small stream of water ran the length of the valley before joining the river; it had been the cause of the valley's existence. The valley was not ancient, for it developed only in the later stages of mountain building; it could not have been any more than forty million years old, but throughout its brief life it had always been a place of exceptional beauty.

It ran almost due east and west and was only a few miles long. Its sides were formed by steep mountains which hemmed it in; it was not wide, the mountain walls being less than a mile apart, and it had a gentle fall, the higher end being at the west. Its beauty was gemlike rather than expansive.

During its existence it had undergone little change. It had started at an elevation of only four thousand feet, but at the great uplifting fifteen million years ago it had been raised to an elevation of ten thousand feet. Subsequent erosion had lowered this to eight thousand, just low enough to make possible one of the features which made it memorable.

On the north wall, which of course received the sun, a thick grove of aspen trees developed about one million years ago to form a thing of joy. The trees heralded spring as it was about to appear, their small gray-green leaves shimmering in the sun. In midsummer their leaves were exquisite, for they were attached to their branches in a peculiar manner which left them free to flutter constantly; the slightest breath of air set the aspen shaking so that at times the entire north wall of the valley seemed to be dancing. It was in the autumn, however, that the aspen came into its true glory, for then each leaf turned a brilliant gold, so that a single tree seemed an explosion of vibrating loveliness. In autumn this valley was a place of beauty unmatched across the entire continent.

But curiously, the valley would take its name from a much different kind of tree, which clustered on the dark south wall where the sun did not shine. It was an evergreen. Now, there were many types of evergreens in the New Rockies; they might be considered the symbolic tree of the region, but the one that grew in this valley was different, for it was not green but a spectacular blue. It was the blue spruce, a tree of dignified proportions and splendid color. It grew much taller than its neighbor across the stream, and larger. And it was not deciduous, so that in late autumn when the aspen stood bare, its golden leaves having vanished one by one, the glory of the blue spruce came into its own. In winter, when clinging snow covered the spruce, allowing patches of blue to show, the valley was a quiet, dreamlike place, so lovely that even passing animals instinctively found refuge here. Throughout the balance of the year the tall spruce trees showed noble coloring, from powdery blue to indigo.

In historic times, the place would be named Blue Valley, a notable setting, well proportioned in all things. If it did not lie at the top of the mountains, it did not hide at the bottom, either. Its stream was capable but never turbulent, and although snow sometimes crowded the floor of the valley, it rarely fell so deep that the valley itself became inaccessible. Under any circumstances this delectable valley, with its gold and blue trees, would have been memorable, but two events made it even more so.

When permanent ice began to form in the highest mountain valleys, it became only a matter of time until some glacier shoved its icy snout into Blue Valley. This happened, and the front edge of the glacier gouged out the bottom lands, widened the base of the valley and scoured the walls of the mountains that enclosed it. Of course, every tree within the valley was destroyed, but ages later, when the ice had receded, the trees reestablished themselves as if nothing serious had interrupted them, and the valley was now much more pleasant than it had been before, since the glacier had carved out a spacious meadow filled on the north bank with aspen and on the south with blue spruce.

Subsequent glaciers broadened the meadow and rearranged the rocks. Each mutilated the trees, but with that fine determination which marks so much of nature, they returned, and by the year 15,000 B.C. the valley had assumed its present form and was a place of enhanced beauty.

The second event happened long before the aspen and blue spruce had given the place its character, and we must go well back in time to understand it. About thirty-five million years ago, a pressure very deep within the mantle sent relatively small amounts of highly liquid magma probing upward at very high temperatures.

It sought out any weakness in the structure of the rock, and was especially inclined to surge into cracks where faces met, expanding them and filling them to the remotest cranny. This had happened often before, as can be seen in any large accumulation of mountain rock: invariably the rock will show where a hot igneous material had intruded itself into interstices, and this has occurred all over the world.

What made this incursion exceptional was that this particular flow of magma contained a high percentage of minerals, sometimes in pure state: galena, silver, copper filled the interstices. The liquid rock that crept into the long pipe underlying Blue Valley contained a large proportion of unalloyed gold.

The end of the pipe it filled lay only ninety feet below the surface of the valley, along the northern flank. It extended downward at an angle of forty degrees for nearly a quarter of a mile. It was not a large pipe, and therefore did not contain any fantastic amount of gold, but it was substantial, and it filled every crevice.

It lay undisturbed for more than thirty million years. When the area rose, it rose too. When minor faults appeared, it adjusted to them. And when the area subsided, the golden pipe fell with it, still ensconced under the north bank of the little stream. In time roots of the golden aspen formed a network above it.

When the first great glacier filled the valley it stripped away some fifty feet of cover protecting the near end of the pipe, but no other change occurred. Each succeeding glacier cut away a little more of the protection until the last one came. Sometime around the year 15,000 B.C. this glacier actually cut away six feet of the pipe and scattered the gold that it had contained along the bottom of the stream for a distance of some two hundred yards.

This same glacier, of course, deposited gravel over the exposed end of the pipe, so that it could not easily be detected, and hid the nuggets of gold that lay at the bottom of the stream. Then trees returned and the gold was buried again, but each autumn when leaves of the aspen turned, this was a valley that was doubly golden.

The third place was conspicuous from all directions, and spectacular, but what was significant about it was hidden, and we shall not know of it till later.

Some sixty-five million years ago—shortly after the emergence of the New Rockies—the river began hauling down an extraordinary amount of rock, gravel and sand, which it deposited in a thick overlay on the flat plains to the east. We have observed this phenomenon before, so there is no need to recapitulate, except to state that at the location we are talking about, a spot to the north of Centennial and slightly to the east, the deposit eventually was more than two hundred feet thick.

When this process was completed, thirty-eight million years ago, the plains to the east were so built up that they blended harmoniously into the lower reaches of the New Rockies, creating a lovely sweep that extended in unbroken beauty several hundred miles into Nebraska and Kansas. This symmetry did not endure, for the New Rockies experienced a massive uplifting, which raised them above the gentle sweep. As a result, the river now dropped more steeply from the mountains, carrying with it many cutting rocks. It surged eastward and for twelve million years dominated the foothills, cutting them away, scraping down hillocks, and depositing on the plains new layers of soil characterized by a rocky, infertile content.

The great inland sea which had once dominated this area had long vanished, so that the building of this new rock had to be accomplished in open air. The river would bring down deposits, which would spread out in fans. Sun and wind would act upon them, and new deposits would form over them. Gradually, disparate components would begin to solidify, and as heavier forms accumulated on top, those on the bottom would coalesce to form conglomerates.

Each year the plains grew a little higher, a little more stable in their footing. Finishing touches were applied about eleven million years ago, when a sandstone rock was laid down, sealing the entire region. This final rock had a peculiar characteristic: at the spot we are talking about, north of Centennial, some variation occurred in the cement which bound the granular elements together. Different from the cement operating in nearby regions, it had been formed perhaps from volcanic ash which had drifted in; at any rate, it created an impermeable caprock which would protect the softer sandstone that rested beneath.

At last the vast job of building was ended. From the period when the New Rockies underwent their secondary uplift, some three hundred and twenty feet of solid rock and soil had been laid down, all protected by the caprock, and had there been an observer at the time, he could have been excused had he concluded that what he saw then, eight million years ago, would be the final structure of the plains.

But it was still the river which determined what the surface of the land would be, and starting eight million years ago, it once more began to tumble out of the mountains with greatly increased velocity, cutting and swirling and spreading far across the plains. It was engaged upon a gargantuan task, to scour away every vestige of the enormous quantity of land that had been contributed by the New Rockies. In some places it had to remove up to a thousand feet of burden; from extensive areas it had to cut away at least three hundred feet. But it succeeded . . . except where that extra-hard caprock protected its monolith.

No matter how wild the torrents that raged down from the mountains, nor how compulsive the flash floods that cascaded across the plain after some torrential downpour, the monolith persisted. It covered an area no more than a quarter of a mile long, two hundred yards wide, but it resisted all assaults of the river. For millions of years this strange and solitary monolith maintained its integrity.

Neighboring sandstone covers were breached, and when they were gone, the softer areas they had protected were easily cut down by the river. Winds helped; meltwater from ice did its damage; and as the eons passed, the river completed its task: all remnants of land deposited by the New Rockies were swept away, except the solitary monolith.

And then, about two million years ago, the central portion of the caprock weakened, cracked during a heavy winter, and broke away. The softer rock which it had been protecting quickly deteriorated—say, over a period of two hundred thousand years—until it was gone.

Two pillars remained, about a quarter of a mile apart, each somewhat elongated in shape; the western was over five hundred feet long and two hundred wide, the eastern only three hundred and eighty feet long and a hundred and ninety wide. The western pillar was taller, too, standing three hundred and twenty feet above its pediment; the eastern, only two hundred and eighty.

They were extraordinary, these two sentinels of the plains. Visible for miles in each direction, they guarded a bleak and silent empire. They were the only remaining relics of that vast plain which the New Rockies had deposited; each bit of land the sentinels surveyed dated back to the ancient times before the mountains were born.

The fourth special place is rather embarrassing to mention, after this parade of fractured cliffs, valleys packed with gold and high monuments of integrity; but eleven thousand years ago, when the main features of the New Rocky Mountain area had long been determined and the land looked pretty much as it looks today, a small, wandering muddy stream joined the river at the spot where Centennial was to be. It came in from the north and in its day must have been a helpful agent to the parent river in scouring off the debris sent down by the mountains. Now it was a miserable thing, carrying little water and serving more as a drainage ditch than a rivulet.

But along its western bank, not far from where it joined the river, its probing fingers had recently penetrated into a pocket of soluble stone lying some seven feet below the surface of the land. It formed a secret cave less than six feet long and only four feet wide. It would scarcely have been noticed except for a dramatic event which would occur in relation to it eleven thousand years after its creation by the meandering stream.

And so the stage is set. One billion, seven hundred million years of activity, including the building of at least two high mountain ranges and the calling into being of vast seas, have produced a land which is ready to receive living things.

It is not a hospitable land, like that farther east in Kansas or back near the Appalachians. It is mean and gravelly and hard to work. It lacks an adequate topsoil for plowing. It is devoid of trees or easy shelter. A family could wander this land for weeks and never find enough wood to build a house.

It lacks water—my God, how it lacks water. Rainfall at Centennial is only thirteen inches a year, when any farmer knows that to produce even miserly corn or wheat requires twenty-one. The extremes of temperature can be unbearable, from one hundred and nine in August to thirty-eight below in February.

It is a land subject to wild whims of nature. Sometimes a score of years will pass with almost no rain, so that crops perish and organized society stands in peril. At sixty- or seventy-year intervals unpredictable winds whip over the prairies, exhausting the land and everything that grows upon it. Duststorms greater than hurricanes and more persistent can sweep the region for months on end, filling all openings with grit. And as if this were not enough, at unexpected times and for unexplained reasons gigantic swarms of locusts can suddenly emerge from the west and darken the sky for three or four days running. They swarm in the air, more extensive than storm clouds, and capriciously they alight, eating every green thing that stands in their path. Then they rise and fly mysteriously on, landing and eating a few more times, then vanishing as inexplicably as they appeared.

But there is one thing about this land. Theoretically, it can be farmed. It is rich in minerals. It is the inheritor of two great mountain ranges; over several hundred million years it conserved deposits sent down by the mountains and is entitled to the richness it possesses. The growing season is adequate for most crops: last frost on May 10, first frost on September 27, with an average 139 frost-free days in between for the prudent farmer. The governing rule is simple.

'If you can lead water onto this land, you can grow anything.'

'Well, you wouldn't try apples or oranges, would you?'

'No, but only because they can be grown better somewhere else.'

Corn and wheat? Magnificent. Sorghum? The best. Garden vegetables? None better.

'Like I said, you can grow anything. But two things grow better here than anywhere else on earth.'

'Such as?'

'Melons of any kind. You name it. And great big juicy sugar beets.'

The land cries for water. The bleakest desert, even the forbidding land about the two pillars, will flourish like a garden if only water can be got to it. Consequently, the crucial problem of this area will be the attempt of man to lead water onto his intractable land. If he can do that, if only he can do that, he will have at his disposal a paradise.

And finally there is the river, a sad, bewildered nothing of a river. It carries no great amount of water, and when it has some it is uncertain where it wants to take it. No ship can navigate it, nor even a canoe, with reasonable assurance. It is the butt of more jokes than any other river on earth, and the greatest joke is to call it a river at all. It's a sand bottom, a wandering afterthought, a useless irritation, a frustration, and when you've said all that, it suddenly rises up, spreads out to a mile wide, engulfs your crops and lays waste your farms.

Its name is as flat as its appearance, the South Platte, yet for a while it was the highway of empire. It was the course of stirring adventure and the means whereby the adventurers lived. Once mighty enough to help build a continent, it is now a mean, pestiferous bother.

'I swear to God, sometimes you can tell where that damned river is only by spotting cottonwoods that line its bank.'

'You're right, and those useless trees drink far more of the water than they're entitled to.'

CAUTION TO *US* EDITORS. Last April, when we started this project, I half warned you on the telephone that my investigations might wander somewhat far afield. But I could not imagine how provocative the history of this little town would prove to be, how involved I would become with the land, the animals, the people. And certainly I did not anticipate that to report to you properly, I would need to start with the origin of the earth.

When you face the problem of dating that origin, you will have to bite the bullet. What I have given you is based upon an earth age of 4,750,000,000 years plus or minus 50,000,000. This is the latest specific estimate I have been able to uncover and is based upon the summary studies of G. R. Tilton and R. H. Steiger, who did analytic work on the Canadian Shield, using lead isotopes.

I have consulted with the leading scientists at Colorado School of Mines, Colorado State and Colorado University and they tend toward a somewhat lesser age. You would not be far wrong if you used 4,600,000,000. You may find it useful to have the principal historical estimates:

Year	Authority	Proposed Origin of Earth
1642	John Lightfoot, professor of Greek	9:00 A.M., September 17, 3928 B.C.
1658	James Ussher, archbishop	October 23, 4004 B.C.
1860	John Phillips	96,000,000 BPE
1869	Thomas Huxley	100,000,000
1892	T. L. Wallace	28,000,000
1892	Sir Archibald Geikie	680,000,000
1897	Jacob Johannes Sederholm	40,000,000
1897	Lord Kelvin	40,000,000
1899	John Joly	100,000,000
1907	B. B. Boltwood	1,640,000,000
1917	Joseph Barrell	1,600,000,000
1947	Arthur Homes	3,000,000,000
1956	C. C. Patterson	4,550,000,000
1960	Tilton and Steiger	4,750,000,000 ± 50,000,000

My own educated guess is that before long we may be tending toward some date like six billion years, but I would not recommend that you stick your neck out in that direction till more studies are in. My figures will prove consistent if you settle upon Tilton and Steiger's 4,750,000,000, which is supported by recent moon data.

As to my datings of classical geologic periods, I have followed the most conservative and generally agreed-upon dates. You should have no trouble with these, as scientists the world over agree generally as to relative datings. There are discrepancies. Ogden Tweto, the foremost expert on the Laramide orogeny, believes the New Rockies began to emerge 72,000,000 years ago, with the process terminating about 43,000,000 years ago. Others have preferred beginning dates like 80,000,000 to 65,000,000 and terminal dates as late as 39,000,000.

But as to the specific relationships between the geological eras, systems and series, there can be no logical protest. The Silurian period follows the Ordovician, and the Miocene epoch follows the Oligocene as surely as Wednesday follows Tuesday. What the precise length of each unit was, and when the whole began, we cannot say with certainty, but we can be absolutely sure of the relative relationships.

It is precisely as if, in the distant future when written records have been lost, scientists want to determine when American constitutional government began. All they have to work on is a marble plaque giving the names of the first sixteen Presidents, the fact that Lincoln ended his term in 1865, and the law that a President was elected for a term of four years.

Washington	Harrison
Adams	Tyler
Jefferson	Polk
Madison	Taylor
Monroe	Fillmore
Adams	Pierce
Jackson	Buchanan
Van Buren	Lincoln

Using these data, the scientists would multiply sixteen by four and subtract that number from 1865; they would thus deduce that our nation started in 1801, which is too late.

Then let us suppose that one clever scientist discovers that Jefferson, Madison and Monroe each served eight years. He might conclude that all did and decide that the nation started in 1737, which is too early.

Let us now suppose that another scholar finds that the two generals, Harrison and Taylor, died shortly after being elected and should therefore not count in the series. There would thus be only fourteen Presidents, each serving eight years, which would give a starting date of 1773, which is better but not yet close to the true date, which was 1789.

However, regardless of the misconceptions of the scientists as they work their way through the data, they do have the proper sequence, and they are refining their judgments. American constitutional democracy started sometime around the end of the eighteenth century and could not possibly have started at the end of the seventeenth.

The Appalachians were incontrovertibly old when the New Rockies emerged; the central part of our nation did lie submerged beneath a great sea for millions of years; and volcanoes in southeastern Colorado did produce rocks aggregating some fourteen thousand cubic miles. On these established matters we can expect future refinements of judgment. But not reversal. The land at Centennial developed pretty much as stated.

THE
INHABITANTS

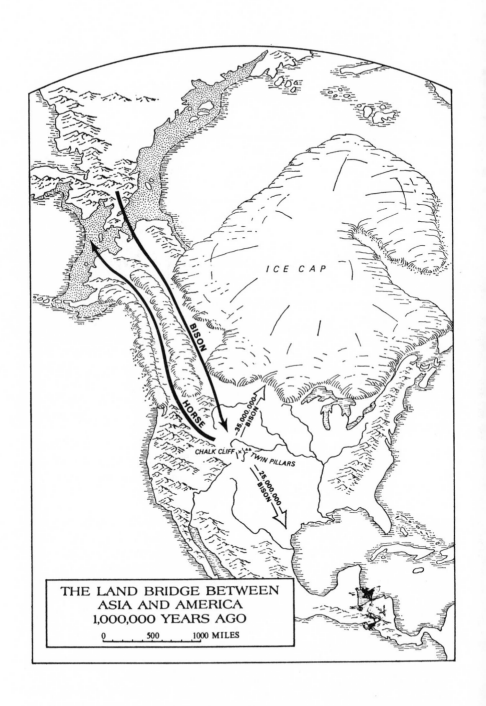

BISON

HORSE

ICE CAP

—35,000,000 BISON

CHALK CLIFF   TWIN PILLARS

—25,000,000 BISON

THE LAND BRIDGE BETWEEN
ASIA AND AMERICA
1,000,000 YEARS AGO

0   500   1000 MILES

Any SEGMENT OF LAND — THE MOON, FOR example—can be interesting of itself, but its greater significance must always lie in the life it sustains.

Toward dusk on a spring evening one hundred and thirty-six million years ago a small furry animal less than four inches long peered cautiously from low reeds which grew along the edge of a tropical lagoon that covered much of what was to be Colorado. It was looking across the surface of the water as if waiting for some creature to emerge from the depths, but nothing stirred.

From among the fern trees to the left there was movement, and for one brief instant the little animal looked in that direction. Shoving its way beneath the drooping branches and making considerable noise as it awkwardly approached the lagoon for a drink of water, came a medium-sized dinosaur, walking on two legs and twisting its short neck from side to side, as if on the watch for larger animals that might attack.

It was about three feet tall at the shoulders and not more than six feet in length. Obviously a land animal, it edged up to the water carefully, constantly jerking its short neck in probing motions. In paying so much attention to the possible dangers on land, it overlooked the real danger that waited in the water, for as it reached the lagoon and began lowering the forepart of its body so that it could drink, a fallen log which had lain inconspicuously half in the water, half out sprang into action.

It was a crocodile, well armored in heavy skin and possessed of powerful jaws lined with piercing teeth. It made a lunge at the drinking dinosaur, but it had moved too soon. Its well-calculated grab at the reptile's right foreleg missed by a fraction, for the dinosaur managed to withdraw so speedily that the great snapping jaw closed not on the bony leg, as intended, but only upon the soft flesh covering it.

There was a ripping sound as the crocodile tore off a strip of flesh, and a sharp guttural click as the wounded dinosaur responded to the pain. Then peace returned. The dinosaur could be heard for some moments retreating. The disappointed crocodile swallowed the meager meal it had caught, then returned to its loglike camouflage, and the furry little animal returned to its earlier preoccupation of staring at the surface of the lagoon.

Its attention was poorly directed, for as it watched, it became aware, with a sense of terrible panic, of wings in the darkening sky, and at the very last moment of safety it threw itself behind the trunk of a ginkgo tree, flattened itself out, and held its breath as a large flying reptile swooped down, its gaping, sharp-toothed mouth open, and just missed its target.

Still flat against the moist earth, the little animal watched in terror as the huge reptile banked low over the lagoon and returned in what under other circumstances might have been a beautiful flight. This time it came straight at the crouching animal, but then, abruptly, had to swerve away because of the ginkgo roots. Dipping one wing, it turned gracefully in the air, then swooped down on another small creature hiding near the crocodile, unprotected by any tree.

Deftly the flying reptile snapped its beak and caught its prey, which uttered high shrieks as it was carried aloft. For some moments the little animal hiding in the ginkgo watched the flight of its enemy as the reptile dipped and swerved through the sky like a falling feather, finally vanishing with its catch.

The little watcher could breathe again. It was unlike the great reptiles, for they were cold-blooded and it was warm. They raised their babies from hatching eggs, while its came from the mother's womb. It was a pantothere, one of the earliest mammals and progenitor of later types like the opossum, and it had scant protection in the swamp. Watching cautiously lest the flying hunter return, it ventured forth to renew its inspection of the lagoon, and after a pause, spotted what it had been looking for.

About ninety feet out into the water a small knob had appeared on the surface. It was only slightly larger than the watching animal itself, about six inches in diameter. It seemed to be floating on the surface, unattached to anything, but actually it was the unusual nose of an animal that had its nostrils on top of its head. The beast was resting on the bottom of the lagoon and breathing in this inventive manner.

Now, as the watching animal expected, the floating knob began slowly to emerge from the waters. It was attached to a head, not extraordinarily large but belonging obviously to an animal markedly bigger than either the first dinosaur or the crocodile. It was not a handsome head, nor graceful either, but what happened next displayed each of those attributes.

For the head continued to rise from the lagoon, higher and higher and higher in one long beautiful arch, until it stood twenty-five feet above the water, suspended at the end of a long and most graceful neck. It was like a ball extended endlessly upward on a frail length of wire, and when it was fully aloft, with no body visible to support it, the head turned this way and that in delicate motion, as if surveying the total world that lay below.

The small head and enormous neck remained in this position for some minutes, sweeping in lovely arcs of exploration. Apparently the small eyes which stood on either side of the projecting nose at the top of the skull were reassured by what they saw, for now a new kind of motion ensued.

From the surface of the lake an enormous construction began slowly to appear, an inch at a time, muddy waters falling from it as it rose. Slowly, slowly the thing in the lagoon came into view, until it disclosed a monstrous prism of dark flesh to which the prehensile neck was attached.

The body of the great reptile looked as if it were about twelve feet tall, but how far into the water it extended could not be discerned; it surely went very deep. Now, as the furry animal on shore watched, the massive body began to move, slowly and rhythmically. Where the neck joined the great dark bulk of the body, little waves broke and slid along the flanks of the beast. Water dripped from the upper part of the body as it moved ponderously through the swamp.

The reptile appeared to be swimming, its neck probing in sweeping arcs, but actually it was walking on the bottom, its huge legs hidden by water. And then, as it drew closer to shore and entered shallower water, there occurred a moment of marked grace and beauty. From the water trailing behind the animal, an enormous tail emerged. Longer than the neck and disposed in more delicate lines, it extended forty-four feet, swaying slightly on the surface of the lagoon. From head to tip of tail, the reptile measured eighty-seven feet.

Up to now it had looked like a long snake, floundering through the lagoon, but the truth was about to be revealed, for as the reptile advanced, the massive legs which had been supporting it became visible. They were enormous, four pillars of great solidity attached to the torso by joints of such crude construction that although the creature was amphibious, she could not easily support herself on dry land, where water did not buoy her up.

With slow, lumbering strides the reptile moved toward a clear river that emptied into the swamp, and now its total form was visible. Its head reared thirty-five feet; its shoulders were thirteen feet high; its tail dragged aft some fifty feet; it weighed nearly thirty tons.

It was diplodocus, not the largest of the dinosaurs and certainly not the most fearsome. This particular specimen was a female, seventy years old and in the prime of life. She lived exclusively on vegetation, which she now sought among the swamp waters. Moving her small head purposefully from one kind of plant to the next, she cropped off such food as she could find. This was not an easy task, for she had an extremely small mouth studded with minute peglike front teeth and no back ones for chewing. It seems incomprehensible that with such trivial teeth she could crop enough food to nourish her enormous body, but she did. It was this problem of chewing that had brought her toward the shore, this and one other strange impetus that she could not yet identify. She attended first to the chewing.

After finishing with such plants as were at hand, she moved into the channel. The mammal, still crouching among the roots of the ginkgo tree, watched with satisfaction as she moved past. It had been afraid that she might plant one of her massive feet on its nest, as another dinosaur had done, obliterating both the nest and its young. Indeed, diplodocus left underwater footprints so wide and so deep that fish used them as nests. One massive footprint might be many times as wide as the mammal was long.

And so diplodocus moved away from the lagoon and the apprehensive watcher. As she went she was one of the most totally lovely creatures so far seen on earth, a perfect poem of motion. Placing each foot carefully and without haste, and assuring herself that at least two were planted solidly on the bottom at all times, she moved like some animated mountain, keeping the main bulk of her body always at the same level, while her graceful neck swayed gently and her extremely long tail remained floating on the surface.

The various motions of her great body were always harmonious; even the plodding of the four gigantic feet had a captivating rhythm. But when the undulating grace of the long neck and the longer tail was added, this large reptile epitomized the beauty of the animal kingdom as it then existed.

She was looking for a stone. For some time she had instinctively known that she lacked a major stone, and this distressed her. She had become agitated about the missing stone and now proposed settling the matter. Keeping her head low, she scanned the bottom of the stream but found no suitable stones.

This forced her to move upstream, the delicate motion of her body conforming to the shifting bottom as it rose slightly before her. Now she came upon a wide selection of stones, but prudence warned her that they were too jagged for her purpose, and she ignored them. Once she stopped, turned a stone over with her blunt nose and scorned it. Too many cutting edges.

Her futile search made her irritable and she failed to notice the approach of a rather large land-based dinosaur that walked on two legs. He did not come close to approaching her in size, but he was quicker of motion, and had a large head, gaping mouth and a ferocious complement of jagged teeth. He was a meat-eater, always on the watch for the giant water-based dinosaurs who ventured too close to land. He was not large enough to tackle a huge animal like diplodocus if she was in her own element, but he had found that usually when the large reptiles came into the stream, there was something wrong with them, and twice he had been able to hack one down.

He approached diplodocus from the side, stepping gingerly on his two powerful hind feet, keeping his two small front feet ready like hands to grasp her should she prove to be in weakened condition. He was careful to keep clear of her tail, for this was her only weapon.

She remained unaware of her would-be attacker, and continued to probe the river bottom for the right stone. The carnivorous dinosaur interpreted her lowered head as a sign of weakness. He lunged at the spot where her vulnerable neck joined the torso, only to find that she was in no way incapacitated, for when she saw him coming she twisted adroitly, and presented the attacker with the broad and heavy side of her body. This repulsed him, and he stumbled back. As he did so, diplodocus stepped forward, and slowly swung her tail in a mighty arc, hitting him with such force that he was thrown off his feet and sent crashing into the brush.

One of his small front feet was broken by the blow and he uttered a series of *awk-awks*, deep in his throat, as he shuffled off. Diplodocus gave him no more attention and resumed her search for the right stone.

Finally she found what she wanted. It weighed about three pounds, was flattish on the ends and both smooth and rounded. She nudged it twice with her snout, satisfied herself that it was suited to her purposes, then lifted it in her mouth, raised her head to its full majestic height, swallowed the stone and allowed it to slide easily down her long neck into her gullet and from there into her grinding gizzard, where it joined six smaller stones that rubbed together gently and incessantly as she moved. This was how she chewed her food, the seven stones serving as substitutes for the molars she lacked.

With awkward yet attractive motions she adjusted herself to the new stone, and could feel it find its place among the others. She felt better all over and hunched her shoulders, then twisted her hips and flexed her long tail.

Night was closing in. The attack by the smaller dinosaur reminded her that she ought to be heading back toward the safety of the lagoon, back where fourteen other reptiles formed a protective herd, but she was kept in the river by a vague longing which she had experienced several times before, but which she could not remember clearly. She had, like all members of the diplodocus family, an extremely small brain, barely large enough to send signals to the various remote parts of her body. For example, to activate her tail became a major tactical problem, for any signal originating in her distant head required some time to reach the effective muscles of the tail. It was the same with the ponderous legs; they could not be called into instant action.

Her brain was too small and too undifferentiated to permit reasoning or memory; habit ingrained warned her of danger, and only the instinctive use of her tail protected her from the kind of assault she had just experienced. As for explaining in specific terms the gnawing agitation she now felt, and which had been the major reason for her leaving the safety of the herd, her small brain could give her no help.

She therefore walked with splashing grace toward a spot some distance upstream. How beautiful she was as she moved through the growing darkness! All parts of her great body seemed to relate to one central impulse, gently twisting neck, stalwart central structure, slow-moving mighty legs, and delicate tail extending almost endlessly behind and balancing the whole. It would require far more than a hundred million years of experiment before her equal would be seen again.

She was moving toward a white chalk cliff which she had known before. It stood some distance in from the lagoon, sixty feet higher than the river at its feet. Here, back eddies had formed a swamp, and as she approached this protected area, diplodocus became aware of a sense of security. She hunched her shoulders again and adjusted her hips. Moving her long tail in graceful arcs, she tested the edge of the swamp with one massive forefoot. Liking what she felt, she moved slowly forward, sinking deeper and deeper into the dark waters until she was totally submerged, except for the knobby tip of her head which she left exposed so that she could breathe.

She did not fall asleep, as she should have done. The gnawing insatiety kept her awake, even though she could feel the new stone working on the foliage she had consumed that day and even though the buzzing of the day insects had ceased, indicating that night was at hand. She wanted to sleep but could not, so after some hours the tiny brain sent signals along the extended nerve systems and she pulled herself through the swamp with noisy sucking sounds. Soon she was back in the main channel, still hunting vaguely for something she could neither define nor locate. And so she spent the long tropical night.

Diplodocus was able to function as capably as she did for three reasons. When she was in the swamp at the foot of the cliff, an area that would have meant death for most animals, she was able to extricate herself because her massive feet had a curious property; although they made a footprint many inches across as they flattened out in mud, they could, when it came time to withdraw them from the clinging muck, compress to the width of the foreleg, so that for diplodocus to pull her huge leg and foot from mud was as simple as pulling a reed from the muck at the edge of the swamp; there was nothing for the mud to cling to, and the leg pulled free with a swooshing sound.

Diplodocus, 'double beams,' was so named because sixteen of her tail vertebrae—twelve through twenty-seven behind the hips—were made with paired flanges to protect the great artery that ran along the underside of the tail. But the vertebrae had another channel topside, and it ran from the base of the head to the strongest segment of the tail. In this channel lay a powerful and very thick sinew which was anchored securely at shoulder and hip and which could be activated from either position. Thus the long neck and the sweeping tail were the progenitors of the crane, which in later time would lift extremely heavy objects by the clever device of running a cable over a pulley and counterbalancing the whole. The pulley used by diplodocus was the channel made by the paired flanges of the vertebrae; her cable was the powerful sinew of neck and tail; her counterbalance was the bulk of her torso, and all functioned with an almost divine simplicity. Had she had powerful teeth, her neck was so excellently balanced that she could have lifted into the air the dinosaur that attacked her in the way the claw of a well-designed crane can lift an object many times its own apparent weight. Without this advanced system of cable and pulley, diplodocus could have activated neither her neck nor her tail, and she could not have survived. With it, she was a sophisticated machine, as well adapted to her mode of life as any animal which might succeed her in generations to come.

The third advantage she had was remarkable, and raises questions as to how it could have developed. The powerful bones of her legs, which were under water most of the time, were of the most heavy construction, thus providing her with necessary ballast, but those that were higher in her body were of successively lighter bulk, not only in sheer weight but also in actual bone composition, and this delicate construction buoyed up her body, permitting it almost to float.

That was not all. Many fenestrations, open spaces like windows, perforated the vertebrae of her neck and tail, thus reducing their weight. These intricate bones, with their channels top and bottom, were so exquisitely engineered that they can be compared only to the arches and windows of a Gothic cathedral. Bone was used only where it was required to handle stress. No shred was left behind to add its weight if it could be dispensed with, yet every arch required for stability was in place. The joints were articulated so perfectly that the long neck could twist in any direction, yet the flanges within which the sinews rode were so strong that they would not be damaged if a great burden was placed on neck or head.

It was this marvel of engineering, this infinitely sophisticated machine which had only recently developed and which would flourish for another seventy million years, that floated along the shore of the lagoon that night, and when the little mammal came out of its nest at dawn, it saw her twisting her neck out toward the lagoon, then inland toward the chalk cliff.

Finally she turned and swam back toward the swamp at the foot of the cliff. When she reached there she sniffed the air in all directions, and one smell seemed familiar, for she turned purposefully toward fern trees at the far end of the swamp, and from them appeared the male diplodocus for which she had been searching. They approached each other slowly, poling themselves along the bottom of the swamp, and when they met they rubbed necks together.

She came close to him, and the little mammal watched as the two giant creatures coupled in the water, their massive bodies intertwined in unbelievable complexity. When he rutted he simply climbed on the back of his mate, locking his forepaws about her, and concluded his mating in seven seconds. The two reptiles remained locked together most of the forenoon.

When they were finished they separated and each by his own route swam away to join the herd. It consisted of fifteen members of the diplodocus family, three large males, seven females and five young animals. They moved together, keeping to the deep water most of the time but never loath to come into the river for food. In the water they poled themselves along with their feet barely touching bottom, their long tails trailing behind, and all kept in balance by that subtle arrangement of bone whereby the heaviest hung close to the bottom, allowing the lighter to float on top.

The family did not engage in play such as later animals of a different breed would; they were reptiles and as such were sluggish. Since they had cold blood with an extremely slow metabolism, they needed neither exercise nor an abundance of food; a little motion sufficed them for a day, a little food for a week. They often lay immobile for hours at a time, and their tiny brains spurred them to action only when they faced specific problems.

After a long time she felt another urge, positively irresistible, and she moved along the shore to a sandy stretch of beach not far from the chalk cliff. There she swept her tail back and forth, clearing a space, in the middle of which she burrowed both her snout and her awkward forelegs. When a declivity was formed, she settled herself into it and over a period of nine days deposited thirty-seven large eggs, each with a protective leathery shell.

When her mission ashore was accomplished, she spent considerable time brushing sand over the nest with her tail and placing with her mouth bits of wood and fallen leaves over the spot so as to hide it from animals that might disturb the eggs. Then she lumbered back to the lagoon, soon forgetting even where she had laid the eggs. Her work was done. If the eggs produced young reptiles, fine. If not, she would not even be aware of their absence.

It was this moment that the furry animal had been watching for. As soon as diplodocus submerged herself in the lagoon, he darted forth, inspected the nest, and found one egg that had not been properly buried. It was larger than he, but he knew that it contained food enough for a long time. Experience had taught him that his feast would be tastier if he waited some days for the contents to harden, so this time he merely inspected his future banquet, and kicked a little dirt over it so that no one else might spot it.

After the thirty-seven eggs had baked four days in the hot sand, he returned with three mates, and they began attacking the egg, gnawing with incisors at its hard shell. They had no success, but in their work they did uncover the egg even more.

At this point a dinosaur much smaller than any which had appeared previously, but at the same time much larger than the mammals, spotted the egg, knocked off one end and ate the contents. The pantotheres were not sorry to see this, for they knew that much meat would still be left in the remnants, so when the small dinosaur left the area, they scurried in to find that the broken eggshells did yield a feast.

In time the other eggs, incubated solely by action of the sun, hatched, and thirty-six baby reptiles sniffed the air, knew by instinct where the lagoon lay, and in single file, they started for the safety of the water.

Their column had progressed only a few yards when the flying reptile that had tried to snatch the mammal spotted them and with expert glide swooped down, catching one in its beak, taking it to its hungry young. Three more trips the reptile made, catching an infant diplodocus each time.

Now the small dinosaur that had eaten the egg also saw the column, and he hurried in to feed on six of the young. As he did so, the others scattered, but with an instinct that kept them moving always closer to the lagoon. The original thirty-seven were now down to twenty-six, and these were attacked continuously by the rapacious flier and the carnivorous dinosaur. Twelve of the reptiles finally reached the water, but as they escaped into it a large fish with bony head and jagged rows of teeth ate seven of them. On the way, another fish saw them swimming overhead and ate one, so that from the original thirty-seven eggs, there were now only four possible survivors. These, with sure instinct, swam on to join the family of fifteen grown diplodocuses, which had no way of knowing the young reptiles were coming.

As the little ones grew, diplodocus herself had no way of knowing that they were her children. They were merely reptile members that had joined the family, and she shared with other members of the herd the burden of teaching them the tricks of life.

When the young were partly grown, their thin snakelike bodies increasing immensely, diplodocus decided that it was time to show them the river. Accompanied by one of the adult males, she set out with the four youngsters.

They had been in the river only a short time when the male snorted sharply, made a crackling sound in his throat, and started moving as fast as he could back to the lagoon. Diplodocus looked up in time to see the most terrifying sight the tropical jungle provided. Bearing down upon the group was a monstrous two-legged creature towering eighteen feet high, with huge head, short neck and rows of gleaming teeth.

It was allosaurus, king of the carnivores, with jaws that could bite the neck of diplodocus in half. When the great beast entered the water to attack her, she lashed at him with her tail and knocked him slightly off course. Even so, the monstrous six-inch claws on his prehensile front feet raked her right flank, laying it open.

He stumbled, righted himself and prepared a second attack, but again she swung her heavy tail at him, knocking him to one side. For a moment it looked as if he might fall, but then he recovered, left the river and rushed off in a new direction. This put him directly behind the male diplodocus, and even though the latter was retreating as fast as possible toward the lagoon, the momentum of allosaurus was such that he was able to reach forward and grab him where the neck joined the torso. With one terrifying snap of the jaws, allosaurus bit through the neck, vertebrae and all, and brought his victim staggering to his knees. The long tail flashed, but to no avail. The body twisted in a violent effort to free itself of the daggerlike teeth, but without success.

With great pressure, allosaurus pushed the giant reptile to the ground, then, without relinquishing its bloody hold, began twisting and tearing at the flesh until the mighty teeth joined and a large chunk of meat was torn loose. Only then did allosaurus back away from the body. Thrusting its chin in the air, it adjusted the chunk of meat in its mouth and dislocated its jaw in such a way that the huge morsel could slide down into the gullet, from whence it would move to the stomach, to be digested later. Twice more it tore at the body, dislodging great hunks of meat which it eased down its throat. It then stood beside the fallen body for a long time as if pondering what to do. Crocodiles approached for their share, but allosaurus drove them off. Carrion reptiles flew in, attracted by the pungent smell of blood, but they too were repulsed.

As allosaurus stood there defying lagoon and jungle alike, he represented an amazing development, as intricately devised as diplodocus. His jaws were enormous, their rear ends lashed down by muscles six inches thick and so powerful that when they contracted in opposing directions they exerted a force that could bite through trees. The edges of the teeth were beautifully serrated, so they could cut or saw or tear; sophisticated machines a hundred and forty million years later would mimic their principle.

The teeth were unique in another respect. In the jaw of allosaurus, imbedded in bone beneath the tooth sockets, lay seven sets of replacements for each tooth. If, in biting through the neck bones of an adversary, allosaurus lost a tooth, this was of little concern. Soon a replacement would emerge, and behind it six others would remain in line waiting to be called upon, and if they were used up, others would take place in line, deep within the jawbone.

Now allosaurus lashed his short tail and emitted growls of protest. He had killed this vast amount of food but could not consume it. Other predators appeared, including the two smaller dinosaurs that had visited the beach before. All remained at a safe distance from allosaurus.

He took one more massive bite from the dead body but could not swallow it. He spit it out, glared at his audience, then tried again. Covered with sand, the flesh rested in his gaping mouth for several minutes, then slid down the extended neck. With a combative *awk-awk* from deep within his throat, allosaurus lunged ineffectively at the watchers, then ambled insolently off to higher ground.

As soon as he was gone, the scavengers moved in—reptiles from the sky, crocodiles from the lagoon, two kinds of dinosaurs from land and the unnoticed mammals from the roots of the ginkgo tree. By nightfall the dead diplodocus, all thirty-three tons of him, had disappeared and only his massive skeleton lay on the beach.

Wounded diplodocus and the four young dinosaurs that had witnessed this massacre now swam back to the lagoon. In the days that followed, she began to experience the last inchoate urge she would ever know. Sharp pains radiated slowly from the place where allosaurus had ripped her. She found no pleasure in association with the other members of the herd. She was drawn by some inexplicable force back to the swamp at the chalk cliff, not for purposes of re-creating the family of which she was a part but for some pressing reason she had never felt before.

For nine days she delayed heading for the swamp, satisfying herself with half-sleep in the lagoon, poling herself idly half-submerged from one warm spot to another, but the pain did not diminish. Vaguely she wanted to float motionless in the sun, but she knew that if she did this, the sun would destroy her. She was a reptile and had no means of controlling body heat; to lie exposed in the sun long enough would boil her to death in her own internal liquids.

Finally, on the tenth day she entered the river for the last time, stepping quietly like some gracious queen. She stopped occasionally to browse on some tree, lifting her head in a glorious arc on which the late sun shone. Her tail extended behind, and when she switched it for some idle purpose it gleamed like a scimitar set with jewels.

How beautiful she was as she took that painful journey, how gracefully coordinated her movements as she swam toward the chalk cliff. She moved as if she owned the earth and conferred grace upon it. She was the great final sum of millions of years of development. Slowly, swaying from side to side with majestic delicacy, she made her way to the swamp that lay at the foot of the cliff.

There she hesitated, twisting her great neck for the last time as if to survey her kingdom. Thirty feet above the earth her small head towered in one last thrust. Then slowly it lowered; slowly the graceful arc capsized. The tail dragged in the mud and the massive knees began to buckle. With a final surge of determination, she moved herself ponderously and without grace into a deep eddy.

Its murky waters crept up her legs, which would never again be pulled forth like reeds; this was the ultimate capture. The torn side went under; the tail submerged for the last time, and finally even the lovely arc of her neck disappeared. The knobby protuberance holding her nose stayed aloft for a few minutes, as if she desired one last lungful of the heavy tropical air, then it too disappeared. She had gone to rest, her mighty frame imprisoned in the muck that would embrace her tightly for a hundred and thirty-six million years.

It was ironic that the only witness to the death of diplodocus was the little pantothere that watched from the safety of a cycad tree, for of all creatures who had appeared on the beach, he was the only one that was not a reptile. The dinosaurs were destined to disappear from earth, while this little animal would survive, its descendants and collaterals populating the entire world, first with prehistoric mammals themselves destined to extinction—titanotheres, mastodons, eohippus—and subsequently with animals man would know, such as the mammoth, the lion, the elephant, the bison and the horse.

Of course, certain smaller reptiles such as the crocodile, the turtle and the snake would survive, but why did they and the little mammal live when the great reptiles vanished? This remains one of the world's supreme mysteries. About sixty-five million years ago, as the New Rockies were emerging, the dinosaurs and all their immediate relations died out. The erasure was total, and scholars have not yet agreed upon a satisfactory explanation. All we know for sure is that these towering beasts disappeared. Triceratops with its ruffed collar, tyrannosaurus of the fearful teeth, ankylosaurus the plated ambulating tank, trachodon the gentle duck-billed monster—all had vanished.

Ingenious theories have been advanced, some of them captivating in their imaginativeness, but they remain only guesses. Yet because the mystery is so complete, and so relevant to man, all proposals merit examination. They fall into three major groups.

The first relates to the physical world, and each argument has some merit. Since the death of the dinosaurs coincided with the birth of the New Rockies, there may have been a causal relationship, with the vast lowland swamps disappearing. Or temperatures may have risen to a degree that killed off the great beasts. Or plant life may have altered so rapidly that the dinosaurs starved. Or the disappearance of the extensive inland sea changed water relationships and dried up lagoons. Or mountain building somehow involved loss of oxygen. Or a combination of changes in plant food doomed the reptiles. Or a single catastrophic sun flare burned the dinosaurs to death, while the mammals, with their built-in heat-adjusting apparatus, survived.

The second theory is more difficult to assess, because it deals with psychological factors, which, even though they may be close to the truth, are so esoteric that they cannot be quantitatively evaluated. Classes of animals, like men, empires and ideas, have a predestined length of life, after which they become senescent and die out. Or the dinosaurs had overspecialized and could not adapt to changes in environment. Or they became too large and fell of their own weight. Or they reproduced too slowly. Or their eggs became infertile. Or carnivores ate the vegetarian dinosaurs faster than they could reproduce and then starved for lack of food. Or for some unknown reason they lost their vital drive and became indifferent to all problems of survival.

The third combines all the reasons that relate to warfare between a declining reptilian world and a rising mammalian one. Mammals ate the eggs of the dinosaurs at such a rate that the reptiles could not keep producing enough to ensure survival. Or mammals of increasing size killed off the smaller reptiles and ate them. Or mammals preempted feeding grounds. Or mammals, because of their warm blood and smaller size, could adjust more easily to the changes introduced by the mountain building or other environmental shifts. Or a world-wide plague erupted to which the reptiles were subject while the mammals were not.

For each of these theories there are obvious refutations, and scholars have expounded them. But if we reject these proposals, where does that leave us in our attempt to find out why this notable breed of animal vanished? We must know, lest the day come when we repeat their mistakes and doom ourselves to extinction.

The best that can be said is that an intricate interrelationship of changes occurred, involving various aspects of life, and that the great reptiles failed to accommodate to them. All we know for sure is that in rocks from all parts of the world there is a lower layer dating back seventy million years in which one finds copious selections of dinosaur bones. Above it there is an ominous layer many feet thick in which few bones of any kind are found. And above that comes a new layer often crowded with the bones of mammal predecessors of the elephant, the camel, the bison and the horse. The dead reach of relatively barren rock, representing the death of the dinosaurs, has not yet been explained.

Long after they disappeared, and after man had risen to the point where he could search out the fossilized skeletons of the dinosaurs, it would become fashionable to make fun of the great reptiles which had vanished through some folly of their own. The lumbering beasts would be held up to ridicule as failures, as inventions that hadn't worked, as proof that a small brain in a big body makes survival impossible.

Facts prove just the opposite. The giant reptiles dominated the earth for one hundred and thirty-five million years; man has survived only two million and most of that time in mean condition. Dinosaurs were some sixty-seven times as persistent as man has so far been. They remain one of the most successful animal inventions nature has provided. They adjusted to their world in marvelous ways and developed all the mechanisms required for the kind of life they led. They are honored as one of the world's longest-lived species, and they dominated their vast period of time just as man dominates his relatively brief one.

Fifty-three million years ago, while the New Rockies were still developing and long after diplodocus had vanished, in the plains area, where the twin pillars formed, an animal began to develop which in later times would give man his greatest assistance, pleasure and mobility. The progenitor of this invaluable beast was a curious little creature, a four-legged mammal, for the age of reptiles was past, and he stood only seven or eight inches high at the shoulder. He weighed little, had a body covering of part-fur, part-hair and seemed destined to develop into nothing more than a small inconsequential beast.

He had, however, three characteristics which would determine his future potential. The bones in his four short legs were complete and separate and capable of elongation. On each foot he had five small toes, that mysteriously perfect number which had characterized most of the ancient animals, including the great dinosaurs. And he had forty-four teeth, arranged in an unprecedented manner: in front, some peglike teeth as weak as those of diplodocus; then a conspicuous open space; then at the back of the jaw, numerous grinding molars.

This little animal made no impression on his age, for he was surrounded by other much larger mammals destined for careers as rhinoceroses, camels and sloths. He lived carefully in the shady parts of such woods as had developed and fed himself by browsing on leaves and soft marsh plants, for his teeth were not strong and would quickly have worn down had they been required to eat rough food like the grass which was even then beginning to develop.

If one had observed all the mammals of this period and tried to evaluate the chances of each to amount to something, one would not have placed this quiet little creature high on the list of significant progenitors; indeed, it seemed then like an indecisive beast which might develop in a number of different ways, none of them memorable, and it would have occasioned no surprise if the little fellow had survived a few million years and then quietly vanished. Its chances were not good.

The curious thing about this little forerunner of greatness is that although we are sure that he existed and are intellectually convinced that he had to have certain characteristics, no man has ever seen a shred of physical evidence that he really did exist. No fossil bone of this little creature has so far been found; we have tons of bones of diplodocus and her fellow reptiles, all of whom vanished, but of this small prototype of one of the great animal families, we have no memorials whatever. Indeed, he has not yet even been named, although we are quite familiar with his attributes; perhaps when his bones are ultimately found—and they will be—a proper name would be 'paleohippus,' the hippus of the Paleocene epoch. When word of his discovery is flashed around the world, scholars and laymen in all countries will be delighted, for they will have come into contact with the father of a most distinguished race, one which all men have loved and from which most have profited.

Perhaps thirteen million years after 'paleohippus' flourished, and when the land that would contain the twin pillars had begun to form, the second in line and first-known in this animal family appeared and became so numerous that in the land about the future pillars hundreds of skeletons would ultimately be laid down in rock, so that scientists would know this small creature as familiarly as they know their own puppies.

He was eohippus, an attractive small animal about twelve inches high at the shoulder. He looked more like a friendly dog than anything else, with small alert ears, a swishing tail to keep insects away, a furry kind of coat and a longish face, which was needed to accommodate the forty-four teeth, which persisted. The teeth were still weak, so that the little creature had to content himself with leaves and other soft foods.

But the thing that marked eohippus and made one suspect that this family of animals might be headed in some important direction was the feet. On the short front feet, not yet adapted for swift movement, the five original toes had been reduced to four; one had only recently disappeared, the bones which had once sustained it vanishing into the leg. And on the rear foot there were now three toes, the two others having withered away during the course of evolution. But the surviving toes had tiny hoofs instead of claws.

One could still not predict what this inconspicuous animal was going to become, and the fact that he would stand second in the sixty-million-year process of creating a noble animal seemed unlikely. Eohippus seemed more suited for a family pet than for an animal of distinction and utility.

And then, about thirty-million years ago, when the land that was to form the twin pillars was being laid down, mesohippus developed, twenty-four inches high at the shoulders and with all the basic characteristics of his ancestors, except that he had only three toes on each of his feet. He was a sleek animal, about the size of our collie or red fox. The forty-four teeth kept his face long and lean and his legs were beginning to lengthen, but his feet still contained pads and small hoofs.

Then, about eighteen million years ago, a dramatic development took place which solved the mystery. Merychippus appeared, a most handsome three-toed animal forty inches high, with bristly mane, extended face and protective bars behind the eye sockets.

He had one additional development which would enable the horse family to survive in a changing world: his teeth acquired the remarkable capacity to grow out from the socket as they wore down at the crown.

This permitted the proto-horse to quit browsing on such leaves as he found and to move instead to grazing on the new grasses that were developing on the prairies. For grass is a dangerous and difficult food; it contains silica and other roughnesses that wear down teeth, which must do much grinding in order to prepare the grass for digestion. Had not merychippus developed these self-renewing grinders, the horse as we know it could have neither developed nor survived. But with this almost magical equipment, he was prepared.

These profound evolutions occurred on the plains that surrounded the site of the twin pillars. There on flat lands that knew varied climates, from tropical to sub-arctic, depending upon where the equator was located at the time, this singular breed of animal went through the manifold changes that were necessary before it stood forth as an accomplished horse.

One of the biggest changes in the antecedents of the horse appeared about six million years ago, when pliohippus, the latest in the breed, evolved with only one toe on each foot and with the pads on which his ancestors had run eliminated. It now had a single hoof. This animal was a medium-sized beautiful horse in almost every sense of the word, and would have been recognized as such, even from a considerable distance. There would be minor refinements, mostly in the teeth and in the shape of the skull, but the horse of historic times was now foreshadowed.

He arrived as equus about two million years ago, as splendid an animal as the ages were to produce. Starting from the mysterious and unseen 'paleohippus,' this breed had unconsciously and with great persistence adapted itself to all the changes that the earth presented, adhering always to those mutations which showed the best chance of future development. 'Paleohippus,' of the many capacities, eohippus of the subtle form, merychippus with the horselike appearance, pliohippus with the single hoof —these attributes persisted; there were dozens of other variations equally interesting which died out because they did not contribute to the final form. There were would-be horses of every description, some with the most ingenious novelties, but they did not survive, for they failed to adjust to the earth as it was developing; they vanished because they were not needed. But the horse, with its notable collection of virtues and adjustments, did survive.

About one million years ago, when the twin pillars were well formed, a male horse with chestnut coloring and flowing tail lived in the area as part of a herd of about ninety. He was three years old and gifted with especially strong legs that enabled him to run more swiftly than most of his fellows. He was a gamin creature and had left his mother sooner than any of the other males of his generation. He was the first to explore new arrivals on the prairie and had developed the bad habit of leading any horses that would follow on excursions into canyons or along extended draws.

One bright summer morning this chestnut was leading a group of six adventurous companions on a short foray from the main herd. He took them across the plains that reached out from the twin pillars and northward into a series of foothills that contained passageways down which they galloped in file, their tails flowing free behind them as they ran. It was an exhilarating chase, and at the end of the main defile they turned eastward toward a plain that opened out invitingly, but as they galloped they saw blocking their way two mammoths of extraordinary size. The great smooth-skinned creatures towered over the horses, for they were gigantic, fourteen feet tall at the shoulders, with monstrous white tusks that curved downward from the head. The tips of the tusks reached sixteen feet, and if they caught an adversary, they could toss him far into the air. The two mammoths were imposing creatures, and had they been ill-disposed toward the horses, could have created havoc, but they were placid by nature, intending no harm.

The chestnut halted his troop, led them at a sober pace around the mammoths, coming very close to the great tusks, then broke into a gallop which would take him onto the eastern plains, where a small herd of camels grazed, bending awkwardly forward. The horses ignored them, for ahead stood a group of antelope as if waiting for a challenge. The seven horses passed at full speed, whereupon the fleet antelope, each with a crown of four large antlers, sprang into action, darting after them.

For a few moments the two groups of animals were locked in an exciting race, the horses a little in the lead, but with a burst of speed the antelopes leaped ahead and before long the horses saw only dust. It had been a joyous race, to no purpose other than the challenge of testing speed.

Beside the grazing area on which the antelope had been feeding there rested a family of armadillos, large ratlike creatures encased in collapsible armor. The horses were vaguely aware of them but remained unconcerned, for the armadillo was a slow, peaceful creature that caused no harm. But now the round little animals stopped searching for slugs and suddenly rolled themselves into a defensive position. Some enemy, unseen to the horses, was approaching from the south and in a moment it appeared, a pack of nine dire wolves, the scourge of the plains, with long fangs and swift legs. They loped easily over the hill that marked the horizon, peering this way and that, sniffing at the air. The wolf serving as scout detected the armadillos and signaled his mates. The predators hurried up, inspected the armor-plated round balls, nudged them with their noses and turned away. No food there.

With some apprehension, the horses watched the nine enemies cross the grassland, hoping that they would pass well to the east, but this was not to be. The lead wolf, a splendid beast with sleek gray coat, spotted the horses and broke into a powerful run, followed instantly by his eight hunting companions. The chestnut snorted and in the flash of a moment realized that he must not lead his six horses back into the canyons from which they had just emerged, for the two mammoths might block the way, allowing the dire wolves to overtake any straggler and cut him down.

So with an adroit leap sideways he broke onto the plains in the direction the antelope had taken and led his troop well away from their home terrain. They galloped with purpose, for although the dire wolves were not yet close at hand, they had anticipated the direction the horses might take and had vectored to the east to cut them off. The chestnut, seeing this maneuver, led his horses to the north, which opened a considerable space between them and the wolves.

As they ran to their own safety, they passed a herd of camels that were slower-moving. The big awkward beasts saw the apprehension of the horses and took fright, although what the cause of the danger was they did not yet know. There was a clutter on the prairie and much dust, and when it had somewhat settled, the horses were well on their way to safety but the camels were left in the direct path of the nine wolves. The lumbering camels ran as fast as they could, scattering to divert attack, but this merely served to identify the slowest-moving and upon this unfortunate the wolves concentrated.

Cutting at him from all sides with fearful teeth, the wolves began to wear him down. He slowed. His head drooped. He had no defense against the dire wolves and within a few moments one had leaped at his exposed throat. Another fastened onto his right flank and a third slashed at his belly. Uttering a futile cry of anguish, the camel collapsed, his ungainly feet buckling under the weight of the wolves. In a flash, all nine were upon him, so that before the horses left the area, the camel had been slain.

At a slow walk they headed south for the hills that separated them from the land of the twin pillars. On the way they passed a giant sloth who stood sniffing at the summer air, dimly aware that wolves were on the prowl. The huge beast, twice the size of the largest horse, knew from the appearance of the horses that they had encountered wolves, and retreated awkwardly to a protected area. An individual sloth, with his powerful foreclaws and hulking weight, was a match for one wolf, but if caught by a pack, he could be torn down, so battle was avoided.

Now the chestnut led his horses into the low hills, down a gully and out onto the home plains. In the distance the twin pillars—white at the bottom where they stood on the prairie, reddish toward the top, and white again where the protecting caps rested—were reassuring, a signal of home, and when all seven of the troop were through the pass, they cantered easily back to the main herd. Their absence had been noted and various older horses came up to nuzzle them. The herd had a nice sense of community, as if all were members of the same family, and each was gratified when others who had been absent returned safely.

Among the six followers accompanying the chestnut on his foray was a young dun-colored mare, and in recent weeks she had been keeping close to him and he to her. They obviously felt an association, a responsibility each to the other, and normally they would by now have bred, but they were inhibited by a peculiar awareness that soon they would be on the move. None of the older animals had signified in any way that the herd was about to depart this congenial land by the twin pillars, but in some strange way the horses knew that they were destined to move . . . and to the north.

What was about to happen would constitute one of the major mysteries of the animal world. The horse, that splendid creature which had developed here at twin pillars, would desert his ancestral home and emigrate to Asia, where he would prosper, and the congenial plains at the pillars would be occupied by other animals. Then, about four hundred thousand years later, the horse would return from Asia to reclaim the pastures along the river, but by the year 6000 B.C. he would become extinct in the Western Hemisphere.

The horses were about to move north and they knew they could not accommodate a lot of colts, so the chestnut and the mare held back, but one cold morning, when they had been chasing idly over the plains as if daring the dire wolves to attack them, they found themselves alone at the mouth of a canyon where the sun shone brightly, and he mounted her and in due course she produced a handsome colt.

It was then that the herd started its slow movement to the northwest. Three times the chestnut tried unsuccessfully to halt them so that the colt could rest and have a fighting chance of keeping up. But some deep instinctive drive within the herd kept luring them away from their homeland, and soon it lay far behind them. The dun-colored mare did her best to keep the colt beside her, and he ran wtih ungainly legs to stay close. She was pleased to see that he grew stronger each day and that his legs functioned better as they moved onto higher ground.

But in the fifth week, as they approached a cold part of their journey, food became scarce and the wisdom of this trek, doubtful. Then the herd had to scatter to find forage, and one evening as the chestnut and the mare and their colt nosed among the scrub for signs of grass, a group of dire wolves struck at them. The mare intuitively presented herself to the wolves in an effort to protect her colt, but the fierce gray beasts were not deluded by this trick, and cut behind her and made savage lunges at it. This enraged the chestnut, who sprang at the wolves with flashing hoofs, but to no avail. Mercilessly, the wolves cut down the colt. His piteous cries sounded for a moment, then died in harrowing gurgle as his own blood drowned him.

The mare was distraught and tried to attack the wolves, but six of them detached themselves and formed a pack to destroy her. She defended herself valiantly for some moments while her mate battled with the other wolves at the body of the colt. Then one bold wolf caught her by a hamstring and brought her down. In a moment the others were upon her, tearing her to pieces.

The whole group of wolves now turned their attention to the chestnut, but he broke loose from them and started at a mad gallop back toward where the main herd of horses had been. The wolves followed him for a few miles, then gave up the chase and returned to their feast.

Mammals, unlike reptiles, had some capacity for memory, and as the trek to the northwest continued, the chestnut felt sorrow at the loss of his mate and the colt, but the recollection did not last long, and he was soon preoccupied with the problems of the journey.

It was a strange hegira on which the horses of Centennial were engaged. It would take them across thousands of miles and onto land that had been under water only a few centuries earlier. For this was the age of ice. From the north pole to Pennsylvania and Wisconsin and Wyoming vast glaciers crept, erasing whatever vegetation had developed there and carving the landscape into new designs.

At no point on earth were the changes more dramatic than at the Bering Sea, that body of ice-cold water which separates Asia from America. The great glaciers used up so much ocean water that the level of this sea dropped three hundred feet. This eliminated the Bering Sea altogether, and in its place appeared a massive land bridge more than a thousand miles wide. It was an isthmus, really, joining two continents, and now any animal that wished, or man, too, when he came along, could walk with security from Asia to America—or the other way.

The bridge, it must be understood, was not constructed along that slim chain of islands which now reaches from America to Asia. Not at all. The drop of ocean was so spectacular that it was the main body of Asia that was joined substantially to America; the bridge was wider than the entire compass of Alaska.

It was toward the direction of this great bridge, barely existent when the true horse emerged, that the chestnut now headed. In time, as older horses died off, he became acknowledged leader of the herd, the one who trotted at the head on leisurely marches to new meadows, the one who marshaled the herd together when danger threatened. He grew canny in the arts of leadership, homing on the good pastures, seeking out the protected resting places.

As the horses marched to the new bridge in the northwest, to their right in unending progression lay the snouts of the glaciers, now a mile away, later on, a hundred miles distant, but always pressing southward and commandeering meadowlands where horses had previously grazed. Perhaps it was this inexorable pressure of ice from the north, eating up all good land, that had started the horses on their emigration; certainly it was a reminder that food was getting scarce throughout their known world.

One year, as the herd moved ever closer to the beginning of the bridge, the horses were competing for food with a large herd of camels that were also deserting the land where they had originated. The chestnut, now a mature horse, led his charges well to the north, right into the face of the glacier. It was the warm period of the year and the nose of the glacier was dripping, so that the horses had much good water and there was, as he had expected, good green grass.

But as they grazed, idling the summer away before they returned to the shoreline, where they would be once more in competition with the camels, he happened to peer into a small canyon that had formed in the ice, and with four companions he penetrated it, finding to his pleasure that it contained much sweet grass. They were grazing with no apprehension when suddenly he looked up to see before him a most gigantic mammoth. It was as tall as three horses, and its mighty tusks were like none he had seen at the pillars. These tusks did not stretch forward, but turned parallel to the face in immense sweeping circles that met before the eyes.

The chestnut stood for a moment surveying the huge beast. He was not afraid, for mammoths did not attack horses, and even if for some unfathomable reason this one did, the chestnut could easily escape. And then slowly, as if the idea were incomprehensible, the stallion began to realize that under no circumstances could this particular mammoth charge, for it was dead. Its frozen rear quarters were caught in the icy grip of the glacier; its front half, from which the glacier had melted, seemed alive. It was a beast in suspension. It was there, with all its features locked in ice, but at the same time it was not there.

Perplexed, the chestnut whinnied and his companions ambled up. They looked at the imprisoned beast, expecting it to charge, and only belatedly did each discover for himself that for some reason he could not explain, this mammoth was immobilized. One of the younger horses probed with his muzzle, but the silent mammoth gave no response. The young horse became angry and nudged the huge beast, again with no results. The horse started to whinny; then they all realized that this great beast was dead. Like all horses, they were appalled by death and silently withdrew.

The chestnut alone wanted to investigate this mystery, and in succeeding days he returned timorously to the small canyon, still puzzled, still captivated by a situation that could not be understood. In the end he knew nothing, so he kicked his heels at the silent mammoth, returned to the grassy area, and led his herd back toward the main road to Asia.

It must not be imagined that the horses emigrated to Asia in any steady progression. The distance from the twin pillars to Siberia was only 3500 miles, and since a horse could cover twenty-five miles a day, the trip might conceivably have been completed in less than a year, but it did not work that way. The horses never chose their direction; they merely sought easier pasturage and sometimes a herd would languish in one favorable spot for eight or nine years. They were pulled slowly westward by mysterious forces, and no horse that started from the twin pillars ever got close to Asia.

But drift was implacable, and the chestnut spent his years from three to sixteen in this overpowering journey, always tending toward the northwest, for the time of the horse in America was ended.

They spent four years on the approaches to Alaska, and now the chestnut had to extend himself to keep pace with the younger horses. Often he fell behind, but he knew no fear, confident that an extra burst of effort would enable him to regain the herd. He watched as younger horses took the lead, giving the signals for marching and halting. The grass seemed thinner this year, and more difficult to find.

One day, late in the afternoon, he was foraging in sparse lands when he became aware that the main herd—indeed the whole herd—had moved on well beyond him. He raised his head with some difficulty, for his breathing had grown tighter, to see that a pack of dire wolves had interposed itself between him and the herd. He looked about quickly for an alternate route, but those available would lead him farther from the other horses; he knew he could outrun the wolves, but he did not wish to increase the distance between himself and the herd.

He therefore made a daring, zigzag dash right through the wolves and toward the other horses. He kicked his heels and with surprising speed negotiated a good two-thirds of the distance through the snarling wolves. Twice he heard jaws snapping at his forelocks, but he managed to kick free.

Then, with terrible suddenness, his breath came short and a great pain clutched at his chest. He fought against it, kept pumping his legs. He felt his body stopping almost in midflight, stopping while the wolves closed in to grab his legs. He felt a sharp pain radiating from his hind quarters where two wolves had fastened onto him, but this external wolf-pain was of lesser consequence than the interior horse-pain that clutched at him. If only his breath could be maintained, he could throw off the wolves. He had done so before. But now the greater pain assailed him and he sank slowly to earth as the pack fell upon him.

The last thing he saw was the uncomprehending herd, following younger leaders, as it maintained its glacial course toward Asia.

Why did this stallion that had prospered so in Colorado desert his amiable homeland for Siberia? We do not know. Why did the finest animal America developed become discontented with the land of his origin? There is no answer. We know that when the horse negotiated the land bridge, which he did with apparent ease and in considerable numbers, he found on the other end an opportunity for varied development that is one of the bright aspects of animal history. He wandered into France and became the mighty Percheron, and into Arabia, where he developed into a lovely poem of a horse, and into Africa, where he became the brilliant zebra, and into Scotland, where he bred selectively to form the massive Clydesdale. He would also journey into Spain, where his very name would become the designation for a gentleman, a caballero, a man of the horse. There he would flourish mightily and serve the armies that would conquer much of the known world, and in 1519 he would leave Spain in small, adventurous ships of conquest and land in Mexico, where he would thrive and develop special characteristics fitting him for life on upland plains. In 1543 he would accompany Coronado on his quest for the golden cities of Quivira, and from later groups of horses brought by other Spaniards some would be stolen by Indians and a few would escape to become feral, once domesticated but now reverted to wildness. And from these varied sources would breed the animals that would return late in history, in the year 1768, to Colorado, the land from which they had sprung, making it for a few brief years the kingdom of the horse, the memorable epitome of all that was best in the relationship of horse and man.

It would be dramatic if we could claim that as the horse left America he met on the bridge to Asia a shaggy, lumbering beast that was leaving Asia to take up his new home in America, but that probably did not happen. The main body of horses deserted America about one million years ago, whereas the ponderous newcomers did not cross the bridge which the horses had used—for it closed shortly after they passed—but a later bridge which opened at the same place and for the same reasons about eight hundred thousand years later.

The beast which came eastward out of Asia had developed late in biologic time, less than two million years ago, but it developed in startling ways. It was a huge and shaggy creature, standing very high at the shoulder and with enormous horns that curved outward, then forward from a bulky forehead that seemed made of rock. When the animal put its head down and walked resolutely into a tree, the tree usually toppled. This ponderous head, held low because of a specialized thick neck, was covered with long, matted hair which itself took up much of the shock when the beast used its head as a battering ram. Males also grew a long, stiff beard, so that their appearance at times seemed satanic. The other major characteristic was that the weight of the animal was concentrated in the massive forequarters, topped by a sizable hump, while the hindquarters seemed unusually slender for so large a beast. The animal, as it had developed in Asia, was so powerful that it had, as an adult, no enemies. Wolves tried constantly to pick off newborn calves or superannuated stragglers, but they avoided mature animals in a group.

This was the ancestral bison, and the relatively few who made the hazardous trip from Asia flourished in their new habitat, and one small herd made its way to the land about the twin pillars, where they found themselves a good home with plenty of grass and security. They multiplied and lived contented lives to the age of thirty, but their size was so gigantic and their heavy horns so burdensome that after only forty thousand years of existence in America, during which time they left their bones and great horns in numerous deposits, so that we know precisely how they looked, the breed exhausted itself.

The original bison was one of the most impressive creatures ever to occupy the land at twin pillars. He was equal in majesty to the mammoth, but like him, was unable to adjust to changing conditions, so like the mammoth, he perished.

That might have been the end of the bison in America, as it was the end of the mammoth and the mastodon and smilodon, the saber-toothed cat, and the huge ground sloth, except that at about the time the original bison vanished, a much smaller and better-adapted version developed in Asia and made its own long trek across a new bridge into America. This seems to have occurred some time just prior to 6000 B.C., and since in the span of geologic time that was merely yesterday, of this fine new beast we have much historic evidence. Bison, as we know them, were established in America and one herd of considerable size located in the area of the twin pillars.

It was late winter when a seven-year-old male of this herd shook the ice off his beard, hunched his awkward shoulders forward as if preparing for some unusual action, and tossed his head belligerently, throwing his rufous mane first over his eyes and then away to one side. He then braced himself as if the anticipated battle were at hand, but when no opponent appeared, he quit his performance and went about the job of pawing at the snow to uncover grass that lay succulent and sweet below.

He stood out among the herd not only for his splendid bulk but also for his coloring, which was noticeably lighter than that of his fellows. He comported himself not with dignity, for he was not an old bull, but with a certain violent willingness; he was what might be called a voluntary animal, eager for whatever change or accident might befall.

For reasons which he could not clearly understand but which were associated somehow with the approach of spring, he started on this wintry day to study carefully the other bulls, and when occasion permitted, to test his strength against theirs. The two- and three-year-olds he dismissed. If they became testy, which they sometimes did, a sharp blow from the flat of his horn disciplined them. The four- and five-year-olds? He had to be watchful with them. Some were putting on substantial weight and were learning to use their horns well. He had allowed one of them to butt heads with him, and he could feel the younger bull's amazing power, not yet sufficient to issue a serious challenge but strong enough to upset any adversary that was not attentive.

There were also the superannuated bulls, pitiful cases, bulls that had once commanded the herd. They had lost their power either to fight or to command and dragged along as stragglers with the herd, animals of no consequence. They grazed about the edges and occasionally, when fighting loomed, they might charge in with ancient valor, but if a six-year-old interposed himself, they made a few futile gestures and retreated. In earlier years they had suffered broken bones and shattered horn tips and some of them limped and others could see from only one eye. Some of them had even been attacked by wolves, if the wolves caught them alone, and it was not uncommon to see some old bull with flesh wounds along his flanks, filled with flies and itching pain.

The old bulls could be ignored. They were tolerated, and on some long march they would fall behind and fail to climb a hill and the wolves would close in and they would be seen no more.

It was the bulls nine and ten years old that caused perplexity, and these Rufous studied meticulously. He was not at all confident that he could handle them. There was one with a slanting left horn; he had dominated the herd three years ago, and even last year had been a bull to conjure with, for he had massive shoulders which could dislodge an opponent and send him sprawling. There was the brown bull with the heavy hair over his eyes; he had been a champion of several springs and had only a few days ago given Rufous a sharp buffeting. Particularly there was the large black bull that had dominated last spring; he seemed quite unassailable and aware that the others held him in awe. Twice in recent weeks Rufous had bumped against him, as if by accident, and the black bull had known what was happening and had casually swung his head around and knocked Rufous backward; this black bull had tremendous power and the skill to use it.

As spring approached and the snows melted, disclosing a short, rich grass refreshed by moisture, the herd began to mill about as if it wished to move to other ground, and one morning as Rufous was grazing in the soft land between the twin pillars, with the warm sun of spring on his back, one of the cows started nudging her way among the other cows and butting the older bulls. This was the cow that made important decisions for the herd, for although the commanding bull disciplined the herd and stood ready to fight any member at any time, he did not direct them as to where they should move or when. It was as if the lead bull were the general in battle, the lead cow the prime minister in running the nation.

She now decided that it was time for her herd to move northward, and after butting others of her followers, she set out at a determined pace, leaving the twin pillars behind. She headed for a pass through the low chalk hills to the north, then led her charges up a draw to the tableland beyond. There she kept the herd for several days, after which she led them slowly and with no apparent purpose to the river that defined this plateau to the north. Testing the water at several places, she decided which crossing was safest and plunged in.

The water was icy cold from melting snow, but she kicked her legs vigorously, swimming comfortably with the current and climbing out at last to shake her matted hair, sending showers of spray into the sunlight. From the north bank she watched with a leader's care as older cows nudged yearlings into the river, then swam beside them, keeping the younger animals upstream, so that if the current did overcome them, they would bounce against their mothers and thus gain security for the next effort.

When the main body of the herd was safely across, the old bulls grudgingly and sometimes with growls of protest entered the river, swimming with powerful kicks as the water threw their beards into their faces. When they climbed onto the north bank they shook themselves with such fury that they produced small rainstorms.

Rufous was one of the last to cross, and he did so carefully, as if studying this particular crossing against the day when he might have to use it in some emergency. He did not like the footing on the south bank, but once the lead cow was satisfied that the cows and calves were safely across, she ignored whatever bulls were left behind and set out purposefully for the grazing lands to which she was leading her herd.

When she reached this spot, less than a hundred miles from the twin pillars, she stopped, smelled the ground to assure herself that it was good, then turned the leadership of the herd back to the bulls, assuming once more the passive role of merely another cow. But if any decision of moment were required, she would again step forth and assert herself, and when she grew too old to assume this task the responsibility would pass to some other strongly opinionated cow, for the leadership of a large group was too important to be left to males.

It was now spring and the calving season was at hand. The sun would rise, as on a normal day, but some cow would experience a profound urge to be by herself, and she would move with determination toward some unknown objective, and if any other cow, or even a bull, tried to interpose, she would knock the offender aside and pursue her course. She would seek some secluded area, even if it were only behind the brow of a low hill, and there she would lie on the ground and prepare for the birth of her calf.

This year a small black cow left the herd as soon as the new grounds were reached, for her time was at hand. As she passed two old bulls they nuzzled her as if to ask what she was about, but she repelled them brusquely and sought a spot not far from the river where trees gave her some protection. There she gave birth to a most handsome black bull calf, and as soon as he appeared she began licking him, and butting him with her head and goading him to stand alone. She spent two hours at this task, then began mooing softly as if to attract the attention of the others, but when they ambled over to inspect her new calf, nudging it with their snouts, she made short and ineffectual charges at them, as if to prove that the calf was hers.

Among the bison that came to inspect the new calf was Rufous, and his nosy intrusion was an error he would regret. The newborn calf liked the smell of Rufous and for a few moments rubbed its small head against his leg. Some intuition told the calf that there would be no milk in that quarter, and he returned to his mother. But the damage had been done.

Now came the days which would be most crucial in the life of this little bison. Within a brief period it had to imprint on its mind the image of its mother, her smell, her feel, the taste of her milk, her look, the sound of her call. Because if it failed to make this indelible and vital connection, it might become unattached when the herd moved and be lost in the strangling dust. If this happened, it would survive only a few hours, for the wolves and vultures, seeing its plight, would close in.

Therefore the mother cow was careful to allow it to nuzzle her, to taste her milk, to smell her urine and to hear her cry. She attended the calf constantly, and when it moved among the other calves that were being born at this time she tried to train him to respond to her cry.

But the calf had proved its inquisitiveness by making friends with Rufous shortly after its birth, and it continued this behavior, moving from one adult to another and failing to establish an indelible impression of its own mother. She tried frantically to correct this defect, but her baby bull would wander.

One of its strongest memories was of the smell of Rufous, and as the days progressed it tried to associate more with the bull and less with its mother, trying even to get milk from Rufous. This irritated the bull, who knocked the confused infant away. The little fellow rolled over in the dust, got up bewildered and ran after another adult bull.

At this point, a fairly large herd of strange bison from the north moved onto the feeding ground, and there was a general milling about of animals, so that the baby bull became lost at the edge of the swirling crush. The two herds were excited enough by their chance meeting, but now they detected strange movement to the west, and this triggered precipitate action on the flank, which quickly communicated itself to the mass. A stampede began, and those calves which had been strongly imprinted by their mothers performed miraculously: no matter how swiftly their mothers ran nor how deftly they dodged, the calves kept up with them stride for stride, their little noses often pressed against their mothers' flanks.

But the handsome black infant had not been adequately trained and had no intuition of where its mother was, nor could it detect her cry in the confusion. It fell behind, far behind, then gave a little cry of joy, for it smelled a reassuring odor. It was not its mother; it was Rufous, lagging behind because he had been grazing on the sweet grass down by the river.

The bull had no intention of caring for a confused baby and rushed past, but the infant, catching a stronger whiff of the familiar smell, joined the gallop and clung to the older bull's flank. This annoyed Rufous, who tried to kick at the pestering calf as they ran, but nothing would divert the baby bull. With a sense of total security, as great as if Rufous had been its mother, it clung to the galloping bull.

But now the wolves which always hung about the edges of a herd, hoping for a bit of luck, spotted the little calf. They had a good chance of picking it off, since the older bull was endeavoring to kick it to one side, so they closed in on the running pair, trying to insert themselves between the baby bull and the mature one.

They failed. Once Rufous recognized their strategy, he became a changed animal. It was his responsibility to protect calves, no matter how bothersome, no matter how distant the retreating herd. Accordingly, he scanned the terrain as he ran and spotted a small embankment which might afford protection.

Twisting his head abruptly to the right, he headed for the rocky bank. As if the young calf had been attached to him by vines, it turned at the same moment, and the two galloped to the refuge. There Rufous turned to confront his enemies, keeping the calf beside him and well protected by his large reddish flank.

The wolves closed in, eleven of them, but they were powerless against his horns and massive head, nor could they slip behind him to attack his tendons because he kept his rear tight against the rocks. If he had not been hampered by this irritating calf, he could have beaten back the wolves and returned to the herd, but with that encumbrance he could do no more than protect himself.

He did manage one other defense. He bellowed, several times, a low guttural cry that seemed to roll vainly across the vast prairies. But he was heard. The bison having outrun their fright, had stopped and were pointlessly milling around when the master fighter of the herd to which Rufous belonged, the large black bull, heard the cry of distress and doubled back to investigate. With him came the bull with the slanting left horn, and the closer they approached to the intermittent bellow, the faster they ran.

They came up to the encircling wolves in a rush, their hind feet digging in like brakes and throwing clouds of dust. In the first moment they perceived what was happening, saw Rufous trapped against the rocky bank with the calf beside him. With lowered heads and flashing hoofs they crashed into the wolves and sent them scattering. The black bull caught one on his horn, tossed him in the air, then stamped on him mercilessly when he fell to earth. The wolf was crushed and the others withdrew.

The three victorious bulls formed a miniature herd, with the calf in the center, and slowly they walked back toward the real herd, which had now stabilized. The calf, exhilarated by the adventure and the consoling smell of his savior Rufous, trotted happily inside the protective triangle.

When the calf regained the herd and the excitement caused by the wolves died down, it felt hungry—and there was the good smell of Rufous. It ran to the bull and tried to nurse, but Rufous had had enough. Lowering his horn, he caught the little fellow under the belly and tossed him well into the air. It uttered pitiful cries and crashed to earth. It rose bewildered, still smelled Rufous and still wanted to join him, but as he approached, Rufous lowered his head and gave the calf another toss in the air.

This time its cries reached the distraught mother; she recognized them and rushed to reclaim the infant she thought she had lost. She licked its coat and nursed it and did her best to bring it to her, but it still remembered the familiar smell of Rufous as they confronted the wolves.

Now the rutting season was at hand. Rufous and the other bulls began a strange but long-inherited chain of behavior. One morning, for no apparent reason, Rufous began suddenly charging at cottonwood trees along the riverbank, tearing into them with wild force as if they were living enemies, then stopping and cleaning his horns against their trunks. The next day as he was walking idly toward the herd he felt an uncontrollable compulsion to throw himself on the ground, twisting and turning in the dust a dozen times until he was laden with sand. Then he rose, urinated heavily in the wallow and threw himself into it again, smearing the muddy urine over his head and body as if to announce to the world, 'When you smell that smell, remember. It belongs to Rufous.'

At this period of the rutting season he did not yet care to confront the other bulls; indeed, he stayed well away from them, as if he were unsure of his capacity to challenge them on equal terms, but he continued to fight the cottonwoods and to wallow excessively. He also stood by himself and threw out guttural threats, ignoring those that were being voiced by other bulls in the vicinity.

And then one morning, on a day no different from others that had preceded it, a quiet brown cow that had been inconspicuous felt an overpowering surge of vitality, and her entire personality changed within the passing of an instant. She became more rhythmic in her motions, gentler in her manner. She left the cows with whom she had been associating and kicked aside her last year's calf when it endeavored to stay close to her, as she had so painfully taught it to do only a year ago.

She sought out the bulls on the edge of the herd and moved from one to the other until she came to its leader. He licked her coat and rubbed his head against hers. Often he rested his shaggy head in the hollow of her back as if it were an accustomed pillow. Wherever she moved, he stayed with her, waiting for the proper time for mating, two huge beasts caught in the throes of passion.

Now the drama of the rutting season began. A four-year-old bull that had not yet mated with any cow left the lesser bulls with whom he had for some time been sparring and marched boldly up to the courtship couple. Ignoring the cow, he took a stubborn stance so that his dark beard was close to that of the black bull. The latter, long prepared for such a challenge but unable to anticipate which bull would issue it, stared for a moment at the intruder.

Then, with shuddering force, the two animals leaped at each other, their shaggy foreheads meeting in a crack that could be heard across the plains. To the surprise of the older bull, this first shattering blow seemed to have no effect upon the young challenger, who pawed the earth, lowered his head and drove with incredible force at the older one's forehead. The black bull was tempted to sidestep and allow the young bull to slide harmlessly off his flank, but he sensed that this opening fight would be crucial, and he intended settling it unmistakably. So he braced himself, lowered his head and took the charge full on his forehead.

For an instant the horns of the two powerful beasts locked, and it looked as if the kinetic force of the younger must drive the older back, but the black bull had reserves of power. His back legs stiffened. His backbone absorbed the shock. And now he began applying pressure of his own. Slowly the younger bull had to retreat. He could not fix his legs.

With a sudden twist, the older bull turned his challenger aside, and as the younger bull's belly was exposed, the old warrior lunged at it. He could hear ribs cracking beneath skin and then the cry of pain. The younger bull withdrew, shook himself to assess the damage, felt his ribs grating, and with no further desire for fight, retreated.

The older bull, victor once more, returned to the cow that he had rightfully won. By this process, wasteful and cruel, cows were assured that they would mate only with the strongest bulls and that the species would be preserved.

But this time it was not to be so easy, for no sooner had the victorious bull turned his back on the herd and resumed his attentions to the cow than he heard a belligerent snort. When he turned, he saw the bull Rufous headed toward him in a slow purposeful march. This was a more serious challenge.

When Rufous stood horn to horn with the older bull, the latter could smell the strong urine in which his challenger had rubbed himself that morning. It was the smell of a mature bull, one ready to assume his place among the leaders of the herd. So the black bull stood very still, made no movement of any kind, and stared into the eyes of his challenger. The two powerful beasts stood that way for more than a minute, then slowly Rufous broke the gaze, lowered his head, and without raising dust, backed away. This was not a good day for extending his challenge. There would be others more propitious.

The black bull did not raise his voice in triumph nor did he make any move to follow Rufous to demonstrate once and for all his supremacy. He seemed quite content to have resolved this particular challenge in this way. He, too, sensed that a more likely day would come, a day he could not escape, and that then the issue would be resolved.

As the rutting season progressed, only three bulls served the cows: the black leader, the bull with the slanted horn and the brown bull with heavy hair over his eyes. Each was challenged repeatedly by younger bulls; each sustained his prerogatives, and it seemed as if the summer would end with those three in ascendancy.

And then, as the mating season drew to a close, Rufous experienced antagonisms he had not felt before. No amount of charging cottonwood trees satisfied him, and wallowing gave him no release. So one bright morning he sought out an old wallow which he had known favorably before. It was a prairie-dog town, where the little squirrel-like animals had piled up much sand. Plodding his way to it, he thrust himself into the soft earth, ignoring the protests of the little animals as they watched their homes destroyed. He wallowed for a long time, till his hair was well filled with dust. Then he rose, urinated copiously and threw himself into it with a fierceness he had not shown before. Now when he got up, his body was well mudded and the matted hair about his head exuded a powerful scent.

With stolid determination he marched back to the herd, seeking whichever older bull was courting that day. It was the ugly brown bull. He was with a fine cow well along in heat, and had it not been for the arrival of Rufous, the two might soon have been mating.

This time Rufous did not waste his time staring into the eyes of his enemy. As soon as he arrived at the scene he lowered his head and charged at the brown bull, but his tactic was not successful because the little bull calf that had adopted him as its mother had caught the scent of the urine-covered body as it passed through the herd and now galloped up to suckle. This interrupted Rufous' charge and allowed the brown bull to slash at him as his attack was aborted. A serious gash appeared on Rufous' shoulder and blood began to spurt out.

This enraged him, and he vented his wrath on his would-be son. With a violent toss of his head he caught the persistent calf and threw it high into the air and some distance away. Without pausing to see where it fell or how, he rushed at the brown bull in such a way as to catch that defender with his head not fully prepared. There was an ugly shock, and the brown bull fell back.

Instantly Rufous leaped at him, boring in with his powerful horns until he struck the right hip of the brown bull. With a ripping sound he swept his horn along the hip, damaging his enemy severely.

This encouraged him, and he swarmed all over the brown bull, jabbing and thrusting and applying constant pressure. It was as if the brown bull were being attacked from all sides, and in time the pressures began to tell. He fell back farther, tried to mount one last counterattack, and failed. Knowing that defeat was inevitable, he backed off and left the area.

Lowing triumphantly, Rufous took over the waiting cow and licked her coat. He was about to lead her into the cottonwoods when the little calf, recovered from its flight, returned to the strong smell of its supposed mother. Sidling up to Rufous, it again tried to nurse, but this time the victorious bull gently nosed him away. He had other matters on his mind.

For the rest of the year Rufous occasionally caught sight of the old brown bull moving along the outer edges of the herd, an embittered elder whose place had been permanently usurped. Never again would the old fellow mount a cow, for if he were to try, the younger bulls would challenge him, remembering that Rufous had humiliated him.

He was free to stay with the herd as long as he wished, and to feed with it and to play with the calves that other bulls sired, but he could have no part in the leadership and certainly no part in the breeding. Some old bulls elected to remain with the herd; many chose to wander off, a part of nothing, afraid of nothing, impregnable to attack, until the closing days when blinded sight and worn-down teeth and blunted horns made them vulnerable. Then wolves moved in. The slashing attacks were sustained, sometimes for three days, with a dozen wolves trying to cut down one stubborn old bull until he could fight no more and the fangs destroyed him.

It was now autumn, and the leader cow sensed that her charges ought to be congregating with the larger herd, so she led them northward, and as they moved ponderously, they merged with larger herds, and then with larger still. Bison seemed to be moving in from all directions until the prairie was black. They stretched to the horizon and blotted out the land, but still more came. They moved in accordance with no plan, but only in response to the ebb and flow which their ancestors had observed.

That spring, during the calving season, the herd to which Rufous belonged had contained only thirty-nine members. In summer, when it joined with another small herd, it numbered about a hundred. After the rutting season it grew to several thousand. And now, on the northern prairie, it contained nearly a million.

In such a congregation the little black bull with the faulty imprinting would have been destroyed had it not clung close to Rufous. It had no chance of locating its mother, for it could not remember her smell, but the strong odor of its adopted father was easy to identify, and the little fellow clung to him.

No matter how sorely Rufous abused his unwanted companion, the latter stayed close. Deprived of its mother's milk, the little bull learned to depend upon grazing seven months before other calves his age, and whereas they clung to their mothers for protection, it developed a wildly independent nature. By the time snow fell it was willing to bang heads with any animal encountered. Having already survived one attack from wolves, it was not even afraid of them. As its hump matured, so its pugnacity grew; it was a tough little bull.

With Rufous it moved freely within the vast herd, sometimes under the leadership of their own cow, sometimes far from her on the edge of the mob. One day when the herd had begun to fragment into the usual smaller units for winter grazing, some hundred thousand bison moved south across the river, and it was fortunate that Rufous and the calf were not in the middle that day. The herd was feeding well west of the twin pillars, heading for the chalk cliff, now forty feet high, and if the bison had approached it normally, they would have separated into two segments, one going west to escape the cliff, the other east.

But on this day a pack of wolves set up a commotion on the eastern flank. This stampeded the bison in that area and they dashed forward. Others, seeing them on the move, joined the flight automatically, and before long a general panic set in until eighty or ninety thousand bison were in motion.

They swept forward irresistibly, overriding anything that came within their path. If a bison stumbled and fell, he was crushed to death by hammering hoofs, and any calf separated even momentarily from its mother was either killed or forever lost.

The center of the stampeding herd drove directly for the chalk cliff, and as the lead animals approached and saw the precipitous drop ahead, they tried to stop, but this they were powerless to do, for the animals surging behind kept coming and forced the first rank over the cliff. Most of them perished in the fall, but those that didn't were soon crushed by succeeding waves of bison as they too plunged over the edge.

The bison on the flanks, of course, easily made their way around the cliff and suffered no fatalities except those few that fell beneath the pounding hoofs. But at the center more than twelve hundred perished and wolves did not have to bother trailing the herd for stragglers.

Rufous and the bull calf were on the left flank that day, and when panic struck they galloped easily to safety on the plains below the cliff. The little bull enjoyed the wild excitement of the chase so much that thereafter he roamed with Rufous, and when their herd reassembled under the leadership of their determined cow, the two moved eastward to the twin pillars, where the self-orphaned bull grew into a stalwart animal.

He had a raffish disposition, and at the age of nineteen months, when he was well formed, with sturdy horns growing out of his jet-black head, he was already seeking adventure. One day he limped back to the herd, badly cut up: his rear left leg was shredded above the ankle; his face was gashed; and his right flank was scored by sharp teeth. When Rufous and the other bulls gathered about him to smell whatever mementos there were of the disaster, they could tell that the blood on his right horn was not his. Sniffing more closely, they detected the smell of wolf, and next morning three of them, wandering east of the twin pillars, came upon a scene of carnage, with three wolves lying dead beside some low bushes which had been broken and trampled.

It had been a notable triumph, but thereafter the young bull would be lame in his left rear leg. He did not limp badly, but when he dug in for a charge against his fellow bulls he favored that leg, and when the charge came, there was a noticeable drag to the left. This did not deter him from fighting with everyone in the herd. Once he even challenged the lead cow when she was leading them north, but she gave him two swift jabs with her horn, indicating that she intended to accept no nonsense from brash young bulls.

He liked best the autumn, when the massive herd coalesced north of the two rivers. In western America two distinct kinds of bison had always existed, wood bison that kept to the hills, and plains bison. The latter were divided into two herds, the northern and the southern, and the land around the twin pillars marked the dividing line. This was because the southern herd usually stayed below the South Platte, while the northern herd stayed above the North Platte. The neutral land between the two rivers was sometimes occupied by a million or two bison from either herd, but they rarely stayed long.

In these years the northern herd, had it ever assembled at one spot, which it did not, would have numbered about thirty-five million animals; the southern herd, twenty-five million. Even such partial concentrations as gathered along the North Platte could number into the two or three millions, and for them to cross the river might require three days. They darkened the prairies; when they moved, the sky was gray with rising dust; they were magnificent and in the whole region at this time they had no enemy except the lurking wolf. They were masters of creation, a force of such magnitude that it could never be diminished, a stable community whose laws were so sound and whose behavior was so reasonable that it could reproduce itself perpetually.

It was this herd, more vast than the eye of a bison could contemplate, that the tough young bull loved, for when he was a part of it he seemed to grow larger. If the herd broke into a gallop, for some unexplained reason, he longed to be at the very heart of it, going where it led, thundering his hoofs, pulled this way or that by the timeless instinct of the herd. Sometimes, at such moments of wild movement, he bellowed for sheer joy.

He found pleasure in milling around the center, fighting whatever young bulls cared to engage him. The fact that he limped deluded other bulls into thinking that here was an easy enemy, and in the first years he was often challenged, always to the dismay of those who did the challenging. For he was not only strong and canny; he could also be downright mean, with sly tricks that other bulls had not learned. It was usual, when two bulls found contact in their first violent charge, for them to remain locked, their great foreheads touching, their back legs pumping in a contest of brute strength. But with a weak leg this jet-black bull knew that he must always lose that battle, so when his stupid and stolid adversary dug in for a traditional contest, he feinted forward, made enough contact to fix his opponent in position, then slid to the side, raking his foe with his sharp right horn.

He startled many bulls in this way, but he himself was also badly scarred in the brawling. Two ribs had already been broken and the tip of his left horn had been knocked off. He bore many scars in addition to the wolf bites, yet he loved the smell of combat when the vast herd assembled.

But when the excitement bred by the giant herd died down, in some mysterious manner the smaller herd of the twin pillars reestablished itself: the lead cow for that year reasserted her dominance and even fractious bulls like the jet-black one fell in line and willingly took up the trek south to their own familiar territory. Then he marched with Rufous, and the two, the younger now as hefty as the older, formed as handsome a pair as even the great master herd could have provided.

Bison had short memories, if any, and the younger bull no longer looked upon the older as his stay in life; indeed, that ridiculous passage in the young one's maturing had been forgotten. To him Rufous was merely the commanding bull of the herd, the one who had not yet been defeated during the rutting season. And here was where the trouble started, for when the jet-black bull was six years old he determined to possess cows of his own; to do otherwise would be ridiculous. And this placed him athwart the prerogatives of Rufous.

That spring the half-lame bull started to train for the extra-rigorous battles he knew lay ahead. He tested his horns against cottonwood trees and bellowed for hours at a time down by the river. He wallowed a good deal and sought fights with younger bulls. With great intensity he watched the three or four older bulls that commanded the cows, and especially he kept his eye on Rufous. It seemed to him that the old tyrant was losing his power.

During the calving season the young bull continued shadow-fighting with trees and galloping suddenly along the edge of the feeding ground, then stopping with dust-raising sharpness, thrusting his horns this way and that. He now ceased any playing around with younger bulls, for he knew that more serious matters were at hand.

When the rutting season began, he became a violent creature, slashing at any animal that came his way. And then, one day when Rufous had singled out a cow for himself, he watched with meticulous care for the right moment to assault him, but while he was making preparatory steps, another young bull stepped forward and boldly challenged the old champion. There was the initial confrontation, the stare, the refusal to back down, the digging in of the hind feet, the colossal charge and the shattering jolt as foreheads crashed.

It was a major fight, a real test of the older bull's power, and he met it with distinction, holding his ground and slowly driving the young challenger back. But when he had humbled the younger bull and given the triumphant bellow of the victor, he found that he was not exactly victorious, for while the two had been fighting, the half-lame bull had skirted off with the cow and was now breeding her in the lush area between the two pillars.

For the rest of that year Rufous and the young bull were enemies. They did not engage in actual battle, for the younger bull sensed that Rufous was so enraged that victory was impossible. In his canny way he bided his time, and when the great herd assembled that autumn he stayed clear of Rufous.

When the time again came for cows to come into heat, the young bull was at the height of his powers, a handsome creature with heavily matted hair and long beard. His forequarters were immense and more than compensated for the inadequate left rear leg. Insolently he muscled his way through the younger bulls, always keeping his eye on Rufous.

It happened with startling suddenness. On the first day of the rutting season he challenged Rufous over the first cow. The two great animals stood glaring at each other for almost a minute and Rufous squared for the initial shock, but when it came he was unprepared for its ferocity. For the first time he backed a little to find a better footing. The second clash was as violent as the first, and again he adjusted his rear feet, but before they found a footing, the younger bull made a feint, followed by a devastating thrust to the other side, and Rufous felt his flank being laid open by a scimitar horn.

For the first time in these fights Rufous was actually hurt, with violent pain coursing through his body. With unprecedented fury he turned upon his assailant and drove at him with such terrible force that he cracked two of the other bull's ribs.

Ordinarily this would have been sufficient to drive a challenger from the field, but the jet-black bull was no ordinary bison. He was an animal trained in adversity and one that would not surrender until death itself intruded. Twisting his side so as to accommodate the pain of the broken ribs, he drove directly at Rufous, staggering him with blows to the chest and flank. Here was no stylized dueling; here was a fired-up young bull trying his best to kill.

Relentlessly he gored and smashed at Rufous, never allowing the older bull a chance to pull himself together. With a mixture of astonishment and panic Rufous sensed that he was not going to defeat this explosive young adversary. Vaguely he acknowledged that a better animal than he had come onto the scene, and with an apprehension of tragedy and lonely years ahead, he began to back away. First one foot moved, grudgingly, then another. He was in retreat.

With a snort of triumph the younger bull charged at him for the last time, knocking him sideways and into confusion. Lowering both his tail and his head, Rufous started running from the battle, disorganized and defeated, while the black bull took possession of the cow he had so clearly won.

The other bison did not react to Rufous as he retreated from the battleground; they displayed neither regret nor satisfaction as he moved disconsolately through their ranks. He had been defeated, and that was that. He was through forever as the commander of the herd and must now make what peace he could with himself.

This proved difficult. For the rest of that summer he stayed apart, taking his position about a quarter of a mile from the edge of the herd. Throughout the autumn he was a lost soul and not even the excitement of the massing of the herds inspirited him. Once or twice he caught a glimpse of the handsome new champion, but the two did not travel together this time, and on the return trip even the lead cow ignored him.

Winter was a trying time. When snow covered the prairies and freezing winds with temperatures far below zero swept in from the west where the mountains stood, Rufous stayed alone, turning his matted head into the storm and doggedly waiting until the blizzard subsided. Then, alone, he faced the problem of finding enough to eat, so he lowered his massive head into the snow, down two or three feet, and with slow side-to-side rhythmic swings, knocked a path in the snow, deeper and deeper, until the frozen grass at the bottom lay revealed. Then he fed, pushing his head into new drifts when the grass in any one spot was gone.

Snow froze in his matted hair. Long icicles formed on his beard. The hair on his cheeks was worn away and his face became raw, but still he stayed by himself, a defeated old bull fighting the blizzard alone until his bones were weary and his face heavy with accumulated ice.

He stayed alive. One night wolves tracked him, and once they attempted an attack, but he was too strong for them, much too strong. Methodically and with old skill he slashed them to pieces when they came near. One wolf he caught on his horn, and before it could get away, he dashed it to the ground and stamped it to a pulp, relishing each repeated thrust of his still-powerful feet. After that the wolves left him alone. An outcast he was, by his own volition, but food for wolves he would not be for many years.

The snow was extremely heavy that year, and in the mountains it accumulated to a depth of forty feet. When spring came and days of hot sun, the melting was sudden and devastating. Huge bodies of water formed and had to find some way down to the plains, so rivulets became streams and streams became rivers, and the South Platte surged out in preposterous flood.

The lead cow, having anticipated this disaster by some intuition, kept the heard at the twin pillars, where the land was high, but since Rufous no longer felt himself a part of the herd, and roamed as he wished, he chose the land that lay beside the river, where the ice was thick and where the grass would be fresh within the next few weeks. He was therefore not prepared when his refuge was abruptly engulfed in water from the mountains, and he delayed leaving for higher ground. He expected that the water would go away; instead it increased.

Now the main body of the flood hit the South Platte, inundating new regions, and Rufous was trapped. Ice floes, broken loose by the flooding, began to pile up about him, and he realized that if he stayed in that area he was doomed, so he struck out for what he remembered as higher ground, but here, too, the water had invaded, with large chunks of ice backing up against the cottonwoods.

Abandoning that possible escape route, Rufous decided to trust his fortunes on the south side of the river, but this meant that he would have to cross the river itself, something he had often done in the past but could not possibly do now. This was a wrong decision, and before he launched into the water he looked about wildly, as if searching for the lead cow to give him directions. Receiving none, he valiantly plunged into the turbulent river, felt himself carried along by its fury, and struck out forcefully for the opposite bank, now miles distant because of the flooding.

He kept his legs pumping, and had this been a normal river he would have mastered it. Even so, he trusted that he was headed safely for the opposite shore and kept swimming. As he did, he lacked the power of mind to reflect that it was the little black bull—the one he had saved and reared—that had driven him from the herd. He knew only that he was outcast.

Down the middle of the swollen river came a congregation of broken logs, ice chunks, large rolling stones and bodies of dead animals. It was a kind of floating island, overwhelming in its force as it swept along. It overtook him, submerged him, ground him relentlessly in dark waters, and passed on.

When the bison straggled over the land bridge into America he encountered a huge misshapen creature that was in many ways the opposite of himself. The bison was large in front, slight in the rear, while the native animal was very large in the rear and slight in front. The bison was a land animal; the other lived mostly in water. The beast weighed some three hundred and fifty pounds as it slouched along, and its appearance was fearsome, for its conspicuous front teeth were formidable and as sharp as chisels. Fortunately, it was not carnivorous; it used its teeth only to cut down trees, for this giant animal was a beaver.

It had developed in North America but would spread in desultory fashion through much of Europe; its residence in the streams of Colorado would prove especially fortuitous, bringing great wealth to those Indians and Frenchmen who mastered the trick of getting its pelt.

The first beavers were too massive to prosper in the competition that developed among the animals of America; they required too much water for their lodges and too many forests for their food, but over the millennia a somewhat smaller collateral strain became dominant, with smaller teeth and softer pelts, and they developed into one of the most lovable and stubborn of animals. They thrived especially in the streams of Colorado.

One spring the mother and father beavers in a lodge on a small creek west of the twin pillars made it clear to their two-year-old daughter that she could no longer stay with them. She must fend for herself, find herself a mate and with him build her own lodge. She was not happy to leave the security in which she had spent her first two years; henceforth she would be without the protection of her hard-working parents and the noisy companionship of the five kits, a year younger than herself, with whom she had played along the banks of the stream and in its deep waters.

Her greatest problem would be to find a young male beaver, for there simply were none in that part of the creek. And so she must leave, or in the end her parents would have to kill her because she was mature enough to work for herself and her space inside the lodge was needed for future batches of babies.

So with apprehension but with instinctive hope, this young female left her family for the last time, turned away from the playful kits and swam down the tunnel leading to the exit. Gingerly, as she had been taught, she surfaced, poked her small brown nose toward shore and sniffed for signs of enemies. Finding none, she gave a strong flip of her webbed hind feet, curling her little paws beneath her chin, and started downstream. There was no use going upstream, for there the building of a dam was easier and all the good locations would be taken.

One flap of her hind feet was sufficient to send her cruising along the surface for a considerable distance, and as she went she kept moving her head from side to side, looking for three things: saplings in case she needed food, likely spots to build a dam and its accompanying lodge, and any male beavers that might be in the vicinity.

Her first quest was disappointing, for although she spotted quite a few cottonwoods, which a beaver could eat if need be, she found no aspen or birch or alders, which were her preferred foods. She already knew how to girdle a small tree, strip its bark and fell it so that she could feed on the upper limbs. She also knew how to build a dam and lay the groundwork for a lodge. In fact, she was a skilled housekeeper, and she would be a good mother, too, when the chance presented itself.

She had gone downstream about a mile when there on the shore, preening himself, she saw a handsome young male. She studied him for a moment without his seeing her, and she judged correctly that he had chosen this spot for his dam. She surveyed the site and knew intuitively that he would have been wiser to build it a little farther upstream, where there were strong banks to which it could be attached. She swam toward him, but she had taken only a few powerful strokes of her hind feet when, from a spot she had not noticed, a young female beaver splashed into the water, slapped her tail twice and came directly at the intruder, intending to do battle. It had taken her a long time to find a mate and she had no intention of allowing anything to disrupt what promised to be a happy family life.

The male on shore watched disinterestedly as his female approached the stranger, bared her powerful front teeth and prepared to attack. The stranger backed away and returned to the middle of the stream, and the victorious female slapped the water twice with her tail, then swam in triumph back to her unconcerned mate, who continued preening himself and applying oil to his silky coat.

The wandering beaver saw only one other male that day, a very old fellow who showed no interest in her. She ignored him as he passed, and she kept drifting with no set purpose.

As late afternoon came on and she faced her first night away from home, she became nervous and hungry. She climbed ashore and started gnawing desultorily at a cottonwood, but her attention was not focused on the food, and this was good, because as she perched there, her scaly tail stretched out behind her, she heard a movement behind a larger tree and looked up in time to spot a bear moving swiftly toward her.

Running in a broken line, as she had been taught, she evaded the first swipe of the slashing paw, but she knew that if she continued running toward the creek, the bear would intercept her. She therefore surprised him by running parallel to the creek for a short distance, and before he could adjust his lunge to this new direction, she had dived to safety.

She went deep into the water, and since she could stay submerged for eight or nine minutes, this gave her time to swim far from where the bear waited, because even from the bank a bear could launch a powerful swipe which might lift a beaver right onto the bank. When she surfaced, he was far behind her.

Night fell, the time when her family had customarily played together and gone on short excursions, and she was lonely. She missed the kits and their noisy frolic, and as night deepened she missed the joy of diving deep into the water and finding the tunnel that would carry her to the warm security of the lodge.

Where would she sleep? She surveyed both banks and selected a spot which offered some protection, and there she curled up as close to the water as she could. It was a miserable substitute for a proper lodge, and she knew it.

Three more nights she spent in this wretched condition. The season was passing and she was doing nothing about the building of a dam. This bothered her, as if some great purpose for which she had been bred was going unattended.

But the next day two wonderful things happened, the second having far more lasting consequences than the first. Early in the morning she ventured into a part of the creek she had not seen before, and as she moved she became aware of a strong and reassuring scent. If it were serious, and not an accident, it would be repeated at the proper intervals, so she swam slowly and in some agitation to the four compass directions, and as she had anticipated, the keen smell was repeated as it should have been. A male beaver, and young at that, had marked out a territory and she was apparently the first female to invade it.

Moving to the middle of the stream, she slapped her tail, and to her joy a fine-looking young beaver appeared on the bank of the creek and looked down into the water. The slapping could have meant that another male had arrived to contest his territory and he was prepared to fight, but when he saw that his visitor was the kind he had hoped to attract, he gave a little bark of pleasure and dived into the stream to welcome her.

With strong sweeps of his webbed feet he darted through the water and came up to her, nudging her nose with his. He was highly pleased with what he found and swam twice around her as if appraising her. Then he dived, inviting her to follow him, and she dived after him, deep into the bottom of the creek. He was showing her where he intended building his lodge, once he found a female to help.

They returned to the surface and he went ashore to fetch some edible bark, which he placed before her. When beavers mated, it was for life, and he was following an established pattern of courtship. The female was eager to indicate her interest, when she noticed that his gaze had left hers and that any fruitful communication had ended.

He was looking upstream, where one of the most beautiful young beavers he had ever seen was about to enter his territory. This female had a shimmering coat and glowing eyes, and she swam gracefully, one kick sending her to the corners of his areas, where she checked the markers he had left. Contented that she was in the presence of a serious suitor, she moved languidly to the center of the area and signaled with her tail.

The young male left his first visitor and with lightning strokes sped to this newcomer, who indicated that she was interested in the segment of the creek he had laid out for himself and was willing to move in permanently. In this brief space of time their destiny was determined.

What now to do with the first visitor? When the new female saw her she apprehended immediately what had happened, so she and the male came to where the young beaver waited and started to shove her out of the delimited area. But she had got there first and intended to stay, so she dived at the intruding female and started to assault her, but the male knew what he wanted. He had no desire to settle for second best, so he joined the newcomer, and together they forced the unwanted intruder downstream, and as she disappeared, chattering in rage, they slapped their tails at her and made joyous noises and prepared to build their dam.

The outcast drifted aimlessly and wondered whether she would ever find a mate. How could she build a home? How could she have kits of her own? Bitterly she sought the next miserable place to spend a night.

But as she explored the bank she became aware of a soft sound behind her and was certain it must be an otter, the most fearful of her enemies. She dived deep and headed for any cranny within the bank that might afford protection, and as she flattened herself against the mud she saw flashing through the waters not far distant the sleek, compacted form of an otter on the prowl.

She hoped that his first sweep would carry him downstream, but his sharp eye had detected something. It could have been a beaver hiding against the bank, so he turned in a graceful dipping circle and started back. She was trapped, and in her anxiety, fought for any avenue of escape. As she probed along the bottom of the bank she came upon an opening which led upward. It could well be some dead end from which there was no escape. But whatever it was, it could be no worse than what she now faced, for the otter was returning and she could not swim fast enough to escape him.

She ducked into the tunnel and with one powerful kick sent herself upward. She moved so swiftly that she catapulted through the surface and saw for the first time the secret cave that had formed in the limestone, with a chimney which admitted air and a security that few animals ever found. Soon her eyes became accustomed to the dim light that filtered in from above and she perceived what a marvelous spot this was, safe from otters and bears and prowling wolves. If she built her dam slightly below the cave and constructed her lodge in the body of the creek, attaching it by tunnel to this secret place, and if she then widened the chimney upward and masked its exit so that no stranger could detect it, she would have a perfect home. To complete her delight she found inside the cave and above the water level a comfortable ledge on which she could sleep that night.

Before dawn she was at work. Moving to all the prominent places on shore and to the ledges in the creek, she stopped at each and grabbed a handful of mud. With her other hand she reached to the opening of her body where two large sacs protruded and from these she extracted a viscous yellow liquid which would become famous throughout the west as castoreum, one of the most gratifying odors in the natural world.

Kneading the castoreum into the mud and mixing in a few grasses to make the cake adhere, she placed it carefully so that its odor would penetrate in all directions, and when she had set out nine of these—for this was a spot worth preserving and protecting—she stopped and tested the results of her labor. She swam upstream and down, and wherever she went she got the clear signal that this stretch of water belonged to a beaver who intended holding it.

She became, that summer, a capable beaver, lively in her pursuit of things she required. The limestone cavern became not only a place of refuge but also a satisfactory home. She built three secret escape hatches, one leading a good twenty feet inland from the bank of the creek, so that if a bear or wolf did take her by surprise, she could dive into it and make her way back to her home before the predator knew where she had gone.

The cycle of her life, however, was still incomplete. By herself she would not build a dam, nor a lodge either, for they were needed primarily for the rearing of young. She could survive in the limestone cave, but without the act of building a lodge with a mate, she was still an outcast.

This did not prevent her from attending herself as carefully as ever. Each day, when the sun was low, she perched on the bank overlooking her domain and preened. She did this by using the two peculiar toes on each of her hind legs; the nails on these toes were split so as to form small combs, and these she dragged through her pelt until even the slightest irregularity was removed. Then she took oil from her body and carefully applied it to each part of her coat, combing it in deeply until her fur glistened in shimmering loveliness. No one saw or applauded this grooming, but it was impossible for her to go to bed until she had completed it.

And then, in early autumn when she had given up hope of finding a mate, a shabby beaver seven years old who had lost his family in some catastrophe, wandered down the river and turned by chance into her creek. He was by no means a handsome creature; indeed, he was not even acceptable, for a long gash ran down the left side of his face and he had lost the two toes on his left hind leg that he needed for cleaning himself, so that his appearance was disreputable.

As he sashayed up the creek he detected the markers and realized immediately that a mistake had been made. The creek spot looked inviting but any flood from the river would wash it away. He looked about for the family which occupied it to warn them of the danger they faced, and after a while he saw the head of the owner breaking through the surface. She swam out to him cautiously and looked for his mate, while he looked for hers. There was a period of motionless silence. He was tired and winter was at hand.

They stared at each other for a long time, for a very long time, and each knew all there was to know. There would be no illusions, no chicanery.

It was he who broke the silence. By the way he looked and moved his tail he indicated that this spot was no place to build a dam.

With a fierce toss of her head she let him know that this was where she would live. And she led him underwater to the entrance of her secret cave and showed him the escape hatches and how she planned to link it to the lodge and the dam, but still he was not satisfied, and when they surfaced, he started to swim to a much safer spot, and she followed, chattering and slamming her tail and halting in disgust as he left her premises.

In the morning he swam back and indicated hesitantly that she was welcome to accompany him if she would consent to build their dam at a proper site.

Again she abused him, protesting furiously and snapping at him, driving him from her water, and that afternoon he came back quietly with a length of aspen in his teeth. Diving to the bottom of the creek, he fastened it to the floor with mud, the first construction in their new home.

It was then September and they set to work with a passion. They labored all night, dragging trees and branches into the stream, weighting them with mud and gradually building the whole construction high enough to check the flow of water. Again and again as they worked he betrayed his doubt that the dam they were building would hold, but she worked with such fervor that he swallowed his precautions.

When the two beavers were satisfied that the dam would impound the water necessary for their establishment, she began tying branches and tree lengths into the bottom, weighting them with rocks and mud and other trees, and it was now that she realized that in the building of the dam she had done most of the work. He was great on starting things, and showed considerable enthusiasm during the first days, but when it came time for doing the hard, backbreaking work, he was usually absent.

She had to acknowledge that she had accepted a lazy mate, one who could not be cured, but instead of infuriating her, this merely spurred her to greater effort. She worked as few beavers, an industrious lot, had ever worked, lugging huge trunks of trees and slapping mud until her paws ached. She did both the planning and the execution, and when the pile from which their lodge would be constructed was nearly finished, and she was eleven pounds lighter than when she started, he indicated for the final time that when the floods came, this would all vanish. She made no response, for she knew that just as she had done most of the building this time, she would have to do it again if floods ever did come.

When the pile in the middle of the small lake behind the dam was completed, they dived to the bottom and began the gratifying task of cutting entrances into it, and providing sleeping levels above the waterline, and places for kits when they came, and digging connecting runways to the secret chamber, and at this planning he was a master, for he had built lodges before.

Only a few days remained before the freeze, and this period they spent in a burst of superenergy, stripping bark and storing it for their winter's food. Where eating was concerned, he was willing to work, and in the end they had a better lodge than any other on the creek, and better provisioned too.

In the early days of winter, when they were frozen in, they mated, and in spring, after she gave birth to four lovely babies, the river produced a flood which washed away the dam and most of the lodge. He grunted as it was happening, but she rescued the babies and took them to higher ground, where a fox ate one.

As soon as the floods receded, she began to rebuild the dam, and when it was finished, she taught the babies how to help rebuild the lodge, which took less effort.

They then enjoyed four good years in their tight little kingdom, but on the fifth, sixth and seventh years there were floods, the last of such magnitude that the whole establishment was erased. This was enough for him, and he spent considerable time upstream looking for a better site, but when he found one, she refused to move. He found her marking the corners of her estate with castoreum and teaching her children how to start erecting a higher and better dam.

He halted at the edge of her territory and watched as this stubborn little creature proceeded with her engineering, making the same mistakes, dooming her dam to the same destruction.

He was now fifteen years old, an advanced age for a beaver, and she treated him with respect, not requiring him to haul logs or do much actual construction on the lodge. He snapped at the kits when they placed branches carelessly, indicating that if he were in charge he would not accept such sloppy workmanship. As he aged, his face grew uglier, with the scar predominating, and he moved with crotchets and limps, and one day while he was helping girdle some cottonwoods, he failed to detect a wolf approaching and would have been snatched had he not been bumped toward the safety tunnel by his mate.

That year there was no flood.

Then one day in early autumn when the food was safely in and the lodge never more secure, she happened to wander up the tunnel into the secret place which the family had so much enjoyed, and she found him lying there on the limestone ledge, his life gone. She nudged him gently, thinking that he might be asleep, then nuzzled him with affection to waken him for their evening swim through the lake they had built and rebuilt so many times, but he did not respond, and she stayed with him for a long time, not fully comprehending what death signified, unwilling to accept that it meant the end of their long and necessary companionship.

In the end the children took the body away, for it was no longer of any use, and automatically she went about the job of gathering food. Dimly she sensed that now there could be no more babies, no more kits playing in the limestone chamber and scampering down the runways.

She left the security of the lodge and went to each of the compass points and to the salient ridges in between, and at each she scooped up a handful of mud and mixed it with grass and kneaded in a copious supply of castoreum, and when the job was done she swam back to the middle of her lake and smelled the night air.

This was her home, and nothing would drive her from it, neither loneliness nor the attack of otters nor the preying of wolves nor the flooding of the river. For the home of any living thing is important, both for itself and for the larger society of which it is a part.

Diplodocus had evolved in Colorado but had died out. The horse had evolved here but had left. The bison had originated elsewhere and had moved in. The beaver had originated here but had emigrated. Was there no inhabitant that had originated here and had stayed? Indeed there was, perhaps the most terrifying creature now living on earth.

For the first four animals that occupied the land about the twin pillars there was self-evident justification. Diplodocus was a magnificent creature that harmed no one; the horse would make man mobile; the bison would make him warm and well fed; and the beaver would make him rich. Even the omnipresent wolf was needed, for he policed the area and kept the herds strong through killing off the old and the weak, while the chattering prairie dog could be justified for the humor it provided. But for the fifth inhabitant no acceptable justification had ever been proposed; the reason for his presence on earth was a mystery.

On a hot summer's day a female eagle flying lazily in the sky watched as a herd of bison left the shadows of the twin pillars and headed north for rendezvous on the far side of the North Platte. The eagle watched with unconcern as the great beasts moved out in single file, for there was nothing of advantage to her in the movement of bison or even in their congregation in large numbers. All they produced was dust.

But as the bison moved north she noticed that at a certain spot each animal shied to the left, even the most aggressive bulls, and this was worth inspecting, so she hovered for some minutes to confirm her observation, then flew in lazy circles till the herd passed.

As soon as the last straggler had come to this spot, looked down and veered, she dropped like an arrow from aloft, keeping her eye on the spot and noticing with pleasure that her deduction had been right. Below her in the dust beside a rock was food.

Increasing her speed, she swooped to earth, almost touching the sand with her wings. At the last moment she extended her talons and grabbed at the object which had attracted her, an enormous rattlesnake some five feet long and very thick in the middle. It had a flat, triangular head and on the end of its tail a curious set of nine hornlike knobs.

The eagle miscalculated slightly, for its talons did not strike the snake squarely. Only one claw of the right foot caught the rattler, well toward the tail, and although the eagle tried to carry the snake aloft so as to drop it on rocks and perhaps kill it, she failed, for the snake, with a violent twisting effort, tore free, and with blood flowing from the wound, immediately coiled itself to repel the next attack.

Seeing that the rattler was in a position to strike, the eagle realized that she could not swoop down and take it by surprise, so she landed some distance away, her feet and wings throwing up a cloud of dust, and with wary, high-stepping movements, approached to give battle.

The snake watched her come and adjusted his position to match hers, but he was not prepared for the kind of attack she made. Uttering a wild cry, she ran directly at the snake, raised her wings, encouraging it to strike at the feathers, then brought the edge of her left wing sharply across the snake's backbone. It was a staggering blow, delivered with all the force the eagle could muster, and it flattened the rattlesnake.

Instantly she leaped upon it, catching it squarely in the middle, so that her claws dug all the way through that part of the snake's body. With a flap of her extended wings she soared into the air, but she did not rise to the highest heavens, for she was working on a plan of calculated cunning. Searching not for rocks but for a terrain quite different, she found what she wanted. She flew with her eyes into the wind to assure herself that it was not strong enough to blow the snake off target when she dropped him. Satisfied, she disengaged the serpent and watched as it plummeted into the middle of a cactus thicket, whose needle-sharp spines jutted upward.

With a thud the rattlesnake fell onto the cactus, impaling itself in a score of places. As it writhed, the jagged edges of the spines cut deep and held fast. There was no way the snake could tear itself loose, and death became inevitable.

Had the eagle realized that exposure to the sun and loss of blood must soon kill the snake, it could merely have waited, then hauled the dead carcass off to its young. But the bird was driven by deep inner compulsion and felt obligated to kill its enemy, so it flapped its great wings slowly and hovered above the cactus spines, lowering itself until its curved talons could catch the serpent again.

This time the eagle flew in wide circles, searching for an area of jagged rocks on which to drop the rattler. Locating what she wanted, she flapped her wings and rose to a great height and shook the snake free, watching with satisfaction as it crashed onto the rocks. The fall did great damage, and the snake should have been dead, but like all rattlers he had a terrible determination to survive, so as soon as he struck the rocks he marshaled his remaining strength and took the coiled position.

The eagle had made a sad miscalculation in dropping the snake onto the rocks, for she had counted upon the fall to kill him outright, but this it had not done, so now she was forced to leave the flat, sandy terrain where she had an advantage and go among the rocks, where the advantage was his. However, since the snake was obviously close to death, she judged that she could quickly finish him off.

But when she sought to deliver the culminating blow with the edge of her wing, he somehow thrust himself about her body and enclosed it in a constricting embrace, fighting desperately to bring his lethal head into contact with some vital part.

She was too clever to permit this. Keeping his head at a disadvantage, she strained and clawed and bit until he had to release his hold. For the moment he was defenseless, and she took this opportunity to pierce him for the third time, and now she carried him very high, kicking him free over the rocks again, and once more he crashed onto them.

He should have been dead, and he feigned that he was, lying stretched out and avoiding the coil. Sorely shattered by this last fall and bleeding from numerous wounds, he made no sound, for his rattles were broken.

The eagle was fooled. She inspected him from the air, then landed on the rocks and walked unsteadily over to carry him aloft for the last time, but as she neared, the snake coiled and struck with what force he had left and plunged his fangs into the unprotected spot where her thin neck joined her torso. The fangs held there for only a moment, but in that brief instant the muscles in his neck contracted, sending a jet of lethal poison deep into her bloodstream. Easily, so easily, the fangs withdrew and the snake fell back upon the rocks.

The startled eagle made no motion. She merely stared with unbelieving eye at the snake while he stared back at her with basilisk gaze. She felt a tremor across her chest and then a vast constriction. She took two halting steps, then fell dead.

The rattlesnake lay motionless for a long time, one wing of the eagle across his wounded body. The sun started to go down and he felt the coldness of the night approaching. Finally he bestirred himself, but he was too damaged to move far.

For a long period it seemed that he would die, there on the rock with the eagle, but just before sundown he mustered enough strength to drag himself into a crevice where there would be some protection from the night cold. He stayed there for three days, slowly regaining strength, and at the end of this time he started his painful trip home.

He lived, as did several hundred other rattlers, some much bigger than he, in the rocks at the twin pillars. They had lived there for two million years, a mass of snakes that found the area good hunting for rats and prairie dogs, with safe crevices in the rocks for hibernation in the winter. When men reached the area the twin pillars would become known as Rattlesnake Buttes, reassuring beacons in the desert when spotted from afar, dangerous death traps when approached too closely.

Rattlesnake Buttes! A thousand westward travelers would remark about them in their diaries: 'Yesterday from a grate distance we seen the Rattlesnake Butes they was like everbody said tall like castels in Yurope and you could see them all day and wundered who will be bit by the snakes like them folks from Missuri?'

The myriad poisonous snakes that infested the buttes served no purpose that man could discern: they terrorized, they ate harmless prairie dogs, they killed whatever they struck, and after a long life they died. Why had they been made custodians of such a deadly poison? It was impossible to say.

The two fangs that folded back against the roof of the mouth when not needed dropped into operating position when the snake wanted to kill. They were not teeth as such, but hollow and very sharp hypodermic needles, so formed that pressure from the rattler's throat would not only deposit the poison but inject it to astounding depths. The poison itself was a combination of highly volatile proteins which reacted with the blood of the victim, producing quick and painful death.

The snakes at Rattlesnake Buttes were apt to leave intruders alone unless the latter did something to frighten them. Bison roamed the area by the thousands, and always had, and as calves they learned to avoid the rattlers. Indeed, even the sound of a rattle, that dreaded clatter in the dust, was enough to make a line of bison move in another direction.

Occasionally some stupid one would put himself into a position from which there was no escape for the rattler, and then the snake would strike him. If the venom entered the bison anywhere near the head or face, it was invariably fatal, but if it struck a leg, there was a fighting chance that the poison would be absorbed before it reached the heart, but the bison would thereafter be lame in that leg, its nerves and muscles half destroyed by the venom.

In the days when horses roamed the area, many a fine steed went lame because it blundered upon a rattlesnake and had taken a shot of venom in its fetlock. But if either a bison or a horse saw a rattler about to strike, and saw it in time, it would take protective action and stamp the snake to death. Sharp hoofs were more dangerous to rattlers than eagles or hawks, so that if the bison tried to avoid the snakes, so, too, did the rattlers keep out of the way of bison—and especially deer, whose ultrasharp hoofs could cut a snake in half.

The rattler that had defeated the eagle in mortal combat took a long time to recover. For the next two years he was in poor shape, able to leave the buttes for only short trips and always gratified when winter came so that he could sleep for five or six months, but gradually he began to feel better, and the gaping wounds in his body retreated into scars. He started to move about, and when the weather was good he joined some of the other snakes in short expeditions in search of mice and small birds.

Then his full vigor returned and he resumed a normal life. For him this had always consisted of matching wits with prairie dogs, those chattering little squirrel-like animals that built intricate subterranean towns.

There was such a town, rather extensive, not far from the buttes, and for a hundred thousand years the rattlesnakes had invaded it.

On a warm day, when the sun relaxed and vivified the muscles that had grown stiff in winter, he set out from the buttes and slithered across the desert toward dog-town. From a distance he could see the little mounds that indicated where the creatures lived, and he noticed with gratification that they were as numerous as ever.

As he approached the town, which contained several thousand dogs, he tried to move as inconspicuously as possible, but from a hillock a sharp-eyed lookout spotted the grass moving and gave a loud chirping sound, which lookouts elsewhere in the town repeated, so that within an instant the whole area was alerted. Where there had been thousands of little prairie dogs sunning themselves and chattering, there were now none and all was silent.

He had encountered this tactic before and was prepared for it. Crawling as close as practical to a concentrated nest of houses, he coiled the long length of his body and waited. The one thing he could count on was curiosity; no matter what threatened, the prairie dog sooner or later had to come out of his safe burrow to inspect. A hawk could be perched at the opening, his feet showing, but the little dogs had to come out to satisfy themselves that he was really there.

So the snake waited, and before too many minutes had passed, from one of the burrows a furry little head appeared. By chance its first glance was directly into the eyes of the snake, which startled it so, it gave one wild cry and disappeared down its hole, but before it had ceased trembling from fright, another dog from another hole came out to see if there really was a snake, and this one was not so fortunate as to look directly at the rattler. It turned first in the opposite direction and before it ever saw the snake, the fangs had sunk into its neck.

There were many burrows in this town, and sometimes the rattlesnakes, caught far from the buttes in bad weather or when the sun was dangerously hot—for a snake, like the great reptiles before him, would quickly perish if exposed too long to the direct rays of the sun—would crawl into the burrows, and even make them their home for extended periods, in which case the prairie dogs would simply leave by another exit.

Sand owls, which built their nests and raised their young underground, also liked to preempt the burrows rather than take the trouble to build their own, and it was not unusual to see within one town the prairie dogs inhabiting one set of burrows, the sand owls another, and the rattlesnakes a third, with each allowing the other to go pretty much his own way.

This rattlesnake had no intention of taking up residence in dog-town. It came only to feed, and when it had caught its prey and swallowed it, there were other areas to visit, down by the river, for example, where mice lived among the roots of the cottonwoods. A rattler would always prefer a mouse above any other food, but they were not easy to catch. There were also birds, especially the young, but catching them required unusual patience, and after his encounter with the eagle this rattler was not much attracted to birds.

As autumn approached, it was essential that each rattler fortify himself with a series of meals upon which he could draw in the months of hibernation, and the hunting became more intense. In those days he practically lived in the heart of dog-town, picking off whatever inquisitive little animals he could, but as the days shortened he felt an irresistible urge to seek protection at the buttes. It was no trivial thing to go to sleep for a series of months during which he would be vulnerable to any foe that came upon him; it was essential that he return to deep rocky crevices which had protected him in the past.

So he started the trek back to the buttes, and as he went he saw many other rattlesnakes on their way, too, and as they convened at familiar places they moved together and sometimes formed intertwined balls of writhing forms, a score of large rattlers twisted together. When men reached this area, as they soon would, they would sometimes in autumn stumble upon such a ball of writhing snakes—'they was as big as a watermillion'—and they would be horrified; memory of the sight would haunt them, and years later they would speak of it: 'I was ridin' a gray mustang, a very steady brute, and all at oncet he shies and like to throw me on my ass and thank God he didn't because there by them red rocks at Rattlesnake Buttes was this ball of snakes all twisted up I like to died.'

Now as the snakes crawled down a path which they had often used before, the old rattler became aware of an unfamiliar creature blundering toward him from the opposite direction. Following his ancient custom, he coiled himself in the middle of the path and emitted a sharp rattle. The stranger, unfamiliar with this warning, ignored it, stumbling directly at the rattler, which made an even sharper sound.

At last the intruder took notice, almost too late.

The snake struck at the thing that stood close to its fangs, but this was to be a unique experience, for deftly the target leaped aside, and from aloft something descended, striking the rattler a heavy blow behind the head. Knocked out of its coil, the snake endeavored in bewilderment to adjust to this unprecedented assault. It formed a half-coil, preparing to strike anew at its assailant.

And then it looked up, and instead of seeing a buffalo or a sharp-hoofed deer, it saw a new creature, standing erect, bearing a heavy weapon not seen before, and the last sensation this rattler had was the sight of the weapon descending toward his head with tremendous force, and the strange cry of triumph from the standing figure, and sharp death.

Man had come to the plains. From the far northwest, from a distant origin, across strange bridges and down green corridors, the two-legged one had journeyed to the buttes, where before only the horse and the camel and the mammoth, the sloth and the beaver and the snake had lived. His first act was symbolic, the instinctive killing of the snake, and for as long as time endured, enmity between these two would continue.

At this watershed of history it might be prudent to look at the land as it then was, for we must remember our inheritance if we are to retain a vision of what it might once more be.

It was a cruel land, that year when man arrived. The New Rockies rose perhaps a millionth of an inch; certainly they did not stand still, for they never had and they never would. They were either rising in birth or falling in decay, and in time to come they might be higher than the Himalayas or lower than the Appalachians. In that year no man could have guessed what their destiny would be.

From the mountains great bodies of water and silt cascaded down onto the plains, as they had been doing for seventy million years. That year there was a flood which killed many bison and swept away all beaver lodges, but at the same time it deposited some of the silt and many of the minerals which would make the area unusually rich when time came for tillage.

The grass grew a little better than usual, making it one of the finest pasture areas in the world, and the bison increased in number, so that when the cows led the northern herd into the yearly convocation the count was at its maximum, around forty million, with thirty million in the southern herd. They darkened the earth in such great numbers, they could never be obliterated.

Beaver had a poor year. The floods killed many in their lodges, especially the kits and one-year-olds. The two-year-old beavers who were expelled from home that year had little trouble finding locations for their lodges, but a lot of trouble finding trees the right size for building their dams; the flood had uprooted too many and swept them downstream.

At Rattlesnake Buttes the animals lived in subtle and long-approved harmony. The little sand owls stole a burrow now and then from the prairie dogs, and occasionally they ate a young dog, but only one that was too weak to survive normally. They also kept the mice in check, but themselves provided food for hawks.

The main problem of the prairie dogs was not the loss of an occasional burrow to the owls, or even the constant depredations of the rattlesnakes, but the fact that in the summer the rutting bulls, frustrated as males often are by the problems of sex, insisted upon wallowing on top of the town where the earth was fine and dusty and then urinating on it; they did a lot of damage and it took time to rebuild a town after such treatment.

The pronged antelope and the wolverine and the sleek deer and gray wolves that watched everything lived together in delicate balance, each needing the other and each dependent upon the land and its abundant grass.

There was another factor which has not been mentioned but which would, in the years ahead, become increasingly important. This land was beautiful.

From the buttes at sunrise a man would be able to look east and see a hundred miles to unbroken horizons, stark meadow after meadow reaching beyond the human imagination. The colors were superb, but the uninitiated could look at them and not see them, for they were soft grays and delicate browns and azure purples.

The vast plains had a nobility that would never diminish, for they were a challenge, with their duststorms, their wild blizzards, their tornadoes and their endless promise, if men treated them with respect. They were a resource inexhaustible in their variety but demanding in their love. In the years ahead they would terrify easterners and Europeans afraid of loneliness, but they would be a haven for all who understood them, and they would be loved in contrary ways and with harsh curses. The great plains—illimitable in both challenge and fulfillment.

If a man looked northward from the buttes he could see the chalk cliffs of Nebraska, those extraordinary white rocks that had once lain at the bottom of some vanished sea. It was infuriating; he could be dying of thirst on the parched plains, yet know that the whole area had once been under water, and there the white cliffs were to prove it. If he poked among them he would find fossil fish and clams, and the only way such things could have been caught in the rocks was for everything to have been under water. Hell, in some places the rock was twenty thousand feet thick, and all of it made under water.

To the south were the cottonwoods, that thin line of useless trees, barely edible for beavers, who would eat any tree that grew. Yet when a traveler saw those trees, broken-branched and torn by storms, his heart skipped a beat, for they marked the South Platte, and wherever it ran, there was at least water, foul though it might be, and some chance that another human being could be in the vicinity, because he needed water too.

It was to the west, however, that the conspicuous grandeur lay, for there the mountains rose in such splendor that when men saw them they gasped. Row upon row the marvelous peaks marched north and south, so many and so varied that the eye could never tire of them. In winter they were white with snow and looked as if they had been pasted against the deep-blue sky. In spring they shone green in their lower reaches and granite-blue above the tree line. In all seasons they were glorious, reaching fourteen thousand feet into the air and visible for more than a hundred miles out in the prairie.

There was one peak visible from the buttes, the largest of all, which captured the affection of every man or woman who saw it from this area.

It was a noble peak of itself and would have been outstanding even if it had no significant features, but up its eastern flank crawled a granite beaver. It was really the oddest thing, but when a man looked at this master-mountain, a thing of obvious majesty, all he remembered was that stone beaver trying to climb to the top. Travelers could see him from a long way off, and from the buttes he commanded attention. This peak should have been called Beaver Mountain, but unfortunately, men are sometimes not imaginative. Other peaks had poetic names like Never-Summer Range, Rabbit's Ear, Medicine Bow, Sangre de Cristo, and one with a perpetual mark of snow in its crisscrossed ravines, the Mount of the Holy Cross. Even Pikes Peak had an alliterative ring, but the best mountain of them all, with a little beaver crawling up its flank, was given the drabbest name of all—Longs Peak.

The Rockies had a characteristic not shared by other ranges of the west, and this both endeared them to people who lived in their shadow and infuriated those who came upon them as strangers. The air surrounding them was so pure that from a distance it was impossible to calculate how far away they were. Of course, the air was just as pure around the ranges to the north, but they were not faced by flat plains across which people traveled, so the phenomenon did not apply to them. If an immigrant came from a flat land like Illinois, he would wake up one morning after crossing the Missouri to see the Rockies as clear as a row of corn on his farm back home, and he would exult and cry, 'Tonight we sleep in the mountains!'

But he could travel westward all the next day, and the mountains would still appear to be where they had been at dawn, and the next night they would be no closer, nor the next either. Distance could not be calculated, and occasionally a man and his wife would become mesmerized by the noble mountains; never had they seen anything so grand and so perplexing. The good part was that close up, these splendid ranges were just as impressive as they had been from a distance. They dominated the plains and served as a backdrop to extraordinary beauty.

It was at sunset that the mountains came into their own, for on some days clouds would rest over them like a light blanket and reflect the dying sun. Then the mountains would be bathed in splendor: gold and red and soft radiant browns and deep blues would color the underside of the clouds and frame the mountains in a celestial light, so that even the most stolid Indiana immigrant would have to halt his oxen and look in amazement at a setting so grand that it seemed to have been ordained solely for the stupefaction of mankind.

The loveliest moment came, however, when the sun had set and its flamboyant coloring had faded. Then, for about twenty minutes, the softest colors of the spectrum played about the crests of the mountains, and the little stone beaver crawled toward the summit to sleep, and many a traveler bit his lower lip and looked away, thinking of a home he would not see again.

Centennial, when it was founded, would stand at the spot where a man could look eastward and catch the full power of the prairie, or westward to see the Rockies. The history of the town would be a record of the way it responded to the impossible task of conciliating the demands of the mountains with the requirements of the prairie. Many would destroy themselves in this conflict, but those who survived, assimilating the best of these two contrasting worlds, would attain a largeness of soul that other men who chose easier paths would not discover.

CAUTION TO *US* EDITORS. Even as I was working on this section a group of leading geologists announced that in their opinion the Pleistocene epoch, which covers the period of the glaciers, should be considered to start not at one million years before the present but two to three million. At the same time another specialist suggested that North America did not experience the five periods of glaciation which I was taught—with five interglacial periods, the last being the one we are in now—but rather a recurring series of shorter-lived glaciers interspersed with many interglacial periods. I tend to agree with each of these opinions, because they are consistent with ideas I have expressed before, that we will probably push all dates back in time. We are older than we used to think. However, in my notes I have respected the established chronology. If your own researches incline you toward the newer dates, use them.

Land bridge. I must also warn you concerning two facts about the land bridge. Its existence cannot be challenged, but it may not have been as vital as my notes make it out to be. A very good geologist told me the other day, 'There is no need to posit this famous land bridge of yours. For much of the time when the exchange of animal life was under way the Asian plate and the North American were in contact and the two continents were undifferentiated. The so-called bridge must have then been two or three thousand miles wide, and glaciers had absolutely nothing to do with it.' Incidentally, do not think of the Eskimo as using the bridge. They got here very late, long after the last glaciation, when there could have been no bridge. No matter. They could get from Asia to Alaska simply by canoeing for fifty-six miles, which is what they did.

Amphibians? Although every text agrees that the sauropods, the family to which diplodocus belonged, were amphibians, the exact significance of this description is uncertain. Some experts like G. Edward Lewis argue that animals as enormous as brontosaurus and diplodocus could not have supported their weight on dry land, considering their crude joints; they must have lived in swamps and lagoons where water buoyed them up. Others point out that the legs, awkward though they were, did persist through millions upon millions of years, whereas unused append-ages, like the human tail, atrophied and vanished. Of seventeen illustra-tions I was able to find of diplodocus, all showed her on land, but Lewis explains that this cannot be accepted as evidence; the artists merely wished to display her total conformation.

Origins of the horse. Some readers may, with scientific backing, ob-ject to a Colorado origin for the horse. They argue that the missing 'paleohippus' of which I write could just as properly have originated in Europe, since there was a well-known European equivalent to the second-generation eohippus. In Europe the little creature was given the totally erroneous name *hyracotherium*, because his discoverers could not imagine him to be related in any way to the horse; they classified him as a forebear of the hyrax, a small shrewlike animal, the cony of the Old Testament. Such experts believe our horse originated in Europe from the hyracotherium. I think not. That eohippus died away into forms with no aptitude for survival. The horse as we know it developed where and as I said. The Arabian, the Percheron, the Clydesdale—all had their begin-nings not far from Rattlesnake Buttes. Crazy idea, isn't it?

Appaloosa. I would advise you not to get involved over the origins of this most beautiful of horses. A group of new scholars is pushing the line that the ancestors of our horse developed in America only as far as mesohippus, which then emigrated to Asia, where it developed into the horse proper, in the form of the Appaloosa, which thus becomes the great ancestor of subsequent breeds. This theory is most ardently voiced, as you might suspect, by Appaloosa owners, but is rejected by others. The Appaloosa is a distinguished animal, one of the great breeds of the world and possibly the most ancient. It has solid-color front quarters, mottled rear, skimpy tail and mane and curiously streaked hoofs. The Nez Percé Indians of western Idaho were responsible for cultivating the strain in North America, and from them a few passed into the hands of west-ern ranchers, who in 1938 banded together to reestablish the breed. They've done a good job, and later on we'll see the effect on a town like Centennial.

Origins of the beaver. You may get some flak regarding the beaver. Some experts have argued that he originated in Europe, or perhaps Egypt, and immigrated to North America rather late. But the greater scholars like Stout and Schultz, both of Nebraska, believe that he origi-nated from American stock dating far back and that he emigrated over the land bridge to Asia to develop collaterally there.

Definitions. It's difficult to find a precise definition of *butte*. A vast upland area is a *plateau*. When bounded on all four sides by cliffs, it's a *mesa*. When the boundaries of the mesa erode to a point at which the height is greater than the width, it's a *butte*. If it continues eroding, it becomes in succession a *monument*, a *chimney*, a *spire*, a *needle*, and finally, a memory.

Eagle-serpent. This enmity is celebrated in many folklores. The pre-eminent visual depiction appears, of course, in the Mexican flag, where a serpent held in the talons of an eagle perched on a cactus serves as the national insignia. Traditionally the eagle (manly virtue) kills the snake (guile and venality); the account I send you, in which the rattlesnake triumphs, is an invention of the western plains, where it occurs in various oral versions.

THE MANY
COUPS OF
LAME BEAVER

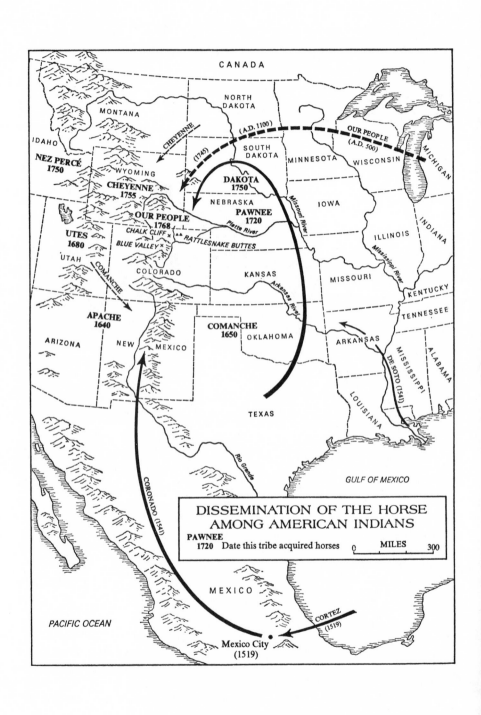

CANADA

NORTH DAKOTA

MONTANA

IDAHO

(A.D. 1100)

OUR PEOPLE
(A.D. 500)

MICHIGAN

NEZ PERCÉ
1750

WYOMING

SOUTH
DAKOTA

MINNESOTA

WISCONSIN

CHEYENNE

(1745)

DAKOTA
1750

CHEYENNE
1755

NEBRASKA

IOWA

INDIANA

OUR PEOPLE
1768

PAWNEE
1720

Missouri River

Platte River

ILLINOIS

UTES
1680

CHALK CLIFF

RATTLESNAKE BUTTES

BLUE VALLEY

COMANCHE

COLORADO

KANSAS

MISSOURI

Mississippi River

UTAH

Arkansas River

KENTUCKY

APACHE
1640

ARIZONA

NEW

MEXICO

COMANCHE
1650

OKLAHOMA

ARKANSAS

TENNESSEE

DE SOTO
(1541)

ALABAMA

MISSISSIPPI

LOUISIANA

TEXAS

Rio Grande

GULF OF MEXICO

CORONADO (1541)

DISSEMINATION OF THE HORSE
AMONG AMERICAN INDIANS

PAWNEE
1720   Date this tribe acquired horses

0   MILES   300

MEXICO

CORTEZ
(1519)

PACIFIC OCEAN

Mexico City
(1519)

Mᴀɴ ᴡᴀѕ ᴛᴀʀᴅʏ ɪɴ ʀᴇᴀᴄʜɪɴɢ ᴄᴏʟᴏʀᴀᴅᴏ, and precisely when he arrived, we do not know. The great land bridge leading from Asia to Alaska was open 40,000 years ago, after which it closed when the glaciers melted and their captured water returned to the sea. It was open again about 28,000 years ago, and for the last time, about 13,000 years ago, closing about 10,000 years ago.

When the bridge was open, perhaps a thousand miles wide, well-developed human beings then living in eastern Siberia could have followed mammoths and other large game from Asia into Alaska. And when the tips of the glaciers began to melt, broad avenues opened, leading in a southeasterly direction, with mountains to the west and broad plains to the east, down which the animals could move, pursued by the men who hunted them.

It is sheer speculation to assume that 40,000 years ago Mongoloid men crossed the bridge and came down the avenues. But it is a certainty that when the bridge opened 13,000 years ago men came down—or were already here—to start the earliest recorded occupation of America. In time their descendants would become known as Indians. Finally, we have good records of a late migration around 6,000 B.C. which did not require any land bridge; these incomers used boats to cross the fifty-six-mile gap of ocean that separates Alaska from Siberia. Today their descendants are known as Eskimo, markedly different from the earlier groups that became Indians.

As yet we have no secure evidence that men actually arrived 40,000 years ago; we have found neither their homes, nor their tools, nor their skeletons. All we have are tantalizing intimations of their occupancy—a carved caribou leg bone in the Yukon, a circle of stones in California, a possible dwelling in Puebla—but one of these days, perhaps before the end of this century, definitive proof may be forthcoming.

Nor do we have proof that the bridge 28,000 years ago brought us men, although it almost certainly did. As of today, all we can be sure of is that man was indubitably here 12,000 years ago, because we have the hard-proof records of his occupancy.

We know where he lived, what time of year he hunted, how he made his spear, where he encountered a great mammoth, and how he killed the animal before the feast began. We are as certain of this hunt as we are that Daniel Boone once shot deer in Kentucky; all we lack is the mammoth's skeleton.

In the year 9268 B.C. at the chalk cliffs west of Rattlesnake Buttes a human being twenty-seven years old, and therefore ancient and about to die, studied a chunk of rock which a younger man had quarried from the mountains. He was a flint-knapper, and his practiced eye assured him that this was the kind he needed, a hard, flinty, gray-brown rock with one facet fairly smooth. It was about the size of a man's head, and most of the memorable rocks he had worked with in the past, those he remembered with affection because of the superb points he had struck from them, had looked like this. He breathed deeply and felt there was a good chance this one might prove productive too.

But he was also apprehensive, for the hunters of his clan had gone almost two months without having made a major kill, and food supplies were low. Scouts had spotted a small group of mammoths, those formidable beasts that stood twice as tall as a man and weighed a hundred times more, but to kill such an adversary required the stoutest spears, tipped with the sharpest points, and it was this flint-knapper's task to provide the latter, for upon his skill depended the security of his clan.

Before he risked breaking into the secret of the rock, he purified himself, for he knew that no man could succeed in a venture of great moment without the aid of gods. Leaving his work space—a flat area at the foot of the chalk cliff—he went to an opening between the trees and there turned his face upward and his body to each of the four compass points, ending with the east, from which the sun came. He engaged in no complicated ritual and uttered no incantation; he merely wished to inform the gods that he was about to engage in a project of importance to his clan, and he solicited their attention. He did not grovel for assistance, because in that large area there was no better knapper than he, but he did want the gods to be aware of his undertaking and to refrain from interfering.

He then went to the running stream that came out of the mountains to the west of the cliff and washed his hands, applying some of the water to his face. He was now ready.

As he walked back to his work area he was indistinguishable, except for his dress, from other men who would occupy this land ten thousand years later. He walked erect, with no apelike bending at the waist. His arms did not dangle and his head was not massive in proportion to the rest of his body. There was no conspicuous ledge of bone above his eyes and his hands were, as we shall see, beautifully articulated.

His eyes had a slight slant, an evidence of his Asian ancestry. His face was somewhat heavier than those of later men, his cheekbones more pronounced, his skin several shades lighter than that which was to come later; it inclined, perhaps, more toward red than yellow, and in this respect was quite similar to the men who would follow.

He had a working vocabulary of twelve or thirteen hundred words, few of which would be intelligible even a short time after his death, for in language swift change was in process. He had considerable powers of thought, could plan ahead, could devise tactics for hunting which required cooperative movements carried out at spaced intervals, and he knew a good deal about animals, the nature of differences between women and men, how to rear children, how to lay by enough food in good periods so that he would have something to eat in time of famine. He worked hard and understood that if he got ahead in his production he would have time for his own enjoyment.

He did not take himself too seriously; he was not lugubrious even when talking to his gods. Often he burst into laughter when his children did something ridiculous. From time to time, in making the projectile points on which his clan depended for their existence, he felt pride in being an artisan, a man trained to accomplish, and such a feeling came over him now.

'If I get a good start,' he told his apprentice, who must soon be making the points himself, 'I can strike . . .' and here he held his ten fingers aloft twice.

What a tremendous statement to have come from the mouth of a primitive man! How totally compelling in its complex range of thought! A man at the dawn of history who could utter such a complicated concept could produce children for whom anything would be possible.

If is a word of infinite intellectual significance, for it indicates actions not yet completed but with the possibility of alternate outcomes. To *get a good start* implies memory of bad starts and how they differed from the good; it implies also that there will be consequences stemming from the *good start* and that they will be consistent with such consequences in the past. The incomplete *I can strike* . . . is the sum of man's experience on earth, the promise of completed action in accordance with known desires. And the ten fingers held aloft twice is an advance in mathematics so profound—an abstract number without a name—that all subsequent analytical thought will be based upon it. To visualize twenty points as being obtainable from a roundish chunk of rock, and to have a number for them and to recognize that that number goes beyond the digits of the hand, is an accomplishment of such magnitude that it must have required man most of the two million years he had so far lived on earth to assemble the experience that would justify such a conclusion.

The knapper who prepared to strike the rock that day had all the innate capacities that future men would have; the only additional component required to produce a complicated society would be a sufficient passage of time and the patient accumulation of memory. But this man had something else which would always be precious in whatever epochs followed: he had an innate sense of proportion, design and beauty, and the degree to which he had these qualities would never be surpassed by any men who followed him on this spot.

Coughing twice, rubbing his fingertips on his chest, he lifted the heavy rock and studied it for the last time. It met his specifications, for it was vitreous, totally homogeneous, without any tendency to fracture along a predetermined plane, and of the same construction along all axes, which would permit it to fracture equally well in all directions.

Making a finished point required four quite different steps, each performed with a different tool. First he must transform the amorphous rock into a truncated cone. Now, obviously the knapper could not possibly have known the mathematical properties of a cone, nor the physical principles governing it, but he had learned from experience that if his rock did not assume a conical shape, it would not yield the flakes he sought, but if it did approximate a cone segment, the flakes would fly off in dazzling sequence.

His first tool was a smallish, rounded rock with curious characteristics. It was ovoid and of a grainy texture, with a certain amount of yield. It was the possession he prized most in his life, for a responsive hammerstone was almost irreplaceable. One morning he had advised his assistant, who was seeking such a stone for himself, 'You must find one that talks back.'

With his hammerstone he knocked away unwanted portions of the flint and coaxed it into conical form. When it was prepared, he worked carefully with his hammer, building the right kind of edge around the top surface. Then, after careful study, he struck one particular spot, and the force of his hammer radiated downward but with a slight lateral effect, and a beautiful flake as long as his hand leaped from the surface of the core. Dropping his hammer, he held this flake to the light and satisfied himself that it contained no telltale lines of fracture. It was fearfully sharp along the edges and as it then stood could have been used for a knife, but he intended working on it later to form a projectile point.

What happened next astonished even his helper. Working rapidly, and revolving the core so that always a new face was exposed, he struck with his hammerstone almost as fast as a woodpecker pecks a dead limb, knocking off one perfect flake after another. Then he paused and worked slowly, building up the edge so that it would catch the hammer blows properly, and when this was done he resumed his woodpecker taps. Nineteen long flakes flew from the core, each sharp enough to butcher a mammoth. In his left hand lay the remnant, too small to be struck for further flakes, and this he tossed aside.

He dropped his hammerstone, threw back his head and winked at his helper: 'Good, eh?' They gathered the flakes and the knapper inspected each one. Three he discarded as offering doubtful promise for future work. They would never make projectile points, but the remaining sixteen had obvious possibilities. Properly finished, they could become masterpieces. Arranging them in a line, he summoned the clan to witness the good luck he had had that day.

The hunters surveyed the potential points and assessed them approvingly. One man, a notable tracker whose spears had started the deaths of several mammoths, grabbed one blade and cried, 'This one for me!' The knapper took it, studied it from various angles and said, 'I'll try.'

When the celebration of the flints was over, the artisan and his helper proceeded to the second step, the critical job of converting these sharp-edged flakes into workable projectiles. Taking a hand-sized piece of mammoth hide, he placed it in his left palm; this precaution was necessary, for otherwise the sharp flint slivers would slice his hand.

He laid aside his hammerstone and reached for his second tool, a clever device made from an antler. It was shaped like a small boomerang, except that at the angle where the two arms met, a knob protruded, about the size and shape of an egg. This was the hammer with which he would shape the flake.

Now, this knob must have contained about one thousand minute faces, indistinguishable one from the other to the untrained eye, but the task at hand was so intricate that the knapper had to swing his hammer with some force, over a fair distance, yet see to it that the precise point on the hammer struck the precise point on the edge of the flint. When it did, a curved piece of flint, reaching all the way around one face of the stone, would fly off. It was an act of incredible skill, of incredible engineering beauty.

He was now ready for the third process. The former flake was fairly close to the shape he wanted, but before it could be called a finished projectile, more precision work was required. Putting aside the hammer, he took an awl made from a single tine of elk horn, rounded on the end, like the tip of a little finger.

Holding the nearly finished point against the hide in his left palm, he applied the tine to minute projections along its edge, and by pressing with great but controlled force, he caused fragments of flint to crack free, and in this way, moving always from one calculated spot to the next, he put a scimitar-sharp edge around the entire point.

When he had worked for about fifteen minutes, pressing but never striking, he stopped and broke into a wide grin of satisfaction and handed the point to the waiting hunter, who showed it to his accomplices. It was superb, perfectly shaped, like a long, slim leaf, balanced, precisely flaked in all areas and with a keen cutting edge. Any huntsman tracking game in Africa or Asia during the preceding two million years would have cherished it.

But the knapper was not satisfied. Grabbing it roughly from the hunter, he prepared for the final process.

Cradling the point in the hide, he used his awl to form a tiny platform at the base, where it would ultimately be lashed by thongs to the haft. When this was leveled to his satisfaction, he took his fourth tool, a chest-punch, formed from the spreading antlers of the elk, with a curve that corresponded to his chest, but with one projecting tine in the middle. Holding the tool against his breast, he brought it to bear on the tiny platform, and with great pressure caused the flint to flake halfway down its length.

Without speaking, for this was a delicate and crucial operation, he used his awl to build another tiny platform on the opposite face, and once more, with the aid of his chest-punch, he forced off a flake running half the length of the point.

When he saw that this intricate move had succeeded, he leaped in the air, holding the finished point aloft in his left hand. Shouting words of triumph, he passed it to the hunter, who, better than most of the watchers, appreciated the tension the knapper had been under during the last moments.

The entire operation had required less than twenty minutes, and only one refinement remained. Recovering the point, the knapper lifted his hammer and with a fine insolence which would have terrified anyone who had begun to value it as a work of art—which it was—knocked a large indentation in the base, so that it could more easily be fastened into its haft by means of mammoth sinews and adhesives. Then with a rough stone he carefully ground away the sharp edges around the base so that the thongs would not be cut when it was lashed to the spear.

At three separate intervals the knapper could have considered his point completely finished, for it was a serviceable projectile that could kill, but each time he had gone beyond to knock away portions of his most meticulous work in order to improve upon some small detail which to another might have seemed trivial. In the midst of any process he could have leapfrogged to the next, but he refused, because he enjoyed his work and knew it to be good. Now-that it was finished, he gave it to the hunter almost carelessly, as if to say, 'I can do as well next time.' Then he laughed raucously, scratched his armpits, and sorted through the flakes to find another likely prospect.

That projectile, later to be named a Clovis point, with its functional design, its exquisite workmanship and its pronounced fluting, would be the finest work of art ever produced in the Centennial region. Men of a later day would have lathes at their disposal and electric drills and computers to assist them in determining slope, but they would produce nothing which in beauty, utility and perfect workmanship would match this Clovis point. Viewed flat, it was a subtle lanceolate, improving upon one of the most satisfying designs of nature. Viewed head-on, it was streamlined with uncanny anticipation of later discoveries. Held sideways, the base seemed like a wafer, so thin did the fluting make it, but when lashed to a haft, the point could penetrate like a bullet.

The rest of its story is quickly told. Next day the hunter took his spear and, with the aid of seven helpers, sought the towering mammoth. A boy trained in agility ran and dodged before the great tusked beast, and when the animal lowered its head to impale the tantalizing boy, the hunter ran with great speed, leaped in the air, landed on the back of the mammoth, vaulted high, and with both hands grasping his spear, brought it down with terrible force into the neck of the animal.

When the mammoth had lowered its massive head to catch the boy, the vertebrae above his shoulders had become extended, so that the point was able to enter and sever the spinal cord. The result was dramatic. The mammoth took one faltering step and dropped dead. Not once in a hundred times could a hunter reach a vital point with his spear; usually death was a long-drawn process of jabs in the side and chasing and bleeding, requiring two or three days. But this was the lucky blow, and the men howled with delight.

Nearly twelve thousand years later the articulated skeleton of this mammoth would be unearthed not far from Centennial, and wedged between two of the neck vertebrae would be found this projectile point, indisputable proof that man had lived in America not the mere three thousand years that some had assumed prior to this discovery, but for a very long time indeed. Thus the Clovis point produced that day by the conscientious knapper was not only a supreme work of art; it would also become a prime fact in our intellectual history.

It was from such men that the American Indian descended. Through the centuries the original stock from Asia, already varied because of the widely separated intervals at which their immigration occurred, underwent many mutations, depending upon where they settled and what luck they had with the natural resources they found. For example, one large tribe lived for some centuries in the Rocky Mountains just west of Rattlesnake Buttes, and there they divided into two, the more adventurous portion proceeding to Mexico, where they developed the dazzling Aztec culture; the less adventurous half remained behind to become one of the poorest Indian families on record, living on roots and barely able to sustain a civilization. We can be sure that the two groups at one time had an equal chance, because they spoke the same language and must have been part of the same tribe, the brilliant Aztecs of Mexico and the somber Utes of Colorado.

Or again, in California two branches of a tribe were offered a fateful choice. One turned a few miles to the east and found an easy highway of riches and good living all the way to Peru, where they built the mighty Inca civilization; the other turned a few miles to the west and found itself trapped on the arid peninsula of Baja California, where its members eked out the most miserable existence known to the world's humans, not even developing anything which could reasonably be called a civilization.

One attractive group of Indians, using a language that no one else could understand and referring to themselves only as Our People, branched off from the prehistoric men who had made the Clovis points and found a good life for themselves east of the Mississippi River. About A.D. 500 they moved westward and took up residence in the forests of northern Minnesota. From there, sometime around A.D. 1100, they moved farther westward onto the northern plains and the Dakotas, and at some point in the latter part of the eighteenth century they wandered tentatively southward to the land along the Platte, taking up a seasonal and foraging residence in the vicinity of Rattlesnake Buttes.

Our People were a tall, slim tribe of Indians with traditions so old they seemed engraved in time. The men tattooed themselves with ashes driven into their skin by cactus needles, three designs across the chest, and when they designated themselves in councils with other tribes they were apt to say 'Our People' and then tap their breasts with their fingertips.

They placed their faith in Man-Above and their reliance in battle on Flat-Pipe, the sacred totem of the tribe. It was a flattened pipe, guarded at all times by its keeper and cherished in the way the ancient Israelites had cherished their Ark. Flat-Pipe was of crucial importance because Our People were surrounded by enemies, and without its consolation, would have long since been overwhelmed.

In the year 1756 a sliver group of Our People, holding tentatively to the land between the two Plattes, faced the latest in the long line of crises which had beset them since the tribe started storing memories. The Indians surrounding them had horses and would soon have guns, and they had neither.

On his ninth birthday Lame Beaver was taken aside by his father Gray Wolf—that is, his real father's oldest brother—and prepared for doleful news: 'You must always remember that Our People are surrounded by enemies. To the north'—and he faced the boy in that direction—'the Dakota, fearful warriors. To the west, the unspeakable Ute, those black evil ones who try to steal our women and our children so that they can become light like us. Never trust a Ute, no matter what presents they bring or how they speak. To the south, the Comanche—they have horses. And to the east . . .' Here he turned the boy toward Rattlesnake Buttes and the prairies beyond. 'Out there, always lurking, always clever, the tribe it is almost impossible to defeat in battle.' He spat. Biting his lower lip, he felt an anger so great that for a moment he could not speak. Then, brandishing his feathered spear toward the east, he snarled, 'The Pawnee.'

He sat the boy on a rock and told him, 'In the morning when you rise. At night before you go to sleep. And especially when you are the lookout on the hill. Always look to the four directions and ask yourself, "Where is my enemy hiding?" '

He said, 'You must never be afraid of enemies . . . or meeting them in battle. The noblest act for a warrior is to touch an enemy in battle . . . to count coup. It would be shameful to die a coward . . . without ever having counted coup.'

Lame Beaver listened. He knew as much about counting coup as did his father. Young boys talked about it all the time, of how they were prepared to rush up to any Ute and touch him with their hand or with a spear and thus count coup. They would even be prepared to face a Comanche on his horse, and brave his lance, in hopes of counting coup, for a man who failed to count coup could have no respected place among Our People. Lame Beaver had boasted to his playmates, 'I would even run up to a Pawnee to gain coup,' but none of them believed this, for the Pawnee would probably have a horse and perhaps a black stick that spewed smoke and killed from a distance. 'I would,' he repeated.

His father Gray Wolf grew silent, and after a long pause, said, 'Only the rocks live forever. A warrior is born for his season and he fights as Man-Above allows. He respects Flat-Pipe and he gains what coups he can. And in the end, if he is lucky, he dies in battle, his hand against the enemy, gaining the greatest coup of all—death in victory.'

He spoke so gravely that Lame Beaver stopped thinking about counting coup in the battles that lay ahead and looked at him. Gray Wolf's face was deeply lined and dust stood in the crevices. His eyes were sorrowful, and in that moment of silent communication Lame Beaver apprehended that his real father, Sun-at-Noon, had been killed. Averting his gaze, he asked, 'Did he die in battle?' and Gray Wolf answered, 'He was trying to count coup on a Pawnee.'

'Did he?' Lame Beaver asked.

'No,' Gray Wolf replied. It would be futile to lie about such a thing, because that night when the warriors gathered at the campfire and reviewed the day's battle, there would be harsh and honest decision as to who counted coup and who did not, and not even the death of a warrior known to be brave, like Sun-at-Noon, would warrant lying about whether he had made coup.

With Our People it was permitted that four warriors count coup on an enemy. The first to touch him shouted for all to hear, 'I first,' and the second, 'I second,' and so on, but when the battle ended these warriors and their witnesses convened, and confirmation was sought, and a warrior might claim, 'I gained first coup on the Pawnee chieftain,' but until someone confirmed this and said, 'I saw him touch the Pawnee and he is first,' the award was not allowed.

Killing the enemy? That amounted to nothing. If it had to be done, it was done, but it did not count beyond whatever coup that might have been involved. Collecting a scalp? That also was nothing, an act some warriors performed when they wanted decorations for their tipi or their saddle. A warrior might kill an enemy and scalp him and still gain no credit if four other warriors had counted coup on him first.

'Sun-at-Noon failed?' the boy asked.

'He tried. The Pawnee had a horse and came too fast.'

'Did you bring his body home?'

'Only the rocks live forever,' Gray Wolf said. 'The Pawnee took his body and scalped him and he is dead.'

The boy sighed, for he knew that if his dead father had no scalp, he could not enter the hunting grounds.

The following stories explain how Lame Beaver gained his own coups and became a great leader of Our People, but never chief.

1. Old Man Staked Out

In the spring of 1764, when Lame Beaver was seventeen years old, Our People met in conclave and decided it was humiliating to exist any longer without horses when the Comanche, the Pawnee and even the Ute had them. It was a situation requiring remedy, for it impeded the tribe in all ways. Not only was it a serious disadvantage in war; Our People also went hungry when the bison wandered too far to be located on foot. Even in moving from camp to camp the lack of horses distressed them, for they had to pack their goods on the backs of women or haul them on dog-travois—the A-shaped wooden frames whose rear legs dragged in dust—whereas the Pawnee, let alone the Ute, could haul theirs on horse-travois.

Therefore a thrill ran through the camp when Cold Ears, with coups to his credit, announced, 'I am an old man. My teeth are breaking. My son is dead and I have no further desire to live. We must raid the Pawnee to capture horses, and when we do I shall stake myself out.'

Our People knew that it was the prerogative of a warrior to die in this manner, and all agreed that Cold Ears should be accorded the privilege. So when the war party was assembled, Cold Ears was awarded a prominent place and he took a public oath which resounded through the camp: 'Three days from now Our People will have horses, for I shall stake myself out and not retreat until we get them.'

Lame Beaver was so inspired by this pledge that he begged for permission to go along, and it was granted, for he was known as a courageous youth. That night, as they set forth, stealthily lest the ever-watchful Pawnee detect them, he felt the excitement of his first expedition against a most devious foe. Stars shone, a good omen, and by their frail light he studied the route against the day when he might have to lead a war party eastward.

To his right ran the Platte, studded with islands, its course marked always by cottonwood trees. He marked each island in memory, and where the stream debouched, and where the beaver had their lodges. He listened to birds and studied how the river looked in that precious hour before dawn. It was his initiation into the precautions observed by Our People when approaching an enemy.

For three days the war party traveled eastward, covering large distances. During the heat of the day they slept in secluded areas, but as twilight approached, they started running at a brisk pace, which they maintained until dark. Then they moved stealthily through the night, after which they ran again, repeating the cycle till well after dawn. Cold Ears, who was past fifty, had no apparent difficulty keeping up and appeared stronger at the end of the third day than he had been at the beginning. He was ready for battle.

Shortly after sunset on the third day Lame Beaver and an older brave were sent forward to see if they could locate the Pawnee camp, which must be at hand, and they crept among the cottonwoods with such skill that they succeeded in evading Pawnee outlooks and approaching to within a quarter mile of the camp. It was located at the spot where the two Plattes began to move together and was in a sense disappointing, for it was not by any means a main camp.

Lame Beaver whispered, 'It's only a hunting party. Not a real camp.'

His companion replied, 'They have horses. Look.'

There were horses, and Lame Beaver noticed with satisfaction that they were tethered at the west end of camp. 'That means, when they move out they'll come this way.'

His friend said, 'Cold Ears should stake himself out there,' and Lame Beaver saw that this would place the old man in direct line with the Pawnee march.

They crept back to camp, and the older man allowed Lame Beaver to speak first: 'Not many Pawnee there.' Then he added, 'But many horses. And they will come our way.'

With that reassuring news Our People did a reckless thing. They went to sleep. They posted a watch, of course, but they had been traveling for three days and were tired. Lame Beaver was much too excited to sleep, and he moved watchfully among the sleeping braves, listening to the night sounds with which he was so familiar: a coyote over there, a deer passing, a beaver slapping his tail, a night owl hooting in the far distance, a soft brush of wings closer at hand. He heard a rustle within the camp and moved to see what had caused it. Cold Ears could not sleep, either. He, too, was listening to the soft symphony of night, the last that he would probably ever hear.

'I'm afraid,' Cold Ears said. This seemed so unlikely that Lame Beaver gasped slightly, and Cold Ears laughed. Pulling the young warrior down beside him, he confided, 'I am always afraid when we fight the Pawnee, because they are so clever. They think up tricks we would never think of, and there is no way to counter them.'

In the darkness he recalled his many confrontations with this wily foe, and whatever he said testified to the superior brilliance of the Pawnee. 'Why were they the first to catch horses?' he demanded, but before he could say more he saw in the faint light along the horizon what looked to be a large boulder. 'Is that lookout asleep?' he asked in dismay. Together they studied the rock; then one shoulder moved and Cold Ears was satisfied that the lookout was alert.

'What happened was that the Pawnee realized they couldn't go down and just steal horses from the Comanche. No better horsemen on the plains than Comanche, and they guard their horses. So what the Pawnee did is what we have to do . . .' He rambled on, reconstructing the ruse by which the Pawnee deceived the Comanche and captured their first horses. 'They not only knew how to get them,' he said with grudging admiration. 'When they got them home they knew how to breed them and make more. They're clever people, but tomorrow we'll take their horses from them.'

'Will they have some new way of defending themselves?' Lame Beaver asked.

The old man understood such apprehension and said reassuringly, 'When I was young I wasn't nervous before my first fight. I was terrified. It was against the Ute, and I shivered all night thinking they'd capture me and drag me back to their camp and make me marry one of their black daughters and raise dark children who would be Ute. But when the fight begins, the fear goes.'

Before dawn Cold Ears moved among the sleeping warriors and whispered to each, 'This is the day we capture horses.' Our People prepared themselves, then crept close to the Pawnee camp, evading sentries with ancient skill, and when all was ready, Cold Ears bade his fellow braves farewell and moved silently forward, stopping behind a hillock on the fringe of the Pawnee camp.

'Man-Above,' Lame Beaver prayed, 'make them come in his direction.'

For some reason the Pawnee were tardy in sending out that day's scouting party, and a warrior standing close to Lame Beaver said with some concern, as if he were a Pawnee depending on bison for food, 'If they do not leave soon, their hunting will not be good.'

With casual indifference, as if they had endless time, Pawnee scouts on the hill to the north started sending signals back to camp that bison were in sight, and activity began. Hunters began assembling at the western edge of camp and prepared to move out from between the low tipis. When they had moved clear of the camp, so that immediate retreat was impractical, Cold Ears disclosed himself and waved his arms to frighten the horses. They saw that he had tied himself to a stake and realized that he was the outpost of a major assault.

A Pawnee chief spurred his horse savagely, lowered his lance and drove directly at the self-tethered enemy, but with great dexterity Cold Ears evaded the lance, caught the shaft with his right hand and with a sudden twist tossed the Pawnee from his horse, slapping him with his left hand as he fell. It was a brilliant coup, one of the bravest in the annals of Our People.

'Get that horse!' Cold Ears shouted, but an alert group of Pawnee braves, aware that the riderless horse might be captured, surged after it, leaving Cold Ears tethered to the ground, and quickly surrounded the runaway, bringing it back safely to their side.

The battle was now engaged, and Cold Ears remained self-pinioned, directing his companions how to proceed, and many coups were counted. But finally the superior speed and wisdom of the Pawnee began to assert itself, and Our People had no choice but to retreat. With bitterness the signal was given.

At this point Cold Ears was required by his own pledge to stay where he was, held to the ground by bison thongs, and fight the enemy so long as his strength lasted. He could be released, but only if some head chief doubled back to untie the thongs with his own hands. When, as in this case, all were preoccupied elsewhere, he was forbidden to release himself.

None of these chiefs could come back to save him; they had enough to do to try to save Our People from a complete rout, so Cold Ears was left alone. Girding himself with the lance he had wrested in the first moments of battle, and with tears of failure in his old eyes, he watched Our People retreat—with no horses. Then he waited.

Three Pawnee urged on their horses and rode straight at him. By some miracle he avoided their lances and succeeded in laming one of the horses with his. The Pawnee stopped to attend their horse, much more important to them than any elderly staked-out brave, and when they turned to resume their attack against him, they saw a remarkable sight.

From the main body of the retreating enemy one young warrior had detached himself and now came running back to make a stand alongside the old man. It was Lame Beaver, and he reached Cold Ears before the Pawnee horsemen did. He ripped away the thongs and stood defiantly beside Cold Ears.

With courage and simple skill the two warriors held off the enemy, knocking aside their lances and fending off the blows with their warclubs. Step by step they retreated, and on the Pawnee's fourth charge Lame

Beaver reached up and actually touched one, counting a clear and un-challengeable coup.

This feat inspirited Our People, and they made a rush to surround Cold Ears and his savior, and when the Pawnee saw how determined these men on foot were, they withdrew their horses and terminated the action.

In this famous battle, which was cherished in the history of each tribe and told to white men a century later, eleven of Our People participated against nineteen Pawnee. Three of Our People were wounded and two Pawnee. No one was killed, of course, but if Cold Ears had not been set free by Lame Beaver, he would have been.

The battle was remembered by Our People not because of Cold Ears' bravery, for old men had staked themselves out before, but because it marked the first public display of courage by Lame Beaver. The Pawnee never forgot it, because it was the opening blow of Lame Beaver's forty-year war against them.

When the war party returned to Rattlesnake Buttes, there was lament-ing. Once again Our People had failed to obtain horses. Nor did Lame Beaver garner any praise for having liberated Cold Ears, for that was a prerogative sacred to chieftains, and for him to have taken this upon himself was presumptuous.

He was rebuked in public, and it was this injustice which rankled and forever deterred him from seeking acclaim or office. The tribe did not declare him ineligible because of his youthful folly; his subsequent be-havior more than erased this first error. It was rather that he discovered for himself the inherent undesirability of becoming a leader; it was an act of pomp engaged in by lesser men who enjoyed bedecking themselves in feathers. He would let others use office to proclaim their feats. He would concentrate on the feat itself, doing what had to be done . . . in silence.

2. Three Against Three Hundred

In 1768, when Lame Beaver was twenty-one years old, he had one of those insights of extreme simplicity which mark superior men. He rea-soned, 'If we want horses, let's go where the horses are.' And it was this that led him on his daring foray against the Comanche.

The vision came to him, as most good ones do, when he was preoccu-pied with hard work in a seemingly unrelated field. It was early autumn and Our People at Rattlesnake Buttes knew that for a safe winter they must lay away much more bison meat than they had so far been able to take. Here again it was that persistent matter of horses. The Pawnee and the Comanche could fan out over vast distances and track down the bison where they were, and even the miserable Ute, when they came down out of their mountain strongholds, had horses for this purpose. But Our People had to track bison in the old way, the way Indians on the northern plains had been doing for a thousand years.

One morning a scout ran in with exciting news. A large herd had been sighted to the northwest and appeared to be moving in the right direction, although one could never tell for sure. Bison rarely moved in a discernible pattern; they milled about like a tornado which could set off on any heading. Still, one had to hope that they would move into a position from which they could be maneuvered toward the chalk cliff. Our People had no alternative but to act upon the supposition that this might happen.

Accordingly, the whole tribe left Rattlesnake Buttes for the laborious trek westward to intercept bison; on the second day scouts brought exhilarating news that the bison were heading southeast. With luck they might be diverted toward the chalk cliff.

As they walked, Lame Beaver became increasingly aware of a tall and lovely girl fourteen years old called Blue Leaf, daughter of Cold Ears, whom he had saved at the stake-out. He had received no thanks for his heroic action, for the old warrior had wanted to die and now his life was needlessly prolonged; many held it against Lame Beaver that he had interfered, because Cold Ears now had to be looked after by his daughter. She, on the other hand, was grateful to Lame Beaver for extending her father's life a few more years and did not complain about the extra work of providing food for him.

It was time that Lame Beaver took a wife, and his father—that is, his real father's second oldest brother—had several times broached the subject, but the young warrior had evaded it. His father offered to arrange a marriage, if necessary, but said that Lame Beaver could also look around for himself. In a desultory sort of way he had been doing that, but up to now he had overlooked Blue Leaf. On the trail in an elk-skin dress she was a handsome girl.

Our People moved a considerable distance westward, three days from camp, and in late afternoon of the third day they spotted the bison. It was a large herd, at least several thousand, and was barely moving. The trick would be to urge it gently toward the cliff in such a way that the bison would not be aware of what was happening. One had to be gentle, yes, but one also had to move with a certain dispatch, for there was always danger that those Ute with their horses might come screaming out of the mountains, cut off a few bison and force the rest to scatter. It required good judgment.

The chiefs decided that the larger body of Our People would swing westward in a great arc and come quietly up behind the herd, not alerting it but maintaining a ready position if the bison tried to retreat over the ground they had just traversed. On the right flank fifteen or twenty braves would operate to keep the herd from moving into the low hills;

theirs would be the easy task. It was the men assigned to the left flank who would have the crucial job, for they must keep the herd from heading toward the open plains, which it would want to do if frightened. The best men would be assigned this job.

Lame Beaver was nominated one of the seven wolves. These were braves who tied recently tanned wolf skins about them so that their bodies were completely masked; in this guise they crept up to the herd, almost touching the animals, which saw the wolves and shied away from them. There was little chance that the herd might stampede because of the wolves, for the bison knew that in a group they could protect themselves.

For two long, waterless days Our People trailed the bison, the Indians in back maintaining a steady pressure, the ones toward the mountains constantly edging the great beasts toward the cliff. Lame Beaver and his six wolf men operated along the left flank to keep the bison from heading for the plains.

On the third day it became obvious that Our People had a good chance of driving the bison over the cliff, and great excitement manifested itself. The seven wolf men were now handed the best bows and arrows the tribe possessed, so that if the grand tactic failed, they could at least salvage something by shooting down some of the animals and thus ensure a meager supply of pemmican for the winter.

The fateful decision of when to stampede the herd was left in the hands of a council, to which Cold Ears, sagest bison hunter of them all, belonged. He said, 'The worst error is to start too soon. The second error is to have men who are afraid at the points. I remember when we had the drive at Red Hills . . .' The council did not wish to hear again about Red Hills; an uncle of one of the present council had failed in courage and the herd had escaped.

'I will take the left point,' Cold Ears said, and everyone knew that this was the crucial one, because if the bison stampeded in that direction and got onto the plains, all was lost. 'Who will take the right point?' This was the one that kept the bison from scattering into the hills and was less dangerous and much less critical, but it nevertheless required a good man. An older chief volunteered for this post, and Cold Ears was satisfied.

So the trap was set. Two elderly chiefs, survivors of many such hunts, were given responsibility for launching the stampede, and they requested that most of the tribe and the dogs be moved into position along the crucial left flank to scare the bison with their noise if the animals tried to head for the plains. Lame Beaver and his wolf men were told what the signal would be, and all was ready.

With a wild cry the two chiefs lunged at the front rank of the bison. At the same instant those in back ran forward screaming and throwing rocks at the rear of the herd. And Lame Beaver and his wolf men fired arrows as fast as they could into the largest bison.

The herd panicked, and for a precarious moment—which terrified the Indians, for their lives depended upon the successful outcome of this hunt—it looked as if the beasts might simply mill in confusion and not run toward the cliff. But the chiefs had anticipated this, and a team of strong-armed young men started throwing large rocks at the lead animals, and after a desperate moment of hesitation, when every Indian prayed to Man-Above for assistance, the great herd began its gallop toward the cliff.

But unexplainedly it started to veer away, toward the plains, and it looked as if all was lost. Our People would garner only the few bison shot down by the wolf men. All the rest of that needed food, those blankets for survival, would escape.

'No! No!' Lame Beaver cried in despair.

Then, from the left point where he had stationed himself, Cold Ears ran forward to confront the bison. With arms waving and thin voice screaming above the thundering of the hoofs, he threw himself directly in front of the escaping beasts and turned them slightly to the west. The animals that followed pounded the fallen man so that his body would not again be recognizable. But the herd had been prevented from escaping to the plains.

Like the tremendous wave of water that thunders out of the mountain when an ice dam breaks, the horde of bison ran down the intended channel, with Our People waving and shouting to keep them in formation. The beasts came roaring down the slight incline, when suddenly those in front tried to stop, furiously grinding their forefeet into the dust and bellowing in fear, but to no avail. The bison coming behind stormed into them and pushed them over the cliff. Then those that had done the pushing were hurled over by those behind. Thus the great herd committed suicide, animals weighing almost a ton crashing down on those heaped up below, breaking necks and legs and backbones, and all marked by billows of dust and pitiful bellowing.

It had become inconsequential how many bison the arrows of the wolf men had killed. Four hundred animals lay at the foot of the cliff, either dead or so injured that they could be killed at leisure by the butcher women. The stampede had been successful beyond hopes; the unneeded carcasses would be left for the Ute, which was about as generous as Our People could be toward them.

Only the very best animals, the tender young cows, were completely butchered. From the others the tongues were taken for ceremonial purposes, and some of the softer cuts about the hump. One had to be careful to collect enough of the guts for making pemmican, and in order to give that winter ration good taste, some proportion of stronger-flavored meat from older animals was advisable, so men who had supervised butchering of such kills before moved among the women and gave advice.

Lame Beaver, watching the wild confusion and appreciating the fact that only the sacrificial bravery of Cold Ears had enabled the drive to succeed, said to himself, 'It is not good to hunt bison this way. The animals at the bottom of the pile are so covered by those on top that even vultures won't be able to get them. It should be done with horses.' Then: 'If you want horses, you go where the horses are.' There would be no more toying with Pawnee, who owned a few horses. He would invade Comanche country, where there were hundreds.

He laid his plans carefully. He would take with him only two companions, but they must be young men he trusted and who would not be afraid to die. For some days, as the tribe lugged huge burdens of bison meat and robes back to Rattlesnake Buttes, with all dogs laden, he studied his companions, and one after another he dismissed them as unlikely to stand the strain of what he had in mind.

Gradually he began to focus on a young brave named Red Nose, stolid, unimaginative, of unquestioned bravery. He saw in him the kind of young man who decides early that he will one day be a chief; from that moment all his actions become subordinate to that desire. He begins to speak gravely, nods cautiously when older men put forth proposals, and deports himself with decorum. Lame Beaver did not like Red Nose; he found him quite pompous. But never had he seen him do a wrong thing, neither an impetuous act nor a foolish one. He was already a sub-chief, a man to be trusted to the death, because his own vanity would not permit him to fail.

One night he went to Red Nose and asked, 'Are you willing to join me in a great feat . . .' He hesitated for the right word. 'Something that would bring horses to our tribe?' Red Nose deliberated for some time, as Lame Beaver knew he would, then said, 'To get horses I would do anything.' They grasped each other's shoulders.

Lame Beaver then directed his attention to an unlikely man called Cottonwood Knee, named after that strange accident which sometimes occurs along the riverbank when a root of a tree which should grow underground takes it upon itself to grow upward for a while, then scampers hurriedly back beneath the earth. He had none of the characteristics of Red Nose: he was plumpish, whereas the would-be chief was lean; he talked a lot, whereas the future sage was taciturn; and his face was an open smile, generous and marked with handsome white teeth, whereas Red Nose preserved the somber countenance of a leader. But Cottonwood Knee had a quality that was priceless for a dangerous mission: he had absolute loyalty to any commitment. He was reliable; just as the Platte River ran year after year, sometimes sprawled out and sometimes a well-defined river, so Cottonwood Knee ambled his fat and amiable way through life. When the Platte was in flood, it seemed to have no central direction whatever, but slowly it pulled itself together and not even Man-Above could restrain it from its course for long.

'Would you be willing to undertake a major adventure?' Lame Beaver asked the chubby man one afternoon.

'Yes,' Cottonwood Knee responded. He did not even ask what it was.

The day came when the three volunteers had to present their plan to the tribal council, and Lame Beaver prudently assigned this task to Red Nose, who discharged it with skill: 'If the whole tribe moved south to make war against the Comanche, they will know about it. They will be prepared. We will lose many braves and not catch many horses. But if we three go down in stealth, if we fail, only three are lost. And if we succeed, we shall have horses.'

After much discussion, permission was granted, but Lame Beaver's father was directed to counsel with the inexperienced warriors, and he said, 'You know, of course, that the Comanche practice terrible tortures on the enemies they capture. They love their horses above all else, and if you are caught tampering with them, you will die horribly. It is said that when a man is taken by the Comanche, he dies eleven times. Their women have cruel ways of torturing a man, yet keeping him alive.

'If your mission fails, wait till the last moment. Then kill yourselves. And if one of you finds himself in a position in which he cannot take his own life, you survivors must promise to kill him before you depart. Is this agreed?'

The three companions looked at each other; they had known of the Comanche reputation for hideous death but they had not wanted to speak openly of it. Now they had to face the prospect, and Red Nose addressed his two comrades: 'If I falter you must kill me.'

Cottonwood Knee said, 'Don't leave me with the Comanche.'

It was Lame Beaver who said it the other way: 'If you are helpless, I promise to kill you.'

Then Lame Beaver's father took him aside and said, 'I have noticed you watching Blue Leaf. Your eye seems to have fallen upon her.' Lame Beaver assented by his silence, and his father continued, 'While you are gone I will speak to her brother and find out how many bison robes.' To this, Lame Beaver made a response which would be long repeated in the tribe: 'Tell her brother that for Blue Leaf, I will give a horse.'

It was a long trek south to the land of the Comanche, with a likelihood at every step that these swift-riding scourges of the plains would spot them, but the three braves were also skilled plainsmen, and they left no tracks, betrayed no presence. Twice, in the later days, they saw Comanche riding along the crests of hills, but even an eagle would have had difficulty detecting the intruders as they hid among the grasses.

They had been away from Rattlesnake Buttes many nights when they came upon signs of a Comanche village, but when they inspected it—with extreme caution—they found to their bitter disappointment that it was a miserable collection of poor tipis with only a few horses; by no means was it a worthy target. The true villages must lie farther south.

Their persistence was rewarded when they came to a swift-moving stream—later to be called the Arkansas—carrying much water and with two islands in the middle. They saw at once that these islands might be of advantage to them, for on the far bank stood a sizable village marked by a sight which gladdened their hearts: a compound hemmed in by woven brush and holding at least ninety horses.

For two days Our People stayed hidden on the north bank of the Arkansas, surveying every action that took place on the south, and Lame Beaver wondered why the Comanche permitted this surveillance. 'Where are their scouts?' he asked several times. It was apparent that the Comanche, having recently driven the Apache from this territory, had grown careless.

The plan they devised was a good one. They would cross to the south bank before midnight, before the next watch took over. They would remain hidden through the darkness, and just before dawn they would assault the corral in this manner: Lame Beaver would knock out the first guard nearest the camp. Red Nose would knock out the other guard nearest the river. And Cottonwood Knee would break down the fencing and drive as many horses as possible toward the north.

Then they would cross to the first island, regroup there, mount three horses and drive the rest with them. To succeed, Lame Beaver and Red Nose would have to scatter the remaining horses so that the Comanche could not quickly follow.

It was Cottonwood Knee who asked the embarrassing question 'How do you know we can ride the horses?' and Lame Beaver replied, 'If a Ute can ride, I can.'

They reached the south bank, and with deepening anxiety, waited for the night to pass. Comanche guards moved about the camp in desultory fashion, not really attending their work. Two watchmen reported to the corral, but to the amazement of Our People, soon departed to spend the night inside their tipis. Lame Beaver wanted to signal Red Nose that there would be no guards at the corral, but Red Nose had already noted this and was signaling Cottonwood Knee. It was agreed that Lame Beaver would divert his attack to the lone guard at the camp, leaving Red Nose free to help Cottonwood Knee round up the horses to be taken and to set the rest loose. But as daylight approached, even the lone guard went in to his tipi. The camp was totally unattended. The road north lay for the moment defenseless.

Working slowly and with precision, Our People took advantage of a situation they could not have hoped for. They tore away a large portion of the fence, selected twenty-nine horses and sent the others quietly scattering. They drove the horses into the river, reached the island, and departed before the Comanche village was aware of what had happened.

It was the cleverest raid Our People ever engineered, for the twenty-nine horses were far to the north of the Arkansas, headed safely for

Rattlesnake Buttes, before the first Comanche warrior crossed the river, and he without a horse.

The three braves were laughing among themselves, overjoyed with the success of their adventure, when Cottonwood Knee reined up with a look of anxiety and said, 'Suppose we got all males!' The three dismounted and satisfied themselves that they had a good mix, and it was in this way that Our People got the horse.

3. Visit to the Sun

The arrival of the horse among Our People changed many things. To take one example, it was now more pleasant to be a woman, for when the tribe moved she no longer had to haul the travois that were too heavy for the dogs. For another, the whole system of wealth was altered, and a man did not have to wait years to accumulate enough bison robes to procure the things he wanted; a horse was not only more acceptable as exchange but also more easily delivered when a transaction was agreed upon.

Hunting the bison changed, too. Three men could search out the herd, covering immense distances, and when they found it, the whole tribe did not have to trudge in pursuit; sixteen swift-riding hunters could trail it and with arrows shoot off the animals needed, then truss up the good parts and haul them back by travois.

The change was greatest for the dogs. They no longer had to haul huge loads on small travois. One horse could haul ten times as much on a big one, and dogs could be kept as pets until the time came for eating them.

Our People, in bringing the horse to Rattlesnake Buttes, unwittingly returned it to the point of its genesis, and there it flourished. A gentler tribe than their neighbors, Our People had an innate appreciation of the horse, attending more carefully to its feeding and care. The saddles Our People devised were an improvement over the heavy affairs used by the Pawnee or the crude wooden efforts of the Ute. The bridles were simpler, too, with a decoration more restrained and utilitarian. Our People adopted the horse as a member of their family, and it proved a most useful friend, for it permitted them to conquer the plains, which they had already occupied but not really explored.

On no Indian did the horse exert a more profound influence than on Lame Beaver. In 1769, when he was twenty-two, one of his fathers approached him again about marrying Blue Leaf but found him far more concerned about a horse than a wife. After the raid on the Comanche camp, the captured horses were allotted according to a sensible plan:

the best-trained mounts went to the older chiefs, who needed them for ceremonial purposes; the acceptable ones went to the middle chiefs, who did the scouting for bison; and the unbroken horses went to the young warriors, who had the time to train them.

Despite the fact that Lame Beaver had masterminded the raid, he was given a nervous, unbroken pinto mare, and when he first tried to ride her she tossed him viciously into the middle of a prairie-dog town. The little animals peeked out of their holes in chattering wonder as he limped after the pinto, failing to catch her on his first tries.

Again and again he sweated with the stubborn pony, not much bigger than he was, and repeatedly she pitched him over her head. Others volunteered to show him how to master her, and they went flying too. Finally an old man said, 'I heard once that the Comanche do it by taking their horses into the river.'

This was such a novel idea that Lame Beaver could not at first grasp its significance, but after his pinto had resisted all other efforts, he and his friends tied her and dragged her by main strength down to the Platte. She shied away from the water, but they plunged in, keeping hold of the thongs, got a good footing, and pulled and jerked until it looked as if her neck might come off before her stubborn feet touched water. Finally, with a mighty jerk, they got her off the bank and into the stream.

She was very frightened, but they kept tugging at her until her beautiful white-and-black-and-brown body was mostly submerged. Then Lame Beaver swam close to her, so that his face was almost touching hers. He began to talk with her, slowly and with a reassuring tone: 'For years and years you and I will be friends. We will ride after the bison together. You will know the feel of my knees on your flanks and turn as I bid you. We shall be friends for all the years and I will see that you get grass.'

When he had spoken with her thus, and quieted somewhat the fear in her eyes, he took off the thongs and left her in the middle of the river. Without looking at her further, he swam to the bank and climbed out. She watched him go, made a half-hearted start for the opposite bank, then followed him, but when she was again safe on land she refused to let him approach.

Daily for two weeks Lame Beaver dragged his pinto into the river, and on the fifteenth day, there in the water, she allowed him to mount her, and when she felt the security of his strong legs about her, she responded and finally ran boldly onto the land and off toward the Rattlesnake Buttes.

From that moment she was his companion, and she liked nothing more than to chase after bison. Since he required both hands to manipulate his bow, she learned to respond to his knee movements, and they formed a team. She was so sure-footed that he did not try to guide her, satisfied that she would find the best course, whatever the terrain. And sometimes, when he saw her running free with a group of other horses, he would catch sight of her straight back and its white patches and he would experience an emotion that could only be called love.

He was therefore disturbed when his father came to him and said, 'The brother of Blue Leaf is willing that you should marry his sister, but he demands that you fulfill your promise and give him your horse.'

Lame Beaver snapped, 'He has his horse . . .'

'True, but he argues that that horse was given him by the council, not by you. For Blue Leaf, he demands your horse.'

This outrageous request Lame Beaver refused. He still wanted Blue Leaf; certainly he had seen no other girl so attractive, but not at the price of his horse. Obstinately he declined even to discuss the matter.

But now the council intervened: 'Lame Beaver promised to give a horse for Blue Leaf. Many heard how he made that vow. He cannot now change his mind and refuse to deliver the horse. It belongs to the brother of Blue Leaf.'

When Lame Beaver heard this decision he was enraged, and might have done something unwise had not Red Nose come to him to speak in low, judicious tones: 'There seems no escape, old friend.'

'I won't surrender that pinto.'

'There will be other horses.'

'None like mine.'

'She is no longer yours, dear friend. Tonight they will take her away.'

Such a verdict seemed so unjust that Lame Beaver went before the council and cried, 'I will not give up my horse. Her brother doesn't even care for the one you gave him.'

'It is proper,' said the elderly chief, 'that men should marry in an orderly way, and we have always given presents to the brothers of our brides. A horse is a suitable gift on such an occasion. Yours must be surrendered to the brother of Blue Leaf.'

On hearing this final judgment, Lame Beaver sped from the council tipi, leaped upon the pinto and dashed from the village, heading southward toward the river. He was followed by Cottonwood Knee, riding a brown pony, and as Lame Beaver was about to spur his pinto into the river, his pursuer caught up with him.

'Come back!' Cottonwood Knee called in the voice of friendship. 'You and I can catch many more horses.'

'Never like this one,' Lame Beaver said bitterly, but in the end he dismounted and allowed Cottonwood Knee to lead the pinto back to its new owner. As Lame Beaver stood by the river, watching his horse disappear, a feeling of inconsolable grief came over him, and for five days he wandered alone. In the end he returned to camp, and Cottonwood Knee and Red Nose took him before the council, and they said, 'We have ordered Blue Leaf's brother to give her to you. She is now your wife.' There was a hush, then Blue Leaf's brother appeared, leading his beautiful shy sister. She stood awkwardly before the chiefs, then saw Lame Beaver standing between his friends. Slowly she came to him, extending her hands and offering herself to him. Few young husbands had ever accepted with such turbulent emotions so lovely a wife.

Lame Beaver now entered a strange world, that of the married man, in which each item of behavior was strictly defined. He could not, for example, ever speak to his wife's mother; that was totally forbidden until such time as he had presented her with some significant present. In moon periods his wife had to live in a special hut along with other women so afflicted, and while residing there, she might not speak to any man or child, lest she bring curses upon them. The consoling compensation was that with marriage he entered upon the warm and infinitely extended companionship of the Indian village, in which a man had three or four fathers and an equal number of mothers, in which all children belonged to all, and where the raising and education of the young was a common responsibility and punishment and harsh words were unknown.

It was a community in which each member did pretty much as he chose and where men who were called chiefs held that office not by heredity but by consent of their neighbors. There was no king, neither in this village nor in the tribe as a whole, only the council of older men, to which any well-comported brave might be elected by acclamation. It was one of the freest societies ever devised, hemmed in only by belief in Man-Above, reliance on Flat-Pipe and the inherited customs of Our People. It was communal without the restraints of communism and extremely libertarian without the excesses of libertinism. It was a way of life ideally fitted to the nomads of the plains, where space was endless and the supply of bison inexhaustible.

It was galling to Lame Beaver to realize that at the next bison hunt he would have to accompany the butcher women on foot, since he had no horse, and he watched with seething anger as lesser huntsmen like his brother-in-law saddled their beasts for the chase. Blue Leaf, observing this, consoled him: 'When the hunt is over you'll get two or three trusted companions and go into the Ute country and capture horses from them. If you did this against the Comanche, you can do it against the Ute.'

'They keep their horses in mountains,' he snapped, 'and I've never been in mountains.'

'I will go to reason with my brother . . . offer him a different horse . . . later, when you make other coups,' and she moved toward the door of their tipi.

Lame Beaver was about to reply when all logic was driven from his mind by a brilliant flash of light. Blue Leaf could not see it, for it came from within his heart, an illumination so transcendent that it would guide him for the rest of his life.

'No!' he cried in exaltation. 'No more brothers. No more council.' Rudely he pushed her away from the door, announcing with fierce dedication, 'We shall have other horses . . . after the Sun Dance . . . many horses.'

The coup which he performed that year was never counted officially, because it had no witnesses, and since he would tell no one what had happened, not even his wife, the tribe had to take it on faith that some extraordinary event had occurred, perhaps even the intercession of Man-Above. They referred to it in tribal annals as 'Lame Beaver's visit to the sun,' and accepted it as a mystery.

Let us look at Lame Beaver on the eve of his journey. He was slightly under six feet tall and weighed one hundred and seventy-three pounds, which gave him a lean, rangy look. He had black hair that he wore in two braids which came to the tip of his shoulders and were bound by bison thong decorated with elk's teeth. He had very dark eyes, deep-set, but because of his diffident nature, not piercing. His skin was a light bronze, not nearly so dark as a Ute's nor so red as a Pawnee's. At this stage he had all his teeth, but some of the corners were beginning to show signs of wear from his habit of eating only jerky during the winter; he did not like the easier-chewed pemmican, considering it women's food.

Since he had walked long distances most of his life, he liked moccasins made of the heaviest bison leather rather than the softer deer or elk even though they were easier on his feet. Most of the time he wore a breech-clout, and otherwise went naked except for his moccasins, but in winter he liked rather heavy full-length leggings whose outer seams were well fringed or even decorated with small feathers. He wore a vest, too, elaborately painted, and a light robe about his shoulders, made from the skin of a young bison.

Once as a child watching the great chiefs convene, he had been awed by their headbands of beads and eagle feathers, and had even gone so far as to fashion a childish one with little feathers picked up on the prairie. Later he recognized that he had no appetite for power and he relinquished its pretensions to others.

When he first experienced the horse and had one of his own, he blended with it harmoniously, adapting his body to the animal's, and he might in time have become as good a rider as the Comanche, but being deprived of the pinto by tribal law, he ceased all identification with the horse and would henceforth consider it only as a means of transport and would allow no deep attachment to develop.

He seemed a cold, self-disciplined man, but he was not. Injustice had graved deep marks on both his heart and his face, and he was capable of furious action. He was careful, however, not to indulge in fits of rage before others or in conditions which might endanger him or any enterprise with which he was connected. He was able to bear much pain, either deprivation of water on long summer marches or the intense cold of winter, and he was about to exhibit this capacity to a degree that would have been totally impossible to most white men living at that period.

As to his intelligence, he was equipped to handle the world he knew. He had an excellent memory, fortified by acute powers of observation. Since his life was lived on a simple level, he addressed himself to simple problems. Since he was not required to bother with a lot of extraneous data from outside sources, he had not developed his reasoning powers to any high degree. He was largely unacquainted with abstract thought and was content to have his small world closely confined by tradition and custom.

He prized the companionship of all people, and was as much at home with children as he was with older warriors. He loved the intimacy of married life and retained close contacts with his three fathers, three mothers and various other relatives. Like most of Our People he was essentially gentle, avoided warfare when he could, but acknowledged that a man's final worth depended on his capacity to count coup. He had not yet killed a man and intuitively drew back from considering in what circumstances he might one day have to do so; he preferred not to think of this. He would face the necessity when it arrived but would not hasten the day. He suffered an inner fear that he might prove cowardly at the moment of trial.

He had a deep sense of identity with living things. Having once seen a fish jump in the river, arching its back in a lovely curve, he often watched the water, hoping to see this phenomenon again. He enjoyed excursions to find lodge poles for tipis and knew well the kinds of trees that yielded such poles. He understood the bison, and he could track elk and deer. He knew where the beaver hid and how eagles could be trapped for their feathers. When his course required him to pass close to Rattlesnake Buttes he knew how to guard against the poison snakes and yet find a place to watch the prairie dogs at play. He liked the wolves and felt that they added definition to the other wild things of the prairie; sometimes he felt a deep identification with the wolf and had often speculated on the desirability of changing his name to Sun Wolf, after a great beast he had seen one day snapping at the sun.

It was this man, still seething with anger at having been deprived of his pinto, who sought spiritual cleansing for the task to which he was about to commit himself. To do what he intended, and alone, would require the control of every faculty he had, and this could be ensured only by offering himself to the sun. After pondering for some days what he must do, he appeared before his wife and announced, 'When the Sun Dance is held, I shall offer myself.'

Blue Leaf shuddered. Lame Beaver saw this and frowned. 'We must both make the sacrifice,' he insisted, without deigning to explain what his ultimate purpose was in committing himself to the sun. He did try to console her, but she withdrew. She appreciated the fact that when a man dedicated himself to the sun, events happened and no one could foresee their consequences.

The Sun Dance, as observed by Our People at that time, was a celebration covering eight days, and it was of such spiritual significance that other villages, oftentimes from far away, were invited to participate. Flat-Pipe was paraded to lend authority, and numerous intricate rituals were observed. On the fourth day stakes were driven into the ground, delimiting a ceremonial area, and on the fifth a sacred place was identified within this area.

It was marked by fourteen willow sticks painted red and protected by a low palisade of cottonwood branches. At the center Flat-Pipe was installed, flanked by two massive bison skulls, on each of which rested a very sharp wooden skewer plus a length of thong. Small boys, imagining the day when they would claim manhood, studied these skulls and shivered.

Two young braves, noted for courage, moved forward, consecrated themselves to the sun, and stepped within the palisade, lifting the heavy skulls, the skewers and the thongs. Presenting these to a group of old men skilled in conducting this part of the ceremony, they waited impassively as the elders tested the sharp points of the skewers.

Now the older men went to the first brave, felt for his back muscle and jabbed a skewer under it. Pushing hard, they forced the wood beneath the taut muscle and out the other side, bringing with it a gush of blood. Testing the skewer for firmness, they secured one end of the thong to it, lashing the other end to the skull, which they placed in the young man's hands. Betraying no evidence of pain, he lifted the skull toward the sun, then threw it to the ground, waiting at attention while the old men repeated the ritual on his companion.

The young warriors now leaped forward. The thongs tightened against the skewers. The bison heads dragged heavily in the sand, almost tearing the skewers through the back muscles, and the braves danced and danced and danced.

Lame Beaver, who had not volunteered for this lesser offering, watched. Women chanted and old men urged the younger on, and for some hours the latter dragged the skulls in a kind of trance, the pain long since numbed by the self-hypnosis. Finally the horn of one skull caught in sagebrush; the thongs tightened and the skewer ripped through the back muscle of that dancer. He collapsed.

On the sixth day it was time for Lame Beaver to offer himself, and he sought out Cottonwood Knee, leading him to the spot where Blue Leaf stood awaiting this terrible moment. Taking his young friend's hand, Lame Beaver placed it in the hand of his wife and said in a loud voice, 'Take her. Get her with child. This is my first sacrifice.' Then he stepped back and watched as Cottonwood Knee led Blue Leaf to a tipi set aside for this highest of ritual purposes. Lame Beaver had sacrificed even his wife, and this proved his eligibility for the ordeal which awaited.

He now confronted his three fathers, holding out to them a pair of sharp skewers and two very long thongs. His oldest father stepped forward, grasped Lame Beaver by the soft flesh of his chest and probed with his fingers until he located his son's left pectoral muscle. Drawing it taut, he reached for a skewer, and after offering it ceremoniously to the sun, jabbed it under the muscle until both ends protruded. The second father did the same with the right pectoral muscle, staring into his son's eyes as the young man accepted the great pain without flinching.

The fathers then lashed the thongs to the skewers and signaled to the watching crowd. A lithe young man leaped forward, grasped the free ends of the thongs and climbed to the top of a pole standing in the middle of the ceremonial area. There he passed the thongs over a deep notch cut into the top of the pole, allowing the ends to fall free. Before he reached the ground, eight strong men had grasped each thong and had started hauling Lame Beaver into the air until he dangled seven feet above the ground, his whole weight suspended from the skewers passing through his breast.

Up to this point Lame Beaver had not uttered a sound, not even when the skewers pierced him, but now when the thongs were lashed and he hung alone, he could feel the dead weight of his body and mumbled, 'This will tear me apart.' But the muscles held. During the first period, while the sun climbed toward the midday point, he felt each stage of pain and at times thought he must cry out to have them halt the ceremony, but when the sun shone on him at noon, he experienced a benign sensation, as if it were banishing the pain because of his bravery, and for the last four hours he existed in a trance, powerful, capable of facing any enemy. In an exaltation of spirit, the memory of which would abide with him the rest of his life, he endured the closing hour and watched with positive sorrow as the sun vanished, releasing him from his ordeal.

His fathers lowered him to the ground and loosened the thongs. Tenderly they drew out the skewers and then rubbed salt and ashes into the gaping wounds, the first to cleanse them, the second to create tattooed cicatrices which would forever mark Lame Beaver as an exceptional member of Our People.

On the seventh day Lame Beaver rested in a special tipi. He had a soaring fever and limbs so pain-racked that he could barely move them, but old men who had suffered the same torture in their youth knew how to tend him, so that on the last day he was prepared for the final ordeal. The various young men who had dragged bison skulls with their backs and he who had made the great sacrifice assembled in a circle around the altar where Flat-Pipe rested and began a solemn dance. To the beat of drums and the chanting of voices they moved, always facing the sun.

They danced this way for eight hours, encouraged by their kinsmen.

Aching with thirst, they kept on until their legs seemed about to explode. Visions of white bison assailed them, and haunting memories. Some staggered and others collapsed, and all the while watchers cajoled them to continue, to remain strong, until at last the sun went down.

That night Lame Beaver returned to his own tipi, where Blue Leaf waited. 'Now I am ready to go,' he said, and she fed him and bathed his wounds and gave him consolation for the sacrifices he had made, and before dawn he was walking alone, quietly, making no noise and leaving no trail, for his solitary confrontation with the Pawnee.

With unbelievable vigor he walked and ran all the way to the confluence of the two Plattes, but found no Pawnee. He continued eastward, well into the heart of enemy country, but they were gone. When he penetrated their permanent villages, these, too, were deserted.

He went to the south toward Kansas and far along the Big Blue River, but they were not hunting there, and then he caught a smell of bison far to the west. He did not actually smell them, of course. They were much too distant for that, but he knew from many signs that they were there, well south of the Platte toward Apache country.

Gambling on his intuition, he made a sweep toward the Arkansas River and came in sight of a Pawnee hunting camp. He remained hidden for three days, exercising the most cruel discipline, for he was alone and without a horse. He required everything to be in his favor if he were to have even a slight chance of success. His spirits were kept alive by his discovery that these Pawnee had several hundred horses.

On the fourth day of scouting he concluded that this night would provide the best possible combination of circumstances, and if a lone warrior were ever to have any chance, this was it. The Pawnee hunters had been riding far to the west—very far for the Pawnee, who customarily kept to the east—and they would come home tired. The camp had been slaughtering for three days, and that, too, was hard work. Tonight he would strike.

Having made that decision, he fell sound asleep and did not awaken till midnight. The stars showed that he had much time till dawn, and he spent it moving into the one position that would enable him to cut out a score of horses and get off to a galloping start toward the Platte. The guard would be at the opposite end of the improvised corral and Lame Beaver would have a brief advantage.

Breathing deeply and recalling his devotion to the sun, he touched his breasts and said, 'I am of Our People. Man-Above, help me.'

He slipped around to the far end of the corral and saw with disgust that the lone guard was not where he had been each previous night but right where he could do the most harm. It would be necessary to kill him; there could be no other solution. But as Lame Beaver was about to move forward to cut the guard's throat, a coyote called, three low notes ending in a higher one. The guard looked in the direction from which the sound had come, and then turned and threw a stone. He threw another, and the coyote called again. Throwing stones rapidly, the Pawnee ran after the pesky beast, and in that moment Lame Beaver dashed into the corral, caught a handsome red horse by the mane, threw himself on its back and hallooed a score of horses northward.

It took some time for the Pawnee to discover what he had done, but when they did, they launched an immediate pursuit.

Pawnee riders, the best of the tribe, chased him all that morning. The sun rose and dew vanished from the low grass. Some of Lame Beaver's horses scattered, but others kept galloping with him. Still the Pawnee scouts hammered across the plains, sending up clouds of dust and ignoring the strays that broke away from Lame Beaver's little herd.

They would have overtaken him except for one thing: the ordeal he had undergone at the Sun Dance was so much more harrowing than a chase across the plains that when his Pawnee pursuers had to stop at a small stream to catch a drink of water, he galloped on, unaware of thirst. Neither dust nor fatigue nor anxiety deterred him; from midafternoon, as he galloped toward the Platte, he seemed to be growing stronger rather than weaker. He realized that at the river he would face a crisis: how could he urge his riderless horses into the water and out the other side?

He was saved by the fact that Red Nose and some braves were searching the riverbanks for beaver. When they saw Lame Beaver speeding across the plains, they were able to guess what was happening. Goading their horses into the water, they sped to his rescue, surrounding him in a protective arc and gathering in the horses.

When the exhausted Pawnee reined up, some distance away, it was obvious that their tired mounts would be no match for the fresh ones ridden by Our People, and they prudently retired, but not before one of their braves made a last heroic effort. Urging his foam-flecked horse, he drove right at Red Nose, touching him with his lance and scoring one of the most gallant coups ever witnessed by Our People. Two warriors tried to knock him down as he passed, but he escaped, and as he rode back to the Pawnee, Our People cheered his bravery.

That night Lame Beaver was acclaimed at Rattlesnake Buttes, for he had brought back not only his own big red stallion, but eighteen other horses as well. One he gave to Red Nose and one to his friend Cottonwood Knee and one fine pinto mare to his wife, Blue Leaf. The others he turned over to the council, almost with contempt, to do with as they wished.

When this was done he washed, ate a long meal of bison liver and hump steak, and told his wife, 'Now we have horses.' From that time on, the warriors who camped around Rattlesnake Buttes rode, and only the women walked . . . except Blue Leaf, who had her own prancing pinto. But Lame Beaver was not awarded a coup, for it could not be ascertained if he had actually touched a Pawnee. Whenever prying ones asked him to explain how he had captured, single-handed, nineteen horses, he said, 'They were a gift of the sun.'

4. Death of Never-Death

In the years when Our People came to occupy the land between the two Plattes, they were surrounded by enemies and life was difficult. But they could depend on one ally, the finest tribe of Indians on the plains, the Cheyenne. They were taller than Our People—in fact, the tallest Indians in America—and braver. They were better horsemen and always more willing to engage in battle. They were sage men and their customs were different: they scorned Our People's practice of eating dogs and abhorred their custom of willingly offering up their women to other men; it was more difficult to count coup among them, too, for they allowed only three of their warriors to count coup on a single enemy, whereas Our People allowed four; and they viewed with special detestation the custom of the Pawnee whereby each year they sacrificed a virgin Indian girl, captured from another tribe if possible, or taken from their own if necessary.

Lame Beaver's father once told him—that is, his real father—'The two things Our People can depend upon are the rising of the sun and the loyalty of the Cheyenne.' Once they had been bitter enemies, and it was no small thing for the Cheyenne to declare war on Our People, who, though they were not flamboyant and did not make a ritual of war, could still be terribly stubborn, and men like Lame Beaver were not uncommon. His grandfather had fought the Cheyenne many times, until one day leading chiefs of the two tribes convened, the Cheyenne bright with paint and eagle feathers, and they had reasoned: 'It is stupid for us to destroy ourselves. We share many things,' and they smoked the pipe, and for a century after that—indeed, for as long as Indians roamed the plains— no Cheyenne ever fought with Our People, and no Cheyenne in distress ever sought aid from Our People without receiving it. Longer than almost any other treaty existing anywhere, any time, the treaty between these two tribes was honored.

This was the more remarkable in that neither tribe could speak the other's language. In fact, each of the Indian tribes with whom Our People came into contact could speak only its own language. Thus Our People could not speak to their enemies the Dakota, nor the Ute, nor the Comanche nor the Pawnee; they could not even speak to their trusted allies.

There was, of course, a sign language which did not depend upon spoken words, but rather on generalized ideas, and all Indians on the plains were conversant with it. Two men from tribes a thousand miles apart could meet at some riverbank and talk intelligently in signs, and in this way communication passed rapidly from one part of the country to the other.

Our People were imprisoned within the most difficult of the Indian languages, so difficult indeed that no other tribe except one related branch, the Gros Ventres, ever learned to speak it. It stood by itself, a language spoken by only 3300 people in the world: that was the total number of Our People. The enemy tribes were not much larger: the Ute had 3600; the Comanche, 3500; the Pawnee, about 6000. The great Cheyenne, who would be famous in history, had only 3500. The Dakota, known also as the Sioux, had many branches, and they totaled perhaps 11,000.

In the year 1776 the Cheyenne chiefs sent a messenger to Our People, their allies, and he said in sign language, 'Comanche in the region between the Platte and the Arkansas are raiding and killing. We are going to make war against them and seek your help.'

There could be only one reply to such a request, and Our People said, 'We will send our warriors with you.' Therefore, in the late summer of that year an army of Cheyenne supported by Our People rode south to teach the Comanche a lesson, but they had traveled only a short distance when scouts reported that the Comanche were aware of their coming and had sought help from their allies, the Apache. This was dread news indeed, for the Comanche by themselves were formidable and cruel, but when allied with the Apache, they would be well-nigh unbeatable.

There was no talk of retreat. The Cheyenne chiefs said, 'If we allow them to invade our land, they will ransack our villages and take our women. They must be taught a lesson, Comanche and Apache alike.' Discipline tightened, and men moved with caution, for to be captured by this dreadful enemy meant more than death.

It was then that the warriors, at night, began to talk about Never-Death: 'I fought against him once. He's a Comanche with a deep scar down his left cheek. When he comes to your part of the battlefield, move away. He is invincible.'

Many reports attested to this. Once when the Pawnee were trying to steal horses, they launched a running battle to distract the Comanche, thus allowing a surprise group to sweep in against the horses, and this would have succeeded had not Never-Death, riding his big black horse, detected the ruse and countered it single-handed. He rode right at the Pawnee, one man against eleven, but his big medicine made their arrows fall harmless. This so terrified the Pawnee raiders that they turned and fled, with Never-Death following them, and when the leading Pawnee saw this, they realized that a miracle of some kind had occurred, and they, too, fled. All the tribes that roamed the plains carried tales of how this ultrabrave Comanche on the black horse possessed a medicine which could not be penetrated by arrows.

Therefore, as the allies approached the Arkansas River, they became more cautious, searching out the best location for their attack, and finally their scouts reported that by crossing the Arkansas and striking the Comanche from the south, they might drive a wedge between the great horsemen and their Apache allies. Then the chiefs consulted. For the Cheyenne there was Broken Hand and Howling Wolf and Gray Beads and Bison Wallow, and for the discussion they dressed in ceremonial gear with headbands resplendent with eagle feathers. For Our People it was Straight Arrow and Jumping Snake and Gray Wolf. Using sign language and drawing many designs in the sand along the riverbank, they devised a clever plan, requiring subtle timing and much deception. They doubted that the enemy would be able to react quickly; they expected to invade the camp itself and create much havoc among the Comanche before the Apache could rally to their assistance. It was a plan that would have done credit to any of the European generals who were engaged in battle in that late summer of 1776, or to any American generals so occupied.

But always the council had to take into account Never-Death, and after much discussion of this imponderable, Gray Wolf had a suggestion. 'Have you among your young Cheyenne three men of great bravery?' They did, of course, and he continued: 'We will assign three of our young men who have conducted themselves well, my son Lame Beaver, Red Nose and Cottonwood Knee, and the six shall have only one responsibility. To fight Never-Death and keep him from striking terror in our braves.'

'Will that be enough?' Bison Wallow asked skeptically.

'It will keep his terror in one place,' Gray Wolf reasoned, and the plan was adopted.

Gray Wolf sought out the three young braves of his tribe and briefed them on his plan, while Bison Wallow instructed his Cheyenne. Finally the eight men convened as a unit and Bison Wallow gave the six warriors their instructions in sign language. 'No matter what happens in the fight, you are to hold back until Never-Death makes his appearance. Big black horse, scar down left cheek, usually dresses for battle in black. We must take him by surprise. You must surround him and engage him . . . only him.'

Gray Wolf then added his advice, also in sign language: 'It is useless to shoot arrows at him. It is useless to try to pierce him with lances. Club him to death. That hasn't been tried yet.'

So the six young warriors cast aside their weapons and armed themselves with clubs, Lame Beaver producing a fine, well-balanced one with knobs, made from a heavy wood. When he swung it in the air, it had a lively *swoooosh* and seemed as if it could deliver a lethal blow. He was satisfied.

Now the grand design was put into operation. The first step required crossing the Arkansas, at this point a deep, dark river. The two tribes rode their horses into the swift water, using a tactic they had learned from the Pawnee: stay on the horse till only his head is above water, then slip off and go the rest of the way holding onto his tail. Once on the other side, the principal chiefs led the main body of warriors eastward along the riverbank until they neared the Comanche camp. A smaller group cut south to intercept the Apache if they should be moving in that area, while Lame Beaver and his special force rode apart, each inwardly terrified by the prospect of encountering Never-Death.

Scouts rode back to inform the allies that prospects were good. The Comanche camp had not moved. The Apache had not yet come into position. 'And Never-Death?' the chiefs asked. 'He has not been seen,' the scouts replied.

So the great battle was joined, and with the initial signal every fine stratagem the chiefs had devised evaporated, because in Indian warfare it was each man his own general, each unit its own command. The Cheyenne started for the Comanche village, but en route they came upon a Comanche riding a slow horse, and everyone tried to count coup on him, and by the time he was dead with eleven arrows through him, the village had been forgotten, because another Comanche was sighted running in the opposite direction.

Things were no better for the southern allies. The Apache had been warned that they must move quickly to support the village, and they would have, except that at the last minute they spotted a small band of Cheyenne who had gotten lost chasing a Comanche, and the whole Apache tribe diverted to annihilate that small band.

Only Lame Beaver, Red Nose and Cottonwood Knee held to the original plan; their three Cheyenne companions spotted an Apache separated from the main body, and chased him for a distance, killing him at last. Breathless, they returned to Our People, whom they accused in sign language of lacking valor. Lame Beaver laughed and replied, 'Anyone who fights an Apache is truly valorous, but we are waiting for Never-Death,' and the Cheyenne said, 'We're waiting for him too,' but in the meantime they sighted another Apache, and off they went. This time they failed to catch him and returned quite winded but delighted with the battle, and Lame Beaver wondered how much help they would be if they did meet up with Never-Death. He knew they would be valiant . . . but exhausted.

The battle now degenerated into a confused melee, with the invaders retaining a slight advantage, but Never-Death had not yet made an appearance. Then came a small body of Comanche led by a large dark man riding a black horse. This was Never-Death, and his arrival so inspirited his allies that they launched a counterthrust against the Cheyenne, gambling that if they could terrorize these warriors, Our People would flee automatically.

But on this day Never-Death was not to have his accustomed effect, for as he was preparing to spread terror among the Cheyenne, Lame Beaver and his five companions rode speedily at him, and a violent scuffle ensued, highlighted by wild battle cries from the exhausted Cheyenne, who anticipated a fine brawl. Never-Death was as powerful as he had been depicted, but did not panic the six warriors. Our People drove steadily against him, but the wild Cheyenne, reveling in battle, sped in and out of the fight until Never-Death's followers unleashed a flood of arrows at them, killing one.

Never-Death supposed that this would discourage the others, and he made a dash for the main battle, but again Lame Beaver intercepted him, while the two remaining Cheyenne, ignoring arrows, slashed at him with their clubs. Never-Death now commanded his troop to evade the pestilential attackers by a wide running sweep, and this would have succeeded except that Lame Beaver spurred his own horse to a gallop, smashed into the heart of Never-Death's group, clubbed him over the head, then dived at him, knocking him from his horse and sprawling him on the ground.

As the two warriors fell, Lame Beaver discovered for himself that Never-Death really was different from other men. His body seemed not human but to be made of iron, and when he struck the earth, with Lame Beaver atop him, he rattled. He was a terrifying creature, and Lame Beaver expected Never-Death to destroy him in some magic way.

Lame Beaver had lost his club and felt powerless to hurt this terrible Comanche, but as Never-Death collected his strength and prepared to kill Lame Beaver, the latter remembered the caution of Gray Wolf: 'Only the rocks live forever,' and he determined that he would fight this Comanche to the death. Doubling his two hands into one powerful fist, he cocked his elbows and brought that fist against the face of Never-Death. The Comanche, stunned by this unexpected blow, fell back, and Lame Beaver struck him again and again. He heard bones breaking in the Comanche's head, and after one final blow he saw that head lying at an impossible angle to the body. He would have fainted, except that his two Cheyenne companions rode up shouting and laughing and proclaiming victory. Kneeling in the dust, he pointed at his fallen adversary and said in sign language, 'Powerful medicine. No more.' The Cheyenne cheered.

Next morning the defeated Comanche and Apache chiefs sought powwow with the Cheyenne, who insisted that Our People participate too. The losers proposed that all prisoners be released, and this was done. They said that they would overlook the destruction of the two camps, and the Cheyenne council members nodded. They said they were offering the Cheyenne twenty horses in exchange for the iron shirt which their great chieftain had worn for so long and which two Cheyenne had stripped from his dead body.

The shirt was produced for all to marvel at, a cuirass made centuries ago in Spain of iron and silver, exhumed from the grave of a Spanish explorer who had died in these alien lands in 1542, and long the treasure of the Comanche. Deep Water, a Comanche chief, said in sign language, 'For your warriors this would be nothing. For us it is the great medicine of our tribe.'

There was a moment of hesitation, which Lame Beaver broke by signaling without authorization, 'Sixty horses,' and without a second's pause Deep Water shouted and signaled, 'Eighty horses,' and the trade was completed.

In this great battle, which stabilized the southern frontier for nearly forty years and was therefore the outstanding Indian battle of half a century, 113 Comanche and 67 Apache fought 92 Cheyenne and 39 Our People. The southern confederacy lost 28 men, including Never-Death; the northern 16, including Gray Wolf.

The victors returned home with the eighty horses from the Comanche, plus another nineteen captured from the Apache. Coups were counted for many nights, none so notable as the one Lame Beaver gained when he grappled barehanded with Never-Death and disclosed the secret of his powerful medicine.

5. Nine Horses Lost

In the year 1782, when Lame Beaver was thirty-five years old, a major imbalance developed on the plains, one which threatened Indian stability until it was corrected. The arrival of the horse was the only other phenomenon which approached it in importance.

That year the Pawnee acquired a substantial supply of guns and for a while dominated all tribes to the west. There had been guns before, isolated examples of some lucky Indian's obtaining a rifle and three or four lead bullets with just enough powder to fire them; but after that explosive celebration, in which his own fingers were liable to be shot off, or his friend's head, only the barren rifle remained. In the end it was used as a club.

But in 1782 the Pawnee got the rifle in earnest through trading with Saint Louis, and acquired the skill to use it. They set forth immediately to impose upon the Platte a Pax Pawnee, and for a while succeeded. Set free from the necessity of riding down their bison by brute strength and shooting them with bow and arrow, they could now stand well back and gun them down at leisure. A war party of six could roam from the Missouri to the Colorado mountains, and move in safety, assured that if trouble did develop with Our People or the Ute, their guns would defend them.

The more remote tribes, learning of the appalling advantage now enjoyed by the Pawnee, had only one desire—to get guns for themselves. But since they had not yet begun to trade with white men, they remained without modern arms. Their world was moving away from them and they were unable to catch up.

'I told you the Pawnee were the cleverest,' Jumping Snake repeated so often and so dolefully that the others wanted to silence him, but he was a senior chief with many coups and his lamentations continued.

Obviously, many councils were held and raids against the Pawnee were planned, but as Jumping Snake reiterated, 'If we got the black-sticks-that-speak-death, we wouldn't know what to do with them. What is their great medicine? Who can tell?'

A number of Our People were then encamped near Rattlesnake Buttes, and early one morning a boy of ten ran up to Jumping Snake and reported, 'A Pawnee war party in the cottonwoods!' The chiefs immediately dispatched scouts to see if this report was true, and they returned with ominous news: 'Fifteen Pawnee. Good horses. Four black sticks.'

The council had to assume that the Pawnee intended trouble, and some advised that the camp be evacuated immediately and reestablished at some point on the other side of the North Platte, and this counsel prevailed. But Lame Beaver and seven of the middle group of warriors were given permission to stay behind to lure the Pawnee on, in hopes of somehow gaining possession of at least one of the rifles.

'We shall need some horses to use as bait,' Lame Beaver said, so they were given sixteen, which included their own mounts, and eight of these they allowed to roam as lures in the direction of the South Platte.

The Pawnee were not marching westward arrogantly, even though they had guns. They kept scouts properly posted, and in time one of them, on a reconnoiter to the north, spotted the horses. He was not so stupid as to imagine that the animals were unattended, and since no men were visible, he concluded that they must be a trap. Soon the other Pawnee were in position to study the situation. Obviously this was a trap, but there was a good chance that whoever had set it knew nothing of guns. This would be a good opportunity to make them permanently afraid of the Pawnee and to get some good mounts at the same time. They laid their plans to snare the horses and terrify their owners.

But as they were doing so, Lame Beaver and his men were constructing contrary plans, and it was obvious that the two must come into violent conflict. The battle started when the fifteen Pawnee fanned out to drive the grazing horses into the river. Lame Beaver allowed this maneuver to develop, because it diluted the force of the enemy, and when the spread was at its greatest, he and Cottonwood Knee made a determined charge at its apex.

They broke through, but now they were encircled by the enemy. This was not accidental; it was an act of special courage, for it distracted the attention of the Pawnee, allowing the other warriors from Our People to attack the two flanks.

Confusion resulted. At first the Pawnee leader thought he might be able to dispose of the two intruders without using his guns, but Lame Beaver and Cottonwood Knee were so wild in their passage, and so disruptive, that ordinary tactics could not contain them and he signaled one of his men bearing a gun to fire.

There was a loud blast, much smoke, and Cottonwood Knee was blown off his horse, his chest shattered. Lame Beaver, seeing the destruction of his friend and knowing from the spurting blood that he must be dead, wheeled his horse and rode hard at the Pawnee who had fired, and that warrior was so preoccupied with his gun that he could not protect himself. Lame Beaver, leaning far out of his saddle, grabbed at the smoking gun with both hands and wrested it from its owner. His momentum carried him out of the semicircle and back toward his own men.

'I have it!' he shouted, waving the gun aloft.

At this Our People on the left flank rallied and started a concerted drive on the Pawnee, who retreated slowly, firing another gun and taking the eight horses and Cottonwood Knee's mount across the Platte with them.

It was an inconclusive battle. Our People had lost nine good horses, which they could not afford, and Cottonwood Knee was dead, a courageous man with many coups to his credit. The Pawnee had been repulsed, leaving two of their men dead and surrendering one precious gun.

Lame Beaver sent a messenger across the North Platte to inform the chiefs that it was safe to return to Rattlesnake Buttes, and while they waited for the tribe to come back and pitch their tipis, they studied the gun. They had seen iron before, and some had knives of it, but they had never seen it in such quantity or so handsomely molded. They found pebbles to run down the interior of the barrel and deduced that these became the deadly missiles.

At this point they cut open Cottonwood Knee to find out what it was that had slain him, and the shape of the bullet confirmed their deductions. They could make nothing of the firing mechanism; its sophistication was quite beyond their understanding at the moment, but one brave did fit his finger against the trigger and conclude that this had something to do with the mystery. They had a gun. They didn't know quite what to do with it, but they were no longer outside the pale.

In this battle fifteen Pawnee faced eight of Our People, and when it came time to counting coups it was agreed that Lame Beaver had gained one, because he had touched the Pawnee who held the gun, but that evening he lost whatever honor he had gained, for as he was helping Blue Leaf raise their tipi he heard an ominous rattle, close to his wife.

Looking frantically about, he saw to his horror a great rattlesnake, coiled and preparing to strike Blue Leaf. Acting instinctively, he leaped at the hideous thing and clubbed at it with the newly captured gun.

He knocked the venomous creature to one side, but saw that it was still capable of striking, so he clubbed it again and again until it lay stretched on the sand beside the tipi.

A crowd, hearing the fight against the snake, gathered, and a woman cried, 'Lame Beaver has killed a great snake,' but a more observant boy said, 'He's broken the stick-that-speaks!'

Hushed warriors gathered in the sunset to stare at Lame Beaver, who stood holding the gun by the end of its barrel, the stock and firing mechanism shattered.

6. New Poles for the Tipi

Our People, dependent upon the bison, had become like the bison. Just as those shaggy animals divided into two herds, one centering on the plains lying north of the North Platte, the other keeping pretty much to the plains south of the South Platte, so Our People were beginning to divide into two tribes, North and South, the former depending upon Flat-Pipe while the southern revered Sacred-Wheel.

Lame Beaver and his small group, now led by Jumping Snake, belonged to the southern group, and although they sometimes ranged far north toward the land of the Crow, they returned always to that congenial land between the two Plattes to pitch their camp near Rattlesnake Buttes. It must not, however, be thought that they lived there. They were nomads, hunters who went where the bison went, and it was of no concern to them what type of land they lived on. In some years they might not camp within a hundred miles of Rattlesnake Buttes; in others they might move far south to the Arkansas. They had no home. They did have a predominant group of bison which they followed, and from time to time, elements of that herd wandered up to the good grass between the two Plattes and Our People followed them.

This constant moving about, increased since obtaining the horse, had one unexpected consequence which caused Our People some trouble. The travois, that primitive but functional invention for hauling goods, was constructed always from two poles used otherwise to support the tipi, and as they dragged for mile after mile across rough terrain, the large ends were gradually abraded until the poles were no longer of sufficient length to use in making the tipi. The Pawnee might have used them, for they constructed low tipis, but Our People liked slim, towering ones, not too wide in circumference at the bottom and gracefully tapered at the top. Long poles were a necessity.

But where to get them? Often Our People would spend eighteen months in the heart of the prairie, where never a tree was seen, not one. And when they did come to a place like Rattlesnake Buttes, all they found was cottonwood, which produced neither long nor straight trunks.

They had to trade for their tipi poles. In the north there were Indians who would give a Pawnee nine short poles for one horse, but since Our People demanded longer poles and better, they received only seven for one horse. They considered this a fair trade, for to Our People the tipi was the center of life.

In the year 1788, when Lame Beaver was forty-one years old and one of the wisest men of the tribe, he noticed with some dismay that the three key-poles of his tipi were so ground down at the butt ends that they no longer permitted the tipi to assume its lofty and dignified form. He was unhappy. For many years now, in fact, ever since his decision not to seek a high station in the tribe, he had found exceptional pleasure in his tipi. It was the most satisfactory in the camp, not the loftiest nor the most garish—for there were others more copiously decorated—but the most congenial. In all its proportions it was correct.

At the end of a long trek he liked to lie back and watch his wife erect it, for she did this with skill and a certain grace, as if to do so were part of her religion. First she gathered the three key-poles and laid them on the ground where the tipi was to stand. Then she lashed the thin ends together with pliant antelope thongs, about three feet from the tips. Thus she had a tripod, which she set upright, the heavy ends of the three poles wedged into the ground, far enough apart to assure stability.

Next she took about a dozen lesser poles, shorter and not so straight, and these she also wedged into the ground, propping them against the point where the key-poles were lashed together. She now had the skeleton of her tipi, its base securely settled on the ground, its top rising far into the air. Her next task was to throw over it the tanned bison hides that would form the covering, and this she did by climbing partway up to the junction of the key-poles and binding a segment of the skin to it.

She allowed the skin to fall naturally, draping it evenly over the poles and making sure that the opening through which people would enter would face east. It was inconceivable that a tipi should be oriented in any other way.

The tipi was now erected save for one other important feature which made it habitable. Taking two extra-long poles, she adroitly fitted their tips into the corners of the bison covering which rested on the very top of the tipi, and these poles she did not fasten in the earth. By swinging them to different positions about the tipi and at different angles, she could determine how much ventilation would come in at the top, or how much would go out if the flap were left open, and in this way ensure both a warm house and a healthy one. The air in her tipi was never suffocating.

When she was finished, Lame Beaver would lift from the travois various parfleches, those boxlike carrying cases made of heavy partially tanned hide, closer to wood than to leather, and from them Blue Leaf would take the cots, her cooking gear and whatever mementos her husband had acquired in his hunting and fighting.

Lame Beaver took charge of building his own cot, for he was proud of it and spent much of his life on it. It had a low wooden frame upon which he placed a mat made of carefully selected and smoothed willow sticks, each one pierced at the ends so that antelope sinews could be passed through, keeping the willow firm and in place. Over this he placed two bison blankets carefully tanned and pliable, and on the tipi wall behind, a medium-sized bison robe which had been worked to the consistency of parchment. On it Blue Leaf, using stick ends for brushes and a variety of pigments for coloring, had drawn memorable scenes from her husband's life; the yellow which predominated came from the bile sac of the bison. She was not an outstanding artist, but she could depict bison and Pawnee and Ute, and these were the things which preoccupied her husband.

The cot had this peculiarity: the willow-stick mat extended for several feet at each end, and these extensions were held in upright position by stout tripods, so as to form two backrests. The exposed wood was highly polished and some of the strands were colored, so that Lame Beaver's cot constituted a kind of throne, with the painted skin behind it and the handsome backrests on either end.

Since no tribe could be at war constantly, or hunt bison when there were no bison, and since there were no books, nor alphabet to print them in if there were, and since no one from Our People could converse with anyone from another tribe, and since there was no need of constant council meetings, Lame Beaver had days and weeks on end of idle time, with no great thoughts to occupy him and no one to share them with if they had mysteriously arisen. He led a bleak, impoverished intellectual life, the highlight coming when younger warriors crowded into his tipi to hear him tell of his adventures in the past.

Then he would seat the most promising young man beside him, and they would lean back against the willow backrests and he would speak to him alone, allowing the others on the floor to listen, and he would relate how he had battled Never-Death and how he had captured the first gun and then destroyed it. He was meticulous in his narration, always giving more than just credit to Cottonwood Knee and Red Nose, the former dead, the latter a considerable chief. He counted no coups that he had not rightfully won, and no interrupter ever had occasion to halt his narrative to ask, 'Who saw you gain that coup?' The coups he counted were part of tribal history and were preserved on the skin his wife had painted.

In the early summer of 1788 he counted one of the great coups of his life, not because of its inherent bravery but because of the extraordinary consequences which flowed from it, not in that year but seventy-three years later.

It started when he was resting one day, watching his wife build the tipi. 'We need some new poles,' he said half out loud.

His wife stopped her work and said, 'We should have traded for them when we were north. We could have got maybe seven poles for one horse.'

'Well, we're not north,' Lame Beaver said, 'but I think I know where there are some good poles, and we don't have to give a horse for them, either.'

She assumed from this that he intended raiding the Pawnee again; he was always ready to test his wits against them, so she decided to stop that line of reasoning before it went further. 'Pawnee poles are not long enough,' she said, resuming her work.

'I would not have a Pawnee pole,' he said. 'Not if a village stood unprotected right over there.' He tossed a stone toward the spot at which some years before he had killed the rattlesnake, and he began laughing at the way he had smashed the first gun. 'Remember that snake?' he called to his wife as she climbed the pole to fix the skin. He made a noise like a rattler, and it was so real that she looked back in old terror. 'Me,' he said.

He had a plan for getting new poles. One of the younger braves, trying to trap beaver, had gone partly by accident, partly by design, well into the mountains and had found a steep valley, one of whose sides was covered with blue spruce, the other with tall, straight aspen. He had told Lame Beaver of this, and at the time the older man had said, 'That might be a place to get some tipi poles,' and the younger had said, 'The aspen were very straight,' but Lame Beaver had explained, 'Aspen rot. You want pine or spruce. How were the spruce?' The young brave assured him they were straight.

Now Lame Beaver sought out the younger man, Antelope by name, and asked him if he would lead a party back to the valley to collect some key-poles. The young brave was eager to do so, but warned, 'It's Ute country,' and Lame Beaver said, 'Everywhere on earth is somebody's country. You just have to be careful,' and the young brave said, 'But I saw signs of Ute in the valley,' and Lame Beaver said, 'I've been seeing Ute signs all my life, and usually it means that there's Ute about.'

They put together a war party of eleven men plus four packhorses and marched westward for one day toward the mountain where the stone beaver tried vainly to reach the summit. The next day they followed one of the small streams which in times past had carried torrential rains and melted ice down from that mountain. They proceeded up it for a while, coming to a fork which led to the south, and this brought them at last to Blue Valley. When they came to it, plains Indians seeing the interior majesty of the mountains for the first time, they stopped in admiration, aware that they were viewing one of the precious sights of their earth.

That day it was magnificent, the dark-blue spruce clustering together on the southern bank where there was no sun, the lighter aspen in many shades of dancing green shimmering on the north bank, and after some moments spent admiring the perfect valley, Lame Beaver dismounted, studied the terrain and said, 'There have been Ute here. They were hunting beaver.' He therefore posted two outlooks and proceeded to the job of cutting key-poles among the spruce.

He had chopped down some two dozen, leaving the trimming of the upper branches to the younger men, when one of the scouts whistled like a bird and indicated that six Ute with horses and guns were coming down the valley from the opposite direction. Lame Beaver weighed this unwelcome information and decided to wait the situation out by simply halting all work and withdrawing into the protective shadows of the spruce. He did this, unaware of three unusual events that had recently taken place near where he hid.

First, in a spring freshet some years ago a boulder tumbling down the stream bed had knocked off the end of a major pipe and brought almost pure gold to the surface. The pipe, with its tip unsealed, had released several nuggets of the highest-quality gold, and these had scattered along the bottom of the stream, where later sediment had partially covered them.

Second, it had not been much later that the Ute in this district had got their first gun and with it a set of equipment for making bullets. They knew how to melt lead and pour it into the iron molds the Pawnee had traded them for beaver skins. Also, they understood powder and how to get a constant supply by trading bison skins south to the Mexicans at Santa Fe. The Ute were now an armed tribe.

Third, some time ago on an exploration down Blue Valley for beaver, a Ute brave responsible for pouring bullets in the mold had spotted the yellow nuggets in the stream bed and had idly picked them up to see if they could be molded into bullets. To his surprise, this could be done without melting, and he made two fine bullets out of pure gold. He had looked around for more of the metal, recognizing it as easier to use than lead, but he found none.

It was this brave, with the iron mold and the two gold bullets, who now came down the valley, carefully watching the stream for signs of beaver. He would have gone right past the hiding enemy had he not happened to see a white chip of wood. Thinking this to be the work of a beaver, he moved inland from the stream, turned a corner and came face to face with Lame Beaver, who knifed him in the throat and took his gun and the parfleche in which he carried his bullets.

When this was done, Our People leaped onto the trail, scaring the five remaining Ute warriors into flight. Seeing that their leader was dead and that they were outnumbered, they turned and fled back toward the head of the valley, where they hoped to find reinforcements.

This gave Lame Beaver and his companions time to load their key-poles and head for lower ground, but before they did so the young brave who had discovered the valley and had led Lame Beaver to it asked him if he wanted the scalp of the dead Ute. Lame Beaver shook his head no, so the younger man neatly lifted the scalp to take back to camp as a souvenir of his first important encounter with the enemy.

Lame Beaver, like most of the serious warriors among the Cheyenne and Our People, never bothered with scalps. Collecting such grisly tokens was not a traditional part of Indian culture; it had been introduced a hundred years earlier by French and English military commanders who, before paying bounty, demanded proof from their Indian mercenaries that they had actually slain an enemy. The habit had become ingrained in the eastern tribes and had slowly spread westward, where some tribes like the Comanche made it a respected part of their ritual.

So now Our People came trailing out of the mountains with four treasures: two dozen key-poles of high quality, a Ute scalp, a memory of the most beautiful valley they had ever seen, and two gold bullets in Lame Beaver's parfleche.

7. Invading the Camp of Strange Gods

In the land between the two Plattes, the temperatures in winter often went down to thirty degrees below zero and stayed there for days, freezing the rivers solid. How did Our People survive?

In the first place, the air was so clear and the wind so calm at such times that the cold was exhilarating rather than exhausting. At zero, if the sun was out, men often played at stick games, wearing nothing above the waist, and at ten below, the weather could be quite pleasant, if there was no wind.

In the second place, the Indians of the plains were accustomed to cold; the Cheyenne had a specific tradition on this point: 'In the old days when we lived far north, before we had crossed the river and survived the flood, we used to go naked all the time and had no tipis. What did we do in winter? We found a hole in the bank and covered ourselves with earth and waited for sunny days when we could gather berries. And men went barefoot in the deepest snow and survived.' Our People also had memories of seasons without tipis, but not of years when they went naked.

But there were also blizzards, when icy cold winds howled for days, depositing so much snow that any man caught out must freeze. What did Our People do then?

They crawled into their tipis, and men sent the women out to close the upper vent, all but a crack, and they directed the women to lay heavy rocks about the edges of the tipi so that snow and wind could not infiltrate. Then all came inside, and a very small fire was lit, wasting only a few precious sticks, and it was kept burning for days, and its heat made the tipi snug, and people inside huddled together and congratulated themselves on being out of the storm, and men talked and women sat in near-darkness day after day and children peeped out and cried the exciting news over their shoulders: 'You can't even see Jumping Snake's tipi from here.'

Winds howled and snow piled halfway up the tipi but there was great warmth within; men went outside only to cut cottonwood branches so that their horses might eat the bark. Once Lame Beaver reflected that each of his children had been born in autumn, having been conceived during blizzards. 'We are like beavers,' he said, 'hiding in our snug lodge while the world outside freezes.'

In the year 1799, when Lame Beaver was an old man of fifty-two, he engaged in an exploit which earned him commendation, for it was a deed requiring courage of a new sort.

In late winter that year scouts reported that two men from an entirely different tribe were making their way up the Platte. They were not red like the Pawnee, from whose lands they came, and they carried with them no Indian artifacts. They were not even dressed like Indians, for their winter clothing was bulky, and they wore no feathers or paint. Their heads were covered with beaver fur and they dragged behind them a travois that slid easily over the snow. Both carried guns, and from their travois projected two other guns, and from this they would have been judged wealthy, except that they had no horses. They were a strange enemy and would bear watching.

Why did Our People not destroy those two white men on first acquaintance? Why had the Pawnee allowed them to traverse their lands? The Pawnee must have watched them every day, as Our People now did. Perhaps it was because these two gods, for so they were called at Rattlesnake Buttes, moved with authority and without visible fear. They moved more like bison than like men, as if they belonged to the prairie and owned it. Scouts kept them in sight every hour and reported always the same thing: 'They moved a little farther west today, and always they seemed to be looking for us. There is a short one, almost as dark as a Ute, and a taller one, not so tall as a Cheyenne, but tall, and on his face he has reddish hair. But it is the smaller one who gives the commands.'

When they reached the confluence of Beaver Creek and the Platte, they halted. They had detected something that pleased them and for the first time they pitched a permanent camp, taking the time and trouble to scrape snow from a flat area and to cut some cottonwood, from which they built a very low shelter. Neither of the strange gods could enter it without stooping.

Our People watched, bewildered, and Lame Beaver, as the most courageous of the Indians, decided to find out more about these gods and their curious tipi. One night, creeping very close, he watched as they unrolled bundles, disclosing small items that shimmered in the light of their torches. Long ago when trading with the Crow for tipi poles he had seen such ornaments.

Another time he saw the taller god trying to catch fish in the river, and he became so intent that he failed to notice the approach of the shorter visitor, and before Lame Beaver could run away, the stranger had come upon him, and stood fast, and stared at him. In that fleeting moment Lame Beaver perceived that these strangers were not gods. They were men like himself, and he hurried back to his tipi to inform Blue Leaf of his discovery.

'Those two, there's nothing special about them.'

'They have four guns.'

'I could have four guns if I traded with the Pawnee.'

'Their skins are different.'

'The Ute skin is different. You can tell a Ute from the other side of the river.'

Blue Leaf paraded all the doubts the tribe had voiced, and her husband refuted each, and finally she conceded, 'If they are like us, and if they are going to live among us, we should talk with them.'

'That was my thought,' Lame Beaver said, and forthwith he walked boldly to where the two strangers waited, and although many in his camp predicted disaster or death, he strode up to them, and looked at them, and raised his hand in greeting.

As he stood there the smaller man began cleverly to disclose the infinite variety of things he had brought up the river. One parfleche had scintillating beads, all in a row and of different colors. A pack contained blankets, not made of bison hide but of some soft and pliant material. Finally the man unfolded a special parfleche, and inside glimmered one of the most beautiful substances Lame Beaver had ever seen, a hard metal like the barrel of a gun, but bright and clean and very white.

'Silver,' the short man said time and again, 'silver,' but when Lame Beaver reached for it, the man drew it back and lifted a beaver pelt. 'Beaver,' he kept repeating, indicating that if the Indians brought him pelts, he would give them shining ornaments of silver. And to prove his good intentions he handed a bracelet to Lame Beaver.

Back in his tipi, Lame Beaver put the lovely thing on his wife's arm, and she moved gracefully with it, allowing the sun to strike its facets, and it was then that he reached his decision: 'I will explore the camp of the strangers to determine what their medicine is.'

So, late on a dark night, he cautiously approached their tipi, but he hesitated outside, gripped by a deeper apprehension than any he had known when facing Comanche. He was entering a new and mysterious world, and his courage began to fail, but he bit his lip and crept inside, compressing himself like a sinew to avoid touching things.

Cautiously he stood erect, scarcely breathing while his eyes adjusted to the darkness. From the earth he could hear the rhythmic sleep-breath of the men and could tell that the smaller lay to his right.

He now faced the most difficult part of his mission. To count coup, he must touch one of them, and characteristically he chose the dark leader. Bending a fraction of an inch at a time, he brought himself closer and closer to the sleeping man until their faces almost touched. He then reached out his hand to place it upon the dark body, when in the dim light he became aware of a terrifying thing.

The sleeper was not asleep! He was wide awake! And in the dim light he was staring directly into the eyes of Lame Beaver.

The two men, each terrified of the other, held this gaze, and then ever so slowly Lame Beaver resumed the movement of his hand and placed it upon the dark face. The hand bore no weapon, no evil intent. Neither man breathed. The hand withdrew, and in that manner the red man first made contact with the white.

Then as Lame Beaver started to withdraw, the man in bed relaxed, and in doing so, made a slight noise. From the other bed the tall man leaped into action, grabbed a gun and would have fired at Lame Beaver had not a deep voice from the first bed cried, 'Arretez! Arretez!'

'What is it?' the man with the gun shouted.

'Il n'a pas d'armes,' and he knocked the gun away.

Slowly Lame Beaver retreated, satisfied that these were men obsessed by the same fears that gripped him, accustomed to sleep as he slept. Had they owned a special medicine, they would not have needed guns, and with this knowledge he returned to his camp.

In the morning he assembled his tribe and disclosed his findings. He assured the chiefs that the visitors were not gods and that they had come in peace. 'They could have killed me, and they let me go,' he said.

He collected all available beaver pelts and threw them onto a travois, leading the horse to where the visitors waited with their alluring goods. But as the trading began, he indicated that he wished no silver trinkets, no gaudy blankets. Pointing resolutely to one of the guns, he let the men know that he would accept nothing less. The younger man demurred, saying to his partner, 'If they get guns, they'll be as bad as the Pawnee,' and he withdrew the gun, but the older man retrieved it and handed it to Lame Beaver, saying in French, 'They'll get guns sooner or later. If they get them from us, we get their pelts.'

As Lame Beaver gained possession of the gun he looked deep into the eyes of the man who had traded it to him, and there was a long moment of silence as each acknowledged that in the previous darkness either could have slain the other but had refrained. No word was spoken, and in this cool diffidence the implied treaty between Our People and the white man was ratified.

8. Two Gold Bullets

In early autumn the straggling cottonwoods which marked the course of every river and stream knew a brief moment of glory, for their ill-formed leaves turned gold and for several days gleamed as if they were aspen, but the winds of the coming winter soon bore them away and the trees were left as bare as before.

In the year 1803, when Lame Beaver was fifty-six, the transformation of the cottonwoods presaged a gloomy time. He did not want to face another winter; the cold had been growing more bitter as the years passed, and he no longer found solace in sitting cross-legged on his bed, regaling younger men with his ancient deeds. Not even the handsome bison skin painted by his wife gave him satisfaction.

His malaise had started some years back when he broke a tooth on a piece of jerked bison. He bit down as always, gave the meat a solid tug, and his tooth came away with the jerky. Next year he lost another, in the same way, and then two more, so that he was reduced to eating the softer pemmican, which he had never liked.

The friends of his youth were dying, too. Red Nose, the best chief of them all, had gone last winter, and Cottonwood Knee was long since dead, slain by a Pawnee rifle. Younger men were in command, and while they maintained the high spirit of the tribe, they handled themselves poorly in negotiation with the Comanche, and so far as resisting the Pawnee was concerned, they might as well have surrendered all the territory to them and been done with it.

He was worried about the Pawnee. They moved ever westward, and soon Our People would be squeezed into a pitiful territory around Rattlesnake Buttes. He was therefore already in gloomy spirits when scouts rushed into camp with the hideous news that the Pawnee had captured a young girl to use in their sacrifice.

'We must take her back,' he stormed, unwilling to consider any alternative. Trade for her? Never. Surrender more hunting land? Never. Horses, pelts, guns? He would listen to no such pusillanimity. 'We will ride east and take her back,' he shouted.

At councils, of which he was not a member, he broke in uninvited and cried, 'We must ride in like braves and take that girl back.' He broke up several intelligent discussions of how this could be achieved without resorting to a war party, but this did not worry him.

'The time comes with the Pawnee when you must face them down in battle,' he stormed. 'It has always been so and always will be. This is such a time.' He reminded the council of how Cottonwood Knee had been slain by the Pawnee in a previous time of decision, but most members of the council had forgotten who Cottonwood Knee was.

In this deep agitation of spirit Lame Beaver went to his wife, and they talked for a long time. She was well aware of what grave thing was on his mind, and what terrible consequences it must have for her. Yet she supported him. He had been a good husband, better than most among Our People, which was high praise, for they, like the Cheyenne, were good to their women and faithful. She had taken pride in his accomplishments and had delineated them on the bison skin, his heroic triumphs set forth in detail. She knew that it would be to her dreadful disadvantage if he proceeded with the plan that she was certain was hatching, but never once did she complain.

'The Pawnee have to be stopped,' he reiterated, and she nodded.

'If they think you are weak, they press on the weakness,' he said, and she knew this to be true.

'They always coveted our land,' he moaned, feeling the empty spaces in his mouth, as if the vanished teeth symbolized the areas already encroached upon by the Pawnee. 'Oh, if Man-Above allowed me to be young again,' he lamented, and she told him that he was still a fine warrior. Then, abruptly, he halted all talk of the Pawnee and turned his attention to his daughter.

Her name, Clay Basket, had been given while they were following bison in the north; a Dakota trader had brought forth a splendid basket made by the Cree. It looked as if it had been woven but was actually of clay. Blue Leaf had liked it and he had bought it for her with a bison robe. No matter that it was her robe and that she had worked on it for many months to make it pliable; he had traded the robe for the basket and it had become her principal treasure, the envy of other women. It was natural that they should name their daughter after this lovely thing, and she had reciprocated by becoming the lithe, poetic creature with whom he now talked.

He told of the tribal journey north and south, of the good days down by the Arkansas and of the delectable valley where the blue spruce grew. He recalled his battle with the huge rattlesnake, when he had sacrificed his first gun to save her mother. And he spoke of the two men who had camped for a while, hunting beaver. He told Clay Basket that they would return. Of that he was positive. And the prospect pleased him, for he liked the shorter man, the dark one without the beard, and felt indebted to him for the gun he now used so expertly. He would welcome such a man into his family.

'When he comes back, Clay Basket, talk with him. He has no woman.

From watching him so carefully, I know this. He'll grow older. His teeth will begin to drop out, too. He'll need a woman to care for him. Think about this when I'm gone.'

'You will not go for many moons,' she assured him.

'You'll have good babies,' he said appraisingly, as if she were a mare. Suddenly he moved about the tipi in great agitation. 'It will all change!' he cried. 'The Pawnee will own everything. The Ute will come down out of the mountain and live like us. And those men will be back to hunt beaver. I don't know,' he moaned to himself, 'I don't know.' He never again spoke to his daughter in a serious manner.

He concentrated on his gun, loading and unloading it, fingering the two gold bullets which he still kept in his parfleche. It was as if he were measuring time by the white man's method and sensed that a new century had begun, one that would swiftly leave him behind with the stark rapidity of its change. He therefore brooded upon lasting things, simplifying the process until only two remained, Blue Leaf and the Pawnee. For him the bison were no more; others could track them now. The beaver and the rattlesnake; others could worry about them from here on. He had never bothered much with the Ute; they were steadfast fighters, but if you stood your ground you could manage the Ute.

As autumn deepened he and Blue Leaf had to acknowledge the dreadful situation that faced them, but he saw no escape, nor did she. She was therefore prepared, spiritually and in all other ways, when he announced: 'When we march against the Pawnee, I will stake myself out.' He was committing suicide for a noble purpose, and she knew it.

The fact that the most famous warrior of Our People was willing to sacrifice himself to teach the Pawnee a lesson sent a surge of patriotism through the tribe, and the vacillating council was powerless to prevent a decision in favor of war. It was determined without their consent and without their approval, but the spirit engendered by Lame Beaver's announcement was so high that all knew that victory was attainable.

Preparation became frantic, for the blow had to be struck before the first blizzard. Young warriors tended their horses and oiled their guns with bison tallow. Lame Beaver spent all his time with Blue Leaf, not telling her of his love but reminding her in many ways of the good life they had shared. 'Remember the wild duck in the cottonwoods?' he asked. Where had that taken place, along what fugitive stream visited once and seen no more? They had walked along so many streams and pitched their tipi in so many valleys that the mind could not recall them, but once there had been a wild duck caught in a cottonwood and he had wanted to eat it and Blue Leaf had wanted to let it go, and it had flown north, days behind the others.

There was the tamed elk, too, that stayed about the camp in the north and the sound of coyotes along the Arkansas when Our People were planning to fight the Comanche, and the sandy places where the children played. They had possessed a universe of endless horizons and sunsets blazing with golden fire.

'Remember when we had no horses?' he asked, and they talked about those burdensome days when dogs and women hauled the travois so that their men could be ready to repel attack. 'We moved so slowly then,' he said.

The day came when the war party was ready to move eastward. It was cold and the leaves had left the cottonwoods. Lame Beaver bade his wife goodbye but ignored his watching daughter. He had his good horse, his rifle, his parfleche; the signal was given, and he left Rattlesnake Buttes for the last time.

Our People moved cautiously toward the confluence of the two Plattes, and there they found nothing, for the Pawnee had settled down for winter a far distance to the east. They continued to march in that direction until they came upon a sizable camp, but whether the Pawnee held the sacrificial girl here or in some other settlement, they could not know; so much time had elapsed since her capture that she was probably dead by now, and all except Lame Beaver acknowledged that fact. He kept saying, 'We shall take back our girl.' He had never seen her and it wasn't clear in his mind whose child she was, but she must be recaptured.

The leaders of the war party decided that this would be the village they would attack, whether the girl was there or not, so once more a clever battle plan was devised.

Lame Beaver's part in the fight was clear. 'I will stake myself out . . . there. I will not fight any warrior who comes at me. I will wait for the great chief, Rude Water, and I will shoot him dead. The Pawnee will panic, and we shall have the girl.' When he spoke these words, no one doubted that he would do exactly as he promised. Around him the battle would form, and if he could demoralize the first Pawnee charge, Our People would have a good chance of victory.

During the night he prayed, but not attentively, for his mind went back to just one thing, insistently: he kept seeing that first wild pinto he had captured from the Comanche and tamed in the river, only to lose it to Blue Leaf's brother. How marvelous that pinto was, how like the wind. Its handsome black and white spots were etched on his mind and he could still recall the placement of each.

'Heigh! Go!' he cried, and the ghost horse leaped across the prairie like a ray of sunlight, illuminating everything it approached.

'Heigh! Heigh!' he called, and the pinto ran on and on into the mountains. Tears came into the old man's eyes and he turned to his gun, but always in the distance there stood the pinto, his colors bright and his mane standing clear.

'Come!' the old man called softly, but the pinto headed for other pastures.

New scouts moved into position, and those who had been watching came back to prepare for battle. Leaders grew nervous, and Lame Beaver took up his rifle and the stake to which he would attach the thongs that now hung loose about his neck.

The war party moved forward according to plan, then waited while Lame Beaver took a position where the Pawnee charge would be heaviest. Finding a stone, he hammered the stake into position, and this noise alerted the Pawnee guards. Shouts went up, and Our People charged the west entrance to the village; with this first violent sweep, the intricate battle plans evaporated, and it was each man for himself.

The Pawnee reacted as had been expected, with a countercharge of their own, and their leaders had covered only a short distance when they spotted Lame Beaver staked out, his rifle at the ready. They expected him to fire, so the first riders swerved to avoid him, but when he held his fire, those behind swept down upon him, and one caught him through the left shoulder with his lance, leaving the barbed shaft behind.

'Agh!' Lame Beaver grunted, for the lance had pierced his left armpit. The pain was so great that he wanted to discharge his gun in fury; instead he wrenched the lance loose, tearing away much flesh and inducing a heavy flow of blood. It was a bad beginning.

Rude Water did not appear in the second charge, either, and once more a Pawnee lancer made a hit, lightly striking Lame Beaver in the left leg. With contempt he wrestled the barb loose, placing the two lances beside him for possible future use.

On the third Pawnee charge Rude Water did appear, a tall, handsome, very red-skinned chief. Assuming that Lame Beaver had been badly wounded, he rode his horse right at the tethered man, whereupon Lame Beaver took careful aim and shot him off his mount. Rude Water was dead.

It took time for Lame Beaver to reload his rifle: he swabbed it, poured in the powder, rammed down the greased wadding, then inserted his second gold bullet and carefully primed it. Taking aim at a lesser chief, he ignited the primer and again shot a warrior off his horse.

The rout of the Pawnee had begun, but it was by no means complete. Mounted warriors in retreat rode over Lame Beaver and two more stabbed at him. He was now bleeding from several wounds, but he took up the Pawnee lance which had caught him in the leg and tried to defend himself with it, but when a fifth Pawnee caught him with a lance from the rear, shoving it completely through his back and out the chest in front, he was finished.

Clutching the exposed point of the spear, he started to fall forward, but halted himself long enough to begin his going-away song:

> 'Only the rocks endure forever.
> The bison thunders
> but I do not see the dust.

> The beaver slaps his tail
>> I do not hear.
> Man-Above still sends the river flowing past,
> Still helps the beaver climb the mountain peak,
> Still turns the aspen golden in the fall.
>> The chiefs assemble
>>> but they speak no words.
>> The enemy begins its charge
>>> and spears are glistening
> Only the rocks . . .'

A tremor passed through his body, stifling his song. With a mighty effort he tried to pull the fatal spear entirely through his chest, but his strength flagged. He fell forward into the dust of battle, facing the corpse of Rude Water, but Lame Beaver did not see his foe. His last earthly vision was of the pinto galloping across the prairie.

This battle had been more bloody than usual, and the death of Lame Beaver infuriated Our People, though why it should have is a mystery, for he went into the fight determined to die. Our People sacked the village and took fifteen Pawnee girls captive; they offered to trade them for the girl destined for sacrifice, but she was long since dead, so they traded for horses—three girls for one horse.

Jumping Snake decreed that Lame Beaver be given a chieftain's burial, and a high wooden platform was built in three cottonwood trees beside the Platte. There, well above ground, the shattered old body was laid to rest. The stake to which he had attached himself was placed beside him, with the thongs of honor drifting loose in the wind. He was covered with a blanket, and on one of the cottonwoods was hung the head of the horse Rude Water had been riding; on another, the tail. The Pawnee lance with which he had defended himself at the last was laid across his body, and young warriors wanted his rifle to be placed there, too, but Jumping Snake said he would keep the rifle. If he didn't, the Pawnee would take it.

There, high above the plains he had loved and the river he had so often followed, Lame Beaver, the man of many coups, found his rest.

He died at the end of an epoch, the grandest the western Indians were to know. In his lifetime an impoverished band of northern Indians had wandered south, hunting the bison on foot and confined by necessity to narrow regions. In their new home they had found the horse and the gun and had developed a wild, sweeping pattern of life which held on to the good customs of the past while embracing the viable new ones now possible.

Our People and the Cheyenne! How few in number, how powerful in essence! Never did they number as many as seven thousand combined, which meant that there could not have been much over three thousand males. Many of these would have been old and more would have been infants, so that there might have been at most one thousand warriors.

Has there ever been in America another group of a thousand men who left so deep an imprint upon the image of the nation? These few men, tall and bronzed, welded to their horses, daring in battle and just in peace, rode across the prairies and into the permanent record of this land. They dominated their period and their terrain. They defended their homes with valor and left their plain not in defeat but trailing glory. In their last days they staked themselves out and parried all lances coming at them.

Cheyenne and Arapaho—for that was the name the other tribes called Our People—were never the majority in any place they occupied; they were always pressed in upon by tribes at least as able: the Brule Sioux and the Oglala Sioux and the Cree and the Blackfoot and the dark Ute and the centaur Comanche, and the cruel Apache and the crafty Kiowa and the far-thinking Pawnee. But their customs were among the finest the Indians of America produced, and their physical bearing the most commanding.

When the Arapaho chieftains met to count coups in the battle against the Pawnee they formed a noble image: they wore the fringed leggings of winter, the vests decorated with quills and elk teeth, and above all, those resplendent headdresses of woven material set with colored stones and adorned with eagle feathers.

'He counted coup upon Rude Water,' a narrator related, 'and upon the warrior who pierced his leg and upon the one who stabbed him through the arm. With his captured lance he counted coup on the Pawnee with the torn shirt and on the Pawnee with the brown horse. He tried to count coup on the warrior who stabbed him through the back, but in this he failed.'

The great chiefs nodded. Thanks to the heroism of Lame Beaver, their eastern flank was secured for a few more years. Not soon would the Pawnee want to invade Arapaho lands after such a defeat. They would be back, of course, in time. The Pawnee would think of some way to retaliate, but for the present the Arapaho could direct their attention to the coming winter. This year they would camp at Rattlesnake Buttes.

While the Arapaho chiefs were awarding Lame Beaver his final set of coups, a gathering destined to have more lasting consequences took place among the ashes of the desolated Pawnee village. In burying their great chief Rude Water, someone discovered that he had been killed by a golden bullet, and then it was found that the lesser chief, too, had been slain by a bullet of gold, and since the Pawnee, because of their trading with whites, knew the value of gold, the discovery caused a sensation.

The bullets were sent with two knowing white men down the Missouri River to the trading post at Saint Louis and there delivered to a dealer who was stunned by their purity and the apparent size of the nuggets from which they had been formed. The white men pestered the Pawnee with repeated questions, but all they could tell was, 'Lame Beaver, big chief of the Arapaho, he fired the bullets.'

In this way the legend was launched that an Arapaho chief named Lame Beaver had discovered a deposit of pure gold from which he made bullets for shooting bison. 'Search the bison bones and you may find his golden bullets. Better still, find out where he had his gold mine and you'll have wealth untold.' A thousand men would tramp the plains and probe the hills, searching for the lost mine of Lame Beaver, the Indian who used gold bullets, and none would have believed the truth: that he shot those bullets without knowing what they were.

In the Arapaho camp a darker side of Indian custom was about to manifest itself, the hideous side that later apologists would want to forget or deny. Because Blue Leaf was no longer the wife of a warrior and co-head of a family, she had no right to a tipi of her own, and women from all parts of the camp now descended upon it to tear it apart for their own use. The two special poles which operated the upper vent through which the smoke escaped went first. They were grabbed by a woman whose husband had long envied them.

The three key-poles which Lame Beaver had cut in Blue Valley went next. They were ripped out of the ground and torn from their bison covering, which caused the rest of the tipi to collapse. The lesser poles went quickly, for it was known that Lame Beaver had the best in camp.

The bison skin was not a prize; it was old and would soon have to be replaced, but the parfleches that Lame Beaver had made were sturdy and much desired. Two women fell into a fight over the larger, and one suffered a cut hand, but the brawling did not stop for that. Quickly the clay basket vanished.

The bed on which Lame Beaver had spent so much of his life passed into the hands of a young wife who had long wanted its painted backrest for her warrior husband, and the beautiful bison rug, covered with paintings of Lame Beaver's many coups, vanished. No one would remember where it went.

Slowly the tipi was ground into the dust of cruel indifference, and at the end of the day Blue Leaf was left with no possessions in the world save what she was wearing. Her daughter Clay Basket had little more, but she at least was assured of a place to sleep at the home of an uncle. Blue Leaf did not even have that, for the law of the plains was clear and immutable: elderly widows who had no man to care for them had expended their usefulness, and the tribe would not allow itself to be impeded by them. For an older woman like Blue Leaf, with no son to protect her and no brother willing to invite her into his tipi, there was no home and there could be none.

That night the first heavy snow fell. Blue Leaf survived the snow by finding a place among the horses, and next day Clay Basket, seeing her pitiful condition, wanted to bring her into the tipi where she had found refuge, but her uncle, Blue Leaf's brother, who had deprived Lame Beaver of the pinto, refused.

On the third night a blizzard struck, and Blue Leaf could find no shelter except among the shivering horses. She had not eaten that day and was extremely weak, but as she crept closer to the horses and they to her, she did not complain. Lame Beaver and she had anticipated that this must be the consequence of his suicide. This had been the fate of her mother and her aunts, and she had expected nothing better.

In the morning she was found frozen to death. In this practical manner the Arapaho living at Rattlesnake Buttes were freed from the encumbrance of an old woman who had outlived her usefulness.

CAUTION TO *US* EDITORS. You have three basic considerations to keep in mind when you introduce any material on Indians in Colorado.

First, although the plains Indians were the most spectacular tribes in American history, they were also the least interesting intrinsically. The Arapaho and Cheyenne arrived very late on the scene. They occupied land which wiser Indians like the Pawnee and more indigenous ones like the Ute had inspected for several centuries and found unproductive. More important, their previous wanderings from east of the Mississippi and north of the Missouri to the arid plains had deprived them of most of their cultural heritage, which they had been forced to leave behind as so much unnecessary baggage. They were cultural nomads whose quality was uplifted by the horse. They must not be depicted in either your illustrations or your text as typical American Indians. Almost any other of the major tribes would serve that purpose more appropriately.

Second, in preparing my notes I fought constantly, though perhaps unsuccessfully, against the temptation to attribute too many consequences to the Indian's obtaining the horse. Everything I say is true, but I sometimes have doubts as to what it means. I think the best precaution is to keep in mind that the arrival of the horse within a tribe like the Arapaho changed not one degree the basic attitudes which the Arapaho had developed over the preceding two thousand years. They were already nomads; the horse merely increased their range. They already had the travois; the horse could merely lug a bigger load. They were already tied to the bison; the horse allowed them to get to him more swiftly and to kill him in a less wasteful way. They already had a society constructed around coup and war party; the horse merely encouraged them to engage in raids which covered more territory. (I am impressed by the fact that with the horse the Arapaho engaged in not one battle which took them into any area which they had not previously penetrated on foot!) The horse merely intensified customs already in existence. There was, however, one minor change which may have been effectuated by the horse: an improved status for women. The burdens they had to carry became smaller; they could accompany the tribe on its farthest excursions; and some women did get horses of their own, which they rode on migrations or to the bison butchering. If Indian men loved their horses, Indian women must have adored them.

Third, you must not depict the plains Indians as having been for any great length of time in the locations where the white men discovered them. I have our branch of the Arapaho arriving in the land between the two Plattes in 1756. Virginia Trenholm, a leading expert on the Arapaho, claims they didn't get that far south until 1790, which is highly significant, because this would put them there somewhat *after* the first French and English fur trappers! I've looked at all the evidence and have concluded that they must have been there somewhat earlier than that; perhaps 1756 is premature, but I think not. If your own researches indicate a later date for their arrival, I do not object. But please do not fall into the error of writing about white men intruding onto areas which the Indians had held from time immemorial . . . at least not on the Colorado plains. The Pawnee had lived in eastern Nebraska for centuries, but in the western areas where Lame Beaver operated they were latecomers. The Ute had lived in the Rockies but had never established any kind of firm foothold in the areas around Centennial. In the period before they had horses, the Comanche were a miserably poor mountain tribe; they moved rather late into position along the Arkansas. The limited area you are dealing with appears to have been devoid of permanently settled human beings from about 6000 B.C. to about A.D. 1750. You are dealing with a very young area, culturally, and it was certainly not one which the Indians had occupied for very long.

Visual images. In depicting the Indian background, do not commit these traditional errors:

Do not show them on war parties in full regalia. I judge from what I have read that Indians in their everyday occupations looked pretty much like students at the Boulder campus of Colorado University today, except that the Indians may have been somewhat cleaner.

On the other hand, don't overdo the cleanliness bit. When I was discussing the Arapaho tipi with an old expert, he listened to my favorable description, then grunted and said, 'You've left out the one thing you could be sure of in an Arapaho tipi.' When I asked what this was, he said, 'If you sat on the chief's bed with that handsome backrest, the one thing you could be sure of catching was lice.'

In the pre-white-man war parties and set battles, few members were engaged and few deaths occurred. The massed charges of western paintings did not occur.

For the pre-white-man era, the paintings of George Catlin are still the best ones to rely on.

For the white-man era, I much prefer the paintings of Charles M. Russell. The Frederic Remington paintings are authentic as depictions of the white man at work on the prairies, but I do not find them sensitive to the Indian.

Don't, for God's sake, perpetuate either in word or illustration or map the legend that the Indians got their horses from the chance descendants of two horses, one stallion, one mare, which escaped from Coronado's excursion and bred like crazy, producing hundreds of colts, all of whom bred just as single-mindedly. Sorry. Coronado had stallions, none of which escaped. The Indians got their mounts either while they were working for Spaniards, or in warfare, or by the time-honored process of after-dark theft, at which they were masters.

If you have your own artist do the illustrations, remember that by the time the Indians got them, horses were much diminished in size and were called ponies, which meant small, compact horses, and the preferred coloring was pinto.

Moral problem. You are then left with the most difficult problem of all. Only when I finished the report did I realize that I had come close to depicting the Arapaho in the late 1700s as the noble savage of Rousseau. I did not intend to do so. I have endeavored at every point to introduce qualifying material by stressing the limitations of his mind, the primitiveness of his social order, the constriction of his language, his harsh treatment of women and his limited horizon. I bring this contradiction to your attention now because it will haunt both you and me during the life of this project. We shall have to make up our minds precisely where we stand on the inherent nobility of the Indian, because the problem will arise later when we least anticipate it. We have got to have our minds clear. To be specific: some ninety percent of American college and university students in 1976 will believe without question, and will vote in accordance with that belief, that the Indians who roamed the west in 1776 had solved all problems of group living and had attained the ecological balance that ought to exist between man and his environment. Will they be justified? Do not try to solve this enigma now. Wait till all the evidence is in. But in the end, you will have to check everything you say or illustrate about the Indian in light of that overriding problem: Was he, in his natural state, inherently superior? In this chapter I have given you as faithful a portrait of one Indian in the closing years of the eighteenth century as I could. That I liked the man and would have loved going hunting with him is obvious. That I have done him abstract historical justice, I do not claim.

Early man. As to the date for the arrival of man into the Americas, we know for certain only that Clovis man operated around Centennial about 12,000 years ago, because we have the projectile points he used and carbonized remnants of his fires.

I am convinced that within this century artifacts and sites will be found dating the North American ancestors of the Indian back to the land bridge of 40,000 years ago. I doubt that you ought to sponsor this date in your magazine but recommend that you do not lock yourself into some date like 10,000 B.C. simply because we have assured carbon dates to support it. Primitive man was in these areas for a much, much longer time than we once thought possible, and do not be surprised if the Calico site in the Mohave Desert northeast of Barstow, California, is confirmed one of these days, pushing the date back toward the year 100,000 B.C.

Spear points. My love for the Clovis point has not blinded me to the fact that there are two other types which some experts have found even more beautiful: the long, slim, beautifully finished Eden point, and the small, exquisitely fluted Folsom. It comes down to this. If you prefer the no-nonsense painting of Giotto and the stark, powerful lines of Romanesque architecture, as I do, you will prefer Clovis. If your taste runs to the more sophisticated beauty of Giorgione and Chartres cathedral, you will prefer Eden. And if you like the delicate arabesques of Watteau and the Sainte-Chapelle, you will choose Folsom. But what I say about the unsurpassed beauty of all these ancient artworks holds true, regardless of which you prefer.

Language. As to the fact that the Ute and the Aztec spoke languages derived from the same root-language, you might want to introduce your readers to glottochronology, the science of dating origins by language attrition. If you need a summary of the studies, I can provide it.

THE
YELLOW
APRON

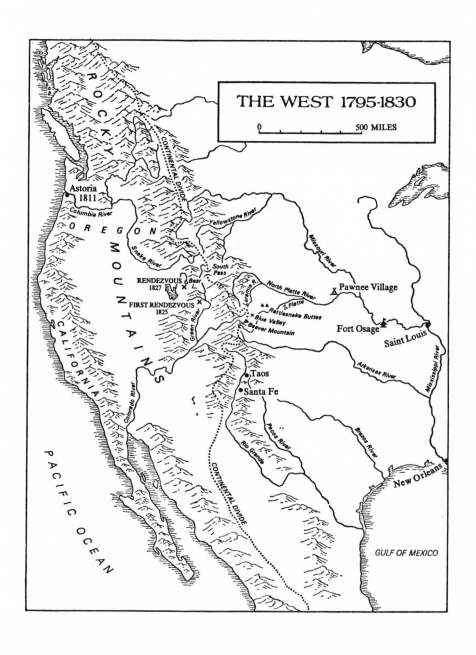

THE WEST 1795-1830

0 _____ 500 MILES

ROCKY

CONTINENTAL DIVIDE

Astoria
1811

Columbia River

OREGON

Yellowstone River

Snake River

Missouri River

South
Pass

RENDEZVOUS
1827

Bear
L.

MOUNTAINS

Sweetwater R.

North Platte River

Pawnee Village

FIRST RENDEZVOUS
1825

S. Platte
Rattlesnake Buttes

Green River

Blue Valley
Beaver Mountain

Fort Osage

Saint Louis

CALIFORNIA

Taos

Santa Fe

Colorado River

Arkansas River

Mississippi River

Pecos River

Rio Grande

Brazos River

PACIFIC OCEAN

CONTINENTAL DIVIDE

New Orleans

GULF OF MEXICO

HE WAS A COUREUR DE BOIS, ONE WHO runs in the woods, and where he came from, no one knew.

He was a small, dark Frenchman who wore the red knitted cap of Quebec, and his name was Pasquinel. No Henri or Ba'tees or Pierre. No nickname, either. Just the three full syllables Pas-qui-nel.

He was a solitary trader with Indians, none better, and in his spacious canoe he carried beads from Paris, silver from Germany, blankets from Canada and bright cloth from New Orleans. With a knife, a gun and a hatchet for saplings, he was ready for work.

He dressed like an Indian, which was why men claimed he carried Indian blood: 'Hidatsa, Assiniboin, mebbe Gros Ventre. He's got Injun blood in there somewheres.' He wore trousers made of elk skin fringed along the seams, a buffalo-hide belt, a fringed jacket decorated with porcupine quills and deerskin moccasins—all made for him by some squaw.

As to where he came from, some claimed Montreal and the Mandan villages. Others said they had seen him in New Orleans in 1789. This was confirmed by a trader who worked the Missouri River: 'I seen him in Saint Louis trading beaver in 17 and 89 and I asked him where he was from, and he said, "New Orleans."' Both sides agreed that he was a man without fear.

Early in December of 1795, in his big birch-bark canoe which he had been paddling upstream for five weeks, he appeared at the confluence of the Platte and the Missouri, determined to try his luck along the former.

The spot at which these rivers joined was one of the bleakest in North America. Mud flats deposited by the Platte reached halfway across the Missouri. Low trees obscured the shores, and swamps made it impossible for traders to erect a post. It was an ugly, forbidding place.

It was Pasquinel's intention to paddle his canoe about five hundred miles up the Platte, reach there in midwinter, trade with whatever tribes he found, then bring the pelts down to the market in Saint Louis. It was a dangerous enterprise, one which required him to pass single-handed through Pawnee, Cheyenne and Arapaho country, going and coming. Chances for survival of a lone coureur were not great, but if he did succeed, rewards would be high, and that was the kind of gamble Pasquinel liked.

Pushing his red cap back on his head, he sang a song of his childhood as he entered the Platte:

> 'Nous étions trois capitaines
> Nous étions trois capitaines
> De la guerre revenant,
> Brave, brave,
> De la guerre revenant,
> Bravement.'

He had paddled only a few miles when he realized that this river bore little resemblance to the Missouri. There progress depended solely upon strength of arm, but with the Platte he found himself often running out of water. Sandbars intruded and sometimes whole islands, which shifted when he touched them. Not only did he have to paddle; he had also to avoid being grounded on mud flats.

It's only during the first part, he assured himself. Not enough current to scour the bottom.

But three days later the situation remained the same. He began to curse the river, setting a precedent for all who would follow. 'Sale rivière,' he growled aloud in Montreal French. 'Où a-t-elle passé?'

A cold spell came and what little water there was froze, and for some days he was immobilized, but this caused no fear. If he could not force his way upstream, he would look for Indians and trade for a few pelts.

Then the thaw came and he was able to proceed. To make a living trading for beaver it was necessary to be at the Indian camps in late winter, when the animals came out of hibernation, their fur sleek and thick. The same animal trapped in midsummer wasn't worth a sou. Beaver trading was a winter job, and Pasquinel knew every trick the Canadians had developed for staying alive in freezing weather.

'Four Frenchmen can live where one Englishman would die,' they said in Detroit, and he believed it. He thought nothing of spending eight months alone in unexplored territory, if the Indians would allow him into their camps. If his canoe was destroyed, he could build another. If his stores were dumped, it didn't matter, for he had invented a canny way of keeping his powder dry. But if Indians proved hostile, he stopped trading and got out. Only a fool would fight Indians if he didn't have to.

Now he entered the land of the Pawnee, reputed in Saint Louis to be the most treacherous tribe. Fais attention! he warned himself, moving so stealthily that he spotted the Indian village before they saw him.

For one whole day he kept his canoe tucked inside a bank while he studied his potential foe. They seemed like those he had known in the north: buffalo hunters, a scalp here and there, low tipis, horses and probably a gun or two—everything was standard.

It was time to move. Methodically he laid out a supply of lead bullets, poured some powder, checked the oil patches required for tamping, and wiped the inside of his short-barreled fusil. His knife was in his belt and his hatchet close by. Taking a deep breath, he paddled his canoe out into the stream and was soon spotted.

Children ran down to the bank and began calling to him in a language he did not know. Grim-lipped, he nodded to them and they shouted back. Three young braves appeared, ready for trouble, and these he saluted with his paddle. Finally two dignified chiefs strode down, looking as if they intended to settle this matter. They indicated that he must pull his canoe ashore, but he kept to the middle of the river.

Angered, the two chiefs signaled a group of young men to plunge into the cold water and haul him ashore. Lithe bodies jumped in, walked easily to the middle of the river, and dragged him ashore. They tried to take his rifle, but he wrested it from them and warned in sign language that if they molested him, he would shoot the nearest chief. They drew back.

Then from the tipis came a tall, fine-looking chief with a very red complexion. Rude Water, they said his name was, and he demanded to know who Pasquinel was and what he was doing.

In sign language Pasquinel spoke for some minutes, explaining that he had come from Saint Louis, that he came in peace, that all he wanted was to trade for beaver. He concluded by saying that when he returned through Pawnee lands, he would bring Chief Rude Water many presents.

'Chief wants his present now,' a lieutenant said, so Pasquinel dug into his canoe and produced a silver bracelet for the chief and three cards of highly colored beads made in Paris and imported through Montreal. Genuflecting, he handed Rude Water the cards and indicated they were for his squaw.

'Chief has four squaws,' the lieutenant said, and Pasquinel brought out another card.

The parley continued all that day, with Pasquinel explaining that the Pawnee must be friends to the great King of France, but have nothing to do with the Americans, who had no king. Rude Water embraced Pasquinel and assured him that the Pawnee, greatest of the Indian tribes, were his friends, but that he must avoid the Cheyenne and Arapaho, who were horse stealers of the worst sort, and above all, the Ute, who were barbarians.

The desultory conversation resumed during the second day, with Rude

Water inquiring as to why Pasquinel would venture into the plains without his woman, to which the Frenchman replied, 'I have a wife . . . north, but she is not strong in paddling the canoe.' This the chief understood.

On the next day Rude Water still insisted on playing host, explaining that Pasquinel could not take his canoe up the Platte—too much mud, too little water. Pasquinel said he would like to try, but Rude Water kept inventing new obstacles. When Pasquinel finally got his canoe into the river, the entire village came down to watch him depart. Rude Water said, 'When you come to where the rivers join, take the south. Many beaver.' The parting was so congenial that Pasquinel had to anticipate trouble.

He paddled upriver all day, suspecting from time to time that he was being followed. At dusk he pitched his tent ashore and ostentatiously appeared to sleep, but when darkness fell he slipped back to his canoe and lay in the bottom, waiting. As he expected, four Pawnee braves crept along the riverbank to steal his canoe. He waited till their probing hands were almost touching his.

Then, with fiendish yells and slashing knife, he rose from the bottom of the canoe, threw himself among the four, cutting and gouging and kicking. He was a one-man explosion, made doubly frightening by the dark. The four fled, and in the morning he continued upstream.

He had gone about fifty miles farther westward when he became aware that he was again being followed. Pawnee, he concluded. Same men.

So once more he laid out his bullets and honed his knife. He judged that if he could repel them one more time, they would leave him alone. He traveled carefully, avoiding mud flats and staying away from shore. He was watchful whenever he knelt to drink or stopped to relieve himself. It was an ugly, difficult game, which the Pawnee stood every chance of winning.

The showdown came at dawn. He had slept in the canoe, lodged against the southern shore, and was bending over to retrieve his paddle when a Pawnee arrow struck him in the middle of his back. A torturing pain coursed down his backbone as the slim arrow tip struck a nerve, and he might have fainted except for the challenge he had to meet.

Ignoring his wound, he grabbed for his fusil, raised it without panic, took aim and killed one of the braves. Ice-cool, he swabbed the barrel, poured his powder, inserted the patch, put in the ball, tamped it down, took aim and killed another. Methodically, while the blood ran down his back, he reloaded, but no third shot was required, because the Indians recognized that this tough little stranger had great magic.

That long winter's day, with the low sun beating into his canoe, was one Pasquinel would not forget. Reaching blindly behind his back, he tugged at the arrow, but the barbed head had caught on bone and could not be dislodged.

He tried twisting the shaft, but the pain was too great. He tried pushing it in deeper, to get it past the bone, but produced a pain so excruciating that he feared losing consciousness. There was no solution but to leave the arrowhead imbedded, with the shaft protruding, and this he did.

For two days of intense pain he lay in his canoe face down, the arrow projecting upward. At intervals he would sit upright and try to paddle his canoe upstream, his back reacting in agony with each stroke but with the canoe moving ever farther from the Pawnee.

On the third day, when he was satisfied that the arrow was not poisoned and when the point was beginning to adjust to his nerve ends and muscles, he found that he could paddle with some ease, but now the river vanished. It contained no water deep enough for a canoe, and he had no alternative but to cache his spare provisions and proceed on foot.

The digging of a hiding place for the canoe called into play new muscles, and their movement caused new pain, which he alleviated by rotating the shaft until the flint accommodated itself. In one day he finished his job. Then he was ready to resume his journey afoot.

Like all coureurs, he used a stout buffalo-hide headstrap for managing his heavy burden. Passing the strap across his forehead, he allowed the two loose ends to fall down his back, where he fastened them to the load he had to carry. Normally his pack would have rested exactly where the shaft of the arrow protruded, so he had to drop the load several inches, allowing it to bounce off his rump.

In this manner he trailed along the Platte to that extraordinary place where the two branches of the river run side by side, sometimes barely separated, for many miles. There, lucky for him, he met two Cheyenne warriors and in sign language explained what had happened at the Pawnee camp. They became agitated and assured him that any man who fought the Pawnee was a friend. Placing him on his stomach, they tried to rip the arrow out by brute force, but the barbs could not be dislodged.

'Better cut it off beneath the skin,' they said.

'Go ahead,' Pasquinel said.

They handed him an arrow to bite on, then cut deep into his back, and after protracted sawing, they cut off the shaft. Within ten days Pasquinel was able to hoist his burden up from his rump and place it over the scar, where it rode not easily but well. Occasionally, as he hiked, he could feel the arrowhead adjusting itself, but each week it caused less pain.

He reached a Cheyenne village in late February 1796 and traded his bangles and blankets for more than a hundred beaver pelts, which he wadded into two compact bales. Wrapping them in moist deerskin which hardened when it dried, he produced packets like rock.

He now divested himself of every item not crucially needed, fastened the buffalo strap across his forehead and suspended the two bales from it. They weighed just under a hundred pounds each. His essential equipment, including rifle, ammunition, hatchet and trading goods, weighed another seventy pounds. Pasquinel, twenty-six years old that spring, and still suffering the ill effects of his wound, weighed somewhat less than a hundred and fifty pounds, yet he proposed to walk two hundred miles to where his canoe was cached.

Adjusting the huge load as if he were going to carry it from house to barn, he satisfied himself as to its balance and set forth. He created an extraordinary image: a small man, five-feet-four, with enormous shoulders and torso, gained from endless paddling, set upon matchstick legs. Day after day he trod eastward, keeping to the Platte and resting occasionally to drink from its muddy bed. He had to guard against wolves, lurking Indians and quicksand. Sometimes, to relieve the pressure on his temples, he squeezed a thumb beneath the buffalo band across his forehead.

He ate berries and a little pemmican he had made during the winter. He deemed it wise not to pitch camp and cook an antelope, for his fire might attract Indians. The worst of the journey, of course, was the spring insects, but he grew accustomed to them at his eyes, taking consolation in the fact that when summer came their numbers would diminish.

As he shuffled along, he muttered old songs, not for their words, which were trivial, but for their consoling rhythms, which kept him moving:

'My canoe is made of fine bark
Stripped from the whitest birch.
The seams are sewn with strong roots,
The paddles carved from white wood.

'I take this canoe and embark
Down the rapids, down the turbulence.
See how it speeds along
Never losing the current.

'I have traveled along great rivers, the whole St. Lawrence,
And have known the savage tribes and their various tongues.'

On one especially trying day he chanted this song for eight hours, allowing its monotony to pull him along. At dusk a pack of wolves came to the opposite bank for water. They must have recently feasted on a deer, for they looked at Pasquinel, drank and ambled off. This caused him to break into a silly song much loved by the coureurs:

'On my way I chanced to meet
Three cavaliers with horses neat.
Oh, you still make me laugh.
I'll never go back home.
I have great fear of wolves.'

In this way he trudged back to where his canoe lay hidden, and when he got there he sighed with relief, for he suspected that he could not have held out much longer; the burden was simply too great. He rested for a day, then dug the canoe out and ate ravenously of the stored food. Tears did not come to his eyes, for he was not an emotional man, but he did give thanks to La Bonne Sainte Anne for his survival.

He loaded his canoe with the rest of the food and the two hundred and sixty pounds he had been carrying and climbed in, but within that day he discovered that the Platte had so little water he could not move. Disgusted, he got out and started pushing the canoe from behind, and in this way struggled down the middle of the river for about a hundred miles. There the water was only inches deep and he was faced with a difficult decision.

He could either abandon the canoe and resume portaging his pelts all the way to the Missouri, or he could camp where he was for six months and wait for the river to rise; he chose the latter. He built himself a small camp, to which Cheyenne reported from time to time, seeking tobacco. Thus the long summer of 1796 passed, and he lived well on antelope and deer, with now and then a buffalo tongue brought in by the Cheyenne. Twice he visited one of the Cheyenne villages and renewed acquaintance with the two braves who had cut the arrow from his back. One of their squaws was so convinced she could work the flint to the surface—she had done this for her father—that Pasquinel submitted to the ordeal, but she succeeded only in shifting the area of pain.

When the river finally rose, Pasquinel bade farewell to the Cheyenne and resumed his trail eastward. 'Be careful of the Pawnee,' his friends warned.

'Rude Water is still my friend,' he assured them.

'With him be most careful of all,' they said.

When he reached the Pawnee lands, Rude Water greeted him as a son, then set eight braves to wrecking his canoe, stealing his rifle and running off with the precious bales of pelts. Unarmed and without food, Pasquinel was left alone, a hundred and fifty miles from the Missouri.

He did have his knife, and with it he grubbed roots and berries to keep alive. He walked by night, relieved in a sardonic way that he no longer had to carry his packs. By day he slept.

But he by no means intended merely to escape to the Missouri, there to be picked up by some passing white men. He was at war with the whole Pawnee nation and was determined to recover his pelts. He calculated that the Indians would appreciate their value and try to make contact with traders, and that the meeting place might be the confluence of the Platte and the Missouri.

When he reached that forbidding spot he made no effort to hail any of the Company boats he saw floating along with their own cargoes of skins. Instead, he hollowed out a hiding place among the roots of trees and waited. Two weeks passed, then three, and no Pawnee. It didn't matter. He had time. Then in the fourth week he saw two canoes coming down the Platte, heavily laden. As he spied on them he felt a surge of excitement, for there were his pelts, just as he had wrapped them.

His joy was premature, for it looked as if the Indians intended paddling all the way to Saint Louis to dispose of their treasure. The two canoes entered the Missouri River, hesitated, and came back to the Platte. Pasquinel was much relieved when the Pawnee moved ashore and set up camp. They were going to wait for a downriver boat.

They waited. He waited. And one day down the Missouri came a pirogue bearing an improvised sign *Saint Antoine*. As soon as the Pawnee saw it they paddled out to flag it down. They had beaver, much beaver.

'Throw 'em aboard,' the rivermen cried.

While they haggled over price, Pasquinel swam into the middle of the stream, came silently onto the Pawnee canoes, turned one over and began slashing with his knife, killing two Pawnee. In the confusion the rivermen saw a chance to make off with the pelts, so they began firing point-blank at the surviving Indians.

Pasquinel swam alongside the boat, shouting in broken English, 'Thees my peltries!' He was about to climb aboard when one of the rivermen had the presence of mind to club him over the head with an oar. He sank in the river.

He drifted face down, afraid to show signs of life lest they shoot at him, and after they disappeared around the bend he swam ashore. Shaking himself like a dog, and pressing water from his buckskin, he looked for a place to sleep. His canoe, his rifle, his store of beads and his pelts were gone: 'Two years of work, I got one knife, one arrowhead in the back.'

He would not give up. If by some miracle he could reach Saint Louis before the pirates sold his furs, he might still reclaim them, and on that slim chance he acted.

He slept a few hours, then rose in the middle of the night and began running along paths that edged the river. When he reached the spot at which the Missouri turned for its long run to the east, he sought out a Sac village and traded his knife for an old canoe. With only such food as he could collect along the banks, he paddled tirelessly toward the Mississippi, hoping to overtake the robbers.

The day came when he detected a new odor, as if the Missouri were changing character, and in spite of his disappointment at not catching up with the pirates, he felt a rush of excitement. He paddled faster, and as he turned a final bend he saw before him the great, broad expanse of the Mississippi, that noble river flowing south, and he remembered the day on which he first saw this stream, far to the north. He had decided then to explore it all, and in the pleasure of meeting an old friend, he forgot his anger.

The Missouri ran much faster than the Mississippi and carried such a burden of sand and silt that it spewed a visible bar deep into the heart of the greater river; as Pasquinel rode the current far toward the Illinois shore, he could see that delicate line in the water where the mud of the Missouri touched the clear water of the Mississippi. For twenty miles downstream this line continued, two mighty rivers flowing side by side without mingling.

Rivermen said, 'The Mississippi, she's a lady. The Missouri, he's a roughneck, plunging at her with muddy hands. For twenty miles she fights him off, keeping him at a distance, but in the end, like the mayor's daughter who marries the coureur, she surrenders.'

When Pasquinel reached the calmer waters of the Mississippi he turned his canoe southward, and within the hour saw the sight which gladdened the hearts of all rivermen: the beautiful, low, white walls of Spain's San Luis de Iluenses, queen of the south, mistress of the north and gateway to the west. When the little town first hove into view Pasquinel halted for a moment, lifted his paddle over his head, and giving the town its French name, muttered, 'Saint Louis, we are coming home . . . empty-handed . . . for the last time.'

In that critical period in central North America a thousand small settlements were started, and some by the year 1796 had grown like Saint Louis into prosperous towns with nine hundred citizens, but most of those would subsequently languish. Saint Louis alone would grow into one of the world's great cities. Why?

Brains. When Pierre Laclède, the Frenchman who started the settlement in 1764, did preliminary exploring to find a perfect site, he naturally chose that spot where the Missouri empties into the Mississippi; logic said that with two rivers the location had to be ideal, except that when he investigated the spot he found mud and brush twenty feet high in the trees. That could only mean floods and he abandoned that spot in a hurry.

Accompanied by his thirteen-year-old assistant, he moved a little farther south and found another attractive site, but it, too, had straw in the branches, so he continued to move south, league by league, and at the eighteenth mile he found what he was looking for: a solid bluff standing twenty to thirty feet above water, with two secure landing places upstream and down. This location provided everything needed for the growth of a major settlement: river port, lowlands for industry, higher sites for homes, fresh water, and to the west an endless forest.

Brains had done it. When other settlements along the Missouri and the Mississippi were under water during recurrent floods, Saint Louis rode high and clear. When other harbors silted up, the river scoured the waterfront at Saint Louis, keeping it clear of sand, so that commerce could continue. In 1796 no one could predict whether it was to thrive or not, but as Pasquinel paddled his canoe into the landing, he was satisfied on one point: 'This is the best town on the river.'

As soon as he landed he started asking in French, 'Have you seen the pirogue, *Saint Antoine*?' A fur buyer said, 'Yes, it was sold for lumber.'

Pasquinel ran to the southern end of town, where a carpenter from New Orleans bought boats as they finished their run and broke them up for timber. *Saint Antoine*? 'Yes. Broke it up two weeks ago.' Where did the men go? 'Who knows? They sold their pelts and they're gone.' Where are my pelts? 'Part of some shipment on its way to New Orleans.' Bitter and without a sou, he moved about the town, cursing Indians and rivermen alike.

Saint Louis would have a confused history, owned by France, then Spain, then France again, then America. Officially it was now Spanish, but actually it was French. Indeed, even the Spanish governor was sometimes a Frenchman, and all of the businessmen. The latter fairly well controlled the fur trade, for they received licenses and monopolies from the Spanish government in New Orleans to trade on this or that river, and it was to them that individuals like Pasquinel had to look for both their financing and their legal permission to trade.

There was a Company, run by a combine of wealthy citizens; there were also private entrepreneurs who were granted monopolies and who then outfitted coureurs, and Pasquinel had worked for one of them. But after the present disaster this gentleman showed no further interest in sinking additional capital in such a risky venture. Pasquinel therefore moved from one French license holder to the next, trying to cadge money to outfit his next expedition: 'You buy me a canoe, some silver, beads, cloth . . . I bring you plenty peltries.' No one was interested: 'Pasquinel? What did he bring back last time? Nothing.'

Along the waterfront a riverman told him of a doctor who had recently fled the revolution in France: 'Dr. Guisbert. Very clever man. He can cut that arrowhead out of your back.' He went to see the newcomer, an enthusiastic man, who told him, 'On your trips you should read Voltaire and Rousseau. To understand why we no longer have a king in France.'

'I know nothing of France,' Pasquinel said.

'Good! I'll lend you some books.'

'I can't read.'

Dr. Guisbert inspected his back, moving the flint with his fingers, and said, 'I'd leave it alone.' As Pasquinel replaced his shirt, Dr. Guisbert gave the flint a sudden push with his thumb, but the trapper barely winced. 'Good,' Guisbert said. 'If you can stand the pain, it's doing no damage.'

He liked the spunky coureur and asked, 'Where'd you get that wound?' Pasquinel haltingly began to explain, and Guisbert became so interested in beaver pelts and Cheyenne villages that the conversation continued for some time, with the doctor saying impulsively, 'One of my patients is a merchant who has a trading license from the governor. Perhaps we can form a partnership, we three.'

And so, staked with the doctor's money and under the protection of the merchant's license, Pasquinel prepared once more for the river.

He bought himself a new rifle, twice the trade goods he had had before, and a sturdy canoe. At the wharf Dr. Guisbert told him, 'You wonder why I risk my money? When I pushed that arrowhead deeper into your back, I know it hurt very much. A man doesn't learn to bear pain like that without having courage. I think you'll bring back pelts.'

On New Year's Day, 1797, Pasquinel reappeared at the Pawnee village to settle affairs with Chief Rude Water: 'If you send your braves to attack me this time, I will kill them and then kill you. But that won't happen, because you and I are trusted friends.' A calumet was smoked, and he told Rude Water, 'Last year we fight. Frenchmen run off with pelts. This year we friends.' Again the calumet was smoked, and Pasquinel concluded the deal: 'I come back, I give you one pelt in five.'

Rude Water assigned four braves to escort Pasquinel to the point where the Platte ran out of water, and there they helped him cache his canoe, bidding him good luck as he departed for alien country.

That winter he traded well with the Cheyenne, but when he had assembled two bales of pelts, a Ute war party stumbled upon him and decided this was a good chance to grab a rifle. For two days he defended himself and was able to survive only because the Ute did not learn quickly how long it took him to reload. In the end one daring brave dashed in, touched him with his coup-stick and retreated, claiming victory. This satisfied the Indians and they withdrew.

This year, remembering the torture of that previous portage, he had planned to lug the pelts downstream one bale at a time: take the first bale down, cache it, come back for the second; cache it, then proceed with the first in a continuing operation. But with the Ute on the move, he judged that he must not risk so prolonged an operation, and he loaded himself as before.

For thirty-two days he staggered down the river, his muscles bulging, his eyes nearly popping from his head. When he reached the hiding place for his canoe, he was in better condition than when he started. Placing the freight in his fragile craft, he pushed it downstream across the sandbars of summer. He had covered less than a hundred miles when he saw with quiet joy four Pawnee braves approaching to help.

Standing ankle-deep in the Platte, he hailed them. 'Many furs,' he said in sign language.

'Big happening!' they said in sign, pointing downstream toward their village. 'We have white man.'

'Who?' They could not explain except to say, 'Red hair, red beard.'

As they neared the village Chief Rude Water came to greet them, holding in his hand a buffalo thong, the far end of which was attached to the neck of a tall red-bearded young white man about nineteen years old. With a neat flick of the halter, Rude Water tossed him forward so that he stood facing Pasquinel, and in this unusual manner the coureur met Alexander McKeag.

'Depuis combien de temps êtes-vous ici?' Pasquinel asked.

'Six months,' McKeag replied in broken French, using a low, gentle voice. 'Captured tryin' to go upstream . . . to trade for beaver.'

'Il y a des castors là-bas,' Pasquinel said.

He showed Rude Water the two heavy bales and reminded him that one-fifth of the pelts belonged to the Pawnee, but when the braves started to rip the bales open, Pasquinel shouted for them to stop. He then tried to explain in sign that it would be more profitable to the Indians if they allowed him, Pasquinel, to sell the pelts in Saint Louis.

'I speak Pawnee,' McKeag interrupted quietly.

'Tell him he'll get more goods.'

In this way Alexander McKeag, refugee from a tyrannical laird in the Highlands of Scotland—whom he had clubbed over the head with a knotted walking stick—started his career as interpreter. He convinced Chief Rude Water that the Indians would profit if they allowed Pasquinel to represent them in Saint Louis, whereupon Rude Water asked, 'How do we know he will bring the goods back?'

When this was translated, the Frenchman said, 'I am Pasquinel. I came among you unafraid.'

The pact was sealed with a calumet, and after Pasquinel had smoked his share, he stepped to McKeag and untied the buffalo thong. 'Dites-leur que vous êtes mon associé,' he said, and in this way the partnership was formed.

Their first venture was a dandy. Pasquinel huddled with Rude Water and said, 'Remember those rivermen? Killed your braves. Stole our pelts.' Rude Water did remember. 'They ought to be coming back down the river about now. Lend me some braves who can swim.'

A war party of nine canoed down to the Missouri and camped there for some weeks, watching several fine boats drift past, *Saint Geneviève*, *Saint Michel*, laden with pelts from the Mandan villages.

And then the boat they waited for appeared, long and ragged, like the *Saint Antoine*, with the same rough men lounging with rifles, waiting for something to shoot at.

'Maintenant,' Pasquinel whispered to McKeag. 'Vous partez. They won't know you.'

So McKeag pushed his canoe into the Missouri and called, 'Hey there! Passage to Saint Louis? I have pelts.'

The boat slowed. The man at the rudder fanned water and another with a pole worked against the current. The leader studied McKeag, saw he was under twenty, and cried cheerfully, 'Sure. Throw the pelts up.' One of the men slipped to the rear, taking a heavy oar with which to knock McKeag senseless once the pelts were aboard.

As the rivermen reached for the bales, Pasquinel put a bullet through the head of the leader. With terrifying calm he handed the smoking rifle to a Pawnee helper, took McKeag's rifle and drilled a bullet into the man lurking with the oar. He then reached for a third gun, but by this time the Pawnee braves were climbing aboard the flatboat, where the remaining crew were massacred. Young McKeag, who had never seen Indians lift a scalp, was shaking by the time Pasquinel got aboard.

'I didn't think we'd kill them,' he said softly.

Pasquinel said, 'L'année dernière ils ont essayé de me tuer.'

'How do you know they're the same men?' McKeag asked.

'That one I know. That one too. The others? Mauvais compagnons vous apportent de la mal chance—Bad companions bring bad luck.'

Young McKeag was impressed by the assurance with which Pasquinel operated; the Frenchman was only eight years older, but he always seemed to know what to do. 'Throw the bodies overboard,' he told the Pawnee, and after McKeag interpreted this, he added, 'Tell them they can have anything on the boat they want.' McKeag protested that he and Pasquinel could use some of the gear, but the Frenchman snapped, 'I want it to look as if pirates had struck,' and he smiled thinly as the braves did their ransacking. When the Pawnee headed their canoes back toward the Platte, McKeag started to wash down the decks, but Pasquinel stopped him: 'I want blood to show—especially the hair—when we talk to the soldiers in Saint Louis.'

Pasquinel defeated and Pasquinel victorious were two different men. This year he brought the pirogue with its cargo of furs to the Company landing like a Roman proconsul returning from Dacia. Seeking out the merchants who had invested in the pirogue, he described the savage attack by the Pawnee, the scalping of the crew, McKeag's bravery and his own gunning down of the Indian miscreants. He displayed the matted hair, the blood, and bowed gracefully when they applauded his defense of their property. He turned his own bales over to Dr. Guisbert.

He began to enjoy himself in Saint Louis. Without money Pasquinel had been withdrawn; with it he became a robust, singing drunk. The lonely discipline of the prairie vanished and he spent his profits lavishly, for the sheer love of spending. He financed vagrants for explorations they would never make, and paid off old debts with bonuses.

After two months of this, he was broke. Sobering up, he applied to Dr. Guisbert for his next advance. The doctor had been expecting the call and did not flinch when Pasquinel said, 'This year, twice as much. I have a partner now.'

*　　*　　*

He and McKeag paddled slowly upstream with enough trade guns for Chief Rude Water to drive the Arapaho and Cheyenne clear off the plains. At the village McKeag saw the white men's scalps and felt sick, but Pasquinel told him, 'The coureur, he ends as a scalp. Vous peut-être, et moi aussi.'

The winter of 1799 was the one they spent at Beaver Creek, meeting for the first time Lame Beaver of the Arapaho. It was that winter, too, when McKeag performed the impossible, learning a little Arapaho so that he could later serve as interpreter for them.

They formed a strange pair, this short stocky Frenchman and this slim red-bearded Scot. Each was taciturn when on the prairie; neither pried into the affairs of the other. Without commenting on the fact, McKeag had now heard Pasquinel tell others that his wife was in Montreal, Detroit and New Orleans, and he began to suspect that there was none. It would never have occurred to him to ask outright, 'Pasquinel, you married?' for that would be intrusive.

When McKeag developed into a competent shot, Pasquinel taught him the one overriding secret of successful trading: 'Keep your powder dry.'

'How do you do that when the canoe upsets?'

'Simple. You buy your powder, then you buy your lead for the bullets. With the lead you make a little keg . . . very tight lid . . . wax on top . . . sealed in deerskin.'

'Why not buy the keg?'

'Ah! That's the secret. You make the keg out of just enough lead to be melted into bullets for the powder. When the powder's gone, the keg's gone.'

He taught McKeag how to use the two-ball mold into which the melted lead was poured to produce good bullets; he gave a further exhibition of his resourcefulness when the Scotsman broke the wooden stock on his rifle. To McKeag it looked as if his gun was ruined, for he could not fit it against his shoulder or take aim, but for Pasquinel the problem was simple.

He fitted the three pieces of wood together, then steamed a chunk of buffalo hide until it was gelatinous. With a bone needle and elk sinew he sewed the skin as tightly as he could about the broken wood, but McKeag tried it and said, 'Still wobbles.'

'Attends!' Pasquinel said, and he placed the rifle with its pliable buffalo patch in winter sunlight, and as the moisture was drawn out, the skin tightened, becoming harder than wood, until the stock was stronger than when McKeag bought it.

One sun-filled morning in May, as they were wandering together north of Rattlesnake Buttes looking for antelope, McKeag had a flash of insight: it occurred to him that he and Pasquinel were the freest men in the world. They were bound by nothing; they owed no one allegiance;

they could move as they wished over an empire larger than France or Scotland; they slept where they willed, worked when they wished, and ate well from the land's bounty.

As he looked at the boundless horizon that lovely day he appreciated what freedom meant: no Highland laird before whom he must grab his forelock. Pasquinel was subservient to no Montreal banker. They were free men, utterly free.

He was so moved by this discovery that he wanted to share it with Pasquinel. 'We are free,' he said. And Pasquinel, looking to the east, replied, 'They will be moving upon us soon.' And McKeag felt a shadow encroaching upon his freedom, and after that day he never felt quite so untrammeled.

In the fall of 1799 Dr. Guisbert staked them for an exploratory trip up the North Platte. It was a difficult journey, past strange formations and along lonely stretches of near-desert. They saw congregations of rock which resembled buildings in some dream city. They saw needles, and passes between red cliffs, and long defiles through ghostly white mountains.

'Impossible country,' McKeag said one evening as they camped among strange towers.

'Il y a des castors,' Pasquinel replied.

When they left the area of monuments they entered territory occupied by a tribe of Dakota, and the Indians sent braves to notify them that they could not continue their march. Pasquinel directed McKeag to say, 'We shall continue. Trading beaver.'

The Dakota, furious at their insolence, withdrew behind a small hill, and Pasquinel warned McKeag, 'Tonight we fight for our trade.' And he showed the young Scot how best to prepare for an Indian fight: 'Be ready to kill or be killed. Then see that it doesn't happen.'

Just before dusk the Dakota swept in on horseback, with every apparent intention of destroying the two intruders. 'Don't fire!' Pasquinel warned McKeag. But Pasquinel did. He sent a bullet well in front of the warriors. Then he took McKeag's gun and sent one harmlessly behind. The Indians wheeled, came roaring back, and this time Pasquinel held his fire altogether. One Dakota touched McKeag, then off they stormed, shouting and kicking their horses.

Next day Pasquinel calmly packed his gear, stowed his rifles and led the way upriver. At the Dakota camp he conducted powwow with the chiefs, giving them presents and assuring them there would be more on the return trip. No word was said of the attack the previous night or of the bullets fired.

When the traders were safely out of Dakota territory, Pasquinel said, 'If you give an Indian a fair chance, you can avoid killing.' He paused. 'In years to come those braves will sit around the campfire and tell about the coup they made on the two white men . . . the whistling bullets.'

He smiled sardonically, then added, 'And you will sit in Scotland and tell of the tomahawks and the arrows.'

In this manner they made their way among the various tribes. At each step they were surrounded, though they could not see them, by thousands of courageous Indians who could have destroyed them. There were skirmishes, but if they held firm and did not run, they were allowed to move westward.

The skirmishes were testings, like the ancient war parties the Arapaho had sent against the Pawnee and the Pawnee against the Comanche. They were moves in an elaborate game by which the white man probed and the Indian reacted, and when word passed through the tribes, 'Pasquinel, he can be trusted,' it was better than a passport. A multitude of coureurs from Montreal, St. Louis and Oregon would in the years ahead traverse Indian country, and for every man who was killed, six hundred would pass in safety.

Pasquinel and McKeag decided to winter at one of the loveliest spots in all America, that trim peninsula formed where the North Platte was joined by a dark, swift river sweeping in from the west. In later years it would be called after a French coureur de bois who had once trapped with Pasquinel, Jacques La Ramee. No finer river crossed the plains; deep and clean, the Laramie formed a haven for beaver. Wild turkey nested and deer came to feed. Ducks sought refuge, and elk. Buffalo used it as their watering spot, and on dead branches, brown-gray hawks stood guard.

In that winter of 1800 the team acquired six bales of superior peltries and were about to head south when a band of Shoshone attacked. The Indians were driven off, but returned to lay siege. A desultory gunfight occurred, but nothing much would have happened except that one Shoshone dashed into camp, astonished McKeag by counting coup on him, and the Scotsman reached for his gun, whereupon the Indian struck him with a tomahawk, gashing his right shoulder.

The wound festered. McKeag became delirious, and any thought of his lugging bales east that June had to be abandoned.

In lucid moments, when McKeag comprehended the dangerous position in which he had placed his partner, he urged Pasquinel to move out: 'Begone with you. I'm bound to die.' Pasquinel did not bother to answer. Grimly but with tenderness he tended his stricken partner.

The wound worsened. It became repulsive and threatened death; its smell contaminated the hut. In one of his lucid moments McKeag begged, 'Cut it off.' Pasquinel replied, 'If you had no arm, how would you fire a gun?'

By mid-July it appeared that McKeag was doomed; again he pleaded with Pasquinel to amputate the arm, and again the Frenchman refused. Instead, he took his ax, chopped a mass of fine wood and built a fire. When it crackled, he plunged the ax in, allowing it to become red-hot.

Without warning, he slammed the incandescent metal against the corrupt shoulder, pinning McKeag to the paillasse as he did so.

There was a stench of burning flesh, a sound of screaming. Pasquinel maintained pressure on the ax until he judged that he had done enough. This drastic treatment halted the corruption; it also permanently destroyed some of the muscles in McKeag's right arm. Henceforth it would be cocked at the elbow. When he realized what Pasquinel had done, or rather not done, he ranted, 'Why didn't you cut it off altogether?' He lapsed into delirium and would probably have died had not Lame Beaver's band of Arapaho wandered by on the prowl for buffalo.

When women from the camp saw McKeag's condition they knew what had to be done, and they sent girls into the stream beds, looking for those plants which were effective in poultices, and soon the swelling subsided.

'Bad scar,' Blue Leaf told McKeag in Arapaho as she tended him.

'He'll use his arm,' Pasquinel asserted when this was translated.

One morning while three Arapaho women were watching him—and thinking he was asleep—they began women's talk about the various braves in camp, and in the robust manner of Indian women, who were never intimidated by their men, they began discussing the sexual equipment of the braves, pointing out any conspicuous deficiencies. Such talk disturbed McKeag, who had been reared in a strict Presbyterian home, and he became even more uncomfortable as the gossip grew rowdier, with even Lame Beaver's capacity reviewed and found wanting.

At this point Blue Leaf came in and the women stopped their talking, but she could guess what the subject of their conversation had been. 'This one speaks our language,' she reminded them, and the three watchers moved to the bed to see if McKeag was awake, and when they were satisfied that he was not, they resumed their chatter and one said that she had seen him when she bathed him and that he seemed even poorer than one of Our People. Blue Leaf silenced them and drove them from the lodge; then she roused McKeag to poultice his shoulder.

Among the Indian girls who gathered medicinal plants was Clay Basket, then eleven and promising to be as pretty as her mother. During the long afternoons she sat with McKeag, learning a little English. She warned him not to call her father *chief*, for he had never been one. She tried to explain why, but could not make herself clear. Instead, she fetched the buffalo hide which recounted his many coups, and there McKeag saw the Arapaho version of Lame Beaver's invasion of their tipi two years before. Looking at the impressive record of Lame Beaver's feats, he told Clay Basket, 'Your father chief . . . big chief,' and she was pleased.

It was now too late for the traders to return down the Platte, so they prepared to winter at the confluence, strengthening the walls of their hut and making pemmican. McKeag was too weak to hunt, nor was it known whether he would ever be able to fire a gun again, for his shoulder remained a gaping wound. He stayed in the lodge, doing what work he could and talking with Clay Basket about why the Cheyenne were trusted allies and the Comanche wicked enemies.

One afternoon Pasquinel returned with an antelope. He was in an evil mood and with a curse threw the animal at McKeag's feet. Then he grabbed McKeag's rifle and pointed to the stock that he had mended with buffalo hide.

'Goddamn! Same thing your shoulder!' He searched for English words, found none, and in frustration, resorted to a method of direct communication which shocked the Indian girl. Pulling his right arm far back, he struck McKeag in the wounded shoulder so forcefully that he knocked him down. Before McKeag could regain his feet, he struck him twice more, then thrust the gun at him, shouting, 'Use it. Take gun. Goddamn, use it.' With that he shoved McKeag from the hut.

McKeag, followed by Clay Basket, walked to the banks of the river, and with considerable pain, placed the gunstock against his right shoulder, but he could not muster the strength to lift his hand to the trigger. Sweat stood on his forehead, and against his will, for he did not want an Indian child to see him cry, tears filled his eyes. 'It's too much,' he groaned.

He would have halted the experiment at that point, but Clay Basket now understood what Pasquinel intended. Either McKeag must learn to function again, or die during the winter. She forced him to lodge the rifle once more against his shoulder. Then taking his right hand in hers, she slowly raised his arm, breaking the scar tissue, until his hand touched the trigger. He bit his lip, held the hand there for some seconds, then let it fall.

Again and again Clay Basket forced the hand up, and there the lesson ended for that day. McKeag refused to speak to Pasquinel, who ignored him.

On the third day Clay Basket lifted the hand easily into position, and when she was satisfied that McKeag could do this by himself, she took the rifle from him, swabbed it, poured in some powder and inserted a ball, as she had learned to do. Ramming the load home, she thrust the gun back into his hands and said, 'Now.'

'I can't,' McKeag protested, refusing to accept the gun.

'Now,' she cried.

She badgered him into taking the gun and raising it into firing position. Slowly she brought his right hand to the stock, placing his forefinger on the trigger. 'Now,' she said softly.

Apprehensive of the pain that was about to strike him, McKeag could not pull the trigger. Clay Basket looked at him with pity, thinking of how her father had hung suspended by his breast for a whole day. When it was apparent that McKeag was not going to fire, she raised herself on her toes, placed her small finger over his and gave a powerful jerk backward.

With a shattering explosion the gun fired. She had poured enough powder to fill a cannon, and when Pasquinel rushed from the lodge, all he could see was a cloud of black smoke and McKeag on the ground.

His wound was opened by the recoil, but Blue Leaf stanched the flow of blood with wet leaves. A week later, when scar tissue had barely begun to form, Clay Basket had McKeag out again with the gun. 'This time I load,' he said, but when he actually held the stock against his shoulder, the pain was too much. So once again the girl slipped her finger over his and pulled the trigger. When he voluntarily reloaded and fired again, she was so proud of his courage, she shyly pressed her lips against his beard.

It was now time for the Arapaho to move on, to locate one more herd whose meat would sustain them through the winter. Lame Beaver came by to say farewell, and Blue Leaf, stately as a spruce, assured McKeag that his shoulder was now mended. Clay Basket, bright in beads, gently touched their faces and told them in English, 'I know you come back.'

The snows came and winds swept down from the north. The river froze and even deer had trouble finding water. From aloft eagles inspected the camp, and the two men sat in their lodge and waited.

There were days, of course, when the winds ceased and the sun shone as if it were summer. Then the partners, naked to the waist, worked outdoors. In their lodges the beaver began to stir, as if this were spring, and elk grazed in the meadows.

But such interludes were followed by storms and temperatures thirty degrees below zero. For three weeks that February the men were snowed under: drifts came clear across their lodge, and like animals they had to burrow out. This caused no concern; they had a comfortable supply of meat and wood. For water they could melt snow—God knows, there was enough of it.

They had no books . . . no loss . . . neither could read. They had no work, no place to go, no problem but survival. So there, deep beneath the snow, they waited. For five hundred miles in any direction there were no white men, unless perhaps some stubborn voyageur from Detroit had holed up in some valley to the north, like them, awaiting spring.

Occasionally they talked, but mostly they sat in silence. Already they had six bales of beaver, worth at least $3600, plus prospects for six more during the coming season. They were rich men, if they could sneak the pelts back through the Indian country.

On the rare occasions when they did speak they used a strange language: French-Pawnee-English. McKeag's native tongue was Gaelic, a poetic language spoken softly. When he uttered words it was with a certain shyness; Pasquinel was more glib. But even so, whole days passed with hardly a word being said.

Then the snowfall diminished and drifts began to melt. Mountain streams grew strong and the river became a torrent. Beaver in their lodges began to stir and moose dropped last year's antlers. Buffalo pawed at the earth and wild turkeys came down from their winter roosts. During warm spells rattlesnakes emerged from deep rocky crevices. One day when the full wonder of spring was about them, Pasquinel said, 'We trade six weeks, go home.'

As they were returning down the Missouri, along that endless east-west reach the river takes before it enters the Mississippi, their rhythmic paddling was interrupted by the appearance of a solitary man bringing a canoe upstream and shouting their names: 'Pasquinel! McKeag! Great news for you.'

Sweating with nervousness, he pulled his canoe alongside theirs and introduced himself: 'Joseph Bean, Kentucky.' His attention focused immediately on the bales, and he said, 'What good luck I bring you. I act as agent for Hermann Bockweiss.' He stopped, as if this startling information carried its own interpretation.

'Qui est-il?' Pasquinel asked.

'Silversmith from Germany. Makes wonderful trinkets for the Indian trade.' Pasquinel shrugged his shoulders, and Bean continued frenetically: 'Came to Saint Louis last January. Heard you were the best trader on the river. Says he will advance the money for your trips.'

Pasquinel replied brusquely, 'No need. I work Dr. Guisbert.'

'Aha!' the American cried. 'That's just it! Dr. Guisbert . . . his partner died and he moved to New Orleans for a rich life downriver.' He explained the new situation in Saint Louis: Pasquinel would deliver Guisbert's pelts to the German, who would sell and send Dr. Guisbert . . .

On and on Bean went, an irritating man, perspiring constantly, but so insistent that the traders had to consider this invitation. When they finally landed at Saint Louis they saw gleaming down at them from the shore the round, plump face of Hermann Bockweiss, silversmith, lately from Munich.

He occupied the house formerly owned by Dr. Guisbert, and in the rooms that had once been devoted to medicine he plied his delicate trade. Using silver imported from Germany and brought up the Mississippi from New Orleans, he fabricated not only the trinkets so loved by the Indians but also the ornate jewelry desired by women as far north as Detroit.

His own childlike enthusiasm enabled him to predict what gleaming device would catch an Indian's fancy. It was he who invented the ear wheel for the squaws, dainty pendants enclosing tiny wheels which revolved, and silver-inlaid tomahawks for the braves. He offered a set of five half-moon pins for women and three wide bands for the upper arm of a man. His specialty was the fish-eyed brooch, an ordinary flat pin upon which he had deposited a score of small, glistening beads of silver; his most impressive item was the silver-chased peace pipe, a stunning affair adorned with pendants of multicolored beads.

At the same time this canny German realized that in the long run his profits would have to come from whatever trade he established with the local gentry, and he had real skill in combining the demands of French elegance with the sturdy approach to silver design he had learned in Bavaria. Indeed, a Bockweiss piece tended to become an heirloom, a subtle blending of two cultures.

His relationship with Pasquinel was interesting. Since Saint Louis still had fewer than a thousand inhabitants, there was no public hotel, and coureurs from the west had to find such lodging as they could in private homes. Most families did not care to board the filthy and profane men, but Bockweiss insisted that Pasquinel and McKeag accept his hospitality. He had two daughters, Lise, the strong-minded one, and Grete, the coquette, and he convinced himself that one day the coureurs would become his sons-in-law. Normally a father in Saint Louis would have preferred his daughters to marry more substantial types, say, established businessmen, but Bockweiss had not made the long journey from Munich to Saint Louis because he was cautious. He was a romantic who relished the idea of probing unsettled prairies and saw that McKeag and Pasquinel fitted the pattern of his new country. So the coureurs moved in to rooms above the shop, and Bockweiss noticed with gratification that Lise was developing an interest in Pasquinel, while Grete confided that she thought McKeag congenial.

There was competition. Local girls, spotting the way Pasquinel spent his money buying presents for anyone connected with the fur trade, thought he might make a good husband. He was generous. He was entertaining. In looks . . . well, he was small but he was not ridiculous. Best of all, he seemed to be lucky.

They made known their interest, but Pasquinel excused himself, as he always did, on grounds that he already had a wife in Quebec. He was willing to give them money, pay for their drinks and bed with them as chance provided, but he could express no interest in marriage.

Lise Bockweiss was not so easy to dispose of. She was a solid, forthright girl with all the domestic qualifications a husband might expect. She also had a sense of humor and could appreciate the comedy in watching the New Orleans French girls trying to catch this elusive trader. She was taller than Pasquinel but she had the knack of making him seem important when she was with him, and from time to time even Pasquinel had the fleeting thought: This one could make 'une bonne femme.'

The four ate together frequently, but between Grete and McKeag little was happening. He was timorous with ladies and blushed as red as his beard when pretty Grete teased, 'I'll bet you have a squaw hidden upstream.' It was not long before young Grete concluded that there was little future for her in wooing McKeag, and she turned her attentions to a shopkeeper who appreciated her.

It was more difficult for Pasquinel to evade Lise. For one thing, her father took a heavy-handed interest in the courtship; he was aware that Lise was seriously considering the coureur and he did not propose to let the Frenchman slip away. Bockweiss could not believe Pasquinel's vague talk of having a wife. He persuaded the coureur to visit with him in his shop, and in the process of explaining how he cast his jewelry he found opportunity to speak of his daughter: 'That one has a solid head on her shoulders. A man would always be proud of that one.'

The silver reached him in ingots, which he melted in a small furnace activated by an arm-powered bellows: 'Lise's mother taught her how to cook . . . good.'

When the silver assumed liquid form, he poured it meticulously into molds shaped like butterflies, or wheels, or arm bracelets: 'It's no easy thing to bring two daughters all the way from Germany, but when they are both angels, especially Lise, it's worth it.'

When the silver cooled, he used delicate files to remove any excess, catching it for reuse later. Then he took the pieces to a buffer wheel, turned by a foot pedal, and as he pumped he said, 'A man with a good business like you ought to marry. I myself plan to marry again next year, but of course, finding a good woman isn't easy.'

He now took the pieces and began the delicate etching and decoration which made a Bockweiss silver piece so desirable. He had large, fat fingers which seemed unsuitable for intricate work, but he used his tools with such skill that he could carve almost any design: 'Pasquinel, let me be frank. I sell a piece like this for ten dollars. I'm going to be a wealthy man. With my daughters, especially Lise, I can afford to be generous. You would have a fixed home here in Saint Louis. A fixed home is something.'

As the time approached for the traders to return to their rivers, Lise Bockweiss took over where her father had stopped. She gave a dinner to which Pasquinel was invited and showed him concentrated attention, after which her father took the Frenchman aside and said, 'As long as the world lasts, women will want jewelry and Indians will want trinkets. You do the trading. I'll make the silver. It will be a good partnership.'

He continued expansively: 'And as your partner, Pasquinel, I would be very happy . . . that is . . . should you at some point in time wish to join my family.' This was said with Germanic gravity and with such obvious regard for Lise's welfare that not even Pasquinel could treat it jokingly. A proposal was being made, one most advantageous, and he was forced to give it attention.

McKeag, watching this from a comfortable distance, since Grete was no longer applying pressure on him, saw that his partner was being maneuvered into marriage, and he began to take seriously Pasquinel's repeated statements that he had a wife somewhere else, Montreal or New Orleans or Quebec. He was not surprised, therefore, when Bockweiss invited him to the shop one day to speak of this matter, but he was taken aback when he found Grete's shopkeeper there, accompanied by a blonde from New Orleans.

'Herr McKeag,' Bockweiss said bluntly, 'this young lady has told us that your partner Pasquinel has a wife in New Orleans. What of that?'

McKeag took a deep breath, looked first at the girl, then at the shopkeeper, and said, 'Pasquinel jokes about this . . . to keep from getting trapped. One time he says he has a wife in Montreal, another time Quebec. I suppose he said New Orleans too.'

Bockweiss laughed nervously, but with obvious relief. The blonde, however, felt that she had been insulted and was not disposed to let the matter drop. 'He told me nothing. I heard it from a New Orleans girl. When I told her that I liked Pasquinel, she said, "No good. He has a wife in New Orleans." '

'Did she know the wife?' Bockweiss asked.

'How do I know?'

'You could ask her.'

'Ask? Ask? She's gone.'

The meeting was inconclusive, and Bockweiss, feeling an impropriety in having raised such a question about a potential son-in-law, yet wanting reassurance as a father, suggested that perhaps McKeag might want to question his partner, but at this the Scotsman rebelled. Blushing deeply, he fumbled, 'I wouldn't know . . . I couldn't.'

So the businessman was deputized to interrogate Pasquinel, and it was a futile interview. The little Frenchman laughed and said, 'This town is too much. I better get back to the Indians.'

'But do you have a wife in New Orleans?' the man pressed.

'No.'

After this reassurance the Bockweiss family concluded there was no impediment. Plans went forward for a wedding, even though the groom had not said definitely that he was entering into the union, and finally Bockweiss put the matter to him bluntly: 'Can we have the wedding before you go back to the plains?'

'Yes.'

It was a charming affair. Normally the local French would have ignored such a wedding, but the Bockweiss family came from South Germany, an area friendly to France, and in addition, were Catholic, which made them doubly welcome in the community. At the celebration, Bockweiss and his daughters made a favorable and lasting impression on the inhabitants, while Pasquinel, looking very short and muscular beside his taller German wife, behaved himself, and the approving news was flashed through the crowd: 'He's turning over whatever savings he has to his wife. Bockweiss has acquired a grant of land from the governor, and she's building a big house.' Before the coureurs left Saint Louis, the new bride assured McKeag, 'We'll always keep one room for you,' but when the canoe was heading west the Scotsman thought, One more freedom gone.

In the late summer of 1803, as they came down the Platte from Rattlesnake Buttes with seven bales of beaver, they heard at the Pawnee village news that was doubly sad. Chief Rude Water had been slain by an Arapaho war party: 'Big devil Lame Beaver, he staked himself out. Shot Rude Water.'

'Pasquinel!' McKeag called. 'You hear that? The Arapaho who helped us up north, Lame Beaver. He killed Rude Water.'

'What happened to Lame Beaver?'

McKeag translated this for the Pawnee, and they replied, 'We killed him.'

Pasquinel shook his head sadly. 'Deux braves hommes . . . morts. Dommage, Dommage.'

Then the Pawnee continued with additional information that proved even more startling: 'Lame Beaver killed Rude Water only because he used special bullets.' And they showed Pasquinel the two bullets.

'They're gold!' Pasquinel cried, letting them drop heavily into a cup.

McKeag interrogated the braves for nearly an hour, trying to determine how Lame Beaver could have obtained gold bullets, and in the end it was agreed that he must have located a lode. Where? No one knew. When? It must have been after the winter when the Arapaho helped cure McKeag's shoulder, because that year there was no evidence of gold bullets.

'Where did he go that winter, after he left us?' Pasquinel asked.

'After buffalo,' McKeag answered. 'Don't you remember? They said, "We've got to find one more herd before winter?" That's what they said.'

'Are there any mountains north of that river?' Pasquinel demanded.

The question was interpreted for the Pawnee, who answered, 'No. Flat. Flat.'

Pasquinel became obsessed with Lame Beaver and his gold bullets. Somewhere this clever Indian had found gold. The trick now was to determine where. Guidance could come only from Blue Leaf; she would know where her husband had found his treasure, so during the forthcoming season they would seek her out and extract the secret. In the meantime, they would carry the two gold bullets to Saint Louis and sell them for the Pawnee.

Unfortunately, when he reached home, Pasquinel's preoccupation with the bullets diverted his attention from the inventive work his wife had completed during his absence. Applying the funds he had left with her, plus others she had wheedled from her father, she had purchased a lot on the residential Rue des Granges. It commanded a comprehensive view of the town; it seemed above the river yet part of it. Here she had built a good stone house with a porch on four sides. The house contained many features suitable for dwelling along the edge of a German forest, yet its outward appearance was completely French, built only of such materials as a frontier town could provide. If a needed brick or fabric was unobtainable, she turned up some ingenious substitute.

And she was the major adornment of the house, a large, capable young woman with zest for whatever was happening in the world. If persons of importance passed through Saint Louis to the western frontier, she wanted to know them, to talk with them of their prospects. In the winter of 1804, for example, she entertained frequently for Captain Meriwether Lewis and his assistant, Lieutenant William Clark, as they prepared an expedition to explore the upper Missouri River, and perhaps points farther. But her special guest was Captain Amos Stoddard, who had been sent to Saint Louis by President Jefferson on a mission of peculiar delicacy. He and his aide, Lieutenant Prebble, made her house their virtual headquarters, and conversation was good.

Pasquinel fitted easily into such entertaining. He was a rough, convivial host, and what he lacked in social grace, he made up for with tales of his adventures on the prairie. Such guests as joined the parties liked to talk with him of Indians, and he expounded views which were more readily accepted by his French listeners than by Captain Stoddard and his aide. 'I have one rule,' Pasquinel often said. 'Never fight the Indian if you can avoid it. Never betray him in a trade. Bring him to you by faithfulness.'

It was remarkable that the French, who had followed these precepts in Canada, would enjoy three hundred years of amiable relations with their Indians, while the Americans, who were sure the ideas were wrong, would breed only agony with theirs. Perhaps it was because the French wanted trade; the Americans, land.

Lieutenant Prebble voiced the prevailing view: 'We found in Kentucky—and everywhere else, for that matter—that the only reasonable way to handle an Indian is to kill him. Trust? He doesn't know the meaning of the word. I say thank God there's a wilderness out there where decent white men will never want to live. I say let's throw every damned Indian into that desert and let them keep it till hell freezes.'

In February, after one such dinner, Lise told her husband and her father that she was pregnant, and they had a private celebration, to which they summoned McKeag, who was alone in his room. There was laughter and prediction as to what the boy would be, assuming, as Pasquinel did, that it would be a boy. Bockweiss suggested that he become a silversmith, to keep the profitable business going, and to everyone's surprise, Pasquinel agreed. 'Keep him in Saint Louis,' he said forcefully. 'Never let him work the rivers.'

He himself spent the winter interrogating voyageurs as to where gold might be found, but none of them knew. He asked Captain Lewis, who said, 'There's no gold in America.' Lieutenant Prebble gave him a book on the subject, but of course, he couldn't read.

On March 9 of that year Pasquinel and the other Frenchmen in Saint Louis watched approvingly as Captain Stoddard engineered a comical, warm-hearted charade. He had been ordered by President Jefferson to inaugurate United States rule in the sprawling Louisiana Purchase recently acquired from Napoleon of France. But there was a complication.

Since Spain had never got around to relinquishing control of the area to France, as she had been obligated to do by one of those treaties which periodically ended European wars, Saint Louis was still Spanish, and French authorities could not legally hand it over to America. It was Stoddard who devised the ingenious stratagem whereby everything could be set right.

'The top Spanish officer in the area must formally cede this domain to the top French officer in the area,' he suggested. 'Then the French officials can, with propriety, yield the territory to the United States.' Few proposals in the brief history of Spain's San Luis de Iluenses had been more enthusiastically received, and through the streets ran Pasquinel, shouting, 'Tomorrow we shall all be French again.'

But there was another difficulty. In the entire area there was no Spanish official; strange as it may seem now, the only Spanish officer in the territory was Charles de Hault de Lassus, a French lieutenant who happened to be serving as the Spanish governor of Upper Louisiana, and if he was required to represent Spain in this transfer, where could a French officer be found to represent the Emperor Napoleon? Captain Stoddard was not only resourceful, but also gallant, and he volunteered to fill the breach: 'For this one day I designate myself as the legal representative of his august majesty the Emperor of France, and on his exalted behalf I shall accept the transfer.'

So on the morning of March 9 a varied crowd surrounded the governor's residence, a squat building on Rue de l'Eglise marked by a flagpole. First in attendance were the Indians assembled from four neighboring tribes to witness the celebration: Delaware, Shawnee, Abnaki, Sac. It was a cold day and they stood in buffalo robes, turning their heads sharply whenever cheers or guns exploded. Second came the French contingent, led by Captain Stoddard, eleven men, including Pasquinel, in Sunday clothes. Third were a few casual Americans, quite dirty and out of place. And finally there was Governor de Lassus, a Frenchman making believe he was a Spaniard in this gracious puppet play.

Very proper and grave, he stepped into the street as drums beat and fifes whistled. At his signal, the Spanish flag was slowly lowered while the battery on the hill thundered an eleven-gun salute. The ensign was folded and retired, with no one shedding a tear, since there were few Spaniards in town.

But now things changed. The new flag of France, Napoleon's tricolor, was briskly unfurled, attached to the halyards and run up the pole. Many guns were fired and fifes played martial airs. Captain Stoddard, loyal emissary of Napoleon, accepted the transfer and led the French contingent in cheers, with Pasquinel tossing his red cap in the air, and for twenty-four glorious hours Saint Louis was again French.

That day and all that night Pasquinel toured his old haunts, declaring, 'Je suis Français. Je serai toujours Français. A bas l'Amérique.' In the morning, bleary-eyed and sad, he invited half a dozen equally depressed Frenchmen to his home on Rue des Granges for breakfast, after which he trooped back to the governor's residence and stood with tears in his eyes as De Lassus, once more a French lieutenant, turned the region over to Captain Stoddard, once again the loyal representative of President Jefferson.

Out of decency a member of the committee cried, 'Three cheers for the United States!' but to his embarrassment no one responded. Pasquinel spoke for the citizenry when he said, 'I'd like to cut my throat.'

That autumn, immediately after his son was born, he and McKeag set off for the Platte, with Pasquinel determined to find the Arapaho gold mine. Wherever they went, he asked for news of Lame Beaver's family, but it was not until June of 1805 that they came upon a Cheyenne war party whose members knew what had happened.

'Blue Leaf is dead. Snow.'

'Dead!' Pasquinel erupted. 'She was too young.'

'She's dead.'

'The girl? Clay Basket?'

'We don't know.'

It was here that Pasquinel announced a decision which gave McKeag his first intimation that ultimately there must be trouble in Saint Louis. The Frenchman said, 'I'm not going back this summer. I'm going to stay here until I find that gold.' McKeag tried to argue that this was inhuman, seeing as how Lise had just had a baby, but Pasquinel replied brusquely, 'Bockweiss will look after her. He'll always look after her, that one.'

Accordingly, Pasquinel cached their pelts, his preoccupation with gold having prevented the partnership from accumulating more than two bales, then led the way over a wide scatter of abandoned campgrounds and empty river basins. The Arapaho seemed to be hiding, maliciously: they were not at Beaver Creek or at Rattlesnake Buttes or at that fine spot where the rivers met. Winter approached and the traders camped at some nondescript place, not even bothering to build a proper shelter.

They did not return to Saint Louis during all of 1805, wasting their time looking for the gold, but in April of 1806 a Ute war party passed on its way to steal horses from the Pawnee, and they advised him that as they came out of the mountains, they had seen signs that a band of Arapaho had moved into Blue Valley.

'Où est-ce?' Pasquinel asked with unconcealed agitation.

A Ute pointed toward the mountain up whose side climbed the stone beaver and said in sign, 'Stream right, stream left.'

Pasquinel and McKeag first saw Blue Valley during an April storm. Rain swept in from the mountain and the area was covered with mist, but as they progressed the sun came out in explosive splendor, and they saw a compact meadow bisected by a stream of crystal water, with many aspen trees to the right and a mass of dark spruce to the left, each needle clean and shining.

'A place for gold,' Pasquinel said, but McKeag just looked. He saw the trees, the lovely sweep of the meadow and the myriad beaver lodges.

'We could trade here for years,' he said, but Pasquinel was not listening.

'This has to be where he found the gold,' he said.

They saw a modest trail leading into the heart of the valley and deduced correctly that this must be where the Ute war party had passed. Following it for about a mile, they saw farther ahead where the Arapaho were camped; running forward to identify himself, Pasquinel saw with delight that this was the band to which Lame Beaver had belonged. When they met the chief, they said they were sorry that Lame Beaver was dead.

'He staked himself out. He wanted to die.'

'Blue Leaf?'

'Her time to die.'

They asked where the Arapaho got their bullets, and the chief showed them a sheet of lead and his bullet mold. Pasquinel asked casually if he could see some of the bullets, and the chief summoned a squaw and commanded her to show the ones she had made that day. They were lead.

As Pasquinel hefted them, McKeag saw Clay Basket coming down the valley. She was now sixteen, tall, shy, but deeply interested when children cried that the white men had come back. When she saw them she stopped, smoothed down her elk-skin dress and adjusted the quills about her neck. Her black hair fell in two braids, and she seemed somewhat pale from the effects of winter, but she was even more bright-eyed than she had been as a child. Walking gravely to McKeag, she placed her hand softly on his right shoulder and asked in English, 'Good?'

He thumped his shoulder and replied, 'Good.' Pointing to Pasquinel, he said, 'He fix.' He delighted the Indians by taking off his shirt and showing them the clever device that Pasquinel had fashioned from buffalo hide, a kind of armor which fitted over his damaged shoulder, enabling him to jam the rifle butt against the hardened hide and fire without fear of the kickback. Clay Basket touched the harness and approved.

May and June of that year were the happiest months Pasquinel, McKeag and Clay Basket had shared. The valley was superb, but the weather had grown so warm that passing Indians no longer had pelts. There was no specific reason for the white men to linger, but Pasquinel still did not know where the gold was, and he did not propose leaving until he found out. He became so attentive to Clay Basket that the Arapaho women, shrewd detectives where sex was concerned, deduced that although it was Pasquinel who had fallen in love with her, it was McKeag she had chosen for her mate.

They were confirmed in their judgment when a young brave who up to now had assumed that he would marry Clay Basket picked a fight with McKeag. It was settled when the Scotsman gave the young man a buffalo robe. Here was an opening for McKeag to pursue his suit, if he wished, but as the women had expected, he did nothing.

In midsummer Pasquinel asked one of the women, 'What will Clay Basket do?'

'Difficult,' she replied. 'Poor girl, she loves Red Beard.'

'Will she . . .'

The woman laughed. 'Red Beard will never take a wife. Everybody knows that.'

'Then what?' Pasquinel asked.

Again she laughed. 'Clay Basket will marry you. Next moon.'

And that's how it happened. With the whole Arapaho nation—at least that part encamped at Blue Valley—knowing that Clay Basket preferred Red Beard, she married Pasquinel, who intended by this device to pry the secret of the gold from her. When McKeag realized the callous thing his partner was doing, he was appalled. It was not the bigamy that distressed him, for many traders had an Indian wife on the prairies to complement the white one back in Saint Louis, but rather the harsh misuse of a young girl. He thought several times of protesting, but Pasquinel was in no mood for moral debate—he never referred to his bigamy; all he said was, 'Now we'll find the gold.'

It wasn't much of a ceremony. Pasquinel had to give her brother a gun and some beads and a pouch of tobacco while Clay Basket watched. She was most beautiful that day, decked in fresh porcupine quills and blue stones bought from Indians who traveled the plains to the south. She tried not to look at McKeag and he helped by staying at a distance. A medicine man pointed to the sky, then to the eastern horizon, and said something that McKeag couldn't translate, and that night when Pasquinel was alone with his new wife he asked her, 'Where is the gold your father found?'

'Gold?' she asked.

'Yes, the gold.'

'What gold?'

He was infuriated by her stupidity, or her deception, he wasn't sure which. He repeated the question and got the same answer, and in frustration, asked, 'Why did you marry me when it was Red Beard you wanted?'

In English she offered an explanation which astonished him. 'That first night, many years ago, when my father crept into your camp at Beaver Creek . . . you could have killed him and he could have killed you. He watched you in those days and loved you—because you were brave. So before he staked himself out at the Pawnee camp he told me, "The dark man will come back. Marry him." In this way I knew it would happen.'

Pasquinel sat silent for some time, then asked, 'Before he died, he told you where the gold was?'

'No,' she said.

He knew she was lying and turned away from her. This distressed her and he could feel her shoulders tensing, as if she were sobbing. He left her alone and crossed the stream to wander amidst the aspen. How incredibly beautiful it was that night, with a summer moon and the sound of an owl in the distance, and after a while Clay Basket joined him, and she placed her hand in his and told him, 'I am your woman. Always I will help.'

'Where's the gold?' he asked.

'I do not know,' she said, but he believed that as she came to trust him more, she would confide her secret. In the meantime, she was a beautiful girl and there was no reason why he should not enjoy her whenever he returned to the prairie. With this idea in mind he led her back to the bridal tipi, and as they crossed the clear stream, they stepped on pebbles hiding the nuggets of gold he sought.

He and Clay Basket would have three children: the famous Jacques Pasquinel, born in 1809; his brother Marcel, born in 1811; and a daughter Lucinda, who would be known by another name, born late in 1827. It was a union that lasted.

But after three years of agonizing attempts to locate Lame Beaver's gold, Pasquinel had to conclude that his wife did not know where it was, though he never ceased believing that somewhere in the hills frequented by the Arapaho there was much gold, and he purposed to find it. If his resolution failed, he had only to recall those two bullets he had held in his hand. They were real and they were gold.

In 1807 when he and McKeag returned to Saint Louis they found many changes. For one thing, the house on Rue des Granges was bigger.

Since Lise enjoyed entertaining, she felt the need of extra rooms, and whatever money Pasquinel had given her over the years she had spent on carpenters. Her father now had two apprentices in his flourishing jewelry business and was sending surplus pieces downriver to New Orleans, but his profits he invested in Saint Louis real estate.

Now came a chain of years when Pasquinel kept increasingly to the prairies, sometimes not appearing in Saint Louis for three years at a stretch. When the partners did come back with their pelts, McKeag studied Lise to see how she was reacting to this strange behavior, but if she felt aggrieved she did not show it. And Pasquinel, when he was on hand, proved an exemplary husband and father, resuming his pattern of life as if he had been absent for only a few days. He loved his son Cyprian and delighted in telling him tales of the west. On Sundays he proudly held his wife's arm as they attended the Catholic church, whose priest he helped with contributions.

He found stubborn pleasure in arguing with those American officers he met at his wife's entertainments, and warned them that if they wanted to hold the west, they ought to be sending out exploration parties to locate the mountain passes. He was amused at their presumptions of knowledge and told them: 'Isn't it strange that a handful of French coureurs who loved these western lands know more about them than your entire government?' One inflated colonel, guarded by six riflemen, took a boat trip of only one hundred and fifty miles up the Missouri, not even coming close to the mouth of the Platte, and when he returned to Saint Louis he was flushed with heroism and a great expert on Indian affairs. Pasquinel listened courteously as he expounded his theories on Indian control, but when the officer began speaking of his own courage in facing the savage, Pasquinel could not control himself. Laughing crudely, he said, 'Colonel, on our trips home from real Indian country, when we get to where you were, we no longer keep lookouts. Because we know we're in women-and-children country.' Lise, instead of being outraged at this rebuke to an exalted guest, winked at her husband, and soon thereafter the colonel left.

As time went on, she viewed with growing dismay Pasquinel's protracted absences. At first she suspected that she might be at fault, that she suffered some deficiency in ardor, and once when he was absent for three years she thought seriously of divorce. She was hurt personally by the gossip concerning her husband which circulated in the city, but kept her reactions to it secret. McKeag was never able to ascertain how much she knew, but it was apparent even to him that the marriage had deteriorated.

It appeared that she had made a fundamental decision: with or without Pasquinel, she would live as good a life as possible and raise her son to be as happy and stable as she was. Pasquinel would always be welcomed, would always have an honored place in their home, but they would not allow themselves to be punished by his irresponsible behavior.

At the conclusion of his visits, Pasquinel, broke as usual, would borrow money from his father-in-law, stock his canoe and head for the Platte, where at some appointed place Clay Basket would be waiting with their two boys. These prairie reunions were tender and even passionate, and Clay Basket would have a tipi ready with the kind of furnishings she knew Pasquinel liked: a willow-reed bed with backrests, buffalo robes on the floor, a reliable flap for emitting smoke.

He loved his Indian sons and spoiled them, bringing them gifts from New Orleans and small rifles for shooting birds. He was especially indulgent with Jacques, who at six could ride his pinto at a gallop. The boy was headstrong, and several times McKeag tried to discipline him, warning him not to speed his pony through places where Indian families were cooking meals, but Jacques rejected such advice, and any further interference by McKeag only served to irritate Pasquinel, who wanted his son to become a fine rider. Marcel was quite different, a chubby little fellow who liked people and was becoming a master in devising tricks to get from them what he wanted.

It seemed to McKeag that the boys stood halfway between the two worlds of white men and Indian, uncertain as to which they would ultimately prefer. Pasquinel brought them white-man toys but steeped them in Indian tradition. They loved their father, but stayed mostly with their mother. They spoke Arapaho primarily, but were at ease in the mélange of French and English spoken when the two men were present.

McKeag was especially disturbed over the fact that throughout the west, both in camps and in Saint Louis, such children were called *breeds* and treated with contempt—half-breeds who had a rightful home in neither race. He suspected that the time must come when this pejorative term would be thrown at young Jacques. Then there would be trouble, for the boy gave promise of becoming almost the archetype of that word: a real two-breed individual.

The first confrontation came during the postwar year of 1816. Pasquinel so enjoyed his Indian sons that he proposed taking them and their mother to Saint Louis with him that year, wanting the boys to see the city. He seemed to have no comprehension of the scandal that would ensue or of the hurt it would inflict on Bockweiss and Lise, and when McKeag pointed this out, Pasquinel's reaction convinced McKeag that the coureur was not insensitive, he just didn't give a damn.

'Don't worry,' Pasquinel said, but McKeag flatly forbade him to take his Indian family to Saint Louis, explaining that it would be especially difficult for Clay Basket.

So Pasquinel compromised. He would take them down the Platte, past the Pawnee villages and onto the Missouri. They would drift down that river as far as the westernmost American fort, recently reopened; Fort Osage it was called. There Clay Basket and the boys would be able to see what civilization was like, with the probability that their visit could be kept secret from Saint Louis.

It started as a happy family vacation organized around the two canoes, and that was what caused the first discord. Since Pasquinel, with his powerful shoulders, could paddle with twice the power of McKeag, it was arranged for Pasquinel and Marcel to ride in the lead canoe with four bales, while McKeag, Clay Basket and Jacques rode in the following canoe with only one bale. Since Jacques, now seven, could handle a paddle, the propulsion of the two canoes would be equalized, but this didn't work, because as a partner for McKeag, Jacques proved quite intractable. If the Scotsman said, 'Shift sides,' Jacques refused to do so, and he did not try to mask his contempt. Before they passed the Pawnee village he began complaining of the fact that McKeag allowed Pasquinel's canoe to get far ahead, and he continued this complaining until Clay Basket was forced to reprimand him, but Indian mothers had little authority where sons were concerned, and Jacques repeated his complaints. McKeag thought it ridiculous to allow a boy of seven to agitate him, but as they approached the Missouri he shouted ahead for Pasquinel to stop.

'You take him,' he said brusquely.

'What's the matter? You can't handle?'

'I cannot,' McKeag said without apology, and the boys traded canoes.

They now entered the swift-flowing Missouri and would have covered the distance to Fort Osage quickly had they not been stopped en route by a guide who pushed his canoe out from the left bank of the river. 'I need help!' he called, and when he drew alongside Pasquinel's canoe, the Frenchman saw that it was Indian Phillips, a lanky, dour-faced half-breed who prowled the backwoods as hunting companion to a unique American.

'He's sick,' Phillips said.

'Where?'

'Morteau's shack.' They followed him along a path leading up from the river, and after a ten-minute walk beneath dense foliage, came to a palisaded hut occupied by a mournful French hunter, Pierre Morteau, who greeted them at the door.

'He's awful sick,' Morteau said, leading the group inside.

In a chair, refusing to lie down although it seemed he must be close to death, sat a gaunt, bearded man in his eighties. He seemed delighted to see Pasquinel and the boys. His breath came unevenly, and his large, frail hands trembled, but when he spoke his voice was crisp, as it had been throughout his life.

He was Daniel Boone, recluse on the lower reaches of the Missouri, who had sworn that each year, as long as the Lord allowed him to live, he would take hunting trips, spring and fall, into the wilderness. This one had gone badly, and it seemed impossible that the gaunt old man could make it back through the woods to his headquarters.

'You want me to take him to Fort Osage?' Pasquinel asked Morteau quietly.

'Not a bit of it!' Boone yelled. 'I walked here. I'll walk out.'

'He looks very weak,' McKeag said. He had no idea who Boone was and asked Pasquinel in a whisper.

'Famous Indian fighter,' Pasquinel said. 'Saint Louis . . . too many people for him.'

'Too goddamned many!' Boone shouted. 'You leave me here. Phillips, damn him, he got me here and he'll get me back.'

The half-breed grinned ruinously, gaping holes showing where teeth used to be. It was his job to accompany Boone on his yearly forays and to bury him if he died. 'I don't want no funeral in Saint Louis,' Boone growled. 'Too damned many people there, a man can't hardly breathe.'

'What can we do?' Pasquinel asked.

'You can tell those dudes at the fort I'm still huntin' ba'ar and I'll be walkin' home soon.' He noticed Clay Basket and said, 'Never cottoned much to Injuns but she looks a good 'un.' Of the boys he asked, 'Breeds?' and Pasquinel nodded.

Boone took Jacques by the hand and drew him to his side. 'Stay on the prairies, lad. Don't let 'em talk you into livin' in no town.' He started coughing and Clay Basket pulled her family away.

'He knows when it's time to die,' she said in Arapaho, and they resumed their trip down the Missouri.

For Clay Basket and her sons, Fort Osage was a marvel, their first acquaintance with the power of the white man. The fort had been built in 1808 on a cliff seventy feet above the Missouri, and from each of its five towers it commanded a vast sweep of the river. Batteries of cannon were trained downward upon the waterway, interdicting any enemy boats that might attempt to force a passage, and from the river, as Pasquinel and his troupe approached, it looked as if each cannon were waiting to blow them out of the water.

'Look at them!' Pasquinel told his sons, and when they had made their canoes fast and had climbed the steep cliff, he asked the guard, 'When do the guns go off?' and the guard said, 'Have your boys here at sunset.'

So as the sun went down, Pasquinel took his wife and sons to the master battery overlooking the western approaches, and they all stood at attention as a sergeant gave orders. The boys gasped as the battery fired and a mighty reverberation echoed down the caverns of the river. 'American guns,' Pasquinel said. He was not much impressed with Americans in general, but he did respect their cannon.

The Indian agent at the fort was Major George Champlin Sibley. His rank was honorary, and he acted principally as the man in charge of the commissary, where rifles and powder could be bought for beaver pelts.

An acidulous, correct gentleman who dressed in western Missouri as he might have done in Washington, he had been respected when he served at the fort in the period from 1808 through 1813, and the Indians in the area had been disconsolate when he had to close it down during the War of 1814. But now that he was back, with the fort flourishing once more, he was actually loved.

'It isn't the major so much,' an Osage explained to Clay Basket. 'It's his wife.'

They had heard about Mrs. Sibley from other sources, always with obvious love; she seemed a remarkable woman, but McKeag, who was perplexed as to why an agent's wife should be so highly regarded, was told, 'It's the noise she makes.' McKeag could make nothing of that, but a Pawnee who had drifted south to the fort told him, 'Oh, what a wonderful noise she makes.'

The party did not see this extraordinary woman until late afternoon on their second day at the fort. At five, some thirty Indians and traders crowded into Major Sibley's living quarters, and McKeag saw that in one corner of the room stood a piano. So the noise, which had so captivated the Indians, was merely a piano. He smiled.

Then Mrs. Sibley appeared, a marvelous little wren dressed in a frail white dress gathered high beneath her breasts, with pink satin slippers on her tiny feet and a pale-blue ribbon in her hair. At fourteen, as the daughter of one of the distinguished citizens of Saint Louis—Judge Easton had been in turn postmaster, judge and congressman—she had formed the habit of slipping out of her parents' home at dusk, riding bareback twenty miles to attend military dances, waltzing all night and riding back at dawn. Many soldiers had proposed to her, but shortly after her fifteenth birthday she married Major Sibley, promising 'to go anywhere on earth with him that he cared to go.' He had brought her to Fort Osage. At first he was fearful lest the Indians frighten her, but at the end of the first week they loved her so that they would have attacked Saint Louis had she requested it.

McKeag continued to smile as she sat at the piano, adjusted her shimmering dress, turned and bowed to the Indians. This so pleased them that they made varied sounds of greeting, whereupon she started playing in dainty fashion a Mozart gigue which had floated up the river from New Orleans.

It was delightful, and Clay Basket clutched her boys to her, indicating to them how much she enjoyed it, but one of the Sac chiefs looked at Pasquinel and whispered, 'Pretty soon now,' and McKeag noticed that all the Indians were bending forward, their eyes ablaze.

What happened next McKeag could not accurately determine, but Mary Sibley launched into a rather livelier tune, and with her left foot, in a most unladylike fashion, began kicking an extra pedal, which activated a large bass drum hidden in the rear of the piano. A French dance resulted, with the drum pretty well drowning out the music. As the Indians cheered, fragile Mrs. Sibley began pumping bellows with her right knee, activating a hidden wind instrument which played 'Yankee Doodle Dandy'—and what with the booming drum and all of her ten fingers banging the keys as hard and as fast as possible, a veritable explosion of noise filled the salon.

Clay Basket thought it one of the finest things she had ever experienced, and the boys were enchanted with the mysterious and multiple noises. Major Sibley appeared, offering sweet punch to the chiefs and whiskey to the five white traders, while his wife passed little cakes to the women and the boys. Obviously the concert could have continued all night without tiring the audience.

'We came across Daniel Boone in the wilderness,' McKeag told the major. 'He seemed near death.'

'He'll be hunting bear by Christmas,' Sibley predicted confidently. He knew Boone and suspected that he was a long way from dying. 'And if he dies, Indian Phillips is there to bury him. Boone wouldn't have it any other way.'

Fort Osage would have been a lively place even without its chatelaine; most traders on their way to the upper Missouri halted there, and there were usually a few adventurers in attendance who didn't know where they were headed. The boys were delighted with the varied activity and each day observed scores of things they could not have seen on the prairies: the shoeing of oxen, the tapping of a beer keg, repairs to a keelboat, Sibley's commissary store with its nails and buckets and brooms. Even Marcel, only five at the time, watched omnivorously as mule trains and river boats unloaded.

There were problems. This was an American military post, painfully un-French and lacking even a knowledge of prior Spanish occupation. The commandant was from Delaware and his men from Kentucky and Tennessee, and they had brought their prejudices with them. Frenchmen they distrusted; Indians they despised, and at meals they tried to abuse Pasquinel by calling him Squaw Man, knowing that this was a term normally used for launching a fight. He accepted it with a laugh, adding, 'You bet. Make one fine wife.' One stranger, seeing his dark skin and Indian costume, made the mistake of calling him 'you goddamned Indian,' which he also accepted gracefully.

'What kind of Indian you think?' he asked. 'Cheyenne, Pawnee?'

The newcomer, guessing him to be a Sioux, said, 'Sigh-ox,' at which Pasquinel jumped about acting like a Sioux at a dance and shouting, 'Me Sigh-ox!' In time the hangers-on at the fort stopped trying to insult him.

But they moved onto very different terrain if by word or act they insulted Clay Basket. She was a beautiful woman, her black hair hanging below her shoulders and her face with the placid composure that high cheekbones and amber skin impart. It was inevitable that in a frontier post like Fort Osage incidents would happen, but when they did, Pasquinel's knife appeared like the fang of a rattler and even drunk men backed off.

That year passions against Frenchmen were already high over the war at New Orleans. Rumors circulated that French in the region had supported the British invaders, so it was not surprising when a newcomer from Virginia, out to survey the frontier defenses, took exception to having Pasquinel at table with him. He announced, 'As a gentleman, I do not relish dining with traitors.' Pasquinel rose and left the table. At this point Clay Basket arrived, leading her two boys in for their meal.

The Virginian, flushed by his victory over the husband, did not intend sharing the table with his squaw, so he said firmly, 'This is for Americans. We don't allow Indians here,' and Clay Basket moved dutifully away. McKeag, who was watching mutely from his own place, grew apprehensive, but still Pasquinel did nothing.

Jacques, however, did not intend coming so close to food without getting any and he pushed his way to the table. The Virginian shoved him off, snapping at him, 'No breeds here. Out! Out!'

In a flash, Pasquinel's knife was loosed and with one terrifying backhand sweep he gave the Virginian a near-mortal gash across the neck. The sight of blood inflamed the others, and they leaped at Pasquinel. In so doing, Clay Basket was knocked down. McKeag, when he saw her fall, reacted automatically, leaping into the brawl with his knife. Someone from the fort fired a pistol and soldiers rushed in to halt the riot. Pasquinel and McKeag retreated methodically, forming a bastion behind which Clay Basket and the boys gathered. In this way they left the mess hall.

Pasquinel had a slight cut across his chest. McKeag had a hand wound, which was easily stanched, and Clay Basket was unhurt, but in spite of this she gave a scream of pain, for she saw that Jacques had suffered a bleeding gash across the right side of his face. Some flashing knife, intended for his mother, had caught him. One inch lower and his throat would have been severed.

The child made no outcry. Putting his hand to the cut, he saw the blood and pressed his fingers against the wound to halt it. His eyes kept moving, imprinting the scene indelibly upon his angry brain: the lights outside the room; the soldiers running about; the cut across his father's chest; and especially his mother's anxiety. He was seven years old that night, and he would remember everything.

In the morning the agent visited the lodge where Pasquinel was staying and said, 'You'd better head north.'

'The others started it,' Pasquinel said.

'I'm sure of that,' Major Sibley said. 'But it's too risky . . . having you here now.'

Pasquinel felt no necessity to thank McKeag for his assistance in the brawl. It was taken for granted that each would support the other, and that kind of partnership required no periodic review. McKeag was distressed, however, when Pasquinel casually announced, 'You take Clay Basket and the boys back to the buttes. I'll take the pelts down to Saint Louis.' McKeag argued that now was not the time to desert the Indian family, since they were already disturbed by affairs at the fort, but Pasquinel brushed such objections aside: 'I'd like to see Lise and the boy.' And it was that summer, after an absence of several years, that he fathered his daughter Lisette.

During Pasquinel's happy stay in Saint Louis, his other family and McKeag paddled west in a canoe burdened with contention. Clay Basket enjoyed being with McKeag and loved anew this quiet, gentle man, but he was mortally afraid of her, proscribed as she was by being the wife of his partner. Young Jacques was abominable, despising each moment of a trip from which his father was missing; he sensed the constraint that existed between his mother and McKeag, and suspected that something was wrong between McKeag and his father. He moved in a world of insecurity and hate, and tried to punish his younger brother for it, but chubby-cheeked Marcel simply laughed at his tormenting.

By the time the little party left the Pawnee village on their journey home, a kind of truce had been arranged between McKeag and Jacques. The travelers would probably have reached Beaver Creek without incident, except that a band of Kiowa, invading from a remote area to the south where guns were not yet common, came to trade with the Pawnee for rifles. In the village was an agent for an English fur company, and he saw the Kiowa as a means to rid himself of troublesome competition, so he offered them two badly worn rifles and a bottle of cheap whiskey if they would pursue McKeag's unprotected group and destroy it. The Kiowa, seeing a chance to obtain two children for their tribe, set out in eager pursuit.

They overtook the canoe at a barren spot in the river. McKeag and Clay Basket were already in trouble, for there was not enough water for paddling, and they looked with misgiving as the strangers approached. Prudently McKeag laid out his armament as Pasquinel had taught, hauled the canoe against a bank and reminded Clay Basket how to load the two guns.

The Kiowa halted a short distance away and launched an arch of arrows, which accomplished nothing. McKeag waited for them to draw closer, and saw that there were six in the party. His first rifle shot would be crucial. Taking careful aim, he held his breath as the warriors crept closer, then fired almost point-blank at the leader, killing him with much display of blood. As the others drew back, McKeag took from Clay Basket his second gun and killed a horse. Its rider fell and became tangled in the reins, and with his first gun reloaded, McKeag could have killed him, but he wisely contented himself with hitting the man in the legs. There was much shouting and confusion, and after a while the Kiowa withdrew. They had the beads and the whiskey; they had tried to kill the trader but that could wait till another day. Placing their wounded comrade on the horse of the dead warrior, they rode south.

It was not until they were out of sight that Jacques displayed the only casualty. A Kiowa arrow, launched at random, had come down in a sweeping arc to strike him in the hand, severing the tip of his little finger. Clay Basket found the arrowhead, sharper than a knife, and McKeag bored a small hole through the shank so that Jacques could wear it about his neck.

A half-breed child only seven years old, he had already been scarred twice, once by the knife of a white man, once by the flint of an Indian.

Pasquinel had such a good time in Saint Louis that he prolonged his visit. Lise surprised him with the information that she had sold the stone house on Rue des Granges in order to build a substantial brick house atop the hill, and when Pasquinel protested that no one would want to climb so high for a family visit, she assured him, 'Soon all the interesting families will live up here. The Presbyterians are even building their church on this level.'

Life with Lise was more enjoyable than he had remembered, and sometimes he wondered why he ever deserted so pleasant a place to endure privation on the prairie. Hermann Bockweiss was doing well with his silver, but Pasquinel noticed that the prudent German was still using his profits to acquire pieces of real estate whose value would grow if the town expanded. It was this possibility that Bockweiss had in mind when he took his son-in-law aside and said, 'Why not stay here permanently? You're getting older. Your son needs you.'

Pasquinel replied that his job was in the mountains trading for pelts. 'No,' Bockweiss reasoned, 'you have a partner for that. Leave the trapping for him.'

Pasquinel gave this idea serious consideration, because it had logic behind it. McKeag with his languages was now the expert trader, and soon young Jacques would be old enough to help. Clay Basket? It didn't matter much about her. Any Indian squaw who had learned to live with one white trader could easily catch hold of another, and as a matter of fact, one of these days McKeag would be needing a wife.

He had every reason to stay in Saint Louis. But in the end he decided against it. In December he was back in his canoe heading west, and when he reached Rattlesnake Buttes the customary emotional reconciliation took place and even little Jacques was happy again.

McKeag marveled at the ease with which Pasquinel switched from one of his families to the other and his lack of compunction about doing so.

But when McKeag compared Pasquinel with other traders who also kept Indian wives, he had to admit that Pasquinel handled this problem with far more grace than any of them. The others always deprived one of their families, but not Pasquinel; he treated both equally. He loved Lise and was proud of the way she ran his house, and after his initial disappointment over the gold, he had come to accept Clay Basket as the superior woman she was. He strove to be a good father, and showed equal affection for his half-breed children and his white.

It was during a visit to his Saint Louis family in the autumn of 1817 that he made a crucial decision. Observing that Bockweiss had developed a large and profitable market in New Orleans and the smaller settlements along the Mississippi for his major silver pieces, he told his father-in-law, 'It's a waste of your time to keep on making trinkets for the Indians.'

'True,' the German agreed. 'But where else would you get them?'

'I don't need them any more. I'm through with trading. Going to trap my own beaver.'

Bockweiss frowned, for he had followed the history of other coureurs who had tried to by-pass the Indians and trap directly. They all ended with arrows through their hearts. 'The Indians will fight you,' he warned.

Pasquinel shrugged. 'Traders also get killed,' he said, recalling his own narrow escapes.

Bockweiss started to argue this point, but when he saw Pasquinel's obstinate determination, he halted. 'How many traps will you need?' he asked.

'For daily use in the rivers, fourteen. For spares, six.'

'I'll buy them,' Bockweiss said, and with the traps taking the place of trade goods, Pasquinel set forth upon the adventure that would lure him and his Indian family deep into the Rockies. When he reached McKeag and Clay Basket he told them, 'No more trade goods. No more trapping. We'll get our own beaver.'

'What will the Indians do?' McKeag asked cautiously.

'They'll fight us,' Pasquinel said. 'They'll probably kill us. But we might as well die rich.'

'Do you know how to trap?' McKeag asked.

'I know this,' and he showed McKeag and his sons a small bottle of castoreum. Early next morning he gave a demonstration of the trapping process.

'Set your traps about four inches under the surface of the water. Fasten one end of the chain to the trap, the other to a stick of dead wood. It must be dead or the beaver will stop there to eat. Then jab another dead stick into the bank so that its end hangs over the hidden trap. And on the end of this stick is where you put your castoreum. Like this. No beaver can come down this stream and smell that without coming over here to investigate. To reach it, he has to plant his feet right in your trap. Slam! He dives for deep water and the weight of the chain drowns him. You come by next day, one beaver.'

In January, February and March, when trapping was impossible, Pasquinel spent his time studying dams, calculating where the hibernating animals would appear when thaws came. While he was so occupied, McKeag took responsibility for feeding the camp, and with his thrifty approach, reckoned a day lost if he fired bullets without bringing down game. Turkey, antelope, buffalo calf, young deer—they ate well. It was also his job to cure hides; he made two good buffalo robes for their beds. To be prepared when Pasquinel started bringing in beaver, he spent much time in winter looking for aspen saplings, which he cut and bent into circles about four feet across, lashing the ends with elk sinew so as to form rigid frames.

McKeag became an expert in skinning beaver: a swift cut from neck to anus plus four quick cuts around the feet, and he had the skin off. With deer sinews attached to a long bone needle, he sewed the moist skin to the frame, using big looping stitches. At times their camp would have thirty skins hung to dry at one time.

McKeag also built the press, a most essential item, since the transport of two hundred pelts in loose form would have been impossible; they had to be compacted. Using stout logs, he constructed a rectangular box with vertical slits at each end. Into this box the sun-cured beaver skins were placed, and when the pile had risen, a long, heavy pole was dropped into the slits so that it rested on the pelts. McKeag now chained the thick end of the pole to stakes sunk in the ground; then he and Pasquinel, with loud exhortations and grunting, swung themselves upon the upraised free end, dragging it slowly down to earth. This compressed the skins into a tight and manageable bundle, but the contraption was more than utilitarian. It was great fun, McKeag thought, to be swinging aloft in the air with his partner, straining together in their joint enterprise and hearing him call, 'Goddamnit, you skinny Scotchman! Pull your weight!' And both of them sweating and shouting and straining to make the free end of the pole touch ground. It was the best part of trapping.

The press could accommodate about eighty pelts, and when these were hammered into a bale, McKeag enclosed them in moist deerskin while Pasquinel sewed the seams. Such a bale was worth more than six hundred dollars and weighed about a hundred pounds, hard as rock and watertight.

They were good trappers, and with the help of the two boys they put together six bales that first year. They experienced no trouble with the Sioux; in fact, the only difficulty they encountered was with the Arapaho, and not because they were hostile, but because they were too friendly.

In the winter of 1818 Pasquinel decided to hole up at Beaver Creek, and using such logs as he could find along the Platte, built a snug sod hut, with logs at each corner and framing the door. He judged correctly that this would be a cold winter, so he directed his sons to bring in branches to line one whole side of the hut. Things looked good until the Arapaho arrived.

On a cold day in January, Chief Large Goose appeared at the door and said, 'Cold. Cold. I stay here.'

'Wait!' McKeag protested, trying to bar the door.

'Warm. I stay here.'

'You can't do this!' McKeag bellowed. He sent Marcel to fetch his mother.

'I stay,' Large Goose said, muscling his way inside. 'I am her uncle.' Nothing McKeag could do dislodged this large Arapaho. The hut belonged to Clay Basket; but he was her uncle, so it belonged to him, too.

When the other Arapaho saw how comfortable Large Goose was finding his niece's hut, another uncle decided to join them: 'I am Red Buffalo. Her uncle.' And he pitched his robes on the floor beside Marcel's bed.

McKeag was outraged. He spent some time arguing with the two chiefs, then informed Pasquinel, 'Hell, they ain't her uncles. They ain't even cousins.' Vainly he tried to make them evacuate, but they pointed out that the winter would soon be over. They would be staying for only two or three months, and they persuaded another uncle to join them, which made the hut warmer than ever.

The three chiefs showed the boys how Indians made tipis and tracked buffalo, and impressed upon them the gallant history of their grandfather, Lame Beaver, and his many coups. Jacques was nine that winter, Marcel seven, when the three chiefs made the boys deeply and indelibly Indian. The boys were breeds no more; they were Arapaho.

Pasquinel saw the value of having the three uncles in the hut to instruct the boys, but he also saw that the voracious men were eating up his stores. They would see a jar of food and take it. Lead bullets were attractive too, and they could not resist tobacco. If they knew a friend whose buffalo robe was frayed, they filched one of McKeag's.

'I cannot support the whole Arapaho nation,' Pasquinel cried one morning when he saw Red Buffalo going off with one of his blankets.

'They are my uncles,' Clay Basket said.

It got so that each autumn, when Pasquinel and McKeag passed through the Pawnee villages, they would ask first where the Arapaho were. 'South Platte,' the Pawnee might answer.

'Good. We'll go to the North Platte,' Pasquinel would reply, and it was at that special spot where the Laramie joins the Platte that the unfortunate events of 1823 occurred.

The hunting for beaver that year was not good. Trappers sent out by the English company had pretty well cleaned out the area and were paying Assiniboin to harass the Pasquinel camp. There were skirmishes, with Pasquinel forced to wound two of the Indians, and the winter was not easy.

What made it worse, Jacques Pasquinel was now fourteen and his father naturally wanted to teach him the secrets of setting traps, and as they worked together McKeag felt that he was being superseded. When the trapping yielded few beaver he grew edgy, concluded that young Jacques was not competent and began making pointed observations to that effect.

Scar-faced Jacques was a hot-tempered youth and did not propose to accept criticism from a man he despised. He wanted to fight, now, but his father dissuaded him; 'McKeag is our best friend.'

'I don't want him for a friend,' Jacques snapped, and in late March when a whole line of traps yielded not one beaver, he waited for McKeag to say something.

'Looks like the traps were set too high,' the Scotsman said.

Jacques leaped for him, but Pasquinel held him back. McKeag interpreted this as support and added, 'From now on I set the traps.'

Jacques broke loose from this father and caught McKeag by the throat. 'I set those traps right,' he said grimly, 'and I'll set them right tomorrow.' He threw McKeag backward, and the Scotsman would have reached for his knife had not Clay Basket intervened. Calming her son, she edged McKeag away.

The fight was merely postponed. Next day when McKeag prepared to set the traps, Jacques contested his right to do so. McKeag pushed the boy aside, and Jacques whipped out his knife. McKeag anticipated this and was ready.

Along the dark Laramie, flecked with cakes of ice, the boy attacked the man, silently but with deadly intent. Each knew how to handle a knife, how to trip and gouge, and each used this knowledge viciously. McKeag, as the older and more experienced man, should have had an advantage, but actually it was young Jacques who dominated, for he offset any immaturity with a hideous determination to kill this enemy.

In the middle of the fight McKeag caught a fleeting glimpse of the boy's face as he made a thrust, and the Scotsman was terrified by what he saw: the awful hatred, the violent rage of an alien face. He had wanted only to teach the boy a lesson; the boy wanted to kill him.

Jacques made a clever feint to the left, threw McKeag off guard, then lunged at him, catching him solidly under the left armpit. Before the inexperienced youth could extract his knife—'Never drive it in to the hilt,' old-timers warned, 'because it's too hard to pull out'—McKeag caught his arm, flipped him over and landed him on his back. With a savage leap the Scotsman landed atop the boy, his knife at his throat. He could have killed Jacques then; perhaps he should have. In later years he would often recall that moment and visualize himself driving the knife home.

Instead, he rose, helped Jacques to his feet, then went into the hut. Even though he was bleeding, he packed his gear and prepared to leave.

He was nine hundred miles from Saint Louis, without adequate provisions, but nothing could persuade him to stay. Pasquinel came running after him, crying, 'McKeag! Are you insane?' But McKeag kept walking south.

Clay Basket came too, begging him to wait, at least to let her tend his wound, and as she was pulling at him, with Pasquinel arguing, he stopped and cried harshly, 'That boy will kill you all.' With that he vanished into the great prairie.

Word passed through the west: 'McKeag has left Pasquinel. He's trapping on his own.' This seemed an unlikely story, but in June of that year Pasquinel arrived in Saint Louis with three bales of fur and McKeag was not to be seen. Later the Scotsman came downriver alone, thin and angry, with only one bale. When he threw the pelts down at the Bockweiss office, the foreman said, 'Mr. Bockweiss wants to see you.' He did not wish to see the German then, and left. But Bockweiss tracked him to his mean shack by the river.

'Can I speak to you, McKeag?' The Scotsman grunted. 'Man to man?' Another grunt.

Bockweiss sat down on a box, cleared his throat, then launched into a discussion which obviously was not the one intended: 'Did my men pay you for the pelts? Good. Do you need an advance?'

'I keep my own money . . . in the bank.'

'I speak to you as a father,' Bockweiss said, dropping his voice. 'McKeag, does Pasquinel have a wife in New Orleans?'

'Ask him.'

'I'm asking you. I'm pleading with you to help me. As a father.'

'Never been to New Orleans,' McKeag said.

'Has he ever told you . . . You know him better than anyone else.'

In flat, unemotional tones McKeag said, 'I've heard him say . . . different times . . . a wife in Montreal, at Detroit, in New Orleans. Also Quebec, I think. He was joking.'

Bockweiss rose and pressed his hands to his forehead. Then he sat down again and said, 'You were at Fort Osage in 1816. When he stabbed that man.' Since word must have traveled to Saint Louis, McKeag nodded.

'Did he have an Indian wife with him? Two sons?'

McKeag pondered this for some time and decided that it was not his duty to report on his partner's Indian family. Without replying, he rose to leave the shack, but Bockweiss caught him by the arm. 'Please, I am a father trying to protect his daughter.' McKeag shook himself free, but Bockweiss barred the way. 'I went to New Orleans,' he said brokenly. 'I met the girl. They were married . . . she had papers . . . the children.'

With unaccustomed force McKeag pushed free of the German. He could not bear to hear ugly stories about Pasquinel, not what he had done in New Orleans or in Saint Louis either. In many ways the Frenchman had treated him badly, and his behavior toward Clay Basket and Lise was deplorable. But Pasquinel was the only solid friend McKeag had ever known and he did not propose to listen to gossip about him, even though the partnership was ruptured. Stalking down to the river, he climbed into his canoe and disappeared.

He became a forlorn man, prowling the prairies. He built himself canoes and kept his traps oiled. Where others failed to make a bale of pelts, he succeeded, and it was said of him, 'He can smell castoreum better than most beavers.'

But he was alone, cut off from the few people he cared about. Some years he did not even bother with Saint Louis. Collecting what pelts he could, he would build his own press and operate it by his own weight, and if some other trapper chanced by, he would sell his bales for a pittance, allowing the stranger to carry them to Saint Louis for large profit.

The English company tried several times to engineer catastrophe for him, but he was trusted by Indians and they could not be paid to damage him. No trapper of that period was more accepted by the Pawnee and Ute, the Arapaho and Cheyenne, than this lanky, red-bearded Scotsman. He gave them honest counsel and helped them conduct their traffic with Americans. In 1825 he showed up in Santa Fe, translating for the Ute, but most often he wandered the land between the two Plattes, wintering sometimes at the Laramie, sometimes at Rattlesnake Buttes.

In the deep winter of 1827, when snow lay fifteen feet in the passes, he spent three weeks in his lodge at the bottom of a considerable drift without once seeing the sky. Then for the first time in his life he thought seriously of death. For the past seven months he had not seen or spoken to a human being, and now in the darkness he did not dare even to speak aloud to himself, as if the sound of a human voice might shatter his universe.

I can still trap for many years, he thought. I seek no trouble with the Indians. I doubt they will kill me, though they could. Perhaps some winter the snow will come extra deep. How it could be much deeper than this would be difficult to say; if a man could survive this winter he could survive anything.

The snow will keep coming and the world will be used up, he thought. There will be no water, no food, no air. How much water there used to be in Scotland! His mind dwelled on this, then returned to the conceit: No air.

Suddenly he felt closed in, as if the air were already consumed, leaving him to suffocate. He visualized himself at the bottom of a great drift, with the tunnel snowed shut, and a fear mightier than any he had ever known gripped him and he thrust himself into the tunnel and began digging furiously, throwing soft snow behind him as a dog does when digging underground. With superhuman effort, gasping for breath, close to suffocation, he burst from his snowy prison to find that the storm had ceased and there was no cause for fear.

Alone as few men have been alone, he stood at the entrance to his tunnel and surveyed his universe. The sun was brilliant. The sky held not a single cloud nor any bird. There were no trees, no tracks of animals, no sound. There was only snow and air, a cold, clear frosty air from horizon to horizon.

Wait! To the west, at a great distance, emerged the shadowy outline of the profound mountain, and up its side with immortal persistence climbed the little stone beaver.

'Aggghhh!' McKeag shouted in a meaningless, almost inhuman cry. 'Little beaver!'

In his lifetime he had slain so many beaver, had lugged so many pelts to Saint Louis, but there climbed his only friend in all the universe. Neither the sun nor the stars nor the rivers nor the trees were his friends, but that little stone animal was.

All that wintry afternoon he watched the beaver, and as light began to fade and vast streaks of color shot out from the mountains, he wanted to delay the night, but the stars appeared and light vanished and the mountain was gone. He stood in the evening silence for some time, as the stars increased.

It was a night of overwhelming beauty, so silent that the fall of a final snowflake would have been audible. He knew that if he wanted to sleep, he must climb back down the tunnel, for to do otherwise would mean death, but still he delayed. The majestic dome of night lowered over the world, and the silence deepened.

With a great crash it ended. There was a cry, a violent cry torn from the soul: 'Oh, God! I am so alone!' It was the voice of Alexander McKeag, forty-nine years old, a permanent exile from his home in Scotland, a voluntary recluse on the prairies.

He heard the voice as if it came from another. He listened, refused to translate its meaning, and after a while climbed dutifully down the tunnel and into his cave of darkness.

That spring the trapper who stopped by to pick up his pelts told him, 'You ought to meet with us at the rendezvous.'

'I don't care for Saint Louis.'

'No! Bear Lake, over by Snake River.'

Another party of trappers passed his way in early summer, lugging their pelts westward instead of to Saint Louis. 'Where you goin' with your pelts?' McKeag asked.

'The rendezvous,' the men said. 'British buyers come up from Oregon.' They pushed westward.

For some weeks McKeag pondered this curious information—a rendezvous, men from Oregon, Scotsmen perhaps. He wondered if he ought to join the trek to satisfy himself as to what it signified, but his decision was made by others.

He was trudging home from an unsuccessful hunt for antelope when he saw approaching from the east an unprecedented number of men. They were riding horses and throwing such a clutter of dust that he could not accurately guess their number; there must have been at least two dozen, and they were not Indians. As they drew closer he saw that they were far more numerous than he had guessed. 'At least fifty of 'em!' he shouted to no one. 'And what are they draggin'?'

Actually there were sixty-three white men, all from Saint Louis, on their way to the rendezvous. They led thirty-seven horses loaded with merchandise for trading, and that remarkable thing he had seen was a heavy brass cannon capable of throwing four-pound iron balls. It was seated on a stout two-wheeled cart drawn by two ugly mules.

'What's the cannon for?' he asked.

'You come to the rendezvous and see,' they told him, and they were off, singing an army song, raising a great dust in the sunset and taking a portion of his imagination with them.

'I'm goin'!' he said aloud that night, and by dawn he was packed.

He traveled north till he reached the North Platte. Holding to its southern bank, he headed west and in a sweeping arc dipped south across a pass in the mountains. That put him on the western slope of the Continental Divide; he was now on land controlled principally by England out of its headquarters in Oregon and by Mexico from its foothold in California. It was beautiful land, open and windswept, with prairies even more bleak than those McKeag knew on the eastern slope. The rivers were turbulent: Sweetwater, Green, Snake, Yellowstone, but the hills were rolling and much less severe than the Rockies. It was an amiable land and McKeag felt an easiness creep into his bones as he crossed it.

Traveling alone, he covered ground swiftly and soon overtook a group of four mountain men who had been working the western slope of the Rockies, north of Santa Fe. They were loud and violent, much given to drink and boastful of their mastery of the mountains. 'How long you been here, Jake?' one asked another. 'Three years,' the man replied. 'And you?' they asked McKeag.

His face grew blank. How many years had he been on the plains? Thirty years, or was it thirty-one? A long time, a long, long time. He would not want to shame these lively men, so he did not answer.

'I asked ya, Red Beard, you a tenderfoot?'

'In the mountains?' McKeag asked.

'What else? The mountains.'

'I've never been in the mountains,' he said. He looked so weather-wise and his clothes so Indian that they couldn't believe this. One of the younger men, well drunk on summer whiskey, grabbed him by the shirt and said, 'Don't you make fun of us, Scotty. We'll break your back. How long you been in the mountains?'

'Never been there.'

'Then how long on the prairies?' the man shouted. 'How long chasin' beaver?'

'Thirty years,' McKeag said.

'Thirty years!' one of them cried in open admiration. 'You musta known Pasquinel.'

McKeag caught his breath. Something in the way the man spoke seemed to indicate that Pasquinel was dead, and in the pain of that moment, McKeag acknowledged to himself that the only reason he was heading for the rendezvous was to meet Pasquinel. 'Is he all right?' he asked in a whisper.

'All right?' One of the men bared his left arm to display a long knife gash, dating back but still lurid beneath the scar tissue.

McKeag fingered the scar, laughed thinly and said, 'He was always good with a knife.'

They traveled together some days till they reached the Green River, and at night they told McKeag of their journey along the Arkansas, of Santa Fe and the western slopes and the high plateau. They seemed to have fought everyone: Comanche, Apache, Mexicans, Ute. 'Of all the Indians we met,' one said, 'the Ute know how to handle their horses in a fight.' They had a high opinion of that tribe and asked McKeag which he preferred. 'Arapaho,' he said, volunteering no reason.

As they swung north toward Bear Lake, where the rendezvous was to be held—the word having been flashed across the whole west, from Oregon to Saint Louis, from Canada to Chihuahua—they came upon six different tribes of Indians heading for the month-long celebration: Ute, Shoshone, Gros Ventre, Snake, Nez Percé, Flathead. The newcomers were showing off their mastery of sign language, a few symbols covering the most meager ideas, when McKeag was greeted by a Ute from the eastern slope, with whom he fell into conversation. A Gros Ventre came up, and McKeag spoke to him in Arapaho. The mountain men were impressed.

'You a squaw man?' they asked.

'Trapper,' McKeag said.

They now mounted a small hill, and from its brow they looked down upon the shimmering lake and the extensive meadows which would house the rendezvous. Already two thousand Indians were camped there and more were drifting in from north and west. 'Last year we didn't have enough grass for the horses,' one of the trappers said.

'You been here before?' McKeag asked.

'Third year. This is better'n goin' to Saint Louis,' the man said enthusiastically, his excitement heightened by actual sight of the locale. 'Scotty, you're goin' to see more hellfire . . . And let me tell you one thing, if that little bastard Pasquinel tries to cut me up again . . .'

'Will he come?' McKeag asked.

'They invented this for him. He won't be sober ten minutes in ten days.'

Another trapper broke in. 'First year he came alone. Drunk all the time. Last year he brought his squaw. Labe here tried to fussy her up. That's when he got his arm cut. Pasquinel had to fight eight different men during rendezvous.'

As they descended the hill, mountain men from various parts of the west recognized the four from Santa Fe and moved in to deliver messages from absent friends. McKeag stood apart, surveying the lake and marveling that so many white men had lain hidden in the hills, that so many warring tribes could convene in peace. He was about to rejoin his group when the air was shattered by a tremendous blast, so powerful that some trappers had their caps blown off.

McKeag looked about to see what had caused it. The men with the cannon had fired a blank to welcome the Santa Fe contingent, one of whom asked, 'What's the cannon for?'

'To scare Indians. Look!' His men had erected a tipi on an opposite hill and around it had piled a formidable collection of logs, on top of which stood a trapper waving a red flag attached to a pole. All the white men stared at the tipi, and scouts moved through the Indian section to be sure they were watching.

The man waved his flag for some minutes. Then a pistol shot was fired and he dropped the flag and ran as fast as he could down into a gully. At the cannon an artilleryman touched a flame to the fuse and jumped back. There was a loud blast, and a four-inch iron ball shot across the intervening land, took one dusty bounce and crashed into the logs, carrying the tipi some distance away, collapsing it.

A trapper from the north, excited by the noise and the good hit, let out a yell, jumped in the air and flung his arms wide in sheer exuberance. 'Alllleeezzzz!' this Canadian shouted. 'Anyone want the apron?'

He whipped out from underneath his Indian blouse a yellow apron. It was about twenty inches wide where the strings were attached, twenty-four from top to bottom, very colorful, very yellow. He swung the apron by one string, bringing it under McKeag's nose. The Scot did not know what it signified, but one of the Santa Fe men did, and he grabbed the other flying string, ripped the apron out of the Canadian's hands and tied it deftly about his own waist. Men in the area stopped to cheer, and one struck up a song, 'Old Joe with a Wart on His Nose.' Soon everyone was singing and clapping hands, whereupon the man wearing the yellow apron danced a few pretty steps and pirouetted like a girl.

This delighted the Canadian, who swooped down upon the dancer, took his two hands and began a jig. Then he slipped his arm around the man's waist and ran forward and backward in long, awkward steps. At the end of this maneuver the man in the yellow apron pushed his partner away, danced lightly about the circle and indicated another man.

This pair danced with some grace, the man in the apron still playing the role of the woman, and after some minutes they tried an intricate waltz, which went so well that the crowd cheered. The man of the partnership bowed and retired, whereupon the man in the apron minced up to McKeag, offering to dance with him, but the Scotsman flushed.

'I can't dance!' he protested, and the aproned man slid gracefully to the next in line, who cut a good figure with jig steps, ending by swinging the 'girl' high into the air, then around in a circle parallel to the crowd, lifting him one moment and dropping him nearly to the earth the next. It was a fine dance, and the Indians stood gape-mouthed, like McKeag.

The clapping had obscured a more somber noise which came from a brawl a short distance away. When it became obvious that a substantial fight was under way, the crowd moved there, and McKeag, pushed along against his will, saw with a mixture of delight and disgust that Jacques Pasquinel, now a husky lad of eighteen, was fistfighting with a man much older and heavier. It was a hard-breathing affair, with each contestant trying to damage the other, and after a series of blows which seemed to be about even, the older man struck one that gave him an advantage which he was eager to follow up.

Drawing back his right arm and cocking it for a major blow, he was about to finish young Pasquinel off when one of the watching trappers shouted, 'Watch out, Emil. The knife.'

Feeling himself about to lose, Jacques had whipped out a long-bladed knife and was ready to close in on his opponent, but a friend of the fighter's had anticipated such a move and had taken out a pistol, which he pointed at the young man's head, shouting as he did, 'Pasquinel! Drop the knife!'

Jacques turned to see who had called his name, saw the pistol leveled at him, and without a moment's hesitation, dropped his knife and broke into a smile. Kicking the needle-pointed knife, he laughed, 'Only play.'

'I know,' the man with the pistol said.

There might have been more words had not a wild shout arisen, whereupon a group of Arapaho on horseback came thundering in. They rode with crazy abandon through the encampment, throwing dust over all the campfires, then doubled back and crossed in the opposite direction. To his dismay, McKeag saw that the two chiefs, Large Goose and Red Buffalo, who had once eaten up his supplies, were in the lead, and he swore that this time they would get none of his gear . . . none. But he suspected that this might be an easier promise to make than to keep, for now Large Goose spotted him and reined his horse.

'Red Beard!' he shouted, running over and embracing his long-absent friend. 'You got tobacco?'

'I have no tobacco,' McKeag said firmly in Arapaho.

'Yes, yes! Where's your tipi?'

'I have no tipi,' McKeag protested.

'You sleep my tipi,' Large Goose cried, embracing McKeag doubly hard.

'You been drinkin'?' McKeag asked.

'Yes, yes! Everybody drinking.' He pointed to the east, where one of the Santa Fe trappers was peddling bottles of Taos Lightning. The world's crudest alcohol was mixed with caramel, a couple of camphor balls, copious amounts of water, pepper and a shredded plug of tobacco. For twenty cents a man could make a gallon of the stuff and trade it for a hundred dollars' worth of furs. The Indian who drank it did not die, but often wished he had.

The Hudson's Bay Company, a Canadian outfit long experienced in the fur trade, did not allow its representatives to sell liquor to Indians, but there was nothing in its rules to keep the Canadians from robbing the Indians in other ways. It sponsored a custom that required an Indian, when purchasing a rifle, to pile beaver pelts as high as the top of the barrel; the Canadians produced a rifle with a barrel twelve inches longer than ordinary, then spread the rumor that it was this extra length that made it deadly.

A Canadian with the strong Scottish name of McClintock had opened a tent by the southern tip of Bear Lake and was buying in beaver pelts as fast as the Indians could unload them, and McKeag gravitated toward this area, wondering vaguely if there might be news from Scotland. After he had waited some minutes for the Indians around the tent to thin out, he edged his way to where a large bearded man in filthy Indian dress and matted hair was speaking rapidly in some north Indian tongue. McKeag caught his eye, and the Canadian stopped his harangue, pushed the Indians to one side and strode over.

'Name's McClintock. You got beaver to sell?'

'Name's McKeag. I sell in Saint Louis.'

'You'll do better with me. Where you from?'

'Wester Ross,' McKeag said, giving the name of a remote and little-known part of Scotland. McClintock had never heard of it. 'Are you from Scotland?' McKeag asked nervously.

'Never saw it. My grandfather, mebbe. Lived in Nova Scotia.'

McKeag was about to leave when the Canadian grabbed him by the arm. 'Did you say McKeag? You the man who used to partner Pasquinel?' McKeag nodded.

'Pasquinel!' the Canadian bellowed, and from inside the tent the familiar, stocky figure of the Frenchman appeared. He was now fifty-seven, heavier, his hair grayed, a couple of front teeth missing. He had a new scar along his chin, but his clothes were the same: Indian dress that Clay Basket had made him, but with more decoration than before, red wool cap. He stood in the sunlight, holding a flap of the tent in his left hand,

and stared at the figure before him. At first he did not recognize Mc-Keag, for he was drunk, and the lean Scotsman felt a pang of sorrow. He was about to retreat, from natural shyness, when McClintock bellowed, 'Pasquinel! It's your old partner McKeag.'

The shroud of drunkenness dropped away from Pasquinel. His eyes cleared and he saw, swimming in space before him, his partner of long ago. 'McKeag,' he whispered softly, 'you come to a strange tent to find me.' He extended his two hands and stepped forward uncertainly. He stumbled and McKeag grabbed him. 'Merci,' the Frenchman said gravely. 'Il y a longtemps.'

Before McKeag could respond to this deeply felt welcome, the area was disturbed by two figures running at great speed toward the tent. 'Father!' the lead figure yelled. It was Marcel Pasquinel, now sixteen, followed by Jacques. They rushed up to their father, and before he could protest, had stripped him of his two knives, each boy taking one and jabbing it inside his belt.

'It's Emil Borcher!' Marcel shouted back over his shoulder. 'If he starts again, we're goin' to kill him.' In a cloud of dust they disappeared, but within a moment they were back again, and Marcel was grabbing McKeag by the arm and swinging him around.

'It's McKeag!' he shouted with real delight. Throwing his arms about the Scotsman, he embraced him warmly, then shoved him along to Jacques, who greeted him with less enthusiasm.

'Last time we were fightin',' Jacques said.

'You're bigger,' McKeag said uneasily. Then grasping for something to say, he asked, 'Is your mother here?'

The brothers laughed at this, and Jacques said, 'Here last year. Too many fights.'

'We're lookin' for a fight right now,' Marcel said. 'Emil Borcher. He started it . . . had one of his friends come at Jacques with a gun.' McKeag thought it best not to say that he had seen Jacques attack Emil with the knife. They ran off, seeking more trouble, and that night when the brothers could not have known that McKeag was listening, he overheard Jacques telling a crowd of young bullies, 'McKeag. He used to trap with my father. I had to drive him out of camp . . . cut him up bad with my knife . . . caught him in bed with my mother.'

McKeag felt so unclean, so humiliated that he wished the ground might envelop him right then to get him out of this evil place. I should have killed him years ago, he thought, and during the rest of the rendezvous he avoided the brothers.

For Pasquinel the turbulent meeting was heaven-sent. He was drunk most of the time, bought enormous quantities of good alcohol from the Canadians, who were allowed to sell it to whites, and danced and fought and chased Indian girls and sought out other Frenchmen to sing the traditional song of the voyageurs, 'A La Claire Fontaine,' that haunting melody with words that caught the full meaning of youth and the start of life:

> 'Sing, nightingale, sing!
> You have the singing heart.
> You have the heart that laughs . . .
> Mine is the heart that weeps.
> > Chante, rossignol, chante.
> > How long, how long have I loved you.
> > Never, never will I forget.

> 'Now I have lost my sweetheart,
> Without any reason at all.
> It was just a bouquet of roses
> That I forgot to give her.
> > Chante, rossignol, chante
> > How long, how long I have loved you.'

Pasquinel bought the singers drinks. He was a generous man, respected for his ability to survive; old-timers knew how often he had stood alone against assailants. He was also the champion singer of love songs, the patron of the rendezvous.

But he was a difficult man, for he attracted trouble. He fought as often as the meanest-minded man at the rendezvous, and when McClintock, his proved friend, remonstrated with him about the behavior of the two boys, claiming that Jacques had raped the daughter of an Arapaho chief without paying, Pasquinel grew furious.

'Lie! Pasquinel always pays.'

'You do,' McClintock assured him, 'but not your son.'

Pasquinel pulled back his right arm, launching a hard blow, which McClintock parried. Immobilizing the stocky Frenchman, he lectured him: 'You warn Jacques to keep his fingers out of my ball and powder. He's a thief.'

'By God!' Pasquinel roared, trying to strike his friend again.

'Tell him, McKeag,' McClintock said, thrusting the pugnacious Frenchman from him.

'How's trappin'?' Pasquinel asked his old partner, forgetting his fight with McClintock as easily as he had begun it.

'The streams are beginning to lose their beaver.'

'Jamais,' Pasquinel roared. 'You just have to go higher in the mountains.'

This started a long discussion, in which several mountain men participated. Those who trapped in the high Rockies agreed with Pasquinel that beaver could never diminish. 'They hide in those lodges all winter making babies,' a newcomer said.

But the Oregon trappers, who had been working the rivers for a longer time, knew that McKeag was right. The beaver were thinning out. 'Always farther up the river,' an Englishman from Astoria said. 'Pretty soon you won't make a bale a year.'

'Ah!' Pasquinel replied. 'Last winter . . . Blue Valley . . . I make six bales . . . no work.'

'I don't know Blue Valley,' the Englishman said. 'I suppose it's fairly high.'

'You climb . . . you climb,' Pasquinel said.

'That's what I mean,' the Englishman said. 'I'll wager there are no streams above it.'

'Well,' Pasquinel began. He stopped, and across his face came a look of bewilderment which all could see, the confession that above Blue Valley there were no more streams. There was a moment of painful silence, broken by his hearty cry, 'Ah! So long as men wear beaver hats, so long we have beaver.'

On the sixth day after McKeag's arrival there was great excitement at the rendezvous. A teamster arrived from Saint Louis. He had come up the Missouri by boat, had disembarked at the Platte, and had brought his cargo over the pass and now to Bear Lake. It was an amazing cargo, so rich and varied as to allure the white man as much as the Indian.

There were penknives and jars of preserved peaches and new pistols and better knives and cloth and beads galore. There were shoes and smoked dried beef and cured pork and bottles of French wine and English brandy and Kentucky whiskey. There were little barrels of candy which the men grabbed for as if they were children, and hard sweet cookies, and forks and hammers and screwdrivers and dried chickens.

Whoever in Saint Louis had packed these twenty-two horses had exercised imagination of the highest quality, for when the goods were unloaded, there was something for every man, something calculated to stir the heart of any woman. When the horses set out, they carried stock worth four thousand dollars in Saint Louis. At the rendezvous they would sell for fifty thousand.

McKeag bought nothing, would not even look seriously at anything. He had so simplified his life that he had all he required; his lead and powder he bought at regular intervals from whoever was passing his lonely camp. To indulge in something like sweetened peaches was beyond his imagination. And yet at this rendezvous he savored something so enticing that he would ever thereafter be its slave.

In the late afternoon he was standing by a tent run by a trapper-merchant from Oregon, an Englishman named Haversham, the only man at the rendezvous in European dress, and Haversham asked, 'Care for a cup of tea?' It had been a long time since McKeag had drunk tea and he said, 'Don't mind if I do.'

The Englishman had two china cups and a small porcelain pot. Washing the cups with steaming water, he took down a square brown tin, opened the top carefully and placed a small portion of leaves in the pot. To McKeag they bore no visible difference from the tea leaves his mother had used, but when Haversham poured him a cup and he took his first sip, an aroma unlike any he had ever known greeted him. He sniffed it several times, then took a deep taste of the hot tea. It was better than anything he had previously tasted, better even than whiskey.

What did it taste like? Well, at first it was tarry, as if the person making the tea had infused by mistake some stray ends of well-tarred rope. But it was penetrating too, and a wee bit salty, and very rich and lingering. McKeag noticed that its taste dwelled in the mouth long after that of an ordinary tea. It was a man's tea, deep and subtle and blended in some rugged place.

'What is it?' he asked. Haversham pointed to the brown canister, and McKeag said, 'I can't read.'

Haversham indicated the lettering and the scene of tea-pickers in India. 'Lapsang souchong,' he said. 'Best tea in the world.'

Impulsively McKeag asked, 'You have some for sale?'

'Of course. We're the agents.' It was a tea, Haversham explained, blended in India especially for men who had known the sea. It was cured in a unique way which the makers kept secret. 'But smoke and tar must obviously play a part,' he said. It came normally from India to London, but the English traders in Oregon imported theirs from China.

'How long would a can like that last?' McKeag asked, cautiously again.

'It'll keep forever . . . with the top on.'

'I mean, how many cups?'

'I use it sparingly. It would last me a year.'

'I'll take two cans,' McKeag said, without asking the price. It was expensive, and as he tucked his small supply of coins back into his belt, Haversham explained, 'The secret in making good lapsang souchong lies in heating the cup first. Heat it well. Then the flavor expands.' McKeag hid the canisters at the bottom of his gear, for he knew they were precious.

The incident in this rendezvous which the mountain men would refer to in their camps for years to come started when Pasquinel got drunk and went among the tents shouting, 'The Hawken is the best goddamned rifle in the world.'

This naturally brought wagers from the Oregonians, who used European guns, which in years past had proved superior to any American product. Recently, however, Jacob Hawken in Saint Louis had begun perfecting a rifle which was to command the plains, and men like Jim Bridger and Kit Carson had performed some commendable feats with it.

The Hawken partisans felt that this was the year to pick up some English money, and a contest was proposed.

Negotiations led to so many arguments about rules and scoring that Pasquinel, drunk and impatient, halted the bickering with an announcement: 'I show you how good the Hawken is.'

He had acquired, on his last selling trip to Saint Louis, a splendid example of Hawken's work; he had been steered to the German gunsmith by Hermann Bockweiss, who had bought him the gun as a present. It had a thirty-six-inch barrel, which the English thought too short, and fired a .33-caliber ball, which they thought too small. Its metal parts were beautifully machined but the woodwork was only average. It was a better gun than it looked.

Pasquinel paraded his rifle for anyone to see, and the crowd expected him to try to perform some difficult feat. Not so. He called for his son Jacques and for an empty whiskey bottle. Placing the boy in a favorable spot, he handed him the gun and walked unsteadily about forty yards away, planted his feet firmly and put the bottle on his head.

It was William Tell in reverse, and men started taking bets as to the four possible outcomes: the boy would miss altogether, would hit the bottle, would wound his father, would kill him outright. The scar-faced lad raised the rifle, took careful aim and knocked off the top of the bottle.

The crowd applauded, but Pasquinel senior was not through. Returning to where men were congratulating Jacques, he took the Hawken and handed it to his younger son, Marcel. Holding the bottom part of the whiskey bottle on his head, he started to walk back to the target position, but now some sensible Englishmen protested that this was insane.

'He's got to learn sometime,' Pasquinel called over his shoulder. Taking his position, he stared at his younger son. Marcel raised the heavy gun, steadied it, aimed carefully and pulled the trigger. The glass shattered, and Pasquinel told the crowd, 'I said it was a good rifle.'

In the closing days of the rendezvous something happened which had a profound effect upon McKeag. One afternoon one of the Santa Fe men was wearing the yellow apron and numerous trappers had taken turns waltzing with him and doing improvised square dances they remembered from Kentucky. After a while he tired, held up his hands and said he had had enough, so the yellow apron was passed to an Englishman from Oregon, and he drew loud applause for his steps in English style. Half a dozen Americans volunteered to dance with him, and he displayed considerable grace as he tried to match their robust movements. It was agreed that he was excellent, but in time he tired, too, and passed the apron on to the first man he saw.

It happened to be McKeag, who was both embarrassed and confused.

He knew little about dancing and certainly nothing about women's steps. He fumbled with the apron, allowed it to fall, then picked it up and tried to fob it off onto someone else.

'Dance! Dance!' the trappers shouted, and someone tied the apron around his middle. Hands forced him into the dancing area and he stood there, looking quite foolish. A Canadian with a fiddle, knowing that McKeag was Scottish, struck up a Highland tune, and from his remote boyhood in the Highlands, McKeag remembered a rude dance.

He began awkwardly. Then his feet caught the rhythm and hesitantly started to respond. His body swayed. His head cocked saucily to one side and he began to recall how the steps went. Slowly and with an almost audible creaking of time's joints, he began to dance, and the terrible isolation of recent years dropped away. In dancing he became whole again.

While he remained preoccupied with doing the right steps, he became aware that another person had moved into the area and he was afraid lest he make a fool of himself with a partner. Then he looked up—it was Pasquinel, drunk and ready for yet another exhibition. McKeag looked at him and perhaps his fear communicated itself, for Pasquinel saw that he was frightened and forgot whatever foolishness he had planned. Slowly his feet began to move in accordance with McKeag's, and gradually the two men evolved a kind of harmony. What resulted could scarcely be termed a dance, for it had little grace and less rhythm, but it was the related movement of two human beings and those who watched treated it with respect.

As the dance reached its climax, with Pasquinel breathing heavily and holding his left shoulder conspicuously low, McKeag closed his eyes and allowed the music to command him, and for the first time in many years felt actually happy. 'I was so lonely,' he muttered to himself, and he had barely said these words when he heard trappers shouting, 'Give him air!' and he looked down to see that his partner had fainted.

When they got Pasquinel stretched out, with McKeag at his head still wearing the yellow apron, he opened his eyes and whispered, 'The arrow . . .'

They called for some Arapaho women to tend him, and McKeag supervised them as they lugged him to a tipi, where they laid him face down on buffalo robes. Gently they massaged his back, feeling the sunken arrow and manipulating it into a position where it hurt less.

During the night Haversham heard of the incident and said airily, 'Simple. Cut the damned thing out.' He was the ebullient type of Englishman who refused to admit that anything was impossible. 'I've cut out many a bullet in me day,' he said enthusiastically. 'Let's have a look.'

He went to the Arapaho tipi and asked a squaw to hold a lantern over Pasquinel's back while he inspected the ancient wound. 'Don't leave it in there a day longer, old fellow,' he said professionally. 'I'll cut it out as soon as we get sunlight.' With that advice he returned to his tent-store and honed a butcher knife to razor sharpness. Then he drank off a bottle of whiskey and fell into a stupor.

He was up at four, building a small fire in which he sterilized the knife. Placing a chair where the sun would strike it, he shouted, 'Bring him over here.'

McKeag, the two Pasquinel boys and three Arapaho women carried the sick man to the operating chair. He was placed on it so that his arms hung over the wooden back. 'Lash 'em down,' Haversham directed, and thongs were tied around his arms, securing them to the chair. 'Legs too,' Haversham cried. When Pasquinel was properly trussed, the surgeon took his knife and neatly slit the back of his shirt, exposing the scar.

McKeag thought, He could of taken if off before he tied him down.

But the surgeon had moved to other problems. Washing his knife in whiskey, he waved it menacingly in the air to dry it. He then gave Pasquinel a large swig of the whiskey and took one himself. Patting the trussed man on the head, he assured him, 'I've done this many times.' With that he stepped behind Pasquinel, studied his muscles, and with deep confident cuts, laid open his back.

Pasquinel made no sound. 'Give him a pistol to bite on,' the surgeon cried belatedly, but this proved unnecessary, for Pasquinel had prepared himself, and the pain could grow many times more excruciating before he would react.

The back was now open and the arrowhead exposed. With the point of the butcher knife Haversham tried to dislodge it, but cartilage had grown about it and held it fast to the backbone and rib. 'A little whiskey,' Haversham called, and some was poured over the fingers of his right hand.

Without hesitation, and with rude force, he jabbed his fingers into the bloody mess, caught the arrowhead by one side and worked it back and forth three times. 'Hold your breath,' he shouted, and Pasquinel, sweat pouring from his face, fixed his eyes stolidly on the horizon.

With wrenching force Haversham pushed the flint deeper into the flesh, twisted it, broke the cartilage and tore it loose from its ancient prison. He thrust it before Pasquinel's nose, and the Frenchman, seeing the mass of blood on Haversham's hand, came close to fainting.

It was five-thirty in the morning and Haversham stayed drunk all that day, refusing to see anyone. Pasquinel, fortified by shots of Taos Lightning, recovered quickly and was stumbling around by nightfall. He was so grateful to the Arapaho women for helping him that he arranged a party and spent much money on drink and presents, but Haversham, the hero of the affair, did not attend. He stayed in his tent, appalled by the realization of what he had done. He had never cut a human being before: there was so much more blood than he had anticipated . . . the arrow had been lodged so tightly. In the end he had wedged his fingers under the man's backbone. He could still feel the bone, and felt nauseated.

As the party grew rowdier, McKeag was approached by one of the

Hudson's Bay men, a voyageur from Montreal, who drew him away from the merriment. 'Is Pasquinel your partner?' he asked. Since the honest reply would have to be 'Yes and no,' McKeag equivocated, and the Canadian asked, 'Is it true that he has a wife in Saint Louis?'

'I don't know.'

'I don't mean his Indian wife. Every man with good sense has an Indian wife—at least one.' He laughed nervously at his joke. 'What I mean,' the Canadian said hesitantly, 'is that in Montreal he has a real wife.'

'I doubt it,' McKeag said evenly.

The Canadian moved so that they were facing. 'She is my cousin,' he said.

McKeag did not care to hear such news and tried to leave, but the Canadian held on to him. 'He left her with two children. We have to pay the money.'

McKeag stared over the man's head, but the Canadian continued: 'You've been in Saint Louis with him. I know it. Does he have a wife there?'

'I know nothing of any wives,' McKeag said stubbornly. He left the man in shadows, and in that way the rendezvous ended.

During the next year, 1828, a series of events occurred, apparently unrelated, which had a lasting effect upon life on the plains. After this climactic year the beaver men would continue to move up and down the rivers for a time, but their disappearance was ordained. The boisterous rendezvous would convene each year for more than a decade, but its doom, too, was sealed, and even Alexander McKeag, so perceptive about beaver, would be involved in these changes without being aware of them.

It started during the winter at Beaver Creek. For some years now the beaver along this stream had been doing poorly. They had no aspen to feed on, and such cottonwood as persisted was poor. Good trees did not exist, for men had cut them down for winter refuges, and even puny trees were difficult to find, for the same men cut them for kindling.

Once there had been a hundred beaver lodges on this creek, each with its own dam, each with its yearly replenishment of kits and two-year-olds. There had been in those days so many beaver that a hungry Indian or a lone trapper could take what he needed without depleting the stock, and all had prospered.

Now the lodges were cleaned out, trapped dry. Year after year the avaricious trappers had raided the dams, drowning the parent beavers, killing the two-year-olds with clubs, leaving the kits without protection or food. The inexhaustible supply was exhausted.

The second event which determined the development of the plains occurred in London, where on a spring morning the young and fashionable David, Earl Venneford of Wye, found that his prized beaver hat had been badly soiled the night before when it toppled out of his landau while he was fondling the left thigh of the Marchioness of Bradbury. He stopped by his hatter to see what repairs were possible, for this was a hat he treasured. It fit him well and had been his favorite since his Oxford days. But now, apparently, its usefulness was ended.

'I could, of course, brush it well and get the sand out,' his hatter said. 'But it's badly worn here, my lord, and if I tried to repair it, you'd never like it. I'm afraid it's gone, my lord, and that's the sum of it.'

'You couldn't replace that worn spot? With new fur?'

'I could, if all you wanted the hat for was shooting in the country, but not for London wear, my lord.'

'Then what's to do? A new beaver?'

'We have a hat here . . . We've been experimenting with Messrs. Wickham. It's a hat we're sure will become the fashion.' He handed young Venneford a handsome deep-blue hat made of some new substance.

'This isn't beaver,' the earl protested. 'I'd not want this.'

'It's a new style, sir. I assure you, it's what all London will be wearing next year.'

'What is it?'

'Silk, my lord. French silk. Stiffer than beaver and easier to maintain.'

Venneford twirled the hat on his right forefinger. He liked the shimmering play of light. Tapping it with his left thumb, he liked the crispness. 'This could be very attractive,' he said. 'I could grow to like a hat of this nature.'

At lunch that day he showed his new acquisition to the ladies. 'It's silk. French silk. Very . . . what shall I say?'

'Fashionable,' the Marchioness of Bradbury suggested. 'It's very fashionable, David, and a heavenly blue.'

When word passed through London that David Venneford was wearing one of the new silk things from Paris—only the silk was from Paris, mind you, the workmanship was by Messrs. Wickham—there was a flurry in the world of fashion. Later when Venneford was married wearing one of the silk hats, of a shimmering silver-gray, a style was set, the fate of the monotonous brown beaver hat was sealed. A whole way of life on the distant plains of America was doomed.

In one of the coincidences of history, the beaver was largely exterminated in the mountains at the exact time when its pelts were no longer wanted in the cities.

'It's not so easy to find pelts now,' McKeag reported to Bockweiss. He stayed in Saint Louis for several weeks, marveling at the changes that had overtaken it as an American city. Grand Rue was now Main Street. Rue de l'Eglise and Rue des Granges were now Second and Third streets, and wherever he went he heard that Bockweiss had bought this or sold that.

Lise Pasquinel, hearing that her old friend was in town, invited him to supper at her big brick house on Fourth Street, and after he had climbed to that height he saw what a splendid view she had. 'The Mississippi runs for you,' he told her, but he became tongue-tied upon finding that Grete and her prosperous husband had been invited too. 'I thought you'd like to meet old friends,' Lise explained, and the sisters were so gracious that they forced him to forget his shyness.

There was much talk of American military action along the frontier, as they now called it, and repeated questions about Indians. After supper Hermann Bockweiss stopped by, bringing the two Pasquinel children. Cyprian, a tall young man, aged twenty-four, appeared in a Parisian outfit: tight trousers, ornate vest, jacket, ruffled shirt, stock, pointed shoes and one of the new silk hats. He was a courteous young fellow and said he was helping his grandfather buy land. Lisette, aged thirteen, was a pert child, pretty in a French way, but firm-chinned like her German mother; she wore a princesse gown with the belt line of the bodice very high and the skirt flaring away in lovely patterns. McKeag could not help contrasting the civilized behavior and dress of these Pasquinel children with that of their half brothers on the prairie; they spoke English, French and German equally well. They were not deceitful enough to act as if they were interested in talking with McKeag; they scarcely knew who he was and were eager to be off.

'Fine children,' McKeag said impulsively as they left. 'Pasquinel would be proud of them.'

This inappropriate observation produced a chill, but without obvious embarrassment Lise leaned forward and asked, 'How is Pasquinel?'

'Hasn't he been here?'

'We haven't seen him for seven years,' she said evenly.

McKeag looked at her without speaking. How pitiful, he thought. No big fight, not even a difference of opinion. Just a fur trapper who got fed up with the city and left one day, a Daniel Boone asking the world to leave him alone. He felt deep compassion for Lise but could find no way to express it. Her brother-in-law broke the silence to ask, 'What's he up to now?'

McKeag reflected. What was Pasquinel up to? From the myriad answers he might have given he chose a strange one: 'They cut that arrowhead out of his back.'

'Did they!' Lise cried.

'How'd they do it?' Grete asked. And McKeag went into such detail, explaining what the rendezvous was like and how the Englishman Haversham sold lapsang souchong, that any tenseness over Pasquinel was eased. Later he said with considerable infelicity, 'I think it was after they cut out the flint . . . Pasquinel was drunk, but he stood stock-still and allowed his son—well, both of his boys—to shoot a whiskey bottle off his head.'

There was another silence, which none of the listeners cared to break. Then Grete's husband asked quietly, 'His sons?'

'Bockweiss knows about the sons,' McKeag said, but as soon as the words were spoken he realized that the old German had sought to protect Lise's feelings by not telling her of the Indian family. Now, having betrayed the secret, McKeag felt that he should complete it. 'They are younger than Cyprian,' he told Lise. 'Marcel has possibilities. Jacques, the oldest, is a terrible monster. What might happen with him, not even God knows.'

Lise listened to this information impassively and refused to comment.

As McKeag started to leave, he noticed again how luxurious the house was, filled with fine things shipped from the east. 'My children will be marrying soon,' Lise said. 'They'll live here at first, I hope, and maybe one of them will want the house and allow me to stay on.' She was a composed, gracious woman, the finest lady McKeag had ever met.

'Thank you for supper,' he said, and the way he spoke was so formal that she reached out and grabbed his hands, pulling herself to him and kissing him on the cheek.

'Alexander! We're old friends!' And she dragged him to a different corner of the house and showed him the room she had built for him. 'This is your room, Alexander,' she cried, pressing her fingers against her tears. 'As long as you live, when you come to Saint Louis you are to come here . . . stay with us. There will be no more living along the river.'

She insisted that he move in that night, sent servants down to the shore to gather his belongings lest he go and not come back, and when his meager equipment was installed she sat on his bed, smoothed out her skirt and said, 'Now tell me about Pasquinel.'

During that autumn of 1828 Pasquinel, Clay Basket, the two boys and their baby sister pitched their tipi among the red-stone monuments that lined the North Platte east of where the Laramie River joined. This was country occupied by the Oglala Sioux, a warlike tribe that Pasquinel liked, and while his sons rampaged with the young braves he held long talks with the chiefs, trying to ascertain whether they knew anything of Lame Beaver's gold. They knew nothing.

He was irritated beyond endurance. He resumed the hard questioning of Clay Basket which he had conducted sporadically through the twenty-two years of their marriage, and one day, as she had reviewed once again her father's life, he recalled something of importance.

'Didn't I see in your father's tipi a buffalo skin with paintings on it? His coups?'

'Yes, my mother painted it.'

'Where is it?'

She shrugged her shoulders and explained again that among her people, when a man died his goods were distributed.

'I know that,' he snapped. 'But who got the picture skin?'

'No one.'

He could not accept this as an answer, and shook her. 'What do you mean, no one?' he shouted, and she explained that at her father's death the painted skin simply disappeared.

After a while he had to believe this, but then he had another clever idea. Let Clay Basket recall the incidents on the skin so that Pasquinel might reconstruct the places that her father had visited. It was a pleasure for her to visualize her mother's beautiful paintings, and she ticked off the scenes.

There was the raid on the Comanche, but that wasn't gold country. There was the victory over Never-Death, but Pasquinel already knew that land.

She went through the litany of courage, but could come up with only seven incidents, whereas even Pasquinel knew there had been eight. He badgered her, charging her with holding back the crucial information because she didn't want him to find the gold . . . wanted to save it for the Arapaho after he was dead.

She punished her brain, trying to reconstruct her father's life, and then, as she was making pemmican, she recalled a small painting in the corner, of her father cutting tent poles and fighting Ute warriors. 'I know!' she called, and Pasquinel came running.

'It was when Lame Beaver went into the mountains to cut tipi poles. He had a fight with some Ute warriors, and I'm sure he took their pouches. And that's where the bullets must have been.'

'Tipi poles, where?'

'Blue Valley.'

'We camped there,' Pasquinel shouted. 'Damn it, we camped there.'

'That's where it was. I remember the story now.'

It was much too late to shift camp to Blue Valley now, but all that winter among the bleak monuments rimming the Platte, Pasquinel visualized Blue Valley, and how the stream cut through the meadow, and where in the hills the gold might lie. Finding it became an obsession many times stronger than it had been when first he held the two gold bullets in his palm.

His life had not worked out well. Had he stayed with any one of his white wives he could have had a reasonably happy time of it; his many children were likable and he supposed they were doing well. But he had wanted to keep running; that's what he was, a coureur de bois. The beaver had been plentiful and he had earned much money from them, but it was all gone now. What he needed was to find that gold—to climax his failures and his indifferent years with a grand exploration and so much wealth that men from Montreal to New Orleans would speak of him with enduring respect: 'Pasquinel who found the gold mine.'

He would leave his Indian sons with the Oglala Sioux. They would be happier there; they were Indians now, and the Sioux would be glad to have two more braves. Yes, he and Clay Basket and the little girl would move south to Blue Valley as soon as the ice broke. The beaver? They could wait. It was getting more difficult to find them, and if he could locate the gold, there would be no more need for beaver.

McKeag, still operating alone, was not gathering many pelts either, certainly not enough to warrant another trip to Saint Louis. In the autumn of 1829 he had to decide where he would trap during the coming winter. He preferred to hole up at Rattlesnake Buttes for the cold months, then work the tributaries of the Platte when the thaw came, but even a cursory examination of those streams satisfied him that the animals were gone. Beaver Creek, which had been jammed with beaver when he first trapped it, had none at all, and the creeks farther west were little better.

He had no alternative but to abandon this congenial country and move into the foothills of the Rockies. With regret he said farewell to an area which had been kind to him and from which he had taken a modest fortune, now safely banked in Saint Louis.

Traveling on foot, he moved to the northwest toward a spot he had marked some years before, a chalk cliff which afforded protection from storms and had likely streams near at hand. There he found enough scraps of wood to erect the outlines of a hut and enough branches to keep a fire going.

It was a bad winter and he was soon snowed under. Drifts covered him and once more he lived at the bottom of a cave. Since he had survived such entombments before, this one did not cause apprehension, and there was one change which brought a measure of contentment. Each day at sunset, after he had crawled back into his tunnel, he brewed himself one small cup of lapsang souchong, and as its smoky aroma filled the cave, it brought visions of Scotland: he saw his mother at the peat fire, his father stomping in from tending sheep. Then, no matter how hard he tried to limit his thoughts, he saw himself in a yellow apron, dancing at the rendezvous, and Pasquinel stepping forward to dance with him— and he could no longer deny how much he loved this difficult man.

They had fought side by side and each had saved the other's life. In long winters they had sat by meager fires, hardly speaking for days at a time. They had been loved by the same woman, that remarkable Arapaho. Above all, they had explored an uncharted continent. They were closer than brothers. They were children of the buffalo, inheritors of the plains.

Pasquinel had taught McKeag the meaning of freedom, of man alone on the infinite prairie hemmed in only by the horizon, and it forever receding. How pitiful the horizons had been in Scotland: a tiny glen dominated by one rich man and all terrified of him and his power. West of the Missouri there were no rich men, only men of courage and capability, and if a man lacked either, he was soon dead.

And yet, as McKeag thought of Pasquinel now, thirty-two years later, he saw all his faults, and he wondered if the Frenchman had ever really known the meaning of freedom. He had cherished the companionship of women, but he had always fled at the first sense of encroachment. He had loved his numerous children, but he had left them for his wives to rear. He had always been a man running away from something, courageous in physical battle, a coward in moral values. He had called it freedom, but it was flight.

McKeag, the tentative one, actually felt compassion for Pasquinel, who had arrogantly directed their ventures. He was sorry that so gallant a man had come to so poor an end, but at the same time he recognized that they were still bound together by the indissoluble bonds of dangers shared and work done. Suddenly he no longer wished to live alone. He wanted to share a tipi with Pasquinel and Clay Basket on the open prairie and to seek with them such beaver as survived.

He spent a week pondering what overt action this decision entailed: At the next rendezvous I will become partners with him again. Fortified by this resolve, he began to look forward to summer, and his snowbound cave became less oppressive.

So on a brilliant, storm-free day in March, as he climbed out to see whether spring was coming to the streams he intended trapping, he felt himself gripped by a force greater than any he had previously known. It was as if a great hand pulled him, and he heard himself cry, 'Pasquinel needs me.' With irrational frenzy he packed what gear he could carry, lashed a pair of snowshoes to his feet and set forth on his difficult journey to Blue Valley.

The drifts were deep and the sun blinding. To invade mountains in such weather was preposterous, but he was convinced that Pasquinel had to be there, so he forged ahead.

Night fell, and he huddled in the lee of a rock, covering himself with snow to keep from freezing, but before dawn he resumed his trek and all that day clawed through drifts.

At last he found the branching stream that flowed down from Blue Valley, and now he was guided by the little stone beaver that climbed the cliff.

As he neared the plateau where the valley rested he had a hideous thought: Suppose Pasquinel is not here? Impossible. He would not think about that.

With a new surge of energy he clambered up the last rocks and looked down into the valley. With immense relief he saw that a lodge had been erected and that signs of life surrounded it, signs the uninitiated might miss: a branch missing from a tree, scuffled snow where an antelope had been shot.

Running as fast as his snowshoes would permit, he shouted, 'Pasquinel! I'm here!'

He was close to the lodge before anyone responded. Then he saw that the door had been torn from its hinges, and Clay Basket stood on the threshold, holding a child in her arms. Clay Basket's face was streaked with blood and she seemed to comprehend nothing.

'Pasquinel!' McKeag screamed into the unechoing snow.

Kicking off his snowshoes, he dashed into the lodge. There on the floor, face down, lay Pasquinel, his body riddled with arrows and his scalp gone. McKeag looked at him dumbly, then knelt to turn the body over, as if it might still contain life.

'Who did it?'

'Shoshone.'

'The boys. Didn't they help?'

'Pasquinel left them with the Sioux.'

He took charge of everything, cutting the arrows from the dead body and preparing it for burial. He washed away the blood and brought in wood to keep the fire going. Before sunset he cleared away a patch of snow and hacked out a shallow grave in the frozen earth. There he buried Pasquinel, man of many wounds, many victories.

That night McKeag recalled that his partner had often predicted that some day the Indians would kill him, and they had. They had caught him kneeling to inspect the stream bed, turning over the gravel to see if perhaps this was where Lame Beaver had found his gold. They shot him full of arrows just as he was reaching for a glistening object. He staggered back to the lodge to protect his wife and child, as he had always protected the weaker in a fight, but they were away gathering wood, and he had died alone, as he always knew he must. In death he had two dollars and eighty cents and owed four thousand; the glistening nugget he had spotted was soon covered over with gravel.

For two uneasy days McKeag stayed in the valley, but then he was pulled by a sense of obligation back to his own traps, to his tunnel under the snow.

'Trap here,' Clay Basket said in a low voice.

'Your sons will care for you,' he said.

'They are gone,' she said. There was a silence, after which she said in a whisper, 'I am alone.'

These words cut McKeag, for they were his words, thrown back at him. In confusion he tried to sort out ideas, but no order prevailed. All he was able to understand was that he no longer wanted to be alone. He acknowledged how wrong it was. He had climbed a mountain of frozen snow to regain a brotherhood he had once known, only to find that such brotherhood was no longer possible.

Could it be, he asked himself, that the mysterious summons he experienced might have involved not Pasquinel but Clay Basket? But he was afraid. He was deeply afraid that he was not meant to share his life with a woman, that he wouldn't know what to do. He was especially afraid that she might laugh at him, as he had heard the Indian women laughing at other men.

For three days he wrestled with this ugly problem and almost convinced himself that he was destined to live alone, but as he looked up at the great mountain and saw the stone beaver forever climbing, he realized that men, like animals, must climb whatever cliff confronts them.

With new courage he returned to the lodge. 'We'll start down the stream today,' he said.

'In this snow?' she asked.

'My traps are down there,' he said.

'The little one?'

'She will be mine,' he said, taking the child in his arms. 'Her name will be Lucinda.'

But as they set forth, and he realized that he was accepting responsibility for these two as long as they lived, the dreadful doubt returned. He put down the child and took Clay Basket by the hands. 'You won't laugh at me?' he asked.

'I will not laugh,' she promised.

CAUTION TO *US* EDITORS. The attractiveness of the rendezvous should not be underestimated. Pragmatic decisions relating to the political and governmental future of the west were made by the Frenchmen, the English, the Scots, the Americans and the Indians who met for informal discussion at these gatherings. It was the town meeting of New England, transferred to the valley and punctuated by gunfire, murder and the screams of Indian women being raped.

I have omitted some of the gorier details: the planned battles against Indians, a drunk whose friends doused him with a bucketful of pure alcohol, then set him ablaze and watched him burn like a torch until he was pretty well consumed, the woman visitor who saw with horror, after one epic brawl, four men playing pinochle and using the stiffening corpse of a friend as their table.

The rendezvous continued from 1825 through 1840, fifteen years in all. In 1831 it did not convene; the wagon train bringing the whiskey from Taos got lost and ended up three hundred and fifty miles off course to the east, where the Laramie River enters the Platte. Name of the mixed-up guide: Kit Carson.

The rosters of those attending each rendezvous have been compiled. Notables like Jim Bridger, N. J. Wyeth, Captain Bonneville, Marcus Whitman and Father De Smet abound. You might want to look into Peter Skene Ogden, the savagely anti-American Englishman after whom Ogden, Utah, was named, and Alfred Jacob Miller, the painter, who did some sketches of the 1837 meeting.

The 1827 rendezvous, which McKeag attended, had a distinguished list of participants: William Sublette, David Jackson, James Clyman and James P. Beckwourth, the famous black. But I think you might want to focus on the group of nineteen hardened veterans who came in from California under the leadership of Jedediah Smith; for me their names form an authentic roll call of the mountain men:

x Boatswain Brown	x Silas Gobel	x John B. Ratelle
x William Campbell	Joseph La Point	x ? Robiseau
x David Cunningham	Toussaint Marishall	Charles Swift
Thomas Daws	x Gregory Ortaga	Richard Taylor
x Frances Deramme	? Pale	John Turner
Isaac Galbraith	Joseph Palmer	Thomas Virgin
	? Polite	

These nineteen had one hell-raising time at the rendezvous; a few days after they departed, they were jumped by a band of Mohave Indians who had been suborned by the Mexican governor of California. Those marked with x were murdered.

On the other hand, the train of sixty-three men who brought in the cannon and the trade goods returned to Saint Louis without incident, carrying with them one hundred and sixty-four bales of beaver, valued at just under $100,000.

Photographs. Should you want authentic shots of a rendezvous, the citizens of Sublette County, in western Wyoming, recreate this raucous affair each year on the first Sunday in July. It convenes at Pinedale, and practically everyone in the area participates in an authentic, emotionally exciting remembrance of the days when beaver were prime and lonely men penetrated the farthest mountains in search of them.

Note: When trappers like Pasquinel and McKeag outfitted in Saint Louis they bought their stores from a son of Daniel Boone, who had set up shop in that city. Daniel himself did not die in that lonely cabin in 1816. He died four years later in 1820, continuing to hunt till the last.

Warning: Do not fall for the popular belief that *bison bison bison* took its American name *buffalo* from the fact that French coureurs like Pasquinel called the animal a *boeuf*, which degenerated quickly into *boeuf-alo*, hence *buffalo*. Good story, but unfortunately the early Latins called Europe's similar beast a *bubalus*, which was corrupted in Late Latin to *bufalus* and from that to *bufalo*. The animal was never known in America during the historical period as anything but buffalo, and most westerners from 1750 to this day would be astonished to find that their regional symbol was really a bison.

Names. A *voyageur* was a man employed by Canadian fur companies to transport supplies, usually by canoe, to and from distant stations. A *coureur de bois* was an illegal, that is, unlicensed, petty trader in the backwoods who carried trinkets to Indians in exchange for pelts. A *trapper* was one who gathered pelts himself, without bothering with Indian intermediaries. A *mountain man* was the later but lineal descendant of any of these types.

River. Confusion surrounds the name *Platte.* Probably no river in history had been called by so many different names—at least thirty-one— of Spanish, French or Indian origin, but in each tongue at some point it was called 'flat' river. In Spanish it was *Rio Chato,* in Pawnee the *Kits Katus,* in French *La Rivière Plate,* so named by the daring Mallet brothers Pierre and Paul in their 1739 exploration. Most wide of the mark was one claim printed in the 1860s that it was named by the Indians a few years earlier in honor of a white woman missionary named Platte. This is patently ridiculous because Nasatir reproduces a French map dated 1796 showing *Rivière Plate* clearly and accurately. But all this is of little moment, for if the Platte is a nothing river, it can survive with a nothing name.

THE WAGON
AND THE
ELEPHANT

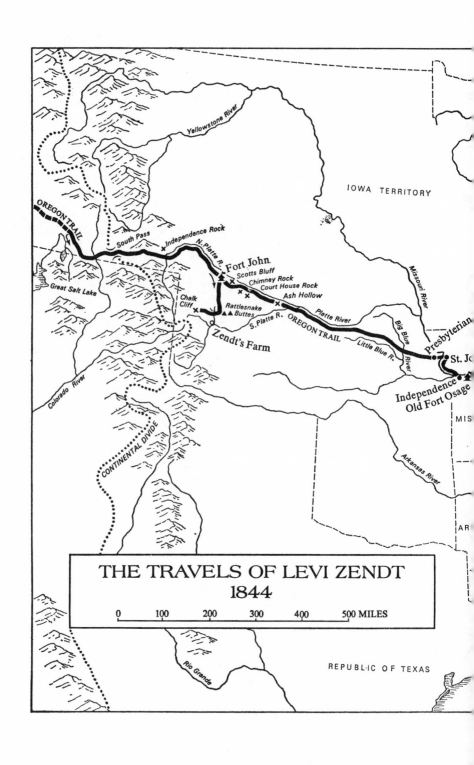

THE TRAVELS OF LEVI ZENDT
1844

0   100   200   300   400   500 MILES

IF IN THE YEAR 1844 A GROUP OF EXPERTS
had been commissioned to identify the three finest agricultural areas of
the world, their first choice would probably have been that group of
farms in the south of England, where the soil was hospitable, the climate
secure and the general state of husbandry congenial. Here sturdy farmers,
well versed in the ancient traditions of the countryside, raised Jersey
cattle, plump black-and-white Hampshire hogs, rugged Clydesdales and
poultry of the best breed.

The experts might also have selected that rare and rich band of black
chernozem that stretched across southern Russia, especially in the
Ukraine. Two feet deep, easy on the plow, and so fertile that it needed
less than normal manuring, this extraordinary soil was unequaled and
constituted an agricultural treasure which the serfs of the area had mined
for the past thousand years without depleting it.

But whether the experts had chosen England or Russia, one area that
would have had to be included was that fortunate farmland lying around
the small city of Lancaster in southeastern Pennsylvania, at the eastern
foothills of the Appalachians. For sheer elegance of land and profitability
of farming, it stood supreme.

It was not flat land. There was just enough tilt to the meadows to
prevent rain from gathering in the bottoms and turning the land sour.
Nor was the topsoil unusually deep or easy to cultivate. If a man wanted
to have a fine Lancaster farm, he had to work. But the rainfall was what
it should be—about forty inches a year—and there was a change of seasons, with frosty autumns during which hickory nuts fell and snowy
winters when the land slept.

The Lancaster farmer did not exaggerate when he boasted, 'On this
land a good man can grow anything except nutmeg.' And on all of it he
could make a handsome profit, for his farm lay within marketing distance of Philadelphia and Baltimore. Corn, wheat, sorghum, hay, truck,

tobacco and even flowers could be got to market, but it was the animals who prospered most and provided the best income, particularly cattle and hogs. Lancaster beef and pork were the standards of excellence against which others from less fortunate regions were judged.

In the divine lottery which matches men and soil—that chancy gamble which often places thrifty men on fields of granite and wastes good farms on incompetents content to reap whatever the wind sows—a proper match-up was made. Into Lancaster County, in the early years of the eighteenth century, came a body of well-trained peasant farmers fleeing oppression and starvation in Germany. Arriving mostly from the southern parts of that country, they brought with them a rigorous Lutheranism, which in its extremes manifested itself as the Amish or the Mennonite faith.

It was the Amish who determined the basic characteristics of Lancaster. They were an austere group who eschewed any display such as buttons or brightly colored clothes, and rejected any movement which might soften the harsh Old Testament pattern of their life. At the age of ten each Amish boy was married to the soil, and to it he dedicated the remainder of his life, rising at four, tending his chores before eating a gargantuan breakfast at seven, laboring till twelve, then eating an even larger meal which he called dinner. He worked till seven at night, ate a light evening meal called supper, after the tradition of Our Lord, and went to bed. He worshipped God on Sundays and in all he did, and when he was old enough to have a black buggy of his own and a brown mare to draw it, as he drove from Blue Ball to Intercourse, he would pause sometimes to give thanks that fate had directed him to Lancaster County, a land worthy of his efforts.

In most other parts of the world the Mennonites would have seemed impossibly rigid, but when compared to the Amish they were downright frivolous, for they indulged in minor worldly pleasures, were expert in conducting business and allowed their children other choices than farming. Some Mennonite children even went to school. But when they did farm, they did it with vigor and were wonderfully skilled in extracting from their soil its maximum yield. When this was accomplished, they became uncanny in their ability to peddle it at maximum profit. Mennonite women in particular were gifted at selling; they knew to the penny what they could demand of a customer, giving him in turn such a good bargain that he was likely to come back. Dressed in demure black jackets, black skirts, white aprons and white net caps, they were prepared to haggle a wagon driver into the ground and to extract the price they wanted, and if they lost a sale they grieved.

In January 1844 one of the most interesting spots in Lancaster County was the rural village of Lampeter. It had been named after a profane and riotous wagoner called Lame Peter who had used that particular spot as a depot when freighting farm produce to Philadelphia. In time all wagoners adopted the custom of laying over in Lampeter, and since they were a rough lot, the main thoroughfare of the village, with Conestogas hitched to every tree, became known as Hell Street.

'Meet you in Hell Street with bells on!' wagoners shouted as they departed Philadelphia on their way home, and when the long canvas-covered wagons jingled into Hell Street, pulled by six dappled horses, each with its canopy of bells—five on the first pair of horses, four on the second pair, three on the third pair—the street echoed with jollity. Many girls who had been leading drab lives on farms in other parts of the county gravitated to the inns that lined Hell Street to listen for the bells of the incoming wagoners.

On a Thursday afternoon, January fourth, a disgruntled wagoner approached Hell Street in silence. His horses lacked the twenty-four brass bells which a proper team of Conestogas should have, and loungers at the inn came into the street to mark this strange arrival. 'He lost his bells!' one of the girls cried, and soon customers had left the bars to stand in the snow around the unhappy wagoner.

'How'ja lose yer bells, Amos?' a fellow teamster shouted.

'That damned left rear,' Amos replied, tying his lead horse to a tree. 'Started to work loose east of Coatesville. Had to be pulled out.'

The Conestoga wagoning fraternity had strict rules: if a teamster got himself into such a predicament that he required help from another, he was obligated to give his rescuer a set of bells. This was the ultimate humiliation.

'You gettin' another set of bells?' an innkeeper asked as Amos moved away from his horses.

'That I ain't,' Amos growled. He was a tall, angular man with a mean scowl.

'You quittin'?'

'That I am,' he replied, and with this he rushed back to the offending Conestoga and began kicking the left rear wheel, at the same time shouting such curses as even Lampeter had not heard for some time. He grew purple in the face, throwing the vilest words he could think of until it seemed that he must scorch the canvas. With a final mighty kick he tried to knock the wheel into the next county, then stood with his arms folded, staring at the wagon and uttering a summary curse that repeated no single profanity but required a minute to discharge. Then, flinging his arms wide and surveying the crowd, 'Anybody can have this bullshit wagon. I never want to see it again.' With that he stomped into the White Swan.

At the edge of the crowd, stamping his feet to keep warm while he watched this remarkable performance, stood a young Mennonite in black suit and flat-brimmed hat. He was twenty-four years old, stockily built, with a reddish beard that started at his ears and met in a neat line just at the edge of his chin. Since his face was already square, the fringe of beard made it look as if it had been framed.

Casually he inspected the abandoned Conestoga. It was old; he could see that. 'Probably been used for forty years,' a farmer near him judged. 'The paint's wore somethin' awful.' The original deep blue of the box had faded to a pastel, while the bright red of the wheels and tongue had become gray-orange. 'That left wheel don't look much,' the farmer said, kicking at it several times. 'Lissen to it rattle.'

As they looked at the worn old wagon a tardy arrival from Philadelphia pulled his Conestoga into Hell Street. With one swift glance he perceived what had happened to his associate. 'My God! Amos Boemer lost his bells,' he shouted, and a crowd left the White Swan to greet him.

'Jacob Dietz had to haul him out of a drift,' one of the crowd explained. 'East of Coatesville.'

The new arrival walked around the old Conestoga, kicked at the wheel and said, 'Told him he should get a new one. Told him last month.'

'Wagon's for sale. If'n you want it.'

'Me? Want a used-up Conestoga?' He laughed and led the way into the White Swan.

The young man with the square beard was left alone in the snowy road. Moving slowly, he walked around the Conestoga, judging its condition, then started for home. He was headed east of town toward one of the finest farms in Lancaster County, just beyond the tollgate. It stood to the south of the road, down a lane marked by handsome trees, now bare of leaves.

From a long distance the stately stone barn—with its red-and-yellow hex signs to ward off evil—was visible, and in the cold moonlight the young man could see the proud name worked into the masonry:

JACOB ZENDT

1713

BUTCHER

As with any self-respecting Lancaster farm, the barn was six times the size of the house, for Amish and Mennonite farmers understood priorities.

As the young man walked down the frozen lane, his heavy shoes making the snow crackle, his attention focused mainly on the trees. Because hickory and oak were so vital in his business, he could spot even a young hickory at a hundred yards, marking it in his mind against the day when it would be old enough for him to harvest.

The Zendt farm contained many fine trees: there was the perpetual woods first harvested in 1701 when Melchior Zendt arrived from Germany; then there was the line of trees along the lane, planted by his son Jacob in 1714, and best of all, there was the miniature forest set out by Lucas Zendt in 1767. It rimmed the far end of the pond and was as fine a collection of maple, ash, elm, oak and hickory as Lancaster County provided. Each tree on the Zendt farm was a masterpiece, properly placed and flourishing.

When he reached the farm buildings, the young man looked briefly at the huge barn, then at the small red building in which he worked, then at the even smaller one stained black from much smoke, then at the various snow-covered pigsties, chicken coops and corncribs. Finally, tucked in among the larger buildings, there was the house, a small clapboard affair. There was a light in the kitchen window, and pushing open the door, he saw that his mother was preparing supper while his oldest brother, Mahlon, read the Bible.

'Amos Boemer lost his bells,' he announced as he hung up his hat. 'He cursed somethin' awful.' His mother continued working and Mahlon kept to his Bible.

'I never heard cursin' like that before,' the young man continued.

'God will attend to him,' Mahlon said in a deep voice, without looking up from his Bible.

'Got into a snowdrift east of Coatesville,' the young man said. There being no response, he went to the washstand and prepared for supper.

But as he washed his face Mahlon observed, 'Amos Boemer is a blasphemous man. Little wonder God struck him down.'

'It was the left rear wheel.'

'It was the will of God,' Mahlon explained.

Now his mother lifted a heavy bell, ringing it for half a minute until the whole farm filled with sound. From the big barn came Christian, whose job it was to purchase hogs and cattle from surrounding farmers; on his ability to buy cheap at the right time depended the financial success of the family. From the pigsties came Jacob; it was his responsibility to see that there was a steady supply of pork. From a clean white building came Caspar; he did the butchering. Levi, the youngest brother, who had watched the arrival of the Conestogas, worked in the two smallest buildings, the red and the one stained black; his job was to make sausage and scrapple, and at this he was so proficient that Zendt pork products brought the highest prices in Lancaster. There was even talk of shipping them in to Philadelphia when the railroad was completed to Lancaster.

The four younger brothers, each with the stamp of Mennonite upbringing, took their places at the two sides of the long table. Their mother, now in her sixties, sat at the end nearest the stove so that she could attend to such cooking as continued during the meal, and at the other sat the oldest brother, Mahlon, a dark and gloomy man in his thirties, feeling the responsibility for this family now that the father was dead.

When the six were seated, they bowed their heads for grace while Mahlon reviewed the evil state of the world and asked for forgiveness for such sins as his four younger brothers had committed during the interval since dinner: 'We are mindful of the fact that Brother Levi has been spending his afternoons on Hell Street, consorting in taverns and making acquaintances with the devil. Guide him to halt this infamous behavior and direct him to attend to his proper obligations.' Levi flushed and could feel the others looking at him from beneath lowered foreheads.

Mahlon had a long list of matters he desired God to take notice of, and at the end he repeated the rubric which had guided this family for the past hundred and fifty years: 'Help us so to live in Thy light that our name shall be respectable in all its doings.' From the five listeners rose a fervent 'Amen.'

It was curious that this supper table contained only one woman. Each of The Five Zendts, as they were called in Lancaster, was of marriageable age and each could be considered a catch. Many farm girls watched the Zendts, especially the four oldest; there was some talk that young Levi was not too stable.

But the Zendt family had always married late, when the stormy passions of youth had been suppressed and when the family as a whole had time to study contiguous farms to ascertain which had desirable fields that might accompany the girl of the family when she married. The Zendt farm had started with sixty acres in 1701 and now contained somewhat over three hundred, and you didn't augment a farm that way by marrying the first girl who came along when you were twenty. You did it by patient acquisition, and if fate determined that you must marry a girl who lived in another part of the county, you sold off her dowry immediately and bought land touching yours. In 1844 there was no better farm in Lancaster County than the Zendts', and with five marriageable sons, by 1854 it ought to be much better.

Mahlon, at thirty-three, had begun slowly to focus upon a certain girl who was likely to receive a substantial amount of land when her father died. He hadn't divulged his decision to anyone yet, least of all to the girl, because a man didn't want to rush into these things, but he kept his eye on her.

Tomorrow was Friday, the last of the three big days around which the Mennonite week revolved: Sunday for worship; Tuesday and Friday for market. At the conclusion of supper Levi shoved back his chair, saying brusquely, 'I'm goin' out to see the souse,' and when he was safely gone Mahlon told his brothers, 'We must all watch Levi. He's getting feisty.' The three other Zendts agreed. In their earlier days each of them had gone feisty at some time or other, had wanted to smoke tobacco, or taste beer at taverns along Hell Street, or ogle the girls, but each had suppressed these urges and had stuck to butchering. It was clear that now they would have to guide Levi through this dangerous period.

Out in the yard he lit a lantern and walked stolidly across the frozen snow to the small red building. Kicking open the door, he surveyed his little kingdom and found it in good order. The sausage machine was clean and placed against the wall. Six baskets of white sausage links were lined up and waiting. The twenty large flat scrapple pans were stacked, each filled nearly to the brim with a grayish delicacy hidden beneath a protecting layer of rich yellow fat. It, too, was ready. It was the souse that needed attention, and when he saw it still on the stove, he knew that he should have worked that afternoon instead of wandering down to Hell Street to watch the wagoners roar in.

Levi liked souse better than any of the other products he made, and he devoted extra attention to preparing it. Throughout the Lancaster area it was said, 'For souse, Levi Zendt.'

He went to the stove and dipped a long-handled ladle into the simmering pot. The thirty-six pigs' feet looked done. He picked up a bone from the ladle, and the well-cooked meat slid off.

'Good!' he said.

He lifted the kettle from the stove and with great skill extracted all the white bones of the hogs' feet, being careful to leave in the gristle, for that was what made Zendt souse so delectable. He then returned the kettle of hog meat to the fire, tossing in six pounds of the best lean pork, well chopped, and six hogs' tongues, also chopped. Throwing two chunks of wood into the stove, he allowed the mixture to cook while he prepared the broth which gave the souse its taste.

Extracting stock from the bubbling kettle, he poured it into a large crock to which he added twelve cups of the sourest cider vinegar the area could provide. 'That'll make 'em pucker,' he said. He then added twelve tablespoons of salt to give the souse a bite, three teaspoons of pepper to make it snap, and a handful of cloves and cinnamon bark to make it sweet. He placed the crock on the back of the stove, keeping it warm rather than hot. Twice he tasted it, smacking his lips over the acrid bite the vinegar and salt imparted, but he crushed two more cloves to give it better balance.

He now laid out twelve souse pans and placed in each of them round disks of the sourest Lancaster pickles and here and there a single small slice of pickled carrot. Then like an artist he adjusted various items to produce a more pleasing design.

After a few minutes he took the kettle of bubbling meat from the fire and with tongs began fishing out the larger pieces of meat, arranging them among the pickles and carrots in the bottom of the pans. It was here that Zendt souse achieved its visual distinction, because the meat came in two colors, white chunks from the fatty parts, red meat from the lean; he kept the two in balance, working rapidly, pulling up smaller and smaller pieces and distributing them evenly.

Finally, when little meat was left, he tipped the crock forward and strained the broth through a sieve, which removed the cloves and bits of cinnamon bark.

'Good!' he grunted.

With care he ladled the broth into the pans of meat, and he had calculated so neatly that when the last pan was filled, the kettle was empty. Before he had finished cleaning up, the gelatin from the hogs' feet had begun to set. By morning the souse would be shimmering hard, filled with tender pork and chewy gristle, clean and sour-tasting.

Links of sausage, pans of scrapple, flats of souse, that's what the people of Lancaster expected from the five Zendts and that's what they got.

When he left the red building he poked his lantern into the small black building, where a flood of acrid smoke greeted him. Covering his nose, he looked up at the rafters where great sausage links hung suspended, brown from the penetrating hickory fumes. They looked just right, but nevertheless he squeezed an end to satisfy himself. It was hard and firm, with just a little grease running out. He smelled it. A strong aroma of burnt hickory, one of the most enticing smells in the world, reassured him.

'It's ready,' he announced to his brothers as he rejoined them.

'We expected it to be,' Mahlon said. He had the Bible open and now asked his four brothers and his mother to join him in their nightly prayer. This being Thursday night, he intoned: 'And help us, O Lord, to be honest men tomorrow and to give good measure and to behave ourselves as Thou wouldst have us, and may no one who comes to us feel cheated or robbed or in any way set upon.' It was a prayer his father had uttered when the boys were young, and his father before him.

Closing the Bible reverently, he said, 'Breakfast at three, Momma,' and the five Zendts went to bed.

Friday for Levi was a day of joy. It was the end of the week and people coming to the market were apt to be in a happy mood, and the Stoltzfus bakery . . . In bed he hugged himself. He could visualize the double stall of the Stoltzfus bakery.

At three the heavy bell rang and the five boys came down to the hearty breakfast their mother had started preparing at two. Scrapple and sausage, a little smoked bacon and some pig's liver and fried chicken, eighteen fried eggs with slabs of ham, some good German bread and two kinds of fruit pie, dried apple and canned cherry, and quarts of milk . . . that was the market-day breakfast for the Zendts.

After morning prayers they all crammed themselves full, for their work was hard and generated tremendous appetites, and when they had pushed themselves away from the table Mahlon said, 'I see that Levi's sleigh isn't loaded yet.'

'I was waitin' for the souse to harden,' Levi said.

'If it had been made on time, it would be hardened, yet," Mahlon snapped.

'It'll be loaded,' Levi said briskly. He would not allow Mahlon to spoil his Friday.

Harnessing his two gray-speckled horses, he brought his sleigh to the small red building and there he gently lifted the various pans and baskets, placing them just so in the sleigh. He then ran to the smokehouse and pulled down the long links of smoked sausage and scooped up four dozen fine smoked porkchops. These, too, he placed in the sleigh, then shouted, 'Christian! Caspar! We're off.'

The three stout brothers drove their sleigh in behind the one containing Mahlon and Jacob, and the procession started down the family lane, beneath the fine trees planted by Grandfather Lucas, and out onto the turnpike leading to Lampeter and on to Lancaster. At the tollhouse a grumbling old man appeared to collect the two pennies, after which Levi whipped up his horses and the Zendt boys were on their way to market.

As they drove down the silent white road they overtook other thrifty farmers on their way to market too. There were the Zuber brothers, noted for the vegetables they grew and the crocheted work their wives did. Coming down a lane west of Lampeter were the Mussers, the three women of the family in black dresses topped by delicate white caps of the filmiest net. They sold preserved goods, none better. The Schertzes and the Dinkelochers and the Eshelmans all fell into line, forming a caravan as rich as any that had ever crossed the sands of Persia, for they were taking to market the best that Lancaster County provided, and that had to be the best that the world produced at that time.

Through the darkness they went. It would take more than two hours to reach the center of Lancaster and the prudent farmers did not hurry their horses; they had no desire to jostle their produce or bruise it.

As day was beginning to break, the sleighs approached the town itself and entered the streets that soon would be filled with customers. But now they were still asleep and the sleighs passed the silent shops of Melchior Fordney the gunsmith, Caspar Metzgar the tailor, Philip Schaum the tinsmith and George Doersch, who worked in leather and bound books. Everyone in Lancaster was known by the work he did. Even two gentlemen who slept late that day had their proper signs out: Thaddeus Stevens, attorney; James Buchanan, lawyer.

Now the caravans began to break up. Smaller merchants, like the Musser women and the Eshelmans, who dealt in poultry, stopped before reaching the center of town and backed their sleighs against the open curb. There, along with scores of others from north and south, they would stand all day in the cold, selling to whoever came down the street.

Important merchants, like Zendt the butcher and Stoltzfus the baker, would ignore the curb sites and proceed directly to a cavernous, exciting building, where they would spread their wares. Only the most prosperous could afford to pay the rent for indoor stall space, the established farmers from Rohrerstown and Landisville and Fertility.

The five Zendts drove their two sleighs to the rear of the market, where the younger brothers began unloading while Mahlon and Christian hurried inside to arrange the stall in the clean, attractive way the Zendts had done for generations. The two brothers washed their hands and put on white coats; then they slipped on raffia wrist covers, and they were ready. With long-practiced skill they laid out the meats: the good steaks, the slabs of pork, the chopped beef, and inside a glass case the scrapple, golden yellow where the grease stood, rich meaty gray below, the sausage smoked or plain, and the trays of glistening souse.

As Levi lugged in his trays, his eyes kept hopping over the double stand opposite the Zendt location. There Peter Stoltzfus was opening a family stall which had almost as long a history as the Zendts'. Three generations had created a reputation for fruit pies and stollen, lebkuchen and shoo-fly and the best crunchy bread in the area. Stoltzfus himself was laying out large trays of gingersnaps and sugar cookies, enticingly arranged, and he waved a greeting to Levi.

'Spring's comin' yet,' he called.

'Good mornin', Mr. Stoltzfus,' Levi replied. He was not really interested in the baker, but he deemed it prudent to keep on good terms with him.

Meanwhile, in other parts of the market scores of families were hauling in the myriad things that would soon be sold: large brown eggs, twelve cents a dozen; butter a deep yellow imprinted into blocks marked with flowers, nineteen cents a pound; apples of all varieties brought up from cold cellars, eighteen cents a peck; plucked chicken killed after midnight, twenty-four cents each; potatoes of the best variety, fifteen cents a peck; the largest turkeys, live and handsome, eighty-five cents; smaller turkeys, forty cents; lovely crocheted bedspreads, one dollar; a bucket of flowers grown indoors, twenty cents.

At Stoltzfus the baker's, prices were slightly higher than at lesser shops, because his reputation was the best: a large mince pie, eighteen cents; a loaf of dark German bread, heavy and crusty, eight cents; gingersnaps with a real bite, three for a penny; chewy black-walnut cookies, ten for twelve cents; a three-tiered cake with lemon icing, twenty-five cents. And with every purchase a smile and a repeated thank you.

The Five Zendts kept their prices on the high side too. Their beef sold for five cents a pound, whereas at cheaper shops it could be bought for four or even three. Pork was a little higher, six cents a pound for unsmoked, seven cents for smoked, but it could be bought elsewhere for four cents. The three specialties that young Levi made were much prized by the Lancaster housewives: scrapple at five cents a pound, sausage at six, and a generous square of souse at four cents. On these prices the thrifty farmers of Lancaster County grew rich.

It was three minutes to seven, and soon the market would be jammed with eager housewives. Levi, hauling in a keg of pickled pigs' feet, looked across at the bakery, and to his dismay, only Peter Stoltzfus stood behind the polished counter. Then the drapes at the rear parted and she appeared.

It was Rebecca Stoltzfus, eighteen years old and a dark, lovely girl. She had a breathtaking complexion and jet hair which she parted in the middle and wore in two braids over her shoulders. She had deep-set eyes and a firm chin. She wore a dark-brown blouse, pulled in tight at the waist, above a sweeping black skirt and black buttoned shoes. Like most Mennonite women, she wore a white apron and a lacy network cap with two strings hanging down over her shoulders; on hers the strings were white, signifying that she was not married. She had a distinct cupid's-bow mouth which made her especially attractive, for it gave her the kind of pout that made men look twice. Her father appreciated the fact that in Rebecca he had an asset which would be perpetually helpful in his business, and he showed her off to best advantage.

Levi, hoisting the keg of pigs' feet into position, felt his mouth go dry. During the past week he had been thinking of little but the Stoltzfus girl; in reality she was even more delectable than in his dreams. He tried to nod, but she was preparing the counter for the rush that now descended upon it.

The citizens of Lancaster swarmed into the market as if food were their sole preoccupation, which in a way it was, for no other region on earth ate as well as the Germans of this county. In the overloaded stalls they could find a hundred varieties of food from Kleinschmidt's walnuts to Moyer's apple butter to Hauser's crisp celery, kept in the icehouse since last September. Special favorites were yellow noodles so thick you had to chew them and jars of crisp pickles.

Levi Zendt helped his brothers haul in replacements as Mahlon and Christian handed out wrapped packages. A housewife from Fertility stopped Levi and told him in a heavy German accent, 'I always feel better when I buy from your brother Mahlon. He don't use no air pump to make his meat look better'n it is. He sells chust as God made it.' She nodded her head knowingly at the stall of another merchant who had the habit of inserting a pump nozzle into his stale meat, injecting it with air to make it look firmer, then sealing the hole with tallow.

'Mahlon wouldn't do that,' Levi assured her.

'I know,' she said warmly. She placed her hand on Levi's and said, 'God will look after honest men.' Levi thanked her and continued with his work.

The Zendts did deal honestly. Strict Mahlon would see the business perish before he would pump air into meat or chop old beef and sell it as new. He tested his scales as carefully as St. Peter is supposed to test his when weighing souls, and if he threw in no added chunks, as some butchers did, he took none away either.

As Levi worked, he kept his eye on the Stoltzfus bakery stall, and the wonderful manner in which Rebecca moved and smiled as she waited on customers created new excitement in his heart. He could scarcely wait till the noon bell rang.

It had been his custom, for as long as he had worked in the market, to have a simple dinner. His mother always packed two slices of dark German bread and gave him a hefty helping of cup cheese to go with it. He cut off a cube of his own souse, and from the Yoder stall he bought three cents' worth of pudding. At the Stoltzfus bakery he always purchased two cents' worth of cookies, and it was then that he had a precious chance to say a few words to Rebecca.

For the last three weeks he had been planning a bold move, to ask her to eat her dinner with him, and now as twelve approached he got everything in readiness. At the Yoder stall he studied the enticing array of puddings: creamy rice pudding with raisins, good chewy bread pudding, cherry pudding with toasted crumbs on top and a delicious apple pudding rich with cinnamon.

'So today what?' Mrs. Yoder asked.

'Cherry,' Levi said, and she dished him out a most generous helping, providing a glass dish and a spoon which he would later return.

He then moved to the Stoltzfus stall, but was dismayed when Peter Stoltzfus stepped forward to wait on him. After a moment of panic Levi said, 'I wanted to see Rebecca.'

'Becky!' Stoltzfus shouted so everyone could hear. 'Levi Zendt to see you.'

With a gentle flowing movement that melted Levi's heart, she left her end of the counter and came down to wait on him, the strings of her cap framing her beautiful face. 'Today, gingersnaps?' He nodded and she counted them out.

He pushed his pennies toward her and gulped, 'Rebecca, how about dinner with me today?'

She looked up brightly, as if she had been expecting just such an invitation, and smiled so that all her teeth showed. 'Yes!' she said. 'Wait'll I fetch my coat.'

She disappeared for a moment, then called to him from a rear exit. He would have preferred slipping out the back entrance, but without his being aware of what she was doing, she maneuvered so that he had to take her directly past the Zendt stall. There, behind the counter, stood Mahlon, staring darkly at his younger brother. Levi did not see this, for he was stumbling along, trying to avoid the sly looks of keepers in the other stalls.

They went out into the snowy town and found a bench by the courthouse. For as far as they could see, the streets of Lancaster were filled with sleighs backed into the curbs, and Rebecca said, 'It's lucky our stalls are inside. Much warmer, eh!' He nodded.

Then she saw his food, that strange combination of souse and cup cheese, and she was about to comment on it when he said, 'You ever tasted my mother's cup cheese? Best in Lancaster.'

Taking a corner of his black bread, he spread it copiously with a yellowish viscous substance that one would not normally identify as cheese;

it was more like a very thick, very cold molasses, and it had a horrific smell. Rebecca was not fond of cup cheese; it was a taste that men seemed to prefer.

'Poppa likes cup cheese,' she said with a neutral look on her pretty face.

'You don't?' Levi asked.

'Too smelly.'

'That's the good part.' He put the piece of bread to his nose, inhaling deeply. He knew of few things in the world he liked better than the smell of his mother's cup cheese. By some old accident the German farmers of Lancaster County had devised a simple way of making a cheese that smelled stronger than limburger and tasted better. He ate her piece, his own, what was left and then licked the container. When he got to his cherry pudding, he offered Rebecca some, and this she accepted.

'Amos Boemer lost his bells yesterday,' he said as they finished.

'He did?'

'He cursed like I never heard before.'

'Maybe that's why he lost them.'

'No. Snowdrift east of Coatesville.' He called it Coates-will.

Rebecca was obviously bored with the dinner, and after a little desultory conversation, said, 'I must get back to help Poppa.' Patting him on the arm in a way that sent shivers through his whole body, she pirouetted away. When she reentered the market, she brought herself to Mahlon's attention again, smiling at him more directly than a mere greeting would have required.

When Levi got back to the stall, Mahlon was dark with rage and would not even allow him to wait on customers while he, Mahlon, had his dinner. Levi, unable to guess what had gone wrong, went back to the sleighs and talked with the brothers working there.

At the end of the day, in accordance with a custom long observed by the Zendts, Mahlon and Christian set aside those bits of meat they would not be taking home, and these they chucked into baskets for the orphan asylum. When the market closed at five, these baskets were placed in Levi's sleigh and it was his job to deliver them, while the other four brothers rode home together.

But this night, as the sleighs left, Rebecca Stoltzfus impetuously broke away from her father and jumped in with Levi. 'I'll help you deliver the gifts,' she cried, and Levi, in a state of euphoria, drove her past his startled brothers.

They rode out to the edge of town, to the orphanage supported by the women of St. James' Episcopal Church; there he found the mistress waiting for him, attended by the girl-of-all-duties, Elly Zahm, who was directed to take the baskets into the kitchen.

'I'll help,' Levi suggested, but the mistress would not allow this.

'You've done enough, bringing the meat. Elly can lug it.'

As the sleigh was leaving the orphanage to enter upon the dark street leading back into town, something happened that Levi Zendt would never comprehend as long as he lived. The nearness of this friendly and beautiful girl and the fact that she had chosen to ride in his sleigh got possession of him, and he started to wrestle with her, trying to steal a kiss. He was rough and awkward, and when she coyly pushed him away, he tore her dress. It was an appalling performance, and she began to scream and leaped from the sleigh. Girls from the orphanage, hearing her cries, ran out to see what had happened.

She fell sobbing into the arms of Elly Zahm. 'He's awful!' she whimpered. Then she managed to faint.

By Saturday morning the news had spread throughout Lancaster and had made its way to Lampeter and along Hell Street to the Zendt farm. When Mahlon heard it he had to sit down. He could not believe that a brother of his . . . He felt sick. Then, in a towering rage, he went to the door and screamed, 'Levi! Come here!'

All morning young Levi had been expecting such a summons. He had fled deep into the smokehouse, attending to the dirtiest work on the farm, cleaning out the flues, hoping thus to escape attention. Pretending not to hear, he continued to work furiously, but soon the door to the house was jerked open and Mahlon's wild voice shouted, 'Come out, you son of the devil!'

In an agony of shame Levi crept slowly down from the flues and along the lines of curing hams and sausages. When Mahlon saw him, black as the fiends of hell, the older brother made as if to strike him, but Levi, anticipating this, grabbed a heavy bar used for moving hams, and brandished it.

'He's gone crazy!' Mahlon shouted. 'He's attacking me.'

'I'm not,' Levi said stolidly. 'You're attackin' me.' But he kept hold of the bar.

The other three Zendts ran up and disarmed Levi. They pulled him into the kitchen and forced him into a chair. Standing around him like a congregation of Old Testament judges, their beards giving them a look of great dignity, they waited for Mahlon to speak.

'You pig!' he roared, thrusting his face into Levi's. 'You child of the devil.'

Levi did not consider himself either a pig or a son of Satan. He was a young man caught up in feistiness, and even though he was confused, he understood that Rebecca Stoltzfus would not have climbed into his sleigh if she had not wanted to. It was in this moment of stubborn confusion that Levi Zendt, twenty-four years old, decided that he would not allow his brothers to bully him.

'I did nothin' evil,' he protested.

That he would dare to argue back when he had obviously done something very evil enraged his brothers, and they closed in upon him so menacingly that their mother started to object: 'Now boys! If Levi says . . .'

'Stay out of this, Momma!' Mahlon warned, and he indicated that Jacob should take the old lady from the kitchen.

When Jacob returned, the four brothers hammered at Levi in unison—shouting that he had taken leave of his senses, that he had humiliated them, disgraced the family name. 'Everyone in Lancaster's talking about it,' Jacob said bitterly.

For some strange reason Levi replied, 'You haven't been to Lancaster. I saw you workin'. . .'

The introduction of logic into such a situation infuriated the Zendts, and burly Caspar charged closer as if to strike his brother, but an anguished cry from Mahlon diverted him. 'Didn't you know,' he asked his youngest brother, 'that I was planning to speak to the Stoltzfus girl myself?'

Levi looked up to see his tall brother's face contorted with shame and anger and hatred, and the younger man began to realize what had happened. Mahlon, thirty-three years old, had finally settled on a girl of good family and with substantial land holdings, but being a cautious man, he had not wanted to commit himself precipitately. He had therefore merely indicated his intentions to the girl, then drawn back . . . to study, to reconsider all angles. And the girl had grown impatient and had used Levi to stir the pot. How well she had succeeded.

'Mahlon was intending to ask the Stoltzfus girl,' Christian explained, in case that fact had escaped the culprit, and in the next half hour each of the brothers repeated that a great wrong had been done Mahlon, the head of the family. No one ever called the girl Rebecca. To them she was merely the Stoltzfus girl, the property of Stoltzfus the baker and heiress to the Stoltzfus acres.

Finally Mahlon handed down the verdict: 'You can never work at the market again, that's clear. You stay here and tend your duties and at the end of the day you come into the market and clean up.'

'How'll I get in?' Levi asked, always the practical one.

'You'll walk,' Mahlon said. 'We'll leave you a sleigh for the cleaning up.'

'You were a disgrace to the family,' Christian said bitterly.

Then Mahlon added, 'And on Tuesday you'll ride in with me and you'll apologize to Peter Stoltzfus . . . and the Stoltzfus girl. Where everybody can see.'

Now Levi dropped his face in his hands, mumbling, 'I don't want to go back.'

'I'm sure you don't,' Mahlon shouted, his pride burning, 'but it's the only way this family can redeem itself. Your apology to the whole market.'

That first Saturday was hell. Levi returned to the smokehouse, finding both refuge and consolation in its murky depths. With studied care he picked the choice pieces of hickory, placing them individually on the smoldering fire and allowing the smoke to pass over him as if it could purify him of the heavy stain he bore.

At dinner he could not face his brothers again; he walked alone through the grove of leafless trees and muttered to himself, 'This is the only place that makes any sense.' Then he visualized himself apologizing to Peter Stoltzfus while Rebecca looked on, and he was so smothered in shame, it seemed to him that even the trees turned away from him.

In the afternoon his mother came out to the sausage machine, bringing a jar of cup cheese and some bread. She told him, 'Mahlon's awful hurt. You must forgive him.'

Without relishing it, he slowly ate the cup cheese, licking it off his fingers and listening as his mother said, 'It don't matter, what happened with the Stoltzfus girl. I knew she was a little flirt the first time I met her. Peter Stoltzfus spoils her crazy, and I hope Mahlon don't marry her. Maybe you done us all a good.'

Sunday was worse. His brothers insisted that he attend church, to let the community view his disgrace, and he had to tag along, sitting in the family pew and feeling the hot stares of the Mennonites, each of whom had heard of what was now being called his assault on the Stoltzfus girl.

'Rape,' a father whispered to his daughters in the row behind. 'The work of the devil here in Lampeter.'

At the close of service he had to run the gantlet of condemnatory glances as Mahlon and Christian paused to explain in loud voices that the whole family was ashamed of what had happened—mortified, Mahlon said—and that Levi was going to apologize to the Stoltzfus girl and her father on Tuesday.

The ugly part came at dinner, when Reverend Fenstermacher and his acidulous wife, Bertha, appeared at the Zendt kitchen for their customary free meal. The minister was considerate enough to say to Mahlon, 'I know I'm expected at dinner, but in view of the tragedy that's overtaken your family, perhaps . . .' He hoped with all his heart that Mahlon would not cancel the invitation.

And Mahlon said, 'You must come! Maybe you can throw some light into his dark soul.' This pleased the Fenstermachers enormously, because they knew how good Mrs. Zendt's cooking was.

In Lampeter the Zendts were known as one of the typical merchant families that kept the best for the market and served the nubbins at home. In a sense this was true. Mahlon never handed his mother any choice piece of beef or the best apples from the orchard; they were reserved for the families of James Buchanan and Thaddeus Stevens. Mrs. Zendt got only the second or third best for family use, but she was such an exceptional cook that from nubbins she produced better results than others did with the best. And when the preacher came, she outdid herself.

It was a splendid board she laid that day. Both the table and the stands along the wall were jammed with the best German dishes. She had never subscribed to the old rule that a table must contain seven sweets and seven sours, but she did believe in a generous variety. For meats she had beef pot roast and frizzled dried-beef gravy, pork loin and leftovers from the last ham. For fowl she had a delicious roast hen and a rooster boiled for many hours and served with dumplings. For vegetables she had whipped white potatoes and candied yams, tomatoes and peas, scallions grown indoors, and lettuce with hot bacon dressing. She had five kinds of sours: onions, red-beet eggs, pepper cabbage, chow-chow and plain cucumber. She had four kinds of sweets: apple-sauce rich and brown, pickled pears, canned peaches and a rich cherry preserve. To start with she had soup with rivels, of course, three kinds of bread, and to close the meal four pies: apple, cherry, lemon meringue and wet-bottom shoo-fly, Mrs. Zendt's specialty made with molasses and cinnamon bread crumbs.

Reverend Fenstermacher, surveying the feast with long-practiced eye, noticed that she had no cake.

When the eight were seated, Mahlon looked to the preacher, and Reverend Fenstermacher was ready. He had been pondering all day what he ought to say when he dined with the Zendts, and his mind was clear. Surveying the bowed heads, he cried in strong German, 'O Lord, we have within our midst this day a sinner, a most grievous sinner, a man who has descended to the level of the beasts, nay, lower.'

That was the opening. From there he reviewed Levi Zendt's pious up-bringing, the sterling character of his father and his mother, who, praise God, was still with us this day, and especially his Grandfather Zendt, who would be suffering tortures in heaven as he contemplated the dis-grace brought upon his family by his grandson, Levi. Reverend Fenster-macher pronounced it Lee-wy, and it was repeated several times until it did sound like the name of a depraved man.

In the midst of his discourse Reverend Fenstermacher used a pro-vocative phrase: he said, 'A man like this should go and live amongst the savages.' The prayer ended on a hopeful note, Reverend Fenster-macher thought, for he did hold out reassurance of salvation if Lee-wy spent the next forty years of his life in dutiful repentance, as he, Fenster-macher, was convinced he would.

All Levi remembered of the prayer was the part about going and living amongst savages, and while the others ate voraciously, he kept his square, stubborn face looking down, refusing food, and thinking of a name he had recently learned: Oregon. At the market one day he had heard men from Massachusetts talking; they had traveled all the way to Lancaster to purchase two wagons. They had said, 'We're heading for Oregon. It's the new world. Great quantities of free land occupied only by savages.'

He had not been sure where Oregon was, but when another group of men and women appeared in Lancaster buying wagons and Melchior Fordney rifles, he had asked them when they stopped at the Zendt stall for smoked meats, 'Where's Oregon?'

'Two hundred and fifty days from here, heading westward all the time. But it's a great country. Malachi here went there by boat. He's our captain.'

Oregon of the savages! Oregon of the free land, the new life!

On Tuesday at eleven, when the market was jammed, both with normal customers and with sensation-seekers who had heard that Levi Zendt was going to apologize in public, stern Mahlon led his youngest brother through the mob and up to the counter of Peter Stoltzfus. In a loud voice he cried, 'Brother Stoltzfus, here is a man who wishes to speak with you.'

Peter Stoltzfus, dressed in white apron, leaned over the edge of his stall and glowered at the man who had tried to rape his daughter. 'Becky, come here!' he called, and from between the curtains masking the back of the stall Rebecca Stoltzfus appeared, so fresh and beautiful in her carefully pressed clothes and so neat in her little white cap with the dangling strings that the onlookers gasped to think that a human beast had tried to defile her. Several women, imagining that they had once looked like that, started to weep.

There was an awkward silence, whereupon Mahlon jabbed Levi in the back and the latter began to speak, in a whisper so low that no one could hear. 'Speak up!' several men shouted.

'I am sorry, Baker Stoltzfus . . .' Levi simply could not go beyond that, and Mahlon grew tense with rage at this new humiliation.

The impasse was ended by Peter Stoltzfus, who leaned down from his stall and punched Levi so solidly in the nose that the young butcher staggered backward, tripped over Mahlon's foot and fell flat on his bottom. The crowd cheered and a man's deep voice shouted, 'Give him another, Peter.'

That was the end of the apology. Mahlon, filled with disgust, abandoned his brother, and the other Zendts returned to their own stall, nodding approvingly across the aisle to Peter Stoltzfus and his daughter. Rebecca stayed at the counter, receiving the condolences of numerous women, and after a protracted moment on the floor, where he was too humiliated even to rise, Levi Zendt pulled himself together, rubbed his nose where Stoltzfus had thwacked him, and left the market.

That night, at five, he loaded the sleigh with the leftovers and drove out to the orphan asylum, where the mistress called him a human beast, directing him to unload the stuff and begone. But as he was working alone, Elly Zahm, the factotum, came to help him. She was a scrawny child, sixteen years old, an orphan whom it had been impossible to place in any private home. She knew how to work and was industrious; normally she should have been picked up as a maid-of-all-duties, but she was so unappealing in appearance, with straggly hair and thin face, that no one wanted her.

She lifted a basket that would have taxed a man, and Levi said, 'Leave that one for me,' but she already had it indoors.

'I heard what they said about you and the Stoltzfus girl,' she said with precise accent. 'I can't believe it.'

Even here! His face grew a deep red and his hands trembled. Was it to be like this the rest of his life: 'What about you and the Stoltzfus girl?' Leaving the baskets behind, he leaped into the sleigh and whipped the horses through the asylum gate.

Wednesday and Thursday were days of deepest anxiety. The Mennonites of Lancaster County were a lusty lot; they were by no means prudish, and their language could be most robust, with words that would have shocked ordinary Baptists or Presbyterians. They particularly liked to use barnyard terms, which made a Lancaster County saloon a rather lively spot, with constant reference to bowel movements, urination and sexual intercourse. It was not through prudishness that the Mennonites turned their back on Levi Zendt; it was because tradition required that sexuality be expressed in words rather than actions. For one Zendt boy to break out of the restraints that had bound the other four was intolerable and a menace to the whole community.

Therefore, without a formal vote, the Mennonites decided to shun him. From that moment he became an outcast. He could not attend church, nor speak with anyone who did. He could not buy or sell, or give or take. He could converse with no man, and the idea of striking up a friendship with any woman was beyond imagination.

'They're shunnin' Levi Zendt!'

'About time. That animal.'

On Friday, when he walked from the farm to Lancaster, no passer-by would offer him a ride. The black sleighs skidded past as if he were a pariah. And when he reached the market, none of the merchants would talk with him. At the end of the day he loaded the gifts and drove out to the edge of town, where the mistress of the orphanage refused to speak to him, but Elly Zahm appeared as usual to help him unload.

'I hear they're shunning you,' she said. He was too anguished to reply, and she said a most peculiar thing: 'They've been shunning me all my life.'

The words made him look up. For the first time he saw this skinny, unlovely child whose hands were so red from overwork and whose eyes seemed so very old. He could say nothing, and left as abruptly as he had the previous time.

But as he drove through the gathering dusk and approached Lampeter, he pulled up at Hell Street and went boldly into the White Swan. 'Is Amos Boemer here!'

The bartender nodded toward a corner, where the tall wagoner sat in a stupor. Levi went over to him, shook him and asked, 'Amos, you want to sell that Conestoga?'

Amos tried to clear his eyes, saw only a dim shape, and mumbled, 'I wanta give the bullshit thing away.'

'How much?'

Now the wagoner's head cleared. 'That wagon was made by Samuel Mummert. Paradise. 1818. It cost two hundred dollars. It's a great wagon.' He tried to stand but could not. 'A man would be crazy to sell that wagon.'

'How much?' Levi asked.

'Twenty dollars and you can kick that bullshit thing all the way to Philadelphia. It ain't worth a nickel.' He fell forward, but as Levi continued to pester him he rose, stared at the intruder and demanded, 'Ain't you the Zendt boy? Goin' around rippin' the clothes off decent girls. Get the hell out of here.' He pushed Levi toward the door, cursing him savagely long after he had departed.

Two weeks later, when the snow was gone, Levi walked down to Hell Street, ignoring the stares that marked his passage. He went to the White Swan and again rousted Amos Boemer from his corner. 'I want to buy your Conestoga,' he said.

'I'm not sure I want to sell. That's a very good wagon.'

'I know. I want to buy it.'

'Twenty dollars and it's your'n.'

'Here's the twenty dollars,' Levi replied, offering him money saved from his wages.

'It ain't got no bells.'

'I don't need bells.'

In that way Levi Zendt became owner of a Conestoga a quarter of a century old. It had been built with great care by one of the best workmen in the area, and had seen much good service on the Philadelphia freight route. It had suffered no broken boards; its toolbox and wagon jacks were usable, and its lazyboard worked. The twenty-four bells were gone, it was true, but where Levi was thinking of going, bells were not desirable.

To haul the wagon he would need six horses, and he had but two, a pair of sturdy grays. During the following week he bought two additional grays from a farmer in Hollinger, but told him to keep them until called for. The farmer said that he would need pay for their boarding, and being in an amiable mood, said, 'You hear of the city feller who wanted to board his horse and he asked his friends what he ought to pay and they said, "The price ranges from one dollar a month to fifty cents to two bits, but whatever you pay, you're entitled to the manure." So this city feller goes to the first farmer, and the farmer says, "One dollar," and the city feller says, "But I get the manure?" The farmer nods, and at the next place it's fifty cents, and the city feller says, "But I get the manure?" and the farmer nods. At the third farm two bits and the same story, so the city feller says, "Maybe I can find a place that's real cheap," and he goes to a broken-down farm and the man says, "Ten cents a month," and the city feller says, "But I get the manure?" and the farmer says, "Son, at ten cents a month they ain't gonna be any manure." ' The farmer laughed heartily. Levi forced a smile and walked back to his farm.

He now had four grays, and he knew where he would get the other two. He would 'borrow' them from his brother Mahlon.

It would be impossible, of course, to go west or anywhere else without one more essential item. He would need a gun. For a Lancaster man to move even across his own farm without a gun was unthinkable. The so-called Kentucky rifle, which had played so powerful a role in the War of Independence and had practically decided the War of 1812, was in truth a Lancaster rifle, invented and perfected in the smithies and shops of this town. Now, in days of peace, the Lancaster gunsmiths made the best hunting rifles in America, and their finest products rivaled those of Vienna.

Levi had never owned a gun. He was a good shot but so far had always used his brothers' guns, and now he faced a dilemma. He had the money, but how could he, under penalty of shunning, march into the shop of Andrew Gumpf or one of the Dreppard brothers and try to do business with them, they being such good churchmen? He devised various stratagems but none seemed practical. He really was an outcast.

Then he thought of Melchior Fordney, who made a very good gun but who was somewhat out of favor with the decent people of Lancaster because he had up to now refused to marry his housekeeper, a Mrs. Tripple, whom they suspected of living with him carnally, without sanctification by the church. Fordney was a strong-minded individual, and if anyone in Lancaster would sell Levi a gun, it would be he.

So on the first of February, Levi quietly slipped out to where Fordney had his gunsmith's shop. An automatic bell jangled as he opened the door and a pleasant woman in black dress and white apron but without white cap appeared: 'Mr. Fordney? He's workin' in back. I'm Mrs. Tripple.'

'Came to see about a gun,' Levi said, almost aggressively.

Mrs. Tripple was accustomed to country lads who took the offensive in such matters, and she said easily, 'You wait chust there. I'll call the mister.'

In a moment Fordney appeared, a brawny man with great square shoulders and features to match. 'Now what is it?'

'I want a good rifle.'

'How much you prepared to pay?'

'I could go as high as twelve dollars . . . but only for a good one.'

'For twelve you get a good one.' Brushing aside two rifles that lay on his workbench, he said, 'Those two, five dollars each, but you wouldn't like 'em.'

Levi hefted one, found it balanced too heavily toward the stock, and said, 'That one I wouldn't like.'

'You noticed?' Fordney laughed. 'A little wood heavy. Now, I have a fine rifle over here, but it's eighteen.'

'Too much,' Levi said. In the rack he noticed an older gun with a most handsome curly-maple stock, well worked with brass fittings. Fifty-five inches long and with an octagonal bluish barrel and a ramrod of well-used hickory, it was a fine weapon, almost the epitome of a Lancaster rifle. Unfortunately, it still carried the old flintlock mechanism.

'Can I see that one?'

'That's a very special gun,' Fordney said.

'Would it cost too much?'

'No. I could let you have that'n for twelve dollars. But it's flintlock, as you can see. Made it for a man nineteen years ago.'

Fordney pulled the rifle down and showed Levi the date etched into the top of the barrel: 'M. Fordney. 1825.' Levi took the gun, fitted it to his shoulder, and said, 'I never felt a better.'

Fordney watched him handle the piece and liked the way he used it. 'Aren't you the young Zendt fellow?' Levi blushed. 'The one they been shunnin'?' He called Mrs. Tripple and told her, 'This here's young Zendt. The colt that acted up with the Stoltzfus girl.'

'She needed some acting up with,' Mrs. Tripple said, returning to her kitchen.

'So the rifle's yours for twelve dollars.'

'I don't know how to work a flintlock.'

'Hold your horses. I'll change the flintlock to percussion.'

'You will!' Levi's voice proved the delight he felt at the prospect of getting such a gun. He put it to his shoulder again and asked, 'Is this gun as good as it feels?'

'One of the best I ever made. Man used it six years, then traded it back to me for a percussion. Stupid ass. I told him I could switch it to percussion, but he said, "I don't never want nothin' that's been altered." So now you get a bargain.'

He told Levi to come back later, but the young man replied, 'I'm not doin' anything,' and Fordney, realizing that he had nowhere to go, said, 'You can watch,' and he rummaged among his boxes to find the bits of gear that would be required to switch the old flintlock over to a new percussion-cap mechanism. Placing each item on the bench before him, he took the beautiful gun he had made so long ago and began disassembling it.

He unscrewed the frizzen spring and removed the frizzen altogether. He dispensed with the flash pan, too, and the hammer that had held the flint. Then with a hard black gum mixed with metal filings, he packed the screw holes and sanded them over. With a file he enlarged, ever so gently, the touch hole and rammed in a graver which would thread it. Into this hole he screwed the drum, adjusting the nipple so that the hammer would strike properly.

Testing the new mechanism many times to see that all parts functioned, he then grabbed a handful of percussion caps—little forms of powder that looked like a man's top hat—and motioned Levi to follow him outdoors. They went to a field, where Fordney swabbed the bluish barrel, poured in the right amount of powder, pushed down the greased patch to form a bind, inserted the ball and then placed the percussion cap on the nipple. Handing the gun to Levi, he said, 'Hit the tree over there,' and Levi placed the stock against his shoulder, felt the sleek brass inlays and sighted along the barrel. Squeezing the trigger with gentle, even pressure, he heard the hammer trip, caught a glimpse of it descending on the percussion cap, saw the momentary flash and felt the powder inside the barrel explode, sending the bullet in a revolving motion straight and true to the limb he had aimed at.

Fordney said, 'The Fenstermacher boy, that's the preacher's son, he told me he could load and fire a gun like that three times in two minutes. I didn't believe him, but he could.'

Levi fired two more shots and then Fordney tried his hand. It was a good gun, subtly balanced, beautifully crosshatched at the wrist. In some respects it was better now than when it had first been sold, for the curly maple was seasoned and the barrel had nested with no chance of gaps.

Fordney handed the gun formally to Levi and said, 'None better. Oh, I have some for twenty or twenty-five, but only because the brassware comes from Germany. This one, all Lancaster.'

As they walked back to the shop Fordney said, 'I'd ask you if you wanted to work with me, seein' as how you like guns, but I suppose you'll be headin' west.' Levi felt it prudent to say nothing, and Fordney added, 'I should have gone west . . . years ago.'

Levi smuggled his rifle home and hid it behind the sausage machine. He now had a good Conestoga, four excellent gray horses and two of Mahlon's he intended to borrow. He had a vague plan of hooking up with the next caravan of people moving west. He would tolerate Lancaster and Lampeter no more. Even if they relaxed the shunning, which they probably would in the spring, he would not live down his disgrace.

He went about his work as industriously as ever, grinding the pork, mixing it with herbs and cramming it into the holder on the sausage machine. When it was filled to the top, he attached one end of a cleaned hog's gut to the spout on the machine, then by cranking a large wheel which operated a screw, he applied pressure on the ground meat and slowly it forced its way into the farthest knotted end of the intestine. When the skin was filled to bursting, he took the open end off the machine and tied it in a tight knot, giving him eight to ten feet of the best sausage. Later, when it had set, the length would be cut to selling size.

He made his scrapple with added care, as if he were just learning the trade, cooking the pig scraps and the cornmeal for hours, spicing them just right and pouring the hot liquid into small deep pans, where a good inch of yellow pork fat would gather on top, airproofing the scrapple so that it could be kept for three months.

He was a good butcher, and he assumed that when he got to Oregon he would continue making scrapple and sausage and souse. There won't be many out there can make any better, he thought.

Each Tuesday and Friday he walked the long distance into Lancaster to clean up the market and drive the scraps out to the orphanage, and on the fourth week after shunning started, he asked Elly, 'Why did they shun you?'

'I have no parents. They called me a bastard.'

'That's not your fault.'

'They let on as if it was.'

'How'd you get here?'

'They found me on the church step.'

He said no more that day, but when the other Zendts were in church, he walked down to the grove of trees and sat for a long time in silence. He straddled the trunk of a fallen oak and looked carefully at each part of the handsome farm his family had accumulated, one building at a time, one field patiently after another. There was no better farm in Lancaster County and he knew it, but it had grown sour—it had grown so terribly sour.

He covered his square, beard-trimmed face in his hands. He was not a man to allow tears, but he did sigh deeply and mutter, 'I will stand no more. On Tuesday morning I will leave this place.'

At the big Sunday dinner he ate as if he had been starving for a week, taking big helpings of everything and ending with two kinds of pie, shoofly, whose sticky bottom he loved, and cherry, the best of all. He was congenial to everyone, and on Monday he volunteered to help his mother make cup cheese, a fact which startled her; when he got to Oregon he wanted to know how it was made.

He noted carefully as she took a couple of gallons of milk and cream that she had allowed to sour and put it on the stove to heat. 'Don't boil it . . . ever,' she warned. 'Just hot enough to ouch your finger.'

He was disappointed when all she did was strain off excess water and place the curds in a bag. 'What happens next?' he asked.

'Oh, tomorrow you can help me again. I crumble the curds and rub in this much soda, and we'll put it in a crock. It'll sour and smell and become runny. Then it's ripe, so you set the crock in hot water till it's warm again, and you stir in some salt and a little water with a squirt of vinegar in it.' She hefted the dripping bag onto a peg over the sink and said, 'Tomorrow you can help me finish.'

Tomorrow he would not be here.

On Tuesday at three in the morning he helped load the Zendt wagons with the last batch of souse and scrapple and sausage he would make. He watched his four brothers drive off to town, and as soon as they were gone he went inside and kissed his mother goodbye. She guessed that he might be running away; his interest in cup cheese had been so unusual that she had tried to fathom why. She knew. She asked, 'Where you goin'?' He replied with another kiss and went out to get his gun and his two horses. He also took the two belonging to Mahlon, plus whatever harness was needed.

He drove the four horses down to the White Swan and hitched them to the Conestoga. He left Hell Street in darkness, driving over to Hollinger to pick up the two horses boarding there. 'That's a fine team of six,' the farmer said approvingly. 'Almost looks as if you'd matched 'em.' As Levi harnessed them to the Conestoga, completing his team, the farmer asked, 'You're the Zendt boy. Ain't they shunnin' you?'

'No more,' Levi said.

By back roads he drove past Lancaster and out to the orphanage. Pulling up outside the gate and hitching his lead horse to a tree, he started toward the house, but remembered his valuable gun lying unprotected in the wagon. Grabbing it, he went inside and bellowed, 'Elly! Elly Zahm! Come down here!'

It was barely dawn but the work girl was up and busy at her chores. She appeared with her arms wet and her skirt tied behind her knees. Her scrawny face was red and her hair unkempt. As soon as she looked at Levi she knew that some powerful thing was afoot, and she was in no way perturbed when he said, 'Get your things. We're goin' west.'

It took her three seconds—one, two, three—to know that her destiny required her to join this man, and his gun and his wagon, and his waiting horses. She had no conception of what was being asked of her, but she knew that there could be no viable alternative. She dashed inside the orphanage and grabbed the few things that belonged to her.

A girl shouted, 'He's taking Elly Zahm . . . with a gun.'

The mistress, not yet dressed, hurried to the front door in her gown, and with one glance, apprehended what was happening. 'Elly!' she screamed. 'Come back here.'

'I am never coming back,' the thin girl said stubbornly.

'That man's a monster.'

'I'm going,' Elly cried, clutching her good dress in her arms as she hurried toward the Conestoga.

'Shall I fetch the police?' one of the girls shouted.

'No!' the mistress snapped. 'He'd kill us all. Let her go. She's nothing but a whore. Just like her mother before her.'

And that would have been the benediction with which Elly left the orphanage had not a tall, lively girl, blond and quite pretty, broken from the crowd of watchers, running to Elly and thrusting into her hand a small bag of carefully saved coins.

'Laura Lou Booker,' the mistress screamed, 'come back here! You're as bad as she is!'

Ignoring the command, the tall girl clasped Elly, kissing her fervently on the cheek. 'You're escaping for all of us,' she whispered, and when Elly tried to return the precious money, Laura Lou kissed her again, whispering, 'Remember what we said. A wife must have a little money of her own.'

Clutching the few dollars, Elly Zahm, sixteen years old, walked resolutely through the gates of the orphanage and climbed into the Conestoga. Levi Zendt, his Melchior Fordney rifle in his left hand, called to his six horses and headed out of Lancaster for the last time.

It was only twelve miles to Columbia, where the famous bridge waited to lift them across the mighty Susquehanna, but because the six grays were new to the wagon and to each other, the going was slow. They d d not reach the river till nightfall, and when they did the tollgate was closed. This required that they sleep on the eastern bank, and as the stars appeared, Elly faced the first crisis of her long trip west.

'We cannot share the wagon till we've been married,' she said. 'I'll sleep under that tree.' Taking a blanket, she prepared to do so.

This Levi would not permit, for he realized that as a gentleman he must allow her to have the wagon, but she had a practical mind and said, "You must guard the wagon. Our things are there.' And she slept beside the Susquehanna.

In the morning Levi asked, 'Would you like it if we found a preacher on the other side?'

'Very much,' she said. 'I want no bastards.'

Levi hitched up the horses and got the Conestoga into line for the crossing. The man in the wagon ahead turned out to be a German on his way to Illinois, and as they waited he came back to talk with the runaways. 'In our schoolbooks in Germany we had pictures of this bridge,' he said, pointing to the engineering marvel. 'Longest bridge of its kind in the world.'

Levi was impressed that so great a thing could have existed so close at hand without his having known of it. He told the man, 'In Germany you have pictures of Lancaster, and in Lancaster we have pictures of Germany,' but Elly pointed out, 'This isn't Lancaster. It's Columbia.'

The fee to cross, for a wagon with six horses, was one dollar, which Elly thought excessive, but the German called back, 'For two dollars such a bridge would be cheap.' And they entered upon the very long covered bridge, with its two separated tracks plus a third for persons walking their horses.

When the heavy wagon reached the western end of the bridge Elly said, 'The minister in that church ought to be up by now,' so at half past seven in the morning they rousted out Reverend Aspinwall, a Baptist minister, who said, 'I couldn't possibly marry you without knowing who you are. You'd have to show me a proper clearance from your church and then get a legal license at the courthouse in York.'

'How far's York?' Levi asked, and Reverend Aspinwall said, 'Twelve miles,' and Levi said, 'That'd take all day.' Elly began to cry, and when Aspinwall asked why, she told him, 'Always they called me a bastard. I don't know whether that's right, because I had no parents. But my children won't have that name.'

'They mustn't,' Aspinwall said. 'Can't you ride into York for your license?'

'We cannot,' Levi said sternly.

'No, I suppose not,' the minister said. He blew his nose and considered the matter. 'Tell you what,' he said. 'There is such a thing as marriage-in-common. You announce to the world that you're going to live as man and wife, and if you have two witnesses . . .'

'Where would we get witnesses?' Elly asked.

Reverend Aspinwall, looking at her unprepossessing face, doubted that she would ever again find a man who might want to marry her. If it were to be done, it had better be done now. Coughing, he said in a low voice, 'Mrs. Aspinwall and I would be your witnesses.'

He called his wife and said, 'Mabel, these young people don't begin to have their papers in order. But they must be married now.'

Mrs. Aspinwall stared at Elly's middle and could see no visible evidence of need. How thin the girl is, she said to herself.

'So I wondered if you and I could serve as witnesses to their intention?'

'Certainly.' She took Elly's hand and said, 'A girl needs someone to stand with her, doesn't she?'

Taking a position in front of his desk and with no Bible, Reverend Aspinwall said, 'In the eyes of man and in the presence of God these two young people . . .' He stopped, looked at Levi and said, 'I don't believe I have your name.'

'Levi Zendt.'

Reverend Aspinwall gasped. 'Aren't you the young man who tried to . . .' He could not force himself to say the word.

'It did not happen that way,' Elly interrupted.

'I heard all about it. The Stoltzfus girl. I know Peter Stoltzfus.'

'It did not happen,' Elly said stubbornly.

'How could you know whether it happened or not?' Reverend Aspinwall asked sternly. 'Has he raped you, too. Is that why you . . .'

'I know it didn't happen because I followed the sleigh,' Elly cried.

'Why would you follow a sleigh? At night?'

'Because I love him,' she said. 'Because I've always loved him. Because he's the only man in this world who has ever been nice to me.' She broke into tears.

Mrs. Aspinwall tried to take the sobbing girl to her bosom, but Elly tore herself away and confronted the minister. 'I saw the whole thing. She flirted with him something awful. She teased him about never going with girls. She was to blame. She did it all.'

There was a moment of embarrassed silence, during which the minister blew his nose and his wife tried to comfort the girl. After coughing several times, Reverend Aspinwall resumed: 'In the presence of God these two young people, Levi Zendt and Elly—your name, child?—Elly Zahm announce their intention to be husband and wife. In the presence of two witnesses, that is.' He coughed again, then dropped into his ministerial voice and prayed: 'God, have tenderness toward these children. Cherish them. Help them, for they are going into territories they do not know. Keep them in Your love.'

With that he raised his hands to indicate that the service, such as it was, had ended, but Elly asked, 'Do we get a paper?'

'Not from me,' Reverend Aspinwall said. 'This isn't a formal marriage, you know. And he's outcast from his own church. I cannot lend it the appearance . . .' He hesitated in embarrassment.

'I can,' Mrs. Aspinwall said.

She went to her husband's desk and took a sheet of paper on which his name and the address of his church had been imprinted. On it she wrote in bold letters:

> On this day Levi Zendt and Elly Zahm appeared before my husband and me and in the sight of God Almighty announced their intention of living together as man and wife, in the state of Holy Matrimony.
>
> *Witness*
>
> Mabel Aspinwall
> February 14, 1843

She handed the paper to her husband, indicating where he was to sign, and with visible reluctance he did so.

'How much?' Elly asked.

'No, no!' Aspinwall protested.

'Here,' she said, handing him one of Laura Lou's dollars. 'It makes it more proper.' She folded the paper neatly, tucked it in her dress, and the trip west was begun.

The journey to York was spent in getting to know the horses. The two lead ones were Levi's own, and they responded well to his direc-

tions. The two nearest the wagon were Mahlon's, and Levi had a pretty
good understanding of what they might do, but the two bought horses
in the middle posed some problems, for they did not feel comfortable
working behind the lead pair and showed their uneasiness at every turn
in the road by pulling against the traces.

Patiently Levi corrected their fractiousness, and at last he had the
satisfaction of feeling them working together. 'This is gonna be a great
team,' he told Elly, who watched with pride as the six handsome grays
moved stolidly forward, pulling the heavy wagon with no apparent strain.

About halfway to York, Levi got his first jolt. A traveler coming eastward stopped to admire the horses and said with visible conviction,
'Neighbor, if you're plannin' to go over them mountains ahead, I'd shed
myself of that Conestoga and get me a smaller rig.' When Levi argued
against this, the traveler said, 'Hell, man, you ain't usin' half that wagon.
You don't need one that big and you're just pullin' dead weight. Ain't
fair to the horses.'

This charge cut Levi, for if there was one thing he tried to be, it was
considerate of his horses. He discussed the matter with Elly, and to his
surprise she sided with the stranger. 'It is half empty,' she said.

'Day'll come we'll need it,' Levi said stubbornly.

'You're gonna kill your horses,' the stranger repeated, cracking his
whip as he moved eastward to the Columbia bridge. When he was gone
Levi mumbled, 'You see his horses, Elly? They need rest and a good
washin'-down, but he has time to lecture me.'

Normally he would have ignored the man, but his growing apprehension was making him testy. He was now married, and come nightfall,
somewhere west of York he and Elly would bed down in the Conestoga
and their life as husband and wife would begin. Certainly he knew a good
deal about horses; the two handsome beasts in the lead had been bred
by him, using a large gray stallion owned by a Welsh farmer in Lampeter
and one of the Zendt mares, but he knew little about women. The five
Zendt brothers had never discussed such matters, and their mother would
have perished rather than speak of husbands and wives. To the boys,
their mother seemed a kind of machine devised for the preparation of
food, and it was impossible to visualize her as their physical parent.

Apart from the usual coarse humor of the barn and the market, more
exciting than informative, Levi knew little except that this was his wedding day and that when night fell, wild and confusing things were due
to happen. The day seemed unusually hot and he began to sweat.

For her part, Elly knew a surprising mixture of facts about marriage,
but not because she had been properly instructed at the orphanage. True,
the good church ladies who supported the place insisted that the girls
receive instruction in the three Rs, in which formal classes were held; but
Elly's more important instruction came because she had the good luck
to be friends with that remarkable girl Laura Lou Booker. They made

a formidable team, one fortifying the other. Laura Lou excelled in numbers and had a scientific curiosity, while Elly was more inclined toward literature, often seeing life as a fragment of some poem. Between them they asked questions, made prudent guesses.

When an orphanage girl attained the age of thirteen years and nine months, a stern-visaged churchwoman met with her in private to advise her of two facts: she was now old enough to have a baby, and God would forever condemn her if she meddled with boys. The precise relationship of these two absolutes was not spelled out.

It happened that Elly and Laura Lou received this information on the same day, and each listened respectfully in the darkened room, but when the instructor was gone, Laura Lou said, 'She didn't tell us much. I wonder if she knows?' It was quite clear to Laura Lou that her body had been fashioned for special purposes, and she proposed to ascertain what they were. She approached the matter as if it were a problem in mathematics, which she handled adroitly, and what she was unable to deduce from the meager information allowed her, she was intuitive enough to guess. Her solutions were not always accurate and she wound up with a somewhat confused understanding of the role of the male, but for a thirteen-year-old girl she did remarkably well. One night in the darkness she assured Elly, 'Men can't be much different from horses.'

The wonderful thing about Laura Lou was her unflagging enthusiasm, her zeal for new experiences. She would study the various men who appeared at the orphanage and would evaluate them in long night sessions with Elly: 'It would be heavenly to be married to that young minister. He's clean and he listens and he eats with good manners and he knows how to laugh.' Of the carpenter she said, 'I do not like thin men. He's too nervous, Elly. He wants to watch us girls but he's afraid to. I simply wouldn't want to be married to him.' It was she who first pointed out the virtues of Levi Zendt, the butcher: 'He's very well built, Elly. Much like a good stallion, dependable and strong. He's shy but he's not crooked.'

One night she said unexpectedly, 'Elly! You're in love with Levi Zendt! I saw it today.' They spent a good deal of time dissecting what a girl like Elly, an orphan with no prospects and less than mediocre looks, would have to do to catch a man like one of the rich Zendts, and Laura Lou concluded, 'I think men like to be loved. Just loved. Just tell them they are more to you than anything else in the world.'

'How do you know that?' Elly asked, eager to keep the conversation going.

'I just feel it,' Laura Lou said. 'Anyway, when I find a man like Levi Zendt, I'm going to tell him I love him, because I don't have any prospects, either. All I have is love.'

'You're pretty,' Elly said.

'Pretty isn't everything,' Laura Lou said, breaking into laughter. When

Elly asked what caused this, she said, 'Remember what they say about Mr. Zearfoss? He keeps his wife Edith for cooking and his sweetheart Becky for nice.' The two girls laughed at the most famous of the local adulterers, after which Laura Lou said solemnly, 'If a man married you for cooking, Elly, and kept me on the side for nice, in the end he'd stay with you.'

'Why do you say that?' Elly asked.

'Because you're the kindest, sweetest girl God ever made, that's why,' Laura Lou said, and now as the wagon rolled toward York, Elly Zahm was determined to be exactly that kind of wife.

As dusk approached they passed through York, a tidy German town in which every house along the main street looked as if it belonged to a banker, and in time they came to a meadowland rimmed by tall trees, and here Levi unhitched the horses. He took a ridiculous length of time to curry them down and find them water, fussing over unnecessary chores, and Elly knew what was bothering him.

Therefore she went about her own work, paying no attention to him. She arranged their belongings in the wagon so that they rode forward, and on the gently sloping floor, made their first bed so that their feet would be at the low part in the middle and their heads at the raised part aft. Then she got out the pan to cook the last of the scrapple Levi had brought along, but after a while she noticed that he was not chopping wood for the fire. 'Where's the wood, Levi?' she called. 'I'm not hungry,' he called back, so without comment she repacked the cooking gear and returned the scrapple to its damp cloth. She knew that he must be starving from the long day's work, but she also guessed why he was not hungry, so in the fading light she made believe she was sewing.

'You'll ruin your eyes,' Levi said when he returned to the wagon, and there was such solicitude in his voice that she almost burst into tears.

'Oh, Levi!' she said in a low voice. 'I do wish I was pretty.' He took her in his arms and for the first time kissed her. 'You're pretty enough for me,' he said gently, and with a maximum of awkwardness and confusion and misapplied strength, Levi Zendt took Elly Zahm as his wife. So many of the guesses she and Laura Lou had made during their nightly sessions were nearly right that the nuptials had about them a pastoral grandeur, and when morning came Levi shouted, 'Elly, I'm starvin'. Fry up that scrapple!' And he ate the whole pound and a half.

The turnpike on which they traveled from York to Gettysburg was one of the busiest and best in the land, forty feet from one grassy edge to the other, with the middle sealed by a good MacAdam, as the recent innovation from Scotland was called. On such a road it was possible to cover thirty miles a day, if you looked after your horses.

It was prudent to be traveling west in winter, before the spring thaw set in and the road began to wash in its weaker sections. As a freighter told them on the outskirts of Gettysburg, 'The trick is to reach Pittsburgh while the roads are still frozen. That way you miss all the trouble. Then you're on hand when the ice breaks up in the Ohio River . . . current runs fast . . . lots of water . . . and it sweeps you right down to Cairo like you're on a magic carpet.' Stepping closer, he asked, 'Mind if I give you a bit of advice, stranger?'

'Go ahead.'

'I'd sell that Conestoga . . . buy me a lighter rig.'

'This suits us just fine,' Levi said.

'Point is, when you get to Pittsburgh you'll need a heavier flatboat. And they cost money.'

'We'll find some,' Levi said.

'I must say you got fine horses, there.'

'I like 'em,' Levi said as he snapped the lines.

The Zendts liked Gettysburg. It was a quiet town in which nothing much happened. A few stores catered to the numerous travelers and the inns served good beer. The land surrounding the town looked as if it would be fine for farming, and the stone fences that crisscrossed it enclosed rolling fields dotted with cattle and horses.

'If a man didn't have his farm around Lancaster,' Levi said, 'this would be a likely spot. I like rolling hills that lead to woodlands.' That night, on the western edge of Gettysburg, they slept in a grove of shagbark hickories, and the stately chestnut trees that boys love, and tall shy walnut trees, last to leaf in spring, first to grow bare in autumn.

'There'll be no wood like this out west,' he mused, and in the twilight Elly saw him picking fragments from the shagbarks. 'If these hickories were in Lancaster,' he called to her, 'they'd be worth a fortune for smokin' hams.' She realized how much more painful this emigration was for him than for her, because he was leaving behind a way of life that had proved fruitful—sausage-smoking, the market stall, hickory trees and walnuts, and stout barns—while she was leaving absolutely nothing she cared for but the affection of Laura Lou Booker. The love that she already felt for her stolid Dutchman intensified, and she determined to make his new life as easy as possible.

'Time for bed, Levi,' she called, and he came to it gladly, for each night she made it more enjoyable.

It was only one hundred and eighty miles from Gettysburg to Pittsburgh, but the road had to climb over several chains of steep mountains and the going became difficult.

East of Chambersburg, Levi had his first trouble with the wheel that had caused Amos Boemer to lose his bells. Customarily, he walked on the left of the wagon, but today, reins in hand, he was riding the lazyboard. This was a piece of strong white oak which could be pulled out from the left-hand side of the wagon. Sitting there, he was able to work the brake and control the reins. Elly was inside tending her chores when he became aware of a slight squeaking behind him. At first he suspected that he might have left a little pressure on the brake, but that was not the case. Inspection of the wheel showed that the iron rim had begun to work loose, and this was a serious problem. It meant either that the hickory in the wheel had warped, or that the iron had expanded under the heat of the road.

'The road's frozen!' Elly said when he suggested this as a reason.

'Feel the iron,' he told her. It was warm.

At the next village they pulled into a wheelwright's, who told them the bad news: 'It's what we call a creeper. A wheel that's weak in every part, but poor in none. Spokes work loose. Hub wobbles. Rim-wood shrinks. And the goddamn rim expands.'

'What should I do?' Levi asked.

'Reset the whole wheel,' the expert said.

'I couldn't just wedge it . . . to take up the slack?'

The man laughed raucously. 'Son, you're travelin' three thousand miles. How long do you think a wedge would last?' He took Levi to the three other wheels and showed him how solid they were. 'As good wheels as a man sees,' he judged, 'but this'n's just a poor wheel.'

'Why?' Levi asked.

'Why does a sow farrow eight pigs that grow into real hogs and one that remains a runt?' the wheelwright asked, laughing at his analogy.

'How much?' Levi asked, cutting him short.

'Two dollars, and you can have the wheel tomorrow noon.'

Levi knew the man was giving him sound advice, and the charge was not excessive; the rim would have to be heated, hammered and slipped over the rebuilt rim while red-hot. As it cooled it would adjust itself to the wood, forming a permanent, trustworthy bind.

'Will it be good for three thousand miles?' Levi asked.

'It's a creeper, son. In that goddamn wheel you have many parts, and right now all of 'em is figurin' out how to wreck you later on. Keep the wood wet when you get a chance. Watch it. And whenever you get to a blacksmith, have him look at it.' He studied the Conestoga and said, 'Whoever built this rig knew the difference between a saw and an ax. He built it good.'

Two days west of McConnellsburg came the first big test, the fording of the Juniata. It wasn't the main Juniata, of course, for that would have required a bridge, but it was a substantial branch and in the last days of winter it carried a good flow of water. When she saw the stream confronting them, Elly cried, 'You mean we take the wagon down into it?' and her husband asked, 'You got any better ideas?'

He walked across the ford and found that the icy water came no higher than his thighs. 'The horses can do it,' he said confidently. 'You stay in the wagon.'

This she refused to do. With her instinct for protecting her man and his property, she wanted to be where she could assist him if the horses reared or the wagon began to slip. And no matter if her skirts got soaked.

So Levi stayed at the left side of the wagon, keeping the reins in his hands, while Elly guided the two lead horses. The descent into the Juniata was steep and slippery, and she fell into the frigid waters, which covered her for a moment. She came up gasping, frightening the horses. They were on the verge of rearing, but she regained her footing and tugged strongly at the head horses' bridle.

'Ho! Ho!' she called, spitting the water from her mouth and guiding the horses to the opposite bank, where the footing was impossible. Again she stumbled.

'You're a pretty sight!' Levi called as he drove the horses forward.

'That water's cold!' Elly called back as she watched the horses straining up the muddy bank, hauling the heavy wagon behind them. As the water ran off the wheels and in rivulets down the horses' flanks, she came back to Levi and said, 'There'll be many rivers before Oregon. We'll learn to do it better.'

'I was glad you were there when the horses started to act up,' he said, and as she clambered inside to change her clothes she felt that their marriage had become a real partnership.

After Bedford they had to make a choice. They could keep to the north and follow the old Forbes Road over the Alleghenies into Pittsburgh or they could hold to the south and use the newer Glade Road through Somerset. 'Forbes Road is twenty miles shorter,' the blacksmith said as he shod the two bought horses, whose shoes were beginning to wear. 'Glade Road's longer and costs more for tolls, but it's an easier way over the top.'

'Are the mountains bad?' Levi asked.

'Mountains are always bad,' the blacksmith said, 'and no matter which road you take, you'll get a bellyful, but if I was doin' it . . .' He hesitated, not wishing to give advice if it wasn't wanted.

'What would you do?' Levi asked.

'I'd whip up my horses and go for the Glade Road and thank God that I'd escaped the Forbes.' He thrust a red-hot shoe into his tank, and when the sizzling stopped, added, 'You're lucky son, to have the choice. Not so long ago there was only the Forbes, and in winter them mountains killed you.'

'We'll follow the Glade,' Levi said, 'because the more mountains we miss, the better,' but even so, before they got to Somerset they found themselves on mountain roads so steep they doubted the horses could pull the wagon up. This was no idle fear, for in two days' journey they passed four wrecked wagons and three dead horses.

At the crest of one mountain, as Levi looked westward and saw what loomed ahead, he lost heart and told Elly, 'My God! These are only the Alleghenies. Three thousand feet high. Do you realize how high the Rockies are?'

'Fourteen thousand,' she said, and they stared at each other.

Should they go on? They did not discuss the problem openly. But each knew that this was the moment of decision. This was their last sensible chance of rejecting the brutal trip to Oregon, the last opportunity for turning back. The fording of the Juniata had been a foretaste of the greater rivers to come; these difficult mountains were but a prelude to the fearsome Rockies.

As the six horses rested from their exertion, the two young travelers judged their own courage, and unfortunately they lacked important information which would have made their decision easier. First, the height of any mountain is significant only in relation to the height of the table-land from which it rises; the low Alleghenies, rising steeply from sea level, were just as high as a ten-thousand-foot mountain rising from a tableland of six thousand, eight hundred feet. Second, a remarkable pass through the Rockies had been discovered by trappers, and it involved no elevation higher than eight thousand feet, so that if a man and his wagon could breast the Alleghenies, they also could conquer the Rockies.

If the Zendts lacked this reassuring knowledge, they had something better. They had youth and they had courage, and now Elly put her hand in her husband's and said, 'We'd better get into the valley before night.'

In spite of the difficult mountains, which the Zendts surmounted better than most, they were by no means lost in a wilderness. Over the entire distance from Lancaster to Pittsburgh, there was some kind of inn available at almost every mile. Often they were rude, filthy affairs, but they did have oats for the horses and hot soup for the travelers. Families avoided the inns wherever possible, preferring to sleep in their wagons rather than risk the bedbugs inside, but when a heavy snowfall hit west of Somerset, blocking the highway, the Zendts did finally halt at Slack's Tavern, where they placed the six grays in a protected stable and themselves in quarters only a little warmer and much less clean.

The room assigned them was shared by four other travelers of dubious cleanliness. Since the bed which he and Elly were expected to use was already occupied by two of the gentlemen, the newlyweds decided to sleep on the floor. Even so, fleas and other insects made sleep almost impossible, and this became the first night of their marriage which could not be termed congenial.

It was a relief to get back on the clean, frozen highway, and on the fourteenth of March, as winter was ending, they came to that spot east of Pittsburgh where the Youghiogheny joins the Monongahela to form a considerable river. Elly burst into the silly song that Laura Lou had taught her:

'The Youghiogheny and the Monongahela,
They run together to the Allegheny,
Where they all join hands, they all join hands
And what do they make? The O-high-O.'

With an excitement that surprised them, they urged the horses on, keeping to the right bank of the Monongahela until they reached a plateau where other travelers had halted to look down upon that mysterious spot, so vital in American history; there, as the song decreed, the dark and turbulent Monongahela came up from the south to join with the quieter Allegheny coming down from the north, forming, at the triangle where Pittsburgh stood, the mighty Ohio.

They caught their breath when they saw the magnitude of the city below them, its dark furnaces standing along the rivers, its powerful smokestacks throwing coal fumes in the air as scores of products were being forged. It was a scene of enormous energy, of boats passing back and forth and trains coughing into tunnels. There were more houses than either Levi or Elly could have imagined, built on hills so steep that no horse could climb them, and over the whole area hung a smoky pall of energy, sometimes hiding the houses and the rivers, sometimes breaking into separated clouds between which the Zendts caught peeks of the activity that marked this amazing site.

'It's like Chimbor*i*zo,' a man at Elly's side cried ecstatically.

'Like what?' she asked.

'The volcano on the equator,' he said, marveling at what he saw below him:

'Endlessly burning, fires of the inner soul
Leap up toward heaven, leaving dark soot below.'

He pronounced *heaven* as if it were spelled *hebm*, and Elly asked, 'Where are you from?' and he told her, 'London. I'm writing a book about our former colonies.' He looked with awe at the scene below and cried, 'Nothing in America is greater than this.' He flung his arms wide and said, 'This is the Chimborazo of the spirit, the American Birmingham, our Birmingham improved upon. Through our mistakes you learn.'

He left his own party and led the Zendts down from the overlook and into the reality of Pittsburgh. Where they saw dirty houses and streets cut off from the sun, he saw unbridled energy and new opportunities for Germans and Irishmen and French expatriates. 'Pittsburgh is the first really good whiskey I've found in America,' he exulted, and Levi wondered what he was talking about.

As Levi guided the large Conestoga on his way to the waterfront, men stopped to show their sons the antique wagon with its high rear wheels, and Levi felt a sense of pride at being the owner of such a rig. But when he reached the rivers at the triangle and saw the magnificent and lacy boats that set forth from that spot on their way to St. Louis and New Orleans, he understood when the captain of the first one he approached laughed at him, saying, 'We couldn't take a wagon like that aboard here, young man. This is for gentlemen and their cargo.'

The second river boat he approached, the *Queen of Sheba*, was even more elegant than the first. It resembled one of the many-layered wedding cakes made by Stoltzfus: the boat's upper tiers were supported by thin white columns and protected by green-striped awnings. Men in gray suits and ladies with parasols lounged on the topmost deck, gazing with languid interest at the busy scene. 'Hello,' one gentleman cried, 'a real Conestoga!' and all moved over to watch Levi rein in his horses.

'Fine set of grays you have, young man,' the gentleman shouted down, 'but they're pulling too heavy a wagon.'

'Where you heading, miss?' a lady called, and Elly replied, 'Oregon.'

This name occasioned such excitement that the gentleman ran down three flights of broad mahogany stairs, and with that impulsive generosity common to the west, insisted that the Zendts join them for refreshment.

'The horses,' Levi protested, whereupon the gentleman commandeered a black boy and handed him five cents. 'You guard these horses,' he said sternly, and the Zendts were whisked aboard and up the palatial stairways to the top deck, where they were surrounded by curious and admiring strangers.

'Oregon!' one of the ladies repeated. Fingering Elly's dress, she said, 'That's a practical cloth for such an excursion. Are you his daughter?'

'His wife.'

This seemed incredible, and a woman asked, 'How old could you be?' Levi noticed that Elly fumbled for an answer and assumed that she did not wish to confess her youth, so he said boldly, 'She's sixteen.' The listeners were aghast. One extremely inquisitive woman discovered that Elly had run away from an orphanage, and she arranged for a collection to be taken—more than seven dollars—and this was given to Elly as a wedding present. 'It's for you, my dear,' the woman announced loudly. 'Not for him.'

The men purchased bottles of champagne to toast the Oregon adventure, and as the glasses passed, there came a moment of solemnity, for not one person in the group had been farther west than Cincinnati, and all they knew of Oregon was that it lay at a great distance.

When talk resumed, the men asked Levi what brought him to the waterfront, and he said, 'I planned to take my wagon to St. Louis . . . on this boat.' The men laughed and pointed to the lower decks of the floating palace, where bales and trunks were stowed in delicate precision. 'You'd have a hard time finding space for a Conestoga down there,' one of the men joked.

'Where shall I go?' Levi asked.

'There's a fellow named Finnerty who'll build you a flatboat. Very good, I'm told. He floats it downstream for you, then sells it at Cairo.' Like everyone in the west, he called it Kay-roe.

'I don't want to stop at Cairo,' Levi protested, for he had been warned against this rowdy town.

'You have to. Because at Cairo your flatboat's useless. To get to St. Louis, you move up the Mississippi. Against the current.' Going to the rail, the gentleman tossed a second nickel to the boy guarding the horses: 'When this young man comes down, lead him to Finnerty, the boat-builder.'

At this point the captain came on deck and said in a strong voice, 'I hear there's a Pennsylvanian on board who wants to ship his Conestoga with us.' When Levi was presented, the captain said gravely, 'Freight steamers will offer to haul you down to Cairo, but they're sad affairs and usually blow up downstream of Cincinnati. Buy yourself a flatboat, but beware of the rascals who run them. If an August sun is shining and they say it's snowing, brush the flakes from your shoulder.' He did agree that Finnerty was the most trustworthy of a bad lot, and with that he bowed, saying, 'I'd be pleased if the newlyweds took lunch with us.'

Elly was eager to accept, for she had never seen luxury of this sort, and as always, she was extremely hungry, but Levi felt obligated to tend his horses, so they descended the stairs. As they approached the dining room, one of the women stood Elly in the doorway to point out the expanse of white linen, the glistening knives and forks, the three glasses for each diner, and best of all, the menu, a folded cardboard decorated with blue curlicues, pink cupids and yellow flowers. It listed a staggering three hundred dishes.

'They have all this food on board?' Elly asked, and the woman said, 'Waiting for you.'

'Oh, Levi!' Elly cried. 'I do wish we could stay.' He started to remind her of their obligations, but she drew close to him and whispered, 'It's my birthday.'

One of the women overheard and soon the stairway was buzzing with the news: 'It's her birthday. We must have a party!' And before Levi comprehended what was happening, he was swept into the crystal room, where waiters fussed about, arranging a birthday table. When the chief steward, a stately black with white hair, bent over Elly's shoulder to ask, 'And what would Madame desire?' she was powerless to choose from that stupendous menu and could only look up at him in bewilderment.

He hesitated just long enough to be polite, then said quietly, 'May I suggest the terrine of duck? It's superb . . . the way our chef does it.'

'Oh, I'd love duck,' Elly cried, and she allowed the steward to fill in the vegetables and oddments that would complete her order.

When the meal was ready to be served, a banker from Baltimore sought permission to ask grace, and since no minister was present, he was encouraged: 'Dear God, when I left home last week I visualized my- self as starting a considerable journey. All the way to Cincinnati. Imagine this girl of seventeen on her way to Oregon. Beloved Father, look after these children, for they are the sinews of our nation.'

Elly opened her eyes and saw the duck resting in its casserole, the lima beans, the candied sweets, the preserved crab apples, the breads, the jel- lies, and at the finish of the feast, the white birthday cake festooned with silver ornaments and seventeen flickering candles. When the meal ended, the banker who had offered the prayer whispered to his neighbor, 'Would you believe it, she ate the whole duck!' And his friend replied, 'Most of the cake, too.'

That afternoon when they found Finnerty he asked only one question: 'Could you get hold of forty dollars?' and when Levi nodded, he adjusted his tobacco to a mouth consisting mostly of gaps and said, 'It works this way. I use only dried timber. I build you the best flatboat on the river. We drift her down to Cairo and sell her for thirty dollars. Net cost to you, ten dollars.'

'How long to build it?'

'Two weeks. Can't take more, because we have to catch the spring floods.'

'And the boat'll be big enough for my Conestoga and the six horses.'

'Big enough for three other wagons. And we'll take 'em if they come along. That way we can earn some money—you and I—fifty-fifty.'

So it was agreed, and as soon as Finnerty got his hands on the money he went to work at a speed that surprised Levi. He had one white helper and two blacks, and they shoved great logs about and borrowed the Conestoga to haul in a load of freshly sawn timber, and there was much hammering and fitting together of boards, and well ahead of schedule a boat forty-four feet long and twelve feet wide took shape.

'I've seen men work,' Levi told Elly, 'but these take the prize.'

The Zendts left their filthy rooming house to watch the three final em- bellishments to their craft. When it seemed ready to go, Finnerty and his helpers built around the edge a combing eight inches high; it was not sturdy, and in a storm would not prevent articles from falling over, but it did define the space and make the huge craft resemble a boat. When this was done, they covered about half its length with a rude house on whose roof the Conestoga would be securely lashed. And at each end of the boat Finnerty rigged a very long pole atop a triangle; the one at the rear was fitted as a rudder, the one in front was for fending off snags, which could be so fatal to shipping.

'We're ready,' Finnerty announced, but when Levi drove his Cones- toga down to the pier he found the roof already taken by two smaller wagons whose drivers had bought passage to Cairo.

'I want to put mine there,' Levi argued, but Finnerty explained in a low voice, 'Levi, they're payin' us for the passage. Naturally they get first choice.'

So the Conestoga was fitted crosswise and forward of the cabin. Elly saw that the other passengers had preempted the good sleeping area, and now she grew angry. Levi had been unwilling to shift the wagons, but she had no compunction about shifting the beds, Finnerty or no Finnerty.

Thrusting her girlish face into the grizzled countenances of men and women three times her age, she announced, 'Mr. Zendt and I will put our bed here, and you can fit yours in as you may.' And down went her bed, smack in the middle.

Finnerty was as capable a boat handler as he was a builder, and early on the morning of April 1 he shoved into the center of the Ohio River, catching the lively current, and started the eleven-hundred-mile journey to the Mississippi. Keeping his position at the rear of the boat, he guided it past the docked steamers and beyond the limits of the city.

Now began the finest portion of the trip to Oregon—the silent, leisurely drift down the Ohio, with its vivid contrasting scenery. To the left lay Virginia, to the right Ohio, and whereas the first was a wilderness with trees coming to the shoreline, except where some adventurous family had chopped out a footing, the Ohio shoreline was a vista of green lawns and meadows, with fine houses showing in the distance.

'I read in a book that Virginia was a rich state,' Elly said, and Finnerty explained, 'It is, but only in the east. Out here, one Ohio's worth ten Virginnys.'

Levi wondered that his wife knew about the comparative riches of states she had never seen, but when they came to Blennerhassett Island she really astonished him, for she asked, 'Isn't this where Aaron Burr committed treason?' and Finnerty replied, 'The same,' and she said, 'It was cruel to place all the blame on Burr when most of it was General Wilkinson's, and the army let him off scot-free,' and Finnerty said, from his deep well of observation, 'The army rarely blames a general.'

'How did you know about Aaron Burr?' Levi asked as the flatboat drifted silently past the scene of infamy, and Elly replied, 'I studied.' Each day he discovered new and pleasing things about his wife.

It was customary for flatboats drifting down the river to lay over a couple of days at Cincinnati to give the passengers a chance to see the German city, where hundreds of hogs and cattle were slaughtered each day to feed the west, and it was here, on a bulletin board, that Levi Zendt caught his first understanding of the schedule that faced him, for a printed poster stated:

ONLY STEAMER TO BLACKSNAKE HILLS AND GREAT FALLS
Robert Q. Fell
CAPTAIN FRAKE
Sailing twelve noon, May 1, 1844
Travelers to Oregon accommodated
Post Seven, St. Louis, Mo.

Levi called Finnerty, showed him the sign and asked, 'Can we get to St. Louis by the first of May?'

'We?' Finnerty asked. 'You can, easy. When we reach Cairo, I head back to Pittsburgh.'

'Will there be steamers at Cairo . . . waiting?' Levi asked.

'Well, let's see. This is April 10. We ought to reach Cairo about April 23. Let's see what shows.' He studied the shipping notices and found that on April 26 the steamer *Ozark Maid*, Captain Shaw, was leaving Cairo for St. Louis, with arrival planned for the early morning of May 1. 'Just what you need,' Finnerty said, but since this allowed for little error, Levi wondered if the flatboat couldn't shove off immediately and skip Cincinnati.

When this proposal was made to the other passengers, they balked. As the women said, 'We been plannin' a long time to see this city,' so the boat was tied up, with Finnerty heading for a saloon he frequented and the other families for the imposing stores that lined the main streets.

Elly went off on her own, leaving her husband on the wharf to guard their Conestoga. He was there when a small steamboat set out from the Kentucky shore, picked its way among the larger craft filling the river and tied up not far from where he sat on a bale of cotton. He watched idly as a double gangplank was lowered and men began hammering timbers onto its sides to build a protected runway. 'Must be plannin' to bring down somethin' pretty valuable,' Levi said to a fellow watcher.

'Horses, probably,' the man grunted, but it wasn't horses at all. It was a group of seven large and handsome steers of a kind Levi had not seen before. They were reddish in color, very broad in the chest, and each had a white face. 'What kind of cattle are they?' Levi asked one of the handlers. 'Seventeens,' the man replied, and Levi asked, 'What's a Seventeen?' and the man explained, 'They belong to Senator Clay. He brought them over from England in 18 and 17.'

'What's their real name?' Levi asked, and the handler said, 'Don't know.' He worked for the senator at Ashland, over in Kentucky a ways, and he approved of the English cattle. 'They give a lot of eatin' beef,' he told Levi, who said, 'I can see that. I'm a butcher. Hogs mainly,' and the man said, 'In this town they slaughter a mighty lot of hogs. That's why the big hotels appreciate our beef.'

The heavy steers waddled off, and for a long time Levi sat staring at the water, remembering those strange white faces that looked so different from the Jerseys and Holsteins to which he was accustomed.

Two days out of Cincinnati a beautiful thing happened. Elly saw it first. She was standing aft with Finnerty, looking idly at the wake left by his rudder, when she saw far to the rear, coming around a bend in the river, two stately luxury steamers moving side by side, and after watching them for a few minutes and noting their rapid approach, she said, 'I declare, Mr. Finnerty, I think they're racing.'

'Race!' he shouted, leaving his tiller to tend itself. He ran back and forth along the flatboat, urging his six passengers to watch the exciting scene that was developing to the rear. They watched captivated as the two large steamers, filigreed like jewels, bore down upon them, and one of the women standing with Elly cried, 'They'll pass us very close!'

They would have to. Finnerty had his flatboat fairly well in the middle of the river, and whereas the two racing steamers could conceivably stay together and pass on one side, it was more likely that they would separate, each keeping as close to the middle of the river as possible.

'One on the left's the *River Belle* out of Cincinnati,' Finnerty shouted. 'Other one's the *Duquesne*, a Pittsburgh boat. Anyone care to bet on the *River Belle*?' There was no response, so he made another proposal: 'Anyone care to bet on the *Duquesne*?' Again there was no response, so he shouted in frustration, 'For Christ's sake, somebody bet. This is a race,' and Elly said, 'I'll bet a nickel on the *River Belle*,' but when she saw his face fall she quickly said, 'All right. I'll make it half a dollar,' and Levi winced at her carelessness with money.

An imaginary line was drawn between the flatboat and a tree on shore, and the other two men were to hold the wagers and serve as judges. Finnerty grew quite agitated as the splendid vessels approached, their decks quivering from the pounding of the engines, their tall smokestacks belching smoke. They seemed about equal, with each straining to the utmost, and as they neared, Finnerty shouted, 'The best part is, sometimes they explode and you can make a lot of money picking up the bodies . . . rescuing people, that is.'

It looked to Levi as if one or the other of these two beauties might explode before his eyes, so furious were the hammerings of the pistons, but with great speed they overtook the flatboat and expertly passed as close to it as possible, each seeking maximum advantage. None of the passengers aboard the graceful steamers could have been more excited than the seven people looking up from the flatboat, and the most delighted was Elly Zendt, for her *River Belle* crossed the imaginary finish line a good six feet ahead of the *Duquesne*. She expected Finnerty to be downcast at his loss, but he remained as delighted as he had been when she first called his attention to the race.

Levi's indifference to the race turned to real concern when the two vessels passed, for the tumbling wakes of the two steamers converged right under the flatboat, tossing it like a cork and straining every timber and rope. For the first time he felt that his investment with a boatbuilder as good as Finnerty had been justified.

Finnerty was undismayed by the danger. Balancing himself against the wildly tossing flatboat, he shouted, 'Look at 'em go!' as the boats approached the bend that would carry them out of sight. Each of the flatboat passengers looked with longing and a sense of exaltation as the great white steamers, more graceful than swans, swept out of view.

Cairo was a miserable site, a small mud flat perched on a large mud flat, which reached out to rest upon a really stupendous mud flat. Here the Ohio emptied into the Mississippi, and someone had decided that this point of land would be ideal as a river port, and it was, except that each spring either the Ohio or the Mississippi came into flood, almost wiping Cairo out. Six years out of seven the little town faced innundation, and this year it looked as if it would be the Mississippi, which was rising ominously.

The residents of Cairo were preoccupied with the building of dikes to hold back the rivers, and the town resembled a fortress sunk below walls, with little attention paid to travelers. It was difficult even to find where the *Ozark Maid*, Captain Shaw, would be loading for the run to St. Louis, and at the height of the confusion Elly ran up to inform Levi that the two families who had shared the flatboat from Pittsburgh had run off without paying . . . anyway, that's what Finnerty claimed.

'Well,' Levi said philosophically, 'at least we can sell the boat and get something back,' but when the time came to do so, the timber men of Cairo pointed to a score of rafts tied up along the muddy waterfront.

'We got more'n we can use in a year,' they grumbled, and they offered Levi ten dollars for his. He was not disposed to accept, and the men showed no disappointment. 'We're doin' you a favor, takin' it off'n your hands,' one of the men said. ' 'Course, you could fit a keel onto it for another thirty and hire ten strong men to pole you upriver to St. Louis. Take about three months.'

Levi laughed and said, 'Sold for ten dollars,' and when the deal was consummated, the men confided, 'Finnerty does this all the time. He knows the most we ever pay is ten dollars.' When Levi shook his head in consternation, one of the men added, 'Wager you the ten that Finnerty told you the other passengers skipped without payin'. He always does that, too.'

Levi looked about the waterfront for Finnerty, but he was gone, shipped aboard a steamer back to Pittsburgh. 'I've got to admit he built a good boat,' Levi muttered grudgingly as they led the horses to the *Ozark Maid*. 'Knew how to handle it, too.'

At eight o'clock in the morning of May 1, 1844, the Negro in the prow of the *Ozark Maid* curled a rope to the shore at St. Louis, where a waiting Negro caught it, passing the end through a large ring embedded in the levee. As soon as possible, Levi leaped from his boat to the one ahead, and from it, to the steamboat and thence to the shore. Leaving the job of unloading the horses to Elly, he dashed along the levee, asking everyone, 'Where's the *Robert Q. Fell*?'

Toward the northern end of the mile-long line of steamboats, and well beyond the range of the trim packets that made regular trips to places like Keokuk and Hannibal, waited a filthy, low-slung, two-deck, stern-paddle steamer with a very shallow draft for clearing mud flats. Twenty years ago it had been built for travel up the Missouri River, and two decades of heavy work on that swift and muddy stream had banged it about.

Few men would willingly embark upon such a leaky craft, except that no other was available for the long trip north, so as various steamers from Mississippi ports docked, other travelers like Zendt ran to the waiting vessel to buy passage. They were met at the stern by a small thin man, Captain Frake, who held a megaphone to his lips: 'If you want passage up the Missouri, get your gear aboard by twelve noon, because sure as hell, that's when we sail.'

'I have a Conestoga and six horses,' Zendt shouted across the dirty water.

'We'll have gangplanks over the side at fifteen minutes to twelve,' Frake replied. 'But, son, you better get her aboard pronto, because at twelve sharp we sail, team or no team.'

'How much?' Zendt shouted.

'How far?' Frake asked.

'Blacksnake Hills.'

'Any kinfolk?'

'Wife.'

Captain Frake calculated how much this traveler could afford to pay, and replied through his megaphone, 'Wagon and horses, thirty-two dollars. Two people, twenty-one dollars. You'll find no better.'

'Agreed,' Zendt called, whereupon Captain Frake ordered a Negro to lower a gangplank to the levee, and Levi climbed aboard, delivering the fifty-three dollars. 'Receipt?' he asked. The dour little captain extended a hand, saying, 'My word's my bond. Get your gear aboard.'

Zendt had three hours to get his wagon ashore and deliver it to the *Robert Q. Fell.* Breathless, he dashed back to the *Ozark Maid,* finding to his dismay that whereas the steamboat itself was neatly tied up, the trailing flatboats were not close to any spot from which they could be unloaded. Later in the day they would be detached and poled to other spots.

'The wagon!' Levi began shouting from shore. 'We have to have that wagon by eleven.'

'Nothing I can do,' Elly called back. Until the men started seriously to shift the flatboats, she was helpless.

'Hey there!' Levi shouted to disinterested men aboard the *Ozark Maid,* 'how do I get my wagon?'

'They'll unload it,' the man said carelessly, waving his arm in no particular direction.

Back and forth Zendt ran, a short-legged Dutchman in a flat-brimmed hat, trying to urge rivermen to work faster than their custom. Ten o'clock came and nothing happened. Eleven o'clock approached and the flatboat was still well offshore. He became desperate and ran the long distance back to the *Robert Q. Fell*, where Captain Frake shouted through his megaphone, 'It's not my concern. This here boat sails at twelve sharp, and you better be aboard.'

'What about my money?'

'You paid your money, and I offer you accommodation in return. It's here waitin', but you better move yourself and get that team aboard.'

Levi ran back to the flatboat and in desperation shouted at Elly, 'Do something!'

'What can I do?' she asked pathetically.

The precious hour passed, the one worth fifty-three dollars to the Zendts, and the flatboat remained stationary. With a burst of speed, Zendt dashed back to the *Robert Q. Fell* and pleaded, 'Captain Frake, wait just a few minutes! We're comin'.'

The captain looked up and down the levee, then back at his steamboat innards and called, 'We'll hold her a couple of minutes.' With a sense of salvation, Levi ran back to the flatboats and saw with joy that the one containing his team was being shifted. 'I offered them two dollars,' Elly called ashore.

'Great idea!' Levi shouted back. He had demanded that she do something, and she had done it. 'How long to unload?' he yelled. Elly consulted with the men and replied, 'About an hour.'

'Oh, my God!' Levi groaned, and back he ran to the *Robert Q. Fell*. 'It'll take fifty more minutes,' he called up to the captain.

'Can't wait more than thirty,' Captain Frake replied, so back Levi galloped to where the flatboat was pulling in to shore. The men operating the craft had no intention of working at extra speed, but they had no objection if Levi and Elly routed out the gangplanks, fastened them in position, led four of the horses ashore, harnessed the other two to the wagon and slowly edged it off the scow.

No sooner did the iron wheels touch cobblestone than Elly backed the other four horses into position, where Levi harnessed them. With Elly walking behind, he whipped up the team, leading his six handsome grays along the levee.

'Fine team you have there,' a man called. 'Care to sell?' Levi did not even reply. His eyes were fixed on the smokestacks of the *Robert Q. Fell*. He became so nervous that he whipped the six heavy horses into a trot, but they had gone only a short distance when a man accompanied by a policeman flagged them down.

'I'm Curtis Wainwright,' the man told Levi. 'I fancy good horseflesh and I'd be interested in that team of six.'

'Not for sale,' Levi said in great agitation.

'You're headed for Oregon?'

'Yes. Get out of the way.'

'Wait a minute, mister,' the policeman said. 'Mr. Wainwright wants to speak with you.'

'My boat! It's leaving without me.'

'Which boat?' the policeman asked.

'*Robert Q. Fell.*'

The two men laughed, and Wainwright said, 'I think you can rest assured that your boat will wait.'

Levi saw that he was trapped, so he turned to Elly and said, 'Run ahead and tell them we're comin'.' The policeman tried good-naturedly to intercept her, but she was off and running, and when she got to the steamboat and Levi saw that she was engaging its captain in conversation, he felt relieved.

'Point is,' Mr. Wainwright explained, 'you really shouldn't take a fine team like that onto the prairies. What you need for Oregon is not horses but oxen. Now, I'll give you two hundred dollars each for those grays, and I'll sell you six oxen for sixty dollars . . . total. You'll reach Oregon a rich man.'

'These are my horses,' Levi said, and without further argument he drove the team along the levee to where Captain Frake's men had lowered gangplanks up which the wagon trundled. As soon as it was aboard, the planks were hoisted and thrown back in a pile.

'You can go now!' Levi called up to the captain, but nothing happened. Two o'clock came, and three and four, and still nothing happened. At five a two-wheeled carriage pulled onto the levee and out of it stepped an army officer in blue uniform with rows of brightly polished buttons. He was about thirty, handsome, with a clipped mustache and an easy manner.

'Halloo, Captain Frake?' he called.

One of the deckhands routed out the captain, who appeared on the upper deck with his megaphone. 'Captain Mercy, how are you?'

'There's a dance tonight, Captain Frake. You won't be leaving, will you?'

'We're leavin' at twelve sharp tomorrow,' Frake replied.

'Good!' the captain called back, and with that he climbed into his carriage, wheeled the horses about and disappeared.

The news that they were not sailing till next day distressed Levi. 'Why did he make us hurry so?' he asked petulantly, and Elly explained that no doubt Captain Frake had intended sailing, as planned, but that something unforeseen had come up. 'No,' Levi said slowly, 'I think he just wanted our fifty-three dollars. He wanted to get us aboard so we couldn't change our minds.' They were so tired they fell asleep without solving the problem or trying the evening meal.

They ate a huge breakfast, then climbed down the gangplank to buy the gear they had failed to get the day before. At various shops along the waterfront they purchased rope and axes and buckets of grease for the wagon and replacements for broken harness and barrels of flour and bacon and all the last-minute things that storekeepers reminded them of. 'You'll want a second rifle,' everyone warned him, but he said, 'I have the best rifle made.' However, a gunsmith showed him a fine used Hawken and assured him, 'This is the best rifle in the world for the prairie,' so Levi bought it for eleven dollars.

It was half past eleven when he and Elly got back to the boat, loaded with gear and guiding a Negro slave boy who trailed behind with the rifle and the buckets of grease. At noon one of the ship's stewards passed along the decks ringing a bell and calling, 'Dinner for all! It won't wait.'

Elly, of course, was hungry, but Levi said, 'I'm going to stay on deck. I want to see them shove off.' A fellow passenger who heard this laughed and said, 'We're not sailing today.'

'We aren't?'

'Not for days.'

Levi found this hard to believe, but at this moment the two-wheeled carriage he had seen the previous night came onto the levee, bearing the same handsome young officer. 'Captain Frake? There's a big dinner tonight after church. All right?'

'We're leaving tomorrow, twelve sharp,' Frake responded, and the carriage disappeared.

So that afternoon Levi and Elly explored the city, restricting themselves to the three oldest streets near the river. With apprehension they passed the large and ominous Catholic cathedral; they had never spoken to a Catholic so far as they knew, but they had heard various Mennonite and Lutheran ministers preach about them, and that taught them enough to be cautious.

That evening at supper a passenger told them, 'At seven I'm going up the hill to the Presbyterian church for worship. Care to come along?'

Elly said she would like that: 'We should give thanks that we've come so far in safety,' and in the pale light of evening they walked past the streets they had visited that afternoon and up to the third level of the city, where on Fourth Street they came to that handsome old church with the white steeple and the picket fence.

From its portico they could look back down the hill and across the sleeping river to the quiet hills of Illinois. In that direction lay home, and never had it seemed so distant, so far beyond recovery.

The service was appropriate. It dealt with Ruth, who had gone into the fields of Boaz, and the minister read those extraordinary lines regarding the trick whereby Naomi caught a husband for her daughter-in-law, Ruth:

'And it shall be, when he lieth down, that thou shalt mark the place where he shall lie, and thou shalt go in, and uncover his feet, and lay thee down; and he will tell thee what thou shalt do.

'And she said unto her, All that thou sayest unto me I will do . . .

'And when Boaz had eaten and drunk, and his heart was merry, he went to lie down at the end of the heap of corn: and she came softly, and uncovered his feet, and laid her down.

'And it came to pass at midnight, that the man was afraid, and turned himself: and, behold, a woman lay at his feet.

'And he said, Who art thou? And she answered, I am Ruth thine handmaid: spread therefore thy skirt over thy handmaid . . .'

He preached for some minutes on this theme, but Levi heard none of the message, for he was speculating, with Pennsylvania Dutch forthrightness, on that curious phrase 'and she uncovered his feet,' and he whispered to Elly, 'I bet she uncovered a lot more than his feet,' and Elly blushed and whispered back, 'It's the Bible way of explaining things,' and he replied, 'I could explain it a lot clearer.'

The minister now turned to his right, where in a special pew reserved for wealthy patrons sat the young captain Levi had seen at the levee. 'One of our sons leaves shortly for the west to do our government's work,' the preacher said, 'and we join his distinguished family in wishing him Godspeed and safe return.' Levi looked at the captain and saw that he sat with a very handsome pair of women, a younger one who must be his wife, and an older woman with silvery hair who could be either his mother or his mother-in-law. They nodded sedately as the minister spoke of their captain, and he looked modestly at the floor. He was wearing a sword whose gold hilt projected at his chest, and now he transferred his right hand to the hilt, gripping it so tightly that his knuckles stood out. He was praying.

Now the minister turned to another section of the church, where a variety of couples sat, men and women in rude dress, and he addressed himself to them: 'These strangers from Vermont go forth to a marvelous destiny, to take civilization and the word of God to distant Oregon. God surely will protect them on their way so that storms and famine and the deadly Indian shall not prevail. To the men I say, "Be strong," and to the women, "Be faithful." And remember that it was Ruth, of whom we spoke this night in another context, who delivered the immortal words which guide all pilgrims:

'And Ruth said, Intreat me not to leave thee, or to return from following after thee: for whither thou goest, I will go; and where thou lodgest, I will lodge: thy people shall be my people, and thy God my God.

'Where thou diest, will I die, and there will I be buried: the Lord do so to me, and more also, if ought but death part thee and me.'

Levi slipped his hand into Elly's, and whereas many of the women in the Vermont group wept, she looked straight ahead and gripped his hand as firmly as if she were a man.

When the service ended the young captain left his pew and passed among the Vermont emigrants, wishing them well and assuring them that he and his sergeant would be accompanying them through the worst of the Indian country and that there was little to fear. As Levi Zendt strained to hear this reassuring news he felt his arm being taken, and turned to see Curtis Wainwright, the man who had tried to buy his horses that morning.

'Hello!' Wainwright said amiably. 'Glad to see you're a churchman.'

'It's a long trip. We need blessing.'

'Yesterday I was importunate,' Wainwright apologized. 'Today I want you to meet our minister,' and he led Levi and Elly to the porch, where the minister was bidding his parishioners goodnight. 'Reverend Oster,' Wainwright said, 'I wish you'd inform these strangers that I'm a man of reasonably decent character. I'm afraid I frightened them yesterday.'

Reverend Oster turned and smiled. Grasping the hands of Levi and Elly, he beamed on them and said, 'This is Curtis Wainwright, responsible citizen and good friend of this church. You can trust him in anything except when he's trying to buy your horse.'

Elly laughed, and Wainwright said, 'The wrong words, Reverend, the wrong words. I was trying to convince them they ought not take their fine horses onto the Oregon Trail. It'll only kill them.'

'In that he's right,' Reverend Oster said. 'Our experience is that you must take oxen, not horses or mules.'

'What's that about mules?' a new voice asked, and they turned to face Captain Mercy.

'Captain Maxwell Mercy,' the minister said. 'I don't believe I caught your names.'

'Levi and Elly Zendt, Lancaster, Pennsylvania.'

'Are you the couple with the Conestoga?' Mercy asked.

'That's ours.'

'We're going west together.'

'When?'

Captain Mercy broke into a laugh. 'With Captain Frake? Who knows! He was scheduled to sail on Wednesday. He may make it by Monday.'

'Why did he make me rush so?'

'He likes to get his freight aboard . . . fare paid.'

'But we're eatin' three meals a day.'

'Cheaper to feed you than to lose you.' He bowed politely to Elly and said, 'Tomorrow buy lots of cloth and three pairs of shoes that fit. And as for the horses, they do not do well on the trail. If you can make a profitable deal, consider it.'

'I love those horses,' Levi said stubbornly, and the men knew that further argument was useless, for they were the kind of men who loved their horses too, and they appreciated his refusal to trade.

'He'll have trouble,' Captain Mercy said as the Zendts left. 'I'm taking mules—army orders—and they'll give trouble enough.'

If Captain Frake had sailed on Friday noon, it is probable that Levi and Elly Zendt would have gone to Oregon without ever knowing that a place like Rattlesnake Buttes in Colorado existed, but the boat did not sail, so on Friday afternoon Levi and Elly strolled along the streets of downtown St. Louis, buying cloth and extra shoes, and as they turned a corner off what used to be Rue de l'Eglise they came upon a building unlike any they had seen before. It seemed to be a store but it was more like a theater. Its front was plastered with signs announcing Mr. L. Reed, Gastriloquist Extraordinary; Master Haskell, Wizzard of the Ages, Thaumaturgist and Metamorphosist; Madame Zelinah-Kah-Nourinha, Fair Lady of Turkey; and Last Time to See the Gigantic Elephant Discovered in These Regions by Dr. Albert C. Koch, now of London.

Levi looked at Elly as if to ask whether she wished to see these wonders; she shrugged her shoulders, and they were about to pass on, when the owner of the museum came into the street and cajoled them with promises of delights they could not even imagine: 'You may never have a chance to see the mighty elephant, because next month we must send it to Europe.'

Since neither Levi nor Elly had ever seen an elephant, except in books, they diffidently allowed the man to sell them tickets, and in they went. It was, as Levi had expected, mostly a theater, with chairs and a stage onto which came a juggler and two pretty girls. Then Mr. Reed appeared; he was worth the whole admission, because standing alone with no equipment of any kind, he could make almost any sound you might care to hear: a roaring alligator, a train falling off a trestle, a trumpeter playing an aria from Donizetti, the explosion of a volcano.

The Zendts were quite captivated by Mr. Reed, and Elly was convinced he must have little bugles and things hidden in his mouth, but Levi asked, 'How could he?' They were about to leave when the manager reminded them, 'You haven't seen the elephant,' and they passed behind a curtain expecting to see a live elephant. Instead, they saw something they would never forget: a truly massive skeleton of a gigantic mastodon that had lived along the riverbank thousands of years ago. They were so astonished that they barely heard the monologue: '. . . ate a ton of hay each day . . . each mighty tusk twenty-two feet long . . . the mother carried the baby in her womb for four years, seven months and nineteen days . . . I want this young lady to lie down beside the foot . . . it could crush her entire body with one savage blow . . . the tail was nine feet long . . . huge, huge, huge.'

The Zendts remained staring at the giant skeleton long after the other spectators had left, Levi in particular being captivated by it. 'How could he find enough to eat?' he kept asking.

'You heard the man. A ton of hay every day.'

'But where would he find it?'

'If he had a trunk to match the rest of him,' Elly reasoned, 'he could stand in one spot and sweep in a ton of grass.'

When they reached the streets they found themselves in a veritable flood, and Levi pondered how he might get Elly back to the boat without being drenched, but she said, 'I'm not afraid of a little rain.' They were about to set forth when they heard themselves being hailed. 'You there! From Pennsylvania! Want a ride back? This is going to get worse.' It was Captain Mercy heading for his nightly intelligence regarding the *Fell*.

When they were inside his carriage he told them, 'I'm being sent west by the army. To select a site for a new fort. Sergeant Lykes, eight mules and me.'

At the *Fell*, Captain Frake warned Mercy, 'We sail tomorrow at twelve sharp. And you better have them mules aboard, because this boat never waits a minute.'

So the Zendts went up the gangplank, and for some time they lingered on deck, staring at the lights of a city which had been hospitable, and Elly saw principally the dark river which was beginning to rise because of the excessive rains, but Levi saw only the elephant, massive and plodding and filling the sky with its premonitory form.

On Saturday, May 4, to everyone's amazement, Captain Frake finally ordered his crew to fire up the boilers, bring in the gangplanks and cast off from the iron rings. At twelve sharp, as he had predicted, the *Robert Q. Fell*, with as full a load as the craft could carry, set out for the middle of the Mississippi and turned its bow upstream.

It was to be a difficult and ugly day, for whereas the steamboat did well in the slow-moving Mississippi, when it reached the mouth of the Missouri, that river was throwing so much water into the main stream and so much mud, that for some hours the *Robert Q. Fell* seemed to be standing still. Captain Frake grew plainly worried, allowed his craft to slip backward some distance, then headed for the Illinois shore. Ordering a major head of steam, he tried again, but his engine could deliver only six knots forward while the river was flowing four knots in the opposite direction.

Cursing the Missouri, he edged closer to the northern bank of the muddy river and fortunately caught a reverse current which helped him enter the main channel. With a final burst of speed he brought his boat into calmer water, and just as darkness fell he pushed ahead to safety— and a sandbank.

They stayed caught on the bar throughout the night, and in the morning all able-bodied passengers were rowed ashore and given heavy ropes to pull. By exerting almost superhuman strength, they edged the boat off the bank and with a cheer returned on board. Elly said, 'It must have taken all the strength you had,' and Sergeant Lykes, in charge of the army mules, said, 'Ma'am, you could hear the muscles poppin'.'

To go up the Missouri was of itself a notable adventure, with sandbars and jagged tree trunks which could rip out the bottom of a boat, and sudden turns and high romantic cliffs on alternate sides. It bore no comparison with the tame Ohio; this was a wild, undisciplined river, with each curve bringing its peculiar problems.

On the fourth day they reached the remarkable twin cities of the lower Missouri, and in accordance with the rule, 'Franklin up, Boonville down,' they stopped at the former city to allow the horses and mules to forage for the afternoon, while the passengers walked inland to the new town which had replaced the old one that had fallen into the river when the land on which it was sitting was undercut by currents. Franklin was a beautiful town of five or six thousand population, with a newspaper, lawyers, good schools and a lively concern for all that happened in the west. From here caravans had formerly set forth for Santa Fe, and the returning freight wagons were often driven by Mexicans who spoke no English. From here, too, men headed for the Yellowstone and the distant forts at the head of the Missouri. Indians of all tribes were common in Franklin; they would stand solemnly at the back of public meetings when local dignitaries discussed Socrates and the philosophy of Edmund Burke.

Elly said, 'It's like Lancaster with common sense,' and if anyone had at that moment made the Zendts a worthwhile proposition, they would have been willing to keep their horses ashore, unload the Conestoga, and let Captain Frake have their passage money. They would remember Franklin as the best of the west, the kind of community they hoped to build in Oregon.

Nine days out, on Sunday, May 12, they passed under the cliff once dominated by Fort Osage and looked up to see the rusted cannon pointing harmlessly down the river they had so long guarded. That afternoon they were in Independence, rowdiest town in the west, and they had been ashore only a few minutes when an ornery Pawnee Indian, liquored up by fur traders, tried to take a pistol from a riverman, who shot him dead. The body was kicked to one side and no law officer made any pretense of arresting the murderer, or even investigating 'the accident.' Three hours later the corpse was still beside the river.

When Captain Frake decided to lay over several days to see if he could pick up Mexican goods for the trip north, it gave Levi a chance to exercise his horses, and when he led the six grays down the gangplank they excited a storm of interest. Many offers were made, for the men of this region appreciated good horseflesh.

'I'll give you three hundred dollars a horse,' one prosperous merchant proposed, but Levi said they were not for sale, not under any circumstances.

He was then approached by a slim, handsome young fellow in his mid-twenties who said with an unusual accent, 'I've just come in from Santa

Fe, and believe me, you'd be a fool to take those valuable beasts onto the prairie. They simply will not last.'

'I don't want to sell them,' Levi snapped.

'I don't want to buy them,' the young stranger replied. 'I am speaking as a friend.'

'Who are you?'

'Oliver Seccombe, Santa Fe, Boston, London, Oxford.'

'What're you doin' here?' Levi asked suspiciously.

'Exploring. Seeing the world before I settle down. Are you by chance headed up the Missouri?'

'I am.'

'To the forts?'

'Oregon.'

'Well met! I'm for Oregon too. Are you by chance a passenger on that disgraceful old tub?' And he pointed with his wrist toward the *Robert Q. Fell.*

'I am.'

'Fellow passenger!' he cried, embracing Levi. 'And is this your good wife?'

'It's Elly.'

'We shall celebrate!' And he led the Zendts to a mangy saloon which sold everything from Taos Lightning to lemon soda. Rapping on the unwashed bar, he cried, 'My good man! Drinks, if you please.'

A thin, sad-faced man who had watched hundreds pass through this room on their way to hopeful adventure came unhappily to stand before the Englishman. 'Whaddle ya have?'

'Whadda ya got?' Seccombe answered, imitating the man.

'For you, horsepiss. For the lady, if she is a lady, lemonade.'

'Excellent!' Seccombe cried. 'In mine a little ginger, and for the lady's husband what do you propose?'

'Him?' The jaundiced bartender studied Levi and said, 'Sarsaparilla.'

'Three whiskeys,' Seccombe said quietly, and with a quick movement he produced a pistol.

Grudgingly the man brought three whiskeys, sloshed them on the bar and said, 'I'm about to throw you out of here.'

Seccombe caught him by the arm and said, 'Before I tried that little trick, my good friend, I would consult with counsel.' He pushed the arm away and added, 'Because otherwise you would find yourself flat on your ass.' When the bartender left, Seccombe told the Zendts, 'When you're an Englishman in the west, you have to establish your reputation fast, otherwise . . .'

'I don't drink whiskey,' Elly said.

'My good man!' Seccombe called. When the bartender appeared, the Englishman laughed disarmingly and said, 'You were right all along. She does want lemonade.'

As they drank he told them of his trip to Santa Fe, the dust, the Comanche, the good times along the road, the great money to be made in western trade. 'But I'm for Oregon,' he said brightly. 'Catch a ship home and write my book, *Travels in the Great West*, with slaughter on every page. How do you spell your names?'

He was an exhausting young man, two years older than Levi but a whole world brighter. When he inspected the gear Levi had assembled for the trip west, he was shocked. 'You've overlooked the one thing you need most,' he said.

'Another gun?'

'Fie on guns. Everyone carries too many. But the hat. The hat!' He said that the one thing the traveler needed was a broad-brimmed hat so wide that the sun could not reach his lips. 'You walk on those prairies for five months, with the sun beating down every day, and your lips burn right off. Madame, you simply must get yourself two sunbonnets, because if you lose one and allow the sun to strike those beautiful lips . . ."

His manner irritated Levi, because he well knew that Elly's lips were not beautiful. In fact, there was little about his wife that anyone in his right mind could call beautiful, and he was perplexed by Seccombe's obvious insincerity. However, the man did appreciate horses, and recognized that the grays were superior. 'Hold out, Zendt,' he counseled. 'In this town you can get four hundred apiece for that group. But I would sell the Conestoga, if anyone makes an offer. Too heavy.'

Seccombe was captivated by Levi's Melchior Fordney rifle, and arranged a test-firing with Captain Mercy and Sergeant Lykes. The men set up targets and fired each other's rifles. Mercy had an expensive Boston weapon, Lykes a standard issue from the Harper's Ferry arsenal, and Seccombe a good English gun; but all agreed that Zendt's Lancaster rifle was the easiest handling of the lot. 'When you decide to sell it, I'm your man,' Seccombe said, balancing the beautiful weapon.

'I'm keeping it,' Levi said.

'On the plains you'll find your Hawken to be the better rifle,' Captain Mercy said. 'I carry two of them.'

'He's right,' Seccombe agreed. 'On the Santa Fe trip I used my English gun for antelope, my Hawken for trouble. You'll do the same.'

From his previous stay in Independence, Oliver Seccombe knew everyone and helped the Zendts purchase their last-minute needs: baking powder, the extra lead for bullets, the dried beef. 'You'll get damned tired of bacon,' he predicted. And when all was in readiness he took them aside and said, 'I've studied you two. You're fine people. Why don't we make it a team to Oregon?'

'We'll need more,' Levi said, so they approached Captain Mercy.

'We'd like to join up with you and Lykes, if we may,' Seccombe said.

'I'd be honored,' Mercy said. 'But I'm not going all the way to Oregon.'

'You could help us get started right,' Seccombe said, 'and at Blacksnake Hills we'll see who else is preparing to go. We'll form a tight party.'

'I don't want to travel with the Vermont people,' Levi said. 'Too churchy.'

'I prefer to give the Psalm-singers a wide berth myself,' Mercy agreed.

So on the five-day trip north to Blacksnake Hills, these five formed a solid team: an army officer on an important commission; his knowledge-able sergeant; Oliver Seccombe, who had already crossed the prairies twice; the patient, hard-working Zendts.

The boat stopped at Fort Leavenworth, where officers boarded to give Captain Mercy last-minute instructions: 'The Arapaho and Cheyenne are peaceful, but watch out for those Oglala Sioux.' A young officer said, 'The Pasquinel brothers are riding with them, and they've caused a lot of trouble.'

Zendt had never heard of the Pasquinel brothers, but he noticed that when the name was mentioned, Captain Mercy firmed his mouth. 'We'll take precautions,' he said.

'Who are the Pasquinels?' Levi asked when the soldiers departed.

'Rough,' Seccombe broke in. 'Half-breeds who lead the Indians on war parties. Last August they cut the Santa Fe trail for three days. Burned some wagons.'

When the boat resumed its tortuous journey to Blacksnake Hills, Levi heard again of the Pasquinel brothers, for a trader who had come aboard at Independence told Elly, 'White men on the prairies can be animals, and Indians can be terrifying, but the half-breed is the worst of both. When those brothers get the tribes roiled up, there's hell to pay.'

'Who are they?' Elly asked.

'Who knows? A French trapper named Pasquinel, I suppose—took himself a squaw, and now we have his bastards to contend with.'

'You ever see them?' Levi asked.

'That I did. Came downriver in 18 and 39 with three bales of buffalo robes, and they led a bunch of Cheyenne who cleaned me out.'

'Why didn't they kill you?' Elly asked.

'Sometimes they kill, sometimes they don't. But if I ever see them again, they won't have the option.' The other trappers who had moved in to listen agreed that on next meeting, the whites would fire first and there'd be two dead half-breed troublemakers.

On reaching Blacksnake Hills, the passengers found that the well-known store run by French trapper Joseph Robidoux had been closed. The proprietor had moved to a new riverfront settlement where he was selling plots for the establishment of a town to be called, after his patron, St. Joseph. He had chosen his site well; it encompassed a projection made by a bend in the river and was protected to the rear by bluffs.

'Capital of the river!' said Robidoux. 'No need to travel any further west.' He told the Zendts, 'Stay here and grow up with a great city.' As soon as he saw the gray horses he said, 'Don't take them beasts onto the prairie. They won't last a month.' He offered to buy the grays at four hundred dollars each and to sell them six oxen to take their place at twenty dollars a head. Levi refused, but that night Oliver Seccombe appeared with a grizzled old man who changed everything.

'This is Sam Purchas,' the Englishman said, pushing forward a wizened man of forty-nine who looked seventy-nine. He dressed like an Indian, except for a huge slouch hat whose brim nearly covered his face, which was notable for a tobacco-stained beard, broken teeth and a nose whose tip had been sliced off by either a rusty knife or the jagged end of a broken bottle. 'He calls himself King of the Mountain Men, and I've hired him to lead us to Oregon.'

'Has he ever been there?' Captain Mercy asked.

'Been there?' the guide snorted. 'Sonny, I been acrost these prairies with all the great ones. Sublette, Kit Carson, Fitzpatrick, the Bents—I've knowed 'em all.'

'But have you ever been to Oregon?' Mercy repeated.

'And they taught me just one thing. Don't never try to reach Oregon with horses draggin' your wagon.' He turned to Seccombe and asked, 'Which one is Zendt?' When Oliver pointed him out, the old guide came up to Levi and growled, 'Sonny, no horses travel with this mountain man. Sell 'em and get oxen.'

This was an order, delivered by Sam Purchas. 'Anybody got any whiskey?' he asked, and when this was provided he reviewed his plans for getting the party to Oregon: 'The whole trick is timin'. We leave St. Joe as soon as these rains stop, allowin' the rivers to fall. But not before there's plenty of grass for the oxen. Too soon, your oxen starve in Kansas. Too late, you freeze to death in Oregon snow.'

As he spoke Elly could not take her eyes from his nose. She very much wanted to ask what had happened, but that would be impolite, so she listened as he droned on: 'I want every man to have two rifles, two pistols, an ax, two knives, a penknife, a hatchet and twenty pounds of lead.'

Captain Mercy protested, 'That's enough ammunition to fight your way inch by inch,' whereupon Purchas looked at him condescendingly and said, 'Soldier boy, that's just what we may have to do.'

Mercy retorted, 'The officers at Fort Leavenworth assured me the Arapaho and the Cheyenne were peaceful this year,' and Purchas snapped, 'I wish they'd give me the same assurance about the Oglala Sioux, the Crow, the Blackfeet and the Gros Ventres. Because they're the ones we have to deal with.'

Captain Mercy said he still thought the armament too heavy, and Purchas lost patience: 'Sonny, I been with 'em all. Kit Carson, Sublette . . .' He went through his litany of recommendations, adding a few names like Bridger and Jackson, and ending, 'And they taught me just one thing. Carry plenty of guns. Me, I carry four rifles, two pistols and this little beauty.' He placed on the table one of the newfangled revolvers. 'Without reloading, I can kill six Indians.'

He told them he had been born in Fauquier County, on a farm owned by General Washington: 'Of course I seen him, many times. We paid him the rent, didn't we?' He had wandered out to Ohio, where he had shot deer to feed the surveying crew of Alexander Hamilton's son, 'Colonel William S., and a fine man he was.' From there he had drifted on to Indiana Territory, where General William Henry Harrison had served as representative in Congress: 'He musta been thinkin' then of goin' into politics, because he plastered every home with free books sent out from Washington, and that's how I got hold of Lewis and Clark's report on their trip to Oregon, and I was lost.'

'You ever been to Oregon?' Mercy asked again, but before Purchas could reply, Sergeant Lykes asked, 'What happened to your nose?'

Purchas pinched his half-nose with his right thumb and forefinger and grinned at the sergeant. 'Sonny, I could tell you that I lost it in one of them river-boat gougin' battles they write about in the St. Louis newspapers— Say, speakin' of newspapers, you might like to see this,' and from a deerskin wallet he produced a clipping from the *New Orleans Picayune:*

> 'Strong as a lion, fearless as a tiger, keen-eyed as an eagle and quick as a panther, Samuel Purchas, greatest of the mountain men and frontiersman extraordinary, departed our city on Thursday last week leading a party of merchants on an exploratory trip to the forts of the Upper Missouri. Sylvestre O'Fallon told this journal, "It's a very dangerous journey, but since we are in the hands of Sam Purchas, we have no fear." We trust that the redoubtable Purchas will get his charges safely home again, for they are among the ornaments of this city.

'That sort of tells you who I am, don't it?' he asked proudly.

Early next morning he brought in a farmer from a settlement downriver, and when Elly awoke she heard Purchas selling their horses. 'Levi,' she called, shaking him, 'get up! They're taking your horses.'

Levi ran out to find Purchas trotting the big grays before a man who obviously was eager to get them. 'Deal's set,' Purchas said brusquely. 'He'll take your horses for five hundred dollars each. Wants the mares to start a line. And he'll sell you eight of the best oxen at fifteen dollars each. My commission is fifty dollars, so it's done.'

The farmer had the cash, more than Levi had seen at one time before, and he had brought with him the eight oxen, big lumbering beasts without a shred of beauty—six for pulling the Conestoga, two for replacements. Purchas knew that Zendt would not want to see his horses go, so he put his arm about him and drew him away, but when Levi actually heard the stranger speak to his horses and start them across the field, he broke loose and ran to them and bade each goodbye, patting their sleek rumps and fighting back tears as they moved eastward.

In a kind of daze he returned to Elly. 'I had to sell them,' he said. She brushed by him and ran into the field in time to see those splendid gray animals disappear over the hill. As she stood there, the morning wind blowing her hair, Levi came to her side and whispered, 'Now we really are alone. Now we can never go back,' and in that moment the Zendts knew what moving west meant—the awful loneliness, the burden of rifles, the strange rivers flowing swift with mud, the unknown Indians lurking, the long, long trails with no homes and no lights at dusk. They had barely started; over half the continent lay ahead, and their courage might have waned, except that Captain Mercy, aware that their grief could be diverted only by new tasks, warned them: 'You'll have to study fast and learn all you can about oxen. These look like good ones.'

When it came time to pack, Levi experienced a stubborn sense of satisfaction in telling Elly, 'They all said, "Get rid of the Conestoga," but now everybody says, "Can we fit this into your Conestoga?" You'd think we were plannin' to open a store.' Captain Mercy, Oliver Seccombe and Sam Purchas had each brought oddments to be tucked in 'out of the way,' they said, until a man with lesser good will might have told them all, 'Go to hell.' But Levi shrugged his shoulders and said, 'Tuck 'em in somewheres,' and the Conestoga creaked.

Friday afternoon Sam Purchas appeared with two heavy wagons drawn by oxen and occupied by two of the dourest-looking families central Missouri had so far produced. 'The Fishers and the Fraziers want to join us' he said by way of introduction, and four lean people stepped forward to shake hands, withdrawing their fingers grudgingly, as if to count them. Mrs. Frazier established the tone of the meeting by asking Purchas, 'That young one? She married?'

'Claims to be,' the mountain man replied.

'I doubt it,' Mrs. Frazier said, and off she went to report her suspicions to the other three.

'They'll be intolerable,' Seccombe predicted, but Purchas silenced him by pointing out, 'We got to have at least three wagons—for defense and to stand the night watches.' So the Fishers and the Fraziers were accepted.

On Saturday morning, May 25, 1844, Sam Purchas chewed his cud, spat in the road and handed down his judgment: 'Time to move out.' But as the three wagons drew up in line, Levi saw with some distress that Purchas, Mercy and Lykes each rode a horse and led two. 'You made me sell my horses, but you kept yours,' he protested.

'We ain't haulin' wagons,' Purchas growled.

The procession wound slowly along the riverbank till it came to a pitiful ferry, which took them aboard, one wagon at a time, for a perilous journey across the Missouri. By noon the party had assembled in Kansas and that afternoon covered the first six miles of the trip west. The oxen moved so slowly that Levi could not hide his impatience, but Purchas reassured him, 'They start slow, but God, how they keep movin'.'

The first crisis on the trip occurred next morning. It was Sunday and the Zendts had their wagon harnessed early. Sergeant Lykes had his mules shaped up, and Captain Mercy was ready, but the two wagons from Missouri showed no signs of life. 'Get the Fishers and the Fraziers up and going,' the captain told his sergeant, but when Lykes went to the wagons and shook them, a voice protested, 'This is Sunday.'

After a long delay, Mr. Fisher and Mr. Frazier climbed out of their wagons to explain that under no circumstances could they travel on the Sabbath. God had ordained this to be a day of rest, and it would be an offense to Him and to their animals if they did any work on Sunday. Captain Mercy replied, 'We have only so many days to get west, and we need the Sundays,' but Fisher and Frazier argued, 'A day of rest will strengthen our animals, and they will progress better than if we violated God's law.' Captain Mercy snapped, 'We've been resting six months. Now we move.'

Levi and Elly Zendt voted with Mercy and Lykes, but to everyone's surprise, Sam Purchas sided with the Missourians. 'A day's rest in seven don't do no harm,' he said. 'I seen plenty of parties that galloped the first half and bleached their bones the second.'

So it was agreed that Captain Mercy's party would travel six days and rest the seventh, but trouble again brewed that afternoon when Mrs. Fisher and Mrs. Frazier, two gaunt women who feared the trip west, came to Captain Mercy to lodge a formal protest: 'Mrs. Zendt ain't restin'.' Captain Mercy looked toward the Conestoga and could see no untimely work on Elly's part. She was sitting quietly, her back to them.

'She's scribblin',' Mrs. Fisher said, and Mrs. Frazier nodded. Then Captain Mercy looked closer and saw that Elly had a pad in her lap and was writing. 'God don't hold with scribblin' on His Sabbath,' Mrs. Fisher whined, 'nor mendin' harness, either,' and she pointed at Levi.

'We'll have to let them observe Sabbath as they see fit,' Mercy said, but the women were not satisfied.

'You must order them to stop,' they insisted. 'They will bring God's wrath upon this venture.'

'Perhaps Mrs. Zendt is writing out her Sunday prayers,' Captain Mercy said, and this seemed to mollify the protestors.

Actually, Elly was writing the first of those many letters she would send back to her friend Laura Lou Booker. Often it had been Laura Lou's unquenchable optimism that had kept alive Elly's courage. Now Elly would repay that kindness by sending her an account of what she was doing and seeing on the Oregon Trail. Laura Lou preserved the letters, and many years later they were printed and widely read; into dry history they breathed the living reality of adventures as witnessed by a seventeen-year-old scrawny Pennsylvania Dutch girl who realized during every moment of that arduous trip that she was heading for a new life:

> May 26, Sunday . . . The funniest thing about our trip is Sergeant Lykes and his mules. He fancies himself a great expert in handling them, but I think they handle him. He has eight of them and says that each is ornerier than the other, which makes a circle. He makes them obey not by pleading, which they ignore, and not by hitting them, which merely makes them more stubborn, but by what he calls his mule persuader. This is a stout wooden pole with a heavy leather cord tied in a circle at one end. He slips the circle over the snout of the mule, then twists the pole ever tighter until you'd think the mule's nose would fall off, and then, as he says, the mule realizes a message is coming. With the mule's head twisted at an impossible angle, Sergeant Lykes gently pats him on the rump and says, 'Now we go this way,' and the mule obeys. Sergeant Lykes told me, 'There must be an easier way to handle mules, but I haven't found it.'

The following days were painful for Levi Zendt. Travelers with horses attached to their wagons moved ahead, throwing dust in his face and disappearing over rises in the road, while his plodding oxen lumbered on, swaying from side to side like ships at sea. Each time he looked at their ungraceful rumps he thought of his gray horses and groaned, but Sam Purchas fell back and reassured him: 'Sonny, come two weeks, we're gonna pass them horse-folks like they was hitched to the ground.'

Three days out from St. Joseph the emigrants arrived at the last organized community they would see before they reached Oregon—the Presbyterian mission to the Sac and Fox Indians—and it was here that Oliver Seccombe's frustration began. He had left England after graduating from Oxford with one determination: to see for himself the noble Indian as he lived in a state of nature before being defiled by the white man. He was assured, by his reading in Rousseau and the romantic philosophers, that this nobility did exist and he wanted to describe it for European readers before it vanished. He had begun his trip to Santa Fe with the most exalted expectations, but his experiences had proved confusing. The first untamed Indians he encountered were the Comanche, and as he rode forward to greet them they unleashed a parabola of arrows, one of which killed the horse of the man riding next to him and several of which came close to killing him. He explained away this unfortunate beginning as a result of regrettable behavior on the part of white Americans, who did not understand the Comanche, but when his party reached the Apache and found them even more murderous, he decided that the noble savage of his dreams lived not in the south but in the freer, colder north.

He was confirmed in this belief when he reached Santa Fe and made a side excursion to the pueblos, hoping that in these ingenious houses he would find his natural man. Instead, he found a miserable congregation of hovels, and upon his return to Santa Fe, discovered that he was infested with lice. He had to shave his head to get rid of the nits and smelled for some days of buffalo fat. His return trip through Apache and Comanche country, with running battles days on end, did little to restore his original enthusiasm, which was almost completely eradicated when the train ran into a war party of Kiowas, who killed two traders. The noble Indian of Rousseau, just and sagacious, must live in the northwestern territories, and now as he started on the Oregon Trail, he dismissed his previous encounters only as a preparation for the great adventure of seeing the unspoiled Indian.

On May 29 he met the Sac and Fox. They came down from the mission building in a party of eleven, well dressed, well fed, speaking English and offering the travelers a selection of blankets, tomahawks and deerskin moccasins decorated with beads. Each item was priced in bits—Spanish silver dollars sawed into eight parts so that twenty-five cents was equal to two bits—and they would not allow the travelers to chivvy them down.

'Those moccasin best quality . . . one dollar two bits,' the leader of the merchants said, and he would accept no less. But while the bargaining was under way, six other Indians arrived on the scene, begging for meat, and when they got none, they stole one of Sergeant Lykes' mules, and when he found out, there was a great to-do until Sam Purchas fired his Hawken in the air and warned the man with the moccasins, 'You get that mule back here or next shot is right through your head.' The Indian believed Purchas, as well he might, for Sam was well known along the trail as a ruthless man, and the mule was recovered.

As the party resumed its way west Seccombe explained that the Sac and Fox were prime examples of what he was talking about: 'They have been corrupted by the white man's religion. All their inherent nobility has been eroded away by Presbyterianism, for which they were not prepared.' In his opinion they would see no real Indians until they reached the Pawnee, of whom he had received good reports.

'Pawnee!' Purchas exploded. 'They would steal Monday in order to get a chance at Tuesday.'

For these emigrants the trail west contained an unfolding series of surprises—it almost seemed as if a superior dramatist had prepared the script best calculated to excite the imagination. Now the first hills appeared, and the travelers began to realize that the going would be difficult, yet the way was eased with excellent grass and good water, from which they could take consolation. Farmers from eastern areas saw the hickory, the oak, the plenitude of walnut and birch, and found themselves in reassuring surroundings, but suddenly at the crest of some hill they would catch a glimpse of landscape reaching to the horizon, infinitely far, with few trees and only scrub grass, and they would catch their breath at the strangeness of the land they were penetrating. The whole trip would be like this, one contrast after another.

At the end of the first week it began to rain, not the way it did back east, but in sullen sheets of water. The rain fell with such intensity that it bounced back up from the earth, and Elly Zendt wrote:

> June 2, Sunday . . . I am writing this at night huddled inside the Conestoga beside a flickering candle. It is raining, but not like any you have seen in Lancaster. It falls in great tubfuls, drowning everything. Sometimes the wagon shakes so that I cannot control my pen, and the wind whistles so piercingly that I cannot think. Levi has put an India-rubber sheet over our wagon, but still the rain drips through. I understand how Noah felt . . .

The rains continued until the emigrants reached the first great obstacle of their course, the Big Blue River coming south out of Nebraska to join the Kansas River. Sam Purchas had warned them in advance of this dangerous crossing: 'You can't get west till you cross it, and it's a killer. Ain't much in October, but in May and June, it sweeps you away.'

When they approached the steep banks through which it normally ran they could not see the sides, for the rains had thrown it into flood, and full-sized trees were roaring along the crest.

'What do we do?' the Fishers and the Fraziers wanted to know.

'We wait,' Purchas said.

'Can't we build a ferry?'

'You put a ferry in that, and before you reach the other shore you wind up back in Independence.'

So they waited. For sixteen interminable days, while late-starting parties from St. Joseph caught up with them, they waited. The only consolation Levi found was that all the horse-people, those who had passed him so blithely, were delayed and fretting the same as he. Each morning the men would go down to inspect the Big Blue, and each afternoon they would study the skies, hoping for some break in the weather. 'Hell,' Purchas told one contingent camped beside the river, 'I come acrost this stream last October and I didn't even dismount. I coulda jumped it.'

'When will it go down?' the leader asked.

'We been here fifteen days and it ain't made no signs yet.'

'Can we get to Oregon? With this late a crossing?'

'Enjoy the heat now,' Purchas said, 'because you'll get lots of snow later on.'

Then, on the evening of the June equinox the river began to recede dramatically, and by morning Purchas called out the good news: 'We cross!'

Captain Mercy and Sergeant Lykes were first over, swimming the mules. Then the Fisher and Frazier wagons were edged down to the water, where heavy logs were strapped to their sides so that they would float. The men dismounted and pushed from behind, but the women remained in the wagons, clinging atop their baggage so their feet would remain dry. Then the oxen were lured into the water, and slowly the wagons sank, sank, sank until it looked as if they must go under. But at the calculated depth they floated, with the bottom eight inches of baggage getting soaked.

Now the moment came when the oxen could no longer feel bottom, and they panicked, but the men swimming alongside comforted them, and soon they were swimming with confidence. To those watching, it was sickening to see the wagons almost submerged in the raging water, but after a tense moment Elly cried, 'They've reached shore!' With much scrambling and snorting the oxen refound their footing and clambered up the muddy slope, laboriously dragging the water-soaked wagons to safety. Seccombe cheered.

Reassured, Sam Purchas led his three horses across, and they took it easily, having often forded such streams; and then Oliver Seccombe and Levi Zendt edged the Conestoga down to the water, where they lashed extra logs to its sides. Levi entered the river, leading the oxen, which did not want to follow. For one dangerous moment they were fractious, but he quieted them, and the big beasts found their footing and proceeded to the spot at which they had to swim.

Something went wrong. Either the oxen grew afraid or Levi gave them bad guidance, but there was confusion and the Conestoga rocked and almost turned over, pitching Elly, in her long and encumbering skirts, into the crest of the flood. That night Elly wrote:

> June 22, Saturday . . . I would not have believed that two men of such exalted station as Captain Mercy and Oliver Seccombe would have leapt into a raging torrent to rescue a girl for whom they have no responsibility. When the wagon tipped and I fell into the river, I thought for sure that I was lost, because Levi was ahead and could not see me go. I was lashing my arms and screaming and swallowing muddy water and I was near dead when these two men disregarding their own safety leaped in to save me. I feel very important, as if God intended me for some significant duty and did not wish to see me lost so young for Him to have risked the lives of two such men on my behalf. The rains have stopped and the sky is clear and this may be the most beautiful night in my life.

If it was God who saved Elly Zendt, it was also God who was responsible for the tremendous falling-out that occurred the next morning. Despite the fact that it was Sunday, Captain Mercy and Sergeant Lykes believed that they should move west in an effort to make up some of the days lost at the Big Blue, but this ran counter to the contract which had been forced by the Fishers and the Fraziers to keep the Sabbath, and they did not intend to break that rule on this particular Sunday, especially since God had seen them safely across the swollen river.

'We have got to move west,' Mercy said firmly.

'We shall not profane this day,' Mrs. Fisher, an unusually acidulous woman, said.

They appealed to Sam Purchas, who listened for less than a minute, then handed down his decision: 'After our delay, anybody don't move west as fast as possible got his brains in his ass.'

Mrs. Fisher wanted her husband to horsewhip Purchas, who told her, 'You get your old man to make one move and he's gonna have more than brains in his ass. Now you get them wagons rollin'.'

The entourage started, with Purchas in the lead, followed by Lykes and the mules, then Captain Mercy on horseback, and the Conestoga, with Elly riding and Levi walking by the left front wheel. It was pretty clear that there was going to be no halting on this day of deliverance, and after a half-hour of wrangling in the wagons the men hitched up and fell tardily in line. They made fourteen miles that day, but the Fishers and the Fraziers spoke to no one.

Purchas now led his group westward a few miles till they encountered the Little Blue, up whose left bank they would travel in a northwesterly direction for nearly two weeks in a long reach for the Platte River, where the real trail west would begin. On July 2 they saw beaver for the first time, a fine small dam with young playing along the banks. On July 4, which they celebrated with much firing of guns and a fine sermon by Mr. Frazier on the grandeur of the American experiment, followed by the most gracious remarks of Oliver Seccombe, who pointed out that England, in losing a colony, had gained a friend. More shooting followed and Elly baked a pie made with dried apples. Sam Purchas got very drunk and kept firing his revolver until it jammed.

The days were pleasant for everyone except Levi, because once more the parties using horses sped forward, while the oxen slogged ahead so painfully slow. 'Let 'em go!' Purchas called reassuringly. 'Your turn will come.'

On July 5 the farmers saw their first buffalo grass, and the next day, their first grama. They studied each, pulling the short stems apart and judging that nothing much could come of such stuff.

On July 7, as they came over the crest of a small sand hill, they halted to look down upon the Platte, the strange and obstinate river they would follow for hundreds of miles. Each remarked upon its curiosities, but only Sam Purchas came close to comprehending it. Elly summarized their thinking:

> July 7, Sunday . . . Like Moses looking into the promised land, we stood on a small hill and looked down at the river which will be our companion for many weeks. How small it appeared! Back east we would

call it a creek, nothing more. The men all remarked how high it ran above the surrounding land. Really, it seems to be laid on top of the earth with practically no banks. And it has so many islands you would not believe it, all cluttered up. The Missouri women made some scornful remarks about it and Sam Purchas spit tobacco and said, 'Lady, you see that cliff way over there? You see that one way back there that we just come down? Well, when the Platte goes into flood, it reaches from cliff to cliff.' We were awed . . .

At last they were on the real road, that remarkable, flat, solid, unbroken highway along which the wagons could move with greater speed and security than along the streets of St. Louis or Philadelphia; some days the oxen made eighteen miles, plodding along a highway as smooth as the National Road. Levi said, 'This must be the best road in America,' and Sam Purchas said, 'Enjoy it while it lasts.'

Now Levi Zendt had his triumph, for with diminishing forage and hard-packed roadways, horses found the pace too much. They began to pull up lame and even to die, while parties who had relied on oxen overtook them and left them far behind. Levi found little to savor in his victory, for whenever he saw an injured horse he wanted to halt and try his hand at treating it, but Purchas was adamant: 'They guessed wrong and now they'll pay for it.'

'What will happen to them?'

'Their horses'll die, and then probably they'll die,' Purchas said, adding, 'And if you'd insisted on bringing your grays, they'd be dyin' now and two weeks from now you'd die.' When they came to a group of three wagons where horse deaths had forced a halt, Purchas would not permit his party to fraternize with them or give them help. 'They made their choice,' he said, but Elly ran to them with food. They were in pitiful shape, having crossed the Big Blue before there was adequate pasture for their animals.

'Their bad luck,' Purchas said. 'They shoulda asked the men who know,' and he forged ahead.

On July 9 they came upon meadows crowded with flowers, yellow and blue, as far as they could see, and Purchas told them, 'Last month this was a desert. Give 'em a little rain, they bloom overnight.' On July 10 there was enormous excitement, for they spotted buffalo tracks, a profusion of tracks which made the wagons bump as the wheels bounced from one depression into the next. And next day came the thing they awaited, real buffalo. Elly wrote:

July 11, Thursday . . . Mrs. Frazier saw them first. Their wagon was in the lead and we heard her screaming, 'They're here! They're here!' and we hurried up and saw below us on the other side of a small hill a herd of buffalo so immense that we could not see the other side. They should be counted not in hundreds but thousands, big and black and all with their heads down grazing. They were moving south, across our trail, and since they were making less than half a mile an hour, it was going to require many hours for them to pass, which meant that we would have to wait most of the day. This was settled by Sam Purchas and Captain Mercy, who got on their horses and rode down right to the edge of the herd and began shooting the younger cows, which are good to eat, the old bulls being not much, and after a while the buffalo turned away and we stopped to butcher the kill . . .

Wherever emigrants went they announced their presence by a constant fusillade, for they fired at anything that moved: antelope, deer, buffalo, prairie dogs, quail, eagles, hawks that watched from the roadside, beaver. Each group that moved west was a perambulating arsenal with guns bristling from every angle. Trains of a thousand wagons would pass without engaging in gunfire with a single Indian, but few made the journey without these doleful entries: 'This day we buried Jacob Dryer of Framingham. He pulled his gun out of the wagon unmindful that it was loaded, and it blew his chest open. He lived six minutes.' 'Baby Helen Dover is dead, to the great sorrow of her parents. A man in a neighboring wagon was riding with his rifle across his knees and it accidentally went off, blowing away the top of her head.' 'Bill Acroyd shot off his right foot and it gangrened and we had to bury him.' For every white man killed by an Indian, and there were almost none, fifty or sixty others killed themselves or their neighbors by accidental gunfire.

On July 12 the three wagons were heading westward in desultory fashion when two Pawnee braves rode up along the north bank of the Platte, and as soon as they came in range Sam Purchas grabbed his Hawken, took aim and put a bullet through the head of one of the young men. His horse reared, his hands fell limp, blood spurted from his forehead and he fell to the ground. Whereupon Purchas grabbed for a second gun and would have shot down the other brave except that Captain Mercy knocked the barrel away, allowing the Pawnee to gallop off.

'You let him get away!' Purchas bellowed.

'You son-of-a-bitch!' Mercy cried, wresting the gun from him.

'Don't nobody call me a son-of-a-bitch,' Purchas snarled, grabbing for one of his knives.

'I'm sorry,' Mercy said quickly. 'I apologize.'

'You better.' Then Purchas appealed to Levi. 'Indians ain't human. They ain't real people, like you and me.' He looked at Seccombe, whose English mannerisms seemed prissy, and added grudgingly, 'Or even him.'

'You killed a man who'd done you no harm,' Seccombe protested.

'He was an Indian,' Purchas said, and rolling back his left sleeve, he showed them the scars on his forearm. 'I been fightin' Indians all my life . . . and they're no damned good. That one the captain let get away will go back and make trouble for us.' He spat tobacco and stalked away, and as he disappeared, Captain Mercy said, 'I'm beginning to wonder if he ever was a mountain man. They have more sense.'

By some miracle the enraged Pawnee did not attack. But the next day they killed a defenseless husband and wife, traveling alone, some miles farther west, so that when the Purchas column reached that spot, they found a boy of six and a girl of four sitting dull-eyed by a burned-out wagon with their scalped parents bloating in the dust.

'We can't take no kids with us,' Purchas warned.

'What the hell do you think we'll do with them?' Sergeant Lykes stormed.

'Leave 'em here. Somebody else'll find 'em,' Purchas said.

'I'll take the children,' Elly said quietly, forcing her way between the two men.

'There will be no children picked up,' Purchas shouted. He took out his revolver and said, 'I am runnin' this wagon train, and we can't be held back by brats.'

Before he could speak further, a rough hand reached from behind, grabbed his revolver arm and threw him to the ground. As Purchas reached for his knife, Levi leaped upon him, tore it away and smashed him across the face with a heavy right fist. 'I'm takin' the kids,' he said. At this point Captain Mercy, who had been outriding, rode up and could only guess at what had happened.

'Mr. Purchas, what goes on here?'

'Them fools want to take aboard two kids.'

'What children?'

'The Pawnee, sir,' Lykes explained. 'They scalped the parents.'

Quietly Captain Mercy looked down, and quietly he said, 'Mr. Frazier and Mr. Zendt, will you please bury the bodies? Mr. Seccombe, will you find some stones for a marker?' When the graves were dug and the bodies placed within them, he directed the two children to stand beside him as he read the soldier's benediction from Romans:

> 'Who shall separate us from the love of Christ? shall tribulation, or distress, or persecution, or famine, or nakedness, or peril, or sword?

> 'As it is written, For thy sake we are killed all day long; we are accounted as sheep for the slaughter.

> 'Nay, in all these things we are more than conquerors through him that loved us.

> 'For I am persuaded, that neither death, nor life, nor angels, nor principalities, nor powers, nor things present, nor things to come,

> 'Nor height, nor depth, nor any other creature, shall be able to separate us from the love of God, which is in Christ Jesus our Lord.'

Closing the Bible, he took a shovel and handed it to the little boy, saying as he did, 'Son, bury your father, who fought the good fight and who died for the sins of others. Bury your mother, who loved you and who turned you over to us for protection. Remember this spot, these hills, for here your new life starts.' He helped the child to toss in the earth, then passed the shovel to the girl. Then he turned the job over to the other men and told the children, 'We are your parents now. God sent us to rescue you,' and he delivered them to Elly, who took them into the Conestoga so that they could not look back upon the graves. That night she wrote:

> July 13, Saturday . . . We have brought the children into our wagon, and they shall be our children from this time on. When they grow up in Oregon and become who knows what, perhaps a doctor and the wife of a minister, what a story they will be able to tell of how they got there, abandoned on the desert and near death only to be saved by God's infinite pity. This is no ordinary trip, for we move within a great dimension . . .

Each of the travelers west carried with him misconceptions of the gravest order, errors which would persist and do great damage. Captain Mercy shared Elly Zendt's impression that what they were traveling through was a desert; he could see no possible use for it in the years ahead and his reports to Washington would be widely circulated throughout the United States and Europe, giving credence to the term 'The Great American Desert':

> The land beyond the Missouri River is barren, windswept, without cover for man or animal and without any possible kind of future promise. Our government should maintain forts at scattered intervals throughout the area and subsequent reports of mine will recommend where and at what distances. But these are merely for the control of Indians and for the protection of emigrants on their way to greener fields in Oregon and perhaps California. No civilized man could live in either Nebraska or Kansas and as for the lands more westerly, perhaps a few Mexicans can survive in Santa Fe, but none other. This is desert, untillable, unprofitable, and unneeded.

Sam Purchas and Oliver Seccombe divided between them most of the existing theories about Indians, and very contradictory they were. Sam was sure the Indians had come originally from Egypt, where they had served the Pharaoh who had persecuted Moses. 'They was sent here as punishment,' he explained, 'and it's our duty to punish 'em . . . every chance we get. God intends it that way.' He proposed executing Indians as long as his rifle fired: 'This land won't be fit for white people till they're all dead.'

Seccombe, like many intellectuals of his day, believed that the Indians were really the cream of Welsh society which at an early period in history had emigrated to America in search of a more natural existence, and he was convinced that somewhere just beyond the visible horizon he would come upon the noble Welshman-Indian he sought. He had acquired this faith when a student at Oxford studying the poetry of John Dryden:

> I am as free as nature first made man,
> Ere the base laws of servitude began,
> When wild in woods the noble savage ran.

This noble savage had not resided among the Pawnee, for the ones he saw were beggars living in low, mean huts, but he felt that this was not their fault. They had been contaminated by French traders, but he felt sure that a little farther west, among the Cheyenne, he would find the type he was seeking. He had high hopes for the Cheyenne, having been told that they were tall and straight and possessed of a superior social organization.

Levi Zendt had begun to acquire his misconception, the strangest of all, that rainy afternoon in St. Louis when he first saw the monstrous elephant of the west; it had haunted him for several nights. Tonight, after he finished helping Elly put the two orphaned children to bed, he volunteered for the early watch, and as he studied the prairie he began to see in the heavens a vast form taking shape among the clouds, and the old sense of terror and mystery took possession of him.

'Sergeant Lykes!' he called. 'What's that?'

'Just the elephant . . . flicking its tail.'

And as soon as the words were spoken, Levi could see the gigantic animal consuming the heavens, and as from a distance he could hear the ghostly voice of Sergeant Lykes telling of the beast that stalked the prairie, striking terror in the hearts of emigrants: 'It's not like them elephants you see in the circus, no sir. It's immense. Taller'n most trees, with tusks that curve back like Turkish swords. It has a trunk that switches like a hurricane and a tail that can flick a wagon off'n the trail. Its disposition is mean—my, is it mean—and when he comes at you, you best run, because he has only one thing in mind, to crush you flat.'

Seccombe, hearing voices in the dark, came up to them, and when he heard what they were talking about, contributed his lore: 'There's about forty of the real big ones between here and the mountains. There was one hiding at the Big Blue, threatening us as we tried to cross. And there's a real monster hiding north of the Pawnee village. But it's farther west, beyond Fort John, where they congregate.' He allowed his voice to drop, conveying apprehension.

The digging up of mastodon bones, like the ones Dr. Koch had exhibited in St. Louis, had given rise to the mythology of an enormous elephant who roamed the plains, and scores of documents of that period testified to the existence of the beast:

> Last night, as we prepared to make camp after a long day, a storm came up worse than any we had seen before. Water so thick you couldn't look through it like to wash us away, and I heard Mr. Stephens say, 'Well, that time we caught a flick of the elephant's tail.' And two women told him they would be quite content to complete the journey without seeing any more elephants.

When Levi came back to the fire after his guard duty, Purchas sought him out to mend the rift that had come between them over the children. As he poured a cup of coffee for Levi, he said, 'You ever seen the elephant, Dutchman?'

'Yep.'

'Where?'

Levi hesitated, not wishing to share any confidences with Purchas, but in the end he said softly, 'I saw him.'

'Where? Come on, where?'

'You know . . .'

Purchas scratched his head, trying to decipher what Levi was saying, and something in the Dutchman's grave manner betrayed the fact that he was thinking of the Big Blue. 'Oh, you mean . . .' and by tipping his right hand toward the flame, Purchas indicated a wagon upsetting in the river. He said, 'Yes, by God, you really did see the elephant.'

And once again Levi felt the despair that had overtaken him at the Blue, when it looked as though Elly would be swept away, and he helpless with the oxen. At that moment he had cried, 'She's gone,' and he had known then how desperately he loved her. Other men, braver than he, had leaped into the flood to rescue her, and in the darkened sky he had seen the brooding elephant that sapped men's courage.

He went to the Conestoga and looked inside. There Elly slept with her arms about the orphaned children; she seemed the summation of all that men love on earth, and in the darkness he bent down to kiss her, but she was so exhausted from that day's decisions, she did not waken.

On July 14 the emigrants took upon themselves a new burden, for on this day they reached the point at which the South Platte flowed into the North. There was much argument as to where this happened, for the waterway was so studded with islands and sand bars that any clear definition of either river was impossible; all that could be said was that somewhere in the vicinity two considerable bodies of water joined.

The junction was like no other in North America; for nearly forty miles the two rivers ran side by side, with only a shallow peninsula separating them. After the travelers had marveled at the phenomenon they became aware that in following the South Platte, they were heading in a southwesterly direction, which took them well away from Oregon.

'We're off course,' Sergeant Lykes finally protested.

'It's the South Platte,' Purchas agreed. 'Heads south to the mountains.'

'We better cross over,' Lykes said. 'Follow the North Platte.'

'You pick the spot, sonny,' Purchas suggested, but wherever the emigrants looked for a possible spot to ford the South Platte, they found only steep banks and quicksand.

'What shall we do?' Captain Mercy asked.

'We'll wander off our course for some days,' Purchas said, 'and pray that we find a good place to ford.'

So now as they drove the oxen, the men kept one eye on the Platte. It was a mean, surly river, offering no invitation to cross, and it was luring them farther and farther from their destination.

On July 15 they met strangers who had seen the elephant. No Oregon for them. They were turnarounds, emigrants who had persevered as far west as their courage would allow, but the elephant had flicked its tail, and they were scurrying back to St. Joseph and civilization—six wagonloads, with only nine oxen surviving.

Levi, the member of Captain Mercy's group who could best appreciate their terror, took one look at the stricken women and said, 'I'll give you my two spare oxen.'

'You'll hell!' Purchas cried, and he enlisted Captain Mercy's support to forestall such stupidity. 'We'll need our oxen,' he warned. 'Mebbe for food.'

'They'll perish,' Levi argued, as the defeated ones listened to the debate which might mean their lives.

'Then they'll perish,' Purchas said coldly. 'They have no right to come onto this prairie unprovisioned.'

'I'm giving them two oxen,' Levi said, and there was such firmness in his voice that Purchas withdrew, but in a moment he was back with a sensible proposal: 'If they're headed back, let 'em take the two kids.'

Everyone but Elly agreed that this should be done, and preparations were made to transfer the children. But she began to cry and protest, and would not listen to their arguments.

In the end the decision was made by Captain Mercy. 'They should go back,' he said, trying to console Elly while Levi carried the two youngsters to the turnarounds.

He delivered them to the apparent leader, then dug into his pants and came up with fifty dollars. Thrusting the money into the hands of the gaunt and weary man, he said, 'This money is for the kids. When they get to St. Joe. And if you abuse them in any way, may God strike your pitiful soul.'

'It'll be for the children,' the man said, and they drove eastward without even thanking Levi for the oxen.

When he returned to the Conestoga, Purchas said, 'Did you give them thieves money, too?' Levi nodded, and Sam said, 'You know they'll kill the kids and make off with it.'

'Don't you trust anybody?' Levi asked.

'Nobody,' Purchas said, 'especially not no turnarounds. No character. The kids'll be dead by nightfall.' Elly heard these words and that night she wrote:

> July 15, Monday . . . I feel as if my own children had been stolen from me. For as long as my eyes could see I watched the sorrowful wagons plodding eastward, taking my son and daughter with them, and when they passed over the final hill and were gone forever I looked about me, and in each direction to the horizon miles away there was nothing, not even a tree or a tall rock, only the road winding to the west, and I felt as if God had deserted me and that I had no friends, no hope, and I think Levi suspected how I felt over the loss of the children, and he was ashamed that he had not sided with me in the argument, and he came to comfort me but I pushed him away, and when night came I felt ashamed, for I remembered how he had given the lost ones his oxen and his money and only because he is such an honorable man, and I went out in the night to find him, but he was wandering somewhere alone, so I came in to write these lines and the gray spots are my tears.

Early on the morning of July 16 Captain Mercy and Sam Purchas rode ahead, determined to locate a likely spot for crossing the South Platte. There was a sense of urgency about their mission, for already the party was much delayed in schedule. According to the wisdom of the prairie, by this date they should have been crossing the Continental Divide, and here they were plodding along, thirteen days short of Fort John, nineteen to reach the Divide. It was frightening, and Purchas, who had seen parties perish in snow, insisted that on this day they had to make their fording.

'How about here?' Mercy asked.

'Let's go in and test the bottom,' Purchas said.

They slipped off their shoes and stockings and waded gingerly into the river, but wherever they stepped the bottom gave way: water eddied under their toes and the gravel washed out. Within moments the water rose from their knees to their waist.

'Whole damned river's in motion,' Purchas said, and they tested two other spots, with equal results. 'Better drive one more day,' Mercy suggested, but Purchas would not hear. of it. 'Today we go. Time's wastin'.'

So they compromised on a spot which was not ideal; the crossing was much too wide, at least half a mile, but it did have a fairly solid bottom. 'The wagons'll sink in,' Purchas said, 'but if we keep them movin', we can make it.'

'You satisfied?' Mercy asked.

'Not exactly, but . . .'

This was not good enough for the captain and he abruptly left the guide and spurred his horse farther west along the riverbank. It was good that he did so, for at a ford which had been used before, he came upon seven wagons backed up, trying to muster courage to try the crossing. He fired his pistol and Purchas came galloping up.

'Good to see you!' the mountain man cried with unaccustomed warmth to the waiting emigrants. 'Trouble?'

When they explained that they had already tried to ford once, only to find the bottom giving out beneath them, he was surprisingly congenial. 'Wait here. We'll have our wagons with you before night, and we'll all get across real easy.'

Alone with Mercy, he explained, 'We need them a lot more than they need us,' and the two men galloped back to speed their wagons.

In organizing the crossing Purchas was invaluable, for only he was familiar with the one system that had any chance of working: 'You ten men, swim to the other bank with them ropes. Two of you stay in the water about twenty feet from shore, and when a wagon reaches you, lash the ropes to it, and you other eight pull like hell and get the wheels up the slope. You men, harness sixteen oxen to that first wagon. You two fellows, can you swim? Good. You swim with the heads of the lead oxen and keep them movin' forward. All the rest, back here with me. Now! Shove her into the water. No matter what happens, keep shovin'.'

With appalling suddenness, the wheels sank up to the hubs, but Sam was ready. Lashing the oxen and shouting to the two swimmers, 'Keep 'em movin',' he gathered a group of husky men to grab the spokes of the wheel. 'Keep 'em turnin',' he roared, and with a mighty effort the combined strength of ox and man broke the wagon free of the clutching gravel and got it started across the river.

Oxen bellowed; men cursed; a woman inside the wagon screamed as water rose about her feet; but Sam Purchas kept the wagon moving until the rope men on the other shore could pull it up the steep and muddy bank. The first emigrants were across.

Allowing no one a moment's rest, for the trick was to keep the oxen working as long as possible, he led the beasts and the men back across the river to the next wagon. Six more times he engineered the passage, until the backed-up wagons were safely across.

'Now ours,' he said. Marshaling all the men, he tried to harness the oxen to the Fisher wagon, but the big beasts had had enough. Without losing patience with them, he told a boy from one of the other wagons, 'Let them graze on this side and we'll save them for the Conestoga.' He summoned Sergeant Lykes and told him, 'We've got to use your mules.'

'That ain't easy,' Lykes said.

'Get a turn on the nose of that big black one,' Purchas suggested, and when Lykes had such a grip with his tourniquet as might have wrenched the mule's head off, he led him into the water and the others followed, dragging the Fisher wagon behind them.

'Can we work it again?' Purchas asked.

'Not with that mule,' Lykes said, 'but maybe that other big one.'

This mule proved a lot more difficult, and the men struggled with the Frazier wagon for more than an hour before they could get the mules hitched to it. The mule, which had had its upper lip practically twisted off, was especially mean, and at one point Purchas asked in desperation, 'Shall I shoot him!' but Lykes said, 'He's only bein' a mule.'

At last they got the wagon across, and then they came back bone-weary, both animals and men exhausted, to try the Conestoga. 'I think we can get one more trip out of the oxen,' Purchas said, and Captain Mercy, dripping and muddy, asked Elly, 'Would you prefer to cross with a horse?' and she said, 'Oh, no. This is my wagon,' and she sat inside, guarding the equipment lest it fall overboard.

The oxen, those great and patient animals, moved wearily into position for the last effort. Seccombe and a man from the strangers' wagons swam from the other shore with extra ropes, then swam back. They looked exhausted, but when they reached land they organized the teams for pulling and stayed in the forefront during the next difficult minutes.

Slowly the huge wagon was let down into the water, where its heavy wheels disappeared in gravel. 'Now!' Purchas bellowed, and every man exerted maximum strength while Levi urged the oxen forward. For a moment it looked as if the wagon might stick, irretrievably, but the combined force of the pullers and pushers got it moving, and just as the sun sank, the Conestoga was pulled onto the northern shore. Of this crossing Elly wrote:

> July 16, Tuesday . . . It was dusk when we finished, and the men, wet and muddy, went to their several wagons and collapsed. Some slept on the ground just as they fell, too exhausted to care for themselves. One of the strangers who swam the river so many times with the ropes vomited for the better part of half an hour with nothing coming up and then fainted. Levi, who swam the oxen across the river sixteen times and the mules four, had nothing to say nor could he eat, but about midnight he did a strange thing. He asked me to put on an old dress and take off my shoes and he led me down to the river and made me go in and duck my head under water and I could hear the river moving sand and gravel and even large rocks along the bottom, and Levi said, 'It's alive and it mighty near trapped us.'

There could be no prolonged rest for the travelers, because the next day they had to hurry across the peninsula between the two rivers and let their wagons down the steep slope at Ash Hollow. When they first saw the hill to be negotiated they felt they had not the strength to accomplish this, but in the end they did.

Once more they handled the strangers' wagons first, then used those men to help lower the Fisher and Frazier wagons. Finally they got to the Conestoga, but in easing it down, the ropes broke, the wagon rushed ahead and the left rear wheel collapsed. It was completely shattered, and the ten wagons had to lay over a day, with all the men trying to improvise a substitute. In the end the Conestoga was able to limp along.

It was now July 18, and although the Mercy party was two and a half weeks behind schedule, they did have before them a hundred and fifty miles of the finest part of the road. It was level, well packed, free of any obstacles or difficult crossings, and passed through some of the finest scenery in all of North America. To travel this section in midsummer, with the days hot and the nights bracingly cool, was a spiritual adventure; on some days the exhilarated travelers would do twenty miles, looking in amazement from side to side as new wonders unfolded. Now buffalo were plentiful and steaks chopped out of the hump were more tasty than beef, while a roasted tongue was a delicacy that the women travelers relished. Levi Zendt, thrifty butcher that he was, thought it shameful to kill a two-thousand-pound buffalo and then eat only six pounds of it, casting aside the rest of the carcass as useless, but as Sam Purchas pointed out, 'Hell, you could kill five thousand of them critters and not leave a dent. They ain't like cattle. They're more like ants, and who cares if he steps on a passel of ants?'

On July 23 the column came in sight of the first great monument of the trail, a pile of whitish rock, standing in such a way as to resemble some dignified building of antiquity. Court House Rock the formation was called, and from a distance it did resemble the massive courthouse of some important city, but each traveler saw in it such comparison as his education permitted. In later years, after the gold rush, it would be fashionable to depict all emigrants as defeated persons, or as people who could not get along back east, or as the scum of our industrial cities, cast out by a society they could not understand and with which they could not cooperate. It may be instructive, therefore, to lift from the diaries of those who passed Court House Rock in summer of 1844 brief passages to show what this particular group of emigrants thought when they saw the impressive monument:

VERMONT HOUSEWIFE. It looked to me like the Temple of Sargon, huge and heavy and close to the ground and very Persian except that it had no carved lions.

BOSTON PHYSICIAN. While others said that it did indeed resemble the courthouse of their home county, I could not drive from my mind the image of Karnak, for this was most Egyptian, save for the columns. I think no man could view these ruins without recalling the impressions of his early reading.

MRS. FISHER, OF MISSOURI. It reminded me of the picture in my Bible of the Tower of Babel. I am satisfied that the buildings of Babylon must have looked much like this.

MICHIGAN FARMER. The emperors of Rome had buildings like this. Looked exactly like the buildings in my schoolbook.

OLIVER SECCOMBE, OF OXFORD. Precisely like the sketches of Petra, but of a less reddish color. If these ruins were in Europe they would be world famous.

ELLY ZENDT, OF LANCASTER, PENNSYLVANIA . . . I was ashamed to tell the others what I thought for fear they would laugh at me, but do you remember, Laura Lou, that framed picture that hung in our schoolroom where Miss Histand taught? Of the Acropolis? And how we used to promise each other that when we grew up we would go see Athens and the first to get there would write and tell the other? Well, I have seen Athens, on the Platte. It is not white as we thought but grayish, and it is not surrounded by men in togas, but Indians on ponies. But the look is the same, and the buildings are even more beautiful than we imagined. I think it may be because the sky is so very blue and so unbroken, not even a cloud showing anywhere. For six hours as we traveled I watched the Acropolis, and from whatever position we were in, it was magnificent. I am sure that when you get to Greece and tell me of the real building it will be something to remember. But I shall not see it, for my Athens lies in the west.

Then came Chimney Rock, a needle pointing skyward; and Scott's Bluff, shame of the west, where early trappers had been accused of abandoning a sick partner named Scott, leaving him to die alone; and then the vast and open land where Indians were on the move.

At dusk one day Sam Purchas caught sight of a war party to the north and he signaled Captain Mercy to proceed with caution, but very soon the Indians disappeared from sight. Nevertheless, that night Purchas insisted that the wagons draw close together and he posted watches. Levi Zendt drew the hours from two till dawn, and as he sat in the total darkness, not even a star showing, he occupied himself with trying to identify the night sounds: far in the distance a coyote's two low notes and a high, over there an owl, to the north a night bird, the soft scuffling of some animal, then a spell of quietness so deep Levi could hear the sound of his own pulse.

Toward morning he heard three birds awaken, and as he listened more closely to their call, he suddenly discovered that they were moving closer to the wagons and on the spur of the moment decided that these were Indian calls. Discharging his rifle into the air, he bellowed, 'Indians coming,' and he was right. Sixteen or seventeen Oglala Sioux came thundering in, a white flag held aloft and barely visible in the pale light of dawn.

I wonder if they'd have showed that flag if I hadn't fired, Levi asked himself as they reined in, throwing dust over the wagons as sleepy men clambered down, each with a rifle at the ready.

'Hello!' the leader of the Indians cried. 'Bacon?'

'Christ!' Purchas whispered. 'That's Jake Pasquinel. Look at the scar down his right cheek.'

When Captain Mercy heard this name he caught his breath, then moved quickly to the fore, calling in a loud voice, 'Jake Pasquinel! Come in! We do have bacon.'

The Sioux were surprised that the white man should have known their leader, and they spoke among themselves in obvious agitation, but before they could react more positively, Mercy called, 'You too, Mike Pasquinel. Come on in.'

This further identification caused the Indians to laugh, and some pushed others forward and there was considerable horseplay before two men in their mid-thirties dismounted and came hesitantly toward the wagons. They were good-looking, tough men, dressed Indian style. They carried themselves with an air of confidence, their hands close to their knives in case of trouble.

Captain Mercy, ostentatiously handing his rifle to Oliver Seccombe, moved forward to greet the two men. They halted, looked uneasily at each other, then resumed walking until they stood facing the captain. Mercy extended his hand, saying, 'Jake Pasquinel, I've heard a lot about you.'

The Indian refused the hand, asking cautiously, 'How did you know my name?' Mercy grabbed suddenly for the man's right hand, bringing it to eye level. 'This finger,' he said, pointing to a missing joint. 'They told me I'd know you by this finger,' and now he ran his forefinger down the scar on the man's right cheek, 'and this scar.' He laughed easily and asked, 'How are you, Jake?'

'Who are you?'

'Captain Maxwell Mercy, United States Army.'

'You come to fight?'

'No, I've come to establish a fort. Permanent fort.'

'Where?' Jake asked suspiciously.

'Call your braves in. We'll smoke.'

So a council took place, there on the open prairie, with Captain Mercy, Oliver Seccombe and Sam Purchas sitting on one side of the ring and the Pasquinel brothers accompanied by two Oglala chiefs on the other. In a long and carefully phrased speech Captain Mercy outlined his mission, assuring the Indians that all the United States government wanted was guaranteed safe passage for emigrants to Oregon.

'You take our land?' Jake asked.

'Never!' Mercy assured him. 'This land is yours for as long as the grass grows and the eagle flies. All we want is one road west.'

Here one of the Oglala broke into wild speech, which everyone allowed to run its course. Then Jake Pasquinel interpreted: 'Wild Horse says that this one, Cut Nose,' and Jake pointed to Sam Purchas, 'cannot be trusted. Evil man. Kills Indians.'

Purchas listened impassively, and then the other Oglala continued the diatribe against him, and after this had been translated, Purchas said, 'You tell the chiefs you Pasquinels have killed a damn sight more white men than I ever killed Indians. You tell them that.' Now Jake remained silent, so Purchas broke into sign language and scattered Indian phrases; the chiefs understood.

The parley continued for several hours, during which pipes were smoked and flitches of bacon were given, and at the end Jake Pasquinel asked, 'So what land will you take for your fort?'

'That is not known,' Mercy explained. 'That's why I'm here.' There was a long silence, broken by Mercy when he said, 'And I was wondering, Jake, if you and Mike would act as my guides for the next three months?'

Mike Pasquinel interpreted this to the sitting chiefs and then to those standing, and the offer caused much consternation, during which Mercy handed the calumet to Jake, as a tender of his sincerity. Jake considered the offer for some minutes, then countered with an act of statesmanship: 'I'm a half-breed. If I serve you, the Indians will say, "Pasquinel, he's a traitor." I won't work for you. But Red Feather here,' and he took the hand of one of the standing braves, 'knows a little English. He will guide you.' Red Feather, a tall young man in his twenties, joined the circle.

Purchas did not like the offer. 'That leaves you free to continue your killin', eh, Pasquinel?'

'The day must come,' Jake said evenly, 'when the killing stops. If you stop, I stop.'

'I wouldn't trust you to stop killin' rabbits,' Purchas snarled.

Jake stared at the trapper, then drew his right thumb across his throat. 'We will kill you yet, Squaw-Killer,' he said.

The nickname Cut Nose had not disturbed Purchas, but when the Indian used this appellation, earned and hated, he leaped to his feet. Mercy pulled him back down. 'We'll take Red Feather,' he said, 'and when we decide on a location, we'll do nothing before meeting with you and Mike and the Oglala chiefs.' Jake nodded without committing himself, whereupon Mercy proposed, 'And at that time we will want you to bring in the Cheyenne and the Arapaho.' Jake said he couldn't speak for those tribes, and Mercy said, 'But you're an Arapaho.' Jake Pasquinel seemed embarrassed at this disclosure of information he supposed the white man did not have. 'How do you know I'm an Arapaho?' he asked.

Captain Mercy pointed to the missing finger, then at the scar. 'That finger you lost in a Kiowa fight. That scar you got at Fort Osage. Jake, in St. Louis everyone knows you. They think you will be the man to bring peace to the prairie.' He told Purchas to translate this, so that all the Oglala would know what he said, and once more Jake Pasquinel looked uncomfortable.

Then Captain Mercy asked, 'This morning, when you were creeping in? If our watchman here hadn't heard you? Would you have shot us all?'

Jake sat impassive, his broad face betraying no line of response. Then he looked up at Levi Zendt and said, 'You have good guards,' and Mercy said, 'We shall keep them posted.'

The Oglala Sioux mounted and drove off. Their backs were to the wagons when they heard a wild shout, 'No! No!' followed by the explosion of a gun. They turned in their saddles to see Captain Mercy knocking into the air the rifle with which Sam Purchas had intended to shoot Jake Pasquinel in the back. Only by a fraction of a second was this prevented, and now Mercy swung his right arm and knocked Purchas into the dust.

'You son-of-a-bitch,' the captain barked. 'We work so hard . . .'

He was interrupted by Jake Pasquinel, who rode back into the crowd of emigrants. Looking down from his horse, he spat at Purchas and said, 'Squaw-Killer, he didn't need to interfere. Shooting at a man, you'd have missed.'

'Nobody spits at me,' the fallen man said, reaching swiftly for one of his knives, but before he could grab it, Jake Pasquinel was well away, laughing at Purchas and deriding him again with the hated name: 'Squaw-Killer!'

On July 29 the column approached that quiet and restful spot where the Laramie joins the Platte, and there in the distance across the river they saw the fort, a major focus of white man's civilization between the Missouri and the Pacific, Fort John, a trading post with three towers, castellated ramparts and adobe walls. It contained a sutler's and a blacksmith shop inside, a score of Indian tipis outside, and everywhere a last reminder of home.

When those inside the fort detected the approach of the column, with Captain Mercy and his mules in the lead, they fired a salute from one of the cannon located in the towers, and Indians clustering below whispered, 'Big noise, he come awake!' They did not like the cannon, having seen at first hand the desolation it could wreak; they preferred that it stay asleep.

For the Zendts the arrival was timely. They required the services of a blacksmith, not only to repair the broken wheel but also to reset the three other iron tires lest they grow loose and rattle off. They also wanted to purchase what dried meat they could to supplement the bacon, and they needed flour badly. Therefore, after driving their Conestoga inside the palisades and delivering it to the blacksmith, they went to the general store, where they found a tall, thin man in his late sixties supervising sales, aided by an attractive Indian woman.

'Levi Zendt, from Lancaster. I'm gonna need a lot of your stuff.'

'Alexander McKeag, Scotland. It's waitin'.'

'This is my wife, Elly. Let her have whatever she needs.'

'This is my wife, Clay Basket. She'll get it.'

They conducted an interesting conversation, two men not given to useless chatter. Zendt spoke of the bad crossing at the South Platte, and McKeag said, 'It's always bad.' Zendt told of how Purchas had killed the Pawnee and how the Pawnee had slain the emigrant couple, leaving behind two children. 'Usually they take the young 'uns,' McKeag said.

Then for some reason he could not have explained, for he was not a curious man, Zendt asked a question that was not routine: 'How did you come to settle here?' and McKeag said, 'I wouldn't have if there was trading posts farther south,' and he told them of the good land he had known at the Buttes and the chalk cliff.

'You say you got a lot of beaver there?' Zendt asked.

'All gone now.'

'Then what's it good for?'

'Farming, I reckon. There's good water, there's good land.'

'Captain Mercy says it's desert.'

'Encourage him to go on sayin' it. That'll keep the bad ones out.'

'Why don't you have your post down there?'

'Nobody comes along down there, that's the beauty of it.'

When Elly had finished her purchases she was surprised to find at her elbow a young Negro boy who said, 'Master, he wants for you all to have dinner with him.' He led her and Levi to the headquarters building, where men were drinking whiskey, and as she entered they rose formally and bowed. A tall man with a heavy beard said, 'Madame Zendt, you do us great honor,' and after a long spell of storytelling, during which the man with the beard said, 'I'd never have that swine Sam Purchas in my compound, let alone at my table. He's a squaw-killer, by God, and that's all he is.'

'He served us well at the river crossing," Captain Mercy said. 'Knows his job.'

'I'm appalled that the army would hire him as a scout.'

'We didn't.' Mercy said. 'He's Seccombe's idea.'

Finally the food was served, and Elly said, 'I was surprised that you had so much good food for sale here,' and Levi said, 'I was surprised at the prices, too,' and Elly said, 'But Mr. McKeag was very helpful.'

'Who?' Mercy asked.

'Alexander McKeag,' Levi said.

At the mention of this name Mercy laid down his knife, looked down at the table for some moments, then rose and excused himself. He left the headquarters and asked the little black boy, 'Where's the store?'

'Yonder,' the boy said, pointing, and with slow, almost painful steps the captain headed in that direction. Stepping inside the store, he saw that the tall man and his Indian wife were preparing to close down for the day.

'Alexander McKeag?' he asked. The thin Scotsman nodded, and Mercy turned to his wife. 'Clay Basket?' She looked up at him, puzzled, and he took her hands and kissed them.

'Who are you?' she asked.

'Maxwell Mercy, of New Hampshire.'

'Why do you kiss my hands?' she asked gravely.

'I am married to Pasquinel's St. Louis daughter, Lisette Bockweiss.'

No one said anything. McKeag moved to the door and closed it, turning the key. He pulled down the window shade, then sat on a pile of beaver skins. 'How is Lise Bockweiss?' he asked.

'The grand woman of St. Louis,' Mercy said warmly, and with this opening he spoke of all that had happened in the city: Cyprian Pasquinel a state senator; old Hermann Bockweiss dead, with choice properties left behind; his daughter Grete and her husband, with many shops in New Orleans; Lise Bockweiss Pasquinel still giving parties in the big red-brick house on Fourth Street.

'Did Lisette grow into a pretty girl?' McKeag asked.

'Ravishing!' Captain Mercy took from his pocket a miniature of his wife, and she was wearing the same kind of French princesse gown as on the first night McKeag had seen her.

Clay Basket said, 'You met my sons on the prairie?'

'Yes,' Captain Mercy said quietly. 'Jacques and Marcel.'

'Are they in trouble again?'

'I think so.' As he said this she drew her hands down her face, and for the first time Mercy saw what a fine-looking woman she was, still slim in her mid-fifties, with streaks of gray in her hair and the handsome high cheekbones that had characterized her father, Lame Beaver. She was a woman of considerable dignity, as notable in her way as Lise Bockweiss Pasquinel was in hers. Captain Mercy took her by the hands and said, 'That Pasquinel, he married beautiful women.' Clay Basket did not smile, for she was thinking of her sons, but whatever thoughts she entertained were broken by a sharp knocking on the door and the petulant cry, 'Yoo, inside! Open the door!'

McKeag did so, and into the store came a seventeen-year-old girl in elk-skin dress and deerskin moccasins. She was tall, had very black hair and features which bespoke an Indian heritage, even though her skin was quite fair. She introduced herself as Lucinda McKeag and said that fiddlers were playing and a dance was in progress.

For the next few nights Captain Mercy gave farewell parties for the emigrants who would be continuing westward, and Oliver Seccombe danced so exclusively with Lucinda that on the last night Mrs. Fisher told Mrs. Frazier, 'I'm sure there's a romance under way,' but if so, it came to naught, for Captain Mercy warned McKeag, 'I don't think I'd want Oliver Seccombe courting my daughter.' When McKeag asked why, Mercy explained, 'He's not altogether reliable.' McKeag was about to ask why Mercy had been willing to travel with a man he did not trust,

but he was interrupted by Sergeant Lykes, who banged loudly for attention, then cried, 'Sam Purchas cannot leave this fort until he tells us how
he lost his nose.'

'One of them gougin' fights you read about in the papers.'

'You tried to tell us that in St. Joe,' Lykes protested.

'Fact is, I was sleepin' with the wife of a river captain and he come
home unexpected and found me where he ought to be, and without
wakin' me or in any way inconveniencin' me, he leaned down and bit off
my nose.'

'You're a horrible man,' Mrs. Fisher said, and Purchas nodded in her
direction, saying, 'Most people in Natchez-under-the-Hill are that way.
Know what happened to my river captain? He tried to bite off the nose
of a Creole gentleman from New Orleans and was shot through the
heart.'

In such reminiscences the night was spent, but early next morning
things grew more serious when word was shouted from the watchtower:
'Pasquinel brothers bringing an Indian war party. Arapaho and Cheyenne.'

Everyone scrambled to the towers to watch the Indians arrive. Out of
respect for a grave occasion, the older chiefs had donned ceremonial
headdress, and since they were coming from the east, the sun framed the
eagle feathers in silhouette. It was summer, and the younger braves wore
only loincloths, their faces hidden in shadow, their bodies glowing bronze
in the morning sunlight.

They sat astride their horses as if they had always lived thus, as if
the pintos were a part of them. Sometimes a horse would become skittish and move sideways for a distance, shifting its hoofs in the dust, and
then the rider would move easily with it, not endeavoring to check his
animal, for he could be confident that the horse would correct itself and
resume its place in line.

How handsome these Indians were that morning, how confident and
self-assured. It was the year in which the two races approached a state
of equilibrium: the Indians still owned the land and still controlled it, the
buffalo were plentiful, and white soldiers had not yet begun to shoot at
Indians they were fearful of, and peace was still possible.

Slowly the chiefs cantered up to the fortress gates, and Elly whispered
to Levi, 'They're so much taller than the Pawnee and the Sioux,' and
Levi replied, 'They sure look better than those Sac and Fox who tried
to sell us moccasins.'

Oliver Seccombe was delighted. 'These are the Indians I've been looking for,' he shouted, climbing down the ladder and running forward to
greet them. The first brave he encountered stared down from his horse
in amazement. What was the silly fellow trying to do? The Indian was
Lost Eagle, grandson of the warrior who had counted so many coups.
He was then thirty-four years old, with broad forehead, deep-set eyes

and very high cheekbones. His coloring was somewhat darker than that of the average Arapaho, so that he looked intensely Indian.

Now he edged his horse past Seccombe, noting with pleasure that his aunt, Clay Basket, was inside the fort. Dismounting, he moved like a stately automaton to where she stood, extending his hands in greeting and saying to her husband in Arapaho, 'McKeag, we come to talk peace, but we are confused about what the army wants.'

Mercy, indicating all the chiefs, said simply, 'I bring you many presents from our Great Father in Washington.'

'Why have we been summoned to a meeting?' Lost Eagle asked, and when Jake Pasquinel finished interpreting, Mercy said, 'The Great Father in Washington requires a fort, somewhere here in the west.'

'You have a fort,' Lost Eagle said, pointing to the adobe within which they had taken seats.

'But the Great Father does not own this fort. Mr. Bordeaux owns it, and the army must have one of its own.'

'Why the army?' Lost Eagle asked, and when Jake Pasquinel translated this, Captain Mercy said gravely, 'Not to shoot. Not to kill. Only to protect.'

'We, too, want to protect,' Lost Eagle said. 'We do not want our squaws killed. Nor our buffalo driven off the range.' He paused, then added significantly, 'Nor do we want our men, like Jake here, shot in the back.'

'I saved Jake's life,' Captain Mercy said solemnly.

'We know you did. Why?'

'Because he is my brother.'

The chiefs accepted this as a form of felicitous address and nodded approvingly. 'We are all your brothers,' Lost Eagle said.

Captain Mercy walked to where Jake Pasquinel stood and took him by the hand. 'But Pasquinel is my real brother. I am married to his sister.' This information caused a storm of discussion among the Indians, and among the whites, too, and in the end Jacques Pasquinel and his brother Marcel detached themselves from their companions and asked if what Mercy had just said was true, and he replied, 'Yes, my wife is Lisette Pasquinel,' and he produced the miniature, and it passed among all the chiefs, Arapaho and Cheyenne alike, and they marveled both at the girl's beauty and at the fact that she was half sister to their Pasquinels.

That evening the various Pasquinels convened: Jake and Mike and their sister Lucinda McKeag and Clay Basket, and Captain Mercy of the St. Louis branch. There was considerable laughter and Jake conceded that the chiefs ought to allocate some of the Arapaho land to Captain Mercy and the Great Father in Washington for a fort. Oliver Seccombe arrived to ask unsuccessfully if he could take Lucinda away for a dance, and there was much frivolity.

But when the time came actually to pin down the land that would be given, Captain Mercy and his aide Sergeant Lykes found themselves negotiating not with Lost Eagle, who had already agreed in principle, but with Broken Thumb, young chief of the Cheyenne, who proved himself to be a man filled with hate engendered by the thoughtless depredations of certain emigrants: 'They kill our buffalo and do not eat them. They cut our trees but bring no presents.' When he spoke, he spoke of war, and Mercy noted that when Jacques Pasquinel interpreted his speeches, an added fury was injected. In his report to Fort Leavenworth, Mercy wrote: 'One Cheyenne who will bear watching is Broken Thumb, his right hand deformed from having been run over years ago by a fur trapper's wagon.'

It was now time for the emigrants continuing to Oregon to move on, and with regret they bade goodbye to Captain Mercy and Sergeant Lykes. Of the departure Elly wrote:

> August 1, Thursday . . . At the fort we saw our first Cheyenne Indians and the first Arapaho. They were tall, handsome men, and Oliver Seccombe said, 'I told you that in his natural state the Indian was a noble figure,' but he changed his tune when he found that while he was dancing with Miss McKeag they had stolen most of his gear. He explained that it was contact with the white man and the influence of half-breeds like Jake and Mike that had corrupted them. With what sadness we bade farewell to Captain Mercy, Sergeant Lykes and their mules. I better than most realized what a fine man Mercy was, for at the flood he risked his life for me. He showed me a portrait of his wife in St. Louis and I was startled at how beautiful she was. I felt the same way about the half-Indian girl at the store. I sometimes think we plain women appreciate beauty even more than men do. I always considered you a real charmer, Laura Lou, and I suspect that you will grow prettier as you age, but as for me . . .

It was now that the elephant began to swish his tail and to threaten with his trunk. To the dismay of everyone, the mended rear wheel quickly showed signs of weakening and on the fourth day west of Fort John it collapsed completely. Sam Purchas and Mr. Frazier studied the wreck and told Levi, 'No hope. Only thing you can do is find a tree trunk and work it as a travois.'

But where to find a tree? They had now left the Platte and were lost in the middle of an endless plain, with never a tree in sight. So Levi and Elly, with two axes, started walking south to where the river ran, and they walked for eleven miles before they found a cottonwood. Levi chopped it down and rested while Elly hacked off the branches. Then they bound the heavy end with rope and proceeded to drag the tree back to the wagon. This expedition required two days, and as they labored their way back Elly asked, 'What if they have gone on without us?' and

Levi snapped, 'How can you think such a thing?' and Elly said, 'Sam Purchas would do anything.'

She had proof of this next night. Because there was no wood, the women of the caravan took it as their job to scour the plains for buffalo chips, those circular flat dried remnants of manure which burned so steadily and gave so good a fire for cooking. Wearing aprons, which they held gathered before them as they walked, they went ahead of the wagons, fanning far out and conducting friendly contests to see who could chuck into her apron the most chips, and sometimes they would run from opposite directions at the same chip, shouting, 'I saw it first!'

Tempers had not been good this day. The men had lashed the tree trunk in such a way that it took the place of the missing wheel, but progress was slowed, and the Fishers even suggested that they and the Fraziers go ahead at their own speed, but Purchas talked them out of this.

Elly Zendt, off by herself and behind a hill in her search for chips, became aware that someone had come up behind her. It was Sam Purchas, grabbing at her and pulling her down. She fought him and scratched at his slashed nose, but he whipped out a knife and grunted, 'You make a sound and I'll kill you.'

He tore at her clothes, and when she was nearly naked he held the knife against the skin below her chin, but when he was about to mount her she uttered a wild scream and tried to kick him away. A bruising fight ensued, with Purchas trying to knock her unconscious. But Levi heard the screaming, rushed over the hill and grabbed her assailant by the throat. If Elly had not interceded, Levi would have killed him.

Before the sun had set the Fishers and the Fraziers had insisted upon moving on. 'We wish to have no further part of this sorry outfit,' they said, and their wagons traveled all that night.

Only the lively spirits of Oliver Seccombe made it possible for the remaining four to operate. 'We must all forget that it happened,' he said airily. 'I assure you that it won't happen again, because if it does, I will personally shoot Mr. Purchas between the eyes. That understood, Sam?'

'Lots of young men have tried to do that, sonny,' Purchas replied.

An abiding tenseness now settled over the diminished camp, but next morning, when the right rear wheel collapsed, their energies had to be united on a common problem. Elly was convinced that Purchas had tampered with it, but she had no proof; besides, the trail had grown so rough that normal wear could have accounted for it.

What to do? After exhausting all reasonable alternatives, Seccombe pointed out that the only way to keep going would be to saw the Conestoga in half, throw away most of the baggage and forge ahead with a two-wheeled cart. Levi was so distraught at losing first his fine horses and now most of his wagon that he could not bear to do the sawing, so Seccombe and Purchas cut the rear half off the wagon.

Now came the difficult part. Elly and Levi had to decide what to throw away, what to keep. The extra barrel of bacon—out! The pans bought with her wedding gift at Cincinnati—out! The extra bolts of cloth —out! The guns and bullets—forward! The flour—forward! The tools and the spare rim—out! With what pain the Zendts watched their treasures discarded—how wretched it was to have dragged these goods two-thirds of the way across a continent and now to toss them aside. Of these decisions Elly wrote:

> August 6, Tuesday . . . When we had finished I was in tears but I did not want that animal Sam Purchas to see me crying, so I went to the great rock that rises up from the plains where names are written and sometimes carved, and I took a piece of stone and scratched on this desert newspaper this message: 'On this day Levi and Elly Zendt cut their Conestoga in half and threw away most of their goods. May the bacon be found by Indians or those in need.' And I signed my name.

The two-wheeled wagon enabled them to move faster, and on the next day they made twenty-two miles, but on August 8, as they were approaching the Continental Divide and the easier downhill portion of the trip, one of the oxen died. This patient animal had exhausted itself at the crossing of the Platte and had managed to survive only by the fierce courage that kept his breed alive. Elly Zendt wept as they lifted the harness from him. To her he was more than friend and loyal servant; he was the stubborn, solemn creature she had grown to love.

On the next day another died, and they felt the heavy burden of travel. 'Now, by God,' Purchas gloated, 'I'll bet you wish you had them two you gave away.'

'You bastard!' Levi yelled. Immediately he was ashamed of himself and walked away. His nerves were in sad shape and not even Elly's attempt at consolation quieted them, but that night Oliver Seccombe came to the half-wagon and said, 'Levi, that man is a bastard. Don't let him rile you.' And Zendt felt reassured to know that Seccombe agreed with him.

On the next day came a moment of triumph, for the small caravan passed over the Continental Divide, and Purchas shouted, 'From here on, downhill all the way!' Elly reflected the reaction of many emigrants when she wrote:

> August 9, Friday . . . I cannot believe it. All my senses rebel at the idea, but it seems true without challenge. From Pittsburgh, which cannot be much above sea level, we have never once climbed a mountain nor even a hill, so far as I remember. The path has been absolutely level, yet now we find ourselves across the Rockies and at the top of a rise more than eight thousand feet high. I wonder if life is not much like that. We go along unmindful and all the while we are climbing a very steep mountain

of insight and understanding. Remember how we used to guess about men and marriage. It was so much simpler than we thought . . .

And then, as if Elly Zendt had been guilty of the sin of hubris, on the night of August 10, when the road lay clear and easy to Oregon, her husband Levi went into the darkness to check his four remaining oxen, and out of the shadows rose the elephant. It was gigantic, thirty or forty feet tall, with wild, curving tusks and beady eyes that glowed. It seemed to Levi to represent all the terror they had experienced and all that might lie ahead on the way to Oregon. It was overwhelming—the menace of that towering creature, and Levi knew that he was destined to turn back.

He returned to the camp, wakened Elly and said, 'I saw the elephant.'
'Where?'
'Out there. We're turnin' back.'

She made no attempt to dissuade him, and before dawn he wakened the other two and told them, 'We're turnin' back.'
'Why?' Seccombe asked.

'I saw the elephant.' That was enough. On this trail, when a man saw the elephant, clear and overwhelming, rising out of the darkness with those beady, flaming eyes, he must heed its warning.

'So you're a turnaround?' Purchas asked contemptuously.

'I saw the elephant,' Levi said, 'and he showed me you with your head hangin' to one side, because in Oregon sure as hell they're gonna hang you.'

For some minutes he lost sight of Purchas, for he was saying farewell to Seccombe. Despite their partnership in a perilous venture, the Englishman showed no regret at their forced parting. 'We'll meet somewhere,' he said nonchalantly. And as if he had no care in the world, this young man started to whistle as he and Sam Purchas headed west for Oregon. Levi thought they were moving with unusual speed, but it was not till some hours later, when he and Elly were well started on their long retreat, that he discovered what Purchas had been up to and why he had left so swiftly.

'The bastard stole my rifle,' he said, and Elly searched the wagon and the beautiful curly-eyed-maple Melchior Fordney was gone. So was her knitted cash bag and her good scissors. They were about to rain curses on the old trapper, but the bitterness of this final indignity was so great that instead of reviling him, they burst into laughter at his pitiful bravado: his constant drawing of knives, his tobacco-stained beard, his bit-off nose, the futility of the man—and as they drove east they laughed, but that night Elly wrote the long letter which one scholar has called 'The Litany of the Loser':

August 11, Sunday . . . We have devised many names for what we are doing in turning back, but the real name is one we have not used. The word is *defeat*, the defeat of all we had hoped for. The horses we loved are lost. The wonderful oxen who were so good to us are dying, and those that live break my heart with their loyal plodding. They can't last long. We have thrown away most of the things we were going to use in Oregon for our new life and even our wagon is a poor thing, cut in half, with only two wheels that cannot continue turning much longer. We have nothing, and now we have lost hope . . .

On August 19 they arrived at Fort John again, this time from the west, and they were relieved to see it, for with only a half-wagon, they had begun to run short of supplies. They headed directly for the store, where McKeag said, 'I never figured you for a turnaround,' and Levi said, 'I saw the elephant.' They talked for a long time, and finally Levi asked, 'That place to the south. Rattlesnake Buttes you called it. You ever think of goin' back down there?'

'Every day of my life,' McKeag said without emotion. 'But I never found a partner.'

'Why don't we try it?'

'Why not, indeed?' McKeag said, and he called out to his wife. When Clay Basket appeared he said, 'This one wants to open a trading post for Indians down at Beaver Creek,' and she said, 'This fort is no place to keep our daughter.' They called Lucinda and the five of them spent no more than fifteen minutes discussing the dangers involved, and all agreed that they would head south as soon as McKeag could turn his accounts over to another.

They were three days out of Fort John when McKeag astounded the Zendts by announcing, 'At the bank in St. Louis, I've got twenty-three thousand dollars, so we'll have them send us up three wagonloads of stock.'

'Where'd you get twenty-three thousand dollars?'

'Saved it . . . when Pasquinel was wastin' his. When word gets out that we have trade goods, the Indians'll come flockin' in, and I can speak most of their languages.'

'I can put in two thousand dollars,' Levi said.

'Where'd you get two thousand dollars?'

'Sold my horses . . . in St. Joe.'

In this manner a solid partnership was formed, the second such in McKeag's life, and he would prove as faithful to the second as to the first. Of the relationship Elly wrote:

August 25, Sunday . . . On a day like this I often wonder if our misfortunes on this trip came to us because we traveled on the Sabbath. I think that perhaps the Fishers and the Fraziers were right and that we should have rested as God commands. And yet when I look at the three people who are traveling with us today I find that they are more Christian than

those we were with before. But Mr. McKeag has no relationship with
God, while Clay Basket and Lucinda do not even know the name, and
since none of the three can read, they cannot know the Bible. Yet God
seems to smile on them so that whatever they do prospers, while on Levi
and me he has frowned . . .

As she was finishing these lines, Lucinda came to the half-wagon and
asked, 'Is it hard . . . to learn writing?' and Elly told her, 'No, but I
think you must start young,' and Lucinda, who was the same age as Elly,
asked, 'Am I too old?' and Elly replied, 'No. I'm sure you could learn,'
and she promised to teach her.

Summer was nearly over, and McKeag explained that since it was too
late to get loaded wagons back from St. Louis this year, they would
occupy the time building a really substantial home at Beaver Creek, on
a rise he remembered where they would be safe from the Platte when it
flooded. From then on they spent each evening planning how the house
should be built and of what.

Clay Basket had noticed that a significant change was taking place in
Elly and suspected that she had not yet told Levi, and one night when
the men were discussing where they might find a supply of straight logs,
she took Elly aside and said, 'We must insist on another room, because
your child will need it as she grows up.'

'How did you know?'

'Indian women watch.'

'I think it will be born in winter. Will that be difficult?'

'If the house is warm . . .' She paused, then added, 'And McKeag
builds warm ones.'

I haven't told Levi yet . . . the disappointments he's had.'

'A child is no disappointment. Maybe that's what he needs most of
all.'

When Elly decided to tell her husband, she discovered that he had
known almost from the first. 'I kept watchin' you,' he said, 'and I noticed little things. But it came clear that day when you were swept away
at the Big Blue.'

'What could you have seen? You were looking ahead.'

'No, at the last moment I turned. And saw you protectin' your stomach
as you fell. That's why, when Purchas made for you that day . . .' His
voice trailed off. 'I would have killed him.'

'Why didn't you tell me?' she asked, as if disappointed that he had
ferreted out her secret.

'Because you're growin' so beautiful. Clay Basket didn't find out because you're fatter. She saw it in your face.' This was true. With her
growing pregnancy Elly had attained a serenity she had not known before, and her thin face was becoming actually beautiful. She would never
again be a scrawny, sixteen-year-old willow stem; she was now a mature

woman of seventeen with a burgeoning loveliness, as if the prairie had called forth a miracle.

'It wasn't really the elephant that made me turn back,' Levi confessed. 'It was wantin' to protect you and the baby.'

That evening while Levi wandered over the prairie, collecting buffalo chips so that Elly would not have to work, she stayed in the wagon, writing to Laura Lou. This letter stands as an epistle of hope and prescience, epitomizing the contributions made by the brave women who crossed the plains in pioneer days:

> August 27, Tuesday . . . To be pregnant takes away the sting of defeat, for just as we shall be starting a new community where the rivers meet, so Levi and I shall be starting a new family. Also, the land we are traveling through is the kind that makes you proud, for it is beautiful in a manner that those of us who lived always in Lancaster could never have dreamed or appreciated. This afternoon we came over a hill and saw before us the two red buttes which have been our target since we left Fort John. They stood like signal towers, or the ramparts of a castle, and they created such a strong sense of home that all of us halted on the hill to appreciate the noble place to which God had brought us. I think Clay Basket had tears in her eyes, for this was where she had lived as a girl, and her father, who must have been a pretty important man, liked to pitch his tent between the two buttes, and as she looked at them she thought of her family, for she told me, 'My mother was called Blue Leaf from the name of a very beautiful tree that grows in the mountains.' Mr. McKeag had often camped alone at the Buttes and told us of how, when the snows came, he might be alone underground for three or four months at a time. And Lucinda, who is trying to learn the alphabet, listened most carefully, for she had not heard these stories before. Levi and I spent only a little while looking at the buttes, because our attention was taken by the mountains to the west, and we both thought that if we were to live within the shadow of such majestic hills we would become like them. It was now growing dark, and the sun disappeared and over the prairie which we have come to love so well came a bluish haze and then a purple and finally the first dark shades of night itself and we were five travelers on the crest of a hill. I feel assured that any family which grows up in such novel surroundings will be strong and different and I thank God that I am pregnant so that I can watch the growing.

Next morning Elly was up early to prepare breakfast, and as she moved briskly toward the small pile of buffalo chips that Levi had gathered for her, she did not heed the warning sound, and as she stopped to lift a large chip, a giant rattlesnake, bigger around than her arm, struck with terrifying speed and sank its fangs deep into her throat. Within three minutes she was dead.

'It's God's mercy,' McKeag said as Levi Zendt came rushing up, too late for even one last kiss. 'It's God's mercy,' the red-bearded Scotsman repeated, as he gripped Zendt by the shoulders. 'I've seen 'em die slow, all swole up. Levi, it's better this way.'

The stocky Dutchman could not be consoled. He had grown to love Elly as few men love their wives, for she had been finer in every way than what he could have expected. Life with her had been a constant unfolding of promise that the better years lay ahead, and to lose her at the moment when a new life was beginning was intolerable.

All that morning he wandered about the buttes, coming back repeatedly to her limp body to touch it, to inspect the fatal dots on her neck, but in the afternoon McKeag said, 'Levi, we got to bury her.' Zendt refused to listen, until the Scotsman said, 'It ain't decent.' Then they took their shovels and dug a narrow grave in the lee of the western butte, and there she lay—Elly Zahm, patient, understanding, loving, the mother of lost children. She had come voluntarily on this great adventure and had won the love of all she met, and now she rested within the shadow of the butte. With her Levi buried her paper, proving that she had been married.

On their way to the river another ox died, and the next day the wagon itself collapsed, both wheels gone. Levi was too numb to do anything about it, but McKeag and Clay Basket lashed his gear onto the backs of the three surviving oxen and chopped the wagon up for wood.

So Levi Zendt reached the west bank of Beaver Creek, where the trading post was to be, bereft of all he had started out with. His sorrow was so heavy that for a long time he could not talk. But as the months passed, he did find some comfort in the task of helping McKeag build two sturdy houses and then a stockade enclosing the whole, with a battlement at the northwest corner, where attacks would come if they came at all. By November the place was secure, and on a cold, windy day McKeag went to the Platte and chopped himself a set of stakes. Taking Levi and the women with him, he paced off plots, each a mile square, three of them on the western bank of the creek, two on the eastern, and he staked out the corners and told his group, 'We're layin' claim to five sections. One for me, one for Levi, one for Clay Basket, one for Lucinda, and one for dead Elly, and we will defend them against trespass.'

But there was no consolation for Levi in the possession of land, and as the winter deepened he grew even more depressed. Clay Basket did what she could to comfort him, but when she heard him ask McKeag, 'Where's the Chalk Cliff you told me about,' she encouraged Levi to seek it out and stay alone for a while, hoping that solitude would enable him to master his grief.

So he loaded a fair amount of gear on his back and walked for two days in a northwesterly direction till he came in sight of the cliffs at whose feet McKeag had once built his refuge. Some of the logs were still there, others could be cut, and he built himself a log-and-sod hut on a spot that men had occupied for the past twelve thousand years.

He became a typical hermit, talking to ducks that settled on the little stream and watching antelope as if they were people. He castigated himself for having brought Elly to this desolate land, for having turned back when the elephant threatened. He convinced himself that if they had pursued their course to Oregon she would now be alive and her son would shortly be born, and he became half mad, with the risk that when the snows covered him, he might cower beneath them and perish.

The snows did come, much earlier than usual, and he spent most of December underground. February was a vicious month and he became a real animal, urinating in a corner of his hut and allowing his excrement to accumulate there—never venturing out, never ceasing to blame himself for Elly's death. If March were to bring blizzards, as it often did, he would soon be dead.

Clay Basket meanwhile was watching the weather, calculating the depth of snow at Chalk Cliff. She could imagine what the imprisoned Dutchman was doing, and when a thaw came in late February she told Lucinda, 'You must take two horses and go to Chalk Cliff.'

'Why should she be the one to go?' McKeag asked.

'He will be ready to come back,' Clay Basket said.

'Then I'll fetch him,' McKeag volunteered.

'He doesn't need you,' she said. 'Only Lucinda can save him.' Her words had the force of accumulated wisdom, for although Indian tradition required that a maiden remain a virgin till the day she took a husband, Clay Basket realized that a human life had to be rescued, and she was willing to send her daughter to a man who had seen no one for many months. Indeed, she suspected that two lives might be involved, for at Fort John she had watched with dismay as Lucinda shifted her attention from one useless trapper to the next. It had then seemed only a matter of time before the child must go off with some old lecher like Sam Purchas, and this she could not permit.

'Go to him,' she said, and Lucinda saddled up two pintos and rode westward.

When she came to the cliff, it took her some time to find where Zendt was holed up. Finally she discovered the hut at the north end of the cliff, and she stood at the entrance, calling, 'Zendt! Zendt!'

It was some time before she got a response, then a bearded, bleary-eyed man appeared, blinking at the sun. 'You are filthy,' she said, and although he tried weakly to stop her, she moved inside to witness the appalling conditions under which he lived.

'Zendt! How could you live like this!' She started to make the place habitable, and as she worked she saw that he was far too weak either to help or to mount a horse for the return trip. So she made him a new bed of clean branches cut from the little willows that the beaver no longer usurped for themselves. She built a fire and made some hot food, which he ate ravenously. Then she unloaded the pintos, and with two buffalo robes, fashioned herself a bed at his feet. He was asleep before she lay down.

In the morning he adjusted his weakened eyes and saw that she had stayed with him, and he asked in a faltering voice, 'Why are you doing this?' and she replied, 'My mother sent me. We love you, Zendt, and do not wish you to die.' And then the despair of recent months overwhelmed him and he hid his face and wept.

She nursed him back to strength, and one day in mid-March, forced him to ride for a short distance, and it was obvious that he was nearly ready for the trip back to the stockade. It was a beautiful day, and they rode some distance into the plains, where she showed him the little stone beaver climbing the mountain. That night when he went to bed, she lay down with him and for a moment he was confused and the memory of Elly Zahm came between them, but he was then only twenty-four and soon the passion of her body overcame him, and for one week, as spring came closer, he experienced untrammeled joy and found new strength.

But if Levi Zendt was a lusty twenty-four, he was also a strictly reared Mennonite—that a pagan Indian girl should share his bed confounded his moral sense. One morning before dawn, as he lay beside her pondering this problem, he chanced to recall the sermon about Ruth which the minister at the church in St. Louis had delivered:

And it shall be when he lieth down . . . thou shalt go in and uncover his feet . . .

and he judged that if it was permissible for Naomi to commit her daughter-in-law, the great-grandmother of King David, to such a mission, it was permissible for Clay Basket to do the same, and the first half of his dilemma was resolved. Gently passing his arm under her sleeping head, he kissed her, thus acknowledging that she had been sent, perhaps by God Himself, to save him.

The time had come when they must return, so they saddled the horses and loaded them with gear, and started the long journey home. Since there had been much snow this year, there was moisture in the ground, and from it sprang a million flowers, gold and blue and brown and red. The prairie was a carpet of buds, a more beautiful face of nature than Levi had ever seen before, more to be cherished than his groves of trees in Lancaster, for the trees endured whereas the flowers flourished for only a few days and would wither as soon as the hot sun struck them in June and July.

Occasionally Levi placed Lucinda on one of the horses and led her along the pathless route; at other times they set both horses free to wander as they wished and in time the animals smelled the Platte and headed south for water, and then the little caravan followed the river until it reached the stockade.

'You're back,' McKeag said, proceeding immediately to show Zendt the improvements he had made during the winter.

'You're thin,' Clay Basket said, and no further comments were made, but Levi Zendt, still wrestling with the second half of his dilemma, asked the McKeag family to sit with him in the sun outside the palisade, and when they were gathered he said, 'Alexander, I want to marry your daughter.'

'High time,' McKeag said.

'But I cannot do so unless she's a Christian.'

'All right, she's a Christian.'

'She must be confirmed . . . and able to read the Bible.'

'I can't teach her. Neither can Clay Basket. Looks like it's your job, Levi.'

'I am not a teacher, Alexander.' This led them to an impasse, which Zendt broke with a remarkable proposal: 'So I have been thinking that when you go to St. Louis to buy our goods, you ought to take her along and put her in school.'

As soon as this was said, everyone listening recognized its merit. Clay Basket wanted her daughter to learn to read. Lucinda had always wanted to see St. Louis. And Alexander McKeag knew that a life as valuable as his daughter's ought not be wasted. It was he who proposed an improvement on the plan. 'I have a room in St. Louis . . . with Pasquinel's St. Louis wife. Clay Basket will take the girl there, and they can live in my room until she learns to read the Bible.'

Within two days they were packed and ready for the long trip to the Missouri. McKeag viewed the trip with pleasure, for he wanted to show his daughter the city that had played such a prominent part in Pasquinel's life. 'And while I'm there, we'll file our claims to the land.'

'Where?' Levi asked.

'I don't know where. But believe me, it's important to have 'em on record . . . with stamps and seals on 'em.'

The idea appealed to Zendt, and he said, 'Before you go I want to stake out a claim at Chalk Cliff.'

'Why do you want that forsaken spot?'

'It was important to me.' So he and Lucinda saddled the best pintos and galloped west to the cliff, where they cut saplings and staked out a square facing the cliff, and when they reviewed their land a great passion overcame them and they made love as they had never done before, wildly, like the primitives who had once inhabited this spot, and without knowing it, they became one with the buffalo bones that lay buried here, and the campfires of ancient people who tipped their spears with Clovis points, and the bones-made-stone of diplodocus, dead more than a hundred and forty million years, and they were part of the flowers that grew during one wet year and lay hidden during ten arid ones, part of the unfathomable mystery of this land and these mountains and this turbulent river. It was love in its perpetual significance, something quite different from what he had known with Elly, and he whispered, 'Be sure to come back from St. Louis. I need you.'

'I need you,' she replied, and at that moment she loved more than he, because she knew by what a narrow margin she had escaped becoming the property of some tobacco-stained lout in search of beaver that no longer existed or gold that remained hidden.

The account of Clay Basket's leading her daughter Lucinda McKeag off the river boat became part of the chronicles of St. Louis. Following McKeag up the hill to Fourth Street, they presented themselves at seven in the morning at the brass-knobbed door of Lise Bockweiss Pasquinel's red-brick mansion. 'I've come for my room,' McKeag announced when Lise recovered from her surprise. 'Not for myself. For Clay Basket and my daughter Lucinda.'

There could have been few people in the world that morning less welcome at the mansion, for Lise Pasquinel was in the midst of the spring social season and was involved with numerous parties relating to her prominent son and daughter. This sudden arrival of people from a distant past could not have been pleasing to her, but when she saw how beautiful Lucinda was and how stately Clay Basket looked in morning sunlight, her heart went out to them and she cried, 'What a splendid family you have, McKeag,' and he, without embarrassment, replied, 'They're Pasquinel's, but I look after them.'

'The room is waiting,' she said with infectious enthusiasm, embracing Lucinda and telling her, 'You're a beautiful child. St. Louis will be kind to you.' She took the trio to a suite of four rooms, but McKeag said he'd lodge along the waterfront while he bought his trade goods. This Lise would not permit. 'You earned much of the money that went into this house,' she said half in jest, 'and you stay here.'

That afternoon she introduced the two women as 'Mrs. Alexander Mc-Keag, wife of my late husband's partner, and her lovely daughter Lucinda,' and she continued this procedure throughout the spring and summer, until St. Louis society had to accept the two Indian women.

She knew what gossips were saying: 'The older woman is really Pasquinel's left-hand wife, which makes Lucinda the half sister of Captain Mercy's wife! I wonder how he feels preparing for the war in Mexico and knowing that his sister-in-law is an Indian.' Lise Pasquinel spoke for her son-in-law when she said, 'It's an honor to have such a beautiful child living with us.

'I consider her my daughter,' she told everyone, 'and she's attending our convent to learn to read.' If eyebrows were raised over the fact that the girl was illiterate, Lise said with disarming frankness, 'She was raised a savage, you know.'

When she was alone with Clay Basket she spoke easily of her life with Pasquinel and relished hearing of how the little trapper had lived on the prairies. She said jokingly that she and Clay Basket were half wives just as Lucinda and Lisette were half sisters: 'There ought to be a name for our relationship.'

One day as they were talking she broke into laughter, crying impulsively, 'The little bastard was fun, though, wasn't he?'

'He was a good husband,' Clay Basket replied. 'My father told me he would be.'

'Your father must have been a wonderful man,' Lise said. 'Mine was, too, you know. It wasn't easy to leave Munich with two daughters . . . come to a place like St. Louis.' She reflected on this for a moment, then added, 'I loved him very much.'

'I loved Lame Beaver the same way,' Clay Basket said, and without voicing their conclusions, the two women reflected on the fact that loving one person completely makes it much easier to love others.

'I know that people here in St. Louis look at me with pity,' Lise confided. 'I can hear them whispering, "Poor Lise. She married a no-good French trapper who deserted her." But out of it I got two wonderful children. Cyprian's married to an excellent girl who helps him in politics, and you met Captain Mercy at the fort.'

'The Indians trust him,' Clay Basket said.

Now Lise frowned and spoke with hesitation. 'Your sons . . . we hear such bad reports of them.' Before Clay Basket could respond, she added, 'I'm sure they're going to bring our name into disgrace, and I'm sure there's nothing you and I can do about it.'

'It's not easy to be half-Indian, half-white,' Clay Basket said.

The conversation was interrupted by a black boy who ran in to report that Captain Mercy had returned on the steamer from Fort Leavenworth. When the child departed, Lise felt required to explain, 'We don't keep slaves, of course. My father wouldn't allow it. But we do hire the boy from next door. He's a slave, so we pay his owners.'

For Clay Basket such explanation was unnecessary. Indians had always kept slaves of one kind or another, most often braves captured from another tribe, but sometimes women, too. These days many tribes traded for black slaves, who worked out rather well.

Captain Mercy's arrival produced new problems. His wife Lisette was delighted to have her Indian cousins staying in the big house, for on his return from Fort John last year he had reported what fine women they were; the trouble arose with the captain. He was so eager that Lucinda have a good time that he kept introducing her to unmarried fellow officers, each of whom fell in love with her, for under Lise's care she grew doubly attractive. There were dances and trips over to Cahokia and picnics on the mysterious Indian mounds back of the city, and best of all, excursions on river steamers. She became familiar with stratagems intended to lure her into some corner for a spate of kissing, and there were at least three young officers who commanded her serious attention. It became popular for the young men to joke, 'When that girl learns to read, she's going to become my wife.'

The *St. Louis Republican* spurred the courtships by printing bits of gossip that made the Indian girl additionally desirable:

> Belle of our season is unquestionably Miss Lucinda McKeag, cousin of one of our leading families, the Lise Bockweiss Pasquinels. Miss Lucinda is not only unusually attractive, with her dark flashing eyes, but she is famed throughout the west as the granddaughter and only heir of Chief Lame Beaver, the Arapaho hero who discovered a gold mine in the Rockies. So as well as being a social delight, she is an heiress. Happy hunting, you young officers on whom the safety of this nation depends. See to it that this young lady remains in St. Louis and let others work her gold mine for her.

Lucinda was not bedazzled by such notices, nor was she swept off her feet by the young officers. She appreciated their attention and found that it was great fun to dance with them while the band played on the river boats, but she also remembered her weeks with that square-faced Dutchman at the foot of the chalk cliff and the more intense kind of love-making that he represented. But then Lieutenant John McIntosh of New Hampshire reported to army headquarters on his way to Mexico, and her attitudes changed.

In the meantime, Levi was having his problems. Left alone at the trading post when the McKeags departed for St. Louis, he occupied himself by building a corral so that when Indians did come to trade they could leave their horses, and one day as he worked he was pleased to see approaching from the east his first visitors. There were about ten in the group, riding carelessly along the Platte and obviously not a war party.

Dismounting casually and leaving their horses to roam, they surprised Levi by speaking English. 'We Pawnee,' they told him, and he was reassured, for by this time the Pawnee were the plains Indians most trusted by the white man; during the remaining years of this century they would serve as scouts for the army and as the agency by which other tribes like the Cheyenne, Arapaho and Sioux would be brought under control.

'McKeag, our old friend, send us here to help guard the place,' they explained. 'He come back summer.' They pitched their tipis along the Platte, and after begging tobacco, settled in easily and shared with Levi such antelope as they shot.

On a July morning as Levi worked in one of the towers, he saw to the north a cloud of dust that came rapidly toward the protective stockade, and within minutes he knew that it was a large war party galloping their ponies. The Pawnee, seeing them approach, grew apprehensive, but the war party came so fast that escape was impossible.

It was Jake and Mike Pasquinel, leading a band of Cheyenne, and without dismounting, the two brothers began shouting in English, 'You Pawnee! Get the hell off this land. It's ours.'

The intruders then dismounted and for a moment it looked as if there might be a battle, but Zendt stepped between the two factions, explaining that the Pawnee were friends of McKeag and Clay Basket. This did not satisfy Jake Pasquinel, who stormed among the Pawnee, yelling at them in Arapaho, which they did not comprehend. He returned to a broken English and commanded them to get out.

Since the Cheyenne outnumbered the Pawnee, the latter had no recourse but to depart, so they gathered their belongings, rolled up their tipis and attached them as travois to their ponies. At a signal from their leader they retreated eastward, to the gibes of the Cheyenne, who counted this a victory over their immemorial foe, and all would have passed easily except that one Pawnee lagged, his pinto proving fractious, and the farther behind he fell, the more abuse he took, until he turned on his horse and shouted something at the Cheyenne, whereupon Jake Pasquinel and two Cheyenne braves spurred their horses, overtook the laggard Pawnee and killed him. One of the Cheyenne leaped to the ground, knelt beside the corpse and scalped it, waving the bloody trophy in the air as he galloped back to the stockade.

'Don't you let Pawnee invade our land,' Jake warned Levi.

'This land is McKeag's,' Levi replied.

'Clay Basket's!' Jake shouted, as Mike stood beside him nodding. 'And when she dies, it's ours. His and mine.' Again Mike nodded.

'And part of it's mine,' Levi said stubbornly.

With snakelike speed Jake Pasquinel caught Levi by the Lancaster shirt he was wearing and jerked him close. Jake was eleven years older than Levi but much quicker. 'This land is ours,' he snarled, 'and on the day we tell you to get off, you get off. Like the Pawnee. You saw what happened when they didn't move.' He released Levi and with his right forefinger tapped the scalp.

The feel of the scalp seemed to infuriate him, and to Zendt's dismay he jerked out a knife and began leaping about the stockade, stabbing at the wooden objects as if he desired to kill them, shouting as he did so, 'It will all go!' He then stood flame-eyed in the middle of the open area, grasping his knife in his right hand, and addressed the Cheyenne warriors, assuring them that this was their land, theirs and the Arapaho's, and that it would remain so forever.

By this time he had worked himself into a frenzy. He leaped at Levi, pressing the point of his knife against the skin at the neck and shouted in English, 'We'll kill you all.' But almost as soon as he had said this, the wild passion departed, and he sheathed his knife and told Zendt reassuringly, 'You can keep the trading post . . . no harm . . . till my mother gets back.'

And with these words he leaped on his horse and led his warriors back to the north. But Mike Pasquinel, hoping to see his mother, stayed behind and helped Levi with the building, and taught him sign language and fragments of the various Indian tongues.

Mike stayed at the store till August, when McKeag returned with three wagonloads of trading goods, and when Levi explained what Mike had done to help, McKeag wanted to thank him. But Mike, disappointed that Clay Basket had not returned, wished no conversation with his stepfather. He rode off to the north without even saying goodbye to Levi.

'The boys have always hated me,' McKeag said sadly.

'Why?'

'Stepsons often behave like that.'

'Lucinda doesn't. To her, you're her father.'

'For boys it's harder. They see another man taking their father's place.'

'Did Jake and Mike love their father so much?'

'They've never loved anyone.'

The trading post prospered, and for a curious reason. Throughout the region it came to be known as Zendt's Farm. During the first summer, when buffalo were plentiful and work scarce, Levi returned to his old habits, and with McKeag's help, started making large links of pemmican, which he considered as nothing but buffalo sausage. McKeag would kill a cow. Using ponies to pull the hide loose, they would tan it and bring back as much meat as they could handle, plus all the intestines. These Levi would clean and knot at one end. Then into the casing he would stuff chopped buffalo meat mixed with salt, pepper, chokecherries, sage, berries and an herb that tasted something like onion. To give the pemmican lightness, he liked to mix in deer meat, if available, and the result was so tasty that word passed among trappers and guides: 'Stop at Zendt's Farm and pick up some of that good pemmican.'

At the farm they kept an increasingly varied supply of goods, thousands of dollars' worth, which they traded with various tribes for buffalo robes, now fashionable throughout the States and England. Instead of the compact bales of beaver which McKeag used to assemble on this spot, large, loose stacks of robes now went to St. Louis, and often in return came letters and newspapers from that capital. On the prairies men invariably referred to land east of the Missouri as 'back in the United States' and to the act of crossing that river as 'leaving the States.' What did they call the prairies? It was an alien land with no name, a place of exile where men worked for a while before 'returning to the States.' That it might one day become part of the United States was beyond their comprehension.

During the winter of 1846 two messages from the States reached Zendt's Farm, creating much confusion. First came a letter from Lucinda, a devotee of phonetic spelling:

Dier Levi,

This is first lettir I rite. I no who God is and Virgin Marie. I luv you.

Lusinda

The temporary exhilaration caused by this epistle was destroyed by a clipping from the *St. Louis Republican* which some well-meaning clerk had included in a package for McKeag. Since the Scotsman could not read, he passed it along to his partner, who read the words with deepening dismay:

> Talk along the river is that our fair city may not be losing the lovely heiress Miss Lucinda McKeag, after all. It appears that a dashing lieutenant who boasts of New Hampshire as his home has been spending a good deal of time away from headquarters while his troop prepares for a punitive excursion into Old Mexico, and we are told on good authority that an announcement of more than passing interest to our community may be forthcoming at any moment. Viva, New Hampshire!

This news distressed Levi, but it did not surprise him. It was what had to be expected when a beautiful girl like Lucinda burst fresh upon a city which always contained more men than women. He was deeply pained but he could not blame Lucinda, for he remembered Captain Mercy and knew how attractive young officers could be.

'What will I do if she doesn't come back?' he asked McKeag.

'Marry someone else.'

These days were not easy for Lucinda. There was much excitement in St. Louis as army detachments went downriver to embark for the war in Mexico, and several of the leave-takings were painful; the young officers had been kind to Lucinda and three had proposed to her, willing to incur the wrath of their relatives back east to whom an Indian was a savage, and she wept to think that they might be killed at war or depart never to be seen again.

But the real problem involved Lieutenant John McIntosh, a delightful young man from Yale University with a dry sense of humor, an intuitive distrust of Indians and a great love for this one. He was twenty-two and she was nineteen, and they made a handsome couple when they danced at the army base or dined together at Lise Pasquinel's. They conducted a stately courtship and each grew more fond of the other, more respectful of personal preferences. Young McIntosh was a man to take seriously, and Lucinda knew that she could be happy with him, but there remained the memory of Levi Zendt and the prairies and prancing pintos, and rides through flowers, and she grew more and more perplexed.

As the time came for Lieutenant McIntosh's departure, he became increasingly eager to formalize their engagement and pressed for a definite answer. It was at this time that she sought counsel with her father's two wives, Lise Pasquinel and Clay Basket, and one day the older women sat with her in a bay window overlooking the Mississippi, discussing her problem.

Lise Pasquinel said, 'Young McIntosh reminds me of Maxwell Mercy when he first came into this room. I was delighted to see him . . . knew at once that he was intended to make Lisette a good husband.'

Clay Basket said, 'It's strange that a half-Indian girl should have so many chances. Three of your men I have liked—Levi Zendt, McIntosh and the young man from Illinois.'

Lucinda said, 'You mentioned Levi first,' and her mother said, 'I met him first.'

Lise Pasquinel said, 'You must weigh one thing carefully. Sooner or later, I am convinced, our army will have to go to war against the Indians. Yes, it's coming. And if at that time Lieutenant McIntosh has a chance to command, it might be taken from him if he has an Indian wife.'

Lucinda considered this for a moment, then pointed out, 'But it's the same thing with your son. His half brothers are Indian,' and Lise said, 'I think of that all the time.'

Clay Basket said, 'St. Louis is nice, but the prairies are free,' and her daughter replied, 'I think of that all the time.'

Lise Pasquinel said, 'There are no goods or bads. There are only choices which lead to satisfaction and those which don't. I know all my friends feel sorry for me, and in a way they're entitled to—deserted as a young wife . . . never remarried. And do you know why? I never remarried because I loved Pasquinel. He was an untidy, untrustworthy man, but love is something, and he gave me many hours of real joy . . . two fine children. And I look at the wives who feel sorry for me, and they never had either.'

'I was lucky,' Clay Basket said. 'I knew two good men and I loved them both.'

In July, when a caravan from St. Louis approached Zendt's Farm, a slow, snakelike procession meandering along the Platte, its wagons raising signals of dust, Levi felt a gripping fear about his heart. 'Can you tell who they are?' he called to McKeag in the tower where the older man watched. Finally he could wait no longer. Jumping on a horse, he spurred it eastward, and when he saw the lead wagon with only two trappers visible, he grew sick with apprehension, but as he dashed on to the second, he saw Lucinda McKeag standing and waving and shouting, 'Levi! I'm home!' And he reined in his horse and sat staring at her, unable to believe that so beautiful a woman could have come back to him.

There was then the problem of how to conduct a marriage with no minister closer than Fort Leavenworth, and neither McKeag nor Clay

Basket had suggestions. 'You're married,' the Scotsman said, and Lucinda didn't care much what happened. But Levi wanted things legal and he recalled that early morning scene at the Columbia ferry and he said, 'If we announce that we're going to be man and wife and two people witness, it's the same as if a minister did it. And,' he added, 'then Lucinda would have a paper.'

So he wrote out a marriage contract which reflected the Mennonite vision of God, and when it was finished Clay Basket said, 'I'd like Jacques and Marcel to witness,' so McKeag saddled up and rode to Fort John, where the brothers were reported to be living with the Arapaho, and after a week he returned with them plus six Arapaho braves.

Jacques, now thirty-seven and as lean as a bush snake, was proud to see his sister looking so beautiful, and there was a tender moment when he greeted her, bringing her hands to his lips. In Arapaho he whispered, 'The man you choose is brave. We tested him.'

Marcel Pasquinel was thirty-five that summer, a pudgy man gifted in languages and gratified to see his sister marrying a real man instead of some Fort John voyageur. Presenting her with an oversized robe made of beaver skins, he said, 'Big enough for both of you to sleep under.'

'Are you married?' she asked her brothers, and they replied evasively. She was delighted that they had come. They seemed as hard and daring as the young officers she had met in St. Louis, and she hoped that perhaps Indians like them and white men like Mercy and McIntosh would be able to find a durable peace on the prairies, for they were equals. But when the time came for her brothers to sign as witnesses she felt deep regret that neither could write. Each signed his name with an X, and she could see that each felt resentment at being cut off from men with education.

Zendt surprised the group by appearing not in his Lancaster clothes but in prairie dress which Clay Basket had sewed for him; henceforth he would wear no other. But what delighted the women, causing them to squeal in unchurchlike merriment, was the fact that he appeared for the first time clean-shaven. He looked quite different, younger and more determined, and his brothers-in-law congratulated him, telling their sister, 'Now he's a true Indian.' And they gave him the name Clear Face, signifying 'One-Without-Guile.'

CAUTION TO *US* EDITORS. Two spellings give difficulty. Where the Oregon Trail comes up from Kansas to hit the Platte River, Fort Kearny was located, but the town that grew up at that site is Kearney, Nebraska, pronounced *Karny*. In northern Wyoming Fort Phil Kearny is located near the town of Kearny. The Oglala Sioux headquartered in western Nebraska near the site of Ogallala, the rip-roaring cattle depot of the late nineteenth century. The beautiful mountain in Colorado, 13,147 feet high, named after these Indians, is spelled Ogalalla, but the small town in Kansas is Ogallah. Don't ask me why.

Politics. You may want to introduce into your text, with a panel of good portraits, facts about the debate which started at approximately this time in Congress. It dealt with the future of lands west of the Missouri. I am impressed by the fact that most congressmen were strongly opposed to our exploring, settling or incorporating the arid regions of the west into the Union. The record is filled with their doleful predictions regarding the west and their refusal to accept responsibility for it. I can dig out the quotes for you, if you should want any.

More instructive, I think, is the fact that only a handful of stubborn men, those who had a vision of the west, kept hope alive for the Trans-Missouri region. Chief of these was Senator Thomas Hart Benton, of Missouri, in my judgment one of the greatest Americans. He would be worth a take-out by himself, as a glowing example of those sturdy Americans who see something their neighbors cannot understand and cling to it with devotion and intelligence. He was a man of staunch character, and the west owes him much.

Here is where the portraits come in. Among the few congressmen who shared Benton's vision, and who were willing to stick their necks out by defending the unpopular view, were these four: Senator John Tyler of Virginia; Senator Franklin Pierce of New Hampshire; Representative James K. Polk of Tennessee; and Representative James Buchanan of Pennsylvania. Each became President, and each, when he assumed office, took steps to incorporate the west. Apparently the way to preferment in those days was to express faith in the Manifest Destiny of the young nation.

Chronology. When you submit your article to researchers, they will probably claim that Fort John ought to be called Fort Laramie, but as you will find in my next report, this change did not occur till 1849. They may also point out that it was traditional for emigrant parties to reach Fort John at least one month earlier than the Zendts got there, and they will be right. If emigrants did not leave Fort John for Oregon or California by early July, they ran the risk of being trapped in mountain blizzards, like the tragic Donner Party of 1846–47. However, the year 1844 was exceptional. One of the first things Harry Truman did when he became President was to ask the Army Engineers to research the principal floods of the Missouri-Mississippi, and their report, which I have seen, assured him that 1844 had the worst flood in recorded history. James Clyman, who left a diary of the Oregon trip he led in 1844, trailed the Zendts by about a week, and after his safe arrival in Willamet Falls (his spelling) he wrote a letter stating that other parties were trailing his by two weeks! That was a bad year.

Inflammatory error. When my secretary, a young woman of unusual intelligence who had been educated in Wyoming, handed me her completed typescript of this chapter, she wore a look of disappointment. 'I keep hoping that you'll correct that bad error you made in your preliminary notes,' she said, 'and here would have been a neat place to do it.' In frank astonishment I asked what my error had been, and she explained, 'Everyone knows that the famous description "A mile wide and an inch deep" applies not to the Platte River, which stole it late, but to the Powder River, which owned it early.' This claim, which I had never heard before, startled me, for in a score of historic documents I had seen this phrase used only with the Platte, but when I told my secretary so, she bristled, and next morning she brought me a book published in 1938 by the Philadelphia novelist Struthers Burt, who loved Wyoming. *Powder River: Let 'Er Buck* told of the heroic exploits of the Wyoming volunteers in France in World War I. They cavorted across the bocage as if it were the plains of Wyoming, and their famous battle cry was adopted by other American units and even by Australians and New Zealanders. The full challenge was, 'Powder River, let 'er buck. A mile wide and an inch deep. Too thin to plow, too thick to drink. Runs uphill all the way from Texas.' Today, wherever rodeos are held, the cowboy who draws the toughest bronco shouts as he leaves the chute, 'Powder River! Let 'er buck!' So do drunks entering strange bars. Intensive questioning in libraries has satisfied me that Wyoming is divided across the middle on this one. Those in the north are sure that the phrase belongs to the Powder; those in the south claim it for their Platte, and each side is ready to fight. My own guess is that the words go far back in history and were probably applied to the Platte years before the Powder was discovered. But I am not brave enough to say so in print.

7

THE
MASSACRE

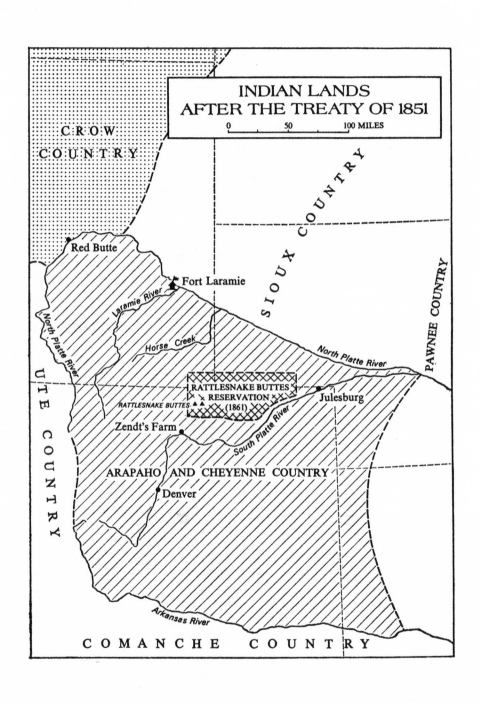

INDIAN LANDS
AFTER THE TREATY OF 1851

0   50   100 MILES

CROW
COUNTRY

SIOUX COUNTRY

PAWNEE COUNTRY

Red Butte

Fort Laramie

Laramie River

North Platte River

Horse Creek

North Platte River

UTE
COUNTRY

RATTLESNAKE BUTTES
RESERVATION
(1861)

RATTLESNAKE BUTTES

South Platte River

Julesburg

Zendt's Farm

ARAPAHO AND CHEYENNE COUNTRY

Denver

Arkansas River

COMANCHE   COUNTRY

IN SPRING OF THE YEAR 1851 AN EXCITING rumor spread across the western plains. Comparing partial information, men convinced themselves that portentous things were afoot.

The rumor started in Washington and moved swiftly out to St. Louis, where it was further augmented. By the time it reached St. Joseph it was raging like a prairie fire, and the father westward it went, the more alluring it became.

'Yessir,' a mountain man affirmed at the Pawnee village, 'the U.S. gov'mint is finally gonna grasp the bull by the horns.'

'And do what?' a suspicious trapper from Minnesota asked.

'We're gonna have a great meeting . . . all the tribes on the plains . . . and we're gonna settle once and for all who owns what.'

A chief of the Pawnee, hearing this heady talk, asked, 'Great White Father, he come? Make peace?'

'He wouldn't come hisself,' the mountain man explained, 'but he would sure send his commissioners and Indian agents. It's gonna be peace.'

The news sped along the Platte as fast as men could ride, and nowhere did it create more commotion than at Fort Laramie, where a small detachment of one hundred and sixty soldiers under tall, prim Captain William Ketchum, accepted responsibility for the safety of an empire. A trader bringing in six wagons of goods for Mr. Tutt, who ran the sutler's store, reported, 'I heard for sure it's gonna happen. Mebbe two hundred, three hundred Indians brought to this fort—right here—for one great powwow.'

'We couldn't handle three hundred Indians,' Ketchum protested. 'Look at us!' He pointed to one of America's most curious military establishments: within a curving sweep made by the Laramie River stood an old adobe fort long used by fur traders and emigrants. Since it was obviously inadequate and probably indefensible, new buildings were being erected along the sides of an impressive parade ground, but at this moment only two were in operation—the sutler's store at the far end and the residential building, a two-storied plantation affair that looked as though it belonged in Virginia. Ultimately, plans called for a palisade to enclose the area, with two tall towers at the diagonal, but it certainly did not exist now, a fact of which Captain Ketchum was painfully aware. Pointing once more to the empty, unprotected space, he complained, 'We could not defend ourselves. It would be a massacre.'

'Well,' the trader said enthusiastically, 'here's where they meet. Three hundred of 'em. Gonna settle all territorial claims. Peace for all time is what Washington wants.' And with this he led his wagons to the sutler's, where the long-needed goods were unloaded.

Captain Ketchum was worried. Sending his orderly to fetch Joe Strunk, long-time mountain man serving as guide and interpreter, the captain said with some bitterness, 'Word from St. Louis is that three hundred Indians will be convening here . . . peace treaty of some kind.' Obviously he did not relish the idea.

'They'd overrun us,' Strunk protested. When he had first heard that the United States was building a fort at Laramie he was pleased. It would help police the various trails that were beginning to crisscross the west. But if the government wanted a real fort in this territory, with no support for six hundred miles, it ought to be a protected fort, not a large open space.

'If the redskins got started, it could be a massacre,' he said dolefully.

'My very words!' Ketchum said.

'They been talkin' peace for the last ten years,' Strunk observed, 'and we got more war across the prairies now than ever before.'

This was not correct. In the middle years of the nineteenth century more than 350,000 emigrants moved along the Platte River from the Missouri to the Pacific, and the bulk passed through Indian lands without encountering difficulty. Something less than one-tenth of one percent of the travelers were slain by Indians—fewer than three hundred—whereas many times that number were killed by their own rifles, or the rifles of friends fired accidentally, or the gunplay of criminals who had joined the procession.

There have been few mass migrations in history so peaceful, and no previous instance in which people of one race passed through lands held by another with such trivial inconvenience. For this good record the Indian was mostly responsible, for it was his willingness to abide the white man that allowed the two groups to coexist in such harmony.

'What we got,' Strunk explained, 'is petty warfare. Crow against Sioux. Shoshone against Cheyenne.'

'And we also have Broken Thumb,' Ketchum said with some distaste as he pointed to a tall, rangy Cheyenne in his mid-thirties who lounged insolently outside the gates of the old fort. 'Broken Thumb!' he called. 'Come over here.'

Slowly the chief detached himself from the Indians with whom he had been talking and very slowly walked the considerable distance from the adobe fort to the new white building. He moved as if he were coming to a fight, a scowl marking his broad, dark face, a gun cradled in his arms. Among the tribes he was a disrupting influence, for he was burdened with a bitter knowledge: he understood what was happening to his people in an age of change.

When he had approached near enough for Ketchum and Strunk to see the contorted right hand from which he took his name, he uttered one word in Cheyenne, 'What?'

'Great White Father says he wants peace,' Strunk said in the same language. 'You want peace?'

Broken Thumb stared at the mountain man, then at the captain, and waved his right hand. It had been crushed when he fell under the wheels of an emigrant wagon while stealing food. 'What is it you call peace?' he asked. 'You give us firewater to drink, and we become a nation of foolish men.' Here he danced a few steps, imitating a drunken Indian. 'And while we are drunk you take our women and drive away our buffalo. Once they were more plentiful than our ponies . . . here where the two rivers meet . . . now where have they gone?'

'Two years ago you brought in thirteen thousand robes,' Strunk reminded him. 'Mr. Tutt gave you many goods—scarlet cloth, beads, looking glasses, that gun you have.' He snatched it to point out the mark on the stock.

Broken Thumb grabbed the gun back and said harshly, 'And this year, what robes? Where have the buffalo hidden? Like us, they cannot stand the white man's ways and have left their old grounds.'

When this was translated, Ketchum assured him, 'They'll come back. I've seen a hundred thousand buffalo along this river, and we'll see them again.'

'If we could have peace,' Strunk asked, 'would you want it?'

For a moment the Cheyenne's broad face relaxed, and he looked at his two interrogators with the eyes of a man willing to negotiate difficult matters. 'We can have peace,' he said quietly, 'if the commissioners come here like men and settle the four big problems . . .' The amiability vanished and he growled, 'But the commissioners never come. Only soldiers. Only fighting.'

'Ask him . . . suppose the commissioners really did come? What four problems?'

Broken Thumb considered for a moment and concluded that he was being subjected to a trick. For years the Indians had sought a meeting with the Great White Father, one where they could smoke the calumet and talk about the prairies and the buffalo and the roads that crossed their lands. They no longer had hope that such a meeting could be arranged. And now Broken Thumb turned abruptly away. 'No more talk,' he said in English. With that he strode from the fort, mounted his pony and splashed his way across the Laramie River toward the area where his tribe was encamped.

Then, in early summer, real news reverberated from the Missouri to the Rockies: 'Yessir, a huge assembly of chiefs at Fort Laramie. End of August. All questions to be settled.'

Trappers employed by Pierre Chouteau and Company in St. Louis, lean hard-bitten men who dressed like Indians and fought them when necessary, penetrated to the Pawnee, the Cheyenne, the Arapaho, the Comanche and the Kiowa with the reassuring news: 'Great White Father sends greetings. You come to powwow, he bring many presents.'

To the northern tribes that clustered along the Missouri—the Mandan, the Hidatsa, the Arikara—went a remarkable emissary, one of the bravest men to operate throughout the region, Pierre Jean De Smet, a Jesuit priest from Belgium, whose word was accepted by all the tribes. 'It will be a famous gathering,' he told them in the many languages he knew. 'The Great Father is sending rich presents, and if you come to Fort Laramie, all things that worry you will be settled.' It was largely due to his persuasiveness that the northern tribes began to weigh the unlikely possibility that real peace might be at hand.

To the fort at Laramie came the most reassuring messenger of all, a major in the United States Army serving as Indian agent with specific powers to set the vast operation in motion. He arrived one July morning, accompanied by seven cavalrymen and a charming woman in her thirties, all of whom had ridden hard from St. Joseph.

'Great news!' the major called before dismounting at the entrance to the fort. 'A treaty to be signed!' When he got off his horse the soldiers at the fort saw that he limped noticeably in his left leg and they judged that this was not the result of some temporary soreness but a permanent thing.

Captain Ketchum came out to greet the arrivals, but before amenities could be concluded, the major cried, 'It's done, Captain! The treaty's to be signed here.'

'What's this about a treaty?' Ketchum asked.

'Supreme Court says the Indian tribes are nations. With nations you have treaties.'

Ketchum frowned and asked, 'How many extra soldiers will they send me?'

'Cheer up! There's talk of a thousand new men. Twenty-seven wagons of gifts for the tribes. Two commissioners and God knows how many interpreters.'

'How many Indians are we to expect?'

'Depends on what luck Father De Smet has. Could go as high as six hundred.'

'We'll need more than a thousand extra soldiers,' Ketchum began.

Then, realizing how rude he was being, he said, 'I haven't welcomed this charming lady to our fort.'

'My wife, Lisette Mercy.'

Before the captain could reply, Lisette had dismounted and grasped him by the hand. 'Think nothing of ignoring me.' She laughed. 'Maxwell's always that way.' And she moved graciously onto the porch of the new building. 'Shall we be staying here?' she asked.

'Yes,' the captain stammered. 'We'll . . .'

'Good!' And with that she returned to her horse and started unpacking her gear.

'Give the lady a hand,' Ketchum called, but before any of his men could reach her, she had her small bags unfastened and on the ground.

'I shall love it here,' she said enthusiastically. 'I can see the Indians, now, hundreds of them . . . on all those hills.'

This was a most unfortunate image, and Captain Ketchum winced. He did not relish the touchy prospect of having six hundred Indian braves on those hills when he might have only two companies of dragoons and one of infantry to defend the place, protect the incoming caravans and serve the commissioners. As soon as he and Mercy sat in his quarters he said, 'I need assurances, Mercy. Will there be at least a thousand new men?'

'Unquestionably!' Mercy replied.

'And there will be twenty-seven wagonloads of gifts? We have practically none left, and Indians will not accept any agreement unless it's solemnized with gifts.'

'I saw the wagons at Kansas City. Knives, guns, food, everything.' He broke into laughter. 'And an amazing special gift for the chiefs. Every time I think Washington is filled with imbeciles, someone there comes up with an idea that dazzles me.'

'What is it?' Ketchum asked suspiciously.

'You'll be astounded,' Mercy said. He then turned to more serious matters. 'We've sent word to all the tribes. Canada to Texas. We want to build one treaty that will encompass everything.'

'Will they all send representatives?' Ketchum asked.

'That's what I'm to find out. Where are the Arapaho and Cheyenne camping?'

Captain Ketchum sent for Strunk and asked, 'Where are the tribes right now?'

'Last we heard, Oglala Sioux west of the fork. Shoshone far to the west of Laramie Peak. Cheyenne down at Horse Creek, the Arapaho at Scott's Bluffs . . .' He was prepared to list six or seven more locations, but Mercy had heard enough.

'Could Strunk and I ride down to the Cheyenne . . . right now?'

'Of course,' Ketchum agreed, and a party of nine was organized.

'You can show Lisette where to put our things,' Mercy said as he transferred his saddle to a fresh horse.

'Where'd you get the limp?' Ketchum asked professionally.

'Chapultepec,' Mercy said without emotion. 'With General Scott.'

'Was it bad . . . down there?'

'Oh, you'd go for days with no action—never see a Mexican—then they'd dig in at some spot of their own choosing, and it would be lively hell.'

'They fight well?'

'Everyone seems to fight well on his own terrain.'

'Doctors can't do anything for the leg?'

'The hip. No, I'll be a major the rest of my life. Crippled . . . and damned fortunate to be alive.' With this he leaped into his saddle as easily as if his hip were sound, and set out for Horse Creek.

The party rode east along the Platte for thirty miles to where Horse Creek began to join the larger stream, and some miles to the south they found the tall, neat tipis of the Cheyenne, arranged, as always, in circles. It was a beautiful, orderly community, with the side flaps of the tipis raised to facilitate the circulation of summer air, and it bespoke the solidity of this tribe.

'Where's Broken Thumb?' Strunk asked in Cheyenne.

'That tipi,' a boy replied, and the men rode there.

Only Strunk and Mercy dismounted; the seven soldiers remained on guard, their rifles at the ready across their saddles.

When Major Mercy stooped to enter the tipi he could not immediately adjust his eyes to the darkness, but after a few moments he saw confronting him five Indians informally dressed, and out of the shadows loomed the faces of the men who would determine Indian activity in this region for the next fourteen years.

In the middle sat a man Mercy already knew—a man with a dark scar down his right cheek and the tip of his left little finger missing. It was his own brother-in-law, Jake Pasquinel, now forty-two years old and tense with the disappointment which comes at that age when a man realizes he has made too many wrong choices. Instead of staying with the Arapaho, among whom he might have achieved real leadership, he had drifted from tribe to tribe, learning many languages badly, fit only to serve as interpreter to men who were far less capable than he. Like all half-breeds he stood with one foot in the Indian world, one in the white man's, and at ease in neither. He was trusted by no one, and suspicion was so constant that he had grown to doubt himself.

To his left, and in the seat of prominence, sat Chief Broken Thumb, twisting the ends of his braids with thumb and finger as if preparing to confront the white man with his string of grievances. Even sitting, he was a tall, impressive man, thirty-five years old and a proved warrior of many coups. Mercy, seeing him for the first time, said to himself, He's like one of those volcanoes in Mexico. You see the ice in the eyes and can be sure the fire smolders below.

The man on Pasquinel's right looked quite different—shorter, much less aggressive and apparently more introspective. He had a most handsome face, lean and hawklike, with prominent nose, exaggerated cheekbones and deep lines cutting vertically down both cheeks. His eyes were deeply recessed and very dark, and his whole appearance was given a somewhat grotesque touch by the fact that he wore a white man's type of hat with moderate brim and very tall crown. It made him look unbalanced, as if both it and the head that wore it were too large for the body that supported them. He did not wear his hair in braids, like the others, but cut straggling-short about his shoulders. The conversation would be far advanced before this reticent chief, then in his forties, would speak, and when he did, it would not be in Cheyenne.

Now Broken Thumb prepared a calumet, keeping it on his knees while he mixed tobacco and kinnikinnick in prescribed amounts. When the pipe was filled and lit, he held it extended at arm's length to the four compass points, then placed his right hand, palm up, at the extreme end of the bowl, drawing his fingers slowly back along the three feet of stem till they reached his throat. There, with a motion parallel to the earth, he brought his hand across his throat, signifying that what he was about to say was sacred and true. This was the oath of the Indian, the solemn promise of the pipe.

As the calumet passed to the other chiefs, Broken Thumb indicated that Mercy was free to speak, and the captain asked, 'Have the messengers come from the Great White Father?'

'They came,' Broken Thumb replied cautiously, pinching his braids.

'And they told you that we can now have peace . . . forever?'

'They told us.'

'And will you send chiefs to our meeting?'

This was the difficult question, the one on which so much depended, and the three other chiefs sat silent, waiting for Broken Thumb to voice their thinking. Reaching for the calumet, he puffed slowly, then held it in his lap, cradled in both hands. Slowly, but with increasing fervor, he gave the Indian's answer to the white man's overture. It was a long speech and was interpreted by Strunk into English, and then by Pasquinel into an Indian language for the benefit of the silent chief to his right.

The White Father wants peace, so that he can send his traders safely through our lands. Of course he wants peace, so that thousands of wagons can cut trails. He wants peace so that his people can kill the buffalo and trap the beaver. But does he want peace strongly enough to deal with us honestly on the matters that divide us?

Here Major Mercy interrupted, intending to ask what the complaints were, but Broken Thumb silenced him imperiously, and spoke with heightened intensity, outlining their grievances. 'Long time ago the white men who came across our land were good people. They wanted to build homes. They had their children with them. There was some fighting, but never much, and there was respect. But in the last two years, a different kind of men. Ketchum says ninety thousand came, and all they wanted was gold. Mean, hungry men with no women, no children. They shoot our people for no reason, the way they shoot antelope. They burn our villages for no reason, the way you burn the nests of hornets. They are ugly men, who have only war in their hearts, and we shall give them war.'

He referred this matter to the other chiefs and two of them supported him enthusiastically, with cries of 'War! War!' Mercy noticed that the chief in the hat remained quietly brooding in the shadows.

'When the Great White Father determined on war with Mexico,' Broken Thumb continued, 'he sent his soldiers across our land, and when they found no Mexicans along the southern river, they wanted to fight us and they killed many of our people. It was not we who started war, Mercy, it was you. We know that you were with the soldiers, because our braves saw you, and now you come here to talk with us of peace. We talk of war!'

Again the two Cheyenne chiefs echoed the defiance, and Mercy sat silent, staring at the floor in humbleness of spirit, because what Broken Thumb said was true. He had marched with his men from Independence along the Arkansas River and down into Texas and Mexico, and in their boredom the men had started shooting down Indians as if they had been turkeys, and villages were burned and squaws violated, and only the iron resistance of men like Mercy had prevented the affair from becoming a total massacre. He suspected that if the Indians knew he had been along, they also knew that it was he who was primarily responsible for halting the disgrace.

'And you must stop selling whiskey to our people,' Broken Thumb continued. 'Mercy, what you are doing is contemptible.' In this sentence Broken Thumb used an Indian word Strunk did not know, and there was much discussion as to its translation. It was Mercy who suggested *contemptible* and when this was translated as *without honor*, the chiefs agreed. 'Because at Fort Laramie the other day I stole a bottle of the real whiskey you drink among yourselves, and it was good to taste. These chiefs have tasted it,' and to Mercy's astonishment he produced a half-filled bottle of whiskey imported from Scotland, which he asked Mercy and Strunk to taste, and it was the best. 'But for us you sell this!' And he produced another bottle, filled with Taos Lightning, and he asked the white men to taste it, and when they refused, well aware of what it was, he thundered in English, 'You drink! Goddamn, you drink!' Mercy took a small taste, and it would have been revolting even had he not known its components.

'Contemptible,' Broken Thumb said with deep bitterness. 'For a small drink of this,' he said with scorn, 'you charge two buffalo robes. With this you take away our squaws and make our children poor. Mercy, are you proud that when your soldiers with their rifles cannot defeat us in battle, you bring this among us to destroy us?'

He put away the bottles, being careful to cork the Scotch, and came to his final point. 'Mercy, you must do something about the sickness, the one you call cholera. It has been so terrible among us. At the Mandan villages they were twelve hundred last year, and this year they are less than forty. White Antelope here has lost six members of his family. Tall Mountain has lost four. My wife and two children are dead. You have brought a terrible illness among us, Mercy, and we must have help.'

'It has killed us too,' Mercy said quietly, and he asked Strunk to inform the chiefs of the tragedies of recent years, of whole families of emigrants wiped out in an afternoon—a man would be driving his oxen, would feel nausea and would cry, 'The fever!' and even his wife would shun him, and within four hours he would die, with the knowledge that four hours later his wife and children would be dead too. When Strunk finished his narration, Mercy said, 'I have ridden this summer from the Missouri River to Fort Laramie and never was I out of sight of some grave. It has been as hard on us as on you.'

'Where did you bring it from, Mercy, you white people?'

'From out there,' he said, pointing to the west, 'from across the great water.'

'Will it go on and on and on?'

'It will end,' he assured them. It had to end. It could not continue like this forever, or the world would be wiped away. A man required assurance that when he rose in the morning he would retire at night, barring some fearful accident against which there could be no reasonable defense. But to rise with the daily expectation that fever would strike, and that a few hours later he would be dead, was too much. 'It will end,' he repeated, 'for you and for us.'

'Will you send medicine?'

'At the forts there will be doctors.'

'Forts?' Jake Pasquinel interrupted.

'Yes, when we have the treaty, the Great Father will need five or six forts . . . here and there . . . you know . . .'

'I do know,' Broken Thumb said coldly. 'You will have many forts, and they will require many soldiers, and the soldiers will need many women, and there will be many bottles of whiskey, and while we are drunk in our tipis you will kill the buffalo.' Here he passed into a kind of trance, and he spoke as if he were seeing a tormenting vision of the future: 'And when the buffalo are gone, we shall starve, and when we are starving, you will take away our lands, the tipis will be in flames and the rifles will fire and we will be no more. The great lands we have wandered over we will see no more.'

'No more,' White Antelope repeated, and the words seemed to inflame Broken Thumb, and he became a man of iron.

'No!' he shouted. 'We want no powwow . . . no peace . . . no surrender. It will be war, Mercy. I have prayed to the sacred medicine arrows and I know this to be true. I shall kill you and you shall kill me.'

He passed from reason into a frenzy, throwing himself about the tipi and waving his mangled hand in Mercy's face, and with a wild gesture he grabbed the calumet and shattered it against a tipi pole. 'It is war!' he shouted, his broad face dark and distorted, his braids shaking like snakes.

It was now that the chief in the hat began to speak. From the shadows he reached out a hand and pulled Broken Thumb down beside him, quietening him and saying in Arapaho, 'No, it will not be war. If the Great Father wants to talk with us one more time, and if he sends a messenger like Mercy to assure us that this time the talk is serious, then we will meet with him. We will come to Fort Laramie and we will listen and try to fathom what he has in his heart. Like my friend Broken Thumb, I know that the treaty will be made and then broken. I have no hope that the white man can ever say something and mean it, because we never deal with the same white man. One makes the treaty, and he goes. Another comes, but he never heard of the treaty. With us it is different. When the calumet passes, every Arapaho now and to be born is bound.'

When this was interpreted, the chiefs assented, and the speaker continued: 'Still we must try. So to you, Broken Thumb, I say, "The Cheyenne will go to Fort Laramie," and to you, Mercy, I say, "Tell the Great Father that Our People are willing to talk with him one more time, because we truly desire peace." '

The speaker was Lost Eagle, chief of Our People, who were camped this summer farther to the east. He had come to discuss with the Cheyenne the message from St. Louis, and for two days he had been arguing, with Pasquinel as his interpreter, that the only hope for the Indian was a lasting treaty with the white man, one that would give the white man freedom to traverse Indian lands and the right to establish forts, and give the Indian a confirmation of his ownership of the land. He was a persuasive arguer, a man who had a view of the future quite different from Broken Thumb's.

His words commanded attention, for he was known as a man dedicated to bringing his people safely through the troubled years that loomed ahead. He was the grandson of Lame Beaver, whose many coups filled the chronicles of Our People.

He now turned to Broken Thumb and said, 'Friend, we stand—you and I—at the edge of a precipice like the ones our fathers used to stampede the buffalo over. But we must not allow ourselves to be stampeded.

The white man's bad medicine has struck us hard. The buffalo are no longer easy to locate. Strangers build forts and farms on our land, and we face many decisions. You are the bravest man I know, Broken Thumb, and often have I followed you to war against Comanche and Pawnee.'

Here he bowed gravely to the Cheyenne warrior, his tall-crowned hat dipping down to hide his face. 'But with our few guns we cannot fight the white man with his cannon. If he loses a hundred men, he sends back east for replacements, but if you Cheyenne lose a hundred, where will you find their replacements? You have seen the thousands who have crossed our prairie, and more come at us every year.'

He paused to allow this reasoning to sink in, then asked for a new calumet, and with it took a special oath that what he was about to say was true: 'If the white man wants to cross our land, he will do so, whether we give him permission or not. If his sons want some of our land to farm, they will take it, either with our permission or with a gun. I say, let us go with Mercy, who is our friend, and listen to what he has to say.'

As he spoke these conciliatory words, Mercy noticed that his interpreter, Jake Pasquinel, was becoming more and more impatient with the tenor of the message, and it appeared to Mercy that Jake was about to explode, but before anything could happen, White Antelope of the Cheyenne said solemnly, 'Lost Eagle, you have never given us bad counsel. How soon will the meeting be?'

Before Mercy could respond, Pasquinel leaped from his seat, flung his arms in the air and shouted in Cheyenne, 'Don't listen to this old woman!' Rushing up to Broken Thumb, he grabbed him by the right arm and pleaded, 'Lost Eagle is a fool. The real Arapaho want war . . . like the real Cheyenne.'

'What's he saying?' Mercy asked Strunk, and the mountain man replied, 'He wants the Cheyenne to ignore Lost Eagle. Wants them to go to war.'

'Jake!' Mercy cried. 'You're talking nonsense!'

The half-breed turned in a flash to confront Mercy, and cried in Cheyenne, 'He comes begging you to attend his meeting. Don't go. The Oglala aren't going. Neither are the Pawnee.'

'Why are you trying to stop them?' Mercy asked angrily.

'Because you white men will use the meeting to steal from us . . . more land . . . more rights.'

'No, Jake. I promise you, this is to be an honest meeting. You and I will be equal. We will listen . . .'

Pasquinel thrust his face close to Mercy's and said, 'Equal? You will always have the cannon.'

'Jake,' Mercy said softly. 'Quiet down. You know the meeting will take place. Lost Eagle has said so.'

'Him!' Jake exploded. 'He speaks for no one.'

Now Lost Eagle rose to stand beside Mercy and face the three Cheyenne chiefs. In the next decades his grave, impassive face, topped by the tall-crowned hat, would be painted by four white artists and photographed by many daguerreotypists, so that the deep lines down his cheeks would become familiar across the country, and he would represent the archetypal Indian chief, the man of unshakable integrity.

Asking Strunk to interpret, he said, 'We will come to Fort Laramie, and the Cheyenne will come too, and so will Jake . . . to help us. And when the paper is ready, Broken Thumb and I will sign it side by side.' Then he added with visible sadness, 'And we shall do this thing because there is nothing else we can do.'

'Do you trust the white man?' Jake yelled at him.

'No, but we have no other choice. We must trust and hope that this time . . .' His voice trailed off. Then he took Mercy by the hand and said, 'Tell the Great Father that we will be there.'

And as Mercy left the tipi the three crucial figures created such a vivid image that it would persist in his mind forever: Broken Thumb, conservator of the old traditions, in his role as leader, twisting his right braid with the damaged thumb of his right hand; Lost Eagle, the man who had a clear vision of what the future was to be like, standing silent, the lines of his face darkened by shadow; Jake Pasquinel, on whom fell the burden of comprehending both worlds, moving in violent agitation from chief to chief, trying to convince them of the danger to which they had committed themselves.

Mercy and Strunk rode back to the fort in confusion. They had been asked to believe that one man, Lost Eagle, could prevail against four. They were to report that the two key tribes, the Cheyenne and Arapaho, would attend in spite of the fact that Pasquinel had reported a rumor that the Pawnee were not coming.

'What do you think?' Strunk asked.

'If Lost Eagle is the grandson of Lame Beaver, as he says he is, the Arapaho will attend,' Mercy said.

When they reached the fort they found bad news awaiting them. Messengers from the Comanche, the great tribe of the south, had ridden in to say contemptuously, 'White man never keeps promises. Why should we waste our horses on so dangerous a trip? And why bring our good horses among those great thieves, the Shoshone and Crow? We will not come.' And that afternoon messengers from the Pawnee reported to Captain Ketchum, 'We already have peace with white man. We will not bring our horses among the Sioux.'

With the commissioners from St. Louis on their way, plus the twenty-seven wagons of gifts coming up from Kansas City, Ketchum was discouraged. On the one hand he did not relish the idea of having five or six hundred warlike Indians pressing in upon his half-fort, but on the other, he could not afford to have the proposed meeting collapse before it started, for he commanded the area, and such failure could only mean a black mark on his record. He therefore summoned Major Mercy, Joe Strunk and his lieutenants to a conference in the new officers' quarters, and was mildly surprised when Mrs. Mercy attended, too.

Lisette Bockweiss Mercy was thirty-six, a woman of great charm, much like her mother, now dead. A tall, exuberant person, she found it easy to accommodate herself to frontier inconveniences; while her husband had been negotiating with Broken Thumb, she had been captivating Fort Laramie. Already her steadfast friend was Mr. Tutt at the sutler's store, who confided the standard complaint about the post: 'You freeze all winter, sweat all summer, and are bored all year. If I have to stay here two more years, I believe I'll go crazy.'

'Nonsense,' she told him. 'My father pitched his camp right where you're standing, and spent a whole year with just one other man.'

'Your father!' Mr. Tutt repeated incredulously. 'I thought you grew up in Boston.'

'You give me a gun and a horse,' she teased, 'and I'll bring you in a buffalo.'

Now, at the conference, she gave sound advice: 'Why not send down to Zendt's Farm to get that marvelous old Indian expert, Alexander McKeag, and send him among the tribes? He speaks all the languages and he could persuade them.'

'McKeag must be in his seventies,' Strunk protested, his pride wounded by the suggestion that some other mountain man might do the job better than he.

'Seventy or not,' Lisette said, 'he'd be most useful.'

So it was agreed that Major Mercy would ride down to the South Platte and speak with McKeag and such tribes as they could conveniently reach on the way back. 'I'm especially eager to get the Shoshone here,' Ketchum said. 'They've been fighting everybody.'

But before Mercy could depart, the first good news broke. 'Here come the Oglala chiefs,' shouted the lookout, and everyone watched with apprehension as they forded first the Platte, then the Laramie. In grave silence they came to the adobe fort, bowed ceremoniously from their caparisoned horses and said, 'The Oglala will come.'

'Thank you!' Captain Ketchum said. He invited them to dismount and led them to his quarters in the new building. 'There will be many presents,' he promised them. 'You will go home with peace—peace for all the tribes.'

This phrase disturbed the Oglala. 'We will not come if the Shoshone come,' they said solemnly.

'Oh, but the Shoshone must come,' Ketchum said briskly. 'Translate that for them and explain why.'

Strunk did his best, stressing the indestructible brotherhood that existed among the tribes. At the end he was sweating, and the Oglala said, 'If the Shoshone come, we will kill them all.'

'Oh, hell!' Ketchum groaned. 'Mercy, get out of here and pick up what's-his-name. McCabe? Ask him if he thinks the Shoshone and the Sioux can meet together.'

So Maxwell Mercy, attended by four good riflemen, rode south to Zendt's Farm, where he found only sorrow. Three weeks before, cholera had carried off both Alexander McKeag and his Indian wife, Clay Basket.

'In the morning McKeag was as well as I am," Levi Zendt said with obvious grief. 'A chill. Nausea. Horrible death. Next morning Clay Basket began shaking. We buried them both down by the river.'

Mercy was deeply saddened by such sudden death, even though a few days before he had rationalized it to the chiefs. He walked down to the river and knelt by the circle of stones marking the graves. He said a short prayer for the quiet Scotsman who had contributed so much to the west. Without rising, he turned toward the mound that covered the Indian woman who had married Lisette's father; he remembered her as she was when she helped run the post at Fort John, soft-spoken and capable. She had been the dutiful wife of two quite different men and had been loved by each. How many squaws, he thought as he prayed, had served in this silent manner, bearing half-breed sons like the Pasquinel brothers and lovely, dark-skinned daughters like Lucinda.

'I hope the treaty we devise will prove good to women like you, Clay Basket,' he said aloud, and on her grave he placed a clump of sage, the only flower growing in midsummer, and scarcely a flower at all.

Lucinda, now twenty-four and at the height of her beauty, volunteered the idea that Levi should go north to act as interpreter, and she showed no fear about running the farm alone. 'I've got the children to keep me busy, and we have three Pawnee who'll stay as long as I feed them.'

As the two men, brothers-in-law of a sort, rode west they talked, and Zendt said, 'My wife's half-Indian, and I try to understand what's happenin', but sometimes I'm plain confused. All day I hear white men complain about the shiftless, no-good Indian. Won't work for a livin'. Isn't fit to own land. And then I look at the land after the white men pass through. What they don't want they just junk beside the trail. Their dead animals decay till the stench fills the prairies. And I say that in some things that count, the Indian is a damn sight better than the white.'

Mercy was inclined to agree, and was prepared to say so when Zendt added, 'I can't figure you out, Mercy. You could have a fancy life back east, but here you are, workin' for this treaty like you were an Indian.'

Mercy rode in silence for some time, looking at the prairies as they swept to the northern horizon, then to the mountains emerging in the west, and finally he said, 'Simple. I love this land. Loved it the first time I saw it, with you and Elly.' The name recalled painful memories and he said, 'She was the soul of the west.'

Levi said nothing, and after a while Mercy snapped his fingers and said briskly, 'What you say about the settlers is true, Levi. A grubby lot. But it's them, not the goldminers, who'll build this land. And when they do, they won't want Indian war parties raiding through their fields or buffalo tearing down their fences. They're going to come . . . can't stop them. The enemy of the tipi is not the rifle. It's the plow.'

'Can the same land hold a farmer and an Indian?'

'My hope is that with this treaty we'll be able to arrange a truce. Land along the Platte for the white farmer. Empty lands like this for the Indian and his buffalo.'

'You think land like this can ever be farmed?' Zendt asked.

'Never. This is desert. And I think that if we can arrange a treaty now, rather than wage a war against the Indians five years from now, it'll cost our government a lot less money in the long run.'

'You're not interested in the money,' Zendt countered.

'I'm interested in justice,' Mercy said. 'You and I have each been close to death, and that clears the air of petty ideas like money and advancement.'

Zendt accepted this as the statement of a reasonable man, and they rode westward into Shoshone country, where they consulted with Chief Washakie, who said that he would not take his braves into the heart of Sioux country, for the enmity between the two tribes had been marked by constant skirmishes and many deaths.

'It is this that we want to end,' Levi explained in broken Ute, a language close to that used by the Shoshone, and he explained with Mercy's help how Fort Laramie would be neutral territory, a safe place for all the tribes to congregate.

'The Sioux will kill us if we venture onto their land,' Washakie repeated.

'It is nobody's land,' Levi insisted. 'The Cheyenne will be there . . .'

'They're worse than the others,' Washakie protested.

But Mercy moved in with compelling reasons. 'There will be much food at the treaty,' he said. 'There will be many presents from the Great Father in Washington. Do you want to deprive your people of this bounty?' When Zendt translated this, Washakie's face broke into a smile and he said, 'If there are to be presents, we will have to come,' and on the spur of the moment Mercy thought to ask, 'We? How many?'

'All of us,' Washakie said. 'If it's a decision affecting all our tribe . . . all of us.'

'How many?' Mercy asked weakly.

'We are fourteen hundred,' Washakie said, and by the time Mercy and Zendt left the area, the Shoshone were starting to collect food and some were folding their tipis.

When Mercy got back to Fort Laramie he found it in turmoil. One of the commissioners had reached the fort early with disastrous news.

'Tell him,' Captain Ketchum directed, and the official from Washington took the major aside and recited a doleful story, whose potential for tragedy he did not even yet appreciate: 'The government allocated fifty thousand dollars for this treaty. Just for the Indians. But instead of commissioning the goods in St. Louis, as we've done for all previous treaties, some clerk decided to buy them this time in New York. Cheaper. And in New York some other clerk decided that while we said the goods had to be in St. Louis on July 1, he felt that July 18 would be just as good, and then he found he could save a little more by using a slower railroad, so maybe they won't get here till September.'

'Oh, my God!' Mercy gasped.

'I left St. Louis early,' the commissioner explained. 'Had some work to do with the Sac and Fox, and when I finally got to Kansas City the presents had arrived, and I thought, "They'll make it in time," but I was there for six days and the wagons hadn't moved a foot.'

'What did you do?'

'Raised hell. Got them started.'

'When will they be here?'

'They're promised for September 15. Probably get here by October 15.'

'You'll dispatch a messenger to Kansas City. Tonight.'

'We've done so,' the commissioner said lamely. 'Believe me, it was the contractors who are at fault in this dreadful thing. We commissioners know better.'

Mercy went to the window and pointed to the meadows beyond the parade grounds, where Indian tipis were already beginning to appear. 'Commissioner,' he said quietly, 'they're beginning to gather. God alone knows how many will be there, but if they don't have food— Look! We have only a hundred and sixty soldiers in this garrison, with a thousand more on their way . . .'

The commissioner coughed. 'Major, I'm to advise you on that, too. The War Department has changed its mind. It needs the promised men elsewhere.' He paused and said, 'Your thousand men are not coming.'

'How many are?'

'Thirty-three dragoons. Escort for the main negotiators.'

Major Mercy left the window and sat down. 'You mean we have thousands of Indians congregating here—most of them braves, eager for a fight—and we have to do with a hundred and sixty men plus a handful of dragoons?'

'That's right.'

'Oh, Jesus!' He stormed from his quarters and ran across the parade ground to the old adobe fort, where Captain Ketchum was meeting with his staff and the mountain men.

Before Mercy could explode, Ketchum asked soberly, 'How many Shoshone are coming?'

'One thousand four hundred.'

Ketchum added some figures and reported, 'That makes over seven thousand for sure, as of this moment, and we haven't heard from the Crow, the Assiniboin or the Hidatsa.'

'You mean ten thousand Indians are coming to this fort?' Mercy asked.

'At least. More like eleven thousand . . . twelve thousand.'

'And we have a hundred and sixty effectives?'

'Plus the commissioners . . . the mountain men . . . and the dragoons!'

'Tell me,' said the commissioner, who had followed Mercy across the grounds, 'how did this miscalculation occur?'

'You tell him, Zendt,' Ketchum directed, and Levi asked an Oglala chief to join them. The chief said in broken English, 'White man always say "Chief, do this" or "Chief, make your tribe do that." Same like Great White Father. But Indian chief nobody. He my uncle, my cousin. Nobody tell him, "Chief, you big man now. You run tribe." He run tribe just so long he do what we want. My uncle, he chief and he have some good ideas, some bad. He talk, we listen, we do. He good man, but he nobody.'

'Don't you choose a chief?' the commission asked. 'Well, for life?'

The young Oglala laughed. 'Chief he lose teeth, he can't bite buffalo, he finish.'

'What does this have to do with ten thousand Indians?' the commissioner asked.

Zendt replied, 'Just this. You can't go to the Oglala and tell them, "Send us your chiefs," because if the chiefs are going to talk about something that affects the whole tribe, the whole tribe will come along. A chief is not a senator. Like the brave says, he's only as good as his teeth. Or as long as he gives sound advice.'

'What will we do?' the commissioner asked Captain Ketchum.

'I don't know what we'll do,' Ketchum said. 'A handful of men against ten thousand Indians . . . no food . . . no gifts. But I can tell you what I'm going to do.'

'What?'

'Pray.' And as he looked out from the fort he saw the tribes from the north drifting in, and no chief rode alone. He was accompanied by his entire tribe, including the children, the dogs and especially the horses— thousands of them.

In all previous American history there had been nothing like the gathering at Fort Laramie that summer, and in the decades to follow there could be nothing to equal it, for in those later years the Indians would be dispersed, and they would lack ponies and tipis and eagle feathers for their war bonnets. But in late August of 1851 they stood at the apex of their power, and as they assembled from all points they were majestic.

First the mighty Sioux came from the northeast, the many tribes glistening in paint and feathers. They had small horses and rode them moderately well; their grandeur lay in the terrible intensity with which they pursued an objective, whether peaceful or warlike. They were the powerful Indians, willing to engage eight different enemy tribes at once, and when they came into camp they brought with them an ancient insolence. Each tribe had its special characteristics—Brulé, Oglala, Minniconjou, Hunkpapa—but all were members of the same warlike society. In their center rode their principal chiefs, who bore aloft an American flag awarded them at some earlier treaty.

From the northwest came the Assiniboin, slim men unbelievably attuned to their horses. They rode like centaurs, man and horse united in one flesh, moving together in subtle grace. To see them coming across an open prairie was to see motion and dust and waving grass frozen together for a moment, then dissolving as the procession came closer. These Indians wore no headdresses; their dignity resided in their solemn character, bred in remote canyons far from the white man.

Up the Platte came the Cheyenne, tallest of the tribes and incomparably the noblest in appearance. They rode their horses well, sat like graven images, with their right hands on their hips, and impressed the assembly with the beauty of their headdresses and the fineness of their garments. They were the nobility of the plains, the men of arrogance and self-assurance. For two hundred years they had defended themselves against any combination, and now they rode as if they possessed the prairies. In war they fought with unparalleled courage, and no other tribe in the Platte region had done more to protect the plains from desecration. Their six leading chiefs—Broken Thumb, Bear's Feather, White Antelope, Little Chief, Rides-on-Clouds and Lean Bear—created a powerful impression of dignity as they rode into camp, for they were tall, slim, handsomely groomed, and their war bonnets were made of finest eagle feathers set in a stout gold-colored webbing decorated with quills. Each chief, because of his raiment, seemed mightier than he was; they formed a compelling phalanx as the sun struck them from the left, their bronzed faces moving in and out of shadow. Behind them, in strict military array, rode the younger chiefs, some almost naked, some in garb only slightly less imposing than their elders'. In the rear, guarding the folded tipis and the children, came the women, tall and dignified, prepared to support their chieftains in whatever decisions were reached.

From the north came the strangers, the Mandan, the Hidatsa and the Arikara, who had come only because of the assurances given by Father De Smet. They were ill-at-ease, so far south, but they came seeking protection from emigrants who were beginning to traverse their lands. They were shorter than the plains Indians but in some ways more knowing, for they had been in contact with the white man since the days of Lewis and Clark.

From the west came the strangest contingent, a small group of one hundred and eighty-three dark-skinned Shoshone, moving cautiously, each with a loaded rifle across his arms. Their arrival created a storm of excitement, and Joe Strunk shouted to the soldiers, 'Watch out for trouble!'

What had happened was this. When the Shoshone left camp in western Wyoming, all fourteen hundred set forth. Their interpreter was Jim Bridger, bravest of the mountain men and one of the most canny; their chief was Washakie, who would play a notable role in subsequent history, and under the leadership of these two men they felt so secure that they traveled for some time in company with a wagon train led by white men, but as they moved eastward, a Cheyenne war party struck from the north, killing a Shoshone chief and his son.

Bridger was appalled at this breaking of an understood truce, and Chief Washakie announced that if there was to be a renewal of ancient Cheyenne-Shoshone warfare, his tribe would refuse to move any farther east. A compromise was struck whereby the women and children were sent back to camp while Washakie led the warriors of his tribe to the meeting, provided military escort were assured from Fort Laramie.

Captain Ketchum, striving desperately to maintain peace, sent Strunk and Mercy to the Cheyenne, exacting from them a solemn promise that they would not further molest the Shoshone, and White Antelope and Broken Thumb gave the assurance, and enforced it. 'No war from us,' Broken Thumb promised several times, and in proof of his good will he told Strunk, 'When Shoshone reach camp, we will give them a feast . . . and make them presents they will treasure.' Mercy shook hands with the Cheyenne chiefs and reported to Ketchum, 'With the Cheyenne there will be no trouble. Broken Thumb has said so, and he keeps his word.'

'Go back and assure the Shoshone,' Ketchum directed, so Mercy rode out with Strunk, and in a mountain pass to the west they found the warriors, tense and suspicious. 'This is to be a convention of true peace,' Mercy assured Bridger, and when this was translated for Washakie, that great chief said grudgingly, 'We will try.' So the Shoshone, led by Washakie on a white horse, with Mercy, Strunk and Bridger at his side, rode cautiously toward the vast encampment, their horses eager to leap forward into battle if necessary, their weapons ready for the command to charge. But when they saw the multitude, and the manner in which Sioux camped by Assiniboin, they relaxed, and in the end they pitched their tipis next to those of their mortal enemy, the Cheyenne.

And from the southwest, when the others had gathered, came the poets of the prairies, the tall, quiet, hesitant Arapaho, less arrogant than the Cheyenne, less imposing than the Sioux. They were handsome men, grave of countenance and stately of mien; they were the philosophers, the artists, the ones who listened when the others spoke, but they were men and women of terrible determination, and if necessary, were willing to hazard their future and the future of their children's children. They were not a tribe to be trifled with, these Arapaho, for they were men and women gifted with an inner dignity that had never so far been subdued. Their chiefs—Eagle Head, Lost Eagle, White Crow, Cut Nose, Little Owl—were sedate men who had come to reason with the White Father, to advise him of their problems and to seek accommodation.

When the tribes were assembled and the days of adjustment completed, the discussions were about to begin when a scout shouted from the northwest sector, 'Here they come! My God, look at 'em.' Riding from the west, with the morning sun striking their faces, came an enormous contingent of three thousand Crow, whom many considered the ideal braves. They were not so dark as some of the other tribes; they were a moody people, vacillating between gravity and exhilaration, and were reported by traders who had dealt with them to be of unusual intelligence. They were a mighty nation, prowling the northern Rockies and holding tenaciously to valleys which had long been theirs.

'They know horses!' the professional soldiers cried admiringly, for although the Crow had ridden eight hundred miles, they now spurred their horses to a canter and they came across the prairie like waves coming to shore. In the forefront rode four chiefs, resplendent in costumes not known among the watching tribes: nine strings of cowries about their necks, long strands of elk bones falling from their temples, breastplates from which dangled scores of ermine tails, and most conspicuous, their hair standing upright in huge pompadours, kept in place by gum from spruce trees.

The four chiefs rode silently, looking straight ahead, but behind them came other braves looking warily from side to side, for they were entering alien land where they might be attacked at any moment. In the center of the horde rode the women, beautifully garbed, while along the flanks, on small black-and-white ponies, rode the boys nine and ten years old, fully prepared to engage the enemy.

At a signal from one of the chiefs, a band of cavalry broke from the rear and thundered to the fore, two hundred men nearly naked, riding their horses savagely. Then, to the surprise of the watchers, each man, keeping one leg wrapped about the saddletree, leaned far down on the right flank of his galloping horse, leaned under the neck and fired a salute from an old flintlock rifle.

Before the crowd could respond, the three thousand Crow reined in their horses, slowed them to a walk, and with the sun exploding on their tired and dusty faces, broke into the song of their nation—a moving chant which told of far mountains—and their voices filled the morning air.

*   *   *

The first decision reached by Ketchum and the commissioners was a sensible one. They convened with Mercy, Zendt, Strunk and Bridger, and asked, 'How many Indians have we on our hands?'

'I'd say about fourteen thousand,' Mercy replied.

'And how many horses?'

'Maybe thirty thousand,' Zendt estimated.

'Impossible,' Ketchum growled.

'Couldn't be less than twenty-seven thousand,' Bridger said.

'We can't feed that many horses,' Ketchum wailed. 'What can we do?'

Mercy told the commissioners, 'When I visited the Cheyenne a month ago I found them camped south of Horse Creek. About thirty-five miles down the Platte. Big meadows, good grass.'

The commissioners asked Bridger what he thought of the place, but he had not come that way. Strunk said, 'Enough grass down there to feed sixty thousand.' Ketchum looked skeptical.

So the decision was announced that all Indians plus a negotiating team would head southeast along the Platte to more adequate pasturage, and the vast assemblage prepared to make the move, which all approved. One hundred and seventy soldiers would go along, leaving a handful to guard the fort that night. But before they left, there was an auspicious sign. Chiefs Broken Thumb and White Antelope walked on foot to the camp of the suspicious Shoshone, where the former said, 'Brothers, we have been at war too long. Our braves did wrong when they killed your people one moon past, and we offer you our friendship.'

Chief Washakie accepted the gesture and embraced the two visitors, whereupon White Antelope said, 'We have come to invite you to a feast —all of you to be our honored guests,' and he led the eighty-three Shoshone across the parade grounds and into the heart of the Cheyenne camp, where a generous feast of deer had been laid out, and word passed through all the camp, Indian and white alike, that the Shoshone and the Cheyenne were feasting in brotherhood, and from each tribe certain chiefs filtered into the Cheyenne camp to see for themselves this miracle, and they arrived in time to see Chief Broken Thumb direct his squaw to rise from her place and walk over to Chief Washakie and present him with the two scalps the Cheyenne had lifted from the dead Shoshone, and as she surrendered them, Broken Thumb said, 'We honored these trophies as memories of a good battle. Now we hand them back to you as proof of our lasting friendship.' And through the camp there were sounds of approbation.

Next morning the monumental procession got under way, this single largest assembly of Indians ever, riding into the sunlight, sometimes in single file, at other times six and eight abreast—Crow and Brulé, Arikara and Oglala, side by side in an amity they had never known before. The line of march, broken here and there by small contingents of American soldiers, stretched out for fifteen miles, and as he saw them go,

Captain Ketchum whispered to one of the commissioners, 'If those Indians got it in their minds, they could wipe us out in ten minutes.'

Fortunately, the Indians had other things in mind, for as the column approached the new campgrounds Major Mercy, riding with the Shoshone, saw bands of Sioux and Cheyenne women rushing ahead to a small plateau overlooking the confluence of the two streams, and there, without consulting the white men present, they swung into confused action, lugging in many poles and unfurling buffalo robes.

'What in hell are they doin'?' Strunk asked, and Mercy looked around till he found Jake Pasquinel.

'Our contribution,' Pasquinel replied, and the men watched in awe as the women constructed a ceremonial bower decorated with flowers, and an amphitheater area in which the formal discussions would be held. It was a creation lovely in appearance, totally Indian in concept and exactly right for the purpose at hand. As with many Indian designs, the amphitheater opened to the east so that evil spirits which might be planning to disturb the debate could escape; the good spirits, of course, would remain behind to guide the deliberations.

Two soldiers, watching the women scrambling up the poles to lash down the last buffalo robes, were astonished that they could work so fast. 'Beat any men I saw in Boston,' one said.

The spirit that emanated from the discussions was as felicitous as the building in which they were held. Probably never in the history of the United States would a plenary session of any kind be convened in which such abundant good will would be manifest. The white men honestly wanted to reach a treaty that would be just and permanent. The Indians sought with open hearts to arrange land and rights in such a way that all could live honorably. The discussions of minor points were conducted, and some of the speeches which were recorded would have done justice to Versailles or Westminster.

It was a Crow chief, Brave Arm, who set the pattern for Indian comment: 'Great Leader, we have ridden many days to hear your speech. Our ears have not been stopped. They have been open, and we begin to feel good in our hearts at what they hear. We came hungry, but we know that you will feed us. As the sun looks down upon us, as the Great Spirit watches me, I am willing to do as you tell me to do. I know you will tell me right and that what you direct will be good for my people. We regard this as a great medicine day when our pipes of peace are one and we are all at peace.'

Major Mercy, speaking for the United States government, said, 'I am directed by the Great White Father in Washington to invite a chief from each of your nations to travel to his home to meet with him. He wants you to ride your horses down to the Missouri River, where a boat will be waiting for you. From there you will go to St. Louis, where you will see our finest city in the west. Then you will board a train and ride across our great country to Washington, where he will talk with you and give you his own solemn promise that this peace is forever, that the lands you get now are yours for as long as the waters flow and the grass shall grow. So as we talk during these last days, each tribe must be thinking, "Which of our chiefs do we want to send to Washington to meet the Great Father?" And on the last day you shall tell us, and we will all start for Washington together.'

It was Lost Eagle who summed up the Indian position, and he did so with the full approval of the Cheyenne and the Sioux and the Crow, for he was known among them as a judicious man: 'It is not for us to tell the Great White Father how we judged his words. You men of the army who have met with us, you commissioners who have smoked the pipe with us, you must tell him how you found us. Were we just in the discussions? Did we listen when you explained why you had to have certain trails? Did we suggest places where you could build your forts? Speak of us as you saw us during these days. And when you have done that, speak also of three things that will exist as long as the sun shines. We must have buffalo, for without food our bodies will perish. We must be permitted to ride the open prairie without the white man's trails cutting us off from old grounds, for without freedom our spirits will perish. And we must have peace. The Crow is willing to sit here with the Sioux. The Cheyenne meet here with the Shoshone. And all assemble with the white man as their brother. We shall have peace.'

While the chiefs were occupied with such discussion, their tribesmen were engaged in lively social activity. Tribal animosities were ignored as one group after another organized feasts and conducted dances. With sophisticated sign languages, tribes swapped stories of bravado and escapades on the plains. The beat of tom-toms sounded through the day and long into the night, with as many as forty or fifty celebrations under way. In normal times such echoes would have sent a spasm of dread down the spines of white listeners, but now they attended the dances and sometimes joined in beating the drums offered them.

The only deterrent to festivity was a lack of food. The wagons were still delayed on their snail-like crawl from Kansas City, and meat became so scarce that the northern Sioux sent bands of young men into the distant Black Hills to hunt, and they returned with some buffalo, but not enough to feed the hungry mob. So the Indians took recourse in the dog feast, from which most of the whites politely excused themselves.

Once a cur had been killed, by being hanged, it was put on a fire and singed. When the skin was scraped clean, the carcass was dressed, cut up and put into a large copper kettle, where it was boiled until the bones were easily removed. Then it was flavored with prairie herbs and dried plums, becoming a succulent dish which the plains tribes considered a delicacy. After observing a sequence of such feasts, Father De Smet noted in his diary: 'No epoch of Indian annals shows a greater massacre of the canine race.'

The lack of food distressed Captain Ketchum, who warned the commissioners, 'If those damned wagons don't get here soon, these Indians will begin to starve. And if I am forced to inform fourteen thousand betrayed Indians that there are no gifts, either . . .' He coughed. 'Gentlemen, I would advise that on this night you write very tender letters to your wives.'

He dispatched Joe Strunk eastward to check on the wagons, but two days later the mountain man returned, glum. 'No wagons in sight,' he said, and Ketchum instructed the commissioners, 'Make your speeches longer.'

Attention was diverted from this lack of food by Broken Thumb, who assembled one hundred of the finest Cheyenne horsemen, telling them, 'We shall remind the white man that while we talk of peace, we remain ready for war. And if he has plans to trick us again, let him know what waits.'

Dressed in war regalia, the hundred braves mounted their ponies and came thundering into the open space before the assembly area, where the negotiators were meeting. There they began a series of intricate and wild maneuvers. The men were armed, some with lances, some with guns, the rest with bows and arrows. Upon the hips and shoulders of each horse were painted indications of the coups that rider had won: a scalp was signified by a red hand, while a horse that had been stolen cleanly in a foray against the enemy was marked by a black horse's hoof.

Under Broken Thumb's direction, the Cheyenne engaged in a maneuver of which they were particularly proud. Congealing in what seemed a hopeless mass of confused horses and riders, they fired their guns aimlessly and shot arrows into the air until Broken Thumb uttered a loud war cry, whereupon one group of riders from the center pushed out to form a circular ring of protection about the whole. Then, with bloodcurdling screams, the horsemen exchanged places, those on the outside turning inward and those on the inside bursting through, each missing the other by inches, an intricate, endlessly moving design.

A principal delight of the gathering was Lisette Mercy. The Indian women were pleased that a white woman had seen fit to attend, and each day they gathered to inspect her. Lisette was a pretty woman whose light hair and many petticoats enthralled the squaws. On some days as many as a hundred would draw their fingers down her delicately rouged cheeks to see if the color would come off. They pried into her petticoats as if they were badgers inspecting a cave. And if she had permitted, they would have plucked her bald on the first day; unfortunately, some squaws had pulled out a few hairs and all felt that they were entitled to do likewise.

Lisette reacted to the encampment as only the daughter of someone like Lise Bockweiss Pasquinel could have done. Since food was scarce, she rode back to the fort to collect all the candy, tobacco and flour she could, plus as many jars of vermilion as Mr. Tutt had in his sutler's shop.

When she returned she delighted the children by drawing red circles on their cheeks. She sang old French songs and in the evening talked with the chiefs, congratulating them on how well things were going.

Because she was a Pasquinel, the Indians thought of her as their special friend, and she was often called upon to calm her half brother Jake when he agonized over the treaty provisions. When he was with her he dropped the rhetoric of war, but voiced a despair that was even more compelling.

'This hasn't been a bargaining, Lisette. It's been a present handed to the white man. He takes what he wants and then gives us back what is already ours. If we voice any doubts, he buys off the old chiefs with baubles and trinkets. In the end, you watch. He'll have everything and we'll have nothing.'

He was a tormented man: 'You and Mike and I have the same father. With you—yes, and with Max too—I can be at peace, but never with the other whites. When I was a boy they gave me this scar. And don't be fooled by Mike. He plays the clown and tries to pretend there's some way out, but when we talk at night he knows our destruction is inevitable.'

During the closing days of the meeting, no one was busier than Father De Smet. Day and night he rushed from one group to another, baptizing babies at a rate not equaled since the days of Galilee: Indians, half-breeds, whites who had been long in the mountains, he baptized them all. He would accept people of any age or any condition, promising each an equal share of God's beneficence. One night, following a day during which he had been especially active, he wrote a report to his superiors:

> During the two weeks that I have passed in the plain of the Great Council, I paid frequent visits to the different tribes and bands of savages, accompanied by one or more of their interpreters. These last were extremely obliging in devoting themselves to my aid in announcing the gospel. The Indians listened eagerly to my instructions. They besought me to explain baptism to them, as several had been present when I had baptized several half-breed children. I complied with their request, and gave them a lengthy instruction on its blessings and obligations. All then entreated me to grant this favor to their infants. Among the Arapaho, I baptized 305 little ones; among the Cheyenne 253; among the Oglala 239; and among the Brulé and Osage Sioux 280; in the camp of Painted Bear 53.

Shortly after he baptized the Arapaho children they fell ill, and the tribe concluded that his religion was false. But among the Sioux he had enormous success, for his description of heaven, where good people go, and hell, where evil ones reside, was much to their liking, for as one chief explained, 'It will be fine to be in heaven and not have to bother about white men, who will all be in hell.'

In spite of Jake Pasquinel's doubts, the terms of the treaty were as just as could have been devised, and for once, all Indian tribes were treated fairly. An effective basis for lasting peace was achieved, one binding not only white and Indian but also each Indian tribe in its conduct with its neighbors. The government gained what it had always wanted: the right to build forts, establish roads and maintain the peace. In return, it bound itself to protect Indians against depredations by whites, while the Indians were obligated to make restitution for any wrongs committed by them.

The government promised to pay the total Indian community an annuity of fifty thousand dollars for fifty years, which the government considered an honorable offer which compensated them for losses so far incurred. A notable feature was a plan whereby the prairie was cut into large segments and allocated to individual tribes, with the understanding that a hunting party from another tribe could follow buffalo wherever they went. Boundaries for the northern tribes were set by Father De Smet, who was acceptable to all, and the southern lines were drawn by Major Mercy and Levi Zendt, who awarded the Cheyenne and Arapaho a generous territory:

> Commencing at the Red Butte, or the place where the road leaves the north fork of the Platte River; thence up the north fork of the Platte River to its source; thence along the main range of the Rocky Mountains to the headwaters of the Arkansas River; thence down the Arkansas River to the crossing of the Santa Fe road; thence in a northwesterly direction to the forks of the Platte River, and thence up the Platte River to the place of beginning.

This meant that 6400 Indians now owned in perpetuity some ninety thousand square miles, or more than fifty-seven million acres. Thus each Indian received fourteen square miles, or about thirty-six thousand acres for a family of four. In later years this Cheyenne-Arapaho allocation would support more than two million white men who, because they understood agriculture and manufacturing, would earn from it a good living.

Why was so much potentially valuable land given to the two tribes in 1851? Simply because both groups involved in making the treaty had false understandings of the land they were dealing with. Still prisoners of the mistaken concept promulgated by Major Mercy, whites believed the plains to be a desert which could not be farmed; Indians were convinced they were useful only for the buffalo. As always, when the significance of a natural resource is misunderstood, any land settlement must end in disaster.

Only two men refused to lose their senses in the general euphoria that marked the final days of treaty-making. The first was Chief Broken Thumb, who knew that no white man could possibly honor a treaty that surrendered lands so spacious. 'Go home in peace,' he told his young braves sardonically, 'but prepare for war. The treaty will soon be broken and soldiers will march out from the forts we have given them.' Seeking Lost Eagle, he called for Jake Pasquinel to translate, and warned, 'Go to Washington, little brother, and humble yourself before the Great White Father, but as you go, remember that when the time comes for you to collect the promised money, there will be a different father, and when you petition him for your annuity, he will cry, "Who is this fool, Lost Eagle? Never saw him before." And there will be no buffalo and no money and no peace, and on that day you will follow me to war. As this campground now gives off a mighty stench from all of us gathered here, so, too, will this treaty.'

The other cynic was Jake Pasquinel, for when Broken Thumb finished speaking, he said on his own, 'Lost Eagle, you are a great fool. When we came here Captain Ketchum promised us two things. Food and presents. Do we have either? You foolish man, they have broken your treaty before it even started.'

Lost Eagle did not know how to answer his critics. He, more than any other Cheyenne or Arapaho, had persuaded the two tribes to accept the new order, but even before the smoke had left the calumet, the first promises seemed to be broken. Still he had faith, and he said, 'If a man like Major Mercy breaks his word, there is no meaning in the world. We will get our presents.'

And he moved among all the tribesmen, advising them to stay at Fort Laramie a few days longer. 'The presents will be here. Major Mercy said so,' and then he went to the major and said, 'Broken Thumb and the others are growing desperate. They are hungry,' and Mercy promised him, 'The food will come.'

And then, after three days of miserable waiting, a scout came roaring in from the east with tremendous news: 'Twenty-seven wagons! Half a day's journey to the east!'

An escort of two thousand Indians fanned out across the plains, and when they saw the loaded wagons, their hubs dragging dust, a soaring hope rose in the hearts of all men, for this was a good omen.

It required the chiefs three days to unload the wagons and distribute the presents: tobacco, coffee so highly treasured, sugar, warm blankets from Baltimore, Green River knives, beads sewn on cardboard from Paris, dried beef, flour, jars of jam and preserves. Feasts were held at which Father De Smet said prayers and men ate till they were sick.

But the real gifts came on the final day! Then Captain Ketchum summoned the principal chiefs and told them, 'The Great White Father in Washington loves his children, and when they have worked wisely with him, he gives them gifts which make them part of his family. To each of you chiefs who have signed the treaty he sends a uniform . . . a full uniform of his army . . . you are now all army officers.'

And from the bales Mr. Tutt broke forth a series of resplendent uniforms, complete with shoes, cap, sashes and swords. A captain's uniform, 'Better than mine,' Ketchum pointed out, went to each of the minor chiefs. For the major chiefs there were the starred uniforms of a brigadier general. And for Washakie of the Shoshone, Lost Eagle of the Arapaho and three others, there were the costly uniforms of major general, the epaulettes shimmering in gold.

At Captain Ketchum's request, the chiefs donned the uniforms, and although some did not exactly fit, the new officers made a fine display, except that before they could line up for a dress review, an Oglala Sioux who had been sent south to scout for meat reported: 'Buffalo on the South Platte!' and the newly commissioned officers dashed off toward Rattlesnake Buttes.

Levi Zendt followed them south at his own pace, satisfied that when they had made their kills they would bring the skins to Zendt's Farm for trading. They did. But the profit that resulted caused no joy, for his attention was diverted by a letter from the east.

Lampeter, Penna.
The Five Zendts

Brother Levi,

I received your letter with the $12 to buy a Fordney gun, yours having been stolen, but there is nothing I can do to help you now, as God has seen fit to visit Lancaster and strike down the blasphemer who lusts after evil ways.

Four times our church directed Melchior Fordney either to marry the woman with which he was living in lust and four times he laughed at the elders. Four times too many for God's patience.

So John Gaggerty, acting on behalf of God, took a broadax and went for sinner Fordney and chopped him down, severing his head, and then he went after the scarlet woman Mrs. Trippet and chopped her down too, slaying her in the scene of her sin. Thus does God revenge himself on the infidel.

I am shamed to report that the courts in Lancaster saw fit to condemn that good man Haggerty for what he done and they hanged him in Lancaster jail. Many good people are outraged, but the courts in Lancaster often seem to do the work of the devil.

Since Fordney is dead, I am applying your $12 against the value of the two horses you stole from me. Your debt is now $88.

Your loving brother in God,
Mahlon Zendt

When Levi finished reading, he told Lucinda, 'Michael Fordney was one of the best men I knew in Lancaster.' And as he compared the gunsmith with his own brothers, he became increasingly irritated. 'Damnit,' he stormed. 'I have four brothers back there, and you'd think Mahlon would tell me whether they were married or had children or what.'

'You never sent him news about yourself,' Lucinda teased.

'But I'm the one away from home. He didn't even tell if Momma is still livin',' and he thought of the farm and the trees and the little buildings in which he had made souse and smoked hams, and he was overcome with homesickness.

Then he laughed at himself and rose and walked around the table to kiss Lucinda. 'What I really wanted to know, if I told the truth, is did he marry the Stoltzfus girl? The mean pig, he didn't even tell me that.'

And suddenly the concerns of Lancaster, Pennsylvania, seemed far away. Here in the west the future of a great part of the nation was being determined, yet his petty-minded brothers knew nothing of it. 'We can draft a good treaty,' Levi growled as he wadded up the letter, 'but when those Lancaster lawyers James Buchanan and Thaddeus Stevens get through with it in Congress, it won't amount to much.' He saw that treaties were made by men of vision like Major Mercy and administered by mean-spirited men like Mahlon Zendt, and he saw little likelihood that any good would come from this particular one.

He was right. When the treaty reached the United States Senate, that body, without consulting the Indians, arbitrarily reduced the payments from fifty years to ten, then contemptuously refused to ratify the whole. It was rejected before it ever went into effect, and the Indians were left with no secure title to their land.

The man who destroyed even the residue of the treaty never realized what he was doing. In 1857 a thin, medium-sized drifter, thirty years old, haunted the waterfront at St. Louis, volunteering occasionally for odd jobs that developed along the levee. When entertainment boats were there he sometimes collected tickets, but more often he held horses for people visiting the boats or helped slaves unload shipments from Pittsburgh.

He was known as Spade Larkin, from his habit of carrying with him a short-handled miner's spade, and it was said that he had already crossed the continent twice, once on his way to the gold fields in California empty-handed and once returning in the same condition except for the spade which he had bought in Sacramento. The spell of gold was upon him, for with his own eyes he had seen men no better prepared than he strike veins which had made them famous throughout California, and it was his determination to do the same when the next field opened.

He explained, 'I seen it time and again. Them as got the gold were them as got there fust.' He had grown up on a farm in southern Ohio, to which he had no intention of returning. 'They's oney two places a man can live properly, St. Louis or San Francisco,' and of the two he preferred the former.

'The day is gonna come—you will live to see the day, all of you—when I step off'n a Missouri River steamer and tell the cabman, "Planters' House," and I'll have money like you never seen—because it's out there, just waitin' to be picked up . . . if you know the right place to dig.

'Sure, I failed in California,' he often confessed. 'Come home with fifty cents and a shovel. But I also come home with an idea. I know how to placer and I know how to dig. I carry this spade so when the next news breaks, I'm off. I got me a piece of paper that tells me where the next big strike is gonna be.' Here he would take from his pocket the oilskin pouch in which he carried his tobacco, and from it he would take a second pouch in which he carried a piece of cardboard onto which was pasted a well-worn clipping from the *Missouri Republican* of 1845:

> Miss Lucinda is not only unusually attractive, with her dark flashing eyes, but she is famed throughout the west as the granddaughter and only heir of Chief Lame Beaver, the Arapaho hero who discovered a gold mine in the Rockies.

Spade was the least surprised man in St. Louis when in 1858 the extraordinary news flashed up and down the Mississippi valley: 'Gold discovered in Nebraska Territory at Pikes Peak!' He left St. Louis that night, carrying only his Sacramento spade and a determination to be first at some new field.

He took a steamer to St. Joseph, now a thriving city to which railroads from the east were delivering hundreds of gold-seekers daily. Some had funds to purchase wagons on whose sides they painted 'Pikes Peak or Bust,' and others could even employ guides to lead their large trains of horses laden with enough equipment for a year.

Larkin and seven men like him proposed to walk to the Rockies. They would ferry across the Missouri at St. Joe, ask directions to the Platte River and then walk the six hundred miles to the new gold fields. They formed a pitiful brigade, plodding along in the dust raised by the thousands who were riding west. They cadged food where they could, cut timber for other travelers who required it and helped wagons across the Big Blue, still a formidable barrier.

When they reached the Platte they lounged like beggars at Fort Kearny for a couple of days, picking up things that other travelers had disposed of because of overweight, and gearing themselves for the long hike west. They had only one bit of good fortune: because they were headed for the Rockies, they did not have to ford the South Platte. By staying close to its southern bank, they were sure to reach the gold fields.

In their passage they came naturally to Zendt's Farm, where stones had been laid across the Platte so that travelers could cross over to buy their last stores for the final push to the mountains, and it was here that Spade Larkin, weighing less than a hundred and thirty pounds because of near-starvation on the route, struck his great fortune.

He and five other foot travelers who had persisted to this point limped exhausted into the crowded stockade, and with one glance Spade saw that this store must be making a mint of money. Quietly he discussed with two of his companions the possibility of robbing it, but there were so many armed Indians camped nearby, and so many gold-seekers crowding in that they abandoned the idea. The other five bought a few necessities for the last stage of their journey and passed on, but for some reason Larkin stayed behind, fascinated by the stockade and the tremendous business it was doing.

'You want to help with the travelers?' Levi Zendt asked the drifter.

'Yeah, yeah!' he said. 'It's gold I'm after, but I need a grubstake, too.' So he got the job of carrying goods across the river to those travelers who could not make it to the northern side, and one day as he was packing goods to ferry across the river he happened to hear Zendt refer to his pretty wife as Lucinda, and in a flash he comprehended that this woman, stuck away in a trading store on the South Platte, was the girl in the newspaper story! He quit what he was doing and moved inconspicuously to the outhouse along the riverbank. Secreting himself within its dark and odorous confines, he brought out his tobacco pouch and carefully unfolded the clipping. There were the heady details: 'Miss Lucinda . . . granddaughter and only heir of Chief Lame Beaver . . . gold mine in the Rockies.'

He returned to work, churning over in his mind various possibilities as to how he might wrest from her the secret of the mine. In the meantime he would go on working as if nothing had changed.

On a winter day in 1860 he returned to the stockade after having gunned down four buffalo cows, from which he had taken the tongues, and as he threw them on the kitchen table he asked Zendt, casually, 'You ever know old man McKeag?'

'My partner. We worked together here for seven years.'

'Is it true you married his daughter?'

'That's right.'

'Is it true that she's the granddaughter of an Arapaho chief?'

'That's right.'

'Where'd she grow up?'

'Ask her.'

So Larkin sidled up to Lucinda as she was darning socks and asked, 'Is it true that you're the granddaughter of Chief Lame Beaver?'

'No,' she said, and Larkin's face fell. Then she laughed and added, 'Because he was never a chief.'

'Oh, but you were his granddaughter?'

'He was a great man,' she said quietly.

'Where'd you grow up?'

'Many places. St. Louis, for one.'

'I mean, when your grandfather was alive?'

'He was long dead before I was born.'

'Where did he live?'

'Just about everywhere between Canada and the Arkansas. He never went south of that because of the Comanche. Remember, I'm an Arapaho.'

'I know.' He hesitated, then plunged ahead: 'Did he ever live in the mountains?'

'Everybody did. Not the real mountains, but the foothills. The first thing I can remember is living in the mountains. Blue Valley, we called it.'

'What were you doing up there?'

Lucinda stopped her darning and looked at the prospector. 'What's all this questioning, Mr. Larkin?' she asked.

'The newspaper said you were the granddaughter of Chief Lame Beaver.'

'Oh, no! Levi! Levi!' When her husband appeared from the kitchen she laughed pleasantly and said, 'Here's another one who's heard about grandfather's gold mine. Tell him the story, because I have to get supper.'

So Levi Zendt told Spade Larkin all he knew about the last days of Lame Beaver, the two gold bullets, the obsession of Pasquinel, and of McKeag's finding him dead in Blue Valley. 'Where is this valley?' Larkin asked, and Levi told him what he had told a dozen others: 'You go up the Platte till you reach the fork. Keep right, then take the first fork left and climb fairly high, keeping the little stone beaver to your left. And there it is, blue spruce on one side, yellow aspen on the other and the creek comin' down the middle.'

'A creek?' Larkin asked.

'Yes. A beautiful creek.'

That night Larkin stole as much as he could carry from the stockade, grabbed his spade and started his solitary hike into the mountains. He was heard of from time to time, prowling the camps that others had pioneered, trying to find a place for himself along streams already overcrowded with men who had got there first. He went as far south as California Gulch, but repeatedly came back to the stream which many had explored without results: Clear Creek in Blue Valley. He pitched his camp there one whole winter, an act of folly, because it was known throughout the mountain area that the stream was barren.

When spring came in 1861 Larkin did not even know that a war was starting which would divide the nation. He had been without human contact for more than six months, and his concern was exclusively with the disintegrating clipping he kept in his tobacco pouch. Now he took it out again, sitting beneath the blue spruce outside his cabin door, and studied its reassuring phrases.

'It's got to be here!' Larkin said. 'This is where Lame Beaver found those bullets.' And with a kind of sullen fury he plunged back into the cold water, slashing at the gravel and uncovering at last a scattering of nuggets.

'Oh, God!' he cried, falling on his knees in the water. 'I knew it was here!'

For six weeks he practiced the most cruel discipline. He had found one of the richest placers in Colorado history, and he kept that fact to himself, panning the gravel and secreting the nuggets, because in California he had learned that when a man found a placer, the trick was to locate the vein which threw off the nuggets, for the nuggets were valuable today, but the vein existed forever.

Desperately he looked upstream of his find, but he discovered nothing. For a while he gave up placer mining and devoted his entire attention to the stream banks, praying that he might find the vein which had produced this splendid gold, but it eluded him. He became frenzied, more agitated than in the earlier days when he was searching merely for such gold as he could find in the stream bed. Now that was not enough. He wanted it all, the mother vein, the lode from which the real wealth sprang.

One day in June he saw with despair that another prospector had climbed the stream and was entering Blue Valley. For a moment he considered shooting the man, to preserve the golden secret, but then he thought that probably the man had a partner, and before he could take decisive action the man, a knowing old fellow who could read signs, was upon him and knew that Larkin had found gold. Methodically the old man cut four saplings and staked out ten feet, the allowable portion of stream bank, and proceeded to set up his sieves.

'Name's Johnson,' he said. 'See you found gold.'

'Found nothin',' Larkin growled.

'Don't see your stakes,' Johnson said.

'They're here,' Larkin said, hastily staking out the area just below his original find.

For two days the men worked side by side, grudgingly, for Larkin wanted freedom to search for the vein, and on the third day Johnson struck a rich deposit of nuggets and went berserk. 'It's here!' he yelled, dancing up and down, and before Larkin could stop him or arrange some deal, he was dashing down the mountain to inform Denver of the great strike in Blue Valley.

Within weeks the valley was lined with claims. Three times Spade Larkin had to fight off claim jumpers, and one newcomer said, 'The prairies are black with people coming out here.' From all over America and parts of Europe disappointed men who had lost out on previous bonanzas streamed in to try their luck on this great concentration. Each pebble in Clear Creek was turned over at least a score of times, and some men like Johnson took out considerable fortunes.

The valley was gutted. The aspen went early for building flumes, and the blue spruce vanished soon thereafter. The beaver were all killed off, and no deer dared venture from the hills. Huts of the most miserable sort sprang up on every side, and a loaf of bread sold for two dollars. Larkin, holding desperately to his original find, watched it decline week by week until it yielded nothing and he was forced into the indignity of descending from the mountain and going to Levi Zendt, brazenly asking the merchant to stock him with goods which he might peddle in the camp.

While he was gone, a man named Foster, from Illinois, a penniless veteran of the California fields, discovered the mother lode. It lay in a place that Larkin had not even considered, and it yielded $19,000,000, none of which accrued to Larkin, who continued to serve as peddler to the valley.

Now huge structures were erected to monitor the mines, and a railroad climbed up for hauling in food and taking down the gold. For three years this garish valley, without a tree or a house worth living in, poured forth its amazing riches, and then the lode ran out. The men departed and the gaunt dwellings stood vacant. The tipple and the trestles rotted in the sun, and the trains ran no more. Blue Valley became a ghost town, one of the ugliest on earth, with not a single feature to redeem it, and Spade Larkin was forced to turn his back on the grandeur he had uncovered and drift along the streets of Denver, telling newcomers that he was the man, yessiree, he was the man that found Blue Valley, and for a beer he would explain how a newspaper clipping, a little clipping from a St. Louis newspaper, had told him the secret that nobody else had ever been able to find, the secret of Chief Lame Beaver's lost gold mine. He became quite tedious.

How did so unsavory a man destroy a document as noble in principle as the Treaty of Fort Laramie? When word flashed to Omaha, St. Louis, Pittsburgh and Boston that Spade Larkin had struck one of the richest of all placers in Blue Valley, a prodigious horde of gold-seekers poured into the west, eager to accomplish there what they had been too late to accomplish in California, and most of them used the South Platte route, which took them past Zendt's Farm, where they spent the last money they had on food and equipment. Each arrival was sure to require a box of physicking pills, a quart of castor oil, two quarts of rum and a large vial of peppermint essence, for only these could cure the 'miner's complaint.' For Levi Zendt these were good years, and like his father-in-law before him, he banked his savings in St. Louis.

For the Indians they were not so good. Some travelers, a trickle at first and then a surge, studied their maps and saw that if they ignored the Platte, which wandered north and south, and chose instead a course due west from Kansas City, they would head straight for the gold fields over flat land and save two hundred miles.

This route was superior in all respects except one: it had no water. Animals perished from thirst and lack of grazing. Men starved to death because the deer and antelope stayed to the north, near the Platte, and the straight line became studded with graves. One party resorted to cannibalism, until only one man survived; Arapaho found him wandering in the waterless country and nursed him back to health.

The new route produced two lasting consequences. First, it brought thousands of emigrants onto land which had previously been considered useless, so that not only did gold-seekers want mining lands in the hills, but truck farmers wanted flat lands from which they could feed the miners. And who owned the lands they sought? A handful of Indians who knew not the meaning of gold or the rules of farming. Bronze-faced men like Lost Eagle kept appearing at the new settlements, complaining of trespass and depredation, and such constant complaining could not be endured for long.

Second, the new route doomed the buffalo. It cut the once-unlimited grazing lands between the Platte and the Arkansas into diminished segments; no longer could huge herds move freely north and south, as they seemed to require for propagation. If the discovery of gold had a devastating effect on the Indians, its effect on the buffalo was fatal. Within a space of time so brief that men would ever after marvel at the depopulation, the buffalo would vanish forever from this region.

Clearly, decisions had to be made, or Indian and gold-seeker would soon be at war. Ironically, the demand for action could not have come at a worse time. In Washington and Fort Leavenworth attention had to be concentrated on the civil war, and few experienced officers could be spared for devising new arrangements with Indians. Men who knew nothing of the west were given the job of managing them, and no attention could be paid as to how it was done.

Without even discussing the situation with the Indians, these men reached an incredible decision: tell the Indians a mistake was made at Fort Laramie, then offer them a new treaty which would give them a small parcel of largely worthless land containing no water, no trees and no buffalo, land whose only redeeming feature was that it could never possibly be desired by white men. And then conclude the new treaty with the solemn assurance that this time when the Great White Father used the phrase 'for as long as the waters flow and the grass shall grow,' he meant it.

The brutal task of persuading the Indians to accept such a one-sided revision was handed to Major Mercy, now at the army's Denver office, and to Indian Agent Albert G. Boone, grandson of old Daniel, who had had his own troubles with Indians.

'I cannot go back to Chief Lost Eagle,' Mercy told his wife, 'and announce that the other treaty is finished. Just because we say it's finished.' He was distressed that his government, without discussion, would void a solemn treaty which he had helped to negotiate, and order him to make it palatable to the persons affected.

'I can't do it!' he said in their Denver home, and Lisette encouraged him in his defiance.

'It's disgraceful, Max, and I'd have none of it,' she told him.

Together they drafted a letter to the authorities at Fort Leavenworth, warning of the consequences. The heart of their letter was contained in four propositions:

I. If the terms agreed to at Fort Laramie are unilaterally abrogated, there will be war across the plains. It may be delayed in coming, but it will be inevitable, and it may strike us just when we are most preoccupied elsewhere.

II. If the Arapaho and the Cheyenne are thus defrauded of their rightful lands, word will spread to all tribes throughout the west, and you must expect the Sioux and the Crow to rise in rebellion, for they will read the signal that their lands, too, will soon be taken from them.

III. If our present agreement with the Indians is now broken, as you propose, the settlers will later feel themselves entitled to take whatever lands we give the Indians this time. The rape will continue endlessly and within a dozen years no Indian will remain in this territory.

IV. Since 1851 the Indians have steadfastly fulfilled all obligations, doing nothing to violate the spirit or regulations of the agreement. For us to break the agreement, as you now propose, is morally wrong and a crime against the principle of treaties whereby civilized nations co-exist. That the agreement should be broken by the civilized partner while being honored by the uncivilized is offensive and the consequences should be weighed.

In reply, Major Mercy received the blunt direction: 'Proceed as ordered.'

In anguish he turned to the one man who shared his views; he saddled his horse and rode up the Platte to Zendt's Farm, placing the wicked proposal before Levi. 'It means war!' Levi said. Lucinda, when she heard of what was afoot, said apprehensively, 'This plays right into the hands of Jake and Broken Thumb,' and Levi posed the most difficult problem of all: 'How are you going to explain this to Lost Eagle? And men like him who staked their reputations on the honest intentions of the white man?'

Major Mercy was too distraught to devise any stratagem for handling Lost Eagle, so Lucinda volunteered to ride out to where the Arapaho were camping and to invite the chiefs to the farm.

When they convened Major Mercy started to explain what lay ahead, but his confusion and embarrassment were apparent to the chiefs. He finally sat down and left the job to Levi Zendt, who fumbled along, not hiding his disgust: 'In Washington the Great White Father, not the one you met, Lost Eagle, but the other one who won't be there much longer. His name is Buchanan and he comes from the town I lived in, but he isn't a very strong man and you can't depend upon him.'

The chiefs looked at each other and were relieved when Lucinda took over.

'Once more they want to change the treaty,' she said. 'They want you to give up all your lands along the Platte, all your lands along the Arkansas, and keep this little corner of land around Rattlesnake Buttes.'

This astonishing statement was greeted by silence. At any time such a brutal proposal would be difficult to absorb, but to hear it coming from three people whom the chiefs could trust was too painful. One chief, Shave Head, rose and stalked from the room.

Finally Lost Eagle asked in a weak voice, 'Is this a message from Major Mercy?'

'It is,' the major said sorrowfully.

'What reason can the Great Father possibly have . . .'

There was to be no answer to this question, for there was a commotion at the door and into the meeting burst the Pasquinel brothers, followed by Shave Head, who had taken them the news.

'Why?' Jake screamed as he rushed up to Mercy. Without waiting for an answer, he turned upon Lost Eagle, shouting dreadful accusations at him.

'Traitor! Old fool who believes everything he's told! Would-be man without balls!' He was so infuriated with the consequences of Lost Eagle's leadership that he spit on him, then whipped about, drew out his knife and gashed himself in the left arm.

Flinging the arm about, he splattered blood on all those attending, even his sister Lucinda, after which he screamed in a fury he could not control, 'It's war. It's death. The terrible day we cannot escape is here.' With that he sped from the room, dashed through the stockade and leaped on his horse, racing to share with the Cheyenne the shameful news.

An ignominious explanation of why the old treaty had to be broken and a new one signed was attempted at a later meeting held at the farm. Agent Boone described in honeyed words the impasse that had arisen. Using the canny type of persuasion practiced by his grandfather, he slowly pointed out that many white men were coming into the area, that they required land too, that the agreement of Fort Laramie had been overgenerous in its gifts because those who wrote it had not comprehended the value of the land—here he paused to stare at Major Mercy, stamping him as a fool—and it was only reasonable that the Great White Father in Washington should ask the Cheyenne and the Arapaho to share the prairie with the white man.

'He wants it all!' Shave Head protested.

Agent Boone ignored this unjust accusation and continued in his bland, conciliatory way. The Great White Father was by no means—not at all—unmindful of his responsibility to his red brothers, and in exchange for their land he was offering them many wonderful gifts: money, each man to get forty acres of new land containing timber and water, farm implements so that they would no longer have to hunt buffalo, seeds and other allurements. His voice fell to a deep religious timbre as he concluded, 'The land belongs not to you but to God. He allows you to have it only so long as you cultivate it. He does not want you to roam over it carelessly. He wants you to settle down and farm it, each man with his own fields.'

'How much is forty acres?' Broken Thumb asked, and the whole party stepped out into the open, but when the dimensions were indicated, the Indians began to laugh. 'Forty acres at Rattlesnake Buttes!' Broken Thumb cried. 'That won't be enough to feed one buffalo calf.'

Agent Boone returned to his deep religious voice, assuring the Indians that to the east, in states like Ohio and Illinois, many American farmers built a good life on forty acres.

'Have they water?' Broken Thumb asked. 'Trees? Good earth?'

'An honest farmer uses what land he has,' Boone replied.

'Where will we find our water?' Broken Thumb demanded.

Boone replied that wherever there was a stream, and wherever timber could be found, the Indians would receive their portion, to which Broken Thumb properly replied, 'But you and I know there are no trees, there are no streams,' and Boone answered, 'But if there were, they would be yours.'

Chief Shave Head asked, 'Will our lands touch the great Platte River?' and Boone replied, 'The Great White Father thinks it best that the Indian lands not reach down to the river, because the white men prefer to travel along the river and trouble might develop.'

'Then where do we get our water?' a third chief asked, and Boone replied, 'I am sure some will be found somewhere.'

It was a pitiful meeting, one of the most shameful the government of the United States had ever engaged in. The only plausible excuse was that the nation was preoccupied with its fratricidal war, but the fact remains that this abominable document was crammed down the throats of two of the finest tribes that roamed the west.

It was accepted only because Lost Eagle pleaded with his people to make one last try to live in peace with the white man. So eloquent was his speech that Agent Boone, in gratitude, handed him a bronze medal containing a bas-relief of President Buchanan, while clever soldiers passed among the other Indians, giving them leftover campaign buttons from the 1856 presidential campaign, each with a grim-faced portrait of the Great White Father, James Buchanan. In subsequent years braves would trade two horses for one of these Buchanans.

Broken Thumb and the Pasquinel brothers encouraged a good half of the Arapaho and Cheyenne to reject the treaty, so they received no buttons and treated with scorn those who had accepted them.

Now came the bad years. The followers of Lost Eagle found themselves crammed onto a reservation one-sixteenth as large as the area they had previously occupied, with no timber and no access to water. 'But,' as government officials liked to point out, 'in times past your people inhabited the lands around Rattlesnake Buttes.' To this, Lost Beaver replied, 'True, but in those days only a few camped here at a time, and the herds of buffalo were so great they could not be counted.'

Today there were few buffalo. In some seasons none wandered into the camp area and real hunger prevailed. It perplexed the Indians to see white men, their bellies filled with food brought from St. Louis, slaughtering what buffalo did remain for only the hides and tallow, leaving the meat to rot in the sun. Indians needed the meat if they were to survive.

The year 1863 was marked by actual starvation; the Indians would remember it as 'the year of hunger.' The buffalo did not appear, and even the most extensive forays to the north failed to find them. The chains of pemmican were gone by early February and the other meager supplies had to be severely rationed. On the streets of Denver half-starved Arapaho children hung about livery stables, fighting for the grains of corn that dribbled from the horses' mouths.

The farm tools which had been promised if the Indians signed the treaty never materialized. Swindling agents stole them, sold them to their friends, and then directed the Indians where to buy them, with 'annuity' money they had never received. Ammunition promised for the hunt was withheld on the logical ground that if the starvation became worse, the Indians might shoot at white settlements in their search for food. Once-proud Arahapo were forced to beg for food from any white they saw, and they would often appear at the side of a wagon train, terrifying the occupants, who expected to be scalped. But this was not the Indians' intent, and during this terrible year they took only such food as they could find. Malnutrition made them highly susceptible to disease, with diarrhea and whooping cough killing off many of the children. Fortunately, some of the older Arapaho died of sheer starvation—those over fifty—and the food they would have consumed enabled the younger warriors to survive.

It was also a year of incipient revolt, for Chief Broken Thumb, now a mature forty-seven and a responsible leader, grew increasingly bitter about the lack of food. In frustration he traveled from one group to the next, trying to determine what the tribes ought to do. Wherever he went he found the younger warriors preparing for war.

'We will not die in silence,' they told him, and he replied, 'If things are not better by next summer, we will have to fight.' At one meeting he said, 'Our first blow will be to kill everyone at Fort Laramie and take the stores.' One young brave warned, 'Not Fort Laramie, it's too strong.' But Broken Thumb called upon Jake Pasquinel to describe developments along the Platte, and Jake said, 'They are moving all soldiers east to fight in the other war. There's practically no one left at the fort.' Another young brave asked, 'Why not take Zendt's Farm too! There's food there,' but Jake forestalled such talk: 'They've been good to us. We'll leave them alone.'

So the talk always came back to an assault on Fort Laramie, and Jake found that the young braves no longer thought of the cannon as demons that roared when they were wakened. They knew that they were four-inch weapons which required three bags of black powder and much tamping, and when they fired they could wipe out a whole band of Indians, but this was starving time and the cannon would have to be faced. Jake assured them, 'There are ways to silence cannon.'

At his office for Indian affairs in Denver, Major Mercy followed the growing agitation with real fear. In vain he endeavored to alert his superiors at Fort Leavenworth to the true state of affairs, but found that they had no time for trivial matters like minor Indian uprisings. Indeed, their concern was how they might siphon off still more troops for the Richmond front, where Union forces were suffering one defeat after another, with enormous casualties. But even when confronted by this indifference Mercy felt obligated to place the facts on record, and he reported:

> I have known these tribes since before the Mexican War, and I assure you that never have they been in more sorry condition. Their buffalo are gone, so they starve. The robes from the buffalo have been sent to St. Louis, so they shiver. Promise after promise of food to eat and guns for shooting smaller game have been made by our government, and broken. I am not disturbed by what I am reporting. I am terrified. If remedial steps are not taken immediately, there has got to be insurrection across the prairie next summer, and all communication will be broken. Such forts as we have will not be able to hold out more than a week.

> Let me cite but one instance, which will be more eloquent than my guessing as to possibilities. The other day I happened to be riding on the left bank of the Platte and I came to a tree in which a platform had been built such as the children of a great Indian warrior build for his burial, and it was obvious to me from the adornments that some notable chief had died, but as I passed I saw the legs of the corpse move, and upon inspection I found that it was my old friend from 1851, Chief Lean Bear of the Cheyenne, a good friend of the United States. There being no food in his camp, he had taken himself away, and had buried himself so that the younger could eat.

> Sir, the Indians are starving to death, and we must do something.

> Maxwell Mercy, Major, USA
> 4 November 1863

A deadly escalation now began, and it would be fruitless to recite each incident that accelerated it. More white people kept crowding into Colorado, and they demanded more land. When a farmer took his land he insisted that Indians and buffalo be kept off. And when the Indians were constantly restricted, without food and sometimes even without water, intolerable things simply had to happen.

On December 19, 1863, two would-be prospectors headed west over the bleak central route from Kansas City direct to Denver. They ran out of water and food and were starving. Two more days and they would be dead. They were men from the Mississippi River region of Missouri who from their youth had both feared and hated Indians, so when in their extremity they saw five Indians riding past, apparently well fed, they had no compunction in gunning down two of them and wounding one of the others as they fled. Their tactic was successful, for on the dead Indians they found some pemmican, which kept them alive. When they reached Denver and recited their adventures, a newspaper reported the affair as one more example of superior American ingenuity:

> Sam Hazel and Virgil Tompkins of Missouri gave an example of quick thinking two weeks ago as they were about to perish at the Kansas-Colorado border. They spotted five Indians about to attack them, and before the redskins could launch their screaming, bloodcurdling charge, Sam and Virgil neatly dropped two of them, and found on their dead bodies enough pemmican to keep going. Nice work, Sam and Virgil. You are the kind of stalwart men this great Territory needs, and let the nervous sisters back east bother about their own problems. We'll take care of the Indians.

On March 26, 1864, a band of Indians from the tribe to which the two murdered braves belonged swept down upon a defenseless farm along the South Platte and killed two white men, lifting their scalps and taking three white women captive. This incident, which had long been feared by settlers along the Platte, threw the white community from Omaha to Denver into consternation, and men talked of forming a militia to control the savages.

On April 3, 1864, another farmer along the Platte found one of his good horses missing and signs that Indians might have been operating in the vicinity. Other farmers said they thought the horse might have been the one they saw grazing on the north bank of the Platte, but Lieutenant Abel Tanner with his group of forty cavalrymen from Denver inspected the site and concluded that it must have been Indians. They therefore authorized a punitive expedition, an abhorrent agency much used in the west, where the phrase meant 'we have no idea who committed the offense, so we shall gun down any Indian we meet.' When Tanner and his men came upon a group of Arapaho whose tipis were pitched a few miles from the established reservation, they surrounded it and executed forty-three men, women and children. When the last tipi was burned, the soldiers divided among themselves the horses and booty that remained. Of this action a Denver paper wrote:

> Forty-three dead Indians for one missing horse might seem excessive to our weak sisters in Vermont and Pennsylvania, the ones who are always telling us how to handle our Indians, but to those of us who have to live with Lo at close quarters, it is clear that only the most stern reprisals will keep him from slaughtering all white men along the Platte. To Lieutenant Tanner, who shows signs of becoming the best Indian fighter in the west, well done! To his brave cohorts, well done, lads, and keep up the good work.

The use of Lo as a description for the Indian was universal in the west and came about because the English poet, Alexander Pope, in his rhymed *Essay on Man*, introduced these thoughtful lines:

> Hope springs eternal in the human breast;
> Man never is, but always to be blest . . .
> Lo, the poor Indian! whose untutored mind
> Sees God in clouds, or hears him in the wind . . .

Many newspapers, such as the *Zendt's Farm Clarion*, recently launched by settlers who had built their homes within the shadow of the stockade, used the whole phrase, Lo, the poor Indian, but more sophisticated papers preferred the simpler Lo.

On June 18, 1864, a band of Indians swept down upon the South Platte road, killed four wagoners, scalped them and stole the provisions they were carrying. For six weeks no traffic passed along the road, no news from the east reached Denver. With merchandise blocked by the Indians, prices soared throughout Colorado, with flour rising from nine dollars a barrel to sixteen dollars to twenty-four in a three-week period. As omens of the evil days ahead, a plague of locusts devoured crops along the Platte and the river rose in flood, submerging a good portion of Denver.

A fearful quiet settled over the region, with white men afraid to venture far from their homes and with streets in the city barricaded against possible invasion. When rumors of a beginning assault flashed through the city, citizens broke into the army ordnance warehouse and commandeered rifles, then patrolled the streets. This was not childish apprehension but an understandable fear that Indians might soon be invading the city. After all, Colorado had fewer than three hundred soldiers to protect the whole territory, and if the Indians wanted to pick off isolated farms, they could do so almost at will.

On July 26, 1864, a rancher living east of the village of Zendt's Farm saw Indians making off with two of his cows, which they slaughtered four miles from his home. This time there was no uncertainty as to what had happened or who the culprits were, so once more Lieutenant Tanner and his riders scoured the prairie and once more they encountered a community of tipis pitched where they should not have been. It was hardly likely that the cow-stealers were lodged in this particular place, but Tanner and his men surrounded it and with a howitzer gunned down forty-seven Indians.

On August 13, 1864, a small band of unidentified Indians overran a peaceful farm some miles east of Denver and slaughtered one of the most attractive white families in the region, Clifford and Belle Barley and their two children. All were brutally killed, their bodies abused and then scalped. Their corpses were hauled in to Denver and put on display under the hand-lettered sign:

THIS IS WHAT AWAITS ALL OF US

UNLESS WE DO SOMETHING

The bodies of the children, dreadfully mutilated, caused men and women alike to burst into tears, and families from remote areas were brought for safekeeping into Denver, where they further inflamed public opinion with their own rumors of Indian horrors. The fear which had lain over the city for some months now crystallized into terror, and men began to talk in whispers of the only alternative they saw before them: 'We may have to exterminate the Indians . . . wipe them out.'

Such whispers reached Lisette Mercy, and she was filled with consternation, for during these bad times she had formed the habit of taking food and clothing to the Arapaho one mile east of Denver. For generations the Indians had camped at this site, near where Cherry Creek ran into the South Platte, and they saw no reason to alter their habits now. Chief Lost Eagle, along with several hundred of his people, pitched their tipis there frequently and met with Denver businessmen who wanted to discuss the future of the area. After all, he had visited President Fillmore following Fort Laramie, and with President Lincoln after the Treaty of 1861. Photographers had taken his portrait with each President, and the one with Lincoln showed two deeply worried men; it was difficult to guess which bore the greater burden: Lincoln, whose nation was being torn apart, or Lost Eagle, whose people were being exterminated.

Lisette Mercy liked Lost Eagle. She found him a compassionate man who desperately wanted to do the right thing but whose ventures seemed always to go astray. He was fifty-four years old now and his influence among his people was greatly diminished; they were listening to Broken Thumb and the young firebrands. The situation had become so desperate that skirmishes were occurring between the followers of the two leaders.

When the Barley massacre occurred Lost Eagle wanted to hurry in to

Denver to explain that it was an irresponsible act, one that decent Indians could not condone, but he was met at the edge of the city by armed militiamen who warned him, 'We don't want no Indians in here, not even you,' and he was turned away from land that he had once owned.

Lisette got to him in his tipi, bringing with her a clipping from the *Zendt's Farm Clarion:*

> The die is cast. By the horrible killings of the Barley family the Indians throw down the gauntlet and challenge us to war. Let us have war, and let us have it now. Nothing less than a few months of punitive raids against the red devils will bring peace. Let us show Lo, the poor Indian once and for all who these prairies belong to. Fight, we say. And fight we would except for the vacuum of leadership in Denver.

'My husband tries his best to make the people see the truth,' Lisette told the old chieftain, 'but we have no leadership, so nothing is done.' They both felt a sense of deepening despair, Lost Eagle because he could no longer direct his people in conciliatory paths, Lisette Mercy because she saw how ineffective her husband was in trying to provide leadership at a time when only a vacuum existed.

In politics, as in nature, a vacuum cannot long be tolerated; and two men were headed for Denver who would fill the void in startling manner. The first was the soft-spoken fifty-five-year-old one-armed general from Vermont, Laban Asher, who had led his volunteers with prudence and gallantry during some of the worst battles of the Civil War. At Vicksburg, the previous year, he had lost his right arm; his associates said that if he had charged more resolutely, he would have been far from where the bullet struck and would have taken one of the heights as well, but in his plodding way, with his arm dangling and blood spurting from beneath the tourniquet, he got his men to the ridge on time, and with far less loss of life than would have been incurred under some of the more heroic generals.

His job was now to bring some kind of order to Colorado Territory while defending it against possible incursions by Confederate adventurers who roamed the west. He was in Denver only two weeks when word reached him that Desperado Jim Reynolds, a Confederate renegade, was storming through the Arkansas River valley, threatening communications and trying to raise levies for an attack on Denver.

'Let there be no misunderstanding,' General Asher said firmly. 'My first duty is to keep this territory in Union hands.' Without hesitation he dispatched what few troops he had to the south, where Reynolds and four of his men were captured and executed.

Belatedly General Asher turned his attention to the Indian problem, with the newspapers and the business leaders supporting Lieutenant Tanner in calling for war and only Major Mercy counseling a more cautious approach.

Intuitively Asher sided with Mercy. He liked him, perhaps because he, too, had been wounded in the service of his country, so that his patriotism could not be challenged; or it might have been Mercy's calm cast of mind that Asher admired. The two men worked well together and began to devise a strategy for moving the Indians away from major trails and providing them with access to water. 'We've also got to feed them,' Asher said one day, 'now and for as far into the future as we can see. They won't become farmers overnight. It'll require two decades to teach them, and if they're to learn, they'll need better land. So feed them we must.'

When news of this proposal leaked out, the Colorado newspapers exploded. The *Clarion* led the way with a savage article:

> Now the dreamer from Vermont tells us, 'You must feed Lo, and be kind to him, and forget that he has slaughtered your fellow farmers like the savage he is.' He tells us this when our food prices have soared because Lo has cut off our freight and mail services. Well, we say to General Laban Asher, 'Go back to Vermont with your one arm and blind eyes and leave the settlement of the Indian problem to real men who understand the issues, men like Lieutenant Abel Tanner, who knows how to shoot them up till they behave.' We say, 'Give Tanner a hundred trusted men on good horses and he will settle the Indian problem in two weeks.' And he won't do it by feeding them at public expense.

'What can I do against such tactics?' Asher asked in his soft voice. He was a New England gentleman who refused to dirty himself with public brawling; he was an army officer who did not know how to respond when newspapers kept calling for the promotion of an inept subordinate like Tanner.

'First off,' Mercy advised, 'send Tanner back east . . . tonight. They're calling for fighters there. Let him fight.'

'No,' Asher said cautiously, 'if I do that, the newspapers will crucify me.' He paced back and forth, and for the first time Mercy noticed that the loss of the arm threw the concerned little man somewhat off balance. He had not yet learned to compensate for the missing limb, and in some strange way this made him insecure. Mercy's limp had made him more daring, as if his spared life had to be used constructively, and now he said, 'General Asher, you have all the right ideas. You must act upon them forcefully.'

But Asher drew back. 'Instinct tells me to play for time. Already some of the Indians are asking for tools for farming. A little more time and this public anxiety will subside. Then we can act.'

There would be no time. In January 1864 there was a man on his way to Denver who possessed a clear vision of how the west was to be and the determination to shape it to that definition.

He was a tall man, six-feet-two, forty-eight years old, broad of shoulder and piercing of eye. He was clean-shaven, and stood so erect that he seemed even taller than he was. He was heavy, from good eating, and he had a strong voice with a peculiar penetrating quality which made it carry over a hundred lesser voices, even if all were talking. He did not speak overmuch, and when he did, it was with a Jovian kind of finality, as if he had long considered lesser alternatives and dismissed them.

He was Frank Skimmerhorn, from some old family of Schermerhorns, no doubt, and he came from Minnesota. There, in the years 1861–62 he had become acquainted at first hand with Indian problems, for the Sioux, irritated by some minor alteration in procedures, had run wild and killed his parents, his wife and his daughter. A farm which had been worth twenty thousand dollars had been left desolated, and he had moved homeless from one Minnesota town to the next, hearing the terrible stories of damage done by the Sioux—a hundred ranches burned, two hundred people scalped, a whole section of the nation in disarray, and all because of a few fractious Indians.

He left Minnesota with his son, satisfied never to return. Rights to his farmland he had sold for fifteen hundred dollars, and with this he had returned to his childhood home in Nauvoo, Illinois, where he tried to piece together for himself an explanation of what he had seen during the Indian uprising, and one night after a church meeting it had all been made clear.

A farmer who had lived in Nauvoo all his life said, 'I never cared for the Mormons. Now understand, I didn't go to war against them the way some of my neighbors did, and I never put fire to their barns. But as a people they don't please me, and their idea of one man having fifty-three wives, which they did. Yes, they did . . .' He lost his thread and leaned against his carriage. 'What was my point, Skimmerhorn?'

'You didn't cotton to the Mormons.'

'Yes. Like I was sayin', I could certainly not be called their defender, but they did have one idea that made a lot of sense, a lot of good common sense.' He paused here to let that sink in, and Skimmerhorn asked obligingly, 'What was it?'

'They had done a lot of serious study about the Indians. Sounded a good deal like you, when they talked. Confused as to who the Indians were and why they behaved in the unchristian way they did. And then it came to them in a prophecy kind of. God sent them a message sayin' that the Indians were really Lamanites, the Lost Tribes of Israel. Yessir, way back in the year 722 B.C. when the Assyrian King Sargon took 'em into bondage . . . ten tribes . . . they never got back to Israel . . . just wandered about the world.'

'That's very interesting,' Skimmerhorn said.

'You know it's true,' his informant continued enthusiastically. 'The Indian medicine lodge, for example, with all that mysterious going-on. What is it really? The tabernacle of the Lost Tribes. And you talk about sackcloth and ashes in the Bible. Don't the Indians mourn by cutting their hair and slashing their arms? Seems clear to me they're Jews.'

'That would explain why they're so hellish,' Skimmerhorn said, grasping his informant by the arm. 'You said they were Lamanites? Now, just what does that mean?'

'I'm not a Mormon, you understand, but I've had my brushes with the Indians, so I listened, and as near as I could make out, the Lamanites were God's name for the Lost Tribes, and because they had known God and turned their backs on Him, he put a powerful curse on them, and darkened their faces, and turned all men against them. Skimmerhorn, if they knew God and rejected Him, it's our duty to hunt them down and slay them. It's our bounden duty.'

For some days Frank Skimmerhorn pondered this matter of the Lamanites, and he asked throughout Nauvoo for other recollections the villagers might have as to what exactly the Mormons had said during their unhappy stay there on their way to Salt Lake City, and he came up with a profound body of confirmation. The Indians really were the Ten Lost Tribes. They had been led to America by the Prophet Lehi and their faces had been darkened because of their sin in rejecting the Lord. To exterminate them was both a duty and an exaltation. They were an abomination to honest men, and the sooner they were wiped from the face of the earth, the better.

In a dream, brought on perhaps by too much listening and too much brooding on this problem, Frank Skimmerhorn saw that he was destined to go to Colorado, where the Indians were causing trouble among the gold-seekers, and put an end to that trouble. It was more than an invitation; it was a command. In the *Clarion* he wrote:

> Patient men across this great United States have racked their brains trying to work out some solution for the Indian problem, and at last the answer stands forth so clear that any man even with one eye can see it. The Indian must be exterminated. He has no right to usurp the land that God intended us to make fruitful. He has no right to chase buffalo over fields that we wish to plough, and the only logical answer to his depredation is total extermination. He and his ugly squaws and his criminal children must be exterminated, and the sooner this Territory gets about the job, the better. Today everyone cries, 'Make Colorado a state!' Only when we have rid ourselves of the red devils will we earn the right to join the other states with honor. Extermination must be our battle cry.

This letter was widely reprinted throughout the gold fields of Colorado, and men of all political persuasions began telling one another, 'That feller from Minnesota, Skimmerhorn, he makes a lot of sense,' and when Skimmerhorn followed with letters detailing how a determined militia could kill off the Arapaho and Cheyenne, others throughout the territory supported his policy of total extermination.

Of the public figures, only three dared speak out against this inhuman proposal. An Episcopal minister in Denver called it murder and got into trouble with his congregation, who had seen the four scalped bodies of the Barley family. General Asher pointed out that it was not the habit of the United States Army to sanction mass murder, and he was excoriated as a coward who refused to face up to facts. And Major Mercy cautioned against so brutal an action as the planned extermination of a body of people, only a few of whom had committed any crime and all of whom had had crimes committed against them. Skimmerhorn of course did not agree and launched a series of savage letters against him:

> Who is this so-called Major Mercy? A limping coward who shot himself in the hip at Chapultepec so he wouldn't have to fight in our present war against the rebels. Who are his friends? All the Indian-lovers in the west, all the lily-livered cowards who are afraid to do God's work in protecting this land against savages. And most important, who are his relatives? The Pasquinel brothers, of shameful report, are his brothers. He is married to their sister and he is more of an Arapaho than they are. I say, 'Colorado should be rid of this cowardly traitor,' and I give him warning that if he continues to spout his defense of the Indian, honest patriots are going to shoot him down in the streets of Denver.

Appalled as Mercy was by such invective, he nevertheless pleaded with his wife to avoid any public comment that might evoke further debate, but she was too much like her mother to allow such rantings to go unchallenged. Trailing Skimmerhorn from one Denver boarding house to the next, she finally found him in a hotel on Larimer Street and castigated him publicly.

Her agitation delighted Skimmerhorn, for it provided him with an additional target. He loosed a blast of his pen at her, and this, too, was carried in the papers, allowing him to recapitulate his basic theory that every Indian in the territory must be slain.

Such inflammatory statements brought the citizens to fever pitch, and they demanded military action. Unfortunately, no federal troops were available in the west, so a local militia had to be conscripted, with Colonel Frank Skimmerhorn as officer in charge. Promptly he declared martial law, promulgating these harsh directives:

> All Indians who wish to remain friendly are to report within twenty days to one of the undersigned locations and lay down their guns.

> After twenty days, any Indian encountered anywhere may be shot on sight.

Any material possessions found on a dead Indian belong to the man who brought him to his rightful end.

Frank Skimmerhorn
Colonel, Special Militia

The day after this order was broadcast, old Chief Lean Bear, whom Major Mercy had rescued from self-starvation, assembled a group of seven Arapaho, old women and old men who knew the folly of trying to fight any further. Under a white flag they marched to a surrender point in Denver, where Lieutenant Tanner shot the old man through the heart and sent the others scattering.

When General Asher heard of this outrage he summoned Colonel Skimmerhorn, intending to give him military hell, but as he spoke he noticed that the colonel was not standing at attention and was indeed smirking. 'Skimmerhorn!' he cried as loudly as his breeding would permit. 'Attention!'

The militiaman ignored the command and said scornfully, 'General, your days here are numbered.'

'Colonel!'

'I have friends in Leavenworth. And influential people in this territory have been sending them reports that you're not the man to deal with the Indians.'

'Skimmerhorn!' the slim general shouted.

'So if you're wise, Asher, you'll pack for a trip to Leavenworth and let me run this Indian war.'

'You'll take no action unless I order it,' Asher said slowly, his voice trembling.

'You're the commanding general,' Skimmerhorn said insolently. 'For the present.'

General Asher was not accustomed to working with men who showed such disregard for military discipline, and he realized that with someone like Skimmerhorn his personal authority had no effect, so he decided to try ordinary reasoning. 'We all know,' he said compassionately, 'that in Minnesota you suffered at the hands of the Indians. But really, Skimmerhorn, you mustn't allow the deaths of your parents . . .'

'Parents?' Skimmerhorn exploded, and it became obvious that he was prey to some kind of insanity. 'Yes, I saw my father shot by the Sioux. I was running from the barn when they killed my mother with a tomahawk. But what of my wife? They shot her twenty times . . . thirty . . . they scalped her. And my daughter. Nine years old . . . curly hair . . . you ever see a child nine years old scalped?' He became a monolithic block of hatred, his face distorted and his hands rigid. 'You leave the Lamanites to me,' he cried. 'I'll discharge God's duty.'

He stalked from the office, leaving Asher slumped in his chair. Pressing his one hand to his forehead, the general had to acknowledge that during this period of civil war he had no way to discipline the madman, and by the time the war ended, Skimmerhorn would be a hero and there would still be no possibility of discipline. His only hope was that Skimmerhorn's friends at Fort Leavenworth might arrange quickly for his recall, because in Denver there was nothing he could do. He had been beaten by an adversary he could not comprehend.

The Arapaho and Cheyenne were required by law to enter a restricted camping area north of Rattlesnake Buttes, and there the pitiful remnant gathered. They had no food, little clothing, no buffalo grazing nearby, few rifles. As a gesture of good intention they turned over to the military the three white women they had kidnapped from a farm.

They were willing to place themselves under the protection of the army because of the persuasive arguments of Lost Eagle, who told them, 'All men would like to stay out with Broken Thumb and wage prairie war as we have always done against our enemies, but I tell you that time is past. General Asher is our friend, Major Mercy is our friend, and he tells me that things will soon be better.'

When the major rode north to inspect the improvised camp, he stopped first at the village of Zendt's Farm, because he wanted to ascertain local reactions. Riding down the main street, he pulled up before the stockade and at the gateway shouted, 'Levi! I need to talk with you.'

From the log house Zendt and Lucinda appeared, and Mercy cried, 'Where is this insanity leading us?' but before Levi could reply, he heard a sound of bugles and in a moment Colonel Skimmerhorn rode up, leading sixteen of his militia, who assumed a military stance at the gate.

'This fort is under arrest,' he announced loudly. 'Zendt, you've been consorting with the enemy and everyone is ordered to stay inside until I give a command to the contrary.' Spurring his prancing horse, he shouted, 'Sergeant, shoot anyone who tries to escape. That's an order.'

Turning to Major Mercy, Skimmerhorn cried, 'I knew I'd find you here. Sergeant, note that Major Mercy was consorting with traitors.'

When Levi heard the extraordinary commands that Skimmerhorn had issued, he tried to argue with him, but from his horse Skimmerhorn replied with scorn, 'I do not converse with fucking squaw men.'

Zendt leaped at him, but Skimmerhorn pulled back and cut at him with his sword. When Major Mercy led the bleeding Dutchman away, the colonel cried, 'Sergeant, take note that the squaw man Zendt attacked me with intent to kill and that I repulsed him with my saber.' Leaving a detachment to guard the stockade, he rode back to Denver, already developing the plans which would rid Colorado permanently of its Indians.

When he was gone, Major Mercy made a fateful decision. Aware that

what he was about to do might involve him in a court-martial, he told
Levi, 'I'm convinced that damn fool had no authority to order my house
arrest, and I propose to ignore it.' Taking Lucinda by the hand, he said,
'That maniac has some crazy idea of wiping out the whole Indian race.
He'll probably start with the camp. I've got to warn General Asher.'

Zendt tried to calm him. 'The Indians in the camp have no guns.
There'd be no reason to attack them.'

'Skimmerhorn might attack anything,' Mercy warned. 'He's convinced
he's doing God's work.'

'More likely he's going to chase down the ones who didn't turn themselves in—Broken Thumb and his young braves.'

This reasoning did not satisfy Mercy, so he devised an escape which
involved Zendt's appearing at the gate while he slipped over the northeast wall. But as he started to head south to alert General Asher, he
changed his mind. Instead, he goaded the horse to the northeast toward
the Indian camp at the buttes.

He reached the buttes at dusk, approaching from the south, and when
he rode to high ground between them he saw in the declivity to the
north a confused mass of tipis thrown helter-skelter across the area
where neat Indian camps had formerly stood. He thought how difficult
it must be for the chiefs who had once led their people across limitless
grasslands to be cooped up in such a depression, with chalk hills hem-
ming them in.

He whistled as a signal to the outlooks who must be hidden somewhere in the rocks, but none appeared, and he realized that this tatter-
demalion group was without organization or guards.

When he had descended almost to the camp, two Arapaho on foot
came to inspect him, and he asked, 'Where are your ponies?' and they
replied, 'All gone.'

They recognized him as a friend of their tribe and took him to the
lodge where the chiefs sat glumly discussing stratagems whereby they
might get food for their starving people. That night Mercy stayed at the
encampment, warning the Indians to give Colonel Skimmerhorn no excuse for attacking them.

'We have no guns,' Lost Eagle said.

'I didn't mean guns,' Mercy explained. 'Skimmerhorn's a madman.
He'll use any pretext.'

'We've done everything General Asher told us,' Lost Eagle said pathetically.

'Steal no cows,' Mercy explained. 'If a white man comes through your
camp, let him go in peace, no matter what he does.'

'Without arms,' Lost Eagle said, 'we couldn't make trouble if we
wanted to.'

Talk turned to more pressing matters. 'When will we get food?' Chief
Black Knee of the Cheyenne asked.

'It's being discussed,' Mercy said lamely.

'Discussed! We're starving, Mercy. Our shame is as big as the earth.'

Every promise made by General Asher had been frustrated by Colonel Skimmerhorn. Every assurance of supplies that he, Mercy, had given these patient men had been countermanded. Two tribes who had been as faithful to their treaties as any in America were being systematically starved, after first being deprived of their land, their buffalo and their guns. Now they were being bedeviled by a maniacal civilian playing at being a soldier, and no one in authority had the courage or the inclination to call a halt. It was the darkest hour in Mercy's life, worse even than when he was left alone at Chapultepec, his companions seeing the blood and thinking him dead.

For the first time he was not proud to be an American soldier. The trickery whereby the ample agreement of 1851 was replaced by the niggardly provisions of 1861 could be accepted. Maybe adjustments were necessary. He no longer accused Commissioner Boone of double dealing with the Indians; white men required land, and they wanted to own the streams along which gold was found, and that was that.

But the present behavior of the American government was despicable, and he proposed saying so as soon as he got back to Denver. To coop up more than fourteen hundred Indians in a rock-rimmed meadow lacking water and to leave them there without food was insupportable, and he was convinced that if the real army in Leavenworth or Washington knew of it, they would demand instant reforms. He must bring the facts to their attention.

He told Lost Eagle, 'Trust me one more time. Hold off any action till I get back.'

'We listen, Mercy,' the old chief said. The lines down his cheeks were deeper now, the eyes more sunken, but the rocklike face was still one of surpassing dignity. In recent weeks he had absorbed much abuse thrown at him by young braves who refused to accept starvation any longer, but the only star he knew was to trust the white man. Men like Major Mercy and General Asher would produce food and some kind of control over Colonel Skimmerhorn.

'Until the new year comes, we will trust you,' he said.

'Where are Jake Pasquinel and Broken Thumb?' Mercy asked as he prepared to depart.

'East, toward Julesburg,' Chief Black Knee said, and he gave Mercy two scouts to guide him to where the dissidents were holed up.

It was snowing when Mercy left Rattlesnake Buttes, and at the rise he looked back upon this forlorn collection of tipis, this assemblage of men and women without hope, and swore that he would try to restore some dignity to them.

How beautiful the Platte valley was that day, white with snow along the banks and shimmering black where the dark waters ran. Ice had not yet formed, and the wagon trail which led from Julesburg to Denver would still be passable. In some ways, Mercy thought, this was the Platte at its finest, for its innumerable islands achieved a certain beauty as their sandy faces lay covered with snow.

We should be able to share a river like this with the Indians, he told himself as the guides led him farther eastward, but when he reached the rude encampment where Broken Thumb had assembled his braves and saw their pitiful condition, he realized that arguing intelligently with them would be difficult.

Dismounting, he limped across the snow-crisp ground and asked a woman for Broken Thumb. Insolently she pointed at a gray-brown tipi which had lost its two poles for controlling smoke. No matter, there was no wood for a fire.

Pushing aside the flap, he said, 'Broken Thumb, I have come to beg you not to make war against the wagons.'

'We're starving,' the Cheyenne said. 'The wagons have food.'

'The next two months are desperate,' he pleaded.

'We're desperate now.'

'Where's Jake Pasquinel?'

'Out trying to find food.'

'Oh, God!' Mercy groaned. He could see Jake doing some foolish thing, bringing the whole wrath of Skimmerhorn down upon him. Jake would come back with beef from a cow he had killed, or beans he had stolen from a rancher who would even now be posting to Denver to complain. As Mercy tried to anticipate the foreboding possibilities, Broken Thumb called for a boy to fetch the piece of paper which the Indians had taken from a wagon heading eastward. One of the young braves had been able to read it, and a summary had passed among all the warriors at the hidden camp. It was a clipping from the *Clarion:*

> At last a military officer in this Territory makes sense. At last a true hero has stepped forward to tell us what we have been eager to hear. On a visit to our fair city Colonel Frank Skimmerhorn told a group of his admirers, 'The hour is at hand when decency and fear of God shall again return to this Territory. The hour is almost upon us when every stinking, sneaking, crawling, sniveling, filthy Red Man in Colorado will be either killed or driven from our boundaries. At the long-awaited hour we shall expect every red-blooded man who loves his home to join us in exterminating once and forever the menace that has threatened us for so long.' Fine words, Colonel. We're behind you. In forthcoming fights we hope our soldiers will not be encumbered with Indian prisoners. And we hope what you said was heard at various stockades around here where Indians are allowed to associate freely with white men and where dastardly plots against our freedom are hourly hatched.

Chief Broken Thumb, now a man of forty-eight without illusions, drew his thin blanket about his shoulders and pointed to the clipping. 'Why do you tell me "Don't make war?" Skimmerhorn makes war, every day.'

'General Asher will take care of Skimmerhorn, I promise you.'

At this the Cheyenne warrior, who knew a good deal about soldiers, burst into derisive laughter. Leaping to his feet and making believe he had but one arm, he minced about the tipi, throwing out contradictory orders and giving a strangely realistic impression of the befuddled general. 'He will do nothing,' Broken Thumb said.

'I will,' Mercy promised.

Before Broken Thumb could respond, Jake Pasquinel broke into the tipi, and when he saw Mercy he moved swiftly toward him and embraced him, a most unusual gesture for this unyielding outlaw.

'Mercy, for God's sake bring some reason into this thing,' he said with anguish. 'These people are starving.'

'I know, Jake.'

'They're . . .' The half-breed's voice choked, and for the first time in his life, Mercy saw one of the Pasquinel brothers unable to speak because of an anguish he did not try to hide. 'Mercy, I promise you,' Jake said, 'if this doesn't stop,' and here he flicked the clipping with the back of his fingers, 'this whole territory is going to explode.'

'You used to want that,' Mercy said compassionately.

'I'm older now,' his brother-in-law said. 'It will be our women and children who will be slaughtered.'

Mike Pasquinel entered the tipi, a nondescript sort of man. He listened for a while, then said, 'Max, we're all going to perish—you and Lucinda and Zendt—all of us, if this is not stopped.' And suddenly Mercy saw his brother-in-law as a man of perception, a kind of God's fool who had watched and laughed all his life and in the end had seen visions of reality. His round, placid face betrayed none of the emotion that marked Jake's, but he spoke with a sorrow that was more compelling than his brother's rage.

'Max,' he pleaded again, 'you're leaving us no escape but to die in battle, and we shall die, every man here.' With his pudgy right arm he swept the tipi, and one after the other of Broken Thumb's men uttered the solemn declaration: 'We shall die.'

Deeply shaken, Mercy left the renegade camp for his long trip back to Denver, and for the first part of his journey he was accompanied by his brothers. They spoke of old days, of how happy Lucinda was at the stockade, of Clay Basket and her remarkable life, and of the irony they felt when gold was discovered at the place their father had prospected so fruitlessly.

'Do you wish he'd found the gold . . . for you?' Mercy asked.

'No,' Jake said. 'Indians don't need gold. They need space . . . and buffalo.'

As Jake left he said, 'It will be war,' and he turned on his horse and rode eastward.

Mike lingered, trying to say many things, but they were too confused and terrible to be voiced, so in the end he reached across his horse and embraced Mercy, 'You are my brother,' he said in Arapaho, and he was gone.

When Mercy reported to General Asher at army headquarters, two grimy rooms at the rear of a hotel, he found himself in real trouble. The general seemed preoccupied as he gathered papers together, but he took time to say, 'Mercy, Colonel Skimmerhorn has preferred serious charges against you.'

'That house arrest,' Mercy said scornfully. 'You know it was improper.'

'Listen to the charges. "Consorting with the enemy in time of war, disobeying a direct order of a superior officer, fleeing to the enemy with national secrets." '

Mercy brushed aside the inflated accusations: 'General Asher, a catastrophe hangs over our heads, yours and mine. I know what I'm talking about. I've been with both branches of the Indians, the friendlies in camp where they ought to be and the hostiles out hiding.'

'You shouldn't have been there,' Asher said firmly. 'Colonel Skimmerhorn ordered you specifically . . .'

'General!' Mercy shouted. 'We are one day away from total insurrection. To hell with Skimmerhorn. How dare he tell you, a general in the United States . . .'

'Max,' the tired Vermonter said, 'look.' He held out a dispatch from Fort Leavenworth:

General Laban Asher
Commanding Officer, Denver

Proceed immediately and by swiftest transport to this headquarters prepared to report fully on steps taken to protect Platte River valley from marauding Indians.

> S. J. Comly, Adjutant
> Fort Leavenworth
> 29 October, 1864

It was a shocking message. After having received scores of appeals from Asher for additional troops to control the Platte, Leavenworth was finally responding—not by sending the needed help but by withdrawing the only man who might bring order to the territory.

General Asher accepted this asinine decision with equanimity. If that's how headquarters wanted to run the Indian war, that's how it would be. Recovering the dispatch and tapping it with sour amusement, he said, 'I'm riding out with six soldiers . . . tonight.'

'Tonight!' Mercy exploded. 'Who'll be in command?'

'Colonel Skimmerhorn.'

'General, he'll destroy everything.'

'And I'm putting you under house arrest, Mercy. You may not leave Denver till I return.'

Mercy was stunned. He could not ignore house arrest imposed by a general of the regular army, yet he saw disastrous consequences if Skimmerhorn were allowed to run wild. 'General Asher,' he said quietly, 'if you turn your troops over to Skimmerhorn, some frightful thing will happen that will damn your reputation forever. The good work you did at Vicksburg with the Vermonters . . .'

'You're under house arrest,' Asher said curtly, and that night, on horseback, accompanied by his guard, he scuttled to the east.

Things could not have worked out better for Colonel Skimmerhorn. He had anticipated that Major Mercy would slip off to warn the Indians, and now he was rid of him, permanently. He had also expected to be placed in command of all troops in the area, and this, too, had happened. But he could not have foreseen General Asher's vacillation, siding one day with him, the next with Mercy, depending on who saw him last. That Asher was now recalled from the area and sent to a distant post could only be a sign that God approved his plan.

He, Skimmerhorn, now had the command, and he proposed exercising it.

On a cold November morning he assembled his troops, sixty-three regular army men under Lieutenant Abel Tanner, whom he gave a field promotion to captain, and eleven hundred and sixteen militiamen under the tactical command of civilian volunteers. Astride his horse, he addressed his troops in few words:

> 'Men of valor! This day we march against the infidel. We are engaged in a noble undertaking. God smiles down upon us as we march forth to rid this territory forever of the Indian menace. Forward.'

Those in the city who realized what was afoot gathered at the edge of town to cheer the heroes as they marched past, and no eleventh-century band of Crusaders setting forth to battle the Saracen could have been more enthusiastically acclaimed. After Skimmerhorn acknowledged the shouts of his well-wishers he sent small detachments ahead to arrest and hold incommunicado all farmers in areas they would be marching through.

They camped that night at Zendt's Farm. Next day, during a heavy snowstorm, Colonel Skimmerhorn performed a military miracle, one that would have done justice to a West Point graduate: he moved his entire body of troops, with five cannon, a score of supply wagons and forty ammunition mules across open land to Rattlesnake Buttes and maneuvered them into position at nightfall without being detected.

It may have been that the Indians were so lacking in food that their men were not strong enough to stand guard that night, but at any rate, Skimmerhorn, under cover of darkness, brought his cannon onto the ridge between the two buttes and directed his gunners how to aim them so as to blanket the sleeping area below. The men loaded their Starr carbines so there would be no delays during the attack and spent their time imagining the booty they could grab when the attack started.

With sound generalship Skimmerhorn divided his command into three segments. The center, under his leadership, would wait till three rounds of cannonfire had struck the tipis and would then move forth in a saber charge, cutting down those Indians who milled about in the confusion. The right flank, under Captain Tanner, whom he could trust, since he had fought Indians before, would circle to the east and come roaring in with a maximum charge to shoot down anyone who tried to escape in that direction. The left flank posed something of a problem, because there Captain Reed, a regular army officer, had to be given command, but Skimmerhorn was not sure he could be trusted.

'Captain Reed,' he said in hushed tones, 'I want to remind you that your job will be to cover the left flank. I don't want a single Indian slipping through your lines.'

'I understand, sir. Will they be heavily armed?'

'Armed? They're Indians. Shoot 'em down.'

'What I meant was, will they be mounting an attack in my direction?'

'Captain Reed! When the cannons fire, there will be great confusion. From the center I expect to compound it. Inevitably in this confusion many of the Indians will rush your way. It's your job to gun them down—all of them. Is that understood?'

'Yes, sir.'

At four in the morning Colonel Skimmerhorn summoned his officers to the ridge where the cannon waited. In solemn tones he told them, 'Gentlemen, we are engaged in a great venture. Much is at stake. If we can win this victory, our glorious nation will be safe for generations yet to be born. Gentlemen, God rides with you. Courage.'

In the motley camp below them at that hour were 1483 Arapaho and Cheyenne, distributed as follows: chiefs 14, other braves of fighting age 389, mature women past the age of sixteen 427, children 653. They were supposed to have no guns, but they did have a few. They also had some four hundred bows, many not strung because deer sinews were growing scarce, and nearly two thousand arrows, a good many of which were not instantly accessible.

The camp mounted no guards that night, for none were needed. The Indians had moved into this cul-de-sac at the express command of the United States government, and here they were supposed to be fed and protected. At last they were at peace.

At half past four a young brave left his tipi to urinate, and according to custom he looked in four directions, seeing nothing. At five Chief Black Knee turned on his tattered buffalo robe, thought he heard a noise toward the buttes, but went back to sleep.

At five minutes after six, just as light was beginning to appear in the east, there was a shattering explosion from the ridge between the buttes, and five cannonballs richocheted through the camp, killing four sleeping Indians and maiming seven.

The Indian who reacted to this surprise assault with greatest self-control was Lost Eagle. He was certain that some terrible mistake had been made—some mix-up of commands—and it was his responsibility to straighten things out. No American soldier would fire a cannon into an undefended . . .

Crash! A second salvo tore through the camp. With trembling hands Lost Eagle rummaged through his parfleche until he found his blue officer's uniform. Putting it on hastily, he hung about his neck his bronze Buchanan. From the honored spot above his bed he took down the American flag which President Lincoln had given him. He put on his high-crowned hat and left his tipi just as the third round of cannonballs ripped through the camp.

About him he saw men and women staggering from wounds and one girl with the right side of her body blown away. The tipis of two chiefs he relied upon were completely pulverized and the men were dead along with their women.

With great resolution he moved among his people, counseling them: 'Wait! I will find out what's happening.' Young men ran up to advise him that many troops were hiding behind the ridge, and in a way this news comforted him, for among them would be Major Mercy, who would know how to correct this awful mistake.

At this moment the central body of troops, under Colonel Skimmerhorn, swept down the slope leading from the buttes and charged headlong into the mass of tipis. Sabers flashed. Pistols fired. One man with a revolver fired six times at six different women, killing four of them. Horses ran over children, and soldiers with burning brands began to fire the tipis.

Amid all the confusion and the screams of terror, Lost Eagle stood before his tipi, waving the American flag and shouting in English, 'Stop! This is a mistake!'

As he was standing thus, Colonel Skimmerhorn spotted him and judged that here was the focus of the rebellion. Spurring his horse, he galloped down upon the old man, swiping at him with his saber, but the blade caught in the flag and ripped it, missing the enemy.

The colonel swung his horse in a wide arc and rushed again at the old chief, who kept shouting, 'Colonel, wait!' The colonel was by no means an adept swordsman and this time he struck Lost Eagle's tall hat, so he whipped out his revolver and would have ridden to within six inches of the blue uniform, so anxious was he not to miss, except that a cry rose on the right flank and an orderly shouted, 'Colonel! Here comes Tanner!'

Down from the eastern bank roared Abel Tanner, followed by his tested Indian fighters. They swept through the camp, killing and slashing and burning. Young girls, babies in arms, old women too feeble to run, braves trying to defend themselves—Tanner's men sabered them all.

Colonel Skimmerhorn, surveying the success so far, was smugly certain that this was going to be one of the memorable victories of the west, but from the corner of his eye he saw with horror that one part of his grand design was not functioning. 'Where is Captain Reed?' he roared, and his orderlies took up the cry: 'Where is Captain Reed?'

Skimmerhorn rushed up to Captain Tanner as the latter was setting fire to the last remaining tipis and bellowed, 'Where is that bastard Reed?'

Where, indeed? Captain Vincent Reed had been born in the city of Richmond, Virginia, of northern parents who were stationed there by the telegraph company. He had attended West Point and he thought he knew something about warfare, having served under General Pope in his long and futile struggle against General Stonewall Jackson. Those men were fighters who would face the enemy till the last bullet was fired, but neither would participate in such a slaughter.

Reed had had his troops in position. He was quite prepared to rush in for the kill, and he had positioned himself so that he would be in the vanguard when his men made their charge against the guns of the young braves threatening the left flank. But when he saw that the enemy had no weapons, that even their bows and arrows were not at hand, and that he was supposed to chop down little girls and old women, he rebelled on the spot, taking counsel with no one but his own conscience.

'It's the signal to charge,' an orderly shouted.

'Stand!'

'Captain, that was the third salvo. Colonel Skimmerhorn has already moved in.'

'Stand.'

He held his horse reined tight, tears of rage in his eyes. He knew that he was doing an unforgivable thing—he was disobeying an understood command in the face of the enemy—but he could not permit his men to participate in this dreadful massacre, not so long as they were his men.

'Goddamnit, Captain,' a sergeant shouted, 'look at 'em! They're escapin'.'

'Let them go, Sergeant,' he said.

'Look at 'em!' the sergeant screamed. 'They're the ones we're supposed to get.'

'Look at them,' Captain Reed said. 'Do look at them, Sergeant.'

And they looked, and there were men who sat their horses at that moment who would all the rest of their lives give thanks that on this day they were under the command of Captain Reed and not Captain Tanner, for the Indians who slipped past them to safety in the hills were old, they were young, they were crippled, they were young men with their arms shot off by cannonballs—and among them all, there was not one gun, not one arrow. They escaped, the most pitiful remnant of an enemy ever faced by a contingent of the United States Army.

It is not pleasant to recite what Tanner's men did that day, but it is necessary. The fighting continued for some time, since those few braves who did have weapons resisted with valor. It was not unusual for one Indian to charge a whole company, determined to kill as many whites as he could before he fell riddled with pistol shots. In its later moments, however, the battle consisted mainly of Skimmerhorn's militiamen roaring across the prairie in pursuit of some solitary Indian who had slipped through the lines. These were run down and lanced with sabers and then scalped.

Three hundred and eighty-seven Indians were slain: 7 chiefs, 108 braves, 123 women and 149 children; all but sixteen were scalped, even the children, for the men sought trophies to prove their victory. All gloried in the order, 'Take no prisoners.' A militiaman named Gropper rummaged through piles of dead, performing atrocious mutilation on the corpses, shouting as he did so, 'That'll teach 'em to kill white women.' Other militiamen, officers and men alike, unsheathed their knives and hacked away at corpses until regular soldiers made them stop.

Old men and women who tried to escape the flaming tipis were thrust back in, and four who volunteered to surrender were stabbed through the neck. The old wife of Chief Lost Eagle was shot eleven times, and survived; she lay quiet among a heap of dead, not even whimpering when one of Tanner's men scalped her. She was blinded by the blood streaming across her face, but she lay there simulating a corpse, and in the night she made her way to the north, bleeding not only from the scalping but from her many wounds.

Lost Eagle, thinking his wife dead, continued waving his tattered flag. Bullets sped past him, and men with lances, and to all he shouted with diminishing vigor, 'Wait! Wait! This is a mistake!' In the melee he wandered to the sector commanded by Captain Reed, and when the troops there saw the American uniform and the pitiful figure wearing it—an old man in a funny hat, with deep wrinkles down his face and glazed eyes that could not comprehend—they let him go.

Captain Tanner's men perpetrated their worst offenses against the Indian children. Many, of course, had been left without elders in the first few minutes of fighting, and as they ran wildly about, soldiers speared them. Others survived briefly, but were shot as they tried to crawl away. Some did escape to the prairie, but they were soon run down by horses and scalped before they stopped breathing. Their bodies would lie unattended to be devoured by dogs and jackals.

Two of the children, a girl and a boy, by some miracle escaped death.

They would be taken alive back to Denver and exhibited in vaudeville theaters, along with the scalps of their parents. Two other children were caught by Tanner's men, and they, too, might have survived, except that as the soldiers held them, Colonel Skimmerhorn rode up and asked, 'What are you doing with those children?' and the men said they'd captured them, and when Skimmerhorn snapped, 'Nits grow into lice,' the men killed them.

On his victorious return from battle, Colonel Skimmerhorn halted his expedition at Zendt's Farm long enough to compose the communiqué which subsequently flashed across America, making him a considerable hero at a time when other campaigns were going badly for the Union:

> Rattlesnake Buttes, Colorado Territory, November 30, 1864
>
> Yesterday at 6:05 in the morning in heavy snow, troops under my command launched a gallant assault against a heavy concentration of Indian warriors who were massing for a general war against the white man. Taking the Indian army by surprise, elements of my force swept in from three sides and achieved a major victory over the savages. Our side killed nearly four hundred Indian warriors while suffering a loss of only seven men. All hands behaved with gallantry except for one deplorable performance which will be dealt with in a special report. Exceptional courage was displayed by Captain Abel Tanner, who engaged the savages under heavy fire and he is hereby commended.
>
> Acts of heroism were too numerous to mention, but recommendations will be forthcoming at the proper time. As a result of this outstanding victory over a savage enemy, peace is assured in this Territory. The attack was doubly justified by our discovery of nineteen scalps of white men in possession of the savages.
>
> > Frank Skimmerhorn
> > Colonel Commanding
> > Colorado Militia

In his communiqué the Hero of Rattlesnake Buttes conveniently overlooked the fact that the real Indian enemies—Chief Broken Thumb, the Pasquinel brothers and their renegades—were still at large. Skimmerhorn had killed the women; the warriors would be heard from later, in terrible fashion.

News of his victory reached Denver the day after the massacre, and when he marched victoriously into the city he found throngs waiting to cheer the man who had saved Colorado from the red devils.

In the brief years since the gold rush, Denver had become an attractive town of 3500, with doctors and real estate agents vying for office space with meat markets and bakeries, and citizens were relieved to know that they were safe from further Indian threats. The ladies of Denver, in silk and brocade, entertained Skimmerhorn in their homes, while three stores on Blake Street gained favorable publicity by extending him credit, which he used freely.

Meetings were held and he was awarded medals from grateful citizens. St. John's convened a special thanksgiving service at which prayers were offered and at which the colonel spoke with becoming modesty. He told of how difficult the battle had been and of the extraordinary courage displayed by Captain Tanner and his men on the right flank.

As to the left flank, ugly rumors had begun to circulate through Denver that Captain Reed had behaved with less than heroism, and some even said he had been an outright coward. Captain Tanner told one newspaperman, 'Far be it from me to question the courage of a fellow officer, but when the bullets started whizzing, he had skedaddled.'

The rumors magnified, and some of Reed's own men began saying that he had been terrified at the sound of the cannon and had tears in his eyes. The issue was joined when Colonel Skimmerhorn filed official court-martial charges against his aide: 'Refusing to obey a lawful command, cowardice in the face of the enemy, conduct unbecoming an officer.' When General Asher returned from Fort Leavenworth to find himself something of a hero for having appointed Colonel Skimmerhorn to a command position from which he could settle the Indian question 'permanently,' he thought first that he would convene a full-scale public court-martial. This would be popular with the territory, which was idolizing Skimmerhorn, but later he decided that with the Union racked by war it would be better to allow Captain Reed to resign silently and bear his disgrace as best he could, and that was his order.

'What should I do?' Reed asked Major Mercy and his wife.

'Fight to the last inch,' Lisette counseled.

'We know Skimmerhorn's a madman,' Mercy said, 'but he's a clever opponent and the people are in back of him.'

'Fight!' Lisette pleaded. When Reed hesitated, she said, 'If you allow them to throw you out of the army now, Vincent, you'll be branded as a traitor. You're finished.'

It was she who planned the tactic whereby the nation first began to question what had really happened at Rattlesnake Buttes. She was tackling a formidable adversary, for in the months of December and January, Colonel Skimmerhorn moved through Colorado like a triumphant Roman consul, giving lectures on how to treat the Indian and conducting church services during which he would utter long prayers about how it was God who chastised those who, having once known His beneficence turned their faces against Him. In these talks he dealt generously with Captain Reed, explaining him as a young man who had served his country well as a paper-work officer under General Pope but who had cringed at the sound of real cannon, and it was that little condescension which was his undoing, for Lisette Mercy had met General

Pope at one of her mother's dinners in St. Louis, and she wrote to him and told him that his aide was being unjustly accused of cowardice—and slowly the Washington wheels began to grind.

The major blow, however, was delivered by her own husband. In February he met a newspaper editor and told him that grave doubts had arisen about the affair at Rattlesnake Buttes—that Chief Lost Eagle had tried to surrender, that no arms of any kind had been found in the camp, and that men under Captain Tanner's command had performed atrocities.

The resulting story tore Colorado apart. Two members of Skimmerhorn's militia horsewhipped the editor of the paper, and leaders throughout the territory rallied to Skimmerhorn's defense. He became more popular than ever and won national acclaim by volunteering to raise a militia which would clean out the Indians in Utah.

But nagging little things kept cropping up, and in March 1865 General Harvey Wade, a slight man who tolerated no nonsense, appeared in Denver with five assistants to assess the grave charges that were being made against the conduct of American troops. The city, having taken Colonel Skimmerhorn to its heart, was very cool toward the diminutive stranger whose investigation might diminish their hero. He treated them the same way.

'This is an impartial inquiry into the general events that occurred at Rattlesnake Buttes last November,' he announced when the panel convened, 'and in particular, into the conduct under fire of Captain Vincent Reed, against whom the gravest charges have been lodged.' At the Denver Hotel, under his skillful questioning, he began to penetrate the miasma engulfing this sorry affair. Within two days he satisfied himself and the board that General Laban Asher had been incompetent and morally supine. The Vermonter left the hearing room a man destroyed, and as he went, he paused to look at Major Mercy, who had predicted such a consequence.

General Wade then proceeded to interrogate the Zendts. 'You're half-Indian?' he asked Lucinda, and when she acknowledged this, he directed the court to take that into account when weighing her testimony. The Zendts told of how Colonel Skimmerhorn had placed their stockade under arrest to prevent them from warning the Indians . . .

'Hearsay, you are guessing at his motives,' General Wade snapped.

Zendt showed the saber cut Skimmerhorn had inflicted on him, and Wade asked brusquely, 'You admit you made a move toward him, don't you?' and when Levi nodded, Wade snapped, 'I'd cut you, too.' But when Levi repeated the insult Skimmerhorn had thrown at him, Wade made no comment.

He summoned Maxwell Mercy and listened intently as the major outlined step by step the insanities of Colonel Skimmerhorn, but in the end he asked three damaging questions: 'Are you half brother to the Pasquinels? Did you seek them out prior to the battle? Did you break house arrest to do so?' Mercy's truthful answers to these questions damaged his credibility with the board, and he knew it.

Then Wade tackled the matter of the battle itself, and here Captain Tanner proved a bulwark of support. He said he had served under many commanders, but none finer than Colonel Skimmerhorn. He detailed the battle plans and the colonel's heroic behavior. He indicated sixteen of his men who would verify his testimony, and one after another paraded to the witness stand to tell of Skimmerhorn's bravery under fire.

Next the city of Denver provided a score of witnesses to testify that if there had been confusion in the command, it lay with General Asher and never with Colonel Skimmerhorn, after which two clergymen volunteered the information that Skimmerhorn was a religious man who had preached in their churches, a man of the most stalwart integrity.

The whole city was backing Skimmerhorn, and farmers from along the Platte were moving into town to give him support if he required it. Members of the militia, who considered themselves on trial as much as their colonel, rallied round, and there was a general feeling that the city might blow up if General Wade and his commission dared condemn Skimmerhorn.

Zendt wanted to know why they couldn't ask General Wade to put Captain Reed on the stand to tell the real truth, but Mercy pointed out that Wade would never allow Reed to testify against the colonel, because Reed himself was on trial as a coward, the gravest charge that could be brought against an officer. Only Lisette Mercy remained convinced that some way would be found to break down this preposterous façade.

She was in a store buying some cloth when she heard a young girl who clerked there saying to a friend, 'If they want the truth, they should ask Jimmy. He says it was horrible.'

With considerable self-control Lisette refrained from asking any questions that would betray her interest. She ran home to tell her husband what she had heard. 'We must find out who Jimmy is,' Mercy said, and Lucinda went back to the store and engaged the girl in conversation. She discovered that Jimmy was the girl's brother, a young member of the militia, and that when telling his sister of what he had seen, he had vomited.

They found Jimmy Clark at one of the barracks, and five minutes' conversation satisfied them that here was a young man of conscience who was revolted almost to the point of losing his sanity by what he had seen at Rattlesnake Buttes, and they got word of his existence to General Wade.

Jimmy Clark's testimony shocked both the court and the nation. Quietly and with considerable patience General Wade led the nervous young man along, step by painful step, halting the interrogation whenever Jimmy wiped his eyes or tried to control his breath.

'You saw men of your command use their sabers on girl children who were running away?'

'Yessir, cut right through them.'

'You saw men whose names you know discharge their revolvers in the faces of little boys?'

'Yessir, four times.'

'You told us of only two.'

'The other time was when these men were holding two children, and Colonel Skimmerhorn rode up and said, "Nits grow into lice," and the men shot that pair too.'

'Now, this next question is most important, Private Clark, and before you answer, I want you to remember that you are under oath.'

'Yessir.'

'Did you see men of your command moving among the dead with knives in their hands?'

'I did.'

'What were they doing?'

'Cutting off the breasts of women.'

General Wade took a deep breath and asked solemnly, 'You yourself saw soldiers cutting off the breasts of dead women?'

'One of them wasn't dead, sir.'

Here Clark started to gag, but all he could do was heave, and General Wade directed a corporal to give him a drink of water.

'Did you, with your own eyes, see men of your unit scalp dead Indians?'

'Yessir, they brought the scalps to Denver and held an exhibition, along with the two children.' Seeing that General Wade was puzzled by this revelation, he explained, 'In the theater.'

'Theater!' Wade roared. 'Sergeant Kennedy, were Indian prisoners exhibited in a public theater?'

'Yessir,' an orderly announced. 'At the Apollo Theater. Admission fifteen cents.'

'Oh, my God,' the general exploded, and for that day the hearings were halted.

Next morning when Jimmy Clark appeared to resume his testimony he was not easily recognizable. It was obvious that he had been beaten brutally. His lips were cut and his eyes blackened. One arm hung limp at his side. When he took the stand, General Wade asked, 'Private Clark, do you wish to tell this court of inquiry what happened to you since we last saw you?'

'I stumbled, sir.'

'You stumbled?'

'Yessir.'

'Is that all you wish to tell us?'

'Yessir.'

'Stenographer, let the record show that this morning Private Clark appeared with his lips cut, his eyes blackened—both of them—with a heavy welt across his chin and with one arm hanging limp. He stumbled.'

There was a spell of quietness in the courtroom, with only the sound of the scratching pen, and then General Wade spoke. 'Only a few questions today. Did you, during the fight, have an opportunity to see the Indian chief known as Lost Eagle.'

'I did, sir.'

'Tell us under what circumstances.'

'It was late in the battle, sir, and this old man came headin' toward me, and at first I thought he was one of us because he had on an army uniform, but it was old style, and then I saw he was an Indian. He was carryin' half a flag and around his neck he had a brass medal, about this big.'

'How could you tell it was a medal?'

'Because when he saw me he supposed I was going to shoot him, and he held out his hands like this, with the torn flag in one hand, and he said, "It's a mistake." '

'Did you also see a Cheyenne chief called White Antelope?'

'I did, sir.'

'Tell the court under what circumstances.'

'Me and Ben Willard—he's a half-breed guide—when we went into the center of the tipis we saw this old man, maybe seventy. You wouldn't believe it. He just stood there with his arms folded while the soldiers shot at him, and he was singin'.'

'Singing?'

'Yessir, in a strong voice. I asked Ben Willard what he was singin', and Ben listened and told me, "His death chant," and the old man chanted, "Only the earth and the mountains, nothin' lives except the earth and the mountains." Then three soldiers came at him at once and gunned him down and one ripped off his pants and cut off his balls, and Ben Willard shouted, "What in hell are you doin'?" and the man said, "Tobacco pouch." '

This testimony produced another silence, after which General Wade coughed, as if he were about to launch into a crucial part of the testimony. 'I understand that you overheard Captain Reed giving orders that day.'

'Yessir, three times. I was servin' with Captain Tanner, and when Reed didn't charge, he grew furious. "Run over there and tell him to get goin'," Captain Tanner told me, and when I reached Reed's command post I told him, "You're supposed to charge," but he said, "Those Indians have no guns, or anything else." '

'Then what did he say?'

' "Stand." '

'Is that all?'

'Yessir, and we stood.'

'What happened the second time?'

'About halfway through the fight Captain Tanner saw that some Indian women were escapin' through a pass in the rocks, and he grabbed me and shouted, "Tell that damned coward Reed he's supposed to stop them," and I ran across the battlefield and told Reed, "Captain Tanner says you're supposed to stop them." And Reed told me, "Let them go through." '

'Did you do so?'

'Yessir. And I did not want to serve with Captain Tanner any more, so I stayed with Reed, and at the end of the battle, when we saw what the other soldiers were doin' to the dead bodies, he asked me, "What's the matter, Clark?" and I told him, "I'm sick," and he said, "We should all be sick this day." '

General Wade coughed again and said in a low voice, 'Now, Private Clark, this court would like to hear specifically why you were sick.'

The young militiaman looked helplessly at the bank of officers and mumbled, 'Well, like I said . . .'

'No, you haven't said.'

Clark appealed to the general. 'I don't know the words, sir. The proper words, that is.'

Wade left his judge's seat and whispered with Clark for a few minutes, then returned to his chair. To the other members of the court he explained, 'I was telling him the words we use.' To Clark he said, 'Now tell us why you were sick.'

'Well, sir, there was this man with a very sharp knife, and he looked around until he found a dead Indian woman, and with his knife he cut away her private parts.'

There was a deathly hush in the room, then General Wade's quiet voice asking, 'And what did he do with them?'

'Jammed them down over his saddle horn, sir.'

'How often did he do this?'

'He went to six different women.'

'And you saw this with your own eyes?'

'Yessir.'

Such testimony seemed so improbable that the members of the court were stunned. Finally a young colonel asked, 'Private Clark, do you appreciate the significance of the oath you took at the beginning of your testimony?'

'I do. I'm a religious man.'

'General Wade, can I have this man sworn again?'

'He's been sworn once.'

'I'd feel easier, under the circumstances.'

So Jimmy Clark was sworn again, and the young colonel asked, 'Did you, yourself, in person, see Colonel Skimmerhorn ride up to soldiers who were holding an Indian girl and an Indian boy and command them to kill them?'

'No, sir. He gave no command.'

'In your previous testimony you said he did.'

'No, sir, if you'll excuse me, sir. What I said was that he rode up to the men and said, "Nits grow into lice," and it was after that the men killed them.'

Jimmy Clark's testimony created a sensation in Denver, but it was unsubstantiated, so General Wade summoned every man who had stood behind Captain Reed that day. The first thirty militiamen refused to testify, or testified in noncommittal ways, but then Wade got to a handful of regular army men, and with revulsion they not only verified what Clark had said but added hideous details of their own, and one man broke into tears, after which General Wade asked in a fatherly way, 'Son, why didn't you step forward like Private Clark and testify to these facts? Why did you make me drag you in here like a criminal and force the truth out of you?'

The man looked dumbly at the general, shrugged his shoulders in a confusion that was obviously painful and said in a whisper, 'I thought it was all an awful mistake.'

The inquiry ended, and Captain Reed was sent back east to a cleaner war, carrying with him a letter of commendation for having behaved in accordance with the highest standards of his profession.

General Wade and the court did not have the power to punish Skimmerhorn, who was not responsible to the United States Army, but they could issue a bitter rebuke to the self-appointed hero:

> Rarely in military history has there been a battle communiqué more mendacious and self-aggrandizing than the one issued by Colonel Skimmerhorn at Zendt's Farm on the day after his attack upon an undefended Indian village whose occupants were unarmed and eager to surrender. Each phrase in that communiqué merits individual analysis, but four will suffice to show the quality of the whole. 'A heavy concentration of Indian warriors' turns out to be 403 men of fighting age and 1,080 women and children. 'Engaged savages under heavy fire' means that Colonel Skimmerhorn's men were free to hack at will, since the enemy had few guns. The 'exceptional courage of Captain Abel Tanner' means that he allowed men under his command to commit the most heinous atrocities which this court has ever heard of. 'Peace is assured in this Territory' means that the prairies are now aflame and war is everywhere, brought on by this man's intemperate action. Special comment must be made about the last sentence of the communiqué, for it is both perfidious and imprecise. The nineteen white scalps used to justify the attack turn out to have been one scalp, very old and possibly not from a white man, and it is unclear whether the savages referred to were the Indians or Colonel Skimmerhorn's own men.

The report, when it reached the streets, evoked a blind fury, and Sergeant Kennedy had to warn General Wade that it would not be prudent for him to appear in public, for there was talk of hanging him, but the little soldier pushed his advisor aside and walked boldly to where his horses waited for the ride back to Leavenworth, reminding Kennedy in a loud voice that the men who might want to hang him were more accustomed to dealing with women and children than with a soldier who stood ready to put a bullet through them if they made a move.

Nevertheless, on the day following Wade's departure, one of Skimmerhorn's supporters ambushed young Jimmy Clark and shot him dead in full daylight at a main intersection.

Some sixty persons witnessed the murder, and saw clearly who had done it—a broken-down prospector who had been paid fifteen dollars for the job—but no one would testify against him. Under the circumstances, the murderer had to be released. He was slipped another fifteen dollars and was seen no more.

This doleful event received scant notice because a hurricane had begun to sweep the prairies. After the massacre at Rattlesnake Buttes, Chief Broken Thumb, who escaped death by refusing to enter the reservation, assumed command of the two tribes, with Jake Pasquinel as his first lieutenant, and the spirit of revenge that animated these men made disaster inevitable.

Major Mercy was dispatched from Denver to offer the tribes any reasonable concessions if only they would lay down their arms and accept a permanent peace guaranteed by Washington, and on a wintry day in a tipi north of the Platte he met with the three crucial leaders for the last time. As at their first meeting, Jake Pasquinel sat in the middle, his face old and scarred and without even a flicker of hope. To his left sat Broken Thumb, lost in a bitter hatred. To Pasquinel's right sat Lost Eagle, smaller now but still wearing his funny hat. How pitiful these men seemed, confused remnants of tribes that had once defined and protected an empire, how lost in time, how utterly beyond rescue.

'You're brave to come here,' Jake conceded bitterly.

'I come with a final offer . . . real peace.'

Broken Thumb and Jake laughed in his face, and the former snarled. 'Get out.'

'I am ashamed,' Mercy began.

'Ashamed?' Pasquinel exploded. 'Hundreds dead—old men and old women, children too—and you're ashamed. Mercy, go before we kill you.'

'Get out!' Broken Thumb repeated.

'Lost Eagle,' Mercy said softly, 'cannot we . . .'

'He is not to speak,' Pasquinel shouted. 'He betrayed us. Everything he said was lies.'

Mercy pushed Jake away and went to the old chief, but no words were spoken, for Lost Eagle had only tears—the time for words was lost.

'Can't we talk reason?' Mercy pleaded, but Broken Thumb refused him the dignity of an answer.

It was Jake who spoke for the Indians now. 'It will be war . . . and murder . . . and burning . . . all along the Platte.'

'Oh, God!' Mercy cried, close to tears. 'It mustn't end this way.'

'Get out,' Broken Thumb said, and he called for braves to take the major away, but Mercy broke loose and came back to Jake and took him by the hands and said, 'It should have ended differently,' and Jake stared at him impassively and said, 'From the beginning it was bound to end this way,' and the braves dragged Mercy away.

The two tribes went on a rampage, looting and burning and belatedly earning for themselves the designation *savages*. With either Broken Thumb or Jake in the lead, they would sweep down on unprotected farms and slaughter everything that lived, even the chickens.

They destroyed the little settlement at Julesburg and overran the army fort farther west along the river. The South Platte became a region of terror, with fiery assaults day after day. The telegraph wires were cut, so that no news seeped in to Denver, and the overland stage stopped running, for on two different attempts it had been waylaid and its passengers killed.

A Denver photographer remembered a portrait he had taken of the Pasquinel brothers, and posters were distributed throughout the west, showing two scowling half-breeds in Indian dress—Jake with a livid scar down his face, Mike with an' evil grin—and from the Atlantic to the Pacific, readers waited avidly for the latest news about the depredations of the 'Half-Breed Monsters of the Plains.'

Finally the killing became so rampant that an army detachment was sent out from Omaha to track down the hostiles. The tribes divided into two groups. One, led by Lost Eagle, surrendered to the army at Fort Kearny; the other, led by Broken Thumb and the Pasquinels, sent a message to Omaha that they would fight to the death.

In a pitched battle, the soldiers closed in on Broken Thumb, and although he could have escaped along the Platte, he chose to stake himself out on ground he had long defended. With seven stubborn warriors he fought till bullets swept the area, then stood upright, and with arms uplifted, began his chant: 'Only the mountains live forever, only the river runs for all the days.' He grabbed what rifles he could from the corpses about him and fired methodically until nine bullets ripped through his chest.

The Pasquinel brothers escaped this battle, and a cry rose from the whole nation set free from its preoccupation with the Civil War: 'The monsters must be slain.' And now a bizarre situation developed. Colonel

Skimmerhorn volunteered to conscript a militia of his former adherents. 'We shall track down the miscreants if their path leads to hell itself!' he proclaimed, and men from all parts of the territory proved eager to march with him again. All Denver applauded when he announced, 'Our punitive expedition sets out from Zendt's Farm tomorrow!'

His opening strategy was draconian. Distributing teams along a three-hundred-mile stretch of the Platte, he waited for dry and windy days, then set fire to the prairie, producing a conflagration so extensive that it burned away all edible fodder from the Platte nearly to the Arkansas. A pall of smoke hung over the area and wildlife for thousands of square miles was threatened. It was one of the worst disasters ever to hit the west, and it accomplished nothing.

Conquered Indians were already on the reservation. The Pasquinel brothers and their renegades knew how to slip through the flames, so even while Skimmerhorn was setting fire to the prairies, they rampaged up and down the Platte, burning farms and scalping the inhabitants.

But finally Skimmerhorn tightened the noose, leaving the Pasquinels diminishing territory in which to maneuver, and one wintry morning along the Platte, about twenty miles east of Zendt's Farm, a detachment of militia surprised Jake and pinioned his arms before he could shoot himself. Messengers were sent to the colonel with the stirring news: 'Jake Pasquinel has been taken.'

Skimmerhorn reached the scene about two o'clock in the afternoon, and within ten minutes, convened a drumhead court-martial. 'Guilty,' the men said unanimously, and no juster verdict was ever reached along the Platte. Two men threw a rope over a cottonwood branch, tied it around Jake Pasquinel's neck and dragged him aloft. The knot had been poorly tied, and for an unbelievably long time he kicked and twisted, strangling slowly as the militia cheered.

That night word of the hanging reached Zendt's Farm, and Levi got a shovel, saddled up a horse, kissed Lucinda goodbye and rode east to cut down the body and bury it. When word of this circulated through the region, it infuriated the Skimmerhorn people, who judged it a rebuke to their triumph, and they were so enraged that a squaw man should have done this thing, they stormed down to the stockade and set it afire.

Stolidly Zendt watched as the flames consumed his home, then had the bitter experience of being turned away by four different neighbors before he found one who would give him and his wife shelter for that night.

Only Mike Pasquinel now survived, a fattish half-breed, fifty-four years old and aware that there was no longer hope of any kind. By keeping to the low bushes that grew along the Platte, he made his way to where his sister had lived, and when he saw the ashes of the stockade, he supposed that she and her family were dead. But he remained hidden, and finally saw Levi Zendt and Lucinda come poking among the ruins to see what could be salvaged.

Cautiously he made himself known to them, and with equal caution they spoke. 'In this village you're bound to be captured,' they reasoned, 'so give yourself up.'

'No!' Mike snarled. 'Find me two guns. I'll fight it out.'

'Mike,' his sister pleaded, 'let's put a stop to the killing.'

For one brief moment Mike seemed to waver. 'Will they hang me?' he asked.

Lucinda was afraid to hazard a guess, so she turned to Levi, who said quietly, 'I think so.'

'No!' Lucinda protested. 'They didn't hang those three who surrendered in Nebraska.'

'They weren't Pasquinels,' Mike said, and with that, old bitterness took control. 'I'll hole up behind that wall. I'll shoot ten before they shoot me.'

It was Levi who made the decision: 'We'll give you no guns, Mike. You're going to surrender, now. Decent men live around here, and they'll see you get a decent trial.'

So they made three white flags from Lucinda's petticoat and held them aloft on sticks and walked slowly down the village's only street, with Levi and Lucinda shouting, 'Surrender! Surrender! We're bringing in Mike Pasquinel.'

As they passed the offices of the *Clarion* a shot rang out and Pasquinel crumpled to the ground. He had been shot in the back by Colonel Frank Skimmerhorn, who had watched each step of the surrender from the *Clarion* window. The editor, having been on the scene, wrote this eyewitness story:

> Vindicated! Colonel Frank Skimmerhorn, who in recent months has suffered contumely at the hands of the lily-livered segment of our population, was completely vindicated yesterday afternoon when he single-handedly shot the last of the Pasquinels as the half-breed was brazenly trying to commit further depredations in this town. Colonel Skimmerhorn can now hang up his guns.

Now that the threat represented by the Pasquinel brothers and Broken Thumb was eliminated, officials sought a true peace. Belatedly they awakened to the fact that in Major Mercy they had someone who understood Indians and who might possibly bring order to the chaos of recent months. Accordingly, they sent him north to deal with Lost Eagle and those few who were camped once more at that fatal spot near the buttes.

When Mercy saw the old man—bent, rejected by his people but still ready to patch up some kind of peace with the white man—he had to control himself severely lest he show his tears, for Lost Eagle appeared with a fragment of the flag Abraham Lincoln had given him and the Buchanan dangling from his neck.

'Was Mr. Lincoln really shot?' the old man asked.

'He was,' Mercy said.

'I am sorry for all good men who are murdered,' Lost Eagle said. At this point his wife appeared, miraculously recovered from her wounds but scarred about the head from being scalped. Unlike her husband, she was in good spirits. 'That day Man Above watched me,' she said, and they both proceeded to outline new plans whereby the surviving Arapaho and Cheyenne would get food and blankets.

'We owe you much,' Mercy said, and in proof he ordered supply wagons to come in from Zendt's Farm, and soldiers actually unloaded foodstuffs, and Lost Eagle told his council, 'See! It really is a new day.'

Two days later, when Major Mercy returned to Denver, toughs from Colonel Skimmerhorn's disbanded militia lay in wait and attacked him, calling him 'Indian lover,' and they beat him so savagely that he lay in the street for several hours before he could summon up enough strength to crawl home.

Lisette heard him fumbling up the steps, and ran down to throw her arms about him and drag him into their house. She did not cry, nor did she panic. With delicate touch she cut away the torn skin and washed him. She helped him to their bed and made him broth, which he could not take through his badly damaged mouth, and after doing all she could with salves and ointments, she said defiantly, 'Maxwell, we still did the right thing,' and with that assurance he fell asleep.

CAUTION TO *US* EDITORS: You are aware, since you sent her, that Carol Endermann spent the last weekend in Centennial advising me of your gratification that the work was going so well and of your disappointment that I was sending you too few scintillating quotes and summary generalizations. She cited three examples of the kind of thing you had hoped to get from me, passages which create the illusion of putting the reader at the heart of the problem:

> The Indian succeeded in his occupancy of the great prairie because he was able to harmonize his limited inner psychological space, hemmed in by ignorance and superstition, with the unlimited outer physical space by which he was surrounded; whereas the white man failed in his attempt to subdue the prairie because he was unable to harmonize his unlimited inner psychological space, set free by the discoveries of science and the liberation of religion, with the limited outer physical space, which he had cut down to manageable size by the wheel, the wagon, the road, the train and the permanent fort.

If an undergraduate student in whom I had faith submitted that, I would write in the margin 'High-falutin', mebbe?' If a graduate student of promise did, I would write 'Pretentious.' If an article in a learned journal, which I was called upon to review, contained it, I would write 'Professor Bates offers us a sophisticated disjunction, each premise of which is false, and the conclusion empty.' And if a trusted colleague uttered it, I would tell him 'Bullshit.'

> The Indian was set free by his discovery of the horse, but because he had no basic philosophy to guide his use of this animal, he allowed it to carry him back into a servitude greater than the one he had known when his only machine was the dog-travois.

This is what we call iridescence without illumination. It was not misuse of the horse that dragged the Indian back to defeat; it was the arrival of the white man on a superior iron horse. But there I go, doing it myself, and it is just as fatuously iridescent when I do it as when another guy does.

> The great mystery of Indian history is not his genesis, which becomes clearer every day, nor his supine submission to the white man, which constitutes his great shame, but the fact that he could not adjust while the black slave did. It is for this reason that we see today the former slave in a position of spiritual command, while the Indian has become the slave. The reason, I think, lies in point of origin. The Indian brought with him from Asia neither a culture nor a religion, whereas the black brought both from Africa—a poor culture and the wrong religion, but nevertheless some structure upon which he could build and a base from which he could relatively quickly learn to operate.

This is double-doming. It's fun. Sometimes it generates a usable concept, and it is invaluable if you're writing a daily syndicated column where you are obliged to appear smarter than your readers and the local editors. But it's only a game; it rarely produces anything solid; and it is intellectually undignified. What's worse, the example given is strict racism.

My strong aversion to this kind of writing stems from the period during which I served with the army in Korea. I was in charge of a billet used by newspaper, magazine and television correspondents, and each Friday the correspondent for a distinguished magazine would lug his typewriter into the bar and groan, 'Well, it's that time again, boys,' and he would type with bold beginning, 'So at week's end the free world could be sure of one thing . . .' And then we would sit around and try to discover what mind-boggling truth the free world had come upon that week. Everybody would throw into the hopper his most glittering generality, and finally some central tendency would emerge and the correspondent would type it out, and it always sounded just dandy, and when it appeared in the magazine it created the impression that only the editors of this journal were in touch with the infinite.

But two weeks later, if one looked back upon the earth-shaking discovery of the previous fortnight, one realized how empty it had been, how largely irrelevant and, usually, how wrong. History unfolds its revealing disclosures in a somewhat more stately pace and most often we do not recognize them as they occur.

I am sorry. I cannot write the way you want me to. I conceive of my job as placing the confused data of history in some kind of formal order, as interestingly as possible, and allowing the user to deduce for himself whatever misleading and glittering generalities he prefers. I would like to think that from my stuff illumination will begin to glow, slowly and without great conflagration, and I suppose that's why my two books have not sold spectacularly well at the beginning and why they are now being quoted by scholars.

Would it not be better if you allow me to submit my material in my customary form and then turn it over to Carol, a damned brilliant girl, to inject the kind of flossy conclusions your readers have come to expect? She can do it and I can't.

In the preceding excerpt there is no sarcasm. Because I realize that during the period I am writing about in this chapter, had the magazine I refer to been in existence, it might have published the following two paragraphs, and they would have been good predictions:

> And so, as the year 1861 draws to its close with the discovery of rich deposits of gold at Blue Valley in the Colorado Rockies, all men concerned with the Indian problem know one thing: that the ore-rich lands ceded to the Indian in perpetuity by the Fort Laramie Treaty of 1851 will have to be taken away from them, and the sooner this reclamation starts, the better it will be for the white man . . . and for the Indian.

> And so, as the year 1864 draws to its bloody close with the massacre at Rattlesnake Buttes, even reasonable men are concluding that the Indian will have to be exterminated, for coexistence of any kind has been proved impossible. Blood will flow across the prairies within six months, and in the end the Indians will be either wiped out or chased from Colorado soil, and the fault will be theirs, because they obstinately refuse to live the way the white man lives, and this cannot be tolerated.

The press. You may want to pay some attention to Peter Held, the editor of the *Zendt's Farm Clarion.* Son of a German printer and an English schoolteacher, he was born in Connecticut, and hauled a Columbian printing press from there to Pittsburgh, to Cincinnati, to Franklin, to St. Joseph, publishing newspapers at each stop. An ardent abolitionist, for economic rather than sentimental reasons, being convinced that slavery was not profitable, he watched through a haze of tar and feathers as his press was thrown into the Missouri by St. Joseph slaveholders, fished it out and hauled it along the Platte to Zendt's Farm, where he published one of the most vigorous dailies in Colorado Territory. His violent animosity to the Indian stemmed from the fact that during his painful hike along the Platte his party was attacked by Kiowas and his younger son killed.

He was a manifest-destiny man and proposed that the United States go to war with Great Britain over Oregon, with Mexico over the lands west of Texas, with France over islands in the Caribbean, with Russia over Alaska, and with Spain over almost any pretext. He saw clearly that irresistible forces of nationalism were in movement which must ultimately throw American settlers into all corners of the continent, and he preached that the sooner this occurred, the better.

In the agonizing sheep wars of his later years he naturally favored extermination of the sheepmen, but in the battle for free coinage of silver he sided with the little man, for he better than most understood how the west was being strangled by eastern bankers and railroad men who held the nation to the gold standard. He was an unlovely, cantankerous, vengeful man, never loath to distort the news to serve his own preconceived ends. You may not care to exhibit him as a prime example of the western editor, but there were many like him.

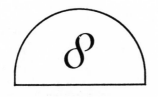

THE
COWBOYS

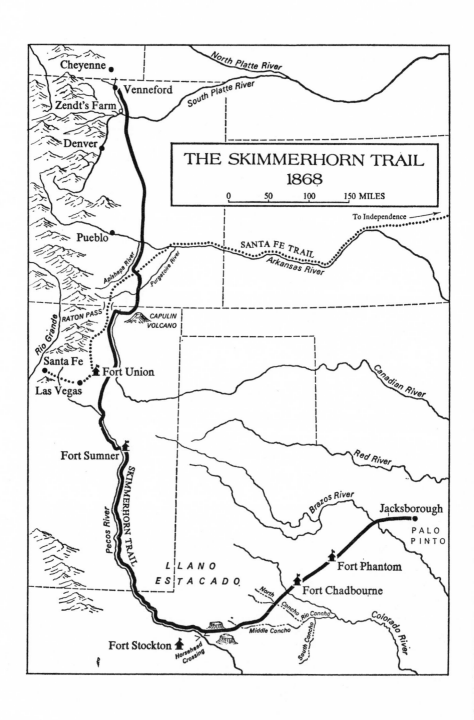

It BECAME A LEGEND OF THE WEST, AND
to this day men swear that it happened just so. An old-time cowboy will
belly up to the bar and assert:

'After General Lee surrendered at Appomattox one of his colonels, an
ol' boy named R. J. Poteet, returned to his family home in southern Virginia to find it burned out. Plumb loco, he headed southwest, windin' up
in Palo Pinto County, Texas, in the fall of 18 and 65.

'That winter he checked out the situation, which was damn near hopeless, and found that the only hand worth a nickel bet was those goddamn
Texas longhorns, which had been runnin' wild and unbranded durin' the
War. They were common as jackrabbits and could be bought for two bits
a head, if you bothered to pay anybody for 'em. More'n likely, you just
went out and slapped an iron on whatever you found. But those same
critters, if you could deliver 'em to the army way north at Fort Laramie
in Wyoming, would bring you four silver dollars each. All you had to do
was gather 'em, head 'em out, and collect your fortune at the end of the
trail.

'So the colonel, he did just that. In the spring of 18 and 66 Poteet
throwed a mixed bunch of three thousand head onto the trail and went
through livin' hell gettin' them acrost the rivers, through Comanche
country and past the Kansas Confederate outlaws who'd kill you
quicker'n look at you just to steal your stock.

'In the fall of 18 and 66—and that was one hell of a dry year, partner
—Poteet got his three thousand cattle as far as Zendt's Farm in Colorado, and there ol' man winter took over. It stormed so bad, with so
much snow, he couldn't do nothin' with his cattle. Caught short only two
hundred lousy miles shy of Fort Laramie and not a goddamn thing he
could do . . . drifts higher'n a tall squaw's ass and the mercury lower'n
a skunk in a hole.

'So with tears streamin' down his cheeks, Poteet pushed his shiverin'

longhorns to them slopes north of Rattlesnake Buttes, and there left 'em
to hustle for theirselves, God help 'em.

'Sayin' a sad goodbye to his poor critters, he beat his way back to
Zendt's Farm and spent that cold winter working for Levi at the new
store Levi built after the stockade was burned to the ground durin' the
Indian troubles, and when spring come the colonel, just to satisfy hisself, left the store and rode out to look for the remains of his poor dead
cattle. Still sore as hell at his loss, he rode over a ridge at the Buttes,
and what did he see? Down in the draws he saw hunerds and hunerds of
his dead longhorns—only they wasn't dead at all, just feedin' and peace-
ful-like on the new spring grass, the cows droppin' perky new calves and
the whole bunch in better shape than when he'd left 'em.

'True as I'm standin', friend, that's how stockmen discovered that the
useless, brown, scrawny buffalo grass and the blue grama was solid feed,
mebbe the best there is, because when winter threatens, this grass sucks
back into its stem all the minerals and such that cattle need, and if they
can only find enough open country where the snows have blowed off,
they'll winter okay. So help me, the whole Colorado cattle industry was
started by Colonel Poteet when he turned them Texas cattle out to die
that day at Rattlesnake Buttes.'

Unfortunately, almost every statement in this version of the legend
was false. The story of abandoned cattle that survived a blizzard winter
first surfaced around 1822 and involved trappers at the rendezvous. It
was repeated as gospel in 1844, but this time dealt with cattle left to die
along the Oregon Trail. In 1846 it was Mormons who deserted them,
and in 1849 the California gold-seekers. Almost every ranch in Colorado, Wyoming or Montana claimed that this climactic event occurred
within its boundaries, and one popular version says it happened as late
as 1879.

In the version just cited, the cowboy got the year wrong, the price of
the cattle wrong and the homesite of his hero wrong. The only thing he
had right was Poteet's name and the fact that he was an extraordinary
man. What really happened was this:

In the late autumn of 1867 Levi Zendt was working at the new store
with his wife. After the Indian raids, they had moved their location
from the old site at the confluence of Beaver Creek and the Platte to
higher ground some distance to the north, selling off at a good profit
much of the land now occupied by the growing town of Zendt's Farm.

As Levi worked he saw a stranger approaching, and from the man's
manner of walking he felt that he had known him somewhere before. It
was Lucinda who recognized their visitor, for she remembered him as
her dancing partner at Fort John in the summer of 1844.

'It's Oliver Seccombe! After all these years!' she cried, and she wanted
to run from the store to greet him, but she was restrained by her recollection of what Levi had once told her: 'When the Conestoga broke in

half, and we were alone on the prairie, he went off whistlin' without a care in the world, and his man stole my Michael Fordney rifle.' So she held back.

It was indeed Oliver Seccombe, come back from Oregon, where he had spent the last twenty-three years, barring two trips to England. It was during the latter of these trips that he had entertained the brainstorm that was to make him rich.

'Levi,' he said with excitement as soon as he was seated in the kitchen, 'in England there are men with so much money . . . they make it in India, Australia . . . barrels of it . . . and they're looking for somewhere to invest it. When I was in Bristol, I kept remembering those empty lands you and I crossed together.'

Sipping a cup of the lapsang souchong old Alexander McKeag had loved, he recalled the vast plains he and Levi had known in the old days. 'I saw them as an ocean of grass, dark and brown, supporting those herds of buffalo . . . Remember?'

Levi did remember—Seccombe's flashy manner when first they met in Missouri, his basic irresponsibility—and he was disposed to have nothing further to do with him. But he also remembered that when Elly was drowning in the Big Blue, it had been Seccombe who leaped into the flood to save her, so he listened as the Englishman said, 'It came to me in a flash. If those plains that Captain Mercy claimed were desert could sustain all those buffalo, they couldn't be desert at all. They had to be some of the best grazing land in the world, only different.'

Lucinda asked, 'What's your plan?'

Seccombe tapped papers in his left pocket. 'I have powers here, and the money to back them up, to acquire a couple of million acres of this land right here—the kind we passed through, Levi.'

'And what will you do with it?' Lucinda asked.

'I have heard,' he said, 'that in Texas, because of the late war, you can buy longhorns—those cattle with horns on their heads like rocking chairs—for twenty-five cents apiece. I want to bring a great herd of them north across the open range, and when I get them here, fatten them up and breed them, and pretty soon I'll have a herd of a hundred thousand feeding on the rich grass, and each year I'll sell off the steers to the army for five and six dollars a head.' He paused dramatically and said, 'That's what you and I are going to do, Levi. You help me get the land, I'll get the cattle and we'll use the money of Englishmen sitting on their fancy bottoms in Bristol.'

He asked for another cup of tea, and as he sipped it he became more relaxed. 'Don't expect you've ever heard of Earl Venneford of Wye? Very powerful man in Bristol and London and a very sporting one. I put the proposition to him and he recognized its possibilities immediately. The Venneford Ranch, we're going to call it, and both Lord Venneford and I are thinking in a big way. Levi, we want to control all the land from the Rockies on the west clear to Nebraska and as far north of the Platte as we can reach.'

'He has enough money to buy all that land?' Zendt asked.

'Well, there's where you come in.'

'Lucinda and I have some savings—in St. Louis—but not . . .'

Seccombe looked toward the doorway to assure himself that no customer had entered. 'It won't cost you anything,' he confided, and from his right pocket he produced a rough map of northeastern Colorado Territory, with the Platte River drawn conspicuously and showing numerous small streams running into it from the north. 'Under the new Homestead Act—' he began pontifically.

'I know,' Levi interrupted. 'I got title to some of my land under that act.'

Ignoring the interruption, Seccombe continued: 'Under this act the trick is to get title only to those parcels of land that control water. Get a hundred and sixty acres of such land, and you control ten thousand acres of range land that has no water,' and here he directed the Zendts' attention to markings on his map. Darting his forefinger quickly from spot to spot, he said, 'I've worked out that there are seventeen crucial spots we've got to have. This stream bank, this junction, this spring up in the hills. When we get them—those few little spots—we'll own the rest of the range without putting down one cent.'

'I don't see what you mean,' Levi said.

'Look! Take this spot where Skunk Hollow joins Beaver Creek. Give me that and I'll give you a hundred thousand acres north of it, because without my water, there isn't a damned thing anyone can do with those acres. Those hundred thousand don't belong to me, but if I control the water, they're useless to anyone else.'

So the Zendts went over the map with him, checking each critical spot: 'Those two parcels along the Platte were taken up by Otto Kraenzel, and I doubt he'd sell. Those two along the creek were taken up by a man named Troxell, and I know you could buy them cheap. Now you're lookin' at Brumbaugh's farm, and I'm certain he won't sell. That next parcel—no one has filed on it, so far's I know.'

'Get Lucinda to file on it tomorrow,' said Seccombe eagerly. 'And how about this section at Skunk Hollow? They've overlooked that, haven't they?'

'I've never been there.'

'That one I'll file on,' Seccombe said, 'and with it I'll control a hundred thousand acres of grass.'

And so they laid their plans. A farm hand would be persuaded to file on this section; his sweetheart, on that; a man out of work, on the one where the creek leaves the canyon, for that would be crucial, because the man who could block the canyon mouth would control the entire canyon of forty thousand acres. By such judicious ownership, Oliver Seccombe and his London backers would spend a relatively small amount of money and gain for it a kingdom larger than many in Europe.

This manipulation had been made possible by one of the finest laws ever passed in the American Congress, the Homestead Act of 1862, whereby the western lands once owned by Indians but now owned by the United States government, were given away in one-hundred-and-sixty-acre parcels to anyone who seriously intended living on the land and cultivating it. Proof of this intention was simple: a man had to build a habitation on his land, live in it for certain months each year, and farm forty of his acres for a period of five years. At the end of that time he got title, and the land was his in perpetuity. In the years following the Civil War, when rootless families threatened to menace stabilized society, they were adroitly converted into self-respecting citizens by the Homestead Act, and much of the greatness of states like Kansas and Minnesota and Colorado stemmed from the application of this wise law.

The land that was not taken up by homesteaders, and much of it was not suitable for farming, remained the property of the government, free for the casual use of whoever could get to it, so that if Oliver Seccombe did succeed in gaining title to his seventeen crucial areas, he had the government's blessing and encouragement to use several million additional acres.

On the morning after his arrival at Zendt's Farm, Seccombe filed for the ultra-critical section at Skunk Hollow, directed Lucinda to file on another good watershed and started to buy up the remaining creeks which had already passed into private ownership. Seven different friends filed for various pieces under his supervision, with the understanding that they would be sold to Seccombe as soon as title was assured.

In one hectic week Seccombe put together a land holding of less than three thousand acres but dominating an area of 5,760,000, larger than Massachusetts and all to be controlled by gentlemen in Bristol, most of whom would never see it.

Now came the problem of how to get the cattle north to stock it, and Seccombe had a plan. 'Levi,' he said one night as they finished supper, 'I've made up my mind. I want you to go down to Texas and bring up the cattle.'

'I don't know anything about drivin' cattle,' the Dutchman protested.

'You don't need to know. You go down there, find an experienced cattleman and allow him to hire his help. You go along to protect our investment.'

'I'm forty-seven,' Zendt said. 'I'm stayin' here,' and to this Lucinda agreed.

'Well, if you won't go, who can we get?'

'By the way, it's a little late to ask,' Zendt said, 'but do you know anything about raisin' cattle?'

'If you live in Oregon long enough, you learn everything,' Seccombe replied with a satisfied smile.

'Speakin' of Oregon, whatever happened to Sam Purchas?'

'Sam!' the Englishman said, recalling his difficulties with that valiant frontiersman. 'The night after he delivered me safely at Willamette, as he was obliged to do by our contract, he treated me the way he did you —stole most of my gear and vanished.'

'What happened to him?'

'Three months later he was hanged as a horse thief.'

'Whatever did he do with my gun?' Levi asked.

'That handsome one he stole from you?'

'Yes. The curly-maple stock.'

'He used it to club a bear over the head. Broke it in twenty pieces.'

An overwhelming sadness came over Levi Zendt. He seldom thought of the past; there had been too much sorrow, too much death. But now he recalled that rifle made so lovingly by a man who had been so brutally murdered; Sam Purchas trying to rape Elly in the dunes; the six beautiful gray horses long since dead in Missouri; the rattlesnake marks on Elly's neck; the terrible pain of digging those graves for the Pasquinels. He propped his elbows on the kitchen table and lowered his forehead onto his fingertips—and for a long moment no one spoke.

Finally Levi said, 'The man you want is John Skimmerhorn. Lives in that house by the river.'

'Skimmerhorn? Isn't he the man who butchered those Indians?'

'His son.'

'The Skimmerhorn I'm thinking about moved to California after the troubles, and wherever he went some newspaper would find out about him and write articles that repeated the testimony given at the army hearings. He left California.' Seccombe tried to recall where he had gone—the papers had reported it, but the name of the town escaped him. 'Would you trust young Skimmerhorn?'

'Very dependable,' Levi said, and they walked down to the river toward the small house in which John Skimmerhorn lived. On the way Levi explained, 'This town supported Colonel Skimmerhorn. To these people he was a great hero. That is, up to the moment he shot Mike Pasquinel in the back—right over there beyond the *Clarion* offices.'

'Then what happened?' Seccombe asked.

'Damnedest thing,' Zendt reflected. 'Nobody blamed him for murderin' those Indian women and children, but when he shot an unarmed man, carryin' a surrender flag, in the back . . .' He paused, as if trying to reconcile these contradictory attitudes. 'I suppose people rejected Skimmerhorn because he broke the basic law of the west. You don't shoot a man in the back—not even a Pasquinel.'

'Those must have been terrible times.'

'We survived.'

'You stayed right here?'

'This was my home.'

They walked in silence for some distance, after which Seccombe said, with incredulity, 'And you'd put our fortunes in the hands of Colonel Skimmerhorn's son?'

'I'd trust him with my life.'

They found Skimmerhorn at home, a reserved, well-built man of twenty-nine, and Seccombe suspected that the obvious tenseness sprang from the fact that young Skimmerhorn could never be sure what strangers might say about his discredited father.

'How'd you like to go down to Texas next month, hire a crew and bring two or three thousand head of longhorns up here?'

'I'd like that,' Skimmerhorn said.

'We're risking a lot of money in this,' Seccombe explained, 'and we need a man we can depend on.'

'John's your man,' Mrs. Skimmerhorn said in a flat Kansas voice.

'I'll pay for the cattle and the crew and give you thirty-five cents for every head delivered.'

'I'll go,' Skimmerhorn agreed at once. 'Not accomplishing much here.'

'How long will he be away?' Mrs. Skimmerhorn asked.

'Down and back—seven, eight months.'

'I'll get Mrs. Weaver to stay with me when the baby comes,' she said.

So three months later on a bright warm day in February 1868 John Skimmerhorn, leading two spare horses, rode into the cattle country of southern Texas and began asking how he might find an experienced trail boss to put together a mixed herd and drive it north through Oklahoma Territory and Kansas, then west to where Seccombe was putting together his ranch.

He received discouraging reactions. One grizzled trail boss said, 'I'll take your critters as far as Abilene, but I'll be damned if I'll take 'em to Colorado.'

'Why not?'

'Last year the Comanche gave us a hell of a lot of trouble in western Oklahoma, and in Kansas them damned Pettis boys like to rob us blind.'

'I just came down through that region. No trouble.'

'You wasn't trailin' cattle,' the Texan pointed out.

'If I'm willing to take the chance, will you?'

'Nope. I'll go as far as Abilene, and that's it!'

Skimmerhorn was unable to persuade any trained hands to risk the dangerous trek through the western parts of Oklahoma and Kansas. As one experienced man explained, 'It ain't only Indians and outlaws. It's also them Kansas farmers. They got the crazy notion that Texas cattle spread disease. Hell, look at our longhorns! You never saw a healthier lot in your life.'

A sense of frustration overtook Skimmerhorn, for all about him he saw an abundance of the very stock he wanted: long rangy cows ready for repeated breeding, lanky steers ready to put on fat once they got settled, hefty prepotent bulls good for years of service in building a herd. Each morning he saw a thousand cattle he was eager to buy, and each night he climbed into his bedroll defeated, for he could find no one brave enough to drive those rugged cattle north through the dangerous country.

One night after he had hobbled his horses and was preparing for a cheerless bed, he suddenly felt as though he were back in Minnesota before the Sioux uprising, before his father had become half mad over the loss of his family. He could swear he smelled the meat and onions his mother usually cooked for supper. Skimmerhorn was not a sentimental man; he had endured too much for that, but this imaginary smell of frying meat became overpowering, and he lost himself in a welter of memories, recalling scenes in Minnesota as he tried to fall asleep.

Sleep wouldn't come. The smell persisted, and he sat up. 'That's got to be meat frying!' he said, climbing out of the bedroll and putting on his pants. He looked about him, but saw nothing. Then around the hump of a hill he saw the glow of a light, and when he came up to it he found a solitary Mexican, forlorn, bowlegged, dressed in very tight trousers that had no proper fly but only a baggy flap that tied with a string.

He was hunched over a meager fire which heated one small pan from which issued the splendid aroma. 'Ah, señor!' the man cried when he saw Skimmerhorn coming at him. 'I not steal.'

'Don't worry,' Skimmerhorn reassured him. 'What're you cooking?'

'Ah, señor. Some ends, only some ends.'

The smell coming from the pan belied this, and Skimmerhorn moved closer. The Mexican was telling the truth. He had only some odds and ends of beef, but with them he had thrown in a few onions, some sage, a couple of peppers, until the resulting combination looked very enticing. Holding the pan up to Skimmerhorn, the kneeling man asked, 'You try, señor?' He spoke with that singsong inflection Mexicans used, and his face was so open and round, so genuine in its invitation, that Skimmerhorn took a small chunk of meat. It was delicious.

'Look!' he said. 'I have some good beef.'

The Mexican beamed. 'With real beef, señor, we have a feast.'

So Skimmerhorn ran for his meat, and thirty minutes later he and the Mexican sat close to a larger fire, sharing a banquet.

'Who are you?' Skimmerhorn asked.

'Ignacio Gómez,' the man said, pronouncing his name most lyrically: Ig-NAZZZ-i-o GOOOO-mez.

'What are you doing?'

'I'm a cook.'

'You certainly are. Where?'

'No work.'

'You want to ride with me? Tend the horses, do the cooking?'

'Where you headed, señor?'

'Who knows?'

The Mexican smiled and said, 'I move my things over to you.' But the only things he had were his frying pan, a dirty bedroll and a spavined horse. When he saw the three sound animals Skimmerhorn had, he cried, 'Oh, señor. You have fine HORRRR-ses.'

In the days following they rode aimlessly from ranch to ranch, asking if any Texans were willing to try the long drive north, and finding only disappointment. They did, however, eat well, and one night when Skimmerhorn came back to camp he found a luscious feast laid out; Gómez had traded his worn-out horse for two chickens, some chunks of beef and a bag of vegetables.

'Ignacio!' Skimmerhorn protested. 'You were robbed.'

'My friends call me NAAAA-cho,' he said, and when Skimmerhorn tasted the stew he said, 'Nacho, I don't know how we'll get our cattle north, but you'll be the cook.' The first member of his crew had been hired.

And then one day on the banks of the Pedernales a trail boss told him, 'I hear tell there's a man up in Palo Pinto County who thinks he has a way of gettin' around the Comanche and the Pettis boys. Man named R. J. Poteet.'

Skimmerhorn made repeated inquiries about Poteet, but most of the ranchers along the Pedernales had not heard of him. Then one day Nacho rode back to camp with reassuring news: 'Poteet? Big man. Knows cattle and how to drive 'em.'

'How many days north?'

'If we ride hard, seven, eight.'

Even though that day was almost over, Skimmerhorn saddled up, and with Nacho trailing behind with the extra horses, set out for Palo Pinto. Toward nightfall on the sixth day he pulled up before a low-roofed clapboard ranch house. Without dismounting, he shouted, 'R. J. Poteet? You there?'

No sound greeted this call, and he repeated it, whereupon into the frame of the open door appeared a spare man of medium height. About forty years old, he had a shock of uncombed sandy hair, tightly pursed lips and narrow eyes that glinted as he surveyed his visitor. He wore a gun and very tight-fitting pants made of striped Mexican fabric, the legs tucked into the tops of his ornamented high-heeled boots. His thumbs were jammed into his broad silvered belt so that his elbows protruded in an awkward way.

'I'm Poteet,' he said.

'I'm Skimmerhorn. Down from Colorado. I want you to put me together a good mixed herd.'

'Why mixed? If you're sellin' beef, steers'll trail better.'

'I'm not just selling. We're starting a ranch.'

'How many you thinkin' of?'

'Two, three thousand.'

'We can get 'em.'

'Can you get them north?'

Now Poteet considered carefully. 'You know that if we tried to push them through western Kansas, we'd be lucky to keep half the herd. I've tried that.'

'What can we do?'

Poteet studied the northerner, trying to gauge his courage. 'That all depends on you,' he said.

'What do you mean?'

'There is another way, but I wouldn't force it on you.'

'What way?' Skimmerhorn asked evenly.

'Two years ago a man called Goodnight did a hell of a thing. Headed two thousand critters far south of here, dead across the desert, then swung them north to Colorado and Wyoming.'

When Skimmerhorn looked perplexed, he added, 'That way, his greatest risk was nature, not Indians or robbers, and the worst came right at the start.'

'Could it be done again?'

'It could.'

'What are your terms?' Skimmerhorn asked.

'Eighty cents for every animal delivered. I pay the crew, you supply the horses.'

'How long before we start?'

'A week to ten days, way the weather's shapin'.'

Neither man had moved from his original position, Skimmerhorn astride his horse, Poteet framed in the doorway, and now the former said, 'Poteet, you're the man I've been looking for. Tomorrow we'll start putting the herd together. Pick your men and we'll head north.'

'We could start buyin' tonight,' Poteet said.

'Let's go.'

'Who's the Mexican?'

'Nacho. He'll be the cook.'

'Not on my trail,' Poteet said firmly, and ignoring Skimmerhorn, he stepped down to face the Mexican and launched into a furious barrage of Spanish, which Nacho answered in kind, until Skimmerhorn feared that a fight might ensue, but at the end of a protracted exchange Poteet came back to the porch and said, 'He'll be the cook. That one knows what he's doin'.'

In Spanish he directed Nacho inside to help Mrs. Poteet cook supper for eight, then he and Skimmerhorn set out to visit neighboring ranches, and long after dark they returned to the Poteet ranch with five lean, poverty-stricken men who were glad to partake of a free meal.

As the men filed in he introduced them formally to his wife, and before the meal was served he placed a bottle of whiskey on the table.

'I'm offerin' four dollars a head, cow or steer, but I reserve the right to reject ten percent of what you offer. And I could use some good bulls too.' Here he banged the table, adding, 'I don't have to warn you that I won't take cows about to drop calves. On the trail I have in mind we can't fool with 'em.'

'What trail you thinkin' of?' one of the men asked.

'The way Goodnight went.'

The men looked at each other, and one asked, 'Llano Estacado?'

'The same.'

Awed silence, then a man named Lem Frater asked in a quiet voice, 'You'll risk it without water to Horsehead Crossing?'

'We'll make it to Horsehead Crossing,' Poteet said firmly, but one cowman turned to Skimmerhorn and asked, 'Stranger, have you any idea of the Llano Estacado?'

'It's a trail that Mr. Poteet says avoids the Comanche and the Kansas outlaws.'

'It does that,' the man agreed, 'but it has one stretch of seventy miles—'

'Eighty, ninety,' Poteet broke in quietly, and all turned to look at him as he twirled his whiskey glass, took a deep swig and said, 'It's an agonizin' trail, the one I have in mind. You start by goin' two hundred miles out of your way. South of New Mexico. And to get there you drive your cattle over a long stretch without one drop of water.'

Skimmerhorn thought of a dozen questions, but stifled them. He must get his cattle north, and the only man he had met so far with any idea as to how to do it was R. J. Poteet. If he said that Texas cattle could cross an eighty- or ninety-mile stretch without water, he said it with reason.

'You payin' in cash?' Lem Frater asked.

'You tell me tonight how many head you're deliverin' tomorrow, and you go home with ten percent of your cash. You get the rest when I see the cattle.'

The men were eager to inform Poteet of their numbers, for they had not seen real cash for many years, but at this moment Mrs. Poteet, a thin, hard-faced woman, entered with a heaping platter of steaks, followed by Nacho Gómez bearing gravy, potatoes and a loaf of freshly baked bread.

'He knows how to cook,' Mrs. Poteet said as she placed the food on the table.

There were only eight chairs, which meant that Nacho had no place to sit, so he supposed he was meant to eat in the kitchen, but Poteet pulled out a box and said in Spanish, 'You sit here,' and Lem Frater said, 'A Mexican? At table?' and Poteet said, 'At this table, yes.'

The steaks were cooked Texas style, which meant they were practically inedible. With the best beef at hand, and the best steaks cut from it, the Texans never let the meat age or become tender in any other way. Cutting it from the fresh carcass, they plopped it into a hot pan and kept it over the coals interminably, according to the ancient Texas law: 'If it's brown it's still cookin', and if it's black it's almost done.'

'Mighty fine steaks,' Frater judged as he gnawed away at the hard and tasty beef.

'Thank you, Lem,' Mrs. Poteet replied. 'He baked the bread,' she said, pointing to Nacho.

'If he can cook that good,' Frater said, 'I wisht I was goin' north with you.'

'I want you to,' Poteet said. 'Early tomorrow mornin' you ride north to Jacksborough and round me up about fifteen hundred head.'

'I better stay here tomorrow,' Frater protested. 'I've got to make my count.'

'I'll count for you,' Poteet said, and no one at the table thought it improper that one man should offer to serve as both buyer and seller, for if you couldn't trust R. J. Poteet, you couldn't trust anybody.

So at dawn Lem Frater headed north to the town of Jacksborough while Poteet and Skimmerhorn moved swiftly to the local ranches inspecting cattle and making their selections. By midafternoon they had picked out and paid for thirteen hundred head plus eighty horses. On the way back to the home ranch Poteet explained, 'I'd like to carry north about twenty-eight hundred head, and twelve cowboys includin' you and me and the Mexican. For each man I'll need twelve horses.'

'So many?'

'We're takin' the hardest trail in the world,' Poteet said simply. 'We won't skimp on the horses, because we'll be ridin' like you never rode before.'

Next morning he began the selection of his crew. He needed nine additional men who could be trusted with serious responsibility, and he knew of only two, Nate Person and a man called Mule Canby. Trailing an extra horse, he led Skimmerhorn to a mean log dugout along the banks of Pinto Creek, where a man, his wife and three children were trying to eke out a living. They were black and had once been slaves in South Texas; freedom had brought them little beyond an abandoned shack and squatter's rights to a miserable plot of land which barely provided the vegetables on which they subsisted.

Tossing one of the children a paper bundle, Poteet said, 'The missus cooked up more steak than we could handle, Dora Mae. Where's your pappy?'

The child grabbed the parcel, smelled it and broke into a joyous smile. 'Mom!' she shouted. 'Meat!'

From the door to the dugout appeared a very thin black woman with flashing white teeth. 'Thank you, Mr. Poteet,' she said effusively yet with dignity. 'The children will love you for this.'

'There's enough for you too,' Poteet said. 'Where's Nate?'

'He's grubbin' for Mr. Goodly.'

'You send Dora Mae to fetch him.' And while the little girl ran to the Goodly place, Poteet asked Mrs. Person how things were going.

'Not bad,' she said cheerily. 'We got the children dressed and Nate gets work here and there. When you and Mrs. Poteet gonna start bringin' me your washin'?'

'One of these days,' Poteet answered.

Nate Person now ran up, out of breath. 'Sorry not to be at home, Mr. Poteet.'

'You're home,' Poteet said abruptly. 'We're headin' for Colorado.'

'When?'

'Now.'

'I don't have no horse, Mr. Poteet.'

'Put your saddle on Baldy.'

Nate turned to study the horse, then said, 'He looks strong,' and Poteet said, 'He is. Get your bedroll.'

And within minutes Nate Person had his roll, his pistol and his saddle. Lifting Dora Mae in his arms, he kissed his wife goodbye and said, 'Tell the boys goodbye for me,' and he was off.

The three men rode along Pinto Creek till they came to a homestead marked by a certain affluence; whoever occupied it understood ranching and had already established a good foothold. 'Canby!' Poteet shouted, and Person said, 'He's yonder,' and across grassland came a cowboy astride a handsome gray.

'Hello, Poteet,' he said gruffly. 'Hear you're buyin' cattle like crazy.'

'We leave for Colorado.'

'Sort of figured you might need me. When?'

'Now.'

'Sounds good.'

Canby jumped down from his horse, an agile, wiry man with bronzed face and stern jaw. Running awkwardly, as cowboys usually do, he cried, 'Emmy, I'm off to Colorado,' but before she could appear, he turned back to Poteet and asked, 'You want to buy my string of horses?'

'If they're any good.'

'Look 'em over while I pack.'

Poteet and Person went to the corral, where Canby had eleven strong mounts. 'Come over here, Skimmerhorn,' Poteet called, and when the northerner reached the corral, Poteet said, 'Canby's from South Texas. Right on the Rio Grande, so don't be surprised at how he dresses. He's stubborn as a mule, but he knows horses and he's got some beauties here. I'd recommend you buy the whole lot.'

'He'll charge,' Person warned. 'He loves his horses.'

'You won't find animals like this in Jacksborough,' Poteet said, and before Skimmerhorn could reply, he added, 'I'd like to use Canby at point. Along with Nate. We'd make him feel good at the start if we met his price.'

'Point means?'

'When you get the cattle strung out on the trail you want your two best men ridin' up front, left and right of the lead steer and a little ahead. If somethin' happens, you don't have time to explain nothin'. Your points must take responsibility on their own. Nate here's the best I ever seen. I trust Canby too.'

'Well, let's buy his horses, if his price isn't robbery.'

'It will be,' Nate predicted.

Canby now appeared, an astonishing apparition. Because of his training along the Rio Grande, where mesquite thorns cut a man to shreds if he was carried into them by his horse, he believed that a cowboy should go dressed against that possibility. Accordingly, he wore heavy chaps and enormous tapaderos, those leather coverings for the stirrup which protect the feet and ankles from clawing brush; many a South Texas cowboy had saved a leg by the leather armor of chap and tapadero. But when a bowlegged man walked in heavy chaps, he looked comical, and Skimmerhorn had to bite his lip to avoid smiling as Canby came toward them.

'How do you like my horses?' he asked.

'The best,' Poteet said honestly. 'How much?'

'Ten dollars a horse.'

Skimmerhorn was surprised that the price was so low, for in Colorado such horses would have brought thirty, but Poteet said, 'You drive a hard bargain.' Canby replied, 'Those horses have hard feet,' and Poteet said grudgingly, 'I'll give you eighty-five for the lot.' Canby, with a slight smile of satisfaction said, 'A deal.' He then went to where Nate Person sat his horse and shook hands. 'You and me ridin' point?'

'Yes, sir,' Nate said.

'Good.' And the four men started back to the Poteet ranch, but before they had gone far Canby said, 'You need another good hand?' and Poteet said, 'I need seven.' Canby suggested, 'You oughta think about Mike Lasater,' and Poteet said, 'Lasater stole horses. Forget him.' But Canby persisted, 'That was a long time ago, Mr. Poteet, and you won't find a better cowboy in Palo Pinto than Mike Lasater.'

'I'm gettin' the others in Jacksborough,' Poteet said flatly, and the conversation ended.

When they reached the ranch they were met by a lanky man with a sour visage, two pistols, a bedroll and a stout pony. 'Mornin', Mr. Poteet. I'm Mike Lasater.'

'I know who you are,' Poteet mumbled, irritated that this semi-outlaw should have imposed himself this way.

'I want to ride with you.'

'I need no hands.'

'Yes, you do, Mr. Poteet. You need a good dozen and you only got four.'

'Five,' Poteet snapped, pointing to where Nacho stood in the doorway, and as soon as he had done this he felt irritated with himself for having been drawn into argument with this renegade.

'You need me, Mr. Poteet,' Lasater insisted. He was a thin, scrawny young man of indeterminate age, but he sat his horse confidently, and before Poteet could rebuff him again he said, 'I'll ride drag. You need a good man back there in the dust.'

'Take him,' Canby said.

'Come along,' Poteet said unhappily, but as he started toward the ranch house he suddenly wheeled his horse and faced Lasater again. 'No gamblin'. No drinkin',' he snapped. Lasater's temper flared: 'Goddamnit, Poteet, if a man is startin' over, he's got to start somewheres. Now you accept me as I am, because I'm the best horseman you'll have on your trail.'

Poteet merely smiled. 'If you're a good horseman, Lasater,' he said quickly, 'I'll be proud to have you along,' and he extended his hand to clasp that of the younger man.

They rode north that afternoon, six men more at ease in the saddle than on their feet, leading thirteen hundred longhorn cattle and ninety-one horses in the remuda de caballos, overseen for the moment by Nacho. At Jacksborough they would hire an experienced wrangler whose job would be looking after the horses for the next four months. They would also hire an additional half-dozen raw cowboys, and since the ones already hired were veterans, the new hands could be farm youths sixteen or seventeen years old eager for trail experience. By the time Poteet had his dozen men, he would have a flexible crew able to work eighteen hours a day, subsist on meager rations and operate as a unit, requiring few words and little exhortation. Their job would be simple: take some twenty-eight hundred fractious longhorns safely across thirteen hundred miles of the west's most bruising country.

Jacksborough in 1868 was a fascinating frontier town built around a spacious square. It was the crossroads of northern Texas, a spot where cattlemen convened from vast and lonely spaces to buy their staples, sell what produce their wives had grown, and make a deal for beef with the army at nearby Fort Richardson.

It was a wild town, with no less than twenty-six establishments licensed to sell liquor, and its inhabitants were not leery of new ideas or radical approaches. For example, when R. J. Poteet entered the smithy of a wagonmaker and said, 'What I want, Sanderson, is a special type of wagon,' Sanderson did not whine and say, 'Well, I don't know . . .' And when Poteet explained, 'At the rear end I'm thinkin' of somethin' like a desk—lot of drawers for keepin' things in and a flat table that will fold out when we stop,' Sanderson studied the idea and said, 'Sounds sensible.'

'Start buildin',' Poteet said.

'You want the drawers to pull out and in, like this?'

'Big drawers.'

'Who said little ones? I ain't no cabinetmaker.'

'I'm gonna leave my Mexican here with you.'

'I don't need no help.'

'He's my cook. And this is gonna be his wagon.'

'Oh! A cook wagon? Why in hell didn't you say so? We could . . . He stopped, studied the imaginary wagon, drew it in the air and said enthusiastically, 'We could hang hooks everywhere. You could carry . . . hell, you could carry . . .' He grabbed a piece of paper and started planning the wagon. 'We got to have two barrels,' Nacho said, 'one flour, one beans,' to which Sanderson replied, 'You goddamned Mexicans couldn't live without beans, could you?'

Finding the rest of the cattle was easy, but choosing six more cowboys was difficult, because every farm boy in the area wanted to ride with them. They were a sorry lot, young fellows with pimples and scraggly blond hair, ill-at-ease with anything except a horse; shy, often unschooled and lost under their big hats.

Skimmerhorn, coming upon a couple of dozen of them waiting in the square, told Nate Person, 'I'd hate to go up the trail with that lot,' and Nate said, 'We all looked that way at sixteen,' to which Skimmerhorn replied, 'Maybe, but we weren't trailing cattle,' and Nate replied quietly, 'I was.' Later he added, 'I guess our job is to take 'em as calves and turn 'em into strong young bulls.'

Poteet did the choosing. He took four gangly boys—Calendar, Gompert, Ragland, Savage—and Skimmerhorn found it impossible to tell one from the other. They were even dressed alike: boots with high heels to prevent the foot from slipping through the stirrup, tight-fitting pants, leather belts with revolver holsters, white shirts, some kind of jacket, a blue or gray bandanna which could be used in a number of ways—over the face as a dust mask, as a sweat rag, a hobble for horses or a signal flag—and a broad-brimmed hat to protect eyes and lips from the blistering sun. And of course, each had his own horse.

The ten hands thus far assembled had the common characteristic of the cowboy: unmounted and walking about the town on foot they were awkward; their high-heeled boots and bowed legs made them almost comic creatures, accentuated by the holsters that banged at their sides, but once in the saddle they became proud lean men. Then their scrawny frames and hat-shaded faces assumed a mysteriousness which fitted exactly the landscape through which they moved. Cowboys were a silent breed, accustomed on the trail to communicate mainly by signals flashed when the trail boss or one of the points waved his hat in special ways.

At work, they talked more with their hats than with their lips, and to their horses, which became in time a living part of them, they spoke with their knees, or not at all, for sometimes in crucial situations it was the horse who spoke to them by the way in which he moved and anticipated danger ahead. Then the wise cowboy heeded neither the trail boss nor the points nor even the man beside him, but only his horse, and many a cowboy returned to camp alive because in a moment of danger he had allowed his horse to take command.

Therefore, each cowboy brought with him three personal possessions for which he remained responsible: his gun, his bedroll and his special horse. From the remuda paid for by the owner he would select his eleven work horses.

To tend the remuda Poteet sought a practiced wrangler. Among the applicants, there was one who seemed to satisfy this requirement, so Poteet went back to Sanderson, who was working sixteen hours a day on the wagon, and was told, 'Real good man with a remuda is Buck, if you can stand his smell.'

When Poteet came within three yards of the wrangler he understood what Sanderson meant, for this unlovely man had worked around horses so much, and was so averse to water, that he smelled worse than a mare in heat. 'He was sort of wonderful,' Poteet explained to Skimmerhorn later that day. 'I figured that if we hired him, his smell alone would kill a rattlesnake downwind at a hundred yards.'

Buck was an older man who had been up the Kansas trail twice. At an early age he had visualized himself as an outcast and now he expected nothing better in life. His extraordinary smell came not only from his habitual uncleanliness, but also from a nervous glandular disorder he could not control. He was an unlikable loner who knew only one thing: horses. 'I wouldn't dare hire him,' Poteet explained, 'except that his job will keep him off to one side, away from the other men.'

'If he can handle horses, take him, smell and all,' Skimmerhorn said.

Eleven men had now been chosen, and the twelfth chose himself. He sauntered into the square one evening, a young man twenty-one years old, extremely thin, wearing a Confederate uniform, a LeMat revolver and a Texas hat. In his left hand he lugged a McClellan saddle, as different from the standard Texas saddle as could be imagined. It was a northern invention, much used by General Grant's cavalry but held in contempt by the south. How a southern veteran happened to have such a saddle was a mystery. It had no horn, a single cinch, practically no cantle, and to the horror of any Texan, was slit down the middle of the seat!

'It's to provide ventilation,' Canby explained to one of the astonished boys.

'Looks like a ball-pincher to me,' the boy replied, amid general laughter.

'Where's the horn?' another asked.

'It ain't a real saddle,' Canby said. A good Texas saddle had a horn stout enough for roping an elephant, and to think that a cowboy would ever use a McClellan wasn't worth discussing.

'M'name's Coker,' the young man said. 'Who's boss?'

'I am,' Poteet said. 'Where you from?'

'South Calinky,' the stranger said with obvious defiance, and when Poteet heard this pronunciation for South Carolina, first state to secede from the Union and foremost in heroic actions, he paid attention. Poteet had served in the Confederate cavalry and knew that no men equaled the South Carolinians, difficult, stubborn, sometimes even hateful, but always dependable. He had once moved with eighteen South Calinky boys, as they called themselves, youngsters barely sixteen, and they had assaulted a northern stronghold held by fifty. Such men. Of the eighteen, eleven had died, charging forward, and when the attack failed, as it had to, two of the survivors halted to run back into the face of terrible fire to toss grenades into the impregnable position. Had they lived, they would have been much like the man who now stood before him.

'What's your name?'

'Buford Coker. They call me Bufe.'

'Where'd you get that saddle?'

'Off'n a blue-coat officer.'

'What's that revolver, a LeMat?' Coker nodded. 'Where'd you get a LeMat?'

'Off'n a gray-coat officer.'

'Your horse?'

'Don't have one.'

'You can ride?'

'Would I have a saddle other?'

'Why do you want to go north with us?'

'I been movin' for some time.'

Desperately Poteet wanted to give this cantankerous young man a job, but he knew that the Confederate might be more trouble than he was worth. Then an idea struck him. 'There might be a place . . .' he began.

'Man at the wagon shop said there was a place,' Coker interrupted. 'You're one hand short.'

'There might be a place,' Poteet repeated without irritation, 'if my top hand thought you'd fit.'

'I'll fit.'

'Mr. Person.' Poteet waited till the black man rode up, then said formally, 'Mr. Person, do you think you could work with this young man?'

Nate studied him, knew that he could be difficult, knew from his Confederate uniform that he might present special problems. But he also knew, from his long acquaintance with Mr. Poteet, that the boss must want to hire the young man, if a justification could be found. So he stared straight into Coker's eyes and said, 'This trail could be just as dangerous as the war you were in, soldier,' and the Confederate replied slowly, without shifting his gaze, 'Nothin' scares me,' and Nate said, 'I think he's a good one, Mr. Poteet.'

There was one more test. Poteet asked Coker directly, 'You think you could work with Mr. Person?'

'I worked with Colonel Biggerstaff, and if you can work with a bastard like that, you oughta be able to work with a gentleman like Mr. Person,' Coker replied, a hint of sarcasm in his voice.

'Mr. Person will give you a horse,' Poteet said, but when the time came for Coker to select his mount, it became apparent to Person that the young man knew nothing of horses.

'You ain't never been on a horse!' the black man cried.

'Don't tell him,' Coker pleaded.

'You'll kill yourself,' Nate protested.

'Pick me a good one, and I'll ride 'im.'

'Son, you're playin' with fire.'

'Pick me a horse,' Coker begged, and Nate ran his judicious eye over the lot. Some were barely broken; they would be tamed by cowboys on the trail. Others were as good as they would ever be, which wasn't much. A few, including the eleven purchased from Canby, were fine mounts, and Nate selected the best of these.

'How do you put the saddle on?' Coker asked.

'Always from the left. Then tighten the cinch.'

'What's a cinch?'

Nate looked at the stubborn young man and said, 'God have mercy on you, Buford, you got courage.'

For two days, while Mr. Poteet and Nacho bought supplies for the wagon, Bufe Coker rode his horse through the fields around Jacksborough, falling off, regaining his saddle and lugging his aching bones to bed in a state of exhaustion. In the afternoon of the second day he went to Person and said, 'Now I know how to ride. Pick me out a real tough one,' and Person said, 'You ain't ready for that, son,' and Coker said, 'I got to learn some time.' So Person lassoed a mean chalk-eyed pinto, the kind cowboys detested, and for the first half hour Coker couldn't even get him saddled. When he did, the pinto bucked him off repeatedly, but each time Coker climbed back on.

'You better call it a day,' Person warned, but Coker said, 'It's either him or me.' Finally he managed to stay on, and the lightness of the McClellan saddle must have pleased the pinto after the heavy Texas saddles, for when he felt the man securely on his back he began to move with a new gracefulness, and for the first time in his life Bufe Coker understood what a horse could be.

When he reined in where Person was waiting, he jumped down with excitement in his eyes and cried, 'I want him,' but Nate dashed his enthusiasm by explaining, 'Son, in an outfit like this you draw for the horses, and you'll take your chance with the rest.'

'But they wouldn't pick a wild horse like this one . . . would they?' Coker asked hopefully.

'Just the kind of spirit a cowboy looks for in a horse,' Person said, but that night he passed among the others and told them, 'At the drawing tomorrow, don't nobody pick the chalk-eyed pinto. Soldier boy seems to think he can handle him.'

At dawn the men made their pick of the remuda, by tradition each in turn choosing a horse, then a second, then a third, until every rider had a string of eleven mounts for the trail.

The Confederate watched with anxiety as Poteet and Person chose first, followed by the men. Ragland, with a sense of comedy, made believe he was going to take the pinto, but at the last moment chose another. So the pinto remained, and when Coker's first turn came he shouted, 'I'll take that one,' and a rewarding partnership was launched.

At six Nacho Gómez drove up with four mules pulling the remarkable new wagon. From the front it looked like any standard long-bedded, canvas-covered prairie wagon, except that from its sides hung suspended an unusual array of pans, buckets, axes and canvas bags. It was from the rear that it seemed so striking, for there a boxlike structure had been fastened in such a way that the back could be lowered and made into a stout table, supported by a folding leg. Behind this collapsible table, hidden from sight until it was dropped, nested seven neat drawers, each with a brass handle, each with a store of useful or delicious items. One drawer was reserved for Mr. Poteet's paper work, one for such medicines as were available, with emphasis on calomel to fight constipation, and various nauseous potions to combat diarrhea. The other five held spices, dried fruits, sugar and the exotic Mexican herbs Nacho intended introducing to his Texans.

Now came the first test of the cowboys as a team. Before the herd could be thrown onto the trail, each animal had to be branded, horses as well as cattle, not only as proof of ownership but also to facilitate sorting in case the herd should become mixed with other cattle on northern sections of the route or at some river crossing.

Poteet said, 'I'll get the smithy to make us some irons, but what brand will your ranch be usin'?'

On this delicate matter Skimmerhorn had been given no instructions, so he said, 'Use a V,' but Poteet said, 'Can't. An outfit down the line's already usin' that.'

'How about Lazy Vee?' But that too had been preempted. So had Bar Vee and Diamond Vee.

'Wait a minute,' Poteet said. 'Didn't you tell me Venneford was a king or somethin'?'

'I don't rightly know what he is,' Skimmerhorn confessed. 'Sometimes they call him an earl, sometimes a lord.'

'In either case he'd have a crown, wouldn't he?' Poteet asked, and when Skimmerhorn said he guessed so, that was enough. 'I've got a dandy!' Poteet cried, and off he went to the blacksmith. Next day he returned with irons for making the handsome brand that would become famous throughout the west, Crown Vee:

Branding day always carried with it a festive spirit, and the testing of the new irons lived up to tradition. Each of the Texans took pleasure in laying his rope over the horns of the cattle or spinning it deftly around their rear legs. Poteet, surmising that Coker had never thrown a rope, forestalled embarrassment by directing him to the dirtiest, dustiest job of all—wrestling with the roped animals and holding them down while the brand was being applied.

It required three days, from first light till fading dusk, to get through all the animals, and even then the job could not have been completed had not local cattlemen volunteered to help. They did so for two reasons: they loved the excitement of hot iron singeing hair, of cattle bawling in protest, of ropers dragging the next reluctant steer into position, of the hullabaloo caused by six teams working at the same time at the same dusty job; but they also anticipated the feast and the drinking that would come afterward, and as they pitched in to help, they kept one eye on Nacho Gómez and his cook wagon.

'Best brandin' I been to in a long time,' one old-timer declared the last night as he chewed on one of Nacho's thickest steaks, set aside for this celebration. 'Good whiskey, too,' Canby added, drawing on a bottle of Tennessee mash which Skimmerhorn had bought from a Jacksborough bar.

'Drink up,' Poteet encouraged the men. 'Last whiskey you'll have for months.'

So the Crown Vee animals were branded, eighteen hundred and ten cows and heifers ready to breed, one hundred and forty-two good bulls eager to breed them, and eight hundred and twenty-six steers, a herd of twenty-seven hundred and seventy-eight, all marked on the left hip, plus one hundred and thirty-two remuda horses and six mules branded lightly on the left shoulder by Nacho and the wrangler. These were the animals on which Oliver Seccombe's dream of riches depended.

On the fifteenth of March, 1868, Mr. Poteet indicated with a wave of his hat that the massive herd should move westward, and the full complement of men, horses and cattle started forward. Far in the lead rode Mr. Poteet, accompanied for the moment by Mr. Skimmerhorn. Behind them rode eight cowboys so spaced that they formed a permanent floating box around the herd. At the front rode the two points, Person to the

left, Canby to the right. About a third of the way back rode the two
swing men. Two-thirds of the way back rode the two flank men, whose
special job it was to see that the main body of cattle did not bunch up
and become overheated, for cattle moving close-bunched generated
a tremendous heat which could actually melt off fat. And in the rear,
where the dust was thickest and the cattle most difficult to handle, for
stragglers must be made to close up, rode the two drags. To the left, in
the humblest position of all, rode Bufe Coker, so stiff he could hardly
stay in his saddle, his bandanna pulled over his face to repel the incredible dust. To the right, escaping some of the dust, rode Lasater.

Far to one side and slightly ahead of even Mr. Poteet, rode Nacho
Gómez in his cook wagon, and well behind him, in a spot where the dust
from the herd could not annoy his horses, came Buck with his hundred
and thirty-two animals. In this established formation the men and animals would move for four months.

They could average fifteen miles a day if conditions were normal, and
that took into account a two-hour break in the hot middle of the day. On
this first break, when the cattle were grazing quietly and Nacho was making coffee, Mr. Poteet spoke to the men as a group.

'The points and the drags will remain the same throughout the run.
The four men at swing and flank will rotate mornin' and afternoon,
clockwise. There will be no gamblin', absolutely none, for it breeds dis-
content and I intend this to be a peaceable trail. There will be no drinkin', and if I catch anyone with a bottle anywhere along the trail, he gets
paid off that instant, less the cost of one horse, which he can take with
him in addition to his own. There are some trail bosses who even forbid
swearin', but I don't see how we can handle twenty-eight hundred bastards like these without it. But keep it down.

'Well, that's the law, easy to understand, easy to keep. Oh, two more
things. Keep your guns in your belt. I want no gunfire, not even in
stampedes. For heading off steers, wavin' a hat is much better. If the
time comes we need guns, you'll know it. And don't abuse the cook. He's
got somethin' you ain't seen yet. Nacho, lay off them beans and show us
your dragoon.'

Leaving his Dutch ovens, the Mexican went to his wagon, rummaged
among his blankets and came back with a fearsome weapon. Basically it
was Samuel Colt's 1848 Third Dragoon, .44-caliber, rounded-trigger-
guard, seven-and-a-half-inch barrel, six-cylinder revolver, heavy and
handsomely tooled. Nacho had picked it up in Mexico, where it had been
lost by some army officer serving with a force left behind by victorious
General Taylor, but what made it especially lethal was that it had been
fitted with a special shoulder stock, which converted it from a pistol into
a carbine. Thus adapted, it could be swept from side to side like a hand-
gun but still controlled like a rifle.

'And I've seen him use it,' Poteet said. 'Three things no sensible man fools with. A rattlesnake, a skunk, and most of all, a cook.' 'Or women,' Ragland added in a whisper. Nacho smiled as he replaced the slaughter-gun, but halted in mid-action when Poteet called, 'Wait a minute, Nacho! Let me see that dragoon.' When the Mexican handed it to him, Poteet deftly opened a secret lock at the base of the stock, tilted it until a few drops ran out, which he tasted as they fell onto his fingers. Then he re-placed the fitting and handed the gun back to Nacho. 'On the ride north with Mr. Skimmerhorn,' Poteet explained, 'Nacho kept that filled with whiskey.'

The hands cheered the Mexican, and he responded by pointing to the coffee, which was now ready. It had been made according to the standard Texas recipe: 'Take two pounds of Arbuckle's best, pour in a little water, boil for two hours, then test by tossing in a clean horseshoe. If the shoe sinks, it ain't quite done.' The meeting ended when Nacho produced a Dutch oven filled with unexpected biscuits.

The cattle were now starting to lie down, which meant they had grazed enough, so Mr. Poteet prepared to hit the trail, but before he did he told the men, 'We have a lot of younger fellows with us this time, so maybe I better remind everybody what a cowboy is. Sometimes he has to fight Indians, and sometimes he requires fancy ridin' and tricky rope work, which I'm sure you can do. At other times, especially in Kansas, he has to protect his herd against outlaws. And when we come to towns, which we don't on this trail, he's supposed to drink his weight in likker and throw his money to the girls.

'All that's to one side, necessary but not important. For me a cowboy is a man who tends cows. All day, every day. Those cows yonder are the reason you're here. And gettin' them up north in one piece is your only responsibility.

'Let's move 'em out!' and the cowboys slowly and with skill got the longhorns onto their feet, back on the trail and properly spaced for the afternoon journey.

That day they made less than nine miles. Not only had they got off to a late start, well after the sun was up, but also Mr. Poteet wanted to have conditions as near perfect as possible for the first night. 'If we can get them safely through these first days and nights,' he told the hands, 'we'll stand a good chance of keepin' 'em from stampedin'.' Knowing that the cattle would be eager to turn back to their home pastures, a very strong instinct, he found a small creek and led them to the other side. There he sought out a meadow which had a well-defined mound between it and the creek, so that any longhorn that might want to run home would first have to climb the little hill. He then had his men quietly circle the meadow, their horses keeping well out from the cattle, so that when a cow or a steer started to edge away from the central mass, some horse-man would be there to nudge it gently back.

Silence was essential during this first critical night. There must be no noise from the camp, not even the sudden dropping of a spoon onto a tin plate or a loud sneeze. The remuda must be kept well away, so that no clatter from the horses could alarm the jittery cattle. Poteet, looking at the sky, was thankful that there were no signs of thunder or lightning, and he trusted that this far south no Comanche would infiltrate to stampede the herd intentionally, with the aim of stealing two or three hundred cattle in the melee.

Poteet stayed up all that night. So did Nate Person. The rest were assigned regular two-hour watches. Two men, riding in opposite directions, circled the herd, singing softly as they went. On each round they would meet twice, dark and silent shapes looming up from the night, nodding as they passed, keeping their horses at a steady walk. In a well-run outfit, it was said, a night rider would move off a hundred yards even to spit, while the lighting of a cigarette or a sudden cough was intolerable.

Within one second after an unusual noise, an entire herd of longhorns could be on its feet, dashing in some arbitrary direction, trampling anything that got in its way. Unmindful of ravines or rivers, of horses or men, they might rush insanely for three hundred yards, then mysteriously subside and sleep the rest of the night, or they might run for thirty miles, nearly killing themselves from sheer exhaustion. Little wonder that a stampede was something to be avoided, for its consequences no man could foresee, and for some, overtaken by a trampling herd or thrown by their horses down some gully, it was the end of the trail.

The first night went peacefully, and Mr. Poteet slept in the wagon part of the morning, while Nate Person used it in the afternoon.

On the second night there was a scare when a poorwill swooped over the restless herd, uttering its mournful cry. Several steers leaped to their feet and at some distance from any of the riders.

'Quick!' Poteet called in a low voice to Lasater, who was riding guard, and the lanky Texan spurred his horse toward the trouble, but he was not needed, because a rugged old steer with a horn spread of fifty inches, named Stonewall by Poteet, muscled his way into the midst of the troublemakers and his resolute presence seemed to settle them.

'A steer like that is worth three cowboys,' Poteet said.

'Where'd you get him?' the cowboy asked.

'I used him twice before,' Poteet said. 'You can trust him . . . like the general.'

'He knew his business,' Lasater said, and the rest of the night went without incident.

On the trail Stonewall pretty much took charge. He was a canny beast, experienced in trail routine, so that no matter where he might be grazing when Mr. Poteet waved his hat, he automatically worked his way to the front, ready to set the pace. By the fourth day the routine seemed well established.

However, it was broken that morning when a young boy, who had been following the cloud of dust thrown up by the cattle, galloped into camp, asking to see Mr. Poteet. Lasater led the boy to the trail boss and listened as the young rider said, 'Mr. Poteet, my mom says please to ride over and see her.'

'And who is your mother?'

'Emma Lloyd.'

'Tom Lloyd your father?'

'Yes, sir.'

'How is he?'

'Dead. Didn't get back from the war.'

Poteet looked across the grasslands, and once more the terror of the southern war assailed him. But he also looked much further back, to the happier days of peace when he and Tom Lloyd were courting Emma Staller, half-heartedly, as cowboys do, and one day Tom had said, 'R. J., I'm gonna marry Emma,' and Poteet had said, 'You're gettin' a great girl.' The Lloyds had settled down and homesteaded a section with good water. Then the war.

'How far is the ranch?' Poteet asked, but before the boy could reply, he added, 'What's your name, son?'

'Jim.'

'Take the herd on, Mr. Person,' Poteet said, preparing to ride with the son of his old friend.

As they came over the hill Poteet saw a sight only too familiar these days: a Texas ranch with good prospects but on the shabby side because it had no man to tend it. A decent effort had been made, that was obvious, but things were run down. Young Jim, for example. He was clean, but his clothes were ragged. His horse was cared for, but his saddle should have been oiled. And the house. How it needed a carpenter!

Seeing Emma Lloyd in these circumstances was painful, but he dusted off his hat and rode up to the house. 'Hi, Emma,' he called easily.

'R. J.! Well, bless me, you look just fine!' she said, wiping her hands on her apron.

'What can I do for you?' Poteet asked. 'Jim here told me Tom didn't get back.'

'Him and many others,' she said. 'I need you to buy my cattle, R. J.'

'I've pretty well got my string, Emma,' he said.

'So Jim told me when he came back from Jacksborough. I sent him there to offer ours.'

'I didn't see him.'

'He got there too late,' she said, and R. J. had to turn away and look at the low hills to the south. He could visualize the boy riding hard through the night and getting there after he had left. In some families the rider always arrives too late, no matter how soon he starts.

'Emma, we have every head we need.'

'I'm sure of that, R. J. But we haven't had a cent of spendin' money in more'n a year. I just got to sell these cattle.'

'How many children you got, Emma?'

'Three boys. Jim's the oldest.'

'I'd like to see 'em.' When the boys were assembled he lit into them. 'Why don't you clean up this place? You're men now, those cattle over there should be in lots better shape. You, Jim, do you ever do the chores to help your Maw? You're men now, and you gotta begin to act like men.'

The boys listened in silence, realizing that Poteet was blustering only because he was under strain, and they were right, for in the end he said awkwardly, 'I'll take your cattle, Emma. How many do you have?'

'Two hundred and ten.'

'I'll take them only on consignment. I'll give you two dollars a head now, plus whatever I get for them at Fort Sumner.'

'Thank God,' Mrs. Lloyd said.

When he handed her the four hundred and twenty dollars—his own not Skimmerhorn's—she asked in a soft voice, 'Would you consider takin' Jim with you?'

'He's only a boy.'

'You just said he was a man.'

'How old are you, Jim?'

'Seventeen,' the boy said with marked determination.

Jesus! Poteet thought. Seventeen years ago Tom hadn't even met Emma. No more had I. The boy can't be much over fourteen.

'He must get away,' Emma Lloyd said insistently. 'Make a life for himself.'

'Can you rope?' Poteet asked. In answer the boy jumped on his horse and sped toward a steer with mammoth horns. Deftly he threw his lariat so that the long axis of the opening fell beautifully over the horns. But having done this, he found he was not yet strong enough to drag in the steer, so that R. J. had to swing into action and rope one of the steer's back feet.

'We'd make a good pair,' Poteet said. 'You can come along, but at the end of the trail you get no wages.' Jim's face betrayed his disappointment, until Poteet added, 'Because I'm payin' them to your maw, now.'

In this way Jim Lloyd joined the trek north. His arrival caused some consternation, since three of the cowboys—Gompert, Calendar and Savage—did not want to work in an outfit that contained thirteen men. 'It's unlucky,' Gompert mumbled, and others were beginning to agree, until Mr. Poteet pointed out that since Mr. Skimmerhorn was not a real member of the outfit, but only the purchaser, the number was not thirteen but twelve, and this satisfied everyone. But that night on their rounds Gompert said to Savage, 'You know, I think he tricked us.'

'How?'

'He said that Skimmerhorn wasn't one of us, makin' twelve. But you watch, if someone else wants to join us, he'll count Skimmerhorn and say, "See, it isn't thirteen. It's fourteen." He's clever.'

'That's why he's boss,' Savage said, and they rode on.

Now came the days of respite, the days of grass and water before the waterless desert. The longhorns were settling down; they were sufficiently far from home to have ceased wanting to return to former pastures and were content to move on to new. Stonewall stepped out each morning with the same sense of adventure that marked the men who were tending him, and at night the risk of stampede grew less and less. The herd was even beginning to gain weight, for the plains were filled with such luxuriant grass that the animals became increasingly content with their march-rest-march routine.

The thirteen men, too, had settled into a team. With the advent of Jim Lloyd, changes had to be made. He was assigned to the left drag, the worst job of all; since prevailing winds were from the northwest, the man riding this position had dust in his face most of the time, but Jim was young and needed the job. Coker moved over to the right drag, which was somewhat freer of dust, and he was glad of the promotion. He still had difficulty riding some of his horses, but on his pinto he had the makings of a real cowboy.

Promotion within the swings and flanks didn't mean much, but at the point positions it did. Nate Person was moved up to scout, and now he ranged far ahead of the herd, seeking alternate routes to water; some days he was scarcely seen and he missed quite a few meals. The control of any string of cattle lay with the left point, for when cattle stampede, in the northern hemisphere at least, they almost invariably veer clockwise. Right point is a dangerous position because the man riding there may be run over, but the left point is determinative. The man in that position must ride fast enough to turn the lead cattle inward upon themselves; this throws them into a milling confusion which gradually tires them out. When Person was promoted to scout, this important job of left point was open, and to it Canby was appointed. In his laconic way he told Poteet, 'I can do it.'

Right point remained to be filled, and Poteet surprised everyone, including the man himself, by promoting Mike Lasater to it. He was a good horseman and he was brave, but he was also a convicted thief and no one had expected Poteet to select him for such important work. 'I'll take care of it,' Lasater said, and he did. He was conscientious and able to anticipate what cattle might do. After several days Skimmerhorn told Poteet, 'You made a fine choice.'

Now, in the evenings, began the after-supper yarning, and Jim Lloyd listened with amazement as the younger cowboys, little older than he, told of their exploits. It was not until several nights had passed that Jim began to suspect that perhaps some of the tales were more invention than truth.

He had the bad luck to challenge the wrong man. The talk was of rattlesnakes, and Canby said, 'There was this man from Illinois and we told him, seventeen times we must have told him, "Don't build your house against them rocks," but he did, in late November, and all during a very hard winter he smiled at us, because we were out in the open and he was snug against them rocks, and we broke our backs gatherin' wood while he was protected against the wind. But come late April, like we expected, we hear this dandy from Illinois inside his house screamin' for help, and we knowed what was up.'

Here Canby halted dramatically, and only Poteet and Person knew what was up, but the others were too trail-hardy to ask, so it fell to Jim Lloyd to say, 'What was up?'

'Heat from the sun had brought the rattlesnakes out from them rocks, and when this dandy wokened up he sees sixty rattlers in his room, with some of them draped over his bed, and he like to died.'

Again a dramatic pause, broken by Jim's question: 'What did he do then?'

'For one thing, he wet the bed. For another, he kept screamin', because there wasn't no place he could put his foot down to escape. Of course, we knew the rattlers was torpid . . .'

'What's that?' Jim asked.

'Half asleep . . . just out from hibernation. So we went in and just swept 'em away like they was dust—shook the covers and flicked 'em off on the floor. We got him out of there, but we wouldn't never go back, not even for his things. We had to send a boy in to fetch them.' He paused and added, 'Sixty rattlers in one little room. That makes you think.'

It was Lasater who told the story that Jim had to challenge. He said, 'I mind when O. D. Cleaver was comin' home from buyin' a milk cow, and if there's one animal on this earth that hates the rattlesnake, it's the milk cow, because as you know, the rattler loves milk better'n anything, and he'll creep up on a cow and suck her dry. Moves from teat to teat, I've seen 'em do it.'

'I don't think a cow would allow it,' Jim suggested.

With deep scorn Lasater stared at the boy, then continued: 'So as O. D. was leadin' his milk cow home he spots this rattler alongside the road, not harmin' anybody and tendin' its nineteen baby rattlers. Like pencils they were, not much. So as soon as the cow sees the mother rattler she lunges at her, and what do you suppose the mother rattler does? She opens her mouth and makes a call, I guess. O. D. couldn't hear the call, of course, but he supposes she made one, for every one of the nineteen baby rattlers scurries across the sand and jumps into mama's mouth and back down into her belly, whereupon Mrs. Rattler glides away to safety just as pretty as you please.'

The story pleased the audience and reminded them once more of nature's inherent mysteries, but Jim Lloyd spoiled its effect by saying, 'I don't believe rattlers can do that. The babies would suffocate.'

Lasater drew back his head as if he had been slapped across the face. 'Are you sayin' it didn't happen?' he demanded.

'I wasn't there,' Jim backed up, 'but I doubt . . .'

Lasater responded by drawing his Colt's Navy and slamming it onto the ground before him, its steel-blue barrel glistening in the firelight. 'Are you calling O. D. Cleaver a liar? He seen it, goddamnit. He seen it, and you're calling O. D. Cleaver a liar.'

'No, I'm not,' Jim apologized. 'If he seen it . . . well . . .'

'That's better,' Lasater said, replacing his revolver.

That night when Jim went to bed the others winked at one another and waited, and sure enough, moments later there came a scream of terror, followed by Jim dashing back to the fire, his face ashen white.

'My God, what is it?' Buck the wrangler cried.

'There's a rattlesnake in my bed!'

'Oh, my God!' Buck cried in equal horror, even though he had been the one to plant it there.

'I kicked my shoes off and slipped my feet in . . .' The memory was too painful, and Buck asked solicitously, 'Did it bite you?'

'I don't think so,' and as Jim started inspecting his ankles by the fire he slowly realized that the others were laughing at him, and instinctively he knew that his future in the outfit depended upon how he accepted this hazing. Keeping his hands about his left ankle and scrutinizing it with care, he said slowly, 'The rattler had a good chance at me, so he was either asleep or dead. I guess he must have been dead, because I don't think Buck would be brave enough to pick up a live one and put him in my bed.'

With a burst of laughter, he caught up a handful of dust and threw it across the fire at the wrangler. When he went back to bed the men laughed and told one another, 'He'll be a pretty good kid,' and they joshed Buck, claiming that the boy had known all along that the rattler was dead. But Jim, lying alone, wondered at the intricacy of the joke that had been played on him. It had started far back in the evening with the first mention of rattlesnakes, and he had swallowed every piece of bait they had thrown before him, so that when he finally felt the snake in his bed he had nearly fainted with fear.

Along with the hazing, which continued for two weeks, the older men were generous in educating Jim regarding trail customs. Once when he returned, hot and dusty, he threw himself on the ground, his head back, his lungs gasping for clean air, but Nate Person caught him by the arm and warned, 'Don't never do that, Jim.'

'What?'

'Throw yourself on the ground thoughtless, that way. Always look first. When a cowboy sits down, nine things can happen to him, and eight are bad.'

'What you talkin' about?' Jim asked in perplexity.

'He can sit on cactus, or embers from the fire, or somebody's plate, or a Gila monster or a scorpion, or steer piss, or cow flop, or worst of all, a rattlesnake. If you're lucky, one time in nine you get a little rest. So you look before you sit.'

The first time he came back to the fire after a twelve-to-two night guard, he went quietly to Canby's sleeping bag and shook him, intending to say, 'Canby, your watch,' but before he could utter a word Canby was bolt upright, jabbing a revolver in his face and cursing him. 'Don't never touch a sleepin' cowboy!' he growled, wakening the other sleepers, the very thing Jim had been trying to avoid.

'I coulda blown his head off!' Canby snarled. 'Goddamn kid comes sneakin' up on me and grabs me like he was a Indian.' He muttered all the way to the herd, and Mr. Poteet warned Jim, 'When you approach the man who's to take your place, let him hear you comin'. Above all, let him hear you call his name. Start about here and say in a low voice, "Canby! Canby! It's Jim. Your turn." And he'll know everything is all right. But for God's sake, don't touch him. You could have been killed.'

They also taught him how to sing during the night watches. 'It's a fact,' Person explained as he rode with Jim. 'Cattle, 'specially them longhorns, stay quieter if they hear a man's voice. So we sing the night through. I heard a fella say, "Singin' hangs a veil of confidence about the herd." They stay content inside.'

The men sang various songs, but the one Jim adopted was the greatest of the cattle songs, the one that struck closest to the heart of what a cowboy was:

> I ride an old paint, I lead an old dan.
> I'm off to Montanny to throw the hoolihan.
> We feed 'em in the coulies and water in the draw.
> Their tails are all matted, their backs are all raw.
>
> Ride around, little dogies, ride around 'em slow.
> They're fiery and snuffy and a-rarin' to go.

He never tired of the words or the monotonous tune. A thousand cowboys would sing this ditty to their restless herds and quiet them. The verse Jim liked best was a dandy:

> Old Bill Jones had a daughter and a son.
> One went to college, the other went wrong.

His wife was killed in a poolroom fight,
But still he keeps singin' both mornin' and night.

Jim, who knew little about girls, speculated on what had happened to the daughter, but it was the wife part that delighted him. He could see Bill Jones and his tough partner swingin' pool cues and bashin' in heads, and he was sorry the old girl was done in. He had seen pool tables and bowling alleys, too, at Fort Richardson, south of Jacksborough.

The strangest song sung by any of the cowboys was that of Bufe Coker, for he favored what had served as a South Carolina anthem:

Hurrah, hurrah!
For southern rights, hurrah!
Hurrah for the Bonnie Blue Flag
That bears the single star.

When Jim rode with him he could hear the rebel singing this old battle song as though Coker were still marching in defense of a lost cause. He would begin to shout the words, and then Jim would quieten him. The opening verse of the song worried Jim:

We are a band of brothers,
Native to the soil,
Fightin' for the property
We gained by honest toil.

'What property you talkin' about?' Jim asked, and Coker replied, 'Niggers, what else?'

Jim once asked Mr. Skimmerhorn about this, he having fought on the northern side, and Skimmerhorn explained that no body of men had ever fought so valiantly for an idea so wrong. This judgment confused Jim even more and he raised the question with Mr. Poteet, who said, 'It's a stupid song, but I marched to it. Who ever heard of a crusadin' army fightin' to protect mere property, and slave property at that?'

As Jim came to know the cowboys better, he discovered how special these men were, these wanderers of the range. They were at ease only with other men; women perplexed and sometimes terrified them. When they told stories of women they spoke with a fifteenth-century gentility and almost always it was the man who appeared foolish or at fault. They held women in a distant respect, and one night when Buck started to tell of a different kind of woman he had met in Kansas, Poteet stared at him reprovingly and indicated by a nod of his head toward Jim that a young boy was present, and Buck ended lamely, 'Well, she was some woman,' and his listeners grinned.

The talk turned to horses, and Lasater told of the legendary horse that roamed the Texas prairies—the fiery-eyed white mustang that no one had ever been able to rope. Several times he had appeared to parties that had lost their way and were perishing of thirst, and with mane flashing in the sunlight, led them to safety. He had done many remarkable things, including the time he had broken through three sets of latches which Mexicans had constructed to imprison him, but his greatest feat was leading a party of women through a prairie fire.

'O. D. Cleaver saw that mustang as he broke through the fire,' Lasater said. 'That pony had chose the only path to safety, and as he finished his job his mane was afire.'

'A fire that big . . .' Jim Lloyd began. But once more Lasater had his revolver out and was demanding, 'Are you calling O. D. Cleaver a liar?'

'No, if he seen it . . .'

'You better be careful, because he did see it and he told me about it, personally.'

On a starry night so beautiful and so mild with the coming of spring that the men lingered long at the fire, Savage, who rarely talked much, said, 'Just over the hill is Fort Phantom . . . that is, the ruins of it.'

'That's a crazy name for a fort,' Canby said.

'That's what it was,' Savage insisted. 'My dad served there when the fort was bein' built in 18 and 52. He said it was the worst fort in the world—hot, dirty, bad food, no water, nothin' to do . . . day after day, nothin' at all.'

'What's the point of your story?' Lasater asked.

'Just this. In 18 and 54 the government finally listened to the complaints and decided to shut the place down, temporary. On the last day as the men were movin' out my dad heard the major say, "It would be a blessin' if this damned place was burned to the ground. Otherwise they'll use it again." So when the major and the men around him moved on, what do you think my dad and six of his friends did?'

'Burn the fort?' Jim asked.

'They spread oil and gunpowder and lots of wood shavings through all the buildings, forty-six of 'em, and burned the whole shebang . . . right to the ground.'

'I don't believe it,' Buck said.

Suddenly Ragland had his revolver out. 'Are you callin' O. D. Cleaver a liar?' he demanded, mimicking Lasater's voice so cleverly that even Lasater had to laugh.

'Let's ride to the top of the hill and see for ourselves,' Savage proposed, and with Mr. Poteet's permission the younger cowboys took their horses, and by a roundabout way that would not disturb the dozing cattle, rode to the crest of a hill from which they could look across the starry wonder of the plains. And down below them stood the charred ruins of a once-great fort. Only the brick chimneys were in place, standing like ghosts guarding the stars.

'You mean your old man burnt this whole place!' Jim asked in awe.

'Him and the others.'

'They coulda been hung.'

'Nobody never found out who done it.'

'That musta been some fire,' Gompert whispered, and the young cowboys rode back to camp.

There the talk was again of rattlesnakes, with Lasater explaining that O. D. Cleaver had seen it with his own eyes: 'This rattler—a huge one, big around as your thigh—chases a prairie dog down a hole. Dog comes out the other end, and as soon as he's safe he calls all the other dogs—and what do you suppose they do?'

'Run like hell,' Ragland suggested.

Lasater ignored the laughter and concluded: 'The other dogs hurried up, started to pile sand into the hole—both openings—then tamped it down with their feet, and smothered that rattler to death.'

'I don't think it would work,' Jim said cautiously. 'I've dug out prairie-dog burrows and there's usually more'n one or two . . .'

'Son,' Lasater interrupted, 'why do you insist on callin' O. D. Cleaver a liar?'

'I . . . well . . . I've dug . . .'

'O. D. Cleaver seen it. He told me about it hisself.'

Skimmerhorn, amused by Cleaver's credentials as an authority on wildlife, asked, 'Where's Cleaver now?'

'He's dead,' Lasater said. 'Shot holdin' up a bank.'

Now the days of caution began, for the time was approaching when the cattle would start their perilous journey across eighty miles of arid wasteland, with no water and little grass to sustain them. It was imperative that during the next two weeks the cattle eat as much as possible and drink copiously so as to be strong when the test came. Therefore Mr. Poteet and Nate Person rode even farther ahead of the herd, seeking good waterholes where grass was plentiful.

The generous land along the Brazos River was now behind them and in its place long sweeps of emptiness prevailed; a rider would come over a ridge with good grass cover and from its crest see before him fifty miles of the brown barren lands that warned him of what lay ahead. The routine tightened and the men trained themselves to drink as little water as possible. They became extra polite in their dealings with each other, and all felt the tension of the ordeal to come.

This feeling was not diminished when they passed Fort Chadbourne, once a notable installation with four hundred men and a German band, now a desolate waste of empty buildings. 'My dad served here too,' Savage explained as they rode past the gaunt ruins. 'Had to be abandoned . . . never enough water.'

Here, at the ruins of Fort Chadbourne, Poteet and his men stood at the edge of vast territories still being explored by frontiersmen, partially protected by small forts. Save for the classic settlements focusing on Santa Fe, there were none of the churches, farms or homes which eastern states had enjoyed for the ninety-two years since Independence. Once again, another huge tract of land waited for adventurous men to join it to America. True, in the hazardous years of 1858–61, the legendary Butterfield Stage had passed through here, taking the route to the Pecos River which Poteet proposed to follow, but the stage had been halted by war. The only sign that it had ever existed was the broken water tanks cached from point to point across the desert. For Poteet and his men there would be no water, and if their courage failed, they and their cattle would perish.

This was the southern edge of the Llano Estacado, the Staked Plain. Its name had come from Spanish explorers who drove stakes as they crossed it, so that they could find their way back across its featureless domain. In 1542 it had broken Coronado's heart, and now it baked in the sun, daring a new breed of adventurers to cross it.

The Llano seemed to have been devised by nature as a fiendish test of man's resolute will. Its difficulty increased by steps, and as each new hazard was encountered, a man would be tempted to turn back, knowing that the next was to be even more difficult.

Step one consisted of the sixty-three-mile stretch from Fort Chadbourne to the north branch of the Concho, a miserable stream which did, however, contain a little brackish water. Along this trail there were a few hidden sources of water to sustain the cattle if the scouts were sharp enough to find them. On an ordinary trail, this stretch would have been known as 'Hell's Reach,' but on this, it was the good part.

Step two covered only thirty miles, from North Concho to Middle Concho, but it contained no water at all between the rivers, and here the handling of cattle would become difficult.

Step three was a reach of eighty miles across barren alkali flats stretching from the Middle Concho to Horsehead Crossing on the Pecos River. Here there was no water and little grass. Traveling at a normal rate, the herd would require nearly seven days to negotiate it, during which time they would have to perish. But if the speed could somehow be doubled or even tripled, the longhorns, drawing upon reserves of energy, might reach the Pecos alive. It was to this desperate gamble that the cowboys now addressed themselves.

'Jim,' Mr. Poteet said, 'it isn't proper to enter this part of the trail without a gun. See if Canby'll lend you one of his.'

So Jim went to the point man and said, 'Mr. Poteet thinks you ought to lend me a gun. But I want to buy it.'

'With what?'

'Money. When I get paid.'

'You ain't gettin' paid. Everybody knows the old man gave your wages to your maw.'

'I'll get money somehow.'

Canby played with his reins, embarrassed by this whole affair. He loved his guns and felt that with eight he had barely enough for the work ahead. Still, it wasn't proper for a boy to head into such country without a gun. It just wasn't proper.

'I might let you have the .22.'

'That ain't a gun,' Jim said.

'You're right there, son.' He slapped the reins against his horse's neck, then pulled her back when she started to move. 'Tell you what, I do have an extra Army Colt's and I could borry it to you.'

'I don't want to borrow it. I want to buy it.'

'What in hell with?' Canby asked in exasperation. 'All right, damnit, I'll sell you the Colt's. Ten dollars and I'll throw in the bullets.'

'I'll pay you some day,' Jim said. 'That's a promise.'

With everything tightened up, the outfit headed into the easy portion of the Llano. The days were hot and dusty, and the cattle grew restive because the grass was hard to find and the water scarce. Poteet and Person again ranged far ahead, finding some holes that had gone dry, others with enough dregs to keep the cattle going.

The trick was to keep the cattle moving forward as rapidly as possible, to divert their attention from the scanty feed; instead of ten to twelve miles a day, the pace was stepped up to fifteen or even eighteen, and in this way the first stretch of the desert was crossed.

At the North Concho the animals drank the brackish water with enthusiasm, and Mr. Poteet kept them there for an extra day, watching as some of the cows stood belly-deep in the creek, as if to let the water seep into their parched hides.

The men had trouble with this water. It gave half of them dysentery; Gompert and Savage became so sick they could not ride their night rounds, so Poteet and Skimmerhorn took their places, riding double shifts. It was Nacho Gómez who saved the day; he brewed up a nauseous concoction of cactus root, tobacco juice, vinegar and rum, guaranteed to tighten the loosest bowel, and after three doses Gompert and Savage were back at work. 'Anything's better'n that,' they warned the others.

The thirty miles between the two branches of the Concho were covered in two days and ended in disappointment, for the Middle Concho contained barely enough water to replenish the cattle. Again Mr. Poteet laid over for an extra day, and this was wise, for some water did return to the creek bottom. He and Skimmerhorn rode well to the south to find the best possible drinking water, and returned to fetch the water barrel, which they filled. Each man looked after his own canteen, while Nacho collected as much as he could for coffee. During the next three days men would gnaw biscuits and drink coffee . . . till the water ran out.

On the night of April 6, 1868, Mr. Poteet gathered his hands for their last hot meal. As they ate he told them, 'We'll pull out at first light and move as fast as possible. You'll have to watch 'em closely. They'll want to come back here for water. I've known longhorns double back fifty miles.'

'Tomorrow night?' Canby asked.

'We travel all night, every night, till we get there.' The men said nothing. 'Mr. Person will scout ahead and make sure we're drivin' for the pass through the mountains. He can borrow any man's horse he needs, because I want him ridin' back and forth, constantly.'

The black man nodded. The distance to water was eighty miles; he would ride nearly two hundred, back and forth, assuring them of their way.

'Now get some sleep,' Poteet concluded.

At midnight Jim and Coker took over the watch, and as they circled the herd Jim could hear the Confederate singing:

> 'We are a band of brothers,
> Native to the soil,
> Fightin' for the property
> We gained by honest toil.'

Once as they passed, Jim asked, 'Was the war tough?'

'Very.'

'As bad as what we face tomorrow?'

'Different,' Coker said, and he rode on singing.

At first light the cattle were moved onto the trail. Now nature had used no subtlety at all. Move two feet from the banks of Middle Concho and you had ground so hard you knew it hadn't seen water for years. Two miles out the alkali began to show, a sickly white deposit over everything. It had a dead, barren taste, neither acid nor sweet, and enough of it in water could kill a cow.

When the sun rose the men caught their first full impact of the Llano, for over the land before them they could see not one tree, nor any shrub of size, nor any trail marking, nor any sign of habitation. It was the most bleak and arid space they had ever surveyed, and it promised nothing.

A man standing on flat ground could see to a horizon 3.2 miles distant. Astride a tall horse he could see an additional 1.2 miles. He was at the center of a circle with the radius of 4.4 miles, so that as the cowboys rode they could survey sixty square miles of the Llano, and on it they saw nothing but their cattle and their own shadows.

By nine o'clock the heat grew intense and the cattle began looking for water, and this search they would continue for the next eighty miles, this endless, patient longing for water that did not exist. The toughest old hand, the rawest youth who was trying to swagger, would at some unexpected moment catch the eye of a frantic cow, and as he drove her back to the panting herd, he would feel his throat choking.

Toward noon Savage cried, 'He's coming!' and far in the west the cowboys saw a light rise of dust and then a horse and then a man upon it, his face white with alkali. They watched as he approached, his horse cantering gently over the flat sands.

Dismounting at the cook wagon, Nate asked for coffee. Holding the cup with both hands and keeping it to his chin as he looked over the edge, he reported, 'We're on the right headin' so far.'

'Any water?'

'None.' He finished his coffee, changed horses and rode off long before the cattle were put back on the trail.

On a normal run it was the head of the column that required special attention, but now, since the cattle might try to double back, it was the rear. So Jim and Coker were strengthened by Mr. Poteet and Skimmerhorn, and for several hours the latter rode with Jim and talked of life in Colorado.

'It's bound to be one of the greatest states,' Skimmerhorn said.

'Better'n Texas?'

'Better scenery. Better chance for a young man.'

'I've heard good things about Wyoming.'

'It'll never be the state Colorado is. Too many Indians.'

'How about Montana?'

'No people.'

Jim was impressed with this man. He wasn't as iron-hard as Mr. Poteet nor was he as good a cowboy, but he was the owner of this outfit, and here he was riding drag. Jim had noticed that no job in the camp was too low for Mr. Skimmerhorn, and if the cook needed more wood, he was the first to volunteer.

'You married?' Jim asked.

'Yes. I have one daughter and a son on the way.'

'What if it's a girl?'

Nothing happened that long day, and for much of the time they rode in silence, each favorably impressed with the other. But on the night march trouble came, for the longhorns were bewildered by this change in tactic and by their lack of water. Again and again strays tried to turn back, so that Jim and Mr. Skimmerhorn were busy all night, riding until they exhausted their night horses and had to get others from the remuda. It was a bad night, and everyone was thirsty, but the men had hot coffee, whereas the cows had nothing.

The second day was miserable, with the men seeing at first hand the effect of this perilous journey on the cattle. Several cows seemed to go half mad and men had to lash at them and beat them over the head, forcing them back onto the trail.

In the late afternoon the cows began lowing, and soon the entire herd was voicing its protest in a surge of sound that rose and fell and entered the heart of every man who heard it.

The sun was unbearable. Men would ride hard and break into a sweat, but the air was so dry that they never became wet. They gulped enormous quantities of coffee but did not have to urinate. Those with dysentery—half the crew—had racking bowel movements but passed no water. And alkali dust covered everything—the eyes of the men above their bandannas and the eyes of the cattle.

Ordinary cows could not have survived this ordeal, but the thrifty longhorn, accustomed to thorns, struggled on doggedly, following Stonewall. In this time of trial each cowboy developed a positive love for that cantankerous old steer, his hipbones jutting out like those of a skeleton. It was as if he alone, among all the cattle, understood why this waterless trek was necessary, and he would do what he could to bring it to a rightful conclusion.

That night was most difficult, especially for the drags. Jim and Coker had been in the saddle now for thirty-nine hours without real sleep or a hot meal and they were desperately tired, but the cattle, scenting no relief ahead, decided to return to the Concho, where they last had water. It seemed to Jim that he spent the entire night at a gallop, bringing steers and cows back into the fold, and often as he dashed into the moonlight, he would be aware of Mr. Skimmerhorn, riding beside him or ahead, working just as hard.

At dawn, the herd having been held intact, Jim collapsed on the ground, and Skimmerhorn said, 'Let him sleep.'

He was there when Nate Person rode back, his dark sleepless eyes sunk deep in his head. He brought good news. 'The gap is dead ahead. Fourteen miles beyond it is the Pecos.'

'Water?' Poteet asked.

'Lots,' Person replied, 'but only at Horsehead is it sweet. Even a short distance north or south . . . almost stagnant . . . pure alkali. It'll kill every cow that drinks it.'

'Is the Horsehead marked?'

'The skulls are still in place.' He referred to the line of horses' skulls fixed on posts that marked the way to the crossing. 'I'll be there to help.' And back he rode to chart the course for them.

The last day was almost unbearable. Thirty-two miles to cover, eighteen to the pass through the mountains, fourteen from there to water, and this could be explained to men, but not to the cattle. One cow, driven mad by thirst, set off on a straight line to nowhere. Jim, knowing this particular cow, tried to turn her back, but she brushed past him as if he did not exist. He called for help, and Mr. Poteet thought of enlisting the aid of Stonewall, but he was too far away, at the head of the column keeping things in order, so the cow was allowed to pursue her way. Jim watched her march into the bleakest part of the desert, stumble, rise again, fall to her knees, rise once more, and fall for the last time as buzzards swooped down to claim her.

'It's all right,' Mr. Poteet said.

'I raised her,' Jim said, tears in his eyes. 'She dropped good calves.' She had been the pride of the Lloyd herd, and he was powerless to save her.

The dreadful routine was now broken. In the distant west appeared a column of dust, and as it drew closer it became a momentary vision of men on horses with a wagon, only to dissolve again into dust.

'What the hell can that be?' Lasater asked, and everyone kept his attention on the dust, thinking that it must be Nate Person, but it was not.

It was indeed a company of men, seven or eight perhaps, leading a wagon drawn by mules.

'There's no army unit around here,' Savage said.

'Could it be the Pettis gang?' Skimmerhorn asked with real apprehension.

'No, they wouldn't range this far south,' Poteet assured him, but he, too, watched the approaching column with concern.

'Move that remuda in closer,' he called to Canby, who rode out to warn Buck. 'Get the wagon, too.' And Nacho headed his mules back toward the column.

These precautions were unnecessary, for when the horsemen were close enough to be identified, they proved to be one of the strangest processions ever to cross the Llano. The man in the lead was a lean, sharp-eyed cattleman, thirty-two years old, named Charles Goodnight, the Christopher Columbus of the prairies. He had been everywhere, the first man to cross these plains with cattle, and now he was going home after having sold his herd at Fort Union.

He knew Poteet. 'You can make it,' he assured the cowboys. 'Your cattle are in bad shape, but they can handle the mountain and then they'll have water.'

He impressed upon Poteet the necessity of keeping his water-starved cattle away from the alkali sections of the Pecos. 'Only at Horsehead is the water good. Station your best men north and south and keep your critters away from the salts.'

'What's in the wagon?' Poteet asked.

'Oliver Loving,' he said solemnly. 'My partner and friend. Killed by Comanche.' He spoke briefly of Loving's character and his knowledge of range life. 'He made me promise one thing. Didn't want his bones buried in a foreign land.'

Goodnight's men had flattened kerosene tins to make a metal covering for the wooden coffin in which they were transporting the body. They had then placed it in a spacious wooden outer coffin and filled the space between with charcoal, so that the body would ride easily.

'We'll bury him in Weatherford, Texas, the way he wanted,' Goodnight said, and he reassembled his men to continue their long march across the desert. 'It's easier,' he said, 'when you don't have cattle.'

Before he left, Mr. Skimmerhorn asked, 'You'll be passing Tom Lloyd's ranch, won't you?'

'Tom's dead.'

'I know. This is his boy.'

Mr. Goodnight looked at the boy and said, 'You must be about fourteen. Good age to be startin' on the trail.'

'What I had in mind,' Skimmerhorn said, 'was that Mrs. Lloyd gave Mr. Poteet about two hundred longhorns . . .'

'Two hundred and eighteen, less one that died this morning,' Jim said.

'And we're taking them to Fort Sumner to sell . . . on consignment, as it were.'

'No market at Fort Sumner. None at all. John Chisum sells 'em all they need.'

Jim's face showed his anguish at such news. His mother needed that money, but Mr. Skimmerhorn continued: 'I've been watching these cattle. I'd like to buy them all—right now. And give you the balance of the money for Mrs. Lloyd.'

'You've got yourself a bargain, sir. Didn't catch the name.'

'Skimmerhorn.'

Mr. Goodnight hesitated. 'You're not old enough to have led the Colorado militia . . .' He stopped.

'At the Rattlesnake Buttes massacre? No, sir. That was my father.'

'I'm sorry to hear it, sir. But if you want to send Mrs. Lloyd the money by me, I'd be honored by such evidence of your trust.'

Skimmerhorn counted out the bills for the two hundred and seventeen longhorns, less the advance that Mr. Poteet had given, and Mr. Goodnight tucked it into his belt. Bidding the cowboys farewell, he headed his cortege eastward toward Fort Chadbourne.

'You trustin' him with all that money for a widow?' Savage asked, and Mr. Poteet said, 'If you can't trust Charles Goodnight, there's no man on earth you can.' Then he interrupted himself to ask, 'What's wrong with that boy?' and he sent Mr. Skimmerhorn to where Jim Lloyd was standing beside his horse, looking at the disappearing column, his shoulders heaving in silent grief.

'What's the matter, son?' Skimmerhorn asked, and the fourteen-year-old boy mumbled, 'I'll never see my mother again . . . nor my brothers.' Skimmerhorn said nothing, for he suspected that this would be so.

They now led the cattle across the last bleak stretch of alkali flats and into the mountains, knowing that when the animals smelled the water ahead they would rush to it. But manipulating them over this final desert was bound to be difficult. The cattle were mad with thirst and could no longer be bullied. A steer cut off on his own, like the cow before him, and like her he died. The buzzards kept steady watch, floating in the cloudless sky, noting each faltering step.

It was now that Stonewall proved himself invaluable; he was a kind of

Old Testament prophet, leading his stricken cohorts to a better land, just beyond the mountains. Perhaps he, sooner than the others, smelled the distant water; at any rate, he kept the animals moving and disciplined those near him if they attempted to break loose.

At the top of the pass, that strange cleft between hills so flat they might have been scraped across the top with a ruler, the cattle sensed that water lay below them in the distant valley and they surged forward with new hope. But as they did so it was the cows, not the bulls or steers, who took charge. Some extra responsibility for keeping life alive animated them, and rudely they shoved the males aside, pushing and knocking until they came to the head of the column, where only the patience of Stonewall kept them in order.

On and on they pressed, mad for water and the continuation of life. Their gaunt necks reached out and their dust-filled eyes peered through the haze as their legs pumped mechanically, driven by the last surges of energy within their shrunken frames.

'Keep up with 'em!' Poteet shouted to his men. 'Keep 'em from the alkali.'

The cowboys started at an easy canter, then found themselves pulled into a gallop by the running herd. Dust rose over the arid plains and buzzards flew higher to escape it. Jim Lloyd, riding drag, had no problem keeping his charges moving forward. They were far ahead of him and it was all he could do with his tired horse to keep up with them.

Now Nate Person rode back from the river, shouting, 'Keep 'em to the south!'

He and Poteet and Skimmerhorn moved to the right point to help Lasater force the stampede away from the bad water, and by skillful riding they turned the herd.

'I think we've got 'em!' Poteet called, for the river was less than a mile away and they were headed in the right direction.

But now a tragic thing happened. Stonewall, having safely brought the herd so far, smelled water and set out for the nearest source, which happened to lie north, just where the alkali was most concentrated.

'Head him off,' Poteet yelled, but it was impossible to turn him. What was worse, the cows were following him and a great pressure developed from behind.

'Stop him!' Person shouted. 'Goddamnit, Lasater! Stop him!'

Lasater, who was closest to the old steer, did not hesitate. Spurring his horse, he rode directly at Stonewall, intending to divert him, but the big steer simply ran down both man and horse, throwing both to the ground. Now only Poteet stood between the cattle and disaster.

Without waiting, he rode hard at Stonewall, and again the big steer tried to run the man down, his old partner Poteet.

When the trail boss saw what the steer intended he reined in his horse and waited till the big brute was upon him. Then, aiming his revolver carefully, he destroyed the wonderful animal. With a last look of astonishment at Poteet, the steer stumbled forward and fell into the dust. Instantly Poteet spurred his horse away from the spot, and with help from Skimmerhorn, held the hesitant cattle and headed them for the good water.

They surged into the stream past the skeleton horseheads and stood there for some minutes before drinking. Then, unlike the men who drank in foolish gulps, they took small sips, lowing as they did, until the whole muddy stream echoed with their joy.

Jim Lloyd and Coker found Lasater stretched out unconscious, but Mr. Skimmerhorn, who listened to his heart and felt for broken bones, told them, 'He'll be all right.' Now Ragland called, 'Poteet's missing,' and everyone tried to reconstruct where the boss had been.

'He was riding like hell when we turned the cows back,' Skimmerhorn said, and they spread out. Canby found him back down the trail a bit, toward the bad water. He had dismounted and was standing beside Stonewall, and as the younger Texans rode by in their search, Canby motioned them away, and they left him there, each cowboy with his own memory of that splendid steer.

The Pecos was a preposterous river. For the past five weeks these men had dreamed of the moment when they would lead their cattle down to it, and for the last three waterless days it had been an obsession. Now here it was, about eighteen feet across, as shallow as six inches in some parts, only a little deeper in others. There wasn't much water, but it kept flowing. Two hundred cows would crowd into the good part and drink like siphons, and minutes later the water would stand at the same level. Jim Lloyd tried it, and it was brakish, tasting of alkali even at the good part. Farther up you couldn't keep the water in your mouth, let alone swallow it.

'Hell, I could jump that,' Ragland said, and he steped back, hunched up his shoulders and pumped his legs like pistons on one of the new steam engines. With a snort he sped across the even upland, tore down the steep bank and gave a mighty roar as he leaped into the hot air brooding over the river.

He would have made it, too, except that he found no secure place from which to take off. He fell two feet short, landed with a resounding splash, fought to maintain a foothold and fell backward in the water. For the rest of the trip, cowboys at night would slap their legs and ask each other, 'Remember when Old Rags said he could jump the Pecos? Hell, he missed by a mile!' Henceforth he would be Old Rags, the highest compliment a cowboy could pay another. It would never be Old Gompert or Old Savage and certainly not Old Buck. That would be inconceivable.

The men led the cows across to the western bank, then camped for three days till everyone recovered, but as they were about to move out, the wrangler, who had his horses to the north, shouted, 'Calvary!' Like all Texans, he pronounced this word in its biblical form. Any soldier on horseback was calvary.

It was a detachment from Fort Sumner, riding out to scout the Mescalero Apaches, who were on a rampage through central New Mexico. 'We want you to drive up the east bank,' a lieutenant shouted.

'Is there grass over there?' Poteet asked.

'Not good, but if you stay over here they'll steal your horses. Keep a sharp eye on your remuda.'

'Much fighting?'

'Nope. Just raids. If you shoot, they shoot.'

When the cavalrymen finished their coffee they disappeared to the south, and Poteet laid plans to keep the remuda closer to camp, with extra men to help guard it. 'An Apache can steal your blanket while you're sittin' on it,' he warned, 'but they're not goin' to get our horses.'

With loud huzzahs the men brought the Crown Vee cattle back to the east bank, no great feat, and started them north. It was a curious trail: the land bordering the river was loaded with cactus, barren of grass and blistering hot. In order for the cattle to feed, the cowboys led them about six miles away from the river, but for them to drink, they had to come back to one of the potable spots, and in this zigzag fashion they stumbled north.

'I'll put this land up against the worst in Texas,' Lasater said.

One night Ragland asked abruptly, 'Is it true, Lasater, that you was mighty near hung?'

'Yep.'

'How come?'

'Me and O. D. Cleaver was fixin' to hold up a bank in a place called Falfurrias . . .'

'They ain't no such place as Falfurrias,' Ragland said.

'North of the border,' Lasater replied. It was important to him that the men acknowledge the truth of his claim. 'You know Reynosa, where we used to pick up the Mexican herds? You cross the river to Hidalgo, which isn't much, and come due north and you hit Falfurrias.'

'Yeah,' Savage agreed. 'About halfway to San Antonio.'

His veracity established, Lasater said, 'Me and O.D. was camped six miles south of Falfurrias, sort of scoutin' out the place, and we figured the sheriff and most of the men would be out of town on Thursday afternoon—somethin' doin' to the north—and we rode into town easy-like, but they hadn't gone. The sheriff spotted us and shouted, "Catch them swine!" and they did, and somebody yelled, "Let's hang 'em," and somebody else yelled, "We can't hang 'em. They ain't done nothin'," and this danged old sheriff shouts, "We can hang 'em for what they was gonna do," and danged if they didn't haul us out to the edge of town and start to string us up when a young feller who musta been either a lawyer or a preacher interrupts in a loud voice cryin', "This is unconstitutional and against the law of God," and the sheriff says, "You know danged well these two was gonna rob the bank. You seen 'em scoutin' the place the last three days," and they tightened the rope, and the young feller draws his gun and says, "Then you gotta hang me too, because I've scouted that danged old bank many a day." So they let us go, and I got just one word for you fellers, "Stay away from Falfurrias," because down there they hang you for what you're thinkin'.'

'How come you took to robbin' banks?' Ragland asked.

Lasater stared at the fire and offered no explanation, so Ragland continued: 'You goin' back to it when we're done?'

'I sure ain't plannin' to,' Lasater said, and Jim Lloyd, sitting near him as he said these words, saw the strange look on his face, as if the older cowboy knew that no man was complete master of his fate, and that sometimes a man found himself caught up in the robbing of a bank when that had not been his intention at all.

It now became difficult to find potable water, for the Pecos became loaded with alkali, and the water holes, which were frequent in the area, could not be used, because they were passing through land claimed by John Chisum, greatest cattle baron in the west. He was so determined to hold on to what he had grabbed that he designated a few holes for the use of his own cattle and directed his men to salt the others.

Some years ago Chisum had accomplished in New Mexico what Seccombe was trying to do in Colorado: by purchasing six hundred strategic acres with water he had established his iron rule over another six million. He considered all this land his and was ready to shoot anyone who dared trespass upon it with intention of staying. His own land would support at best twenty cows; he ran upward of forty thousand on land that rightfully belonged to the general public, but if one of that public tried to build a cabin anywhere on the vast reaches, or tried to water his cattle at a Chisum well, he faced the barrel of a gun.

'We're now on John Chisum land,' Poteet warned the men as they moved north. The range, farther than a man could see in ten days of travel, was Chisum's because he said so. Scores of good men would die before this unique theory of land ownership could be successfully challenged.

After the cowboys had learned to grapple with this problem of no drinkable water in the Pecos and none in John Chisum's wells, they were confronted with another trying situation. For some time the older hands had noticed that two or three of the cows were growing distressingly fat, and one morning they woke to find that one of them had thrown a calf. They looked at Jim.

When Mr. Poteet heard of the matter he said, 'Well, Jim. The drag takes care of the calves. That's the rule.'

'How?' Jim asked.

'You kill 'em.'

'I what?' Jim asked, his face turning white.

'Tell him, Nate,' and Person took Jim and Coker aside and said, 'Every outfit that trails cows has this problem. Calves. They can't possibly keep up. You'd lose cow and calf.' He shook his head and told the drags, 'It's your job to kill 'em.'

'But how?' Jim pleaded.

'Some shoots 'em. Some bangs 'em over the head with a club.'

'But I . . .' Before the boy could speak Person left, taking Coker with him.

Jim went to where the cow was suckling her newborn, and one look at the white snout and the eager lips of the calf as it found the teat undid Jim completely for his task. He touched his revolver but could not take it from his holster. He looked about for a club and was gratified when he found none. Finally, in despair, he lifted the calf and took it from its protecting mother, who followed him almost to the camp.

'I can't kill a calf, Mr. Poteet. I raise 'em.'

'Put the damned thing down,' Poteet shouted, 'and get rid of it.' He turned away in disgust, and Jim appealed to the others, but no one would help. He was ashamed of the tears that came into his eyes, but he would not put down the calf. Finally, off to the left he saw Nacho driving his team to the next stop and he ran to him.

'Let me put the calf in your wagon . . . just for a while. I'll think of somethin',' so Nacho hid the calf, but when they stopped and the men were eating, the calf bawled, and Mr. Poteet started to say, 'What in hell . . .' but he stopped. There were some things a trail boss was wise not to hear.

So Jim fed the calf and tended it, and when another was born the job of destroying it was given to Coker, but he proved no more valiant than Jim. 'Hell, I can't use a LeMat that was carried by a Confederate colonel to kill no calf,' he said, and his found a place with Nacho, too.

But when a third was born and Jim could not kill it, Mr. Poteet had had enough of first-time drags. 'Out those calves go, and you two men finish them off,' he snapped, but Jim found reprieve in an unlikely quarter. Nacho in his singsong voice said, 'Mr. Poteet, I theenk I got some-theeng . . . sometheeng goood,' and he asked permission to keep the calves till they got to Fort Sumner, and Poteet gave grudging consent.

Three days shy of Fort Sumner the Apaches struck, but they did so with such cunning, crossing the Pecos after midnight and moving with the stealth of coyotes, that three of the horses were on the west bank of the river before anyone realized they had been stolen, and the cowboys wouldn't have known it even then except that a bay horse much loved by Gompert whinnied, and he leaped up from his sleeping bag with a wild shout, 'They're stealin' my horse.'

The cowboys couldn't believe it. The Apaches had come right into the camp, had passed the remuda where the three guards waited, and had stalked through the space between the sleepers and the cook wagon, leading three good horses away with them.

'We didn't see nothin',' the wrangler reported on behalf of the guards, and Nacho said the calves had kept him awake and he had heard nothing. Gompert wanted to organize a posse to ride after the Apache and shoot it out, and Lasater and Coker were eager to go, but Mr. Skimmerhorn counseled prudence.

'Apaches have been stealing horses for centuries,' he said.

'They could of killed us in our sleep,' Lasater said.

'Why in hell didn't they steal the calves?' Poteet asked.

During the next two days the cowboys were unusually sensitive to their surroundings, and twice the younger fellows thought they saw Apaches on the western hills, but nothing came of it. Jim Lloyd, inspecting the landscape with extra care, made the acquaintance of a bird that he would always remember as the symbol of the drive, a doughty, quick, amusing creature that stayed on the ground much of the time, tilting his head from side to side while his crest of brown and white feathers glistened in the sun.

It was the roadrunner, a member of the cuckoo family, with an extensive tail which balanced beautifully as he ran across open spaces looking for insects. He was a friendly, curious bird, and he made the cowboys laugh, for his crest rose and fell according to his interest in things at hand. Often he would halt, look up at Jim and cock his head, fluttering his tail to maintain balance.

Jim was surprised to find that it was Lasater, the robber, who most appreciated the animals they encountered. 'Mom told us that God sent the roadrunner to show us the way through difficult places,' he said, and this started a lugubrious fireside discussion of mothers and other noble women the cowboys had known. Tale after tale of frontier heroism unfolded, invariably with some gallant woman at the core of the action.

'They was this woman down along the Rio Grande,' Canby said. 'Husband killed in the war with Mexico. Big ranch to care for, thousands of cattle and no one around her but a bunch of greasy damned Mexicans . . .'

Nacho Gómez was cleaning up after the night meal and listened with rapt attention. He liked stories of brave women.

Canby's tale went on and on, but never too long or tedious for his listeners. The stars of spring rose high in the heavens and Jim thought how sad it was to see Orion go to bed in the west, taking the long sleep till next winter.

That night as he and Ragland rode the two-to-four, listening for Apaches, they traveled at their regular, monotonous speed, but each time as they passed in the darkness they stopped their singing to exchange a few words, the subject continuing to be women.

FIRST PASS: 'Jim, you ever kissed a girl?'
  'Nope.'
SECOND PASS: 'It can be rather satisfyin'.'
THIRD PASS: 'But parts of it can be mystifyin', too.'
That was the lesson for the night, and Jim brooded upon it till his watch ended. Two nights later he and Ragland resumed their discussion, which became more specific.
FIRST PASS: 'Jim, you ever been in a whorehouse?'
  'Nope.'
SECOND PASS: 'Jim, you know what a whorehouse is?'
  'Nope.'
THIRD PASS: 'We get to Las Vegas, you're gonna find out.'
In this fragmentary but highly gratifying manner Jim Lloyd was introduced to the mysteries of life. God, sex, money, acquiring a ranch and, above all, how to handle women were explained to him by the night riders. Once as he passed Gompert on the ten-to-twelve that young cowboy sort of summarized the whole subject.
FIRST PASS: 'Jim, don't you believe everthing Old Rags tells you.'
SECOND PASS: 'There's one hell of a lot Mr. Smart-ass Ragland don't know.'
THIRD PASS: 'Always remember, the finest woman you'll ever meet was your maw.'
  'I know.'
FOURTH PASS: 'Of course, other girls can be pretty nice, too.'
  'I know.'
FIFTH PASS: 'Of course, Jim, I'm speakin' only of nice girls.'
  'So am I.'
There was a sense of relief when the column reached Fort Sumner, a dismal outpost on the Pecos, established to keep the Mescalero Apaches in line. When the commander heard that Poteet's group had lost only three horses, he laughed. 'We keep a line of old crocks over there so the braves can practice stealing. Makes 'em think the old days are still here.' He told Gompert, 'If you lost only one horse, it was cheap,' but Gompert wanted to know if he could ride out with a scouting party, to see if he could recover his horse.
  'Son, forget it! You'll have real problems on your hands if the Comanche decide to move westward.'
  'Where are they now?' Poteet asked.
  'Our scouts have them spotted way to the east. North of Texas in the Indian country. But they could be moving west. I'd take my cattle over to the west bank. Forget the Apaches and keep an eye out pretty firmly to the east.'
  Now Nacho Gómez sprang his surprise regarding the calves. Asking for a horse, he spoke with some of the soldiers, then rode directly west into Apache country. Some hours later he returned with a dozen Mexi-

can farmers leading a horse laden with trading goods. Going to his wagon, he produced the three calves, and the Mexicans groaned with delight. 'A bull!' one cried, and Mr. Poteet watched as Nacho entered into frenetic bargaining.

The Mexicans offered chickens, long strings of garlic, onions, peppers and bundles of herbs none of the cowboys could identify. Nacho accepted each with a delighted grin, turning to inform the cowboys, 'Now we feast!' In the end the Mexicans appointed three riders to follow the herd north, to collect any additional new calves, and the leader said to Mr. Poteet, 'Pray God there will be bulls! For then we can start our own herd.'

On the first night out of Fort Sumner, Nacho prepared a chicken stew with potatoes and gravy, which Mr. Skimmerhorn pronounced one of the best he'd ever eaten, but Canby, Gompert and Savage refused it. 'We don't want no Mexican grub,' they complained. 'We want real food,' so Nacho took down a Dutch oven, cut off six big steaks, two per man, put the oven in the fire, piled coals on the lids, and when the chewy meat was nearly black, served it to the grumblers.

'That's decent food,' Canby said as he chewed the tough meat.

The same thing happened next night when Nacho served a kind of chili, hot and meaty and very tasty. Again Mr. Skimmerhorn complimented the Mexican, and again Canby and his colleagues complained that they didn't come on no cattle trail to eat Mexican grub, and where were the steaks? Sad-eyed, Nacho again got down the oven and crisped up half a dozen steaks, and the cowboys were satisfied.

Wanting to get back in their good graces, Nacho decided to give them an extra ration of biscuits. He was especially good with biscuits, for which he kept a large crock of sourdough fermenting in the back of his wagon. He had started this crock working back in Jacksborough: flour, water, some sugar, a little vinegar, some clean wood ash and some salt. When it was well fermented he threw away about two-thirds—'To keep the crock happy'—and refilled it with flour and water.

Sourdough wouldn't breed unless the temperature was just right, so on very cold nights Nacho took the crock to bed with him; on unusually hot days he kept it in the wagon wrapped in a wet cloth.

To make his biscuits he took from the crock a good helping of sourdough, mixed it with flour, water and salt, and pinched off nubbins, which he placed around the bottom of a Dutch oven, maybe forty biscuits to one baking.

Nacho's biscuits were the best the men had ever eaten, and he told them his secret: 'More coals on top than on the bottom.' He achieved this by placing his oven in dying embers and heaping upon the lid the liveliest coals he could find. In this way the biscuits came out brown and crisp on top, well done on the bottom and just about perfect inside.

It was not unusual for him to bake eighty for a meal, so that each rider could have six or seven, but this night he outdid himself.

Knowing that the treat he had for them would be appreciated, he baked up three ovenfuls of biscuits, many more than a hundred, and told the men, 'For that young bull Mr. Poteet traded, look what we got!' And he opened four jars of the finest sagebrush honey, dark and aromatic and tasty.

The men ate ravenously, and Canby said, 'For a lousy Mexican, you are one great cook.' The chili and the chicken stew were forgiven. Men broke open the crusty biscuits, drenched the feather-light insides with honey and ate them like Christmas candy.

Two days later, as they were crossing the Pecos prior to the march into Colorado, Poteet allowed his herd to get separated. The first half was safely across the river and had started toward the low mountains that lay ahead, but the trailing half was having trouble negotiating the steep bank into the stream.

At this vulnerable moment Bufe Coker, well to the east chasing strays, looked across the Pecos and saw some twenty Comanche sweep out from behind a mesa, where they had been hiding, and launch an attack on the forward half of the herd.

For just a moment Coker sat transfixed, staring at the superb horsemen, checking to see how many had guns, how many lances, and he was stunned by the magnificence of these half-naked warriors. Quickly he recovered his senses and fired a warning shot from his LeMat, but the Indians ignored him, concentrating their attention on the forward half of the column.

Now Coker spurred his horse, galloping back to the rear of the herd, but what he saw there dismayed him. Jim Lloyd and Ragland had been helping at drag, and when they saw a skirmish developing on the north side of the Pecos, they drove their horses into the river, with Ragland yelling, 'Here we come!'

Mr. Poteet, anticipating such foolhardy response, left the fight for a moment and bellowed, 'Get back there and protect the rear!' They turned in midstream to find Coker cursing at them from the shore. 'Our fight will be here,' he yelled. And as they scrambled back to dry land he shouted, 'Bring the cattle in close. If they stampede, we're finished.'

On the north bank a savage struggle ensued, with Poteet in charge and Canby firing like a machine as the Indians surged past in one attack after another. Mr. Skimmerhorn and Nate Person stayed up at point, drawing much of the Indian fire and alternately riding back to keep the startled herd from milling. 'Sweet Jesus!' Nate yelled. 'I sure wish we had Stonewall now.'

Coker, watching the fight, shouted to Lloyd, 'That nigger can handle hisself,' but Jim was watching Mr. Skimmerhorn, noting the cool yet desperate way in which the northerner held off the Indians when they bore down upon him. 'Everything he's got is at stake,' Jim muttered as he watched Skimmerhorn reloading.

It would be a long time before Jim could forget what happened next. Seven Indians detached themselves and rode furiously right at the central core of white men, trying apparently to chop down Mr. Poteet, whom they spotted as the leader. He stood coolly firing his revolver as they approached, then took up his rifle, firing point-blank at the Indians and diverting their attack.

In a violent turn to the north, the Indians bore down on Canby, who kept firing with both hands. One Comanche with a vicious chop of his hatchet caught Canby on the right shoulder, tearing away cloth and skin down to the elbow. For one desolate moment Canby stood erect with a revolver in his right hand; then cloth and flesh and blood enveloped the hand and the revolver vanished. The Texan stared at his nearly severed arm and calmly said something to Savage, who was fighting beside him.

A band of Comanche now forded the river and spurred their horses to attack the rear guard. 'Don't fire too soon,' Coker shouted, and the three guardians waited until the Indians were well upon them. Then Coker and Ragland started firing furiously, and Jim heard the Confederate yelling, 'Fire, Lloyd, fire!' And in a kind of daze the boy began using the pistol Canby had given him, thinking all the while of Canby's arm. Twice more the Comanche bore down on Jim and might have killed him except that before the third charge, Bufe Coker rushed over, firing rapidly and killing two Indians. The rest fled.

The herd had been held together. No horses, no cattle had been lost. One Indian was dead on the north bank, three on the south, and suddenly Jim Lloyd realized that he had been at the center of the fight.

'Old Jim just stood there and fired like he was a veteran,' the cowboys said admiringly, and Jim said to Nate Person, 'Boy, was I glad to see you comin' back across that river,' and he pretended not to hear when Gompert told Mr. Skimmerhorn, 'Did you see Old Jim blazin' away at that Comanche chief? Hell, he couldn'ta been three feet away from you, Jim, when you killed him.'

The words blazed through. 'I killed him?' Jim asked.

'I sure as hell didn't,' Coker said. 'I was busy with them braves.'

The young cowboys were turning the corpse over with their boots and Jim could see once more the chief's face during that last charge: terrifying, very close. 'I think Nate Person shot him,' Jim said. But he knew that he himself had fired the shot—had killed a man.

Canby's arm was in pitiful shape. Nate Person thought it ought to be amputated right then, but Canby bellowed, 'Christ, not my shootin' arm.' Next day it began to fester, and even Jim could see that there wasn't much chance to save it. They put Canby in the wagon and Jim rode with him for most of that day, fetching him water and lighting his cigarettes, and he told the southerner, 'You better let 'em cut it off, Canby. It's festerin' bad,' but Canby said, 'I might as well die as lose my gun arm.'

The column was now eleven miles to the east of Las Vegas, that wild, inviting frontier town, and the men begged Poteet to lay over and allow them a spree, but he said, 'No. No leave in Las Vegas.' When the men asked why, he said, 'We can't leave the herd unprotected, and we've got to push on to the doctor at Fort Union.' He nodded toward the wagon, where Canby lay in delirium, and the men complained no more.

There was a saying on the trails: 'If a man gets sick or wounded, only two things he can decently do. Get well or die quick.' It looked as if Canby would do the latter, for since he refused to have his arm cut off, it was poisoning his entire body. Two days later Mr. Poteet made up his mind. He told Nacho, 'Lash your cooking gear to the backs of horses. I'm taking the wagon into Fort Union with Canby.' There an army doctor would know what to do, and Poteet and Skimmerhorn rode off, leaving command of the outfit to Nate Person.

On the second afternoon Poteet and Skimmerhorn returned to camp with the wagon, but without Canby. 'The doctor took one look at the arm and said, "Off it comes." ' Poteet explained. 'Canby fought like hell, and it took three men to lash him down before they could get the chloroform to him.' No one spoke, and he added, 'We paid him off and he'll go back to Texas.'

'His horse is here,' Buck said.

'We bought his horse,' Poteet said. 'Mr. Skimmerhorn paid him well,' and no more was said by anyone.

It was about five-thirty in the afternoon. Never before on the trip had they camped at such a beautiful spot, with low mountains to the north, dark-blue piñon trees everywhere, and to the west the high snow-covered peaks of New Mexico. It was a valley of protection and peace, and while Nacho Gómez began putting his gear back in the wagon Mr. Poteet turned to Nate and asked, 'Are you well rested?' The black man said he was, and Poteet said, 'Men, we've had a hard trip and Canby's misfortune weighs upon us all. With Mr. Skimmerhorn's permission I have brought you a change of diet.' And he uncovered six bottles of whiskey.

As the men cheered, Poteet added, 'Mr. Skimmerhorn has agreed to guard the remuda. Mr. Person and I will watch the herd.' Forgetting even Nacho's good cooking, the cowboys opened the whiskey bottles and sat about the fire till midnight, drinking and telling more and more outrageous stories with less and less clarity until one by one they fell asleep.

Through the night Mr. Poteet and Nate Person rode guard, and as they passed each other in the darkness the black man said invariably, 'Evenin', Mr. Poteet,' and Poteet said softly, 'Evenin', Nate,' and they rode in this manner till two o'clock, when Poteet said, 'My horse is weary, Nate. I'll ride in and fetch a replacement,' and when he returned,

Nate asked, 'Are they givin' that boy whiskey?' and Poteet said, 'Three things a man's got to learn to handle—a gun, a glass of whiskey and a girl. He don't learn by readin'.' And they rode through that starry night, thinking of poor Canby with his arm gone, and of dead Comanche and of their good luck so far. And whenever they passed, Nate said, 'Evenin', Mr. Poteet,' and he replied, 'Evenin', Nate.'

At dawn the hands awakened from their stupors, as sorry a lot as ever proposed to herd cattle, and Mr. Poteet said, 'We'll move north,' and Nate said, 'Mr. Poteet, I like good whiskey just like anybody else,' and Old Rags said, 'Well, there ain't none left,' and Mr. Poteet glared at the gangling young man and said, 'Nate, I am sorry,' and he went to Mr. Skimmerhorn's sleeping bag and produced a half-full bottle, handing it to the black man.

Nate guzzled a huge drink, blinked his eyes and told Jim Lloyd, 'That is good.' He took three more real belts, then became glassy-eyed and looked around for a place to lie down. Mr. Poteet guided him to the wagon, helped him in and took away the bottle, and all that morning Nate rode inside, his mouth agape like a stranded sunfish.

Six days later the herd reached Raton Pass, that high and difficult route from New Mexico to Colorado, and there, blocking their way, stood Uncle Dick Wootton, one of the wildest pioneers of the west. He had done everything, traveled everywhere. His name appeared in the lists of the earliest trappers attending the rendezvous in western Wyoming, and now in his later years he had come upon what he called 'a good thing.'

By chicanery so devious that no one had yet deciphered it, he had cajoled the territorial governments of New Mexico and Colorado into allowing him to build, with Indian and Mexican labor, a rude passageway through the mountains, following Raton Pass and making of it a toll road, which he guarded with a gang of toughs carrying Winchesters.

'Ten cents a head,' he told Nate Person, who was scouting ahead.

'We're bringin' a lot of head,' Person explained.

'Then you'll pay a lot of ten centses,' the old reprobate replied.

Nate rode back to tell Mr. Poteet, whose thin lips tightened, making his jaw muscles stand out. He said quietly, 'Mr. Person, I'll borrow your extra gun, if I may.' And off he rode.

His meeting with the old robber was conducted with high formality, as if heads of state were discussing tariffs. Poteet said, 'You know, Uncle Dick, ten cents a head is too much.'

'It's my road,' the old man said, 'and that's my charge.'

'But I'm bringin' through two thousand, nine hundred and fifty head.'

'We'll do the countin'. You do the payin'.'

'For that number it oughtn't to be over six cents a head.'

'For any number it's ten cents.'

'Uncle Dick, you're being downright unreasonable.'

'I'm bein' downright practical,' the old trapper said. 'I built the road. You'll pay for usin' it.'

'You miserable son-of-a-bitch!' Poteet cursed. Then, reviling him Texas-style, he threatened to put him out of business.

'You can't talk to Wootton like that,' one of his henchmen said.

Drawing his guns, Poteet said, 'One of you makes a move—just one —and I'll blow this miserable old bastard to hell.'

The men backed off, and Poteet kept his guns on Wootten and said, 'I'm goin' back down that pass and find me another way through these mountains.' He cursed the pirate for a full minute, thrust his guns back in their holsters and rode back down the pass.

Assembling his men, he told them, 'This herd will never go over that pass. I will not be made a fool of.'

Skimmerhorn argued that the cattle were here, ready to go, and he felt sure that Mr. Seccombe would understand and be willing to pay the two hundred and ninety-five dollars. 'Not while I'm trail boss,' Poteet snapped, and that discussion was closed.

Calling Nate Person to his side, he said, 'Nate and I are goin' to scout this whole state till we find a pass north. Bring the cattle east after us.' Again Mr. Skimmerhorn demurred. 'Why not camp here till we're sure we've found a pass? Then, if there is none, we can still use Wootton's . . .'

'Mr. Skimmerhorn!' Poteet shouted. 'I am in command! Take those cattle east to the volcano! Now!'

In a fury he rode eastward with his black guide, and together they probed all the high country leading in to Colorado, finding nothing. His temper in no way abating, he ordered Person to ride back and see that the cattle kept moving eastward while he proceeded to the various mountains, probing, testing and still finding nothing.

Nate told the cowboys, 'The old man's in such a rage. At this rate we could go all the way east to Kentucky!'

'Stay with him,' Skimmerhorn said. 'He'll work out something.'

So the black man rode back, but it was two days before he could find Poteet, for the wiry Texan had ridden far into Colorado over a rocky pass that cattle could not possibly use. Nevertheless, when Person met him riding south he was grinning.

'We've got it, Nate,' he exulted. 'On the way in I found nothin', but on the way back, a smooth, level turnpike. And we'll tell every cattle-man in Texas about it. We'll break that old bastard's heart.'

They rode back to where the herd was approaching Capulin, that splendid volcano, dead for nine hundred thousand years, a perfect peak except for one side knocked off during the last eruption. He directed the men to bring the cattle up past the west side of the volcano, heading them due north, and as the last of the strays passed into Colorado, Mr.

Poteet turned west toward where Raton Pass stood far in the distance and shouted, as if the old robber could hear him, 'To hell with you, Dick Wootton!'

At the end of the first full day in Colorado they came to the Picketwire, the western river with the most delicate name. It was properly El Rio de Las Animas Perdido en Purgatorio. In Coronado's time three difficult and greedy Spanish soldiers had revolted and struck out on their own to find the cities of gold. Sometime later the main body of explorers came upon them, naked and riddled with arrows, and one of the priests explained solemnly, 'God struck them down, using Indians as his agents, and for their disobedience their souls remain in purgatory.'

The River of the Souls Lost in Purgatory! French trappers had shortened it to the Purgatoire, and practical men from Indiana and Tennessee, adapting the sound to their own tongue, called it Picketwire. It was not a difficult river to cross, and three days later they reached the stream they had been seeking, the Apishapa, whose name was far less romantic in origin than the Picketwire. It was a Ute word meaning *stinking water* and it was well named, for the water had an unpleasant taste, but it was potable and it led toward the end of the trail.

Poteet was quite willing to follow the Apishapa, because this kept the outfit well east of Pueblo and Denver—two hellholes where cowboys were concerned—and they were on this safe eastern course when Nate Person came riding back in some excitement. 'Santa Fe Trail!' he shouted. 'Dead ahead,' and when they came to a rise they looked north and saw it. Heading west along the ancient trail was a procession of some magnitude: first came a detachment of cavalry, then seven wagons, followed by horses and livestock, and finally guards bringing up the rear. It was a recapitulation of the west, of all the wagons that had passed this way since Spaniards first developed the road, and the young Texans, who had seen nothing like it before, watched with delight as the procession crossed their trail.

Mr. Poteet rode ahead to ask the cavalrymen why they were escorting the train, since the Comanche were so far to the south, and the captain in charge said condescendingly, 'Kansas outlaws.'

'Not this far west, surely.'

'They've been driven out of Kansas,' the captain said. 'Last month they raided into New Mexico.'

'The Pettis boys?'

'Yes.'

'Hell,' Mr. Poteet said in disgust. 'I thought we were safe.'

'On this trail you're never safe,' the captain said haughtily, as if he were addressing a lowly private, and rode off toward Santa Fe.

That night Poteet warned the hands that they were heading into dangerous country. 'Worse than the Comanche, because these men abide by no rules. They're outlaws and they're killers.'

'Who are they?' Jim Lloyd asked the younger cowboys, and Gompert said, 'Confederates. Like Old Coker and his damned McClellan saddle.'

'They're men who fought and lost,' Coker snapped. 'Just like me.'

'How did they get to Kansas?' Jim asked.

'How did Old Coker get to Texas? They walked till they got a chance to steal some horses.'

'They're killers now,' Coker said.

'If they come at us, Coker, will you join 'em? You're a Confederate.'

'So's Poteet. You think he'll join 'em?' And so the younger men joshed and argued as they headed for outlaw country.

The Apishapa emptied into the Arkansas River in a valley that showed great promise of becoming good agricultural land. 'A man could raise crops here,' Savage said approvingly as the Crown Vee cattle headed for the lush grass that lined the bottomlands.

'This is the last good drink the stock get till they reach the Platte,' Skimmerhorn warned, and the men allowed the animals to graze and take it easy for a day.

Crossing the Arkansas was the most difficult feat on the trail, for this river ran dark and swift and was cut by sand banks which presented special problems. Mr. Poteet and Nate spent half a day trying to calculate where the safest spot would be, and they finally decided upon a relatively narrow area some miles east of the Apishapa, and there they led their cattle into the cold, fast-running water.

It was a lively crossing, with two horses being swept downstream when they lost their footing, and no sooner were they recovered than a cantankerous steer they called Mean Red decided, in midstream, to head back for the south shore, and he took half a hundred steers and young bulls with him. They ran into the bunch being brought across by Jim and Coker, and there was a frightful milling in mid-river, with weaker animals going under, and all of them bawling and slashing about with their monstrous horns, and Mr. Poteet on shore shouting, 'Kick that red steer in the face! Turn him around!'

What should have required forty minutes consumed four hours, and tempers were totally frayed when the herd finally assembled on the north bank. Eleven cattle had drowned in the panic. 'Some cowboys!' Poteet lashed out. 'You, Coker! When you saw that red steer messing things up, why didn't you shoot him?'

'You told us not to use our guns,' Coker snapped back.

Poteet's face reddened and he was obviously ready for a fight, eager for one, perhaps, and it was clear that Coker would accommodate him, but Mr. Skimmerhorn broke it up by saying, 'We were lucky to make it without losing more than we did,' and Poteet walked over to the remuda and gave Buck hell for not having the horses in shape.

'He's worried about the Kansans,' Lasater said. 'And so am I.'

Soon Poteet came back and unrolled Canby's bed things. He had been

guarding them against the day when he met the one-armed man somewhere, but now he passed out Canby's guns. A second revolver to Jim
Lloyd. One to Coker, the others to the swing men. He gave one Win-
chester to Nate Person and the other to Mr. Skimmerhorn. The .22 he
kept for himself.

'Some people have deceived themselves by trying to buy the Pettis
boys off . . . giving them a share of the cattle,' he said. 'We won't.'

Four men rode guard that night, and next day Poteet moved the remuda and the cook wagon to the left flank. He posted an extra guard on
the right flank and the day passed without incident, but shortly after
dawn on the second day north of the Arkansas, all hell broke loose.

A band of sixteen Kansas outlaws led by the two Pettis boys swept in
from a nest of low hills and launched a full-scale attack against the cattlemen. The Kansans had fine horses, which they handled well. Driving
straight at the cattle, they tried to cut the herd in half. If this tactic succeeded, they could shoot the men tending the rear portion and make off
with many cattle and horses. But Bufe Coker greeted them with such
heavy fire from his LeMat that they had to swing well south of the rear,
which put them on the left flank, where they had a free run at Nacho
Gómez and the remuda.

When Mr. Poteet and Skimmerhorn saw what was happening, they
rode breakneck to help, but their support was not needed, for Nacho
had unlimbered his Third Dragoon and stood before his cook wagon,
feet apart, with the deadly weapon at his shoulder. His aim was not
good: one volley went over the heads of the Kansans, a second into the
dust beneath their horses' hoofs. But he created such a racket and waved
his carbine with such fury that the Kansans decided to leave him alone.
Before they could get to the remuda, Poteet and Skimmerhorn were
throwing showers of lead, and the invaders swung in a wide curve to
the head of the column, where Lasater waited grimly.

For about forty minutes the fight continued in this manner, and miraculously no one was killed, neither outlaw nor cattleman. Twice Jim
Lloyd caught a glimpse of the Pettis boys, mean-looking mustached men
wearing suspenders and derbies, who waved their pistols as they rushed
past. They were killers, and Jim knew that if the cowboys wavered even
a little, the Kansans would override them and shoot them all.

It looked as if the Texans had won a victory, for the outlaws were
withdrawing to the east, but then the younger of the Pettis boys wheeled
his horse about, gave a mighty shout and led a final charge, right into
Jim Lloyd, killing his horse and wounding Jim in the left arm.

Coker saw that Jim was defenseless, and before a new attack could
gun the boy down, he spurred his horse right at the oncoming Kansans
and exploded his LeMat shotgun into the men's faces. There was a foun-
tain of blood, a human head flying in bits over the landscape, a horse
galloping madly with a tottering driver, and finally a body falling to earth
not far from the cook wagon.

After the Kansans withdrew, the weary cowboys sat on the ground, breathing heavily as each man reloaded. Mr. Skimmerhorn had hurried to Jim Lloyd and found him loading his two revolvers, while blood ran down his left arm in a trickle. His bravery was reviewed at the campfire: 'Old Jim just stood there and took the full charge. Why in hell didn't you fire at 'em?' He said, 'I was too scared.'

Coker did not join in the discussion. He was shaken by the killing of the outlaw and finally confided to Ragland, 'I have killed my brother.'

'Jesus,' Ragland told the others. 'The Confederate killed his own brother,' and Mr. Poteet left what he was doing and went to Coker and asked, 'How can you say he was your kin?' and Coker said, 'Any man who fought northern tyranny was my kin,' and he dug a grave at the foot of a small hill and buried the outlaw, raising above his head a flat piece of wood from the cook wagon, on which he scratched:

HERE LIES

A CONFEDERATE SOLDIER

NAME UNKNOWN

KILLED IN FAIR FIGHT

BY A BEAUREGARD LEMAT

OF SUCH IS THE KINGDOM OF HEAVEN

For two nights Coker could speak with no one and then on the third he said at the fire, 'I won't go back to Texas. I'll take my pay and keep movin'. I hear Australia's a good place.'

Such talk created gloom in camp, for as they approached the end of the trail, each man wondered what he could find to do next. Lasater, wishing to halt such speculation, turned to Coker and asked, 'How'd you get that gun, Coker?' and the Confederate said, 'Same way's I got the saddle.'

"And how was that?' Lasater probed.

'It was in the Shenandoah Valley. Stonewall Jackson was dead and they were pressin' us on all sides, and there was this Confederate colonel we were followin' and he had this real good pistol which he was always polishin', and we all knew about it 'cause it could fire nine ordinary bullets, and then a sawed-off shotgun, all in this size.' He passed the deadly weapon among his companions and they marveled at its complexity and its deadly concentration of fire power. It had two barrels, a small one for bullets and a very large, blunt one for the buckshot.

'I kept pretty close to the colonel, figuring he was bound to get hit sooner or later, and each time we attacked the Yanks, I kept urgin' him on, "Go to it, Colonel! Move up closer!" And he kept makin' a hero of hisself and I kept on his heels, and after a while I noticed that a man from North Calinky was doggin' him too, and I could see he had his eye on that LeMat, and if there's one thing I can't stand, it's a North Calinky man. They got no character, no courage and when the colonel was finally hit, the North Calinky man jumped for the LeMat, but I had the presence of mind to forget the revolver and attend to the competition. I swung the butt of my gun around and just about knocked his head off, and only then did I stoop down to pick up the LeMat.'

'And the McClellan saddle?'

'About the same. A Yankee colonel lookin' for glory, so we let him through and a Georgia man shot him and his horse fell practically in my lap, so I took the saddle.'

'It's a pitiful saddle,' Lasater said. 'Damned hole down the middle.'

'I ain't had no trouble with it.'

'That's right,' Lasater said generously. 'You sure rode down that Confederate and blew his head off.'

'I did it in sorrow,' Coker said. 'I thought he'd killed Old Jim.'

Ragland broke into untimely laughter and the men turned toward him. He looked to check whether Mr. Poteet was listening, then confided, 'Old R. J. thought hisself so smart, takin' us acrost that desert to escape the Comanche and the Kansans. Hell, we run right into both. Might just as well have come straight north and saved ourselves the trouble.' But as Lasater pointed out, 'Doin' it your way, we face the Indians and the outlaws on their own land, where they'd have reinforcements. Doin' it R. J.'s way, we got 'em at the end of their string,' and the others agreed.

Only now did Jim begin to pay attention to the strangest man in the outfit. Calendar had ridden with the longhorns for over a thousand miles, yet no one really knew him, a silent, thin man of twenty who acted as if he were fifty. Twice Jim had shared night watches with him, and the man had not spoken a word. As he sang to the restless cattle, he did so in a voice so low they could hardly hear him, as if he were taking from them a reassurance he needed rather than the other way around:

> 'The grass is green, the hills are brown.
> I'm gonna leave this goddamn town.
> The gals won't pester me henceforth.
> I'm cuttin' out, I'm headin' north.'

He sang in a whisper, and Jim, listening close to catch the words, asked, 'Where'd you learn that song? I don't know it.' But Calendar passed on without comment, singing softly to himself:

> 'Got my rope and got my saddle,
> Think it best that I skedaddle.
> I don't want no shotgun weddin'.
> Colorado's where I'm headin'.'

But now as they reached the bounteous plains of that territory, with deer and antelope plentiful, Calendar came into his own. He had a rifle made by Christian Sharps of Harper's Ferry, a handsome blue-steel affair that laid a bullet accurately at two hundred yards. Six cowboys would ride out for deer, but only he, stalking silently in his own way, would come back with venison.

'How do you do it?' Jim asked one day.

'I look,' he said, and it was obvious that he wished no further questions.

Buck the wrangler was an outcast because of his awful smell; he really had no choice. But Calendar ostracized himself deliberately because he preferred being alone. He wanted to be on the prairie with his Sharps rifle and a good horse, and that was all. He did nothing to offend the other cowboys, but he did avoid ordinary human contacts. The west contained hundreds like him, silent men who could shoot straight and survive anywhere.

One morning as the cowboys were heading north onto that great empty plateau which fills the area between the Platte and the Arkansas, they saw a mass of low shapes on the horizon.

'What's that?' Poteet called to Person, and he shouted back, 'It can't be Indians.' Everyone brought his guns into position and watched as the shapes moved closer. They spread over a huge area, and finally Person galloped back, shouting, 'Buffalo!' and soon a gigantic herd of black beasts bore down upon the cowboys.

They were coming from the northwest and heading for the southeast, and the front of the column, if it could be called such, was about four miles across—four miles of milling buffalo. Behind the leaders the mighty herd covered the earth for a score of miles, a massive black-brown unit that seemed to move with a single purpose.

'Hold the cattle!' Poteet shouted as the great beasts came down upon them.

The buffalo were now less than a hundred yards away, coming at the men at an angle. The cattle, bemused by such a moving mass, seemed hypnotized, and slowly, without the men's being aware of what was happening, the buffalo herd parted slightly, the leaders going north and south of the longhorns. The Texans, with all their herd and horses, were encapsulated in the midst of the buffalo.

For hours this incredible movement of animals continued. At times Jim could reach out his hand and feel them passing beneath it, one by one, large hairy creatures with handsome bearded faces and dark, piercing eyes. The animals became familiar and then tedious. They were so docile that the men began tugging at their horns and patting their rumps as they went past, and still they came, the last remnant of that enormous herd of thirty million that had once roamed the land between the two rivers.

'Ain't they ever gonna pass?' Savage called.

When the final straggler was gone, the Texans were silent, as if they had just come from church, until Mr. Poteet said, 'I never saw anything like that before,' and Mr. Skimmerhorn said, 'You may never see it again,' and Ragland said, 'Why, you think they're goin' somewheres?' and Mr. Skimmerhorn said, 'Yes, to their death.'

No one could believe it. 'Took four hours to pass,' Ragland said, and Savage asked, 'How would you know, you ain't got no watch,' and Ragland said, 'I can tell.'

Calendar suddenly spurred his horse, galloped onto a little hill, dismounted, dropped to one knee, and with great precision aimed his Sharps at a buffalo and sent a bullet into the spot where the neck joined the body. The stricken animal twisted to the right, tried to control its legs, then collapsed in a spasm. It was a perfect kill.

'What in hell did you do that for?' Poteet raged when Calendar rode back, abandoning the carcass.

'Man's got to know how to use his gun,' Calendar said, and that's all he would say. Jim rode guard with him that night and tried vainly to engage him in conversation. No use—the thin Texan attended his rounds, singing in his whispery voice:

> 'She was bright and she was pretty,
> Sweetest gal in Kansas City.
> But her maw was a real terror.
> I'm headin' north to hide my error.'

The presence of the buffalo, so many for so long a time, and the firing of Calendar's rifle, had baffled the longhorns, and they showed signs of unrest. Jim, as he circled them singing his own song, could see that they were going to be troublesome, and Mean Red, the steer who had turned back in the river, started once to head for open country, but Calendar anticipated the move and rode at him briskly, waving the Sharps in the steer's face until the brute turned back.

'Nice ridin',' Jim said as they passed, but Calendar made no answer.

They prevented trouble that night, but on the next the damnedest thing happened. Mr. Skimmerhorn, returning from his ten-to-twelve guard, dismounted and stepped smack in the middle of Coker's McClellan saddle. His foot got trapped in the opening and he kicked to free himself, but the saddle could not be shaken off, and he stumbled into the fire, knocking over the coffeepot. There was a sharp clatter—and the cattle were off.

It is said that no man has ever seen the start of a stampede. He hears an unfamiliar noise, sees a blur, and within one second three thousand cattle who appeared to have been sleeping are on their feet, galloping.

'Stampede!' Calendar shouted, just once. Then, tight-lipped, he sped into the night.

'Stampede!' flashed through the camp, and each man leaped out of his blankets, grabbed for the bridle of his night horse and set out automatically in the direction of the greatest noise.

'Where's my saddle?' Coker shouted in the darkness.

'Get the damned thing off my foot,' Skimmerhorn yelled, and the two wrestled for a moment, finally freeing Skimmerhorn. Then each leaped for his horse, and only Nacho Gómez was left alone in the camp.

This was a strange and wild stampede. Mercifully, the land was flat, so there was no danger of plunging down a sudden arroyo, but being flat, it also encouraged the animals to run, and all that night they did so, not in one direction, but in a hundred.

Each cowboy settled upon some fleeing group of longhorns, thinking that he was working the main body, but each fought with only a fragment. Lasater, riding like a ghost demented, turned a large bunch into a milling circle, effectively stopping them, only to find that as he did so, a much larger herd swept past, luring his group behind them.

Gompert managed to intercept Mean Red and some six hundred of his followers, but this accomplished nothing, because they represented only a small portion of the herd, and besides, he had no one to help him hold them, and when another group roared past, their hoofs thundering on the hard earth, Mean Red and his longhorns joined them, and were seen no more that night.

By two in the morning R. J. Poteet's longhorns were scattered over a large portion of middle Colorado. There seemed no discernible order in the cowboys' attempts to reassemble them; Poteet and Person, well schooled in such affairs, were as powerless as the novices, riding first here, then there, cursing the while.

'Bring some discipline into this!' Poteet shouted at his black assistant, and Person, futilely trying to chase down several hundred cows and young bulls, called back, 'Yessir!' All that night, to Poteet's disgust, groups of cattle and cowboys rampaged across the flat prairie, and when dawn broke, the animals were scattered in at least fourteen different groups. Poteet, surveying the scene in the beautiful pale light that comes before sunrise, could only say, 'Christ!'

He then began to direct a sensible effort at bringing the far-flung cattle back to one spot. 'Person! Get that bunch over on the horizon! Coker! Bring in those strays and get a center started.'

It was noon before the exhausted cowboys succeeded in reassembling the herd, and when Poteet made a rough count, he concluded that some two hundred were missing. 'Where can they be!' he asked the men, for the prairie was so flat that any rise could be seen for five or six miles, and after riding out in various directions, the cowboys reported, 'No cattle anywhere,' and then Jim Lloyd, who was always gazing at the horizon in search of birds or antelope, cried, 'Look!' and there on a distant hill the missing cattle were grazing, their black silhouettes showing against the first rays of the sun.

'Fetch 'em,' Poteet cried in disgust, and Jim and Calendar rode in silence for at least seven miles to bring back the docile creatures. When they approached camp, Mean Red, who had led them on their escapade, broke into a trot, delighted to rejoin the herd and ready for the next gallop.

'That one we get rid of,' Poteet said, but before anyone could ask how, Nate Person rode back from a scouting trip to the north with the ominous news: 'Indians.'

'Oh, Christ!' Poteet said. 'Not again!' And for the first time on this trip the cowboys saw R. J. wilt. For a moment his shoulders sagged, but just for a moment. 'All right! All right!' he shouted. 'Form up.' And he placed his men at strategic positions from which they could repel the Indian attack. The preparation was unnecessary.

Across the prairie came a file of bedraggled Indians on fleshless horses. They were led by an old chief, a dumpy little fellow wearing a tall-crowned hat with a single feather. 'They ain't Comanche,' Lasater whispered.

They were Arapaho, emaciated and without spirit. 'Food,' the old chief pleaded.

'We got no food,' Ragland replied.

'Food. We are starving,' the old man pleaded a second time.

Mr. Poteet rode up and asked, 'What's he want, Gompert?'

'Food. Says his tribe is starving.'

'They look it.'

Poteet left the Indians to talk with Skimmerhorn. 'They're your cattle,' he said. 'Let's give them one,' Skimmerhorn said, and Gompert, overhearing the decision, yelled, 'Let's give 'em Mean Red!' and the cowboys applauded, so Mr. Poteet rode back to the Indians and said, 'Mr. Skimmerhorn here says . . .'

'Did you say Skimmerhorn?' the old man asked.

'Yes,' Skimmerhorn replied.

'I am Lost Eagle.'

The two men sat their horses, uneasy, each looking directly into the eyes of the other, saying nothing, and after a while Mr. Skimmerhorn rode closer and extended his hand to the old man, and indicated three steers the Indians could have.

'We are not beggars,' Lost Eagle said. 'We are starving. There is no way left for us to feed ourselves,' and he rode to each of the cowboys, shaking his hand and thanking him for his generosity.

That was how Mean Red left the herd. The nights were peaceful now and daytime work was kept to a minimum, for Mr. Poteet was in no hurry to cover the last two hundred miles. 'He don't fool me none,' Ragland told the men around the campfire. 'He's lollygaggin' so's them critters'll put on weight.'

In these last days Jim had his first good chance to study the plains of Colorado, and everything he saw pleased him: the golden-brown color, the gently rising sweeps, the hidden swales, the rounded hills, the limitless horizon darkening at the edges, and day after day the cloudless sky, an arc of blue enclosing an untouched paradise. 'If I ever saw land made for cattle,' he told Savage, 'this is it.' He liked especially the crystal air, thinner than the humid atmosphere of Texas and infinitely cleaner. A man could breathe this air and feel each particle creeping into his lungs, bringing health.

As trail's end came closer, so did the men. Intense friendships sprang up where before there had been only courteous respect. 'I got to say that for a nigger, Nate Person knows his horses,' Coker admitted, and Ragland, no great lover of Mexicans, paid a similar grudging tribute to Nacho Gómez: 'He sure knows how to make crusty biscuits.'

They spoke often of Mule Canby, and when they did, Jim felt remorse at not having paid Canby the ten dollars he owed him for the Army Colt's. 'How will he earn his livin' with only one arm?' he asked.

'Lotsa men with one arm make it,' Coker said. 'You disqualify all the men with one arm or one leg, hell, you'd have to throw out half the men in South Calinky. We had a bad war.'

'Speakin' of one leg,' Lasater said, 'they was this pretty little gal in San Antonio had only one leg. All the women felt sorry for her. "What's Letitia gonna do with one leg?" And you know, all the men felt sorry for her too, so as a result little Letitia got more . . .'

Here Mr. Poteet interrupted, indicating with a nod that Jim Lloyd was in the audience, and Lasater ended lamely, 'She got more attention than most gals with two legs.' Jim felt he understood what Lasater was leading up to.

There was a lot of joshing, too. Again and again cowboys recalled Old Rags 'tryin' to jump the Pecos and fallin' flat on his ass,' and Ragland protested that if he had had a fair run at the river he could have jumped it . . . 'but you saw for yourself how the bank was slippy and downhill.'

'Hell, on the best day you ever lived you couldn't jump that river,' Savage responded. So a small wager was arranged, and Mr. Poteet and Mr. Skimmerhorn were given the job of stepping off eighteen feet, with a clean level approach, and a heavy starting line was drawn in the earth, and Savage said, 'One inch over that line and you lose.'

So Ragland backed way up, scrunched up his body, yelled, 'Here we go!' and came tearing down the approach, arms and legs flying in all directions. As he approached the line, he gathered his strength in one mighty effort and sailed a good six inches beyond the far bank of the river.

'My God! He done it!' Lasater shouted, and now the men entered their endless and tedious review: 'It's true that Old Rags fell in the Pecos when he tried it in Texas, but up here, with a fair chance to run . . . hell, he cleared it and then some.'

Jim, watching the cowboys in these final days, experienced a sadness he could not control. He saw things clearly. If this particular group could be held together, each man lending strength to his companion, they could build themselves a good life. Even Lasater might be kept in line, but when they broke up and each had to fend for himself, troubles might well overtake them. Not Mr. Poteet or Nate Person. They were grown men, solidly constructed; you could trust them anywhere, and they'd get the job done.

But Lasater? Wild, splendid Lasater who would risk anything. He was bound to run into trouble, for basically he was weak. Jim prayed that Mr. Poteet would allow Lasater to stay with him for the trip back to Texas.

And Ragland, he was sure to get himself mixed up with women and make a mess of one affair after another . . .

Then he began to think of the animals left dead on this trail. His own cow, wandering bereft across the alkali flats . . . Stonewall shot dead at the moment of triumph . . . the cattle drowned at the crossing . . . the dead buffalo . . .

God, he wished he could ride forever with these men. Just keep riding toward some distant horizon behind which the Comanche and the Kansans and the unfordable rivers lay. But it could not be. Trails end, and companies of men fall apart.

What would he do, a fourteen-year-old boy on the loose in a vast new territory? Something would turn up. He liked animals, and something would turn up.

On the last night watch before they reached the Platte, the two-to-four, as he rode with Coker he asked, 'Was it really your brother, the one you shot?' They made a complete circle, and Coker said, 'He was my brother and you're my brother.' They made another complete circle while Jim pondered this, and on the next turn Coker said, 'If two fellas eat dust in drag position for four months, that makes 'em brothers, don't it?' Jim weighed this, and on the next turn Coker said, 'If you ever need help, Jim . . .' He left the rest unspoken, and the long night passed.

On the night of July 12, 1868, Mr. Skimmerhorn announced at the last campfire, 'Tomorrow we reach our pasture,' and the cowboys reacted in a way that surprised Jim, for each man broke out fresh clothing, used his hands to press his bandanna free of wrinkles, even polished his saddle. For the first time Jim realized how vain these men were, what pride they had in their profession, and when dawn of that last day broke, each man rode a little straighter and spoke with a quieter precision, for they had accomplished a considerable feat and they knew it. They had herded nearly three thousand longhorns thirteen hundred miles, with minimum loss, and they were proud.

When word of their approach reached Zendt's Farm, the villagers became so excited at the prospect of receiving cattle from Texas that everyone walked out to watch. The cowboys, with a larger audience than expected, outdid themselves in crisp commands and boldly waved signals. Lasater even unholstered his revolver, using it to signal the lead steers into the water.

The crossing was so easy it seemed an afterthought. 'Not much like the Arkansas,' Ragland said scornfully, but Mr. Skimmerhorn pointed to the farthest banks of the valley and told him, 'You thank your stars this river isn't in flood. It reaches from there to there.' But Ragland wasn't listening. He had spotted a pretty girl.

'You did it, John!' the newspaper editor shouted as the cattle climbed up the north bank.

'He did it,' Skimmerhorn called back, giving credit to Poteet. 'What's more, he's gonna do it for us again.'

Ahead, to greet them as they forded the river, stood Oliver Seccombe: 'Well done, men. The cattle look fine.'

The crowd separated to let the herd through and Nacho Gómez drove his wagon past the ladies and on to the final camping ground. When Buck brought his remuda across, Mr. Poteet assembled the cowboys, who were pleased for another chance to posture among the townspeople, and told them, 'Each of you is to pick one horse from the remuda. A present from Mr. Skimmerhorn. The other horses,' he said, raising his voice so that the townsmen could hear, 'will be sold, tomorrow noon.'

'Where?' the horse-hungry locals asked.

'We'll bring 'em in town, so look 'em over.'

Insistently, as if they had a corporate will of their own, the cattle pressed north and the men followed. The last river had been crossed, the last danger repulsed.

Jim Lloyd had stayed on the south bank with Coker, who, wishing to display his horsemanship, made a great show of rounding up the strays, but Jim, behaving more sedately, scrambled his horse up the north bank, and as he came over the brow he found himself looking into the eyes of a young girl, the most astonishingly beautiful girl he had ever seen.

She had a dark complexion, black eyes and ebony hair, which she wore in ribboned braids. She was almost as tall as he, and her face had that brazen look which challenges men. When he stared at her, she stared back, her eyes like pools of clear water at the far edge of the Llano. He sat very tall in his saddle and smiled down like a conquistador. She broke into a disrespectful laugh, and when he was past he asked Mr. Skimmerhorn, 'Who's that girl?' Skimmerhorn turned in his saddle and said, 'That's Levi Zendt's daughter. She's part Indian,' and Jim said quietly, 'I'm goin' to marry her,' and the herd moved on.

CAUTION TO US EDITORS: Please, please make your artist exercise restraint in illustrating this section. I have studied forty-seven photographs of groups of cowboys in the years 1867–68–69, and not one appears in chaps, tapaderos or exaggerated hat. All wear working clothes, plus high-heeled boots and bandanna. The Denver Public Library has nine photographs of R. J. Poteet in the early years before he put together his big ranch northwest of Jacksboro, and he is not gussied up. He shows no flamboyance but a good deal of solid character.

Do not allow your artists to portray these cowboys as big men. Most of the good ones were slight. Boone McClure of that admirable Panhandle Plains Historical Museum just south of Amarillo is my authority for the statement: 'We had this convocation of famous living cowboys, and three were picked as most representative. I'm only five-feet-six, and every one of those men was no taller than I.'

Few towering cowboys like those depicted by John Wayne and Joel McCrea, existed in those early days. From various photographs which contained reference points I have calculated the height of our thirteen men. We know that John Skimmerhorn was tall, like his father, say 6-1, but he was not a Texas cowboy. R. J. Poteet was not over 5-6, with Canby, Person, Calendar and Savage coming in at about that level too. Nate Person was a mite taller, but Gompert, Nacho, Coker and Buck were all 5-4 or less. Lasater might have run to 5-7, but only Ragland had any real height, 5-10 at the most generous. Jim Lloyd was a special case. At fourteen he was only 5-5, but he added some inches later.

Be careful how you handle John Chisum on that gigantic spread along the Pecos River. Don't confuse him with Jesse Chisholm, 1806–68, after whom the greatest of the cattle trails was named, posthumously, as a matter of fact. Recent motion pictures have been making our Chisum a notable hero of the west. The facts do not support this. Tough? Yes. Fearless? I wonder. He never carried a gun on the theory that the code of the west forbade the shooting of an unarmed man, and he knew that a lot of people wanted to shoot him. He hired others to do his killing for him, and some say Billy the Kid was in his employ when finally shot. In protecting his assumed acres, he was ruthless, and in disciplining Mexicans he suspected of encroaching on the land he didn't own, he was pitiless. I've read all that's available on Chisum and find him at best an unlovely man. If you wish to cut him from the text, feel free.

On the other hand, I have tried to be restrained in depicting R. J. Poteet. In retrospect he seems better than I have said, a trail-hardened man who engaged in every aspect of range life without ever having been charged with a bad performance. In the 1870s he shot bandits and in the 1890s endowed a college. In the 1880s he ran squatters off his land, but in the 1900s gave land he owned for the founding of five different towns. He was the first to import to the prairies really good breed bulls from England, the first to bring in Black Angus cattle, the first to experiment with irrigation.

A nice touch. In later years Poteet confessed that whenever he was on a dangerous trail he allowed Nate Person to carry the outfit's money. 'Not only was Nigger Nate the best hand I had, but if the outlaws did ride us down, there was little likelihood they would search Nate for the money, he being black and they being from the south.'

Trouble spot. Records of several long drives to the north indicate that many trail bosses took the eight cowboys who enclosed the herd—two points, two swings, two flanks and two drags—and rotated each man through each of the eight positions, clockwise, and some reader familiar with this may give you flak. R. J. Poteet argued that he wanted his top experts at the two points, with the best man riding left and the next best right. He also had a rule that if young or inexperienced cowboys wanted to ride with him, they had to prove themselves by making their first trip at drag, and so far as I can ascertain, he never wavered from this routine.

Technical point. Although Jim Lloyd riding left drag would eat dust during the westward leg of the journey, when the trail turned north, as it did once the Pecos was reached, the prevailing northwest wind would throw the greater burden on Bufe Coker riding right drag.

Caption material. R. J. Poteet has a passage in one of his letters which you might want to use: 'I was always impressed by the fact that although we Texans held the Mexican in contempt, our profession and its vocabulary were borrowed from Mexican experience in running cattle south of the Rio Grande. Chaps from *chaparejos,* lariat from *la reata,* sombrero, mesquite, latigo, tapadero, bandanna, buckaroo from *vaquero,* corral, rodeo, remuda, ranch from *rancho.* While coosie, a word we use for cook, came from *cocinero.*'

Tell your artist to observe that the northern Texas cowboy invariably tied his lariat to his saddle horn, but a man from the Rio Grande, like Canby, would dally his, that is, give it a couple of twists around the horn, relying on friction to hold it. Dally comes from the Mexican *dar la vuelta,* 'to give the turn.'

Llano Estacado. Be careful what you say about this and how you show it on your maps. Few problems in American history are more sticky, because delineation of the area varies radically from one source to another; it probably extended as far south as the route we follow, but some experts claim it halted farther north. The derivation of the name is totally confused, six major theses having been advanced: (1) Spanish legend says stakes were driven to mark the only trail across the desert. (2) Indians claim that their ancestors drove stakes to guide an unknown Great Chief who would come from the east to deliver them from their enemies. (3) Josiah Gregg, famed historian of western commerce, says the stakes marked the course between water holes. (4) Later travelers believed the stakes had been set and adorned with buffalo skulls to mark the route of the Butterfield Overland Mail. (5) Naturalists, asking the irritating question 'In a land without trees, how did they cut stakes?' explain, 'From a distance the yucca looks like a stake.' (6) Herbert Bolton, the noted historian of the west, is probably closest to the truth when he says that one translation of the Spanish noun *estacada* is *palisade,* and in the western reaches of the area there were many spectacular bluffs resembling palisades, tilted and glowing in sunlight.

Cattle. Even though I have used a cattle drive originating in Texas, and even though most novels and films have done the same, you must remember that the principal ranches of Wyoming, Montana and even Colorado received the major portion of their cattle not from Texas but from Oregon. The early emigrants traveling westward along the Oregon Trail took with them many first-rate British-bred cows and bulls, and on the Pacific Coast these animals proliferated. Consequently, the typical cattle drive of this period consisted not of scrawny longhorns coming north from Texas but of sleek, well-bred cattle heading east from Oregon.

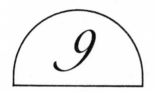

THE
HUNTERS

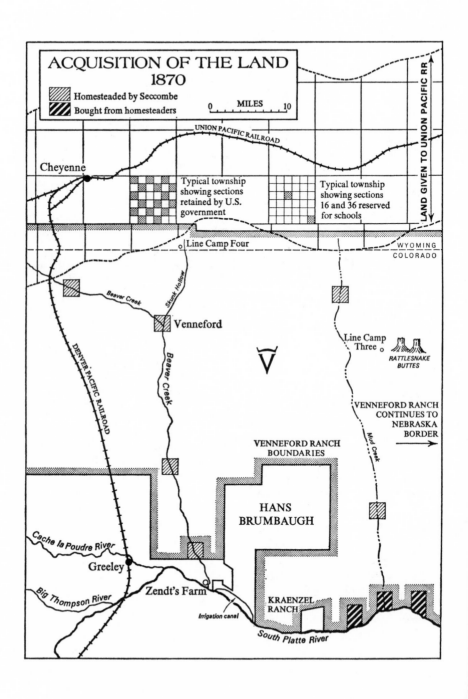

ACQUISITION OF THE LAND
1870

Homesteaded by Seccombe
Bought from homesteaders

0   MILES   10

TWO OF THE MOST SIGNIFICANT CONTRI-
butions to the use of land in Colorado were made in 1859 by a thirty-two-year-old Russian. He was a goldminer with the good German name of Hans Brumbaugh, and he happened to be a Russian because in the year 1764 his great-grandfather, a German farmer, listened when Catherine the Great, the German princess ruling Russia, issued one of the most enticing colonization promises in history: 'Any German subject consenting to settle in my Russia will be given land practically free and will be insured freedom of worship, freedom from taxation, self-rule within your own German settlement, freedom to conduct education in your own language and perpetual freedom from military service.'

The Brumbaughs read this glowing invitation posted on the door of their little church in Hesse, where crops had failed for six years and war had ravaged the countryside for seven. They walked to the Baltic port of Lubeck, took ship to St. Petersburg, and sailed down the Volga River till they found a treasury of arable land at Saratov. The Volgadeutsch they were henceforth called, and for thirty-four years they enjoyed a prosperity and a freedom greater than they could have hoped for. They experienced the usual difficulties of all immigrants—learning Russian, mastering local systems of agriculture, preventing their daughters from marrying Russians—but they were happy, and few would have returned to Germany had they been given the opportunity.

But not even empresses live forever, and when Catherine finally died in 1796, her promises to her German settlements were forgotten, and in time the Volgadeutsch marched in Russian regiments just like other peasants, and their schools were nationalized and the old concordat became a scrap of paper. It was then that stubborn peasants like Hans Brumbaugh began to yearn for the freedom which had been stolen from them.

At age seventeen he started making himself a nuisance to the Russian authorities, so that his mother had to warn him, 'Hans, be careful. The Czar's men will hang you.' At nineteen he was with a group that attacked a military convoy, and that night he left the Volga and clawed his way out of Russia and back to Germany. At twenty-six he had the bad luck to buy a farm in Illinois from a man who did not own it, and when the rightful owner forced the sheriff to dispossess him, he decided to quit that state.

In January of 1859 he heard of the discovery of gold in Jefferson Territory, as Colorado was then calling itself, and he walked across Missouri and Nebraska, a husky, stoop-shouldered, obstinate man willing to face weather that would have killed an ordinary traveler. Like thousands of others, he stopped briefly at Zendt's trading post to acquire provisions for the last stage of his journey to Pikes Peak. He was pleased to find in Levi a fellow German, and for the better part of two days they talked in that language; Levi's long stay in Pennsylvania had corrupted his mother tongue as much as the Brumbaugh family's exile in Russia had altered his. A purist would have shuddered at what they called *German,* but each made himself understood.

As they talked, Brumbaugh complained of the high prices Levi was charging, but Levi explained, 'What I bring in from St. Louis has to be expensive. But what I grow here you will find to be cheap,' and Brumbaugh saw that this was true. During his last day at the post he inspected the land Levi was using along the Platte.

'Good land,' he said.

'Where there's water,' Levi replied, and this remark caused Brumbaugh to examine the benches up from the riverbed, and he listened attentively when Levi said, 'Nothin's ever been grown up here, it bein' so far from water, but if you could get water to it, I'm convinced it's the same land as that fruitful stretch down by the river.'

Brumbaugh proceeded to the gold fields, lost himself in the frenzy of Pikes Peak and found not even one nugget. At the end of three months, his supplies gone, his stomach empty and his temper frayed, he developed the first of his significant ideas. He was seated with a group of eleven miners endeavoring to entertain each other with stories, and it occurred to him that they were talking so avidly in an attempt to divert attention from the fact that they were starving.

They had money. They had energy. But there simply was no food other than flour at twenty-two dollars a barrel and bacon at six dollars a pound, and as one of the men gallantly opened a last can of beans, passing it out among the ravenous miners, Brumbaugh said to himself, Folly! Men more interested in gold than food. The real money is in the farm.

That night he left Pikes Peak, one of the dreariest spots he had ever seen, and three days later, passed the bend in the Platte where the city of Denver was burgeoning. On the fifth day he was back at Zendt's, asking, 'How can I get hold of some land?'

Levi said, 'For a farm?'

'Yes.' And there followed those intricate maneuverings which were becoming common throughout the west.

Levi explained how things stood in 1859: 'It's impossible to say who owns the land. McKeag and I staked it out long ago, but we're still not a legal territory. In law it still belongs to the Indians, so you can't squat on it and say, "This land is mine," because it isn't yours. It's theirs.'

'You have land,' Brumbaugh pointed out.

'Correct. It was land owned by my wife's mother. Full-blooded Arapaho. She gave me a paper, which I filed in St. Louis, showing that I had paid her for it.' Levi stopped to recall the solemn day when the transfer was made. Clay Basket had ridiculed the idea, but old Alexander McKeag, who couldn't read or write, had a Scotsman's reverence for legal documents, and he insisted that the paper be drawn, witnessed and filed, even though at that time there was no proper place for filing. He himself had carried it to St. Louis for deposit with an official of the Missouri government, witnessed by Cyprian Pasquinel, the congressman.

'So I claim about eight hundred acres,' Levi concluded, 'and I have a legal paper proving it, but whether it'll be recognized when things get straightened out, I don't know.'

'What can I do?' Brumbaugh asked.

'You can squat on Indian land and hope that when law comes this way, title will pass to you, or you can buy some of my land and hope that the title I give you will some day be honored.'

'How much an acre?'

Levi considered this for some time, then said tentatively, 'For good land along the river, where we know things will grow, ten dollars an acre. For barren land on the benches, two dollars.'

'What I'll do,' Brumbaugh replied, 'is buy twenty of your good acres at two hundred dollars and borrow the other forty from the Indians.'

In this way the farm of Hans Brumbaugh was started, and in the spring of 1859 he was planting vegetables, including a large crop of potatoes. Harvesting them as early as possible, he sold some to Levi Zendt and carted the rest to Denver, where he made more cash than he could have trying to find gold fields. Potato Brumbaugh he would be called henceforth, the canny Russian who had quit the gold fields to go where the real money was.

The second significant thing he did had consequences more far-reaching. By the middle of May in that first season, when it became apparent that the land was good for vegetables, he was in the store one afternoon when the latest contingent of miners came through, eager to buy food, and they spoke so much of impending civil war that Brumbaugh had a sudden vision of what would probably happen. 'Levi,' he said when the men were gone, 'there's gonna be a war east of Mississippi and precious little food will trickle out here. If you sell me more river land, I can slip in an extra crop. I'll grow twice as much, and you'll make a fortune selling it.'

'I have no spare river land,' Levi said regretfully.

Brumbaugh, a compact, determined man, sat hunched over the end of a box, drawing designs with his finger. 'They tell me,' he said cautiously, 'that you have thousands of acres you haven't mentioned.'

'I do,' Levi replied frankly. 'Over at Chalk Cliff. So dry it won't even grow weeds.'

'How'd you get it?'

'From the Indians. My wife's father . . .' He decided not to go into that intricate web. 'You can have land up there if you want, but you won't grow anything on it.'

'And you say your river land's all gone?'

'Mine is. The Indians still have some.'

'Oh, no! If I have to work as hard as I work, I want to own the land. And I want title to it. I got robbed once.'

'You'll get title when we become a legal territory.'

Brumbaugh was not listening. With a dirty finger he had drawn on the box the outlines of the Platte River and the projection of his land lying along it, and as the lines squiggled through the dust they assumed a reality, as happens when men who love land look at maps. This *was* the river, this *was* his land, and slowly within the evening darkness the top of the box became alive, and on it there was water and grass and growing vegetables, and it was then that Potato Brumbaugh glimpsed the miracle, the whole marvelous design that could turn The Great American Desert into a rich harvestland.

Next morning he got up before dawn, scouted the reach of the Platte River as it ran past his land and satisfied himself that it could be done. But to make sure, he marked a spot high in a cottonwood tree which stood at the eastern end, then retreated to the far western end and watched it as he walked slowly along the riverbank. Yes! The river did drop perceptibly in its journey past the Brumbaugh land. His daring plan was practical. So he ran to his shack, grabbed his shovel and pickax and went to work.

Starting at the extreme western tip, he began to dig a channel which would bring water from the Platte, not onto his low-lying land, which was already well watered, but onto the first bench, which was arid. He would lead this small man-made arm of the river down the middle of that bench, thus trebling the size of his arable farm, and at the eastern end he would allow the unused water to find its way back to the Platte.

So Brumbaugh harnessed the river and nourished the land. And in the hot summer of 1860 he produced an enormous crop of vegetables, which were sold mainly in Denver. The once-arid land on the bench proved exceptionally fertile as soon as water was brought to it, and Potato Brumbaugh's farm became the wonder of Jefferson Territory. As he had foreseen that wintry night on Pikes Peak, it was the farmer, bringing unlikely acreages into cultivation by shrewd devices, who would account for the wealth of the future state.

When Brumbaugh drew water off the Platte, he unwittingly established himself as the first man to tap this river for irrigation purposes, so that even a century later when the judges of the supreme court of Colorado, or even the Supreme Court of the nation, were called upon to adjudicate water rights relating to the river—rights of indescribable value —they had to come back to one basic consideration:

> Priority in the use of water deriving from the Platte River dates to Hans Brumbaugh, who first constructed an irrigation ditch in the year 1859. His rights to this water and the rights of all owners of his land into the endless future must be respected, and all later claims are hereby declared subservient to his.

At the end of the 1860 growing season Potato Brumbaugh came to the trading post and plopped two hundred dollars on the counter. 'Levi, can you forward this to St. Louis and have the bank there send it along to my wife in Illinois? I want her to join me.'

When his wife and children stood at the western end of the holding, near the spot where he had dug the ditch, they were overwhelmed by the size of the farm he pointed out. It seemed bigger than a county in Illinois, and as they stepped onto it for the first time, it was fortunate that they could not envisage the incredible obstacles they would face in trying to hold on to it.

The relationship of a man to his land is never easy. It is perhaps the noblest relationship in the world, after the family, and certainly the most rewarding. But the land must be won, it must be revered, it must be defended.

On the afternoon of 1868 when John Skimmerhorn delivered his twenty-nine hundred and thirty-six head of cattle to the emerging Venneford Ranch, he happened to look across the milling longhorns and see young Jim Lloyd, still riding drag, but now more like a man than a gangling boy, and it occurred to Skimmerhorn that if he was given control of the Crown Vee cattle, he would require some tested young fellow to look after the far reaches of the ranch.

Accordingly, he spurred his horse and rode to where Oliver Seccombe was eying his new longhorns. 'Mr. Seccombe,' Skimmerhorn said, 'if you acquire the land . . .'

'I've already acquired a good deal of it. I haven't been idle while you were on the trail.'

'Does it extend as far as you proposed?'

'Farther.'

'Then you'll need some trustworthy hands, and there's none better than the boy who came north with us.'

Skimmerhorn signaled for Jim to join them, and Seccombe was surprised at his youth. 'You're still a kid!' he protested.

'If you drive cattle from Jacksborough across the Llano,' Skimmerhorn said, 'you're no longer a kid.'

Seccombe shook his head and was about to dismiss the idea, when Skimmerhorn added, 'This boy has fought off Kansas outlaws and killed a Comanche chief.'

'He has?' Seccombe asked in disbelief. 'Hell, he can't be more than fourteen.'

'He can be anything from fourteen to fifty,' Skimmerhorn said. 'Part of the reason your cattle got here, sir, was the courage of this boy.'

'He's hired,' Seccombe said.

Jim Lloyd's first ride across the vast domain with which he would be associated for the remainder of his life was an exploration in grandeur, for on the morning when he and Skimmerhorn set forth to position the line camps, they started by riding westward. A hawk flew before them, uttering a wild 'Scree, scree' very high in the heavens and flying in three distinct ways: motionless soaring, hovering to inspect the land below, and then the awful swift dive when any small victim was spotted. No birds on earth, not even the eagle or the falcon, were more majestic than these hawks of the west, ranging endlessly over the prairie.

Skimmerhorn had decided that to manage the ranch properly, five line camps would be needed, each with a rude hut sleeping six men, plus a stone barn for horses, and he wanted to number them from east to west. Selecting a bleak and lonely spot north of Chalk Cliff, he said, 'Here's Camp Five.' Its back was to the mountains and it overlooked an immense stretch of empty land. He staked out a protected site, to which Jim would later return with the construction crew. 'You'll be able to find it,' Skimmerhorn said. 'Just keep your eye on that little stone beaver climbing the face of the tallest mountain.'

Skimmerhorn wanted Line Camp Four convenient to the new Union Pacific Railroad, and this required that they expand into Wyoming Territory. At first the new land was much like the old, completely empty, but toward dusk one day they saw to the east that low piñon trees had somehow established themselves in spite of wind and drought; they dotted the land with attractive specks of dark green. Their shapes were twisted and they did not grow high, nor were there enough of them to form a forest, but they did create a scene of great natural beauty.

'This'll be a fine spot,' Jim said approvingly, but Skimmerhorn delayed decision, for as the sun set he caught a glimpse of something farther east that attracted him. Before dawn he was in the saddle, and as the sun came up he and Jim entered one of the notable areas on the ranch—a hillside covered with piñon trees and marked by wind-eroded pinnacles that looked like gnomes marching from the pages of a German fairy tale. On a southern exposure, protected from the wind and overlooking an infinite expanse of prairie, Skimmerhorn located his camp.

'All the cowboys'll be wanting duty up here,' he predicted. 'But not because it's beautiful.' As he spoke, the whistle from a train on the Union Pacific sounded to the north, and he laughed. 'When we build this camp, Jim, we'll have hell keeping the men out of Cheyenne,' and that night when they spread their sleeping bags Jim could see in the west the lights of that hell-raising railhead city.

They left the piñons and rode toward Rattlesnake Buttes, west of which they located Line Camp Three. It would be a favorite of those cowboys, for here they could scale the red buttes and generally enjoy themselves in one of the rugged areas of the west.

But it was on the eastern reaches, when they were searching for sites from which immense prairies could be controlled, that Jim caught once more that feeling of Colorado's dormant grandeur. He had first experienced this sensation on the morning after the fight with the Kansas outlaws, when the immensity of the prairie exploded before him. Then the emptiness was a new sensation; now it was home. And as soon as he rode east and reached those limitless horizons, with not a tree or a trail in sight, he sensed that he had found his universe, and said, 'Mr. Skimmerhorn, when you give the men their jobs, I'd like to work out here."
Skimmerhorn laughed. 'You like this?'

'This is good country,' Jim said.

They located Line Camp Two about halfway to the Nebraska line, and Line Camp One at the mouth of a canyon in an area so bleak and forbidding that only someone like Jim could appreciate it. 'We'll put our strongest cattle out here and let them fend for themselves,' he suggested, but Skimmerhorn, kneeling to inspect the sturdy grass that covered the area, said, 'No, this grass is so rich it'll do wonders for our weakest cattle. As soon as we get back to headquarters, Jim, I want you to ride into Denver and file for a homestead on this site. Mark off your boundaries now.'

And Jim did, using piles of stones to approximate the corners of the hundred-and-sixty-acre plot to which he could gain title if he successfully lied about his age. A considerable joy welled up as he placed the final corner. 'This is to be my land!' he cried, and Mr. Skimmerhorn said, 'Not exactly. You homestead it, but when the patent comes through, you sell to the ranch.'

'I don't want the money!' Jim protested. 'I want this canyon.'

'The rule is,' Skimmerhorn explained, with some coughing, 'that our cowboys file on the critical homesteads, then deed them back to the company.'

'I've always wanted my own land,' Jim said stubbornly.

'So have I,' Skimmerhorn confessed. 'In the years when my father drifted from one place to another . . .'

'You have yours.'

'Half an acre,' Skimmerhorn said contemptuously. 'I wanted land like this.' And he swept his right arm through a far reach, then dropped it. 'Fellows like you and me, Jim, we'll get our land by managing it for others.'

They rode home by following the Platte, and for the first time Jim came to appreciate this extraordinary river. In some places it reminded him of the Pecos, and he told Skimmerhorn, 'Old Rags could jump this,' but at other times he saw its power and its tattered magnificence. 'Just as you think you see it,' he said, 'it changes completely. It must be the only river in the world that's more islands than water.'

On one of the islands Jim found the bird which, even more than the soaring hawk, would epitomize for him this strange new land. It was a frail thing, walking delicately through marshes on slim yellow legs. It was attractively colored, with touches of yellow and brown and flecked gray, but what distinguished it was its remarkable bill, a long thing which turned up sharply at the end. Jim had never seen a bird like this and he laughed with pleasure as it tiptoed along the shore of the river, dipping its curved beak into wormholes.

'What is it?' he asked.

'Avocet.'

'Never heard of it.'

'It patrols the river,' Skimmerhorn said, and they watched the antics of the bird until night fell.

One morning Jim rose early and looked west to the mountains, and the day was so unsullied that they could see the Rockies from a distance which Skimmerhorn calculated to be a hundred and fifty miles. 'That's what's good about this territory,' Skimmerhorn said. 'You don't find air like this in St. Louis.'

So Jim Lloyd returned to Zendt's Farm and homesteaded his quarter section at the mouth of the canyon where Line Camp One was to be, but when he reached the land office he found three other Venneford cowboys going through the paper work to acquire other choice sites, and he asked them, 'You takin' out the land for the ranch?' and the men whispered, 'Ssssh! Don't let anyone hear you say that. It's illegal.' Jim knew the whole arrangement was illegal, but like the others, he needed the job.

From the moment of his arrival in Colorado, Oliver Seccombe had worked fifteen and eighteen hours a day, piecing together a ranch whose Crown Vee brand would be respected throughout the west. During the six months that Skimmerhorn had been absent, Seccombe had assembled the crucial holdings, and now, with a relatively small outlay of British capital, he had his empire consolidated.

It had required a good many more than the seventeen sites he had confidently assumed would do the trick, and it had taken more money than he had anticipated to buy up abandoned holdings, but his cowboys had homesteaded some of the choicest sites for him, and there was that stroke of luck in Elmwood, Illinois.

In 1871 he had gone back to Illinois to buy some good British bulls, Shorthorns and Angus, and had persuaded two of the farmers to come west with their animals, bringing them by railroad as far as Cheyenne. While they were in the area, he conceived the idea of asking them to homestead two quarter sections for him. They saw no harm in this and agreed to sell him the homesteads once they were proved up. When they had signed the papers—they never saw the land they were acquiring—he had the further idea of proposing that as a gesture of good will to their friends and relatives in Elmwood, they get sixty or seventy of them to take the train trip west, at Seccombe's expense, with each taking up a homestead for the benefit of the Venneford Ranch. The good people of Elmwood, eager to see the west, flocked out for a few days and then flocked right back home, but not before filing claims in Denver. In this unorthodox way Seccombe picked up an additional sixty-nine strategic holdings.

By 1872 the Venneford empire was fairly well completed—there were a few farms along the Platte it still needed—and it stretched a hundred and fifty miles from east to west, fifty miles from north to south, for a total of 5,760,000 acres. But it should never be said that the Venneford Ranch *owned* so much land; its actual holdings were rather modest:

17 parcels purchased outright	3,100 acres
37 cowboy homesteads, beneficially controlled	5,920 acres
69 Elmwood, Illinois homesteads, beneficially controlled	11,040 acres
Total ownership, real and beneficial	20,060 acres

This meant that of the open range referred to by the Venneford cowboys as 'our land,' Seccombe and his absentee masters actually owned, by one device or another, less than one half of one percent. Nor was there any permanence to their control. Each railroad that entered the territory would gobble up its share of the range; any town established in the area would eat up more; homesteaders would nibble away at the edges. Each year the total would diminish, until by the end of the century the ranch would be whittled down to reasonable size, say three-quarters of a million acres. Seccombe was right when he said, 'We're borrowing the land.'

Who owned this borrowed land? It belonged to the United States government, and until it was claimed by some adventurous homesteader, it was free for anyone to use. Even in this year of 1873 when the Venneford Ranch was operating at maximum efficiency, if you came out from

Iowa and announced that you intended to run two thousand head of longhorns on their open range, you were absolutely free to do so, with two *if's*.

If you could get your cattle to water along one of the creeks, which would prove impossible, since all the good watering spots were preempted by the Venneford people. And *if* you could escape being shot. No one ever knew who did the shooting; certainly it was not Mr. Seccombe, and for sure, not Mr. Skimmerhorn, who raised hell with Seccombe about the things that were going on.

What happened was that when you brought your cattle onto the grazing lands, a Venneford cowboy would ride up and warn you not to trespass on his watering rights, and if you persisted in claiming your rights to the open land, one day you became shot. That was the phrase they used: 'Poor Waddington. Running his cattle north toward Skunk Hollow. He became shot.' In eleven such incidents no one ever saw who did the shooting, nor were there even suspicions. But eleven would-be intruders became shot.

Take the case of the two ranches along the Platte east of Zendt's Farm. Close in was the farm belonging to Potato Brumbaugh, his wife, their daughter and two sons. Farther east, and therefore less protected, lay the ranch of Otto Kraenzel. Each commanded an influential stretch of riverbank, and if either fell into the hands of uncongenial cattlemen, the whole open range might become vulnerable. It was therefore essential that the Venneford people obtain these two ranches.

Realizing that Hans Brumbaugh, with his successful irrigation project, would be the more difficult to persuade, Oliver Seccombe first approached the Kraenzels. They didn't want to sell. They liked the Platte valley and foresaw a bright future. Seccombe pointed out that if they sold to him at a good price, they could take the money and homestead elsewhere in Colorado; he would help them locate a favorable site.

They refused to discuss the matter, told Seccombe it was no use arguing any further, regardless of price. So he bade them an amiable farewell and caught the train at Cheyenne for business in Chicago.

In his absence a Mr. Farwell arrived in Cheyenne. First he rode down to visit the Kraenzels, offering them a very good deal indeed, and then he rode up to the Brumbaugh ranch, where Hans and his wife assured him that under no conditions would they be interested in selling.

Mr. Farwell came back with two assistants, whom he called Gus and Harry, and the trio did their best to convince both Kraenzel and Brumbaugh to sell, but neither was interested. During the last discussion Mr. Farwell, a dark man in his forties who spoke with a gentle voice, said, 'I'm sorry that negotiations have broken down.'

'There never were any,' Brumbaugh said.

Mr. Farwell ignored this and said, 'I'll wait for two days at Zendt's place. If you change your mind, come in and we'll settle this easily.'

'There's nothing to settle,' Brumbaugh said, and Kraenzel said the same.

'Then I suppose that's all there is to it,' Mr. Farwell said quietly. He indicated that Gus and Harry were to depart and he shook hands with the stubborn ranchers. For two days he waited at Zendt's, and when nothing happened he rode off toward Cheyenne, with Gus and Harry trailing behind.

Two nights later Otto Kraenzel was gunned down and his ranch house set on fire. Mrs. Kraenzel and the two children escaped. They were so terrified, so eager to be rid of this dreadful place, that when they got to Denver they authorized a lawyer to sell the establishment, cattle and all, if a buyer could be found, and they were seen no more in the west. Oliver Seccombe, not being in the area, sent a telegram to Denver commissioning a lawyer he knew to acquire the vacated Kraenzel ranch, which solidified the Venneford holdings along the river.

When news of Kraenzel's murder sped through the community, the killers must have expected Potato Brumbaugh to hightail it off the Platte; if so, they underestimated the stoop-shouldered Russian, for having once fought off the Volga Cossacks, he now had no intention of surrendering either to fear or to Mr. Farwell, wherever he was. Instead, he sent his daughter to town with a message for Levi Zendt: 'If they kill me, you'll be next,' and Levi suspected that this might be correct, but the request placed him in an awkward position. Brumbaugh was accusing the Venneford people of trying to assassinate him and his family, and Levi was a partner in the Venneford operation. It was he, Levi, who was being accused of murder.

He sent the Brumbaugh girl back to the farm and sought out Skimmerhorn. 'John, did you hire outsiders to come in here and kill Kraenzel and Brumbaugh?'

'God! No!'

He spoke with such conviction that Levi had to believe him. 'Did Oliver Seccombe hire anybody?'

'No, Levi! He wants to round out his holdings, but not with bullets.'

'Then our duty is clear. Somebody in the operation is trying to run Brumbaugh off his land. I'm getting my guns to help him defend it.'

Without awaiting an answer, he turned and left, a stubborn, smallish man fifty-three years old, but at the gate he did hesitate, as if he expected a response, and John Skimmerhorn called, 'Wait. I'll go with you.'

The enemy, whoever they were, struck that night, but they were met by such a hail of bullets from the Brumbaugh house—seven guns firing from all sides—that they failed to set any buildings on fire and killed no one, even though numerous bullets ripped through the house.

The next night this ugly, unidentified war resumed, but toward dawn Potato Brumbaugh had had enough. Stooped like an ape, he gathered his family together and said, 'They're over behind that hayrick. There's five of us to go out and get 'em, and these two friends to guard the house.'

'I'm goin' with you,' Levi said, but Brumbaugh would not allow it. Light was just beginning to break when they ventured forth—a husband, his sharpshooter wife, his daughter, aged thirteen, and his boys, twelve and ten, all wielding big guns, all determined to drive the enemy off or die.

It was a brutal six minutes, with gunfire coming from many directions, but after the Brumbaughs worked their way safely across the open space leading to the barn, Potato surprised everyone. Running forward under protecting gunfire from his sons, he set fire to the hayrick, and as flames rose he bellowed, 'Over there, goddamnit, over there!' And his wife and daughter ran speedily to a vantage point and killed a man as he tried to escape the flames. The others rode off and were seen no more.

Levi went to the dead body, expecting to find Farwell or Gus or Harry, but the corpse was not of anyone previously seen in the area.

When Oliver Seccombe returned from Chicago he was met by Zendt and Skimmerhorn, who told him, 'Outlaws killed Otto Kraenzel and drove his family off the land,' and Seccombe said sanctimoniously, 'Yes, I heard of that sad affair.'

'Next night they started on Potato Brumbaugh's place,' Skimmerhorn said, 'but Levi and I helped the family. They killed one of the outlaws and drove the others away.'

Levi was staring directly into Seccombe's face as these words were said, and the man never flinched.

Seccombe placed his arm about Skimmerhorn's shoulder and said, 'You did exactly right, John. Ranches around here must be protected from nightriders.' He then rode down to offer the Brumbaugh family the assistance of three ranch carpenters to help repair the damage, and Brumbaugh said, 'I'd be glad to have them,' and within a short period the farm was restored.

After that Seccombe visited the Brumbaughs frequently, bringing the children presents from Cheyenne, and after a while it occurred to Brumbaugh that he was spying on his irrigation, so he switched his canvas dams and outlets to other places so as to confuse the Englishman. One day when he caught Seccombe surveying the hayricks he said, 'That's to feed cattle when the winters get cold,' and Seccombe said, 'Last winter I hardly wore a coat,' and Brumbaugh said blandly, 'With all your cattle, you better hope it stays that way.'

Later he saw Seccombe instructing his cowboys how to dig irrigation ditches, and by one device or another he let Seccombe know that he was no longer welcome to visit the Brumbaugh farm. 'I'll keep my ideas to myself,' he told his wife, 'and let Oliver Seccombe do the same.'

In this way the traditional antagonism of the prairies was launched: the rancher who wanted the range kept open against the farmer who required fenced land which he could control. It was a warfare as old as the first human family: 'And Abel was a keeper of sheep, but Cain was a tiller of the ground . . . and it came to pass, when they were in the field, that Cain rose up against Abel his brother, and slew him.'

Levi Zendt, watching the growing friction, told his wife, 'Like always, the Bible was right. In a fight for land, the farmer will always kill off the rancher, because the farmer's tied to the land and he'll fight to protect it.'

During the early summer of 1873 three hunts were organized, and when they ended, the face of the west was permanently altered and any hope of retaining old patterns of life vanished.

The first started in Omaha, Nebraska, and came at a dramatic time, for the Panic of 1873 had already cast its shadow across the money markets of New York and Chicago; prudent men were beginning to draw in their investments, but the men and women involved in this outlandish affair were so wealthy and so protected that the panic could not touch them.

Leader of the hunt was one of the lesser dukes from Austria. He was accompanied by a grand duke from Russia. They were joined by French and English military attachés and by seven generals who had served with more or less distinction in the Union armies during the Civil War, among them a charismatic firebrand named George Armstrong Custer, a temporary general during the Civil War but now returned to the rank of captain. Seconded to serve Custer was young Pasquinel Mercy, a lieutenant from Fort Laramie, who knew where to find buffalo.

In the second echelon of the party, below the dukes and the generals but providing most of the money to pay for the special train, the servants, the boxcars of liquor and the twelve cooks to prepare the banquets, came a group of French and British financiers interested in the west, and among them was a member of the Venneford enterprises sent out to inspect the holdings of the noble earl in the American west. He was Henry Buckland, fifty-one years old, an importer of silks from India with offices in Bristol, and traveling with him was his daughter Charlotte, aged twenty-one.

Buckland was a handsome, florid man of substance, both bodily and financially. He had left home as a young man to work aboard an India-bound ship and had loved the subcontinent, finding himself more at home in Bombay than in Bristol. He had built for himself an impeccable business reputation. He had married the daughter of a cousin of Earl Venneford of Wye, and this happy union, somewhat above his station, had projected him into the front ranks of Bristol society.

It was natural, when Venneford launched his adventures in America, that Henry Buckland be invited to participate, and it was equally natural that he should be the first British member of the combine to visit the American establishment.

His being along on the formal hunt was an accident. The organizers, hoping to snag a titled Englishman to augment the Austrian and Russian luminaries, had invited Lord Venneford, on the not preposterous theory that an English earl was at least the equal of a grand duke, but Venneford could not break away from duties at home; instead, he recommended his trusted associate, Henry Buckland of Bristol.

Charlotte Buckland's presence was not an accident. A headstrong, unpredictable girl of more than average beauty, she had during the past few years become increasingly troublesome to her parents. When she was nineteen—an age when her mother was already married—they had tried to arrange a most acceptable engagement to one of Bristol's more promising young men, a member of the Pollard family notable for the excellent teas it imported from Ceylon and India. The match was totally appropriate, for it would have linked two families which had distinguished themselves in the India trade, and it had the warm approval of Lord Venneford.

But Charlotte simply did not like young Pollard and abused him shamefully, letting it be known throughout Bristol that under no circumstances would she consent to marry him. And after casting him aside, she began flirting with a variety of men, including a naval officer and a married barrister, and her behavior was creating something of a scandal. It was high time that she was removed from Bristol, and the unexpected invitation to her father to join the Omaha hunt could not have come at a more opportune time.

'I'd love to go, Papa,' she cried, emphasizing the word *love,* which she pronounced *lovv,* with that musical force that well-trained English girls often used. Indeed, she sang her sentences, and in so charming a way that she sometimes seemed a delicate bird infected with spring. She was tall and blond, and laughed easily. She had proved to her own satisfaction that she could entice men, and she liked their company.

She left England in the spring of 1873 with a sense of keen excitement, as if in the new world she would find a fulfillment which she had missed in the old. She had no desire whatever to visit India, 'that *dread*ful place filled with *cob*ras and fat *ra*jahs.' She believed that India should be reserved for the capable young men of her family who understood trading in silk.

Longhorn cattle? Now, that was something else! She had seen an early photograph of some two dozen steers on her father's ranch—well, he owned a goodly share of it, even if it was in old Venneford's name—and from the first had been fascinated by those incredible horns, jutting out at right angles to the animal's face and reaching for seven feet, with a double twist on the way. 'I should love those animals,' she assured her father. Also, the distances involved on the ranch intrigued her. She figured that if one end of the ranch were placed on Bristol, the other would reach right across England to Dover and ten miles into the English Channel, and to have so much land under one management seemed quite preposterous.

New York delighted her, with its plebeian vigor, and Chicago was a joy. She visited the burgeoning stockyards and for the first time saw her family's beef on the hoof, but the horns of those steers were decidedly disappointing. 'They're so dreadfully short,' she complained. 'Hardly longhorns at all. Look more like docile Herefords.' She had often been to Herefordshire, the county that bordered Wales to the north, and knew the handsome red-and-white cattle that formed the specialty of that area.

It was the trip west from Chicago that gave Charlotte her introduction to what she called 'the real America,' and by the time she reached Omaha and the beginning of the Union Pacific she was in love with the sprawling land that seemed to encompass so many of her attitudes. It was bold, and innovative, and unafraid and often given to excess. She liked the men—those ruddy, well-fed merchants talking in hushed whispers about the panic. They were disturbed by it, but not afraid. She liked the hearty voices, the lack of affectation and the open manner in which the men ogled her. By the time the train reached Nebraska she and her father had been invited as house guests to four different establishments, and she wanted to visit each.

At Omaha the Bucklands were submerged in a sea of undirected activity, for the entourages of the two dukes descended upon the city, and junior members were making outrageous demands: 'The grand duke simply must have a bath twice a day, and the water must be hot, do you hear, hot!' There was also the matter of special foods and cooks to prepare them. The seven American generals had their problems, too, but each had a bevy of subalterns to solve them, while French and English businessmen encountered much difficulty in acquiring even basic necessities. The confusion was compounded by the four ubiquitous American journalists who wanted to talk with everyone, two photographers who were laboriously taking pictures which would be treasured a hundred years hence, and a German watercolorist who made lifelike pictures of the mélange. He dashed them off with bewildering facility, seven and eight a day; in time they would be worth five thousand dollars each, but now he handed the less appealing ones around as souvenirs, keeping only the best for the book that a German publisher had commissioned.

This was the American west, the land of Indians and buffalo, the dream world of millions of Europeans who saw it as an escape from the routine of their city-pent lives. No detail was lacking in interest, and when Charlotte Buckland saw on the streets of Omaha a cowboy, a Chinese railway worker and a Pawnee Indian, she brought all three into line and had her photograph taken with them.

(There she is, standing between the Chinese and the Indian, a slim, beautiful English girl with a mischievous look that can be seen even now as she flirts with the cowboy. She wears a long dress, a summer blouse with ruffled sleeves, a large hat, and about her trim waist a heavy leather belt. Off to one side in the picture, photographed by accident, stands Lieutenant Pasquinel Mercy, whom she has not yet met.)

'I am Lieutenant Mercy,' a young man said, stepping forward. 'I have been commissioned to watch after you.'

She left the Indian and the Chinese and went over to Mercy, extending her hand. 'I'm Charlotte Buckland, and over there's my father, having apoplexy trying to buy an extra trunk from that horrid little man.'

They went to where Buckland was arguing, and within a few moments Lieutenant Mercy had the purchase arranged. He then took them on a brief tour of the station and showed them the train on which they would soon be embarking. As he did so, a well-worn little engine with a beehive stack puffed into the station, and Charlotte cried, 'Look at that darling little thing! Is it going to pull us all the way to Wyoming?' And Mercy, with obvious pride, pointed to a black monster coming down another track and said, 'That's ours.'

'Papa!' Charlotte cried. 'Look at that giant beetle coming to consume us.' The way she pronounced the word *consume* captivated Mercy, and he said, 'If it is a beetle, it must have wings,' but his metaphor was awkward, and Buckland stared at him, but Charlotte, appreciating what the young officer had been attempting, cried, 'It does have wings! It does! And we shall fly to Wyoming.'

As she said this she pirouetted through the station, coming back to her father and grasping him by both hands. 'I shall never leave here, Papa. I feel it. I shall fly with my black beetle, and I shall be gone.'

It was nearly dusk when the amazing entourage finally packed itself aboard the special train and the new black engine pulled the seventeen cars westward. What a dinner was served that first night—from oysters to iced creams! The two dukes were graceful in acknowledging the applause of people lining the tracks and frequently they halted the train, dragging this or that Civil War hero to the back platform with them as torchlights began to flare in the countryside.

Charlotte was flirting easily with Lieutenant Mercy, who seemed a most congenial young man, and brave too, with his stories of fighting Indians, when she became aware that a stranger was standing at her elbow, awaiting an opportunity to speak with her. It pleased her to make believe she did not see him; instead, she talked to Mercy with unusual animation, singing her sentences joyously, then halting abruptly, looking up at the stranger and saying, 'I am most awfully sorry. Did you wish to speak to Lieutenant Mercy?'

'I wished to speak with you, Miss Buckland,' the man said. 'My name's Oliver Seccombe and I am general manager of Venneford Ranch. I've come to take you to the Platte.'

She did not know the word. 'Is that the town where the ranch is?'
'It's a river,' he said.

'What a flat, ugly name for a river. Platte. Sounds as if somebody dropped a plate in a dishpan.'

Seccombe smiled. 'The name's appropriate, for it is a flat, ugly river, isn't it, Lieutenant Mercy?'

'Not at Fort Laramie,' Mercy said. 'Up there it's rather fine.'

'The ranch doesn't extend to the fort,' Seccombe explained.

Charlotte, not entirely liking his manner, did not ask him to join them. 'You'll find my father over there, with the Russian duke,' she said.

'I've spoken to Mr. Buckland,' Seccombe said quietly. He was fifty-five years old that summer, a lean, capable Englishman who had bowed and bent and sprung back in all the storms America could throw at him, and he did not intend to allow this ill-mannered daughter of a Bristol silk merchant to confuse him now. 'If you need me,' he said softly, 'I shall be happy to assist you. For the present, you seem to be well cared for, and I shall go to bed. Busy day tomorrow.'

The long ride across Nebraska required two days, what with stopping to inspect items of interest and a long wait while the horses were unloaded so that the two dukes could caper across the prairies, with Pawnee scouts shouting like Indian warriors as they rode. Seccombe thought the Pawnee looked silly, undignified, but the dukes apparently loved it, so on the second day a mock battle was staged between the Pawnee and Lieutenant Mercy's young officers. The riding was superb, and as planned, after a sharp encounter the soldiers sent the Indians scampering across the prairie. When they rejoined the train the Pawnee were laughing, destroying any illusion that the fray could have been serious, but General Custer, as he insisted upon calling himself, quickly corrected that.

A thin man with flowing mustaches, he told the dukes of his feat in 1868, only five years ago, at Washita River in Kansas. 'It was touch and go,' he said, drawing the battle lines on paper, 'but in the end my cavalry swept around this point and taught the red men a lesson.'

'How many did you kill?' one of the dukes asked.

'Two hundred, three hundred.'

'A stirring victory!' the Russian duke cried, and he asked his aides if they did not agree that this was indeed a stirring victory. They did. Then Custer said modestly, 'These plains will never be safe until the red devils are exterminated, and by that I mean exterminated.' The dukes nodded solemnly. A newspaperman overhearing the conversation winced. He knew that Custer had reported that he had slain 103 fierce warriors, whereas the official investigation, held later that year, had shown the Indian dead to number thirteen men, sixteen women and nine children.

On the third day—after the train passed Julesburg and was well into Wyoming, skirting the Venneford Ranch, which touched the tracks on the south—the unbelievable happened. It could never have been planned, and it was no part of the arrangements or even the hopes of the seven generals, for their intention was to disembark at Cheyenne, ride north on horseback to Fort Laramie and hunt the buffalo from there.

But as the train puffed westward, a remnant of the last herd to occupy the land between the two Plattes stumbled its way along the railroad tracks, and the engineer, blowing his whistle loudly all the while slowed down almost to a standstill as the train cut a path through the middle of the herd. The buffalo, still confused by trains although they had seen them for six years now, started to mill around and in the end wound up within touching distance from the train windows.

This was simply too good a chance to miss! The dukes unlimbered their rifles. The generals got down their Winchesters. Even Charlotte Buckland was offered a heavy Civil War gun, which she refused.

It was almost impossible to miss a buffalo. Indeed, at some points it was necessary to wait for him to move off a few feet so that one could aim at a vital organ; otherwise the gun went off with the muzzle caught in the hair, which merely blew a hole in the beast's stomach without really finishing him off.

The firing continued for nearly half an hour, with animals dropping on either side of the train, depending upon which windows were crowded with sportsmen, and in this manner some sixty or seventy buffalo were slain.

There was a brief interlude of excited chatter as they all compared notes on their kills. Suddenly someone noticed, moving parallel to the coach, a splendid bull with massive head held low, great shoulders and a sloping rear well adapted to fast charges. He could hardly have been important in the servicing of cows, for surely younger bulls must have driven him away by now, but he had a notable dignity which the German watercolorist tried to catch. 'What an animal!' he cried as he rapidly started to sketch the sloping shoulders and drooping head.

Charlotte could not remember later who uttered the cry, but someone shouted, 'It's for Miss Charlotte,' and a special gun, an Austrian one with a powerful sight, was handed to her, but again she refused.

'Please!' the Austrian duke cried. 'You may never have another chance . . .'

'She doesn't want it,' a quiet voice said, and Charlotte saw with relief that it was Oliver Seccombe. He took the heavy gun and handed it to one of the Russians.

'I'll take him!' the Russian duke bellowed, but the pace of the bull matched exactly the speed of the train, and for more than a minute the grizzled old veteran moved beside the window, close enough to be touched but too close for a sporting shot.

'Have the engineer speed up!' the Russian roared, and an equerry ran forward to deliver the message, but it was not required, for now the old bull started to veer away and the men standing behind the grand duke cheered and an American general shouted 'Now!' But at that moment someone bumped the Russian, so that his bullet did not strike a vital organ; it may even have ricocheted off the horn, for the old bull snorted, kicked his hind legs and galloped off toward the open prairie.

'Don't let him escape!' one of the generals cried, and nineteen guns blazed from the slowly moving train. The old bull quivered, tried to maintain his balance but collapsed in the dirt. He had been running with such force that his body scraped along the ground for fifteen feet, raising a pillar of dust.

'The best bull of all,' one of the Russians said, 'and we saved it for last.' Seventy-three buffalo had been shot, a perfectly splendid accounting, all agreed. By this time the train, now unimpeded, started speeding up—leaving behind to rot some fifty tons of choice meat, along with hides that could have been fashioned into seventy-three of the finest robes.

The portrait of the old bull was never finished. The German watercolorist, watching the noble beast go down under the blizzard of bullets, had no stomach for depicting his death. He crumpled the paper, and cleaning women at Cheyenne found it on the floor with the other rubbish.

The second hunt occurred in response to national policy. It started in April of that year, in the town of Jacksboro, Texas, where in the handsome public square a man named Harker appeared leading three stout wagons and a group of four extremely tough skinners. When his convoy halted he let it be known that he would consider signing up one buffalo hunter, if the man was unusually good with the rifle. Everyone he spoke to said, 'Amos Calendar's your man,' and after he heard this four times he said, 'I better see Calendar,' and he went in search of him.

He found him on the north edge of town, living alone in a miserable shack. Calendar was then twenty-five years old, an extremely thin, clean-shaven recluse without even a dog to keep him company. His only possessions seemed to be the clothes he wore and two fine rifles invented by Christian Sharps and now manufactured in Hartford, Connecticut.

'Name's Harker,' the buffalo hunter said.

'Mine's Calendar.'

'Hear you been up the trail to Colorado.'

'Twicet.'

'See any buffalo?'

'Millions.'

'How long ago?'

'Five years.'

'Aha!' Harker cried. 'I'm the man who knows where they are now.'

'Meanin' what?'

'They tell me you can shoot.'

'That's right.'

'Care to prove it?'

Calendar showed no desire to demonstrate a known fact, so he remained inside his shack, but Harker was insistent, so he took down his oldest Sharps, the one he had carried on the Colorado trail. With studied insolence he took out a paper cartridge, hefted it for weight, pulled down the lever on his rifle and inserted the cartridge so that a tail of paper extended backward from the chamber. Then, with a sudden upward flick of the lever, he closed the breech in such a manner that a sharp knife sheared off the loose end of paper, exposing in the chamber a heavy charge of black powder, ready to be ignited whenever a spark was thrown upon it.

'I see you're usin' the old-style cartridge,' Harker said with an edge of contempt.

'Because I like 'em,' Calendar replied defiantly.

He opened a minute chamber into which he placed a fulminate of mercury primer, which, when the hammer exploded it, would send a flash of fire down a tube to discharge the exposed powder. It was as complicated a system as had ever been devised for a rifle, and was beset with drawbacks. It had only one virtue: it worked.

'What are you goin' to hit?' Harker asked.

'Anything you say.'

Harker looked about for a bottle, found one and walked a considerable distance before placing it against a tree. 'Try that,' he called.

Calendar raised his Sharps, felt it nestle against his shoulder, and experienced not the slightest doubt that he would strike the bottle, for he had molded the bullet at the end of the paper cartridge; he had tied the banknote paper to the bullet with silk thread; he had weighed precisely the amount of powder; and he knew to a fraction how each part of the gun would act.

'I'll shoot off the top,' he said. Carefully, yet with familiar ease, he steadied the gun, pulled back the rear trigger to move the sear into hairtrigger position and moved his finger to the forward trigger. With ever so slight a touch he depressed the forward trigger, and several remarkable things happened.

Because the powder lay exposed in the chamber, and because no breech could be made airtight, a dangerous body of flame shot upward through the loose fittings, temporarily blinding the shooter. Also, because the breech was loose-fitted in another direction, a fair supply of powder backfired into the face of the operator. But most important, the Sharps was so well made, and with such a heavy barrel, that the bullet had to leave the muzzle at great speed and with perfect direction. If Calendar aimed right, the bullet went right.

Smack! There was no crash of broken glass, just the crisp sound of the top being blown off. 'You can shoot,' Harker said as he returned to the shack. 'You want to work for me on a buffalo hunt . . . a real buffalo hunt?'

'Well . . .' Calendar said. He had no need of work. Doing odds and ends around Jacksboro, he made enough to keep alive, for his wants were few. He didn't drink. He had no woman. He didn't have to plow, so he needed only one horse. And he made enough money to care for his guns; he didn't even need to buy cartridges, since he made his own.

But Harker had a persuasion that Calendar could not resist. 'See that thing sticking out of my saddlebag? That's a new Sharps. Brass cartridge.'

'It is?' Calendar asked, unable to mask his surprise. He had heard of this mighty gun, .50 caliber, 70 grains of powder, 475 grains of lead in the bullet. It was supposed to be a monster and only a few test samples had so far been made.

'How'd you get aholt of one?' Calendar asked, studying the weapon as it rested in the saddlebag.

'Friend bought it for me. You come out with me, Calendar, that rifle's yours. Go ahead, take it out.'

Once Calendar had the black-steel rifle in his hands, once he had inspected that enormous barrel—thirty-five inches long, twenty-three pounds in weight—he was lost. 'You'd have to fire this'n from a tripod,' he told Harker. 'Man couldn't hold this.'

'We've got a tripod,' Harker said. 'And we've got the cartridges.' He handed Calendar three beautiful brass tubes. No more dangerous paper cartridges, no more flash from loose powder, no more backfire into the face.

And then Harker, like Mephistopholes, whispered the magic words that made resistance impossible. Handing Calendar an intricate tool on which he had been working, he said softly, 'At night, when the hunting's done for that day, you'll sit around filling your own brass cartridges . . . molding the lead bullets . . . fitting them in place.'

Calendar studied the improvised tool: one hook removed the primer from the head of the spent cartridge, another plunger seated the new primer; a clever device straightened the cartridge; another crimped the edge to fasten the end of the bullet; at the far end there was a bullet mold into which hot lead would be poured; on the side was attached a powder measure. With such a gun, and such a tool, with three or four dozen cartridges to be reloaded, a bar of lead for casting bullets and a can of black powder, a man could shoot his way from here to hell.

'How much is the gun?' Calendar asked, his eyes dancing.

'Nothing. You shoot for me all summer . . . I got four of the best skinners you ever seen. You keep 'em busy, and at the end of the season that gun's yours.'

'I don't go out with no man's gun but my own,' Calendar said. 'How much?'

'Forty-nine dollars, and the double trigger, four dollars more.'

'Wouldn't be no good without a double trigger.' He looked at the gun, studied Harker, who seemed remarkably unpleasant. 'I got fifty-three dollars, mister. I'm buyin' the gun, and I'm leavin' with you this afternoon.'

So off they went to hunt buffalo—Bill Harker, as tough a plainsman as ever lived; Amos Calendar, veteran of the trail with R. J. Poteet; four ugly, dirty skinners; two wagon men to haul the skins; and a cook. They left Jacksboro about dusk and made camp well outside of town. Heading in a northwest direction, they crossed the Trinity River, the Wichita, the Peace and the Red, which put them into Oklahoma Indian territory, where they had no right to be.

Harker warned them, 'Keep a sharp eye for Comanche,' and a night guard was posted. God help the Indian who stumbled into this camp, because these men were killers. They hated Indians, sheriffs, missionaries, schoolteachers, buffalo, deer, antelope and other things yet to be identified.

On their third day in Oklahoma they sprang into action, for Harker was right. With some innate sense he knew where the buffalo were, and he led his deadly team right to the edge of a herd. From a slight rise they looked down on at least six hundred animals.

'We work this way,' he told Calendar. 'You're probably the best shot, so you edge your way downwind while I move in from this side. You shoot first and knock down whatever animal seems to be leading the pack, but don't kill him. If we can knock down the leader, the rest will mill around inspectin' him and we can pick 'em off at our speed.'

The big thing, as Harker explained, was to achieve a stand. That happened when the hunter succeeded in dropping but not killing the leader; then he could remain in one spot and shoot at leisure, bagging as many as seventy or eighty beasts while they milled about their fallen leader, uncertain what to do or which way to go. 'There's nothin' in this world stupider than a buffalo,' Harker whispered as they prepared to attack the herd. 'Wound one of them, the rest will gather round. I killed sixty-seven once, just like that.'

Calendar crept into position downwind of the herd and watched as the animals continued to graze unmindful of danger. Take it slow, he told himself, creeping ever closer. He was now within sixty yards of the stragglers, but he did not want them. It was his responsibility to knock down the leader. You aimed not for the heart, because even with two bullets through the heart, a buffalo bull could run a hundred yards, throwing the herd into panic. What you did was aim for the lungs, because then the bull fell to the ground in lingering and unfrenzied dying. Then the other buffalo would gather to watch in quiet confusion.

Now Calendar was close to the leaders and he could discern which of them had to be shot first. Looking back to where Harker waited with his own Sharps, Calendar signaled that he was about to begin.

Methodically he cocked his rifle, inserted the brass cartridge and listened as the block moved snugly back into position. He set the trigger, adjusted the monstrous gun in its tripod and aimed at the lungs of the lead animal. Stroking the front trigger lightly, he heard a *whoosh*, not the crack of the normal rifle but the heavy push of a cannon.

The bullet sped accurately and with tremendous force. Striking the lead buffalo in the side, it penetrated both lungs, and the bewildered animal dropped to the ground. The rest of the herd began their invariable ritual of milling around, sniffing the fallen beast, then standing still as though waiting for a decision. During this time, which might last as long as forty minutes, the hunters had the herd at their mercy. A stand, it was called, and the trick was to pick off the waiting animals with a clean shot, lodged between the horn and the ear so as to produce immediate death, a swift sinking to the ground without even a muted bellow of pain. Despite the noise of the rifles, which somehow the buffalo never learned to heed, the animals remained unaware of danger.

Working methodically, Harker and Calendar killed nineteen buffalo, reloading with care and shifting their tripods from time to time. But on the twentieth shot Harker had the bad luck to fire low, striking an old bull in the right rear leg and causing him to thrash about, dangling the useless leg and bellowing. This put the whole herd into a frenzy, and one cow, sensing the danger at last, started off at a gallop, taking the remaining animals with her. It was no use to shoot blindly at retreating buffalo; cartridges must not be wasted.

Now the skinners moved in, men skilled with knives. They worked in pairs, throwing the carcass on its back and slitting the belly from tail to throat. Ropes were attached to the skin, and horses pulled the heavy robes loose. The carcass, of course, was left to rot, but a good robe with the flesh cleaned off might bring as much as three dollars. Properly tanned, it could go as high as twelve.

'We nearly had ourselves a stand,' Harker said that night as he and Calendar made up the cartridges for the next day. 'We would of had it, but I hit that damned bull in the leg.' He had aimed right, had fired right. 'Musta been a light charge of powder,' he surmised. 'Hell, in this business, anything can go wrong.

'We're doin' God's work, you could say,' he told the men. 'I heard General Phil Sheridan in Austin, and there's no man knows the west like General Phil. And he said that the west will not be worth a damn till every buffalo is killed. Every one.'

'What was his thinkin'?' one of the skinners asked.

'Hell, it's clear. We wipe out the buffalo, the Indian has got to go on the reservation, where he belongs. When they start to starve, what choice do they have but to obey?'

The buffalo men considered this for some time, and Harker explained,

'When you face an enemy they's two things you can do. Kill him or starve him. The ministers and the newspaper people and them damn fools in Washington won't let us kill the Indians off, like we should, but by God, if we eliminate the buffalo, like we're doin', we can sure as hell starve 'em into submission.'

The slaughter continued—twenty-three . . . thirty . . . sixteen, and on one memorable day, fifty-seven, killed in two lots, one in the morning and another in the late afternoon when everyone thought the day was finished.

The line of carcasses alerted the Comanche to the fact that Texans had invaded their territory, and an assault was launched, with many Indians riding swiftly at the three wagons, but Harker had his men ready.

He and Calendar, with their Sharps reloading in seconds, sat stolidly behind one of the wagons, resting their small cannon on the framework, and carefully picked off one Comanche after another. The same practical principle applied as in hunting buffalo: take it slow, pick off the leaders, throw the tribe into confusion.

Whoosh! While Harker reloaded, Calendar drew a sight on a young brave who was shouting orders, and he fell in a heap.

Whoosh! It was very much like a buffalo stand—resolute gunners working professionally and bringing down the enemy.

When nine bodies lay scattered through the sage, the Comanche withdrew. In previous forays they had often encountered stubborn resistance from white men, but never this quiet, deadly fire.

'We showed 'em!' Harker exulted that night. 'A few more days like this and we'll have this territory cleaned of buffalo and Indians both.'

'They oughta give us a medal,' one of the skinners said.

'General Sheridan suggested that,' Harker said. 'I was talkin' with him at his hotel and he told me, "Harker, they oughta cast gold medals for men like you. One side a buffalo, other side an Indian. You're doin' the work of civilization." What he meant, as I heard later, was that when we get through, the plains'll be a decent place for proper settlers.'

This observation was digested by the men, none of whom had much use for civilization, and after a while Calendar made one of the few comments he was to utter this summer: 'Proper settlers is sometimes more of a pain in the ass than Indians . . . or buffalo either.'

As he said these words he was looking at the open prairie to the west, and on the next day, when he was far ahead of the wagons, he came upon his big chance and he knew exactly what to do about it.

He was in Colorado Territory, north of the Arkansas, when some sixth sense warned him that buffalo might be grazing ahead. Dismounting, he crept over the brow of the hill and saw below him several hundred large animals, one of the last major remnants of the southern herd. For a moment he considered riding back to alert Harker, for it would take two guns to handle this herd properly, but some movement among the animals to the north warned him that he had no time to spare.

He therefore crept back over the hill to get his rifle and tripod and four dozen cartridges. Crawling slowly to the buffalo, he positioned himself downwind but in a location from which he could knock down the leader. Adjusting his tripod, he sat behind it, his thin legs spread like a V, his eye at gun level.

Patiently, and without visible excitement, he dropped the lead animal with a shot through the lungs and watched as the others began to mill around. Blowing into the breech, he reloaded and killed the first of the standing buffalo. Time after time he fired with sober calculation, killing his buffalo with precision. On the twenty-sixth kill he uttered his only words: 'I think I got me a stand.'

It looked as if he could fire at the animals forever, but there was a limitation and he knew it. If he fired any faster than once every forty seconds, the barrel of his rifle would accumulate so much heat it would expand, thick as it was, and it might not cool to its former accuracy.

So he worked slowly, feeling the barrel after each shot. He wished to hell he had a canteen of water and more bullets. Thirty-two, thirty-nine, forty-three. The huge beasts fell in the dust and still the herd could not comprehend what was happening. Can't be nothin' stupider than a buffalo, Calendar thought. They deserve to die.

And then, as he fired his forty-sixth shot, help came. Harker, hearing from a distance the slow, rhythmic firing, guessed that Calendar might have himself a stand, and now he came creeping over the hill with a canteen of water and five dozen more bullets. When Calendar saw him he was so delighted that tears of gratitude almost came to his eyes.

'Jesus!' Harker whispered. 'Have you got yourself a stand!' He gave Calendar the water and watched as the hunter cooled off his rifle. When Calendar, in sign language, asked if Harker wanted to go back for his own rifle and join the kill, the boss shook his head. 'It's your stand,' he whispered. 'Let's see what you can do.'

So Calendar, still sitting with his legs at a V behind the tripod, methodically shot a fifth dozen, then a sixth, then a seventh. 'Christ, you got eighty-five, eighty-six buffalo down there,' Harker said.

'Eighty-four,' Calendar said, watering the barrel on the outside, pouring some down the inside and letting it flow through the open breech.

Still the stupid buffalo made no move. Seven dozen of their mates lay dead and they were unable to adjust to that fact, because none of the dead had thrashed about or bellowed.

'Eighty-five, eighty-six,' Harker counted. 'Take it easy, and you got your hundred.'

It was unlikely that the skinners could handle so many. The surplus would be left to rot with their hides on, but the gun was cool now and Calendar might as well try for a record. He killed two more of the big animals, then gunned down a medium-sized cow, but on his ninetieth shot the cartridge must have been defective, for it struck far short of the herd, ricocheted and hit a cow in the rump.

She bellowed, shook her leg and started to gallop. Before Calendar could fire again, the herd was gone, leaving eighty-nine dead.

The third hunt can be reported briefly. In the late summer of 1873 those few Arapaho still trying to survive on the cramped remnants of the reservation at Rattlesnake Buttes ran so short of food that they faced actual starvation. The government said it wanted to help and even sent messages of commiseration, but the financial panic restricted funds in the east and no money could be spared to feed Indians. Chief Lost Eagle, now an old man of sixty-three with breaking teeth, made one last appeal, sending a delegation to Major Mercy in Denver, and the major rode out to the reservation and cursed the deprivation he saw, but he had neither the power nor the money to alleviate it.

So it was decided by the younger braves to try one last buffalo hunt, even though this would take them from the reservation and across lands on which settlers had begun to appear. Lost Eagle was too old to lead the foray, so command devolved to his son Red Wolf, and the remnants of the once-mighty Arapaho set forth.

What a pitiful lot they were. Their horses were lank; if buffalo were sighted, the horses would scarcely be able to keep up with them, let alone overtake and ride them down. The braves were in worse condition —emaciated, sullen men who could not comprehend what was happening to them. No white man in the path of these Indians had much to fear; one rifle blast would scatter the lot.

They went south, entering upon that land between the Platte and the Arkansas, and there they searched for buffalo. Each morning weary scouts rode to the four compass directions and saw much rolling land, all empty. Somewhere there had to be buffalo. They had heard reports of the train whose engineer had run into the middle of a herd. But they could find none.

Two long weeks they spent in the saddle, chasing illusions and finding emptiness. They grew so weak from lack of food, they could scarcely ride, but still they searched, and in the end they might have perished, actually starved to death on their prairie, had they not stumbled upon an area north of the Arkansas where the carcasses of eighty-nine buffalo lay rotting in the sun.

The men were so famished that one actually ate some decayed meat, but Red Wolf saw the folly of this and spurred his horse so that he stood between his men and the meat. Holding his right hand aloft, he gradually drove them back, and after a while the one who had eaten was gripped in dreadful pain, dying with foam on his lips, and the others acknowledged the wisdom of their chief.

He took no consolation. Astride his horse he looked down at the slaughter, nearly a hundred buffalo slain and not even the tongues removed. Some hunter had killed so many that his skinners could not keep up, and twenty of the animals were left to rot with their hides untouched.

'What kind of men are they?' Red Wolf cried in anguish. 'That they kill the food we need and do not even eat?'

And he suffered the ultimate indignity, the mortal shame of the leader: to lead a people and be unable to feed them.

It was at that moment that his evil luck changed. An outfit came over the hill at the Arkansas, trailing cattle up the Skimmerhorn Trail to Wyoming, and the trail boss took pity on the starving Indians and gave them two old steers.

Red Wolf allowed his braves to slaughter one of the longhorns, then exercised severe discipline as he made his ravenous braves save one to drive back for the women on the reservation. Revitalized by this accidental food, the hunters scoured the prairie, convinced they must encounter buffalo, but none were to be found; between the Platte and the Arkansas, there were no more buffalo.

Red Wolf, sitting beside his horse on the last night of the hunt, told his men, 'The old days have passed. We shall hunt no more forever.' The younger men asked what they would do instead, and Red Wolf said, 'Through hunger the Great White Father has made us submit to his command. We must leave the buttes and go to some smaller reservation, as he directs.'

The young braves protested: 'This is our land. It was given to us for as long as the waters flow and the birds fly.'

'The White Father wants it, and we must go.' He never deviated from this harsh decision, and as soon as he returned to Rattlesnake Buttes, bringing back from the hunt the drying meat from one old Texas steer, he advised his father, 'Lost Eagle, now we must go,' and that old chief fingered his Buchanan and agreed.

They sent a messenger to Denver to inform Major Mercy that they were now prepared to surrender their lands forever, and he sent a telegram to Washington, and a commissioner was sent out who held long powwows, assuring the Arapaho they were making the right decision and that in their new home, far to the north in Dakota, there would be ample food and a secure home 'for as long as the grass shall grow and the eagle fly.'

So in late summer the last group of Arapaho departed. They rode north on spavined horses, wrapped in tattered blankets. The gaily painted buffalo hides that recalled the history of their people were gone; the garments of elk and porcupine quill were gone; the young braves riding ahead to scout for buffalo were no more. The ancient ways were lost.

As they reached the crest of the white hills which marked the northern border of their truncated reservation, Chief Lost Eagle, wearing his hat with the turkey feather, paused to look back upon the buttes and the Platte and the prairie, and there was no sadness in him: 'Often in the past Our People were forced to make a new life in a new land, and always we had the courage to succeed. We were here at the buttes less than six generations and now we move to something different. This time I do believe the White Father will keep his promises. In Dakota we shall grow strong again.' He kicked his pony, and the Indians vanished forever from the spacious lands they loved so deeply and had protected so well.

The *Clarion* could express no sorrow at their passing:

> Yesterday we went out to the buttes to witness the departure of Lo from our fair land. Good riddance. They left Colorado for the last time riding mangy ponies, most of them stolen, we feel sure, and wearing blankets which would have profited from a good washing. They were a miserable lot of flea-ridden, filthy, ignorant, disgusting animals, and our only regret at watching them go was that Colonel Frank Skimmerhorn could not have been here to see his prophecy fulfilled.

> We hear that on the other side of the mountain the Utes are kicking up trouble again. We warn them that if they stick their noses over this way, we will shoot them off. They'll get far worse from us than they ever got from the Arapaho. Colorado will never merit statehood until we complete the job of exterminating these vermin.

When Oliver Seccombe watched the Arapaho depart, he realized that this was the moment to appropriate the good grazing lands around Rattlesnake Buttes, and by the judicious acquisition of two key parcels of land, he secured the whole area for the Venneford Ranch. Ninety-nine hundredths of the former Indian lands were actually public property, open to everyone, but Seccombe and his men made sure that no one could get to them.

That summer of 1873 was to be an exciting one for Oliver Seccombe. Henry Buckland was proving himself to be a shrewd and sensible businessman, and he required little instruction before grasping the essentials of any operation. After a visit to one line camp, he put his finger on the permanent problem: 'Land, Seccombe! We must own our own grazing land . . . have it secure in our possession.'

He was pleased with the devices Seccombe had used to acquire control of water, but even so, the total seemed inadequate. And then good fortune struck for the Englishmen. The Union Pacific Railroad volunteered to help them out.

Back in 1862, when the United States government had determined that a railroad was needed to bind the nation together, Congress hit upon a clever device for financing such a major undertaking. The nation was too poor to pay for the road out of tax funds, but there was an ingenious way to finance it. From the center of the main track, reaching out ten miles on each side, the government would give the railroad land, with no charge of any kind. This land in its original barren condition would be worth about twenty cents an acre, but with a prosperous railroad running through it, it might become worth as much as four dollars an acre. By selling this land to would-be settlers, the railroad would earn back more than the cost of building the road. The western range would be settled; the nation would have a link to the Pacific; towns would appear—and all at no expense to the taxpayer. It was one of the sagest devices ever invented by Congress.

Furthermore, Congress added an adroit stipulation: the railroad would not receive all the land ten miles out from the track; it would get only every other section, with the nation holding on to the alternate sections, and thus sharing in whatever increased values might accrue. It was a happy solution, made more palatable by the rule that two sections in each township must be set aside for public education. In later years, when the Union Pacific gleaned a fortune on the sale of land the government had given it, jaundiced critics would cry, with some justification, 'We gave our soul away to the railroad,' but in 1862 there had been no viable alternative, and in the long run, little harm was done.

It worked this way. Back in 1785 when the surveys of Ohio and Indiana were being conducted, it was provided that an American township be composed of thirty-six square miles, each called a section. They were numbered in a way which ensured that two sections with contiguous numbers would also have contiguous boundaries:

6	5	4	3	2	1
7	8	9	10	11	12
18	17	16	15	14	13
19	20	21	22	23	24
30	29	28	27	26	25
31	32	33	34	35	36

The railroad received the odd-numbered sections, sixteen in each township, with the federal government retaining the even-numbered, except for 16 and 36, which the state could sell or lease to provide funds for area schools.

Now, in 1873, the railroad was preparing to sell off a number of its odd-numbered sections, all the way from Omaha to Utah, and Henry Buckland, during his visits in New York and Chicago, had laid the groundwork for a massive purchase of these sections. He had till the end of August to decide whether his Bristol confreres wished to acquire sixty running miles of land on the south side of the railroad track, a stretch reaching from Line Camp Two to Cheyenne. Since the land was ten miles deep, six hundred square miles of range were involved. By purchasing only the odd-numbered sections, 192,000 acres in all, the Venneford people would acquire physical control of the even-numbered too, or nearly four hundred thousand secure acres. If the Bristol merchants could come up with the cash, the permanence of the cattle operation would be ensured for decades to come.

So Buckland held a series of tough, inquisitive reviews with Seccombe and Skimmerhorn. 'We have an empire within our grasp,' he said. 'Let's see if we can afford it.'

The three men went over the maps and figures until they had the data memorized, and consistently Skimmerhorn came back to one basic fact: 'If we have our water safe on the Platte, and we do, and can get hold of this land up north, we control everything in between. We have to have it, no matter the cost.'

Buckland was distressed by the fact that proffered land did not reach all the way east to Line Camp One. 'We'd be unprotected on that end,' he complained, and Skimmerhorn introduced him to the facts.

'We're unprotected there right now. We're unprotected over by the mountains. Within a short time, Mr. Buckland, homesteaders will begin claiming those lands. We have only a few years more of open range.'

'It's our land!' Buckland protested.

'Only because we say so.'

'We run our cattle on it. We look after it.'

'But the time is coming, Mr. Buckland, when there won't be open range. When I went back to Indiana for that last load of bulls, a man named Jacob Haish showed me something he'd invented. A fence.'

'Cattle will go right through a fence,' Buckland said.

'Not this fence,' Skimmerhorn said, and onto the table he tossed a piece of crude barbed wire, not the sophisticated product that would soon burst onto the market, but a primitive affair, with deadly spikes.

'Farmers like Potato Brumbaugh will soon fence their lands with wire like this,' Skimmerhorn predicted. 'And homesteaders on the Nebraska end will fence theirs . . .'

'And finally, we'll have to fence ours,' Buckland interrupted.

'If we own any,' Seccombe said.

'We must own it,' Buckland snapped. 'As much as we can.'

And then his two managers became aware of a fact that would dominate the rest of their business lives. Venneford Ranch was not run by Oliver Seccombe or by John Skimmerhorn. Lord Venneford had little say in it, nor did prosperous men like Henry Buckland. It was run by a faceless clerk called Finlay Perkin, and until he gave permission for the American ranch to buy the railroad lands, they could not be bought.

'What's he like?' Skimmerhorn asked, as Buckland prepared the message for Perkin.

'He's a Scotsman.'

'That's all we need,' Seccombe said. 'A Scotsman running an English ranch.'

'They have a saying in Scotland,' Buckland explained. 'If you have three sons, and one is especially brilliant and of good character, keep him in Edinburgh, for there the competition is fierce and he'll need all the fiber he has. If your second son is brilliant, but lacking in character, send him to America, where anything goes. And if your third son has tremendous character but no brains, send him to England, where the lack will never be noticed. Finlay Perkin is a third son. He came to Bristol.'

The new transatlantic cable to England had become a fast link to home, and the three plotters took a good deal of time drafting their message so that it would seem enticing to a clerk in Bristol:

PERKIN VENNEFORDS BRISTOL

OPPORTUNITY PURCHASE UNIONPACIFIC TWO HUNDRED THOUSAND ACRES FREEHOLD GIVING EXCLUSIVE CONTROL EQUAL AMOUNT GOVERNMENT LAND ONE DOLLAR TWENTYFIVE AN ACRE STOP SECCOMBE SKIMMERHORN CONCUR STOP AUTHORIZE

BUCKLAND

Within a day Finlay Perkin answered. He said he had reason to believe that the railroad was not ready to sell now, but that an option could be had for ultimate sale at no more than sixty cents an acre.

'We can't offer them less than half!' Seccombe protested, but when he and Buckland went to Omaha with an ironclad proposal—option money delivered in New York within two days, total sum in escrow in an Omaha bank—the railroad signed at fifty-five cents an acre and seemed glad to be rid of the land.

On the way back to the ranch Seccombe asked, 'How could Perkin, in Bristol, have known what American railroad men in Omaha were thinking?' and Buckland replied, 'Perkin knows everything.'

Charlotte Buckland had accompanied her father to the negotiations in Omaha, and now as the train rolled westward, with fascinating people crowding the parlor cars, she felt more than ever that she belonged to this vibrant land where a man could buy two hundred thousand acres of land in an afternoon, and she began studying Oliver Seccombe with increased interest.

He was a handsome man, about the same age as her father but infinitely more vital. He obviously needed a wife. He was older than she and would not live forever, but there were other parts of the world she had not yet explored, and she was prepared to make some of those future journeys as a widow, if necessary.

Young Pasquinel Mercy had wooed her with some ardor, and she liked him, but he seemed much the same as the bright young men who filled the British army; his tales of Wyoming were their stories of India, and both were boring. What excited her was not barracks life but the full swing of a new world: Cheyenne, Denver, Salt Lake. The names entranced her, and by the time her train reached the borders of Wyoming she had convinced herself that ranch life in the west was what she wanted. Looking at her father, paunchy and dozing in the sun, satisfied her that the one thing she did not want was to return to Bristol.

She therefore focused her attention on Oliver Seccombe, and before he was aware of what was happening, he was in love with her.

They got off the train in Cheyenne, now a cleaned-up, booming young city with the whores out and the churches in. There, in the railroad hotel, they waited for the horses that would take them down to their inspection of Line Camp Four, and in the interval they explored Cheyenne, meeting numerous attractive Englishmen who had come to try their luck at ranching. One morning, with the air crisp and the sun radiant, she clasped Seccombe's hand and cried ecstatically, 'Oh, Oliver, I do wish I could stay here forever,' and she waited for him to say, 'You can, you know.' But he remained silent. There followed delightful days visiting with English ranchers and listening to their euphoric accounts of how they would make their millions. 'It's fabulous,' a young fellow named Tredinnick cried. 'Really, Charlotte, all you do is lead the cattle onto the land, and the bulls take care of the cows and the cows take care of the calves, and each year you ship the surplus off in a great goods train to Chicago and pocket the gold. It comes rolling in.'

'Have you sent any shipments east?' Buckland asked.

'Not yet, but Harry over there has.'

They talked with Harry, a young man from Leeds, and he had shipped cattle east. 'At a simply staggering profit. This year, of course, what with the panic, prices won't be so fantastic. But you can't help making money, bundles of it.'

These enterprising Englishmen had not forced their way into Wyoming and Colorado; they were here because Americans simply did not have surplus money to develop their own country. Foreign investment was essential if the west was to develop. So the British, with an excess of funds from trade with their great empire, were invited to do what Americans were incapable of doing, and Charlotte was constantly surprised at the imaginative way they applied their capital. She felt especially proud of Oliver Seccombe.

But she supposed that he feared marrying a girl so much younger, and she began making clever and even bold observations to the effect that difference in age was not disqualifying. Once, as they inspected Freddy Tredinnick's herd, she said quietly, 'I notice the good ranchers build their stock from young cows and proven bulls.' As soon as she said this she blushed.

'I'm not a proven bull,' Seccombe parried. 'I'm just an old one.'

She teased with him like this for several days, always thinking that he was holding back because of her age and never once detecting the real reason for his restraint. Erroneously she deduced that he was fearful of his sexual competency with a partner so young, and she concluded that this was a problem which only she could resolve for him, so on their last night in the railroad hotel, after the Negro servants had closed the doors and overfed Henry Buckland had plodded off to bed, she said goodnight to Seccombe, and they went to their separate rooms. She prepared for bed, waited till the halls were quiet, then slipped along to Seccombe's door, opening it gently. She stood so that she was silhouetted against the light burning in the hall. Hearing Seccombe gasp, she went to his bed and whispered, 'It's not complicated, Oliver, not when you're in love.'

Next day, on the ride down to Line Camp Four, Seccombe could not refrain from congratulating himself on his good luck in snaring a girl like Charlotte Buckland—wit, wealth, family association with the Vennefords, and above all, an affection for the west. When she saw the camp, with its piñon trees and eroded pillars, she cried, 'This is the Colorado I dreamed about,' and he said wryly, 'We're still in Wyoming.'

This unkind remark sprang from the deep apprehension he felt toward any permanent involvement with this attractive girl. She was wrong in assuming that he held back because of anxiety over their difference in ages. He knew that she thought he was forty-eight, three years younger than her father, when he was really fifty-five. But he also knew that his vitality was not impaired. When she contrived opportunities to be alone with him among the piñon trees or in the secrecy of the barn, and she managed several, their enjoyment of each other was complete.

Nor was his affection for her passive. He loved the sound of her voice, her British manner of singing words and giving a lilt to her sentences, so refreshing after the years of flat American accents. When she said, as they were halting for a picnic, 'The curve of that hill reminds me of the strangest thing, the lovely terraces of Bristol,' he would see again the noble sweep of Georgian stone houses he had known as a boy.

She reminded him of his Englishness, and whereas he had been content in America, growing to respect its extraordinary diversity from Santa Fe to Oregon, he did remain English at heart, and it was good, in these later years of his life, to have that heritage refreshed.

'You're slow in proposing, Oliver,' she said one afternoon as they returned from the barn. 'I should like to live here, to know that each summer we could come out to this camp.'

'I'm too old,' he said, although he had just finished proving that he was not.

He was restrained not by age but by a sensible conviction that if he got too entangled with the Bucklands, he would face disaster. He was far more worried about Henry Buckland than he was about Charlotte, because the canny merchant had begun to ask those penetrating questions which the curators of the Venneford Ranch could not answer.

For some years Seccombe, in an effort to keep his Bristol investors happy, had been declaring cash dividends when none had been earned. In 1872, for example, he had paid a tidy eight percent by the simple device of buying 6626 mature longhorns from L. D. Kane in Wyoming and turning around and selling 2493 of them to packing houses in Chicago for beef. He entered the sale on his books as a profit, as if it had been 2493 calves raised on the ranch that he had sold. There had also been unusual expenses connected to the acquisition of land, items he did not want to appear on the books, like the train fare for the spurious homesteaders from Elmwood, Illinois. Oliver Seccombe had not misappropriated any Venneford money for his own use, but he had diverted much of it into channels that he could not now explain satisfactorily.

Buckland, becoming increasingly suspicious of Seccombe, started to make cautious inquiries among the ranch hands. One day at Line Camp Four he showed Skimmerhorn a report which had been assembled by Finlay Perkin. The Scotsman had lifted from the Venneford records an account of every animal the investors had paid for. It was an impressive list:

To Henry Buckland:

When you reach the ranch you should find these cattle on the premises:

1868	delivery by R. J. Poteet, Texas	2934
	purchase from L. D. Kane, Wyoming	4817
1869	delivery by J. J. Stoat, Texas	2404
	purchase from John Skene, Colorado	4419
1870	delivery by R. J. Poteet, Texas, two lots	4559
	purchase from L. Y. Frame, Wyoming	6697
1871	delivery by R. J. Poteet, Texas, two lots	4816
	purchase from K. N. Kennedy, Illinois	86
1872	delivery by R. J. Poteet, Texas, two lots	4831
	purchase from L. D. Kane, Wyoming	6626
	purchase from K. N. Kennedy, Illinois	93
	Total stock acquired	42,282

It would be desirable for you to check on the presence or absence of every animal listed, especially the expensive Shorthorns acquired from Illinois.

Finlay Perkin

When Skimmerhorn saw Perkin's suggestion, he could not suppress a smile. 'Sir,' he said disarmingly to Buckland, 'God himself doesn't know where all those cattle are.'

And for the first time a Bristol member of Venneford Ranch Limited realized that running a herd of Texas longhorns on a ranch containing more than five million acres was not the same as importing bolts of silk from India, or investing in consols, where a paper certificate proved that you had actual possession of the consols. Running cattle on a great western ranch was a little more imprecise.

With this discovery, Buckland's questioning became more detailed, and now John Skimmerhorn faced his second moral problem as manager of the ranch. The first one had come when he had helped Potato Brumbaugh fight off the gunmen. This one centered, as it would on every western ranch owned by absentee Englishmen, on the phrase *book count*.

Mr. Buckland pointed to the two purchases made from L. D. Kane, of Wyoming. 'They total eleven thousand head of cattle. A good many dollars are involved. Now, I feel sure you counted them as you got them.'

Skimmerhorn smiled nervously. 'You see, sir, that's what we call book count.'

'If you count, you count.'

'But when you buy in that number . . . After all, Kane didn't have his cattle penned up.'

'Where were they?'

'Book count means that there ought to be that number of cattle and that they ought to be somewhere.'

'Good God!'

'You're dealing with honorable men. If Kane says he has . . .'

'I wouldn't accept that kind of statement from the most prestigious merchant in India. If he says he's sending me three hundred bolts . . .'

'Cattle are not bolts of silk,' Seccombe interrupted.

'I'm beginning to think they're invisible.'

What Skimmerhorn did not tell Buckland, hence the moral question, was that he and Jim Lloyd had always had grave suspicions about the various book counts passed along to the Venneford Ranch. Finlay Perkin's figures showed that the ranch had paid for more than forty-two thousand head of cattle; Skimmerhorn doubted that more than twenty-five thousand were on hand now. And there was also the matter of how Seccombe paid dividends.

Skimmerhorn did not consider Seccombe dishonest, although the Englishman did do irregular things. He was a man of vast ideas and enthusiasms who behaved as if he had forty-two thousand head of cattle, when in reality he had only twenty-five. And every year, in his tight little Bristol office, Finlay Perkin would add up the absent stock, accept

Seccombe's estimate of how many calves should have been produced, and the truth grew even further from reality.

Some day this miserable bubble would burst. Skimmerhorn judged it might happen when the outlying portions of the ranch were lost, or when fences framed in the actual land owned. Then the cattle could be counted, and the deficit would be astonishing. In the meantime, Skimmerhorn would keep meticulous records of each transaction in which he was personally involved, and if Finlay Perkin ever wanted to see his books, their facts would stand forth with crystal clarity. Under no circumstances could Skimmerhorn betray Oliver Seccombe; he would not alert Henry Buckland to the inherent falsity of the Venneford accounts. But he would not allow Seccombe's manipulations to contaminate him. Through the bitter experience of being the son of Colonel Frank Skimmerhorn, John had learned how fatal a lack of discipline could be. He had made himself into a man of terrible, rock-hewn integrity, unafraid of Comanche or Kansas outlaws, not hesitant to help gun down the rustlers trying to steal Potato Brumbaugh's farm, and he would remain that way.

When Skimmerhorn left the camp, Henry Buckland remained as perplexed as ever. What it means, he reflected, is that in the cattle business the investor has to trust the manager. And he supposed he would have to trust Seccombe, in spite of doubts about book count. The fellow was congenial, and if he was what Charlotte wanted, she could do worse.

And so the last days at the camp became a period of drift during which three people moved toward decisions about which each had apprehensions. Buckland's concerning the stability of the ranch were never dispersed.

Charlotte, seduced by the loveliness of Line Camp Four, was satisfied that come autumn Seccombe would propose to her, and she began inspecting the northern range as if she were already its proprietor. It was certainly not the life she had planned for herself, but it was acceptable.

Oliver Seccombe still felt that close association with the Bucklands could be dangerous for him. He'd had a very bad moment when Henry started boring in on details. Who could calculate to a bookkeeper's satisfaction the number of cattle on a range so large? True, he had sold off breeding stock to get the funds to pay dividends, but many managers in Wyoming and Colorado were doing that, and if in the years ahead the calf crop was even average, the losses would easily be made up. But to give specific figures? Who could be sure that some bull found every cow in heat, or impregnated her successfully if he did. Who could possibly know how many calves were born dead on a ranch with more than five million acres? Or how many were killed by wolves? Or stolen by rustlers!

Somewhere beyond the horizon Venneford had forty-two thousand cattle. Hell, that number could now be sixty thousand, or even seventy, if the calf crop was good. As low as twenty-five thousand, as Skimmerhorn had suggested? Impossible. The cattle were out there, and when they were needed they would be found.

As he rode south with the Bucklands to ranch headquarters, they in a buckboard, he on horseback beside them, he decided to take the risk, to marry this challenging English girl and to get her father back to England as quickly as possible. Give me six good years, he said to himself, and I'll get this thing straightened out.

When the Bucklands were installed at headquarters, he rode in to Zendt's Farm to consult with practical Levi and imaginative Lucinda, especially the latter. Perched on a stool in their kitchen, with a cup of hot coffee clutched in his hands, he confided, 'It looks as if I might marry.'

'Good!' Levi cried. 'I've often wondered . . .'

Lucinda did not speak. Instead, she rose, walked to the stool and kissed the Englishman as if he were a member of her family. Pulling one of his hands from the cup, she grasped it, then said, 'It's time.'

'One of the English girls at Cheyenne?' Levi asked with a boy's excitement.

'Buckland's daughter.'

'She's not much older than Clemma,' Levi blurted out, and Lucinda glared at him.

'She's twenty-one,' Seccombe said. 'And I'm . . .'

'Older than I am,' Levi said bluntly. 'You must be insane.'

'Wait a minute,' Lucinda said. 'No man is ever too old to need a wife. God created us . . .'

At this moment Clemma Zendt came in, a marvelously beautiful girl of eighteen, and she passed through the kitchen like a summer breeze, recalling flowers. She said nothing, nodded toward Seccombe, then hurried by on some important mission of her own. She seemed very young, and Seccombe was especially aware of this.

'Don't be an old fool,' Levi counseled. 'If you need a wife, get one your own age among the English families in Cheyenne.'

'Does she love you?' Lucinda asked.

'I think so.'

'Do you do well in bed?'

'Yes.'

'Then marry her.'

That was her position, and she held to it. She invited the Bucklands to dinner, and when they were seated and the roast pig was on the table—purchased from Potato Brumbaugh—she said as she poured the lapsang, 'I hear you and Oliver are getting married.'

'Yes,' Charlotte said, although the matter was by no means settled.

'Good. Levi, fetch a bottle of wine,' and a startled Henry Buckland drank to the good health of his future son-in-law, a man four years older than he.

The wedding was held in Cheyenne at the home of Claude Barker, an Englishman who was putting together a mighty ranch along Horse Creek. It was a gala occasion, with champagne imported from France and singing and croquet on the lawn under torchlights.

The English community wished the newlyweds well, pleased that others from back home were settling in the territories. The affair was marred only by one slight incident. Henry Buckland, in talking with Claude Barker about the latter's new ranch, heard Barker say, 'I bought a good share of my stock from L. D. Kane.'

'Book count?' Buckland asked.

'Of course. The man's a bounder. Probably didn't have half the cattle he said, but what could I do? I needed his water rights.'

'Who is Kane?'

'Chap out from London. More money than brains.'

Buckland thought, He has brains enough to keep on selling cattle he doesn't have. And when he returned to Bristol he discussed this matter with Finlay Perkin, who for the first time began to view the fine figures in his books with some skepticism.

In 1875, when the buffalo were finally exterminated and the hunters went out no more, Amos Calendar appeared at Zendt's Farm driving a large four-wheeled army wagon, his unneeded Sharps across his knees.

He was collecting buffalo bones, to be used back east for the making of fertilizer. He scoured the prairies, returning to haunts where he had slain the animals and gathering their whitening bones for delivery to the nearest railway. Selecting a spot north of Line Camp Four, he received permission from the railway to accumulate bones there until he had a carload. Then he fanned out across the prairie searching for skeletons, and travelers would report in various towns: 'I was goin' down this hill when what do you think I seen? This big wagon drawn by two mules with a skinny man holdin' the reins, a big gun acrost his knees. And the wagon was filled with bones.'

Alone, always alone, Calendar became the hunter again, and gradually he built up at his depot a gigantic mound of bones. At intervals he placed some specially large skull on a stake with this message scrawled across its white forehead: 'These bones is mine. Calendar.'

Having shot the last of the buffalo, he now seemed determined to remove from earth all visible signs that the great animal had ever existed, as if God had commanded, 'You made the mess. Clean it up.' In due course he ranged westward toward Line Camp Five, where at Chalk Cliff his keen eye detected signs that here buffalo had once jumped to their death. For the buffalo hunter, a stand was what he dreamed of; for the bone picker it was the site of an ancient jump, because if he found such a place, he could dig it for days, exhuming the skeletons of hundreds of long-dead animals.

As Calendar was probing at the base of the cliff, Jim Lloyd came by on one of his inspections. He had not known that Calendar was in the area, but seeing him brought happy recollections of their drive north in '68.

'Huntin',' Calendar said when Jim asked what he had done after that. 'That run out, now I'm bone collectin'.'

'Pay well?'

'Maybe nine dollars a ton.'

'These bones are pretty light,' Jim said, hefting a desiccated skull.

'They add.'

'You taking these?'

'I thought to.'

'Go ahead.'

But that night when Jim stopped by to see Clemma Zendt, he reported Calendar's activities to her father, and next day a curious Levi rode out to Chalk Cliff—and this led to a discovery which eventually rocked intellectual circles throughout the world. For as Levi stood by, watching Calendar as he unearthed a hoard of bones which would require weeks to exhaust, he happened to look at a series of purplish rocks exposed at the base of the cliff, well below the level where the buffalo bones were, and protruding from this rock he saw what he first supposed to be part of a buffalo.

'That was some buffalo!' he said, amazed at the size of the projecting bone.

'That ain't no buffalo,' Calendar said. 'Never saw no buffalo bone inside a rock.' With the destructive urge that seemed an inherent part of his character, he lifted a large rock and was about to smash the strange bone, but Levi restrained him.

'This could be something important,' he said.

'What?'

'I don't know. But Lucinda was readin' in a magazine . . .' He stopped. 'You leave that bone there,' he said. 'I'm goin' back to town.'

When he reached home he asked his wife for the magazine with the story of the professor from Harvard, and with some excitement he thumbed through it and found the article he was seeking. It told of the work being done by Professor Horace Wright at Harvard in Massachusetts. Working upon principles developed in England, he had been digging in New Jersey clay pits and had come up with the bones of animals dead for millions of years. Woodcuts showed what the monstrous creatures may have looked like, and as Levi studied them he recalled that gigantic skeleton of the elephant he and Elly had seen at the museum in St. Louis.

That same night, unable to drive the visions of these ancient animals from his head, Levi rode to the telegraph station in Greeley and dispatched a telegram which was to become famous:

PROFESSOR HORACE WRIGHT
HARVARD UNIVERSITY
CAMBRIDGE, MASSACHUSETTS

BELIEVE ON MY FARM COLORADO HAVE DISCOVERED BONE OF PREHISTORIC
ELEPHANT STOP HAVE NOT MONEY EXCAVATE BUT OFFER YOU PRIVILEGE

LEVI ZENDT

Professor Wright, always on the search for fossils, roared out to Cheyenne by the earliest train, and there is no other verb that could more accurately describe his arrival. He was known to his contemporaries, and especially to his adversaries, as Horrible Horace, a huge, arrogant man educated in Germany and married to the daughter of a New England textile millionaire. He never visited a site; he invaded it, with two assistants and if at all possible an equal number of newspapermen and photographers. He wore formal clothes, including striped pants, even when at work on a dig, and although he had been photographed numerous times at various dramatic excavations, he was never shown without a top hat.

He delighted in convening the press wherever he worked and announcing to them: 'Gentlemen, we have this day uncovered one of the most remarkable secrets in the history of mankind.' He was hated by those who worked for him and despised by his rivals at Yale. He was insufferable, pompous and brilliant, and he did more for the advancement of paleontology than any other man in the history of American science.

At Cheyenne he hired four wagons, two tents and a cook, and like an emperor, moved south to Chalk Cliff. Levi Zendt and Jim Lloyd were waiting for him, and when they saw a cloud of dust to the east Jim said, 'Maybe the army is escorting him,' but it was only Horrible Horace traveling in customary style.

He ordered his driver to draw the wagon close to the cliff, and majestically dismounted, a man over six feet tall plus his top hat. Striding with sure instinct to the spot where Levi had found the bone, he ignored it. Dropping to his knees, he spent fifteen or twenty minutes inspecting the basic rock from which the bone projected, and as he poked and probed, he grunted with deep satisfaction, like a hog finding acorns.

He summoned his assistants and pointed out to them the characteristics of this base rock, then asked in haughty tones, 'Well, gentlemen, what is it?'

'Morrison?' one of the young men asked hesitantly.

'Of course it's Morrison!' he exploded. 'You dunderheads, look at the purple color, the alternate clays, the texture. What else could it be but Morrison?'

Even now he did not bother to look at the bone itself. Instead, he

summoned the lone newspaperman he had bullied into coming down
from Cheyenne, and proclaimed, 'Sir, you may inform the waiting world
that here on the property of this good man,' and he placed his right arm
benignly about the shoulder of Levi Zendt, 'I have discovered the bones
of a great dinosaur . . .'

'Elephant?' Levi asked.

'Infinitely older.'

'How old?' the reporter asked.

'One million years . . . two million.'

'You haven't looked at the bone yet,' the reporter pointed out.

'My good man,' Professor Wright said condescendingly as he kicked
at the base rock. 'This is Morrison. Do you understand that? Morrison!'

'Who's Morrison?' the reporter asked.

'It's a formation!' Realizing that he was antagonizing the press, he
abandoned Levi and placed his encompassing arm about the reporter.
'It's a purplish formation of clay and rock. It exists in a small belt
throughout the west, and where you find Morrison, you find dinosaurs.
Now this one . . .'

At last he attended to the bone, and as he did so his jaw dropped.
'My hammer,' he said in a whisper, and when he had it, he tapped ever
so delicately at the rock which embedded the bone, then moved along
the face of the cliff, returning to the men with a look of positive awe
upon his face. All the pomposity was gone and he became a man staggered by good fortune.

'My God!' he said. 'It looks as if we have a complete dinosaur.'

The reporter asked, 'Would that be a good find . . . important?'

'It would be notable,' Wright said in a low voice.

'What can I call it? What name?'

'That we cannot tell,' Wright said.

He worked like a demon, calling for flour and old newspapers, from
which he made a heavy protective paste in which to envelop the bones.
In the days that followed, newsmen and photographers came from all
parts of America to watch, and every new visitor who saw the imposing
chalk cliff assumed that the bones lay imbedded in it, and they were
surprised to find Professor Wright laboring away in the purplish deposits
at the base of the cliff.

'This is the Morrison,' he explained over and over, and he laid out
stakes to indicate the incredible extent of the skeleton on which he was
working. 'Maybe seventy feet,' he said, and even the most skeptical
visitor had to be impressed.

Finally the day came when he felt prepared to issue a formal communiqué, so he assembled the press and visiting scientists and stood
before them in a black suit and top hat. 'Gentlemen,' he said gravely,
'I have the honor to announce that on this site I have uncovered the
complete articulated skeleton of a dinosaur which reached to the length
of seventy-seven feet and weighed in the vicinity of thirty tons. Not a

single bone is missing, and this must stand as one of the supreme finds of all times.'

He went on to disclose that the skeleton, when excavated, would go to a museum in Berlin. 'But,' someone asked, 'if it's as great a find as you say it is, and it was discovered in America, why do you allow it to go to Germany?'

'The world of science is international,' he proclaimed. 'Museums in Germany aided me when I was starting. Now I shall aid them.'

This launched somewhat of an argument, which ended when Levi Zendt pointed out that the skeleton actually belonged to him, since it was found on his property, and he agreed with Professor Wright. He, Zendt, had come from Germany—that is, his family had—and it was only proper that he send a gift back to the home country.

'Thank you, my good man,' Wright said. 'I knew I could count on you.'

So the notable skeleton was shipped off to Berlin, which led a Denver politician who had graduated from Yale to ask, 'What else would you expect from a Harvard man?'

The next summer, at Rattlesnake Buttes, Horrible Horace uncovered a striking set of titanothere bones, accompanied by complete skeletons of camels, mammoths and dire wolves. But what gained greatest attention, especially from ranchers in the west, was his discovery in subsequent years of handsome skeletons of four of the progenitors of the horse: eohippus, mesohippus, miohippus and the crucial, determinative merychippus.

When this learned tyrant ended his excavations, men knew that in ages past the land of Colorado had been shared by gigantic dinosaurs beyond their imagining, and bison with unbelievable horns, and titanotheres and animals not yet visualized, and men became aware of the fact that the earth which they had been assuming was theirs had always belonged to other creatures, too.

Perhaps the most lasting local effect of Professor Wright's frenetic invasion came in something he casually said to Jim Lloyd as he was packing up after his dig at Rattlesnake Buttes. He had found a little treasure, an articulated skeleton of eohippus, the tiny creature who had grown into the horse, and as he contemplated it he said, 'In their day they must have been as common as rabbits.'

Jim repeated this to men at the ranch, and sometimes when they saw a jackrabbit tearing across the brown grass, they thought of older days and other grasses, when tiny horses were as common as rabbits.

What Jim Lloyd hopefully referred to as his 'love affair with Clemma Zendt' was not going well. It had never gone well. From the start it had been a ridiculous thing, scarcely involved with love at all. To speak

accurately, it had been nothing but a fatuous obsession, but each year
it deepened.

It had begun that July day in 1868 when Mr. Seccombe had accepted
Jim as one of his new cowboys. As Jim rode out of Zendt's Farm that
morning to finish the drive, he carried with him a vision of this ravishing
Indian girl, and he knew that he needed her. The punishing ride north
from Texas, the gunfights that had changed him from a boy to a man and
the suspicion that he might never see his mother again made him hunger
for friendship, so as soon as he had delivered the longhorns to Venneford, he rode back to the village, presenting himself at the store.

'Name's Jim Lloyd,' he said with becoming embarrassment. 'I wondered . . .'

He could not finish the sentence. He couldn't come out and say, 'I'd
like permission to meet your daughter,' and he became additionally
flustered when her older brother banged his way through the store, asking brusquely, 'What do you want, sonny?'

Mrs. Zendt, an understanding woman with dark skin and laughing
eyes, had observed the encounter that morning and could guess what
Jim's mission was, so to rescue him from further embarrassment she
asked, 'Did you wish to open a charge account?'

'That's it!' Jim cried, and she explained how she would set aside a
page in her store ledger for him, and the solemn attention he paid to her
instructions made her realize how old this apparent child really was.
'Fourteen going on fifty,' Skimmerhorn had said.

Knowing that he wanted to see Clemma, she said casually, 'Would
you care to have a cup of coffee . . . in the kitchen . . . with my
daughter?'

'Yes!' he blurted, and for the first time he met with Clemma.

What a delectable child she was that year, thirteen and blossoming,
with red in her cheeks and a sly grin. When she had detected him smiling
at her as the longhorns forded the Platte, she knew that he would seek
her out; she also knew intuitively what tricks to use if she wanted him to
return. So, affecting to have no interest in him, she positioned herself
so that he could not keep his eyes away from her. And when he did
look, she twisted her head in such a flirtatious way that his mouth fell
open in amazement at her charm.

Mr. Skimmerhorn had told him, 'She's part Indian,' and now he saw
that this fact showed in her high cheekbones and squarish chin. Her
eyes were quite dark and her black hair hung in braids through which
were intertwined porcupine quills, in the old fashion. But there was
something else, indefinable, that said she was Indian: the total ease with
which she moved.

What he could not see was that she also had the Indian woman's sense
of humor, a mocking view of life which she had acquired from her

mother and which she now directed at her first suitor. She would make Jim's life miserable, but also refulgent.

During the next two years whenever he was in town he tried to talk with her seriously, but she rebuffed him, for she could see him only as an awkward cowboy with few graces, and she was already beginning to set her heart on something more polished and congenial. She studied the strangers who stopped by the store on their way from Omaha to Denver and derived from them her definition of what a gentleman ought to be. As a consequence, she thought of Jim as a child much younger than herself.

At sixteen Jim decided to do something that would convince her of his seriousness. He chose a Sunday, and in his best clothes rode into the village and tied his horse to the railing in front of the store. There he waited till the Zendts returned from church, and when he saw Levi he walked boldly up to him and asked, 'Could I speak to you, Mr. Zendt?' and when the storekeeper nodded, Jim followed him into the parlor. Clutching his hands behind him, he said, 'Mr. Zendt, I wish to court your daughter.'

Levi did not smile. After all, he had married Elly when she was but little older than Clemma, so the idea of formal courtship was not preposterous. He treated Jim with dignity, but pointed out, 'James, I see no evidence that Clemma is eager to be courted by you or anyone else. Have you settled the problem with her?'

'No, but I will.'

'In such matters, James, it's best to arrange things first with the girl.'

'I thought that out of respect for you and Mrs. Zendt . . .'

'We appreciate your good manners, and Clemma will, too.'

But when he sent Jim to her, she laughed at him. 'Who'd be thinking about such things?' she teased, refusing to take him seriously, so that he fled from the store in confusion.

During the next three years Jim returned often, waiting hungrily for a glimpse of Clemma, but she persisted in ignoring him. This in no way diminished his ardor; his obsession intensified, and when through sheer boredom she allowed him to walk with her one day through the cottonwoods and actually kiss her, he became dizzy. For months thereafter he could remember that kiss; it had burned its way into his mind. He became convinced that Clemma Zendt had been created for him, that only she could fill the other half of his life.

The other cowboys, a robust crowd, found his behavior mulish and told him, 'You better forget that Indian gal and do yourself some good in Cheyenne,' but the idea repelled him, and they began to think he might be effeminate. Then R. J. Poteet came back up the trail with another consignment of longhorns and with him came Bufe Coker, who had decided to try his luck in Colorado.

'Don't you underestimate Jim Lloyd,' he told the Venneford hands.

'He killed his man at age fourteen.' And the cowboys treated the moon-struck young man with more respect.

In 1873, when Jim was nineteen, he decided it was time to propose formally. He had a good job, some savings and quarters at the ranch in which to house a family. Again he chose a Sunday, and again he dressed in his best suit, but this time when the Zendts returned from church he ignored Levi and Clemma and went directly to Mrs. Zendt.

'I truly believe that Clemma's happiness depends upon marrying me,' he said gravely.

'That could well be, Jim.'

'Won't you reason with her, Mrs. Zendt?'

'Jim, if she doesn't . . .'

'Can't you people see I'm a responsible person?'

'Of course, Jim. You'd make a wonderful husband . . .'

'Then please speak to her.'

Mrs. Zendt was embarrassed, not by Jim's awkward proposal but by what she was forced to tell him. In decency, Clemma should have broken the news, but she had never taken Jim seriously and it had not occurred to her that she owed him this courtesy. So the task was left to her mother.

'Jim, marriage right now is impossible. Clemma's going to St. Louis.'

Jim sat silent. His eyes seemed to lose focus, as if someone had clubbed him over the head with the butt of a rifle. Then, as if from a distance, he heard the words again: 'She's going to St. Louis the way I did when I was her age. For an education. To make a lady of herself. And like me, she'll come back.'

And that's the way it was. Miss Clemma Zendt, age eighteen, held a parasol over her head as they rode in Jim's wagon to Cheyenne, where she took the Union Pacific to St. Louis. There she boarded with her cousin, Cyprian Pasquinel, the elderly white-haired congressman, who enrolled her in the convent school her mother had attended back in 1845. Her letters home were infrequent.

After she had been away two months, Jim arrived at the store with a solemn proposition: 'If Clemma's getting this good education in St. Louis, and if I'm going to marry her some day, don't you think I'd better educate myself right here?' Levi and Lucinda thought this a first-rate idea and proposed that he take lessons from Miss Keller, the middle-aged schoolteacher. So three nights a week, when he was not obliged to be out at Line Camp One or Two, Jim would ride over to the Stumper Farm, where Miss Keller boarded, and do his lessons.

He learned American history and mathematics and some poetry, and most especially, a sense of the continuity of man and his limitless poten-tial. Miss Keller, a New England woman in her thirties, did not suffer from limited horizons; to her the lessons of Rome and London were as pertinent as those of New York and Chicago, and she believed that by and large those men and women who were openly committed to some worthy goal achieved more than those who were reluctant to associate themselves with anything.

It was from her that Jim first became aware of the gross injustices under which the west suffered. 'It's like this, Jim. At the end of the Civil War my father bought a farm in Kansas for nine thousand dollars. He paid five in cash, got four in a mortgage. At that time there were x number of dollars in circulation.'

'What do you mean by x?'

'From algebra. You remember. An arbitrary unknown.'

'Sure.'

'Well, every year since then the population in America has increased, but the number of dollars has remained at x. Do you comprehend what this means?'

'That to pay back his mortgage, your father has less and less chance to get any of those dollars.'

'Exactly! The system makes the rich get richer and the poor get poorer.'

She spoke also of the railroads. 'They got this fantastic amount of land from the government, from the west really, from you and me, and when they had their monopoly, they charged us anything they wished. Did you know that it costs an Illinois farmer two dollars to ship his steer a thousand mlies? It costs a Colorado farmer four dollars. Same with wheat, same with lumber, same with trade goods coming this way. We are crucified by the railroads, who ought to be our servants.'

She spoke especially of silver, which Jim had never thought of. 'Do you know why this nation is collapsing in panic? Right now? Because the people holding gold dollars won't allow silver dollars to be cast. They don't want you and me to be able to buy a silver dollar from the government with one hundred pennies of work. They want to force us into buying gold dollars from them at one hundred and seventy pennies of our work. This nation is staggering to its knees because no money is circulating.'

Sometimes she became enraged when spelling out an injustice: 'Do you know why Englishmen own the ranch you work on? And those other big ranches in Wyoming? Because there's not enough cash circulating in the United States. Americans like you and my father can't get your hands on money to buy land and run cattle. My father would just love to own Venneford Ranch . . . if he could borrow the money from Chicago bankers the way Englishmen borrow from their London banks.'

So Jim studied the books she provided, books he could never have stumbled upon by himself: Darwin's *Origin of Species* and *Descent of Man*; Alfred Russel Wallace's *Natural Selection*; Matthew Arnold's *Culture and Anarchy* and Mark Twain's *Roughing It*.

With such guidance Jim made of himself an educated man with a grasp of what was happening not only in New York and Washington but also at Venneford and Line Camp Three.

The news he got from St. Louis was not good. Travelers returning to Denver sometimes stopped off in Zendt's Farm to report on how Clemma Zendt was capturing the heart of the gateway city: 'She's attending dances every night, it seemed to us. Very popular with the young officers.'

One night after class Jim stopped at the store and told the Zendts, 'I'm worried. She doesn't answer my letters . . .'

'Jim!' Lucinda said, pouring coffee and arranging a plate of doughnuts. 'I was the same way! Ask Levi.' She laughed and kissed her husband. 'I'm sure he must have thought I'd never come back to a little town like this . . . after having known St. Louis.'

A delightful smile came over her face as she recalled those days, and she reached for her husband's hand. 'So many young men,' she mused, 'but I came back to my dear little Dutchman.'

Clemma also came back, in the summer of 1874, a tall slim girl with her black hair coiled on top of her head, and except for high cheekbones, no evidence that she was part Indian. She was a lady now, nineteen years old and beautiful in a new way. She had a certain languor and seemed ill-at-ease in her father's store. Gratuitously she dropped hints of having been to Chicago and of a visit to New York to see the family of a young officer serving in the forts south of St. Louis.

She found Jim Lloyd ridiculously stiff and not much fun to be with, for he either spent their time together proposing or airing his newly acquired knowledge of things that did not interest her. She asked him once if he drank, and he did not realize that she was intimating that she wanted a whiskey. Instead, he said with awkward firmness, 'Bufe Coker drinks a good deal, but he's a southerner.'

When the time came for her to return to St. Louis for her final year, she made no pretense of concern for Jim's feelings and did not even volunteer a kiss, but seeing the despair in his eyes, she leaned from the train window, took his hand and said gaily, 'Don't look so glum, Jim. I'll be back.'

On this small shred of hope Jim lived for three months, but at Christmas he could no longer deceive himself. Sitting in the Zendt kitchen, he confided that Clemma had not once written to him, whereupon Mrs. Zendt broke into tears.

'She wrote to us!' she said bitterly, showing the letter to Jim. And there it was:

Mom,

Lt. Jack Ferguson and I were married on December 10. He lives in New York and is very nice. I am going to have a baby soon.

Clemma

There was another letter, from Cyprian Pasquinel, and it was brutally frank, the letter of a relative who could not comprehend what had happened under the roof of his hospitality:

Of all the young men who courted her in our home, she chose with unerring instinct the weakest officer the United States Army has ever stationed in this district. If he stays with her a month after the baby is born, I'll be the most amazed man in Missouri.

When this harsh estimate was shown Jim, he sat silently in the Zendt kitchen, drumming his fingers on the table. Twice he tried to speak, but there were tears in his eyes and he seemed afraid lest his voice break. Finally he pushed back his chair and said something the senior Zendts would never forget: 'She'll need me. I must go find her.' He withdrew what money he had in the bank and late that afternoon returned to the ranch, where he saddled his horse, riding all night to reach Cheyenne in time to catch the morning train for St. Louis, where he sought out Cyprian Pasquinel.

'Turn away from that girl, young man,' the congressman advised.

'You say that only because she's an Indian,' Jim countered, willing to grasp at any straw.

Pasquinel laughed at him. 'That's unworthy, and you know it. Her mother is a member of our family. So is Clemma. Simple fact is, she's inherited all the weaknesses of her uncles. And you know what happened to them.'

'That's cruel!' Jim protested, but the congressman stuck to his guns.

'Forget that wild Indian girl,' he counseled. It was to no avail. Jim spent more than a week searching St. Louis for her, wandering through all parts of the city, hoping to pick up a trace of her—along the waterfront, in the hotels, through the mean streets. But he did not find her.

The winter of 1875 passed, and no one in Zendt's Farm could even guess where Clemma might be, or whether her baby was safely born, or whether it was a boy or girl. The Zendts wrote letters to friends in Chicago and New York, and Cyprian Pasquinel made inquiries at the War Department in Washington. All that he discovered was that Lieutenant Ferguson had been dismissed from the service for embezzling government funds. He had taken his discharge in New Orleans and had not been heard from since.

And then in the spring of that year an army officer was dispatched to Denver to check on the western forts, and one afternoon he stopped by the store to tell Lucinda, 'I knew your daughter in St. Louis. She was lucky to get shed of that Ferguson.'

'What happened to him?' Lucinda asked quietly.

'Living with a French girl in Boston, I think.'

'And Clemma?'

'You mean . . . you haven't heard from her?'

'No.'

'I am sorry. You haven't heard then that the baby died?'

'No.' All her Indian stoicism revealed itself in this brief word. Lucinda had no sense of shame, no reticence. Her daughter had vanished and she would be grateful for any information.

'I have no idea where she is,' the officer said, and Lucinda nodded.

When Jim heard this news he was distraught and announced his intention of trying once more to find her, but Levi forestalled him: 'James, I shall never forget how you put everything aside to search for her, but that was enough. You've done all that could be expected and now you must put her out of your mind.'

'Can you put her out of yours?'

'No, but I'm her father.'

'I'm to be her husband,' Jim said. And instead of forgetting her, as he should have done, he became more obsessed with the belief that he was meant to find her, to care for her. Whenever he came to town he asked the Zendts if they had heard anything, and he convinced himself that one day she would write him, and would wait somewhere for him to rescue her.

Jim let it be known that he had no interest in meeting girls, and not much in other kinds of social life, either. He directed his energy toward the ranch, and became so proficient that he received attractive offers from several English corporations running large herds to the north, but he preferred to stick with Seccombe and Skimmerhorn, two men he trusted.

He intensified his study of nature, analyzing the habits of birds and small animals, but found his greatest delight in supervising the Crown Vee Herefords. He became known throughout the industry as 'Jim Lloyd, the Hereford man,' a name in which he took restrained pride.

In 1876 everything connected with Zendt's Farm reached a climax. To begin with, Congress at last agreed to accept Colorado into the Union as the thirty-eighth state, and it was decided that entry should be made on August 1, just after the hundredth anniversary of the nation.

Statehood should have come much earlier, in 1866, as a matter of fact, and it would have, except that southern sympathizers in the territory, combining with those who still revered Colonel Skimmerhorn for his gallant victory at Rattlesnake Buttes, proposed that the constitution of the new state contain a proviso ensuring that in Colorado, so long as the state endured, only white men should be allowed to vote. Since there were practically no Negroes or Chinese in the territory, and certainly no Indians, the only reason these patriots could cite for such exclusion was that it sounded fashionable.

'Sort of makes us modern,' they said, and their fellow citizens enthusiastically adopted the proposal. The national Senate and House accepted it, too, on grounds that the people of a state ought to be able to choose whom they wished to share their responsibilities with.

President Andrew Johnson, however, made short shrift of the bill when it reached his desk. He vetoed it with a sharp rebuke, basing his decision not on the moral problem of discrimination but on the practical fact of population decline plus the results of a recent plebescite which contradicted earlier mandates:

> Colorado, instead of increasing, has declined in population. At an election in 1861, 10,580 votes were cast. At the election in 1864, the number of votes cast was 6192; while at the election held in 1865, the aggregate of votes was 5905 . . . It is not satisfactorily established that a majority of citizens desire state government. In an election held for the purpose of ascertaining the views of the people, 6192 votes were cast, and of this number a majority of 3152 was given against statehood.

Perhaps a divine counselor sat at Johnson's elbow when he penned these words, for had he admitted Colorado at that time, her two senators would surely have voted against him in the forthcoming impeachment—they said so—and he would have become the only President to be removed from office. At any rate, in 1866 Colorado remained a territory.

Now, in pleasanter times, and with the offending proviso eliminated, Colorado was to become a state, and there were celebrations from border to border.

There were also elections! The new state would be entitled to two senators, who would be chosen by the legislature, since it was felt that the general public was not qualified to vote directly for such an august position, and one congressman; seeing that he was of a lower order, the public would be permitted to vote for him directly.

As the time for statehood approached, a sensible movement started in the little town of Zendt's Farm. It was the schoolteacher, Miss Keller, who launched it, and no sooner had she uttered her suggestion, than it caught the imagination of everyone: 'Zendt's Farm is no name for a town that's destined to be a city. Let's celebrate the double birthday and rename ourselves Centennial!'

The idea was so popular that it was two days before anyone thought to ask, 'What will Levi say? After all, he founded the place.'

He thought it a great idea. 'Never did like Zendt's Farm,' he said. 'As a matter of fact, I don't like the name Zendt. Everyone I knew with that name either was stingy or ornery, except my mother. And she was born a Spreichert.'

Lucinda said she thought the name Centennial was perfect, and that afternoon dated a letter to Cyprian: 'Centennial, Colorado, June 9, 1876,' the first appearance of the name in any document.

So the decision was made, and the town of Centennial was born. A flamboyant celebration was arranged at the river to usher in the second hundred years of American independence and the birth of the new town. Steers donated by the Venneford Ranch were roasted, and patriotic speeches were made, predicting a notable future for both the nation and the town, but festivities were dampened when word arrived on the train from Cheyenne that on an undistinguished battleground in Montana, Colonel George Armstrong Custer with all his men had been massacred by the Sioux and vengeful Cheyenne.

Pasquinel Mercy was among them, chosen specifically by Custer to be his aide after the buffalo hunt on the Union Pacific. When a young cowboy ran into the midst of the celebration, shouting the awful news, Mercy's pregnant young wife, Laura Skimmerhorn, fainted, and some celebrants began to stare accusingly at Lucinda Zendt.

The nation was now a hundred years old, the town thirty-two, dating from that August day in 1844 when Levi Zendt and the McKeags arrived to establish their trading post. In the case of both nation and town, all major strands of future development had been identified; history would consist of their slow maturing. For the nation: what to do about race? how to control expanding business? how to distribute the growing wealth? For Centennial, history would be what it always had been: how could man adjust to his harsh surroundings? how could he use his land creatively?

CAUTION TO *US* EDITORS: As a southerner I have always shared the westerner's suspicion of railroads. Had I been either a rancher or a farmer in the west, I would have been quite bitter about the insolent way in which the railroads treated me. Discriminatory rates, arbitrary rulings on cattle and feed grains, refusal to provide service and arrogant indifference to my problems—all of which we endured in the south—would have been infuriating, and I would have enrolled myself among the agitators. The abuses stemmed from the fact that the owners of the railroads never saw themselves as servants to an expanding nation; they were men trying to squeeze the last penny of profit from a good thing, and to accomplish this, they subverted legislatures, perverted economic law and persecuted anyone who tried to hold them to a more honest discharge of their duties. As a result, even today westerners buy airplane tickets with actual relish, and out here the current call for public support for the railroads falls on deaf ears. If Commodore Vanderbilt did indeed say, 'The public be damned,' what the descendants of that public now say to the railroads is unprintable.

Diplodocus. The dinosaur excavated at Chalk Cliff in 1875 became known as diplodocus, and some years later along the border of Colorado and Utah an expedition financed by Andrew Carnegie dug up two beautiful specimens. One now rests in a handsome setting in the Denver Museum of Natural History and is the gem of that collection. Carnegie was so delighted with his find that at his own expense he had molds made for each separate bone in the skeleton, hundreds of them, and circulated plaster casts to various museums throughout the world, so that people everywhere could enjoy 'his dinosaur.' A later cast from the molds, this time in cement, now stands at the entrance to the museum at Vernal, Utah, not far from where the original diplodocus roamed 136,000,000 years ago, and it is enormous.

Triceratops. The lands around Rattlesnake Buttes proved rewarding to many teams of excavators. Starting in 1873 and continuing through the rest of the nineteenth century, scientists dug a startling variety of bones. In the twentieth century, teams from Europe and eastern universities have continued the work. This year, in Pleistocene clay beds I myself found the jaw of an eohippus; it shone in my hand like a little jewel, and just north of Chalk Cliff, in a classic Morrison deposit, I had the thrill of finding an entire armored collar that triceratops carried about his neck, erecting it into a formidable defense whenever some predator attacked. It is very exciting, I can assure you, to hold in your hand the remnant of a giant lizard who stood 70,000,000 years ago where you now stand.

Warning. You understand, and your caption writer must too, that no human being has ever seen a dinosaur bone. What I uncovered that day from triceratops was not a bone, but rather the petrification of a bone that had once existed. All so-called dinosaur bones are in fact stones formed within the matrix of the original bone. What happened was this: When the original bone was buried, water containing silica seeped into it, and ever so slowly the silica was deposited within the bone. In time the bony structure dissolved and was completely replaced by stone, in such minute detail that from the appearance of the stone we can today deduce with total accuracy even the cell structure of the original bone, and can indeed diagnose what diseases the bone may have suffered. No one has ever seen a bone of diplodocus, but the stony recollection of that great beast is even more exciting and beautiful than I have been able to describe.

Records. The 89 buffalo that Amos Calendar killed in his stand did not by any means constitute a record. Authenticated reports of that period cite the following one-day kills: Charles Rath 107, Doc Zahl 120, Orlando A. Bond 293. Witnesses saw Tom Nixon kill 120 in forty minutes, but in doing so he ruined the barrel of his Sharps. Jim Cato, famous buffalo hunter working out of the Texas Panhandle, is credited with having shot 16,000 buffalo during the great extermination.

Guns. It would be impossible to overestimate the emotional significance of guns to the westerner. If you want your head blown off, elbow your way into a crowded bar and mention gun control. One popular legislator wins perennial reelection with a simple slogan which he plasters over the car bumpers in his district: 'The west wasn't won with a registered gun.' The weapons mentioned in this report are especially favored by collectors. Pasquinel's fine Hawkens sold for $17.68 in 1826; today it would bring around $1,200. Levi Zendt's beautiful Melchior Fordney cost him $12 in 1844 but would now be worth $600. Buford Coker's 1863 LeMat originally sold for $50; today it would fetch $1,000. And Amos Calendar's buffalo Sharps cost him $53 in 1873; today it would be worth $1,250.

Book count. It may seem improbable that operations as carefully financed and supervised as the great English and Scottish ranches could have allowed themselves to be bilked by fraudulent or misleading accounting, but the records are replete with instances. In 1882 the Holly and Sullivan Ranch was sold to Arkansas Valley Land and Cattle Company with 440,000 acres and a book count of 17,000 head of cattle. Fortunately, the buyer insisted on a downward escalating clause which depended on the actual count of the cattle, should one be made. The true count proved to be 8683. The Niobrara Land and Cattle Company carried 39,000 cattle on their books; in liquidation they could find only 9000. These errors came about principally because managers made rough estimates of their calf crops: 'We have 1000 cows and it stands to reason 85 percent will drop calves, so next year we'll have 1850 critters.' On the open range the true calf drop figured no more than 70 percent, so each year the gap between actual count and book count widened.

Intemperate press. As editors required by libel laws to watch your words, you may find the quotations from the *Clarion* somewhat inflammatory. Where Indians were concerned, the Colorado press felt few restraints, and one finds in the files numerous invocations to genocide. Editorial policy called for the extermination of the Indian, and that did not mean removal; it meant killing every Indian within the state borders.

Colorado. Warn your cartographer to be wary when mapping this region. The state was put together late by joining three vertical strips of unassociated territory—western, central, eastern—each with its separate dramatic history. 1492 Spain lays vague claim to entire area (Columbus); confirmed 1541 (Coronado). Western and central strips remain Spanish till 1821, then Mexican Empire; 1823 Republic of Mexico. *Western*: 1848 Mexico cedes to U.S. as consequence of war; 1850 Utah Territory. *Central*: Mexico till 1836, then Republic of Texas; 1845 Texas joins U.S. and retains northern lands; 1850 Texas sells lands to U.S., which immediately divides them between Territories of Utah (north) and New Mexico (south). *Eastern*: Spanish till 1682, then France (La Salle); 1763 back to Spain by treaty; 1800 back to France (Napoleon); 1803 sold to U.S. (Louisiana Purchase); 1805 Louisiana

Territory; 1812 Missouri Territory; 1819 vague claim by Indiana but legally Unorganized Territory. In 1854 central and eastern strips combined, but immediately divided horizontally among Territories of Nebraska (north, including Zendt's Farm), Kansas (central) and New Mexico (south); 1859 illegal and abortive Jefferson Territory proclaimed; 1861 Colorado Territory with boundaries of present state; 1876 statehood. Name *Colorado* derives from Spanish and can mean either *red, colored* or *a dirty joke.*

10
A SMELL
OF SHEEP

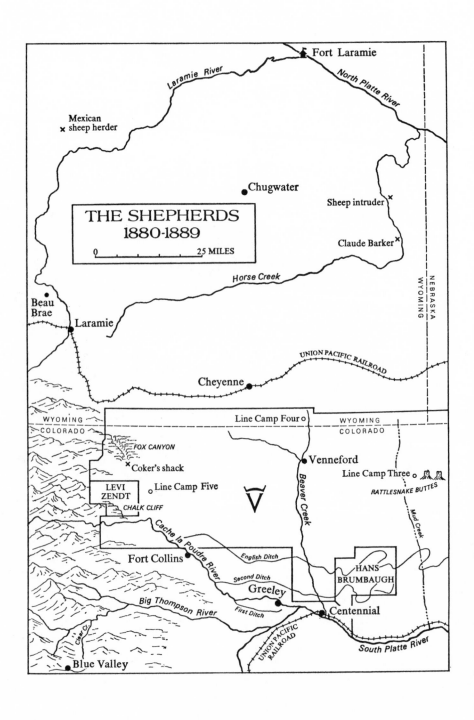

THE SHEPHERDS
1880-1889

0   25 MILES

Fort Laramie

Laramie River

North Platte River

Mexican
× sheep herder

Chugwater

Sheep intruder ×

Claude Barker ×

Horse Creek

Beau
Brae

Laramie

UNION PACIFIC RAILROAD

Cheyenne

NEBRASKA

WYOMING

Line Camp Four ○

WYOMING
COLORADO

WYOMING
COLORADO

FOX CANYON

× Coker's shack

Venneford

Line Camp Three ○

LEVI
ZENDT

○ Line Camp Five

RATTLESNAKE BUTTES

CHALK CLIFF

Beaver Creek

Mud Creek

Cache la Poudre River

Fort Collins

English Ditch

HANS
BRUMBAUGH

Second Ditch

Greeley

Big Thompson River

First Ditch

Centennial

Clear Cr.

UNION PACIFIC RAILROAD

South Platte River

Blue Valley

IF ANY SECTION OF THE UNITED STATES ever enjoyed a true golden age, it must have been the cattle regions of the west in the early 1880s. There had been previous fine periods. The New England shipping industry in the 1840s had been magnificent, with whalers sailing distant seas and merchant vessels opening the Orient. The prosperity of cotton plantations in the early 1850s, when British markets were begging to buy, and slaves were docile and great ships from all parts of the world put in to rivers like the James and the Rappahannock to load bales, certainly deluded their owners into believing that cotton was king. And the hectic 1870s, when eastern manufacturers controlled the nation, sending their finished products out on the new railroads at huge profits, buying their raw materials cheaply from the south and west, working their labor fourteen hours a day and controlling the money market to suit their purposes, were a heyday long remembered.

But none of these earlier periods of exuberance surpassed the euphoria that settled over the west in the dazzling eighties. In those years winters were mild and cattle proliferated; investments in land produced enormous dividends; and citizens of all types saw before them a constantly expanding horizon. Like the men in earlier decades who had basked in the sun of fishing, or cotton, or manufacturing, the ranchers of the west truly believed that their golden age must continue forever, for if gold dazzles, it also blinds.

No group prospered more than those canny British who had long before spotted this part of the world as one ripe for development and hungry for investment. In later years it would be popular to lampoon these foreigners as 'remittance men,' as if incompetent third and fourth sons were exiled to the west on small monthly payments to keep them out of trouble and, more important, out of sight. Many American dramatic companies, flitting from town to town on night trains, kept in their repertoire plays which made fun of these remittance men, relying on strange accents and unfamiliar customs to draw derisive laughter, but the truth was otherwise.

The sturdy merchants of Bristol sent out only first-class men to check on their considerable investments at the Venneford Ranch. The tight-fisted marmalade millionaires of Dundee did their best to run their great Chugwater Ranch effectively, and they did not dispatch nincompoops to do the job. In Texas the Matador Ranch, largest of all, was run primarily by shrewd investors from London, while over at Horse Creek the merchants of Liverpool were putting together a fine ranch under the leadership of Claude Barker. The most beautiful ranch of all, Beau Brae on the west bank of the Laramie River, was owned and managed by ultra-cautious Scottish businessmen from Edinburgh, and they intended to make money.

The Englishmen who supervised the railroads, protecting British investments there, were excellent people, and those who operated the mines were even better, for a more courageous type of man was required. The irrigation men were prudent, while those dealing primarily in land were bold. They brought their women with them, or sent for them after a short stay in America, and during these years along the Colorado-Wyoming border, English and Scottish patterns of life predominated. The land between the two Plattes could not properly be called an English colony, for the local political leaders were apt to be Dutchmen or tough-minded Kentuckians, but socially the area was an outreach of London-Edinburgh-Dundee-Bristol-Liverpool, and the hard-working Britishers were determined to enjoy themselves.

In September of 1880 a group of young American ranchers, educated at Harvard and Yale, accompanied Claude Barker of Wolf Pass on a ride down from Cheyenne to visit with Oliver Seccombe on a matter of some importance. Venneford was now almost a village, with sturdy buildings erected by the ranch carpenters and stonemasons. There were barns and corrals, of course, and a long, low range of sheds in which boss hands like Skimmerhorn and Lloyd worked, but the center of activity was the three-story red-stone Gothic mansion erected by the Seccombes. It was an imposing residence, resembling a castle on the upper reaches of the Rhine, and it became famous throughout the west.

Three rounded towers soared above the corners of the large house, with a four-sided battlement rising at the fourth corner. The roof contained eleven chimneys and was broken repeatedly by dormers. The ground floor was surrounded by a pillared veranda, while all doors leading into the house were made of heavy oak studded with brass fittings. It was possible to sleep eighteen guests in comfort, with four Negro servants to attend their needs.

'What we have in mind,' Claude Barker told the Seccombes, 'is a club . . . a gentlemen's club. We've selected a suitable corner in Cheyenne, and we'll keep the membership exclusive. All of us here, plus a few others with the right kind of background.'

'What are you calling it?' Charlotte Seccombe asked.

'The Cactus Club,' Barker said.

'Oh, that's delicious!' Charlotte cried, but her husband was more interested in the list of proposed members. They were all substantial cattlemen, except for the manager of the Union Pacific Railroad; of the initial twenty members, fourteen would be Americans, six British. Socially they were impeccable; in ranching, the most powerful.

'Will only twenty families be able to support such a club?' Seccombe asked warily. He and Charlotte were sorely overextended by the building of their mansion; true, she had put up most of the money, but he had had to sell off more Crown Vee stock to scrape up his share, and he did not relish the idea of added expense right now.

'We have a subsidiary list,' Bill Warsaw, one of the Americans said, and he showed Seccombe forty additional names, some less glittering socially than the original but all capable of putting up large sums of money.

'These are great years for cattle,' Barker added enthusiastically. 'Ranchers have money.'

'If you enlarge the list to include this second category,' Seccombe said, 'we'll come in."

Papers of incorporation were filed on September 22, 1880, and the famous Cactus Club of Cheyenne was founded. It retained that name only briefly, for at an early meeting Seccombe proposed, 'Cactus seems rather repelling. Let's call it simply the Cheyenne Club,' and the change was made.

Its rules were rigid. They were patterned after the fine clubs in London, to which most of the British members belonged, and their purpose was to create an ambience in which a conservative cattleman could feel at ease, protected from grubby merchants, importuning businessmen and small-time farmers. Fireplaces in the various rooms were decorated with blue-and-white tiles depicting scenes and quotations from Shakespeare, and the members who occupied these rooms were expected to conform to the highest standards of decorum. Offenses which called for immediate expulsion included:

DRUNKENNESS IN THE PRECINCTS OF THE CLUB TO A
DEGREE OFFENSIVE TO MEMBERS.

CHEATING AT CARDS.

THE COMMISSION OF AN ACT SO DISHONORABLE AS
TO UNFIT THE GUILTY PERSON FOR THE SOCIETY
OF GENTLEMEN.

In addition to these major abhorrences, the rules decreed, perhaps optimistically, that no wager of any description be made in the public rooms of the club, nor any loud or boisterous noise on the premises. In view of the ebullient nature of the younger members, and the burgeoning and heady state of the cattle industry, both a blind eye and a deaf ear became the distinguishing marks of the Rules Committee. But upon any palpable breach of social etiquette, particularly one that might reflect upon a member's behavior toward the fair sex, the board showed no hesitancy in cutting the hair that held the Damoclean sword.

The cost of belonging to the Cheyenne Club was high, but membership ensured amenities. There were billiard rooms, games for cards, three tennis courts, access to a polo ground, a library stocked with books from Paris and London and an incomparable dining room supervised by chefs with international experience. The menus were extraordinary, and included the choicest viands and game from the region, fresh oysters from the Atlantic and fish from the Pacific, the finest cheeses and delectable fruits, a side table piled high with a Viennese pastry cook's most mouth-watering confections, and a wine cellar that was to become the object of envy in many London clubs.

But what gave the Cheyenne Club its real significance was that from its rooms the government of the territory was dictated. Here all decisions were made relating to land ownership, the rights of irrigation, the laws for branding cattle, the regulations for banks. Wyoming Territory was a democracy; its constitution said so and it had a legislature to prove it, but the members of the legislature who mattered were all members of the Cheyenne Club, and what they decided at private caucus within the club mattered much more than what they said in open meetings of the legislature. Wyoming was a splendid, unpopulated state admirably suited for the running of cattle, and the membership of the Cheyenne Club proposed keeping it that way.

In protecting their interests they could be ruthless. Take the roundup law, for example. With nineteen-twentieths of the state an open range, cattle from one ranch could wander for a hundred miles without being detected, so when the cows had calves it was essential that some kind of general collection of animals be held, to enable each ranch to identify and brand its stock. Without this safeguard, a small-time rancher with a few cows and a flexible sense of property could round up cattle fifty or a hundred miles from any ranch headquarters and slap his iron on thirty or forty unbranded calves in no time, and after a few years of this he would wind up with a sizable herd, all reared by someone else.

'What kind of cattle do you figure is best for Wyoming?' a rancher asked one day at the Cheyenne Club.

'Without question, the Cravath breed.'

'Don't believe I know it.'

'It was developed by Dan Cravath on his little place on the Laramie.'

'What are its characteristics?'

'Extreme fertility of the cow. Dan had only twelve cows bearing his brand, but every year they each had five calves. And this can be proved, because each year he branded sixty, sure as hell.' The members had to laugh over their wine and cigars, for all had been victimized by rustlers like Cravath.

To halt the depredations of such men, the big ranchers bullied the Wyoming legislature into passing a law without parallel. Henceforth it would be illegal for anyone except owners of the big ranches to conduct a roundup. At their roundups any calves not specifically belonging to one of the big ranches would be thrown into a common lot and sold, the proceeds to go for the hiring of officers to enforce the law. Thus big cattlemen like Oliver Seccombe and Claude Barker were legally deputized to police the range, to their own enrichment.

Now the little man like Dan Cravath, who had been running a few head on public property, would be squeezed out of business. Of course, Cravath was entitled to look on at the big roundups, but if his calves were not properly branded, they would be taken and sold. He would thus be paying the salaries of the officers whose job it was to drive him out of business, and the majesty of the state could be called upon by the big ranchers to toss him in jail if he protested.

The members of the Cheyenne Club did not abuse their privilege. A few difficult mavericks like Dan Cravath and Simon Juggers north of Chugwater were shot, but everyone knew that they had been stealing calves and it was conceded that the range was better off without them.

The members had a strong sense of stewardship where the range was concerned. They had opened it to cattle, cleared it of predators and supervised it, and whereas a distant government in Washington claimed to own it, effective ownership resided in these tough-minded men. At one hearing before the United States Senate, R. J. Poteet, the prominent rancher from Jacksboro, testified as follows:

LAMBERT: Tell us in your own words what a rancher means by the doctrine of contiguity.

POTEET: We've always held in Texas, and throughout the west generally, that a rancher has the right to run his cattle on any part of the open range that lays contiguous to his holding.

LAMBERT: Do you define *contiguous* as a matter of a mile or a hundred miles?

POTEET: Well, east and west, I've seen my cattle wander a hundred and fifty miles. North and south, they've gone halfway to Kansas, that's better'n a hundred and sixty miles. And they did so because the open range was contiguous to mine.

LAMBERT: Aren't you claiming, Mr. Poteet, that the range contiguous to your barn reaches from Canada to Mexico? (Prolonged laughter.)

POTEET: You know, young man, I'd never thought of it that way, but you may be right. I remember in 18 and 69 when I trailed a bunch of cattle from Reynosa in Old Mexico, across the Rio Grande and up to Miles City, Montana. Using the western trail, we traveled getting on for two thousand miles, and in all that time we crossed only two roads, the Santa Fe Trail along the Arkansas and the Oregon Trail along the Platte. We saw no fences, no gates, no bridges. We swam our cattle across so many rivers that my left point, fellow named Lasater, said, 'Them critters has swum so much water, they's growin' webbed feet.' I guess our contiguous range did reach from Canada to Mexico, and it would be a good thing for this nation if it did so again.

Members of the Cheyenne Club quoted this testimony with approbation, for it represented their thinking.

The glory of the club was the social life that centered upon it. Charlotte Seccombe exclaimed one night, 'At dinner this evening we had four peers of the realm sharing oyster stew with us. You couldn't better that in London!'

And it wasn't only Englishmen who graced the dining hall. The lovely Jerome sisters, daughters of a New York banker, came out from the east. Clara, the older, would marry Moreton Frewen, the Englishman who maintained his castle in northern Wyoming. Jennie, the younger, would marry Randolph Churchill and become the mother of the great Winston.

Bankers from all parts of the United States flocked into Cheyenne to look into the cattle business, and as they dined at the club and heard what the enterprising Englishmen were accomplishing, they felt an irresistible urge to invest their own funds, so that Boston financiers began to appear on British boards, and millionaires from Baltimore and fiduciary agents from Philadelphia, and in due time each of the new investors had to be initiated, to his sorrow, into the meaning of that subtle phrase *book count*.

Whenever John Skimmerhorn watched Oliver and Charlotte Seccombe hitch up their four bay mares for the drive to Cheyenne, he felt a pang of fear. 'What'll they buy this time?' he would mumble to himself. He did not begrudge the couple their mansion, although as an austere man he felt it pretentious, nor did he mind the extra work when delightful people like the Jerome sisters and their suitors stayed at the ranch. Indeed he told his wife, 'It's sort of fun to have dukes and earls on the place. Makes our cowboys spruce up a bit.'

What did worry him was the fact that each year Seccombe sold off more of the ranch's basic stock. Each year the discrepancy between actual count and book count widened.

'Jim,' he asked Lloyd one autumn when the Seccombes were frolicking in Cheyenne, 'how many breed cows do you estimate we have?'

'No one can say. They're scattered . . .'

'How many? You're a damned shrewd man, Jim, and I know you have your guess.'

'I'd say . . .' Jim stopped. He was thirty years old and most satisfied with his job. It was precisely how he wanted to spend his life, and he could look forward to many more years of employment. As he had neither wife nor children, the Venneford Ranch occupied his whole attention, and he would do nothing to endanger his position.

'You're not puttin' this down in a book somewheres, are you?' he asked suspiciously.

'Nope.'

'You're not aimin' to use it against Seccombe? Him spendin' so much of the ranch's money?'

'I'm asking your opinion!' Skimmerhorn snapped. 'You run the cattle. I have the right to know.'

'Okay then,' Jim flashed. The two men were on tricky ground, and each knew it. As boss hand among the cowboys, Jim had to have a horseback opinion on everything, and he had one, but he did not want his information used to Seccombe's disadvantage.

'If I was in court, properly sworn, I'd say we have about twenty-nine thousand, countin' everything.'

'Book count says close to fifty-three thousand.'

'The book is wrong.' He was angry, both with the questioning and with the facts. For some time he had known that the books were badly inflated, and he also knew that sooner or later someone from Bristol would discover that fact, and there would be hell to pay.

'Jim, I'm on your side,' Skimmerhorn said placatingly.

'You don't sound it.'

'What I think we should do is this. Every six months you and I will submit to Seccombe, in writing, our best guess as to the actual condition of the herd. Everything. New bulls, cows, calves, steers.'

Jim nodded.

'We'll give them to Seccombe. What he does with them is his business. But I think we're obligated—'

'I've been doin' it,' Jim broke in, and he went to his desk and produced a ledger with honest estimates. When Skimmerhorn studied it he had nothing to say. He thought some of the figures too pessimistic and with pen and ink altered them upward, initialing his estimates.

When he was through he looked up at Jim and said, 'Sometimes I think you were lucky, Jim, not to get married. She's killing him, that one.'

Jim flushed and looked away. It was clear to him that Oliver Seccombe was in way over his head, with the headquarters mansion a monstrous weight around his neck, but never once did Jim think that Seccombe would have been better off unmarried. When he watched Charlotte greet the boss with a kiss and when he saw how proud Seccombe was to introduce his wife to their guests, he knew that whatever cost the Englishman paid was worth it. He saw Charlotte as a high-spirited woman, never afraid of skittish horses, and God knows she spent a lot of money. But she was laughter and a bright breeze and the dip of a bird's wing. And to Jim Lloyd, without a woman of his own, these things were more important than book count.

The reassuring success Potato Brumbaugh was having with his irrigated fields should have satisfied him, for his produce was bringing premium prices in Denver, but instead it exasperated him, for during every planting season and every harvest he compared the trivial portion of his irrigated land against the massive proportion of arid land, which produced nothing, and the imbalance infuriated him.

He made two experiments. First, he tried planting his arid land, but with a rainfall of less than fifteen inches a year, all he got was a luxuriant stand of foliage in May, when the last rains fell, and withered vegetables in September, when the land lay gasping in the sun. For three successive years he spent considerable money and effort, producing nothing except the hard-won conclusion that without irrigation his benchlands were useless, except to grow native grass for the grazing of cattle.

His second experiment proved what irrigation could accomplish. Purchasing six galvanized buckets from Levi, he plowed up a small corner of his dry benchland, planted it with varied crops, then directed his wife and children to haul water all summer to keep the plants alive. It was hard work, but in September the family had melons and corn and half a dozen other things that had been waiting only for water.

'The soil is even richer than down along the riverbed,' Brumbaugh said, and the idea that hundreds of acres of productive land were going idle grieved him, and he began to brood.

He stalked along the Platte, a stoop-shouldered man in his forties, powerful and with enormous energies. Catherine the Great had been wise to import such men to her wasteland along the Volga and the later Czars had been fools to let them go, for these were the kind of men who loved the soil, who lived close to earth, listening to its secrets and guessing at its next wants. It was inconceivable to Potato Brumbaugh that nature intended those superfertile lands to lie unused, and he tried to fathom ways to bring them under cultivation.

'There's lots of water,' he grumbled as he watched the Platte flow past. 'I could pump it up.' But he had neither the pump nor the power. 'We could carry it up,' but even that year's small experiment had exhausted the resources of five strong people.

He strode along the river for so long, and with such intensity, that he became the river. He moved with it, felt it in his bones. He sensed each nuance of the flow throughout the year and slowly he began to visualize this noble river as a unit, an exposed artery with channels flowing out and back in from all directions. It held the land together and made it viable.

One day he developed an image of himself standing on dry land and pulling the river and all its tributaries up by the roots, and what was left was an empty canal, and from that conceit he began to formulate his concept of the Platte.

'It's not a river!' he told his family with excitement dancing in his eyes. 'It's a canal, put there to bring water to land that needs it. We could go into the mountains and force the lakes to empty their water into little streams, and they'd bring the water to the Platte, and the river would carry it right to us. We could dig our own lakes, down here on the dry land, and imprison the flood water that comes during the spring and release it later as our replenishment.' He was only a peasant, but like all men with seminal ideas, he found the words he needed to express himself. He had heard a professor use the words *imprison* and *replenishment* and he understood immediately what the man had meant, for he, Brumbaugh, had discovered the concept before he heard the word, but when he did hear it, the word was automatically his, for he had already absorbed the idea which entitled him to the symbol.

'The Platte is merely a canal to serve us,' he repeated, and with this basic concept guiding him, he directed his attention to the best way to use the beneficence the river provided. For three weeks he struggled with the problem, and then by a stroke of good luck he met some farmers in nearby Greeley who were grappling with the same problem, and together they saw what needed to be done.

Well to the west of Centennial rose a river which fed into the Platte, and it bore one of the most musical names in the west, Cache la Poudre. It had been named by some French trapper who had hidden his powder there during an exploration of the higher mountains, and its pronunciation had been debased to Cash lah Pooder. Usually it was known simply as the Pooder, and during the first years of the white man's occupancy it had been ignored.

However, when farmers entered the area the Cache la Poudre assumed major significance, for it contributed to the flow of the Platte twenty-nine percent of the total. The Platte itself accounted for only twenty-two percent of its final flow, the rest coming from streams much smaller than the Poudre, and it did not take canny farmers like Potato Brumbaugh long to realize that in their Pooder they had a flowing gold mine.

Shortly after Brumbaugh tapped the Platte in 1859 for his small ditch, Greeley farmers took out from the south bank of the Poudre a small ditch, First Ditch, that irrigated the rich lands between the Poudre and the Platte, the ones lying close to the new town. This was a puny effort, not much larger than the private ditch dug by Brumbaugh, and it did nothing for the important accumulations of benchlands to the north.

It was Brumbaugh's idea to cut into the north bank of the Poudre, far to the west, and to build a major canal, Second Ditch, many miles long, that would follow the contours of the first bench, bringing millions of gallons of water to dry lands, including his own. Some farmers in Greeley, called upon to share in the cost, predicted disaster and refused, but others recognized the potential value of such a project and subscribed their fortunes to its building.

Through the early years it was known as 'Brumbaugh's Folly,' for it cost four times what the Russian had predicted, and some estimates for siphons and conduits had to be multiplied seven and eight times, so that the cost of throwing water upon an acre of land rose appallingly, and many advocated that the wasteful project be abandoned. Banks would lend no more money and only the stubborn courage of men like Brumbaugh, his friend Levi Zendt and a few of the religious men of Greeley kept the ditch going.

'I can't understand them,' Brumbaugh cried in frustration as one after another of his partners withdrew. 'What if it cost ten times as much as I said? Does that matter? Suppose we get water on our dry land and each acre produces thousands of dollars? Who cares about original cost?'

It was the end product that mattered, always the end product. If fearful men had set out to build the Union Pacific, they would have quit, and if cowards had been called upon to pioneer an Oregon Trail across two thousand miles of unmarked land, they would have retired. But there were always men like Potato Brumbaugh who saw not the disappointing canal but the irrigated field, and if it cost an extra two thousand dollars to build the canal, that cost was nothing—it was absolutely nothing—if from it came water that ultimately would irrigate a thousand acres for a hundred years.

It was also Brumbaugh who visualized the great fishhook at the end of the Second Ditch. The canal had gone eastward as far as practical, but it still carried a good head of water, in spite of the smaller ditches draining from it, and Brumbaugh suggested, 'Let's lead it back west,' and he encouraged the surveyors to find new levels which would permit the water to return toward its point of origin.

'He's takin' the water back to use it over again,' cynics joked, and when Brumbaugh heard the jest and contemplated it, he realized how sensible the critic's idea was, and out of his own pocket he employed a water engineer from Denver to study what actually happened to water diverted from a river, and the expert, after measuring the Platte and the Poudre at many sites, concluded that whereas Brumbaugh's Second Ditch did unquestionably take out a good deal of water from the Poudre, seepage allowed more than thirty-seven percent to drain back into the Platte downstream. The water was used, but not used up, and the engineer calculated that with more thrifty procedures, as much as fifty percent of any irrigation water would find its way back to the mother river, available for use again and again.

'It's what I said!' Brumbaugh cried with as much joy as if the returned water were coming back to his advantage. 'The whole river is one system, and we can use it over and over.' He went from one community to another, expounding his views, showing farmers how the Platte could be plumbed as an inexhaustible resource, but one shrewd man in Sterling pointed out, 'You say you send half the water back, and that's true, but you also use up half, and if we keep using half of half of half, we dry up the river.'

'Right!' Brumbaugh shouted. 'We use it up as it is now. But if we build tunnels up in the mountains and bring water that's now wasted on the other side where it isn't needed over to our side where it is . . .'

'Now he wants to dig under mountains,' one of the Sterling men said, and again Brumbaugh shouted, 'That's right. That's just what I want to do. When the Platte flows past my farm I want it to be as big as the Mississippi, and when it leaves Colorado to enter Nebraska, I want it to be bone-dry. This valley can be the new Eden.'

To accomplish what he had in mind, Brumbaugh had to devise a miracle which would have disheartened a lesser man. 'What do you want to do?' a lawyer asked him one day. 'Change the laws?'

'That's exactly what I want to do,' Potato cried. And with the assistance of an impecunious but brainy lawyer from the Greeley colony, he set out to do it.

The law governing rivers, Riparian Rights, had accumulated through several thousand years of experience in countries of ample rainfall like England, Germany and France. The law was clear, and fair, and simple: 'If a river has historically run first past the farm of A and later past the farm of B, A is allowed to do nothing which will diminish the flow of the river as it passes B.' This was a perfect law for the governance of the flour mill that A proposed building. He was free to lead the river down a millrace, and over his mill wheel and have the water do his work, just so long as he saw that the other end of the millrace returned to the river, so that the level when it passed B was in no way impeded. It was also an ideal law when B was a fisherman and used his portion of the river only for catching salmon; it was essential that the river keep to its proper level, and A was permitted nothing that might modify that level.

The average rainfall in the parts of England where Riparian Rights were codified was more than thirty-five inches a year, and a farmer's big problem was getting excess water off his land. He had no reason for stealing any of it from the river, and if all lands throughout the world enjoyed thirty-five inches of rainfall a year, Riparian Rights would serve handsomely.

But what to do in a country like the drylands of Colorado, where the average rainfall was under fifteen inches a year? Here a river was ex-

actly what Potato Brumbaugh said—an exposed artery determining life
and death. To take a few inches of the Platte and lead it onto arid land,
making that land blossom, was not stealing. It was something else not
yet defined by law.

'We must have a new law,' Brumbaugh grumbled month after month,
and in time he found in a small Greeley law office a man who saw even
more clearly than he that a new land required a new law. Joe Beck was
a Harvard graduate who had never been able to earn a nickel, because
he was always heading off into strange directions. Brumbaugh, when he
first saw Beck, knew that here was his man, and he offered him a solid
fee.

'Change the law,' he told Beck. And the seedy lawyer proceeded to
do so.

He devised a brilliant new concept of a river, taking most of his ideas
from Brumbaugh's apocalyptic visions: 'The public owns the rivers and
all the water in them. The use of that water resides in the man who first
took it onto his land and put it to practical purposes. If A lives at the
head of the river and has watched it flow past year after year without
putting it to any constructive use, and if B lives far down the river and
at an early date conceived a plan for using it constructively, then A
cannot at some late date step in and divert the river so that B no
longer has the water he used to have . . . First-in-time, first-in-right.'

It was called the Colorado Doctrine of Priority of Appropriation, and
it never caught on in states like Virginia and South Carolina, with their
myriad rivers and plentiful rainfall like Europe's, but the arid western
states adopted it, because they knew there could be no alternative. Rivers
existed to be used, every drop of them, and they were best used in
orderly procedures.

Encouraged by this victory, Brumbaugh reached out to all portions of
the Platte, visualizing new ways of using the water effectively. He followed the Poudre to its source, then climbed over the mountains and
down into the valleys that fed the Laramie River, which flowed north
into Wyoming.

'What a waste!' he muttered as he watched the clear, icy water leaving Colorado. He saw how easy it would be to dig a diversionary tunnel
—'Fifty thousand dollars,' he told Joe Beck, falling short in his estimate
by two hundred thousand—and through it divert millions of gallons of
water now being wasted on Wyoming drylands.

'That goddamned Russian is a menace!' the farmers of Wyoming and
Nebraska growled, and they hired their own lawyers to fight him. These
men told the courts, 'Leave these matters to Brumbaugh and he wouldn't
allow a drop of water to flow out of Colorado.'

The accusation was just. He wanted to divert every drop of water
falling west of the mountains into the Platte, then use every gallon for
irrigation in Colorado. In time even the judges of the United States Su-

preme Court would have to wrestle with his visions, and a lawyer from Wyoming would ask the Court, 'What is this man trying to do? Restructure the whole west?'

If the question had been put to Brumbaugh, he would have replied, 'Yes. The only task big enough for an honorable man is the restructuring of his world.' He would not have understood the word *restructure* when the lawyer first threw it at him, but he would have caught the meaning quickly, for long ago he had developed the concept.

One afternoon he took his son Kurt aside and said, 'Report to Joe Beck in Greeley tomorrow and start to read law.' His son, then eighteen, demurred on the grounds that he wanted to work the farm, but Potato saw the future clearly: 'The man who knows the farm controls the melons, but the man who knows the law controls the river.' And it was the river, always the river, that would in the long run determine life. So Kurt Brumbaugh mastered the nuances of law regarding rivers, especially the Platte, and in time he was arguing his father's cases before the Supreme Court.

Potato himself kept to his farm, and when he saw that the water provided by the Second Ditch was fully utilized, he combined with some far-seeing Greeley men to build a Third Ditch, but this time his vision exceeded his capacity, and he ran out of money. He and Joe Beck tried to tap every bank in Chicago and New York. 'All we need is four million dollars,' Brumbaugh said disparagingly, but it was not forthcoming, so he took passage on a Cunard liner and went to London with various introductions obtained through the good offices of Seccombe. After two days of hectic oratory, Potato got his money. When he first saw the sweet, clear water running onto his land from the English Ditch, he had another idea: 'In Russia on land like this we grew sugar beets. Why can't we grow sugar beets here?' And he put in motion a whole new set of headaches for the local farmers.

In 1881 a revolutionary change came over Centennial. For the past twenty years the citizens had been calling for a railroad to build its track into the town, but they had been ignored. The Union Pacific, in its thrust westward from Omaha to bind the nation together, had pulled a rather neat trick: along its entire route only two large centers of population existed, Denver and Salt Lake City, and it managed to miss both.

From the earliest days people knew that the Union Pacific ought to build a shortcut from Julesburg along the Platte to Denver, but this the railroad refused to do. 'If a man wants to travel from Omaha to Denver,' said the managers of the road, 'let him ride our line to Cheyenne and take the other road down to Denver. As for shipping cattle, to hell with cattle.'

But now the rival Burlington Railroad announced plans to build a new line directly to Denver, through the vacant land well south of the Platte, and suddenly the Union Pacific burst into all kinds of energy. Starting from the parent line at Julesburg, the rails were thrust westward at a galvanic rate: ten, eighteen, twenty-two miles a day. Skilled construction crews who had learned their jobs elsewhere, the Irish and the Chinese, moved in with practiced skill and fairly skimmed the tracks across the prairie. Like a great centipede the rails jumped westward.

When the railhead reached Centennial, citizens watched the laying of tracks with as much excitement as if it were a circus, and three local girls ran off with members of the construction gang. Hans Brumbaugh's younger daughter, a flaxen-haired woman of twenty-three, was more prudent, and when the surveyor attempted to seek her favors, she insisted upon marriage.

The tracks ran along the north bank of the Platte, and formed a fine, solid edge to the town. The railway station became the focus of civic life, with several trains a day in each direction and a telegraph office from which messages of grave import could circulate throughout the town. Social life centered on the Railway Arms, the large hotel which the railroad built adjacent to its station.

On land donated by Levi Zendt, architects who had built other such establishments along the Union Pacific swept into town and in a few breath-taking months erected a major hotel, with many rooms, three different dining areas and a long bar. It cost the railroad $18,000 to build, and in 1883 alone it made a profit of $31,000.

Centennial was now linked to all the major cities in America, and the Venneford Ranch could ship its cattle direct to whatever market it deemed best. Boxcars of goods could be imported, and few men or women in town would forget the excitement that arose when word flashed that a cattleman named Messmore Garrett was bringing in four boxcars of steers which he proposed running on the open range.

'There is no open range,' men said. 'Venneford has it all.'

'They don't own it. It's open if'n this guy Garrett can get to it.'

'How in hell's he gonna get to it, answer me that.'

'He wouldn't be comin' if'n he didn't have an idea on that score.'

The telegram said simply:

BAGBY CENTENNIAL

ARRIVING THURSDAY FOUR CATTLECARS OF STOCK

MESSMORE GARRETT
CARY MONTANA

So when the freight pulled in on Thursday afternoon, most of Centennial was at the station to see who would be handling the Garrett steers. The train whistled twice east of town, then chugged in and came to a halt. Mailbags were thrown down and messages exchanged, but the citizens focused their attention on four boxcars, from the first of which stepped a slim cattleman in his late thirties. He wore the customary large hat, but even so, women could see that his hair was slightly graying. His eyes were deep-set and commanding, and he walked with a firm step as he strode forward, extending his right hand and introducing himself. 'I'm Messmore Garrett. Who's here to help unload my stock?'

Watchers looked at the various experienced cowboys and were astonished when none of them stepped forward. Instead, Amos Calendar shuffled to the front, wiped his nose with the back of his sleeve and said, 'I'm Calendar.'

'Bagby hire you?'

'He did.'

'Glad to see you. Let's drop those chutes.'

Calendar went to one of the cars, which had now been detached from the rest of the train, and threw a chute into position. Someone inside the car slid the door open, and from a crowd of cowboys came the awed cry, 'Jesus Christ! Sheep!'

Down the ramp ran hundreds of woolly sheep, dirty from their long ride, inquisitive and hungry. One ram ran to where the cowboys stood, and they recoiled from it as if it were a rattler. 'Get away from me!' one of the cowboys yelled, almost as if he were a woman, but the ram pushed on, brushing against the cowboy's leg. As it pressed onward, the man gave it a mighty kick in the head, all the time cursing as only a cowboy could. 'The damned thing touched me,' he told his mates with obvious revulsion.

By nightfall word had sped across northern Colorado and well into Wyoming, carrying the dismal news that sheep had entered the cattle country. John Skimmerhorn, appalled at the event, cabled Bristol:

> PERKIN EIGHTEEN HUNDRED SHEEP INVADED
> OUR RANGE STOP ADVISE IMMEDIATELY
>
> SKIMMERHORN

The answer was brief: GET THEM OFF. In fact, it was the only sensible answer that could be given, for it was an established fact that cattle and sheep could not use the same pasture.

'The sheep is a filthy beast,' cowboys averred that night as they tried to get the smell of the new arrivals from their nostrils. 'A steer won't touch grass that sheep have walked over. The woollies leave a smell. Christ, I can smell it now.'

'What's worse,' another said. 'The sheep crops the grass so close, a cow can't get nothin' for two years after.'

'It ain't only that,' the first cowboy said. 'The sheep has a sharp hoof, and he cuts the grass below the stem, right down into the root.'

'Mostly, though, it's the smell,' a third man said. 'My uncle could walk into a restaurant and if they'd cooked mutton within three months, he could smell it. Cattle ain't dumb. They know that smell kills.'

So the war began. In self-protection against the woollies the cattlemen felt they had to drive the sheepmen off the range, and they were ruthless in their determination. At the Cheyenne Club the big ranchers compared notes, and some thought the way to protect the range was to shoot the sheep from ambush, but others reported success from clubbing them to death after dark. One rancher along the Laramie River got his cowboys to herd the woollies over a precipice. 'We killed more'n a thousand that way,' he said.

But others preferred poisoning. 'Usin' saltpeter or blue vitriol on the grass,' a Chugwater man said, 'takes care of a hell of a lot of sheep and you don't lose any cattle.'

Claude Barker, a notably serene man, said little about the problem, but when sheepmen invaded his range, two of them were shot, leaving one survivor to drive the remnants of the herd back north.

On the Venneford Ranch the problem became acute. Oliver Seccombe was on his way to England when Messmore Garrett arrived with his first four loads of sheep, and decisions had to be left to Skimmerhorn, who used every device he could think of short of murder to dislodge the sheep. He had no success. Calendar moved the first flock onto the range east of Rattlesnake Buttes, and Buford Coker, the South Carolina Confederate, led a large bunch to Fox Canyon northwest of Line Camp Five.

Skimmerhorn was restrained in dealing with the two intruders because he knew them both, had served with them on the Texas cattle drive. He liked Coker and had a grudging respect for Calendar's ability to protect himself. 'One thing I've got to warn you about,' he told his cowboys at a meeting convened to deal with the trespassers. 'Those two men know how to shoot. Calendar especially isn't going to be scared by threats of gunplay. You behave yourselves.'

The well at Fox Canyon was poisoned and quite a few of Coker's sheep died before he could rescue the others. Calendar's flock was attacked by a running pack of savage dogs who had been maneuvered into the area by men on horseback. Calendar coolly shot most of the dogs, but only after they had done much damage. Grass in the draw which was used as a corral was set afire from all directions, and some two hundred sheep burned to death, but Calendar and Coker stuck to their job, and Messmore Garrett shipped in more sheep.

He was a resolute man. At the local bank, where the tellers found it repugnant to serve him, he deposited ten thousand dollars and let it be known that he wished to buy land for a sheep ranch, his own headquarters, that is, while he ran his sheep on the public domain.

'It's a goddamned disgrace,' the banker said at a dinner held by cattlemen in the Railway Arms. 'That range has been out there for a thousand years, and the only person who has cared for it in all that time is the cattleman. Legally I suppose it belongs to the government. But it's our range. That damned Messmore Garrett better not try to buy land from me.'

The cattlemen were especially outraged when employees of Garrett rode in to the land office and signified their intention of taking up homesteads. 'You know it ain't for them!' they exploded. 'It's just Garrett tryin' to get aholt of some land. Sure as hell, the day they prove it up, they'll turn and sell to him. The law oughta stop them.'

Three members of Garrett's family applied for homesteads, but their papers were lost. They applied again, but a lawyer intervened on behalf of the local citizenry to fault one of the applications, and the two others had to be sent to Kansas City for verification. They, too, were lost.

Garrett made no public complaint. He hired a Denver lawyer who had fought such cases for years, and with glacierlike pressure that expert tied up some parcels of land from which Garrett could, although with difficulty, organize and run his sheep ranch.

The big breakthrough came when the lawyer filed papers at the courthouse for the purchase of two thousand acres of land at Chalk Cliff from Levi Zendt.

The whole pressure of the cattle industry fell on poor Levi, and his store was set on fire, the second time he had suffered this incendiary form of debate. The fire was extinguished, not by the fire company, whose members refused to fight any fire on property belonging to a sheepman, but by Garrett and his friends. Next day the *Clarion* reported:

> The store of Levi Zendt, who seems to prefer the company of sheepmen to that of honest men, caught fire. Unfortunately, it was put out. We remind our readers who have the welfare of this region at heart that this is the same Levi Zendt who protected the Pasquinel brothers when they were burning and murdering along the Platte. People from Pennsylvania seem to require a lot of learning.

Zendt ignored both the fire and the news report, but when a group of cowboys wanted to know how he could sell decent land to a sheepman, he told them, 'Indians sold me that land, to help me get started. I allowed Venneford to use it, to help them get started. I sold Brumbaugh other land, to help him get started. And you're damned fools to ask such a question.'

They reported this at the ranch, and Skimmerhorn rode down from headquarters to reason with Levi. 'It's criminal to bring sheep onto a cattle range,' the foreman argued. 'They destroy. They use up. They're no better'n a bunch of hoofed locusts.'

Levi countered that in his life—he was now sixty-two—he had seen many new ideas evolve and always men said they destroyed the world as it had been. 'Maybe the endless range that you know, John, is a thing of the past. Maybe you ought to buy some of that barbed wire I have and fence your land and know what you're doin'.'

'But, Levi, you own shares in Venneford. You're cutting your own throat.'

'I don't think too much of your cattle shares, John.' And onto the table he tossed the contract he had made with Messmore Garrett, giving him land for his sheep. 'Fact is, John, I'd like to sell my Venneford shares. If you know anyone who wants to buy them.'

Skimmerhorn did. Next day Jim Lloyd appeared at the store and said, 'Mr. Zendt, I hear you got some Venneford shares for sale.'

'I sure do.'

'I'd like to buy 'em.'

'You'd be a lot smarter buyin' sheep shares. I could get you some.'

Jim drew back, aghast. 'I'm a cattleman. I run cattle.'

'If you know what you like, stick to it,' Levi said. 'You can pick up my Venneford shares at the bank.' Then, lowering his voice, he said, 'Lucinda and I have been wondering—do you ever hear anything about Clemma?'

'Never,' Jim said.

'No more do we,' Levi said. Then, briskly: 'Jim, you'd be doin' this part of the country a service if you warned your cowboys to leave Coker and Calendar alone. Those men have only so much patience.'

'They're not my cowboys,' Jim protested. 'The troublemakers are comin' down from Wyoming.'

'Better warn 'em to stay home, Jim. There's gonna be trouble else.'

The warning was to no avail, and three nights later someone got among the Calendar sheep and clubbed more than a hundred to death, breaking their heads open with violent, shattering blows.

In the golden summer of 1883 Chief Lost Eagle, then a frail old man of seventy-three, had his third and last portrait made standing beside a President of the United States. In 1851 he had stood with Millard Fillmore following the great treaty of Fort Laramie, and ten years later he had been photographed with Abraham Lincoln. Now Chester Arthur was vacationing in Yellowstone Park, in an effort to bring the needs of that noble area to the attention of the nation at large. Such a trip into wilderness was a daring venture, requiring the services of seventy-five cavalrymen, many teamsters and scouts, and one hundred and seventy-five pack animals. In passage the President proposed to stop over at the Indian reservation in northwestern Wyoming.

There he met the famous Shoshone chieftain Washakie, who had a grievous complaint, lodged with vigor and ancient contempt: 'Why did the Great White Father allow the Arapaho to trespass onto my reservation?'

President Arthur looked to one of his aides for explanation, but none was forthcoming, and Washakie, now a man in his eighties, continued: 'You know the Arapaho eat their dogs. You know we have fought them for a hundred years.'

Here an aide informed the President that the Ute, of which the Shoshone were a segment, had indeed fought the Arapaho for a century, and it was true that the Arapaho did eat dogs. 'Disgusting,' the President said.

The protest continued for some time, after which a scout was found who could explain: 'The Arapaho have no right to be here . . . none at all. They were expelled from their reservation in Colorado and taken to the Dakotas, but they didn't like it there.'

'Who required that they like it?' the President asked.

'So when food ran out, they were allowed to come down here.'

'They should be sent back,' the President snapped.

'But they've been moved around too much, sir.'

The President agreed to listen to the Arapaho side of the story, and Chief Lost Eagle was brought to see him. He presented a pathetic figure, a withered little old man in a tattered army uniform, with a big bronze medal about his neck and on his head a silly high-crowned hat, a turkey feather sticking up from the band. He was bowlegged from years in the saddle and he spoke in a high voice.

'We have traveled far,' he said, 'and at last we have a home. We wish to stay.'

'What's the medal?' Arthur asked, and General Phil Sheridan, a man who hated Indians and who had coined the classic phrase 'The only good Indian is a dead Indian,' moved forward to inspect the bronze.

'President Buchanan,' Sheridan reported, repressing a snigger.

The entourage moved in, each man wanting to be photographed with the funny little Indian, and he posed for some time, realizing that his appeal to the Great Father had not been taken seriously. 'If I could speak with the President again,' he pleaded, but the cavalrymen kept pressing in to have their pictures taken, and by the time Lost Eagle was able to break away, the President had gone.

'Over here! Over here!' the scouts were calling in Shoshone, and Lost Eagle, who did not understand that language, was left alone until a soldier started pushing him. 'Over here, Grandpa,' and he was maneuvered into a group containing Washakie and the other Shoshone.

'Arapaho,' one of them muttered, but now the photographer was shouting at them to remain very still, and he had barely taken the picture when a wild shout arose from a distance and a group of young Indian braves galloped onto a large open field, where President Arthur sat under a canopy. It looked as if the young men were going to attack the President, but at the last moment, from another corner of the field, a company of cavalrymen, led by a boy blowing a bugle, rushed forward to engage the Indians in mock battle. There was a furious discharge of blank ammunition, with horses whinnying and eleven Indians, trained for the purpose, falling off their horses and sliding in the dust as if they had been killed. After ten minutes of shouting and fine horsemanship and an infinity of firing, the brave cavalrymen drove the Indian savages from the scene and saved the President.

The young Indians who participated were congratulated by both President Arthur and General Sheridan for their fine riding, after which they were allowed to get mildly drunk. Senator George Vest, of Missouri, and Robert Lincoln, son of the late President, agreed that it had been a memorable display, and then the last of the joking cavalrymen insisted upon being photographed with Chief Lost Eagle, and again he patiently posed while the group made fun of him.

Of all the men who were photographed that day, the chief's life had come closest to the American ideal, closest in observing the principles on which this nation had been founded. He was immeasurably greater than Chester Arthur, the hack politician from New York, incomparably finer than Robert Lincoln, a niggardly man of no stature who inherited from his father only his name, and a better warrior, considering his troops and ordnance, than Phil Sheridan. His only close competitor was Senator Vest, who shared with him a love of land and a joy in seeing it used constructively.

But the group laughed at him, would not listen to his petition, and failed even to realize that he was presenting them with a grave moral problem, not of much magnitude, but perhaps of greater intensity for that reason. By the time the presidential party left Wyoming, Chief Lost Eagle was dead.

The coming of the railroad affected the white man as profoundly as the horse had changed the Indian. For example, in the early summer of 1884 Levi Zendt was confounded by a telegram which the stationmaster handed him:

ARRIVING UNION PACIFIC FRIDAY AFTERNOON TO STUDY INDIAN TRIBAL LAW

CHRISTIAN ZENDT

In confusion he showed the message to Lucinda, who asked, naturally, 'Who's he?'

'I don't know. I had a brother Christian. He bought cattle and was so stupid he never heard of an Indian, let alone law.'

'Could it be his son?'

'Nobody ever told me who has sons.'

Lucinda decided it must be one of Levi's nephews, most likely a son of Christian. He was probably studying law somewhere and had caught on to some fancy idea about Indians. Having suggested this, she became grave: 'Should I leave while he's here?'

'No!' Levi exploded. 'Why should you?'

'I am Indian.'

'That's what he's comin' out to study. Cutthroat Indians. Let him see a real one.'

'What about my brothers.'

'Look!' He pulled his wife by the arm. 'When they kicked me out of Lancaster my family thought me worse than your brothers. I was lower than a murderer. They've got no right to be put off their feed by Pasquinels.'

'Does your family know that I'm your wife?'

'I haven't told 'em.'

'I think I'd better go to Denver.'

'You stay here. It's time they knew.'

So when the afternoon train chugged in from Julesburg, with many of the townfolk at the station, for its arrival was still a novelty, Levi and Lucinda were there to greet Christian Zendt, whoever he was. Down the steps, carrying a small carpet suitcase, came a tall, blond, square-faced boy about twenty-three years old.

'You must be Uncle Levi,' he said brightly, with an unpretentious grin. 'And this is Mrs. Zendt.' Then he looked at her closely and asked, 'Are you a real Indian?' And when she nodded graciously, he cried, 'This is better than I'd hoped for. It's truly wonderful!'

All the way to the farm he talked like a magpie. Graduated from Franklin and Marshall. Yes, son of Christian Zendt, but he was dead now. Three years ago. Enrolled in the law school at Dickinson. Yes, the other three brothers were still living, all with kids. His mother had been one of the Mummerts of Paradise . . .

'The old wagon makers!'

'The same.'

'Did Mahlon marry?'

Yes, but very late. He courted the Stoltzfus girl for about fifteen years. He was afraid to marry, right out like that, and she was afraid to lose him, because he was the only man her age left, and she lost her looks and every Tuesday and Friday they stared at each other across the market, she in her stall selling baked goods and he in his selling meat and both families getting richer, and finally the three brothers got together and said he had to marry her, it was unfair otherwise, and he took to his bed with fear, so Christian and the other two brothers went to the Stoltzfus girl and proposed for Mahlon, and they were married, 'And when I last saw them, they stood side by side in the meat stall and one of the Stoltzfus boys had taken over the bakery.'

'Any children?'

'One every year for five years.'

The more Levi and his wife saw of this ebullient young man, the more they liked him. He sat enraptured as she told how her uncles had tied buffalo skulls to their backs and had danced in swirling dust until the thongs broke through their back muscles. She told also of her brothers and how they had escaped the massacre, and Levi shared the pain when Christian broke in: 'Dear God, Aunt Lucinda! You don't mean Skimmerhorn set up the guns on purpose and mowed them down?' She said that was exactly what she meant.

He had a wonderful freedom from false nicety. 'Tell me about the deaths of your two brothers. We hear a lot about them back east. I never dreamed they were my uncles!'

She laughed bitterly, then told how one had been hanged, how the other had been shot in the back by Frank Skimmerhorn, and how Levi, defying local hatreds, had buried them both. They talked a good deal about tribal law, and Levi was astounded at how much his wife knew. Her knowledge was not codified—that would be the task of trained men like Christian—but it hung together, and for the first time Levi understood that Indians were governed by customs as rigid as those which bound the Mennonites of Lancaster County.

One night Lucinda told Levi, 'It's not proper, a young man like this talking with us all night. He ought to be meeting some of the girls.' When Levi saw how easily this youngster of twenty-three handled the young ladies and with what grace he bandied their flirtations, he recalled his own barbarity at that age.

When the time came for Christian to return to Dickinson, four Centennial families with daughters sought to give him farewell parties, and he accepted, kissing the girls and their mothers goodbye. At the station he told Levi, 'You should visit the family. I'm sure they'd welcome you.'

'I'm not so sure. I'm still the outcast.' He was standing with his arm about Lucinda as he added, 'Don't tell them I married an Indian. They wouldn't understand.'

'I never see them.'

'You don't?'

'No, when I wanted to go to college they raised Cain, Mahlon worst of all. Even my father ridiculed me. To hell with them all.'

When the train chugged in from Denver, Lucinda kissed her nephew goodbye and said, 'Come back. Come often. Lots of people in this town would be pleased to see you, Levi and me most of all.'

He swung onto the train, blew kisses at the girls—and returned to his studies. Three times that winter Lucinda brought up the question of Levi's going back home for a short visit. Each time he said, 'Not unless you come too,' and she replied, 'Lancaster's not ready for an Arapaho Indian.'

So he dropped the matter, but she raised it a fourth time: 'A man ought to see his kin. Levi, you can't imagine how you perked up when Christian was here. You have a right to know how the trees are doing.'

Often through the years he had wondered how those stately trees had grown, and whether the barn still sat with its hex signs among the meadows, but before he could respond, she made another comment even more compelling: 'I cannot forget that when they left Jake Pasquinel's body on the gallows, you stepped forward to claim it, because he was my brother. From that day I would have walked through hell for you, Levi. A man ought to stick with his kin.'

She bought him a large suitcase and some new clothes. She purchased the ticket, Centennial to Omaha to Chicago on the Union Pacific. Change stations at Chicago for Lancaster on the Pennsylvania. She took him down to the station an hour early and introduced him to others who were going as far as Chicago. But she would not accompany him.

The trip was so uneventful. He could not believe that he had once struggled for a half year to cover the same distance, and on Wednesday morning when the train pulled into the cavernous station at Lancaster, he was awed by the change, but then he saw his three bearded brothers waiting for him, and time seemed not to have touched them. Mahlon, still tall and dark, had acquired neither weight nor congeniality. He looked as if he were there to collect the remaining eighty-eight dollars Levi owed him for the stolen horses. Jacob looked pretty much the same, and Caspar, who did the butchering, was the powerful man he had been forty years ago. To the farmers of Lancaster the passage of years meant little; they tended their business and allowed others to worry over intrusions like the Civil War and financial panics.

The brothers remarked on Levi's lack of beard and congratulated him on having been able to manage a train trip all the way from Colorado. They piled him into a wagon pulled by two handsome bays and off they went to Lampeter, where Levi discovered that Hell Street was quieter now, but as they approached the ancient lane and the tall trees, he saw that the farm was unchanged. There stood the towering barn with its colorful hex signs and the reassuring pronouncement:

JACOB ZENDT

1713

BUTCHER

The lovely trees were more stately and the little buildings were just as he had left them. He wondered how many miles of sausage and acres of scrapple had come from that red shack since he left.

'We have a stall in Philadelphia now,' Caspar explained. 'We take the train to Reading Terminal. Very large business.' Levi was pleased to hear the Pennsylvania German accent again: *werry larch busy-niss.*

At the house, so small when compared to the barn, Levi met the Zendt wives, and there was Rebecca Stoltzfus, totally changed. She was plump and white-haired and very stolid. Only the cupid's-bow mouth was the same, and in her expanded face it looked rather ridiculous. He held out his hand and she shook it formally.

'Things are good at the market,' she said.

'Who's runnin' the bakery?' he asked.

'My brother,' she said.

The Zendt women had a traditional family dinner waiting, a display of food that staggered Levi, who recalled the many years he had lived on pemmican and beans. The table and the groaning sideboards contained a full seven sweets and seven sours, eight kinds of meat, three kinds of fowl, and six kinds of cookies, including the ones whose memory had tormented him when he was starving: crunchy black-walnut made with black molasses.

He wondered if any people were entitled to so much food, so much of the world's goodness. And as he surveyed the farm and saw the ample supply of water and the infinity of trees and the lush grass where one acre would support a cow, he was struck with how easy life was in Pennsylvania and how brutally difficult in Colorado, where you had to dig a ditch twenty miles before you could tease a little water onto your land.

It was the trees that moved him most deeply. He loved to walk in the woods or sit at the picnic area in the grove: Yes, that's a hickory. How many of them I chopped down to fuel the smokehouse. And the oaks, they haven't grown an inch in forty years. And the good maples and the ash and the elm. We had a treasure here and never knew it.

On Friday evening the children found him sitting beneath the trees, tears in his eyes. 'You feeling tired, Uncle Levi?'

'I was thinkin' of the time I needed a tree to save my wagon,' he told them. 'And I had to walk many miles to find one.' They knew he had to be lying.

At family prayers Levi was astonished, there could be no other word for it, by the minute detail with which Mahlon told God what to do. At each grace the tall, acidulous man would direct God's attention to evildoers, to men who had stolen money from the bank, to girls who were misbehaving, and Levi began to understand why so much violence had been permitted in Colorado. With God kept so busy in Lancaster prying into petty problems, how could He find time to watch over real crimes like those of the Pasquinel brothers and Colonel Skimmerhorn?

From time to time the family dropped discreet questions about his experiences in the west. They knew that the girl he had abducted from the orphanage at gunpoint had died.

'Killed by a rattlesnake,' Levi said without inflection.

'Any children?'

'She was about to have one when she died.'

'Did you remarry?'

'Yep.' He let it go at that.

By Saturday it was obvious that Levi Zendt was not happy at the family farm and that his brothers were ill-at-ease with him. He did not belong to the family, and no one was grieved when he announced that on Monday he would head back for Colorado. 'Chicago, then St. Joseph, Missouri. There's a stage that runs out of there along the old road that Elly and I took in the Conestoga . . .'

'That would be interesting,' Caspar said frigidly.

At Sunday dinner the Zendt women put on a lavish display, not only to send Levi west on a full stomach but also to welcome Reverend Fenstermacher—son of the older preacher—on his regular eating visit. Levi dreaded the prospect, but the minister proved much different from his self-righteous father.

'Forty years ago, when I bought my rifle from Melchior Fordney, he boasted that you could fire one of his percussion guns three times in two minutes,' Levi said.

'That was my brother. He died at Antietam.'

'Was the war hard on Lancaster?'

'On boys like my brother . . . very hard.'

Fenstermacher offered a grace marked by a deep sense of God's benign presence and the fellowship that sprang from it. At the end he pointed to the table and said to Levi, 'Your family intends that you shall not forget the bounty of Lancaster.'

Levi put his fork down and said, 'It's strange, but when we were starving on the plains I never once thought of a dinner like this. I thought only of special things. The bite of sour souse, the rich stink of cup cheese, and black-walnut cookies. Does the souse still sell well?'

'Better than ever,' Mahlon said, 'especially in Philadelphia. Caspar's wife makes it now, same way you did.'

Then, for some perverse reason, Levi decided to show his family their sister-in-law. Coughing, he produced a photograph of Lucinda, one in which she looked very dark. He said, 'You haven't seen my wife,' and passed it to his left. He could tell who was holding the picture by the look of shock that came over each face. Finally the Stoltzfus girl said, hesitantly, 'She's very . . . western.'

'She's an Arapaho.'

'What's that?' Caspar asked.

'Indian. She's half-Indian.'

This was greeted with gasps, which Levi ignored, directing his attention to the meats. From somewhere came the question, 'What's her name?'

'Lucinda McKeag.'

'Doesn't sound Indian. Sounds Scotch.'

'That wasn't her real name. McKeag picked up her mother when her father died, and she went along.'

There was enough in that sentence to preoccupy the Zendts for some moments, after which Levi volunteered, 'Her real name was Pasquinel.'

This information was greeted by silence, during which Reverend Fenstermacher knitted his brow. At last he asked quietly, 'Was she related to . . . Wasn't there a Pasquinel family we read about?'

'There was. The old fellow was a mountain man. His sons were known as the Pasquinel brothers.'

'Those?' several voices asked almost tremulously.

'Yep. Lucinda's brothers were a mean pair. They hanged one. Shot the other in the back.'

'The half-breed murderers?'

'The Indians suffered more murders than they committed, but the Pasquinels were killers.' Levi helped himself to apple butter and preserved cherries. 'I had the unpleasant job of cutting the older boy down from the gallows. At the time I thought it was merciful he was dead, but reflectin' on what we did to his tribe, I'm not so sure we hung the right people.'

Reverend Fenstermacher coughed, but Levi was started and nothing, not even food, could stop him. He told of the Indian fights, of the years of drought, of locust swarms, of the gold-mining camps. Every incident he referred to was alien to the Zendts, and in a way ugly, but as he unfolded the epic of life in the west it began to acquire a certain grandeur, and the very magnitude of it made them at least listen with respect.

One comment on the sun dance reminded him of young Christian Zendt, and prompted him to say, 'You ought to get that boy back here. He may prove to be the best Zendt of all.'

As the meal ended, Mahlon said unctuously, 'Reverend Fenstermacher, since it may be a long time before we see our brother again, would you please give our family a special blessing!' The reverend, having anticipated such an invitation, had certain things he wanted to say.

'Dear God, Who watches over us, You have heard me say a hundred times in church, "God moves in a mysterious way, His wonders to perform." Nothing in my experience has been more mysterious than the manner in which You took Brother Levi west and placed him among the Indians and gave him an Indian wife and Indian brothers. You chose him from among the five Zendt brothers to do Your work on the frontier, and he has done it well. He has been our emissary, and we have all been remiss in not sending him money to aid him when he needed it. We have kept our love from him. We have not even bothered to acquaint ourselves with what he was doing. God, forgive us for our indifference.

'But Levi was in error, too. He did not share with us his adventure in settling the wilderness. He did not report to us either his struggles or his victories. Especially was he afraid to bring his wife Lucinda here to visit with his family, afraid lest we embarrass her because she was Indian. Does he think we are so poor in spirit? When he returns home let him tell his wife that we send her our love, that we know her as our sister and that our home is her home, now and forever. Does he think that we do not know tragedy also? The Civil War that struck so many families here was just as deep a sorrow to us as the Indian wars were to him. We are all Your children, God. Truly, we are brothers in Your family and as we share our tragedies so we share our triumphs, and it is love that binds us together. Amen.'

There wasn't much the Zendts could say after that. It was obvious that any preacher who would insult the richest Mennonite family in Lampeter, and at their own table, had no bright future in the Lancaster area, and the goodbyes after dinner were restrained. Levi went down to the grove, to sit among the trees, and it occurred to him that just as the Arapaho had dragged buffalo skulls through the dust, punishing themselves, so white men dragged behind them enormous skulls of another kind. The Indians were smart enough to allow their burdens to rip free; the white man seldom did.

The return to Lancaster had been unbearably painful. He had not said a dozen words to Rebecca Stoltzfus, the girl who had changed the direction of his life; he knew no more about her now than when he stepped off the train. He had discussed nothing of gravity with Mahlon, who seemed as distasteful now as he had forty years ago. He had not even been gracious enough to ride in to Philadelphia to see the family stall in Reading Station, because he had been so wrapped up in his own memories that he didn't really care what was happening to the family.

It had been a terrible mistake to come here, and he left without being able to improve relations with his family in the way Reverend Fenstermacher had hoped. He was not sorry to go, and the Zendts were even less sorry to see him board the train.

At St. Joseph, Levi changed to the stagecoach, which would take him slowly west; and as the ferry carried them across the Missouri, he relived the journey of forty years ago. He felt he had been correct in leaving Lancaster, for now he knew that nothing had changed in the intervening years: he had found no significance other than tables piled ridiculously high with food. And as they chugged along, everything he saw added to his excitement—the muddy river, the black boys along the waterfront, the creaking ferry, the brooding threat of Kansas, the highway west. How he wished that Elly and proper Captain Mercy and bright Oliver Seccombe were with him now, just starting out with their teams. Even crafty Sam Purchas—he would want Sam too.

But after the coach was well into Kansas and had climbed past the Presbyterian mission, it came to the Big Blue, and Levi called to the driver to stop, and he climbed down to inspect this puny creek, this mere trickle of water in August, and he was aghast to think that this miserable pencil line across the landscape had once been a forbidding torrent where he had nearly lost his wagon and his wife.

It was incredible. Memory was playing him false. Then the image of the buffalo skulls returned, and he visualized himself dragging across the prairies his painful burdens of remembrance. But his robust sense of reality reasserted itself, and he began to laugh at himself. 'I missed the whole point!' he cried. 'My brothers were uneasy because they feared I was comin' back to claim my share of the farm. It's part mine, but let 'em keep it.' He continued laughing. 'Never once did they ask about the dinosaur. Biggest thing ever discovered in the west. Must have been in the Lancaster papers.' He shook his head and chuckled. 'They'd have asked about the dinosaur if it was something good to eat.'

When he climbed back into the coach a man from Nebraska, staring at the river, said, 'Hell, you could spit across that,' and Levi laughed and told him, 'Not in the spring of '44, my friend.' And heavy skulls tore from the sinews of his mind, and he told the man, 'Right now, though, you're right. A good man could spit across it.'

When Levi reached Centennial, neighbors persisted in questioning him about the east, and at first he rebuffed them, but finally he spoke for all westerners when he said, 'Back east, wherever you look, you see something. The world crowds in on you. I can't tell you how homesick I got for the prairies, where a man can look for miles and not see any-thing . . . not feel crowded. Out here the human being is important . . . not a lot of trees and buildings.'

Other people were also returning from their travels. When Oliver Seccombe came home with his wife after their six months in England, he found Venneford Ranch in trouble. On the extreme outer edges, over toward Nebraska, squatters were building sod huts on the open range which had long been preempted by Crown Vee cattle. Along the Platte, immigrants from states like Ohio and Tennessee were taking out formal homesteads, as if by doing so they could gain access to the range. Committees were actually visiting the ranch headquarters to see about buying ranch land for the building of small towns.

'We need towns in this state,' they argued, and Seccombe told them, 'Not on our land you don't.'

Worst of all, the sheepmen led by that damned Messmore Garrett were more and more digging in and running their sheep on what had always been considered cattle territory. The situation was becoming in-tolerable, and on his first day home Seccombe ordered Skimmerhorn and Lloyd to ride out with him to warn Garrett's men: 'Vacate or suffer the consequences.'

They rode east to where Amos Calendar had parked his lonely wagon—bed, commissary, refuge from storms for months on end—and it was some time before they could find the lean **Texan**. He rode toward them with his rifle across his saddle and grunted a meager hello to Skimmerhorn and Lloyd.

'I'm Oliver Seccombe,' the Englishman said. 'You're trespassing with your sheep. This is cattle country.'

'It's open range,' Calendar said.

'I'm warning you to get your sheep out of here.'

'I'm stayin' till Mr. Garrett tells me to move.'

A dog now ran up, a collie-type with white and black hair. 'Good-looking dog.' Seccombe said. 'You ought to get him out of here, where he'll be safe.'

'Rajah's safe anywhere,' Calendar said slowly. 'Long as I got my Sharps.'

The ranchers were getting nowhere with this difficult man, but Seccombe was determined to deliver the warning: 'If you don't move the sheep, Calendar, we'll move them for you.'

'You tried that before and failed.'

Seccombe flushed. 'What do you mean by that?'

'Them gunmen who tried to kill me didn't come from Brazil.'

'Are you suggesting that I . . .'

'I ain't suggestin' nothin'. I'm simply tellin' you that if any of you sonsabitches fire at me, I'm gonna fire back.'

'Let's get out of here,' Seccombe said, spurring his horse and starting west.

They headed for Line Camp Four, among the piñons, and as they rode Skimmerhorn said, 'I better explain Buford Coker, Mr. Seccombe. He's a hot-tempered Confederate from South Carolina. He's not like Calendar at all. As you've seen, Calendar likes being alone. Coker don't. He's gone in to Cheyenne and spent a lot of time at Ida Hamilton's House of Mirrors, and last time I saw him he'd persuaded one of the girls, Fat Laura . . .'

'I've heard of Fat Laura,' Seccombe said.

'Well, you'll find Fat Laura in the sheep wagon with him. Or maybe in a shack. Coker's building himself a shack at Fox Canyon.'

'Building!' Seccombe exploded. 'That's cattle country. We let him build, we'll have half the sheepmen in the west . . .'

Coker was building. He and Fat Laura had hired two men to come down from Cheyenne and build them a substantial shack at the mouth of Fox Canyon. It was not elegant, but it was sturdy, and when Seccombe saw it he wanted to shout, 'Skimmerhorn! Have that thing torn down!' for it was a visible warning of what would happen across the range if corrective steps were not taken, and quickly.

At the door of the new house stood Fat Laura, a Virginia woman in her late twenties and obviously a graduate of Ida Hamilton's academy. In her teens she must have been pretty in the buxom, bucolic way that cowboys appreciated, but ten years of hard life and constant movement from one brothel to the next could not be disguised, and the accumulation of forty pounds gained through the only activity she really enjoyed had made her a slattern. She was six inches taller than Coker and thirty pounds heavier, and why he had associated himself with her remained a mystery.

But here she was, a Cheyenne castoff, living on the edge of nowhere with a sheepman. A woman could hardly sink any lower, Seccombe thought, and he had no desire to enter into conversation with her. He let Skimmerhorn do the talking.

'Where's Coker?'

'Out.'

'Which direction?'

'Make a noise, his dog might bark.'

'You living here permanent?'

'Looks like.'

She was a repulsive woman with fat lips and heavy eyes and faded hair. She had no intention of informing these men as to Coker's whereabouts, and now she stood gross and ugly in the doorway as if daring them to enter.

'I have a gun,' she said, 'so don't start nothin'.'

'We don't shoot ladies.' Skimmerhorn laughed. 'But tell Coker to get his sheep off this land. And get that shack off it, too.'

'I homesteaded this shack.'

'You what?' Seccombe shouted. 'A Cheyenne whore homesteading cattle country?'

Fat Laura stared at him with her basilisk eyes and said nothing, but from behind the doorjamb she produced a heavy shotgun. Bringing it forward, she plopped the butt end in the dust, then leaned her fat bosom on the barrel.

'You tell Coker to get off this land,' Seccombe warned, and Fat Laura's huge face broke into a contemptuous smile.

'Up your fancy ass, Englishman.'

The three ranchmen rode back to headquarters, bewildered as to what they must do next. If Venneford sat by supinely while sheepmen invaded the range, and if they made no protest when immigrants squatted on the outer edges of the ranch and homesteaders took up government land, pretty soon the whole intricate structure would begin to fall apart, the trend would accelerate and a noble way of life would be lost.

'Thing I cannot understand,' Seccombe said as they approached headquarters, 'is how a decent man like Levi Zendt could sell his land to sheepmen.'

'There's a theory going around,' Skimmerhorn said, 'that the open range is ended. Zendt told me he thought sheep were a better investment, especially with a man like Garrett supervising.'

'Garrett!' Seccombe exclaimed. 'Isn't there any way to run that scoundrel off the range?'

Skimmerhorn ignored the question and continued with Zendt's reactions: 'He says maybe we ought to consolidate around the land we own. Fence it in and concentrate on about half the cattle we now run.'

'But this is cattle country!' Seccombe said. 'It belongs to us.'

Skimmerhorn was reluctant to point out that for the past seven hours the riders had not once been on Venneford land. They were on open range, land that belonged to anyone; it was cattle country only because the cattleman had always said so.

Confusing days followed. This was the finest time of year, late August before the first frost, with calves grown sturdy on rich grasses. A man should be enjoying these days, and Charlotte entertained numerous visitors at the castle, with her usual flair and merriment, but Oliver Seccombe enjoyed none of it.

He could not comprehend how the citizens of Centennial could permit sheepmen to invade their land. 'The animals are filthy,' he said to the banker. 'Look at the pitiful men who work them. This fellow Calendar, a miserable hermit talking to his dog. And that wreck of a man, Bufe Coker, living with his Cheyenne harlot. Hell, he's slept with sheep so long he probably can't tell the difference.'

All cattlemen believed the accusation that the lonely sheepherder engaged in sexual intercourse with his charges, and many funny stories circulated regarding this supposed custom: 'You hear about the Englishman countin' sheep in Wyomin'? "One, two, three, four. Good mornin', Pamela. Don't forget. Tea at five." '

'Look at a sheepman when he comes to town,' Seccombe said bitterly to the editor of the *Clarion*. 'He walks alone. His eyes are downcast. He's ashamed to speak up to people he meets. In a bar he stays at the far end, drinking with no one. He's an outcast and he knows it. His smell alone, sleeping with those woollies, would make him a lonely man.' He shook his head mournfully, then brightened.

'On the other hand, you take a cowboy. Frank, honest, clean-cut. He sleeps with girls, not sheep, and his joy shows. He's never alone. Likes a crowd. In a bar he heads right for the middle, where the people are, and when he speaks to you he looks you in the eye. The cowboy is a clean, fine man. I've seen thousands of them. But the sheepman is craven. They ought to be run out of here.'

The Old Testament bothered Seccombe. It was full of sheep and shepherds, and he began to wonder if perhaps the Jews were not also contaminated people. 'They spent all this time worrying about pork,' he told Charlotte's guests at dinner one night, 'when their real problem was mutton, and they didn't recognize it.'

'Abraham was a shepherd. David was a shepherd. Joseph was a shepherd,' one of the guests pointed out.

'Yes!' Seccombe cried. 'But when Our Lord was born you didn't find

Him looking for a sheep pen. He was born with the cattle, where He belonged. I could have little respect for Him if it had been otherwise.' His tirade was proof of his total adaptation to American customs, for certainly in his native England, where there was no inbred resentment of sheep, fine spring lamb was as welcome on the discriminating table as beef.

'Don't forget, Oliver,' an argumentative guest said, 'that the first man born on earth tended sheep, Abel, and when he handed God one of his sheep, God accepted it and blessed it.'

'God was careless that time,' Seccombe growled. 'It's a sad day when I hear sheep being defended in my own house,' and he stiffly excused himself and headed for the Cheyenne Club, where he could associate with men dedicated to cattle and the proper use of the range.

He found little levity. Claude Barker was bitter against the invasions made by sheepmen on the north end of his Horse Creek ranch, and the Chugwater people felt the same. 'This country is goin' to hell,' Barker protested, and various plans were proposed for counteracting the drift.

'All we're asking,' Seccombe said, 'is to have things go on as they were. We don't need cities out here, and sheep, and homesteaders trying to grub out a meager living. This land should be kept open. It was made for cattle the way Chicago was made for people. There's an honesty about raising cattle . . . a dignity . . .'

The younger ranchers allowed him to finish his speech, knowing that it meant nothing. When the difficult decision of what specifically to do had to be faced, Seccombe would board a train and head for business out of town. He was not much for difficult decisions, and sure enough, two days after this first planning session he found reasons for visiting bankers in Kansas City.

He was at work in that city on the afternoon that the five-thirteen Union Pacific pulled into Centennial from Denver. The usual inquisitive locals and wide-eyed children were at the station to watch the train arrive, and they remarked on the various local people who disembarked, making shrewd guesses as to what they had been up to in the capital. But as the last of the customary passengers had left the train, a man whispered, 'Hey, look!' and everyone turned toward the rear car, where two slim men in black suits and broad-brimmed hats were alighting. The older stepped onto the platform, looked cautiously about him, beckoned to the other to follow. When they were free of the train, a porter handed down two valises and pointed to the Railway Arms, saying in a voice loud enough for the watchers to hear, 'Over there, Mr. Pettis.'

'The Pettis boys!' someone cried in a hoarse whisper, and all other arrivals were ignored as men drew back while the two visitors walked solemnly through the station and across the road to the hotel. There they registered boldly as Frank and Orvid Pettis.

For the next two days Centennial buzzed with speculation as to what had brought these two aging gunmen to town. The Pettis boys! What a travesty of language! They had never been boys. At fourteen they were vicious killers, and now at fifty-seven Frank was a black-toothed, scrawny man with sharp, battle-worn eyes. Orvid, in his fifty-second year, was a hardened assassin living out his years with the small funds he received for one or another routine murder.

Yet they were known as the Pettis boys, and their arrival in any frontier town signified that someone with a grievance to settle had grown impatient with the law. They had never been apprehended in coldblooded murder; they were too clever for that. Even when they were arrested, with every item of evidence pointing to their guilt, as in the Pueblo murders, where they were seen at the crime and where their footprints matched exactly those found at the site of the triple assassination, clever lawyers were brought in from Kansas and the jury exonerated them.

The pitiful aspect of their lives was that whereas they had done much work for men with money, they got little for themselves. They killed and threatened and evicted, but they never lived well. When they came to a town like Centennial they had funds for the purchase of horses and their hotel bills were taken care of, but when the job was done, whatever it was, they would move on to a similar town, buy a couple of horses, eat free at the hotel. But they did not prosper. From the cattle they stampeded on the Skimmerhorn Trail in the years from 1868 through 1880, they made barely enough dollars to subsist on, and thirteen of their equally underpaid men were shot. They now lived in a small town in western Kansas, always ready for a telegraphed invitation.

A few days later they rode out of town, two dark and silent men heading east. 'They're after Calendar,' boys whispered, and one gallant fellow only fifteen years old, who had grown to respect that somber sheepman, jumped on his horse and rode out to warn him. 'Calendar! Calendar!' he was shouting long before he reined in his sweating horse, 'Pettis boys are after you.'

But they were not headed in his direction. After a long detour to the east, they cut north, left Colorado and went deep into Wyoming to a draw leading into Horse Creek, where a sheepman was herding some two thousand woollies. They shot him from ambush, then stampeded the sheep into the quicksand river, where they floundered, bleating piteously, and perished.

They then rode far west, beyond the Laramie River, to a remote spot where a Mexican was tending twelve hundred sheep. Seeing that he was alone and unarmed, Frank Pettis said, 'Let's gunnysack him,' and they threw a bag over the shepherd's head, tying it about his waist. They lashed him to a rock and he had to listen as they methodically clubbed his sheep to death. The sad cries of sheep beaten but not yet dead so affected the poor man that he began to whimper in sympathy, and Orvid said, 'Let's put him out of his misery,' and each of the brothers emptied his revolver into the sack.

The boys then swung south in a long loop which brought them finally to Fox Canyon, where they spent a day secretly observing Buford Coker's new shack.

'There's the whore,' Frank whispered to Orvid as Fat Laura appeared at the doorway.

'I don't want to kill no woman,' Orvid replied.

'She ain't no woman,' Frank said, and as they watched they saw, coming from the north, Wyoming way, a man riding full blast toward the cabin, shouting, 'Coker! The Pettis boys is on the loose! They're killin' sheepmen!'

'Son-of-a-bitch!' Frank mumbled. 'Just when things was goin' good.'

They continued to watch as the man galloped up to the cabin, dismounted and began talking agitatedly with Fat Laura.

'We better knock them off,' Frank said with professional judgment. 'We don't want three guns against us.'

'Three?' Orvid asked.

'I bet that whore can fight like a cornered badger,' Frank said, indicating with his right shoulder the fact that she was already going for her rifle.

'Here goes,' Frank said. 'I'll get the man. You get the whore.'

With no more talk, the two killers edged themselves closer to the cabin, and at a signal from Frank, they fired. The man dropped with a bullet through his head, but Orvid had less luck with Fat Laura. He merely shot her through the left shoulder. He saw blood spurt out, so he knew he had winged her well, but she was not dead, for she succeeded in crawling back into the shack.

'You missed!' Frank said with disgust. 'And look!'

There, edging his way down the draw behind the cabin, was Bufe Coker, shouting encouragement to his woman: 'Hold on, Laura. I'm comin'.'

Dodging bullets, he made his way to the back door of the cabin and in to where Laura leaned against the wall, blood dripping from her shoulder. Ignoring the bullets that zinged through the shack, he tended the fat woman, binding her wound and giving her assurance that it could not be fatal.

'We'll hold 'em off till help comes,' he said. 'Who are they?'

'Kellerman said they was the Pettis boys.'

'Where's Kellerman now?'

'Out there, dead.'

'Hell. We could've used him.'

'Will they kill us?'

'They got to come in here to do it.' He gathered his guns, giving one to his woman, and began shoring up the front door with furniture. He was preoccupied with this task when he heard Fat Laura scream, 'No! No!' and he looked out in time to see his dog Bravo run toward the house.

'Back! Back!' he shouted, and if the dog had been working sheep he would have obeyed, but he sensed that Laura was in danger and continued running toward her.

With one shot Orvid Pettis killed the dog. Fat Laura looked at Coker with a dumb, animal-like emptiness in her eyes, and tears rolled down her ravaged face. 'They mean to kill us all,' she said.

Coker consoled her, 'We've lots of ammunition. And lots of guns. If Kellerman knew about this, so do others, and they'll be along to help.'

So they dug in, returning fire only when one of the Pettis boys moved his position, and for that whole day gunfire blasted spasmodically, with no apparent effect.

Then, in late afternoon, sheep began wandering into the area, and as each one appeared, inquisitive and shy, Orvid Pettis shot it. The noise would cause other sheep to investigate, and whenever one came into range, Orvid shot it through the head. His marksmanship was uncanny and caused Fat Laura to whisper, 'He can kill anything he puts his mind to.'

'Not you or me,' Coker said grimly, and with well-aimed shots he kept the killers at bay.

But shortly before sunset Frank Pettis worked his way around to a rock from which he commanded the front of the shack, and while Orvid blasted away at the back, he drew a perfect bead on the window, then waited with extraordinary patience for thirty minutes until someone inside the house moved accidentally into view.

It was Fat Laura. Pettis pulled his trigger and a bullet ripped through the window and into her head, killing her instantly.

'Oh, my God!' Coker groaned. 'Laura! Laura!' He crawled along the floor to where she lay in blood and cradled her head in his arms. At the House of Mirrors she had been the girl who tended the other girls when they were sick. She had taken care of cowboys down on their luck and had given Coker three hundred dollars to help build this cabin. She had loved the place and had planted a few hopeless trees to shield it from the wind, and if she was not a good cook, she was enthusiastic, and now she was dead.

'Better come out, Coker, or we'll burn you out,' Frank Pettis cried.

'Come get me, you bastards,' the South Carolina man shouted back.

'We're gonna burn you out,' Frank warned.

'I ain't no woman. You can't kill me.'

'Is the whore dead?'

It was an ill-matched fight. Never once did Bufe Coker get a clean shot at either of the Pettis boys. With practiced skill they hid behind rocks, shooting only when they had a good chance of hitting him, and he was powerless to punish them in return.

Night fell, a dark and moonless night, and he could not check on what they were up to. He had to stay awake to protect the cabin, and he spent the hours moving from front to back, firing at unexpected moments to assure them that he was on guard. They could take turns sleeping, but not he.

About three in the morning he decided that Orvid was asleep, for he recognized the different sounds made by their guns, and he made a desperate move. Firing twice from the front window, he ran quickly to the back and out into the night, blazing away at the spot where he thought Orvid might be resting. No luck. Orvid was not there, and Coker barely made it back to the cabin. He fired madly at the shapes closing in on him but apparently hit nothing.

'Coker,' came the warning voice. 'You got till dawn to come out. Then we burn the place.'

The next two hours were quiet. And as dawn brightened, Coker could see the prostrate body of Fat Laura sprawled in her own blood. It made him sick to see her hair matting in the gore that surrounded her, but she was too heavy for him to lug onto their bed. 'Jesus, Laura,' he whispered.

With the first ray of sun Frank Pettis sent a fusillade at the front of the house, moving constantly closer, and while Coker was occupied shooting back, Orvid succeeded in sneaking to the rear and setting the shack ablaze.

For thirty minutes Coker fought the fire, stopping at intervals to shoot at shadows, but he was powerless to halt the flames. And all the time Frank Pettis was shouting, 'Come on out, Coker, or you'll cook.'

So in the end the South Calinky man grabbed his LeMat, checked the chambers of the sawed-off shotgun and waited till the flames crept about his legs. Then, instead of coming out the front door, he burst through the window, firing at the spot where he supposed them to be, but they were not there.

In the moment before Coker leaped, Frank had cautioned his younger brother, 'He'll try to jump us from the window,' so when Coker came out, he sprang right into the fire of two deadly rifles. He took seven shots in the face and chest and collapsed before the chambers of the LeMat were exhausted.

'Better throw them damned sheepmen in the fire,' Frank said, and they picked up the stiff body of the man who had brought the warning, swung him back and forth a couple of times and lofted him easily into the flames. Then they lifted Coker high in the morning air and with a powerful toss sent him arching into the embers of his cabin.

'That'll learn 'em,' Frank said.

When the various murders were discovered, sheep owners appealed to the governors of both Wyoming and Colorado for protection, but were told that no evidence was at hand that these crimes had been directed against sheepmen as such. As for the Pettis boys' having been employed by cattlemen to settle range differences, that suggestion was abhorrent to any right-thinking man. As a matter of fact, there was not a shred of proof connecting the Pettis boys with the killings, and it seemed more probable that the crimes had been committed by itinerant Mexican sheepmen. The *Clarion* summarized local opinion when it editorialized:

> It is offensive to the decent citizens of this city when malicious and ill-founded rumors are circulated to the effect that two law-abiding visitors from Kansas are accused of the most heinous crimes. No substantial charge of any kind has been leveled against them, and none can be proved. We would remind our readers who the five victims were. A Mexican, a Confederate who took arms against the Union, a woman of bad character and worse performance, a troublemaker who ran about the countryside spreading rumors, and a miserable outcast charged with having committed abominations with sheep he was supposed to guard. While we do not condone murder, we cannot but feel that the area is the better off for the departure of these unfortunates, and the sooner others like them leave, the happier decent citizens will be.

Messmore Garrett, having a clearer understanding of what had happened and what might happen, armed himself and rode out to Amos Calendar's sheep station, where he said, 'They'll get you next . . . or me. You any idea where they might be holing up?'

'I do.'

'Tell me and I'll get them.'

'That's my job. You watch the sheep.'

So Calendar rode in to Centennial and sent a boy up to the headquarters to fetch Jim Lloyd. When the subforeman came down, Calendar said, 'Jim, they killed Coker.'

'I know.'

'He was your friend.'

'He certainly was.'

'They're holed out in the saloon at Blue Valley.'

'What are you goin' to do about it?'

'With your help, I'm gonna kill 'em.'

'My help?'

'He was your friend, wasn't he?'

Jim licked his lips. He wanted to avoid gunfire, but Bufe Coker had been his friend. In the fight with the Comanche, Bufe had saved his life. In the worse fight with the Pettis boys, Bufe had saved him again. They were more than friends, they were brothers, and Jim could recall what Bufe had said on that last night they had ridden the two-to-four: 'If two fellas eat dust in drag positions for four months, that makes 'em brothers, don't it?'

'I'll go.'

And as they were riding west toward the mountains, they were joined by a most unexpected volunteer. They heard their names called: 'Jim, Calendar!' It was Potato Brumbaugh on his favorite horse.

'You after the Pettis boys?'

'We are.'

'I'll join you.'

'Why?' Calendar asked.

'When they tried to burn me out, Zendt and Skimmerhorn helped me.'

'Was they the Pettis boys?'

'Sure. Didn't you know that? The cattlemen in Wyoming hired them.'

No stranger posse ever rode the trail: an aging Russian farmer not directly involved, a young rancher-businessman who hated guns, a deadly marksman lugging a buffalo Sharps, who knew that he must strike first or not at all. The three rode west till they reached the trail leading up Clear Creek to Blue Valley, and there they cut far to the north over rough country.

'The Pettis boys never sleep,' Calendar warned. 'The slightest change attracts their attention. No one must see us.' This was a long speech for Calendar, but each phrase was packed with meaning; a casual traveler stopping by might say, 'Saw three fellows on the trail,' and that would be enough to alert the killers, so that when the strangers reached town they would be gunned down, just on chance.

So the three avengers dismounted and led their horses to the upper rim of the valley, where they could look down into the former mining camp. Tethering their horses, they started the descent, going slowly and very carefully lest even the snap of a twig betray them.

It was about five in the afternoon when they reached the level of the old camp, and there they waited till dusk. What an ugly place it was, Jim thought, as he studied the dirty stream that ran past his feet, the weather-stained boarding of the old mines, the dismal saloon, the few houses. Once he had heard Levi Zendt describe the valley as it had been when Alexander McKeag and Clay Basket occupied it, and he thought, They must have been thinking of a different place.

When dark settled over the valley, Calendar quietly slipped into the main street and with infinite patience scouted the saloon. When he came back his eyes glowed with excitement. 'They're in there!' And then he explained the battle plans: 'I'll take care of Frank. The one with the mustache. Jim, you've got to get Orvid. He's a killer, Jim, and either you get him on the first shot or he'll get us. Potato, you fire at Orvid, too.'

He showed his accomplices how the two gunmen were standing, and Jim interrupted: 'I don't shoot no man in the back.'

'It won't be in the back, not when I'm through.'

'Calendar, I will not shoot a man in the back.'

For the first time in all the years that Jim had known him, Calendar touched another person. Placing his hand on Jim's arm, he said, 'I promise, it won't be in the back.'

Through the darkness the three men crept toward the saloon. Finally they stood at the door, and in the silence Calendar looked at each man. He took a very deep breath, then did a most extraordinary thing.

Kicking open the door, he uttered a wild, terrifying scream that might have come from a pack of maddened coyotes. It was unearthly, hellish, a scream of such intensity that everyone in the bar, including the Pettis boys, automatically turned toward the door and grabbed for their guns.

As they did so, Calendar fired his buffalo gun right at Frank Pettis, blasting a great hole through the outlaw's chest. At the same moment Jim Lloyd fired five times at Orvid Pettis, who stumbled and fell forward, to intercept full in the face an enormous load of buckshot fired by Potato Brumbaugh.

Less than ten seconds after Calendar's scream, the three intruders had backed out of the saloon and disappeared into the night. No one volunteered to pursue them, considering their devastating fire power, nor did any of the witnesses try to identify them. Everything had happened so swiftly that men could not even agree as to how many gunmen there were: 'They was four, I seen them, and one was black.' 'No, they was two, the shotgun and the little fellow with two revolvers.' No one saw three men.

When the avengers were gone, two comments were made, and each passed into the folklore of the ghost town. One ashen-faced man, staring at the body of Orvid Pettis, asked in a whisper, 'How we gonna know which was which? This'n ain't got no head.' And the bartender, gaping in horror at the ghastly hole made in Frank's chest by the buffalo gun, said, 'I could pass a stein of beer through there and not get the edges wet.'

Spring, in 1886, was unusually dry, and years after the disaster residents of the area recalled: 'Spring was mighty dry that year and the summer that followed was even drier.'

Otherwise it was a fine summer, with long even days that produced exhilaration and cool nights made for visiting. On the eastern range Amos Calendar tended his sheep, seeing no one for weeks on end, talking only to his dog Rajah, a singular animal who listened so intently and with so much joy in human companionship that he seemed capable of talking back.

Along the river Potato Brumbaugh pursued his various objectives, forging a farm that was practically a demonstration of how to apply water to land, how to make the desert blossom. He now shipped carloads of melons to Denver, raised sweet corn and was making a big success of his sugar beets, which for the time being he fed to cattle, since there was no sugar factory in the region. 'A strange place,' he complained. 'A land capable of growing the best beets but the men too lazy to build a plant to make sugar. In Russia we had a plant forty years ago.' He intended doing something about this.

In town Levi Zendt was coming to the end of a fruitful life. His many projects had prospered modestly; his son was doing well and only the absence of his daughter Clemma disturbed him. He was sorry that the area no longer contained Indians, for he felt deprived when day after day passed with no blanket-shawled Arapaho coming to his store to sit and watch proceedings. 'This land was made for Indians,' he told Lucinda one day, 'and without them we are all cheated.'

The man in town whose fortunes were taking a dramatic turn for the better was Messmore Garrett. His determination to protect his land and to extend his sheep holdings had been so persistent and so valiant that the bankers had begun to respect him, and even the *Clarion* declared a truce in its war against sheep.

In fact, the paper had become noticeably more tolerant of many things, including Englishmen, as demonstrated by the gracious article it ran in late June:

> A recent visitor to our offices lent grace and a good deal of dignity to our modest surroundings. It was none other than the venerable Earl Venneford of Wye, come to Centennial for the first time to inspect his far-flung holdings. The Earl, a handsome, thin, gray-haired man in his seventies, spoke with an accent that would lend distinction to the Denver stage. He could play Hamlet's uncle or King Lear as well as those who customarily essay those roles, although his voice might be a little weak for the mad scene in the latter play.
>
> When we asked how the ranch was going, he replied like any eastern banker, 'We always seem to be buying more cattle than we sell.' But his most memorable response came when we asked admiringly, 'What kind of cloth is in your jacket?' For the information of our readers it was a heavy bluish-gray with what appeared to be little sticks of sagebrush woven in. 'It's Harris tweed, from the Hebrides,' he told us. 'Cured by leaving it in horsep—.' He invited us to test the truth of this last statement by smelling the cloth, and from our long acquaintance with stables we are prepared to affirm that the noble Earl was telling the truth.

Venneford spent three weeks at the ranch, then rode in a comfortable wagon up to Line Camp Four, where he reveled in the piñon trees and erosion sculptures, but he felt himself really at home only when he reached the Cheyenne Club, with its afternoon polo games and delightful tennis. The long summer evenings he spent outdoors playing croquet by torchlight, a game at which in spite of his years he was most adept.

Charlotte Seccombe was with him constantly, assuring him of the progress of his ranch and introducing him to the other British ranchers in the area. At times the club seemed an adjunct of some military club off St. James's Street, so many Englishmen with military connections kept appearing, but mostly it was the hearty cattlemen of Wyoming who clustered around Venneford to talk about mutual problems. Claude Barker was there with his tales of fending off sheepmen from Horse Creek, and the sturdy Scotsmen from Chugwater gave their own accounts of that feud.

But when the festivities were over, and Lord Venneford was preparing to board the train for Chicago and New York, where the boat would be waiting, he struck fear in Oliver Seccombe's heart by announcing in a thin, reedy voice, 'I've seen wonders I never expected to see. Oysters in Wyoming! The beauty of Line Camp Four! The charm of my hostess! And God knows what else. The only thing I haven't seen is cattle, so as soon as I reach home I shall be sending Finlay Perkin out to look into that. He shall be wanting a strict accounting. Of that I'm sure.' And without further formality, he strode onto the train and disappeared.

It must be said in his favor that in no way did Oliver Seccombe seek to incriminate his wife. He did not accuse her of forcing him to waste money, nor did he ridicule the castle she had built at headquarters. He had enjoyed thirteen years of happiness with her and found her now as exciting and unpredictable as when he first courted her. She still sang her words with a delicious accent; she still laughed at the contrarieties of life and had never once complained that existence in Colorado was less than she had hoped. She loved the range and was an exemplary ranch wife.

It was true that she wasted money, but principally it was her own. That Oliver had 'begged and borrowed a bit from the ranch,' as he put it, was his decision, not hers, and no matter what defalcations Finlay Perkin might uncover, they would rest on Seccombe's head and not his wife's.

'Why is Venneford sending Finlay Perkin out?' Charlotte asked.

'We've spent somewhat more than we can account for,' he evaded.

'What do you mean?'

'Book count. We ought to have a lot more cattle on the land than we do.'

'That's easy to explain. Cows sometimes don't have calves.'

They rode by wagon back to Line Camp Four, and there he forced her to face up to the difficult problems that would be raised when Perkin arrived with his notebooks and papers.

'He'll have a list of every cow we ever bought, and he'll want to tick off each one.'

'Will that be possible?'

'Not with a thousand cowboys could he do it.'

'Then, what's the worry?'

'He'll niggle away until he turns up every discrepancy, and in the end he'll see that somewhere around twenty-four thousand cattle have disappeared.'

'What in the world . . .'

'They have disappeared, Charlotte. No one's stolen them, like that, but they just aren't here. And how can I explain that to a man like Perkin?'

How indeed? He arrived at Cheyenne on September 15, 1886, and insisted that he be taken immediately to Line Camp Four. He was a small, wispish man sixty-six years old, accompanied by so much luggage that it required two porters to lift it off the train and into a special wagon. In the past eighteen years he had never once been outside Bristol, not even to visit his parents in Kincardineshire or the bankers in London, yet from reading reports and studying maps he had an exact knowledge of Wyoming and northern Colorado.

'Ah yes,' he said thinly as he sat in the carriage, hands folded, looking left and right. 'This is the Union Pacific and our lots eighty-one through eighty-seven lie just over there. Yes, this is the deep well we drilled in 1881, and I see it's still pumping. This, I take it, is the new Glidden barbed wire. Is it standing up well?'

He knew to the quarter mile when they should be turning south to reach the camp, and as he approached it he recognized new fencing and pastures from which cattle had been removed. 'It's a pity,' he said, 'a great pity that the government won't sell us these intervening sections.'

'We have the use of them anyway,' Seccombe said with an attempt at airiness.

'Using is never the same as owning,' Perkin said abruptly. 'Ah, this is the gate to the camp itself.'

When the carriage drew up before the cabin, he did not even look at the living quarters but went directly to the low stone barn, inspecting its woodwork and the stalls for the horses. 'Splendid building,' he said. 'In 1868 when Skimmerhorn recommended wood I counseled stone. See how it's stood, as good today as when it was built. Clinger did a fine job.'

'Who?' Seccombe asked.

'Clinger. The stonemason from Cheyenne. Expensive, but in the long run the cheapest. Tell me, before we go in, do you happen to have any of the Illinois Shorthorns pastured nearby?'

'They're off east.'

'Very good.'

During three days of preliminary investigation, everything Perkin wanted to see was either off east or off west, but this absence apparently did not disturb him. He simply noted in his books that the Illinois Shorthorns were for the moment grazing to the east.

He wanted to know everything, and quickly demonstrated that he comprehended much more of the intricate maneuverings of ranch management than Seccombe. His questions were quiet, never provocative, and never abandoned until he had a specific answer which he could write in his book.

'He is on to every discrepancy,' Seccombe told Charlotte the third night as they went to bed.

'He seems to be building a case against you, Oliver. I had the strong feeling that he was recording your answers so that later on he could show them to Skimmerhorn and Lloyd and invite them to contradict you.' To this Seccombe had no response, for he, too, had guessed the nature of Perkin's game.

'Tell me, Oliver, will those two support you?' No reply. 'I mean, can we trust them to be fair?' No reply. 'What I mean, Oliver, is, will it be to their advantage to betray you . . . No, that sounds as if you were guilty of something evil. What I mean is . . .'

'I know what you mean. Skimmerhorn and Lloyd are two of the most honest men in ranching. That's why we've done so well . . . if it weren't for that damned book count Bristol's been relying on.' He paced the floor. 'Why can't they realize that on a ranch this big, you can't go around earmarking every cow?'

'That's what Perkin wants.'

'That's what he'll never get.'

'Then you trust Skimmerhorn?'

'I'd better. He has our fate in his hands.'

They had estimated Perkin correctly, for he was patiently building a document against them. It would be meticulous and just, but it would be terribly damning. What they had not anticipated was his thoroughness when it came to cattle.

'We'll ride down to headquarters,' Seccombe suggested on the fourth morning.

'No,' Perkin said, 'we'll start over at Line Camp Five.'

'What do you wish to see there?'

'I'm going to count the cattle,' he said matter-of-factly. 'We'll start west and work over to the Nebraska border.'

'You can't count . . .'

'That's been the trouble, Seccombe. You may not be able to count, but I can, and I propose to start tomorrow. Assemble the cowboys.'

And when the cowboys reported at Line Camp Five, not far from where the dinosaur bones had been found, Seccombe discovered that Perkin's luggage consisted mainly of cans of special blue paint developed in Germany, and a dab of this paint was to be placed down the spine of every living animal on the four million acres of Venneford Ranch, insofar as Perkin could catch them.

When word was passed, the cowboys began to laugh. Perkin showed no displeasure. 'If we paint each cow, then we won't be tempted to count twice,' he explained. 'By the time we reach Nebraska we'll know exactly how many we have.'

'We'll miss thousands,' a foreman protested. 'You can't ride up every draw. Half our cattle may be in Wyoming right now, looking for good grass. We ain't got much left here.'

'It will be your job to search the draws and if necessary ride into Wyoming,' Perkin said calmly, and for five weeks this prim little man rode in a buckboard eastward across the great prairie, dabbing blobs of German paint on such cattle as could be rounded up and brought before him. He was tireless. Cowboys who had been in the saddle all their lives grew exhausted in the warmth of this unusual autumn, merely following Perkin and his buckboard.

By the time he had worked his way to the Nebraska border he had used up gallons of paint and had been up every draw on the ranch, seen all the watering places, the homesteaded areas and the government sections interspliced with the Venneford holdings.

'You were wise to run the sheepmen off those eastern edges,' he said approvingly, and he praised the fencing program. 'I like to see our own land protected.' But it grew painfully apparent to everyone that no matter how many Crown Vee cattle were daubed with paint, the grand total was pitifully short of what the Venneford outfit had presumably purchased.

'We'll ride back to headquarters,' Seccombe proposed during the last week in October, but Perkin astonished him yet again by saying, 'No, we'll go directly back to Line Camp Five.'

'But why?'

'I want to run a test. We'll inspect all the cattle we find there. Check the paint. See how many we overlooked the first time, then correct our figures accordingly.'

It was a hilarious undertaking, one that cowboys sang about for years afterward:

> Finlay Perkin is a-jerkin'
> One end of an empty rope.
> His bright blue paint has grown quite faint
> The little guy has got no hope.

The song was accurate, if unkind. When the buckboard reached Chalk Cliff the cowboys corralled some two hundred Crown Vee steers, and not one bore a sign of paint. There were sniggers as the little Scotsman inspected each animal and recorded it as a new find. But after he did this for each of the two hundred, it occurred to him that for the first inspection to have missed every one of these steers was unlikely.

'We've had no rain,' he said reflectively.

'None,' Skimmerhorn said.

'Catch me some more animals.'

So they moved to a different area and rounded up another three hundred, and not one of them showed any paint, either. 'The chemist assured me the paint was waterproof,' he said with no intimation of complaint. He was merely reporting what he had been told.

'How about sun-proof?' Skimmerhorn asked.

'On that he didn't commit himself,' Perkin said, so they got some boards and he painted stripes, and the sun that autumn was so strong that after a few days the stripes began to disintegrate, and the costly, time-consuming experiment proved worthless.

'We're back to book count,' he said primly. 'We know there ought to be fifty-three thousand cattle and we hope there are more.'

'It always comes back to book count,' Seccombe said.

Now, at last, they rode to headquarters, and after one look at the costly mansion Perkin knew that he had a substantial case, whether German paint lasted or not.

'I should like to check the books on your buildings,' he said in clipped accents. 'Barns first.'

Seccombe was able to prove how the red barns, the most handsome in Colorado, had been paid for, and the corrals and the storage areas. But when it came to the castle the accounts were in deplorable shape.

'Now, these funds, if I interpret correctly, came from the account of Henry Buckland, your wife's father in Bristol? Good, that can be checked. But these funds over here?'

Seccombe fumbled, and never once did Perkin hurry him or in any way agitate him. If Seccombe drew back from explaining exactly where the funds had originated, Perkin said nothing, made notes and passed on to the next item. His thrust for the jugular was insatiable. He knew that grave misapplications had occurred, but he could not easily penetrate to the specific defalcation, and until he could do so, he had no case, and he knew it.

Then abruptly he left the house and started probing into the irrigation expenses. He could see no reason why Venneford should have spent so much money bringing water onto land that didn't need it, and the more he saw of the ditches and the useless meadows, the more concerned he became, until Skimmerhorn prevailed upon him to visit Potato Brumbaugh, who reacted with enthusiasm: 'Mr. Perkin, look at those grasslands. Look at those stacks of hay for winter feeding.'

'But in this climate we've never needed hay for winter feeding,' Perkin pointed out. 'This is a waste.'

'Mr. Perkin!' Brumbaugh shouted. He pronounced the name Berkin, much to the Scotsman's irritation. 'The winter will come when that hay will be gold. On my farm I have almost as much hay as you do, and the winter will come when I shall sell it for dollars uncounted.'

When the interview ended Perkin asked acidly, 'Who is that man?'

'The most successful farmer in these parts,' Skimmerhorn said. 'A Russian.'

'A Russian!' Perkin exclaimed. 'What's he doing here?' And Brumbaugh's evidence was discounted. The irrigation project was an indefensible wastage of Bristol funds.

On the fifteenth of November, Finlay Perkin knew all he required to know, and that night, in fairness to the Seccombes, he told them frankly the results of his investigation: 'Lord Venneford sent me here to ascertain certain facts. I've done so. You've wasted our money. You've accepted cattle without counting them. I have a strong suspicion that you've been in concert with the sellers. And it's clear that you've sold off our calves and cows to pay for this monstrous castle. I'll present my findings to his Lordship, and I must warn that he may decide to start legal proceedings. Certainly, if he seeks my counsel, I shall advise him to do so, for if I ever saw fraudulent conversion of corporate funds, it's here.' With that he went to bed.

He was not able to catch the train at Cheyenne, for that night the thermometer dropped crazily to several degrees below zero, most improbable for that time of year. 'We'll go tomorrow,' Seccombe advised, but before morning a howling storm attacked, depositing seven inches of snow and piling it in drifts.

'In November it melts quickly,' Seccombe assured his visitor. Certainly he did not want to keep the unpleasant little man a day longer than necessary, but that afternoon the storm increased, throwing down another six inches. On the third night seventeen inches fell. From the northern borders of Montana to the Platte the west was snowbound, and it would remain that way through a long and disastrous winter.

The burden of the blizzard fell principally on Jim Lloyd, for it was his job to keep the cattle alive, and he proceeded in his efforts to do so. In the first hours of the storm he rode to Potato Brumbaugh's farm and told the Russian, 'I'm buying all your hay.'

'Smart move,' Potato said. 'We're due for a long, hard winter.' He would not give Jim all his hay, for he had a few cattle of his own and his bones warned him that this snow was different, but he did sell a portion, keeping the brown piles, now under two feet of snow, on his place till Jim sent his men to haul them away.

When Jim presented the bill on the afternoon of the first day, Finlay Perkin said furiously, 'One little storm and you panic.' To his surprise Jim fought back, briefly but with silencing effect: 'It's my job to feed those cattle. I'm gonna do it.'

On the second day, when drifts had closed the roads and were beginning to cover the windward sides of the ranch buildings, Jim saddled his strongest horse and tried to visit the longhorns in nearby pastures, but he was unable to breast the accumulations of snow. No matter what direction he chose, he could not get far from the ranch, and during that whole day he saw no cattle.

On the third day he had difficulty getting his horse from the stable.

A howling wind had sent the snow whipping across the countryside until it encountered some stationary object; then drifts piled to an amazing height. At the headquarters they reached ten and twelve feet.

On the evening of the third day Jim saw his first cattle. They had come down from the north, moving stolidly with the storm, keeping the wind to their backs. In this way they hoped to stumble upon feed and, more important, water.

The first freezing beasts packed up against a fence, and when later arrivals pushed in behind them, those in front broke down the fence and drifted eastward. Jim tried to halt them, threw out thin supplies of hay from the barns, but they pushed on, always keeping their heads away from the whipping wind. For days they pressed on, till the storm abated, eating nothing, drinking nothing, never resting until they came upon a fence or some other immovable object. At that perilous moment they would begin to pile up, and if not led to safety, many would perish as one heaped upon the other.

'They're drifting with the storm!' Jim told the hands. 'We've got to stop them!'

So the cowboys scattered across the frozen ranch, miles from food or water, and tried valiantly to head off the slowly moving cattle. It was heartbreaking work. The frostbitten men struggled through drifts, their horses deep in snow, and when they did get to the cattle, they could only try to head them in directions which seemed safer than those they were pursuing.

To feed them was impossible. 'We'll have to wait till it quits,' Jim advised Skimmerhorn, and he reported the situation to Seccombe and Perkin.

'Will the loss of cattle be serious?' Perkin asked.

'We could lose them all,' Skimmerhorn said bleakly.

'Oh, dear!' Perkin said. And he canceled his trip back to Bristol. If the blizzard posed a threat of that magnitude, it was his job to stay on the spot and provide what help he could.

He proved surprisingly resourceful. When no thaw came and cattle at the far reaches of the ranch would surely starve, it was he who proposed, 'Load boxcars with Brumbaugh's hay and ship it out to Julesburg. Hire men to distribute it from there.' And when the railroad, sensing that the ranchers had no alternatives, upped the freight rates, it was Perkin who fought them, threatening to write letters to the *London Times*. To Jim this seemed a futile gesture, but it had prompt results in Omaha, since the railroad had to depend substantially on financing from London, and realized that a condemnatory letter in the *Times* might adversely affect bond issues.

But as before, the principal burden fell on Jim Lloyd, and it was he who took teams into the remotest corners of the great ranch, succoring cattle wherever he found them. Thousands of head had wandered down from Wyoming, and he fed them, too, when he came upon them along the Platte. He guessed that perhaps as many as ten thousand Crown Vee longhorns had wandered into Nebraska.

'We won't see them till spring,' he told Perkin when he returned to headquarters.

'But will we find them?' Perkin asked.

'Maybe a thousand,' Jim said.

'You mean nine thousand may die!' the little clerk asked.

'They're probably dead now,' Jim said dolefully.

The Crown Vee animals who had stayed on the ranch survived, thanks to Jim's heroic efforts and the hay he had prudently stored up, and when Perkin accompanied Seccombe to the Cheyenne Club in early January and heard the stories of total disaster that had overtaken some of the Englishmen ranching in Wyoming, he began to appreciate the good management at Venneford.

'There's never been a storm like it,' Claude Barker said. 'For fifty miles you can't see where Horse Creek is—frozen solid and covered over from bank to bank. If the thaw doesn't come soon, we'll be wiped out.'

'No,' Perkin assured him. 'Our man Jim Lloyd told me he had three or four thousand of your cattle down on our pastures.'

'Thank God. They getting any food?'

'Jim's feeding them some hay.'

'Thank God.'

By mid-January it looked as if the freak storm had worn itself out. A series of warm days began to melt the snow, and on the trip back to the ranch Seccombe said, 'Two more days of this and the snow will be off the grass. Then you'll see the cattle recover.'

'Oliver,' the little Scotsman said, 'I am deeply impressed by the men you've hired. They know cattle. Better yet, they love them. Crown Vee came out better than any of the others, and I shall take this into consideration in my report.'

The two men reached headquarters in a state of suspended animosity. Charlotte had a piping-hot dinner waiting, and Perkin told her, 'Your husband turns out to be a prudent rancher,' and she replied stiffly, 'We're so pleased that you could see for yourself what running a ranch involves.' And disregarding her attitude, he said gallantly, 'I'll be leaving Friday, and taking with me the kindest memories.'

Again he did not leave. That night a wind unprecedented in western history roared in from the arctic, dropping the thermometer from a benevolent fifty-three above to a gelid twenty-two below. The moisture which had accumulated from the melting snow froze into an impenetrable layer of ice.

'This is most grave,' Seccombe said when he saw the glistening shield.

'Why?' Perkin asked nervously, unable to comprehend what had hit the ranch.

'The grass is sealed off. No cow can reach a blade of it. If this doesn't melt within two days . . .'

Instead of melting, the ice became even thicker, for the thermometer dropped to minus twenty-seven.

Then, on the night of January 15, the great blizzard of 1887 struck. It piled sixteen inches of snow atop the layers of ice, creating drifts which covered barns and obliterated roads and dropping the temperature to a historic forty-five degrees below zero. All pasturelands were buried beyond the capacity of any animal to penetrate. With no hay in storage, no feedcake available, most ranchers in western America sat impotent by their hearths and prayed for the storm to abate, while millions of cattle froze to death or starved.

For five terrible days the intense cold continued, with more snow each night. The entire prairie was encased in ice, and anguished ranchers were forced to acknowledge that their dangerous gamble of running cattle on an open range, with no stores of feed to succor them in case of storm, had come to an end.

The cow was the animal least fitted to fight a blizzard. The buffalo had learned to swing his massive head and push away the snow. The horse would paw down through the snow, finding grass beneath. Sheep would eat snow if water was lacking. Turkeys roosted in trees to escape the drifts, and chickens pecked till they reached ground and gulped snow to form water. The cow never learned any of these survival tricks; up to its belly in snow, it would die of thirst.

Jim Lloyd had a cowhand from Texas called Red, who fancied himself as a roper. He walked with an exaggerated swagger and kept his thumbs locked in his belt, the way he had seen older men do. He was twenty-two and could be one of the best if he settled down. During one respite in the blizzard Red volunteered to ride the north boundary to report on what was happening. This was sheer bravado, and Jim allowed him every opportunity to change his mind. Not Red! He saddled up and headed east, taking pack rations and a flask. He was gone for nine days, and when he got back he was gaunt and red-eyed.

Finlay Perkin suggested that he come into the kitchen at the castle and report on what he had seen, and he sat there just like the tough cowboy he wanted to be, gripping his coffee cup with both hands and talking in clipped sentences. But then as the phrases came out, his lower lip began to tremble and he had to put his cup down. For long moments he could not speak.

'I seen . . .' He looked helplessly at Seccombe. 'I seen in that draw by the three piñons . . .' He could not go on.

After a period of silence he began again. 'I seen dead cattle piled one on top of another till they seemed to fill the whole draw. I seen Pine Creek lined with what musta been a thousand carcasses. I seen over by the draw that runs into Line Camp Two a whole field of ice with horns and noses sticking out, musta been five hundred longhorns buried there in the first storm. I seen . . .'

He couldn't continue. Dropping his red head onto the table, he remained silent, too tough to cry, too choked to speak. His listeners looked away, and after a while he mumbled, 'Half our herd must be dead.'

It was. But even so, Crown Vee came off better than most, solely because of the unflagging efforts of Jim Lloyd and his feeding teams. When the icy snow did not abate, he encouraged the carpenters to convert the ranch wagons into rude sleighs, and these he drove to all parts of the ranch, hauling hay. He worked eighteen and twenty hours a day, and sometimes when he came unexpectedly upon a herd of longhorns who had perished in some draw, their bleak faces still turned hopefully away from the wind, he came close to tears.

Across the west these were days of anguish, when tough cowboys like Texas Red could not contain the tragedy they saw, when gay and gallant ranchers like Claude Barker at Horse Creek surveyed the situation and said, 'Well, that's the end of the ranch. It was a good thing while it lasted.'

The open-range cattle industry as the ranch barons had enjoyed it in the golden years of 1880 through October of 1886 was gone forever. No more could a man run his cattle wild through the clement winter, depending upon them to forage grass from the lightly frozen ground. No more could a man boast of owning five million acres of unfenced land and cattle so numerous he could not count them. The old days were dead; the Englishmen who had done so much to pioneer the west would be going home. New ideas would be needed: fences, new types of cattle, new systems of control.

At no ranch were the consequences more bizarre than at Venneford, where during the dreadful days three mutually suspicious people were imprisoned within a castle—Oliver, Charlotte and Perkin, each in his separate corner tower. They met only for meals served in the drafty dining room—each keeping a watchful eye upon the other, each aware that the basis of his life was shifting, each pondering how best he could adjust to new requirements. The wind wailed and the ice formed, and each remained in his cell, like monks in a crumbling monastery a thousand years before.

Oliver Seccombe was now sixty-nine years old, a man whose life was fairly well used up. It was ending in decay, with an ugly lawsuit threatening, and he saw no escape from almost certain catastrophe. He would have to surrender his position at the ranch, the lovely days at Line Camp Four among the piñons, his position as squire of the region. Leaving Charlotte's castle would be no sorrow; it had been an expensive demon. But leaving the ranch would be, for this was his creation. Without his persistent enthusiasm it could never have come into being, and it was ironic that he should have been an agent of its destruction. The only consolation he had was that even after the collapse, Charlotte would possess enough money of her own to survive on, and somehow she would be able to find a good life. As for himself, Perkin had quite openly suggested that he resign. Well, ranchers in Argentina were always making inquiries among the Englishmen in Wyoming, and perhaps he could hook up with one of them. His deepest regret would be the loss of the Cheyenne Club, that amiable group of gentlemen, that Athens of the west, where the food was good, the wine better and the talk best of all. Damn, he would miss that club.

Charlotte Seccombe had no such elegiac thoughts. Shrewd girl that she was, she realized something that neither her husband nor Perkin had yet thought about. With the tremendous losses suffered by all ranches during the blizzard—as high as ninety-three percent in some parts of Montana—the discrepancy between Finlay Perkin's book count and the actual number of cattle on the range was wiped out! It simply did not exist! In October 1886 Finlay Perkin could point to his ledgers and say, 'You paid for so-and-so many cattle, but you have only so-and-so many. You must have stolen the difference.' But in March 1887 Seccombe could reply, 'The missing cattle died in the storm.' As the bartender at the Cheyenne Club had cynically observed during the worst of the winter, 'Forget the dead cattle, gentlemen. Doctor your account books.' She perceived that Perkin would have no case in court, even though he might make things unpleasant with the Bristol directors. So she began to treat him with studied contempt, inventing various ways to demean him. She laughed at the wrong time and took delight in contradicting him or even making him look foolish. Twice during the blizzard, when they were locked inside the castle with poor food and inadequate heat, she brought up the subject of the paint. 'We lost a great deal of money and effort on that foolishness,' she said. 'The paint cost little,' Perkin said defensively. 'True, but the hours the cowboys wasted! They could have been cutting fall hay!' As for her husband, she had only the kindliest thoughts, but they were condescending. She saw that he had not the acumen of Perkin, nor the integrity of Skimmerhorn. He was a man gifted with words and initial action, but never one to see a difficult situation through to the end. As she had observed once to Jim Lloyd, whom she respected as a man of courage, 'Oliver has never done a dishonest thing in his life.' When Jim looked up in surprise, she added, 'He's always hired someone else.' She hoped Oliver would come out of this impasse in one piece. Perhaps resigning would be the honorable solution. If not, there were other alternatives, both for him and for her.

On Finlay Perkin the blizzard had a profound effect. Up to now, the cloistered little Scotsman had known a horizon delimited by Kincardineshire and Bristol. But in the storm he found himself at the center of a turbulent world where great fortunes could be dissipated overnight, where nature in one vast sweep of her hand could wipe out an area as large as Europe. But he knew it was more than the blizzard. Ranchers who had fallen into sloppy ways will complain that the storm ruined them, he mused as he shivered in his tower, but they were doomed long before the weather changed. Book count, overgrazing, careless management, stubborn refusal to look at new ways of operating—damn, damn, what a wasted world! He understood what should have been done because he was discovering that he liked cattle. He also had a keen appreciation of land; like Jim Lloyd, he had a feeling for what it could be made to do, what it would balk at. He saw Wyoming and Colorado as empires, scarcely touched so far as capacities were concerned. And most of all, he had evolved a very solid sense of what the cattle ranch of the future ought to be. He was aware that Oliver and Charlotte suspected him of compiling a dossier against them. Far from it. He held them in little consideration; Seccombe had no doubt abused his prerogatives and perhaps had misappropriated Venneford funds for the building of this ridiculous castle, but he was no longer of any central concern. The important thing was to encourage Seccombe to resign as soon as possible. He saw that with the interposition of the blizzard, and the wiping away of whole ranches, it would be petty and unfruitful to make a case at law over the disappearance of a few thousand Crown Vee cattle. He caught himself: What am I saying? A few thousand cattle? He must have diverted twenty thousand. More than six hundred thousand dollars snatched from under our noses. And because of the blizzard, we can't do a thing about it. Our job is to build solidly for the future. Six years of honest operation and we'll have a million back . . .

It was late March when the thaw finally came, and as Jim Lloyd moved about the ranch he saw that many of the emergency measures he had taken had worked. He felt that he had learned from this dreadful year many secrets for the successful handling of cattle, and he was therefore surprised and even a little irritated when Finlay Perkin, with his snooping ways, subjected him to intensive interrogation.

'Did we pay a reasonable sum for our irrigation ditches?'

'Of course. We dug most of them ourselves.'

'Did this Russian, Potato Somebody, profit from the ditches?'

'Mr. Seccombe got the idea from him!'

'Did Mr. Seccombe ever sell any of the hay?'

The little clerk hammered at one point after another, and in time Jim deduced that he was trying to force accusations against Mr. Seccombe, and after this line of questioning had continued for a while Jim got mad and snapped, 'Listen, Mr. Perkin, I work for Mr. Seccombe, and he's one of the best bosses a man ever had. I'll not say a word against him.'

'I would never want you to,' Perkin said evenly.

'You sure sound as if that's what you wanted.'

In some dismay Jim took his problem to Mr. Skimmerhorn, who

slapped his leg and said, 'Damn! He followed the same line with me.'

'What's he up to?' Jim asked. 'Why's he testing Mr. Seccombe after what we've been through?'

Skimmerhorn pondered this for some minutes, drumming with his fingers on the headquarters table. 'The logical conclusion,' he said slowly, 'is that he hasn't been testing Mr. Seccombe at all. He's been testing us.'

'What have we done? Saved his cattle, that's all.'

'He was testing to see whether we were loyal to the man we're working for.'

'I was. How about you?'

'I'm loyal to my boss till the moment he goes to jail.'

'You think Mr. Seccombe may go to jail?'

'Not after the blizzard. Could Mr. Perkin possibly go into court and say to the judge, "Some of our cattle are missing." If the judge owned any, he might reply, "Hell, all of mine are missing." Perkin has no case and he knows it.'

'I don't like that little son-of-a-bitch,' Jim said, and he was not on hand when the Scotsman said goodbye.

Seccombe and his wife took the clerk to Cheyenne, where at the railroad station Perkin said his farewells. 'You did a remarkable job, Oliver, bringing us through that blizzard. You have our thanks.'

'But you're determined to press the lawsuit?'

'Not if you resign, Oliver. You're almost seventy. Resign.'

The train pulled into the station. The conductor cried, 'All aboard for North Platte, Grand Island, Omaha!' and Charlotte bade the little clerk a restrained farewell. Oliver shook hands with him formally, then led Charlotte to the Cheyenne Club.

He found there an autumnal mood, as if the end of an era were at hand. Instead of the vivacity that had always marked the card rooms and the bar during March, when winter was ending and polo about to begin, he found solemnity.

'Claude Barker? Wiped out. Hasn't a sou.'

'Moreton Frewen! Dreadful shape, poor fellow. Said something about South Africa.'

'The Chugwater people? No celebrations in Dundee this year. Someone said their losses were so heavy they may run sheep.'

And so the mournful litany went: thousands of head of cattle starved; on some ranches ninety percent; no more money from Boston; seventeen club members, mind you, seventeen of our most secure men, eliminated —gone bust.

The club itself was in sad shape. More than half the members had lost heavily and were relinquishing membership. The dining rooms, which had once been so gay in spring, were desolate areas where bleak white tablecloths served only to remind the few diners of their fields covered with snow. Even the room in which the Seccombes stayed seemed shabby.

How sad, how infinitely sad it was. Oliver bore it for two days, then told Charlotte with gray despair, 'It's all ending so poorly, so very poorly.'

'Forget that little worm,' she snapped. 'He's powerless to hurt us.'

'It's not Perkin, it's me.'

'There's nothing wrong we can't put right. What's book count? If we'd had the damned cattle, they'd have frozen.'

He was dismayed to realize that she had no comprehension of the anguish he was feeling or its cause, and he tried to explain: 'When I watched Jim Lloyd in the blizzard . . . and Texas Red . . . and saw them taking command, doing the things a cattleman ought to do.'

'They're paid to do it. It's their job.'

'Even Claude Barker rode through the storm thirty miles to summon help . . . lost two fingers . . .'

'Claude Barker is a silly, ineffectual man, and if he'd stayed home, he wouldn't have frozen his fingers.'

He said no more. There was an acceptable way for men to behave if they presumed to run cattle, and he had failed. All heart was gone out of him and much of his strength. He longed for the cleanliness of the great ranch he had put together, but when they returned to the preposterous castle which had diverted so much of his energy, he brooded, barely hearing Charlotte's efforts to cheer him up, avoiding the staff, snapping at Skimmerhorn, drinking each day more heavily and far into the night hours.

Then one day in April, when the sun gave signal that winter was ended, he seemed rejuvenated and moved about the mansion as if he had reached a significant decision. When he came down from his tower he told Charlotte, 'I'd like to see how the grass is doing,' and he walked far to the east, where he could see the limitless plains of the empire he had created.

It was Jim Lloyd who heard the shot echoing in the thin spring air. He could not imagine rustlers so close to the main buildings, but he saddled his horse and rode over the rim of the hill, where he found a white-haired man lying on the prairie, his face against the earth. After a while he rode back to the castle, calling in a soft voice so as to cause no panic, 'Mrs. Seccombe! Mrs. Seccombe! I think you'd better come.'

Levi Zendt received one more letter from his family in Lancaster. It was written in brother Mahlon's cramped, ungenerous script:

Brother Levi,

We have just heard the most exciting news. The United States government is passing a law which permits any white man who married an Indian woman under pressure I mean when he married her to help keep the peace before there were soldiers to shoot the Indians, why he is free to divorce her. All you have to do is go to the postoffice and tell them that you had to marry the Indian and they will tell you how you can get divorced and it wont cost you nothing.

This is a fine chance Levi to correct a bad thing because as you know your brothers and me have been mighty ashamed of you being married to that Indian, and she being sister to the Paskinel murderers, and we have kept it very quiet unless the people in Lancaster heard about it. Now you can make everything right. Just go to the postoffice.

Your brother,
Mahlon

Levi was so appalled by the letter that he threw it down, then stared at it, unable to believe that another human being could write in such manner of a woman he had never seen and about whom he knew nothing, except that she was an Indian. He shook his head in disgust, then lifted the sheet of paper by one unsavory corner and with his left hand applied a match to it. He did not want it about where Lucinda might stumble across it, but as it was burning close to his fingers his wife passed, tall and graceful, and she saw the fire and asked, 'What are you doing?'

'Burning an old bill,' he said.

'I hope it's paid.'

'Long ago,' he replied, and the ashes fell to the floor.

But he could not protect her from the indignity of the new law. One morning as he was sweeping out the store he heard her laughing, and when he turned to see her standing in sunlight, she was holding a printed broadside. It explained things pretty much as Mahlon had reported, except that the husband who wished to be free should go to the court-house, not the post office. She thrust the handbill at him, and after reading only a few lines he crumpled it, uttering several Mennonite obscenities.

'I'm sorry you saw it,' he said.

'You knew about it?'

'Trust Mahlon. That bill I said I was burning, it was Mahlon telling me of my wonderful opportunity.' He put his arm about her and said softly, 'This is a disgraceful thing for the government to do. The last in a long line . . .'

'They're confused,' Lucinda said, feeling very Indian in her resentment. But as a woman, she could not resist testing the man with whom she had lived for so long, through so many divergencies and trials. 'You can get rid of me,' she whispered.

He had led her to a chair, and as she sat he stood before her, a heavy-set Dutchman nearing seventy, a man who had wanted her more than anything else in life. 'Get rid of you!' he repeated. 'If you were back in St. Louis again, I'd crawl on my knees to fetch you.'

She looked up at him and smiled, and reached out her hand.

* * *

As soon as Finlay Perkin returned safely to Bristol, he drafted one of the sagest documents ever to come from the cattle country. It was addressed to the Venneford directors, but with his customary prudence he saw fit to send copies to Skimmerhorn and Lloyd. After a brilliant analysis of the industry as it would have to operate following the blizzard, he gave these instructions:

> 1. We must get rid of the stupid idea that we can supervise a ranch of four million acres. Sell off all land east of Line Camp Two. Sell off all land north of the Colorado-Wyoming border.
>
> 2. Hold back Line Camp Four, with the short trees, and sell it as a separate parcel to some rich industrialist in Cheyenne.
>
> 3. When our holdings are compact, fence them in.
>
> 4. Settlers who want to erect towns on our property should be given every opportunity to buy personal holdings, and we should contribute free land for the town hall, the churches, the school and a small business district.
>
> 5. Sheep are an abomination. Keep them out.
>
> 6. Grow more hay.
>
> 7. John Skimmerhorn is to be manager. Jim Lloyd is to be his assistant. The young cowboy known as Texas Red is to take Lloyd's old job. These are tested men, of proven loyalty. We should rely upon their guidance for many years.

And then he added, out of the blue as it were, an eighth directive which would in the long run be more determinative than any of the others, making Crown Vee the famous ranch of the next forty years:

> 8. I believe our ranch will best prosper if we speedily submerge our longhorns and Shorthorns and change over completely to Herefords. From what I saw of our range, and its climate, the Hereford will thrive and we will prosper therefrom. I am sending by Cunard liner and Union Pacific a fine Hereford bull I saw at Leominster and six of the best Hereford cows. Skimmerhorn is to consult with T. L. Miller, of Beecher, Illinois, and acquire others.

He ended with a clerk's summary, a sensible conclusion to the disaster of 1886–1887:

> 9. We have expunged from our books thirty thousand cattle, presumed to be dead in the snow. This represents a loss of three-quarters of a million dollars, but we are prepared to absorb it in the faith that from a proper second start we can quickly recover. I feel certain that Skimmerhorn and Lloyd must have their own private guesses as to how many cattle we actually have. For the moment we shall enter the figure as twenty thousand, but if that is too high or too low, Skimmerhorn must

inform us immediately, for never again do we wish to rely upon book count.

When the first carload of Herefords reached Centennial, Jim Lloyd's life assumed a new direction. He was at the station, of course, when they arrived, and after the planks were carefully laid and the first two cows descended and he saw those handsome white faces and reddish bodies, the sturdy legs and the long, straight backs, he knew that *real* cattle were at last coming under his care.

But when the bull came down, Jim and all those watching caught their breath, and you could hear sighs, for here was one of the finest animals England had so far produced, King Bristol, close to a ton in weight, with a flawless white face and ponderous red body. His horns sloped down at a sharp angle, ending well below his eyes. His forehead was ample, studded with bone and covered with white curly hair. His snout was a healthy pale pink and his mouth drooped as if he had a surly disposition, while down the back of his neck ran a heavy line of twisted white hair.

What made him most memorable, during those first few minutes, so that people throughout Colorado would soon be talking of King Bristol, was the majestic way he walked, flexing the knees of his forelegs, pulling the hoofs far back, then plopping them down heavily, as if he owned the earth. The cows had come down the ramp tentatively, for to them this was a new, untested land; but the bull came clumping down as if to occupy an empire.

He took possession of the ranch, siring calves from each of the six Hereford cows and from eighteen of the longhorns, too. From his pure Hereford offspring came four bulls, three of whom would be kept for the herd; the bulls from longhorn cows were castrated to be sold later as fat steers.

But the half-longhorn, half-Hereford heifers were kept, and bred back to Hereford bulls, and their offspring were three parts Hereford, one part longhorn; and after five such crosses, Crown Vee had cows that were thirty-one parts Hereford, one part longhorn, and at that point, biologically speaking, the famous longhorns of Texas were extinct so far as Venneford Ranch was concerned.

How beautiful the Herefords were! In the morning when Jim went out to check them in the distant pastures he would delight as a line of heifers turned to face him, their white countenances shining in the sun, their red flanks swollen with unborn calves. No domesticated cattle had ever had the capacity to generate love in a man's heart the way a string of Herefords could. They were clean beasts, easy to handle, responsive to good treatment and astonishingly able to fend for themselves in unfavorable conditions.

'Herefords will survive where others will perish' became the axiom of the unprotected range. The cows were good mothers too, but most of all, they were beautiful and well suited to range conditions in the west.

'They stand on the range as if they had been carved there,' Jim told Skimmerhorn one morning as they surveyed the new calves. 'A calf one day old looks ready to fight a wolf.'

But the stunning animals were the great Hereford bulls. King Bristol became the most famous stud in the west, with other ranchers hauling cows long distances on the chance they might throw a bull his equal. He grew extremely heavy, walking like a mountain from one valley to the next, and Jim never tired of seeing him flex those massive knees, drawing his hoofs in, then throwing them forward to eat up the next reach of earth.

His sons, too, were fine bulls, and some built distinguished reputations on other ranches, but none really compared with the massive progenitor. He was indeed a king, and other ranchers, buying his offspring, would stand for some minutes, just looking at the old fellow and admiring his perfect configuration, his massive head, the down-drooping horns and the heavy snout.

'A child can lead him,' Jim assured the visitors, and sometimes he would allow Ellen Mercy, John Skimmerhorn's granddaughter, to bring the great bull to the fence. But the thing that pleased Jim most about the Herefords was, as he said, 'they look so right on the land.' It was as if the clever breeders of Herefordshire, starting a hundred years earlier, had bred this unique animal from Old English strains for the specific purpose of filling the western ranges in America.

The ranch made its income in two ways. It castrated nineteen-twentieths of its male calves, allowed them to wander over the range and sold them at age three to packers in Chicago, receiving cash in return. The heifers were kept on the ranch to breed, but each year ranch owners from all parts of the west visited Venneford to buy Crown Vee heifers for upgrading their own stock, and a few were released at good prices. Also, from time to time Venneford sold young bulls to start Hereford herds in other areas. Thanks largely to the pioneering efforts of the Venneford people, and Jim Lloyd's scrupulous attention to honest breeding, the Hereford became the noble animal of the west, and there were many like Jim whose hearts beat faster when they saw the range area populated by 'white-faces.'

Some people claimed afterward that the bishop in Chicago had done it on purpose, because, as they pointed out, his father had tried to ranch in Nebraska and had failed. But there seemed little likelihood that any churchman could have been so malicious.

The Union Church on Third Street required a new minister, and the bishop in Chicago sent a glowing report about a serious young man named Bluntworthy who had done a good job in rural Iowa. The bishop did not confide, however, his personal opinion that young Bluntworthy was one of the most gawky and naïve clergymen who had ever served under him. The congregation voted to invite him to preach a trial sermon, and a committee of six, including John Skimmerhorn, Jim Lloyd and three other ranchers, was directed to meet the train, take the reverend to his hotel room and produce him for the Sunday service.

The more they talked with the tall shy man, the more they liked him. His theology seemed sound; he had a reassuring attitude toward pastoral work; and he loved farms: 'I was brought up on one and feel that towns like Centennial, representing as they do the best of urban and rural, will form the backbone of this nation.'

'You couldn't have ideas much better than that,' Skimmerhorn said approvingly, and at the church, even before Bluntworthy began to preach, committee members passed the word, 'We've found our man,' and the banker's wife elbowed her way into the group to insist that the new reverend dine with them. He accepted with a smile which avoided unctuousness.

When he opened the service with prayer, his delivery was firm, and when the first hymn was sung, his voice could be heard, not too strong but right on key. Men who had been worried about their chance of finding the proper minister prepared to contribute with extra generosity to the collection plates, but then Bluntworthy spoiled everything when he began to preach.

'My text stands close to the heart of every true Christian, for better than any other it epitomizes the spirit of our Lord. It comes, fittingly, from the last chapter of the last Gospel, John 21.'

A rancher in the front pew who knew his Bible muttered, 'Oh, no!' but Reverend Bluntworthy in his firm, clear voice lined out the message: ' "Jesus saith to Simon Peter . . . Feed my lambs." ' A whisper passed along the pews. ' "He saith to him the second time . . . Feed my sheep." ' Skimmerhorn and Lloyd looked at each other in confusion. ' "He saith unto him the third time, Simon, son of Jonas . . . Feed my sheep." '

From this unfortunate beginning Bluntworthy launched into a perfervid oration about sheep as the symbol of humankind, Jesus as the shepherd, and the world as a great meadow in which right-thinking men took it upon themselves as a holy obligation to *Feed my sheep*. He must have used this exhortation fifteen times, increasing the volume of his voice until at the end of his sermon he implored every man in church to go forth and become a shepherd.

The collection was one of the bleakest ever taken at Union Church, and in the closing hymn only the minister's voice could be heard.

It was a custom in Colorado churches for members of the committee to stand in the doorway with the minister as parishioners left, but three of the members refused. 'The man must be a fool,' one said, and his neighbor muttered, 'He'd have been smarter to use Exodus 22, verse 1 for his text. There God said that if one of His people stole an ox, he must give back five oxen. But if he stole a sheep, he had to give back only four. God understood.'

The banker's wife sent a boy to inform Skimmerhorn and Lloyd that her husband had been called to Denver and she could not therefore have the minister to dinner, and half the congregation left by a side door so they wouldn't have to shake hands with the perplexed visitor, who was left standing alone.

Finally Jim Lloyd took his place beside the clergyman, and some semblance of decency was maintained, but when the parishioners were gone, Jim was left with the bewildered minister. 'Let's have dinner at the hotel,' Jim said. 'You can catch the evening train.'

'I had hoped to meet . . .'

Jim felt he owed the man some kind of explanation, so as the meal was being served, with several ranch families staring balefully at Bluntworthy, he said, 'The Lord may be partial to sheep, but this is Hereford country.'

As these words were spoken, Reverend Bluntworthy was about to put a forkful of food into his mouth, but his right arm froze and over his face came first a look of puzzlement, then pained comprehension, and he put down his fork and said, 'I don't feel hungry. In fact, I may be sick, if you'll excuse me.'

'You can rest in your room,' Jim said. 'The five thirty-eight will come in over there.'

The Crown Vee Herefords suffered from one major weakness which afflicted all American Herefords: they were cat-hammed, and whenever Hereford men met with other stockmen, especially Black Angus breeders, they had to suffer the jibe: 'Up front you have a good-looking animal, but it's awful cat-hammed.' To this charge, there was no rebuttal, for whereas the forequarters were sturdy, they tapered off too quickly, producing a hindquarter much like a cat's, lean and scrawny. This not only made the Hereford fore-heavy, but it also cut down on the steaks he could provide, and that's where the money lay.

'We've got to eliminate those cat-hams,' Jim told Skimmerhorn. 'You ever seen a Hereford bull with real strong hindquarters?'

'No, but they must exist.'

So the two cattlemen began their search for the young bull that would correct the deficiency, but with no success. Exhausting local sources, Jim went as far as Indiana, where the Hereford was popular, but those bulls were as cat-hammed as his.

'Looks as if we're stuck with what we've got,' he reported when he reached home, but he continued looking, and one day he came up with a good idea: 'Let's write to Mrs. Seccombe, in Bristol. She could go right into the Hereford country and try to find us something.' So Jim wrote to the widow, and he and Skimmerhorn waited impatiently for her to reply.

One afternoon as Jim was passing time with Levi Zendt at the store, he noticed how the old Dutchman walked, picking up his feet and planting them solidly, and he burst into laughter. 'What's so funny?' Levi asked.

'You walk just like King Bristol.' Jim chuckled, and he imitated the great bull, and Levi understood the joke but did not laugh.

'If I was you, James, and I was thirty-four, I wouldn't be content to be in love with no herd of cows, white-faced or not.'

Jim flushed. Others had teased him about tending his Herefords so lovingly, and he asked, 'What would you do, Levi?'

'Find me a girl and get married.' And instantly Jim replied, 'If I could find Clemma, I'd get married.' And Levi asked, 'After all these years?'

Yes, after twenty years Jim Lloyd still believed that one day a stranger would come to Centennial with news of Clemma's whereabouts, and he would hurry there to claim her. No stranger came, but one afternoon the army officer who had been stationed in Denver years before did return to the area, and as a courtesy he stopped by Centennial to pay his respects to the Zendts.

'Yes,' he said expansively, after informing them of his duty along the Canadian border and of his adventures in pacifying Indians, 'believe it or not, I've met your daughter. Actually talked with her. I was waiting to change trains in Chicago and went into this little Irish restaurant. Kilbride's Kerry Roost . . .'

As soon as Lucinda had the name properly written down she sent a messenger up to the ranch to inform Jim Lloyd, and he rushed down to discuss the startling news that Clemma had been located. And once more he made plans to seek her out.

'James!' Levi reasoned when the cowboy told him he was going to Chicago. 'She's known where you were all these years. If she'd wanted . . .'

'Don't you care for your own daughter?' Jim cried. 'All you ever think about is your son. Because he's here, helping you. Well, Clemma's not here, and she needs me.'

Levi saw no sense in further argument, no reason to explain to this irrational cowboy that he thought of Clemma every night, even prayed for her in Mennonite German.

So Jim caught the night train to Chicago, and as soon as he landed in that busy city, hurried to Kilbride's Kerry Roost, where the white-haired, lugubrious owner remembered Clemma Ferguson: 'Fine-looking girl. Good waitress.'

'Where is she now?'

'Owner of a fancy restaurant came in here for lunch, saw her, offered her a better job.' He shook his head mournfully, as if to indicate that bad luck hounded him.

Jim found her working in an oak-paneled restaurant near the railway station used by the Union Pacific. From the doorway he watched her as she managed her customers with that raffish smile and naughty good humor he had loved years ago. She seemed smaller and her eyes were deep-sunk. She was older, much older, but strangely, she did not look worn out.

He waited till she paused in her work, then walked firmly toward her, extending his hand. 'It's me, Jim Lloyd. You're to come home with me.'

As gaily as if she had talked with him only a day ago, she said, 'Jim! How nice to see you again.'

'You're to come home,' he repeated.

'Sit down. I'll bring you a menu.' She deposited him at one of her tables, and after a decent interval, handed him a printed menu offering many dishes.

Later she came swinging back, treating him as if he were a first-time customer. 'The lamb's good.'

'I don't eat lamb.'

'Of course not. The veal here is very good. Crown Vee calves only.' She was laughing at him, and before he could order she had moved deftly away to tend another customer.

When she returned, with her order pad open, she asked, 'What is your desire?' and the words sounded so awful that he threw the menu down, then quickly recovered it and said, 'I'll take the veal.'

'You'll not regret it,' she said professionally, and after he had finished the excellent meal, unable even to speak a dozen words to her, she presented him with a bill, and he caught her hand.

'Please!' she whispered. 'Mr. Marshall watches me.' She took his money and returned with his change.

'When can I see you?' he pleaded.

'I work here every night.'

So every night he walked from his quarters near the railway station to the restaurant and tried unsuccessfully to engage her in serious conversation. On the fourth night he grew desperate, and finally thought of something which he hoped would pierce her armor: 'Your parents can't live forever. Don't you want to see them?'

'I see lots of people,' she parried, but he could see that she was affected.

'Not too much idling, there,' Mr. Marshall warned as he walked by.

'What keeps you here?' Jim whispered when the owner had moved on.

'Wait for me outside,' she said in a low voice.

She led him to her cheerless room, where she tried to convince him that return to Centennial was impossible: 'I like the city. I never want to go back to that tiny town.'

'You like this?' And with a wave of his hand he indicated the drabness of her flat. 'Surely you can remember the good land?'

She cut him off. 'Here in Chicago it doesn't matter if you're an Indian. Life is better when no one knows who you are.'

The bleakness of such reasoning was so contrary to the warm love he had known on that Texas farm with his mother, and so alien to the friendships he had experienced on the trail north with Poteet that he could not accept it. 'You must come home. Where people love you,' he pleaded.

She replied, 'You know I'm grateful to you, Jim. Coming all the way to Chicago just to talk with me.'

'I went to St. Louis, too.'

For a brief moment she appreciated the stubborn love this cowboy must always have had for her, and she was tempted. 'I'd marry you . . . if I could. You know that. But I already have a husband.'

'Ferguson? I was told he left you.'

'He did. But we're still married.'

'Get a divorce. That's no problem. We'll go to court tomorrow.'

This innocent phrase had a terrifying effect on Clemma. She drew back, and a real look of terror came into her eyes. Without another word she ran past him and out the door, and for three days Jim could not find her.

Eager for any clue to her strange behavior, he went to the Kerry Roost to ask the mournful proprietor, 'Has Clemma been here?'

'Nope.'

Jim stayed at the counter, explaining that things had gone well with them until the mention of divorce sent her flying away.

'She's never been divorced, so far as I know,' Kilbride said.

Jim toyed with his coffee cup, trying to re-create the scene. 'I did mention divorce . . . said she could go into any court . . .'

'Well,' Kilbride broke in. 'That explains it.'

'You mean court?'

The Irishman seemed hesitant to explain, but Jim reached out and caught him by the wrist. 'Has she ever been in court?'

'Just that once . . . when the judge gave her a year.'

'You mean in jail? A year?'

'It wasn't her fault. Even the judge admitted that. It was that fellow Harrigan who gave her the bad checks to cash.'

'Where is he?' Jim asked, instinctively reaching for his belt, as if he were once more carrying Mule Canby's army Colt's.

'He skedaddled . . . and she went to jail.'

'Jail!' Jim repeated with all the anguish he would have experienced if the sentence had been his. 'God, I've got to find her.'

But as he started for the door the weary Irishman said quietly, 'Young bucko! Finish your coffee.' And when Jim returned to his seat at the counter the old man leaned forward to confide, 'I've seen all sorts in my time, and I've learned one thing. If a girl takes it in her mind to run away, no man on earth can stop her. I couldn't keep Clemma in my restaurant, and you can't keep her in your bed.'

With each word Kilbride spoke, Jim's tired and muddled brain visualized a headstrong young woman with high cheekbonès and squarish jaw; she was fleeing the prairie as if braves of an alien tribe were pursuing her, and there was no mortal way of stopping her.

With a pain so great he could not contemplate it, nor seek relief, he walked through the desolate streets and back to his lodging. There he packed his bag, then caught the train for Omaha. As the wheels rattled through the darkness he slowly began to gain control of his emotions. I'll be a fool no longer, he pledged. There's always the ranch. And a man never knows enough about Herefords. I'll work. I'll work.

He believed he had found the solution to his problem, and that he was at last free of Clemma. But then the rhythmic clacking of the wheels reminded him of the girl's teasing laughter, and all his bold defenses crumbled. Covering his ears to stifle her taunts, he confessed: It must have been my fault. If I had been able to bring her back to Centennial . . . And as dawn broke over the prairie, he could see in the flaming clouds the figure of an Indian girl, running and laughing.

After Oliver Seccombe shot himself, his young widow, not too surprised by this action, faced a series of perplexing decisions: Where to live? How to dispose of her castle? And especially, where to look for a new husband?

Her confusion was unraveled, as she might have expected, by old Finlay Perkin. Anticipating her troubles, he wrote:

> You must come to Bristol. The directors will buy your castle, deducting such moneys as they feel you owe them. And as for the ranch, I want to assure you that I have every confidence in Skimmerhorn and Lloyd, two trustworthy and loyal men. They are ideally prepared to look after your interests.

It was a strange letter. 'Your interests.' Why had he spoken as if the ranch belonged to her?

When she arrived in Bristol she understood. Earl Venneford was a very old man, and he had sold all his stock in the ranch except one large block, which he intended deeding to Charlotte, whose mother had been related to him. When Charlotte visited him to pay her respects she found him painfully thin, bundled up in tweeds, but bright of eye.

'You're a spunky girl,' he said. 'I'm giving you my share of the ranch.

I want to think of those wild acres as belonging to someone who will appreciate them.' He asked what her plans were, and when she proved vague, he said, 'Find yourself a good man . . . someone who's served in India . . . or an army man with African experience. How old are you?'

'Thirty-six.'

'Prime of life. Woman's never better. Has some sense to go along with her beauty, and you always were a beauty, Charlotte.' Then he asked bluntly, 'Was it Seccombe who stole our money out there?'

'He stole nothing. He managed the ranch well, and if the blizzards hadn't come . . .'

'I've found that blizzards usually do come,' he said.

Later that afternoon, when she informed her father that through the kindness of the old earl she now owned a substantial portion of the ranch, he surprised her by confiding that one day she would own a great deal more, because it was he who had bought the shares the old earl had disposed of. 'When I die, you'll own nearly half the stock.'

'Is it a good investment?' she asked.

'Excellent. Of course, you'll never make any money running cattle— too much book count.'

'Where will the profit come from?'

'Land. Each year that enormous spread of land will become more valuable. Never sell, even if you have to borrow money to pay the taxes, because that land is gold.'

He advised strongly against her ever returning to Colorado. 'Keep out of their way. It's a man's job, and your job is to stay here, rely on Finlay Perkin and collect your dividends.'

'What if Perkin dies?'

'He'll never die,' Buckland said. 'He'll wither down to a little lump, but he'll still be able to scratch a pen.'

When she met with the old factotum she found him as vital as ever, a wisp of a man with only one concern in life: to keep the distant ranch profitable. 'Miss Charlotte,' he said in an effort to erase the bitterness which had marked their last encounter, 'one day you'll own a great ranch . . . that is, a fair portion of it. I hope to serve you as faithfully as I have served your predecessors.'

'I couldn't get along without you,' she said, and having placed her confidence in the little Scotsman, she turned to her major problem.

She spent her time in Bristol society, renewing old acquaintances and learning afresh how pleasant life could be in the placid west of England. She was more handsome than ever, in a horsy way, and since she was known to be an heiress, she became an attractive target for bachelors, either eligible or ineligible, who were seeking rich wives.

Most of them seemed interchangeable, like the parts of those new guns, where you could switch stocks and barrels and sights and never know the difference. There was one widower of forty-eight, home from

India, but his life was dictated by his regiment, and when Charlotte was invited to dine with some of his fellow officers in London, it was painfully obvious that she was there on approval. Her being a good horsewoman enhanced her chances of acceptance, but her strong views on justice for Indians rather shot holes in her score, and by the time the evening was over, she knew that she had failed her tests. She was not for the regimental mess in India.

And then, in rapid-fire succession, two deaths made her desultory courtships seem unimportant. The old earl died peacefully one day, and scarcely was he buried when Henry Buckland, a much younger man but grossly overweight, dropped dead. It fell to Charlotte to supervise both funerals, and in this distressful time it was Finlay Perkin who helped her most. He was a canny gnome, and on the way home from her father's funeral she confided, 'I've received a perplexing letter from Colorado. All about cat-hamming and what I must do to avoid it.'

She showed him Lloyd's letter, which he immediately saw as a way for diverting her from her sorrow. 'What we must do, and promptly, Miss Charlotte, is search the countryside for a good bull.' So he took her from one farm to another; they found many bulls, but none with the characteristics they sought. And then one afternoon, as they rode home in disappointment, Perkin startled her with a proposal she could not have anticipated.

'When we do find our bull, Miss Charlotte, I think you should take him out to Colorado.'

'I never expect to see the place again.'

'I know, your father told me he advised you to stand clear. But I'm afraid he gave bad advice.'

'How?'

'Isn't it obvious, child? Bristol's not for you. The men you've been wasting your time on . . . you'd marry none of them. Go back and find yourself one of the Englishmen working the ranches in Wyoming—daring men like Moreton Frewen and Claude Barker.'

She did not respond to his counsel on marriage, but his mention of the west lingered most hauntingly. At times she would be looking at some cultivated, rock-walled English field and would see instead the sweeping prairie. Flakes of snow would fall and she would see a blizzard. Life in western America had a majesty, and the memory of it possessed her.

And then one day she and Perkin found their bull, and one sight of it made up her mind. She wanted to watch it grow on the prairie. She was homesick for Colorado. That night Perkin wrote to Skimmerhorn:

> I feel every confidence that he is the bull we seek. He is from an admirable strain of dams, and I have always believed the inherent quality of a bull to be derived from the female side. In the rear he is most heavy,

like his dam, and Charlotte has given him the appropriate name of Confidence. She has decided to bring him to you.

When she arrived with this excellent animal at the Centennial station, there was none of the awe that had greeted King Bristol, for the young bull lacked every characteristic which had made that noble beast so predominant: he was not heavy; he did not stride with kingly grace; he lacked space between his emerging horns. He had only two conspicuous qualities—extremely substantial rear quarters with never a hint of cat-hamming, and a prepotent power to stamp upon his offspring, especially his bull calves, the physical attributes he possessed.

'Cat-hamming is ended,' Skimmerhorn said, leading the young bull to a dray. Then, turning to the new owner: 'Miss Charlotte, it will seem so natural, having you in the castle again.'

'I'll be traveling in Wyoming,' she said.

Her search for a husband in Wyoming proved fruitless. The kinds of young Englishmen she had once known had long since vanished, expelled by the blizzard and the economic disaster that followed. The levity and the long evenings of croquet were gone, and several times she had the dismal feeling that her return to the west had been a mistake.

On her ride back to Venneford she realized with a pang that the ranch no longer owned Line Camp Four, where she had spent so many delightful days. It had been sold to a Cheyenne merchant, who used it several weeks each year. She considered buying it back, but took no steps to do so, for she was at odds with herself, unable to determine anything.

One day as she was walking idly out to inspect Confidence, she happened to see Jim Lloyd approaching from the other direction, and for the first time she noticed how straight he was, how lithe. She had rarely spoken to him but did remember that morning when he came to report her husband's suicide. He had been gentle and perhaps more stricken than she by the death of his long-time boss. Beyond that she knew nothing except that he had come north as a boy of fourteen and through the years had been mixed up in some way with an Indian girl.

Actually, she knew him best through the letters of Finlay Perkin, who held him in the highest regard. What were the phrases? 'Absolute trust . . . sober good judgment . . . fine man with Herefords.'

'Hello, Mr. Lloyd,' she said as he reached the corral fence. 'How's the bull?'

'He's doing great, ma'am,' Jim said.

'As good as you hoped?'

'Better. He's . . . he's . . .' She wondered what word he was groping for and was surprised when he said, 'He's voluntary. Moves right out. That's a good sign in a bull.'

'He's certainly not cat-hammed,' she said.

They began to talk about many things, and she was impressed with his broad knowledge. He had read widely, had studied economics and was capable of expressing strong opinions. He was really much better informed than Mr. Skimmerhorn, who stuck pretty much to ranching. But she also detected that he was an isolated man, extremely lonely, and she sensed that if these were critical years for her, trying as she was to settle upon patterns she would follow for the rest of her life, they were doubly crucial for this cowboy. For her, finding a new husband was merely following a style of life; for him, taking a wife could be life itself, the acceptance of another human being; and she supposed that she was the only means whereby he could escape from the prison of loneliness in which he had immured himself.

So one afternoon she said, 'Mr. Lloyd, would you care to have dinner with me tonight?'

'I'd be most obliged,' he said, and at six promptly, he appeared at the door of the castle.

'I had in mind about eight,' she said, and he replied, 'I work early, ma'am.'

So she hurried up the cook and they sat in a kind of regal splendor in the round dining room, and she asked him how the sales were going, and then they got into differential freight rates and the possibility that if a sugar-beet factory ever started in the area, the beet tops might be utilized as feed for the Venneford cattle.

Suddenly she asked, 'Are you still involved with that Indian girl?'

He reddened and said, 'I wanted to marry her. She wouldn't have me.'

It was growing late and Jim excused himself, but next day Charlotte saw him at the loading chute and said, 'Last night was so pleasant, James. Could you come to dinner again tonight?'

'No,' he said, and when she showed disappointment, he added, 'Because I'm inviting you to Centennial for a bite.'

At six he was at the door with a polished rig drawn by two bays. They rode quietly into town and dined at the Railway Arms, where several townsmen greeted them, then turned away to discuss the impropriety of an English gentlewoman's consorting with a cowboy.

The same thing bothered Jim. In later years it would become accepted for heiresses or wealthy widows inheriting ranches to socialize with cowboys, but in 1889 such a relationship bore the marks of scandal, and Jim was a very proper man. He was also worried by the fact that he was two years younger than Charlotte, and that she had more money than he, more power at the ranch.

Offsetting these doubts was her beauty and her lively interest in the west. She was fun to talk with, always ready for an adventure, and she maintained a certain organization in her life. She really was a superior woman, Jim concluded, and he acknowledged his good luck in having excited her interest.

And so in this unresolved fashion they drifted through the mild winter and spring of 1889, dining here and there, working together, reading the same books and checking the same figures. It could have continued this way for a long time, but recently Charlotte had turned thirty-seven, and although the prairie she had learned to cherish was still expansive, her own life was closing in. She had rejected Bristol and would never return there. India was out. Africa, too. All that remained was her future in Colorado, and she had better get it organized.

So on a day in June she arranged a picnic, and even though she no longer owned Line Camp Four, she and Jim trespassed there, among the piñons and eroding spires, and it was after speaking of her regret at having allowed this heavenly spot to be sold that she said boldly, 'If we don't marry, James, then in the years to come we'll have other regrets.'

He was playing with a pine needle, holding it between his thumbs to make a whistle. Blowing a long, sweet blast, he dropped his hands and without looking at Charlotte, said, 'You're right.'

'Then what shall we do about it?'

'Get married, I guess.'

Impulsively she thwacked him over the head. 'Damn it! Are you proposing?'

'Yes!' he cried happily. Grabbing her around the waist, he hoisted her high in the air and carried her into the little stone house he had built twenty years before.

When their engagement was announced, there was much discussion of how that canny Texan had arranged 'a good thing for hisse'f.' The ladies wondered how a rich gentlewoman like Charlotte could demean herself by marrying a poor cowboy, but the town banker confided, 'You got it all wrong, ladies. Jim Lloyd's no pauper. I'd call him one of the best catches in town.' When the women asked how this could be, the banker explained, 'Because he saves his money, that's why.'

The wedding was to be held in the Union Church soon after the Fourth of July, but on the first of that month the Union Pacific brought an unexpected guest to Centennial. It was Clemma Zendt Ferguson, only thirty-four years old but with the look of a tired and defeated woman.

As soon as Jim Lloyd heard she was in town he rushed to her parents' home and found her in the kitchen. 'I've got my divorce,' she said dully. 'I'm ready to marry you now.'

Ignoring everything that had happened in recent months, Jim swept her into his arms, and as he kissed her his heart felt as if it were expanding. 'I'm so glad you've come home,' he said.

That one embrace settled all problems for Jim. He realized that he was under serious obligation to marry Charlotte, and normally he could have done nothing to embarrass that fine woman. He knew also the advantages she would bring him, and whereas the community might view with distaste the marriage of a wealthy gentlewoman to a cowboy, he trusted that she would never use that whip against him. She was an honorable woman, and she would make a good wife. But to be with

Clemma was to be with the earth he loved, with the Indian west that he revered. She was a total vision of life, and to win her, any sacrifice would be justified.

'Will you marry me right away?' he asked.

'Yes,' she replied, acknowledging at last that for two decades this simple option which could have saved her life had lain before her, without her being able to appreciate or accept it. Now, at the end of a long trail, she was prepared to marry the man she should have married years before. His obvious love convinced her that she had been right in burying her fears and returning to Centennial.

Embracing her again, he excused himself with the remark, 'I have some work to do at the ranch.'

'I'll bet he does,' Levi said as he departed, and when Clemma asked what this meant, her father replied, 'He has some heavy explaining to do. He was supposed to marry Charlotte Seccombe next week.'

And as he said these words he noticed that Clemma showed no surprise or remorse, as if Jim's obligations were no responsibility of hers. 'She's a lot like the Stoltzfus girl,' Levi said to himself, and he was not happy with the comparison.

At the ranch Jim found Charlotte preparing her wardrobe for their wedding, and without any attempt at finesse he said, 'Clemma's back.'

Charlotte continued laying out her clothes, and said nothing.

'She's back,' he shouted. 'And I'm going to marry her.'

Charlotte did not even pale. She simply pulled Jim around by the arm and asked, 'You're what?'

'I've got to marry her. It's her only salvation.'

Charlotte did not ask, 'And what about me?' Instead she said quietly, 'James Lloyd, our wedding is six days from now. Take those days to think this over. But bear in mind one thing. Clemma Zendt will ruin you. She's a drifter. She cannot control herself. And you deserve better than that.'

He tried to explain, to protest, but she would hear none of it. 'Please leave now,' she said firmly, a very proud and resolute woman. 'Ride your horse, James, and do some thinking.'

She escorted him to the door, and felt inclined to shove him out, when a much wiser tactic came to mind. Holding him by one hand, she gave him a long kiss and told him, 'You're a man worth having, James Lloyd. And I intend to marry you.'

For two days he rode to the corners of the ranch in a fever of indecision. Twice he went into town to talk with the Zendts, and as soon as he came within the presence of Clemma he felt his heart pounding, and once when she kissed him goodbye it seemed as if all the passion of Colorado were compressed in her lithe and poetic body.

His mind was made up. Clemma was the only woman he would marry. But as he rode east of town to that crossing of the Platte where he had first seen her, a captivating little Indian girl of thirteen, he suddenly realized that all through the years he had continued to think of her as that fairy-tale child. He really knew nothing of her as a woman, or what had touched her in St. Louis and Chicago. And at last he had to face the truth: that he was in love with an obsession which he himself had cultivated.

However, on the fourth day, still indecisive, he returned to the Zendts' to find that Clemma had been drinking, seeking to fortify herself against the charge circulating in the town that she had come home to take Jim away from Charlotte Seccombe. The accusation of course was false, since she could not possibly have known of the marriage plans, but when Jim tried to explain this, she repeated what she had predicted in Chicago: 'They just don't want Indians in this town.'

'Ridiculous! Your mother . . .'

She was no longer listening. Across the prairie the evening train whistled, and he could see that the sound tormented her, and that she was no longer a story-book Indian princess of thirteen but a tragic and haunted woman of thirty-four.

On the evening of July 4 the Zendts were in their kitchen when a knock sounded on their screen door. 'Come in,' Levi called, and he was surprised when Charlotte entered. She nodded to the senior Zendts and asked if she could speak to their daughter alone. When they left, she shifted one of the chairs so that she could sit facing Clemma.

'I want you to leave on the morning train,' she said firmly.

'He wants to marry me.'

'I'm quite sure he thinks he does.'

'And I want to marry him,' Clemma said softly.

'Do you? Really?'

'I should have married him years ago.'

'Positively,' Charlotte said with real eagerness. 'You should have married him while I still lived in England. You should have married him the year of the blizzard, when he was promoted. You should have married him a thousand times . . . but you didn't.'

'I always meant to come back . . .'

'But you didn't. You never had the courage.'

Clemma poured herself a small drink and felt better when it was downed. 'I don't want to hurt you, Mrs. Seccombe,' she said.

'We're not talking about me,' Charlotte corrected. 'We're talking about your hurting James Lloyd.'

'Jim?' Clemma cried, and something in the way she said the word—as if he were inanimate—made Charlotte realize that this woman had never once considered Jim as a human being with rights and feelings of his own. She, Charlotte, had considered Jim's estate most carefully; she would do nothing to demean him, would not even marry him if she thought she might in any way destroy or even imperil his manliness.

'Yes, Clemma, we're speaking of James Lloyd . . . a real human being. Long ago you'd have destroyed him if he'd been one shade weaker.'

'I never meant . . .'

'I know you didn't,' Charlotte said softly. 'Even now you mean nothing wrong.'

'But you're older than he is, Mrs. Seccombe. How can he love you the way . . .'

'He can't. He'll always love you. But with me he can make a life for himself. With you . . .' She hesitated, knowing that whatever she said next would be of crucial importance. 'How long would you stay with Jim?'

'Well . . .'

'How long?' Charlotte asked with great force. 'How long before the morning train took you away again?' There was no reply, and she added, 'For the sake of a man who at last has a chance to build a life for himself, get out of here.'

She left Clemma seated in a chair, staring at the floor, a small glass in her hand. As Charlotte came onto the porch she told the older Zendts, 'I advised her to leave.'

'You were wise,' Levi said. He was an old man now, entering his seventies, and he could sustain no illusions about his daughter; he supposed that she would leave in the morning and that they would never see her again.

She did leave. Jim Lloyd, weighing feed, heard about it from one of his cowboys who had delivered steers to the morning train. For two days he roamed the prairie, riding out to where Line Camp Two had been located, then up toward the Nebraska border, where he had long ago homesteaded that excellent piece of land at the mouth of the draw.

When his turbulent spirit came under control, he could see again that eternal prairie and his relationship to it. Bending low over the withers of his horse, he muttered, 'You work. That's what you do. You work the land and make it feed your cattle. And after a few short years they bury you in the earth, and what has happened in between doesn't matter a hell of a lot. Just so long as you keep close to the earth.'

With a comprehension that would last for the remainder of his life he rode back to the castle and said simply, 'I abused you, Charlotte, and I apologize. If you'll have me, let's get married.'

'I will indeed have you,' she said. 'I fought for you, and together we'll build something this state will be proud of.'

He clasped her hand, then said, 'Before we ride in to see the minister I want you to have this paper. It's my wedding present to you. I bought it two weeks ago.'

When she inspected the paper she found it to be the deed for the retreat among the piñons at Line Camp Four. He had spent all his savings to buy it back from the man in Cheyenne. 'It's proper that you should have it,' he said. 'I built it years ago . . . for someone like you.'

CAUTION TO *US* EDITORS: There is no way you can exaggerate the cattleman's contempt for the sheepman. When Charles Russell, the famous cowboy artist, first went from St. Louis to Montana, he could find no work on a ranch, so for two weeks he helped run sheep. Subsequently he completed over 3500 works of art, in which he portrayed every known kind of western animal: rabbit, bear, buffalo, you name it. But never once did he depict a sheep. In later years he became a lush, and when he was tanked up there was no way you could offend him except to claim that he had once herded sheep. That he would not tolerate.

I witnessed two vivid exhibitions of the old animosity. The Rotary Club at Centennial invited me to lunch, and my host, Morgan Wendell, asked my forgiveness in advance. 'This is hardly a proper day to take a guest,' he said, but I didn't understand. Before the meal the president apologized, saying, 'Gentlemen, we must exhibit our sense of fair play. After all, a lot of people share Colorado, and we must live together. Once a year, to prove our brotherhood, this club serves lamb.' Six members rose and strode from the hall, including a grizzled veteran who had been sitting beside me. As he left he growled, 'I'm seventy and I'll be goddamned if any man will ever accuse me of eating sheep.' Three men at my table remained in the audience, but refused to touch their food. After the meeting they would go to some restaurant and have real food, and Morgan Wendell, a man with a college education, was among them.

Another time I was doing some investigation on the loneliest part of the prairies, at a ramshackle house which had broken the heart of homesteaders, who had abandoned it. An old squatter now occupied it, making his meals from cans. When I asked him who lived on the big ranch I passed, one with good water and a fine set of buildings, where the occupants were probably making a fortune, he said, 'You wouldn't want to bother with them . . . sad case . . . they run sheep.'

Warning. In Wyoming the range wars were a lot more virulent than in Colorado, but even though they do provide good illustrative material, I would advise against referring to them. Frank Horn was such a vile killer that after he was hanged, they skinned him and tanned his hide and from it sewed articles which they gleefully exhibited in the local drugstore. Frank Canton was a fascinating Jekyll-Hyde, churchgoing cattle detective by day, a moonlighting range murderer at night, always in the employ of members of the Cheyenne Club but never so careless as to be caught.

I would especially advise against dabbling in the Johnson County War, in which a Pullman train of Cheyenne Club types rode north with a massive arsenal to end, once and for all, the cattle rustling. Like an invading army, they shot up the countryside, checking off names from the list they had prepared in advance. There are some great photographs of the invasion, including one showing the entire army as its members awaited trial in Cheyenne. They were set free, of course, on the historic principle that the men who had been shot were probably better off dead. The cattlemen had a just grievance; local juries refused to find their neighbors guilty of rustling even when caught in the act, and vigilante action seemed the only recourse. Today, in ranching Wyoming, tempers are still high over the affair, with evidence being fabricated and suppressed on both sides, and it's wisest to stand clear until the gunsmoke clears, which will probably not occur until sometime around 1995.

Irrigation. When I last flew over the Platte east of Centennial, I could not believe my eyes. It was late August, at the end of the driest period of the year, and for miles at a stretch, the riverbed was dry. Not a drop of water. Then suddenly for ten or fifteen miles it would become a flowing river, after which it would go dry again. What was happening was Potato Brumbaugh's dream in action. Indeed, the dream had been exceeded, because with improved conservation techniques, the Platte was recovering not the thirty-seven percent of diverted water that he had predicted, but almost fifty percent. Each drop, as he had foreseen, was being used six or seven times and in obedience to such a well-conceived plan, when the Platte finally reached the exit point, it was carrying exactly the 120 cusecs which the Supreme Court had directed Colorado to deliver to Nebraska. No other place in the world uses so wisely every drop of water to which it is entitled by law.

Blizzard. In Montana the 1887 storms were even more devastating than in Wyoming, and if you want illustrative incidents or woodcut pictures of the disaster, they abound. Curiously, for Colorado south of the Platte the worst year was 1886, and you will find accounts which cite that as the bad year, but do not alter your text. For the area north of the Platte, things happened as I describe. In the winter of 1949 the worst blizzard in history struck the Wyoming ranches, exceeding even the one of 1887. This time government records and newspaper photographs documented events. (1) Cowboys had to lash themselves together with rope before attempting to negotiate the fifty feet separating bunkhouse from kitchen; (2) a helicopter flew 220 miles north from Cheyenne and saw no barns or houses, since all were submerged in snowdrifts; (3) the wind was so fierce and the snow so close to sleet that ice particles blown into the noses of cattle suffocated them; and (4) some ranchers could reach their horses only by digging tunnels from kitchen to barn.

THE
CRIME

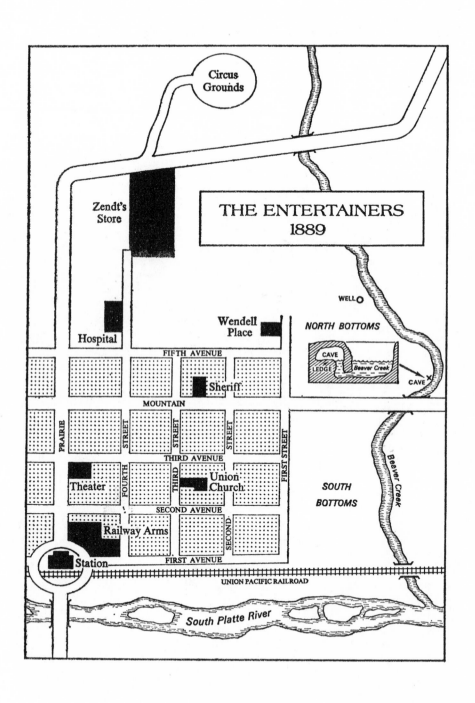

THERE WAS A DARK SIDE TO WESTERN history, and many a family that later attained prominence did so only because some enterprising progenitor had known when to strike and how to keep his mouth shut.

Two men, long-tested friends, would enter a valley together, prospecting for gold; one would emerge with an ironclad claim to the mine they had discovered, leaving the other six feet deep with a bullet in his back.

Or three men, trusted partners in numerous difficult deals, would ride into an arroyo, and one would be dry-gulched, with the desirable result that profits could be split two ways instead of three.

Such things happened in towns, too. In the summer of 1889 Centennial witnessed a grisly affair which affected the way the town developed. It began in Minnesota when a Mr. Soren Sorenson went to his bank, withdrew his funds, placed them in a small black bag and told the banker, 'It's too cold here. Gonna try my luck in Colorado.'

'The American cowboy is the dumbest man on earth and the rancher who employs him is even worse.'

The speaker was a forty-eight-year-old sheriff named Axel Dumire, a small, lean man with a bulldog jaw. He wore twin holsters for the Colt .45s he wanted people to see when he stalked the town. He had Texas-style boots, filigreed with silver, and a Texas hat, even though he had never been in that state. He did not wear a jacket of any kind, preferring a heavy red-flannel shirt, whose sleeves were kept up by elastic arm bands, and a leather vest.

He had reached Centennial after service in a long series of west Kansas towns, where his soft-spoken ways, good humor and flinty resolution made him respected if not feared. Only rarely had he found it necessary to draw his guns, and then he held them hip-high, walking steadily forward and relying upon his determination and obvious willingness to shoot it out to force his opponent to back down. So far he had succeeded.

After the spate of killings in the range wars between cattlemen and sheepherders, the citizens of Centennial felt they should import a lawman to quieten things down, and Axel Dumire had done just that. His calm persuasion had encouraged the warring sides to make peace, and his reputation as a tough enforcer had kept killers out of town. The big job was done, but the little jobs were never done.

'There's always a circus comin' to town,' Dumire said one June morning as he studied the handbill for Cartright's Sensational Congress of Heroism and Courage . . . Scores of Wild Animals . . . Most Thrilling Act in the World . . . Daring Dan and the Apache.

'You ever seen Daring Dan?' he asked the loungers on the porch of the Railway Arms. 'He's legitimate. Best shot I ever saw. Wait till you see what happens.'

'Sounds as if you admire him,' one of the men said.

'I do,' the sheriff confessed. 'I admire any man who can do what he's done.'

'What's he done?' the man asked.

'Pay your money and see.' He resumed his conversation with the other men. 'It's the rabble that follow the circus that gives me trouble. The cheats, the three-card monte experts and that damned thimble game. Our cowboys just throw their money away, with never a chance of winning.'

'Don't you always say ranchers are just as dumb?'

'They are. A man with a good education accepts responsibility for runnin' a ranch worth a million dollars and then comes to the circus and allows some fast-talkin' con artist to sell him one-third of Yellowstone Park—and you know what clinches the sale? The crook offers him the middle third, where the hot water is, so's his cows can graze through the winter without danger of the place freezin' up.'

'Nobody's that dumb!'

'I could name one right here,' the sheriff said, staring at a tall, thin cattleman who was listening from the edge of the group. 'He went into one of the girlie tents. Saw this pretty octoroon with nothin' on. For twenty-five cents he was allowed to pat her on the ass and for seventy-five cents more he could pluck a hair out of her front.' The men turned toward the tall man and began laughing. 'Yes,' Dumire said, 'we're speakin' of you, Joe.' The tall man blushed and offered no defense.

'So this year I intend to keep the circus reasonably clean, and if I have to deputize some of you men for the next two days, I want your help. First man I'm goin' to call on, since he's had experience, is you, Joe.'

This evoked even louder laughter, but the tough little sheriff rose, went to the tall cattleman and pinned a badge on him. 'Set a thief to catch a thief,' he said, 'and you keep out of those tents.'

The Cartright Circus traveled by train, and on Saturday morning the six o'clock freight that hauled milk to Denver brought the five brightly colored cars to Centennial, where they were cheered by most of the town's children and a good many of their elders.

The big tent occupied one car, and from it the roustabouts piled out briskly, enlisting the help of local young men to raise the canvas on the vacant lot north of Zendt's old store. A manager of sorts also appeared, moving among the crowd and warning them, 'Please stay clear of the other cars. The most ferocious animals in the world are sleeping there, and were you to arouse them . . .' He allowed the townspeople to imagine what might follow.

At a quarter to eight exciting things began to happen. A lion in one of the cars roared, and people standing near could feel the air vibrate, and then from the first car a charming woman in her early thirties appeared, with a professional savoir-faire that captivated the local men. Nodding in various directions, she walked along the cars, entering the one with the animals. Her arrival occasioned much bellowing and snorting within the car, and after some moments of this she appeared at the door, asking in a soft voice, 'Is there, perhaps, some young man on the platform who would like to help me with the lions?'

The question caused an explosion of shouts and encouragings, and finally a gawky youth who worked on Potato Brumbaugh's sugar-beet farm stepped forward. Hesitantly he moved toward where the woman waited, and when he reached her she held out both hands and helped him onto the step.

'What is your name?' she asked.

'Milton.'

'Milton is a very brave young man,' she said to the crowd. She led him inside, and shortly after he had disappeared a horse or a zebra started kicking the wall of the car furiously and the lion roared, and after a while Milton appeared at the door, his face radiant.

'Thank you, Milton,' the woman said in a delightful, low voice, and as he was about to leave, she kissed him.

Axel Dumire, watching these proceedings with a practiced eye, told his tall deputy, 'The bad actors ain't appeared yet,' but then he saw emerging from the second sleeping car a pair of men whose very appearance bespoke craftiness. They came into the bright summer sunlight like slugs from beneath a rock, and what they saw reassured them: a lot of cowboys, a lot of local boobs waiting for games, and especially a group of businessmen on the lookout for something good.

One of the men was thin, hawk-eyed. The other was comfortably fat, bulging from a coat two sizes too small. Harry and Meurice, they called themselves, and with the blandness of rattlesnakes leaving hibernation, too torpid to do damage, they surveyed the crowd, spotted the sheriff and walked up to him.

'Mornin', Sheriff,' Meurice, the fat man said 'What's the rules?'

'No monte, no shell game, no sellin' ideas.'

The thin man smiled benignly. 'You make it rather difficult, my good man.'

'I'm not your good man,' Dumire said quietly. 'And I'll be watching you every moment.'

The fat man did not alter his attitude. With a smile dripping with duplicity, he said, 'With the amount of murder goin' on around here, I'd think you'd haul your fancy boots off to where the criminals are, but I suppose they're buyin' you off.'

Dumire did not change his expression. 'They are, Meurice, they are. But this weekend they promised to do no killin', so's I could watch you.' The two men bowed formally, then Meurice took Harry by the arm and began to circulate among the crowd.

That Saturday Dumire and his deputies kept the circus reasonably clean. There were the usual complaints from cowboys who had bought things that didn't exist, and the sheriff tried to force restitution, but usually the complaining cowboy could not find the man who had swindled him. A couple of side shows operated, to no one's serious disadvantage and to the total amazement of the younger cowboys. There was an acceptable amount of pickpocketing, and some rather incandescent sales opportunities were offered to gullible ranchers, but by and large Axel Dumire kept the thing in bounds.

'It's a pretty fair circus,' he conceded as he found the free seat provided by the management. Across the way sat John Skimmerhorn, too cautious to be taken in by the grifters, and not far away Jim Lloyd. In the cheap seats he saw Amos Calendar, who rarely appeared in town, sitting alone, of course.

The circus acts went off handsomely, with the lions roaring at the right time. The tightrope walkers were exceptional, threatening to fall and calling forth screams of horrified delight from the women and children, but Sheriff Dumire told the men around him, 'If you appreciate guns, wait'll you see Daring Dan.'

Intermission came, and the sheriff caught sight of Harry and Meurice working a swift thimble game, with gape-mouthed cowboys refusing to believe that the pea was not under the thimble they had bet on. The sheriff smiled and walked the other way. 'To this day I cannot understand how those men shift that damned pea. You ever played the game?' he asked one of his deputies.

'Nope.'

'Give it a hand.'

The man took off his badge, and while Dumire stayed in the shadows, walked up to the table where Meurice talked like a Gatling gun while Harry shifted the three thimbles, depositing the pea very obviously under one of them. Dumire chuckled as his man put down fifty cents and indicated which thimble held the pea—it had to be there, because the deputy had seen it go under. To Dumire's discomfort, Harry lifted the thimble and there the pea was. Handing over the money which Dumire's man had won, Meurice smiled generously and said in a loud voice, 'You beat us that time, Deputy,' and the crowd laughed as the officer withdrew.

The second half of the performance contained the best acts, and excitement rose as the time for Daring Dan and the Apache approached. The gaslights were turned down and the ringmaster appeared with his megaphone. 'Ladies and gentlemen,' he said in deep, dulcet tones, 'we bring you now the greatest act in the history of the circus. Not Rome nor Babylonia nor the crowned heads of Europe . . .' He delivered an introduction that rose in hyperbole, and at the end he was shouting at the top of his powerful voice, 'Daring Dan and his tribe of wild Apache . . .'

Into the center of the arena, riding a large white horse, came a man in his fifties dressed in an exaggerated cowboy uniform, with woolly chaps, brocaded vest and silver-tassled hat. He was a good rider and wore, like Sheriff Dumire, two guns.

Now an assistant rode out and started throwing large glass balls in the air, which Daring Dan, using the gun in his right hand, shot down. It was a fine exhibition and the crowd cheered.

From the band came an ominous roll of drums. The assistant scurried off, and into the arena came 'the thundering horde' of six Apache, making up in noise and horsemanship what they lacked in numbers. They circled Daring Dan, discharging both arrows and gunfire at him. Gallantly he stood them off, but they overpowered him, and women screamed in real terror as one Apache drew back his tomahawk and actually chopped off the white man's right arm. Blood, in the form of red liquid carried in a sack, spurted down the arm and across the Indian's face, and to a wild cascade of trumpets and drums, the six Apache rode off, bearing the severed arm in the air.

A hush fell over the tent as two army doctors in white rushed in to operate on Daring Dan, while the ringmaster said in churchlike tones, 'Ever on guard to protect brave men, the good surgeons of our devoted army come to the aid of the dying man—they halt the bleeding, they mend the wound. Oh, glory be, they effect a miraculous cure!' His voice rose to a tremendous crescendo as he shouted, 'Daring Dan walks again!'

The doctors disappeared and the ringmaster's voice lowered as he explained, 'Driven by a courage that few men have known, Daring Dan refuses to admit defeat. He dedicates himself to the task of learning to fire with his left arm, which he had never previously used. Watch, watch as this courageous man . . .'

'Jesus Christ!' came a voice from the cheap seats. 'It's Canby?' And from the more expensive seats across from the sheriff, Jim Lloyd shouted, 'It *is* Canby!'

It was Mule Canby, who had done pretty much what the ringmaster was saying. Deposited at Fort Union in the spring of 1868 by Poteet, he had found himself with no right arm and no profession. He had trained himself to fire with his left hand, and was now one of the top marksmen of the world, a fact which he proceeded to prove with a display that was remarkable.

Again the six Apache attacked him as the ringmaster intoned, 'But this time Daring Dan is more than a match for them,' and as they kept their pintos galloping in a circle around him, he stood undaunted and picked the Indians off, one by one, the braves falling skillfully from their ponies and sliding in the dust.

'Yeah, Canby!' Calendar shouted from the darkness, with Jim Lloyd taking up the cry as the entire audience rose to cheer their resurrected hero.

It was traditional, when a circus played Centennial on a Saturday, for it to lay over on Sunday and cooperate with the local churches in the holding of a joint community service on Sunday night. The circus band played hymns. A choir made up of circus men and women sang, and the local women served a dinner to which the circus people were invited.

Early Sunday morning Sheriff Dumire appeared at the circus train to announce that he was putting Harry and Meurice in jail until the train pulled out that night, and they went off peacefully with him. Dumire had given them a fairly free run on Saturday and they understood that he did not want them cluttering up things on Sunday.

Jim invited Calendar and Mule Canby to ride out into the country with him; John Skimmerhorn wanted to come along, so the four old trail hands lit out for Rattlesnake Buttes, and as they rode slowly through the blazing heat, Canby told them snatches of his life following the loss of his arm.

'It's like the fellow said with the megaphone.' He started to give details, but stopped. 'You'll hear it tonight. I deliver an inspirational message. What I say isn't all true. The fellow wrote it for me, but mostly it's true.'

He told them of England and especially Germany, where they were crazy for Indians and the west. 'The emperor himself wanted to know how I shot so well with my right arm.'

'How do you?' Jim asked. 'It's wood, ain't it?'

'It's a secret,' Canby said. 'Took me four years to get it right. I tell you, you tell the next circus, then anyone can do it.'

'I wouldn't tell,' Jim promised.

'It's a secret.'

'Tell me one thing,' Skimmerhorn said. 'When you hold the gun in your wooden arm, you do the shooting, don't you? There's not somebody else firing at the balls?'

Canby looked at his old companion in dismay. 'You think I'd let someone shoot for me?' He smiled grimly. 'I suppose you doubt my left hand, too?'

A hawk flew by, one of those splendid birds that nested near the buttes, and Canby dropped his reins over the saddle horn and whipped out his revolver with his left hand, but Jim moved over and pushed the gun down.

'Don't shoot it,' and the four men watched the hawk as it wheeled and dived like a guide leading them across the prairie. The old bond of fellowship that had existed on the long ride north reasserted itself, and Canby asked Calendar, 'How'd a cattleman ever come to herdin' sheep?' and Calendar replied, 'I like workin' alone.'

They rode up the slope leading to the buttes, and at the top of the rise, looked down on a hundred and fifty white-faced Herefords, all of a size, all grazing in the summer sun, the red bodies blending with the brown grass, and Canby could see that Jim was mighty proud.

'They sure look better than the longhorns we herded,' he said, and they dismounted at the buttes, where Canby gave an exhibition of shooting rattlesnakes left-handed. Then they headed homeward along the Platte, where Jim showed Canby the marshes in which the avocet hid, and the Texan said he'd never seen such a bird and did Jim want one to stuff. He took out his gun, but Jim said, 'No, let him go. He's huntin' worms.'

'I won't be seein' you tonight,' Calendar said. 'I been away two days already.' He shook hands with Canby, awkwardly reaching out first his right hand, then his left. Obviously he wanted to say more but could not find the right words, and he rode silently eastward toward his sheep.

When he was gone, Jim rode beside Canby and said hesitantly, 'Somethin's been botherin' me . . . ever since that day we started across the Llano Estacado.'

'It's been botherin' me, too,' Canby said.

'You mean the ten dollars I owe you?'

'For the Army Colt's. I never forget a gun.'

'Well, I have the money for you. I've always kept it to one side,' and from a deep pocket he handed Canby a ten-dollar bill.

The Texan studied it carefully: 'There was days back there when I wondered if I'd ever have ten dollars of my own,' and he tucked the bill into his wallet.

So the long day ended, and Jim and Skimmerhorn were asleep in the Railway Arms at two in the morning when they heard wild screaming in the street below and saw the glare of flames and heard Sheriff Dumire shouting, 'Get down here, everybody! The circus train's on fire!'

When Jim reached the train there was little he or anyone else could do. The second sleeping car had caught fire, and with no one awake to sound the alarm, the rushing of the wind had whipped the blaze into an inferno.

'Anybody in that car?' Jim shouted.

'There's people in back, fightin' to get out,' one of the circus men yelled.

He and Jim tried to approach the flaming car but were unable to breast the fire that leaped from the forward windows. The circus man, exhibiting a bravery that confounded the watchers, dashed into the flaming space between the end of the burning car and the car that followed. Working frantically, he managed to uncouple them. Then he signaled the engineer, and when the engine moved slowly forward, the rear cars were left behind, out of danger.

As soon as the engineer halted the train, the circus man leaped among the flames and uncoupled the other end of the doomed car. This time, when the engineer pulled forward, the first sleeping car was also out of danger.

The fatal car was isolated, and for one terrible moment Jim and Sheriff Dumire saw at one of the windows, like a dim moon behind the glass, the fat and tortured face of Meurice. For a brief moment it hung there, then fell backward into the flames. When he disappeared, another frenzied face took his place momentarily.

'Canby's in there!' Jim screamed, and he broke away from the crowd and grabbed a coat and threw it about his face and fought his way to the rear door. With strength he had never shown before, he burst the door open and rushed in among the smoke and flames. Courageous townsmen followed, hauling out four unconscious men, but Canby was not among them.

The fire now raged the length of the car, throwing pillars of twisting light, and Sheriff Dumire, assisted by two deputies, dragged Jim to safety, his eyebrows burned off and his hair smoking.

The tragedy had a profound effect on Centennial. Of the fourteen dead, twelve, including Mule Canby, were buried in the town cemetery, for no families could be located. Reverend Holly, from the Union Church, volunteered his services for the burials, then convened a special prayer meeting at which he extolled the spirit of the entertainers who toured small towns: 'With their tricks and sly games these nameless people, despite the difficulties of their life, brought levity to us. They amazed us with their daring skill, and we will not soon forget how a man with no right arm trained himself to shoot so accurately. In the age of Jesus and Paul, circuses like the one we saw wandered through the Roman Empire bringing diversion to the people. We thank these dead for having entertained us. It is proper that they rest with us.'

His words reminded the citizens of Centennial of the harsh existence these wanderers had known, and they were therefore in a mood to receive with special affection the Maude and Mervin Wendell Theatrical Troupe and Thespian Exhibition when it arrived in late July.

From the moment Mervin Wendell appeared at the door of the train from Omaha, he was recognized as an actor, and probably an important one. He stood on the upper step with his left arm held behind his back, his right folded across his chest. His legs were spread in a wide stance, and his right shoulder was conspicuously higher than his left. A broad felt hat covered dark hair which showed in ringlets beside his ears, and his gaze was imperial, with a touch of adventure and glowing spirits, as if to proclaim, 'A new town! A new opportunity.'

The effect of his grand arrival was somewhat tarnished by a red-faced conductor who thrust a bag into his hand with the warning, 'Don't you ever try that again.'

Mervin made no attempt either to hide or to explain the conductor's behavior. Instead, he descended the steps majestically, then extended his right hand upward to lead a very beautiful lady in her early forties down the steps, saying as he did so, 'Come, my dear. I see our hotel just over there.'

Maude Wendell graciously accepted her husband's courtesy, then directed her attention to the interior of the train, from which appeared their son, a child with golden hair kept long, and a most fair complexion. Since they would be doing scenes from Shakespeare, it was necessary that he be able to play girls' parts as well as boys'.

When the three were on the platform, with two battered suitcases, Mervin Wendell turned to a stoutish man and woman who had descended from a different car and were now looking after large cases containing the troupe's costumes. 'Watch sharply, Murphy,' Wendell said, as if the man and his wife required help in identifying the cases.

Going to where the trainmen had unloaded the boxes, Wendell kicked each imperiously, advising Murphy, 'Take them to the theater.' Having said this, he turned his back on his assistant, only to find himself facing Sheriff Dumire, whom he had known unfavorably in Kansas.

'Good evening, Mr. Wendell,' Dumire said with studied propriety.

'Ah!' Wendell cried, as if delighted to meet an old friend. 'Sheriff Dumire! Accept from me a pass to tomorrow's entertainment,' and from his pocket he produced an ornately embellished card, entitling the bearer to pass free into one performance of the Maude and Mervin Wendell Theatrical Troupe and Thespian Exhibition.

The Wendells proposed to offer their talents to the citizens of Centennial in two resplendent evenings: the first, a group of eleven scenes from Shakespeare, edited somewhat to fit the talents of the troupe; the second, a gala evening of olios, recitations, solos and imitations. Philip Wendell would recite 'The Faithful Drummer Boy of the Rappahannock,' and dressed as a girl, would give the moving 'The Blind Girl Addresses Her Harp.'

Maude Wendell would be seen in a series of declamations chosen from her greatest theatrical triumphs here and in Europe, specifically, 'Portia's Address to the Court' from Shakespeare's *Merchant of Venice;* 'Farewell of the Parthian Mother to Her Son about to Fight Wild Beasts in the Roman Colosseum'; and 'Selections from "Mazeppa" by Lord Byron.'

The two highlights of the evening, however, were reserved for Mervin

Wendell. At the end of the first half 'Mr. Wendell, standing alone on the stage and accompanied by no one, will imitate a Union Pacific freight train leaving Centennial and delivering its cargo at Denver. You will hear the slipping of the drivers, the snorting of the locomotive going through a tunnel, the whistle, the application of brakes and the safe arrival, after which the entire company will pose in a moving tableau showing the dead members of the Cartright Circus entering heaven.'

The closing of the second half promised to be even better, for then 'Mervin Wendell, accompanied by his son Philip on the triple drum, will represent the Battle of Fredericksburg, with the pickets firing, the attack of the northern troops, the rattle of southern musketry, the roar of cannon from both sides, the bursting shells, and with the participation of the entire company, bugle calls and the triumphant charge to victory.'

The entire company consisted of the three Wendells, the two Murphys and a young man of angelic beauty named Chisholm, who looked as if a zephyr would blow him away.

'I've seen Chisholm before,' Sheriff Dumire warned his deputies. 'Keep him away from cowboys, and especially sheepherders.'

It wasn't that Axel Dumire scorned the arts. He appreciated Shakespeare and intended seeing the first night's performance, on the sensible grounds that not even Mervin Wendell could damage the Bard, much. 'He's very good as the gravedigger addressing Yorick,' Dumire admitted, 'but watch him. I don't think he has a penny, and whenever he finds himself in that condition he'll try anything.'

Discreet inquiries at the Railway Arms revealed that the proprietor had wanted the troupe to pay in full in advance, and that Wendell had proposed compromising the bill, paying half when they registered, and half when receipts from the two engagements, as he called them, were in. The hotel man said he would be at the box office the first night and collect the balance, a procedure he had found advisable in such circumstances. Mr. Wendell acceded gracefully to this proposal, saying, 'I cannot imagine a more just policy.'

On the first night the crowd was not large, the average citizen of Centennial being less enthusiastic about Shakespeare than Sheriff Dumire. At fifty and seventy-five cents admission, the take for that evening was just enough to cover the hotel manager's lien, but Wendell was far from downcast. 'A splendid performance,' he assured his troupe.

On the second night the hall was packed and the handclapping enthusiastic, to which the three Wendells responded magnificently. 'Really,' Wendell cried exultantly between acts, 'I've rarely played before a more enthusiastic audience. Wasn't it superb, Maude?'

Mrs. Wendell was now forty-two, and for the past nine years had been moving from one small town to another, from one medium-sized city like Omaha or Salt Lake to the next, keeping her fragile family intact, nodding when Mervin, two years her junior, glowed with enthusiasm over trivial triumphs, and wondering what they might try next. Once they had been leading actor and actress for the good companies—Langrishe's in Denver, for example—and for a brief time had enjoyed rural triumphs in the Black Hills of Dakota, where they were hailed as the first couple of the American stage. But in recent years they had barely stayed alive; a dozen times their trunks had been impounded, and now the sheriff had handed her, as the responsible member of the troupe, the latest telegram:

SHERIFF
CENTENNIAL COLORADO

ATTACH FOR NUMEROUS UNPAID BILLS ALL EQUIPMENT BELONGING MAUDE AND MERVIN WENDELL TROUPE PLAYING YOUR CITY

SHERIFF ED BANCROFT
GRAND RIVER NEBRASKA

'This ends the tour,' she told her husband as she showed him the telegram.

'How tactless!' he cried in feigned moral protest. 'To present this in the middle of a performance.'

'Mervin,' she said with great control, 'face up to it. They have us backed against the wall.'

'Darling,' he whispered, trying to reassure her. When he spoke this word he meant it in its real sense, for Maude Wendell was his life. In those rare moments when he looked at himself as he really was, he was forced to admit that he had always been a man of limited talent. Oh, he could imitate trains as well as Major Hendershot and he was rather good at bird calls. But when he tried to act Shakespeare or Dion Boucicault, he was barely acceptable. He had never had the brilliant quality of young Chisholm or Mike Murphy's robust sense of comedy.

And yet Maude De Lisle had married him when she could have chosen others. She had carried him with her in the years when she enjoyed triumphs and had stayed with him when their life deteriorated to drab hotels. He treasured this loyalty, and if on the one hand he was a rather pathetic actor, he was on the other a faithful husband who adored his wife and let her know it. Once in a little town in South Dakota when they were offering the balcony scene from *Romeo and Juliet*, he had looked up at her and found her more radiant than Shakespeare's lines. He had stood dumb at the foot of the balcony while Murphy threw him the cue: 'But soft! what light through yonder window breaks?' Instead of repeating it, as he should, he accepted it as if some disembodied voice had said it, and responded with the one that followed: 'It is the east, and Juliet is the sun!' And the play had gone on.

'What's the trouble?' Murphy now asked, always alert to the probability of disaster. Over Mervin's protest, Maude thrust the telegram at the Irishman.

'Inform Chisholm,' Maude said acidly. 'If you can find him.'

'Wait!' Mervin pleaded, but the decision had been made. This troupe had absorbed too many reverses. The bond required to hold the members together had been too eroded by sheriffs and hotel managers and railway conductors.

Now Maude announced her decision: 'This, dear friends, is truly our closing night. I don't know what you are going to do, but we are going to settle here, in this town, and'—she looked knowingly at her husband—'I feel sure something will turn up.'

Among those who heard this declaration, in addition to Sheriff Dumire and the actors, was young Philip Wendell. He had been standing in shadows, as he often did when he sensed that older people were in trouble, and he had heard the whole conversation from the moment that Dumire entered. He could guess what the telegram said, and he had a sure understanding of what it meant. He was precocious and knew that this time his mother intended what she said. This was the end of the tour.

And then he saw, with deep pride, his beleaguered father rally his forces. 'Come, now!' the gallant actor cried. 'If it is the last, let's make it the best.' And the child watched as Mervin went to the Murphys, offering them encouragement, and to young Chisholm, to whom he said, 'Play as if the kings were out there.' It was so like his father to say *kings*. One would not be enough.

Then Mervin saw his son and came to him and took his hands and asked, 'You know?' The boy nodded, and Mervin hugged him and said, 'Make it the performance you'll never forget.' Philip got into his girl's costume, and when the curtain was lowered after his mother's performance as Lady Teazle, in a scene from *The School for Scandal*, he slipped into his place and sat with his harp between his knees and his eyes closed to indicate blindness. Running his fingers lightly over the strings, he began to sing Tom Moore's heartbreaking song of old Ireland:

> 'The harp that once through Tara's halls
> The soul of music shed,
> Now hangs as mute on Tara's walls
> As if that soul were fled.'

At this point it was customary for him to play passionately and address the harp as if it were a friend, but on this night Philip barely touched the strings. He stopped his singing, and looking at the harp with closed eyes, began to recite the familiar lines: 'Why must I play an instrument I cannot see? I feel the strings and hear them echo . . .'

The emotion of this night was too much for him, and the planned words died away. He played a few chords and forgot the sequence of his apostrophe. Instead, he started to sing the entire Moore ballad, and its effect upon the audience was profound. He was a blind girl. He was at the heart of a doomed Ireland singing at its wake:

> 'Thus Freedom now so seldom wakes,
>   The only throb she gives
> Is when some heart indignant breaks,
>   To show that she still lives.'

When he finished, the audience cheered and whistled, and he stayed at his harp, his eyes closed, praying that this moment of acceptance might never end. Finally young Chisholm came onstage and led him off, and in the wings Chisholm started to cry and embraced the boy and told him, 'You will never forget this night. You were a triumph,' and Philip's mother came and took him away.

So the last number came, and Philip, in his costume as the Little Drummer Boy of Fredericksburg, beat the triple drums as if the entire Union army marched to his command, and Mr. Murphy was splendid as the dying sergeant, and Mrs. Murphy blew the bugle in her right hand while her left waved a flag; she represented the Spirit of the Eventual Triumph of Right over Wrong, meaning the north over the south, and young Chisholm was heroic as the lieutenant who led the charge, and through it all Mervin Wendell, unaided by any mechanical device, as the program promised, exploded shells, imitated Minié balls whining at the enemy, operated a Gatling gun and almost became the ammunition train.

At the final tableau, with Mrs. Murphy still blowing her bugle and waving her flag, the audience burst into cheers, and as the curtain fell, Mervin Wendell asked that question which haunts touring companies on their infrequent nights of triumph, 'Why can't it always be like this?'

Sheriff Dumire, having participated in many such closing nights, was as gentle as possible, but he was also firm. No, the Wendells could have nothing, absolutely nothing, not their costumes, nor their drums, nor even Philip's harp. He surmised that in a dozen states like Iowa and Nebraska they had defrauded merchants, and the citizens of Colorado required protection. The tour was indeed ended.

So the six actors sat in the darkened theater, discussing what they would do next. Young Chisholm looked forward to a bright future; he was only twenty-two and looked sixteen. He could trade on his looks for years, and in the morning would be off to Denver. The Murphys had known an endless chain of disastrous nights, but they had always been able to find some traveling company that needed a good Irish comedian with a wife who could double on trumpet. They thought they'd head back to Chicago.

The Wendells would stay in Centennial. 'But what can we do?' Mervin pleaded. Since the age of twelve the stage had been his home, and he knew nothing else. 'What work can I do?' he repeated aimlessly.

Before she could respond, unexpected help arrived, in the form of a man they had not seen before. He came hesitantly through the back door of the theater, a place to which he was not accustomed, and made his way tentatively to where the family sat. He was a tall man, ungainly and shy. Since the stage was dark, the Wendells could not see his clerical collar or the Bible which he carried in his two hands.

'I wonder if I could help,' he asked gently, and at these words Mrs. Wendell's shoulders slumped and she leaned back against a box and said, 'We need a great deal of help.'

'I know,' he said. 'The hotel has taken possession of your things.'

'They can't do that!' Mervin cried. 'I paid in advance.'

'For the room,' Maude said with much tiredness. 'We ate like pigs.'

'Excuse me,' the man said, 'my name's Holly. Reverend Holly from the Union Church.' He went to each of the Wendells, extending his hand in greeting, and said to Philip, 'You ought to be in bed, young man. Tonight you'll sleep at our place.'

'Why are you doing this?' Maude asked.

'This town was deeply moved by the circus deaths. We were reminded that actors and jugglers and clowns . . .' Sensing that he had used an infelicitous grouping, he stopped. 'Many of us would like to help.'

He boarded them for three days, then announced that he had found them a permanent place, a furnished house owned by a Mr. Delmar Gribben, a member of his congregation.

'How will we pay the rent?' Maude asked.

'For two months there will be no rent. After that you'll have the money, for the railway station needs a part-time man to handle baggage, and the job is yours, Mr. Wendell.'

'Does it pay?'

'Of course it pays! Mr. Wendell, this community wants you and your family to reside with us. We need more people. We need you.'

So the Wendells deserted a theater which had long ago deserted them and gratefully moved into the Gribben place on First and Fifth, that is, at the far end of First Street just after it crossed Fifth Avenue. The rambling house faced the open space of North Bottoms and the eastward curve of Beaver Creek. That Sunday evening, at the informal worship services Reverend Holly enjoyed conducting, the three Wendells secured for themselves a place in the affections of Centennial.

It was the custom, at these night services, for musical members of the congregation to offer solos and duets. Hymns were preferred, such as 'The Old Rugged Cross' and 'Work, for the Night Is Coming,' but Mervin suggested to the pastor that he and Maude, assisted by their son, offer the group a moving song with which the family had had some success when worshipping in states like Ohio and Indiana. Reverend Holly was delighted and Mervin consulted briefly with the pianist. Yes indeed, she knew the proposed song. It was, in fact, one of her favorites.

So she struck those deep, rich chords which signal the opening of Septimus Winner's outstanding triumph, 'Whispering Hope.' This notable song had been published in 1868 under the pseudonym Alice Hawthorne, the author feeling, and rightly so, that its extraordinary sentiment would seem more appropriate if the composer was thought to be a lady. It had swept the nation, primarily because the legato notes sung by the soprano invited the bass or baritone to boom out a patter accompaniment, while the third voice, if there was one, could engrave delicate arabesques. It was a song predestined for Maude and Mervin Wendell, and they knew how to exploit it. In a clear, sweet treble Philip lined out the lush words:

> 'Soft as the Voice of an Angel,
> Breathing a Lesson unheard,
> Hope with a gentle Persuasion,
> Whispers her comforting Word;
> Wait till the Darkness is over,
> Wait till the Tempest is done,
> Hope for the Sunshine Tomorrow,
> After the Shower is gone.'

As the child sang the melody, his mother, in a strong contralto, sang a close harmony which moved alternately above and below the note her son was singing, uniting occasionally on a single note to produce an effect of such delicious accidentals that the audience sighed at its sheer loveliness.

Now came the good part, the chorus. While Philip and Maude continued as they were, singing their soprano and alto versions of the words *whispering hope*, Mervin broke in with a deep, rumbling baritone, singing three and four words while they sang one. He produced such a powerful effect that when the chorus ended, the audience started to applaud, even though it was in church.

'I think we have heard *sursum corda*,' Reverend Holly said. 'As this gifted family sings our old favorite it sounds more like a hymn than the hymns we sing,' and with this benediction the Wendells became citizens of Centennial.

Henceforth, on any occasion when the citizenry gathered, they were asked to sing, and 'Whispering Hope' was bound to be called for. How stable, how strongly bound they seemed when they united in this song, their voices separate yet blending. 'They're a lesson to us all,' Reverend Holly said many times. He actually preferred the other number by Septimus Winner, also published under the name of Alice Hawthorne, which the Wendells offered, 'Listen to the Mockingbird.' The words of this song lacked the purity of 'Whispering Hope,' and there was a certain repetitiousness about them. Mervin preferred singing it while sitting in a chair, his right hand pressed against his forehead, his eyes fixed on an imaginary fire:

> 'I'm dreaming now of Hallie, sweet Hallie, sweet Hallie,
> I'm dreaming now of Hallie,
> For the thought of her is one that never dies;
> She's sleeping in the valley, the valley, the valley,
> She's sleeping in the valley,
> And the mockingbird is singing where she lies.'

At this point the audience heard the mockingbird in the distance, for Philip in the wings gave a fine whistling imitation of the bird, but before he ended, his mother walked onstage, whistling as fine a series of bird calls as the west had ever heard. She was phenomenal, sliding up and down the scale, doing robins and nightingales and thrushes and even hawks, while her husband sang:

> 'Listen to the mockingbird,
> Listen to the mockingbird
> The mockingbird still singing o'er her grave . . .'

When the last chorus was reached, the Wendells really let go. Now Philip walked out from the wings, whistling his heart out as the mockingbird, while his mother shrilled a score of wild bird notes and her husband expressed his grief in deep, passionate notes.

One member of the audience was not impressed. Sheriff Dumire kept close watch on the Wendells and asked himself, What are they using for money? They were dressing well, eating regularly and moving from one party to the next. On Sunday mornings when the collection plate was passed, Mervin made a show of dropping a heavy coin, a quarter or perhaps even a half dollar, into the metal plate, where it echoed, and he had been seen at the livery stable looking at a type of horse which could only be used to pull a carriage. Something was wrong.

So Dumire casually dropped by the railroad station to ascertain what salary Mervin was making, and the agent told him, 'We only had a half-time job for him. Gets four dollars a week. He said something about a second job.'

Dumire watched Mervin even more closely and satisfied himself that he had no second job. 'He can't be living on four dollars a week. Not the way they eat.'

His suspicions intensified, but his freedom to investigate became hampered by a development he could not have foreseen. Since it was summer, young Philip had no school to attend, and with the sheriff's office only three blocks from his home, he had fallen into the habit of spending time there, sitting quietly on the porch, watching carefully as the sheriff came and went. One day Dumire, eager to know what the family was up to, invited the boy into the dark-paneled office, but as Philip sat there, clearly overcome by hero worship, the sheriff was reluctant to question him.

'I like men who have jobs,' the boy said as his eyes followed the tough little sheriff.

'Your father has a job.'

'Not a very good one. Not a real one like yours.'

Such admiration pleased Dumire, and on his duty walks through the town he began to look for the boy. It was obvious to him that Philip was striving to do all the things he had been deprived of during his years of traveling with the theater, and one evening the sheriff watched him in the empty lot across from the Gribben house, and the boy was throwing stones with commendable accuracy. 'Good shot,' he called. 'Where's your father?'

'He's visiting with the Wilsons. They give him sandwiches.'

During another inspection tour Dumire saw the boy swimming in the creek, kicking well and diving deep without fear. 'You're not afraid to stay under, I see,' he called. 'By the way, where's your mother?'

'At the church.'

He began to look forward to the boy's visits to his office, and was pleased when Philip told him, 'You're the bravest man I ever met.' He was amused when Philip asked, 'Mr. Dumire, why is the bottom of your face so brown and the top so white? Do you use make-up like my father?'

'No!' Dumire laughed. 'Sheriffs and cowboys wear big hats . . . to keep the sun off their heads. That's how you can tell a cowboy. Down here brown, up here white.' Next day Philip appeared wearing a large hat.

One morning the boy was perched beside Dumire's desk, watching him file papers, when the station agent ran in with a telegram from Julesburg. Dumire read it, frowned, then tossed it professionally to Philip, as if he were a deputy:

BOARD UNION PACIFIC 817 AND ARREST CHARLES KENDERDINE ALIAS HARVARD JOE ARMED AND DANGEROUS

SHERIFF BAGLEY

Dumire permitted the boy to follow him down Prairie as he headed for the station, and although the sheriff was not tall, he carried himself with such authority that he imprinted upon Philip's mind an image of how a man ought to look: clean, hard, devoid of frills. In his life backstage he had seen few such men.

Number 817 pulled into the station; Dumire climbed aboard. Philip could see him, hands over his guns, arguing with a seated man, and in a moment Harvard Joe, much taller than Dumire, came dutifully down the steps, allowing himself to be guided through the main streets to the jail.

Philip waited for the sheriff in his office, and when the courageous little Kansan returned, the boy said with beaming affection, 'You can handle those guns.'

'It wasn't the guns,' Dumire said. 'It's knowin' what to say so you don't need them.'

At this moment a man Philip knew as his landlord, Mr. Gribben, entered the office and asked, 'Sheriff, can I speak with you for a moment?'

'Certainly,' Dumire said.

'Alone?'

Dumire indicated that Philip must go, and he did, pausing to stare curiously at Gribben as he left.

'I want to speak with you, Axel. On an ugly business.'

'Business often gets ugly.'

'I want to warn you about somethin', but I must first state that under no circumstances will I press charges.'

'Just information?' Dumire asked.

'That's right.'

'Because the facts would prove you a fool?'

'They would indeed. Sheriff, the Wendells are workin' the badger game.'

This was the clue Dumire had been waiting for. If they were running a badger game, everything became clear. 'Tell me about it.'

'I'm speakin' of my own case,' Gribben said. 'And two or three others I've watched, although on them I could be wrong.'

'You met her at one of the socials,' Dumire suggested. 'She thanked you for letting them use your house. Brushed against you. And in your hearing Mr. Wendell said he had to catch the night train to Denver?'

'How did you know?'

'There's only one way to work the badger game. The wife gets the target steamed up, the husband says he's got to leave town, and some way or another she lets you know you can take her home, and just when you got your pants off and hers down, in storms the outraged husband with a revolver. How much did they blackmail you for?'

'The house.'

'The what!'

'The house. Reverend Holly had pleaded with me that since it was vacant and since they were a Christian family, it was my duty . . . You know that Holly. Well . . . they grew to like it. Now it's theirs.'

'Have you gone completely idiot?'

'It was either the house or a scandal, and my wife . . .'

'You gave them the house?'

'Yes. I went over to Greeley with them and switched title to their

name. "For one dollar and other valuable considerations." Miserable
son-of-a-bitch actually handed me the dollar in front of witnesses. So
now it's theirs.'

'What do you want me to do? Arrest them?'

'God, no!' Gribben cried. 'My daughter's getting married. She wants
them to sing at her wedding.'

'What do you want me to do?'

'Watch them. Catch them. And run them out of town.'

Dumire considered this for some time, then asked, 'Was Mrs. Wendell
in this too? I mean . . . of course she was the bait, but was she a real
partner?'

'Her? Hell, her old man was so wobbly with that gun that I could of
settled with him for fifty bucks. It was her that brought up the house,
conducted all the negotiations. She's the brains.' He reflected on this,
then added hesitantly, 'Did you see how their kid stared at me when
I came in? I wouldn't be surprised if he was in on it too.'

He was. But not in the way Mr. Gribben suspected. He had been
asleep that night, but he had heard a strange voice, like the others he
had heard on previous nights, and he had peeked through a small opening in the door and had watched as his mother unbuttoned Mr. Gribben's pants and allowed him to unbutton her blouse, and he could pretty
well guess what was going to happen next, except that at the critical
moment his father rushed into the room, waving a pistol and making
a fiery statement about honor. There was a long argument, with Mr.
Gribben trying to get his pants back on and getting them stuck on one
leg, and there was discussion about a house, perhaps the one they were
living in, and when Mr. Gribben left, cursing at them, his father fell into
a chair and said in a hoarse voice, 'We can't do this any more, Maude.
It's too dangerous,' but his mother did a little dance around the room,
touching the walls and crying, 'The kind of house I've always wanted.'

It could have been damaging for a child of ten to absorb what Philip
had seen. His mother's amorous play with Mr. Gribben could have been
fearfully disturbing, and his father's exhibition with the gun might have
distressed the boy, but to him, what happened was merely an extension
of the plays the family had performed. This was confirmed when he saw
the pistol his father brandished: it came from the theatrical company
and had a trigger which made a click, but no hammer. And the words
his father had said when he burst into the room were not real words.
Philip knew them well, and could have recited them, for they came from
a play the family had done in Minnesota, the one in which Philip played
a girl perched on his mother's lap when his father tore into the room
and cried,

'Shame, shame! My honor is defiled. I will not tolerate for another moment such disgrace. I will destroy the man who has wronged me.'

The ridiculous speech posed no difficulty for Philip, but he did lie awake that night, comparing his father with Sheriff Dumire, and he decided that he preferred men who carried real revolvers and who did not shout about using them, but did use them if they had to. He also liked men who spoke in their own words—in short sentences which they meant.

Consequently, in the days that followed he kept even closer to the sheriff. He did not like men like Mr. Gribben. He wanted to be like Sheriff Dumire, who stood with dignity, and Mr. Gribben had been ridiculous, jumping around the room on one leg, his pants all twisted, while he shouted 'Don't shoot! Don't shoot!' as if that old revolver had ever been able to shoot.

After Gribben's visit the sheriff became even more friendly with Philip and showed a deeper interest in his family. He wanted to know what they were eating, where they bought things, and Philip told him. Dumire particularly wanted to know if his mother and father ever had guests, men coming there for dinner, or such like.

And at this point young Philip held back. He knew that Mr. Gribben and other men had come to the house, but he suspected that this was a family secret and none of Sheriff Dumire's business. So when these questions were asked, he acted dumb, as he had in the play when he was the good bandit's little girl and the evil king was asking her where her father was. 'I don't know,' the little girl had said, and all the while her father, the good bandit, had been hiding in the trunk, the very one she was sitting on.

'I don't know,' Philip said. 'Mr. Holly, the minister, came over the other day. He wants us to sing at the wedding of Mr. Gribben's daughter. He said Mrs. Gribben wanted it very much, and there would be five dollars for us.'

Dumire attended the wedding, held in the ballroom of the Railway Arms, and he listened while the three Wendells sang and women wept. He was not able to remain for refreshments because an urgent message arrived calling him to Greeley, and he was therefore not present when a Mr. Soren Sorenson, in town for a couple of days and staying at the hotel, happened to pass the hall where the wedding reception was being held. Hearing the music, he wandered in, even though he did look out of place carrying a black bag, and he found himself standing beside Mrs. Wendell, a remarkably handsome woman, who offered him several glasses of punch and who expressed obvious disappointment when her tall and attractive husband informed her of his bad news: 'Dash it! I've got to catch the night train to Denver. Those damned bankers.'

Philip was standing at the window of his bedroom when he heard his mother and Mr. Sorenson coming up First Street, chatting gaily, and when they entered the house he would have moved to the chink in the door to watch what unfolded, except that when the pair closed the front

door behind them, Philip saw his father slip quietly onto the porch, holding the stage revolver and waiting for a signal to rush into the room to
protect his honor.

Philip now moved to the door to watch the playful wrestling, and
heard Mr. Sorenson's heavy breathing and saw what his mother was
doing to encourage him to undress her. He wondered what signal she
would use to alert his father, then noted that during the heat of the
wrestling she found an opportunity to brush her white arm against the
window curtain, and Philip knew that soon his father would burst in
with the stage pistol and start reciting his lines.

But on this night something went wrong. Philip was watching Mr. Sorenson as his father rushed into the room, and to the boy's surprise, the
visitor showed no fright, didn't even bother to pull up his pants. Instead,
he said, 'What in hell is this? The old badger game?'

Philip knew that now his father must begin to recite his lines, but when
he tried, the visitor brushed him away. 'Put that toy down and let me out
of here,' he said contemptuously, reaching for his black bag, and Philip
saw that his father was most eager to obey, except that his mother cried,
'Don't let him get away!' and there was a scuffle, during which Mervin
dropped the gun, and the visitor would have escaped except that Maude
grabbed the fake pistol and clubbed him over the head, knocking him to
the floor, where she clubbed him again and again.

The man lay very still, and Philip watched as his father knelt down,
saying in an awful voice, 'My God, Maude! You've killed him.'

She had. The two Wendells, with their son watching impassively behind the door, argued for several terrifying minutes as to what they might
do, and Mervin was all for calling the sheriff and charging the dead man
with having . . .

'Stop it!' Maude snapped. 'Dumire'd know in a minute.'

'Then what can we do?' Mervin asked piteously.

'We must hide the body. Get rid of it. No one knows he was in town.'

So Philip watched with detached interest as they pulled the man's
pants back on. He saw his mother help swing the limp body onto her
husband's back, and then he went to the window to watch his father
stagger across the field with it. Mervin Wendell was gone a long time,
during which Philip watched his mother tidy up the place, removing any
signs of struggle. She was as methodical as if she were preparing for a
party, and when her husband returned she asked him matter-of-factly,
'What did you do with it?' and he said, 'Threw it down the well,' and
she cried, 'Jesus Christ! That's the first place Dumire'll look,' and they
stared at each other in horror.

It was in that moment that Philip first saw his good friend Dumire as
a potential enemy of his family, and he knew intuitively that only he,
Philip, could protect his parents from the sheriff's investigations. It was
much like the play *The Bugler Boy of Bruges*, in which he had been the

instrument of his family's salvation, and now as he listened to the real tragedy in the other room, he knew that his mother was right. If the body were left in the well, Dumire would find it. But he knew a safer place, one which not even Dumire could ever discover. It was exactly like that scene with the bugler boy, when his father was going to hide the king's money in a trunk which the evil counselor would be sure to spot. It was Philip, that is, the bugler boy, who thought of the windmill.

So he left his hiding place and entered the room and automatically recited his line from that play, 'Father, I know where you should hide it.'

His parents turned to look at him, a ten-year-old boy with ringlets, and they were so involved in their own drama that they saw nothing ridiculous in accepting advice from him.

'I know where you must hide it,' he repeated, and this slight change in words, warning them what they must do, moved them to action. Mervin reached for his coat and said, 'Let's go,' but Philip said, 'No. Just Mother and me.' He knew that in this great crisis his father could not be trusted.

'I know where to put him,' he repeated calmly as he and his mother got a rope and went to the well. 'They'll never find him.'

At the well they hauled up the bucket, which showed dry, as Philip had expected. He climbed into it and allowed his mother to lower him, while he held on to the end of the extra rope. He felt the bucket strike a soft body, then slide off to gravel. Climbing down, he tied the rope tightly around the dead man's chest and under the arms. Then he sat the corpse upright, so that when the rope was pulled from above, it would not slide down and off the legs.

Signaling his mother, he climbed into the bucket and waited for her to haul him aloft. When he joined her he said, 'Now we must pull strong,' and together they hauled the body up and out of the well.

When it lay beside their feet, Mrs. Wendell asked, 'Now what?' and Philip replied, 'We must carry him to the creek,' and his mother cried in near-despair, 'Dumire will look there!' and Philip assured her, 'Not where I'm going.'

As they lugged the heavy body Philip warned his mother, 'Don't let it drag! Dumire will see the marks. He sees everything.'

When they had maneuvered the corpse to the point where Beaver Creek takes its big bend to the east, they stretched the body out and Philip undressed. Standing naked beside his mother, he told her, 'Now we must get him into the creek,' and he jumped into the water, making a soft splash.

Working alone, his mother found it difficult to manipulate the dead weight, but her son directed from the stream, 'Push him, Mother. Closer, so that I can grab his leg.'

Mother and son worked on the heavy burden and finally got it into the stream. 'You'll never be able to handle it,' Maude Wendell whispered in her first sign of panic, but her son reassured her with the kind of knowledge boys acquire: 'Things weigh less in water.' And she watched in mute anxiety as her golden-haired son wrestled with the corpse and slowly dragged it beneath the surface.

He swam down to that opening in the limestone bank which a little beaver had discovered sixty thousand years ago, to the mouth of that mysterious cave she had loved so dearly and in which her babies had romped. It remained as she had left it, a secret place which only beavers had known until this exploring child, swimming alone, had found it, and occupied it, and christened it his underwater castle.

Guided by some instinct of self-preservation, as if he had perceived even then that one day this secret cave might be of value to him, he had told no one of its existence, not even Sheriff Dumire that day when he asked, 'Was it fun, diving in the creek?' He had told no one, and now he held his breath as he brought the dead body to the entrance.

Fighting against his lack of oxygen, he used all his power to force the corpse into the cave, but failed. He had to surface for air, and as he did so he heard his mother ask desperately, 'Did you hide it?' Before he could reply, his mother screamed, for the corpse, its lungs still filled with air, had floated up behind him. The dead man's face stared accusingly from the water.

'I need more breath,' Philip said, grabbing the body as it floated away. 'This time . . .'

He dived again, dragging the buoyant body behind him, and by conserving his energy, he reached the entrance to the cave in good condition. Working with speed and precise knowledge of what he wanted to accomplish, he forced the body through the opening and found with satisfaction that it fitted in the cave nicely, and was so protected by the lip that it could never work itself free.

With bursting lungs he returned to the surface, and this time his mother saw with relief that no face followed in the waters.

'He's hidden forever,' Philip announced, breathing deeply. His mother reached down to help pull him from the stream. Grasping her hands, he drew himself onto the bank and dressed, kicking bits of dirt over the area where the corpse had lain. 'If it rains before Dumire starts searching,' he told her as they returned to the house, 'everything will be washed clean. He's gone to Greeley, and before he gets back the signs will disappear.'

When they reached the house they found Mervin sitting in the room where the murder had been committed, Mr. Sorenson's black bag on his lap and a happy grin on his face.

'Guess what?' he cried maniacally as they entered the room. 'Look at this bag!' And from it he allowed many five- and ten-dollar bills to filter through his fingers to the floor. 'I've counted to three thousand, and there's more.'

The bag contained fifty-five hundred dollars, the small fortune that Sorenson had brought to Colorado for the purchase of irrigated land, and now it belonged to the Wendells.

'What we must do,' Maude said quickly, grasping the situation, 'is keep this hidden. We mustn't spend even one dollar of it.' Philip was awed by his mother's cool thinking, for when Mervin argued, 'It can't be marked,' she countered, 'Probably not. But if we start spending lavishly, Dumire will become suspicious.'

And Philip listened with admiration as his mother spelled out the strategy her endangered family must follow. 'Mervin, see if you can gradually get more work at the railway station. I'll pass the word that I could take in a little washing. Philip, you must earn us some money by finding yards that need tending.'

The plan seemed too complicated for Mervin to follow, and he asked whiningly, 'Why don't we just leave this town? Find some safe place in South Dakota?'

'No!' his wife said with great firmness. 'I will run no more. We have a very good thing in this town, and I intend to protect it.'

It was not till dawn that Mervin finally asked, 'At least tell me what you did with the body.' But Maude and Philip just looked at each other and shook their heads. 'It's best that we tell no one,' Maude said.

Luck continued to smile on the Wendells, for on the third day of Sheriff Dumire's absence a night rain fell, just enough to smooth away marks and wash down the sides of the well. When the sheriff did return, it was at least a week before anyone noticed the absence of Soren Sorenson. He had left luggage at the hotel, it is true, but he had warned the desk man that he might be absent for some days, looking for land.

But after several weeks an inquiry arrived from the Minnesota police, and Axel Dumire launched a formal investigation. The hotel staff remembered Sorenson, a middle-aged Swede with a pleasant disposition who tipped well. He carried the normal luggage plus a small black bag which he liked to keep near him.

This suggested to Dumire that the man might have brought a substantial amount of cash, and a telegram to the bank in Sorenson's hometown established that he had withdrawn fifty-five hundred dollars, which he had taken with him in hopes of acquiring the best possible piece of land if he offered cash on the barrelhead, as he put it.

As bits of evidence began to coalesce, Sheriff Dumire assembled a fairly clear picture of what must have happened to Sorenson. He had come to Centennial, had tried to buy part of Potato Brumbaugh's farm and failed, had gone to the Indian woman, Levi Zendt's widow, to see if she wanted to sell off some of her dead husband's holdings and had failed again.

He had gone to two other irrigation farmers and they had suggested that he try a little farther east toward Sterling. It was logical to think that he had gone to Sterling, but there was no evidence of this, absolutely none, and he began to wonder if Sorenson had made the acquaintance of the Wendells.

He watched the family carefully, and could detect no sign of misbehavior. Mervin was now working full time at the station, and Maude was doing laundry and a little sewing for local ladies. Even Philip was working at odd jobs, but he still found time to stop by the sheriff's office.

'Your father unload any baggage for a Swede?' Dumire asked the boy one day.

'Maybe. He unloads a lot of stuff.'

'He ever mention any Swedes?'

'No.'

Despite all his questioning, Dumire could in no way establish that Sorenson had ever been acquainted with the Wendells. Accordingly, he telegraphed Minnesota that all leads in the Centennial area had proved futile and that Soren Sorenson had probably headed east for Sterling. In reply he received the startling news that Mrs. Sorenson had received a letter from her husband, postmarked Centennial, informing her that whereas he had found nothing yet, and whereas the local farmers were advising him to move east to Sterling, he was convinced Centennial was where they ought to settle and he would remain at the Railway Arms till he found something.

Dumire doubled his efforts, and the thought came to him that perhaps Sorenson had gone out on the prairies alone and had met with someone like Calendar, a renegade type who was already suspected of having gunned down the two Pettis boys. He saddled a horse and rode out to see Calendar, but he could tell him nothing.

'Who's the boy?' Dumire asked when he saw a blond-haired boy of about eleven in the sheep wagon.

'Mine.'

'Your son?'

'Yep. Jake. Born in New Mexico.'

'When were you ever married?'

'Well, not exactly married.'

'How'd the boy get here?'

'With some cattlemen.'

Sheriff Dumire looked at the toughened little boy and thought, If any child could work his way north, this one could. He left the sheep range satisfied that Calendar had not done away with Sorenson.

But as he rode back to Centennial, the image of that boy lingered in his mind, and he thought of Philip, also mature beyond his years, and he began again to concentrate on Philip and something the child had said about tending yards led Dumire to a hasty calculation of the money the Wendells were earning. Mervin Wendell had started to work full time shortly after Soren Sorenson disappeared. Maude had begun asking for work at the same time. And young Philip had started doing odd jobs.

'It's a scheme!' he cried aloud. 'As sure as I'm alive, it's a dirty scheme. That family got hold of the fifty-five hundred dollars, somehow, and they've all taken jobs to provide a way to ease the bills into circulation without causing comment.'

He made meticulous inquiries at all stores, but found to his disappointment that the Wendells had not accelerated their expenditures. Their joint wages more than justified their purchases. He discovered nothing, but he did succeed in alerting Maude Wendell as to his suspicions, for when she went to the butcher to buy liver, one of the cheaper meats, he said, 'You wouldn't like some fine beef?' and she replied, 'That's a little expensive for us,' and he said, 'That's what I told Sheriff Dumire.'

She did not change expression, but she did say, 'He can afford the higher cuts,' and the butcher agreed: 'He gets a good salary. And he likes his beef.'

When she got home she said nothing to her husband, for if he learned that Dumire was interrogating people he might panic and do or say something stupid, but when Philip returned after weeding and running errands for Mrs. Zendt, she took him for a quiet walk on the open land near the well and warned him, 'Sheriff Dumire suspects us,' and he said, 'I know. He's been asking me all sorts of strange questions, but I tell him nothing,' and she said, 'You ought to stop seeing him,' and he told her, 'That would make him more suspicious.'

So he continued visiting the sheriff. One day he said, 'Do you notice how I've changed?' and Dumire studied the child, then slammed one hand onto his desk and cried, 'You got your hair cut.'

'I wanted it short, like yours,' Philip said. And the more he was with Dumire, the more he respected him. The sheriff was not the kind of man to get mixed up in badger games, neither as perpetrator nor victim, and if he were by accident involved, he would not panic.

But much as he respected Dumire, he saw that the sheriff was playing a game, yet somehow it was not a game. His parents were participating in another play, but it was not a play. Real, terrible things were happening, like that tornado he had experienced in Kansas, and he knew that he was at the vortex. Ugly things had taken place, perhaps the ugliest, and only he could keep them in balance. He was no longer a child, nor a play-acting girl, nor a sissy with long hair. He was responsible for his family, and never, never would he reveal even the slightest clue that might endanger it.

The conflict in which he was embroiled—abiding respect for Dumire and the necessity to protect his parents—became almost unbearable. An adult would have been excused had he crumbled under such pressures;

Philip was able to maintain his balance solely because of his childish ignorance of possible consequences.

So now he and the sheriff began to joust with each other on a much more serious level. The sheriff was convinced that this boy knew what had happened to Soren Sorenson, and the boy knew that Dumire must be kept from penetrating that secret.

The first break for Dumire came when a chambermaid at the hotel, who had already been questioned four times, told the sheriff, 'Now stop suggestin' that I stole that black bag. Mr. Sorenson had it himself when he stopped by the wedding.'

'He what?'

'You were there. I seen you. He looked in, just the way you did. He wasn't invited, but the door was open and he heard the Wendells singin' that beautiful song . . .'

Quietly Dumire asked the maid to go over what she had said, and he satisfied himself that on the night of the Gribben wedding, Soren Sorenson must have somehow got involved with the Wendells.

That was all he needed. He was certain that Sorenson must have struck up a conversation with Mrs. Wendell, had 'accidentally' overheard that her husband had to leave on the night train to Denver and had fallen prey to their scheme. Somehow it had gone awry and Sorenson had been murdered.

For two weeks he kept this deduction to himself, praying that he might find someone who had seen Sorenson leave the wedding party with Mrs. Wendell, but there were no such witnesses. 'Damn it!' he cried, banging his office desk. 'She walked that man right up Prairie and east on Mountain at ten o'clock on a moonlit night and no one saw them. I can't believe it.'

No one had seen them. He walked the distance a score of times, trying to picture where the two had moved, and how. He then tried walking along the railway tracks and north on First Street, but he knew Mrs. Wendell would never have taken Sorenson along the deserted bottoms, for he would have become suspicious. No, damn it, she had led him boldly along the main streets, and no one had noticed them. It was incredible.

So he resumed working on the boy, using the most roundabout and clever lines of questioning, never suspecting that Philip was anticipating every move, and then late one day as he was asking the boy about some trivial thing, Philip looked at him in the inquisitive way he had looked at Mr. Gribben that morning. What was it Gribben had said: 'Did you see how their kid stared at me?' With Dumire's recollection of these words, everything became clear.

Slowly he rose from his desk and pointed his right forefinger at Philip. 'You know!' he said in a low voice. 'You know all about it. You've known from the start. You knew about Mr. Gribben.'

Philip merely stared at him. Neither the twitch of an eye nor an increased rate of breathing betrayed any inner turmoil. He looked up at the sheriff with innocent blue eyes and asked, 'What are you talking about?'

For a moment the sheriff was disarmed. Then he began to shout. 'You know what I'm talking about, goddamnit! You were there and you saw it all.'

Philip did not change expression. Sitting demurely, with his hands in his lap, he repeated his question: 'Mr. Dumire, what are you talking about?'

'Murder!'

At this word Philip looked aghast. Tilting his head up so that he could see better the frenzied man towering above him, he asked, 'Murdered Mr. Gribben? I saw him this morning.'

'You little bastard!' Dumire had not introduced the name Sorenson, hoping to trap the boy into using it, but Philip had been too clever for that. Mr. Sorenson did not exist until Sheriff Dumire said he existed.

'Get out of here,' Dumire said, grinding his teeth.

'But I did see him,' Philip insisted as he rose.

'Did you see Mr. Sorenson?' Dumire shouted.

'Who is he?' Philip asked with blank innocence.

'Get out,' the sheriff said, kicking open the door.

Philip told no one of this exchange. Knowledge of it would only frighten his parents, and they were scheduled to sing that night at the church. The family went early to enjoy the supper, after which Reverend Holly said prayers and introduced the choir, which sang several hymns. 'And now,' he said with obvious pleasure, 'what we've all been waiting for! The Wendells to give us one of their beautiful renditions.'

He beamed as the Wendells took their place beside the piano. Then he nodded to Sheriff Dumire, sitting across the worship hall, and beamed again as Philip addressed his boyish soprano to the rich opening lines:

> 'Soft as the Voice of an Angel,
> Breathing a Lesson unheard . . .'

When Mervin, who must have done the actual killing, came in with his booming baritone, it was too much for Sheriff Dumire. He left before the concluding prayer.

Early next morning he rode over to the courthouse in Greeley to consult with Judge Leverton, an acidulous man who became furious when he learned the nature of Dumire's visit. 'How dare you come to me with shabby details of a case you can't prove? And take me into your confidence on something that could later come before me judicially? I ought to throw you in jail.'

Dumire ignored the rebuke. 'I'm merely asking your advice, sir.'

'For advice, sheriffs go to the district attorney.'

'You know more law than he does.'

'I'll give you some of it. You're in contempt of court.'

'Just one question. Will you give me a search warrant?'

'On such evidence? I'd be impeached.'

'Judge Leverton, I know they have the money.'

'On what possible evidence?'

'Because it's the only logical solution.'

'Get out of here! Before I have you arrested.'

On the ride back to Centennial the rebuked sheriff started once more to review the facts; something Judge Leverton had said came into his mind: 'Hell, Dumire, without a corpus delicti you have no right to even suggest murder. Sorenson could be enjoying himself in Texas.'

That was the fundamental problem. Find the corpse, then prove the guilt. But where could it have been hidden?

He now directed his whole attention to the territory around the Wendell house. If they killed him in there, he asked himself, how did they dispose of him?

One morning as Maude Wendell left home to deliver a basket of laundry, she noted with concern that a man was loitering in the empty field opposite their house, and when she looked closer she saw it was Sheriff Dumire, pacing off distances and moving ever closer to the old well.

When he saw her leave the house he nodded, and she returned the gesture, then walked down First Street as if Dumire were not there. Do not look back! she told herself firmly, but when she returned at noon she found her husband in the front room, peeking through the curtain and trembling. 'Look!' he told her in frightened whispers, and he pointed to where Dumire and two assistants were carrying a long ladder to the well.

Mervin stayed at the window, calling out to his wife the progress being made by the sheriff and his men. 'My God!' he shouted. 'Dumire's climbing down the well.'

At this tense moment Philip banged his way through the back door, asking, 'What do we have for lunch?' When his mother did not answer, he came into the front room. Seeing them transfixed at the window, he pushed his way in beside his father, just in time to see Sheriff Dumire's head disappear down the well.

Breaking into a laugh, he assured his father, 'He won't find anything.'

'How can you say that?' Mervin cried, leaving the boy and reaching for his wife's hand.

'Because I know,' his son said. 'Where's lunch?'

His parents could not tear themselves from the window, and soon they saw Dumire climb out of the well and indicate by a shrug of his shoulders that nothing unusual had been deposited there. Mrs. Wendell sighed and missed what happened next at the well, for her attention was diverted to the room behind her, where a loud clump indicated that Mervin Wendell had fainted.

But Sheriff Dumire had found something, a shred of cloth, and he bore this triumphantly to the Railway Arms, where he showed it to the maids, hoping to establish that it had come from some article of clothing Sorenson had worn, but in this attempt he failed. The cloth had been ripped from the shirt young Philip Wendell was wearing when he descended in the bucket, and although Dumire had the evidence firmly in his possession, he would never be able to trace it to Philip's shirt, for after the boy had trailed the sheriff to the hotel and discovered from a porter the nature of Dumire's questioning, he understood at once what the sheriff was trying to establish, and he scampered home, found his torn shirt and burned it.

The next day Philip experienced his one moment of terror. He had been playing east of town with some boys, and as they returned home they noticed a commotion on the little bridge that carried Mountain over Beaver Creek. 'The whole town's there!' one of the boys shouted, and they ran to see what was happening.

'Sheriff Dumire's up to something!' a woman cried. 'I think he's found the missing Swede.'

And Philip saw with dismay that the small creek was filled with boats carrying men who were dragging the bottom with grapples. In the lead boat stood Sheriff Dumire, calling orders, and as Philip watched in horrified fascination, the boats passed close to the spot where the entrance to the underwater cave lay submerged.

'See if the body could be caught under the edges,' Dumire directed, and long wooden probes poked unsuccessfully along the bank.

'Try down here,' Dumire called, and as his boat drifted downstream he happened to look up at the bridge, where an ashen-faced boy stood with his trembling chin pressed against the railing.

'Hello, Philip,' the sheriff called.

'What are you looking for?' the boy shouted.

'Things,' Dumire replied, and his boat drifted safely past the telltale cave. For a moment the boy feared he might faint, but then a woman at his elbow shouted, 'You ain't findin' much, are you, Sheriff?' And the boats disappeared beneath the bridge.

With that crucial day behind him, Philip could direct all his acting skill toward getting back into the good graces of the sheriff, and so persuasive was he in flattering Dumire that within a few days he was once more running blithely in and out of the office. In the late afternoons he would listen with open admiration as the sheriff explained what had been happening in town that day. 'You have so many different things to take care of,' the boy said admiringly. Once he asked Dumire if he had any children of his own, and the sheriff said 'One,' and that was all. He obviously did not care for any further questions on that subject, and Philip said, 'I wish I was your son.'

Dumire did not acknowledge the compliment, but inwardly he felt gratified that this boy liked both him and his job. There had been those who didn't. Back in Kansas his wife had asked in a complaining voice, 'What difference does it make if one man gets away?' And he had replied, 'All the difference, if you're the sheriff.' And six days later, when he rode back into town leading the handcuffed killer, he discovered that his wife and son had left, and he had not seen them since.

With sudden tenderness he asked, 'What are you gonna be when you grow up, Philip?'

'A sheriff,' Philip said promptly.

'Why?'

'A sheriff has to be brave and think about things.'

'That's right,' Dumire said encouragingly. 'I've been doing a lot of thinking, and you know what I found?'

'What?' Philip asked innocently.

'Mr. Sorenson came to your house and he did something that wasn't very nice to your mother, and your father killed him. Then he got scared and threw him down the well.' He paused for this to take effect, then asked, 'You know how I found out about the well?'

'What well?' Philip asked.

'On the crossbeam that holds the pulley that holds the rope, I saw marks of a second rope. Your mother let you down into the well in the bucket, didn't she, and you tied the rope around Mr. Sorenson's body, and then she pulled you back up in the bucket, and you helped her pull the dead body up. And I know it happened that way, Philip, because the rope left its mark. And of course, when you were being pulled up, a rock caught on your shirt and ripped off this piece of cloth.'

From his desk he produced a triangular piece of red-and-gray cloth. Philip looked at it and said nothing. He had never worn that shirt to Sheriff Dumire's office, so he felt no great worry at seeing the scrap of cloth. Sweeping it up in his right hand, Dumire tossed it back in the drawer. 'I'm not going to search your house for the shirt, Philip, because by now you've probably burned it.'

The two antagonists stared at each other, and Dumire asked quietly, 'Where did you hide him, Philip?'

The boy looked at the sheriff and said nothing.

Then Dumire made a mistake, a bad mistake. He said, 'You can tell me, Philip, because you're just a child. The judge can't do anything to you.'

Philip looked serenely at the older man, his resolute little jaw jutting out, and he said nothing, but into his eyes came a look of hurt. He was dismayed that Sheriff Dumire could think he was keeping silent to protect himself. If the sheriff knew so much, didn't he also know that Philip was protecting not himself but his parents? The boy's eyes fixed on Dumire's, and the sheriff felt the rebuke.

'Now, Philip,' he said lamely. 'I didn't mean that a boy should tell on his parents just so's he could go scot-free. I wouldn't advise that . . .

never.' Philip stared at him, and Dumire asked, 'Is there any way we can make a deal?'

The boy replied, 'I still want to be a sheriff. They have to think all the time . . . like you.' And he ran home.

But next day he was back in the office when Dumire received the warning telegram from Kansas:

THREE FORMER MEMBERS PETTIS GANG HEADING YOUR WAY TO KILL CALENDAR

The sheriff sprang into action at once, dispatching telegrams to towns along the Union Pacific and receiving word from Sterling that three men corresponding to the description had got off the train there, had hired horses and were heading west.

He was planning what steps to take when Jim Lloyd rode in to town from Line Camp Three, followed by the young Calendar boy astride a big horse. 'Sheriff!' the boy called. 'They're tryin' to kill my pop!'

'The boy rode into camp this morning,' Lloyd explained. 'We're getting up a posse to help you.'

'Let's go!' the sheriff said, and from Centennial he conscripted Potato Brumbaugh, always ready to join a posse, and two good riders.

He left the Calendar boy with Philip, thinking how their young lives had followed similar patterns—at an early age each had been required to face and conquer hazardous situations. Perhaps that was why men in the west grew so strong. They had to start fighting so young.

The posse rode east till they came to Calendar's beleaguered sheep wagon, where they found the sinewy Texan bleary-eyed from lack of sleep, a Sharps buffalo gun in his hands, and one dead Kansas gunslinger on the rise overlooking the draw.

'How did your son get through?' Dumire asked.

'He rode,' Calendar grunted, and Dumire could visualize the cautious preparation, the sneaking through darkness, the sudden lift onto the horse and the mad dash across the prairie.

'Where are the gunmen?' he asked Calendar.

'Follow their blood. I winged one in the leg.'

'Where'd they go?'

'West. Tryin' to catch a train and get out of here.'

Dumire led the posse back toward Centennial, and they entered town just in time to intercept the two killers, who had planned to catch the afternoon train to Denver. They had abandoned their horses and were hiding near the railway station when the posse arrived. As soon as Dumire and his men appeared, Philip leaped into the middle of the street, shouting, 'They're behind that store!'

Without hesitation Dumire spurred his horse and rode right at the two bandits. Bullets flew at him, but he kept going and gunned down the bandit with the wounded leg. The other escaped.

Now a manhunt occupied the town, and citizens with guns stalked warily down one street after another. Finally, at the intersection of Fourth Street and Fifth Avenue, up toward Zendt's store, Philip spotted the fugitive, and as he did so he saw with horror that Sheriff Dumire was walking blindly into a trap. Two more steps and the bandit would have a target he couldn't miss. Indeed, he was already leveling his gun.

For one moment Philip hesitated. If Dumire were to die, the secret of Soren Sorenson would die with him, for no one else in town had shared in the sheriff's guesses. If he were dead, there would be peace, and the Wendells could slowly start to spend their bundle of bills. But it was unthinkable that Dumire should die.

'Sher-iff!' the boy screamed with all the force he could command. Dumire jumped back and began firing. He killed the outlaw, but in doing so, took a fearful blast, which shattered his chest.

For three days the town of Centennial awaited news from the hospital. The citizens knew that Axel Dumire had represented a strong force for good in their town, and with this final elimination of the Pettis gang, they could hope that the peace this region deserved had finally arrived.

On Friday prayers were said, and Reverend Holly, his voice shaking, announced that for the closing of his service he had asked the Wendells to sing once more that divine song of hope. 'For there is hope,' he said. 'As long as God loves just men, there is hope.'

So the Wendells took their accustomed places beside the piano and their sweet voices united in that anthem of countryside hope. Never did they sing better, but toward the end, when Philip was singing the arabesques his parents had invented for him, his soprano voice broke, as if manhood were approaching, and he pressed his hands against his face so that people in the front rows could not see that he was crying, and he prayed, 'God, don't let him die.'

That night Sheriff Dumire told the doctor he wanted to see young Philip, so a deputy was sent to the Wendell house, and Mervin asked with intense excitement, 'Is he dead?' and the deputy said, 'He ain't got long. He wants to see your son,' and as the boy left the house, his mother stepped before him and gripped his hand and would have spoken to him or kissed him, but he needed no strengthening from her. Breaking away, he ran to the hospital.

There, in a small room lay Axel Dumire, attended by two nurses and a doctor. He indicated that he wanted them to leave, then said hoarsely, 'Philip, I'm dying . . . where did you hide the body?'

The boy stared at him in the old, innocent way, and the sheriff became angry. 'It can't hurt anybody now, goddamnit. Where did you hide it?'

The doctor, hearing the loud voice, came back in, but Dumire motioned that he was all right, and again they were alone. 'I have a right to know,' he pleaded. 'It's my job.' Philip said nothing.

Now a strange light of memory came into the dying man's eyes. 'By God, I remember!' he cried weakly. 'That day . . . You were swimming in Beaver Creek. Alone. You must have found something . . . a hiding place . . .'

Philip stared down at the sheriff as the latter fought back a strangling cough. He saw Dumire's body wrench in pain as he tried to hold the ends of life together for a few crucial minutes. 'It had to be in the creek!' Dumire said in a low whisper. His eyes grew bright as he put together the final pieces of the puzzle. 'You lugged the body from the well to the bank of the stream. You were too smart just to weight it down and throw it in, because you knew I'd drag for it. But somewhere . . . a place that no one else would know . . . maybe in the bank . . .'

The sorrow Philip felt for the dying man as he wrestled with death and truth drained blood from his face, and when Dumire saw that ashen countenance, he recalled the frightened boy he had seen on the bridge: 'That day we were dragging the stream! You grew terrified when you saw me so close to the bank. Philip, I know where the body is!'

He uttered these words triumphantly, for at last all pieces fitted together. 'You don't have to speak, son.' Never before had he called Philip that. 'You don't have to betray anyone. Just nod if I'm right . . . tell me . . . tell me . . .' His plea became an imploring moan which brought the doctor and nurses into the room.

They found Dumire dead, and clutching his hand, a young boy with golden hair, sobbing.

From the moment of Dumire's death, the fortunes of the Wendell family improved dramatically. Mervin's full-time job led to a promotion. Maude's doing laundry and mending in turn led to dressmaking and a solid acquaintance with the better families of the region, and Philip's reliability in doing odd jobs opened the path to friendship with the high school principal and, ultimately, a scholarship to the university.

Better yet, with Dumire gone, no one was left who could link the Wendells with the disappearance of Soren Sorenson, and with that basic fear removed, Mervin was free to start feeding into the economy the bundles of bills he had acquired in the small black bag. He did so with circumspection, a five this week, a ten next month, and the amounts were so restrained that they seemed in no way out of line with what the family was earning.

Best of all, at the bottom of Sorenson's bag of money Mervin had found a letter which the Swede had obviously intended mailing to his wife:

> A wise choice might be a small irrigated farm near Centennial plus about five thousand acres of drylands, on the chance that one of these days we'll learn how to grow wheat on it. I'm convinced it can be done.

So I'm thinking seriously of buying the Karpitz place north of town, with its forty irrigated acres, for about three thousand dollars. Then pick up all the drylands we need for twenty-five cents an acre.

Before burning the letter, a prudent move, Mervin copied down the relevant data, and after Sheriff Dumire was safely buried he rode north to talk with Adam Karpitz, and found him eager to sell. Mervin himself was no judge of land, but he felt safe in relying on Sorenson's conclusions as to its potential and his recommendations as to price.

Mervin's original offer was so low that Karpitz laughed, but gradually the two reached an agreement, but before closing it Mervin consulted with Reverend Holly, asking him, 'You know values around here. Is Karpitz asking a fair price?'

Holly studied the figures and said, 'I'd be glad to buy it at that price myself . . . if I had the money.'

'I don't have the money either,' Mervin said. 'But I'm thinking of applying to the bank for a mortgage.'

'Anyone in town would be willing to go your mortgage, Mervin. Few men have made the impression on Centennial you have. Your church work and all.' And it was then that Reverend Holly gave Wendell the idea that got him fairly started. 'Why bother with the bank? Why don't you see if Karpitz himself would carry the loan? At less interest.'

So he went back to Karpitz and propositioned him, and the farmer said, 'I like you, Wendell, did from the first time I heard you sing in church. How much can you put down?'

Mervin named a conservative figure, and Karpitz said, 'Too low. Tell you what, I'd like to keep the farm till about this time next year. That gives you one year to come up with one thousand dollars more. Beg, borrow or steal, anything but commit murder.' The two men laughed, and Mervin let it be known around town that his family was engaged in the task of saving a thousand dollars to use as down payment on the Karpitz place, and when people heard this, it was amazing how many openings the family encountered. Each day for eleven months they worked overtime, and the whole community followed the progress of their savings.

Every Wednesday night they met at the Union Church and listened to Reverend Holly, whose faith in them had got them started. And frequently he asked them to sing the old favorite, because as he said, 'A family is always entitled to hope.'

The rendition was somewhat different now, because only Maude and Mervin sang, and wonderful as they were, with their voices sliding up and down the scale, the obbligato of young Philip was missed. There were many inquiries as to why he did not sing; the real explanation was that he had warned his parents the night after Sheriff Dumire's funeral, 'I'm not going to sing high any more.'

Mervin told the congregation, on the side, 'You know how it is when voices change. He's beginning to be a little man.'

CAUTION TO *US* EDITORS: The laws of libel or a sense of propriety may keep you from using this story. That's up to you. I will affirm that it is correct, even to what might seem the most intimate details. How could I have uncovered such a macabre tale? Two days after I delivered Miss Endermann to the plane in Denver, I stumbled onto the cave in which the body had been buried eighty-five years earlier. I watched Morgan Wendell rush down to it when it was accidentally uncovered, and later took from it what I judged to be a human bone. During my subsequent work in Centennial, I heard various rumors about the Wendell antecedents and did some investigating in Denver on the theatrical couple who brought the family to Colorado originally. I became very much like Axel Dumire, piecing small bits together, and when I had a fairly complete dossier I went to see Morgan Wendell, with whom I had struck up an amiable but casual acquaintance. Placing my findings before him, I watched as he nearly fainted. First he thought I was trying to blackmail him at a crucial time in his political career; remember that this was early October of an election year. When I assured him that that was not my purpose, he assumed that you had sent me out to do a hatchet job on him for your November issue, which would hit the stands just prior to election day. After explaining what lead time was on a magazine, I convinced him that nothing I uncovered could possibly be printed till two months after the election. When he was satisfied on this point, he collapsed into a chair, poured himself one hell of a whiskey and talked to me for three hours. I did not have a tape recorder, but I took copious notes, none of which would be accurate enough to defend you in a libel case, should you decide to break the story. The important thing he said was this: 'My father, Philip Wendell, who was responsible for our family fortune, was a man with ice water in his veins. I never saw him flustered, never heard him raise his voice, never knew him to be diverted from the main topic at hand. He was almost brutally honest and a master of understatement. I thought he had no feelings, but when his final illness overtook him in 1951 he became extremely talkative, and for five days during a December blizzard he insisted upon telling me, only me in a wintry room, about his days with the traveling troupe, of the crime his family had committed and of the one really great man he had known, a small-town sheriff named Axel Dumire.'

Theater. If you illustrate this chapter or one like it, do not be misled by the grubbiness of the Maude and Mervin Wendell Theatrical Troupe. Since Centennial was on the main railroad from Omaha to Denver, it had a rich opportunity to see in its small theater most of the great actors and actresses of that day. In the 1889 seasons Lillie Langtry, Sarah Bernhardt, Helena Modjeska, Edwin Booth and Thomas Keene played there. Nine different Shakespeare dramas were offered, including four starring Booth, but the artistic gem of the period was the Divine Sarah in *Camille*. Of it the critic from the *Clarion* said:

> Bernhardt faded away like a delicate flower afflicted by some deadly blight, exhaling a radiant fragrance to the last. Some deaths in the theater are beautiful in their gradual dissolution. Others come like the soft approach of a summer evening. But there is no death so sublime and moving as that which claims this ever-hopeful consumptive.

Shortly after the dissolution of the Wendell Troupe, Centennial was visited by the Italian Opera Company, with a full repertoire and three stars of the first magnitude: Adelina Patti, Madame Albani, Francesco Tamagno. Greatest acclaim, however, was reserved for that perennial play *The Count of Monte Cristo*, featuring James O'Neill, heavy-drinking father of the future playwright.

12
CENTRAL
BEET

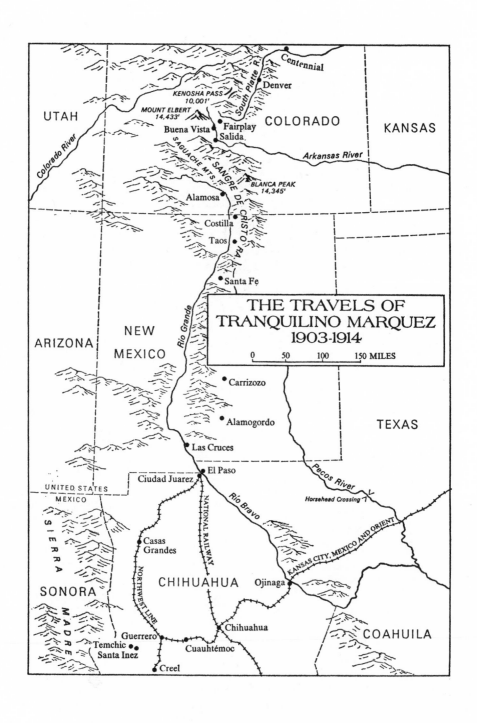

THE TRAVELS OF
TRANQUILINO MARQUEZ
1903-1914

0   50   100   150 MILES

THE TROUBLE WITH SUGAR BEETS, A MAN could never find anyone to do the thinning.

For example, Potato Brumbaugh had learned that it was prudent to deep-plow his fields in late October, so that winter snow would water them and winter freezing aerate the compact soil and break up the clods. In March a brisk sequence of disk, harrow and drag would have the land moist, firm, level and ready to seed. And at this point the job looked easy.

Unfortunately, the seed of the beet was both small and unreliable. It would have been all right if Brumbaugh could plant one seed here and another twelve inches down the row, with a reasonable expectation that each would germinate and produce its one-pound beet, but that he could not depend upon, for the seeds were capricious; one would germinate properly and the very next one, alike in every outward aspect and nurtured in identical soil, would not.

So on April 25, when the likelihood of frost had diminished, he had to plant his sugar beets the way a housewife plants radishes: he sowed the seed heavily along the whole length of his rows, using about twenty-four times as many seeds as he really needed. This heavy overplanting was necessary to offset high losses in germinating and the early death of weak plants that did germinate; insects, weather and carelessness could cause losses as high as seventy percent.

On May 26, therefore, he had in his carefully tended rows not one plant every twelve inches, the way he wanted, but a continuous line of young plantlings, eight for every one he intended keeping. If all eight were allowed to mature, they would be so crowded that none would have space or food to produce a usable beet. So he had to do what the housewife did: take a long-handled hoe and chop away seven out of every eight plants, leaving one strong plant to produce its beet.

Blocking and thinning it was called, and tedious work it was, for it required a person to move slowly over the entire field, hour after hour, hacking away at the unwanted plants. No owner had the time to block his whole acreage by himself, for the job had to be done within a brief, specified period, lest the unwanted plants grow so tall that their roots would suck away the nutrition required by the one which had been selected to produce the beet.

A lot of men and women with hoes were needed to block a field properly, and they had to be reliable, for they were required to work fast and to exercise judgment.

'Some farmers block their plants ten inches apart,' Brumbaugh instructed the Italian immigrants who appeared by the trainload to work the beets, 'but I like mine a little farther apart, about a foot. Keep this stick with you to show how far apart the plants should be.'

The Italians were excellent workers, with a sense of soil and a quick comprehension of what Brumbaugh wanted. They understood when he said, 'I've been chopping beets so long, I can hack out the unwanted ones with one swipe of the hoe. More better you use two chops . . . like this.'

The Italians worked well, but wouldn't stay on the job. They didn't like transient work or the loneliness of sugar-beet plantations. Time and again a fine crew would spend one spring with Brumbaugh, but come late summer they would hear about the steel mills down in Pueblo and off they would go for work where they could have their own little house in an Italian community with its priest and a good restaurant, and the sugar beets would see them no more.

'Giuseppe,' Brumbaugh pleaded with the head of one family, 'why can't you stay north with me?'

'Ah, I like to be with the others. Some singing. A priest you can rely on. No, I'm going to Pueblo.' And off he went, leaving Brumbaugh with no one to block his beets, or thin them, or pull and top them at harvest.

German immigrants were arriving in New York about this time, so the beet farmers around Centennial paid the train fare for sixty families, and they were some of the best help Brumbaugh ever had. He enjoyed talking with them in German, even if they did laugh at his Russian pronunciation, but they posed a serious problem: they loved the land, and within two years of arriving at the Brumbaugh farm, they wanted land of their own, and left to grow their own beets.

The next experiment had a more fortunate outcome . . . at first. Brumbaugh, at his wits' end, proposed to a group of his sugar-beet neighbors, 'Why not the Russians? When I lived on the Volga they knew more about sugar beets than anyone.' So the community imported numerous German-Russian families—Emig, Krakel, Frobe, Stumpf, Lebsack, Giesinger, Wenzlaff—and when these sturdy men and women got off the train at Centennial they took one look at the spacious fields and knew intuitively that they had found a permanent home.

They were splendid people, hard workers, thrifty, intelligent. Ten minutes of instruction told them all they required about their new job, and

when Brumbaugh saw them whisking down the rows, chopping out unwanted beets with one swipe, he knew he had solved his problem.

Not quite. The Volgadeutsch yearned for land even more than the
Germans, and within eighteen months each family had begun to pay in-
stallments on a farm of its own, and with sorrow in his big square face
Potato Brumbaugh watched them pack up their few belongings and leave.

He was cooperative. When Otto Emig informed him that he was buying the Stupple place, Brumbaugh said, 'Karl, that farm's too small to
work profitably. You ought to pick up fifty more acres while you can.'

'I have no money,' Emig said.

'I'll lend you some. I don't want a good farmer like you to start on too
small a plot.' In this way he helped some dozen of the Russians get their
foothold, hardy men and women with large families who would lend
much character to the northern plains. Strasser, Schmick, Wiebe, Grutz-
ler—they all owed their mortgages to Potato Brumbaugh and they were
grateful, but still Brumbaugh found himself with no one to block his
beets.

He imported Indians from the reservation and they were all right during the spring when they could work with horses, but when it came time
to hoe, they vanished. He tried impoverished white men drifting westward
from states like Missouri and Kansas, but they stole, got drunk and trampled the young plants, leaving six-inch gaps in one row, fifteen in the
next. They seemed determined to prove why they had become derelicts
and why they would remain so.

'Get them out of here!' Brumbaugh thundered. 'I'll block the beets
myself.' But when the useless drifters were gone and he attempted to farm
the fields, he found that whereas he might be able to block a large field
at the age of seventy-seven, he could certainly not take the next step and
thin it too.

Thinning was the brutal part, the stoop-work. It required a man to
bend over hour after hour, demonstrating judgment, accuracy and the
ability to endure prolonged discomfort. Again the trouble lay in the seed,
for instead of a single seed, beets have a cluster of from three to five enclosed in a hard, rough shell. When planted, the cluster produces not one
plant, but three or four or five. The shell is too hard to be broken and no
way has been found to encourage one of the plants to grow and the others
to die.

'What you have to do,' Brumbaugh told his various workers, 'is go
down the row that's been blocked and look at each of the bunches we've
left standing. You'll see that each bunch is really three or four or five
plants. Each could produce a beet, but if they all did, none of the beets
would be worth a nickel. So what I want you to do is leave the biggest
plant and pull the others out. And be sure to get the root.'

He could not avoid this imprecision: 'Guess the good one and kill the
others.' In the end, it had to be a matter of personal judgment. With his

practiced eye he could pick the strong plant, and had he the strength to thin his entire acreage, he would produce the best crop in Colorado, but this crucial task he had to leave to others—to the guesswork of untrained hands. He used to shudder when he saw them ripping out the good plant and leaving in its place another that could never produce a big beet.

'Can't you see which the good ones are?' he used to rail at the thinners in the early days. He stopped when he realized that they couldn't see, that to them one plant looked pretty much like another, and he began to wonder if the sugar-beet industry could survive when it had to depend upon such unreliable labor.

Yet he was gentle with his workers, for he knew that thinning beets was among the most miserable jobs on earth. Hour after hour, bent double, eyes close to the earth, back knotted with pain, knees scabbed where they dragged along the ground. He had great respect for a man, or more likely a child, who could thin beets properly, and he brooded about where he would find his next crop of workers.

It was his son, Kurt, now in his prosperous forties, who solved the problem. Kurt had become Colorado's leading legal expert on irrigation; in Washington he had defended the state before the Supreme Court and in Denver had helped draft the state laws governing the use of water. Because of his knowledge he had been the logical lawyer for the sugar-beet financiers to look to after they had collected the large amount of capital required to launch Central Beet, for they intended to construct a many-tentacled company, with factories in all areas. In time this combine would dominate the western states.

A sugar beet was worthless until a sugar factory stood nearby. A mature beet was a heavy gray-brown lump of fiber hiding a liquid which with great difficulty could be made to yield crystallized sugar. In the late eighteenth century chemists in Germany, where there was no sugar cane, perfected an intricate method of making the beet surrender its sugar, but the industry had staggered along until Napoleon Bonaparte, faced by the loss of cane sugar due to the British blockade, decreed, 'Let us have beet sugar!' and the French discovered how to provide it.

Because the beets were so heavy, and transporting them so costly, it was obligatory that the factory be near at hand, and it fell to a committee of three men in Central Beet to determine where the factories should be located. An engineer, a soil expert and Kurt Brumbaugh, as the irrigation man skilled in finance, visited every likely area from Nebraska to California, choosing sites. They made some mistakes, and lost thousands of dollars in the process, but mostly they chose well, and never did they select a better site than on that day in the spring of 1901 when they announced, 'Our biggest plant in northern Colorado will be erected this summer in Centennial. A plant capable of slicing nine hundred tons of beets per day. When finished, it will be able to handle the entire crop from this area.'

The E. H. Dyer Construction Company of California moved in its skilled engineers and the Union Pacific started building a spur down which the beets would arrive and along which the bags of sugar would depart. It was a massive operation, located east of town on Beaver Creek, for the extraction process required much water.

When the factory was completed in 1902, and the first wagonloads of Potato Brumbaugh's beets were delivered, the slicing began, then the carbonation process, then the crystallization. Soon across Centennial drifted the rich, distinctive smell of wet-pulp fermentation. Some citizens thought it acrid or even putrescent, and after a couple of seasons of sugar-making they left town, unable to stand the new odors. But most found it to be the smell of progress, a decent, earthy aroma of beets turning themselves into gold.

Messmore Garrett, who welcomed any scientific addition to the community, observed, 'It's an earthy smell . . . organic . . . crisp. I like it.' In time, most people living in Centennial grew to welcome the yearly arrival of the sugar smell. Charlotte Lloyd said, 'It sort of cleans out the nose, like the smell of good manure. I feel better when the campaign starts.'

Mature sugar beets were harvested during October and early November, for they had to be out of the ground before the heavy frosts of late November. This meant that they began arriving at the factory about the first of October, with the slicing under way every day till the middle of February. This period was known as the campaign, and it was an exciting time in the beet country, for not only did the rich smell permeate the countryside, but the top ten farmers of each district were announced, and to be one of the top ten in Centennial was a coveted accolade in American agriculture.

Each farmer's yield per acre was determined by taking the total weight of beets delivered to the factory, less the weight of dirt he had allowed to cling to his beets, less the weight of excess tops he had failed to chop off, divided by his total acreage. Toward the end of each year the officials at Central Beet announced their findings, after which the ten winners were photographed. Their pictures would appear in the Centennial paper, suitably captioned: 'Our Top Ten, They Can't Be Beet!' And then these leaders were feted at a large banquet in Denver.

In 1904 it was suspected that the Centennial championship would go either to Potato Brumbaugh, who had won the two previous years, or to Otto Emig, who had some good acreage along the Platte east of town. Brumbaugh growled, 'If Emig wants to win, he's got to do better than seventeen and a half tons to the acre.' Some listeners considered this boastful, and Emil Wenzlaff challenged him: 'You never made seventeen and a half, Potato, and you know it.'

'Wait till you see the figures,' Brumbaugh said confidently. He was an old man now, and when he grinned at his competitors, his mouth was yellow and wrinkled at the corners. The other farmers could not believe that a man his age could have thinned so large a portion of his crop, for he was thick-set, and bending must have been painful. However, since he could find no competent help, he had had no choice but to tend the fields himself.

As he compared notes with others who hoped for the championship, he invariably ended with one question: 'What are we going to do about help?' He listened as the other farmers proposed various solutions: 'More Germans, but this time get the dumb ones who don't want to send their kids to school.' 'Why not try the Indians again? They're not doing anything up there on the reservation.' 'What we need is someone who enjoys doing stoop-work and doesn't want to buy his own farm.' But where to find such workers?

Otto Emig, whose beets looked the best of the lot, argued, 'Central Beet would never have spent so much money building that factory if they didn't have a plan in mind. They'll find us workers somewhere.' The solution to this problem was to come from a man not associated with the factory.

Jim Lloyd, at Venneford, had been delighted with the arrival of the sugar factory, because it provided an alternative source of feed for his white-faced cattle. It was pulp that was important to him.

'I love to smell that pulp come out the chute,' Jim said. 'I like the way my Herefords go for it.'

When the heavy sugar beet was sliced and pressed, and its precious liquid drained off, there remained a moist, grayish mass called pulp. It was an excellent fodder for cattle; especially when mixed with heavy black low-grade molasses, another by-product of the sugar process.

'Pulp and molasses!' Jim Lloyd said admiringly. 'Whenever I cart a load of that up to the feed yards, you can almost see the Herefords spreading the news. They'd walk miles for it.'

Jim was therefore much concerned about keeping the Centennial factory operating, and he knew that without reliable help for the local farmers during the blocking and thinning seasons, the whole thing was going to go bust. Germans, Indians, Italians, Russians, poor whites—none of them was a solution. 'We've got to find someone who can be trusted to thin properly and who'll stay on the job.' He decided to talk to Kurt Brumbaugh about an idea he had.

In December heady news spread through Centennial. Otto Emig had apparently performed a miracle.

As soon as it became apparent that some farmer stood a chance of winning the championship, experts from the factory went to that man's farm with a steel chain to measure the exact number of acres he had harvested, and the results at Otto Emig's farm indicated that he had set a new record: 'Seventeen point seven tons to the acre!'

Emil Wenzlaff carried the news to Brumbaugh. 'That's what he done, Potato.'

'He's a good farmer,' Brumbaugh admitted grudgingly. He could not believe that Emig had done so well on those bottom lands. He must have fertilized each plant by hand.

Potato had enjoyed many successes in his life and it would have been generous of him to concede victory this year to Otto Emig, but he was a fearful competitor and at seventy-seven needed victory as keenly as he had at twenty-seven.

And then the final figures were released! In a long article in the *Clarion*, with photographs, it was revealed that Potato Brumbaugh had set a new record! Seventeen point nine tons to the acre, a figure so high the other farmers could scarcely believe it.

Of his victory Brumbaugh said, 'The right soil, the right water, the right seed, this Platte Valley land can grow anything.'

'And the right thinning," Otto Emig said generously.

'Where will we get our thinners next year?' Potato asked.

In late February 1905 Kurt Brumbaugh sprang his surprise. He announced that following a suggestion provided by Jim Lloyd, and as a result of extensive investigation, Central Beet had come up with the ideal solution to the problem. Its field men had located the world's best agriculturists, men and women—and children, too—who could grow fuzz on a billiard ball. One hundred and forty-three of them would arrive on March 11 prepared to make the Platte Valley hum.

All the beet growers of the region were at the station when the train pulled in, and it was a day memorable in Colorado history. Down the iron steps leading from the cars came a timid, frightened group of men, women and children. They were small, thin, shy and dark. They were Japanese, and not one of them spoke a word of English, but the waiting farmers could see that they were a rugged people, with stout, bowed legs and hands like iron. If any people on God's earth could thin sugar beets properly, these were the ones.

A representative from the Japanese consulate in San Francisco stepped forward, a bright young man in dark suit and glasses, and he said in precise English, 'Gentlemen of Centennial and surrounding terrain. These are all trusted farm families. You can rely on them to work. In consultation with Mr. Kurt Brumbaugh of Central Beet, we have assigned them as follows.'

And he began to recite that extraordinary series of lyric four-syllable names: Kagohara, Sabusawa, Tomoseki, Yasunori, Nobutake, Moronaga. As he did so, the families stepped forward, shoulder to shoulder, and bowed low from the waist, even the smallest children. Each family was then assigned to one of the Russian farmers, a curiosity which the editor of the *Clarion* duly noted:

> Yesterday at the Union Pacific station a miracle happened, an amazing event which could have occurred only in the United States, where people of diverse races and religions live together in perfect harmony. A group of one hundred and forty-three sons and daughters of the Sun Goddess arrived in our fair city and were promptly assigned to work with our finest Russian farmers, and this at a time when Japan and Russia are locked in mortal combat on the other side of the world. Since the Japanese speak no English and no Russian, they have placed themselves in the hands of their worst enemies. But such is the miracle of America that no one present at the station yesterday had the slightest fear that the local Russians would in any way treat their Japanese workmen poorly or with injustice.

The editor was right. This was a most happy union of Japanese who knew how to farm with Russians who loved the soil, and during that war-torn year, peace and amity reigned along the Platte, primarily because the Japanese were the best sugar-beet workers in the world.

To Potato Brumbaugh were assigned the Takemotos: father aged twenty-seven, mother aged twenty-five and strong as a Hereford, daughter aged seven, son aged six, son aged three. They rose before sunrise, had a meal of rice plus whatever they could find to go with it, and went out into the beet fields with the wife carrying a small basket containing cold rice balls, each with a sour pickled plum in the center, and a bucket of cold tea. They worked till dusk with a tenacity that Brumbaugh had not seen before.

Mother and father would take their hoes and start blocking, each to his own row. Behind Mr. Takemoto crawled his elder son, thinning the clumps. Behind Mrs. Takemoto crawled the seven-year-old girl, thinning her row. All day the baby watched the workers, pulling away any half-rooted plants they had missed. Since the parents could block a little faster than the children could thin, at the end of each row the elders would put down their hoes, drop to their knees and thin back down the row till they met their children. At each such meeting there would be a brief pause while the parents brushed away dirt from the round little faces or said something reassuring. Then it was back to the hoes and the thinning.

From March through October, there was no spoken communication between Potato Brumbaugh and this remarkable family. In pantomime he would show them what he wanted; after that they took charge, and by mid-September it was pretty clear that he stood a good chance of winning the championship again.

He told his son, 'Kurt, the best thing you ever did for Central Beet was to bring in the Takemotos. One of them is worth six Russians. No wonder Japan won the war.'

And then he noticed two chilling things. The Takemotos were obviously acquiring money, and they were looking at land. How could they get hold of that much money? When Brumbaugh had allowed them a small plot by the river, he expected they would grow a few vegetables for their own use; instead, they had cultivated the land with extreme frugality, depositing on it all the Takemoto sewage, and were producing so many fine vegetables that Mrs. Takemoto was peddling the surplus through the village.

Where did they find time to do this? From sunup to sundown they worked in Brumbaugh's fields, but they rose an hour early and in the darkness tended their vegetables, and in the moments after sunset they did not sit around resting after that day's work. All five of them were down by the river, watering and hoeing and cultivating. When Brumbaugh indicated in sign language, 'In America we don't use human manure,' Mr. Takemoto replied in excited gestures, 'In Japan we do, long, long time.'

'Well, quit doing it here!' Brumbaugh indicated, and they did. Each morning when they came to work and each night when they went home, the Takemotos carried a bag in which they gathered horse manure, or any other that had fallen, and their garden flourished.

On Saturday afternoons and Sundays, Mrs. Takemoto, accompanied by her son, who was picking up a few words of English, trailed through town, offering her enormous vegetables for sale and accumulating cash, which the family deposited at the local bank.

'They come in here every Saturday morning,' the banker told Brumbaugh, 'and without saying a word they plop their money down and I give them a slip. He checks it and she checks it and then they check it a third time with me, and then they write something in their gobbledegook and they bow and go out.'

What really frightened Brumbaugh was that on Sundays the Takemotos, all five of them, inspected farms in the region. He saw them first one hot day in September, the father kneeling in the soil of the old Stacey place, the mother checking the irrigation gate, the children playing with stones. In August they were up at the Limeholder place at the end of the English Ditch, inspecting the soil and the water. Later he saw them at the abandoned Stretzel farm, beyond Otto Emig's excellent land, and in October, when the beets were topped and delivered and Brumbaugh was on his way to another championship, the ax fell.

Takemoto and his wife, and the three children, appeared at the Brumbaugh ranch, bowing low. Mrs. Takemoto, who apparently handled the money, placed a bankbook before Potato, and by means of gestures easily understood, indicated that they had decided to buy the Stretzel farm. They sought help from him in arranging the legal details.

Brumbaugh was seventy-eight that October and he feared that he had not the strength to break in a new set of help or till the fields himself. He judged it terribly unfair that this family had stayed with him less than a year, and he needed them more now than he had in March. He was tired, and there had been frightening spells of dizziness. A prudent man would quit the farm and the irrigation board and retire to Denver to live in ease, but to Potato this was simply not an option. He loved the soil, the flow of water, even the sight of deer in the far fields eating their just share of the crops. He had taken this once-barren land and made a garden of it, plowing back year after year the beet tops which helped keep it strong. Some farmers, eager for the last penny, sold their beet tops to Jim Lloyd as forage for his Herefords, but Brumbaugh would not consider this. 'The tops belong to the soil,' he told young farmers. 'Plow them back and keep the land happy. Cart manure from the ranches. Everything depends on the soil.'

It had been Brumbaugh who devised the clever system of importing boxcar-loads of bat manure from the recently discovered deposits at the bottom of Carlsbad Caverns in New Mexico. This new-type fertilizer was dry and compact and easy to handle. It was also preternaturally rich in mineral deposits; where it was used, crops grew.

Because of his own preoccupation with manure and its relationship to land, Brumbaugh had followed carefully the efforts of the Takemotos to enrich their soil, and whereas he had not always approved of their methods, he did applaud their determination. Therefore, when Takemoto sought his help in finding a farm for himself, Brumbaugh was ready to assist.

He loaded the family into a wagon and drove them to town. The banker, whose wife had for some time been buying vegetables from Mrs. Takemoto, said judiciously, 'These people have a fine reputation, Potato. Look like top-quality risks. But they don't begin to have enough money to make a down payment on the Stretzel place.'

Of the Takemotos, only the six-year-old son had acquired any mastery of English, and now he stepped forward as the interpreter. Jabbering in Japanese, he explained to his father that the banker could not lend the missing funds, then listened as his father spoke with terrible intensity.

Turning to the banker, the boy said, 'He not want money you. He want money him,' and the child pointed directly at Brumbaugh.

'Me?' This was too much. The family was deserting him, and they wanted him to finance their flight. 'No!' he roared. 'You leave me alone . . . helpless. Then you want me to pay . . .'

When the child interpreted this, it had a profound effect on Mr. Takemoto. Ignoring the banker, he turned to face Brumbaugh and his eyes misted. He spoke directly to Potato in Japanese, as if he knew the Russian would understand, and he made walking gestures with his fingers, and after a while the child broke in and said, 'We not leave you,' and he made the same walking gestures across the banker's desk, saying, 'We walk thin beets you. We walk thin beets us.'

Brumbaugh understood. This incredible family was proposing that for the next year they would work two farms—Brumbaugh's during the good hours, their own during the dark—and to accomplish this they were prepared to trudge twice a day the miles between.

This was in the fall of 1905, when the Russo-Japanese bitterness had not yet subsided, but in Centennial the two men looked carefully at each other, an aging Russian who had known great success in this land, a bulldog little Japanese who longed for a chance to equal it, and each knew he could trust the other. If Takemoto said he would tend Brumbaugh's beets, he would, and after a while the Russian said to the banker, 'Call Merv Wendell in here,' and in a few minutes the prosperous real estate broker joined them.

'Merv,' Brumbaugh said, 'two months ago you quoted me a price of four thousand dollars on the Stretzel farm. I offered you three-five, and you said you thought they'd take three-seven. Well, Mr. Takemoto here is offering you three-seven as of this minute, and, Merv, I don't want him to suffer any fancy business at your hands.'

'Potato!' the real estate man cried in honest dismay. 'Do you think for one minute . . .'

'I know what you tried with Otto Emig,' Brumbaugh cut in sharply. 'No fancy charges this time. Three-seven.'

'Of course, of course!' Wendell agreed. 'And you're getting one of the best farms in the area,' he said unctuously to Takemoto.

'He don't understand English,' Brumbaugh growled. 'But I do. And you see he gets it, fee simple, by tomorrow night.'

'Yes, sir, Mr. Brumbaugh, yes, sir. And when you want to sell your place . . .'

'That'll be many years, Merv.'

'We aren't getting any younger, are we?'

'I am,' Brumbaugh said, and before he left the bank he signed Takemoto's note for three thousand dollars. Looking down at the six-year-old child who had negotiated the deal in a language he had first heard only eight months ago, he thought, I've never felt safer about signing a note. If the old man can't pay, the boy will.

Next morning he visited Kurt at the sugar factory and told him, 'I want you to issue Goro Takemoto a contract for twenty-five acres of beets, and I want you to see that he gets some good seed.'

The sugar industry was an ingenious interlocking arrangement whereby many disparate elements were forced to depend upon one another in creating a sophisticated whole. The factory could not exist without assurance that farmers would supply it with beets, and the farmers had no alternative but to sell their beets to the factory; there simply was no other market.

The interdependence went further. Land produced the beets, but the tops were plowed back to enrich that land. Extracting sugar produced the by-products of pulp and molasses, which could be fed to cattle, whose manure came back to keep the land productive.

Because of this interdependence, the industry found it logical to operate on a system of binding contracts, and each January the farmers waited anxiously for a visit from the company field man to sign that precious slip of paper which guaranteed that all beets raised on the allotted acreage would be purchased as from October 1, with the first payment coming on November 15.

With this contract the farmer could go to the Centennial Bank and borrow the money he needed for seeds in March, planters in April, thinners in May and his general expenses through October. Come November 15 his first check would arrive: twenty-five acres of beets, sixteen tons to the acre, six dollars a ton equals $2400.

The check was never made payable to the farmer. Invariably it read something like this: 'Centennial Bank, Mervin Wendell, Otto Emig,' a shrewd precaution which ensured that the bank would recover its loan, Mervin Wendell would collect on his mortgage, and Otto Emig would receive whatever was left over.

The system was a tribute to intelligence: procedures were spelled out clearly, financed with adequate capital, and administered justly. But what Potato Brumbaugh, with his philosophical inclination, relished was the higher intricacy of beet production, for to him this proved the limitless capacity of man. One night when the Russian farmers were bemoaning the growing number of Japanese in business for themselves, he grew impatient: 'Keep your eye on the beet. A hundred years ago it was a little round red thing that weighed three ounces. It was an annual, which meant that each year it produced the whole cycle: leaves, root, stalks, seeds, and it gave damned little sugar . . . less than one percent. Well, some smart Germans took that red thing and changed it to white. They multiplied the size until it weighed over a pound. They turned it into a two-year plant, big root this year. If replanted, seeds next year, which meant that all the first-year energy could go to making sugar. This increased the sugar content from less than one percent to fifteen percent and maybe pretty soon sixteen or seventeen. If men can do that to the beet, they're smart enough to find us workmen to help grow it.'

It was a pretty speech, and it told the Russians things they hadn't known before, but as Otto Emig whispered to Emil Wenzlaff, 'You notice he didn't say where we'll find men for stoop-work when our Japanese leave.'

Everything was under scientific control except the one element which determined success or failure: where could the farmer find a labor force willing to do stoop-work without wanting to buy farms or educate children to the point where they no longer wished to thin beets? The whole intricate structure, so vital to the west, threatened to collapse around this insoluble problem.

And then one day Potato Brumbaugh rode up to Venneford to sell his crop of hay, and he warned Jim Lloyd, 'After this year there may not be any hay for your Herefords.'

'Where you gonna sell it?'

'I may have to quit growing it.'

This improbable statement confused Lloyd, because he knew that a beet farmer had to grow hay; beets were so voracious in sucking minerals from the soil that no field could grow them continuously. If this was tried, the minerals would be used up, allowing sugar-beet nematodes and other insects to infest the field, stunting the beets or even killing them off. So when a provident farmer dug his beets in October, next year he planted that field in barley, then alfalfa for two years and then potatoes. Only in the fifth year would he dare to plant beets again.

This meant that a man would divide his farm into enough segments to practice this rotation, and the maximum land he could apply to beets in any one year would be one of those segments. The others had better be growing hay, or something like potatoes or barley. So if Brumbaugh intended to go on with beets, Jim knew he had to grow hay too, and he told Potato so.

'I mean I'm going to quit farming altogether,' Brumbaugh said. 'I can't find anyone to stay on the job, and neither can Emig or Wenzlaff.' He recounted for Jim his disillusioning experiences: 'My Germans thinned beets two years, then bought their own farm. My Russians stayed eighteen months, and *pooooof!* They had their own place. And those Japanese! they bought a farm in eight months. What we've got to find is someone who loves farming but hates farms.'

As Brumbaugh spoke these words, Jim was leaning on a gate to a field dotted with Crown Vee cows and their sleek, gentle calves. Even after all these years Jim was fascinated by the Hereford, constantly seeking to improve his herd, always trying to deduce why certain of these cows dropped strong calves.

'This bunch of calves from the same bull?' Brumbaugh asked.

Jim nodded. 'That calf by the fence . . .' He never completed his sentence, because as he stared at the calf he remembered a day almost forty years before when he had known another calf—on the burning alkali flats east of the Pecos when he and R. J. Poteet were herding longhorns. A calf had been born and R. J. had ridden back to the drags and ordered them to kill it. Jim had been unable to do so. 'I raise calves,' he had told Poteet, 'I don't kill 'em.'

And with the connivance of the chuck-wagon cook—what was his name, Mexican of some kind—he had saved the calf and later the cook had traded it to Mexican squatters farming land near the great Chisum ranch, and he could still see the joy shining in the eyes of those peons when they got their hands on that calf—the round, dark faces, the heavy black hair, the white teeth, the brown hands offering chili beans and chickens.

'I've got it!' he said. 'Mexicans!'

South of the Rio Grande, known in Mexico as the Río Bravo, lay the huge state of Chihuahua, with its capital of the same name situated near the middle. One hundred and twenty-five miles west of the city rose the steep, dark mountains of the Sierra Madre, rich in gold and silver.

Dropping out of the mountains like a slim thread of spun silver came the Falls of Temchic, graceful and lovely in themselves but made more so by the valley into which they fell. The Vale of Temchic ran eastward from the mountains, a delicate enclave surrounded on three sides by rocky forms so unusual they seemed to have been placed in position by an artist. North of the Río Temchic stood the four guardian peaks: La Águila, El Halcón, El León, El Oso—Eagle, Falcon, Lion, Bear. Along the south side rose great masses of granite, looking like ships or sulking prehistoric animals.

For some three thousand years this valley had been the home of the Temchic Indians, a tribe of the Tarahumare, those slim, deerlike people who occupied the mountains, living with a minimal culture, so primitive were they. Old accounts claimed that the Temchics had been a handsome, gentle tribe, but this cannot be confirmed. Unfortunately, the valley they had chosen for their home contained one of the world's major silver mines, and although they never discovered how to mine the ore, Spaniards exploring the region in 1609 did, and the Temchics were promptly rounded up, forcibly converted to Christianity and pressed into an underground slavery so terrible that by the year 1667 not a single Temchic existed, either above ground or below.

Legend said that the silver of the waterfall fell an equal distance into the earth, where it crystallized into a rich vein penetrating deep. Certainly the Temchic mines reached far down, and to bring the ore to the surface was always a problem. Long, slim tree trunks were let down into the bowels, and bare cross beams about three feet wide were nailed to the trunks, forming a suicidal ladder without railing or protection and rising almost vertically.

Up these dreadful ladders the Temchics had been forced to climb, lugging enormous baskets of ore. Year after year they lived underground, and their death knell sounded in vanishing screams as they plunged one after the other, weak and unsteady, from the tall ladders. 'The last Temchic died yesterday,' the report of 1667 related, 'but we have the consolation of knowing that they all died Christians.'

The vale was lovingly referred to as Temchic plateada—Silvery Temchic—and when the original Indians were gone, the Spanish operators of the mines corralled the gentle Tarahumare from the Sierra Madre, but they perished at an appalling rate, so that it was scarcely economical to continue using them. One Spanish engineer reported to Madrid: 'They take one look at the deep pit and the ladders and fall to their death. I do not believe they fall through vertigo. I believe they throw themselves into the pit rather than work in darkness when they have been accustomed to the mountain peaks.'

Their place in the valley was taken by that strange and often beautiful race of mestizos—part Indian, part Spaniard—which would come to be known as Mexican. By no means could they be called Spaniards, for that blood had been seriously diluted, but on the other hand, they were not Indians, either, for a semi-European culture had displaced the Indian language, the Indian religion and the Indian way of doing things.

They were Mexicans, a new breed and a stalwart one. They were people capable of enormous effort when they saw it was needed, capable of either a compelling gentleness when generously treated or savage retribution when outraged. Many bloodlines converged in them: in Mexico's colonial period the land contained about 15,000,000 Indians; among them came 300,000 Spaniards and 250,000 blacks from Africa, and out of this mix arose the Mexican. Since the Spaniards were dominant, and since only they had the guns and books and churches, the culture quickly became predominantly Spanish: language, military organization, religion, ways of doing business were all Spanish, so it was understandable that the new people should boast, 'Somos españoles,' but they were not. They were Mexicans, and often the Spanish blood was a mere trickle.

On the other hand, since the Spaniards killed off a large percentage of the Indians and since they subjugated the blacks unmercifully, in large parts of Mexico a Spanish culture did prevail, and it was not preposterous for people there to claim somos españoles. But it was more accurate to speak of the entire population as mestizo. Certainly, in the Vale of Temchic in the year 1903 the thin, underpaid workers were considerably more Indian than Spanish.

They worked like mules. Some of the miners would be underground for days at a time. They ate little, for they were paid little. They were lashed and beaten as few workers in the world were in this relatively humane period, and when in desperation they went to the authorities for relief, they were repulsed by rural police, who took positive delight in shooting them, and by the parish priest, Father Grávez, who explained that it was God's will that they should work in the mines and that if they agitated for higher wages, they would displease both God and Don Luis. The latter was the more important.

General Luis Terrazas owned Chihuahua, not only the city, but the entire state. Starting in 1860, he had led a minor military assault against an undefended building, and as a consequence, had ordained himself colonel. With four thousand dollars he bought himself a ranch comprising seven million acres on which he ran cattle ultimately worth twenty-five million dollars. With this as his leverage, by the year 1900 he owned three banks, four textile mills, numerous flour mills and sixteen other critical businesses with a cash value of more than twenty-seven million dollars. He also owned the Temchic silver mine, and his managers would be very angry if the miners interrupted production, thus causing him to lose income. The managers, therefore, instructed the rural police to gun down any troublemakers, and warned Father Grávez that Don Luis expected the priest to keep the valley peaceful.

It was by nature peaceful. On each side of the tumbling Río Temchic, small huts, not much larger than doghouses, lined the stream. Up the slopes, set well back from the mule trails, stood the commodious white houses of the German and American engineers who operated the mines for General Terrazas. As a result of some historical accident, all the American families came from one small region in Minnesota, and they were treated so generously by Terrazas that they came to think of themselves as his chosen agents and fell into the habit of brutalizing the Mexican workmen almost as severely as did the rural police.

'They're really nothing but animals,' the American engineers were fond of saying as they supervised a work schedule of fourteen hours a day, seven days a week. 'When they do get off work, all they do is run to their huts and womanize. They don't need extra time.'

In some respects the American wives were worse than their husbands, monopolizing the time of the miners' wives, using them as servants and paying them seventy-five cents a week for working ten hours a day, seven days a week. 'It takes four of them a whole day to do what one white woman would do in fifteen minutes,' the wives told each other in justification, 'and if you don't watch them, they'll eat you blind.'

Even so, Temchic was a place that people loved. It was an enclave protected from snow in winter and from extreme heat in summer. It could have been an ideal setting for the establishment of a mestizo paradise, except that silver lay hidden, and the engineers wanted it. Things would have continued to go well, thanks to the surveillance of the rural police and the church, if it had not been for a lean, long-legged, mean-visaged troublemaker whom the miners followed, but whom the engineers named contemptuously Capitan Frijoles, Captain Baked Beans, the Windy One. 'I wish the rurales would gun him down,' the principal engineer said when he heard that Frijoles was talking again of a strike. 'What the hell does the man want?'

What Frijoles wanted was one day off a week, no more than twelve hours' work in the mines each day, more food, and a doctor for women who were having babies.

Captain Mendoza of the rurales visited Frijoles and warned him, 'Such talk is revolutionary. If I hear you make such claims—ever again—you'll be taken care of.'

Father Grávez also visited Frijoles and explained to him that 'God gives each of us our work to do, Capitan, and your work is to bring silver out of the earth. God watches what you do. He knows your excellence and one day He will reward you. Also, General Terrazas needs the silver for the good works he does in Chihuahua.'

This line of reasoning impressed Frijoles at the moment, but later when he tried to recall one good thing General Terrazas had ever done for the people of Chihuahua, he could think of nothing. The general spent his money on big houses and bigger ranches and automobiles for his many children and trips to Europe and the entertainment of European businessmen and the paying of bribes to politicians in Mexico City. 'Perhaps,' Frijoles told his fellow workers, 'when he's finished with all that, one of these days he'll get around to us.' The miners suspected, from past experience, that this might take a long time.

So the agitation continued, and people in power resolved to destroy this troublesome Frijoles. The rural police saw him as a growing danger, and Captain Mendoza gave the simple order, 'Shoot him.' The engineers saw him as a disturbance in their good relations with General Terrazas, and they agreed, 'Get rid of him.' Father Grávez, and especially his superior, the cardinal in Chihuahua, saw Frijoles as an attack upon the order of the church, and both said, 'He must be disciplined.' General Terrazas saw him clearly as the opening wedge of all kinds of demands from workers who wanted to work only seventy-two hours a week, and he passed the word, 'Eliminate him.' And in Mexico City, President Porfirio Díaz, an old dictator aware that tremors in the north were beginning to threaten his beloved country, saw in Frijoles, the long-legged revolutionary up north, a portentous threat to the stability of the nation. 'Kill him now!' the old man advised, for he had learned to recognize an enemy when he saw one.

On a bright day in February, Captain Mendoza personally led a band of his rurales, hardened men accustomed to shoot without asking questions, into the village of Temchic, intending to arrest Frijoles. On the way back down the valley the revolutionary would be set free, and the gunmen, fourteen of them, would shoot him down, 'as he was trying to escape.' This Ley de Fuga, the Law of Flight, saved both jail and court costs.

'Don't shoot him here,' Captain Mendoza instructed his men. 'It always makes the women scream, and we don't want any agitation.'

As he entered the town he stopped at the office of the engineers and assured them, 'You'll have no more trouble with Frijoles,' and they thanked him, for engineers the world over wanted workmen to tend their jobs, work long hours and keep their mouths shut. 'We'll have him out of here in fifteen minutes,' Mendoza assured them.

It was a long fifteen minutes. Frijoles, anticipating that his enemies might strike, had prepared his cohorts for this day, and now as Mendoza and his henchmen turned the corner leading to the mine, they were met by a fusillade which killed the captain and three of his lieutenants. A pitched battle ensued, and when the rurales ran back down the valley, they left seven of their men dead on the banks of the Temchic.

A convulsion swept Mexico. This was revolution, the defiance of established authority, and all responsible people in the nation recognized the danger. An army battalion from Chihuahua was dispatched to Temchic, but was ignominiously defeated by Frijoles and his resolute miners. A new army was convened at Durango, with reinforcements moving in from Torreón, and this, too, was defeated. Generals long accustomed to terrifying farmers on open land discovered that they could not throw unlimited forces against Temchic, because they couldn't be crowded into the narrow defile. This time it was seventy soldiers against seventy miners, and the latter were fighting for their homes and a new way of life.

The war strung out from February till October, with the miners organizing their village as a redoubt capable of withstanding almost any assault. The American engineers and their families were sent down the valley under armed escort, and were now in Chihuahua city, giving interviews which explained that Frijoles and his gang were insane demons bent on destroying Mexico. The Germans were gone too, all except one quixotic young man who elected to stay with Frijoles and the miners. 'We'll take care of him when this is over,' the other Germans said, and they assured General Terrazas that it would soon end, because, as they explained, 'Frijoles isn't even educated.'

Then, in late October, a very brave young captain named Salcedo grew impatient with the pusillanimous behavior of the fat generals and devised a daring plan for climbing the Sierra Madre and sweeping down from the west while the generals moved up the valley and in from the flanks. The plan worked, and by the end of October the revolution at Temchic was doomed.

At this point the men around Frijoles made a desperate decision. He must escape—somehow he must get out of the valley to lead the revolution in other parts of the country. They had no doubt that the evil old order whereby one man could own seven million acres of land and dispose of it as he wished would vanish. They would be dead, but in that new day men and women would not work fourteen hours a day, seven days a week. So they devised a plan whereby four of them would set up a diversion to distract Captain Salcedo. They could not hope to escape; surely they would be shot—but their deaths would provide Frijoles with a chance to scurry into the mountains and on to the real revolution which lay ahead.

The strategy succeeded, and by dawn Frijoles was far into the mountains. When he stopped to rest on a log beside the river, he could hear in the distance the cannonade of government troops overrunning his village. When he chanced to look up he saw a file of nearly naked Tarahumare Indians passing, thin, swift runners from the highest mountains, and his eyes filled with tears of rage. For a moment he looked at them as they ran, silent men confused by the appearance of a stranger in their land, and he wondered why over the past generations the miners and the Indians had not somehow united in a common struggle for justice, and then the shadowy Tarahumare were gone, and he realized that never in the history of Mexico could such a union have occurred, for the Indians were Indians and the miners were Mexicans, and there was no chance of mutual understanding.

When Temchic was subdued—with German and American engineers reinstalled in their big houses—a matter of discipline arose. Nineteen of the rebellious miners had been captured alive, along with three women who had supported them, and it was decreed in Mexico City that they should be publicly shot as a warning to other potential troublemakers. Then someone had the creditable idea that it would be better if the doomed men and women were executed not by soldiers or rurales, who did a good deal of that sort of thing, but by ordinary villagers from the region, as if to show the world that sensible Mexicans shared no part of the miners' revolution and did indeed reject it.

Captain Salcedo, who had emerged from the final assault as some kind of national hero, was therefore commissioned to move into a village of farmers three miles down the valley and conscript a firing squad. In the selecting he was to be assisted by Father Grávez, whose church stood in the village and who could identify the men best suited for such service.

Like Temchic, Santa Ynez clung to the sides of the river, but there the resemblance stopped. Its houses were the white adobe habitations of men who worked the soil, and not the dark hovels of miners. Nor could it boast commodious houses on the hill, for no Germans or Americans would want to bother with its meager riches. It did, however, contain one spot of excellence that surpassed anything the mining town could provide, the Spanish colonial church of Santa Ynez with its two historic doors.

They were massive and made from wood which Tarahumare Indians had lugged down from the Sierra Madre. They had been carved by some forgotten priest who had learned his art in Taxco to the south, and depicted two scenes from the life of Saint Agnes, as she was known in Europe, the saint whose holy day came on January 21, when nights were bitter chill, as the poet Keats had said in his poem.

The left door showed Ynez, the radiant child of thirteen, holding in her right hand a sword, the instrument by which she was martyred, and at her feet a protecting lamb which signified the purity of her life. The right door showed her entering into her heavenly marriage with Jesus. But it was the combination of these two doors, each complementing the other, that epitomized the town's youthful innocence. It was a clean town, perched high in the Sierra Madre and protected on three sides by the pinnacles of those mountains.

It was a village to be loved, especially on the saint's day, when the population convened in darkness to sing before the doors of the church. All waited in silence, watching eastward for the first rays of the sun. When it appeared, farmers' voices joined with those of their wives and children in the traditional birthday song, 'Las Mañanitas,' honoring the little girl they loved:

> 'This is the birthday song
> Sung by King David.
> Because this is your day,
> I sing it to you.
>
> If the night-watch at the corner
> Wants to do me a favor,
> Let him dim his lantern
> While I whisper my love.'

'We need one reliable man to act as sergeant,' Captain Salcedo explained as he marched into the village with the priest. He was a trim man, with a small mustache and highly polished brown German boots which made a formidable impression on rural people.

'Tranquilino Marquez,' the priest said without hesitation. 'Solid man, twenty-three years old, married to a good woman named Serafina, with two children.'

'He won't give us trouble?' Salcedo asked. 'No speeches or anything like that?'

'Tranquilino?' Father Grávez asked. 'Utterly reliable. Works his small plot. Pays his rent to General Terrazas like a good citizen.'

Captain Salcedo summoned Tranquilino, and when the young farmer stood before him, taller than average, thin-faced, barefoot, straw hat deferentially in hand, the officer knew intuitively that here was the stolid, obedient type that made Mexico strong. 'You're a fine-looking man. You're to stand at the right end,' he said enthusiastically. 'Sort of a sergeant. I'll give the command but you'll see that your men are in line.'

'To do what?' Tranquilino asked.

'Oh! We're executing the rebels. You've fired a gun, of course?'

'Yes. But I don't want to shoot . . .'

'It's your duty! You don't want rebels destroying your farm . . . your family?'

'I sell corn to those miners.'

'Tranquilino! Mexico must rid itself of these criminal men. Explain it to him, Father.'

So Father Grávez took Tranquilino aside and explained everything in clear, simple terms: 'The mines belong to a good man, Tranquilino. General Terrazas does many fine things for Mexico, and if we allow strikers to steal his silver . . .'

'They didn't take silver.'

'Of course not. But when a workman strikes and doesn't produce what he's supposed to produce, it's the same as stealing. He deprives General Terrazas of things that are rightfully his.'

This made sense, and what Father Grávez said next made even more sense. 'It's just as if you lived on land belonging to the general and you refused to grow corn for him. Wouldn't that be stealing from him?' Tranquilino had to agree that it would be, and never in his life had he stolen from anyone or given the rurales cause to discipline him.

Step by step Father Grávez explained why it was necessary for the farmers of Santa Ynez to shoot the miners of Temchic, and in the end Tranquilino was convinced. Those men who had listened to Frijoles were a menace to Mexico and had to be exterminated.

But when Father Grávez took Tranquilino to headquarters, the head of the American engineers came into the room where Salcedo was choosing his firing squad and said, 'We're still short eleven men in the mines. We'd better take a dozen or so of these farmers and convert them to miners,' and Father Grávez, always subservient to the authorities, said, 'There's no better man in the region than Tranquilino here,' and the engineer turned to Tranquilino and said, 'Good. You can start in the mines right after the executions.'

'It's an opportunity,' Father Grávez explained. 'You're given your food and you don't have to farm any more.'

Tranquilino wanted to say, 'I like to farm. I don't want to work down in a mine and never see the sun.' But he sensed that if he said this, with Captain Salcedo and the engineer and Father Grávez listening, he would be in serious trouble. Things were happening too fast, and he wanted to talk with Serafina, who understood complexities better than he, but instead he was handed a gun and marched up the valley to Temchic, where two dozen other confused farmers had assembled, and he heard Captain Salcedo saying, 'Men, you are to line up on Tranquilino here. He's your sergeant.'

And they lined up, that bright, hot October morning, and the nineteen rebels were led out, ordinary men like Tranquilino, and behind them came three women with rags tied across their lips, for women are apt to scream, and the farmers heard Captain Salcedo giving directions: 'We'll shoot them in batches of six. Now, men, when I give the word "Fire" you're to shoot at the prisoner opposite you. Right at his heart.'

On the first fusillade all the farmers fired at the prisoners standing toward the ends of the line, with the result that two men in the middle were left standing. Captain Salcedo had to leave the firing squad, march across the open space, and kill the survivors with his revolver, standing very close to them and shooting into their faces.

The second time the same thing happened, and after Salcedo had fired point-blank at the two surviving miners, he berated the farmers, telling them that they would make a sorry lot of soldiers. He explained that he would now divide the firing squad into six groups, each being responsible for the execution of one of the miners. 'And this time, if one of those six men over there is left standing, I personally will shoot the lead man in the squad that was responsible.' He stalked down the line, punching his forefinger at each of the six leaders, striking Tranquilino first. There could be no doubt that Salcedo meant what he said, and this time there were no survivors.

'Good!' he congratulated the farmers. 'Now bring on the last man and two of the women.'

When the trio was moved into position against the wall, Tranquilino saw with relief that his group would be responsible for the man. He could not fire at a woman, and apparently some of the other farmers felt the same way, for their bullets went high, very high, leaving pockmarks in the wall and one defiant woman standing. In her anguish her bandage had slipped loose, and she started cursing Salcedo and the engineers, and in the end Salcedo had to shoot her in the face.

Grimly he returned to the farmers. 'This last one is Frijoles' wife. She was worse than he was. If there is one bullet high on that wall, I'll bring in soldiers and shoot the lot of you. Now get ready.'

The woman stood with her feet apart, her back pressed against the wall. She was mute, but her fiery eyes blazed curses at her executioners, reminding them of empty bellies and years lost in the mines. Before Captain Salcedo could give the order to fire, Tranquilino Marquez threw down his gun, uttering just one word, 'No,' and like falling stalks of wheat the other rifles fell into the dust.

In a rage Captain Salcedo rushed across the open space and executed Frijoles' wife. Then he stormed back and would have shot Tranquilino, but the thin-faced farmer was saved by Father Grávez, who stepped before him in intercession, saying, 'He's a good man, this one. Spare him.'

As the twenty-two corpses were hauled away, Tranquilino Marquez walked down the valley like a ghost. The echo of his rifle still sounded in his ears, the staccato fire of Captain Salcedo's fierce revolver. He heard the woman screaming, and the saving voice of Father Grávez. But most of all he heard those terrible words which sentenced him to a life underground: 'He can start in the mines right after the executions.' They would be coming for him soon and he hurried his steps.

He started running, and when he reached his adobe at the far end of Santa Ynez, he burst into the room, threw his arms about his young wife and cried, 'They're coming after me.'

Serafina Marquez had watched the executions from the crest of a small hill and had seen her husband throw down his rifle, and then after Father Grávez saved his life, she had seen Captain Salcedo talking agitatedly with the new captain of rurales, and it was clear to her that the captain was ordering the policemen to arrest Tranquilino as a troublemaker and shoot him as he tried to escape. She had already decided what must be done.

'You must go north, Tranquilino.'

'Where?'

'Go over the fields and catch the train at Guerrero. This instant!'

'Go where?"

'Cross the Río Bravo. There's always work across the river.'

'The children?'

'We'll stay here. We'll do.'

'But—Serafina!'

'Go!' she screamed. And in three minutes she had packed him a parcel of food and given him all the money they had saved. 'You can send us some when you find work. The way Hernandez does with his wife.' And she shoved him out the door.

It was not a minute too soon, for down the Vale of Temchic came the rurales, asking directions to the home of Tranquilino Marquez, troublemaker.

One of the notable features of northern Mexico was the network of plodding railroads which crisscrossed the area. In Chihuahua one improbable line called the Kansas City, Mexico and Orient entered from southern Texas to peter out at a railhead hundreds of miles short of its announced destination at the Pacific Ocean.

The main line ran north from Chihuahua to the border city of Ciudad Juarez, where a bridge carried it into El Paso. A third line was the most interesting, and the one destined to be a focus of history in this period. It, too, ran from Chihuahua to Ciudad Juarez, but along a route well to the west, through such picturesque towns as Cuauhtémoc, Guerrero and Casas Grandes, which had been an important center a thousand years ago, with ancient pyramids and ruined streets still proving how great the pre-Columbian Indians had been.

It was for this Northwest Line that Tranquilino Marquez headed, traveling mostly at night. He came at last to the vicinity of Guerrero, where he hid for two days, finally slipping into town at dusk to buy much-needed food. That night he traveled north to where the railroad stopped to take on wood for its furnaces and water for its boilers, and there, where no guards watched, he climbed beneath one of the freight cars and fastened himself to the iron rods that ran the length of the car. In this precarious way he rode to Casas Grandes, where some farmers headed for the United States detected him.

'Come on!' they whispered, kneeling to see how he had kept himself from the wheels.

'We ride inside!' one of the men said in a low voice, and they dragged him out and showed him how to force open doors on the freight train.

'At Ciudad Juarez we climb down before the police catch us, and an hour later we're across the border.'

In those days no papers were required to move from Mexico into Texas, but as the men prepared to cross the river the leader warned them, 'If they ask you, say we're on our way to Arizona.' Tranquilino asked why, and the man said, 'In Texas they hate Mexicans, and if they think we're staying there . . . trouble. So we always say Arizona. In Arizona they don't give a damn what happens.'

At the northern end of the bridge a jaded customs official asked the men, 'You bringin' any guns?' They were obviously bringing nothing but their clothes, so he let them through, for at that time the United States needed field workers.

Some of the immigrants headed northeast to the prosperous parts of Texas, and a few went directly west to Arizona, en route to California, but one who had been north before took Tranquilino aside and whispered, 'The good jobs are in New Mexico. You stay with me.'

There followed one of the quietest periods of Tranquilino's life. From October 1903 till March 1904 he wandered north through the majestic state of New Mexico, seeing roads and valleys of a beauty he could not have imagined, with fields leading gently up the sides of mountains until snow-covered crests were reached. Always he was in the companionship of men who spoke Spanish, and although the only jobs he could find were menial, they did pay cash, and he learned the sweet secret of Mexicans who worked in the United States:

'In any town, Tranquilino, you can go to the post office and tell the man "Giro postal," and you give him your money and he gives you a piece of paper which you send to your wife. He'll write her name on the envelope and she'll get the money.'

For six months he went from one post office to the next, asking for the giro postal, and without once knowing whether she received the money or not, he sent Serafina and the children every penny he earned, taking out only what he needed for the most meager necessities. Las Cruces, Alamogordo, Carrizozo of the beautiful hills, Encino, Santa Fe, Taos, Costilla—in each town the postmasters sold him the 'giros' and addressed his letters, as they did for hundreds of other workers.

New Mexico was so elegant a state, and so congenial to Mexicans, that he thought of living there permanently—bringing his wife and children north to build a home somewhere in the Santa Fe area if he could get a job on one of the ranches, but in March 1904 this dream was postponed when a man came to the area around Costilla, asking, 'Any Mexicans here want a real fine job growing vegetables at Alamosa . . . up in

Colorado?' And he offered such phenomenal wages—four dollars a week besides food and lodging—that Tranquilino and several others jumped at the chance.

They were taken by wagon north to where Blanca Peak guarded the road, then west to the irrigated lands around Alamosa, where Tranquilino saw that magnificent valley reaching off to the north, with the Sangre de Cristo mountains to the east and the Saguache peaks to the west. He felt privileged to work in Alamosa, where numerous storekeepers spoke Spanish, and he began to think that Colorado was an even better place than New Mexico, until he became aware that many citizens of the small city cursed Mexicans, and accused them of all sorts of evil.

Certain Americans in western states, having lost their Indians and with few blacks at hand, naturally turned to hating Mexicans, and they devised many tricks to torment the dark-skinned strangers. The sheriff in Alamosa arrested Mexicans for even the most trivial offenses, and judges sentenced them harshly and without the semblance of a trial. Storekeepers charged them higher prices than they charged white customers, and there were many places like barbershops and restaurants into which a Mexican could not go. Their money was welcome, but they were not.

But even after three ugly brushes with the law over charges he could not understand, Tranquilino, a quiet man seeking to avoid trouble, told his Mexican jailmates, 'It could be worse. If I wasn't here, I'd be down in the silver mines at Temchic, or more likely dead.' And he gained a reputation in Alamosa as a reliable man. He was the first at work, the last to leave, and he never lost his good humor.

'Hello, Mr. Adams! Yes, Mr. Adams! Right away, Mr. Adams.' He did not behave in this manner because he was subservient. He did so because he was glad to have a job, because he was grateful for the raise to five dollars a week, which enabled him to send even more money to his wife in Santa Ynez.

Some of his fiery companions chided him with being afraid to stand up for his rights, but he told them, 'I have all the rights I need. I stay away from the sheriff and I haven't been in jail for eight months.'

He was now in this third year of sending money back to Mexico, and he still had not learned whether his wife was getting it or not, so in October, when the crops were in, he told Mr. Adams, 'I'm going down to Chihuahua,' and Mr. Adams, not unhappy to have one less hand to worry about through the workless winter, told him, 'A fine idea, Tranquilino, and next spring your job will be waiting.'

There was a train to El Paso, and for a small fare he was able to ride to the border. There he walked over the bridge and was greeted amiably by the Mexican officials. 'Santa Ynez,' he told them, and a lieutenant said in reply, 'Watch yourself, my friend, and stay clear of the revolutionaries who are pestering that region.'

'I just want to see my wife,' Tranquilino said. 'I haven't heard from her in three years.' He went out to the yards of the Northwest Line, where scores of other men coming home from the United States were waiting to catch a boxcar heading south.

On the way to Guerrero, Tranquilino learned for the first time of the serious troubles erupting throughout Mexico, and he heard first-hand reports of how Colonel Salcedo, the hero of Temchic, was dominating the area, a cruel man in leather puttees who shot field workers if they uttered a word against General Tarrazas or President Díaz.

But he also heard romantic tales of Capitan Frijoles, who was hiding somewhere in the Sierra Madre, tormenting the government troops with audacious sorties, and he felt a sense of elation to think that the rebel, whom he had never seen, was still alive.

Then, when the train was well south of Casas Grandes, Tranquilino had his first experience with real revolution. Someone had mined the tracks of the Northwest Line, and although the engine passed over the dynamite safely, along with the car that carried the wood for the furnace, the following cars were ripped apart, killing the men riding within, leaving Tranquilino's car edging the fiery spot.

Survivors climbed down to survey the wreckage, and soldiers moved in from a headquarters to the south. Everyone was placed under arrest, and later in the day Colonel Salcedo, now in full control of his district, stormed onto the scene and began questioning suspects. Man after man told the same story: 'I am coming home from work in Texas, Mi Coronel,' and it was obvious that they were telling the truth.

Salcedo grabbed Tranquilino roughly, stared at him without recognizing him and snapped, 'You? What's your story?'

'I'm coming home from Colorado.'

'Where's that?'

'North of Texas.'

'Where are you going?'

Tranquilino was on the verge of saying 'Santa Ynez,' but he judged correctly that this might arouse suspicions or even a recollection of the insurrection which had occurred there. 'I'm getting off at Guerrero,' he said, and Salcedo passed on.

The colonel's men, however, identified three revolutionaries, who were lined up against a wall and shot. 'Let that be a lesson to you men coming back to Mexico.' And after a while the track was mended and the train resumed its way to Guerrero, where Tranquilino left it, heading overland on foot for the beautiful Vale of Temchic.

As he passed the four guardian peaks and entered the southern end of Santa Ynez, children began to yell, 'Tranquilino Marquez is coming home!' And a crowd surrounded him and boys yelled, 'Victoriano! It's your father!' And a shy, small child whom Tranquilino did not recognize stepped forward, wearing good clothes that his father had paid for with the giros postales, and the two stared at each other like strangers.

It was a prolonged, gentle visit. The children looked healthy; Serafina had spent her money wisely. In a box she had each of the envelopes from the strange towns: Alamogordo, Carrizozo, Taos, Alamosa. A neighbor who could read had deciphered the names for her, and she had said, 'They sound like towns in Mexico.'

Father Grávez was pleased to see Tranquilino and told him, 'You are a man of some nobility—alguna nobleza—because for three years you have never once failed to send money to your family. There are others . . .'

Tranquilino discovered that he enjoyed talking with the padre. 'Is it true,' Grávez asked, 'that in Estados Unidos you work only six days a week and have part of Saturday off?' When Tranquilino explained the working conditions and the availability of medical services for everyone . . . 'You have to walk four miles to the doctor and if you have the money, you must pay,' he explained, 'but when Guttierez lost a leg, nobody charged him anything and an Anglo woman in Alamosa gave him crutches.'

'It should be that way,' Father Grávez said.

Tranquilino asked the priest whether it would be a good idea to take Serafina and the children to Colorado, and Grávez said, 'No, women and children should stay close to their church,' and Tranquilino argued, 'They don't blow up trains in Colorado,' and Father Grávez admitted with some sadness, 'Perhaps the time may come when you will have to take your family north. But not yet.'

As the weeks passed, with only vague echoes of the trouble in the north, Tranquilino discovered anew what a jewel he had in Serafina Gómez. She had a disposition like the clotted milk he ate in Alamosa, gentle, lambent, always the same. In her youth she had worked in the fields like a burro, and now, even though Tranquilino supported her well, she continued to work as hard, but for different and larger purposes. She tended the sick and cared for children whose fathers were killed in the mines. She helped at the church and was called upon by Father Grávez in any emergency. Mexico had millions like her, if it ever discovered a way to release their energies, but for the present, they slaved in mining towns like Temchic or tended gardens in small villages like Santa Ynez.

She was embarrassed when she told Tranquilino that she was pregnant. 'You won't be here to see the baby,' she said, and in the intimate conversation which followed she whispered a secret to her husband: 'When you were gone and no money had arrived and we were near to starvation, for everyone was afraid to befriend us, a man crept to the door at night bringing us food and a few pesos. Who do you think it was?'

Tranquilino named three of his friends, but it had not been they. 'It was Frijoles,' she said. 'He came to bless you for refusing to shoot his wife. I hid him for three days.' Nothing more was said, but now the revolution seemed very close to the Marquez family.

It was an easy trip back. He crossed the border in the last week of 1905, worked in Carrizozo a few days, then drifted up to Taos, then on to Alamosa, but when he reached there, he found that Mr. Adams had already hired a full complement, so he wandered north to Salida, where he tried to find work on a lettuce farm, but they didn't need anyone, so he went over the mountains to Buena Vista, where he lodged with a Mexican family and worked on the road for a couple of weeks. After this he went on to the high town of Fairplay, where he tried to find odd jobs.

There he met a fellow Mexican who was living in Denver—Dember, the man called it—'best city in the world,' and in the wake of this man's enthusiasm he continued his way east across the great mountains and came at last to that final ridge from which the traveler could look down on the city of the high plains.

Denver! What a mecca for the Mexican worker! Here, in the winter months when work in the fields had ended, men gathered from all parts of Colorado, and when the snow fell deep in the streets and avenues, the Mexicans huddled together with good songs and beer and dances and toasted tortillas and talk of home.

Denver! It was a city perched a mile high, loved by ranchers who brought their cattle to the winter show, loved by lonely men out on the drylands who came in for a good steak dinner, but loved especially by the Mexicans, who could lose themselves in the small streets where Spanish was spoken.

'This is ten times better than Chihuahua city,' Tranquilino told the men he was drinking with.

'You ever been to Chihuahua?' one asked.

'No. But this is better.'

He spent two months in Denver, earning money at eight different jobs. But life in the golden city was expensive, and he found himself with little left over to send south. Then one night in a cantina where there was much singing, he met Magdalena, a young woman of twenty-two who could have had any man she wanted, and she invited him to live with her. She had a job in a restaurant and together they could eat well.

'Why me?' he asked in real perplexity.

'Because you're good-looking . . . and kind,' she said. 'I'm tired of fighters. You're like your name. It would feel good to come home to a man like you.'

She was altogether different from Serafina, whom he never mentioned. Magdalena had a turbulence of spirit, a wildness in her love-making. She liked to be with men, but she was afraid of them and was at ease only with Tranquilino. When it came time to pay the rent for their room, she discovered that he had been sending giros postales to his wife in Old Mexico, and instead of becoming angry, she kissed him feverishly, crying, 'That's why I need you, Tranquilino. Because if I was your wife and you were away, you'd send me money, too.'

At times he grew frightened as to what might happen to them, because he could never do what some men did: they had one wife in Sonora or Sinaloa, but they got married just the same in Denver—part of the year in Mexico with one wife, part in Denver with the other. Father Zapata, who ran the mission on Santa Fe Street, came to talk with them one afternoon.

'It's not right, what you're doing,' he said gravely. 'Magdalena, you're a fine beautiful woman and you're entitled to a home . . . to children. Porfirio has sent me to ask you to marry him. He's a good man, and he'll make you a fine husband.'

To the priest's surprise, the girl broke into violent sobbing. 'I'm afraid,' she said.

'Of what?' the priest asked.

'Of what's going to happen,' she said. 'My father and brothers have gone to the mountains. They're outlaws with Capitan Frijoles. All of Méjico . . .' She could not continue. With a terrible clarity of vision she could almost foresee the nation in its madness, and she was afraid.

Father Zapata, who was a good priest working with almost no funds and little encouragement, brought Porfirio Menendez around to the house. He was a tall, silent man who worked on a farm north of Brighton, and he needed a wife. He said, 'The farmer wants me to live there permanent. I have a house with inside running water.'

Tranquilino told him, 'She's the best woman I've seen in Colorado. She's nervous but she's a very good woman.'

'Will you have me?' Porfirio asked, but she would give no answer.

On his next visit Porfirio brought Father Zapata again, and the two men convinced Magdalena that she should marry and move to the farm, which she did, but three weeks later Porfirio was back, distraught and begging help from Tranquilino. 'Did she come here?' he asked pathetically.

'Not to me,' Tranquilino said, and because he was concerned about this girl he accompanied Porfirio to the priest, who told them, 'She passed through here a few days ago. On her way to the Sierra Madre to join her father and her brothers.'

That night Tranquilino and Porforio walked the streets together, and they came to the park which overlooked the new capital, and boys started to tease them because they were Mexicans, but Tranquilino said in his bad English, 'You go away now. We are not happy.' This brought additional jeers, and after a while a policeman came and told the men, 'You'd better move out. We want no trouble here,' and they continued to walk the streets, and finally Porfirio broke down and cried, right in the middle of Santa Fe Street, and when he regained control he said, 'I'll never see her again. She was going to have a baby. I think it was yours.' And the two men parted.

*   *   *

In the closing years of the last century the Union Pacific Railroad performed an outstanding service for the nation, and nowhere was its contribution more salutary than in Centennial.

It decided, in its own self-interest, that the easiest way to earn a profit was to acquire a large number of customers, especially farmers who might want to ship their produce by rail. Accordingly, it hired two groups of special assistants. One group traveled to Europe, extolling the virtues of settling in states like Colorado and Utah. These men did a splendid job of explaining American patterns of living and the opportunities for a good life in the west. They were responsible for the immigration of many trainloads of Germans, Czechs, Poles and Irishmen, who settled the plains; they were particularly successful in enlisting people from the Scandinavian countries.

The second group was less dramatic in its operations, but in the long run, more effective. These men traveled through the west itself, issuing a flood of roseate pamphlets, always with photographs, showing what could be done by a hard-working farmer with forty or sixty acres of good irrigated land. Millions of these publications circulated throughout America and Europe, and if a man had even a shred of interest in the soil, his expectations were bound to be aroused, for the corn raised by Farmer Bigley, who had emigrated from Illinois, stood seven feet tall and the melons produced by Farmer Wright were so big they could scarcely be lifted.

The pamphlet for Centennial was one of the best, and much of what later generations would know about the town came from it. In thirty-two well-written pages this pamphlet provided a storehouse of information about the town and the rich agricultural land that surrounded it. Temperatures for each month were given, with rainfall to match. Length of growing season was spelled out, with the warning:

> Crops which can be grown without concern in states like Virginia and Pennsylvania cannot possibly be grown in Centennial, for the growing season is restricted, but one glance at our photographs will assure even the most skeptical that crops of a much different kind and of greater commercial value can easily be grown.

The Centennial pamphlet was exceptional because the railroad had commissioned two atypical people to write it. The unadorned facts were provided by the elderly schoolteacher Miss Keller, who loved the land she was writing about and showed her enthusiasm. With no exaggeration she laid these facts before the reader; she built a portrait of a territory rich in history but even richer in promise.

The flamboyant salesmanship of the pamphlet came from a much different individual. When the railroad agent arrived in town, looking for someone to do the pamphlet, he had stayed at the Railway Arms of course, and while lounging in the bar, fell into conversation with a man of such outgoing enthusiasm and such an apparent knowledge of agriculture that he knew immediately that this was the man he sought.

The man was forty-nine years old, tall, handsome, well mannered and with the bearing of a gentleman. He expressed through a choice use of words a very lively interest in the visitor's proposed project and a most sympathetic comprehension of what needed to be done.

'This, sir,' he said gravely, his finely chiseled face close to the agent's, 'could be the new Garden of Eden. Wherever I have been able to bring water onto the soil, my crops have flourished. I say flourished, sir, and I mean nothing less.' Here he reached out and with his left hand took the stranger by the arm. With his right hand he painted an imaginary portrait of largesse: 'I see a land teeming with industrious peasants from Europe, each man a king in his new empire. If he will but apply himself to land as I have done, he will see it augment yearly . . .'

'I don't believe I caught your name,' the railroad man interrupted.

'Mervin Wendell, sir. Agriculturist.'

'You may be the very man I'm looking for, Mr. Wendell.'

'I would be honored to be of service,' Wendell said.

'We're contemplating a real estate operation . . .'

'You have the advantage of me, sir. Your name?'

'Norris. Omaha.'

'Mr. Norris. Let's sit over here. Just what did you have in mind when you said *real estate?*'

From this accidental but auspicious beginning, one of the soundest Centennial businesses was born: MERVIN WENDELL. *Slap Your Brand on a Hunk of Land.*

The first step would be the pamphlet, which Wendell would supervise. 'No finer pen exists in the west than that of Miss Keller,' he assured Norris, 'and we can depend on her to provide the facts. But the presentation of them . . .' He felt that this required his special attention, and he began by requisitioning a railroad photographer to come to Centennial to take a series of bold, exciting pictures. The captions, similar to those in all railroad pamphlets of the time, told the story of irrigation:

> Palatial home of Messmore Garrett, who runs sheep in the Centennial district.

> Elegant home of Mervin Wendell, well-known agriculturist, who arrived in Centennial nine years ago penniless.

> Imposing bank of Centennial, owned locally and the source of loans at low interest.

> Hans Brumbaugh, immigrant from Russia. Observe the size of the squash he has grown on his irrigated land.

> James Lloyd, who arrived from Texas without a penny, standing beside his herd of white-faced Herefords.

The pamphlet contained twenty-four photographs of palatial homes, thriving businesses and outsized vegetables. The last picture in the booklet showed Mervin Wendell's fine office on First Avenue facing the railway station.

The strange thing about this pamphlet was that it contained no hyperbole. The palatial homes shown had been built by men who arrived on the scene with no money. The crops of the farmers were exactly as pictured. And any hard-working newcomer who bought irrigated land in the years from 1896 through 1910 acquired a bargain whose value would multiply with the years. This was bonanza time, when the last of the great irrigation ditches were being dug, when desert land was being made to blossom.

Mervin Wendell's real estate business flourished. Using Union Pacific funds at first, then reinvesting his substantial profits, he patiently acquired for himself a collection of the choicest acres. Whenever a new area was opened up, and the railroad delivered fifty or a hundred eager buyers, he sold off the poorest land first and managed by careful investment to hold back the best for himself.

He now owned not only the Karpitz farm, which had been his first purchase, but also some four thousand additional acres, not all of them irrigated, to be sure, but all of them capable of producing some kind of crop. He became, indeed, the largest landowner in the district, if one counted only cropland, and if his fields received enough rainfall, he would soon be the richest.

The 'elegant home of Mervin Wendell' was not a new structure. He had taken the place won from Gribben in the badger game, and imposed upon it a new façade, a wing to the north, a new porch, new cement walks and a bright new iron fence. Its size had been doubled and it was, as the photograph claimed, elegant.

The citizens of Centennial took pride in the way the Wendells had handled themselves. Starting with practically nothing, this engaging couple had worked in the community, had helped others and had been exemplary citizens. Apart from the renovation, they did not spend money conspicuously. 'Every nickel that man earns he puts into land,' the admiring banker reported. Long before the Union Pacific arrived with its plan for a real estate operation, Mervin Wendell had acquired enough land to launch one of his own.

As Maude Wendell grew older, she grew more gracious. As an actress heading her own company, she had always had a flair for clothes and a dignified manner, but now, with middle-class stability, she blossomed and became the social leader of the community. She exerted this leadership not by virtue of her income, which was becoming substantial, but because she was a relaxed woman with a sincere interest in the community and what it wished to accomplish. Dinner at the Wendells' became the highlight of any week, and the *Clarion* duly noted the sedate but delightful entertainments given there.

Few of the leaders of our intellectual and social community were absent on Thursday night when Maude and Mervin Wendell entertained at their refurbished home on First Street. The sideboards groaned with refreshments hastened in by train from Chicago and California. One saw on the library table the latest magazines from New York and even one from London. A string quartet from the college at Greeley played Mozart, but as always when this gracious couple entertains, the highlight of the evening came when they were persuaded to give their delightful rendition of 'Listen to the Mockingbird.' This reporter never heard a finer whistler than Maude. She brings distinction to this community. They closed the evening by demand with the duet which has become their trademark, 'Whispering Hope.'

The reporter did not share with his readers the one contretemps of the evening. Some guests, recalling the old days, wanted young Philip Wendell to join his parents in the duets, but he refused. They then asked him to play the violin, but again he proved surly, whereupon Mervin Wendell said sharply, 'Play for the people,' and the fair-haired young man, now approaching twenty-one, glared at his father and stomped from the room.

'He's behaving like a ten-year-old,' the banker muttered, and his wife said, 'He's always been turned around. When he was ten he behaved like a grown man.'

The Wendells were not happy with the way Philip was developing. A student of music at the university in Boulder, he demonstrated a solid comprehension of classical works and had trained himself to be a violinist of some skill, but when he was home he refused to perform at his parents' entertainments. If Mervin persisted, he made excuses and retired to his room. Nor could he manifest any interest in the family real estate business; Mervin told his associates, 'I really don't know what's going to become of Philip.' Maude understood that her son's involvement in the murder of Mr. Sorenson had affected him much more deeply than they had recognized at the time, but she never spoke to him about the burden he was carrying.

The senior Wendells certainly did not allow the murder to trouble their consciences. From her seat at the dining-room table, Maude could look out the window and see the spot on Beaver Creek where her son had concealed the corpse, but she felt no morbid preoccupation with it. She was free to look at it or not, as her fancy dictated.

Philip's main problem was with his father, whom he saw with increasing clarity as a pompous, vain poseur. Once he confided to a girl in Boulder who had a similar problem with her father, a lawyer in Denver, 'If he told me that tomorrow was Thursday I'd check to see whether it was Friday or Tuesday. He's incapable of telling the truth.'

For Mervin, the passage of time had erased completely those moments of agony following the murder. He could no longer recall having pitched the corpse down the well, nor of having fainted when Sheriff Dumire came up empty-handed. Indeed, he had come to treat the event as a family joke. 'Come on,' he would say if he ever saw Maude looking out the window in the direction of the well. 'Tell me where you hid it.'

If Philip ever chanced to hear this, he would wince and stare at him harshly, and Mervin could guess what the boy was thinking. 'All right, all right. You think I'd blab the secret . . . get drunk at the Railway Arms . . . All right, if that's what you think, don't tell me.'

On January 17, 1904, he said brightly at breakfast, 'This is my birthday, Philip. Today you must tell me where you hid it.' Philip left the table and was not seen again that day.

The one man Mervin Wendell fooled completely was Mr. Norris of the Union Pacific. After the Centennial pamphlet was published and the railroad began receiving inquiries about the purchase of land along the Platte, Norris returned to town at the end of a trip during which he had encouraged other communities along the line to publish pamphlets as enticing as Centennial's.

He visited Miss Keller, and told her, 'You should be proud of that effort. Your text is being copied by all the railroads that run into the west. A beautiful piece of writing, Miss Keller.' Then he added, 'Of course, you and I were lucky to stumble upon an experienced farmer like Mervin Wendell to pull the thing together.'

'He's never farmed,' Miss Keller said.

'He's known as an agriculturist,' Norris protested. 'He talked with me at the highest level of authority.'

'He can discuss anything at the highest level,' Miss Keller said. She was not being derogatory but merely descriptive, like the good teacher she was.

'You mean Mervin Wendell never farmed?'

'He was an actor . . . and a good one. Take him to Omaha and he'll explain to your president how to run the railroad.' She was an old lady now, but she loved the nonsense of life. Rising, she went to Mr. Norris and with her left hand grasped his arm. With her right she drew great windy pictures against the wall of her little room. 'Mr. President,' she said in a cathedral voice, 'I see your Union Pacific probing into the mountains, crossing Berthoud Pass to unite Denver and Salt Lake. I see hordes of people . . .'

She laughed and returned to her chair. 'There's a church social tonight Mr. Norris. I haven't attended one for a long time, but I'm inviting you . . . as my guest. It's time you heard Mervin Wendell sing.'

As Wendell and the Union Pacific continued to bring farmers into the Platte Valley, and when all of them wanted to grow sugar beets as their sure cash crop, it became obligatory that a stable labor supply be found, and in early March of 1906 Potato Brumbaugh, in his customary bang-bang way decided to do something about it.

Climbing into his six-cylinder Model K touring Ford—he would naturally be the first in Centennial to own an automobile and he would want a big one—he thundered down to Denver, asked where the Mexican quarter was, and pushed his way into the cantina where laborers were whiling away the last of the good winter days.

'Evening,' he said.

'Alloo,' one of the Mexicans replied suspiciously.

'I'm Potato Brumbaugh. Grow beets at Centennial. I have three good jobs open. Good pay. Good house.'

The men looked at him suspiciously. The girl serving beer eyed this old man with his suspenders and belt but did not smile.

'Well?' Brumbaugh said. No response.

He stood in the middle of the smoke-filled cantina and his eye fell on a hollow-cheeked man sitting alone in a corner. This man had black hair hanging down to his eyes, and the general look of a man who knew how to work. Ignoring the others, Brumbaugh walked over to him, extended his hand and said, 'It's a good job. You better come.'

The quiet man looked at the big hand being thrust at him, reflected for a moment, then grasped it and rose. 'What do you like to be called?' Brumbaugh asked, and so far as the man could recollect, this was the first time in his life that any Anglo had ever asked his preference on anything.

'Tranquilino,' he said.

'You got two friends?'

Tranquilino looked about the cantina, then nominated two likely men. Brumbaugh went to each and made an offer of employment. To his gratification, the men accepted and asked when Brumbaugh wanted them. He said, 'Right now,' meaning within the week, and the men said, 'Good,' and indicated that they were ready to go.

'Where shall I pick you up?' Brumbaugh asked.

'Here,' the men said.

'When?'

'Now.' Yes, they meant now. When Brumbaugh asked what they would do about their rooms, they said, 'We'll be back in November,' and it was arranged. They left the cantina for a few minutes, reappearing with small bundles. 'We go,' they said, expecting to walk to the railroad station. When they saw the automobile and realized that they were to ride in it, they shouted for the others in the cantina to come see.

An impromptu fiesta was held in the street, after which the three men climbed into the Ford, and Brumbaugh headed north.

The ride was even more exciting than the automobile, for Brumbaugh drove as if the highway had been built for him. Tearing down the middle of the road, he swore right and left at anyone or anything that threatened to encroach, and when he reached open countryside north of the city, he proved himself a terror to dogs and chickens. The three Mexicans loved the boisterousness and joined Brumbaugh in shouting at pedestrians and cats. In this joyous manner they went to work.

At the end of the first week Brumbaugh was afraid to tell anyone else what good workers Mexicans were, lest they be stolen from him. The men liked farming, understood problems of soil and were not averse to doing stoop-work. They had been employed to work from March to November, and what they were asked to do made no difference. They were meek people, Brumbaugh noticed, not at all like the pushy Russians, who hated to be told what to do, nor the industrious Japanese, who stared as if their eyes would pop out when a new procedure was being explained in a language they could not understand. You told a Japanese farmer once, he never forgot.

The Mexicans liked to be told three times, not because they were slow to learn but because they wanted to be absolutely certain they knew what the boss wanted. Once they felt that they and the boss had agreed on what was needed, they performed stolidly and well. Because the men had no children to help them, the way the Russians and Japanese did, they evolved their own back-breaking way of blocking and thinning beets. It was ingenious and effective, founded upon the short-handled hoe. Tranquilino, for example, blocked and thinned two rows simultaneously. Squatting with his left knee firmly on the ground between the two rows, he kept his body weight on the bent right leg. This left his right hand free to chop with the hoe, now one row, now the other, while his left hand thinned the multiple clumps as far ahead as he could reach. Next he dragged the right knee forward, while his left leg bent to support his body for the next chopping-thinning operation. This duck walk was an art which allowed his deft hands to chop and thin an acre of beets during each twelve-hour day. Of course his back ached. Of course his knees grew scabs, but always he told the others, 'It's better than climbing poles in the silver mine.' And he began to visualize how much easier his work would be when he had his children to trail behind him, doing the thinning.

Those Mexicans are awful good, Brumbaugh concluded, and he noticed that Takemoto had found four of them, as had the one Italian farmer who had stayed north. But what gave Brumbaugh the greatest reassurance was his discovery that the Mexicans showed no signs of wanting to save money to purchase their own farms. On Sundays they did not go prowling the countryside looking for abandoned land, but sat resting in the shade near their shacks. They were content, and Potato Brumbaugh began to think that maybe at last he had found his ideal workers.

And when the Mexicans came to him, asking his help in sending their *giros postales* back to their families, he felt a positive bond of affection for them. 'Hell,' he finally confided at a small meeting of farmers, 'we got a gold mine in them Mexicans. This fellow Tranquilino working for me. Of every dollar I pay him, he sends ninety-three cents down to his wife and kids. I can't figure what he lives on. I don't know any Russians or Germans ever helped their families that way.'

As the summer wore on, Brumbaugh discovered the other solid qualities possessed by Tranquilino Marquez. He tended cattle well, could lift more than either of the other men, had a quicker laugh when an accident befell him. He was a tough, wiry man, and from time to time Brumbaugh muttered to himself, 'He's as good a man as I am . . . without the learning.' He therefore proposed that Miss Keller teach Tranquilino to read and write, but the Mexican refused to assume the heavy burden of literacy.

'You take care of the giros for me,' he said. 'That's enough.'

Brumbaugh also offered him a small piece of irrigated land to grow vegetables on, but again Tranquilino was reluctant to be trapped into unnecessary responsibilities. 'I watch your land,' he said. 'Got no time watch my land too.' And he protected Brumbaugh's interests with affection; nothing belonging to the farm went unattended. The magnificent Model K was polished until it glinted; the cattle were moved joyously at the slightest pretext, so much did Tranquilino enjoy playing cowboy on a borrowed horse. But the Mexican's special contribution was his meticulous attention to irrigation, for whenever Brumbaugh's turn came to draw water from the ditch, Tranquilino was on hand, inserting his canvas dams, cutting holes in the bank and leading the water onto all parts of the field.

In October, when the beets were harvested and delivered to the factory, Brumbaugh offered Tranquilino a special deal: 'Stay with me over the winter. I'll call the carpenter and have him make your shack winterproof.'

'Oh, no!' Tranquilino said. 'I want to be with the others in Dember.'

'What are you going to do about money?'

'Money? You send Serafina the giros. She has money.'

'But you?'

'Me?' Tranquilino asked, raising his palms to heaven. 'I find a little money.' And with the others he was off to Denver, but not before assuring Brumbaugh, 'we be back to tend your beets.' Then, hesitating, 'You come get us in automobile?'

The city of Denver, which had shown itself capable of withstanding almost anything, from gold-rush murderers to Colonel Frank Skimmerhorn's volunteers, displayed no eagerness to make concessions to Mexicans who had begun to invade the place during the winter months. They were a stubborn, quiet people who did not want to be bankers or schoolteachers. They spoke Spanish and intended to keep on speaking it. They ate strange food like tortillas and chili beans, and they did not hunger for steak. Their cantinas were dusty and noisy, and they wanted them kept that way. In each a naked bulb hung suspended from the ceiling by a cord, and they did not want a lampshade. Above all, they preferred to settle quarrels in accordance with their custom.

In a society where a young man, to prove his manhood, is required to have sexual intercourse with a maximum number of young women, and where a brother is obligated to kill any man who violates his sister, there are bound to be disturbances on a Saturday night. Often they were settled with flashing knives. To shoot a man from a distance would be unmanly; to rely upon a mechanical tool like a revolver instead of one's own face-to-face bravery would be cowardly.

To the western Anglo, accustomed to gunning down his foes from afar, the use of a knife was abhorrent and even shameful. There was something noble and dignified in being able to pump six quick lead bullets into an enemy at sixty paces, but to grapple with him at close quarters, he with his knife, you with yours, was somehow contemptible. In a year when Denver had sixty-seven shootings, many from ambush, no complaint was made, for this was the honorable pattern of the west; but when one Mexican—a short, hot-tempered fellow who worked for Brumbaugh—knifed another for fooling around with his sister, a cry of moral indignation swept the city, and newspapers warned the Mexicans that Denver was not about to tolerate any descent into barbarism.

The Mexicans did not have an easy time in Denver, but they had made a section of it their own, and many began bringing their families up from Chihuahua and Sonora. The settlement in the heart of the city grew, and even more than semi-Spanish cities like El Paso and Santa Fe, it became the mecca of Mexican laborers. In the beet fields north of town they could find work during the summer; in the cozy cantinas of Denver they could pass the winter, surviving as best they could.

No Mexican enjoyed Denver more than Tranquilino Marquez. Returning to the mile-high city after long months in the beet fields was a journey to an earthly paradise. Bringing what little money he had saved after sending Serafina her giros postales, he would burst into the familiar cantinas on Santa Fe Street and buy beer for his old acquaintances. The hot food, the noisy Spanish songs warmed him; when his money was gone and the blizzard whistled down from the high Rockies, he would huddle in some warm corner and tell the crowd, 'Winter's the best part of the year.'

In late 1909 events began to unfold which would exile Tranquilino from this congenial refuge. The trouble started with Potato Brumbaugh, and as so often happens in such affairs, the difficulty arose not from a lack of affection but from an excess of it. Brumbaugh had always liked Marquez, recognizing him for the superior workman he was, and now he wanted to make a significant gesture to prove his appreciation.

However, the generous-hearted Russian was absolutely incapable of understanding Marquez as he was: a sober, quiet, illiterate peasant quite content with present conditions. Brumbaugh wanted him to go to school, wanted him to farm his own little plot of land. Potato had a clear concept of what relationship a farmer should have to his land, and a German-type industriousness was fundamental. He would teach the Mexican how to live, and as a first step he dangled before Tranquilino an alluring opportunity.

Throwing his arm about the Mexican's shoulder, he said in a mixture of German, English and Spanish, 'Tranquilino, you are my best friend on earth. I don't like to see you wandering back and forth . . . Centennial . . . Denver . . . Chihuahua. You must have your own home. Go back to Old Mexico one last time to fetch your family. I'll build a little house over there and it's yours rent-free as long as you live.'

Once more Tranquilino drew back. 'I like Dember,' he said. 'When winter comes, I like Santa Fe Street . . . music . . . Mexican food. House up here, no friends, cold weather. I like Dember.' And he refused the offer.

But in 1911, when the November beet check was in, Brumbaugh faced up to the fact that he was not paying his Mexican help their fair share of the income from his land, and he was not the kind of man to profit improperly from the work of others, so he told Tranquilino, 'You are my son,' and he meant it, for when he had forced his own son, Kurt, to study law and thus into the management of Central Beet, Potato had inadvertently driven the boy from the farm, and he was now a stranger to the land, a young man alienated from his beginnings.

'I need you with me,' Potato told Tranquilino with some embarrassment. 'I am an old man and I need help. Bring your wife and children. You can work this land as long as you live.' So Tranquilino set out for Old Mexico.

In the early years of the twentieth century the Venneford Ranch underwent a dislocation which could have had disagreeable consequences had not Charlotte Lloyd been understanding as well as tough. It had started with a confidential letter from Finlay Perkin, addressed to her alone:

> You and James Lloyd have been married three years now, and I deem it imperative to bring a rather difficult matter to your attention, even though I am sure that you must be aware of it. The Bristol owners consider it most unwise for John Skimmerhorn to be retained as manager while you and your husband, major stockholders, reside on the premises with full ability to run the operation. It is not only a waste of money but it also threatens antagonisms between the two men. Skimmerhorn is

only fifty-four and can easily find himself another job. We could give him the best recommendations. I therefore recommend that you dispense with his services immediately.

When Charlotte read the letter she recognized its propriety. As Perkin had intimated, she had for some time been pondering the situation.

It was a nagging source of irritation to her to watch the daily activities of the ranch, knowing that her husband held only a secondary position. She owned forty-six percent of the shares, but Jim was almost a lackey, taking orders from John Skimmerhorn. It was galling to see her mild-mannered husband playing such a poor second fiddle, and she had often contemplated moves to correct this imbalance.

Now shrewd old Finlay Perkin had provided the opening, and she jumped for it. Running out to the calving shed, she told Jim, 'Just got a letter from Bristol. They have a great idea. You're to be general manager.'

'What about Skimmerhorn?' he asked instantly.

'He'll find something.'

Turning off the hose with which he had been washing down the shed, he asked, 'Is Bristol thinking of firing Skimmerhorn?'

'Not exactly firing . . .'

'Charlotte,' the wiry Texan interrupted. 'John Skimmerhorn gave me my chance to learn ranching. When we got the cattle here, Seccombe didn't want to hire me but Skimmerhorn insisted.' He paused to recall the greatest debt of all. 'In the middle of Llano Estacado, when we were nearly dead of thirst, he bought my mother's cattle.' He turned away so that his wife could not see the moisture rising to his eyes.

'What does all that mean?' Charlotte asked.

Slowly and with great force he said, 'It means that John Skimmerhorn cannot be fired.'

'But . . .'

'Charlotte! He can never be fired from this ranch. Never!'

'Are you content to take orders the rest of your life from another man?'

'He's not another man. He's been like a father . . . He's . . .' He fumbled, then said with finality. 'You can fire me, Charlotte, but you cannot fire him. And if Bristol insists, they'll lose us both.'

His wife could think of many practical arguments, but she knew that he would override them, and in a way she was gratified to have seen this side of Jim. She had lost respect for her first husband, Oliver Seccombe, because he had grown so morally flabby that he stood for nothing.

Her second husband, this resolute Texas cowboy, was stating once and for all that the life of John Skimmerhorn was not negotiable, and although she did not agree, she loved him the more for it.

So she bided her time, and about eleven months later Jim Lloyd received a letter which he described to his wife as 'a bolt out of the blue.' It was from R. J. Poteet, in Jacksboro, Texas, and said:

> A group of English financiers is putting together a large ranch west of here and they've asked me to come in with them. I have some cash saved up, so I can handle it from that end, but I'm getting too old to manage so large a property and I told them frankly I wouldn't come unless they'd allow me to hire someone else to do the heavy managing, and the only man I'd trust with the job is your manager and our mutual friend, John Skimmerhorn. I would never make a move like this behind your back, so do I have your permission to open the matter with him?

It was sort of providential, Jim thought, that Poteet's offer should arrive just when Charlotte was getting restive again about having the older man around, and he sent Poteet a telegram to the effect that if the Jacksboro job was advantageous for Skimmerhorn, the Venneford people would release him.

Three days later R. J. Poteet, sixty-four years old, but still slim and wiry, got off the Union Pacific and greeted his three old trailmates, Skimmerhorn, Lloyd and Calendar, who had been brought into town by the other two. They went into the bar of the Railway Arms and retold ancient tales.

In this mellow mood they rode to the castle, where Charlotte had platters of steaks waiting, and Mrs. Skimmerhorn drove up to chat with Charlotte while the men talked business, and about nine o'clock that night R. J. Poteet called the ladies in and said, 'I have the distinct pleasure of announcing that as of this moment, John Skimmerhorn has been hired to manage the big new spread being put together by our friends from London. Mrs. Skimmerhorn, how soon do you think you can get your goods packed?'

When Charlotte said she would help, as would some of the other wives from the ranch, Mrs. Skimmerhorn judged it could be done in four days. 'Do it,' Poteet said, and more drinking followed, and Amos Calendar came close to intoxication, relaxing in good-humored fellowship for one of the few times in his life. 'Yeah,' he chided Poteet. 'You was takin' such care of little Jim Lloyd, like he was a baby. And you was so careful to protect him when we was fightin' the Pettis boys.'

He stopped and winked at Jim. 'Well, did you hear about your little fellow? He creeps up into the mountains and he kicks open the door of that old saloon and he pumps hot lead into them Pettis boys . . . *yungh . . . yungh . . . yungh . . .*'

'Was it you who shot them?' Poteet asked, but Jim would not reply.

At the railway station next day Poteet accidentally let the cat out of the bag. As he was about to board the train he told Jim, 'One of the luckiest breaks I ever had. There I was, tryin' to find a manager and out of the clear blue sky comes this letter from this lawyer fellow in Bristol, England. Never heard of him, and he says that he's heard from his London sources and might I be in the market for a good manager? Wasn't that lucky?'

'Yep,' Jim replied slowly. 'Imagine—a total stranger.'

He never disclosed to Charlotte that he knew how Skimmerhorn had landed his new job. He was going to, but on the day everyone gathered at the train station to see the couple off on their long trip to Texas, Skimmerhorn took him aside and said, 'You really didn't have to do it, Jim. But since we've been partners for so long, I want you to know I appreciate it.'

'Do what?' Jim asked, for he could not think of anything he had done to warrant such thanks.

'The two thousand dollars Charlotte gave me . . . to buy into the new ranch.'

'It's only what you're due,' Jim said, and that evening as he drove north with Charlotte he realized how much he loved this energetic, headstrong Englishwoman. He was about to kiss her when she reached over impulsively and kissed him.

'You'll be the best manager the ranch ever had,' she said.

And he was. He combined the enthusiasm of Oliver Seccombe with the cautious good management of John Skimmerhorn. Under his tutelage, Crown Vee Herefords were prized throughout the west, a fact in which Charlotte and Jim took great pride. The ranch didn't make much actual profit; that would come later, Jim said, when the reputation was better established and they could charge more for their bulls and heifers, but it didn't lose money either, and for eighteen years the Lloyds improved the holding and gave it vigorous leadership. And then, one day in early 1911, they received their last letter from old Finlay Perkin. He was ninety-one that year, still capable, still preoccupied with the workings of the ranch:

> My ninety-first birthday reminds me, James Lloyd, that you, too, are growing older and you must attend to the problem of your successor. Bear in mind that John Skimmerhorn had a substantial apprenticeship before he assumed the reins, and that he in turn gave you careful instruction. The board wishes that you write them very fully on this matter by return mail. There are several young men related to members of our board who would like to try their hand running a great ranch, but I believe the best results come when an American brought up in the tradition assumes control. Twice you have referred to young Beeley Garrett, and I have made some judicious inquiries through our Wyoming connection. He seems a solid man with a responsible business sense. I am aware that he has been connected with sheep, and normally this would disqualify him in your country, but in England that has never

been the case. Include in your letter an assessment of young Garrett. He comes from a strong family, and that is always reassuring, I think.

So Jim determined to put his affairs in order and reviewed what he knew of Beeley Garrett. The name was an odd one, derived from the Garrett habit of giving first-born sons the family name of the wife. He was in his late thirties, and although he had started life running sheep for his father, he had later received a thorough grounding in Herefords on the ranch at Roggen. He was married to Levi Zendt's granddaughter, an irreverent dark-haired girl with five-eighths Indian blood and the appearance of an Arapaho princess.

Levi Zendt had had two children: Clemma, who had run away, and Martin, who had stayed at home. Like his sister, the boy had experienced difficulty in adjusting to an Indian heritage, and for a while it looked as if he might respond to local taunting by turning outlaw, as the Pasquinel brothers had done. But one summer he happened to visit the Arapaho reservation in western Wyoming, and while there he met this delightful Indian girl who had neither care nor inhibition. On the spur of the moment he persuaded her to run away with him, and after they were married he discovered through her his comprehension of what it meant to be an Indian. They had a daughter named Pale Star, and it was this lively girl that Beeley Garrett had married.

Jim Lloyd, obedient to Finlay Perkin's advice, sought Garrett out and asked if he might like to accompany the Venneford cowboys on their spring roundup, and Garrett guessed immediately what was in the wind. 'Crown Vee has got to find somebody to run that place when Lloyd retires,' he confided to Pale Star. 'And with luck, it could be me.'

'Why not invite them to supper?' Pale Star asked teasingly. 'I don't want Lady Charlotte to discover late in the game that I'm an Arapaho.'

It turned out to be a relaxed, amusing party. When the two men retired to talk ranching, Pale Star said, 'I insisted on this supper, Mrs. Lloyd. I wanted to be sure you knew I was an Indian.' Charlotte laughed heartily and said, 'Dear girl! I've been following the ins and outs of your family for three generations.' Growing more serious, she added, 'I knew your Aunt Clemma . . . not well . . . but very intensely.' And Pale Star said, 'Grandfather Levi told me that when you cotched Jim Lloyd, it was the best thing that ever happened in these parts.'

While the women talked, Beeley Garrett was trying in a bluff, casual manner to let Jim know that he understood the fundamentals of Hereford management: 'I think a ranch does best if it sticks to the great bulls. Anxiety IV, The Grove III. But most of us think that the best bull of all was Confidence, the one you Venneford people found in England. He ended the cat-hamming.'

'We got the best beef cattle in the west out of Confidence,' Jim said. 'It looked a mite less finished when the live steers were lined up, but weight for weight it butchered out forty pounds more of edible beef than anything you had at Roggen. And that's where the money is.'

Spring roundup in these years was an exhilarating time. The Venneford Ranch was down to half a million acres, but the lands it had disposed of were still largely unfenced and in the spring cows from as far away as Wyoming or Nebraska would wander onto the Venneford land to drop their calves. The only feasible way known to prevent rustlers from stealing calves and slapping a spurious brand upon them was to hold a general roundup and branding.

This was made possible by a trait which all young animals possessed, cattle to an extreme degree. If you take a newborn calf from its mother, and place it at random among a hundred other bawling Herefords, in a surprisingly short time that calf—by smell, sound or some mysterious instinct—will find its way back to its mother.

For example, suppose that if the mother bore the Crown Vee brand, and an unmarked calf ran to her, that calf had to belong to the Crown Vee ranch. By the same principle, if a calf bearing a rustler's brand ran up to a Crown Vee cow, you knew that dirty work had been done and that you had a court case, unless some hot-handed cowboy shot the rustler first, in which circumstance an obliging coroner would certify death from natural causes.

But this remarkable capacity of the calf to identify its mother faded quickly, and if you were tardy in your roundup, and your calves had already weaned themselves, they did not then run to their mothers, and the rustlers could brand such animals with impunity, for there was no way you could prove they were yours.

Each of the large ranches sent out three or four chuck wagons identical to the one devised by R. J. Poteet years before. Each contained a jar of fermenting dough; each offered pancakes, beans and freshly cut steaks cooked in Dutch ovens.

The traditional camaraderie existed, too. The wagons would move into an area about ten miles square and for two days men from various ranches would converge on that section of the range and round up cattle from the draws and the valleys. Fires would be started, and irons from six or seven ranches would heat side by side. As the cows were herded in, the calves were separated from their mothers by men on highly trained cutting horses. Then an older man like Jim Lloyd or an expert hand from another ranch would move among the calves and with a deft throw of his rope catch one of the little fellows by a hind leg and drag him bawling to where the cowboys worked. Two men would wrestle the calf to the ground, and then the team would spring into action. From the fire one man would take the brand and press it onto the hair, hard enough to mark the skin, but not so hard as to cause a deep wound. Properly branded, the mark would be recognizable till the death of the animal, and if it were subsequently altered by a rustler's running iron—

and very skilled the thieves became in converting a V into a W, for instance—the animal need only be slaughtered and its skin exposed to prove the alteration.

At the same time that the calf was being branded, it was also castrated if it was a bull calf intended for beef. The testicles were carefully tossed into a bucket, for rocky mountain oysters were featured at every roundup.

As soon as the branded calf was released, he would go bawling away to seek his mother, and it was always somehow satisfying to even the toughest cowhands to see the mother and child reunited.

After two days the chuck wagons would move to a new location, perhaps as far east as Line Camp One. At night, when stars came out and the fires burned, men from surrounding ranches visited together, and talk would invariably go back to the old days, and men would recall how Old Rags had failed to jump the Pecos at Horsehead Crossing, how Oliver Seccombe had shot himself through the head, and how Nate Person was the best nigger ever rode a horse, and how Mule Canby had 'taught hisse'f to shoot with a wooden arm.'

This year the first two nights of the roundup were spent on the silent, empty plains northeast of Sterling, where the night sky arched from east to west without disclosing one tree or a road leading anywhere or any sign of human habitation. Jim Lloyd doubted if he had ever seen the prairie in better condition; wildflowers abounded and the grass was rich. When he saw the silhouettes of his Herefords in the moonlight he recalled the good years he had spent on this land, and he was content to be passing the responsibility on to a man like Beeley Garrett. He could rope. He handled a horse well. He knew a good calf from a weakling. And his judgment coincided with Jim's on which of the bull calves to hold back for breeding purposes. It was unlikely that Venneford Ranch could find a better manager, and the good thing about him was that even though he had grown up with sheep, he had lost the smell. He had become a real cattleman.

Jim asked him if he'd like to walk out toward where the horses were, and Beeley said, 'Sure,' as if he hadn't an idea in the world what Jim was up to.

'I ain't gettin' any younger,' Jim said.

'None of us is,' Beeley allowed.

'You got a lot of good years ahead of you, Beeley.' Garrett made no reply, and Jim said, 'Thing I like about you, Beeley, you were raised with sheep but you had the intelligence to switch to cattle.'

To the son of a sheepman, this was an insult, but Beeley decided to hold his temper. The job had not been formally offered yet, and he wanted to hear the details. 'I like Herefords,' he said quietly.

They listened to the cowboys singing the old songs, and Jim said, 'You ever notice, Beeley, there's a thousand cowboy songs and there ain't one sheep song.'

But now Beeley was getting mad. He didn't need a job. He'd be glad to work at Venneford, understand, but he'd be damned if he'd allow any man to throw manure on his father's grave.

'Sheepherdin' is for Mexicans,' Jim stumbled on. 'Or maybe Indians.'

'Goddamn it,' Beeley shouted, 'it was good enough for my father! You take your Herefords and shove 'em!'

'Beeley!' Jim cried, shocked that any words of his should have given offense. 'I wouldn't for the world say anything bad against your old man. Christ, there never was a finer person in Centennial than Messmore Garrett. I was proud to have him as a friend.' Then, as if to make amends for his blundering: 'Beeley, I'm offering you a job. Will you take it?'

'Yes. But no more talk of sheep.'

'Beeley,' Jim said in real remorse. 'Charlotte and I eat mutton just to prove we got no animosity . . . once a year, that is!'

He extended his hand, which Beeley grasped, and they stood for a moment as the cowboys sang:

> 'Old Bill Jones had a daughter and a son
> One went to college, the other went wrong.
> His wife got killed in a poolroom fight,
> But still he keeps singin' with all his might.'

Jim placed his arm around Beeley's shoulder and said, 'How do you figure the old lady got killed in that poolroom? What was she doin' there in the first place?' Beeley could provide no logical explanation.

In the last weeks of 1911 Tranquilino crossed the Río Bravo at El Paso, and when he saw the crowds of refugees in Ciudad Juarez, he realized that open warfare had begun. And the deeper his train penetrated into Chihuahua, with frightened people climbing aboard the flatcars at every halt, each one with his tale of terror, the more disturbed he became.

'The way things are going,' he told a bewhiskered man sprawled out next to him, 'my wife could be in danger.'

'Everybody's in danger,' the man said. 'And we'll continue to have trouble until somebody shoots Salcedo, the bloody colonel.'

'Is he that fellow with the shiny brown boots?'

'You know him?'

'I saw him shoot Frijoles' wife.'

'You did!'

For a moment Tranquilino became a hero and he was encouraged to review the incidents that had terminated that first rebellion at the Temchic mines.

'And he ordered you shot, too?' the bewhiskered man asked.

'Yes, but Serafina guessed what was happening and sent me off to Estados Unidos.'

'How is it up there?' some of the men asked.

'Fine.'

'They treat Mexicans poorly?' the man with the whiskers asked.

'No.'

The man appeared to be a schoolteacher, and he pulled from his pocket a dirty wallet from which he took a well-creased clipping. It came from a Texas newspaper and was in English, so none of the others could read it when he showed it around:

> Hilario Guttierez, a Mexican working on a farm near Eagle Pass, made approaches to a white woman yesterday and was duly lynched.

The man translated the article, then asked Tranquilino, 'How do you like that?' and Tranquilino said, 'Well, if he hit the woman and threatened her . . .'

'My stupid friend,' the man shouted. 'He did not hit her. He smiled at her. Maybe he said, "Ay-ya, muchacha!" And for this he was lynched.'

'In Colorado we wouldn't say that to an Anglo woman,' Tranquilino assured him.

'Stupid!' the man shouted again. 'The word I'm talking about is *duly*. It means *in the natural course of affairs*. Since he was a Mexican, he was naturally lynched. What else?'

'What else?' Tranquilino asked. The man was making no sense to Tranquilino, who was relieved when the fellow left the flatcar at Casas Grandes.

At Guerrero, where Tranquilino got off, the situation was tense. Colonel Salcedo's government troops had recently swept through the area, burning and killing, and farmers were beginning to arm themselves with pitchforks and scythes. 'If Salcedo comes this way again, it will be a different story,' one old man promised, and Tranquilino thought, It'll be different, all right. Two hundred dead instead of twenty.

When he arrived at the Vale of Temchic and saw the four guardian peaks, with mists rising from the morning fields, he recalled the happy years he had known in this place, but when he reached Santa Ynez and witnessed for himself the deterioration of Mexican life, with the whole valley huddling in terror, he understood what the men on the flatcar had been talking about. His feelings were intensified when Serafina gathered the children to welcome him, and the oldest boy started telling him about Colonel Salcedo's raid down the valley.

'He started at the waterfall,' Victoriano said. The people of the valley liked to give their children heroic names; the other boy was Triunfador. 'At the mines he shot every man who had asked for less work, and in

Santa Ynez he shot a man and a woman who had spoken against the church.'

'What did they say?'

'That it was wrong to spend so much on decorating the church when men were starving. Colonel Salcedo stood the two people against the church doors and shot them.'

'I hope you kept your mouths shut,' he told his Victoriano, an eager boy of fifteen.

Tranquilino went to see Father Grávez, now white-haired and stooped, and asked him why Salcedo was still seeking revenge on the valley, and the priest said, 'He's a madman, but all of Mexico seems to be mad these days. Did you hear that General Terrazas had to flee? Yes, he's in exile, in Texas.'

'But he owned Chihuahua,' Tranquilino said.

'He thought he did. I thought he did. Years ago, when he was on a trip to Los Estados Unidos, a newspaperman asked him, "Are you from Chihuahua?" and he replied, "I am Chihuahua," and he was. Once the American army asked if he could provide them with five thousand horses. I understand they laughed when they asked this, knowing it to be impossible that one man should have so many horses, but General Terrazas replied, "What color?" ' The priest shook his head.

'Why did he run away?' Tranquilino asked. He could not visualize any man less likely to run away than General Terrazas.

'They're all running away,' Father Grávez said. 'Don Porfirio, Don Luis, Colonel Fabregas. They're all in El Paso.' Again he shook his head. 'It's pitiful when a strong man comes to the end of his days and has to run away. It means everything he stood for was wrong.'

'Was Terrazas wrong?' Tranquilino asked.

'To abuse the people you rule is always wrong,' the priest said. 'Reflections from the sun shining on the rifles got into my eyes for a while,' he confessed. 'When I ordered you to work in the mines, Tranquilino, I was very wrong. I have wanted to beg your forgiveness.'

'Me? Forgive you? Father, in Dember, I lived with a girl who wasn't my wife. I want your forgiveness.'

'You should take your family north, Tranquilino. Your son Victoriano is hotheaded, and he's going to find himself in great trouble.' He hesitated, then added, 'We all will. I told the American engineers they had better go. Now.'

'The men on the flatcar said the same thing,' Tranquilino reported. 'If the trouble comes, what will happen to you?'

'That could be a problem,' the old priest said. 'I always sided with the government troops. Last time when Colonel Salcedo shot the two freethinkers, he left bullet scars on the beautiful doors of our church, and I didn't even protest. My only excuse can be that I knew no better. No one ever told me any better.'

For the first time in his life Tranquilino felt like sharing his deepest thoughts with another human being. He had never done this with his wife, nor with Potato Brumbaugh, two people he loved, but now vast changes were afoot and he felt the need to speak. 'You know, Father Grávez, in Colorado we do not work seven days a week. At sunrise and at sunset we have time for ourselves. We don't step in the gutter when the strong man walks past, not even the sheriff. And we get paid. And when a man breaks his arm, as Hernandez did, someone takes him on a horse to the doctor and he pays nothing.'

Flies buzzed in the whitewashed rectory, and Tranquilino concluded, 'It was never right for men to work so long in the mines, climbing those narrow ladders and falling to their death, and leaving no money for their families. Maybe it was the thought of those narrow ladders and the men climbing them day after day like ants that made General Terrazas run away.'

'Tranquilino!' the old priest pleaded, 'Keep such things to yourself! And get your family out of this valley.'

But Tranquilino did not move fast enough, for late one afternoon a horde of barefoot men in blue blouses knotted in front came over the hills into Temchic, assembled all the American engineers, fourteen of them, and shot them.

On stolen horses they galloped down the valley to Santa Ynez, where they called for the priest who had for so many years defended the conditions imposed by the engineers. 'Come out, you miserable old . . .' They used a fearful word, and the old man appeared at the carved door of his church, prepared for death, but before they could kill him, Tranquilino Marquez ran out of his house and thrust himself in front of the priest, protecting him with his body, and there was a moment of confusion until a tall man rode up to ask, 'What's the delay?'

'This one. He won't let us have the priest.'

'Shoot them both,' the man ordered, but before this could be done, Serafina Marquez screamed, 'No, Frijoles! That's Tranquilino.'

Colonel Frijoles dismounted and strode over to the resolute farmer in front of the priest. 'Are you Tranquilino Marquez?'

'Yes.'

'The one who refused to shoot my wife?'

'Yes.'

'My brother!' the revolutionary cried, embracing his unknown friend. But with this gesture he pulled Tranquilino away from the priest, and as he did so, he ordered his men to seize the old man. Quickly Father Grávez was thrust against the doors of Santa Ynez, where Salcedo had executed the two freethinkers.

'Shoot him,' Frijoles ordered.

'No!' Tranquilino protested. 'It's murder . . . like your wife!'

At this impiety Frijoles swung his hand and knocked Tranquilino to the ground, and he lay there as the fusillade echoed, adding its quota of pockmarks to the already scarred doors.

Only then did Colonel Frijoles kneel down and lift Tranquilino to his feet. In apology he said in low tones, 'He sent too many of us to die in the mines . . . too many.'

'But he repented.'

'Today everyone in Mexico is repenting. It's too late.'

Frijoles dined that night with Tranquilino and his wife, the woman who had shielded him for three critical days, and at the conclusion of the meager meal he said, 'Send your wife and the two young children to Colorado. You and this boy I need.'

So it was arranged, and Serafina took Triunfador and the girl across the hills to Guerrero, where, like many others, they caught a boxcar on the Northwest Line, leaving the war-torn country at El Paso. They found their way to Centennial, where Potato Brumbaugh gave them the shack Tranquilino had occupied. Now the positions were reversed: she and the children worked sugar beets in Colorado and wondered what was happening in Santa Ynez. The only difference was that she did not send Tranquilino any giros postales, for she had no idea where he was, but Brumbaugh showed her how to save her money at the bank, which she did.

Tranquilino and his son were not at Santa Ynez. When word of the massacre of the fourteen American engineers from Minnesota, and the murder of Father Grávez, had flashed across Mexico and southern United States, an outcry had been raised, and the Mexican government, such as it was, felt obligated to prove that it did not countenance such barbarities. It placated the North Americans by sending Colonel Salcedo into the Vale of Temchic to exterminate the entire population. They also burned both Santa Ynez and the visible structures at the mines and produced photographs to prove how complete their pacification had been.

This dual action—Frijoles' murder of foreigners and Salcedo's destruction of the valley—led to a point from which retreat was impossible. Now two resolute and remorseless adversaries, the self-appointed colonels, rampaged back and forth across northern Mexico, using the trains as their cavalry.

There had never before been anything quite like this, and there never would be again—two armies who moved only by train. Tranquilino and his son Victoriano joined a group of wild-eyed, fearless peasants who crept north to the tracks at Guerrero, where they waited until a government-occupied train stopped to take on water. Then, with howls and blunderbusses, they stormed the flatcars, massacred the soldiers and took possession of the train, sending it north toward Casas Grandes. From time to time they would order the engineer to halt, and they would sweep out like locusts to destroy some remote hacienda that had belonged to General Terrazas, killing all they found, then setting fire to the buildings and dancing to the flames as they drank the general's wine. At such celebrations Tranquilino could always identify which of the peasants had worked in Los Estados Unidos. They wore shoes.

Sometimes their train would be riding along when government troops would ambush it, firing directly onto the flatcars, killing scores. The train would chug on ahead, and slowly the cars would be hauled out of rifle range; then they would count the dead, throwing the bodies off the cars as the train moved on.

The most dangerous spot in this weird caravan was the solitary flatcar which ran in front of the engine. Its purpose was to detonate any mines before they could damage the engine, and a hardy group of men rode this car, aware that they might be blown to bits at any moment.

Colonel Frijoles, who was taking the train north to combine his forces with those of a redoubtable warrior new to the field—a man named Pancho Villa—asked Tranquilino if he and Victoriano would volunteer to ride the first car. Without hesitation Tranquilino said he would do so, but he refused to allow his son to share this considerable danger, and that was why Victoriano was riding in the fifth car when the federal troops sprang their ambush on a curve south of Casas Grandes.

They had hidden a large mine under the track, and Colonel Salcedo, who crouched beside the man who would plunge the handle to explode the dynamite, whispered as the train approached, 'Remember. Let the first car go past. At my signal, blow up the engine.' The flatcar containing Tranquilino and the other brave men did get safely past, but the man with the plunger failed to respond quickly to Salcedo's signal. The mine did not destroy the engine; it caught the following two cars instead.

There was a tremendous explosion, with bodies flying in the air, and for one anguished moment Tranquilino thought the blast had struck the fifth car, but that was not the case, and with relief he looked back and saw that it was still on the tracks.

However, the trailing cars were now motionless, and federal riflemen began picking the rebels off, one by one. In despair Tranquilino watched as man after man twisted when the bullets struck him, or fell sideways in twitching movements.

'No!' he screamed, but the procession of bullets went savagely on, and he saw Victoriano leap sideways as the bullets ripped into him. Six or seven must have struck him, tearing him this way and that until his body crumpled and fell.

'Get the engine forward!' Frijoles shouted, and the train moved north —an engine, a tender and one flatcar in the van. The whole body of troops on the abandoned cars behind had to fight off the soldiers as best they could, and with whatever weapons they could improvise.

From that moment on, Colonel Frijoles and survivors like Tranquilino Marquez became avengers without pity. They failed to make contact with Pancho Villa, but they did succeed in assembling a new train and more men than they needed. They rampaged up and down the Northwest Line on their iron cavalry, destroying and killing. Tranquilino, who had once been unable to see a woman shot, or a priest, now participated in frenzies of slaughter in which whole haciendas were wiped out.

They knocked three government trains off the line, and once when two of Frijoles' engines passed near Casas Grandes, Tranquilino saw, for one dramatic moment only, the girl he had known in Denver—Magdalena. She was standing in the door of a boxcar, rifle in hand, bandoleers of cartridges across her breast. Their eyes met for an instant and he recognized her, but she had seen too many men on the trains. They all looked alike.

'Magdalena!' he bellowed, but she could not hear him.

There were many women aboard these trains, fierce creatures who had no fear of death and who consoled the men who did. At times it seemed as if they were the ones who kept the revolution going, this chaotic, haphazard movement of an outraged people who would endure no more persecution. Sometimes the rabble army would come to a hacienda where servant girls had been constantly mistreated—younger sons of the ranch demanding bed partners as they willed and the girls forced at gunpoint to comply—and the men attacking the hacienda might waver in the face of gunfire. Then the women took charge, disregarding the bullets, and when the walls were breeched and lacy bedrooms invaded, it was the women who dragged out the soft-skinned white mistresses and lined them against the wall.

It was one of these vengeful women who came to the train while it was stalled at Casas Grandes, with electrifying news: 'One day's march to the east, Colonel Salcedo's men are trapped without a train or horses.' She was a soft-spoken, gray-haired woman of fifty, carrying a jar of honey. It seemed unlikely that she was lying, for men whispered, 'Her husband and sons were hanged. She is thirsty for revenge.'

So a raiding party was organized, with this woman, still holding her jar of honey, serving as scout and Frijoles himself in command. They forayed eastward and the woman led them to a small valley where Colonel Salcedo had been forced to hole up, awaiting reinforcements, and when Frijoles saw that Salcedo was indeed among the troops, he became frenzied and led three suicidal charges into the mouths of the guns, and the federal soldiers were overwhelmed and slain one after another, but Salcedo was kept alive and taken prisoner.

He was a brave man. His thin mustache did not quiver when he faced his mortal adversary, and he stood firm in his polished German boots. Apparently Colonel Frijoles had long anticipated this moment, for he knew precisely what he wanted to do. With his own hands he stripped Salcedo of all his clothes save the gleaming boots. Then he staked him out on a level piece of ground, where the sun would strike him evenly and roast him to death. Each hand was lashed to its own stake; each ankle tied to its stake, with all ropes pulled taut. He would be dead by nightfall.

But for the woman that was not enough. Into each orifice of the naked man's body she trickled a thin stream of honey: eyes, ears, nose, mouth, anus—all were well smeared so that the savage ants of the desert would find them. And then the woman and Frijoles withdrew to watch the sun and the insects go to work, and when the screams were most agonized, Tranquilino asked, 'Can I shoot him?' and Frijoles said, 'No.'

CAUTION TO *US* EDITORS: Do not panic if your western agricultural experts refuse to believe that the sugar beet was originally an annual. It was. Prior to 1800 it produced beet and seed the same year, with all its energies going into the reproductive process and little into the generation of sugar. German botanists forced it to behave itself and to spend its major energies during the first year in the making of sugar. Today, if you want seed, you dig the beet up at the end of the first year, tend it carefully through the winter and plant it like a bulb the second year.

Ecology. While I was in Centennial there was a great stink, if you'll forgive the pun, about the effluent going into the river and the smell from fermenting pulp that crept over the town. Agitated ecologists launched a movement to drive the factory from town. I beg you not to go overboard on this. When the 1973 beet campaign started and I first smelled the pulp, I wanted to dynamite the factory, for it is a most pungent and pervasive odor, but by December, when I left town, I had grown not only to respect it but even to like it. For me it became the smell of the land at work, the sweet, heavy smell of the earth's produce readjusting itself to new utilities. This country can make a damned fool of itself if it tries in a nice-nelly way to eliminate all evidence of the fact that we are animals who inhabit a natural world. I abhor scented toilet paper.

Racial mix in Mexico. Few data in my report will be more controversial than my figures on the basic population of Mexico. Let me underline the pitfalls, and you may prefer to edit out this material. I will not protest if you do so. (1) Most educated, upper-class Mexicans prefer to believe that an extremely large number of Spaniards entered Mexico, stayed there and provided some seventy or eighty percent of the bloodlines. (2) Revolutionary Mexicans prefer to think that only a few Spaniards arrived and that their blood was quickly submerged by indigenous Indian blood. (3) Most Mexicans prefer to forget the black infusion altogether, and if the matter does come up, confess to the arrival of 'a few thousand Negritos.' (4) Those special pleadings are, I suppose, self-evident, but a more vital dissension is not. Scholars whose persuasions are antithetical to Spain's, or anticlerical, always want to show that the original Indian population of Mexico was enormous, for this permits them to proceed with an explanation of how the evil practices of Madrid and the church killed off the indigenous population. (5) Anti-United States leaders also like to visualize the original Indian population as enormous, because this provides justification for a very large population now. In some peculiar way this is interpreted as a rebuff to the population experts, most of whom happen to be from the United States. (6) Sentimentalists argue in favor of a large Indian population.

Estimates of population. The figures I give for Mexican population are conservative. Anti-Spanish theorists claim there were as many as 25,000,000 Indians in prosperous condition when Cortez arrived. Pro-Spanish theorists argue that not more than 4,500,000 lived in Mexico at that time. A good many serious scholars seem to be centering on the figure 20,000,000, but I consider even this too high. As to the blacks, the figure 250,000 is secure and is derived from slave-ship records. As to my figure of 300,000 Spaniards, most scholars consider this about 150,000 too high. They are basing their judgment, I believe, on those few Spaniards who came to Mexico and actually *stayed* there. I think we must also count those who came, worked, fathered a dozen children and went home, because it is their contribution to the gene pool that we are concerned about, not where they died. Taking that into consideration, I stand by my figure of 300,000.

Significance. This is not a peripheral question. In the western states, from Texas to California, it is obligatory that citizens of all ancestry decide once and for all what they think about Mexicans, both in Mexico and in the United States. Spanish-speaking people will continue to form a significant minority in American life, and in a town like Centennial the misapprehensions as to what Mexicans are, what they signify and what they can become are an appalling mixture of misinformation and prejudice. As a beet farmer told me, 'Our biggest problems are nematodes and Mexicans, and we know more about the former than the latter.'

Illustrations. Before you decide on any photographs for this period, please study the Union Pacific real estate pamphlets, for Centennial. The shot of Potato Brumbaugh standing in suspenders and belt beside his squash, with that delightful grin, tells the whole story. The contraption lower left is the portable canvas dam he used for irrigation.

The Platte. Had I been writing this report for pleasure, I would have chosen as my subject the Colorado, most dramatic of American rivers. Had I been primarily concerned with history, I'd have chosen the Missouri, jugular vein of American expansion. Instead, I was assigned the South Platte, but as I studied it I became aware of the majesty this mean, intemperate river can often assume. In 1973, just before I started work in Centennial, the Platte went into one of its periodic floods. It swept away bridges, flooded whole towns, laid the countryside waste and killed at least nine people. Once twenty-four inches of rain fell along its flank within one three-hour period. In 1965 Mud Creek, which is empty most of the year and which for the past half century has produced an average of 1.6 cusecs a year, threw into the Platte in one afternoon 466,000 cusecs! When you have seen the river in these manifestations, you remember it with respect.

13
DRYLANDS

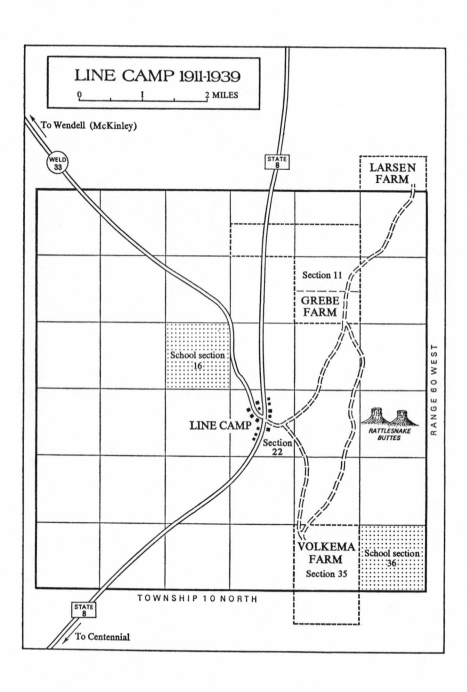

LINE CAMP 1911-1939

0   1   2 MILES

To Wendell (McKinley)

WELD
33

STATE
8

LARSEN
FARM

Section 11

GREBE
FARM

School section
16

RANGE 60 WEST

LINE CAMP

Section
22

RATTLESNAKE
BUTTES

VOLKEMA
FARM

Section 35

School section
36

TOWNSHIP 10 NORTH

STATE
8

To Centennial

BY THE YEAR 1911 NORTHERN COLORADO had evolved a system of land use which had to be judged one of the most advantageous in the world. Had it been allowed to develop unimpeded from that time on, it would have converted this part of America into a preserve of beauty, ensuring a neat balance between the needs of man and the dictates of nature.

How appropriate it was. The vast plains were reserved for cattle, sixty or seventy acres to a cow-and-calf unit. It was true that barbed wire tended to enclose each man's land, but since ranches ran to seventy and eighty thousand acres, an owner could ride many miles across his property without encountering a road, a house or a town. The range was shared by deer and antelope, but anchored the soil so that even the stiffest wind did little damage. Only thirteen inches of rain could be expected each year, barely enough to keep things going, and if a rancher allowed his stock to overgraze an area, it could take five or six years for the grass to recover.

Cowboys prospered on the plains and created their own culture. For example, Texas Red, one of the heroes of the 1887 blizzard, became so proficient with his lariat that the Crown Vee ranch issued challenges to the cowhands on neighboring spreads, and rustic competitions were held, often supplying contestants for the famous Cheyenne Frontier Days and those other rodeos which flourished throughout the west.

Crown Vee also produced Lightning, the notorious bucking horse that succeeded in keeping riders off his back for nine years. Texas Red, the man who came closest to staying aboard for the regulation ten seconds, said of this cantankerous beast, 'Never was a horse that could sunfish the way he did. Straight in the air, then roll over with his belly up, then down with all four legs thrashing and his backbone in a knot.'

The best thing about the ranches, however, was the careful superintendence they gave the range. 'All in this world we got to sell,' Jim Lloyd often instructed his men, 'is grass. The Hereford, handsome though he may be, is just a machine for converting grass into beef. If you look out for the grass, I'll look out for the Herefords.'

There was a built-in conservatism in the rancher. He wanted things left as they were, with him owning his eighty thousand acres and with the government intruding as little as possible. All he wanted from Washington was free use of public lands, high tariff on any meat coming in from Australia or Argentina, the building and maintenance of public roads, the control of predators, the provision of free education, a good mail service with free delivery to the ranch gate, and a strong sheriff's department to arrest anyone who might think of intruding on the land. 'I want no interference from government,' the rancher proclaimed, and he meant it. In return, he would look after his grass, share some of it with the wild animals and protect one of the greatest natural resources of the nation—the open range.

The rancher's partner, although any rancher would have been offended if someone had suggested that a Russian or a Japanese was his companion, was the irrigation farmer who took the lands along the rivers and cleverly led water onto them, creating gardens out of deserts and multiplying fiftyfold the value of the land in one summer. These men used small amounts of land for which the rancher could not profitably compete, and with sugar beets they brought into the community an assured supply of cash which helped maintain the services which only towns and villages could provide.

It was a fruitful symbiosis: the rancher utilizing land which got little rain and the irrigator concentrating on those marginal lands where irrigation could be utilized. Neither trespassed upon the other and neither tried to lure away the workers employed by the other. No self-respecting cowboy would chop sugar beets, while the average beet worker was terrified by a steer.

Like the rancher, the irrigator was a conservative and despised any intervention from government. What he wanted principally from Washington was the maintenance of a very high tariff against cane sugar, Cuban especially. Had there been a free sugar market in these years, the cane growers of the Caribbean could have supplied all of America's needs, and at a much lower price than Central Beet, using beets, could have matched. The sugar-beet industry was not really feasible, economically speaking, but it was close enough to the margin to warrant the protection given it, and the one requirement for being a senator from Colorado was to have the muscle to keep a high tariff on cane sugar. Integrity, hard work and statesmanship were desirable, but familiarity with the sugar beet was essential.

The irrigator expected a few other services: a constant supply of immigrant labor from Mexico, protection against labor unions, a very low tariff on cheap nitrates from Chile, good roads from farm to factory, low railroad rates and an ample supply of currency, but for the most part the irrigation farmer considered himself an independent man who faced the risks of agriculture alone, and the character of a society depends more upon what men think of themselves than upon what they really are.

The few towns that sprang up on the plains were geared to the needs of rancher and farmer. Banks, hardware stores, department stores and railroad stations adjusted to the cycle of the land. Each year, on November 13 and 14, the days prior to the issuance of sugar-beet checks, the community throbbed with excitement, and merchants totted up their account books to see what each farmer would owe when his check came through, and stores selling dresses redid their front windows. It was the same when one of the great ranches was shipping a trainload of cattle to Chicago; the whole railway system seemed to gird itself for that event, and men went to the station to see the stockcars loaded with steers.

This spacious way of life was possible only because the population of both the United States and Colorado was low. In 1910 the nation had 91,972,000 citizens, Colorado had 799,000, Denver had 213,000, Centennial had 1,037. A farmer could locate his beet field fifteen miles outside of Denver, and no one cared, because no one coveted his land. The Venneford Ranch was still allowed to keep hundreds of thousands of vacant acres, primarily because no one had visualized any better use for them than the running of cattle.

So for a few years around 1911, northern Colorado was as placid as it had ever been, and life in towns like Centennial was close to ideal. Then came Dr. Thomas Dole Creevey, and this agricultural stability was shattered.

Creevey was built like a duck, a round, chunky little man about five-feet-five with a large head and heavy glasses. He wore a suit which seemed too small and a vest whose two bottom buttons could not possibly fasten. He had unbelievable energy and an honesty which beamed from his animated face. Like most dedicated men, he had made one big discovery which consumed his life: he was a true believer, one who had seen the answer, and he had the power which such total dedication generates. Above all, he was a likable man whose enthusiasm infected his listeners. Men trusted Thomas Dole Creevey and were never abused in that trust. Of course, sometimes a farmer using his methods failed to duplicate his results, but even then they never charged him with fraud, because if they did, they knew that he could come onto their land and prove that what he had said was true.

He was a revolutionary, a man with a wildly disruptive idea, and when he put his plan into operation, the easy monopoly of rancher-irrigator would no longer exist. It was natural, therefore, that the men who had been monopolizing the land feared him, for his announced mission was to challenge them.

*   *   *

In the small Iowa town of Ottumwa, Dr. Creevey was about to enter into his peroration. He was addressing an assembly of farmers who had gathered in the school auditorium to hear the new apostle of the west, and as he looked down into this collection of intelligent faces, this gathering of men who wanted to know the facts behind the rumors, he felt inspired, and whenever this happened he spoke in a lower voice than usual, allowing the force of his ideas to take the place of rhetoric:

> For the past hundred years they have lied to you. They have said, 'Everything west of the Hundredth Meridian is a desert.' This is not true, and I have proved it. In a few minutes we will lower the lights and I will show you what a man can grow on that desert. I will show you tall spires of corn, and huge potatoes, and fields of wheat unmatched.
>
> It was the great Jethro Tull working in the fields of England in the years 1720–1740 who made the discovery upon which your future and mine depends, that whereas many crops can be grown with forty to sixty inches of rain a year, equally fine crops—not always of the same plants —can be grown by careful procedures where the rainfall is only twelve inches a year.

Here he explained how Jethro Tull had worked this miracle, and his words were so persuasive that the Iowa farmers began to be convinced, and Earl Grebe leaned over to Magnes Volkema and whispered, 'Do you think it can be done?' They listened intently as Creevey explained how Tull's principles could be adapted to states like Kansas and Colorado, and they experienced a flush of excitement when the doctor stopped dramatically and called to the auditorium janitor, 'Bring in the stereopticon!'

The machine was set up and the lamp lit. Then, as the janitor inserted the hand-colored slides, Dr. Creevey showed the Iowa men what he had accomplished on a fourteen-inch-rainfall farm in western Kansas. It was a startling exhibition, a demonstration of how man's ingenuity and perseverance could triumph over obstacles. There were scenes of the land before Dr. Creevey took over, and several photographs of contiguous land untouched by Creevey which remained as empty at the end of the experiment as at the beginning. Best of all were the autumn shots of the harvest he had made on this bleak soil: corn, wheat, potatoes, tomatoes and rich fields of lucerne.

The stereopticon was turned off and the lights turned up. In his final exhortation he addressed the farmers with honesty and common sense:

> You saw the corn. I raised it with my own hands, but I must warn you that corn is not a good dry-land crop. If you are set in your ways and insist upon growing corn and feeding it to your hogs, do not move west. I doubt that potatoes are an appropriate crop, either. But if you want to raise wheat, for which there will always be an unlimited market of hungry humans, then the west is your destination. If you want milo for

tilth, and lucerne for your neighbor's cattle, then the free west is the place for you.

But, gentlemen, do not come west unless you want to work. Do not join me if you want to plow your field once and let it go at that. If ample rain has made you lazy, stay home. Because on those fields only the man who works from sunrise to sunset can make his fortune.

I said fortune, and I mean fortune. Every man in this room is entitled by law to 320 acres of God's finest dry-land farm. All you have to do is go there, register your claim in the land office and go to work. I can hear you asking, 'What's in it for him?' and I'll tell you what's in it for me. I am employed by the railroad and by a consortium of real estate companies who own land in the west, and after you've taken your homestead and got your hands on some land, we will sell you additional land, the best in the area, for eight dollars an acre. What are you paying for land in Iowa? One hundred and fifty dollars an acre, and most of you can't afford to own your own farms. Come west with me and for one-twentieth as much you'll be twenty times wealthier.

He spoke with conviction, and when he came to his conclusion, many of his listeners leaned forward:

When I say 'Come with me,' I mean it. I'll tell you what I'm going to do. With the assistance of the Rock Island Railroad, which wants to see the west developed as much as I do, I am going to invite two men from this audience to visit my demonstration farm to see for themselves what can be done. All they have to pay, and I mean all, is their meals on the train and in the hotel. And if their wives pack them a big enough lunch, they won't even have to spend that. Now, whom do you nominate to come out with me and make the report?

Amid good-humored banter, Grebe and Volkema were selected, and were handed passes from Ottumwa, Iowa, to Goodland, Kansas. A few days later they disembarked into a forbidding wonderland. When Dr. Creevey piled them, and one hundred and twenty-nine other visitors, into the railroad's autobuses and drove northward, they were appalled by the bleak aspects of the land: no trees, no streams, no signs of rain.

In the bus Earl Grebe sat near Dr. Creevey, and found himself confused: on the one hand, he could see the arid quality of the area to be tilled and knew from his Iowa experience that only a miracle would permit wheat to be grown here; but on the other hand, he was subjected to the wild enthusiasm of the round little agriculturist: 'When I see land like this, gentlemen, my heart explodes. What a challenge! What a promise! I assure you that I can take land exactly like this and make it produce twenty-six bushels of wheat to the acre.'

'Have you ever done it?' Grebe asked.

'Done it? I'm doing it now. That's what I'm taking you to see.'

'On land like this?'

'Not as good as this. Gentlemen, within the hour you will see my miracle. You will see the Word of God come down to earth and made real. I started dry-land farming on that sacred Sunday morning when I was staring out the church door at the bleak and empty plains of my youth. Nothing grew on those plains, and I heard the minister reading from the Book of Genesis, "And God blessed them, and God said unto them, Be fruitful, and multiply, and replenish the earth, and subdue it." And the word of God descended upon me at that moment, and I understood.'

Grebe was looking at Dr. Creevey as these words were spoken, and he observed the sincerity in the man's face. Then Creevey added, 'And subdue it! That is what God wants us to do with this land, and I shall show how each of you can go forth and subdue your portion.'

When the autobuses drove into the yard of Dr. Creevey's experimental farm, the visitors knew that they were in a special place, for the farm machinery was clean and the barns were in order. But the group did not linger there, for Dr. Creevey was eager for them to wander over his fields and see for themselves what could be accomplished with dry-land farming.

They walked several miles. Some fields were fallow, some were growing grains Grebe did not recognize, and some were about to be plowed. The pattern bore no relationship to what an Iowa farmer would be doing with his land in September, and Grebe quickly realized that if anyone were to dry-farm, he must listen to the experience of someone like Creevey, because this farm in western Kansas was flourishing. Much more of it lay fallow than would be permitted in Iowa, but the fields that were working were performing miracles.

The other visitors were equally impressed, and all wanted to hear Dr. Creevey's secrets. So after their inspection they assembled in one of the barns, where a blackboard was set up before rows of benches, and when they were settled, a representative from the Rock Island Railroad rose, and with a piece of chalk in his hand, said, 'Gentlemen, I am going to place upon this board the one irrefutable fact about this wonderful farm you have just inspected.' With that he wrote a huge 14. 'There it is, gentlemen, the basic fact you must remember as long as you are with us. On this land, only fourteen inches of rain falls a year. We have no irrigation, no tricks. Only the genius of this man, Dr. Thomas Dole Creevey.'

The little doctor walked to the board, his vest unbuttoned and his eyes flashing. 'I affirm,' he said in his lowest voice, 'that any man in this room who follows the principles I have delineated can move onto any land in the west, if it have topsoil and at least twelve inches of rainfall a year, and duplicate what you have just seen.'

Bursting with enthusiasm, he jumped around before the blackboard, jabbing his right forefinger into the faces of men in the front row as he laid forth the ten principles which would revolutionize the west.

'One, the whole secret is to catch, store and protect from evaporation whatever rain falls on your land.

'Two, you can never catch and store enough in one year to grow a good crop. Therefore, you must allow about sixty percent of your land to lie fallow. If you've been farming eighty acres in Iowa, plan to farm at least three hundred and twenty out here. And allow most of it to rest and accumulate water.

'Three, you must know your soil. Don't move a foot west of Iowa without an earth auger. It looks like this and enables you to bore beneath the surface and see what's going on. How deep the topsoil is, how wet.

'Four, keep a mulch of some kind on your fields throughout the year, for this will prevent what moisture you do get from evaporating. You must never allow even one drop of rain to escape.

'Five, whenever it rains you must do two things. Fall on your knees and thank God. Then jump up, harness your horses to the disk and turn the field over while the last drops are falling. This will throw a mulch that traps the water. If you wait till tomorrow before you disk, half the water will evaporate.

'Six, plow in the fall. If you keep a small family garden, you will naturally want to plow that in the spring, but plow your big fields in October and November.

'Seven, plow at least ten inches deep. Then disk. Then harrow.

'Eight, plant your wheat only in the fall. Plant only Turkey Red.

'Nine, after a field has lain fallow for a year, it's a fine idea to raise a crop of lucerne or milo and plow it under. This roughage aerates the soil, adds nitrates and enriches.

'Ten, farm every day of your life as if next year would see the drought.'

As he finished his decalogue he clasped his hands in front of his round belly and bowed his head. He knew that he was asking inexperienced men to engage in a dangerous gamble, and some would be so faltering in courage that they would fail; for them he felt deep sadness. But he also knew that some of his listeners were men of determination like the pioneers who had settled this land originally; for them he felt an abounding joy. They were about to enlist in a great adventure, and he knew they could succeed.

In the quiet barn he delivered his challenge: 'I do not offer you men an easy life. I offer you riches if you will work. I do not promise your wives a life of ease. I do promise them partnership in the last great challenge of this land. And to husband and wife I offer that divine promise so beautifully expressed in Isaiah 35:

> The wilderness and the solitary place shall be glad for them; and the desert shall rejoice, and blossom as the rose. It shall blossom abundantly, and rejoice even with joy and singing . . . Strengthen ye the weak hands, and confirm the feeble knees . . . for in the wilderness shall waters break

out, and streams in the desert. And the parched ground shall become a pool, and the thirsty land springs of water . . .

In the next three days Dr. Creevey demonstrated each of his principles, showing how to use the earth auger and the mulch and the system of summer tillage. Since it did not rain during their visit, one morning he said, 'We shall make believe that rain falls at ten o'clock, because you must fix in your minds what to do when it does.'

So at ten a small sprinkler was hauled onto one of the fallow fields, and four horses dragged it back and forth for an hour to show how far the water would penetrate. As soon as they left, Dr. Creevey shouted, 'Rain's over!' and he hitched four other horses to his disk and proceeded to turn over barely four inches of the moistened soil, throwing it to the bottom of the furrows where its water content would be protected from evaporation. He then unhitched his team, fastening them to a harrow, with which he smoothed the roughened field. In this way the rainfall was conserved.

'When I plow this field in October,' he told the men confidently, 'and plant it with Turkey Red, I am assured a crop, even if no moisture falls during the winter, for I have trapped the moisture down there and it lies waiting. The only thing that can injure me is a sudden hailstorm.'

At the end of his exposition he placed before his visitors his farm accounts for the past five years, and they could see for themselves what he had accomplished on this Kansas farm, on the one near Denver, Colorado, and on the one in California. There were the rainfall records; there were the crops harvested; there were the funds deposited in the bank. One hundred and thirty-one farmers were satisfied that it could be done, and more than ninety were prepared to follow in his footsteps. Their plows would tear apart the sleeping west. Of the ten principles Creevey had expounded, nine would have permanent applicability; only one was defective, and this only because he had failed to take into consideration the interaction between it and a natural phenomenon which swept the plains at rare intervals.

During the first twenty years of his experiments, the nature of this fatal deficiency would not become apparent, but when it did, it would come close to destroying a major portion of the nation.

On the train back to Ottumwa, Earl Grebe was preoccupied with the task of convincing himself that he ought to leave his farm in Iowa and take the risk of dry-land farming farther west. He was a cautious man, and the idea of leaving the fields on which he had been raised was distressing, but since he had worked them for some years without moving any closer to ownership, he was receptive to any solution which promised improvement. Magnes Volkema was certain that Colorado was the answer.

'Look at the pictures,' he told Grebe. 'Same kind of land, same kind of results.'

They studied the sixteen-page pamphlet which Creevey had distributed as they boarded the train. It detailed the rich future that awaited any man who bought a dry-land farm in the vicinity of Centennial, Colorado. The wheat was tall. The furrows were straight. The pages were filled with photographs of expensive homes that had been built by enterprising men and women who had moved west. Pages of statistics showed what the rainfall was and how long the growing season, but the persuasive portion of the brochure came in the words of the man who had compiled it. The photograph showed a frank, sincere businessman in a dark suit, sitting at his desk beneath a shiny new sign which said:

Slap Your Brand on a Hunk of Land

MERVIN WENDELL

RANCHES AND ESTATES

Wend Your Way to Wendell

Below the reassuring portrait were the words: 'In 1889 I arrived in Centennial penniless, but through the prudent purchase of irrigated farmland, I now own the palatial residence portrayed on the opposite page. You can do the same with your dry-land farm.' The photograph showed a fine new mansion at the corner of Eighth Avenue and Ninth Street, with Mervin Wendell standing on the lower step and looking up fondly at his handsome wife on the porch. It exuded success and stamped Real Estate Agent Wendell as a man to be both trusted and emulated.

Grebe and Volkema were particularly interested in the map of the region open to the lucky families who moved west, for it showed where the proposed new town would be located. 'Line Camp,' the brochure said, 'soon to be the Athens of the west. The school will be housed in this fine building, facing this edifice in which the civil officials will maintain their headquarters.' The photograph showed the two stone buildings built there by Jim Lloyd back in 1869. They were sturdy and clean and the years had not marked them. They sat solidly upon the plains, lending an impression of permanence and promise.

'The land office will be housed here,' the brochure promised, 'and all you have to do is go onto the prairie, locate the 320 acres you prefer, and claim it for your own. Three years to a day from the moment you step foot on your chosen land, it's yours, and you'll have a paper signed by the President of the United States to prove it.'

'Can you imagine owning 320 acres like the ones Dr. Creevey had?' Volkema asked. 'A man could make his fortune on that.'

Grebe was looking at the photograph of a dry-land farm operated by a man named John Stephenson, who, the caption maintained, had come to Centennial penniless in 1908, had purchased some land from Mervin

Wendell and now lived in a palatial home. The land looked good and the wheat was tall.

'He wouldn't dare lie about this, would he?' Grebe asked suspiciously.

'No! When we get to Centennial and ask, "Where is Stephenson's farm?" Mr. Wendell'd be in real trouble if there wasn't any such farm. This is real, Earl. People are making their fortune out there, and you and I ought to be part of it.'

So the two men studied the seductive publication, and the more they saw, the more convinced they became, so that by the time their train reached Ottumwa they were not reporters, they were missionaries, and each man went home to talk to his wife and neighbors.

Alice Grebe was a tall, thin young woman of twenty-two. She had been reared on a farm east of Ottumwa, one of seven children of deeply religious parents, and Earl had met her at church. He had courted her over a period of three years, and when he formally proposed, at first her parents seemed reluctant to let her go, even though their home was crowded. But her father and older brother launched an inspection of Earl's life and came away satisfied that he was worthy to join their God-fearing family.

The wedding had taken place only the year before, with three members of Earl's family in attendance and nineteen of Alice's. As she stood before the minister she looked more dedicated than radiant, for she was not a beautiful girl. Her quality lay in her capacity for work and her desire to found a Christian home. The women of Ottumwa who watched as she pledged her vows concluded that here was a girl who would give her husband little trouble and much support. She was, indeed, an ideal wife for a young farmer, and the fact that she preferred rural life enhanced this promise.

This first year of marriage had been close to perfect, because each honestly sought to be a good partner; their only disappointment stemmed from Earl's inability to acquire a farm of his own. Iowa prices were simply too high, and the young couple had to content themselves with leasing a farm owned by a banker in town. They inspected several farms up for sale but could not meet the required down payments and had resigned themselves to working for others when Dr. Thomas Dole Creevey arrived in town.

Alice Grebe had been the first to see the announcement and it had been she who had encouraged her husband and Magnes Volkema to attend the first night's lecture. On the second night, when Dr. Creevey promised to get down to specifics, she and Vesta Volkema had sat near the front, and it was partly because of their visible enthusiasm that the audience had nominated their husbands to take the trip west to investigate Creevey's experimental farm.

'It's all he promised,' Earl reported as they sat together after supper. 'Look at these photographs of the land we get free in Colorado.' When she saw the alluring pamphlet, and the friendly countenance of the real estate man who was volunteering to help them acquire land around the new town he was planning, she experienced the same excitement that had gripped her husband when he had first seen the publication.

'It looks just fine,' she said, turning the pages.

'You wouldn't believe what Dr. Creevey accomplishes on land just like this,' Earl said, and he went on to explain Turkey Red, that fine winter wheat imported from Russia, and the clever new ways of trapping moisture.

She was not listening. Her eye had fallen upon the one photograph Mervin Wendell had fought against including in his pamphlet. 'You've got to show them what the land looks like,' the railroad agent had insisted. 'I don't want women looking at those bleak empty spaces,' Wendell had said with the prescience that marked his dealings. 'You show a bunch of Iowa women those prairies, and they'll panic.' Against his better judgment the dry-land photograph had been included, and now as Alice Grebe looked at it, she had a premonition of the loneliness she could expect and the dread silence at night with no human being within earshot, and she was no longer sure they should embark on this adventure.

'Are you all right?' Earl asked, seeing her grow pale.

'Of course,' she said weakly. 'It looks to be wonderful land.'

'I want to move west,' he said. 'I want to work where I can own my own place.'

It was the timeless cry of the man who dreamed of moving on, of leaving old patterns which circumscribed less venturesome men. It had been voiced at every stage of American development and had motivated the most diverse types of men: the renegade trapper, the devoted Mormon, the feckless son, the daring entrepreneur, the young woman without a man or a prospect of one, the housewife who wanted better things for her husband. It was the authentic vision of the pioneer American, the dream of freedom and more spacious horizons.

In the early years of the twentieth century this eagerness to move westward reached its height. New immigrants from Europe who did not wish to be trapped in city slums caught the train to Chicago and from there to the wheatfields of Dakota and Minnesota. Old residents of the Atlantic seaboard who sensed that this might be the last chance for a man to live more freely heard of unclaimed lands in Colorado and Montana and made the break. Young ministers, middle-aged hardware merchants and old roustabouts joined the movement, while a score of different railroads sent persuasive men into all towns preaching the doctrine of free land in the west. It was a conscious movement and the people who participated were among the finest and strongest citizens America had yet produced.

Alice Grebe stifled her fears. If her husband longed to hazard new fortunes, like the hero of a book she had just finished, she must encourage him. And in the last days of summer, 1911, two families from Ottumwa reported to the station for the journey west: Earl and Alice Grebe and a crafty older pair already familiar with emigration, Magnes and Vesta Volkema, accompanied by their two teen-age children. A few men in the crowd that bade them farewell said, 'I wisht I was younger so's I could go along,' and Vesta Volkema told some of them, 'You're younger right now than I am.'

They went to Omaha, and caught the train there which would take them to Centennial, where Mervin Wendell would be waiting. And as they sat in the coach through the long night while the train crept westward through Nebraska and across the border into Colorado, they talked of their bright future.

'It's a new start,' Alice Grebe said with an animation she did not wholly feel. 'Like the ox-cart women of a hundred years ago. It's really quite thrilling.'

'It's a chance to pick up a few easy dollars,' Vesta Volkema said. 'I want to get hold of as much land as possible as quick as possible. Sell at a profit. Then on to California.'

'I see it as an opportunity to establish a home,' Alice Grebe said. 'Our own town . . . maybe watch one of our sons become mayor.' She leaned forward as she spoke, as if eager to begin this new contest with the land, and once she reached out to touch her husband's hand, reassuring him that she was ready for whatever the new challenge presented. 'I can hardly wait to see our new home,' she said.

'Our families will build the church,' Alice said prophetically. 'And we'll put our books together to build a library.'

'You're looking too far ahead,' Vesta teased. 'What I'd like to see is a good grocery store.'

'We'll get one,' Alice said. She had been valedictorian of her class in Ottumwa, a very bright girl who should have gone on to college, her teachers said. She read books by Upton Sinclair and visualized an always-better society. In her graduation address she had declaimed: 'We are the builders of tomorrow. We are the new pioneers.' At the time she drafted those words she had been only vaguely aware of their import, but now as the train rattled toward Denver and the great mountains she felt as if she were the very spirit of a pioneer movement, and she reveled in the excitement of what lay ahead.

'It's so thrilling!' she whispered to Vesta. 'There can't be another pair on this train as fortunate as we.'

But when dawn broke and she saw those interminate plains west of Julesburg, those prodigious reaches of loneliness, gray-brown to the horizon without tree or shadow, the enormousness of their adventure overcame her, and she fell into such a trembling that Vesta had to grasp her hands and quieten her.

'Earl! Come here!' Vesta called, and when Grebe sat with his wife he said, 'She's only nervous,' but Vesta sized the situation up more accurately. 'She's pregnant,' she said matter-of-factly, and when she confronted Alice, the girl confessed that she had known for several weeks but had told no one lest the trip west be canceled.

'It's an omen,' Earl told the group. 'Just like the Bible says: "Be fruitful, and multiply, and replenish the earth, and subdue it." Those are the first words God ever spoke to man.' He sat with Alice's hand in his and looked out at the lonely land. 'We shall multiply,' he said, 'and we shall subdue.'

Mervin Wendell rose early that morning. In the years when he sold irrigated farmland, he had learned to be at the station whenever settlers arrived, for he had found that in their first hours in Centennial they were likely to require his reassurance in a variety of ways, and if he signed them up early, they stayed signed. Now that he was trying to peddle drylands, it was even more important. He therefore shaved by the new electric light which graced his mansion, then doused himself with real French eau de cologne shipped in from Boston. He trimmed the hair about his ears, using his wife's scissors, and slipped into his western outfit: whipcord trousers, Texas boots adorned with silver, pale-blue shirt with string tie, a wide-brimmed hat. Reviewing himself in the mirror, he felt satisfied that his figure was as good as ever and his jaw line still firm and in its way commanding.

The Negro cook waited with Mervin's regular breakfast: sourdough pancakes, two eggs, three strips of bacon and a pot of hot coffee without cream or sugar. He liked the batter for his cakes to be kept watery, so that the resulting cakes were thin and very brown on each side. 'Thick pancakes that taste like a blotting-paper sandwich are not my style,' he explained, and this morning they were done his way.

When he had eaten, he went upstairs to kiss his wife goodbye, advising her, 'I'm hauling our first load of homesteaders out to Line Camp, and I won't be back till late. Each man will want to tramp over his land, and I'll be busy.'

He went downstairs and climbed into his new six-seater Buick, which he idled for some minutes before venturing out onto Eighth Avenue. The quiet purr of the motor pleased him, and slowly he engaged the clutch, releasing it with skill so that the gears meshed properly. With a restrained touch on the horn, he announced without ostentation that Centennial's leading citizen was about to move down the street.

On this morning he was to experience a nasty shock, for when he reached the station he found Jim Lloyd and Old Man Brumbaugh already there, and he discovered that they proposed addressing the new settlers as they left the train.

'What about?' he asked with visible dismay.

'About land,' Brumbaugh said shortly.

'What about it? They homestead legally. I sell them additional land, which I own. What's wrong about that?'

'The use of the land,' Brumbaugh said with impatience. 'Have you no conscience?'

'It's good land for wheat,' Wendell said pugnaciously, glaring at Brumbaugh. 'It's been proved you can grow wheat out there.'

'The sod crop,' Brumbaugh said contemptuously. 'Any soil in the world will produce a crop first year the sod's broken. You know that.'

'It's the years that follow the sod crop that will break these people's hearts,' Jim Lloyd broke in. 'What are they going to do, Wendell, when those roaring winds blow out of the Rockies? You've seen what they can do to irrigated farms. What in hell would they do to dry-land crops?'

Wendell licked his lips and asked placatingly, 'What kind of speech will you make to our visitors?' He did not try to override his two antagonists; from past experience he had learned that where land was involved, these men could be difficult. However, he did keep stored in the back of his mind a strong telling point against them, and if they tried to make real trouble for him, he intended using it.

'We're going to warn the newcomers to go back home,' Brumbaugh growled. 'We don't want them to commit suicide on this barren land.'

'You've done pretty well on "this barren land." ' He mimicked Brumbaugh's pronunciation, and the old Russian grew angry.

'I had water,' he said, turning away from Wendell and leading Jim Lloyd to a different part of the station platform.

They were talking together when the train pulled in, and they watched as this batch of families that Wendell had assembled from all parts of the nation came hesitantly down the steps. They were a handsome lot, men and women in their late twenties and thirties mostly, skilled farmers ready for the new challenge. Potato Brumbaugh felt his heart warming to these adventurous people, especially the women, on whom the terrors of the new life would fall so heavily. 'Tears come in my eyes when I see them,' he told Lloyd. 'The government should prevent this.'

One of the couples overheard this remark, and the woman shivered at the words and drew her husband closer to her.

'You settling here?' Brumbaugh asked them.

'Yes,' the husband said.

'What's your name?'

'Grebe. Earl Grebe.'

'Listen to an old man, Earl . . .' Before he could issue his warning Mervin Wendell's clear, reassuring voice sounded through the morning air.

'Over this way, ladies and gentlemen. I'm Mervin Wendell, the man who's been writing to you, and I've rented these automobiles to carry you to your new homes.'

He moved in deftly, a figure of distinction and reassurance, saying precisely those things which the new families wanted to hear: 'The land commissioner is in his office at Line Camp. He has plats of the new town we are going to build. More important, he has the surveyors' maps showing the townships and the sections from which you can choose free land.' As he reminded them of the opportunity they faced, his voice assumed a kind of grandeur, and he held out his hands like an Old Testament figure leading his people toward a promised land.

The effect was somewhat destroyed, however, by Potato Brumbaugh, who muscled his way to the head of the crowd, seeking to warn them against the mistake they were making: 'Good farmers, listen to me. You cannot make a living on the drylands. Men tried in the eighties.'

'They did not try Dr. Creevey's new method,' Wendell said coldly.

'You'll get good crops the first year, and you women will think you've found a paradise.'

'They have,' Wendell broke in.

'But that's just the sod crop, and you know it. Think ahead to the dry years.'

'If we plant the way Dr. Creevey told us,' an Indiana farmer said, 'there won't be no dry years.'

'Some will be terribly dry,' Jim said. 'And you've never seen the like of our Colorado windstorms.'

Mervin Wendell saw that Brumbaugh and Lloyd were beginning to have an effect on the newcomers, so he decided that the time was proper for him to counter their arguments. 'Ladies and gentlemen,' he said quietly, 'these good men have every reason in the world to discourage you from claiming land that is rightfully yours. Mr. Brumbaugh came to Centennial years ago without a penny. He took up his free land to grow sugar beets, and now he's a millionaire. Jim Lloyd, that cowboy over there, also arrived without a cent. He took up grazing land for his cattle, and now he's a millionaire too.' Wendell dropped his voice and added slyly, 'Of course, he married the boss's daughter, and that never hurts.' He watched with aloof amusement as the two men squirmed.

'The situation is obvious, isn't it?' he asked with scorn. 'These men have all the land they need and now they wish to keep you from getting yours. Every word they utter is self-serving, because they want to keep everything for themselves.'

The charge was devastating, and Brumbaugh realized that anything further he might say would have no effect. He walked away from the young farmers and would have left the station except that a tall young woman ran to him, touching his hand. 'Are you convinced we're wrong?' she asked earnestly.

'You're dead wrong,' he said.

'Why?'

'Because you're destroying the grass. You're tearing up the sod. It's impossible to farm the land you'll be choosing.'

'Dr. Creevey does.'

'He spends his whole life on the project. He has every kind of support from the railroad. But when the bad years come, even he will be wiped out.'

'You're sure the bad years will come?' the young woman asked.

Brumbaugh looked at her, and she appeared to be the type of woman he had known decades ago on the Volga, hard-working, dedicated, whose soul would be shattered by the experiences that lay ahead. 'Are you pregnant?' he asked bluntly. When she nodded in shy embarrassment, he said quietly, 'May God have mercy on you, because the land won't.'

'You've prospered, they say.'

'My farm was near water. Yours won't be.'

Mervin Wendell called for the women to follow him, and the Grebes started to move away, but Brumbaugh caught Alice by the hand. 'Go back home," he warned her. 'The land out there . . . it's fine for dogs and men. It's hell on horses and women.'

'Over here!' Wendell called. 'You, young lady. In this car.'

And it was from the rear seat of a fancy Buick that Alice Grebe first approached her new home. Mr. Wendell, at the wheel of his own car, drove east on Prairie, then north past Little Mexico, where adobe hovels astonished the newcomers, and then northeast toward the proposed village of Line Camp. When the caravan crossed Mud Creek and entered the great plains, several women gasped at the total emptiness, for not one living thing could be seen except grass, not one sign of human occupancy except the winding road.

'My God, this is desolate!' Vesta Volkema cried.

'Not when it has barns and windmills and lovely homes dotted across the horizon,' Wendell said brightly. And now it became clear why he had crowded all the wives into separate automobiles; he did not want their disappointment to contaminate their husbands. The men would be looking at the soil, trying to estimate its worth, and if left alone, would reach favorable conclusions . . . or at least not negative ones. And later they would persuade their womenfolk to accept the decision.

'Wait till you see Line Camp!' he said enthusiastically.

'What's it like?' Vesta asked.

'A paradise!' he assured her.

He had purchased a section of land—640 acres—from the Venneford people for the establishment of a new town centered upon old Line Camp Three, long abandoned. With the land, he acquired the stone barn and the low-built one-story stone house which had been used by generations of cowboys when they worked the Venneford cattle. The buildings were the best part of the purchase, and with them as a focus, the surveyors had platted a western town, centered upon the intersection of State 8 and Weld 33.

A newcomer to Line Camp had three choices. He could buy land and live in town, or close to it. He could homestead for three years and get a half-section, 320 acres, free. Or he could start to homestead and after fourteen months buy the land from the government for $1.25 an acre.

Mervin Wendell encouraged as many people as possible to do the last, for as soon as they got legal title to the land, they were free to sell it, and he was prepared to buy as much as possible from them at $1.75 an acre, intending to sell it to later arrivals at $7.00 or $8.00. It was to his interest that as many as possible of the newcomers occupy their land for fourteen months and then quit, for in their failure lay his success.

With this first drylands group he was doubly sure that many would lose heart. The tall girl who had been talking with Brumbaugh—she wouldn't stay long. Nor the minister's wife, nor the young woman with two children. He had often bought homesteads from such defeated people for 25¢ an acre, and he would do so again.

So his tactic would be to encourage the families as fulsomely as possible while they were signing up for their free land, then to commiserate with them when they wanted to flee the area. He would work principally on the women, reassuring them at first, sympathizing with them when the bad years struck. And in this manner he would acquire huge holdings in the area, hovering always like a jackal about the edges of a camp, picking up the strays.

With horns blowing, the rented automobiles drove into the space between the two stone buildings, and Mervin Wendell climbed atop a wooden box to explain procedures: 'This will be your new town. That stone barn is being converted into a first-class general store, where you will be able to purchase almost anything you could in Chicago. That round thing over there will climb ninety feet into the air and serve as the elevator where you will store your vast crops of wheat. Down there is where the railroad station will be. And this low building houses the land commissioner, who is going to give you all the acres you require. The free land extends in every direction, but I'll tell you frankly, if I was choosing, I'd take one of those half-sections in the northeast sector, up beyond Rattlesnake Buttes.' Here he broke into an easy laugh, explaining to the women, 'When Indians lived here, the Buttes had rattlers. Today no Indians, no rattlers. Today mostly Baptists, and they're trouble enough.' At this joke the wives laughed nervously.

'The automobiles will sally forth in various directions, and you are free to inspect the land for as long as you like. When you've made your choice, you come back here and speak to my good friend Walter Bellamy.' From the interior of the building, he summoned the land commissioner, and a curious young man appeared, thin as a reed, red-haired, awkward and with a green shade protecting his pale-blue eyes from the incessant sun. He was twenty-four years old, a college graduate from Grinnell in Iowa. He was shy and deprecatory of his ability; he had come west to find escape from family pressures, and he loved the quiet job he had stumbled into as land commissioner. To watch people, day after day, choosing and settling upon new land would be exciting.

'Show them the maps,' Wendell said unctuously, and the surveys were unrolled: Township 10 North, Range 60 West, with the town of Line Camp occupying Section 22, and with Sections 16 and 36 reserved for the school district.

The farmers could see that most of the half-sections in this township were spoken for; what they could not detect was that most of them belonged to Mervin Wendell, who was ready to sell them at a profit. The free land lay farther out, and for some reason he could not have explained, Earl Grebe focused on land which lay to the northwest, and when he discussed this with the group, he found that another family, the Larsens, had done the same, so they procured one of the cars and drove along country trails to that section of the free land, but when Earl bored in with his earth auger, he brought up a very dry sample that showed a tillable depth of less than six inches.

'This isn't for me,' he announced, and he went off on his own, and at the northeast corner of the township he found a half-section that had everything he required: rolling land for good drainage when the rains did come, a topsoil fourteen inches deep, fairly good moisture already in the soil and a view of the two red buttes to the south, with absolutely nothing but low hills visible in any other direction. He saw this as a majestic land, worthy of a man's best efforts.

'Alice!' he shouted to his wife. 'Look at this!' And he showed her the dimensions of the land the government would be giving them. It seemed a vast holding, 320 acres, with enough to leave a large part fallow year after year, and a protected hillside behind which a house could be sheltered.

Alice stood by her husband, staring at the huge land they were about to occupy, and whether it was a chill or her pregnancy or a foreboding of what the years might contain, she began shivering, for this seemed to her the bleakest land that God had ever given His children to plow. Earl, sensing her fright, placed his arm about her and promised, 'It's our task to subdue this land and make it ours.'

He handed her his notebook and asked her to jot down the designation of their new home: 'Township 10 North, Range 60 West, Section 11, the south 320.' When the figures were written, Alice found in them a sense of reality, and her apprehension abated somewhat. Bending down, for she was slightly taller than her husband, she kissed him on the cheek and said, 'I'm all right. The place is so empty, it seems filled with ghosts.' To Earl such a statement was incomprehensible, and he made no reply.

The Larsens found a good piece of land in Township 11, a little farther north, but the Volkemas located a fine half-section to the southeast and staked out two additional half-sections to which they were not entitled. When the group reassembled outside the land commissioner's office, Alice asked, 'What are you going to do with the extra sections?' and Vesta said, 'Don't worry about that, I have the chalk.' This reply made no sense at all, so Alice turned and asked Mrs. Larsen, 'What does she mean?' and Mrs. Larsen said, 'She looks as if she knows what she's doing.'

With the others watching, Mrs. Volkema directed her son, aged seventeen, and her daughter, eighteen, to take off their shoes. With her chalk she wrote on the inner sole of each shoe: 'Age 21.' Then the two children put their shoes back on and accompanied Vesta into the land office, where Commissioner Bellamy waited with his maps.

'Have you located the land you prefer?' he asked formally.

'We have,' Earl Grebe replied, and he proceeded to designate what he and Alice had chosen. Papers were signed, and Bellamy said, 'You have staked your claim as of this date. Within six months you must give me proof that you have taken up actual residence on your land. If you fail to do so, you forfeit your claim. On the other hand, if you pitch a tent today and take up residence, three years from this date the land is yours, fee simple. Are these terms understood?'

'How do we inform you that we've taken residence?' Grebe asked.

'You come in here and tell me so. You put your hand on that Bible and swear to your occupancy, and that's good enough for the government, because we know you're all Christian persons.' And in this simple manner Earl and Alice Grebe filed their intention of homesteading.

With the Volkemas the routine was somewhat different, for after Peter and Vesta had filed for their 320 acres, they nudged their son to step forward. 'I'm filing on the 320 north of my father's,' the boy said, and Walter Bellamy's jaw dropped a couple of inches, for the law required that a homesteader be twenty-one, and this downy-cheeked lad looked as if he were about eighteen.

But before Bellamy could protest, the Volkema girl stepped forward, a slim child who could not possibly be over twenty-one, and she filed on the 320 south of her parents'.

'Are you young people over age twenty-one?' Bellamy asked and they, knowing that they were standing above the 'Age 21' written in their shoes, replied 'Yes, sir.'

This was too much for Bellamy, so he produced his Bible and made them place their hands on it, after which he asked in a funereal voice, 'Do you solemnly swear in the presence of Almighty God that you are over age twenty-one?'

'I do,' the boy said.

'I am,' the girl said.

'Well, there's nothing more I can do,' Bellamy shrugged, and he entered their claims. The Volkemas now had a grasp on 960 acres, and they intended acquiring much more.

The Homestead Act of 1862 as amended in 1909 required a settler to erect a house at least twelve feet by fourteen feet, and this was customarily referred to as 'a house twelve by fourteen.'

The Volkemas, therefore, carved a little wooden house twelve inches by fourteen inches, and four weeks later when they appeared at Bellamy's office to announce their occupancy of their land, they assured him that they had a house twelve by fourteen. So did their son. So did their daughter. And Bellamy had no alternative but to enter their proof of occupancy.

The Larsens chose an alternate course. Some years before, Mervin Wendell had directed his carpenter to build the flimsiest possible kind of house, twelve by fourteen feet, on a sledge which could be hauled from one homestead to another. He rented it to newcomers—five dollars for twenty-four hours—and with it perched on their claim, they could swear that they had on their half-section a house twelve by fourteen. As soon as their assertion was recorded, the sledge could be hauled to the next homestead.

The Grebes would not engage in such deception. For them to have sworn to a lie would have been inconceivable, for they believed that God inspected all they did and that only through His assistance could something like their present venture succeed. So they refused Mervin Wendell's offer of the house-on-the-sledge and Vesta Volkema's kind gift of the carved house. Theirs they would build the honest way.

Earl purchased two wooden doors, two door sills and three window frames. The carpenter delivered them to the half-section, where Grebe and two boys from the village were cutting sod for the walls and collecting flat stones for the floors. When the materials were assembled, Grebe and the boys rode into the low hills north of Rattlesnake Buttes to find lodge poles and rafters, and at the end of two months of arduous work, the Grebes had themselves a soddy.

It was not a neat-looking house, for the earth was uneven in form and color, but it was surprisingly snug, a low, compact refuge which gave solid protection from the wind and such occasional rain as might fall. When the house was ready for occupancy they invited a clergyman from Centennial to bless it, and he appeared with Walter Bellamy in tow, and a solemn service was held.

It was exciting, this launching of a new life, but that night Alice Grebe suffered the consequences of the heavy obligations she had undertaken. Toward evening she fell ill, and before anyone could be summoned from the neighboring ranches, she miscarried. Her husband was grief-stricken. He sat with her through the remainder of the night as the first winter wind whipped at the soddy, and when dawn broke he walked heartbroken across the plains to the Volkemas'.

When they heard the sad news, Vesta went back with Earl. She assured him that Alice was a strong woman and would produce numerous future children. There were no complications that she was aware of, but consulting a doctor might be a prudent safeguard. The nearest one was in Centennial, and Walter Bellamy volunteered to take Alice in to town, and as Vesta had predicted, the doctor found nothing wrong, and that night Alice was back in the soddy.

'You must see that she doesn't fall into a depression,' Vesta had warned, but of this there was no fear, for Alice herself had foreseen that danger and now plunged directly into the tasks of making this soddy into a true Christian home.

There was a library at the college in Greeley, and from it she procured books by Edith Wharton and Lincoln Steffens and a new treatise on dryland farming by a Dr. Widtsoe. She studied this with care, in order to help her husband, and took much consolation in the portrait of Jethro Tull, a stout Englishman in a copious wig who had proved that a family could be successful on a dry-land farm.

'It seems so strange,' she told her husband, 'to be growing things I'd never heard of six months ago. What is milo?'

'A sturdy type of sorghum.'

'What's sorghum?'

'A sturdy type of sugar cane.'

'We don't make sugar.'

'We plow it into the ground. Roughage. Aeration.'

'And lucerne? Never heard of it before.'

'That's a sturdy form of alfalfa.'

'Everything in this land must be sturdy,' she said. 'I'll be so, too.' And two months later she was pregnant again.

When the spring crops of 1912 were well up, and a bountiful harvest seemed assured, she heard a strange rattling in the fields, a sound she could not identify, and she ran to the door of the soddy to behold a devastating hailstorm sweeping eastward from the mountains. The ice pellets were as large as hen's eggs and they fell with such terrible force that she had to retreat from the door lest the hail strike her and endanger her child.

In the eleven minutes the storm raged across the prairie, it knocked flat every growing thing. When it passed, the fields were desolate, and that night Earl Grebe wondered if he would make a crop at all. The Volkemas came by to see what damage the Grebes had suffered; by a trick of nature the storm had concentrated on a small path to the north of Line Camp, so that the Grebes were pretty well wiped out while the Volkemas were practically untouched.

'I've had a lot of experience with hail,' Vesta said, 'and thank God this storm came early. Tomorrow you'll plow under the dead crops and still have time to grow summer wheat. The milo and the lucerne will fertilize the fields and all you've lost is some time and some seed.' She and her husband helped with the plowing, and whereas the summer crop was not as good as the winter one would have been, the Grebes did make some money that year.

It was the sound of the coyotes that tormented Alice, and one lonely night in October when her baby was about to be born and Earl was helping out on another farm, she heard the ululating cries in the darkness, and they sounded to her like the voice of doom. She fell to violent trembling and was seized with a strong premonition that something fearful was about to happen, but she steeled herself against the night, and kneeling beside the bed, she prayed for strength to bring this pregnancy to its proper conclusion.

'Oh, God, help me through this dark autumn. Help me to be strong.'

When Earl reached home he found his wife on her knees beside the bed. 'I'm having the baby early,' she whispered.

'Right now?' Earl cried.

'No. Maybe three hours . . . four.'

'I'll fetch Vesta,' he said.

When Magnes and Vesta reached the soddy, they found Alice so far advanced in labor that any thought of taking her to Centennial was vain. 'Do you know what to do?' Earl asked Vesta, and she said, 'It's nothing,' and she produced her book of home medicine. With much fumbling and more mess than necessary, Alice Grebe was delivered of her baby, a boy whom she named Ethan, after a character in a novel by Mrs. Wharton.

For Alice, the hardship of life in the soddy was relieved by the constant variations she saw in the prairie. 'At first I thought it was all emptiness,' she once told Vesta. 'Then I started watching birds, and the hawks and the redwings became more beautiful than the flowers back home. I heard the meadowlarks and one day I watched the courtship performance of the sage grouse . . . the males had their white chests all puffed out . . . and I could see strange-looking yellow air sacs on their necks, while their tails were spread sort of like a peacock. It was something.'

Near the Grebe soddy a town of prairie dogs had existed for more than three thousand years, and it accommodated itself easily to the arrival of human beings, the antics of the little animals providing much amusement for Alice. More dramatic things happened, too, like the sudden, heart-catching sight of antelope as they leaped mysteriously from the buttes, dashing past the soddy to disappear to the north, winged things, fragile and fleet.

In October 1912 the last surviving buffalo in Colorado drifted into Blue Valley. It was an old cow that had been hiding in the hills back of the mining camp. How she had escaped wolves, hunters and starvation, no one knew, but she had struggled on, the last of the herd.

She was a heavy beast and required much grass during the year. She would have preferred ranging the plains, as her ancestors had done, but with the coming of settlers and the establishment of towns like Line Camp, this was no longer possible. She therefore hid in the mountains, foraging on the lush vegetation which appeared in remote valleys.

In summer she ate as much as she could; in winter she lived off her fat plus such dried grasses as she could uncover beneath the snows. In blizzards, she still used the ancient tactic: stand firm, lower the head and swing it back and forth like the bucket on a steam shovel until the grass was exposed.

The winter of 1913 brought much snow, and she had worn herself out pushing it away, but when she got down to the grass, it was good, and she had survived nicely. A warm spring followed and a rich summer, and she was fat. She had not enjoyed foraging alone, for she had always been a gregarious creature, but during the recent years of loneliness she had grown accustomed to her lot.

And then, by an unfortunate accident which might not have occurred had she been younger and able to detect the danger, she came over the crest of a hill at dawn to find herself in the backyard of a hunting lodge.

'Jesus Christ!' Jake Calendar called back to his friends. 'A buffalo!'

He and four other men had come hunting the mountains—for deer or elk; if nothing better, antelope, with always the chance of a bear. Now, at Calendar's cry, they all rushed to the window, and saw near the top of the hill behind the cabin a buffalo—and it was a big one.

'Throw me my gun!' Jake said in a low, controlled voice. He stood watching as the old animal, sensing no danger, kept coming down the hill.

Inside the cabin the four other hunters slipped into their shoes, not even bothering with pants, and within a few moments went outside, each with a loaded high-powered rifle. Silently the men lined up and took sight. 'Take it slow,' Jake warned. 'It ain't easy to kill somethin' that big.'

'One . . . two . . . three!' Jackson Quimbish did the counting, and when his voice uttered the last number, the five men fired in unison.

Quickly they reloaded and fired again.

Reloading for the second time, they blazed away once more at the astonished old cow. At the first fusillade she had stopped, then stubbornly had plodded on, keeping her massive head directed toward the creatures she could not see.

Since she was coming head-on, the hunters could not easily strike her in a vital spot, but the second five shots did some damage, and she stumbled, kicking up dust. Her eyes were blurred, but still she kept moving forward, an old, old cow, heavy in her knees. She was not afraid and showed no inclination to turn away from her adversaries, but she had no concept of how to cope with them. She merely kept moving forward.

The last fusillade struck her from two sides and her legs began to cave in. She tried to take a deep breath, but something stuck in her lungs, and in desperation she started to fall forward. Now her whole massive body surrendered and she tumbled into the autumn dust, sliding sideways down the hill for a few feet, then coming to rest against rocks.

When the sportsmen reached the body, five men in nightshirts and Jake Calendar barefooted as well, they judged that fifteen shots had struck the animal, but as Jake pointed out, 'Six, seven must have hit her in the forehead, and hell, anyone knows that with all that matted hair and bone, you can't kill no buffalo by hittin' it straight on.'

In 1914 the plowmen's championship was held on a bright October day on a ranch some miles north of Little Mexico. Farmers convened from all parts of northern Colorado to compete, and Line Camp was represented by Earl Grebe, who stood a good chance of carrying off first prize.

His four horses were in fine condition, their harnesses oiled and polished and their bellies filled with just the right amount of oats. Earl himself was well rested and prepared to do his best.

There would be nineteen competitors, and the field they would plow was an eighth of a mile square, with enough gentle dips and swells to provide a good test. The ground had never been plowed before; it was virgin sod and would not turn easily. Rules required that the nose of the plow must cut at least seven inches into the soil, so that weak horses would be of little use, for it required four of the strongest to cut that deep into unbroken sod.

The plowmen were required to demonstrate their skill with three farm implements: plow, disk, harrow. With the first the men had to cut to the proper depth, maintain an absolutely straight line and turn uniform furrows. With the disk they had to chop the sod. With the harrow they had to pulverize it and smooth it. Only experienced farmers could perform these various tasks, converting rough virgin earth into a tractable soil ready for the planting drill.

The plowmen worked simultaneously, each on his assigned portion of the field, and time was a factor, although not the determinant one. If two men plowed equally well, the one who finished first won, but no points could be gained by galloping the horses through the tasks, for crooked furrows did not count.

It was an exciting contest, one which drew several hundred spectators, many placing bets on their favorites. When the nineteen teams of horses were lined up behind the shining plows, with the disks and harrows waiting behind, one caught a sense of the prodigious undertaking the men of the west were engaged in: from Minnesota to Montana, from North Dakota to the plains of Texas, land that had never before felt the plow—not even the forked stick of the Indian—was being broken.

At ten o'clock the men in charge called the contestants to order, and the nineteen stalwart farmers grasped the handles of their plows, the reins draped about their necks. 'Men,' the starter shouted, 'it don't need me to tell you no rules. Plow deep, plow straight, and change your hitches to the disk and harrow as fast as possible. You've got to pull each piece of machinery back behind the line before you unhitch. Ready? Go!'

It was difficult for the spectators to ascertain who was winning, because only the judges could allocate points, and they kept their conclusions to themselves, but from the lovely straightness of Earl Grebe's furrows and their extraordinary uniformity, it was clear that he had a good chance.

But at the far end of the line there was a Swede with almost no neck, a little rock of a man, and his ability to identify with his horses was uncanny; with them, he formed a team of five, sturdy, hard-working animals who knew what they were about, and it was a joy to watch them move up and down the furrows in unison. The man's name was Swenson, and he could use the disk just as capably as he used the plow.

But when it came to harrowing, no one could excel Earl Grebe. He was capable of putting a fine finish on the roughest terrain, and as the contest neared conclusion, the spectators knew that the winner would be Grebe or the little Swede.

There was silence as the four judges walked back and forth along the plowed stretches, comparing the evenness of the earth and the uniformity of the topsoil. 'I think Earl has it,' Vesta whispered as the judges convened, and Alice kept her fingers crossed as the chairman stepped forward.

'The winner! Ole Swenson of Sterling.'

Alice looked down at the ground to hide her disappointment, then felt this to be an unworthy escape. Looking up with a bright smile, she winked at Earl as the judges proclaimed him the runner-up. He won the affection of the crowd by stepping back and patting his horses, giving them all the credit for the good work.

There was much cheering, and money prizes were handed out, and other farmers congregated about the two winners, congratulating them on jobs well done, and Walter Bellamy moved from one group to another, saying with obvious delight, 'Wasn't it splendid? A little town, Line Camp, winning second place? I'm really very proud.'

Two witnesses to the contest were not impressed. When the others had departed, they remained behind, staring at the plowed strips, each covered with harrowed earth almost as fine as the grains from a river bottom.

'It's unnatural,' Potato Brumbaugh grumbled as he inspected the soil. 'This land was intended for grass. If they abuse it this way, there'll come a day of reckoning.'

Jim Lloyd stooped down to compare the uncut sod with the plowed, and what he saw appalled him. 'It'll take five years for this to grow grass again,' he said angrily. 'They must be insane.'

'It wouldn't be so bad,' Brumbaugh growled, 'if they didn't harrow it at the end. If they left the clods unbroken, maybe the land could save itself. But this way! Good God, all they're doing is manufacturing dust.' He kicked at the offending soil and sent its pulverized fragments spinning in the sunlight.

'We had a good system here,' Jim said, 'and they couldn't recognize it. They had to tear the sod apart.'

'One thing I'm glad about,' Brumbaugh said with resignation, 'I won't be here to see the reckoning. I've worked harder than those horses to till this earth, the right way. I'll be glad to be in my grave when the wrong way comes to grief.'

His lament was not heard by those who should have listened, for they were all now at the Railway Arms, discussing the victors and the good fortune that had come to wheat farmers generally. As Ole Swenson, the winner, proclaimed in his toast, 'If them Germans and others keep fightin' in Europe, sure as hell we're gonna see two-dollar wheat. So come November, I'm gonna break an additional 640 and plant it in Turkey Red. If the war keeps on long enough, we'll all be rich.'

Toward the end of November 1914 the Grebes became eligible to prove-up their half-section, for they had complied with the three major requirements: they had lived on the land for three years; they had built a house twelve by fourteen; and they had cultivated the soil. For five dollars Walter Bellamy would advertise in the local paper his intention of awarding the Grebes title to their farm, and in due time they would receive from Washington a legal paper, signed by President Wilson himself.

'You understand,' Bellamy told them when they gave him the five dollars, 'that President Wilson himself doesn't do the signing. It looks as if he did, but I'm sure he has a girl in the White House who can imitate his signature. Stands to reason, he'd wear out his fingers.'

On proving-up day the law required the applicant to bring to the land commissioner's office two trusted friends who would testify that to their certain knowledge the said Earl Grebe had lived on his land and cultivated it. Grebe chose Magnes and Vesta Volkema, and when the three stood before Commissioner Bellamy, he warned them, 'I shall interrogate each of you in private. You will be sworn on the Bible, and what you say will be recorded.' He pointed to Grebe and told the others to wait outside.

Bellamy took his job seriously and made the transfer of government land an impressive ritual, one that conferred dignity as well as title.

'What crops did you raise?'

'Wheat, milo, lucerne and a little speltz for the cows.'

'During 1913 what months were you in residence on your claim?'

'Not a day off it.'

'In 1912 what other members of your family resided there?'

'My wife, Alice. My son Ethan. But he was there only the last two months.'

'Where had be been previously?'

'Not born yet.'

'Have you a house at least twelve by fourteen?'

'Bigger.'

'You may stand aside, Mr. Grebe.'

Bellamy then summoned the witnesses, each by himself, and probed into this history of the Grebe holdings, and after a while he called all three before him. 'I find that Earl Grebe did stake out a legal claim on his half-section, did occupy it, did cultivate it and did erect thereon a residence. If you have twenty-two dollars, Mr. Grebe, I will give you a receipt and the land is yours, fee simple and forever.'

'When do I get the deed?'

'That will be sent you by President Wilson. The land is yours.'

It was the custom in Colorado for a successful claimant, on the day his ownership was affirmed, to invite his witnesses to the local hotel for dinner, but Grebe was so relieved at gaining actual title to his land that he felt expansive. 'Mr. Bellamy,' he said, 'I'd be proud if you'd join us.' Bellamy, a bachelor who usually ate alone, accepted eagerly, and this inspired Mrs. Volkema to whisper to him during dinner, 'You know I have a daughter with 320 acres in her own name. One of these days Magnes and I will be heading for California, and who knows? She may inherit our land, too.' Mr. Bellamy chewed away on his fried steak and appeared not to have heard.

The dinner was made memorable when the waitress interrupted to inform the guests that it was snowing outside, the first real moisture of the new planting season. The farmers left their drinks to gather at the window and watch with approval as flakes covered the earth and accumulated in drifts. 'It's going to be a good year,' Magnes Volkema said. 'Maybe the best we ever had.' The two families now owned their farms and were prepared for the good fortune that the war was bringing them. This snow, enriching the earth, was an augury.

As soon as Earl Grebe had legal title to his land, he became an inviting target for Mervin Wendell's real estate manipulations. The gracious, elderly man with the exquisite manners started to frequent Line Camp, making judicious but not secret inquiries about the Grebes: 'Is a refined lady like Alice Grebe satisfied to live in a soddy?' 'Mrs. Grebe seems the nervous sort. Maybe she'd like to sell the place and move to some town where life would be easier?' 'Is this fellow Grebe adequate as a farmer? What I mean is, should he continue on the land or is he merely wasting his effort?'

So he watched for those times when Earl was plowing in the far corners; then he would stop by the soddy to ask Alice if she missed Ottumwa and whether she wouldn't prefer to live in a place like Centennial, with real houses and where she could walk to the store.

'I like it here, and besides, it was you who encouraged us to take this land in the first place,' she said.

'But if you came to town, you wouldn't have to live in a soddy.'

'Are many farmhouses you visit cleaner than this?'

'Oh, Mrs. Grebe! You misunderstand. I have the greatest respect for women like you. Backbone of the nation, I always say.'

Getting nowhere with her, he turned his attention to Earl, pointing out that if he cared to sell his half-section, there were houses in Centennial which he, Wendell, owned and which could be rented for a nice figure.

'Matter of fact,' Grebe replied, 'what I'd like to do is homestead another half-section.'

'That might be possible,' Wendell said blandly.

'But I thought the law won't allow it.'

'There could be ways,' Wendell said quietly as he drove off.

When it became obvious that the war in Europe would expand, and possibly involve the United States, the urge to break new land became irresistible. Even the weather cooperated, sixteen inches of rain in 1914, seventeen inches in 1915. Yield rose from a normal eighteen bushels an acre to a phenomenal thirty-one. As Ole Swenson had predicted, 'If the war keeps on long enough, we'll all be rich.'

For the Grebes such prosperity posed problems more perplexing than those of adversity. They now had money, but Alice wanted to spend it in building a real house; Earl wanted to buy more land. In this he was encouraged by Mervin Wendell, who now returned with the second half of his attack.

He drove up early one morning, smiling and affable, to congratulate Mrs. Grebe on the fine job she and her husband were doing. 'You've made this place a little haven in the wilderness,' he said approvingly. 'No wonder you wish to stay.'

'We aim to keep it neat,' she conceded.

'Where's Earl?'

'Breaking new sod at the far end.'

'He's a prudent man.' Picking his way carefully, Wendell started to cross the fields already plowed, but he had not gone far when Earl saw him and came down one of the long, straight rows he had turned earlier that day.

'Morning, Mr. Wendell. What brings you out?'

'Opportunity, Earl. It always strikes for a worthy man.'

Grebe could make no sense of this, but like the other farmers, he had grown accustomed to Wendell's flamboyancies, and nodded. 'What opportunity?' he asked.

'Right up there.'

Grebe looked in the direction indicated and saw nothing. Empty land stretched unimpeded in low sweeps and rises, none of it yet touched by the plow. It had once belonged to the Arlingtons, but like so many others, they had quit homesteading.

'It's my land,' Wendell said. 'A whole section. Young Arlington had his own 320. You know. "Do you swear by Almighty God that you are over age twenty-one?" "I swear I am over twenty-one." ' He broke into a deep, reverberating laugh. 'So right here, adjacent to your holding, we have 640 acres of the choicest drylands.'

'And you propose to sell it?'

'I do. In the hands of the right man, this land could produce thirty bushels.' Placing his right arm about Grebe's shoulder, he indicated that he considered Grebe just the man to achieve it.

'How much?'

'You're looking at five dollars an acre.'

'Too much.'

'It does sound high, Earl, but with wheat the way it is, this land can make your fortune. Talk it over with Alice.'

'It's too much,' Grebe said flatly.

'Now, Earl,' the older man said persuasively, 'you're caught in what I always call "the trap of knowledge." ' When Grebe looked bewildered, Wendell explained: 'You know too much. You know the Arlingtons commuted their land after fourteen months by paying Mr. Bellamy a dollar twenty-five an acre. And you know that I bought it from them at one seventy-five an acre, showing them a neat profit. Yes indeed, a very neat profit. And you think I ought to restrict my profit and sell you the land for something like three dollars and twenty-five cents an acre. But, Earl! The value of this land . . . your land . . . Larsen's land . . . it's gone up, what with the war and the prospect that we'll soon be involved. Earl, this land is worth a fortune!'

'Too much,' Grebe reiterated, but Wendell, before he drove off, stopped to warn Alice: 'Your husband has a chance to make real money —to move you onto the finest avenue in Centennial, into the biggest mansion. All he has to do is plant another section in wheat. Right now. I'm offering him the land very cheap, Mrs. Grebe, very cheap indeed.'

When Earl returned to the soddy, she asked, 'How much did he want?'

'Five dollars an acre.'

'Too much.'

'That's what I thought.'

'How much could we afford to go?' she asked.

'No. We're going to build you that house you've been wanting.'

'Earl, if you have a real chance to better yourself, grab it. I can wait. What kind of figure would be reasonable?'

'About three dollars and forty cents.'

'Have we the money?'

'We could put down fifteen hundred. I think Wendell would carry our mortgage for the rest.'

So they discussed all aspects of the deal: the benefit from farming not 320 acres but a sprawling 960, the possibility of allowing fields to lie fallow for two years, the certainty that with rain the yield could go as high as thirty-six bushels an acre, the certainty that with a continuing war, prices must rise.

They convinced themselves, and when Mr. Wendell returned a few days later to check on their intentions, he cut his price to $3.60 an acre and they bought. He gave them a mortgage for one thousand dollars, which he volunteered to carry himself.

Earl Grebe now had a farm many times larger than he could reasonably have hoped for; from the northwest corner to the southeast it was a distance of two and a half miles, and he could plow his straight furrows so far that when Alice stood at one end she could scarcely see him when he turned his team at the other. All the farmers were plowing these deep, continuous furrows, and there were places in northern Colorado where one field blended in with the next, with scarcely any break intervening, for a distance of forty miles. And when these fields were disked and harrowed, the land presented the appearance of an endless table, flat and uniform, the surface of the soil consisting of fine dust. When rains fell, this silvery silt was locked to the soil, making a splendid soft surface in which to plant wheat. No fields were flatter or more uniformly pulverized than Earl Grebe's.

Walter Bellamy, working in his land commissioner's office, was beginning to raise irritating questions about the practices of the farmers in his district. He had been reading books which argued that if a man plowed not in one unbroken line—'Up hill and down dale,' as he phrased it— but in wavering lines which followed the contour of the land, leaving strips of unplowed land, more water would be trapped, there would be less likelihood of soil blowing if a high wind came and there would be much less erosion.

'What's erosion?' Grebe asked.

'It's when a stream starts running downhill and picks up speed. You know, it eats away the soil and forms a gully.'

'I learned how to stop that when I was a boy.' He knew the problem but not the word. 'We placed rocks in the path and slowed down the water.'

'Yes, but the water still escaped. If you'd plow around the hills and not down them . . .'

Grebe could not help being impatient with someone who had never farmed, and when Bellamy persuaded a man named Rumson to plow the new way, Grebe and the other farmers in the area journeyed to Rumson's farm and saw for themselves how ridiculous the whole thing was. The man's furrows went this way and that and were so uneven that no self-respecting plowman would have owned them. And in that year's contest Rumson didn't even bother to enter, and a good thing, for the judges would have disqualified him. Furthermore, with nineteen inches of rain, who needed the extra catchment, provided there was any?

It was during the winter of 1917 that Alice Grebe came at last to accept prairie life. As she told Vesta Volkema, 'People around here speak of a soddy as if it were despicable or fit only for animals. It's really adobe, nothing more or less, and Spanish people have been living in it for centuries. In Arizona, I'm told, they prefer it.'

Their soddy was comfortable—cool in summer, warm in winter—and the charge that it bred lice and bedbugs was a lie. 'If you keep after the corners,' she told Vesta, who had never lived in a soddy, 'it breeds nothing. And the walls don't sweat.'

In February she and Earl bought a load of lumber and added a lean-to to the eastern end of the house, and with thin slats, partitioned it into a large kitchen and a small room for the two children, Ethan and Victoria. It was a snug, comfortable house, and in summer flowers grew on the sod roof, where birds gathered to pick the seeds.

If the Grebes' soddy was one of the most congenial homes at Line Camp, it was primarily because Alice made it so. She seemed to grow taller and thinner as the years passed, and more determined to make her family's western venture a success. She had a tenseness which she never lost, but she had learned to control it and directed her energy to problems in the community when her work at home was finished.

Mervin Wendell had worked diligently to sell his lots in the town of Line Camp, and the settlement flourished, with dwellings for more than three hundred people. In addition to the two stone buildings, there was a church, a bank, a newspaper, a fine hardware store and a commodious hotel with a wide veranda containing six rocking chairs.

What Alice Grebe wanted for her community was a library and a larger church, and she became, as the banker complained, 'quite pestilential' in pressing these needs upon her neighbors. She organized suppers, started a summer fair, made the plowing committee give a portion of the prize money for books, and in time watched both the library and the church grow.

Across America women like her goaded their communities into attaining the goals which distinguish a civilized society from an uncivilized. It was always women who insisted upon libraries, and parks, and public nurses, and better schools, and newer churches, and paved roads. It was women with nervous energy, like Alice Grebe, who argued with bankers and merchants and came away with funds to do the good things that were required. One of the conspicuous differences between small towns in the United States and those in less-concerned nations was that American women insisted upon improvements, upon charitable works and upon the proliferation of cultural activities. How bleak Line Camp would have been without the proddings of Alice Grebe, how lonely and austere—an accidental cluster of buildings lost in the great plains. With her efforts it became a civilized little town whose signboard at the western entrance was not ridiculous:

BIGGEST LITTLE TOWN IN THE WEST

WATCH US GROW!

Potato Brumbaugh was wearing out. It was the year 1915 and he was eighty-eight. The body he had used so unstintingly was showing signs of protest, and recently he had suffered a stroke which paralyzed the left side of his body. It was pathetic and in a way indecent to see this stocky old man with uncontrollable tears in his left eye, for he had never been a man to tolerate weakness. And to watch him unable to walk was a reminder of the ultimate failure of all men.

Every day he would ask Serafina Marquez to place him on the lawn in front of his house, where he could watch the river with which he had wrestled for so long, and it became apparent to her that whereas he could scarcely speak, his mind was not impaired. It was obvious that he was deep in thought. He liked to have visitors, especially Jim Lloyd, to whom he felt deeply attached. They would sit together and watch hawks perform over the river, those magnificent birds that flew so differently from all others. If one of the hawks uttered his peculiar cry, Jim would see by the change in Brumbaugh's face that the old man had heard. He was much like a hawk himself, Jim thought, a man off on his own individual course, a man always fighting for the upper air.

Several times Jim wheeled the old cripple down to the river itself, where they watched avocets probing among the rushes, and Brumbaugh indicated that he had never known that shy bird well. Now he found amusement in the way the stilt-legged creature shoved his inquisitive upturned beak into hidden places, coming up with surprising treats.

Once, with the fingers of his right hand, Potato made dancing little movements, mimicking the avocet, and Jim suspected that he was wishing he could move about as easily as this bird. He saw tears come into Brumbaugh's right eye, matching the permanent ones in his left.

Brumbaugh was much distressed that his friend Tranquilino still lingered in Mexico, and often he summoned Serafina and her two children to sit with him. He had increasing respect for Triunfador, for the boy had labored hard to take his father's place and was a strong hand in the field. But he loved Serafina, this stately, quiet woman who bore the accidents of life with such dignity. For three years she had worked the beets with her two children and saved her money. She was thirty-one years old now and growing more beautiful as the years passed. She moved, Brumbaugh thought, with the grace of a young antelope.

More than once Brumbaugh had pointed at Triunfador, managing to say, 'School,' but Serafina told him in Spanish, 'He's needed on the farm. School is for Anglos.' With some impatience Brumbaugh indicated that the Takemoto children were going to school, but Serafina said, 'They have different customs,' and she refused to allow her son to get mixed up with such matters.

The girl Soledad was four now, old enough to help with the beets, and she gave promise of being even more graceful than her mother. She had dark, luminous eyes and very black hair which hung down her back in two pigtails. Brumbaugh often invited her to sit on his lap, but he was unable to control his leg muscles and she kept sliding off. She preferred to sit on the ground at his feet, watching him intently and now and then rewarding him with a grave smile. Pointing to her, he mouthed with great difficulty the word 'School,' but Serafina laughed and said, 'She's a girl!' Again Brumbaugh noted that the Takemoto girl was going to school, and Serafina dismissed such foolishness by retreating to her former remark, 'They have different customs.'

Like all original thinkers who approach the end of their lives, Brumbaugh was forced to acknowledge that he had never thought radically enough. The really bold ideas, those which form the foundations of concepts, had frightened him, and he had backed away from them. Now, in the warm summer of 1915, his mind leaped from one construct to the next. Immobilized physically, he ranged the world intellectually, and at the end of one probing day he said to himself, I'm like an old apple tree, too worn out to produce fruit. Hammer a few spikes into the trunk and the tree begins to yield like a four-year-old. It's been reminded that this might be the last season.

He was irritated that men like him had not yet produced a beet seed which would grow not five seedlings, four of them useless, but only one. With such a seed, the stoop-work of thinning would be eliminated, because any plant which survived could be depended upon to grow its one beet without competition from its four useless neighbors.

It's possible to find such a seed, he thought. You look at a field of sugar beets, here and there you find a clump with only one plant. That seed did it. The problem is to conserve that seed and breed thousands more like it.

He had been much impressed by what this man Warren Gammon in Des Moines had been able to accomplish. This was the sort of thing men ought to be doing in all fields, for it required only imagination. Gammon had recognized the Hereford as a noble animal; however, it had long, sharp horns which looked fine on bulls—very masculine and powerful—but which had two drawbacks: they made the animal difficult to handle, and during shipment the horns of one steer often gouged the flanks of another, which damaged the meat, producing a lower price at slaughter. Of course, the horns could be sawed off, but what the rancher really needed was a polled Hereford, one born without the ability to grow horns, and this fellow Gammon had made up his mind to produce it.

Brilliant man, Brumbaugh mused as he looked across the field at his own hornless stock. How had Gammon produced this new breed of cattle? By the penny postal card! Patiently he had mailed printed cards to every Hereford grower in the United States, asking if the recipient happened to have in his stock any bull or cow which lacked horns genetically.

Brumbaugh could remember the day in 1903 when he had received his card of inquiry. He had appreciated immediately what Gammon was trying to do and had inspected his own cattle; finding no hornless animals, he had taken the trouble to visit all other herds in the district, and at Roggen he had found one such Hereford and in Wyoming another. He had bought them with his own money and shipped them off to Des Moines. Gammon was able to locate only fourteen polled Herefords throughout the United States, but from them he succeeded in creating a whole new breed of animal, one that saved millions of dollars for farmers.

There must be seeds like that, the old man told himself. We were just too damned lazy to find them.

He wanted very much to share his ideas with someone, so he sent for Takemoto, and the proper little Japanese came into the yard and bowed. Despite Brumbaugh's inability to speak, the two farmers nevertheless managed to converse. 'Children?' Brumbaugh asked, and from his pocket Takemoto produced report cards for his first three children, and while he could not read them himself, he knew what they showed. Brumbaugh, who remembered his own pride when his son Kurt did well in school, could see the high grades when Takemoto held the cards before him.

'Seed,' he said painfully, and with his right hand he indicated that somehow seed must be developed which would produce only one plant.

'Shinningu no,' Takemoto said. *Shinningu* was his pronunciation of *thinning* and the two men nodded: with proper seed the stoop-work of thinning would be no longer necessary.

'You are the only man who respects farming,' Brumbaugh wanted to say. The words refused to form themselves but the idea did, and Takemoto nodded. If he did understand farming, Colorado-style, it was only because he had emulated Brumbaugh.

'Eighth . . . section,' Brumbaugh mumbled. 'Arroyo . . . I give.'

This good news Takemoto understood instantly, and that afternoon he returned to the yard with a lawyer and his oldest son to serve as translator. 'This fellow tells me, Potato, that you want to give him that eighth-section by the arroyo,' the lawyer said.

If Brumbaugh could have moved, he would have embraced the little Japanese. If a dying man says he's going to give you some land, get it in writing. He thought back to his father's days along the Volga when the Czarist forces were stealing land from the Volgadeutsch. How terrible the loss of land could be to a farmer, how joyous its reception.

'Yes,' Brumbaugh said painfully, and the paper was drawn, with two neighbors called in to witness. At the conclusion of the transfer the Takemoto boy bowed and said formally, 'You have been so generous to my family, Mr. Brumbaugh, that my father insists upon paying the fees.' Brumbaugh understood, for he was a proud man too.

But his main concern was always with the river. Day after day he studied the Platte, seeing it for the thing it was: the canal that brought water from the mountains into the hands of men who knew how to use it. How beautiful that river was! In the course of his travels to London he had seen four great rivers—Missouri, Mississippi, Hudson, Thames— and he had comprehended the peculiar qualities of each. All rivers, he supposed, had special responsibilities, but there was none quite like the Platte.

Look at it now, in midsummer! A duck had a hard job finding enough water to light on. An avocet scarcely found worms. For at this stage the Platte was out of its channel. It was inland, working . . . irrigating beets. The river itself was nothing but a dry, empty line on the map, all of its water having been appropriated by crafty men like Brumbaugh. Never did the Platte look so useful as when it left its channel, entered the canals and worked up on the benches.

But in recent years it had been going dry too soon in the summer. It was not receiving enough water, and Brumbaugh wanted to correct this. How?

He had diverted from Wyoming and Nebraska every drop of water they would allow, and those states were castigating him in the Supreme Court. He had tapped rivers that normally went elsewhere, and still the water was insufficient.

How infuriating it was! Land which looked like baked sand became the Garden of Eden if only it could get water. You could draw a line with a pencil: on one side, a waterless barren; on the other, an irrigated luxuriance.

This man Creevey was all wrong. He was destroying the land with his fatuous notion that crops could be grown without water. The last three years had been lucky years. The settlers were producing good crops, but they'd had above-normal rainfall, and sooner or later the averages must reassert themselves. Years would come with lower than normal rain, and the dry-land farms would produce nothing.

Get my record book, Brumbaugh indicated to Jim Lloyd when the latter paid one of his regular visits, and when the book was in his lap, with Jim turning the pages, Brumbaugh proved what he was talking about. The established average for Centennial was thirteen inches of rain a year, yet here was a year in which twenty-three had fallen.

'Good, good!' Brumbaugh grunted. He could remember the twenty-one-inch year too, and the nineteen. But then his face clouded and he pointed to the dreadful years: seven inches and crops burned; six inches and nothing growing; five inches and a Sahara.

At this point the old man made a *whooshing* sound, and Jim feared he was suffering a new attack. Not at all. He was merely trying to indicate windstorms. How they had blown in those dry years, whipping the world before them, raising tall pillars of dust.

'Sooner or later we'll have the winds again,' he assured Brumbaugh.

'Only . . . one . . . thing . . .' The words formed with terrible effort as Brumbaugh pointed to the mountains standing so clear and beautiful in the west. The two men paused to stare at those great sentinels which pinned down the western edges of the plains, and they saw them in radically different ways. Jim Lloyd recognized them as distant entities which he had never really known. He had visited them occasionally, and he had climbed into their heart that night he and Brumbaugh had gone after the Pettis boys, but they formed no real part of his life.

'Remember the Pettis boys?' he asked the old man.

The old Russian's thoughts were far from such irrelevancies. He was staring at the mountains in a bold new way, seeing them for what they really were, a barrier thrusting itself into the heavens, impeding the natural circulation of clouds and knocking water from them before it could cross their crests and fall upon the eastern slope. It was the Rockies that had caused The Great American Desert; it was the Rockies that kept Potato Brumbaugh from getting as much water into the Platte as he wanted.

Now, at the very close of his life, he understood them for the implacable enemy they had always been. They were not the exquisite sculpture they seemed to be when a traveler first saw them from far out on the plains. They were the barrier, hard and rocky and almost impermeable. But they could be subdued.

Pointing with his right forefinger, Brumbaugh declared war. 'What . . . we . . . do . . . tunnel.'

Jim considered these strange words and repeated the crucial one: 'Tunnel?' Brumbaugh blinked his eyes. 'They're already working on a tunnel,' Jim said. 'The trains will go . . .'

'Water,' Brumbaugh said.

There was a long silence, at the end of which Jim rose and walked down to the edge of the river. He watched the avocets for some time, and after a while he came back and pushed the old man's chair to a spot from which he could watch the birds too.

'You're saying that we should build a tunnel underneath those mountains, bring the water that falls on the western slope—the water that isn't needed on that side—through the heart of the mountains and . . .'

Brumbaugh's right eye flashed with youthful exuberance. Lloyd had understood. With considerable excitement the old man pointed at the dry bed of the Platte.

'And you want the water we get that way to be thrown into the Platte?'

With a sweep of his right arm Brumbaugh indicated to the east the great prairie that could be brought into cultivation by such a scheme. It was a vision that had been maturing in his mind for the past half century, but he had been unable to formulate it. Now he saw the whole intricate system: water—water through the heart of the mountain—untold quantities of water to feed the thirsty plains.

'But to dig a tunnel through the heart of those mountains,' Jim protested. 'It would have to be . . . how long? Fourteen miles? Twenty?' The very thought of the task frightened him.

It did not frighten Brumbaugh. Trying frantically to express himself in words that would not come, the old man was able to utter just one, but it explained everything: 'Boom!'

If a man had enough dynamite, and enough brains, no tunnel in the world was impossible.

Jim was so impressed with Brumbaugh's vision that he reported it to a writer at the *Clarion*, and that young man wrote a long article, with maps and photographs explaining how Potato Brumbaugh proposed diverting from the other side of the mountain all the water Centennial would ever need. The Denver papers caught Brumbaugh's heroic image of a new agriculture on the plains, and they reported the theory, adding four learned explanations as to why it wouldn't work. Most telling was the argument that mountains were porous, as every miner learned to his sorrow when water collected in his dig, which meant that whereas the water could be led into them from the west, it would seep away before it reached the eastern end of the tunnel. When Jim read this negative report, Brumbaugh merely brushed his right hand back and forth as if to dismiss it, but when Jim laughed, the old man brushed his hand more firmly, and finally Jim understood: 'If there are holes in the mountain, cement them.'

So during the last days of his life the stubborn Russian kept his eyes fixed on the mountains. In his long years he had encountered many powerful opponents: Cossacks, land thieves, the Pettis boys, those heart-tearing years of five-inch rain, the governors of Wyoming and Nebraska, and now the mountains. They could be conquered. The water the mountains held back from the Platte could be recovered through the tunnel.

And as he looked at those majestic heights he experienced the sensation that overcomes most fighters. He was pleased that his adversary was a worthy one. He had a feeling that the great masses of granite pushing their heads into the clouds would be gratified if he did penetrate them and bend them to his purpose.

But one day toward the end of August, as he sat facing the sunset, congratulating himself that he had at last solved the problem of the

Platte, he discovered that he had missed the major point. The river was part of a totally different system from the one he had imagined, and to understand how that system functioned required a whole new set of constructs.

He made this shattering discovery while reflecting on a line from a poem his minister had quoted at a funeral some years before: 'Even the weariest river winds somewhere safe to sea.' It had been offered as consolation, a reminder that even the most pain-racked life finds ultimate release, and the image it presented had appealed to Brumbaugh. He had imagined himself as that portion of the Platte which had been induced to run through his farm, irrigating his fields and then returning to the Platte—which ran into the Missouri, which ran into the Mississippi, which emptied into the Gulf of Mexico, which returned safely to the greater sea.

'Rubbish!' he cried, forming the word painfully. It wasn't like that at all. Neither the poet nor the minister had had a glimmering of what it was all about.

What happens, he told himself, is that from the Pacific Ocean a wandering drop of water is drawn upward into a cloud, and that cloud rises and the water is frozen into a flake of snow, and the cloud moves east away from the ocean and across California, and when it reaches the Rockies their peaks clutch at it and the snowflake falls on a slope, where it melts and runs into the Poudre, and it tumbles into the Platte and I draw it off for my irrigation, and it goes back to the Platte, and then into the Mississippi and into the Atlantic, and somehow at the southern end of South America the two oceans balance out their water and my drop comes back into the center of the Pacific and it rises into another cloud and again it freezes into a snowflake and once more the flake falls on the Poudre. And this goes on forever and ever. There is no rest, neither for the river nor for the man. And the man is entitled only to as much water as he can borrow from this endless cycle. And when he has finished his work of struggling with the river, he does not go to some eternal rest. His body becomes the dust upon which the next snowflake falls, and he finds himself part of the endless cycle.

Toward five, when Serafina came to wheel him back into the farmhouse, she saw that he was dead. She was not given to excessive lamentation, for she had seen much death, and from the satisfied look on Brumbaugh's face she concluded that he had died neither in pain nor in disappointment. She and Triunfador laid the body out, after which the boy went in to town to inform the police that the old man was gone.

Italians, Russians, Germans, Japanese and numerous Mexicans attended his funeral, all of them indebted to him for instructions and mortgages. Jim Lloyd, as the old man's best friend, took charge of the burial and was deeply moved when the young minister said, 'At such moments we find consolation not only in the Bible but also in the words of our great poets, and never has the passing of an energetic man like Hans Brumbaugh been better summarized than in these beautiful words of Swinburne:

> From too much love of living,
>   From hope and fear set free,
> We thank with brief thanksgiving
>   Whatever gods may be
> That no life lives forever;
> That dead men rise up never;
> That even the weariest river
>   Winds somewhere safe to sea.

Today we can visualize our tireless old fighter safe at rest.'

During the celebrations which filled the last weeks of 1918, when, as the *Clarion* put it, 'American victory over the German hordes was confirmed and the honor of Europe salvaged by our brave doughboys,' Mervin Wendell experienced his first premonition of death.

For some months he had not been in good health, for his efforts during the war years had been titanic. As War Bond chairman for northern Colorado, he had appeared on platforms in places as distant as Omaha and Salt Lake City. He wore a modified uniform of his own design, featuring leather puttees and a Teddy Roosevelt hat, and spoke on such subjects as 'Our Daring Adventure at the Somme' and 'We Are Strong Because We Are United.'

At the Wendell mansion on Eighth Avenue he and Maude entertained most of the dignitaries who visited Colorado—Secretary of War Baker, General Pershing's relatives from Wyoming, General Barker of the British army, whose father had run the big cattle ranch at Horse Creek—and he had often sat up late talking with them about strategy and the ultimate triumph of Allied arms.

He retained his old-time gift of mimicry; on tour his accent was principally Oxonian. With his dashing uniform, most of his listeners considered him an officer in the British Royal Dragoons, of whom he spoke frequently and with a certain intimacy ever since he had spent a long evening with a colonel of that regiment reviewing tactics. He collected a great deal of money for the war effort, and Maude Wendell, as the gracious chairlady for the Red Cross, supervised the rolling of interminable lengths of bandage.

But his principal effort was reserved for the manipulation of his extensive land holdings, which now totaled more than fifty-five thousand acres of better-than-average land scattered about forty-three farms and ranches which he had acquired at panic prices. All his holdings in Line Camp were now sold and he had pioneered a new community to the north. It was named McKinley, 'after our martyred leader,' he invariably explained with a quiver in his voice. He had seen McKinley once in Chicago and considered him our greatest President.

He had made a real killing on his McKinley operation, having learned from his experience at Line Camp not to sell too quickly but to hold on till the town became established and its future assured. He had spent most of 1917 hauling prospective buyers to the northern settlement, and since wheat was then at $2.29 a bushel, he had little trouble peddling really sizable acreages to farmers from the east.

His pamphlet on McKinley outdid anything he had previously offered, for the photographs and text were downright shameless. One group of pictures featured the steady progress of Farmer Earl Grebe, from Ottumwa, Iowa, who had come to Line Camp penniless in 1911 and who had recently picked up another half-section, making 1280 acres in all:

> Notice the rural mansion in which Earl and his lovely wife Alice live . . . all paid for by $2.00 wheat, 36 bushels to the acre. The small building to the left is the sod hut in which the Grebes lived while they were getting started. Prudent custodians, they now use the 'soddy,' our affectionate name for such memorials of the past, as a place to entertain admiring visitors from the east. The photographs on the opposite page show what Earl Grebe has grown on his farm, which is located less than twenty miles from the land you will be purchasing.

The wheat shown was from the Grebe farm, but the large melons, apples and sugar beets had all been photographed on irrigated land along the Platte.

In late 1918 Mervin Wendell was expended. Everything he had put his hand to had prospered and he was the richest man in Centennial or any town north to the Wyoming border. He now had only one concern: to live past his seventieth birthday. And he took every possible precaution to see that he did so.

His heart had weakened, so he canceled all speaking engagements, but he did appear on the platform at victory celebrations. He also drove up to McKinley when the new school was dedicated, and he showed up at his office in town occasionally, directing his son Philip, now a stable married man of forty, in the intricacies of real estate. For the rest, he guarded his health, halting smoking altogether and drinking only occasionally.

He was delighted when the New Year came and passed, for he considered this a major milestone. 'I'd have hated dying in 1918, when so many other things were happening,' he told Maude, who seemed to grow younger with the passing years. She laughed at such a statement and assured him he would see 1920. 'That's a nice-sounding year,' he said. 'I should like to welcome a new decade.'

It was not to be. During the second week of January he fell seriously ill, a complication of heart trouble and mild pneumonia. It was precisely the kind of terminal illness he would have chosen for himself, for it allowed him to lie in bed, unscarred and unafflicted by any loathsome disease. Each afternoon he held a kind of court in his bedroom, expatiating on all sorts of subjects.

'Those frail-hearted persons who fear we have overcultivated the plains will live to see ten farms where one is today. Mark my words, they'll live to see three-dollar wheat . . .

'The nation has suffered enormously from the prattering of Woodrow Wilson. At the Ludlow troubles he should have sent in twice as many troops and shot down twice as many miners. Colorado would have been much the better for it . . .

'The theater will never die. Mark my words, it will never die. I remember when the great Edwin Booth came to Centennial in 1891. The Union Pacific deposited his red-and-gold private car where the grain silos stand now, and it rested there for three days while he regaled us with *Hamlet, Macbeth* and *Richard III.* The car contained two baths— complete bathtubs I mean—and a library that would have done justice to an emperor. The Union Pacific brought in tubs of oysters in ice and gave a public dinner for three dozen. I was invited, of course, being of the theater . . .

'I have the greatest respect for the rancher. He made Colorado what it is, a great free state. If I have been at odds with him from time to time, over land policy, it was only because he was endeavoring vainly to keep land from the people. The people, sir, that's where the strength of a nation lies. But we all owe the rancher the respect Mr. Lamson at the bank accords him. He said to me not long ago, "Wendell," he said, "when I look out of my office door and see four men waiting for me, it's easy to decide who to see first. The rancher, for he is nature's nobleman. Then the irrigation farmer, for he is a long-time citizen and to be trusted, even if he is apt to be Russian. Then the dry-land farmer, because you never know where he came from nor how long he's going to be around. And if the fourth man happens to be a Mexican, I tell him, 'We already have a janitor.' " '

On the evening of January 16 he grew quite weak, but he assured his family, 'I feel confident I'll make it,' and on the seventeenth he admitted a large number of well-wishers to his bedroom, regaling them with stories of when he had toured in the Dakotas with the lovely Maude De Lisle, who finally consented to be his wife and who had been his helpmeet during all these years. He went off into a flowery oration about the joys of conjugal bliss, during which his son left the room.

'It's a passage from a play we gave in Minnesota,' Philip told his wife. 'He'll be doing the balcony scene from *Romeo* next,' and sure enough, toward five in the afternoon Mervin told the group how once in South Dakota he had looked up and had been so overcome by his wife's beauty that he forgot his lines. He then recited the whole scene, Juliet's lines as well as his own.

He died on the nineteenth, and all the Colorado newspapers carried obituaries recalling his unique contributions to the state. His funeral was a triumph, with dignitaries from varied walks of life paying tribute to his capacity for progress and his love of humanity. Many persons whom he had helped volunteered stories of his generosity, and the day was topped by the announcement of a delegation from McKinley that this new community wished to change its name to Wendell.

In Line Camp there was some feeling that the honor should be theirs, because the odd dual name was not liked by the residents, and a considerable movement got under way to effect a legal change before McKinley could do so, but in the end the northern community won out, and McKinley became Wendell, with the approval of the editorial writer of the *Clarion:*

It is proper that northern Colorado have a town named after its most illustrious son, for he did much to develop this section of the state. His vision in sponsoring the radical concepts of Dr. Thomas Dole Creevey when others insisted that dry-land farming could never succeed came to fruition during the late unpleasantness when the region north of Centennial became the 'breadbasket of the world,' in his happy phrase. On Tuesday next there will be a celebration in McKinley as the name is changed officially to Wendell, and all of us who profited from the leadership of this great man should pay him tribute by being in attendance. We are assured that Governor Gunter will be there to honor the man who served as his statewide chairman in a previous election.

Colorado's retiring governor, Julius Gunter, did attend and so did the Grebes, for they of course believed that Mervin Wendell was largely responsible for their good fortune. He had met them at the train that first day in the fall of 1911 when they arrived to try their luck at dry-land farming, and he had cooperated whenever they sought to buy more land. He had contributed a free plot for a library and another for a Sunday School.

The Grebes invited Vesta and Magnes Volkema to join them at the inauguration of the new town, but Vesta said, 'That windbag? He stole the land he gave us for the library, and he stole the land he sold you, and the only reason he didn't steal our homestead was that I was too goddamned smart for him. This crazy husband of mine came within one hour of selling us out.'

Alice said, 'I thought you wanted to sell . . . and move to California.'

'Still do,' Vesta said. 'But not for twenty-five cents an acre. And not to that oily son-of-a-bitch Wendell.'

Such language did not please Alice Grebe, who felt that hard work on the farm was coarsening Vesta, and at the ceremonies, when a mixed quartet sang 'Whispering Hope' in honor of Mervin Wendell, she wept.

Potato Brumbaugh had had every intention of providing for Tranquilino Marquez and his family. He did give the Takemotos eighty acres of good irrigated land and would have done the same for Tranquilino if the Mexican had been at hand during his final days. Unfortunately, Tranquilino was chasing across northern Mexico with Pancho Villa and did not get back to Centennial until 1917, when Brumbaugh was long since dead.

Tranquilino returned to a miserable situation; there could be no other word for it. With Brumbaugh gone, he had no regular job at the farm and no settled place to live. He had to take his wife and two children and find such seasonal work as he could, which meant that his family had to live in one hovel or another. His wages were so low that he could save no money; when November 15 came, and the beet checks were distributed, he received so little that it was impossible to take his family to Denver, where there was at least a congenial Mexican community in whose warmth they could lose themselves during the bitter winter months.

Instead, each November, when they were kicked off the beet farm on which they had been working, they would take what money they had and move into one of the disgraceful shacks that had grown up at the northern extremity of Centennial. Little Mexico, the area was called contemptuously, as sad and filthy a collection of dwellings as had ever been allowed to exist in the west. Here the unwanted workers hid themselves during the winter. How they existed during blizzards no one could explain, for the walls were made of slats, with gaping cracks where the wood had warped, and the floors were of mud which froze when water seeped in from the edges. There were no health facilities, no paved roads, no schools, no amenities of any kind and no plans for any.

The farmers of Colorado, having come to depend on Mexican labor, considered it not only natural but right that these illiterate people should toil from March through November at rip-gut wages, then shift for themselves through the cold months, with inadequate food, inadequate heat, polluted water and festering social conditions. The merchants of Centennial, depending upon the Mexicans for the agricultural stability of the region and welcoming whatever surplus coins they had, saw nothing immoral in condemning this labor to a rural ghetto where they were expected to say nothing and make no demands. And if a Mexican sought to enter a barbershop, a restaurant or a store where fine clothes were sold, he might be chastised. Even the churches condoned this brutal system, for not even a mission was maintained. Protestant churches could perhaps be excused for this indifference, for as their elders said, 'The Mexicans don't belong to us,' but the attitude of the Catholics was less understandable, because the workers were members of that church. Of course, a so-called 'Mexican Mass' was held each Sunday, but it convened at six in the morning, when upper-class Catholics would not have to mingle with Mexicans. Even this was restricted to domestic workers who served the better families, and had a mere beet worker wandered in, the priest would have been astounded, for in Centennial a field worker was considered little better than an animal.

They were an outcast tribe, with a strange language and even stranger customs. 'They name their sons Jesus,' the children of Centennial giggled, and that alone was sufficient to disqualify them.

And it was not only the townspeople. Every rancher whose spread lay to the north had to pass Little Mexico on his way in to town. Every complacent ranch wife from Line Camp or Wendell had to see this ghetto, and no one cared.

It wasn't that Little Mexico was ignored. The police were there a good deal, settling fights between residents, and Sheriff Bogardus considered it his major responsibility to keep the place in order during the winter so that field workers would be in good shape when spring planting commenced. In fact, a prime requisite for a Centennial law officer was that he be able to handle Mexicans and keep them from irritating their employers. The little settlement also came in for repetitious comment in the *Clarion*, where every reporter tried his hand at composing items intended to be amusing:

> On Friday night as usual there were two stabbings in Little Mexico, but nobody died. Sheriff Bogardus arrested four participants but saw no reason to incarcerate them, since our courts are already clogged with problems emanating from that metropolis.

There was one man who might have served as spokesman for the Mexican community, an itinerant priest named Father Vigil—Veeheel—but unfortunately, he came from New Mexico, where he had been corrupted by the Penitente movement, that strange, John-the-Baptist-type of desert fanaticism in which devout members pierced their backs with cactus thorns to display their penitence, and when he sponsored such carryings-on, the respectable Christians of northern Colorado made it clear that they would not tolerate such behavior. There were proper ways to worship God, and penitential exhibitionism was not one of them.

It therefore fell upon Sheriff Bogardus to break up such demonstrations, because if the Mexicans coalesced around this inflammatory religion, next thing they would be forming a labor union, and the massacre of the coal miners at Ludlow had shown what could be expected then. So one of the most compelling cries that could be uttered in the police station was: 'The goddamned Penitentes are out again!'

Then the sheriff and his deputies would leap into their cars and roar out to the fields north of Little Mexico, where ecstatic worshippers with thorns through their flesh were dancing and moaning and establishing relationships with God. Clubs would swing, and hoarse-voiced men would shout, 'You can't do that on Colorado property,' and sooner or later frail Father Vigil would move in to protest and some officer would belt him across the mouth and he would fall to earth, bleeding.

'Why can't they worship like everyone else?' Sheriff Bogardus asked one Sunday after the Penitentes had given him a passel of trouble. 'Why can't they be Baptists or regular Catholics?'

It was curious that a state so advanced in all other directions should have been so permanently blind in its understanding of Mexicans. Colorado was where sensible labor relations were first worked out, where old-age pensions would be developed, where education was generously supported, where colleges proliferated and churches abounded. Colorado was a state where good ideas flourished, yet on this great basic question of human rights it remained purblind. It could never admit that for farmers to use labor for personal gain and then to dismiss that labor with no acceptance of responsibility was immoral. And any Anglo brave enough to raise the question ran the risk of having his teeth kicked in.

For more than half a century this condition prevailed. No church, no crusading newspaper, no band of women sought to correct this basic evil, and across Colorado, Anglo children who once had been raised to believe that Indians were not human were now raised to think that Mexicans were even less so. As one popular children's book stated: 'By the time Billy the Kid was twenty-one years old, he had killed one man for each year of his life, not counting Indians or Mexicans.'

It was to this kind of Little Mexico that Tranquilino Marquez moved permanently in late November 1921, with his wife, Serafina, his hotheaded son Triunfador and his lovely daughter Soledad, now thirteen years old. They found a shack of unbelievable decrepitude and filth, which they proceeded to clean up. Serafina performed miracles with scissors and needle; she would have done even better had a sewing machine been available. And Triunfador obtained, in a way that his father thought best not to inquire about, some lumber for shoring up the falling sides of the building. When they were through, the place could not have been called a house, for it offered practically no protection from either rain or wind, but it was a shelter, and there the family settled down.

They were not the kind of people to attract attention, so they had no reason to fear raids by Sheriff Bogardus, nor was Tranquilino disposed toward the Penitente movement, so there was no danger of his being clubbed by the deputies. The trouble lay with Triunfador, tall and sinewy, like his father; hard as iron, like his mother. He was now twenty and well instructed in the methods of sugar-beet cultivation. He was not able to read or write, but he had an unusual ingenuity and a determination to better himself.

Trouble started when he found an abandoned shack close to State 8, the rural highway leading from Centennial to Line Camp. Without seeking permission from the authorities, he took it over and installed a phonograph, three tables and some chairs. He made it a congenial place for the unemployed laborers to congregate and soon he was selling candy bars and soda pop.

It did not take the farmers of Centennial long to discover that in La Cantina, as it was called, lay the seeds of rebellion. 'You let them damned Mexicans start congregating like that,' a Russian beet farmer warned Sheriff Bogardus, 'and first thing you know, we got labor unions and all sorts of trouble.' When a second complaint was filed, Bogardus saw his duty.

Looming in the doorway, his pistols protruding from his holster, he announced, 'This place is closed.' Saying no more, he withdrew, confident that no Mexican would defy such a clear-cut order.

Triunfador did not intend to close down, for he saw in La Cantina a nucleus around which a better way of life could be obtained for his people. 'La Raza,' he said when speaking of his fellow Mexicans. The race, the whole Spanish race, both those from New Mexico, like Father Vigil, and the peons from Old Mexico, like his father. They must not live like animals, the members of La Raza, hibernating in their winter hovels like rattlesnakes. They must devise something better, something finer even than the back streets of Denver. He would not close.

'Goddamnit!' Sheriff Bogardus bellowed the next morning, after farmers had complained that 'them damned Mexicans are still at it.' 'I told you to close this joint. Now you get the hell out of here.' He started kicking the furniture around, and some men, who had already experienced his violence, left. But not Triunfador. Standing behind his improvised bar, he stared at the sheriff and said nothing.

'You!' Bogardus shouted. 'I told you to get out of here.'

'This is my place,' Triunfador said, with heavy rising emphasis on the final word.

'This is my plAAAAce!' Bogardus mimicked. He glared at the young man who was defying him, and with a sudden reach of both hands, grabbed Triunfador, jerked him across the bar and threw him out the door and into the gutter.

That afternoon he returned with a court order directing him to padlock the place, and when Triunfador, against his father's admonition, ripped off the padlock, a passing farmer hurried in to the sheriff's office to report, 'Well, Sheriff, them Mexicans tore down your paper. We got trouble.'

Bogardus and three assistants speeded out State 8 and wheeled their vehicles to the door of La Cantina. 'You son-of-a-bitch!' the sheriff bellowed. 'Who in hell do you think you are, defying a court order?'

He ordered his deputies to haul the revolutionary off to jail. Next morning Triunfador was arraigned before the judge in Greeley, a man who owned a farm himself and recognized insurrection when he saw it. Leaning across the bench, he admonished Triunfador: 'Young man, you're a visitor in this country and you must obey our laws. You have no license to operate a house of amusement, no license to play music and certainly no license to sell either candy or soft drinks. Furthermore, you have no right to be on that property, and you have defied a court order. Sixty days.'

During his time in jail Triunfador did not know that he was being defended by a robust woman he had never met. Father Vigil, outraged at the sentence, did what he could to arouse public indignation, but he was ineffective, and one night in a shack at Little Mexico he confessed his impotence: 'The judge won't listen. The sheriff is a bully. The newspaper laughs at us. The priest is more useless than the Anglo ministers. Not even the professors in Greeley will attend. Doesn't anyone in Colorado care?'

From the shadows a workman said, 'Charlotte Lloyd. One day she brought my children clothes.'

'Mrs. Lloyd!' some of the others muttered, and next morning Father Vigil stood before the castle, knocking at the great oak door.

After a while a formidable woman greeted him, Charlotte Lloyd, almost seventy now but still straight as a soldier. As major stockholder in a famous ranch, she was a woman who accepted no nonsense, for she had proved that she could handle a man as easily as a horse. She had a weather-beaten face and a hearty laugh. 'Come in,' she said abruptly, leading him into a large room from whose walls the heads of stuffed moose and buffalo stared down. 'What nonsense are you up to?' Before he could answer, she asked, 'Aren't you the one who sticks darning needles into people?'

Father Vigil was confused, but he sensed that he was in the presence of someone who might help, so he persisted. 'I come to you about injustice,' he said.

'World's full of it,' Charlotte replied.

'The Mexicans.'

'Never had much use for 'em,' Charlotte said. 'What's happening to 'em now?'

He burst into an impassioned series of questions: 'Is it fair to work our people all summer and then force them to sit like puppets in the dark all winter? Are we not entitled to a cantina where we can have music?'

'Everyone's entitled to music.'

'Is it fair that we have nothing, nothing?'

'Doesn't sound fair at all. Be specific.'

He was, and the more he said, the more furious Charlotte became. 'This is outrageous,' she fumed, reaching for her hat.

With Father Vigil, she visited the Roman Catholic priest in Greeley, the editors, the licensing board in Denver, the sheriff, and wherever she went she asked one simple question: 'Aren't you ashamed of what you've been doing?'

When word of Charlotte Lloyd's interference reached the beet farmers, there was consternation. 'Father Vigil's putting her up to this,' the farmers said. 'He's preaching revolution.' So the farmers started a backlash. 'Charlotte Lloyd is nothing but a damned fool. Not a brain in her head. But this Father Vigil. He's got to go.' Petitions were circulated, calling for the deportation of the priest to Mexico, and when the signatures were presented to the judge, he summoned Father Vigil to the bench; unfortunately for the cause of justice, Charlotte Lloyd came along, and a rather hectic legal scene ensued.

JUDGE: You know, Father Vigil, you're only a guest in this country and Sheriff Bogardus has the power to send you back to Mexico if you don't behave.

CHARLOTTE: He absolutely doesn't.

JUDGE: Are you contradicting this court?

CHARLOTTE: Father Vigil's a citizen of New Mexico. He's an American.

JUDGE: He is?

CHARLOTTE: His ancestors have lived here for the past four hundred years. I chanced to look up the ancestors of Sheriff Bogardus and they came here in 1901. If anybody gets thrown out of this country, maybe it should be Sheriff Bogardus.

JUDGE: May I ask, Mrs. Lloyd, are you a citizen of this country?

CHARLOTTE: Give up my British passport? Are you crazy?

The judge leaned back. It was incomprehensible that Father Vigil, this unlovely man who stuck thorns in people, should have been an American longer than anyone else in his court that morning. Emig, Osterhaut, Miller—they had been serfs on the Volga at a time when the Vigils had already occupied New Mexico and southern Colorado for centuries. It was most confusing.

The judge denied every request Charlotte made, and Triunfador was ordered to close his cantina for good. When the decision was promulgated, Charlotte appeared to accept it with good grace, and she commiserated openly with Triunfador. The judge and sheriff, pleased with having fended off this difficult Englishwoman, started to terminate proceedings, whereupon Charlotte asked innocently, but in a loud voice, 'By the way, Harry, who owns those shacks?'

A hasty recess was ordered, during which the judge explained in a whisper, 'You know damned well, Charlotte, that Mervin Wendell built them. Now his son owns them, but it would be most embarrassing if this appeared in the paper. Philip does many good things in this community. Matter of fact, he's promised us a new library.'

'Then I will expect him, this afternoon, to sell me for one hundred

dollars the shack where Triunfador has his cantina, and I propose renting
it to Triunfador for one dollar a year. I'm sure you and the sheriff can
convince him to sell. Otherwise, I take my story to the *Denver Post.*'
　'That's blackmail,' the judge protested.

Charlotte smiled, and in this roundabout way Triunfador Marquez
obtained his license to operate a cantina, which became, as the Anglo
farmers had predicted, a center for Mexican agitation. Core of the place
was the phonograph with its stack of records imported from Old Mexico.
Could the beet farmers have heard the songs which emanated from this
creaky machine, they would have been terrified, for they were the songs
of revolution. One of the most popular was 'La Adelita,' that heart-
pulsing ballad of the woman bandoleras:

> Oh, if Adelita ran off with another,
> I would follow her by land and sea.
> If by sea, in a ship of war.
> If by land, in a military train.

Many of the songs spoke of the brave years when men caroused across
the state of Chihuahua aboard the military trains. Tranquilino often sat
in his son's establishment, listening to ballads which told of this excursion
or that:

> I boarded the train in Chihuahua
> Seeking the war of Pancho Villa
> But there was that girl in Durango.
> Ay, me! I am not a brave one, not me.

But the song which gave deepest gratification to the Mexicans was 'The
Corrido of Pancho Villa,' for in its verses the Mexicans won the war of
1916. They simply kicked hell out of the inept Americans under General
Pershing:

> On February twenty-third
> President Wilson sent six thousand Americans
> Into Mexico to hunt down Pancho Villa
> Through all the hills and mountains.

The bouncy ballad, sung by a double quartet of male voices, told in many
stanzas how Villa tantalized the Americans, leading them into one ambush after another until they had to retreat in ignominy, leaving Villa
triumphant.

> Valiente, valiente Pancho Villa!
> Conquistador y sus Dorados!

It was some time before Tranquilino confessed that he had been one of the Dorados, the golden ones who had swept across Chihuahua and Sonora and Durango. When the ballads were playing on the phonograph he would close his eyes, and whenever the phrase 'el tren militar' occurred, he would open them and smile at the men watching him, and they would nod out of respect, knowing that he had been on such trains and they had not.

> Oh, brave Pancho Villa! How you fought!
> How you drove the hated Yanqui from our land.
> We adore you and your Golden Ones.
> Oh, Pancho Villa, teach me how to fight.

Sheriff Bogardus kept a close watch on La Cantina and made arrests whenever singers grew raucous or someone threw a pop bottle onto the road. He suspected that the new amendment forbidding alcohol in the United States was being flouted, and numerous raids were made. Whenever news of a shipment reached him—for bootleggers driving down from Canada to deliver their goods to homes in Centennial sometimes dropped a few bottles off in Little Mexico—he ignored the sales in town and arrested Triunfador, and on Monday morning the *Clarion* would carry a sarcastic notice:

> Triunfador Marquez, the would-be mayor of Little Mexico, was arrested again last Saturday night, dispensing bootleg alcohol of a deadly variety from his esteemed emporium. He is now in jail.

Those frequent arrests of his son caused Tranquilino much anxiety, for although he had been a considerable revolutionary in Old Mexico, in Little Mexico he had always been an exemplary citizen, and he often upbraided his son.

'Last time you were in jail,' he said to Triunfador, 'Sheriff Bogardus, he came to see me and asked, "Why can't Triunfador be a good Mexican? Work in summer and keep his nose clean in winter?" '

During his stays in jail Triunfador was frequently visited by Father Vigil, and to his surprise he found the Catholic priest to be a man of profound vision. He foresaw a day when Mexicans in states like Texas and Arizona would come into their own, finding a satisfactory level of life, neither high nor low but just. To prepare for that day he started teaching Triunfador how to read and gave him primary-school texts imported from Old Mexico. In them the prisoner learned about Mexican history and the traditions of his land. In more advanced books he studied how the dictator Porfirio Díaz had sold every worthy item in Mexico to the highest bidder, whether he be Mexican, Spaniard, Yanqui or German. He was delighted when he read of General Terrazas, dictator of

Chihuahua, for his father had told him of how they had burned the Terrazas ranches, and he began to comprehend what it meant to be a Mexican.

He had no desire to return to the land of his birth; indeed, he barely remembered it now. It was like a bad dream, for he recalled something his father had told him: 'On the trains you could tell which of us had worked in America del Norte, for we had shoes.' It was better in Colorado, infinitely better than in Chihuahua. He loved America and its relative freedom and the opportunities it gave people. He could even borrow money from the soda-pop distributor, and he had bought on credit the lumber for the extension to his cantina.

But some things that happened in America enraged him, like the incident in October 1923. That summer his father and mother had worked for a Russian named Grabhorn, and they had slaved extra-long hours at the beets. When the crop was harvested, Tranquilino had served as beet-fork man—'the widow-maker' this fork was called, for it pulled a man's guts out, lifting thirty-two pounds of beets and tossing them high into the wagons—but he had justified the extra effort by explaining that when the check arrived on November 15, he would have additional money which he would give to Triunfador to help enlarge the cantina.

On the last day of October, Mr. Grabhorn made the telephone call. All the Anglo farmers knew how to do this—Immigration Service Denver Colorado. You didn't have to give your name, either. You just whispered in the phone, 'I'm a loyal American and it turns my stomach to see what's happening to this country. At the Rudolf Grabhorn farm in Centennial seven miles east on Weld 17, two Mexicans are working without proper papers, Tranquilino Marquez and his wife Serafina. They ought to be sent back to Mexico, where they belong.'

So three or four days before the checks arrived, immigration officials swept down upon the Grabhorn farm, arrested Tranquilino and his wife, and shipped them back to Mexico. Grabhorn, of course, escaped paying their wages and pocketed the money they had so painfully earned. Come next March, he would hire a different family. As for Tranquilino, once he and his wife were thrown across the border at Ciudad Juarez, they were free to slip upstream a few miles, wade across the Rio Grande, and walk right back to Centennial, where they could hire themselves out to some other farmer.

This extraordinary procedure was condoned because neither Colorado nor national laws cared to face up to the problem. Colorado farmers were allowed to employ wetbacks, as they were called, without fear of punishment, but the wetback himself was illegal, and could suffer both punishment and deportation. Whenever the matter came before the legislature, it was quickly brushed aside on the grounds, 'We need them.' They were needed, but they were not wanted, and it was for this reason that evil tricks like the one played on Tranquilino Marquez were allowed.

When Triunfador heard of how his parents had been abused, he stormed about his cell. 'They were robbed! And the government helped!' He vowed he would gain revenge, but it was then that Father Vigil spoke most persuasively. 'You must subdue your passions, my son. You must control them and bend them to your purpose. There is simply no good in raging or cursing or making threats. The whole judicial system is contrived against us, and there is no way we can fight back. What we can do . . .'

'Yes! What in hell can we do?'

'We can submit ourselves to the goodness of God.'

'I don't believe in God.'

Father Vigil said quickly, 'But you must believe in the compassion of the Lord Jesus Christ. When a powerful man submits himself to the love of that great soul, he gains power.'

'What do you want me to do?'

'Gain control of yourself.'

Triunfador considered these words for several days. He knew very well what Father Vigil was proposing—that he, Triunfador Marquez, on the day of his release from jail forgive the sore injustice Rudolf Grabhorn had visited upon his family, forgive the persecutions of Sheriff Bogardus and submit himself to the discipline of Jesus Christ.

'I'll do it,' he told the priest.

'I knew you would.'

He left the jail on Saturday afternoon, and that night he fasted. On Sunday morning he rose early and went to the fields north of Little Mexico, where a large crowd had gathered. There he stripped to the waist and allowed Father Vigil to insert cactus thorns beneath the sinews of his back while his sister Soledad stuck four into the skin about his temples. Bleeding from many places and shuddering with pain, he reached down and lifted a heavy cross, a replica of the one upon which Christ was crucified, and with it upon his bleeding back he started the long walk to his Golgotha.

He had covered only a short distance when a group of Anglo farmers rushed into town with the frightening news: 'Those goddamned Mexicans are at it again. They got some horse's ass lugging a cross up the hill.'

Sheriff Bogardus and his men hurried out of town and up State 8 to where the procession was winding up a hill much like the one Jesus had climbed in Jerusalem. With clubs swinging, they smashed their way into the heart of the crowd, where one deputy slugged Triunfador and dropped him to the ground. As he struck the earth, the thorns cut deeply into his forehead, bringing forth much blood, but he did not feel the pain.

'I am one,' he muttered to himself. He did not know what this meant, nor what its spiritual ramifications might be, but he sensed that from that stricken moment he was going to be a greater man than he had ever been before.

And he was. He attained that marvelous stability that some men achieve when they find a balance between heaven and earth. He held himself taller, and could look the sheriff in the eye, or the judge, or the Anglo ministers who belatedly were trying to do the right thing, and meet them as an equal. People in the district began to say, when a problem arose, 'Ask Triunfador. He has a good head on his shoulders.'

When his father and mother made their way back from Old Mexico, he had a shack prepared for them, but before he would permit them to take work with any beet farmer, he sought advice. Waiting in the door of the cantina till he saw a new Dodge coupe coming down the road from the Venneford Ranch, he ran onto the highway and flagged it down. 'Mr. Garrett,' he apologized to the driver. 'I need your advice.'

'You in trouble again?' the Venneford's manager asked.

'Not me, Mr. Garrett,' Triunfador said, 'my father.' He reported what had happened last October with Rudolf Grabhorn, and Garrett said, 'I can believe it. He's a mean-hearted son-of-a-bitch.' When Triunfador asked what farmer could be trusted, Garrett said, 'Klaus Emig. Honest as they come.' So that year the Marquez family not only worked for Emig, but got paid too.

One thing worried Triunfador—his sister Soledad. She was sixteen now and very beautiful, with black eyes and long braids. When he was occupied with other things she sometimes supervised the cantina, playing records for the customers, and men were beginning to grab at her, and he wondered what might happen to her. In a place like Little Mexico she could find herself in serious trouble.

And then, one hot July day while Triunfador was absent picking up some freight at the Centennial railway station, the Venneford Dodge pulled up before the cantina. This time it was not Beeley Garrett but a tall, good-looking younger man who walked into the café and introduced himself. 'I'm Henry Garrett. Father wanted to know if the old couple took the job at Emig's?'

'They did,' the slim girl behind the counter said suspiciously.

'It's hot. I need a cold drink.'

'We're not bootleggers,' the girl snapped.

'I meant a Coke,' Garrett apologized. 'Or something.' As he drank he listened to the phonograph. 'That's a saucy tune,' he said. 'What is it?'

' "Serian las Dos," ' she replied. 'Just a popular song.'

Two Mexican girls were singing a series of lilting words, and apparently they were nonsense syllables, because when Garrett asked Soledad what they meant, she listened for a while, then shrugged her shoulders. 'That stuff? Who can say?'

Garrett bent down to hear the words more clearly, for he knew a little Spanish, and when he looked up he saw Soledad smiling at him. 'That part says, "Girls today no longer know how to eat tortillas. As soon as they marry a fellow they want white bread and butter." ' She laughed at the song, and in that moment Henry Garrett acknowledged how barren his life had been, how devoid of laughter, and he lingered to hear the music, the first Anglo ever to have entered the cantina as a customer.

In these years the Venneford Ranch continued as one of the best-run cattle operations in the west. Jim Lloyd, who knew as much about Herefords as any man then alive, gave overall supervision, but the day-to-day management was left to Beeley Garrett, who had a solid sense about ranching, and to his son, Henry Garrett, who was learning fast. The ranch didn't earn as large dividends as the majority stockholders in Bristol might have wanted, but as Garrett assured them in each annual report, 'The value of land continues to rise, and by holding on to your acres, you become richer every year. Also,' he added, 'the herd is constantly improved and there continues to be a lively demand for Venneford bulls.'

Charlotte Lloyd spent most of her energy supervising the refurnishing of her plaything, the Venneford castle, and at one time astonished her neighbors by importing from France an enormous organ, which she installed in the circular room where she did her entertaining. Her parties, to which she invited guests from Denver and Cheyenne, recapitulated the grace of the old Cheyenne Club. She remained an Englishwoman, on a temporary visit to the west, likely to return home at any moment, and she followed carefully the education of her many nieces and nephews as they fumbled their way through the better English schools.

She delighted in having them visit her in Colorado, and nothing pleased her more than those days when she would bundle a flock of children into carts and drive north to Line Camp Four, where she had been so happy with two such different men, Oliver Seccombe and Jim Lloyd. 'I first saw this lovely place in 1873,' she told the children. 'It looked much as it does today, and I had a cart with two horses, just like the one you have.'

She was seventy-two years old, but her enthusiasms ran as high as they had been when she first saw these splendid plains and decided to make them her own. Only one irritation marred her supervision of the ranch. She and Jim Lloyd were beginning to argue about the Herefords, each in his own strong-minded way.

Charlotte saw these noble animals, which had after all been developed not far from her home in the west of England, as the finest exemplars of the animal kingdom, and she was proud of exhibiting them at stock shows around the nation. She therefore wanted them groomed and polished and fattened, in order for them to make the most spectacular appearance. She imported breeders from Herefordshire and instructed them to produce a more compact animal, tighter-boned and more appealing in the head.

These men did wonders. Taking the original Crown Vee Herefords, a rangy breed, they bred them into more handsome forms which won ribbons across the country. 'A Crown Vee' became synonymous with the best, and Charlotte delighted in attending shows, dressed in fine tweeds, and having her photograph taken with this great bull or that champion steer. She was sometimes called 'The Queen of the West,' and wherever she went, there was lively talk in which the values of the Hereford were defended against lesser breeds like the Angus and Shorthorn.

Jim Lloyd was not enthusiastic about displaying his Herefords in the hope of winning ribbons. He had begun to suspect that the whole stock-show routine was a presumption, which, if persisted in, would destroy the Hereford breed. He especially doubted the qualifications of the visiting English breeders, who in his opinion were leading the Herefords into every wrong direction.

'They're breeding the animals too small,' he complained. 'They're so taken by the beauty of the head, they're forgetting the strength of the body. I like my range animals big and brawny and tough and able to forage for themselves in bad winters. I don't want a damn beauty queen, and I'm terrified of these blue ribbons because they encourage ranchers to do all the wrong things.' When he reflected on the matter he had to confess that what really irritated him was a trivial thing; the English breeders, who were doing a great job copping prizes, called their animals *Her-ri-fuds* in three fancy syllables instead of the honest Texan *Hur-ferd*. It galled him when a breeder exulted, 'Our Herrifuds won another blue rosette at Kansas City.' What Jim wanted was some big, burly Hurferds tending to the breeding duties on the far reaches of the ranch.

He lost the argument. In October 1924 one of the English breeders heard from a friend near Bristol that the next in line of great bulls had been born, Emperor IX, and whoever got hold of him would probably dominate the breed for years, the way Anxiety IV and Confidence had done in their generations.

It seemed unlikely to Jim that a man could look at a bull calf four months old and make such a prediction, but he approved when Charlotte decided to buy the little fellow at the astronomical price of nine thousand dollars. And when Emperor IX came down the ramp after his long trip from England and stared left and right, like a real-life emperor occupying a defeated kingdom, he won the hearts of everyone.

He was a stunning animal, a prepotent bull with the precious capacity of stamping only his better qualities on his progeny. He spent half the year servicing cows brought to him from distant ranches, half in the show ring winning more blue ribbons than any other bull of the twentieth century. He became a gold mine for the Venneford Ranch, and as Charlotte pointed out repeatedly, 'He'd never have earned a penny for us unless he'd established his credentials in the show ring. Every time he wins another ribbon, his fee goes up.'

But Jim was noticing something that others had missed. Emperor IX, splendid though he was, kept producing bulls which were slightly smaller than he, and it seemed to Jim that these bulls were in their turn producing wonderful-looking offspring, but just a fraction of an inch shorter than he thought they ought to be.

He brought this to the attention of the English breeders, but they dismissed him almost with contempt. 'What we're after is a shorter, more compact animal who'll produce better beef. Emperor IX is exactly what we needed, and his performance excels anything we hoped for.'

The Emperor and his offspring continued to dominate the shows, continued to glean blue ribbons for their owners, and no one was happier with the results than Charlotte, for they justified her long faith in the ranch. She was certainly the premier stockwoman of America, and if Jim Lloyd had been interested in playing that game, he could have been one of the leading stockmen, but he withstood the lure of the show ring and never had his photograph taken with his winners. He preferred tending the everyday Herefords out on the range. 'I've never seen anything prettier in my life than a line of white-faces walking over the brow of a hill at dusk as they come in for a drink.' He had hoped for a son who might share his instinct for range cattle, 'the real ones that make the beef,' but his only child was a daughter who cared little for the ranch.

He had looked to Beeley Garrett for support, but Beeley was preoccupied with the financial problem of keeping a large ranch solvent; where the cattle were concerned, he surrendered to Charlotte. Henry Garrett, Beeley's son, who would take over the ranch one day, was simply a businessman with little sense of cattle, so the protection of the one thing that made ranching viable, the animals, was left to Jim.

He decided to force a showdown with Charlotte and her English advisors, for he considered it criminal to take a splendid beast like the Hereford and consciously diminish the very characteristics which made him great . . . and do this merely to satisfy a few opinionated judges. As they gathered at the corral to look at the bulls, he asked, 'Can't you see we're ruining the breed?'

'Emperor IX is the top Hereford in history,' Charlotte snapped.

'Emperor IX is a runt. The day will come when scrupulous cattlemen will breed out of their herds every strain of that bull.'

'What nonsense are you talking?' Charlotte demanded. Turning to her breeders, she sought their support.

'The general judgment is that Emperor's saving the breed . . . bringing it into conformity to modern necessities.'

Jim took a deep breath, not because he felt any need for courage but because he felt a sudden lack of air. 'I despise watching nature altered to suit a passing fad. I don't like seeing a breed I've loved . . .' He felt that *loved* might sound ridiculous in such context, but upon reflection, judged it to be the word he wanted. 'I can't stand by and watch a breed

I've loved messed up. I think we should leave animals alone . . . and the land too . . .'

He paused to take another deep breath, for he was losing his temper. 'I do feel most deeply, my dear Charlotte, that for this ranch, to send forth a generation of dwarfs . . .' He grabbed at the corral gate, failed to reach it and crumpled in a heap. From the earth he tried one last time to protest, but words did not come, and before they could carry him back to the castle, he was dead.

After the funeral, Emperor IX won blue ribbons at Denver, Kansas City and Houston, confirming his domination of the field. He came to represent the sleek conformation the judges had decided to sponsor, the compact look that new-type ranchers wanted for their herds. It was acknowledged that he was the bull of the future.

It seemed that with the death of Jim Lloyd, who had protected the land, luck left the region. The previous year, 1923, had been a disaster for dry-land farmers, for only six inches of rain had fallen, which meant that even the best fields produced only about two bushels of wheat an acre, not enough to pay for the plowing, and land-poor men like Earl Grebe now found they had barely enough money to pay their store bills.

In 1924 things were no better, for even though nine inches of rain did fall, the drought of the preceding year showed its effects, and the good fields produced slightly under four bushels an acre.

A sense of defeat spread through the area, for if such conditions continued, many farmers would be driven out of business. They would not produce enough to make interest payments on their mortgages, and banks would foreclose. For the lack of a few dollars of ready cash, a man stood to lose a farm worth many thousands. It was a crazy system, one devised by idiots and administered by bankers, but it was the way America was run, and the individual farmer could do nothing about it.

Now the dreadful word *mortgage* struck at the heart of the Grebe family. In the good years, when money was plentiful, they had bought a half-section from Mervin Wendell and had considered themselves clever in talking him into accepting a thousand-dollar mortgage at five percent per annum.

'It's like finding money,' Earl had explained enthusiastically. With four hundred acres planted to wheat which sold at two dollars a bushel, the Grebes had a gold mine, and when the cash came in they had built what the brochure called 'their mansion.' They had also paid off their mortgage, but as soon as this was done Mervin Wendell came by with the good news that he could sell them an adjoining 320 acres. He also extended them the courtesy of another thousand-dollar mortgage, but when the papers were drawn he did not restrict it to the land he had just sold; he applied the mortgage to the entire farm.

Now, in the bad years, they owed Mervin Wendell's son Philip one thousand dollars at a time when there were simply no dollars in circulation, and certainly none coming their way. The interest was only fifty dollars a year; if they continued to pay that, nothing bad could happen to them; they did not have to reduce the principal. But pay the interest they must, even though the debt had been contracted when dollars were plentiful and was coming due when they were rare.

'It's so unfair,' Alice Grebe told her family as they gathered to discuss the threat which hung over their home. 'He switched the mortgage from the land, which we could give back if we had to, onto the house, which is our very life blood. Earl, you must do something about this.'

He visited Philip Wendell in his offices near the railroad station and explained the error. 'Your father must have meant to put the mortgage on the land,' he said, but the new head of Wendell Ranches and Estates proved adamant, polite but adamant.

'I'm quite sure, Mr. Grebe, that my father never made such a careless mistake. Times being unfavorable, you look back upon the event in a way which best supports your interests. I'm sure rain is coming back to these parts, and all you have to do is pay off the mortgage, and this unpleasantness will be forgotten.'

That night Earl Grebe assembled his family and spoke to them in harsh, grave words. His wife Alice was thirty-five years old that autumn and seemed prepared for whatever trials might lie ahead. She was still a tense woman and her energy had not flagged. Their son Ethan, an intelligent boy who duplicated many of the virtues of Mrs. Wharton's hero, was twelve years old and eager to work. Their daughter Victoria was a tall, quiet girl like her mother, but their son Tim, two years old, was a boisterous little fellow. He sat on his mother's lap as the discussion began.

'He means to take this farm from us,' Grebe said. 'I could see it in his eye. In everything he did.'

'Was he so harsh?' Alice asked.

'He's already foreclosed on three farms, Alice, and he intends making us the fourth.'

'He wouldn't transfer the mortgage to the land?'

'He looked me in the eye, never blinking, and said he was sure his father never made such a mistake.'

'We should have had a lawyer,' Alice said, biting her lip to keep from whimpering.

'I did not think you required a lawyer when dealing with an honest man.' He was sweating, and Alice said, 'Victoria, make us some lemonade.'

'Sit still! There will be no more lemonade. This family is going to eat grass if necessary, but we're going to accumulate that thousand dollars and pay him off. Our life depends on it. Alice, you start. Tell us right now how you can save money.'

'Oh, dear!' she said falteringly. For some time now she had been conducting her home as frugally as possible. She was about to say that no
further savings could be effected, but then she saw her husband's stern
visage, the goodness of his character shining through, and she knew that
she must do even more.

So she began to enumerate the little things that could be done: 'We'll
buy no clothes for anyone. No toys for Christmas. No candy. We'll eat
a lot of mush, the way we did in the soddy. And we don't need curtains
or brooms or anything like that. I'd feel happier, Earl, if you gave me
no money at all, because I do grow careless. You buy the things and
handle the accounts.'

Each of the two older children stated what he or she would surrender,
and when Earl's turn came he said harshly, 'I'll sell the two bay
horses . . .'

'Oh, no!' his wife protested. 'They're the heart of the farm.'

'I must sell them,' he said.

The prospect of Earl's selling the two bays was more than Alice could
face, and she broke into tears, dropping her head onto the table and
shuddering as she had done years ago. Her shoulders contracted for some
moments, and Earl said to Victoria. 'Comfort her,' and he continued
with his account of what expenditures he would eliminate. When he finished, his wife said weakly, 'Earl, for God's sake, don't sell the horses.
We don't have to give at church. Victoria can . . .'

'We will all bear down, Alice. We will pay back this unjust debt. The
fault is mine, but we must all share it.'

So the Grebes went onto a regimen so spartan that only their neighbors who were in similar straits could comprehend. They were encouraged by two unexpected events. Vesta and Magnes Volkema, who had
never allowed a mortgage on anything they owned, came voluntarily, and
Vesta said, 'We have some savings. If that miserable bastard tries to
sheriff you out for the mortgage money, we'll pay your interest.'

'I'm glad to see you're cutting back expenses, Earl,' Magnes said. 'If
we get any rain at all, you'll get out from under.'

The other appreciated visitor was Dr. Thomas Dole Creevey. At his
own expense he was visiting the dry-land areas hit hardest by the two-
year drought, and he was not even close to surrender. At the school
auditorium he said in his low, powerful voice, 'Don't lose heart! Don't
listen to the ranchers when they gloat "We told you so!" Never in the
history of this state have we had three bad years in a row. Men! Look at
the statistics! In region after region across this nation two bad years have
always been followed by five good ones. Look at the facts!'

He became his old evangelical self as he scribbled the reassuring figures on a board. Montana, two bad years followed by six good ones.
North Dakota, two very bad years followed by five excellent ones. Utah,
where they kept careful records, the same. 'Five years from now,' he

promised them, 'I'll be lecturing somewhere in Kansas, and I'll write on the blackboard, "Colorado, two bad years in 1923–24, followed by five excellent ones." It's the law of nature.'

He visited Earl Grebe's farm, making numerous borings with the earth auger, and he proved that down deep a residue of moisture existed. 'This soil is ready for snow, Earl. You have your surface well prepared to accept it. For God's sake, when it comes, disk it at once and trap the moisture in here. You've a great farm, Earl, and you'll see thirty-bushel wheat again. On that I give you my solemn promise.'

And two days after he left, snow came, and then more snow, and then more, until it was clear that the drought had ended. Vesta Volkema, who was becoming quite rowdy as she grew older, told the Grebes during a family dinner, 'Our little bastard Creevey warned God to get off his ass and get some snow moving,' but before the two families started to eat, Alice Grebe asked if she might open the meal with grace, and the other five bowed their heads as she began, 'Dear Lord, from the depths of our hearts we thank . . .' She could go no further, for she fell into a fit of weeping and Vesta had to take her from the room for a while.

The moisture came and the crops were saved, but in the late spring of 1925 something happened which went unnoticed by everyone in town except Walter Bellamy, who was now the town postmaster, the land commissioner's office having had to close down. It was in May, on a cold, blustery day such as spring often brought to Colorado, and he was looking toward the mountains when he noticed an unusually heavy gust of wind sweep eastward across the prairie. It came from such a direction that its path lay along furrowed fields, with never a windbreak or a strip of unplowed land to temper its force, and as it moved, it began to catch up from the earth small grains of soil and collections of tumbleweeds and shreds of Russian thistle which had come in with the Turkey Red, and as it whipped through Line Camp, Bellamy thought that if such winds became frequent, especially during years with little snow, they might do real damage.

Increasingly apprehensive, Bellamy convened a meeting of the district farmers and invited an expert from the Agricultural College in Fort Collins to explain how they might protect their fields from either wind or rushing summer rains by plowing in a different pattern, but fifteen inches of rain had already fallen this year, with more expected, so no one paid much attention to what the professor said. Bellamy did insist, however, that the new tenant who was farming the land he had acquired east of Line Camp start to plow in the new way, and although they grumbled at 'fancy-pants ideas of men who never farmed,' they did agree to plow along the contours, but since there was neither wind nor flood, they accomplished nothing, and in the fall of 1925 Bellamy saw to his disgust that they had reverted to long, straight furrows, uphill and down. Any force left in his argument vanished that October when his tenant won the plowing contest with a set of the straightest, evenest furrows a judge ever saw.

On December 31 Earl Grebe had the satisfaction of carrying seven hundred dollars in cash into the office of Philip Wendell. 'That leaves only three hundred dollars on the mortgage,' he said with a certain grimness.

'I told you last year we'd get rain,' Wendell said evenly. 'Next year looks just as good.'

'If it is, we'll burn the mortgage.'

'I'm sure you will,' Philip said. 'My father had great respect for you and Alice.'

Why the Grebes and families like them now fought to stay on the land was a mystery. They could see that Line Camp had reached its peak and was beginning to die. In 1924 the local newspaper had folded, and even in the good year of 1925 two major businesses closed down. The tall white grain elevator stood half empty and the railroad which was supposed to have reached the town went into bankruptcy without laying a yard of track.

Alice Grebe, who had done so much to make the town habitable, was among the first to realize it was doomed, and twice she begged her husband to pull up stakes now, sell out and move to California. But men like Grebe could not bring themselves to admit defeat. 'Look, Alice!' he pleaded. 'I own more than a thousand acres. We have this good house. When things turn around . . .'

Alice suspected they might never turn around. For reasons she could not have explained she saw that prairie towns such as Line Camp must become vacated ghosts populated only by gusts of wind, yet she was powerless to act. 'We'll make the best of it,' she said with little hope, for she saw that the Grebes and the Volkemas had, through vanity and hope, locked themselves onto a land that was dying and to a town that was vanishing. At the end of 1925 two more stores shut down, and the population fell below one hundred.

Imprisonment at Line Camp proved especially bitter to Vesta Volkema, who watched her vision of California vanish in dust. Once at the Grebes' she came close to tears, confessing, 'Magnes was right that time when he wanted to sell our damned acres for twenty-five cents each. Hell, we'd have been better off if we'd given them away.'

'You still could,' Alice said excitedly. 'We all could. Just give them away and get out.'

'No,' Magnes said. 'You get trapped on the land. It reaches out and holds you.'

Then, as though to test the courage of the immigrants, the years 1926 and 1927 turned even more brutal, and farm income dropped so low that sometimes it seemed as if the Grebes would starve on the rich land they owned. For two long years they went to not one picture show in Greeley, nor to any church supper, for they were too poor to contribute a covered dish. They were paupers, worse off than the meanest family in Little Mexico, and Alice sometimes wondered if the providential years they had known when they first broke the sod would ever return.

Yet even during these painful years her love for her husband increased, and she bore him two more children, a third son and a second daughter, and the burden of providing them with a reasonable start in life fell solely upon her. She went days without food to ensure their getting the nourishment they required. She dressed them well, too, making over the clothes which had been worn by their brothers and sisters. She did much sewing, often working until her eyes were heavy, and she spent hours playing with the youngest three in the old soddy, telling them of former days and of how the family had worked together.

Her only consolation was the church, and it was a powerful support. Sometimes when the minister brought in a speaker from the college at Greeley, and Earl was too dead-tired to attend, she would walk by herself along the back path to Line Camp, and ask pertinent questions, and then return home alone, carrying only a small flashlight. Occasionally Mr. Bellamy arranged meetings, like the one in which an actress from Denver reported on the New York plays, and on the very special one, *The Great God Brown*, in which she had played a role. By popular demand, she recited some of the scenes from that play, a bright, lovely young woman, and Alice thought how proper it would be if Mr. Bellamy were to marry such a girl.

And then in 1928 everything conspired to help the Grebes: there was ample rain, much snow and a warm spring. Earl made an astonishing forty bushels to the acre, and it sold at $1.32 a bushel. The mortgage was paid off and every Grebe child received a new outfit, with Ethan, now sixteen, getting his first long trousers.

One evening that autumn, the Volkemas and the Larsens came over to dinner, and after the meat was taken away but before the dessert was brought in by Victoria, Earl Grebe cleared his throat, rose and asked his wife to produce the bottle of champagne. When the glasses were filled he asked Ethan to bring in a bucket, and when it was placed before him on the table, he brought from his pocket the mortgage paper and a box of matches.

'The Grebe family has been through a dangerous time,' Earl said. 'We might have lost our farm except for the support our neighbors gave us, but all that's past.' Striking a match, he held the flame to the bottom edge of the mortgage, and everyone at the table watched with fascination as the dangerous paper burned.

When it was ashes, Alice Grebe lifted her glass and said, 'From here on out . . . only good times . . . for all of us.'

*　　*　　*

Early spring on the great plains is the most hellish season known in the United States. Wet snow falls and for days the thermometer growls at the freezing point, now down, now up. No blossoms grace the roadside and such birds as do brave the weather huddle in the grass, their feathers ruffled, for April and May can often be fifteen or twenty degrees colder than February and March.

It was a miserable time, and the woman from Utah who wrote the song about springtime in the Rockies obviously lived on the western slope. Only the red-winged blackbird gives the period any distinction; even the hawks try to avoid the cold. There is much truth in the saying, 'Colorado has only three seasons—July, August and winter.'

In 1931 in Colorado a new misery was added. During the last week in March a strong wind began blowing from the northwest, and it continued for five days. There had been winds before, but this one was ominous, for it kept low, hugging the earth, as if it intended to suck from the soil what little moisture had been deposited by the inadequate snows that year. Walter Bellamy, studying the direction and force of the wind, predicted, 'If this keeps up another week, it'll be like losing seven inches of rainfall.'

It did keep up. What was worse, it started a howling sound which echoed across the empty plains. It was low and mournful, like the wailing of a wounded coyote, and it persisted day and night. The decibel strength was never high; it was not a roaring wind that deafened, but it had a penetrating quality that set the nerves on edge, so that at some unexpected moment a farmer, or more often his wife, would suddenly shout, 'Damn the wind! Doesn't it ever let up?'

In June the howling subsided, and residents of the lonely homes across the prairie looked back with wry amusement at the way they had responded to it. 'It really set my nerves jangling,' Jenny Larsen confessed. 'Wasn't it strange, the way it kept up, day after day?' Alice Grebe, to whom this question was directed, said nothing, for there had been days in May when she thought she might go out of her senses, and she was afraid.

The men spent June in drilling their augers into the soil to calculate just how much damage the wind had done, and their conclusions were pessimistic. 'If we don't get one more good gully-washer,' Magnes Volkema predicted, 'we're going to be in real trouble.'

None came. Instead, in late June the wind returned, this time with terrible consequences.

Alice Grebe was working in the yard, trying to ignore the whistling when she happened to look west toward the mountains, and there, coming directly at her, was a monstrous cloud forty thousand feet high and so wide it filled the sky.

'Earl!' she cried, but he was in the far fields turning a mulch in case rains came.

As she watched the onslaught, she felt happy on the one hand, for the rain would drench the fields, but on the other, she was afraid, for the winds might be violent. 'Don't let it do much damage,' she prayed.

Her prayer was unnecessary, for this was not a damaging storm. There was no rain, no wrecking winds, but it did bring something Alice Grebe had never seen before: a universe of swirling dust, a blackness that blotted out the sun, a choking, all-pervading silt that would seep through every wall and window.

When the mighty duststorm, silent and terrifying, first engulfed her, she thought she would choke. Spitting dust from her dry lips, she ran indoors to protect her children, and found them coughing. She sat with them for two hours, two of the strangest hours she had ever spent, for although it was midday, the sky was dark as night, and a weird gloom covered the earth.

Then the storm passed, leaving piles of dust everywhere, and after a while Earl returned to the house, spitting and stamping his feet. 'That was a wild one!' he said as he entered the kitchen.

'What was it?' Alice asked in real perplexity.

'Just a duststorm.'

'It was terrifying. Like a tornado with no wind.'

'There wasn't much wind, was there?'

That night the neighbors gathered to discuss this phenomenon, and Walter Bellamy drove out to meet with them. 'We may be in for some real trouble,' he said. 'I received a newspaper from Montana yesterday. They've had a succession of such storms.'

'Oh, dear, no!' Alice cried involuntarily.

'Now, Alice,' her husband said. 'If it's not hail and it's not a tornado, I guess we can survive.'

That became questionable when the next towering storm rolled in, vast black clouds of dust sweeping even the redwings and the hawks from the sky. It was a paralyzing storm—no wind, no moaning, no rainfall, just the terrible presence of dust seeping into every crevice, irritating every membrane.

'I cannot tolerate this,' Alice whispered to herself, but she refrained from showing her fear lest she frighten the children.

'What's happening, Mommy?' her five-year-old daughter asked as dust invaded the kitchen.

'It's a storm, dear, and storms pass.'

This one took five hours to go by, and when it was over, the citizens of Line Camp were shocked at its consequences, for in outdoor areas as much as nine inches of dust had accumulated against walls and fences, and in the houses a film of dust perhaps an eighth of an inch thick had seeped in through walls and closed windows.

Nothing had escaped. Vesta Volkema said, 'I opened my refrigerator door and there was dust on everything.'

That summer there were nine such storms at Line Camp. Never had the residents experienced such dreadful occurrences, and men began each day by looking westward. At dawn the sky would be clear. At eleven there would be a faint shadow below the mountains. By three in the afternoon the great, silent, towering form would creep through the sky, bringing the dust of Wyoming across the land, picking up the dust of Colorado and carrying it into Kansas.

It was toward the end of this year that a macabre story started circulating: if a man murders his wife during a duststorm, there will be no jury trial, because his act will be understandable.

Many farm women did find it impossible to live with the dust, and several in the Line Camp and Wendell area had to be carted off to mental institutions, for it was no easy thing to sit alone in some remote cabin and listen to the soft moaning of the wind and feel the choking dust come creeping at you, covering your shoes and your stockings and lying ever so lightly on your apron and choking your nose, and all this happening in broad daylight, except that it seemed like gloomy night.

'Save me! Save me!' the Lindenmeier woman had screamed as she ran four miles across the prairie. Like a wild woman she burst into Vesta Volkema's kitchen, and Magnes had to tie her down and haul her in to Greeley.

In every respect the year was a disaster. Even Earl Grebe, acknowledged as the best farmer in the district, could make no more than six bushels to the acre, and he had to sell it at thirty-three cents the bushel, about half the lowest previous price in this century.

'At that price, I'm giving it away,' he told his family, but before they could comment, he added, 'What else can we do? We can't eat it all.'

In 1933 no farmer in the district harvested a single bushel of wheat, and the same applied in 1934. In farmhouse after farmhouse there was not a penny of income during these two years, and some came close to starving. Farmers killed their livestock for lack of fodder to give them, and then found no market for the meat because no one had money to buy it.

And the duststorms kept returning, one after another, in high, billowing grandeur, sweeping the world before them. Dust became a constant presence that choked and strangled. Children wore masks over their noses as they went to school, and many farm wives wore caps night and day to keep the dust from their hair.

But even in the third year of the dreadful affliction, farmers whose lives were being slowly blown away were able to make grisly jokes. Visitors to Magnes Volkema's farm were astonished to find his plow resting upside down on top of his barn. 'It's the only way I can earn any money,' he explained. 'As the fields blow out of Colorado, I plow them for their new owners in Kansas.'

Vesta said, 'What little money we do get we spend on cinnamon.' This seemed so preposterous that the people to whom she said this stepped back to study her. 'We mix it with the dust and make believe we're eating cinnamon toast.'

At the store in Line Camp they told of the chickens who thought that what was covering them was snow and froze to death. Another farmer saw a hawk flying into the storm with a red-winged blackbird going ahead to brush the dust out of his eyes. When it came time for one farmer to pay his mortgage, he complained, 'I don't know where to go. The paper is in Philip Wendell's safe in Centennial, but my farm's in Nebraska.'

This problem of mortgages, however, was not amusing. For the lack of forty dollars to cover interest, many a farmer lost land worth thousands, and the government seemed powerless to prevent such tragedy. Nineteen farms in Line Camp were foreclosed by Philip Wendell; sixteen others were sold by the sheriff to pay back taxes, sometimes amounting to only a few dollars. By legal trickery, often of the most venal sort, some of the hardest-working men and women of America had their land stolen from them. Of the nineteen farms foreclosed by Wendell, the average price he had to pay per acre was sixteen cents.

In most respects 1934 was the year of hell. The wheat crop was zero. At the Grebe farm, that rich and wide land which had supported its people so well, a family of six children and two adults had to live on sixteen dollars a month, and there were many days when they ate only one meal. The younger children lacked milk and vitamins. The older children were in the midst of their education, and it was cut out from under them; sometimes their mother would cry herself to sleep as she contemplated the ruin of their bright young lives.

But she grieved most for her second son, Timmy, twelve years old and at that age when a boy entering adolescence discovered so many things he wanted to do. And there was not a penny he could have . . . nothing . . . nothing. 'Oh, God!' she wept one wintry day as she watched him swinging off to school. 'How can this nation allow such things to happen?'

And then, in the fall of the year, Mr. Bellamy, tall and thin as ever, heard some good news. Calling together all the deprived young boys of the area, he told them about an exciting development in Denver: 'In the January stock show there's to be a new event: "Catch It and You Can Keep It." '

'What's that?' Timmy Grebe asked.

'It's not for sissies,' Bellamy warned. 'Twenty boys . . . just like you . . . you'll go into the big arena with thousands of people watching. And all you'll have is a halter attached to a ten-foot rope. A bugle will sound, and they'll release ten calves. And you boys, if you're lucky enough to make the trip, will chase those calves, and wrestle them to the ground, and the boy who fixes his halter around a calf's head and leads it away unaided will win that calf.'

'He will?' Timmy asked.

'He'll bring the calf home, and feed it, and next winter he'll take it back to the stock show, and if it wins the judging, it'll be auctioned, and the money, lots of it, will be his to keep.'

Eleven boys sat silent, dreaming of such an event, but Mr. Bellamy dampened their ardor somewhat by saying, 'So the big problem is, where can we borrow some calves to practice with?'

The local families had none, but one of the boys had a logical suggestion. 'Mrs. Lloyd helps people,' and all agreed to ask her for the use of some of her calves.

Six of the boys piled into Mr. Bellamy's car and drove to Venneford, where Mrs. Lloyd met them formally in the room with the moose heads. 'To what do I owe this pleasure?'

It had been agreed that Timmy Grebe would make the presentation, so he coughed, sat forward in his chair and explained about the calves. 'A splendid idea!' the severe old woman said, and forthwith she summoned Henry Garrett and told him to deliver four sturdy calves to the Grebe farm. 'Boys should be active,' she told her visitors as she served them sandwiches and cinnamon buns. As she watched them wolf the food she thought, My God, are they really so hungry?

With the four Crown Vee calves Bellamy taught his boys how to tackle the frisky animals, wrestle them to the ground and slap the halter over their noses. It was difficult work, and since a boy had to have a certain weight in order to keep the calf down, it began to look as if Timmy Grebe, a year younger than the others, might be too light. 'He might better wait till next year,' Bellamy told Alice Grebe, but she pleaded that he be allowed to try.

'You can't imagine what this has done for him, Mr. Bellamy.'

'I can guess. Well, if he wants to try . . .'

The next night Timmy did not appear for family dinner, but his parents could guess where he was. They had seen him heading for the Volkema farm, and knew that he would be in a stall, wrestling with a young steer twice the weight of the calves that would be used.

Crash! The steer slammed him against the boards, but up he rose to try again.

Slam! The steer flashed his hindquarters, sending Timmy spinning around the wall, but he regained his feet, hitched up his pants and tried again.

The steer butted the twelve-year-old into a corner. With his right hand in the animal's face, Timmy backed him away.

Then, with a flying tackle, Timmy wrapped himself around the steer's head and neck, and for a wild two minutes boy and Hereford rolled and slammed around the stall. They made so much noise that Vesta Volkema came out with a lantern to see what was happening, and when she saw Timmy bleeding from several wood burns, and the astonished steer shaking its head wildly, trying to throw the boy clear, she started to laugh and jabbed the Hereford with a pitchfork, causing it to back into a corner, where the boy could safely let go.

'Get home with you!' she said, after satisfying herself that no bones had been broken.

He walked home through the November evening as content as he had ever been. Above, in the clear sky, he saw Orion, battle-bound between the Dog Star and the Bull, and as he watched, he heard geese from Canada flying south, signaling to one another as their multiple Vs wandered back and forth. When he entered the kitchen, dark spots and bruises about his face, he told his mother, 'Maybe I won't catch me a calf, but I sure ain't gonna be scared.'

In January, Mr. Bellamy selected Timmy and the Larsen boy for the contest, and drove them to Denver in his own car. The city was magnificent, with official buildings decorated with red, green and orange lights, and stockmen clustering about the Albany Hotel, and the famous rodeo champions from states as distant as Texas and Oregon strutting through the lobbies.

There was nothing in America quite like Denver's National Western Stock Show, for here the quality of the west's prime industry was determined. It had a daily rodeo, of course, but it also had hard-nosed judgings of Herefords and Black Angus, and how a man's bull did in such contests affected the success or failure of his ranch. Men would borrow their wives' curling irons to dress their animals and use shoe polish to make hoofs glisten. Morning, afternoon and night there were shows, and races and exhibitions and judging and baking contests, but that year the thing most people wanted to see was the Catch It, Keep It contest.

As the twenty boys waited in the dark bowels of the arena, like gladiators of Rome about to face the animals, a long-time rodeo hero saw little Timmy and talked with him. 'You're the youngest and the lightest, aren't you? I'll bet I know what you have in mind. Run like hell for one of the smallest calves. But that's not a good idea, because all those older boys will dive for the little calves too. And they'll knock you galley west. So when the whistle blows, dash down there and grab the biggest, because the other kids will leave him alone.' He stared at Timmy. 'You ain't scared, are you?'

'I ain't scared.'

'Then grab for the biggest.'

Timmy listened carefully, and it was fortunate he did, for as the rodeo hand had predicted, everyone made a jump at the smaller calves, and big boys muscled the younger away. Timmy, in the meantime, had made a flying leap at a rowdy Hereford, and to his delight, bore the surprised animal right to the ground. How much smaller the calf was than the steer he had practiced with in the Volkema barn—this was going to be easy!

But it wasn't. No Hereford calf was ever easy to push around, not even for a grown man, and as Timmy lay with the calf's head locked in his arms, he found to his dismay that whereas he could keep the Hereford pinned down, it required all his weight to do so, and he had no possible chance of applying the halter. Oh, Jesus! he prayed. Let me hold him.

But he felt himself growing weaker and the white-faced calf growing stronger. The other nine calves had been led away and now everyone in the auditorium focused on the gallant fight between the little boy and the rambunctious calf.

'Hold on, kid!' the crowd began to roar, and the rodeo hand slipped along the barrier and shouted, 'Throw your leg over his neck! Kid! Throw your leg!'

With a titanic effort Timmy tried to get his left leg across the calf's neck, but the sturdy Hereford was too strong. Slowly, slowly the struggling animal began to break free. Oh, Jesus! the boy pleaded. Don't let him get away. I need him!

But the inexorable weight of the calf was too much, and to the groans of thousands of adults, Timmy felt the calf break loose and scamper free. He lay in the dust while a bigger boy tackled the rebellious whiteface and led him off.

'Tough luck, kid!' a man shouted as Timmy stood up, dusted himself off and started the long walk to the exit, without a calf.

He went into a corner of the waiting area and bit his lip to keep from crying. He stuck his little jaw in the air and kicked at the wooden siding. I wasn't scared, he told himself, but in this he found no consolation. He'd had a calf, but it had escaped.

'If you want to cry,' a voice said, 'let her go.' It was the rodeo hand, and he sat with Timmy and told of the many times he had been knocked against the wall and lost the prize.

They were sitting there when a roar went up from the arena. The rodeo man, fearing that one of his friends had been hurt by a Brahma bull, ran to the entrance, stood there for a while, then walked back to where Timmy sat, still biting his lip.

'It's you, kid,' the rider said. 'It's you they want.'

'Me?'

'Yep. Get yourse'f out there.' And he led Timmy back to the arena, where another roar rose from the crowd, while he stood bewildered, still holding back tears.

Then he heard the loudspeaker booming and felt the searchlights playing in his eyes. 'Because you put up such a terrific fight, Timmy Grebe, Charlotte Lloyd of the Crown Vee Hereford ranch wants to award you a calf, anyway.' A wild cheer rose from the crowd as a spunky white-face was led in. 'Take him home, Timmy. You earned him.'

As the little boy led the calf across the arena thousands of people cheered, and when he got to the exit the rodeo man was waiting to congratulate him. 'I'm going to call him Rodeo,' Timmy said.

Timmy's victory gave the trouble-stricken community of Line Camp something to talk about, but it brought no money into the Grebe household. Salvation was to come from a most unexpected quarter. The driver of the school bus was stricken with a hernia; he had been holding down three jobs to feed his family. Ethan Grebe was given the job temporarily; it paid almost nothing, but it did pay cash, and with this the family could buy more food.

It hurt Alice and Earl to have to take from their son money which should have gone for a college education, but as Earl told Alice, 'The times are so mixed up, we have to adjust to everything. One of these days we'll be growing wheat again.'

But not that year. The duststorms continued, and Timmy had to build a special lean-to in order to protect Rodeo from being smothered. Fences were especially vulnerable. The terrible force would send a horde of tumbleweeds across a field; they would be imprisoned by some fence, and when the next storm hit, the weeds would catch so much dust that the fences would vanish and cattle would roam for a score of miles.

What affected Alice Grebe the most was the constant noise—the awful moaning of the wind as it swept across the prairies. On some days its high intensity drove her to a frenzy, and Vesta proposed that she be sent to Denver, to get her off the prairie before she had a breakdown. Earl would have wanted to do this but the Grebes had no money. They literally had no money beyond the few dollars that Ethan brought in, and during the summer recess they did not even have that.

And then Alice did reach the breaking point. It was a very dry August day, with the earth parched and breaking, when she heard her youngest daughter, Betsy, making a curious sound. She ran into the yard, not able to guess what might be happening, and saw to her horror that a huge rattlesnake had come down from the buttes seeking water. He was only a few feet from the child, a monstrous snake almost six feet long and very thick, with an evil-looking head and a black tongue which kept probing the area ahead. His skin was scarred and dark, and his rattlers were rough. As Alice watched, he moved toward the baby.

She would never be able to explain how she found the courage, but she grabbed a hoe and thrust herself in the space between her child and the rattler. With awkward chopping strokes, she hacked away at the huge serpent, driving it back and cutting it whenever it tried to attack her. With a fury she had never known before, she fought the snake for some minutes, countering its thrusts with savage swipes of the hoe, then, after one swift strike of the venomous head, which almost caught her on the leg, she cut it in two and watched in horror while the halves writhed, as if each had a life of its own, as if together they might yet attack both her and the child.

She stood leaning on the hoe, unable to move. She could hear the prattle of her child behind her, but she could not take her eyes off the dead snake. She was still standing there like a statue when Earl came in from the fields.

'What're you doing, Alice?' he asked as he approached her.

She could not answer . . . just stood there. And then he looked down and saw the severed snake, as hideous in death as it had been in life.

'Oh, my darling!' he whispered, lifting her like an infant into his arms.

He put her to bed, and that night Vesta Volkema said, after she had tended her, 'Earl, I'm going to take her to my place. She's at the end of her rope.'

'What will I do about the children?' he asked.

'What will we do about anything, goddamnit!' she shouted. 'Your wife is destroying herself. You look after the children.'

They were not left alone. The next day Victoria called out from the window, 'Car coming!' and up the lane came a large black auto driven by an elderly woman whom the girls did not recognize. When it jolted to a halt, the woman climbed out, dragging two baskets. 'I'm Charlotte Lloyd,' she said. 'Police told me my friend Timmy Grebe was here without a mother.'

'We have a mother,' Timmy said.

'Of course you do,' Charlotte said quickly. 'But she's gone away for a while, hasn't she?' Before the boy could answer, she embraced him and said. 'You're champion bull-dogger, aren't you?' and from one of her baskets she produced a large plate of brown sticky buns.

She acted as if she were a member of the family, taking from her baskets things the children had not seen for years. Among her goodies was a tin of canned oysters, which the youngsters were afraid to try. 'Got to try everything,' she said, showing them how to place the strange food on crusts of bread. For three weeks she visited the farm daily, tending the children and entertaining them with stories of strange places she had seen.

She was eighty-three years old that summer, but as lively as when she had first crossed Nebraska on the shooting expedition with the grand duke. She was still interested in the land and chided Earl Grebe for plowing the way he did. 'You have a man right here in Line Camp who knows the answers,' she said.

'Who?'

'Walter Bellamy. Heard him give a fine talk in Centennial last winter.'

'He couldn't plow a straight line,' Grebe protested.

'Exactly, that's his virtue,' she said, and she arranged for Bellamy to come to the farm and invited the Volkemas and others to listen as the postmaster explained again what the error had been.

'From the mountains to the border of Nebraska—you have one unbroken sweep of plowed land. The wind gets started as it comes down off the hills and begins to pick up the harrowed soil. It gets bigger and stronger and all the time it picks up more of our soil, until half the state is in the air.'

'What should we do?' Magnes asked.

'Tie the soil down. You've got to tie it down.'

'How?'

'Never plow in a straight line. Never plow with the fall of the land. Plow across it. Never plow all the land. Leave strips of grass, and for God's sake, burn your harrow. Leave the soil in clumps too big for the wind to lift.'

The farmers began to see that he was right, that if an endless corridor of plowed and harrowed land lay in the path of the wind, it could roll that land up, mile after mile, and carry it away like a thief. But if the topsoil were tied down, one way or another, the wind could blow over it as before, and accumulate nothing.

'This land will come back,' Charlotte insisted. With her own money she arranged for a symposium to be held in Line Camp, and in her black car, with the Grebe children to accompany her, she drove in to Centennial to pick up the featured speaker. The farmers who had emigrated from Ottumwa were astonished to see him, for it was Thomas Dole Creevey, now an old man who had lived to see the desolation he had fathered. Few men would have had the courage to come back to the scenes which had disproved their cherished theories, but he did. He wanted to see for himself what had gone wrong; he wanted to identify the corrective steps to be taken by those who followed.

He was not so fat now, but his ill-fitting clothes were even more unkempt. He stood before the men he had misled and told them, 'I gave you ten principles, and only one was erroneous, the seventh. "Plow at least ten inches deep. Then disk. Then harrow." All wrong. What I didn't foresee were the great winds. In every other respect my theories were correct, and future years will see these plains teeming with wheat.'

'What should we do now?' Earl Grebe asked.

'Pray for rain. Throw away your harrows. Never have an endless chain of plowed fields that the wind can get at.'

'How deep should we plow?'

'Three inches, maybe four. But keep the ground covered.'

'Is your farm at Goodland producing?'

'It's blown away,' Creevey said. 'When the rains return, it will return.' He said that in spite of everything that had struck the plains, he still believed in those great words which God had delivered to man during their first meeting in Eden: 'Replenish the earth and subdue it.' He concluded, 'To do this we must study the earth more than we have. We must be more careful to attune ourselves to its eternities. If at periods it produces great winds, we must learn how to live with them.' He assured his listeners that the plains were not intended to be a desert and would again be rippling with wheat.

Charlotte Lloyd drove him back to the station in Centennial, where he boarded the train to meet with other drought-stricken farmers. On the way back to Line Camp, when her black car climbed to the top of a hill from which she could see the seared plains that had once been a part of the Venneford Ranch, she felt a great dizziness, so that the plains and sky became one, and she lifted her foot from the gas pedal, allowing the car to drift slowly off the road and into the parched fields, where she was found next morning, her hands still gripping the wheel.

The unabated optimism of Dr. Creevey did little to help the men whose farms were being sold for taxes, and Philip Wendell was picking up some terrific bargains at forced sales. Farms were going for a dollar an acre . . . fifty cents an acre . . . and in some cases, for a used car that would enable the owner to reach California.

At the Grebe farm there was one bright note. In November, Alice returned much improved. Vesta Volkema's salty attitudes had teased her back to reality, and with Ethan driving the school bus again, at least a little money was coming to the family. In fact, Earl said that things were beginning to look up.

Then, in March, a blizzard swept across the prairie and snow piled the roads; what was worse, a gale bearing no snow howled down from the mountains. Farmers shouted to their wives, 'Ground blizzard!' This meant that what snow had fallen would now whip across the open plains, engulfing anything it encountered.

Ethan Grebe had already started on his afternoon drive north delivering children to Wendell when the blizzard struck, and there was no logical way for him to escape it. He thought of turning and trying to run back to Line Camp, but the road was too treacherous for that. He therefore plunged ahead, satisfied that he had enough gasoline to keep the children warm even if he were forced to pull up for an hour or two.

But then the winds whipped a fearful burden of snow across the prairie and within minutes the windward side of the bus was banked with snow. The wheels were unable to move.

Ethan kept the motor running for three hours, trusting that farmers at either Line Camp or Wendell would launch rescue parties. He led the children in singing and made them huddle together. As the gasoline gauge dropped and night fell, it became obvious that pretty soon the bus would be completely buried in snow, with no possible way of keeping the children warm.

Biting his lower lip, he looked at the nineteen frightened faces and made his decision. 'I know where we are,' he said slowly. 'Three miles to the Rumson farm. They'll bring help. Now, Harry, what are you going to do while I'm gone?'

'Mind the door,' he said.

'That's right. No one must leave. Now you wait here.'

And he was off into the heart of the ground blizzard. Nineteen children were in his care and he must do everything within his power to save them, whether it seemed a reasonable act or not. He had not been out in the storm more than three minutes before he realized that this blizzard was overpowering. It was not abating, and the winds roared at him with such force that he could barely move, but on he plodded. He walked three awful miles, and by the time he reached the Rumson gate he was so near death that he could not force it open, but with his last strength he created a banging, and a dog heard him and barked, and the children were saved.

President Roosevelt himself sent a message to the Grebes, praising them for having reared such a son, and Alice treasured it, but often when she read it she wondered why the government did nothing to help the farmers that produced such young men. 'They don't grow by accident, you know,' she told Mr. Bellamy.

In the months following Charlotte Lloyd's death, decisions had to be reached concerning the Venneford Ranch. The majority owners in Bristol were suffering from the world-wide depression as much as anyone else, and they had no surplus funds to sink into a distant venture which had never paid substantial dividends. They had watched their ranch shrink from five and a half million acres to something like ninety thousand, and with every shrinkage their American managers had assured them, 'With a tighter operation we can begin to show real profits,' but such profits had never been forthcoming.

In 1887 it had been the great blizzard and in 1893 the nationwide panic and in 1923–24 the first drought. In 1925 they had written to Beeley Garrett, who was managing for them:

> It seems that the western cattle business is always going to prosper next year, if only conditions remain stable, but stable conditions have not been known since the industry began. Every messenger we have sent from Bristol to Venneford has returned with gallant tales of how exciting the life is on the range, and what a great bull Emperor IX is, and we have concluded that this immense industry is run for the pleasure of cowboys and bulls, and to the disregard of investors.

Now, in this summer of 1935, they were fed up. They wanted to sell their remaining holdings and were offering them at a bargain. Charlotte Lloyd had been the principal stockholder in America, so it was natural that her heirs should be offered first chance to buy, but here a problem arose. She and Jim had had only one child, a daughter Nancy, who had married the grandson of Major Maxwell Mercy, the congressman. Nancy and Paul made a dashing couple, but they had been somewhat reckless, like old Pasquinel, from whom Paul was descended, and in attempting to fly over the Rockies in a small plane, they crashed near Blue Valley and were killed.

They left behind a frail daughter named Ruth, who was cared for by her grandmother, Charlotte, and it looked for a while as if the awkward girl might never marry, for her nervous mannerisms discouraged men. However, the year before Charlotte died, she took the Garrett boy aside one day and told him bluntly, 'If you ever expect to manage this ranch, young Henry Garrett, you'd be well advised to marry that girl,' and he did. To show her approval, Charlotte had given the young couple a wedding present: her shares in the ranch. In her will she gave them the money to buy the stock still owned in Bristol, and when it was delivered to the castle, Beeley Garrett said, 'For the first time in Venneford history this ranch is controlled by Americans, who should have controlled it from the beginning.'

Beeley continued as ranch manager, but the pressures of drought and wind and depression were telling on him, and he often indicated that he wished to retire from management and move to Florida. In this he was supported by his wife, Pale Star Zendt, five-eighths Indian and as lovely as all the women of her family. She had grown to dislike northern winters, and Beeley told her, 'We'll stick it out a few more years. Maybe in that time Henry and Ruth will become more solidly united than they seem now. You can't run a ranch with a wobbly couple at the head.'

In the fall of 1935 Beeley faced a difficult decision. With cattle prices the lowest he had ever seen them, he had to make up his mind whether to ship a load of steers to Chicago in the blind hope that he might earn even a dollar a head profit on them, but his chances were not bright. His accountant submitted the disheartening figures:

> The best Herefords America has ever produced are selling in Chicago for $14 a head. Our figures show that we spend $11 a head to grow them. This means a profit of $3 each, which is not bad for these times. But for us to ship the animals to Chicago costs us $6.10 a head, so that for every Hereford we sell, we lose $3.10. And the more we sell, the more we lose.

Garrett could not believe that this preposterous situation could long continue. He remembered good years like 1919, when even a mediocre Hereford brought $58.75. In a relatively bad year like 1929 he had sold his steers at $55.35. The precipitous drop of the 1930s was unconscionable, and the nation must be going crazy if it thought that cattlemen could continue to market their beasts while losing money on each head. To sell choice steak at twenty-three cents a pound was ridiculous, and he felt certain that prices to the rancher would soon rise.

He therefore decided to take the gamble and send two hundred prime head to Chicago, hoping that by the time they reached the slaughterhouse the price would be up to $30.00, where it ought to be. He talked some of his neighbors into taking the same risk, and a cattle train was put together with animals from as far away as Fort Collins and the ranches south of Cheyenne.

As soon as word leaked through the district that a cattle train was being assembled, the participating stockmen were besieged with offers of assistance from young men in the area. Beeley Garrett, with his headquarters not far from Centennial, where the train was forming, was especially vulnerable. From dawn till midnight awkward young men came knocking at his door, cowboy hats in hand: 'Hear tell you're sendin' some cattle east. I'd sure like to help.'

'Your name.'

'Chester—Otto Emig's grandson.'

'I knew your grandfather. Have you tried the Roggen people? Otto had good relations with them.'

'Nothin' out there. They sent me here.'

'I'll take your name, Chester. You're a fine young man and maybe we could use you.'

One after another the young cowboys came to the door, begging for a job that paid nothing and for which they had to pack their own food. Of course, they would get a chance to visit Chicago, but what allured them was that after the cattle were delivered, each cowboy received a free ride home on a Pullman.

But it was not this enticement that drove Dr. Walter Gregg, a young professor at the college in Greeley, to apply for a job. 'It's imperative that I get to Chicago,' he pleaded with Garrett. 'To attend a professional meeting.'

'Is it that important?'

'It's crucial. They've asked me to read a paper. It could make all the difference . . . in my career, that is.'

'If it's that important, why not take the train?'

'We've absolutely no money.'

'I'd like to help, Dr. Gregg, but the idea of a college professor . . . riding a cattle train . . .'

'Please,' the man begged. 'The leaders in my field will be there. My whole future depends on this.'

'I'll take your name, Professor. You may hear from me.'

On the day when the decision had to be made, Beeley was visited by an unlikely candidate, Jake Calendar's son Cisco, a thin, taciturn young man with yellowish hair. He was probably the best cowboy among the applicants, but he had a surly attitude which irritated Garrett.

'Hear you're lookin' for a couple of hands to ride the cattle cars,' he said in a mumbling sort of way.

'It's the other way around, young man. A lot of people have been here applying for the job.'

'Add me to the list,' he said insolently, not bothering to take the cigarette from his mouth. Beeley felt an almost uncontrollable urge to punch him, but he refrained because Calendar had about him an air of absolute authenticity. He was obviously someone who loved the range and knew animals. He was a challenge, and for reasons Beeley could not have explained, he felt drawn toward the youth. Perhaps it was because Calendar represented the real west, a throwback to the great days.

'Tell you what,' Garrett said on the spur of the moment. 'I'll take you. Now you run over to the college and find Professor Gregg and tell him the train's leaving tonight at six.'

'Ain't got a car,' Calendar said.

'Use the pickup.'

He watched as the young man slouched over to the Ford, banged open the door and jiggled the gearshift. In a moment the pickup roared, the wheels spun in gravel and the cowboy was off to the college.

At the train Professor Gregg was so profuse in his thanks that Garrett felt ashamed. What a rotten time, he said to himself. College professor with no money to travel.

He was not surprised to see that Dr. Gregg carried a large suitcase, but he was certainly astonished to find that Calendar was lugging along a paper bag with one clean shirt and a razor, plus a large guitar. He had never thought of the Calendars, those outcasts of the prairie, as musical.

Professor Gregg, of the sociology department, and Cisco Calendar, aspirant guitarist, were able to board the cattle train because of the 36-Hour Law. This required any cattlemen shipping livestock a considerable distance to provide attendants to water and exercise the animals if the total trip exceeded thirty-six hours.

This law had been forced through legislatures by animal-protection societies whose agents submitted reports of what had happened in the horrendous days of 1910 through 1928. Then cattlemen would shove huge numbers of animals into unventilated cars and ship them off to Chicago. If all went well, the cattle train reached the stockyards within thirty-six hours, which was about the maximum time cattle could survive without water. But if for any reason the train had to be sidetracked, it might lay over unattended for two or three days in blazing sun or cold wind, and the cattle, with no water and no chance to move, would die by the score.

In accordance with the 36-Hour Law, Dr. Gregg and Cisco Calendar would ride the caboose and during a normal trip might never see the animals they were supposed to be tending. The railroad had every incentive to get the train into Chicago on time, and the evil old habit of sidetracking without regard to the welfare of the animals was forbidden. Of course, if an unavoidable delay occurred, then Gregg and Calendar would become important, for they would have to unload the animals, see that they moved about and provide them with water.

'Nineteen trips out of twenty, nothin' happens,' the brakemen assured the two guardians. 'Sit back and enjoy the ride.'

There were nine men in the large caboose, with sleeping bunks for five. There were four regulars in the train crew and five volunteers like Calendar. It was around this somber young man that the others gathered, for when he unlimbered his guitar and started singing, everyone listened.

He had a reedy voice that spoke of western campfires, and he knew all the songs the old-time cowboys had sung—'Aura Lee,' 'Buffalo Gal,' 'Old Blue, 'Old Paint'—and the two new songs which were so popular on the radio, 'The Last Roundup' and 'Wagon Wheels.' But the songs that captivated the men were two that scarcely seemed to be songs at all; they were fragments of human experience, deep and moving.

The first told of a wrangler who allowed that there wasn't a horse alive he couldn't ride. So the boss offered him a ten-spot to try his luck with a strawberry roan, a mean-looking cayuse with a battered frame:

> 'He's got spavined old legs and small pigeon toes,
> And a pair of pig eyes and a long Roman nose,
> He's got little pin ears, they're all split at the tips,
> In the middle he's lean but wide at the hips . . .'

The wonder of this song was its intimate knowledge of men and horses, the way it spoke lovingly of actual life on the range, and Cisco brought out all the inner essence of the relationships. This was a real cowboy trying his luck with a real horse, and in the end it was the horse that won.

> 'When my stirrups I lose and also my hat,
> And I starts pullin' leather as blind as a bat,
> And he makes one more jump, he is headed up high
> Leaves me settin' on air way up in the sky.'

'I think that must be the best western song I ever heard,' Professor Gregg said; he was interested in the west and intended one day to write about it. He asked Cisco to sing the words again and wrote down passages in a notebook. 'It carries its own credentials, a song like that,' he said, and Cisco had no idea what he was talking about.

The trainmen wanted Cisco to sing their favorite, 'Red River Valley,' and when he struck the first chords they leaned back in approval. It was a sentimental song, the lament of a cowboy who had known for a short time a girl who must leave the valley. It was hard to know how a young fellow like Calendar could comprehend the longing that an older man felt about a woman, but he made the song his. Again, he was not a singer but a man who had worked in the valleys and who had met an attractive woman, perhaps the only one he had ever known:

> 'Come and sit by my side, if you love me.
> Do not hasten to bid me adieu.
> Just remember the Red River Valley
> And the cowboy who loved you so true.'

No one spoke. Each listener was silently comparing the song against his own experience, and no additional comment was necessary.

After a while Dr. Gregg said, 'You ought to sing professionally.'

'I aim to.'

'You ought to see what you can do in Chicago.'

'I aim to.'

'I'm really very excited about your potential,' the professor said. 'Your voice has an exceptional quality . . . an authenticity.' To these words Calendar made no reply whatever, so the professor continued: 'To be truly successful, Cisco, you have to visualize what it is you want to convey. You'll be singing to people who've never seen a campfire. You ought to get yourself a Stetson . . . Texas-style boots . . . a red bandanna.'

'I got no money for such,' Cisco said.

'I know a place in Chicago, they might give it on credit,' Gregg said. 'In art you've got to give yourself every advantage.'

The train braked to a halt and voices outside the caboose shouted, 'This goddamn train is infested with hobos.' And the crew piled out with baseball bats and started knocking drifters from beneath the cars, and Gregg looked out the window and saw one man run past with blood streaming down his face, and for a moment the running man looked up in an appeal for help, but Gregg was powerless.

When the train resumed its trek eastward he could not eat. The four crewmen who ran the caboose were not evil men, but when they had gone after the hobos they had swung their bats with actual glee, as if knocking helpless men over the head were sport. It was sickening.

Calendar was the only one who understood what had happened to Gregg, and he went to him with half a sandwich, but the professor still could not eat. 'What's the matter?' Cisco asked. 'You never see a man clubbed before?' He took Gregg's hand and passed it over his head so the professor could feel the knobs.

'These are hateful times,' Gregg said.

'We've had worse,' Calendar replied, and he resumed singing.

In the thirty-fourth hour the train pulled into the stockyards, and Dr. Gregg for the first time saw for himself just how hateful the times really were, for when the Venneford Herefords were unloaded and auctioned next day, he found that the handsome animals fetched only $13.87 each.

When word of the sale got back to Centennial, and the various ranchers discovered that they had literally given their animals away, earning no profit whatever for their years of labor—the baling of hay, the wintry rides, the watch over pregnant cows, the dusty roundups—a sullen grief settled over the community. Men grew stubborn and swore revenge against a system that had defrauded them so sorely.

Then came the wintry day in November 1935 when the Grebe family had to admit they could no longer hold on to their farm. It was true that they had paid off their mortgage, but they owed an accumulation of back taxes; the bank was dunning them to repay a small loan they had been forced to make in order to buy food; and the garage would no longer give them gasoline on credit. The debts were trivial—less than a thousand dollars—but paying them was impossible, totally impossible. Earl Grebe did not have one dollar, and with no gasoline for his tractor, he would be unable to produce crops even if the duststorms did abate.

On some days the family ate so little that their survival was a mystery, and if Vesta Volkema had not brought them food, the Grebes would have suffered grievously. But this generosity created its own problem, and one evening when Alice saw her neighbor coming across the prairie, she burst into tears and protested to her husband, 'Oh, Earl! It's so terribly unfair. Vesta's able to help us because she stole her land and saved her money. We bought ours honestly and used up all our funds.'

Her husband would not tolerate such an accusation against the goodhearted Vesta. 'She's the one person in this world we can trust,' he said. 'If these dreadful things are happening to us, it must be God's will.' And when Vesta reached the kitchen she found the Grebes and their children kneeling in prayer.

The family was prepared, therefore, when Sheriff Bogardus rode up to nail the notice to their front door: 'Sheriff's Sale for Taxes.'

'What will it bring?' Grebe asked.

'If the auctioneer has a good day . . . if people come out . . . farms like this have been bringing . . . maybe fifteen hundred dollars.'

'Jesus!' Grebe cried. 'After I pay the debts, it leaves me almost nothing.'

'That's the way it is, these days,' Bogardus said.

Surprisingly, it was Alice Grebe who showed fortitude in this crisis. She had stayed indoors when the sheriff delivered his message, but she knew what was happening. The land her husband had cultivated with such care was lost. The soddy in which they had known so much love was gone. The new house with its bright curtains would be no more. The animals would be sold and the implements for which they had saved so strenuously. What was worse, the children would be forced to leave the only home they had known. They would gather their things and leave this place . . .

'Oh, God!' she whispered to herself before Earl entered the kitchen. 'What will happen to that good man?' She felt that she could adjust to this defeat, but what would such a catastrophe do to him?

She moved to the sink, pretending that she was doing dishes, so that she could appear composed when he came into the room, for she was determined to give him support, but when he walked into the kitchen his feet dragged across the linoleum, the slogging drift of a man totally defeated.

She threw herself into his arms and collapsed in tears. 'We've worked so hard,' she sobbed. 'We've never wasted money.' She kissed him tenderly and led him to a chair. She poured him a cup of coffee and said gently, 'I wonder if I dare take the sign down before the children see it?'

'No,' he said firmly. 'It's the law. We owe the money and there's no way out.'

'How can a nation support a law which takes away a man's farm? Especially when it's the nation that's gone wrong, not us?'

'The bank has to be paid.'

'But it's the banks that refuse to circulate their money.' She was not argumentative, merely bewildered by this savage turn.

When the children came home and saw the notice they started to cry, and she felt it her responsibility to shield them from as much pain as possible. 'We'll live somewhere else,' she said brightly as she prepared toast and cocoa. From the bare shelf she took down her last jar of jam and they had a mournful picnic, after which she suggested that they all walk down to the Volkemas' to discuss what must be done.

'Put on your scarfs,' she said. 'We don't want to freeze.' At this unfortunate word, Victoria remembered Ethan and started to cry, but her mother caught her by the hand and said, 'Now, Vicky. Watch the children and we'll go across the fields.' But as they went past the barn Timmy broke away and ran to where Rodeo was fattening and he flung his arms about the handsome Hereford and stayed there till his mother dragged him away.

'I won't give up Rodeo,' he mumbled.

'There's no need to,' she said quietly. 'We'll find a way.'

What a sad procession they formed as they walked across the beautiful low hills that separated them from the Volkemas': Earl in front walking with slow tread; Alice behind; then Victoria and the two girls; then Larry and in the rear Timmy, looking back now and then toward his steer. Winter hawks accompanied them in the blue sky and to the north they saw a small herd of antelope.

When they reached the Volkemas', they broke the news abruptly. 'We're being sheriffed,' Alice said matter-of-factly, and Vesta broke into tears.

Not Magnes. He wanted to fight, to destroy something. He started cursing, and when his wife shushed him, he ignored her and cried, 'I know the man we need. Jake Calendar.'

'You stay away from Jake,' his wife warned.

'If anybody has the courage to stand up to these bastards, Jake does.'

'I don't want to go to jail,' Grebe protested. 'Losin' the farm's bad enough.'

'It's got to be stopped!' Magnes shouted. Grebe tried to quieten him, but his sense of outrage was so great that no reasoning had effect. 'I'm gonna see Jake Calendar, and I'm gonna see him right now,' the infuriated man said, and he was gone.

Vesta prepared a meal for her distraught neighbors and tried to console the children. She saw that the family failure was having its severest impact on Timmy, and tried to divert his attention with idle talk about Rodeo. 'He's doin' good,' he said, but there the conversation ended, for Victoria asked, 'If we get thrown off the farm, Timmy, what'll you do with Rodeo?' and he ran from the house to keep from bursting into tears.

On the day of the sale Sheriff Bogardus and three deputies arrived to maintain order. In the Dakotas ugly things had been happening at these forced sales, and Bogardus was determined that this one, unfortunate though it might be, must go off smoothly. As he toured the premises and stared at each of the sullen farmers, seeking to intimidate them, he told his followers, 'It's gonna be all right. I think we can handle whatever they may have in mind.'

'Un-unh!' one of his assistants groaned. 'You spoke too soon.'

And everyone turned to watch as a shifty-eyed man in his late fifties sauntered into the yard to look over the equipment Earl Grebe had put together over the years. He was accompanied by two young men as lean and surly as he, and the trio paid no attention as the crowd whispered, 'It's the Calendars. Everything's okay.'

'Hiya, Jake!' Sheriff Bogardus said with unnecessary effusiveness. 'Fine day for the sale.'

'Best,' Jake said, continuing his slow inspection.

'Hiya, Cisco. How was Chicago?'

'Okay,' the younger of the boys said as he kicked the tire of the tractor.

News of the sale had been widely circulated, and buyers had come in from Kansas and Nebraska, for here was a chance to get nearly thirteen hundred acres of first-class farmland, with a prospect of making real money when rain returned to the plains.

The auctioneer was a tested man, Mike Garmisch of Fort Collins. He had an ingratiating way of pulling a crowd together and chivvying them into bidding a little more than they had intended. 'It's a fine day for a fine farm,' he said for openers, and after a few jokes that stayed well clear of the day's tragedy—dispossessing a man for the lack of a few dollars—he got down to the business of the sale.

'We have here a good house, a very strong barn and one thousand, two hundred and eighty acres of prime, rolling drylands. Friends, you give this land one year of proper rain, it's gonna be a gold mine—a gold mine, I said.'

He invited any bid above one thousand dollars, and a real estate man from Kimball, Nebraska, offered fifteen hundred. By slow steps this rose to three thousand, two hundred. Then an investor from Kansas bid three thousand, four hundred, and the bidding stopped.

'Three thousand, four hundred once . . .'

At this point Jake Calendar and his sons elbowed their way through the crowd toward the successful Kansas bidder, and as they moved, slowly, like rattlesnakes, Sheriff Bogardus caught sight of a little boy throwing a ball against the barn. Choosing this as an excuse to avoid a showdown with the Calendars, he said in a loud voice, 'We can't have that boy disrupting our sale,' and he motioned to his three deputies, who silently filed out behind him to halt this misdemeanor.

When the lawmen were gone, Jake Calendar zeroed in on the Kansas bidder and grabbed him by the throat. 'Did you make that last bid?' Calendar asked in a grim whisper.

'Yes.'

Holding the man in his left hand, Jake produced a huge pistol. Thrusting it against the Kansan's temple, he issued his ultimatum: 'If you don't withdraw that bid, I'm gonna blow your fuckin' head off.'

The visitor paled and looked about for the sheriff. Unable to locate him, he tried to find the deputies, but they were gone too. There was only that monstrous pistol touching his head.

'I understand you want to reconsider your bid,' Calendar said softly.

'I do. Oh, indeed I do.'

'He wants permission to reconsider,' Calendar announced to the crowd. 'Floyd, Cisco, step over there and help the auctioneer.'

The two young Calendars, pistols drawn, elbowed their way to the podium, where they stood glaring at Mike Garmisch, who said in a quivering voice, 'Gentlemen, I'm advised that the bidder from Kansas was under some kind of misapprehension. Is that right?'

'Indeed it is!' the Kansan said eagerly. 'I understood that the farm implements were included in this part of the sale.'

'They certainly are not. It states that on the notice.'

'In that case I withdraw my bid.'

'Gentlemen, we want to run the fairest sale possible, and if this good man thinks he has in any way . . .' The two Calendar boys nudged him and he stopped the palaver.

'The gentleman from Kansas withdraws his bid. Does the gentleman from Kimball, Nebraska, wish to stand by his?' One flourish of Jake Calendar's horse pistol satisfied the investor from Kimball that he, too, had misunderstood the terms of sale.

'Gentlemen, the only fair thing will be to start over,' Garmisch said, his throat very dry. 'Do I hear a bid?'

'Five dollars,' Vesta Volkema said in a clear voice.

'Five once, five twice, five three times—sold! To Mrs. Volkema for five dollars.' The words came in one gasp.

When Sheriff Bogardus and his deputies heard the gavel fall, they left the law-breaking boy and wandered back into the sales area. A representative of the bank rushed up to Bogardus, complaining that the bank had been defrauded of its money.

'In a sense that's right,' Bogardus agreed. 'You're entitled to the total proceeds of the sale, after taxes.'

'But since the farm only brought—what was it?—five dollars.' The sheriff shrugged his shoulders. He had no intention of bucking forty angry farmers, most of them with concealed guns, not when they were led by the Calendars.

'Where the hell were you?' Auctioneer Garmisch asked the sheriff, for he, too, had been bilked of his fee.

'Enforcing the law,' the sheriff said, pointing to the miscreant boy with the ball.

Difficult as these years were, they were not devoid of the rowdy humor that had always characterized western life.

In 1935 Denver society was bedazzled by the visit of Lord Codrington, announced as the scion of a family who had long been associated with Colorado ranching. He was a charming man, from Oxford he said, whose gracious manners won him entry to the very topmost levels of Denver society, where he courted several marriageable heiresses and lent both amusement and dignity to the better clubs. He ran up some bills, but not many, ordered suits at various tailors patronized by his hosts, but not an excessive number, and in the end was discovered to be a complete fraud, a Cockney sailor off the Cunard Line who had mastered his accent studying Ronald Colman movies while his ship plied the Atlantic.

His downfall was a six-day wonder, with the cream of Denver society made to look like asses in the local press. The photographs, taken earlier by bored cameramen dragooned into covering for the society page, now made front page, top and center: 'Mrs. Charles Bannister, leader of Denver society, presenting Lord Codrington to the Delmar Linners at the March Fete.'

And then the affair took a typical Colorado twist. No one in Denver would bring suit against Lord Codrington. As Mrs. Bannister said, in an interview which brought chuckles and a sense of restored propriety: 'Who did he hurt? He was utterly delightful and provided everyone with a sense of joy during a rather bleak period in our lives. He did me no harm.'

Her husband, Charles Bannister, said pretty much the same: 'I'm certainly not going to bring charges against a man who bilked me out of three suits. I pay a lot more than that these days without getting half the entertainment.'

When the police bustled the errant lord out of town, with a warning never to appear within the precincts again, at least two dozen leaders of Denver society appeared to bid him farewell as he stepped aboard the train which would whisk him to Chicago and deportation. Three young women ignored the flashing bulbs to kiss him goodbye, and Delmar Linner, father of one of the girls and a leading banker, told reporters, 'He looks a damned sight better in that suit than I ever did.'

At about this time Centennial became the butt of a prank by a group of high school students, who had been complaining about poor food served in the cafeteria. They erected over its portals a sign which infuriated some, evoked hilarity in others. Unfortunately, all the perpetrators were offspring of Republican families and a regrettable political overtone was cast over the affair, where none was intended. The sign read:

ALFERD PACKER MEMORIAL CAFETERIA

And when the teachers saw it, all hell broke loose, the local Democratic leader claiming that to erect such a sign on a building paid for by taxpayers was an insult to Franklin D. Roosevelt, not a favorite figure in the area. The leader of the Republicans had the wit to snap back, 'Nonsense! That sign has no national significance whatever. It merely recognizes, and belatedly at that, a thoughtful citizen of Colorado who performed a public service for which we should all be grateful.' And so the confrontation raged, until some children from Democratic families tore the sign down.

Alferd Packer had been a mountain guide, as mixed up as the spelling of his first name, and late in 1873 for a grubstake he volunteered to lead a hunting party of twenty into the western mountains. When a blizzard struck he got lost with five of the members. The party was snowbound for three months. They ran out of food, so Packer, as the man responsible for the leadership and survival of the group, began eating his fellow sportsmen.

When the spring thaws came Alferd Packer returned, picking his teeth and showing no signs of ordeal, but later the skeletons of his companions were found, each skull showing signs of having been smacked with the sharp edge of an ax.

The macabre episode might have passed unnoticed into history as one more macabre affair along the Continental Divide, except for the memorable charge made by the judge when he sentenced Packer. Whether the judge actually said these words cannot now be proved, but they have passed into the folklore of the state, providing Colorado with its one indisputable folk hero. Said the judge, 'Alferd Packer, you voracious, man-eating son-of-a-bitch. They was only seven Democrats in Hinsdale County, and you ate five of them.'

This affair made Packer the patron saint of the Republican party, and small wallet cards were printed up bearing his well-fed, handsome, bearded face accompanied by the legend: 'I admire the example set by the great Alferd Packer and wish to be a member of his club. In proof of my fidelity to his sterling principles, I agree to eliminate five Roosevelt Democrats.' It must be pointed out that Packer escaped punishment, for a clever Republican attorney proved that whereas the supposed crime had been committed while Colorado was a territory, the case had been tried under the criminal laws of the new state, and any fair-minded man would have to agree that that was unfair.

Contributions to public hilarity were also made by the Mexican community. In 1920 Pancho Villa, having made a fool of General Pershing, was about to launch a similar campaign against the Mexican government. They bought him off with a spacious ranch in Durango, where he ruled like a feudal lord, even resuming his less provocative original name, Doroteo Arrango.

However, many citizens remembered not his victories over the Americans but his brutal assassinations of Mexicans, and one hot afternoon, July 20, 1923, as he was driving in his new Dodge, he was ambushed by seven ancient enemies. When colored postcards of his disemboweled body were placed on sale, little white arrows pointed to forty-seven bullet wounds.

Villa was buried in his favorite city of Chihuahua, but one night in 1926 persons who had suffered at his hands invaded the cemetery, dug up his coffin and made off with the skeleton. The official history reports the grisly denouement: 'Being carried off his skull to New Mexico, vile opportunists there continue to sell it six or seven times each year to rapacious norteamericanos.'

Two of his skulls landed in Denver, brought there by tourists, and controversy arose as to which had once been the real Pancho Villa. Skull One was large and round and looked as if it might once have belonged to the legendary bandit. Skull Two, however, had been sold for twice the amount of Skull One, and therefore had to command respect. Furthermore, it had been sold by a woman who offered written affidavits proving that she was the one legal widow of Pancho Villa and was selling the skull only to help educate Pancho's children, whereupon the owner of Skull One produced a newspaper clipping from Old Mexico: 'There are no fewer than twenty-seven women with papers proving each to be the only true wife of Pancho Villa, and of these, sixteen have skulls to sell.'

Once more the argument was resolved in a manner which did credit to Colorado. The Anglo owners of the skulls agreed to put the decision in the hands of men from the area who had fought in Villa's army. They were brought to Denver to compare the skulls, and Centennial was proud when their own Tranquilino Marquez boarded the train to serve on the jury. The old soldiers looked at the two skulls, and in few minds was there any doubt that the bigger and rounder skull—that would be Skull One—conformed to the remembered physiognomy of their martyred leader, but there was that nagging problem raised by the fact that Skull Two had cost more and had come with a written documentation.

A judgment worthy of Solomon was handed down: 'Skull One is undoubtedly that of Pancho Villa, the mature man. But Skull Two, somewhat smaller, is also his, at the age of sixteen.'

*   *   *

After the disastrous sale of his cattle in Chicago, Beeley Garrett had put his foot down: 'Your mother and I have no intention of spending another winter in this God-forsaken climate. Come October, we'll go to Florida for good, but before we go, we do wish you'd get things straightened out with Ruth.'

'They're all right,' his son said evasively.

'Don't be a damned fool, Henry. What you and Ruth have can barely be called a marriage.'

'It'll work out,' Henry insisted. On this topic he was reticent, and he was much relieved when his parents actually packed their car.

For some years he had been making major decisions regarding the ranch, and under his tutelage Venneford bulls had strengthened their reputation as the blue-ribbon bulls of the west. Purists noted that each generation was a fraction of an inch shorter than the preceding, and they suspected that the dwarfism which Jim Lloyd had feared was operating, but Venneford publicity masked this deficiency, and the great Crown Vee bulls with their ponderous stride and drooping horns continued to bring top price at the auctions.

When Beeley and Pale Star climbed into their Cadillac for the long drive south, Ruth was not present to bid them goodbye. She was feeling poorly, and Beeley said, 'I'll give you two years, Henry. Get your marriage squared away or I'll have to take the ranch back. It's too valuable to let you ruin it.'

When his parents were gone, Henry had ample time to survey his situation, and the more he considered Ruth and her peculiar behavior, the more worried he became. Shortly after their marriage she had begun to act strangely, and before long she was another of those nervous, self-condemning, withdrawn women who haunted western ranches.

Beeley had said of her, 'She ought to leave Venneford and live out there on the drylands for a year. Let her see what some women endure without complaining.'

'A week in one of those tipis would drive her truly crazy,' Pale Star had said. She considered her daughter-in-law's behavior disgraceful. 'You've been very patient with her,' she had told Henry. 'Don't let her ruin your life.'

Now, alone, Henry wondered if he had in some way failed Ruth when her parents were killed in the plane crash. If so, there were no amends he could make. When he considered his wife's withdrawal, her complaining, her inability to pursue any interest, and especially her lack of affection toward either him or their children, he was bewildered.

It was in this mood that he started making regular halts at La Cantina on his way home from Centennial. In fact, he was finding much ranch business to do in town, and often instead of sending one of the cowboys to fetch a bucket of red paint to touch up the barns, he would ride in himself, then park his Dodge at La Cantina while he had a cold drink.

He never indicated that it was Soledad Marquez that he was stopping by to see, but when he entered the smoky, noisy room he always cast one swift, encompassing glance to ascertain the situation. If she was present, he sat and stared at her. If she was not there, the men could see that his shoulders sagged a little.

She had known, of course, from the first moment, that he was attracted to her, and this gave her enormous satisfaction. It was like the time when the family spent the winter in Denver and a singer up from Old Mexico had taken her on his knee and sung to her. It had signified nothing, really, yet she treasured the remembrance.

She knew that Henry Garrett was married, had children and was a Protestant, so there could be nothing in this for her. She also knew that her brother Triunfador watched her closely and had openly threatened to send her back to Mexico if she gave the gringo any encouragement. But in spite of these impediments she caught herself listening for the sound of the Dodge coming from Venneford as it carried Garrett into town on one or another of his missions.

Without betraying emotion, she listened as the car sped south, knowing that on its return it would not go by so swiftly, but would halt. Smiling to herself, she would clean the tables or make some refritos, and after a while she would retreat to her room, in the new section of the building, where she would comb her hair and tend her ribbons.

For half a year this desultory exchange continued; only once had the two touched hands, that day when he started to change records at the machine and she had reached for the needle. The effect had been electrifying, like the touch of disparate wires in the box which ignites the distant explosion.

One surprisingly warm day in January 1936 Henry drove into town, and when she heard the reassuring signal of his car, Soledad reacted in a new way. When he returned later and stopped for a drink, his first swift glance told him that she was not there. He drank his Coke, listened to the 'Ballad of Pancho Villa,' whose words he was beginning to know, and waited till the Mexicans threw General Pershing out. Disappointed at Soledad's absence, he climbed back into his car and drove north.

He had gone only a short distance when he saw Soledad standing boldly beside the road. Braking to a stop, he clicked open the door and she jumped in. With one wild sweep of her arms she embraced him, and whispered, 'Over there. Down the road.'

They drove westward along a trail that led to a broken dam which had once impounded the waters of Beaver Creek. When the car stopped, facing a swamplike area crowded with birds, she threw her arms about him again and kissed him passionately. They sat there a long time, indulging their hopeless affection for each other and watching the redwinged blackbirds as they alighted deftly on the tips of long-dead rushes. They spoke of conditions as they were, without magnification or vain hope, and they acknowledged how dangerous a game they had entered into.

'My brother might kill you,' she said. 'They are required to do that in Mexico, you know.'

'I'm not afraid of your brother,' he said. And then came the question which so tantalizes men in love with girls they cannot marry: 'How is it you're not already married?'

'I've been waiting,' she said, offering no further explanation.

They contrived to meet in strange places, and once when Ruth Mercy Garrett was in Denver, Henry actually spirited Soledad into the Venneford castle, where in one of the towers they pretended no longer. In a flood of passion they undressed and lay on an ancient buffalo robe brought there by Oliver Seccombe.

They made love for two hours, and when they crept out of the castle, praying that no one had seen them, their lives were tangled and lost. Now, when Garrett entered the cantina, he made no attempt to hide his savage disappointment if she was not there. They drifted into playing certain records, particularly 'Serian las Dos,' about the girls who no longer were content to eat tortillas.

In this accidental manner Henry Garrett became the first Anglo in Centennial to discover that the Mexicans had their own sweet, stable patterns of society, and that in some strange way they tended to find a happiness with nature that the Anglos missed. There were not many men in the region as totally stable as Triunfador Marquez, not many young women who vibrated to the whole of life the way his sister Soledad did. Off to a wretched corner by themselves, living in hovels, these quiet people arranged a world that gave them dignity and a kind of rude repose. In places like Denver, Santa Fe, San Antonio and Centennial they evolved a placid, self-sustaining pattern of life, creating values of peace and joy which in years to come the Anglos would seek and not find.

A marvelous symbiosis of English and Spanish culture might have evolved in these decades if it had been encouraged or even permitted to flourish, but there was almost no Anglo who could even comprehend that such a thing was possible, so the two races lived apart in deepening suspicion.

Still rejected by white Catholics, the Mexicans turned inevitably to exotic religions, and Henry Garrett would never forget the wintry Sunday afternoon when the Children of God in the Mountains outraged the honest citizens of Centennial by appearing with a brass band in the public square to conduct religious worship.

Soledad Marquez was there in a long white dress decorated with cheap red roses purchased from the J. C. Penney store. She was exquisite, there was no other word for it, Henry thought, a slim vision of a strange way of life. She marched arm in arm with two other girls almost as pretty

as she, and they were followed by other trios of men and women, and as
they swirled their way in a great circle around the square, the band
played and they chanted the hymn that best summarized their hopes:
'Con Cristo en el Mundo Otra Vez.'

The hymn had a compelling rhythm and many verses, all telling of
how life would be when Christ returned to the earth the next time:

> 'There will be justice then,
> And bread for all.
> And I shall have a new dress,
> And my sister shall have shoes.'

It would be such a different world when Jesus came back and looked at
the injustices under which his children labored. Then his brown-skinned
Mexicans would stand free of their oppressors, and there was even a
crude verse about the beet workers:

> 'With Christ in the world a second time
> There will be no short-handled hoes,
> There will be no telephone in the night,
> "Send Gómez back and steal his pay." '

Fortunately, the Anglos who watched the rhythmic procession did not
understand the words, but they nevertheless sent for the sheriff, and he
watched for just long enough to convince any sensible man that if these
Mexicans kept this up much longer, there was bound to be trouble.

'All right, all right!' he said amiably as he moved down the line, pulling people away. 'We don't conduct religious services in the street in this
town. That's what we have churches for.'

He wanted no trouble, certainly not on a Sunday, and he did nothing
to cause any. He merely tugged and pulled at the marchers, breaking up
their pattern while three of his men hustled the band onto a truck.

He had started in the middle of the procession and now the leaders
were coming past him. 'You there,' he called as he grabbed at the girl
on Soledad's right. 'You nuts stop this.'

He yanked the girl away, and this left Soledad alone, facing Henry
Garrett. To the established rhythm of the hymn she sang:

> 'With Jesus in the world a second time,
> Oh, things will be so different!'

He never saw her again. That night her brother bundled her into a car
and sent her out of Colorado.

When Garrett stopped at the cantina, looking for her, Triunfador told him bluntly, 'You'd better not come in here any more, Mr. Garrett. This is for Mexicans.'

'Where's Soledad?'

'It was you who forced her to leave.'

'Where . . . is . . . she?'

'Mr. Garrett, go home to your wife. She's crazy. But she's an Anglo.'

'I love your sister.'

'Well, she's gone. And what can we do about it, either of us?'

January 1936 was a time of great excitement for Timmy Grebe. His steer Rodeo had filled out handsomely and both he and Mr. Bellamy, who was coaching him, felt that the beautiful big Hereford might even have a chance to win top prize among the steers at the Denver show.

'It would mean a great deal to your parents, I needn't tell you,' Mr. Bellamy said as he helped Timmy groom the steer. 'The big restaurants in Denver like the publicity. They buy the prize steers and pay over a hundred dollars for them. To get their names in the papers . . . so that cattlemen will eat at their table, knowing the steaks will be good.'

Better than Mr. Bellamy, Timmy Grebe appreciated what the prize money would mean to his family. There never had been a year worse than this one. The whole world had gone wrong, Timmy thought, and he listened with dismay whenever his family gathered to discuss what might be done.

For his father he felt the deep shame that only a son could when he watched a man he loved unable to do anything right. 'The banks certainly won't lend us money,' Earl said, 'not after that sale.' They were grateful to Calendar, a man they scarcely knew, for having given them a second chance. 'But we still have no money to operate,' Grebe said to his family. 'What in decency can we do?'

For his mother Timmy felt only a deep burning compassion. It caught at his guts to see her working so hard, to see her gaunt thinness and the lack of joy in her deep-sunk eyes. Oh, dearest God, he prayed each night. Let me win so that I can give her the money.

Once he left his bed around two in the morning and went to his mother, and he lay beside her for some time, telling her that he was going to do something for her, but he felt her trembling the way she used to do, and he crept back to his own bed bewildered, for she had said not a word to him.

The week before the Denver show he cut school altogether and stayed at home, polishing the hoofs of his steer, grooming him and trimming his hair. The animal looked so handsome, his white face gleaming against his red body, that on the last afternoon Timmy grabbed him around the neck and whispered, 'Last year I didn't do much, but I sure wasn't scared. You aren't scared, are you?' Rodeo chomped away, his big bland face and wide eyes indicating that he had never known fear.

Mr. Bellamy arranged for a local farmer to truck Rodeo down to Denver, and Timmy said that he would ride inside with the steer, to be sure that Rodeo did not bump against the sides, and he ran home to fetch blankets to place against the wood. When he got there he found his mother in the kitchen, rummaging among the cutlery, and he barely had time to shout, 'I feel it, Mom. I'm going to win.' She looked at him in a blank way he had never seen before and said in a hollow voice, 'We are past the stage of winning.' He wanted to talk with her, but the truck was waiting.

It was an exciting ride in to Denver on that cold January day. Rodeo shifted his feet to maintain balance while Timmy watched the blankets to be sure his steer did not bruise himself. The driver stopped at a diner in Brighton and asked Timmy if he'd like a Coke. When they went inside, the man announced to other stockmen who had gathered there, 'I'm hauling the champion into Denver, that's what I'm doing.'

One of the men said, 'Aren't you the kid that got the special calf last year?' and for the first time in his life Timmy had that rare joy of being remembered for something he had done, and he nodded quietly.

'I'd like to see what you've done with that steer,' the man said, and Timmy led them all to the rear of the truck, where they inspected Rodeo, and several said, 'You know, you just might have the champion there,' and Timmy climbed back in beside his Hereford.

Judging the steers would take place at ten the next morning, and at five Timmy was in the stall with Rodeo. He gave the big steer a bath, then shampooed his coat and washed away the suds. He dried him with a pair of towels, then combed and curried for an hour. He had wax for the hoofs and a small pair of scissors to cut away stray hairs. When the bell rang at five to ten, Rodeo was in the handsomest condition possible, and when Timmy led him into the ring, the beautiful Hereford moved with weighty grace, plumping his powerful feet in stately rhythm. Several stockmen's wives, who knew a good steer when they saw one, applauded.

The judging required almost half an hour, for other boys had done an equally good job with their calves, and some of their steers were heavier than Timmy's, but none were of such perfect conformation, and in the end the judges agreed unanimously that Rodeo was champion. If Timmy had not cried in defeat last year, he certainly was not going to do so in victory. Clenching his teeth, he stood quietly, holding the halter in his left hand, but when the official photographs were taken and the noise was over, he could no longer contain himself, and with a cry of joy he threw his arms about Rodeo's placid neck. It was this photograph, taken accidentally by a lingering newsman, that would soon flash around the world, a compelling shot of triumph and heartbreak.

Timmy wished that his parents had a phone, because he wanted to inform them immediately of his victory. Even more, he longed to tell his mother that he would be bringing her at least one hundred dollars—that is, if the auction went as expected.

It did. When Timmy led Rodeo into the auction ring the man in charge took the loudspeaker and said, 'Gentlemen, most of you were here last year when this boy Timmy Grebe put up a great fight in the Catch It, Keep It contest. He failed, but he was awarded a calf anyway, and that judgment has been justified, for here he comes with the best steer in his class.' Then he dropped his voice and added, 'I don't need to tell you that he is the brother of Ethan Grebe, our heroic bus driver.'

The audience cheered and Mr. Bellamy, who had come down for the sale, smiled proudly. The bidding was lively, a contest between the Albany Hotel, the cattlemen's headquarters, and the Brown Palace, the place where rich people went for their steaks. In the end it was the Brown Palace that won with a bid of $145. After the auctioneer's modest fee, Timmy would take $140 back to his family.

He rode home with Mr. Bellamy, and when they reached Brighton he insisted upon stopping at the diner where they'd had Cokes the day before. Loungers were delighted to greet the champion. When he reached Line Camp he told Mr. Bellamy, 'I'll walk home. I could never have won without your assistance.' He liked big words but had been afraid to use them before this night, but now he was a champion, taking real money home to his mother.

Mr. Bellamy understood that on this night the boy wanted to be by himself, so he drove him to the point where the path started and watched with satisfaction as young Timmy started walking north over the prairie.

There was a moon, and the night was gentle. In all directions the great plains stretched silently and for the first time Timmy understood why his father had loved this land, this cruel yet compelling emptiness. It commanded attention, and there were still ways to control it. When the rains came back this would be mighty again, and he and his father would wrestle with it, for it was the noblest part of earth.

When he reached the slight rise from which the farmhouse first became visible, he was disturbed that no light was showing, because when one of the children was out, the Grebes always kept a lamp burning. But he remembered that his mother had been distraught that morning—the wind and the dust and the loneliness had finally worn her down—so it was not surprising if she had forgotten, but as he neared the house he saw the gate standing open, and this was something his father never allowed.

He became frightened and started to run and when he came upon the hideous scene he screamed. He just stood in the yard, screaming, and no one there to hear, and he continued screaming for timeless minutes, a boy torn out of his mind.

Then he started running again, mumbling and sobbing and striking himself with his fists, and he came at last to the Volkemas', and Magnes heard him first, thinking him to be a coyote howling in the night, but then Vesta heard him and she lit a lamp and cried, 'I do think it's a boy down there. It's Timmy,' and she opened the window and heard his terrible wailing cry, 'Oh, oh! They're all dead.'

'What must have happened,' said Sheriff Bogardus after the bodies had been hauled away, 'when Timmy seen her in the kitchen as he was driving off to the stock show, she was hunting for a butcher knife. Well, she found it, and I judge she killed her daughter Victoria first. Cut her head nearly off. Then she went for the two other girls, Eleanore and Betsy. The boy Larry must have seen some of this, because he started to run away, but she caught him in the yard and stabbed him many times. That musta been the first body that Earl saw when he came in from the fields, and when he went inside and saw the three girls and his wife still with the butcher knife . . . because it was in her hands when we found her . . . Well, he went sort of wild too, and he grabbed a shotgun and held it pretty close to her head and fired. Then he went back to the yard, picked up his son and laid him where we found him, then put the muzzle in his own mouth and pulled the trigger.'

There were pictures of the bodies, of course, decently covered with sheets, and they were accompanied by that chance shot of Timmy Grebe embracing his prize Hereford. To the easterner this display was a gripping contradiction: a little boy triumphing at the moment when his family was being slaughtered. But to the westerner, who had known the great winds and seeping dust, it was a self-portrait. The bad years were ending, but they had exacted a terrible cost.

Timmy went to live in the stone house with Mr. Bellamy. The Grebe place was sold to Philip Wendell, who was buying up any farmland that was being vacated by discouraged homesteaders, and he paid the going price: three thousand dollars for 1,280 acres plus the house, with the soddy thrown in.

Wendell had a clear vision of what lay ahead for this region and the courage to back his judgment with such money as his father had accumulated. He saw that in spite of the recent disasters, Dr. Creevey had been right. These apparent drylands could grow wheat, enormous quantities of it in any year when the normal thirteen inches of rain fell.

'You don't plow this land deep,' Wendell told the farmers he employed to work his fields, 'and for certain, when you do plow, you never, never harrow. We don't want fields that look like billiard tables. We don't want those long, straight rows. Nobody who works for me will ever again compete in those silly plowing contests. On our land we're going to plow

along the contours. And we are certainly going to leave strips of unplowed grass, big wide strips in every field to slow down the wind.'

He saw now that the Line Camp families could have survived the
great drought of 1930–36 if only they could have prevented their fields
from blowing away. 'They might've had one or two years on skimpy
rations, but they could've survived. Look at the Volkemas. Never borrowed money. Spent every cent they earned for more land. Now they
have four thousand acres and they're in great shape.' He had tried to
buy the Volkema farm, and Magnes had been willing to sell, but Vesta
had snapped, 'If we wouldn't sell to your crooked father in bad years,
why should we sell to you when times are good?' and he had countered,
'I thought you wanted to leave for California,' and Magnes had said,
'California's the land beyond the rainbow, and we haven't had many
rainbows here.'

Philip Wendell worked on one abiding principle: the rain would come
back. The Grebe farm, for example, would once more produce thirty
bushels to the acre. Maybe not in 1937, but in 1938 for sure. He therefore scraped together extra money to engage in one great gamble, after
which he would quit and move to Florida, the way other rich people in
the state were doing.

He now controlled some sixty thousand acres, most of it inherited
from his father, and if two rainy years came side by side, he would plant
so much wheat that the people in these parts would be stunned. He
didn't mean three hundred acres. He was thinking of thirty thousand
this year, and thirty thousand the next, on land that had lain fallow.

This strategy was based on fact and intuition. It was a fact that high
winds could be controlled. It was a fact that hail struck only one year in
five. It was a fact that rain must return. Where his brilliance lay was in
his intuition that before long the world was going to want wheat, lots of
it, and that prices would have to rise to two dollars a bushel.

Figure it out, he argued with himself. If I risk thirty thousand acres
and grow thirty bushels to the acre, I'm looking at nine hundred thousand bushels of wheat. And if something big happens to drive wheat up
to two dollars, we're talking about a million and a half dollars. Those
people in Denver can't even imagine such figures.

What was the 'big thing' he hoped for? He never specified, but he
sensed that with Adolf Hitler, Benito Mussolini, Josef Stalin and that
idiot Roosevelt making fools of themselves, something was bound to
happen. What it would prove to be he could not guess, but he knew
that in any crisis, people needed wheat, and he would be in a position
to supply it.

In the fall of 1937 he planted an incredible number of acres in wheat,
being careful to keep his fields scattered and never to use the same
plowman more than once. He did not want anyone to discover the great
risk he was taking, for he had found that bankers and their associates

liked to knock a man in the head when he was too far extended. When the seed was in the ground, he started to pray.

He told his wife, 'If God will give us just twenty inches of snow, we'll make it.' He studied the weather, watched every cloud, and by the first of April, concluded that the gamble had failed. The rainfall was below average and he was not going to make much more than nine bushels to the acre. Yet he was not discouraged, for the price of a bushel of wheat rose to a gratifying ninety-one cents and at the end of the spring harvest he said to his wife, 'We got by. We may not have made much, but at least we didn't lose.' She was relieved, for the pressures upon them had been great, and she supposed that with his lucky break he would quit the gamble. But not at all.

In the fall of 1938 he planted not thirty thousand acres, but forty. If moisture failed him this year, he might go bankrupt, and again he prayed for snow. Even the slightest flurry consoled him and when a real blizzard blew in for three hours, piling the snow deep, he ran into the midst of it, relishing the wet flakes as they struck his face.

He became almost maniacal, doing ridiculous things in the hope that they might bring rain or snow. He burned automobile tires, believing that their smoke activated clouds, and he hired an airplane to scatter grains of sand from a high altitude. Ironically, a good sixteen inches of rain did fall before the end of the growing season.

Near to collapse, he fell onto the davenport in the front room of his mansion in Centennial one day in March and told his wife, 'I couldn't stand the anxiety of another year like this. I've had dizzy spells. I'm a living corpse.'

'You promised this'd be the last year,' she said.

'You don't need to remind me,' he told her. 'I'd never go through this again.'

And as soon as the crop was harvested and sold, at a modest profit, he started making plans to unload his land and quit the wheat business altogether. He talked with a variety of buyers and found a banker in Denver who wanted to speculate in dry-land farming. As the gentleman explained, 'I think that with enough land, I can get not only a wheat crop but substantial payments from the government—soil bank, contour plowing, things like that.'

In a way Wendell felt regrets at not being in on the killing which he knew had to come. 'We'll live to see three-dollar wheat,' he told his wife, but she replied, 'No backing down,' and he assured her, 'Not me. I'm willing to let someone else make the profit.'

He would be far from destitute. Take that farm he had picked up from the Grebe boy after the tragedy. He had paid three thousand for it and a banker from Chicago was offering twenty. Not all of his deals had worked so well, but he would quit Centennial with more than a million dollars, which wasn't bad for a boy who had reached town with a traveling theatrical group.

He spent July and August working out the details of the transactions which would move his property into the hands of others. No specific deals were concluded, because the men he was negotiating with were on vacation, but come September the arrangements would be terminated quickly.

'We're out from under,' he told his wife with real relief during the last week of August. 'I feel years younger, and we should have a great time in Florida. Morgan's going to love the beach, and I'm told the University of Florida is almost as good as Colorado.' His son was eleven at the time and excited at the prospect of living in a tropical climate.

And then, on Thursday night, the last day of August 1939, rain began to fall, and when Philip Wendell went to bed he told his wife, 'Just our damned luck! I'm selling the farms tomorrow, and tonight it rains.' From their bedroom window he looked at the rain, a real downpour that would fill the fields prior to the fall planting. 'Well,' he said, 'our bad luck is somebody else's good luck. In my bones I know this is the beginning of a wet cycle. Somebody's going to make the millions, and I wish it were us.'

'Philip, go to sleep.'

He couldn't. All night he tossed uneasily, brooding about the fortune he was throwing away, the retreat he was making just when the drylands were about to come into their own. It wasn't fair. His parents had committed murder to gain a foothold in this town and with a sure nose his father had sought out the good lands. Old Mervin Wendell had sensed the destiny of this region and now his son was throwing away the advantage.

For some reason he could not later explain, Philip Wendell rose from his bed while the rain was still falling and dawn was not yet at hand. He went downstairs to review the sales papers he would be signing tomorrow, to assure himself that he had gotten top dollar for each of the parcels, and when he turned on the radio he heard the electrifying news from Europe:

At dawn this morning, Friday, September 1, Adolf Hitler marched into Poland. Protected on the flanks by the treaty signed recently with Soviet Russia, the Germans are on their way to Warsaw. Polish forces are reported to be fighting gallantly, but . . .

The first thing Wendell thought, recalling the many Russians he had done business with, was, Sooner or later, he'll have to fight Russia.

From this intuition he never wavered, and on it he began to construct the probable course of events: the stalemate, the American involvement, Japan up to something in the Pacific, the confusion which must entangle all nations.

'This could go on for years!' he muttered, pacing up and down, listening to the reassuring rain. 'America's got to stumble in. And everybody will want wheat. The rain and the war! It's what I knew would happen.'

Without consulting his wife, he began calling real estate men in the region, rousing them from bed and offering to buy whatever dry-land farms they had on their lists. 'I'll bring the check before nine o'clock,' he told them. 'I know that's early, but I want to close the deal.' When one of the agents said, 'I have some fine irrigated farms, Philip,' he snapped, 'They're for men afraid to gamble. Real men fight the drylands.'

His wife, hearing his raised voice, came down in her nightgown to find her husband telephoning, one after another, the men who had been planning to buy his farms: 'Deal's off, Garrett. I've decided to hold on to the land.' Pause. 'Yes. I know we shook hands, but we signed no papers. The deal's off. Going to farm it myself.'

'What are you doing?' his wife asked in dismay. Morgan, having been awakened by the noise, came sleepy-eyed into the room and asked, 'What's happening, Daddy?'

'The world's changed,' Philip said. 'Overnight, everything's changed.' He flicked on the radio, and they heard the solemn announcements from London, and Morgan said in awed tones, 'Golly, it's a real war!'

His mother, now able to view this day's events from her husband's perspective, took his hand and whispered, 'If the war lasts long enough, we could become . . .'

She was not allowed to finish her sentence, because Philip was speaking to his son. 'The earth gives you nothing, Morgan. It simply sits there and waits. It neither loves you nor hates you, but it does cooperate with men who are not afraid. Your grandfather bought nineteen farms and made eighteen of them pay because he understood land, and so do I, and so must you. Dust, drought, war . . . they're nothing. It's the land that counts, and starting today, you're to learn everything there is to know about it. Because this time the land is going to make us rich . . . very rich.'

CAUTION TO *US* EDITORS: This table, compiled for me by Walter Bellamy, shows what happened to agriculture at Line Camp in selected years. It is unique in that his crucial figures for rainfall refer not to the calendar year, like other tables, but to the actual growing season. Thus '1923 . . . 6″ ' means that the winter wheat which was harvested in the spring of 1923 had enjoyed during its entire year from May 1922 through April 1923 only six inches of moisture from rain and snow combined. These figures apply only to Line Camp. In a town like Centennial near the South Platte, moisture and yield per acre could have been much different.

Year	Inches Rain	Bushels Per Acre	Value Per Bushel	Value Head Cattle	Year	Inches Rain	Bushels Per Acre	Value Per Bushel	Value Head Cattle
1880	13	9	$1.05	$ 14.	1932	7	2	$ .37	$ 22.
1883	11	8	1.00	27.	1933	6	0	.65	16.
1896	14	9	.64	15.	1934	5	0	.84	15.
1911	15	8	.86	27.	1935	7	0	.90	14.
1913	19	18	.75	37.	1936	5	0	1.00	30.
1915	17	31	.87	46.	1937	12	10	.91	32.
1919	17	15	2.02	59.	1940	19	19	.62	38.
1923	6	2	.82	27.	1944	18	27	1.35	63.
1927	7	2	1.09	36.	1947	21	36	2.23	90.
1930	11	9	.61	51.	1952	13	30	2.11	177.
1931	8	6	.33	37.	1973	17	34	5.78	298.

Denver. You might want to do a nostalgic take-out on Denver as the mecca of the Mexican beet worker during the depression years. A good deal of animosity developed in this period, with Denverites claiming that the rural areas used the beet workers all summer, then threw them onto the Denver taxpayer during the winter. The problem was aggravated by the fact that many Mexicans preferred the congenial society that was possible in Denver, with specialized restaurants, cantinas, dances. But even if he did get to Denver, the lot of the Mexican was not idyllic, for he was penned into a narrow district between Jews on the one side, Italians on the other. The causeway near the railroad station was known as 'the longest bridge in the world, runs from Mexico to Israel.' Fights between the groups were constant. Even so, many older Mexicans now living in rural Colorado think back upon those winters in Denver as the happiest in their lives.

Depression. I have been reluctant to use this word in my report, because in Colorado the phenomenon had a contradictory application. On the plains where duststorms struck, this period was one of the bleakest in American history and not even dramatic exaggeration could convey the anguish of some of the stories from that period. On the other hand, in the high country back of the Rockies there remain to this day people who ask, 'What depression? We had no dust, no drought. We could always butcher a beef or go out and kill an elk or a deer. We saw no hobos, no unemployed. We didn't buy new cars, but no one starved. We never saw anyone selling apples, and with us there were no sheriff sales.' On large spreads like the Venneford Ranch, cowboys often had to go without wages, but they kept their bunks, their horses, their jobs and some very good food. It was places like Line Camp that had the heart kicked out of them. I have photographs of nine communities like it that are now ghost towns, of more than a hundred isolated farms whose once-proud houses are falling into ruin. My photographs of the deserted churches, white and stark against the sky, are almost too painful to look at. On the plains there was a depression, and the visible consequences terrify the beholder even today.

Scandal. You may feel obligated to cover the one occasion in which Centennial achieved nationwide publicity, all of it bad. In the spring of 1948 the Patriotic Order of the Women of the West, Centennial chapter, announced an All-American Citizenship award for high school seniors. By every criterion the prize had to be awarded to an outstanding athlete-scholar-leader, Jesus Melendez, but when his name appeared in the *Clarion* as the nominee, a Mrs. Wentworth Carver, president of the statewide P.O.W.W., stated flatly, 'The true American ideals of this great nation were generated by those gallant forebears of English stock who settled our eastern seaboard, and it was not the intention of our society to bestow its medal upon some Mexican immigrant who is probably in our state illegally to begin with.' Well, as you may remember, the whole nation got into the act, heaping ridicule on Mrs. Carver, but national scorn was not needed to reverse the damage she had done. Philip Wendell, an extreme conservative, excoriated her statement and Walter Bellamy pointed out to a reporter from the *Chicago Tribune*, 'The Melendez family has lived in Colorado much longer than Mrs. Carver's family has lived in the United States. Besides, his older brother Fidel gave his life for this nation at Anzio.' The most telling blow, however, came from the schoolchildren of Centennial. Acting on their own, they passed a resolution drafted by one of the Takemoto girls: 'If Jesus is denied the prize, it must not be awarded at all, because no one else in this school is half as worthy of it as him.'

NOVEMBER
ELEGY

```
                                                                   ⎧ John Garrett
                                            Messmore Garrett       ⎨ 1810–1881
                                            1849–1904              ⎩ Prudence Messmore
                          ⎧ Beeley Garrett                           1814–1887
                          ⎨ 1870–1938                               ⎧ Patrick Beeley
                          ⎪                 Jane Beeley             ⎨ 1806–1856
                          ⎪                 1855–1914               ⎩ Helen Garrett
          ⎧ Henry Garrett ⎩                                          1810–1880
          ⎨ 1895–1958                                              ⎧ Levi Zendt
          ⎪               ⎧                Martin Zendt            ⎨ 1820–1887
          ⎪               ⎪                1849–1911               ⎩ Lucinda McKeag
          ⎪               ⎨ Pale Star Zendt                          1827–1890
          ⎪               ⎪ 1874–1939                              ⎧ Red Wolf
          ⎪               ⎩                Prudence Wolf           ⎨ 1831–1897
          ⎪                                1866–1936               ⎩ Pale Star
┌──────────────────┐                                                1842–1912
│ PAUL GARRETT     │
│ 1927-            │
└──────────────────┘                                               ⎧ Maxwell Mercy
          ⎪                                Pasquinel Mercy         ⎨ 1811–1891
          ⎪               ⎧                1850–1876               ⎩ Lisette Pasquinel
          ⎪               ⎪                                          1817–1883
          ⎪               ⎨ Paul Mercy                             ⎧ John Skimmerhorn
          ⎪               ⎪ 1877–1933                              ⎨ 1838–1906
          ⎨ Ruth Mercy    ⎩                Laura Skimmerhorn       ⎩ Martha Deal
          ⎪ 1906–1973                      1858–1903                 1841–1908
          ⎪                                                        ⎧ Tom Lloyd
          ⎪               ⎧                James Lloyd             ⎨ 1834–1864
          ⎪               ⎪                1854–1924               ⎩ Emma Staller
          ⎪               ⎨ Nancy Lloyd                             1840–1891
          ⎩               ⎪ 1890–1933                             ⎧ Henry Buckland
                          ⎩                Charlotte Buckland     ⎨ 1822–1888
                                           1852–1935              ⎩ Evelyn Buckland
                                                                    1827–1866
```

I SPENT THE MONTH OF OCTOBER 1973 searching Centennial for some man or woman whose life epitomized the history of the west. I wanted to send the *US* editors in New York a kind of capstone to our project, a detailed and intimate portrait of what westerners were doing and thinking about in these critical years prior to our national birthday celebration.

At first I focused on Centennial's black barber, Nate Person, grandson of the only black cowboy ever to have ridden point on the Skimmerhorn Trail. The story of how this family achieved its position of love and leadership in my small western town was an American epic.

Then I shifted to Manolo Marquez, descendant of those redoubtable Mexicans, Tranquilino and Triunfador. He had a fascinating story to tell of breaking through prejudice and winning a solid place for himself. But these were special cases, and their association with Centennial began rather late in its history. I needed someone more deeply rooted in the community, and more typical. And then, on the last day of the month, I found my perfect prototype.

Early in the morning on November 1 I was breakfasting in a corner of the large room at Venneford Castle. Three moose heads, long undusted, stared down at me as I chatted with Paul Garrett, forty-six years old, tall and graying at the temples. He was one of the most perceptive men in Colorado, and a leader in many fields.

What attracted me to him especially was his combination of seriousness and self-deprecating good humor. For example, as I finished my tar-flavored cup of tea he told me, 'My family has always favored that strange-smelling stuff. My grandmother, Pale Star . . . She was an Arapaho Indian you know . . . she said it tasted to her like charred jockstrap.'

'Who were your grandparents?' I asked, and he produced from his cluttered desk a standard breed book in which he kept track of his prize Herefords.

'I've already studied the history of the Venneford bulls,' I told him, but he said, 'Not this one,' and he opened the book to a page which he had filled out about himself, as if he were a Hereford. It showed his ancestors back to the fifth generation, and after I had studied it for a few minutes, I was confirmed in my earlier opinion that here was the man I needed to complete my report.

The Garretts had started in sheep, it is true, but they'd had the good sense to shift over to cattle. Paul had army people like the Mercys in his ancestry, and frontiersmen like Pasquinel. One branch of his family had been English, so he would know that interesting aspect of western development, and another branch was Indian.

'Garrett, Messmore and Buckland were of English stock,' he told me as I put the book down. 'The Lloyds were a Welsh family that emigrated to Tennessee and Texas. Patrick Beeley was a hard-drinking Irishman. Pasquinel and Mercy were French, and writers usually ignore the French influence in western history. Zendt, Skimmerhorn, Staller and Bockweiss were Germans. Deal was Dutch, but originally he spelled his name a different way. Red Wolf and Pale Star were full-blooded Indians. Lucinda McKeag, whom everyone seemed to love, was the daughter of a squaw named Clay Basket, about whom the mountain men wrote in their diaries.'

'Pretty mixed up,' I said.

'Damned near incestuous,' he confessed. Then he slapped the breed book and said, 'If you follow the history of the really great bulls, you'll find many instances of very close in-breeding. My case, the same way. A son of Lucinda McKeag married the daughter of her brother. Messmore Garrett married his first cousin. And Henry Buckland, father of the formidable Charlotte you've spoken about so often, married his niece, if you please.'

Before I could respond to this last bit of information, the telephone rang and an elderly Mexican serving woman shuffled in to report, 'It's very important.' And she handed him the phone from his desk.

It was the new governor of Colorado, eager to share some exciting news: 'At my ten o'clock press conference this morning I'm announcing your appointment as head of our executive committee responsible for the state centennial celebration.' This was a greater honor than a stranger might have appreciated, because Colorado alone of the fifty states would be celebrating in 1976 not only the two-hundredth birthday of our nation but also the hundredth anniversary of the state.'

'This fits in perfectly,' I said when I heard the news. 'What I'd like to do, Mr. Garrett, is to follow you around a bit. For a couple of weeks. Listen in as you conduct your business . . . give my editors a feeling for what a westerner is doing these days. If you wouldn't mind, I wish you'd carry this tape recorder with you when I'm not there. Just in case there's something you'd like to get off your chest.'

'A month ago I'd have said no,' he replied. 'It isn't easy, Vernor, when your wife dies. Not even when you haven't been really married, which was my case, as you may have heard.'

'I've heard a good deal about you,' I said. 'I'd like to know more.'

'If the tape recorder works, you may know a helluva lot more.' He insisted on my staying for lunch, and as we ate beneath the moose heads, word of his appointment penetrated to various corners of the state, and his phone began jangling, with citizens from the western slope of the Rockies demanding to know if they were to form part of the twin celebrations, or if they were as usual to play second fiddle to the greater concentrations of population along the front range. 'Of course you're counted in,' he assured them. 'First thing I do tomorrow is drive across the mountains to consult with you. Get your crowd together. Decide what you want, and I'll have dinner with you tomorrow night . . . in Cortez.'

On November 2 he got me out of bed early, filled his gray Buick at the ranch gasoline pump and headed for the mountains. There had been rumors that gas rationing might be imposed, and perhaps a speed limit of fifty miles an hour. 'Impossible speed for the west,' he muttered as he settled the car into its normal cruising speed of eighty. By the route we had planned, the day's drive would cover some six hundred miles, but with the excellent roads that crisscrossed Colorado, this was a short trip for a western driver. Cutting onto the interstate west of Venneford, we roared south toward Denver, skirted that city and headed into the high passes at ninety miles an hour.

We had gone only a short distance when Garrett saw something which had always pleased him. It demonstrated the imaginative manner in which Colorado had confronted some of its problems, for in the building of the interstate the engineers had to cut through a tilted geologic formation, and instead of simply bulldozing a path through the little mountain, they had made an extremely neat cut which exposed some twenty geological strata. A park had been built around the multicolored edges, so that schoolchildren could wander across the steep slopes of the cuts and actually touch rocks which had formed two hundred million years ago. They could inspect the purple Morrison formation in which the dinosaurs had been found, and could see how layers of sea deposit had been thrust upward when the Rocky Mountains erupted. 'This is one of the best things accomplished in Colorado in the past twenty years,' Garrett told visitors, 'and it cost practically nothing. Just some imagination.'

He loved driving, for he responded to the motion of the car as it leaned gracefully into the well-banked curves. There was a kinesthetic beauty about pushing a quietly running automobile through the mountains, and it helped him sense the quality of the land he was traversing. Looking above him as he sped along, he saw once more the noble peaks of Colorado. Often he had astonished eastern visitors by asking, 'You've surely heard of Pikes Peak. How many mountains in Colorado are higher? Give a guess.'

Many easterners had never heard of Colorado's other mountains, and they were always surprised when he told them, 'We have fifty-three mountains higher than fourteen thousand feet—many, many more than any other state. Pikes Peak is a mere hill. It's number thirty-seven on the list—only 14,111 feet high.' Even Longs Peak, which his family had always called Beaver Mountain, was no more than fifteenth on the list. This was truly a majestic state.

He kept his foot well down on the throttle as we roared toward Eisenhower Tunnel, highest major tunnel in the world; it would take us deep beneath the Continental Divide and at its western end bring us into some of the loveliest valleys on earth. Here new ski centers were being developed, and he stopped briefly at several to alert the proprietors that he expected them to contribute some topnotch sports events for the celebration.

At Vail, where we halted for midmorning coffee, sixteen local leaders met with him, showing him the imaginative plans they had developed for the centennial. He liked the people of Vail and was impressed with their energy. Some years ago the ecologists had feared that the proliferation of ski resorts might ruin the mountains, but he had supported the ski runs, for he saw mountains as places for recreation, a locale in which city people could escape their pressures, and he had been right. A properly planned ski resort did not scar the landscape; it made the rewards of nature available to more citizens—but only if enough primitive area was held inviolate. Whenever the Vail plans threatened the wilderness, Garrett would have to oppose them.

'If you want new runs along the highway, I'll support you,' he promised. 'But on your plans to commercialize the back valleys, I've got to oppose you.'

Since he had championed the resort in previous applications, the Vail people accepted his veto, and as we left he assured them, 'We've got no budget yet, but when we get one, I'll allocate funds for planning. You're on the right track.'

We now doubled back to Fairplay, a beautiful village surrounded by mountain peaks, and there Garrett encouraged the leaders to come up with their own ideas. Then we crossed a series of trivial bridges which always pleased him, for under them ran those minute rivulets which formed the headwaters of the Platte. Here, high in the Rockies, these clear, sweet streams ran through alpine meadows; it seemed impossible that they could coalesce to form the muddy serpent that crawled across the plains.

Then came one of the most enjoyable parts of the drive, a long leg south through those exquisite valleys that so few travelers ever saw, with giant mountains on both sides and the road pencil-straight for fifty miles at a time. He drove at ninety-five and felt his heart expanding as the Sangre de Cristo Range opened up before us to the east. He had known Tranquilino Marquez before the old man died and had once heard him tell of the impression this desert road had made on him when he first came north from Old Mexico to work in the Centennial beet fields. 'It was like the finger of God drawing a path into the mountains,' the old man had said.

At the end of the valley we turned west and soon found ourselves driving along a river not often recognized as a Colorado stream. It was the Rio Grande, tumbling and leaping as it dropped out of the mountains, and as he watched its whirlpools he reflected on the crucial role his state played in providing water for the nation. Four notable rivers had their birth in the Colorado uplands—Platte, Arkansas, Rio Grande, Colorado—and what happened there determined life in neighboring states like Nebraska, Kansas, Texas, New Mexico, Arkansas, California, and even Old Mexico. Colorado was indeed the mother of rivers.

Now Garrett flicked on an invention which in recent years had given him much delight, a cassette player built into the Buick, one into which the driver inserted a small plastic cassette containing ninety minutes of music recorded on tape. Two speakers at the rear of the car provided a stereophonic effect, and as the car headed west for the Spanish country, the cassette poured forth a flood of luscious sound. The sensation of driving ninety-five miles an hour over flawless roads, with towering mountains watching over you while music reverberated through the car was a sensuous joy.

Today, and for some time past, Garrett played only Chicano songs. Some years ago he had formed the habit of taking his lunch, when in Centennial, at Flor de Méjico, the restaurant owned by Manolo Marquez, and there he had grown acquainted with the flamboyant folk music brought north by the Chicano beet workers, and the more of it he heard, the more he loved the rowdy, rambunctious rhythms. Now 'La Negra' echoed through the speeding car, a saucy, tricky beat. After that came 'La Bamba,' in which a girl singer with a provocative voice shouted, 'Soy capitán, soy capitán, soy capitán.' That was followed by 'Little Jesus from Chihuahua,' which he had grown to like very much, but then came the finer songs, the ones that caused him involuntarily to slow down.

'Las Mañanitas,' the birthday song with that totally strange beginning 'This is the song King David sang,' captivated him, and he always sang along. 'It must be the strangest birthday song in the world,' he told me, 'and the best.'

As for 'La Paloma' and 'La Golondrina,' they were songs of such ancient beauty that he wondered if any country had ever produced such appropriate popular music to summarize its contradictory longings: 'If a

dove should fly to your window, treat it with charity, for it is really me.'
No self-respecting American would dare write words like that, nor elect
them as a national symbol if he did.

Now the Buick was crawling along at forty-five, toward Wolf Creek
Pass, for the tape had come to that strange song which had possessed
him in recent months. No other person he had spoken to in the Anglo
community had ever heard of it, and only a few Chicanos knew it. 'Dos
Arbolitos' it was called, and he had it in two versions. The first, which
now drifted dreamily from the speakers, was played by an orchestra of
forty violins and a few wind instruments; it was quite unlike usual Chicano music, for although it bespoke a deep passion, it also had a sweet
gentleness. The melody was simple, with delightful rising and falling
notes and unexpected twists. It was the song which first awakened him
to the fact that Chicano music was something other than 'La Cucaracha'
and 'Rancho Grande.'

It was this song that had lured him on his first trip to Mexico, when
he had driven those desolate miles to Chihuahua and those flower-strewn
miles farther south. Places like Oaxaca had been a revelation to him,
and he had come home with two records of 'Dos Arbolitos,' one the
stringed version which he had just played and another in which two
voices, male and female, sang the sentimental words:

> 'Two little trees grow in my garden,
> Two little trees that seem like twins.'

The Buick had dropped to a mere forty while Garrett joined the singers,
tilting his head back and barely watching the road. When the song
ended, he leaned forward and reversed the tape until he felt it had returned to the starting point of the violin version, then released it to play
again. Once more 'Dos Arbolitos' sounded, and he sang with the violins.

We had a very late lunch at Pagosa Springs at the western end of
Wolf Creek Pass, where he met his first delegation of Spanish-speaking
citizens. He told them he wished he could address them in their own
language, but whereas he understood Spanish when they spoke it, his
attempts to respond were laughable.

'Let us laugh,' one of the Chicano leaders suggested, so he said a few
words. 'It's pretty bad,' the Chicano agreed.

He told them that in the forthcoming celebrations there would be an
honored place for Chicanos. 'We've heard that before,' they said with
some bitterness.

Montezuma and Archuleta had recently started a mock-serious separa-
tist movement, seeking to join New Mexico, since distant Denver never
gave a damn for their interests. 'That's all changed,' Garrett assured
them. 'The governor himself wanted me to come down here to tell you
of our plans.'

'Him, yes,' the Chicanos said. 'But what about his successor?'

'Those of us on the front range have learned our lesson. We know you exist.'

He made little impression on the suspicious men of Pagosa Springs, so late in the afternoon we headed for Durango, pausing there briefly before continuing to our final destination, Cortez, not far from that historic spot where four states meet, the only place in America where that happens. In Cortez we had a late dinner with leaders of the Chicano minority and talked with them late into the night.

On November 4, which was a Sunday, we made several extended tours with the Anglos of Cortez, and they showed us their plans for a ceremony at Four Corners, a bleak point in the desert but a place with considerable emotional appeal. 'I can imagine lots of Americans wanting to drive this way,' Garrett said, 'if we have something to offer them when they get here.'

On November 5 we headed back to Centennial by the northern route, and once more we roared along the spacious highways while Chicano music thundered from the cassettes. Again Garrett slowed down when it came time to sing along with 'Dos Arbolitos,' but after a while he turned off the machine, and during the long haul from Grand Junction to Glenwood Springs he discussed the difficult problem he would face the next day.

It was election day and Colorado would be the first state in the nation to face up to the future, for it was electing an officer of a new description. His title was resounding, Commissioner of Resources and Priorities, and his task was to steer the state in making right industrial and ecological choices. It was appropriate that Colorado should be the state to experiment with such a concept, for its citizens had always been pioneer types, willing to sponsor change. Colorado had led the nation in old-age pensions, proper funding of education, liberal labor laws, and it had been the state which turned down the 1976 Winter Olympics as destructive to the environment.

When one looked at the original settlers, men like Lame Beaver of the Arapaho, Levi Zendt of Pennsylvania, Potato Brumbaugh from Russia and Charlotte Buckland from England, it was no wonder that traditions of individualism had been established. Now the state would lead the nation in trying to define an acceptable use of its resources.

The new officer had already been dubbed the Czar, and tomorrow the first man to occupy the crucial office would be elected. Like most Coloradans, Garrett felt that the Republican party represented the time-honored values of American life and could be trusted to place in office men and women of probity who would remain above temptation. Whenever a Republican officeholder turned out to be a crook, as one or another did year after year, he explained away the affair as an accident.

On the other hand, he felt that in time of crisis, when real brains were needed to salvage the nation, it was best to place Democrats in office, since they usually showed more imagination. And when one Democrat after another proved colossally stupid, he termed that failure an accident too.

He was always willing to split his ticket, not wishing to be like the old beet farmer at Centennial who said, 'Me! I vote for the man not the party. Harding, Coolidge, Hoover, Landon, Willkie, Dewey, Eisenhower, Nixon, Goldwater.' For example, Garrett had voted for both John Kennedy and Lyndon Johnson, but looking back, suspected that he had made a mistake each time.

The preceding night, while we were watching television in his motel room, he found his politics becoming confused. Julie Nixon Eisenhower was shown defending her father. 'Fight, fight, fight. My father will never resign,' the attractive young lady proclaimed, and Garrett judged it to be improper for a father to use his daughter in such an undignified way. 'If he wants to defend himself,' he had growled at the television, 'let him do it himself . . . not hide behind his daughter's skirts.' He had voted for Nixon, had met him twice in Denver and had liked him, but now he told me, 'I'm beginning to wonder if the man can ever extricate himself from the morass he's fallen into.'

He found himself equally bewildered when he considered his choice on Tuesday. The Democrats had nominated for commissioner a lackluster man from the western slope, and it would be fairly easy to vote against him, except that the Republicans had chosen a man from Centennial, and to Garrett he was simply unacceptable.

The candidate was Morgan Wendell, born the same year as Garrett and a graduate in the same class from the University of Colorado. He was a wealthy man, his father having made a killing in wheat during World War II, and in business relations he was quite reliable. He had done well in college and had served the state in various capacities. It looked as if he would win handily, so that whether Paul Garrett voted for him or against him was of little moment.

But Garrett prized his vote. It seemed to him the noblest ritual of American life, and he had never failed to vote, nor had he voted carelessly.

The Buick slowed perceptibly as he asked himself, What is it about Morgan Wendell I don't trust? He put aside the secret gossip which had circulated within the Garrett family. Paul Garrett's grandfather, Beeley Garrett, had told the family, with Paul listening, that a Mr. Gribben, before he died, had confided that Maude and Mervin Wendell had stolen their first house from him by working the badger game.

'What's the badger game?' Paul had asked.

'It's when a man gets caught with his pants down in somebody else's bedroom and is afraid to admit it.' Grandfather Garrett had continued with the part of the story that worried Paul: 'We had a Swede come to town about that time, man named Sorenson, and he disappeared. A lot of his money was missing. Something that Sheriff Dumire told me at the time made me think that he suspected the Wendells of having done away with the man. I know for a fact that Dumire was on to something, but before he could settle it he was killed in a street fight.'

That was rumor, and Paul dismissed it as something that had happened more than eighty years ago. What possible difference did it make now? But the next charge was not rumor, and it was a harsh one. Paul's own father related the details when Paul was twelve years old.

It was on the first day of World War II, back in 1939, and the Garretts were having their usual early breakfast when the phone rang. It was Philip Wendell, the real estate man, and he had called to inform Paul's father that a deal they agreed upon—Henry Garrett would buy back four thousand acres which had once belonged to Crown Vee—was called off.

'But we shook hands on that deal, Philip,' Henry Garrett said. There was a brief silence, and then he said, 'Of course. There's nothing signed. You never brought me the paper. But doesn't your word mean anything?' Another silence, followed by Henry Garrett's shouting, 'You miserable son-of-a-bitch!' after which he slammed down the phone.

Returning to the breakfast table, he trembled for some moments, then turned to Paul, saying, 'Never in your life have anything to do with a Wendell. He went back on his word.'

'What does that mean?' Paul had asked.

'He shook hands with me, promised to go through with a deal at a price agreed upon. Something's happened whereby he can make a little more money, so he refuses to honor our agreement.'

'What could it be?' Paul's mother asked, but her husband ignored the question, and she left the room. Turning to his son, he shook hands formally and said solemnly, 'If you shake hands on anything, Paul, and then break your word, I do not care ever to see you again. The association of men is founded on honor, and no Wendell has ever understood that basic truth.'

'Henry,' his wife called. 'Listen to what the radio's saying!' And when the fact of war was known, Philip Wendell's revoking of his promise was understood. 'If he plants all that land in wheat,' Ruth Garrett said, 'he'll be very wealthy . . . if the war continues.'

'Let him have it,' her husband said with smoldering fury. 'Paul, never earn money that way. It's not worth it.'

From that time Paul Garrett had watched the Wendells with deepening interest, and he concluded that his father was right. The Wendells, none of them, had any basic sense of responsibility. At the university Morgan Wendell had done everything to ingratiate himself with older men in power—professors, athletic coaches, fraternity leaders, he had toadied to them all—but no one ever knew what principles he stood for, and on this program he prospered.

And in his adult life he had continued to prosper. Now he stood on the threshold of becoming an important official of a great state, and perhaps Paul Garrett was being overly cautious in wondering if he could vote for such a man. As we drove eastward toward the Eisenhower Tunnel he grabbed the tape recorder and started dictating, as if determined that I have an exact account of what he was disclosing:

> I don't trust him, Vernor. It's as simple as that. It's not the things his grandparents did . . . and I haven't told you that whole story because it really doesn't concern you. And it's not because his father was a sneaky operator, because I don't believe the sins of the father are visited on the heads of the sons. It's just that he's a low-grade individual without principle. He's a technician. He can perform. He can keep things from getting tangled. But in a crisis he'll have no base from which to operate. He believes in nothing. At the university he took no classes that made him think. He's never stretched his mind, because he's never faced himself . . . or the facts . . . or the future. And I think democracy can't function unless it's led by men and women who know what kind of people they are. How can you solve an equation if x is never known?

When we reached the interstate leading back to Greeley he drove at a hundred and five, telling me, 'Tomorrow I'll get up at dawn and figure this thing out. I'll saddle Bonnet and ride over to look at the Herefords.'

On Tuesday, November 6, Garrett did not get to the polls till late, because when he returned to the castle following his long ride, he was deeply agitated. For some time he sat alone, his head in his hands, pondering not the election, for on that his mind was fairly made up, but the painful confrontation he faced regarding his beloved Herefords. When he had seen those stalwart beasts in their distant pastures and watched as they moved slowly toward him, white faces shining against red coats, he felt a knife-thrust of pain as he recalled the vicissitudes he and his family had brought upon this noble breed. The Garretts had always acted in good faith where the Herefords were concerned. Great-Grandfather Jim Lloyd had loved them almost as dearly as he had loved his own daughter, and the ranch had always bought the top bulls, but somewhere things had got onto the wrong track, and now they must be corrected.

'I'd rather cut off my right hand,' Garrett said, and he meant it. He was about to make a phone call to Montana when he heard footsteps on the porch, and when he went out he found to his astonishment that Morgan Wendell, the presumptive Czar, was standing there.

'I had to vote early,' Morgan explained. His manager had told him, 'Be there at seven. I'll have photographers on hand, and we'll make all the afternoon papers.' He had stood by the voting machine with his wife, both of them smiling.

'I trust you're going to vote, Paul.'

'Never miss.'

'I hope you'll vote for me.'

'Isn't this rather late to be campaigning?'

'I'm not campaigning. It looks as if I'll win safely, and I don't give a damn how you vote.'

Garrett had made no move to invite Wendell into the castle, a place the real estate man had rarely visited, but this sharp rejoinder brought him to attention. 'What's the reason for the visit, Morgan?'

'Something very important, Paul.' The candidate hesitated, and Garrett said, 'Come on in,' and Wendell said, 'Thanks.'

As Garrett ushered him into the big room with the moose heads, Wendell said abruptly, 'Paul, you and I have never gotten along well, and I suppose that when you do vote, you'll vote for Hendrickson.' Garrett shrugged his shoulders but said nothing. 'What I'm here for is to tell you that I need your help . . . need it badly.'

'You just said you didn't give a damn.'

'On the voting . . . who cares? But on the morning after I'm elected—and I think I will be—I'm going to require some first-rate brains to help me out. No, don't interrupt. Brains are not my long suit. But sensing what's happening in the world is—anticipating what troubles people.'

'How does this involve me?'

'Most directly. The great problem in the next decade in Colorado will be to save the state. I really mean that. To save the forests, the trout, the elk—and especially things like the rivers and the air we breathe.'

Paul Garrett leaned back and studied his visitor. 'You know, Morgan, for the first time in your life you're talking sense.'

'I've learned it from men like you,' Wendell said. 'The first appointment I want to give to the press is my deputy, Paul Garrett.'

'It's a job I'd have to accept . . . if offered.'

'I knew you'd say that.'

'But, Morgan, I won't take it just to provide a façade for you. When you speak about ecology it's the popular word, the in-thing to do politically. And I have no objections, because men have to get elected. But when I use the word it summarizes my whole life. I may not be an easy man to live with.'

'That I understand,' Wendell said. 'Let's leave it this way. You make every decision about our natural resources just as you see it, and when you become totally intolerable, I'll fire you with a "Dear Paul" letter and replace you with someone a little more congenial. I judge we can tolerate each other for at least three years, and in that time the basic task can be started.'

'Sounds workable,' Garrett said. Then he thought of something that might prove disqualifying. 'You know, Morgan, that I'm testifying at the Calendar trial this week. It could prove sticky.'

Wendell lowered his head, for this was unpleasant news. The Calendar trial was bound to agitate voters across the state, and to have his deputy take sides was bound to be unsettling. 'Couldn't you duck that one, Paul?'

Garrett laughed. 'You see, even before you make the appointment you're asking me to draw back. Morgan, the Calendar trial is at the heart of all we've been talking about. Of course I can't duck it. Of course I'm going to embarrass you.'

'Maybe I could delay announcing your appointment. That would be reasonable.'

'Anything is reasonable,' Garrett said. 'Anything on God's earth can be given a reason. But if you delay, I won't accept the appointment. Can't you see, Morgan, I will always be a thorn in your side, because the protection of this state will invariably irritate people whom you want to placate . . . whom you must placate. It's going to be a dogfight every inch of the way. We know that. Question is, can we live with it?'

Wendell contemplated this forthright declaration of difference, then said, 'Your job will be to protect all the natural good things of this state, and I know you'll do it. My job is to see that industry gets a fair shake so there will be jobs and tax rolls. You conserve the water. I want every drop I can get for new cities and new factories. It will be difficult, and you want to make it worse by getting mixed up in the Calendar affair . . . infuriate every hunter in the state.'

'You wouldn't want me, Morgan, if I weren't committed on such issues.'

Morgan Wendell, facing the first difficult decision of his future administration, took a deep breath and said something which took Garrett completely off guard. 'Paul, do you know who my favorite American of all time was? Warren Gamaliel Harding. Because he came along at a lush period of our national life, when we had a comfortable margin for error. And he proved how horrible an elected official can be. He's a warning for all politicians. On the day we take office we all think of President Harding and we say to ourselves, "Well, I won't allow myself to be as bad as that." Harding keeps the ball game honest, and I judge him to be one of the most useful Americans who ever lived. I'm not going to be the Colorado Harding.'

'I'm having lunch in town,' Garrett said. 'At the Marquez place. Join me.'

So the first public appearance the Czar made was in the Flor de Méjico, with a man who was known to be cool toward his candidacy. It did Wendell a lot of good in the district, but shrewd politician that he was, he saw something that day which would aid him even more. He had an unusual gift for sensing what was going on in his vicinity, and as he entered the restaurant with Garrett he noticed that Paul hesitated in the doorway and looked in all directions, then walked to the table, plainly showing his disappointment.

Later in the meal Wendell was watching Garrett out of the corner of his eye and saw his future deputy's face brighten. Looking toward the kitchen, Wendell saw Manolo Marquez's daughter come in with an armful of dishes. Townspeople knew that she had been married in Los Angeles, but after only two weeks, she had returned home with a scar down the side of her face and grounds for divorce. Well, I'll be damned! he said to himself. Old blue-blood Garrett and a Chicano girl! That could make me very popular with the Chicano voters in the southwest. I will be damned.

That afternoon when Paul Garrett went into the secrecy of the polling booth and looked at the two names confronting him—Charles Hendrickson, a man who lacked every qualification that Democrats sometimes had, and Morgan Wendell, a man without the basic character expected in Republicans, he felt a great nausea. I'll be damned if I can vote for either of them, he decided, and after pulling the lever for one of the Takemoto boys who was running for school board and another lever for a German woman, he left the booth without voting for Czar on either ticket.

On the following day he began his series of inspection tours, those brief trips during which he simply looked at the land he would be protecting. His journeys east through the drylands sometimes brought tears to his eyes as he surveyed that chronicle of lost hope, but he was even more deeply distressed by what he saw along the front range from Cheyenne down to the New Mexico border:

> When I was a boy we had an old book, *Journey West* by John Brent of Illinois. He came this way in 1848, and I remember his writing in his diary that one morning, while they were still one hundred and five miles east of the Rockies, they could see the mountains so clearly they could almost spot the valleys. Look at them now! We're ten miles away and we can't see a damned thing—only that lens of filth, that curtain of perpetual smog. What must be in the minds of men that they are satisfied to smother a whole range of mountains in their aerial garbage? This must be the saddest sight in America.

South from Cheyenne, clear across Colorado, hung a perpetual veil of suspended contamination. The lens appeared to be seven hundred feet thick, composed of industrial waste, especially from the automobile. Week after week it hung there, stagnant. Had it clung to the ground, it would have imperiled human breathing and would have been treated as the menace it was, but since it stayed aloft, it merely blotted out the sun and dropped enough acid to make the eyes smart twenty-four hours a day.

From Centennial, Beaver Mountain was no longer visible, and whole days would pass with the cowboys at Venneford unable to see that majestic range which once had formed their western backdrop. Men who used to stand at the intersection of Mountain and Prairie, inspecting the Rockies to determine the weather, now had to get that information from the radio.

Garrett was especially perturbed about what had happened to Denver, once America's most spectacular capital, a mile-high city with the noblest Rockies looking down on the lively town, made prosperous by the mountains' yield of silver and gold. Now it was a smog-bound trap with one of the worst atmospheres in the nation, and the mountains were seen no more.

There were days, of course, when the contamination was swept aloft by some intruding breeze, making the peaks visible again for a few hours. Then people would stare lovingly at the great mountains and tell their children, 'It used to be this way all the time.'

During the past ten years Paul Garrett had often had the dismal feeling that no one in Denver gave a damn. The state had succumbed to the automobile, and any attempt to discipline it had seemed futile. Year after year, two citizens a day were killed by cars throughout the state, and no one did anything to halt the slaughter. Drunk drivers accounted for more than half these deaths, but the legislature refused to punish them. It was held that any red-blooded man in the west was entitled to his car and his gun, and what he did with either was no one else's business.

The west had surrendered to the automobile in a way it had once refused to surrender to the Indian, for the car in one year killed more settlers than the redman did during the entire history of the territory. The concrete ribbons ate up the landscape and penetrated to the most secret places. And if by chance some valley remained inviolate, the snowmobile whined and sputtered its way in, chasing the elk until they died of exhaustion. No place was sacred, no place was quiet, in no valley was the snow left undisturbed.

Paul Garrett, pondering these problems in the early days of November, made a series of promises: 'As Deputy Commissioner of Resources and Priorities I'm going to switch to a small car. I'm going to drive slower. Day and night I'm going to tackle the Denver smog. And I'm going to ban snowmobiles in every state forest.' Even so he feared that such measures might be too late, and he muttered sardonically, 'Pretty soon, if you want to see the unspoiled grandeur of Colorado you'll have to go to Wyoming.'

On Friday, November 9, Paul Garrett faced up to a most disagreeable task. He shaved carefully, dressed in a conservative business suit, and with his razor, trimmed some of the gray hair about his ears. This would be his first public appearance since the announcement of his appointment to the new position, and he wanted to make a good impression.

He drove to the Federal Court in Denver, where the trial of Floyd Calendar was to start. The judge was a small, alert man with a well-known sense of humor, and the contesting attorneys were men who typified the forces at stake in this case. The district attorney, representing the conservation forces of the nation, was a former athlete who could not in the slightest degree be termed a bleeding heart, while the defense attorney was a famous outdoors man, well known as a hunter and a rancher.

The accused was something else again. Floyd Calendar was a mean-looking, thin, heavily bearded man in his early sixties. He wore no tie and his suit seemed several sizes too large, even though he was a tall man. He had one tooth missing in front, which made his normally surly countenance almost sinister. Even so, he represented hunters, men who loved the outdoors and ranchers who sought to protect their livestock.

Calendar was involved in two serious crimes: shooting bald eagles, our national bird, from a plane and killing bears, an endangered species, in 'a cruel and unfair manner.'

The first prosecution witness was Harold Emig, from Centennial. The government lawyer wanted to use him to establish the kind of man Floyd Calendar was.

'He was a guide,' Emig said. 'First public job he had was putting parties together to shoot prairie dogs.'

'Are prairie dogs edible?' the prosecutor asked.

'Oh, no! You just shoot prairie dogs for the fun of it. Floyd knew where all the dog towns were. There aren't many these days, you know. And for a dollar a head he would take us out there, and we'd rim the prairie-dog town. We'd be on the west, you understand, so's the sun would be in the critters' eyes, and Floyd had drums and whistles and he knew how to make the little fellows stick their heads up, and when one did we'd blaze away.'

'How many dogs would you kill?'

'Well, on a good day when Floyd's whistles were working, each man would get maybe ten, twenty . . . that's not countin' probables.'

'What did you do with them?'

'Nothin'. A prairie dog ain't good for nothin'. You couldn't eat 'em. It was just the fun of seein' a little head pop up from the hole and blasting it with a well-aimed shot.'

'Does Mr. Calendar still conduct such hunts?'

'No, sir. After a while the dogs were pretty well cleaned out, and he turned to rabbit drives. You get sixty, seventy men with clubs and you range over a pretty large area, always closin' the circle, and in the end you have an excitin' time, everybody clubbin' rabbits to death.'

'I thought that was stopped some years ago.'

'Yeah. *Life* magazine slipped a photographer into one of Floyd's hunts and took pictures of the men . . . I was in the middle of one of the shots. Well, it sort of irritated a lot of women back east . . . grown men you know, clubbin' jackrabbits that way, but they never seen what damage a rabbit could do.'

'Then what did Mr. Calendar do?'

'Well, he came up with a real fine idea. Lot of men in pickup trucks and special huntin' dogs, and we'd go out onto the prairie, far away from everything, and we'd turn up some coyotes, and we'd chase after 'em for mebbe ten miles and then we'd let the dogs go and they'd zero in on a coyote.'

'Then what?'

'Then the dogs would tear him apart.' There was a pause in court, and Emig added, 'It was necessary, of course, because coyotes eat sheep.'

'Your sheep?'

'No.'

'Mr. Calendar's sheep?'

'No. We just went along for the fun.'

The prosecution now called a new witness, Clyde Devlin, a dynamiter. 'What we done, there wasn't no more prairie dogs, and the coyotes was used up, so Floyd, he kept lookin' for anything sportin', and his mind fell on the rattlers up at the buttes. We bought small sticks of dynamite and threw them into the dens. Killed a lot that way, but the fun was standin' around with shotguns and blastin' the others as they crawled out.

'But the reason people was willin' to pay money for the dynamitin' was the fun of seein' Floyd handle rattlers. He had a way of pinnin' 'em down with a forked stick, then pickin' 'em up by the tail and snappin' 'em like a whip. The rattler's head would fly off. I seen him whip sixteen snakes in one day, and nobody else had the guts to try even one. Me? I wouldn't get near 'em.'

The prosecutor turned to the first serious charge. Calling to the stand Hank Garvey, pilot of a small plane stationed at Fort Collins, he asked, 'When, in your opinion, Mr. Garvey, did Mr. Calendar first direct his attention to eagles?'

'We were flyin' one day, about five years ago, and in the distance we seen this eagle come off a dead tree, and we both watched it flyin' for some time, and Floyd said, "Hell, Hank, with the right attention a man could stay on that eagle's tail and blast him right out of the sky." So we spent a whole week makin' dry runs, seein' if we could spot eagles and close in on them, and we found it was right easy. Eagles don't fly half as fast as they show 'em in the cartoons.'

'When did the idea . . . I mean, whose idea was it to do this commercially?'

'That came natural. Floyd and I knew a lot about hunters, him bein' a guide and all, and we knew how tough it was for a hunter to bag his-self a eagle. Some very good shots tried for years without ever gettin' close to one, let alone hittin' it. And this bugged 'em, because on their walls they would have the head of a rhinoceros from Africa and a tiger from India, but they wouldn't have their own national bird. There was a blank spot on their wall, and they were hungry to do somethin' about it, because nothin' looks better, when it's mounted right, than a bald eagle.'

'When did the commercial aspect begin? Your first customer, that is?'

'One day when we were practicin' on dry runs we came so close to a big bird that Floyd cried, "Shit, a man don't even have to aim. If he can point a gun he can get hisself a eagle this way." So there was this dude from Boston. Had one of everything in his game room except a eagle. Even had a Kodiak bear, and wanted a eagle so bad he could taste it.

'He told Floyd before takeoff, "I don't think you can get a eagle this way, but if you bring me onto one, I'll give you five hundred dollars." Then he turned to me and said, "And there'll be a little somethin' in it for you." So we were bound to locate a eagle.'

'Did you?'

'We cruised for a while west of Fort Collins and didn't find nothin'. So we sorta drifted down over Rocky Mountain National Park, where we turned up a big, beautiful bird. The dude wanted to fire as soon as we saw it, but we didn't want to shoot him over the park, because we might run into trouble when we landed to pick it up.

'So I swung the plane south of him and we worked him north, out of the park, and when he was over plowed land I moved in real close.

'Now, the eagle and the plane fly at about the same speed, so it was just like the bird was standin' still. And that's where we made our big mistake on our first try. I got too close. Hell, you could of killed that eagle with a broom.

'So when the dude does fire he practically disintegrates the eagle. We spent the better part of a hour pickin' up the various bits and pieces, and when we hauled them in to Gundeweisser, the taxidermist, he looks at the pile and asks, "How do you want this job made up? As a duck or a eagle? I can play it either way."

'He turned out a masterpiece. Spread-eagled, talons projectin', glass eyes flashin'. The dude was delighted and sent us the picture you have over there. When we showed it to Gundeweisser, he said, "That eagle's two-thirds plastic, but he'll never know." So after that I kept the crate a little farther away so's the gun blast didn't tear the bird apart.'

'How many did you kill from your platform in the sky?'

'Somethin' over four hundred, but me'n Floyd never shot a single one. Always some sportsman who wanted our national bird on his wall.'

Taxidermist Gundeweisser confirmed these figures. 'The boys brought me their eagles because I'd perfected the knack of making them look extra ferocious—talons extended. I was able to do this because I bought only first-class eyes from Germany—hard glass with a flash of yellow. I mounted over four hundred eagles, and nobody ever wanted the bird just looking natural. Always had to be in the act of killing something, talons extended.'

One of the state naturalists was now called, and he testified that he and his associates had been watching Floyd Calendar for some time. 'National publicity on the eagle thing scared him off that line, and we never saw the plane again. What he directed his attention to was bears. There was almost as good a market for bears as there was for eagles, and he devised a sure-fire way of helping an eastern hunter bag his bear.'

'Explain it, if you will.'

'He learned to trap bears. He probably knows more about bears than any man in America. At the beginning of each season he'd trap eight or ten beauties and hide them in cages deep in the woods. When some sportsman came along Floyd would charge him one hundred dollars for the hunt, two hundred if he bagged a bear. He would take the sportsman to one of several cabins in the woods, and about a quarter of a mile away he would have one of his bears in a cage. At five in the morning he'd sneak out and let the bear loose and at five-fifteen he and the sportsman would start trailing it, and by five-thirty the bear would be dead. I investigated three dozen cases like this, and never did the hunter suspect what Floyd had done. He handed over two hundred dollars and was delighted with the deal.'

'Then what happened?'

'Well, every now and then Floyd would release a bear that would take off in some unanticipated direction, and there'd be no chance of trailing him. So he adopted the practice of not feeding the caged bears for two weeks prior to releasing them. Now there were few escapes, because the bear would stop to eat, and the sportsman could creep up and gun it down.'

'We'd like to hear what Mr. Calendar tried next.'

'Ranger Quarry will explain that.'

A very young man took the stand, with a collection of gadgets to which the clerk gave numbers. 'Mr. Calendar was still not satisfied, for an occasional bear would still get away. We have evidence that his new plan was inspired by an article in *National Geographic* in which I detailed experiments I had made in Canada on the hibernating habits of bears. In the article, which now I'm sorry I wrote, I explained how we attached to the bear a very small radio device, like this. Wherever the bear went, it sent a signal, which betrayed his position at all times. Then I put one of these direction finders in my cap, and I could move about and always know where the bears were.

'Well, Floyd Calendar discovered who manufactured the broadcasting and listening devices, and after that whenever he captured a bear to be used later, he planted one of these transmitters around his neck. Then when a sportsman came into the mountains to get himself a bear, all

Floyd had to do was let the bear loose, listen to where he was going, and zero his hunter right onto the scene without any chance of failure.'

'Didn't the hunter realize what was happening when he got to the dead bear and saw the broadcast device?'

'No. Because Floyd never let him shoot at the bear till he—Floyd, that is—was all set for a running start. Then, while the hunter jumped in the air with joy, Floyd ran in, bent over, and with one quick swipe, tore the little transmitter from the bear's neck, and no one was the wiser.'

Now came the turn of Paul Garrett, who was introduced as deputy to the commissioner. Spectators in the courtroom leaned forward as he took the stand, because feelings ran high in this case, and some citizens felt that it was unfair to confront Calendar with an official like Garrett.

'I've known Floyd Calendar all my life,' Garrett said under questioning. 'Knew his father, too. And my family knew his grandfather.'

'Tell us about Mr. Calendar and turkeys.'

'About ten years ago I lured a family of wild turkeys onto the north edge of my ranch. We fed them, protected them, and after a while we had quite a colony. The wild turkey is a very sensitive bird, almost extinct in these parts, and we watched our brood very carefully, because they're our real national bird.

'But apparently Floyd Calendar was watching them too, because after they reached a certain number they began to decline, and we could find no sign of coyotes. We worried about this until a friend of mine in Massachusetts sent me a copy of a form letter he'd received from Colorado. Here it is.'

The judge instructed the clerk to read it, and the spectators were either amused or outraged when Floyd Calendar's mimeographed letter to his clients was divulged: 'I can make you a guarantee that no other guide in America can make. Come to the Rockies and I'll show you how to bag both of our national birds, a baldheaded eagle and a wild turkey.'

'Where did he get the turkey?' the prosecutor asked.

'From my protected sanctuary. When I saw the letter I staked one of my men out to guard the turkeys, and sure enough, here comes Floyd Calendar with a hunter from Wisconsin, shooting my turkeys.'

'Now, Mr. Garrett, there are rumors circulating as to what you did then. Will you tell the court.'

'I became very angry and waited till I saw Calendar go into Flor de Méjico, that's the restaurant run by Manolo Marquez, and I went up to him and I said something like . . .'

'We don't want to hear "something like" what you said. What did you say?'

'As well as I can remember, I said, "Calendar, if you ever set foot on that turkey range again, I'll kill you. If I'm there when you come, I'll do it there. If I miss you when you sneak in, I'll come into this restaurant and get you while you're eating." '

'Did you say, Mr. Garrett, that you'd get him while he was eating?'

'I did. I was very angry.'

This early confession of his threat took some of the sting out of the cross-examination, but the defense attorney made a good deal of the fact that a man who would be working with sportsmen in his new job had threatened to shoot one of them in a public restaurant. By the time the interrogation ended, Garrett did not look good.

The last prosecution witness was a Centennial man who had had several run-ins with Calendar, and his testimony was devastating: 'With Floyd Calendar, killing became an end in itself. He hated everything that moved—prairie dogs, rattlers, antelope and, like you heard, bears and eagles. I think if you gave Floyd a free hand, when he got through with the animal kingdom he'd start on Negroes and Mexicans and Chinese and Catholics and anyone else who wasn't exactly like himself. He hates anything that intrudes on his part of the world, and considers it his duty to wipe it out. To call him a sportsman is obscene. He's a one-man ecological disaster.'

The defense attorney, of course, objected to this whole tirade, and the judge ordered it stricken from the record.

When the first defense witnesses appeared the general tenor of the trial became clear, for they were ranchers and hunters who testified that bald eagles carried away young lambs and should therefore be exterminated. They also testified that Floyd Calendar was one of the finest men in the west—everyone said he had been kind to his mother—and on that edifying note the court recessed over the weekend. One rancher, as he left the courtroom, told Garrett, 'You have a nerve, testifyin' against a real American,' and Paul was relieved to know that he would be required to testify no further.

On Saturday, November 10, he worked on the ranch, riding north to inspect the wild turkeys. They were most handsome birds, big and heavy. They always looked as if Pilgrims with long guns should be chasing them for the 1621 Thanksgiving, and Paul was delighted that they shared the ranch with him.

He also rode over to a corner of the range he had set aside for a prairie-dog town. Slowly the little creatures were making a comeback, sharing their burrows with sand owls. Their return was not an unmixed blessing, for one of Garrett's horses broke his leg in a burrow and had to be shot. The ranch foreman wanted to bulldoze the town out of existence, but Garrett refused permission: 'You preserve nothing without encountering some disadvantages. If we keep this dog town, horses will break their legs and rattlers will come back. But in the large picture, things balance out, as they did two thousand years ago. The trick is to preserve the balance and pay whatever price it costs.'

The fact that he had sought the company of turkeys and prairie dogs reminded him of how deeply he was afflicted by the permanent American illness. A deep depression attacked him, which he could identify but not explain, the awful malaise of loneliness:

> I've never understood why so many Americans are so committed to loneliness. I know it runs in my family. When Alexander McKeag, who could be called an ancestor because he held Pasquinel's family together, spent the winter of 1827 alone in a cave, speaking to no one, he was succumbing to our sickness.
>
> And when my other ancestor, Levi Zendt, turned his back on Beaver Creek and chose the dreadful isolation of Chalk Cliff, he was behaving like a typical American.
>
> Sheepmen like Amos Calendar elected to live by themselves. Like their prototype Daniel Boone, they preferred living alone 'rather than with all them people.'
>
> Only the white Americans did this. The Arapaho always combined in large communal societies. Chinese railroad workers lived in colonies, and so did Chicano beet workers. The Japanese clung to their communities and so did the Russians. It took the American to build his ranch far from everything, his farm where no one else could see him. Why?

Garrett had assembled various theories about this American preference for isolation. When a Pilgrim was thrown onto the shore at Plymouth he faced only wilderness, and from it each man had chopped out his own little kingdom. He had to wrestle with loneliness, learn to live with it and overcome it. If he could not do this, he could not survive. Traipsing off to the town meeting was not the basic characteristic of New England life; it was going back afterward to the loneliness of one's own cottage.

It had been the same with all subsequent frontiers. If a man was inwardly afraid of loneliness, he had small chance of adjusting to the terrible isolation of the Kentucky forest. A predisposition for living alone became almost a requirement for survival in America, and even now, Garrett thought, the world held few places so lonely as the average American city.

The prairie had intensified the challenge, for there the emptiness was inescapable; even the sheltering tree was absent. A family moving west could anticipate fifty days of travel without encountering a sign of human habitation, and the wife whose husband decided to settle in Wyoming had to face an endless expanse of nothingness.

And there had been that ultimate in isolation, the snowbound mountain men passing the winters in some forgotten spot, allowing the drifts to cover him during the silent months, reading nothing, conversing not even with animals, who were also in hibernation. This was a form of exile difficult to comprehend, but there were always men who sought it.

The only heroes I had as a boy were loners. The isolated defenders of the Alamo. Nathan Hale operating alone and taking his punishment solo. The pioneer mother defending the Conestoga wagon after her man was slain. The Pony Express rider pointing the nose of his horse west and going it alone. These were my symbols.

This had an effect on every aspect of American life. One courageous man building a solitary log cabin and calling it home. Any self-respecting family must live apart . . . by itself . . . in its own little cabin, and any unfortunate who failed to achieve this alone-ness was either pitied or ridiculed. The unmarried elder sister became the focus of pity because she had to live with others. Any son-in-law who had to live with his wife's parents was an object of ridicule.

When the west was opened, people did not live in communities. One ranch was thirty miles from the next. During the period of Indian raids no one gave the remote settler hell for trying to make it alone. He was cheered for being brave enough to face the Indians on his own.

As a consequence of all this, Americans became the loneliest people on the face of the earth. We're even lonelier than the Eskimos, who live in close units. We're much lonelier than the Mexicans, who occupy the same type of land to the south, for Mexicans retain the extended family in which people of all ages live together in reasonable harmony.

There were compensations, Garrett had to admit. Living alone meant that men had to be more ingenious, which led to inventiveness. Old patterns had to be surrendered, so revolutionary new ones could be more easily accepted. Forward-seeking led to the development of the brash, resolute, outgoing man. The world needed him, but he evolved at a terrible price in loneliness.

For Garrett was also aware of the heavy social cost. Americans were both wasteful and cruel with their old people, especially their older women. Three factors conspired to produce a plethora of elderly women. First, as in all nations, females tended to live about five years longer than males. Second, custom encouraged a man to marry a woman somewhat younger than he. Third, American tradition required the man to work himself to death to support his woman, so that many men died prematurely. Adding these data, the average wife could look forward to about fifteen years of widowhood.

Other civilizations had grappled with this phenomenon. The American Indian who used to live at Rattlesnake Buttes solved it by depriving the widow of everything, even shelter, and encouraging her to starve to death. Asian Indians adopted a crueler solution: the widow was expected to climb the funeral pyre of her husband and burn to death. Arab nations developed the sensible device of multiple wives. In America, Garrett saw, the survivors were condemned to infirmity and loneliness.

Men fared only slightly better. Some of the loneliest men Garrett had ever known were the heads of corporations, trusting no one, confiding in no one, living out their lives in quiet despair, each wealthy man immured within his own castle.

What the hell am I doing living in a castle? he asked himself as he returned to ranch headquarters. Since the death of his wife he had been terribly lonely, felt himself no better off than the widows and the tycoons he had been pitying. He had a fine ranch, a profession he loved and now a responsible job with the government, but these did not compensate for his increasing sense of isolation.

About three o'clock that afternoon he took a shower, shaved and climbed into his car. When he left the ranch he could not have said where he was heading. Vaguely he wanted to hear Cisco Calendar sing some good western songs, for Cisco was the best in the business and was home again from his television show in Chicago. He also wanted to assure Cisco that his testimony against Floyd indicated no grudge.

But Cisco was not the main reason for the trip to town. What he really needed was to see Flor Marquez, to make up his mind about that long-legged, dark-haired divorcee. She had first caught his eye during his visits to her father's restaurant for some good Chicano food. It could not be said that he watched her grow up, for he was too preoccupied with other things to notice a Chicano girl, but he was aware that she had married a dashing fellow from Los Angeles, and of course it was a general scandal when she returned home after two weeks with a scar along her left cheek.

She had referred to her marriage only once: 'How can a girl tell that a guy is a total creep?'

She was in the restaurant when Garrett arrived. 'Let's go see if Cisco will sing tonight,' he suggested, and she was eager for an excuse to leave the restaurant. They walked west on Mountain, then down Prairie and along the railroad tracks to where Cisco lived in an old clapboard house. He was sitting on the porch, as he usually did in the afternoon, just watching things go past. Like his older brother, he was tall and lean, with the face of a man long accustomed to outdoor work.

'Hiya, folks,' he said amiably, without getting up.

'Came by to tell you I'm sorry about the run-in with Floyd . . . in court, that is.'

'He's a mean one. Anything you said was probably true.'

'I only testified about the turkeys.'

'How they doin'?'

'Checked them this morning. There they were, fat and sassy.'

'Come on over tonight,' Flor said. 'Give us some songs.'

'I just may do that,' Cisco said.

They knew it was unnecessary to say anything more. If he felt like it, he would stop by Flor de Méjico around ten and entertain his neighbors. Flor knew that in places like Cleveland and Birmingham he could command thousands of dollars for a night's performance, but when at home he liked to associate with the people from whom he had learned his songs, the Chicanos and the cowboys.

Garrett and Flor walked back to the Railway Arms, where they stopped for a couple of beers. They were aware that townspeople were watching them, and that there had been a good deal of talk. Gossips claimed that Flor was his mistress, but a waitress who knew her said, 'That hot tamale ain't gonna let no man in her bed without a license.'

She was wrong. In various rooms in various towns Flor Marquez and Paul Garrett had been lovers for some time now, each wary of the other, each uncertain of what the future could be. On this afternoon, when each was feeling desolate with loneliness, they separated at the hotel, then found their way by back paths to a motel, where they stayed through the early evening.

About nine they slipped away, at different times and by different paths, to join me at the restaurant. Flor arrived first and made a desultory effort at helping her father serve the dinner crowd, and after a while Garrett drifted in, as he often did, to play the juke box.

At ten there was a commotion. 'Cisco's coming!' a boy at the door shouted, and in came the lanky singer with his guitar. Nodding to various friends, he made his way to where Garrett and I were sitting, then invited Flor to join us. He drank beer for about an hour, answering the questions of well-wishers who wanted to know about Nashville and Hollywood, and finally he took up his guitar, plucking a few notes.

Without warning he struck a series of swift chords, then placed the guitar on the table. 'What would you like to hear, Paul?'

It really didn't matter, for whatever Cisco Calendar sang evoked the west. If he sang of buffalo skinners, he called forth images of his own grandfather during the big kill of 1873, with his Sharps .50 firing until it was too hot to handle. If he sang of the dust bowl, he reminded listeners of his own father, Jake, who had gone broke in 1936 after watching his farm blow away; when his wife wouldn't stop nagging him, he blazed away at her with a shotgun and spent a year in jail.

And if Cisco sang of cowboys, people could hear in his high, nasal complaint the rush of the tumbleweed or the harsh dissonance of a rattler coiled in a sandy path. He could sing of the hawk and the eagle and the Indian's pinto and make the listener see these creatures, for he had in his manner a terrible reality, the art of a man who had absorbed a culture and found its essence.

'I'd like to hear "Malagueña Salerosa," ' Garrett said, and Cisco looked at him.

'That's a tough one to start with.'

'I didn't say it was easy.'

Cisco lifted the guitar and played the unique chords which framed this love song, perhaps the finest written in North America in the past fifty years. It was difficult to sing, requiring a command of Spanish-type falsetto, but Cisco respected it as the best of his Chicano repertoire:

> 'What beautiful eyes she has
> Beneath those dark brows ...
> Beneath those dark brows ...
> What lovely eyes ...'

The Chicanos in the restaurant applauded as he sang a passage in high falsetto. After finishing the song, he placed the guitar on the table and bowed to the applauders. 'I am singing this song for my good friend Paul Garrett and my better friend Flor Marquez, who are in love.' Recovering the guitar, he played a long passage based on the theme of the song, then sang tenderly the exquisite conclusion:

> 'I offer you only my heart ...
> I offer you my heart
> In exchange for my poverty ...
>
> She is pretty and bewitching
> Like the innocence of a rose ...'

With the last word he strummed the guitar softly and bowed again. He avoided the popular pitfalls like 'Cool Water' or 'Ghost Riders in the Sky' or 'Bury Me Not on the Lone Prairie,' apologizing, 'Those songs are for the boys with strong voices. I'm after somethin' different, altogether different.'

As he unraveled bits and pieces of the songs he really loved, he built a portrait of a west that no longer existed but which men wanted to remember. Single phrases often evoked a whole era: 'Beat the drum slowly and play the fife lowly.' Or 'On a ten-dollar horse and forty-dollar saddle, I'm off to punch them Texas cattle.' Or 'His wife, she died in a poolroom fight.' Or 'Clouds in the west, it looks like rain. Derned old slicker's in the wagon again.'

He sang for several hours—the last of the real cowboys, the last of the buffalo men. He had enjoyed great popularity in Europe as well as in the eastern cities, but he felt most at ease in the restaurant of Manolo Marquez, who had fed him free during the bad years. Here he had learned most of the good Chicano songs he sang, like his very popular translation of 'The Ballad of Pancho Villa,' which American audiences appreciated for its outrageous nationalism.

But the highlight of any Cisco Calendar performance always came late at night, as it did now. Nodding to Garrett and Flor, he played the famous opening chords of the song they waited for. The words were as taut as Homer's and strove for the same effect: the beginning of a memorable saga:

'Twas in the town of Jacksboro in the year of '73, ⊚
A man by the name of Crego comes steppin' up to me,
Says, "How d'you do, young feller, and how'd you like to go
And spend one summer pleasantly on the range of the buffalo?" '

The song had excellent touches—the smell of the west, the Indians, the
tense narrative, the petulant cowboys:

'It's now we've crossed Pease River, boys, our troubles have begun.
First damned buffalo that I skinned, Christ, how I cut my thumb!'

Now Cisco became something larger than life, an epic figure chanting in
the darkness of the wild, free days that were no more. Sitting very
straight, and moving his hands as little as possible, he approached the
end of his song with the inevitability found in Greek tragedy:

'The season was near over, boys, Old Crego he did say
The crowd had been extravagant, we were in debt to him that day.
We coaxed him and we begged him, but still it was, "No go!"
So we left his damned old bones to bleach on the range of the buffalo.'

'The Buffalo Skinners' was the name of this splendid song. Its composer?
No one knew, but the music hammered with the beat of buffalo hoofs on
the prairie. Its lyricist? Some nameless Texas cowboy, down on his luck,
who had tried his hand at buffalo-skinning during the year of the last
great hunt.

'Well, that's it,' he said as he finished. 'If I was you two,' he said
quietly to Flor and Garrett, 'I'd get married and to hell with them.'

I did not see Garrett on Sunday, for he spent the day with Flor, talking seriously about the problems that would arise if they did marry. He
was Episcopalian and she Catholic, but that was of no consequence to
either of them. He had two children, and they were at a difficult age . . .
well, all ages were difficult when a widower sought to remarry, because
the children rarely approved, no matter whom he chose. The young Garretts had already stated that they would not like the idea of a Chicano
stepmother. The principal objection, of course, had been removed by the
death in February of Paul's mother, Ruth Mercy Garrett. She had been a
tense, unlikable woman who had always known of her husband's protracted love affair with Flor's great-aunt, Soledad, and because of it she
despised Chicanos. When she heard that Paul was seeing Flor Marquez,
a divorcee to boot, she put on a terrible scene, accusing her son of trying
to hasten her death. She was so irrational that Paul could not discuss the

matter with her, but he honestly believed that his mother might indeed have a heart attack if he married Flor, especially after she bellowed at him, 'You're just like your father! You're carrying on with that Mexican hussy merely to spite me, the way he did.' Now she was gone and no one deplored her passing, not even her grandchildren, whom she had tried to pamper but who saw her for what she was—a miserable, self-pitying, self-destroying woman.

One of the real obstacles was Manolo Marquez, for he saw little chance that an Anglo-Chicano marriage might succeed. The few he had witnessed had turned out disastrously, and he doubted that Flor and Paul would do much better. Flor respected what he had to say, because while she was preparing for her first marriage he had predicted that it couldn't last two months, and it had crashed after only eleven days.

'He's a flashy macho,' Manolo had warned his daughter. 'But you wouldn't recognize the type because you don't hang around poolrooms.' No description could better fit her unfortunate husband, a strutting would-be hero with ideas about the rights of the male in marriage so bizarre that one couldn't even be amused by them. Flor was humiliated that she had been such a miserable judge of human behavior and felt little confidence in her belief that Garrett might be different.

But all doubts withered in face of the fact that she and Paul loved each other, wanted each other and felt like better people when in each other's company. Sex with her first husband had been an appalling affair, without feeling or fulfillment, but to share a bed with Paul Garrett was totally satisfying. He was not afraid of letting her know that he needed her.

On this Sunday, for example, when they had made their way to the motel again, he told her, 'I'm so lonely I can hardly bear it. I stay up there in the castle surrounded by acres of empty land, and they insulate me from everything. If I couldn't see you in the restaurant, I'd go batty.'

It became obvious to each that they ought to get married. What held them back? It simply was not the custom in Colorado for Anglos to marry Chicanos. To marry an Indian was acceptable, but a Chicano? No!

Paul spent Monday away from Flor, trying to sort out his convictions. He applied himself to the job of getting the centennial commission functioning, and since one of his plans called for widespread use of radio, he needed to know what that medium was doing, and the more he heard, the more disgusted he became. On this day he wanted a tape of the major noon broadcast from the local station, and here is the complete transcription:

FIRST MALE ANNOUNCER: Well, folks, it's high noon and the train is chuggin' in from Poison Snake and Sheriff Gary Cooper is a-waitin' at the station.

SECOND MALE ANNOUNCER: It's time for news, all the news, the straight news, delivered without fear or favor, the news you want when you want it.

FEMALE QUARTET (*singing in close harmony*):

> 'From north from south,
> From east and west,
> We bring it first,
> We bring it best.'

FIRST MALE ANNOUNCER: Yessiree, like the girls just said, we bring it best. Remember you heard it first on Western Burst.

MALE AND FEMALE QUARTETS (*blending*):

> 'The news, the news, the news!
> Here comes the news.'

SECOND MALE ANNOUNCER: But first a brief message which is sure to be of interest. (Here followed two minutes of singing commercials.)

FIRST ANNOUNCER (*breathlessly*): West Berlin, Germany. This morning Chancellor Willy Brandt announced a radical shift in his cabinet.

SECOND ANNOUNCER (*gravely*): Oakland, California. At a special press conference called hurriedly this morning the management of the Oakland Raiders announced that Choo-Choo Chamberlain would—I repeat would—be able to play Sunday against the Denver Broncos.

MALE AND FEMALE QUARTETS (*blending*):

> 'No matter when the stories burst,
> You hear it here, you hear it first.'

FIRST MALE ANNOUNCER: Stay tuned for all the news, the news in depth, the news behind the news.

MALE AND FEMALE QUARTETS (*blending*):

> 'All the news, the news you need.
> Yes indeed. Yes indeed.'

FIRST MALE ANNOUNCER: Next complete news coverage one hour from now.

SECOND MALE ANNOUNCER: Unless, of course, there is some fast-breaking news development anywhere in the world. If there is, you know we break in right away, regardless of the program. Because Western Burst is always first. All the news, the news in depth.

Resignedly, Garrett leaned forward and clicked off the set. Radio and television could have been profound educative devices; instead, most of them were so shockingly bad that a reasonable man could barely tolerate them. In one spell last winter television had offered him an automobile that talked, a housewife who was a genie, a village idiot who could move forward and backward in history, and eighteen detectives involved in forty-seven murders. When one station did run the B.B.C. series *Six Wives of Henry VIII*, the newspaper announced the first episode as a western, *Catherine of Oregon*.

There was the same illiterate cheapening in every aspect of life. One local restaurant had a big sign advertising its specialty, 'Veal Parma John.' Another proclaimed, 'Broken Drum Café. You Can't Beat It. Our Chicken Has That Real Fowl Taste.' A refreshment booth featured 'Custard's Last Stand,' while a motel sign flashed 'Just a Little Bedder.'

One gap in Colorado's cultural life perplexed him. The state had no major publishing program, and whereas its history was perhaps the most varied and vital in the west, there were few local books to celebrate it. This was the more remarkable in that two neighboring states, Nebraska and Oklahoma, each had a university press which produced really fine volumes on western themes; Garrett was pleased that they kept him supplied with the books he needed but thought it deplorable that Colorado, a richer state with a better subject matter, published almost nothing, as if it were ashamed of its history.

He did not propose any radical moves in this area, because some years ago he had burnt his fingers badly trying to modify western taste. Denver had a City-and-County Building which faced the gold-domed capitol across a lovely plaza; together they formed one of the most attractive state centers in America. It had become traditional each Christmas to decorate the former building with an appalling collection of green, red, orange and sickly purple lights, and to leave them in position for the January stock show. One French architect, when asked his opinion of the decorations, exclaimed, 'The ultimate flowering of early Shanghai Whorehouse.' After unrelieved ridicule had been heaped on the display, Garrett spearheaded a movement to replace it with something more appropriate, and a high-salaried decorator was flown in from New York to take charge. With an international taste he threw out the garish lights and substituted muted colors which blended with the dark Rockies towering beyond, but when cattlemen from various parts of the state descended on the city and found the lights to which they had been accustomed missing, they raised hell, disrupted a session of the legislature and informed the city that 'if Denver don't think enough of us to decorate the building properly, we'll move our show to Omaha.' In panic the city fathers tore down the new lights and reinstalled the awful old ones, so that now Denver had one of the few unique Christmas displays in America. Flamboyant beyond description, it evoked no sense of Christmas, but it did exemplify a cattle show, and every Colorado rancher knew which of those two celebrations was the more important.

Wherever he looked Garrett saw this same lack of art, this failure of taste. He wondered what the state had to celebrate, except superhighways. Even the mountains were being abused. Brooding over Denver each night was a gigantic neon-lit cross occupying the whole face of a mountain. It had been placed there as an advertisement, and the majority of people in the city liked it, because, they said, 'it puts the mountain to some practical use. Also, it reminds us that we are one nation under God.'

One of the first decisions his committee would have to make involved the application of an enthusiastic group who wanted permission to carve the whole front side of Beaver Mountain with likenesses of Buffalo Bill on his horse and Kit Carson shooting an Indian. Considerable popular support was being generated for the project on the ground that 'if the mountains are there, they ought to be put to some use.' Garrett hoped that among the young people of the state he would find support in opposing this, even though he was powerless to remove the cross already in position over Denver.

> I sometimes think that in the west we have produced only two serious works of art: the Clovis point engineered with such obvious love by primitive man twelve thousand years ago and that wonderful arch along the waterfront in St. Louis.
>
> The more I study the Clovis point, the more convinced I become that it was brought into being by a true artist. His basic job was predetermined by practicality, but in its final stages it was executed with love. It is perfectly obvious that the point could have been left rougher and still been capable of killing a mammoth. But the maker went beyond that requirement and made it a work of art as well. The Clovis is as graceful as a butterfly wing, as lethal as a Thompson machine gun. Those first men set high standards for those of us who follow, and only rarely do we attain their level.
>
> That arch in St. Louis does. It is appropriate that it stand as the gateway to the west. Many of my ancestors debarked at that spot on their way to Colorado—Levi Zendt, Lisette Pasquinel, Major Mercy, Frank Skimmerhorn—and the arch represents the spiritual forces that impelled them.
>
> I can't conceive how the city of St. Louis had either the imagination or the determination to erect such a monument. It's perfect. A soaring symbol of the best in American life, and I suppose if it had been put to a popular vote, it would have been defeated on the grounds, 'Who needs an arch?'
>
> All of us need an arch. We need symbols that are bigger than we are. We need emotional reminders of who we are and what we represent. I hope to God our committee can come up with something for 1976 that will recall our simple past . . . the tread of feet across the prairie.

During this November of 1973 the nation was in sad disarray. Watergate, gasoline rationing, a crumbling Atlantic alliance, confrontation with the Arabs and a runaway inflation with wheat at $5.78 a bushel as a result of the mismanaged deal with Russia created a sense of lost direction. In no part of government was the chaos more apparent than in the commission responsible for planning the nation's bicentennial. So inept was the leadership from Washington that it seemed America was afraid to celebrate its birthday lest citizens gather in the street; only the energy and enthusiasm of certain state leaders could save the anniversary, and no one had a more imaginative proposal than Paul Garrett, chairman of the Colorado commission.

'What is our nation's principal contribution to world art?' he asked his committee when it met on the afternoon of November 13. 'The motion picture. And what kind of movies do we make better than anyone else? The mythical western.' And he proceeded to unfold a plan that would cost little and produce much.

'What we're going to do,' he explained, 'is go back in the files and find thirty or forty of our best western films. We'll arrange a gala festival in every town that has a theater. Charge no more than maybe fifty cents a night. Encourage everyone in the state to see the whole shebang. And we'll teach more about the spirit of the west than we could in any other way.'

He insisted that his committee join him on a ride north to Cheyenne to see a film which had been highly recommended by French critics. None of the others had even heard of it, but as we sped through the starry night with the prairie opening out on either side, he spoke enthusiastically of what the festival might accomplish.

'I must warn you, I have strong ideas about films. Best heroic western I ever saw was John Wayne in *Red River*. It was spoiled somewhat by the ridiculous plot which called for Montgomery Clift to whip Wayne in a fist fight, but apart from that, it was a masterpiece.'

He also liked *The Covered Wagon* and other old-timers which few had seen. It was when he reached the recent movies that he ran into trouble. For example, he wanted to be sure that *McCabe and Mrs. Miller* ran during the first week to set a standard of honesty for the festival, but two of the committee had seen it and found it to be insulting. 'Nothing but whores and cheap grifters,' one complained, to which Garrett replied, 'And who did you think populated our first towns?' One of the other members pointed out that John Wayne had objected to the movie most strenuously, on the grounds that it impugned the standard characters of the west, whereupon Garrett said, 'We're honoring Wayne as an actor, not as a critic.'

He especially recommended two Indian pictures which none of the committee had seen. 'On these you can trust me. They're marvelous depictions. *Cheyenne Autumn* tells about the tribe on its long march north to Fort Robinson and what happened there in 1878. It'll break your heart. And I do want people to see *A Man Called Horse*. Wasn't big at the box office, but it comes closer to Indian life than anything else I've seen.'

The committee wanted some preparation for what they were to see in Cheyenne, because Garrett's sponsorship of *McCabe* worried them. 'Have no fear,' he said. 'I'm taking you to a masterpiece.'

And he did. It was *Monte Walsh*, a low-budget picture starring Lee Marvin, Jack Palance and Jeanne Moreau, and it unfolded with such simplicity, such heart-ripping reality that a strange mood developed. Everyone who had any knowledge of the old west sat transfixed by the memories this film engendered, but those who had known the region only secondhand felt irritated at the wasted evening. Masterpieces are like that; they require an active participation and offer nothing to those who are unwilling to contribute.

Monte Walsh had its principal effect on Paul Garrett; he was bowled over by the integrity of the cowboy played by Marvin and the haunting tragedy of his love for the hanger-on, played by Jeanne Moreau. Garrett was nervous all the way back to Venneford, and on Wednesday morning he said to me, 'Damn it all, Vernor, she's a Chicano, so let's do it the Chicano way!'

We waited till evening, then rode in to Denver, seeking out a night club that had imported a mariachi band from Old Mexico, and he propositioned the leader, who said, 'Why not?'—and it was arranged.

The band played at the club till two in the morning, then shared with Garrett the tamale dinner he paid for. They drank some good Mexican beer and at three-thirty piled into the bus he had rented, all fourteen of them.

It was nearly dawn when we reached Centennial, and the driver parked in an area where the bus would attract no attention. Then the mariachis assembled at the railway station, where the leader told Garrett, 'It was never this cold in Mexico,' and he assured them, 'When you start to play, it'll warm up.'

No one in town had yet spotted the band, but now the leader gave a signal and with an explosion of sound the mariachis began 'La Cucaracha,' the song of the poor little cockroach who couldn't negotiate very well because he had no more marijuana to smoke.

Lights went on in all the streets leading off Prairie as the mariachis marched north, then turned east on Mountain, where they played the ear-shattering 'La Bamba' and then 'La Negra.' By the time they reached Third Street two members of the police force were running after them.

'It's all right,' Garrett assured them. 'Just listen.'

The mariachis had now reached Flor de Méjico, and under Garrett's direction they formed a large semicircle and launched into 'Las Mañanitas,' the birthday song. They played half the stanza without voices, then six of the players blended harmoniously in that most gracious and tender song:

> 'This is the birthday song
> Sung by King David.
> Because this is your day,
> I sing it to you.'

There were four verses to the song, and the men sang with such delight that it seemed a true serenade from a man to the woman he loved. When it was finished, Garrett signaled to the conductor, who beat twice with his right arm, and the mariachis began their gentle rendition of 'Dos Arbolitos.' A light appeared in an upper window and Flor Marquez looked down.

'What goes on here?' the reporter from the *Clarion* asked, for by now the noisy musicians had half the town awake.

'I'm serenading the girl I'm going to marry,' Garrett replied.

'Is that an announcement?' the newsman asked excitedly.

'Ask her.'

So the reporter went to a spot beneath the window and asked, 'Can I report that you and Mr. Garrett are getting married?' Flor had tears in her eyes, for women are not often serenaded by a band of fourteen, but she replied in that lovely phrase of Chicano insolence, 'Si, ¿como no?'

On Thursday morning, November 15, Garrett met with some ranchers from the northeastern corner of the state, who wanted to discuss range management, and after he left them he reflected upon the regrettable sheep wars that had marred the area at the beginning of this century. Many lives had been lost defending the theory that where a sheep had trod, no cow would graze, but today most of the cattlemen occupying land that used to belong to the Venneford Ranch ran cattle and sheep side by side, and each prospered.

Take Hermann Spengler, for example. His grandfather Otto had killed a sheepman in 1889 and no jury in the area could be found to convict him, because of the general opinion that death by gunfire was too good for any man who would bring sheep onto the open range. Today Spengler ran seven hundred Herefords and two thousand sheep. They grazed together on the same fields and complemented each other nicely, the coarse manure of the cattle blending with the more concentrated manure of the sheep to keep the grama grass flourishing.

Even so, one amusing custom still operated throughout the district. A man might run five thousand sheep, but if he had even six steers, he called himself a cattleman, and in all the area around Centennial, there were thousands of sheep but no sheepman. That was a name of opprobrium that no prudent man would take upon himself.

As noon approached, Paul Garrett began to feel uneasy, for this was the third Thursday of the month, and on this day the cattlemen of the region convened at the Railway Arms for lunch in the old-style upstairs dining room. They called themselves the Sirloin Club, and they met in close-knit grandeur, the last of their breed. Czar Wendell would be there, and Hermann Spengler and Dade Commager; and young Skimmerhorn, who ran a big herd of French Charolais. I would be an invited guest.

The room we met in was decorated with photographs of the historic figures of the region: Earl Venneford of Wye, looking natty in his Scottish tweed, had been photographed at the railway station; Oliver Seccombe was seated in his carriage on an inspection tour of Line Camp Four among the pines; the Pettis boys had been photographed in rocking chairs on the veranda of the hotel; and Otto Spengler stood with legs apart, hefting a double-barreled shotgun. One of the finest pictures showed R. J. Poteet fording the Platte River with Nate Person riding behind. This was a room dedicated to cattlemen, and soon the hotel would be torn down, since modern travelers preferred antiseptic motels at the edge of town.

Paul Garrett had never been wholly accepted by the Sirloin Club, since one of his ancestors had been responsible for introducing sheep into the area, and regardless of Paul's lifelong devotion to Herefords, the contaminating smell could never be completely removed. Now that his engagement to a Chicano was known, the time-honored antipathies against Mexicans might be revived, and he was apprehensive about his reception.

He need not have been. When he entered the room the cattlemen cheered and Dade Commager embraced him, slapping him on the back and proposing a toast: 'To Paul, who's doing what should have been done years ago.' Morgan Wendell, having satisfied himself that Garrett's marriage to a Chicano would be highly popular in Denver and the southwest portions of the state, proposed a toast of his own: 'To Paul Garrett, public servant extraordinary.' And all joined in.

Now the ritual began. At twelve-fifteen on the dot we took our places at three oilcloth-covered tables, and tumblers of ditch—bar bourbon and Platte water—were circulated. Wendell raised his glass and cried, 'Gentlemen, to the open range!' All drank, and Hermann Spengler proposed, 'To the Hereford.'

Waiters now came in with large baskets of French fried potatoes, which they emptied onto the middle of each table, forming golden pyramids, over which they sprinkled handfuls of salt. The doors swung open and the waiters reappeared with huge trays. Before each of us they placed a sizzling platter containing nothing but a monstrous sirloin cut from some super-steer at the Brumbaugh feed lots.

Steak and potatoes, the food of real men. Hands reached into the golden stacks to grab potatoes, and knives cut into tender steak. For the first few minutes there was not much talk, then Wendell recalled the time the club had entertained a senator from Rhode Island. The members had been most attentive to him, for on a matter of vital concern he held the crucial vote, and things looked promising until the sirloins were served. In a quiet voice he had asked, 'Could I have some catsup?'

There was a ghastly silence. To these men, putting catsup on a sirloin was like dumping cigarette ashes in holy water. No one knew what to say, but everyone was adamant that no bottle of catsup would disgrace that table, even if the supplicant was a senator commanding a vital vote. The impasse had been broken by Wendell's father, a steely-eyed man: 'Senator, as you know, your vote is crucial to us, and there is nothing in the world we would not do for you. I think we've given you ample proof of that. But I would rather see horse piss sprinkled over my steak than see this table profaned by a bottle of catsup. No, Senator, you may not have catsup.'

'How'd he vote?'

'He was a good sport. Never allowed the bill out of committee.'

Now the steaks were gone, and one of the ranchers turned to Garrett with an embarrassing question: 'They tell me, Paul, you're thinkin' of meddlin' with your Herefords. Believe me, don't do it.'

'Haven't made up my mind,' Garrett said. Of the eighteen men at the tables, sixteen ran Herefords, and any defection by a rancher as important as Paul Garrett would have serious consequences for them, for if word got around that Crown Vee was dissatisfied with its white-faces, the whole market might become unsettled.

The waiters reappeared with coffee and apple pie, and as the meal ended, Hermann Spengler gripped Garrett by the shoulder, saying, 'I'd be honored, Paul, if I could attend the wedding.' Others, hearing this remark, expressed a similar interest, so Garrett said, 'We're being married tomorrow at two . . . in her father's restaurant.'

'We'll be there,' the ranchers promised.

The next day we all gathered in Flor de Méjico as Father Vigil, now an old man speaking in a whisper, conducted the service. When Garrett placed the ring on Flor's finger he felt a surge of tenderness for his beautiful bride, and at the end of the ceremony he embraced Manolo Marquez, thanking him for having raised such a splendid daughter.

I did not see either Paul or Flor over the weekend, for they had gone to Line Camp Four on their honeymoon, but on Saturday he telephoned me with a startling piece of news.

'Vernor? Have you heard the decision in the Floyd Calendar case?' His voice was agitated and he was obviously furious.

'Did the jury find him guilty?' I asked.

'They acquitted him on every major count,' Garrett stormed. 'The law of the west. "No man is guilty of anything, unless he's an Indian." But guess what they did find him guilty of?'

I had had no experience with western juries and offered no opinion, so Garrett continued: 'Operating a zoo without a license. He'd held his bears in cages for periods of more than thirty days.' He uttered a string of profanities, then added, 'Now guess what his fine was. For killing four hundred and thirteen bald eagles, two hundred bears wired for sound and eighty-one of my turkeys . . . a fine of fifty dollars.'

'Go back to your honeymoon,' I told him. Laughing, he hung up.

Late that afternoon he must have turned on his television, for when he returned to town he handed me a tape which he especially wanted me to hear:

> When President Nixon started to speak to the newspaper editors I was much encouraged, and told Flor, 'Great! Just what he ought to be doing. If he'd explained all this six months ago, we'd have had no Watergate.' But then I heard him say to the American public, 'The people have to know whether their President is a crook. Well, I'm not a crook. I've earned everything I have got.' I felt sick. How undignified. How damned awful. I snapped off the television and sat with my head in my hands. My world seemed to be coming apart. Shortage of gasoline. Rampant inflation. Plants in Denver closing down for lack of raw materials. Spiro Agnew, a man I had trusted, kicked out because of his own misbehavior. And now my President proclaiming that he was not a crook.
>
> I told Flor, 'No man should ever find it necessary to make such a statement in public. It's like a doctor assuring everyone in Centennial that he doesn't give his patients strychnine. Who in hell said he did? A President of the United States buttonholing a bunch of editors and telling them, "I'm not a crook." Who said he was?' And Flor said, 'You must admit he started the rumor.'

Early Monday morning Paul and Flor drove back to Venneford, where Bradley Finch, one of America's leading experts on water supply, waited to take Garrett to a meeting of the Water Board. It was to be held at a research station near the headwaters of the Cache la Poudre, and Garrett said, 'I think Professor Vernor would be interested in seeing what we're doing,' and Finch said, 'Come along. Might as well start to worry now as later.'

When I asked him what this meant, he said, 'Our citizens seem to be rather worried about gasoline rationing. That'll be child's play compared to what's going to happen when we start rationing water.'

'Will it come to that?' I asked.

'It already has. When you see our analog model, you'll understand.'

'What's an analog model?' I asked.

'It's easier to demonstrate than to explain.'

As we drove up the beautiful canyon of the Poudre, Finch told Garrett, 'This is your first appearance as a member of the board, Paul, and it's crucial. We're looking to you for leadership. You've got to make some very tough decisions, and you mustn't show yourself as wishy-washy.'

'You make it sound ominous,' Garrett said.

'It is.' As we parked the car before a low building hidden beneath tall evergreens, Finch concluded, 'You and I will have to decide who shall live and who shall not live. It's as serious as that.' Before he could say more, other members of the Water Board spied the new deputy and gathered to congratulate him.

'I don't even understand the questions, let alone the answers,' Garrett protested.

'You will, by lunchtime,' Welch assured him.

We assembled in an austere room, one wall of which was painted white. Bradley Finch, as chairman of the board, said briefly, 'Our technicians worked all last week to get a slide show ready for you, Garrett, and I think we'd better plunge right in.'

He darkened the room, and a young woman, who was introduced as Dr. Mary White from Cal Tech, said, 'I'm to give the presentation, Mr. Garrett, and if you have any questions, press that buzzer at your desk.' Forthwith she unfolded the dramatic story of water, as it affected all the western states. Slide after slide developed the inevitable theme: population, agriculture and industry were all growing so fast that available supplies of water simply could not keep pace. States like Colorado, Arizona and Utah faced permanent drought conditions.

Garrett pushed his buzzer and the slides halted. 'You keep mentioning the word *aquifer*. Define it for me.'

The lights went on, and Finch said, 'Dr. Welch, I've heard you handle that question rather well. Care to take a crack?'

Dr. Welch went to a blackboard and drew a heavy, solid line from left to right. At one end he wrote 'Rocky Mountains,' and at the other 'Nebraska.' Beneath the line he wrote in bold letters 'Platte River.' 'This is us,' he said.

With red chalk he drew three dramatic lines leading away from the Platte. The first he labeled 'Towns and Other Social Use.' The second he labeled 'Agriculture.' The third was 'Industry.' 'These are the agencies which want our water, and right now they're prepared, among them, to take away far more than we can provide.'

Finch, himself an engineer from M.I.T., interrupted. 'That shows you rather well the basic problem, Garrett. The three outgoes already exceed the various inflows. Your job . . . that is, the job of our committees . . . well, we have to apportion our available water.'

'What's the aquifer?' Garrett repeated.

Dr. Welch resumed. 'The only inflow we have, really, is fourteen inches of precipitation on the plains out here. Pitifully small. Just barely enough to keep life going. And lots of snow up here in the mountains. It all winds up in the Platte . . . or the Arkansas . . . or one of our other rivers.

'Now, as the water comes down the river system, several things happen. Some of it we can see—like the Cache la Poudre outside this building. And some of that is diverted into dams and irrigation ditches. And some of the diversion seeps into the ground and creeps back into the Platte.'

'That sounds like one of Potato Brumbaugh's theories,' Garrett said.

'But what even he failed to take into account,' Welch said, 'was the water we can't see. And having missed that, he missed exactly half the equation.'

Deftly he sketched in the various inflows into the great system: the snowfall, the rainfall, the dams, the ditches. Then, with a broad stroke of his chalk, he laid down two boundary lines about five miles north and south of the river, and with hasty, sweeping movements filled in the space between so that the river and its intricate relationships could no longer be seen.

'That's your aquifer,' he said. 'Underground and invisible. Four million years ago, when the Platte was being carved into the silt thrown down from the Rockies, there was this impermeable basement of shale and limestone. On it rested deposits of highly permeable gravel and sand, in some places two hundred feet thick, and as you can see, up to ten miles wide. For millions of years this catchment lay hidden, covered over by whatever topsoil came along. It now forms a lens whose interstices can be filled with water. It's really a massive subterranean reservoir, and it acts as the balance for our entire Platte system.'

The lights were turned off, and various slides were flashed on the wall to indicate the operation of this mysterious phenomenon. As Garrett traced the intricate manner in which water seeped down into the aquifer and then escaped upward through springs and artesian wells and filtration—this constant coming and going of the water that sustained all life—he could not help thinking of old Potato Brumbaugh, who had lived his life sitting on top of the great reservoir without comprehending either its existence or its operation. He had plumbed all the secrets except the biggest.

'We must think of the aquifer as the permanent invisible counterpart of the visible river. Had we left it alone, it would have served us forever, but unfortunately, some years ago we began to sink wells into it, and now it's in grave danger.'

Dr. White resumed her slides, showing how ranchers, like Paul Garrett, had sunk artesian wells into the aquifer and were drawing off millions of gallons of water that should have been left in the subterranean system.

'This invention,' she said, flashing onto the screen a photograph of an ingenious watering device, 'has done more harm to the Platte River than anything else in history, for it has almost destroyed the aquifer.'

On the wall appeared the photograph of a flat, treeless, open range. In the middle stood a steel tower resting on self-propelled wheels. To it came electricity and water, and it moved ceaselessly in a circle, throwing a fine spray of moisture from a set of nozzles on top. Twenty-four hours a day this tower could revolve, watering an immense area.

That was not all. Eight to thirteen such towers could be linked together, side by side, each with its own motor, each moving around the circle at the appropriate speed. The combined towers thus formed a vast arm reaching out a quarter of a mile and irrigating an area containing one hundred and twenty-five acres. These were the fairy circles that I had seen on my first tour in Garrett's plane.

The lights went on, and Finch said, 'So that's our aquifer. And it's in peril. Not only are present demands on it depleting, future demands threaten to exhaust it. Detlev Schneider has some news on that front.'

Schneider, trained in demography at Oxford, was a robust man with an effusive sense of humor, and as he spoke, Garrett reflected on one of the most reassuring aspects of Colorado; it enlisted help from the best sources in the world: Oxford, Cal Tech, M.I.T., Harvard, Stanford.

'We face a real dilly,' Schneider was saying. 'Because Colorado is such a popular state, fifty thousand newcomers want to move in each year. We'd like to welcome them, but we haven't enough water. And within the state itself, twenty thousand of our rural people a year want to move into Denver. Love to have them, but no water. We also have scores of industries that want to establish their headquarters here. Executives want instant skiing, and we need their tax dollars. But we simply don't have the water.'

Harry Welch interrupted to say that the Colorado legislature had been handed a bill denying permission to anyone from outside the state to move into Colorado. 'We'll set up checkpoints at the borders and turn them back,' he said.

'Completely unconstitutional,' Schneider retorted. 'Any American citizen can move anywhere he likes.'

'But not into Colorado,' Finch said. 'The analog model takes care of that.'

In a small room at the rear of the building stood a pegboard forty feet long by five feet high, simulating in minute detail all aspects of the Platte system. The river was represented by a heavy copper wire, to which came smaller wires for the contributory streams. Soldered to these were thousands of electrical resistors of varying strength, duplicating the water-bearing properties of the region. Just as rocks impeded the flow of water through the aquifer, resistors impeded the flow of electricity through the model.

At each junction of four resistors a capacitor was attached, storing electricity the way porous rocks and dams stored water. With everything operating, this complex electrical system reproduced every attribute of the river and the aquifer, and any flow of water that came into the real system was reflected in the model.

'But what about the outflow?' Garrett asked, and Schneider explained, 'You see these small light bulbs scattered about the plan? And these little resistors? They draw off electricity in the same way that irrigation ditches and wells withdraw water.'

As Garrett inspected the model, Finch said, 'It shows you the Platte as it is today. But it can also show you what will happen five years from now if we continue to increase the demand for water. Let's see what Harry Welch was warning us about with his red outgoes.'

The electrical input, representing precipitation, was kept constant, but a large light bulb representing increased demand by communities of new people was turned on. 'Watch the oscilloscope,' Finch said.

There, on a screen placed to one side of the model, were graphically shown the effects of the new demand: a shadow-line which had been depicting the even flow of the river dropped dramatically toward the bottom of the screen, forming a deep cone of depression. 'It proves what we predicted,' Finch said. 'Look downstream. Real shortages down there, but we still have a river.'

Schneider said, 'But now let's increase the demand for industry too,' and he turned on various bulbs. The line on the oscilloscope dropped ominously toward the bottom of the screen.

'At this point agriculture is hurting like hell,' Finch said.

'Now let's crank in five years of drought,' Schneider said, 'such as we've often had.'

Instead of adding new bulbs to simulate increased demand, current was diminished in the mountains, indicating low snowfall, and other current was stopped to show decline in rainfall. The oscilloscope line vanished; the Platte no longer flowed.

The model was turned off. 'There you have it,' Finch said. 'If we encourage the population of Colorado to increase, and invite more industry, and continue to deplete the aquifer with agricultural pumps, we shall destroy the state. Your job, Garrett, is to see that this doesn't happen.'

'Do we still have options?' Garrett asked.

'Yes, but you must explain them to the citizens. For example, if we continue to steal water away from our farms, onions will have to cost ten dollars apiece.'

On the drive home, a much-sobered Garrett reflected on his new job as protector of resources: 'I thought the task was to provide the people of Colorado with good air to breathe. Now I've got to see that they have water to drink. And when the soil experts get through their indoctrination, I suspect my principal job will be to ensure that we have earth to till. This nation is running out of everything. We forgot the fact that we've always existed in a precarious balance, and now if we don't protect all the components, we'll collapse. I never knew my great-grandfather, Jim Lloyd—he died before my time. But I've heard my Grandfather Beeley tell how Lloyd loved the earth and never wanted to do anything to disturb its balance. He wouldn't allow one extra steer to graze on a field that might be damaged by close cropping. We've got to get back to that sense of responsibility toward the earth. When I think that the people of this state didn't give a damn when Floyd Calendar shot eagles and bears and turkeys—just for the hell of it, just to titillate some eastern sportsmen . . .'

On Tuesday, November 20, it was the farmers and the financiers who had to bite the bullet. The climactic meeting of Central Beet was held in Denver, with Paul Garrett and Harvey Brumbaugh present as board members, and they sat in silence as the dismal figures were paraded.

'The beet industry,' droned the chairman, 'has fallen on evil times. So many people covet our land for so many new purposes that the farmer can't afford to reserve it for beets. He's got to sell to the subdividers, who build new towns for people from the east. And even if he did hold on to his land, he couldn't find anyone to work his fields or harvest the crop in the fall.' He continued his painful litany until he reached the obvious conclusion: 'And so, gentlemen, we have no alternative but to close down our plant at Centennial. We won't lose money, because a real estate developer from Chicago has made us a most attractive offer. He wants to build ninety-seven Colonial-type houses.'

Harvey Brumbaugh was the first to react. As the owner of a large feed lot where young steers were assembled for fattening, he had relied on sugar-beet pulp and molasses as a convenient source of feed. Now he would have to look elsewhere and absorb the cost of shipping.

The chairman listened to this complaint, then said, 'The time may be at hand when the cattle industry will be forced to quit Colorado. Our state is so beautiful, and so many people want to live here, that I suspect ranchers like Paul Garrett will no longer be able to run their cattle economically. A whole pattern of life is vanishing, gentlemen. We're just the first to feel the pinch.'

The chairman did not say so, but all present realized that in some forthcoming meeting, say within three years, the first topic on the agenda would be: 'Shall we dissolve the company altogether?'

It was incomprehensible to Garrett that this great institution, which had once dominated life in Colorado—'We live and breathe as Central Beet directs,' the farmers had said—should be on the verge of collapse. Even when he was a boy, as late as 1936, Central Beet had dictated to banks and school boards and sheriffs' offices. For thousands of farmers and small-town businessmen, Central Beet was Colorado, and to watch it fall from that high estate was painful.

'What went wrong?' Garrett asked Brumbaugh as they rode home together.

'We didn't pay enough attention to the relationship of land and people,' Brumbaugh said. 'I glimpsed something of the problem when I developed the feed-lot concept. Take the young cattle off the land, herd them in lots and stuff them with feed for market. Well, that idea seems to have run its course. You know what I'm thinking right now?'

Garrett turned to look at the man who rode beside him. Harvey, like his great-grandfather, Potato, had a far-ranging mind, one that was ever willing to investigate new potentials. Now Brumbaugh said, 'I have a suspicion that before long we'll be raising cattle the way they raise those new-style chickens. Never touch the earth. Live in sanitized pens from birth to death. Cowboys will be city fellers with college degrees, dressed in white aprons. They'll ship manure away in desiccated pellets.'

Excited by his vision of the future, even though it entailed hardship for him, Brumbaugh continued: 'Time's got to come when we can no longer afford to keep cows in Colorado. First they'll move to Wyoming and Montana, but land prices are rising there too. Know what's going to happen?'

Garrett had been thinking, for some time, that ranching in Colorado was doomed, but he had not deduced where the business would go, and he listened with fascination as Brumbaugh said, 'Within a few years we'll be raising most of our cattle on cheap land back in states like Indiana . . . close to the feed supply. On the other hand, I've heard some good reports on cottonseed cake as feed for Herefords. I may move my whole operation to Georgia . . . or maybe Alabama.'

Garrett was impressed by the facility with which Brumbaugh could leap from one alternative to the next, without allowing sentiment to intrude where it could serve no useful purpose. He wasn't able to do that. If the time came when he could no longer afford to run Hereford cattle, a large part of his life would be shattered, and with these gloomy thoughts of change and the flow of life he dropped Brumbaugh at the feed lot and drove north.

On Wednesday Paul faced an ugly necessity, one he had been postponing for some weeks. Now he must meet the people concerned and report the bad news.

When it was announced that he would be chairman of the Centennial Commission, a delegation from Blue Valley in the heart of the Rockies visited him with an elaborate plan for making that historic area a focus for the celebration. When he first studied the proposal he had been offended by its garishness and its pandering to every base item in Colorado's history, but as the days passed and he heard further details, he was downright revolted. The men and women of Blue Valley did not seem to know that in 1976 a great state and a greater nation would be celebrating their birthdays and that what was required was a rededication to the principles that had made them outstanding in the first place. In Blue Valley they wanted a carnival.

With reluctance he drove into the high mountains to visit the ugliest town in America. As he reached the top of the steep ascent and looked down into the valley he felt compelled to record his thoughts:

> This used to be one of the loveliest spots in North America. That stream was crystal, filled with beaver. Those bare flanks were covered with trees. Deer and elk abounded, and the mountains stood like sentinels protecting it. My ancestors discovered the place, and that old Indian I told you about found gold here.

> Well, no spot anywhere in the world, no matter how lovely, can withstand the discovery of gold . . . or oil. Look at this abhorrent thing—no trees, a fouled stream, no wildlife except dogs left to die by summer visitors. The old opera house rotting, the railroad trestle falling in—and those goddamned neon signs.

Before the first open sewer had been laid down the middle of Main Street, the town of Blue Valley had been a disgrace. For sheer destruction of nature, it took the prize in a state which had so often defiled its finest treasures. Not a single redeeming feature had been built into the town, and those that remained stood as memorials to man's greed and insensitivity.

'The whole damned thing should be burned to the ground,' Garrett mumbled as he drove into town. But then he slammed on the brakes and studied the problem anew, spotting here and there some old building which might be restored for travelers to gawk at:

> The mind of man is provoked to speculation by ruins, and the paintings of Hubert Robert that show the desolation of Rome, or the dark, powerful etchings of Piranesi showing the ruins of those somber castles excite us. Maybe the committee's right. Maybe we could salvage something that would remind the city traveler of the past.

He looked disconsolately at the awful modern excrescences that monopolized the town—the hot-dog stands built like hot dogs, the Moorish motels, the towering neon signs, the trash in the gutter, the preposterous architecture, and everywhere the assault on taste and judgment. Even the ski slope, built at enormous expense, was contaminated. In winter, candy-bar wrappers lay frozen in the snow. In summer, they mingled with beer cans and broken bottles:

> It's beyond redemption. Everything about it is wrong. Look at how the highway stupidly crosses and recrosses the stream, which can no

longer be seen. The only possible salvation for this place would be to hire gigantic helicopters with huge dredges to fly over it, day after day, and fill the whole valley with earth and hope that within a couple of hundred years the eroding stream might create something lovely again.

The worst awaited him in the town itself, where a group of men representing saloons and motels had gathered to outline their ideas for the centennial.

'What we have in mind,' the spokesman said, 'is the re-creation of scenes which will inspire the visitor and give him a feel of the old west. We're gonna take that building on Main Street and false-front it into a Wells Fargo station. Every day at noon a band of outlaws—we can hire eight cowboys at a price we can afford—will hold up the stage, and a big gun battle will last for about five minutes. Jeff, tell him about the hangin'.'

'Well, we figure that for less than a hundred dollars we can erect a gallows over there, where we have lots of parkin', and at three each afternoon we'll enact the hangin' of Dirty Louie and Belle Beagle. Now, we know that the actual execution took place about four miles up the stream—charge was claim jumpin', and her bein' a whore and all that— but we figure no one'll complain if we move it into town.

'The highlight comes at seven o'clock each night. We're gonna rename the saloon "The Bucket of Blood" and come sundown we're gonna re-enact the shootin' of the Pettis boys. We've contacted Floyd Calendar and he's agreed to play the part of his grandfather—Amos Calendar, the one who gunned them down—'

'Say,' a motelkeeper asked Garrett, 'wasn't one of your kinfolk involved in that shootin'?'

'Yes. And so was Harvey Brumbaugh's.'

'Do you think that on the actual anniversary we could get you and Brumbaugh to join Calendar and come down the Main Street blazin' away? We could have television and it'd make every station in the country.'

The dismal plans went on and on—the whores, the dry-gulching, the bank robbery, the runaway stagecoach. As Garrett listened he wondered if these men had any comprehension of western history. Did they think it was all murder and mayhem? Didn't they know that ordinary men and women also settled the west, and that most of them had deplored the very excesses this committee wanted to celebrate. Jim Lloyd had left a brief memento of his foray into the mountains in search of the Pettis boys:

From that moment on I have never handled a gun. I have found even the shooting of a rattlesnake abhorrent, and I recommend to all my descendants that they keep away from firearms, for I have found that they do far more damage to good men than to evil.

At lunch the committee presented its one good idea. The chairman said, 'We've saved this till last, because we know you'll like it. What we're going to do is put a big billboard on every major road leading into the state. We'll tell the tourists, "Come to Blue Valley and Eat Like the Pioneers Ate." ' With this he snapped his fingers, and the cooks brought out the sourdough bread, the beans and onions, the johnnycake and the elk meat.

It was an imaginative concept, and Garrett was loath to discourage the men. Such a meal, served on red-checked oilcloth in a rough surrounding, might prove popular with tourists. The other proposals were offensive, and Garrett wanted nothing to do with them, but he had to concede that these men would do no worse damage to the valley than their predecessors had already done.

Grudgingly he told them, 'If you can scrape up forty or fifty thousand dollars to clean this town up . . . and build some false fronts . . .'

'Then you'll play your grandfather in the big shoot-out?'

He smiled. 'As chairman of the statewide committee, I mustn't show any partiality.'

'Of course. We're gonna call our show "Ghost Town Lives Again." '

'I wasn't aware you'd ever been a ghost town.'

'Well, we fudge the history . . . a little, here and there.'

On Thursday, November 22, Garrett took Harvey Brumbaugh aside before the beginning of the committee hearing and told him, 'Blue Valley has made us an offer we can't refuse. We're to wear revolvers, stalk down Main Street, and gun down the Pettis boys again.'

'I can hardly wait,' Brumbaugh said, brushing aside the levity. 'Let's get your lynching party over with.' He sat erect in the chair reserved for him, placed both hands on the table and said, 'I suppose you gentlemen have reached a conclusion?'

'We have,' the chairman said. 'Harvey, much as it pains me . . . well, the health problem . . . the smell . . . the future plans for Centennial . . . We've studied everything and we can reach only one conclusion.'

'You want me to move my feed lot out of here?'

'We do,' the chairman said placatingly. 'Now, we don't want you to move too far. Ten, fifteen miles maybe. The workers at the lot want to stay with you.'

'How soon?' Brumbaugh asked coldly.

'We're not going to rush you. Eight . . . nine months.'

One member said brightly, 'We hear you've taken an option on some of the Volkema land out at Line Camp. That would be just great.'

Brumbaugh pushed himself away from the table to survey carefully the ecologists who were driving him out of business, and when his eyes met Garrett's he gave a slight wink. 'Gentlemen,' he said slowly, 'I may have a surprise for you.'

He was imposing that morning—fifty-six years old, tough-minded like Potato Brumbaugh, and one of the wealthiest cattlemen in the west. He had prospered by being ready at any moment to make unpalatable decisions. The citizens of Centennial had considered him crazy when he sold his bottom lands along the Platte, but he had seen earlier than they that sugar beets were a dying proposition. They had predicted failure when he devised his plan for buying young steers and fattening them scientifically, absorbing the risks of the market, so that if prices went up he made a fortune, which he could easily lose if they dropped. He was the new type of westerner, the revolutionary entrepreneur, and for some time he had been anticipating the day when ecological considerations would force him to abandon his huge feed lot. Indeed, the closing down of the sugar-beet plant, with its resultant loss of pulp, would make a change of location desirable for him, so as an opportunist in the good sense of the word he welcomed the committee's decision.

Garrett could not anticipate what his long-time friend was about to do, so he listened attentively as Brumbaugh said, 'For some months past I've been weighing the merits of a change, and your decision this morning forces my hand. I think we'd better call in the press.'

The chairman coughed nervously. 'Are you sure this is the time?'

'Quite sure,' Brumbaugh replied, winking again at Garrett, and as the men waited for the reporters, Brumbaugh asked, 'Aren't you weighing some rather serious decisions of your own, Paul?'

Garrett flushed, then said, 'None that I know of.' In fact, he was perplexed on many points, but he did not care to discuss any of them with his neighbors.

'I mean about your Herefords.' Garrett tried not to betray emotion, and Brumbaugh continued: 'I heard in Montana the other day that Tim Grebe was heading down this way, and in our business, when Tim Grebe shows up, it means only one thing.'

'He could be heading for Denver,' Garrett said evasively.

'They said he was coming to Venneford,' Brumbaugh said, staring at Garrett.

Now the reporters filed in, and Brumbaugh addressed them: 'For some time the citizens of Centennial have opposed, and rightly so I think, the continuance of my feed lots on the edge of town. Reasons of health, sanitation and odor have been advanced, and I concur. Gentlemen, I'm in a position to announce that starting immediately, I shall move.'

The chairman interrupted to say, 'Mr. Brumbaugh is taking his lots out to Line Camp. So we won't really lose the benefits of his operation, only the smell.'

This brought smiles, which Brumbaugh halted with an announcement that stunned his listeners: 'I'm dividing the lots into two halves. One part will locate west of Ottumwa, Iowa. The other part, northeast of Macon, Georgia.'

'Can Centennial survive?' the reporter from the *Clarion* asked. 'Losing Central Beet on Tuesday, Brumbaugh Feed Lots on Thursday?'

'Centennial's always survived,' Brumbaugh said. 'It'll adjust to this new situation.' After allowing this harsh conclusion to be digested, he added, 'Newspapers and radio stations should be preparing citizens for the time, perhaps not far distant, when even the famous cattle ranches in this area will have to close down. You can't run Herefords on land worth two thousand dollars an acre. Especially if your aquifers run dry and you have to import hay. I'm taking my feed lots to where the rain is . . . to where hay is abundant. If you take away my beet pulp, I have to go to the cottonseed cake.'

That was a gloomy night in Centennial, for many families were hit by the dual loss. 'Is the town finished?' descendants of the pioneers asked. 'Are we to go the way of Line Camp and Wendell?' The town banker, who saw two substantial accounts vanishing, told his wife, 'It's possible for every banking need in this town to be supplied from Greeley, or better yet, Denver. All we're left with is a holding operation, and that has never appealed to me. I think we'd better reconsider that job offer in Chicago.'

It was on November 23 that the hardest blow for Garrett fell. Early that morning a large red Cadillac sped south from Cheyenne, pulling up at the Venneford Ranch. It was driven by Tim Grebe, now fifty-one years old, a handsome, florid-faced cattle salesman from eastern Montana. After the slaughter of his family he had lived with Walter Bellamy, the former land commissioner, who had sent him to the agricultural college at Fort Collins, where he had graduated near the top of his class. He had been hired by a large Hereford rancher in Wyoming, and some years ago had left that job to become managing partner in a very large ranch put together in Montana by a Texas oilman. He had gained fame as an innovator and in recent years had traveled widely throughout the west, helping ranchers revitalize their herds, introducing new methods and new types of exotic European cattle.

He had trained himself to be a master persuader, and as he put down his teacup he looked directly at Garrett and spoke with that gentleness which had earned him a leading position in the industry: 'Paul, I'm an old Hereford man myself. I can remember the psychological wrench I suffered when I had to give up my herd, and I understand how men feel when they finally decide to protect themselves.' And from his papers he produced that famous newspaper photograph from the year 1936. It was enclosed in plastic and showed a fourteen-year-old Timmy embracing a Hereford.

'I remember that,' Garrett said. 'I was nine,' and he remembered, too, the other events of that fatal day. Tim Grebe exploited his photograph for that very reason; when ranchers recalled the gruesome deaths at Line Camp, they were more apt to be receptive to Grebe. He was no longer a big-shot rancher from Montana with brash ideas and the million-dollar Texas bank account. He was a country boy who had survived his own hell.

'So when I come to reason with you, Paul, I come as a friend who's been through the mill. Let me tell you,' and he accented the word *you* slightly, 'what your real position is.' And he ticked off each of the problems that had been concerning Garrett.

'First, your Herefords are not entirely freed from the dwarfism introduced by Charlotte Lloyd and her fancy experts. You clung to the Emperor line too long. Great bulls for exhibiting in hotel lobbies during the stock shows. Fatal when it came to breeding. To eliminate the errors Emperor introduced, you've got to have new blood.

'Second, your Hereford yearlings don't weigh enough. You've watched ranchers who've switched to the exotics shipping their steers off to market eight weeks ahead of you and saving all that feed.

'Third, and this isn't of top importance, because of light pigmentation the Hereford has always been subject to eye cancer and udder burn. You can eliminate both these faults with a simple crossbreeding.

'Fourth, your cows, when they do have calves, never produce enough milk to fatten them.' He paused and lifted his empty cup.

'Want some more of that tea?' Garrett asked quietly. Skillfully Grebe had identified each weakness Paul had been pondering.

'That's a great tea. Sort of smoky. What's in it?'

'Special blend my family's been drinking for generations. Cured with tar.' He sipped from his own cup, then said with awkward sincerity, 'I appreciate your coming.'

'Let's look at your problem from a detached point of view, and believe me, Paul, you can consult anyone you wish, and if they're honest, they'll tell you about the same. So I invite you to check up on every statement I make.' He drank deeply of the hot tea and continued.

'If you stick to pure Herefords, Paul, it'll take years to tighten up your herd, and even then you'll have made no progress on the big items that mean money. So I say bluntly, "You've got to crossbreed." You've got to introduce new blood in new ways, painful though the thought may be.'

'I'm prepared.'

'Good. Now, you can do it in two ways. The Curtiss people have some truly great bulls and they'll sell you semen for artificial insemination. Pick the right breed and the right bull, and you can turn your herd around in five years. First year you get half-bred cattle. Second year you get three-fourths. Third year it's seven-eighths. And in the fourth year you get fifteen-sixteenths, which in our profession counts as full bred. I've used A.I. and it works. You breed more of your cows, and you breed them in the first estrus cycle, which means ninety-six more pounds per calf at the end of the growing season as compared to the cow that gets caught only in the fourth estrus cycle.'

He leaned back, allowing Garrett time to digest the arguments of the opposition. 'If you want to go A.I., I can put you in touch with two fine young men who work for Curtiss, and they'll have the semen out here the minute you want it. But I earnestly advise you to consider my way.'

'That's why I asked you to come down,' Garrett said.

'Good. Paul, I'm going to hit you with a blizzard of revolutionary ideas, so fasten your seat belt. I want you to buy, from me, if you like the breed I've elected, sixty young bulls, thirty of them half-bred at four hundred and fifty dollars each, thirty of them three-quarters bred at six hundred each. That's an initial investment of thirty-one thousand, five hundred and it sounds like a lot, but let me show you how you can amortize it overnight. I want you to sell every one of your Hereford bulls to the bologna manufacturers—they're paying top dollar these days because they want tough, tasty old meat. I can get you a very good contract, and you wind up owing me less than ten thousand dollars, which I'll spread out over three years.'

'What's your thinking on specific breeds, Tim?'

'It's all here in the book,' Grebe said, handing Garrett a pamphlet with numerous photographs showing the results of crossbreeding Hereford cows with bulls of the various European breeds imported recently into Canada. But before Garrett had a chance to leaf through the pages, he said, 'One of the very best crosses, of course, is one you know well, Hereford and Black Angus. The dark pigmentation of the black bull eliminates eye cancer and udder burn. And you get a handsome calf, body jet-black like the Angus, face snowy white like the Hereford.'

Now he let Garrett turn the pages. 'Briefly, the story on the Europeans is this. The biggest animal is the Chianina from Italy, a white bull, but I don't like the color of the Hereford-Chianina calves, and I don't think you would either. Most popular has been the Charolais, and with the Hereford they throw a beautiful tan cross, but it has many weaknesses. Hottest new item is the Maine-Anjou, a French animal, black-and-white, very good on milk production and beef. But the beast I like—and I've put my money where my mouth is—is the Simmental, that big reddish animal from the Simme Valley in Switzerland. I'm not going to sing its praises, because you've seen the literature, but as an old Hereford man I will tell you this. Because the Simmental's basic coloring is so close to the Hereford, you can have a Simmental-Hereford cross and the calves will retain a red body and a good white face.' He showed Garrett color photographs of sixteen such crosses, and the calves looked so much like Herefords that sometimes Garrett could not detect the cross.

'I'm not concerned with color,' Garrett lied. 'What else will the cross do for me?'

'It will introduce hybrid vigor. Any cross will improve a Hereford ranch ten percent. Any fine European will improve the herd fourteen percent, simply because it introduces new strains of resistance. And the best Simmental will improve it eighteen percent.

'Your cows will give more milk. Eye cancer and udder burn will be diminished. But the big difference will be that the Simmental has never been bred to look good in hotel lobbies. It's a draft animal, big and rugged, and it shows in the calves. Look at these figures!' And he showed Garrett the comparisons:

Measurement	Hereford	Simmental Cross
Weight of calf at birth	70	87
Weight at 205 days	410	575
Weight at 345 days	940	1129

'And those extra pounds mean extra dollars. On the same amount of food, the crossbred will give you nearly two hundred pounds more per animal, and that's profit.'

He waited for Garrett to study the chart, then said confidentially, 'I think that because of your fine reputation as a cattleman, I might be able to get you a couple of rabbits.'

'Rabbits?'

'Haven't you heard about the latest development in Canada?' Garrett hadn't, so he explained. 'As you know, none of the European exotics can ever be imported into the United States. Hoof-and-mouth disease. So we bring them into Canada and export sealed and frozen semen from there. All those great bulls you see in the pamphlets live in Canada. We have none in the States.

'But a team of brilliant Canadian veterinarians have developed a system that frankly amazes me. They do it with rabbits, and it goes like this. They identify the finest Simmental cow in the world. They inject her with hormones, so that she produces not one or two ova but scores. Then they inseminate her with the very best bull in the breed, so that instead of producing one superior calf a year, like an ordinary cow, she is prepared to produce sixteen or seventeen at one shot.

'Of course, her womb wouldn't be big enough to accomplish this, so as soon as the ova are fertilized, she is cut open—perfectly harmless operation—and the fertilized ova are stripped away from her tubes, and we have a dozen or so potential calves from the two greatest parents in the world.

'But we don't want them in Canada, we want them in the United States. And here's where the rabbits come in. We take female rabbits ready to conceive and place in their uterus the inseminated Simmental ova, which grow there just as well as they would in the uterus of a cow. The rabbits are then flown to the United States and operated upon. The ova are taken from them and placed into any substantial kind of cow who happens to be at hand. Doesn't have to be a Simmental, because the characteristics of the future animal are in the ovum, not in the substitute mother.

'In due course the ersatz mother produces her offspring, and it's a pure-bred Simmental, as beautiful as any reared in Switzerland.'

Garrett sat back. Such manipulation of nature was beyond his comprehension, and the image of a two-pound rabbit carrying a potential two-thousand-pound bull in her womb was preposterous. 'Is it legal?' he asked.

'Well,' Grebe replied, 'it may not be for long, but I'd like you to import three of four of these rabbits, because I haven't told you the best part. Each rabbit is impregnated with two ova, and they go into the mother cow, so that time after time what you get is not one Simmental but twins. We've found a way to make cows produce twins about eighty percent of the time. So with four rabbits you ought to get seven calves for sure and maybe eight.'

The ideas were coming too fast for Garrett to absorb, so he strode about the room for a while, then asked, 'Is the Simmental-Hereford cross a good one?'

'I think it's the best,' Grebe said. 'But, of course, I may be prejudiced.' Watching Garrett carefully, he realized that now was the time to repeat the clinching argument required to close any sale. 'The good part is, the Simmental looks like a Hereford. Before long you'll like the new animals the way you did the Herefords.'

'That I doubt,' Garrett said. For some minutes he looked up at the moose heads, then made his decision. 'I'll take thirty of your best bulls, Grebe. Fifteen half-bred. Fifteen three-quarters. I'll keep thirty of my best Hereford bulls, and we'll split the herd. See which does best.'

'Splendid idea,' Grebe said quickly. 'You want to come to Montana to pick them out?'

'I'll trust you, Tim.'

'If you do, I've got to see you get the best deal.'

When he was gone, Garrett went in to tell his wife, 'I've done it. We're selling off half the Hereford bulls.'

She had never understood much about ranching and could not appreciate the gravity of her husband's decision, but she was aware of his feeling for the white-faces, and she said consolingly, 'We'll get to like the new ones just as much.' This was little reassurance, so after kissing her he left the castle and saddled his horse, riding to the far fields.

How history repeats! he reflected. A century ago it was English millionaires using textile profits to buy great ranches and introduce Herefords. Today it's Texas oilmen and Chicago doctors using tax dollars to buy the same ranches and introduce things like Simmentals. They're still absentee landlords buying the land for investment.

When he reached the fields where his bulls were grazing he began the painful task of deciding which would be kept, which sent to the bologna factory, but after inspecting nineteen bulls, he had condemned only one and reprieved eighteen. 'To hell with it,' he growled. 'I'll let someone else do the picking.' Riding off, he turned for one last look at the great beasts, their horns drooping down beside their eyes. They had never looked better. 'Christ,' he muttered, 'I hope I'm doing right in selling them.'

Early Saturday morning, November 24, the governor sent Garrett, by special messenger, a confidential, prepublication copy of a report assembled by a team of research scientists working out of Montreal, Canada, with the notation: 'What can we do about this?' With fascination Garrett read the study. He had heard rumors of its compilation and had wondered how his state would fare. He had expected Colorado to do moderately well, but the results staggered him.

The scientists had posed a simple problem: 'Of the fifty states, which ones provide the finest quality of life, and which the poorest?' They had isolated forty-two criteria which any sensible citizen would accept as relevant. Garrett looked at the list and tried to rate Colorado:

How many dentists per 1000 population?
How many hospital beds per 1000?
How many miles of unpolluted streams per 1000?
How many books in public libraries per 1000?
How many square miles of national park or forest per 1000?
How many tennis courts per 1000?

When scientists arranged the states in order, Garrett found to his astonishment that Colorado led the list! California came next, then Oregon, Connecticut, Wisconsin and Wyoming. The bottom slots were occupied by those southern states which until recent years had refused to spend money on parks and playing fields and library books because they were afraid that blacks might want to use them too.

The rating would raise a serious problem for Colorado, for when it was published across the nation, as it would be, thousands of people who had only vaguely thought of moving to the state would now be inspired to do so, and there would be a flood of immigration and a corresponding torrent of local protest.

Garrett was about to put the report aside, figuring that its problems would have to be faced by others, when he saw that the governor had flagged one of the footnotes. It said:

> Colorado would lead the comparisons by an even greater margin were it not for its shocking abuse of one of its greatest resources, the Platte River. As it passes through Denver, this stream is treated as a public sewer. Its condition is appalling, and it creates the suspicion that there has never been in either the Colorado legislature or the Denver city council one man or woman who cared. We recommend that Colorado send a commission to San Antonio, Texas, to study in detail what that city has accomplished in utilizing its trivial river. The imaginative creation of an old-style Mexican village, La Villita, could be duplicated by any city determined to salvage its history, and Denver with its great resources could do even more. That it allows its river to be devastated within its boundaries is a disgrace.

By the middle of December this criticism would hit the local papers and editorials would begin asking questions as to why Colorado tolerated the continued abuse of the Platte:

> And the critics will be right, Vernor. Damn it, they're right. The earth is something you protect every day of the year. A river is something you defend every inch of its course. All the men who tried to save the river are dead now, and what have fellows like me done in the past twenty years? We are judged only by the future, and men like me have allowed the river to go unattended . . . to our disgrace.

He then did something that would cause his neighbors to wonder if he were sane. He decided not to go to the Colorado-Nebraska football game, even though he had tickets!

'Flor!' he called. 'How about phoning Norman? And ask him to get the plane ready.'

'We have to leave for the game.'

'We're going to skip the game.'

'What about our picnic?'

'We'll take it with us.'

'But the tickets?'

The absolute apex of the social year in Colorado was the Nebraska game. Good tickets could be sold for two hundred dollars a pair, or even more if the day was good, and for a Chicano woman to be going to this almost sacred rite was something so special that even Flor, who had little sense of vanity, had to be pleased. Since Denver had no opera, no regular theater and no grand balls, the whole cultural scene was compressed into one football game, and Flor was right to wonder why her husband would waste their tickets.

'Call Sam Pottifer,' Paul said. 'I think he'd grab at them.'

While her husband shaved, she called Pottifer, a Chicago millionaire who had recently bought a large spread in the foothills west of Centennial, and he was amazed that at the last minute such good fortune should befall him. As a newcomer, he had been trying vainly to get a pair of tickets, but not even his wealth enabled him to break so quickly into the magic circle of those who possessed season tickets.

A lawsuit dealing with the value of these tickets was being watched by important families in the state. It had gone through the lower courts and was now being adjudicated in the supreme court. A man named Colson and his wife had seats on the forty-yard line, which they had owned for some thirty years. Mrs. Colson died, and the university, deciding that Colson now needed only one seat, arbitrarily took the other one away from him and awarded it to someone who had been waiting eleven years. Colson's suit was for a mandamus ordering the university to give back his second seat on the logical grounds that the deprivation condemned him to bachelorhood in that 'no self-respecting woman of the type I might want to marry would consider me if she knew that I had only one ticket to the university football games.'

So Flor's picnic lunch, which should have been consumed from some tailgate in the shadow of the stadium and shared with the first families of the state, was stowed in the Beechcraft, and at ten the newlyweds were aloft, heading due west for the high Rockies.

'Where are we going?' Flor asked excitedly.

'I have to survey the Platte and report to the governor.'

'The river's down that way,' Flor said, pointing south.

'Not the part we want to see.'

Below them, there was no sign of the Platte, only the peaks, one after another in mighty congregation. The perilous passes were already blocked with snow, and herds of elk were gathering where only a short time ago summer campers had pitched their tents. It was a world of whiteness, and if a plane crashed here, and some did each winter, it might lie hidden for months before it was discovered.

The plane turned south to enter the area where small mining villages had once flourished, and at Fairplay a small stream, barely noticeable, wandered through the snow.

Garrett directed his pilot to follow this fork of the South Platte across level areas eight thousand feet high and down the cascades as it tumbled to the plains.

In the distance Flor could see the smog hanging like a cloud over Denver, and she thought they would fly into it, but instead the pilot turned west again, to fly up the valley of another fork. This branch penetrated to the very highest mountains, a little stream lost among peaks.

It was the confluence of these two forks that formed the South Platte, and for about an hour Garrett and his wife flew up and down them, finding not a single error in their utilization. So long as the streams kept to the mountains, they were pure and free; it was when they mingled with men that the abuses began.

At the approaches to Denver the Platte became a squalid thing, compressed between unkempt banks; it was one of the ugliest stretches of river in America, not much better than the Cuyahoga, which caught fire in Cleveland one day because of its cargo of filth and oil. Garrett, looking down at the river and the smog asked Flor, 'If Colorado is first on the list, what must the others be like?'

Northwest of Denver lay the university town of Boulder, and Garrett directed his pilot to fly over the huge gray stadium, and saw the approaches to it clogged with thousands of automobiles. He wondered how the game was going. Each year Colorado enthusiasts vowed that this time they would defeat Nebraska, and each year their hopes were dashed: 1970, Nebraska 29 Colorado 13; 1971, Nebraska 31 Colorado 7; 1972, Nebraska 33 Colorado 10.

Garrett, staring down at the frenzied scene of which he had so often been a part, both as player and spectator, reflected that if the most superior intellect on Mars had landed in the United States to study its educational system for a year, that brain could not have understood the accidental development whereby America's state universities had become operators of professional football teams. The universities were judged not on their libraries or their research centers or their courses in philosophy, but only on their capacity to buy a football team, most of whose members did not come from the home state or reside in it. Often they were not even true students connected with the university; they were young men dedicated principally to the job of landing contracts with acknowledged professional teams after their so-called graduations from the institutions of which they had never been a real part. Garrett, who had been a tackle at Colorado when the team was truly amateur, could laugh at the system now:

> It's the craziest pattern ever devised. Here you have the citizens of two great states growing apoplectic about a football game played not by their own people but by hired thugs imported at great expense from all over the United States. A large percentage of the players are blacks who would not be welcomed if they wanted to stay in the state after their playing days were over. They're coddled and paid and pampered, then thrown out on their ass. And for one Saturday afternoon in November the prestige of two states depends upon their performance. And the whole damned thing is done in the name of education!

North of Boulder they intersected the valley of the Cache la Poudre, and the plane turned back into the mountains where Garrett pointed out the lakes built by Potato Brumbaugh. When the Beechcraft climbed to an altitude of fourteen thousand feet Garrett pointed down to the tunnel Brumbaugh's men had dug under the mountains in order to steal a river from Wyoming so that the Platte could be more fruitful.

The plane turned eastward, following the braided Platte as it moved toward the Nebraska line. The river seemed an infinite chain of wooded islands strung along the merest thread of water, for the irrigation ditches had drawn off almost every usable inch of moisture. At Julesburg, near the Nebraska border, the Platte was a bare trickle, exactly the way Potato Brumbaugh had planned, but as the river crossed the state line, waters escaping from the irrigation ditches returned, so that in the end Nebraska received its lawful share.

'This is the part that never ceases to fascinate me,' Garrett told his wife as the plane continued into Nebraska. Pointing ahead, he showed her the North Platte and the South running side by side for almost forty miles, each refusing to surrender its identity. Because he wanted a faithful transcription of what he was about to say, he again took up the tape recorder and said:

> During the Korean War, I took one leave in Southeast Asia and saw their rivers—Brahmaputra, Mekong, Ganges, Irrawaddy. But I can tell you that no rivers I have ever seen moved me the way those two down there do. Look at them, two lovers yearning to come together, yet afraid. Isn't that the damnedest thing, really? And here, at North Platte, where they finally join, how excellent.

The plane traversed the site several times, with Flor pressing her face against the window to see the union of the rivers. Then, impulsively, Garrett said, 'We'll fly to the Missouri,' and the plane hit top speed, following the twists and turns of the Platte as it crossed Nebraska, past Fort Kearny where the Oregon Trail wagons had rested, past the Pawnee village where Pasquinel and McKeag had first fought the Indians, then traded with them, and on to that mysterious, wooded, swampy, useless spot where the Platte surrendered its identity and lost itself in the Missouri. Garrett, imagining scenes in which his ancestors must have participated at that forlorn confluence, looked down and said to Flor, 'No one in Colorado will believe it, but this river is more exciting than football.'

The week had been one of tension, but Sunday was given over to frivolity. On that day hundreds of spectators would gather at the spacious ranch of Sam Pottifer to watch the Appaloosa exhibition, and whereas Paul Garrett could conceivably skip a Colorado-Nebraska football game, it would have been inconceivable for him to miss the Appaloosas. If a stranger had asked him, 'Paul, what are you proudest of in your life?' he would have been entitled to give various replies: high government position, leading Hereford breeder, his conservation work with turkeys and prairie dogs and buffalo, but most certainly he would have replied, 'The fact that I helped rescue the Appaloosa from extinction.'

It was somehow gratifying for Garrett that he spent so much of his time and money on the Appaloosa for this lovely breed of horse had originated in the Rattlesnake Buttes area about a million years ago, and was now considered by many to be the oldest continuing strain of horses. 'To have revived this particular breed,' Garrett wrote in one report, 'is to have helped nature remember her best.'

When the land bridge existed between Alaska and Asia, this horse had emigrated from Colorado to the old world. There it had flourished, and ancient art was replete with depictions: Cro-Magnon man painted the Appaloosa on the walls of his cave; Chinese artists loved to display this unique animal; Persian miniatures show him to advantage, his dotted hindquarters flashing in gold and silver; and many of Europe's greatest painters, like Titian and Rubens, showed the animal in battle scenes.

Not a big horse, he was lively, strong, had great endurance and was easy to train. He liked people and from the first seemed to enjoy showing off, for many of the Lippizaners of Austria had originated from this breed.

His survival in America was a miracle, nothing less. He returned to this continent by accident—three or four of the horses brought over by Cortez and the early Spaniards being Appaloosas. In the new world he died out, except for a rare few that were taken far north of Arizona, where some time around 1715, they fell into the hands of the Nez Percé Indians of Idaho. These famous horse traders recognized them as superior animals. By careful husbandry, the Nez Percé produced a large number of Appaloosas, which they used as cavalry in their running fight with the United States government.

When the Nez Percé were finally defeated, the incoming missionaries handed down three decrees: 'You must stop dancing, because it leads to debauchery. You must not wear beads and feathers any more, because they remind you of battle. And you must sell your spotted horses, because when you gallop them over the prairie you think of war.' So the Nez Percé Appaloosas, named for the Palouse Indians in Idaho, were taken from their owners and sold indiscriminately throughout the west.

During the first two decades of the twentieth century different ranchers began to notice among their herds stalwart horses with dots on their hindquarters, and one or two experts, remembering old paintings of the frontier, suspected that these might be the famed speckled horses of the Nez Percé. They began buying up such animals whenever they appeared on the market, and through a process of meticulous breeding, assured the continuation of this beautiful species.

It was not until the 1950s that the story was completed. Then owners began to assemble large numbers of Appaloosas. Garrett and some friends from Idaho found an old Nez Percé chief who remembered how his tribe had bred Appaloosas:

This old fellow had no teeth, could barely talk. But he loved horses, especially the spotted breed that had carried Chief Joseph and the Nez

Percé warriors in their fights against our cavalry. I remember him, almost too weak to stand, running after one of my mares and holding her as he said, 'You watch the pregnant mare carefully till she is a hundred and fifty days. Then you place her in a corral painted with black dots. Seeing these dots day after day, she gets them on her mind. During her last week you take a bucket of black paint and dip your right hand in and place it on her right hip and say, "Dots, dots, appear, appear." Then with your left hand you do the same on her left hip, repeating the same words. If you have painted the corral properly, and if you make good fingerprints on the hips, she will always throw a colt with Appaloosa markings. But I have noticed that this magic works only if she is an Appaloosa mare to begin with.'

When Garrett first organized his Appaloosa Club he did so out of his love for the handsome horses, but he had owned his string only a short time before he saw that he and his friends would find their greatest joy in recalling the heroic days when Nez Percé warriors used them as war ponies. The club therefore encouraged its members to acquire trappings and costumes that would evoke Indian life of the last century. Garrett would accept no one into the club who was not willing to provide himself or herself with an authentic Nez Percé costume, and he sent each prospective member this message:

It is obvious that with the sleazy modern materials available in any five-and-ten a rider can produce a pretty handsome costume. And with the flashy colors available in make-believe leather, we can deck our horses so they look like Christmas trees. While such effects gain applause in a parade, they are not exactly what this group is striving for. We ride our Appaloosas in honor of Chief Joseph and his Nez Percé heroes, who, when they were allowed to own these horses, kicked the living hell out of the American cavalry. We ride in honor of the great Arapaho and Cheyenne horsemen who once owned the land we occupy. Above all, we ride out of respect for our national heritage, so when you ride with us, you will ride as an Indian or keep the hell out.

It was against this background that he had presented Flor Marquez with a wedding present: an authentic Nez Percé costume made by Broken Paw's wife in Idaho. As Paul tore away the protecting paper, Flor saw for the first time the exquisite gray-white elk skin tanned so that it was heavy as brocade, but infinitely softer, all decorated with porcupine quills and elk's teeth and silver. When she slipped into it, donned a headband of iridescent cowrie shells and twisted silver strings into the braids of her black hair, she looked completely Indian.

When Garrett saw her, he caught his breath, then embraced her. 'You're a true Nez Percé princess,' he whispered.

The Crown Vee cowboys had loaded the seven Venneford Appaloosas in gooseneck trailers, and at ten we all began the short drive west to the

Pottifer ranch. There was sun on the plains, snow in the mountains, and from various parts of northern Colorado tourists had gathered to see the curious and moving exhibition put on by the dentists, doctors, lawyers and merchants of the region. A newsman, sent out from Chicago with a camera crew to cover this unusual event, asked Garrett why grown men and women would play at being Indians, and I recorded what he said:

> My wife and I are Indians. Now, those others, as you point out, aren't. But we all have this in common. We respect our Indian heritage. There's not a phony in that bunch. Not one imitation dress or saddle. But to be perfectly honest with you, the secret is the Appaloosa. If you've never bred this amazing horse, you can't begin to imagine the excitement that comes over a family when their Appaloosa mare is pregnant. You wait for the birth with anxiety . . . yes, a real anxiety. What kind of foal will it be?

We took the camera crew to the Venneford trailers, where Garrett's horses were being unloaded: a gray stallion with black spots like a leopard; three fawn-colored mares with blankets of stars over their hips; a big male with reddish circles covering his hindquarters; and two delicate mares of such beautiful black-and-white configuration that watchers applauded as they came gingerly down the ramp.

> When you breed Appaloosas you deal with the mystery of nature. You never know what you're going to get, but when you see horses like these, each different, each magnificent in its own way . . . Mister, there are about two hundred possible colorings for an Appaloosa, and you ask me my favorite combination. I've narrowed the choice down to twenty-seven, and every morning when I look at one of my own horses I say, 'That's the best color.' And the next day I'll choose the stablemate.

The riders mounted, thirty-one men and women dressed in authentic Nez Percé costumes, and the cameramen expected some kind of dazzling exhibition, but none evolved. The horsemen simply rode back and forth as Indians might have done on their range two hundred years ago, and after a while, from the ravines to the west, a group of twenty additional riders appeared, each on an Appaloosa of a different marking, and they rode down the slopes not as enemies galloping to attack a camp, but as visitors from another tribe, and the two groups commingled and from time to time some rider in exquisite costume would appear at the crest of a ridge and stand silhouetted against the mountains. Cameras would click, and when Paul Garrett and his wife, he on the leopard-spotted stallion, she on a black-and-white mare, cantered easily down a slope, the crowd cheered.

Of course, at the end of the leisurely exhibition, a group of fifteen cowboys dressed like American cavalrymen of the 1880s did appear from the south, firing carbines, and the Nez Percé did flee, starting their long trek through the mountains, as they had done in the past, and when the last Appaloosa disappeared behind the ridge, the plains were empty and the watchers felt as if they had shared, for those brief moments, in the history of their land.

On Monday, November 26, Garrett was approached by an assistant professor from the university who wanted to question him about the baleful influence of British imperialism on the prairie. The young man had mastered the relevant figures:

'Earl Venneford of Wye put together a ranch of five million, seven hundred thousand acres. Of these he actually owned, legally or illegally, only twenty thousand acres, for which he paid, I calculate, not more than sixty cents an acre for a total of only twelve thousand dollars in cash.

'In addition, he laid out something like a hundred and fifty thousand for his cattle, equipment and supplies. Now, I'm willing to admit that his partners later on did add additional cash to pay for land they had been using, so that in the end the British put in a total, let's say, of three hundred thousand dollars.'

'What's your point?' Garrett asked.

'Look at the profits Venneford and his gang made.'

'I don't think they were a gang. They were a group of businessmen who operated within the laws of this country.'

'Be that as it may,' the professor said. 'I calculate that Venneford took out of this state not less than thirty thousand dollars a year for thirty years. What's that? About a million dollars. At the end of that period he sold his holdings of three hundred thousand acres at around ten dollars an acre, or three million dollars, plus another million for stock and equipment.'

'You've done a lot of research,' Garrett said with some admiration.

'Thus, on an original investment of three hundred thousand dollars the British picked up a neat profit of four million seven hundred thousand dollars, or a whopping 1566 percent.'

'That seems to work out,' Garrett said. 'But one of my ancestors in that period invested rather liberally, and his returns were not nearly so good, as I can attest.'

The professor ignored this remark. 'Nor was ranching the only form of investment. Englishmen owned coal mines and gold mines and irrigation ditches and railroads and insurance companies. In fact, Colorado was a colony of Europe, and it remained so until about 1924. Year after year thousands of European-controlled dollars funneled into the plains while millions of dollars in profits made their way back to Europe. It was an example of economic imperialism at its worst.'

'Was it?' Garrett asked.

'The facts speak for themselves.'

'I wonder if they do? Colorado borrowed European money and on it paid a handsome interest, but in the end Earl Venneford had his dollars and we had a state. It's my opinion that Colorado could have afforded to pay Venneford ten times as much for the use of his money, and still come out way ahead. The men in London who built the irrigation ditch did get their interest, year after year, but a thousand farmers got land that paid them infinitely more. I'd say the best investment America ever made was to allow Englishmen to develop our plains for us. No price would have been too great to pay for railroads and mines and irrigation. In the Venneford deal, which I know pretty well, it was the state of Colorado that made the killing.'

'But the economic control? The imperialism?'

'Venneford tried to keep out sheepmen and lost. They tried to keep out farmers and lost absolutely. They tried to hold their five million acres and every damned year they lost more and more. No English battleship ever sailed up the Platte to blast hell out of the Russians and the Japanese who were cutting the English throats.'

'Russians? Japanese?'

Paul Garrett rarely cursed, but now he could not refrain. 'Goddamnit, Professor. Don't waste my time if you haven't done your homework. Who in hell do you suppose stole the land from Venneford—the Methodist Church?'

This was such a *non sequitur* that the professor fumbled for a moment. 'What . . . I mean, there were no big Russian or Japanese investments.'

'Potato Brumbaugh? Goro Takemoto? They were the most insidious imperialists ever to hit this neck of the woods. Almost as bad as Triunfador Marquez, that damned Chicano.' The professor looked shocked. 'Don't worry, Doctor. I married his granddaughter.'

The interview was ending in confusion, and Garrett thought he ought to give the man some solid data. 'Seems to me, Professor, that two salient facts saved us in Colorado. Europe was a long way off, and America was a strong, self-confident nation. We never permitted warship diplomacy. We never wavered before European military threats. Small countries today don't have that security, and sometimes they're badly abused. There is such a thing as imperialism, but in Colorado it didn't operate.

'The other advantage we had, we were a people with a free system of education. The clever British could come here and run ranches and build ditches and do everything else, but they couldn't keep our bright young men from learning the tricks of the trade. European investment bought us time to learn what we had to learn. They were great teachers, men like Oliver Seccombe . . .'

'Who was he?'

Garrett stopped in disgust. This scholar knew all the figures, all the profit-and-loss statements, but he knew none of the men. What could Garrett say about Seccombe, that brilliant, uneven man? That he put together a great ranch? That he introduced Herefords to the west? 'He shot himself, at the age of sixty-nine, in that field over there.'

The interview left a bad taste in his mouth, and when the scholar was gone he poured himself a heavy drink, even though he was opposed to daytime alcohol. He was gulping it down when Flor came in to announce that her brother had shown up unexpectedly and insisted upon interrogating him. Before Garrett could ask on what, into the room burst a fiery young man of twenty-three.

'What are you going to do?' he shouted at his new brother-in-law.

'About what?' Paul asked quietly. He did not like Flor's brother, and was disgusted with the way he had dropped out of college after one week with the complaint 'None of the professors are relevant.'

'I'm speaking about La Raza,' the young firebrand shouted.

'Keep your voice down, Ricardo,' Paul snapped, and immediately he was sorry that he had lost his temper.

'Aren't you offering me a drink?'

'It's over there.'

This interview was going even worse than the one with the professor, and Garrett could think of no way to save it. For some time young Ricardo had been seeking a fight, so let it come.

'I've been sent to warn you that this state will not be allowed to hold any kind of centennial celebration unless La Raza has a dominant say in what's done. After all, this state belongs to us . . . historically.'

'Your request makes a great deal of sense,' Garrett conceded. 'Have you been told that the first thing I did upon being appointed was to visit Cortez? And invite two Chicanos onto the committee?'

Young Marquez ignored this attempt at conciliation. 'We demand that your reactionary committee issue a press release admitting that the principles of Aztlán will govern the entire celebration.'

'What are the principles of Aztlán?'

'I have them here.' Paul reached for the paper, but the young revolutionary pulled it back, for he wanted to read it aloud: ' "Those who have stolen from La Raza the land of Aztlán—the states of Texas, New Mexico, Arizona, California and Colorado—confess their crime and admit that the brown people of the continent own these states and by rights must govern them.

' "False owners who came from nations like Russia, England, Italy and Japan to steal these lands from La Raza confess their crime and submit to just demands for indemnity. If La Raza decides that these thieves may continue in Aztlán, they must surrender all political control to La Raza and live here as immigrants, bound by the laws of Aztlán." '

The young man read on and on, inflamed by the beauty of his words and the simplicity of the solutions they outlined. When he was finished,

Garrett asked, 'I can see how your plan might have appeal in Arizona and New Mexico, but do you really think the Anglos in Texas are going to move away and give the state to you?'

'They'll be allowed to remain,' Ricardo said. 'But only if they submit themselves to our laws.'

'Will you be able to supply a group who can write the laws?'

'We have the inspiration,' Marquez replied.

'Sit down,' Garrett said.

'I prefer to stand.'

'Then excuse me while I sit. Ricardo, don't you think it strange that your people have missed chance after chance at self-education?'

'Anglo education is not relevant.'

'I was making a comparison the other day. No, listen. You may find this interesting. The Takemoto family came here about the same time as the Marquez family. The five Takemotos of this generation have had ninety-seven years of free education. That's almost twenty years for each one. As a result, they're doctors and legislators and dentists. The Marquez family also has five in this generation, and all of you together have had thirty-eight years of education. And it's been waiting there, free.'

'The Takemotos are slaves to the establishment,' the young man said contemptuously. 'We Chicanos don't want to be servile dentists and all that crap.'

'Then become lawyers,' Garrett said, 'so that you can fight for your people.'

'The whole court system is crap,' Marquez shouted.

'Lower your voice, Ricardo. What I'd like to do is pay for your university education. I'm interested . . .'

'You're trying to buy me off. Subvert the revolution. I know how my grandfather slaved in your fields . . .'

It seemed more than strange to Garrett that a young man whose sister had just married an Anglo should be abusing that very Anglo as an enemy of the race. It showed distorted thinking, but in the back of his mind Garrett suspected that if he were in Ricardo's place, he would be tempted to behave much like him. He felt a real empathy with his brother-in-law.

'Learn their system, Ricardo. Beat them over the head with it. I'm on your side, you know.'

'You're the enemy,' Marquez said. 'And I'm warning you now. We're going to destroy your celebration if you try to organize it without us.'

'You weren't listening. I said I'd already brought two Chicanos onto the committee.'

'Ah! Them! The faithful old biscuits.'

'What do you mean—biscuits?'

'Brown on the outside. White on the inside. Traitors to La Raza.'

'Whom can I appoint? That you would accept?'

'The leaders of the revolution, that's who.'

'Would they serve?'

'Yes.'

'Good. Have them see me on December first and I'll appoint them.'

'But we shall insist on gaining control of Texas.'

'Ricardo, my dear brother in blood, that will be a long time off. The problem is, what can we do now, you and your sister and I? Because Flor and I want you to live with us.'

'You can't buy me off, Garrett.' And he left the house, gunning his old Ford down the lane.

On Tuesday Garrett was awakened by a cry which always made him feel good: 'Jenny's headin' north.' It came from the yard below his window and signified that once more he would have to take down his shotgun with the rubber pellets.

'Come on, Flor. Jenny's heading north.'

They dressed hurriedly, laughing as they did, and as they ran out through the kitchen, each of them grabbed a shotgun and a handful of special bullets. It took a fairly determined stand to turn Jenny around, and one shotgun blast never did the trick.

In 1960 Garrett had purchased sixty buffalo from breeders in Canada and had trucked them onto his spread. Jenny, a female weighing more than half a ton, had kicked out the sides of three trucks before the Canadians got her tranquilized for the trip south, and when she was released onto the Venneford acres she tried to revenge herself, knocking two men flat.

She seemed to have a built-in radar beamed to her old home in Canada, because each year when the time came that buffalo traditionally migrated, she would stand in the middle of the prairie, sniff in various directions, then start to walk north, ignoring fences, roads, railroad tracks and state boundaries. The only way she could be turned about was to take a position about twenty-five feet ahead of her and fire a blast of rubber pellets smack in her face.

The first shot accomplished nothing. She merely blinked, lowered her head and kept coming. It was the second and third shots, which looked as if they might blast her head off, that finally delivered the message. She would stop, shake her head as if flies were bothering her, turn around and come home.

'She's still headin' north,' one of the cowboys said as the Garretts reached the pasture, and there stood the shattered fences through which Jenny had walked with her accustomed insolence.

'We can head her off north of the road,' the cowboy suggested, and he drove the jeep at a good speed in the direction of the errant buffalo. After twenty minutes they saw her, head down, plodding away in response to some ancient impulse. They watched her for a few minutes, laughing at her determination. When she came to a fence she barely paused, applying her great bulk and pushing it flat.

'We'll have to go up to the other road,' Garrett cried, so they went farther north and took their stand directly in front of the lumbering old cow. She must have seen them, but on she came.

Paul fired right at her face, but she merely swept her head from side to side. 'Fire, damnit!' he yelled to his wife, and Flor banged away with a second shot. Jenny hesitated, so the cowboy sent a blast right at her. She shook her head, looked about, then turned resignedly and started back to the Crown Vee pastures, where the other buffalo were grazing peacefully.

Tim Grebe kept his promise. He arranged a deal for the sale of Garrett's bulls to a bologna factory, but when the butcher phoned to complete the details, Garrett lost heart and said, 'Sorry, I've changed my mind. I couldn't possibly sell you the bulls.' He then summoned his foreman and said, 'There's got to be some smaller ranch around here that could use thirty good bulls. Sell them for whatever you can get. Give them away, if you have to.' He'd be damned if he'd sell prime Herefords to be ground up for sandwich meat.

When the foreman left, Garrett stormed about the castle in a state of anxiety. He had made a major decision and already it was haunting him. Once he grabbed me by the arm, saying earnestly, 'You can see my position, can't you, Vernor? I can't run this ranch as a hobby. And if the Simmentals will bring in more money, I've got to consider them.' I nodded.

Then he snapped his fingers and shouted to Flor, 'It's time I visited the family. I've had some of my best ideas when I've been up there,' and within fifteen minutes he and Flor had packed and we were speeding north to the reservation in western Wyoming where the remnants of the Arapaho tribe were sequestered.

Each year, from the time he was a small boy, Garrett had visited his Indian relatives, taking them presents. Most of his friends in Colorado overlooked the fact that he was part Indian, five thirty-seconds, if you traced it out on the chart in the breed book.

'I've never been a professional Indian apologist,' he told me as we sped along the great empty roads of Wyoming, 'and I've always refrained from trying to capitalize on that heritage for political effect, but I do sometimes feel like a true Indian. At least I'm sympathetic to their problems, and if I were twenty years younger, I suppose I'd be one of the gun-toting activists.'

As we neared the reservation he became moody, and I could see that he was now regretting his impulse. On his previous visit he had found his various aunts and uncles caught in despondency, and now as we drove onto the Indian lands he said prayerfully, 'God, I hope they're in better shape this time.'

They weren't. Aunt Augusta, bitter and ancient, launched her mournful litany the moment we arrived: 'Government says we can have a recreation hall, but the damned Shoshone want it on their land and we want it on ours, and we may have to go to war against them.' The old Arapaho-Ute antagonism was as venomous as it had been in 1750. The Shoshone were an offshoot of the Ute and nurtured the animosity that had always existed between the two tribes, made permanent by that unfortunate mistake in 1873 when President Arthur gave permission for the remnant of the Arapaho to share the reservation formerly occupied only by the Shoshone. There was enough land for two tribes, more than enough, but not when those tribes were mortal enemies.

In spite of her complaining, Garrett had always enjoyed Aunt Augusta, and now she demonstrated why: 'Our whole trouble stems from the Bureau of Indian Affairs. Did you know the agent is so terrified of us that he won't sleep on the reservation? He sleeps in town.' She narrated several outrageous stories about the bureau, then said, 'It all began when General Custer was head of Indian Affairs.'

I assumed that her mind must be wandering, for so far as I knew, it had been Custer's job to fight Indians, not govern them, but then the sly old lady winked and said, 'In 1876 General Custer left his office on the way to Little Big Horn and said, "Don't do anything till I get back." ' There was a long pause, and then Flor comprehended what the old woman was saying, and burst into laughter. 'That's right!' the old woman said. 'He never came back, and they've not done a damned thing since.'

Then she resumed her lament. 'Did you hear, Paul, what happened to Sam Loper's boy?'

On our way to Loper's shack Paul explained, 'He's my cousin, some way or other. His real name is White Antelope, but the government said it was silly for a grown man to be named after an animal, so he cut it down to Lope and added an r. Same way with Harry Grasshopper. Had to change his to Harry Hopper.'

Sam Loper was an older man, and his son, like so many Indian youths, had taken to heavy drinking. A week before, as he staggered home from an all-night party, he had fallen into a small ditch, not two feet deep, and drowned.

Now his father sat in his jumbled kitchen, swilling coffee and beer. And Flor wanted to weep as she listened to his narrative: 'The boy left a wife and three children, but she drinks heavy. Ain't sober days at a time. The kids—where in hell are they?'

We stopped by the Mission of Christ and asked the young director, 'Can't anything be done for the Loper family?' and he shrugged his shoulders.

'The awful problem is that no girls in America, and I mean none, are better brought up than these Indian girls. At nineteen they must make God smile in satisfaction at His handiwork. They study here at the mission and they're clean, devout, abstemious—filled with the excitement of life. Then they marry. And who do they marry? The tall, good-looking young men on the reservation . . .'

'Do Arapaho ever marry Shoshone?'

'Unthinkable. And what happens to these promising young men who play basketball so well when they're nineteen? They drift. They lose interest. They have no future, no hope. So they start drinking, and often after the first baby comes, the utter chaos of their lives becomes unbearable. They start beating up their young wives. Yes, the girls come to me with horrible bruises and broken teeth. So the only contact the wife is able to maintain with her husband is to join him in drinking, and whole families stay drunk week after week.'

'I know,' Garrett said impatiently, for he had heard this dismal story too often. 'But what can we do about the Loper widow?'

'Nothing,' the missionary said. 'She's a lost alcoholic and I cannot even approach her.'

'The children?'

'The boy will become like his father. The two girls, if I remember them, will be as beautiful as their mother, and at age twenty-eight they'll be hopeless alcoholics.'

As always on his trips to the reservation, Garrett spent his last moments in the small cemetery where Sacajawea was buried, and this time the visit would be doubly meaningful, for he wanted Flor to see the grave of the Indian woman most revered in American history, the tall and beautiful Shoshone who had led Lewis and Clark to Oregon. But he was not prepared for the emotional punishment he himself was to undergo, for while Flor studied the monument he wandered to another part of the cemetery, and there he saw a new gravestone, that of Hugh Bonatsie, who had died in the spring. Across the stone was engraved the message: 'To live in the hearts we leave behind is not to die.' The words were banal, perhaps, but the carving that accompanied them was not. There on the face of the stone, chosen for its redness, were etched the things Bonatsie had loved most in life: a white-faced Hereford bull and two cows.

On the way south from the reservation Garrett drove slowly, for he was assailed by an anguish so complex that he wanted me to preserve it accurately:

> The way we react to the Indian will always remain this nation's unique moral headache. It may seem a smaller problem than our Negro one, and less important, but many other sections of the world have had to grapple with slavery and its consequences.

There's no parallel for our treatment of the Indian. In Tasmania the English settlers solved the matter neatly by killing off every single Tasmanian, bagging the last one as late as 1910. Australia had tried to keep its aborigines permanently debased—much crueler than anything we did with our Indians. Brazil, about the same. Only in America did we show total confusion. One day we treated Indians as sovereign nations. Did you know that my relative Lost Eagle and Lincoln were photographed together as two heads of state? The next year we treated him as an uncivilized brute to be exterminated. And this dreadful dichotomy continues.

Looking at that reservation as it exists now . . . what in hell can a man say? It seems clear the Indian never intended to accommodate himself to white man's ways, so that our grandiose plans of 'fitting him into white society' were doomed. He formed an indigestible mass in the belly of progress and had to be regurgitated. Like Jonah, he came out about as well as he went in. It seems inevitable that his land had to be taken from him. The white man was in motion, the Indian wasn't. The whole thrust of our national life placed us in opposition to his requirements, and even though we signed the land treaties with the best intentions in the world, the wisest of the white men knew, at the very moment of signing, that the papers weren't worth a damn. Before the ink was dry, the Indian was dispossessed.

We drove in silence for some time, crossing the great prairies once controlled by Paul's ancestors, and finally Flor pointed out that when her husband spoke of the Indian problem, especially when he became intellectually excited, he always referred to himself as part of the white establishment which had committed these crimes against the Indian part of his inheritance:

No! When I come to Wyoming and lose myself in these empty prairies . . . I think this part, right here, is the most beautiful section of America. Look! Not a house, not a fence, not a road except the one we're on. When I'm here I'm an Arapaho. And I'll tell you this. I'm immensely impressed with the cultural persistence of my people. We may find, and very soon, too, that if the white man wants to survive on the prairie, he'll have to go back to the permanent values of the Indian. Respect for the land. Attention to animals. Living in harmony with the seasons. Some kind of basic relationship with the soil. An awful lot of the white man's progress will come to grief when the next dry spell comes along.

Again we drove in silence, with Flor vainly trying to imagine what her life would have been like in those days. She probably had in her veins a much larger proportion of Indian blood than he, yet their tradition was totally alien to her, while Paul could easily become an Indian once more. Her reverie was broken when he lifted both hands off the wheel and slammed them down on the horn-rim, sending wild surges of sound across the prairie:

This trip's been worthwhile, Vernor. I may not know what I think about Nixon or Agnew or Watergate, but at last I know what I think about the American Indian. Every reservation in this nation should be closed down. The land should be distributed among the Indians, and if some of them wish to continue living communally, they should be encouraged, like the Pueblos in New Mexico. The rest should enter the dominant culture, to sink or swim as their talents determine. The way my family had to. The way Flor's did in Old Mexico. Many good things will be lost, but the best will persist—in legend, in remembered ways of doing things, in our attitude toward the land. I can no longer support a system which keeps the Indians apart, like freaks of nature. They aren't whooping cranes, to be preserved till the last one dies out. They're part of the mainstream, and that's where they belong.

At dusk on November 28 we took motel rooms in Douglas, home of the fabled jackalope, half-jackrabbit, half-antelope. Local taxidermists were so skilled at grafting small deer horns onto the heads of stuffed jackrabbits that many visitors, including Flor Garrett, believed the mutant existed. A huge statue in the town square confirmed her belief, and when she asked where a live jackalope could be seen, Paul broke into laughter.

'You're precious,' he told her. 'A typical tourist. What the United States ought to do right now is take the money we're spending in Southeast Asia and on space shots and build a barbed-wire fence around the whole state of Wyoming. Declare it a national treasure and allow only five hundred thousand visitors a year. When you come through the gate, the officer ties a little broadcasting radio around your neck, the way Floyd Calendar did with his bears, and they'd keep track of you, and after seven days a message would go out, "Paul Garrett, driving a gray Buick with a beautiful Chicano girl. He's been inside a week. Kick him to hell out." '

Flor pointed out that whereas he had wanted to dissolve a small Indian reservation, he now wanted to initiate a huge Wyoming reservation, and she thought this contradictory, but he said, 'Not at all. Human beings cannot be kept in a state of preservation, but irreplaceable natural resources can. I say, "Declare Wyoming a national park and treat it as such." ' After dinner he bought her a small jackalope, and as he presented it to her formally, he announced to the diners in the restaurant that she was now protector of this rare creature.

On Thursday, November 29, we drove to the spot which Garrett loved most in America, the one he visited at least twice each year. It was of little consequence, really, and even though it had at one point played a specific role in American history, it had not been a major one; few

Americans could ever have heard of it. But the site had been preserved
with such intelligence that it stood as an example of almost flawless
restoration.

It was Fort Laramie, still standing in silence at the spot where the
swift dark Laramie River emptied into the North Platte. Wild turkeys
still roamed the fields where the Indians had camped during the Treaty
of 1851, and elk could sometimes be seen on the range where the Oglala
Sioux had hunted. In the soft limestone west of the fort the deep ruts of
wagon wheels could still be seen, where straining forty-niners had
dragged their covered wagons.

The old buildings had been preserved if their walls were sound, or
reconstructed if only their foundations remained, and not a false note
had been struck. There were no mighty cannon or ramparts filled with
dummy soldiers firing at nonexistent Indians. Only the materials available in the 1860s and 1870s had been used, and the sutler's store where
the emigrants had bought their last food before heading west for Oregon
still offered Arbuckle's coffee and those handsome white blankets of the
Hudson's Bay Company.

Not many visitors came to Fort Laramie, for it was in no way spectacular, but scores of men and women who loved the west made pil-
grimages to its clean, well-ordered acres to recapture the reality of
American settlement:

> Down there is where Pasquinel and McKeag had their winter headquar-
> ters. Lame Beaver and his Arapaho spent one winter over there. Levi
> Zendt and that remarkable girl, Elly Zendt . . . she's the one whose
> diaries you read. The wagons came down that hill and camped on the
> other side of the Laramie. The great convocation you read about . . .
> 1851 when all the Indians came here. The Crow came in from the north-
> west over there. It must have been a tremendous sight, the whole Crow
> nation on horseback. And this building over here is where McKeag and
> Clay Basket had their store. That's where my great-great-grandfather
> Maxwell Mercy, first met them. This other fine building . . . Old Bedlam
> it's still called. That's where my ancestor Pasquinel Mercy served before
> he went to Little Big Horn with General Custer.

Our visit ended on a bitter note, because as Garrett was about to leave
the fort, he saw on the bulletin board an announcement that any letters
mailed there would be posted with the handsome three-cent stamp honoring Francis Parkman, and if there was one man in American letters
Garrett despised, it was Parkman:

> Honoring a man like that! He debased the Oregon Trail with one of the
> feeblest historical books ever written. He had no comprehension of what
> the trail signified, no compassion for the Indians who roamed it and no
> generosity for the emigrants using it. He could turn a phrase rather
> well, but in human understanding he was pitifully deficient. He made

fun of Mexicans, ridiculed Indians, heaped abuse on hardworking farmers from the midwest, lacked any comprehension of Catholic culture and, worst of all, failed to understand the prairie. He judged all life by the meanest Boston yardstick, and almost every generalization he made about the west was wrong.

Some of his phrases fester in my mind. He called Chief Pontiac, one of America's best-balanced Indians, a 'thorough savage to whom treachery seemed fair and honorable, the Satan of his forest paradise.' I remember one passage in which he excoriated the farmers passing through as little more than animals, concluding, 'Most of them were from Missouri.' But the one that best sums up his miserable view of life stated that he divided the human race as he saw it, into three divisions 'arranged in the order of their merit: white men, Indians and Mexicans,' and he doubts that to the Mexican can be conceded the honorable title 'white.'

I'll tell you one thing, Vernor. If you ever send me a letter bearing Parkman stamps I'll burn the damned thing unopened. I don't want him in my house. What I resent most is that by getting his book published first, he scared away other writers infinitely better qualified. He never looked at the plains, nor the Platte, nor the Arapaho, nor the beaver, nor the coureur de bois, nor the bison. Of course, I'm speaking as an Arapaho, but I'll promise you this. If I run into him on the Happy Hunting Grounds, I'll scalp the son-of-a-bitch.

As we crossed the state line to enter Colorado, Garrett breathed deeply, saying, 'It's so good to be home.' Over dirt roads we drove to the ruined town of Line Camp, where only the grain elevator and the two stone buildings erected by Jim Lloyd more than a century before remained. Where was the sign that boasted WATCH US GROW? Where were the library and the bank and Replogle's Grocery Store? Where was the tractor agency that used to sell sixty tractors a year? And worst of all, where were the homes that had been so painstakingly built, so painfully sustained during the years of drought?

They were gone, vanished down to the building blocks of the cellars. A town which had had a newspaper and a dozen flourishing stores had completely disappeared. Only the mournful ruins of hope remained, and over those ruins flew the hawks of autumn.

Our car pulled up before one of the low stone buildings and Garrett got out to knock on the door. For a moment it seemed that no one was there. Then a very old man with fading reddish hair and deep-set eyes came to the door. He was eighty-six, but he moved and spoke with youthful enthusiasm, almost as if the excitements of life were just beginning.

'Paul Garrett, come in! Tim Grebe told me you'd married a beautiful Chicano, and I see she's as pretty as he said. Come in! Come in!'

He led us into the office from which he had once helped give away a hundred and ninety thousand acres of drylands, and he had watched as the defeated had abandoned the land. Now only he survived. With firm voice he spoke of those distant years, of the good rainfall at the start of the pestilential years. His memory was acute, and he could recall most of the families.

'What was the worst thing that happened in those years?' Garrett asked. In whatever celebration Colorado organized for its birthday, he would insist that the tragic times be remembered too, for they were a part of history that should not be denied.

Bellamy pondered this question for such a long interval, staring out the low window of the stone house, that I supposed he had not heard. 'Was it the Grebe tragedy?' Garrett asked.

'No,' Bellamy said brusquely, as if he had already dismissed that possibility. 'That was an accident, without cause or consequence. But there was one terrible moment. The farmers were starving. The dust was finger-high inside the houses. Everyone was losing hope. Then Dr. Thomas Dole Creevey visited us. What a godlike man! He visited with every farmer he had persuaded to come here. He walked over the land and assured us that the good years were bound to return. He confessed his mistakes and was especially helpful with the wives, for he gave them courage.'

'What was so terrible about that?' Garrett asked.

'When the meetings ended, he came in here, alone. He fell into that chair you're sitting in and asked for a drink of water. When I placed it on the table before him, he shuddered. Then, without touching the glass, he uttered a piercing shriek and covered his face with his hands. After a moment he looked up at me and whispered, "May Christ forgive me for what I did to these men and women." Then he pulled himself together and Miss Charlotte drove him back to Centennial, but he refused to touch the water.'

On the short drive home to Venneford, Garrett studied the great rolling fields sown in winter wheat. He could see that every prediction made by Dr. Creevey half a century ago had been fulfilled. Wheat prospered on The Great American Desert, and vast farms like that of the Volkema brothers earned huge profits, for the owners had learned not to plow deep and never to harrow.

A new law helped, too: if any farmer saw that because of poor management his neighbor's fields were beginning to blow away, with the inevitable consequence that other fields in line would blow away too, the observant farmer was allowed by law to plow his neighbor's field correctly. The cost of doing this would be added to the taxes of the remiss farmer. If any farmer persisted in his sloppy husbandry, his land would be taken away from him, for it imperiled the entire district. Never again would fields be allowed to blow away.

The old two-part system that had prevailed at the end of the nineteenth century—rancher and irrigator—was now a tripartite cooperation:

the rancher used the rougher upland prairie; the irrigation farmer kept to the bottom lands; and the drylands gambler plowed the sweeping fields in between, losing his seed money one year, reaping a fortune the next, depending on the rain. It was an imaginative system, requiring three different types of man, three different attitudes toward life, and Garrett was honored to have found a niche within it.

How powerful the land was! Continuously men did strange and destructive things to it, yet always the land endured. It was the factor which limited what men could accomplish; it determined what the irrigated fields would produce and how many cows could be grazed on a section. Even when men walked upon the moon, they remained attached to their native land by electrical impulses, and to the land they must return.

To be engaged in the protection of this land, as Potato Brumbaugh had been in his long wrestling with the river, or Jim Lloyd in his guardianship of the grasslands, was an honorable occupation, Garrett felt, because each generation was obligated to leave the land in a position to defend itself against the next generation.

As the car approached the castle, Garrett reflected on the grand circularity of history. On that hill to the west the good men of Centennial had once beat up the Chicano Penitentes for their weird practices, and the other day a crowd of young fellows from the town had thumped the Jesus Freaks for behaving differently from decent Methodists or Baptists. Last week a judge in Denver had announced from the bench that if Colorado still had any red-blooded men, they'd go out in the streets and thrash the Hare Krishna, who offended law-abiding citizens with their yellow robes and crazy cymbals.

At the castle we found Arthur Skimmerhorn pacing beneath the moose heads: 'Forgive me for letting myself in, but I had to see you, Paul.' Without waiting for an acknowledgment, he blurted, 'Have you sold those Hereford bulls?'

'Why?'

'I want to buy them.'

'I told the foreman to get rid of them.'

'Has he sold them?'

'We can find out soon enough.'

Skimmerhorn listened apprehensively as Garrett rang the foreman: 'How about those thirty bulls I told you to sell? . . . A man in Kansas is trying to make up his mind . . . Did you make a promise of any kind to him? . . . It doesn't have to be writing . . . You gave him an option? . . . Till when? . . . He was supposed to make up his mind yesterday and he didn't bother to call? . . . Ring him right now and tell him we sold them to Skimmerhorn in Colorado.' He replaced the phone and told Skimmerhorn, 'They're yours. And I'm delighted they'll be staying close to home where I can watch them.'

'Thanks, Paul.'

'I thought you'd switched to Charolais.'

'I did. Got the results they said I'd get, too. Bigger calves. More money. With your Simmentals you'll do the same. Those fancy boys don't lie.'

'Then why the eagerness to buy my Herefords?'

'Well,' the young rancher said with a touch of sarcasm, 'they tell the truth but they're not obliged to tell the whole truth. Look at my figures.' And from his pocket he produced a folded sheet which summarized the fuller story: Hereford cow–Charolais bull. Calves so big they could only be born by Caesarean section, fifteen percent. Calves so big they had to be born with the help of calf-puller, nineteen percent. Calves dead at birth or shortly thereafter, fourteen percent.

'What it means,' Skimmerhorn said, 'is that you do get extra money when you sell your steers, but you waste it all on veterinary fees. So I figure, if I'm working extra hard just to pay the vet, why not run cattle I really like?' He accepted the drink Garrett proffered and slumped into one of the chairs beneath the moose heads. Twirling his glass, he confessed, 'I've done very well with the Charolais. No complaints, and I'm going to keep some of those big bulls . . . to tighten up my herd, you might say. But when I haul your thirty Hereford bulls over to my ranch, and then pick up some good white-face cows at the Nebraska sales, well . . . I'll feel I'm an honest man again.'

'I can drink to that,' Garrett said.

On the last day of November, Paul Garrett was wakened early by a cowboy shouting, 'The Simmentals are here!'

There, waiting by the barn, were cattle trucks which had hauled the thirty red-and-white bulls nonstop from Montana. At first Garrett wanted no part of introducing them to their new home, for this was Hereford country and they were trespassers, but then he felt ashamed of himself. 'If we're experimenting with Simmentals, we'll do it right,' he said to me, and he went down to assist with the unloading.

The new bulls were big, full-bodied, and they looked as if they could care for themselves, but they were flabby, more like dairy cows than range Herefords. One of the hands cried softly, 'Moo cow, moo!' But then he saw the boss and scurried off.

'Pete!' Garrett called. 'Come back here. They may look moo-cow, but they'll be paying your wages. Show them respect.'

So the Simmentals were unloaded, and Garrett could see that Tim Grebe had sent him thirty strong bulls. They'd do well on Crown Vee land, and maybe the balance sheet would look better in a year or two. But when the animals moved out to take possession of land which for a century had reverberated to the hoofbeats of Herefords, Garrett felt sick to his stomach, and that afternoon he went in to Centennial alone, to drink at the bar of the Railway Arms. Next year it, too, would be gone.

And as he drank he grew increasingly mournful over the fate of Centennial. It had known a hundred good years and now was perishing. The sugar-beet factory, the feed lots, the Hereford ranches—all the old patterns of life were dissolving.

He banged his glass on the table and grabbed at a stranger. 'This was a good town, a great one,' Garrett shouted at him. 'Do you know that Edwin Booth played in our theater, and Sarah Bernhardt? William Jennings Bryan stopped here, and so did James Russell Conwell and Aristide Briand.' The man was obviously unfamiliar with these names, and pulled away.

A freight train, one of the few that still came through town, sounded its querulous whistle, evoking a new set of memories. Garrett left his table and went over to the stranger, saying compulsively, 'Listen to that, pardner. That's the Union Pacific. I remember the day, thirty-four years ago this month, when Morgan Wendell . . . he'll take office in January . . .'

His phrases dribbled off, but not his memories. He left the bar and went out onto the veranda, and cold air reminded him of that distant time. Morgan Wendell had come to the ranch and said, 'Let's go down and see it today!' and they had hitchhiked their way to a point along the Platte some miles east of Centennial. There they waited along the shore, two boys twelve years old skipping stones across the water, watching the hawks.

Then Morgan had looked at his birthday watch and said, 'It'll be pulling out of La Salle about now,' and they left the river and stationed themselves as close to the railroad tracks as possible. ♦

In the west they heard the purring of a giant cat, the swift movement of some immense creature across the prairie. It was like nothing they had heard before, a singing rush of air, and Morgan called, 'Paul! Here it comes!'

It was the *City of Denver*, that majestic gold-and-silver streamliner that left Denver each afternoon at four-fifteen, speeding almost nonstop to Chicago. It bore down upon them, its mighty engines humming. It had been built without a single protrusion—a sleek, perfect thing. Its thirty cars could not be differentiated, for flexible doors enclosed what in former days had been open space between them. This humming, lovely thing moved as a unit, swift and unbelievably quiet.

'Oh!' Morgan whispered as it bore down upon him, ninety miles an hour, a flashing drift of gold on its way to Chicago. He sighed as the last car leaped onward, vanishing in the distance.

It was the finest train that had ever run, a marvel of grace and utility. But it had dominated the prairie only briefly. It was the most civilized form of travel thus far devised, but after less than three decades its elegance was no longer appreciated and now it gathered rust.

Garrett stared across the silent tracks and saw, on the far side of the Platte, automobiles whizzing by in one unbroken chain, filled with men and women who had left Omaha that morning and who would sleep in Denver that night, ghosts of the Interstate, most of them zombies who set their speed at ninety and ignored all of America except the big cities, where tonight's motel was totally indistinguishable from last night's.

'Look at the stupid bastards,' he said to no one. 'They haven't even seen Grand Island, where the rivers join, or Ogalalla, where the cowboys rioted, or Julesburg, where a third of a million emigrants swam the Platte . . .' He stayed for some minutes watching the unceasing flight down the Interstate. Soon the drivers would be safe in Denver, and each year that city would grow larger, uglier and less congenial.

'Those bastards would be afraid to detour for an hour at Line Camp,' he mused. 'Afraid to see American history staring at them.' And he knew that with the continuing exodus, one day soon Centennial would become the next ghost town. Kicking at the rotting boards of the veranda, he said gloomily, 'Well, we've had a good hundred years. Perhaps another hundred years from now people with sense will start coming back to these towns.'

About nine that night Cisco Calendar was told by friends that Paul Garrett was sloppy drunk in the Railway Arms, so he called me and we took charge. We led Garrett unsteadily to Flor de Méjico, where we forced him to eat a chili-size—toasted bun, hamburger with onions, all smothered in hot chili beans and covered with melted cheese—after which Garrett sobered a little and asked Cisco to sing 'Buffalo Skinner.'

'Don't have my guitar,' Cisco said.

'Get the damned thing,' Garrett said, and a boy was sent to fetch it. Then the diners quietened as Cisco sang of Jacksboro, Texas, in the spring of 1873. He sang many other songs, so aching with the memory of the west that Garrett lowered his head on the table, lest his neighbors see his reddened eyes.

After a while Cisco put the guitar aside and told Garrett, 'I know how you feel, Paul. I could live anywhere in America . . . anywhere in the world, I suppose. All I need is my guitar and a Sears Roebuck catalogue for buyin' a new pair of jeans now and then. But I keep livin' in that old clapboard house my grandpappy built. You know why?

'A man needs roots. Specially a singin' man tryin' to catch at the heart of people. He needs to know where his pappy worked and which families his mom did washin' for. When he walks down the street it's got to be his street. The rootless guys I sing about are interestin' only if they've lost one place and are lookin' for another. Like they say, Paul, a man springs from the soil but he don't spring far.

'I live in Centennial because at night, when I'm through workin' I can jump into my pickup and be up in the Rockies inside of an hour—pitch my tent in Blue Valley up beyond the crud, beside a real stream of water, and wake up with trees in my eyes, and maybe in the high country an elk starin' at me. Paul, that's somethin'—that is truly somethin'.

'But what I like even better, I head the pickup east and in fifteen minutes I'm lost on the prairie with nothin', absolutely nothin', visible to the horizon except maybe a jet airplane thirty thousand feet high streamin' from New York to L.A. I pitch my tent the way men been doin' out there for ten thousand years. And when you do that you are alone . . . Man, are you alone! And somethin' seeps into your soul you simply can't pick up in Chicago or Dallas.

'I live in Centennial because it's maybe the best spot in America . . . could even be the best remainin' spot on earth.'

'Could be,' Garrett said. 'It damn well could be.'

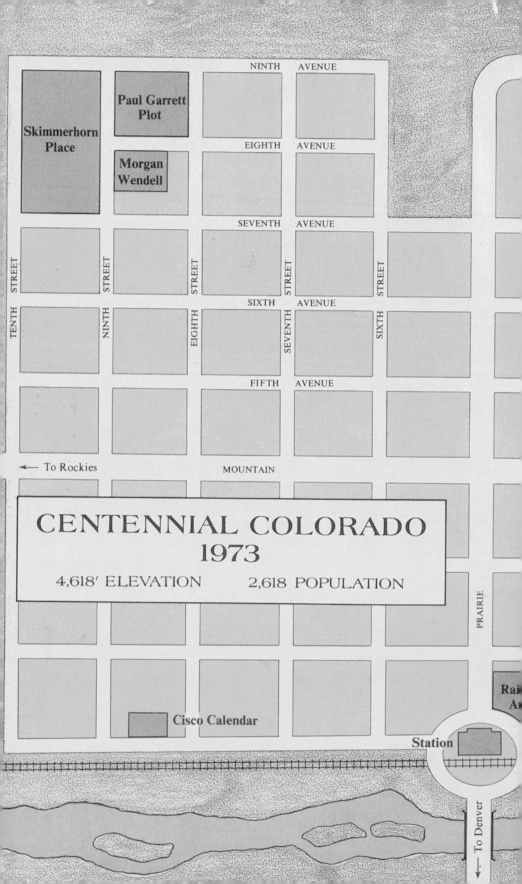

NINTH AVENUE

Skimmerhorn Place

Paul Garrett Plot

Morgan Wendell

EIGHTH AVENUE

SEVENTH AVENUE

TENTH STREET

NINTH STREET

EIGHTH STREET

SEVENTH STREET

SIXTH STREET

SIXTH AVENUE

FIFTH AVENUE

← To Rockies   MOUNTAIN

CENTENNIAL COLORADO
1973

4,618′ ELEVATION   2,618 POPULATION

PRAIRIE

Cisco Calendar

Station

Rai
A

To Denver →